STEPHEN KING

THREE COMPLETE NOVELS

CARRIE

'SALEM'S LOT

THE SHINING

STEPHEN KING

THREE COMPLETE NOVELS

CARRIE

'SALEM'S LOT

THE SHINING

WINGS BOOKS
NEW YORK

This 2002 edition is published by Wings Books, an imprint of Random House Value Publishing, by arrangement with the Doubleday Broadway Publishing Group, divisions of Random House, Inc., New York.

Wings Books® and colophon are trademarks of Random House, Inc.

Printed in the United States of America

Random House
New York • Toronto • London • Sydney • Auckland
www.randomhouse.com

A catalog record for this title is available from the Library of Congress

ISBN 0-517-21902-6

9 8 7 6 5 4 3

CONTENTS

CARRIE

This is for Tabby, who got me into it—
and then bailed me out of it.

PART ONE

BLOOD SPORT

News item from the Westover (Me.) weekly *Enterprise,* August 19, 1966:

RAIN OF STONES REPORTED

It was reliably reported by several persons that a rain of stones fell from a clear blue sky on Carlin Street in the town of Chamberlain on August 17th. The stones fell principally on the home of Mrs. Margaret White, damaging the roof extensively and ruining two gutters and a downspout valued at approximately $25. Mrs. White, a widow, lives with her three-year-old daughter, Carietta.

Mrs. White could not be reached for comment.

Nobody was really surprised when it happened, not really, not at the subconscious level where savage things grow. On the surface, all the girls in the shower room were shocked, thrilled, ashamed, or simply glad that the White bitch had taken it in the mouth again. Some of them might also have claimed surprise, but of course their claim was untrue. Carrie had been going to school with some of them since the first grade, and this had been building since that time, building slowly and immutably, in accordance with all the laws that govern human nature, building with all the steadiness of a chain reaction approaching critical mass.

What none of them knew, of course, was that Carrie White was telekinetic.

Graffiti scratched on a desk of the Barker Street Grammar School in Chamberlain:
Carrie White eats shit.

The locker room was filled with shouts, echoes, and the subterranean sound of showers splashing on tile. The girls had been playing volleyball in Period One, and their morning sweat was light and eager.

Girls stretched and writhed under the hot water, squalling, flicking water, squirting white bars of soap from hand to hand. Carrie stood among them stolidly, a frog among swans. She was a chunky girl with pimples on her neck and back and buttocks, her wet hair completely without color. It rested against her face with dispirited sogginess and she simply stood, head slightly bent, letting the water splat against her flesh and roll off. She looked the part of the sacrificial goat, the constant butt, believer in left-handed monkey wrenches, perpetual foul-up, and she was. She wished forlornly and constantly that Ewen High had individual—and thus private—showers, like the high schools at Westover or Lewiston. They stared. They always *stared*.

Showers turning off one by one, girls stepping out, removing pastel bathing caps, toweling, spraying deodorant, checking the clock over the door. Bras were hooked, underpants stepped into. Steam hung in the air; the place might have been an Egyptian bathhouse except for the constant rumble of the Jacuzzi whirlpool in the corner. Calls and catcalls rebounded with all the snap and flicker of billiard balls after a hard break.

"—so Tommy said he *hated* it on me and I—"

"—I'm going with my sister and her husband. He picks his nose but so does she, so they're very—"

"—shower after school and—"

"—too cheap to spend a goddam penny so Cindi and I—"

Miss Desjardin, their slim, nonbreasted gym teacher, stepped in, craned her neck around briefly, and slapped her hands together once, smartly. "What are you waiting for, Carrie? Doom? Bell in five minutes." Her shorts were blinding white, her legs not too curved but striking in their unobtrusive muscularity. A silver whistle, won in college archery competition, hung around her neck.

The girls giggled and Carrie looked up, her eyes slow and dazed from the heat and the steady, pounding roar of the water. "Ohuh?"

It was a strangely froggy sound, grotesquely apt, and the girls giggled again. Sue Snell had whipped a towel from her hair with the speed of a magician embarking on a wondrous feat and began to comb rapidly. Miss Desjardin made an irritated cranking gesture at Carrie and stepped out.

Carrie turned off the shower. It died in a drip and a gurgle.

It wasn't until she stepped out that they all saw the blood running down her leg.

From *The Shadow Exploded: Documented Facts and Specific Conclusions Derived from the Case of Carietta White,* by David R. Congress (Tulane University Press: 1981), p. 34:

It can hardly be disputed that failure to note specific instances of telekinesis during the White girl's earlier years must be attributed to the conclusion offered by White and Stearns in their paper *Telekinesis: A Wild Talent Revisited*—that the ability to move objects by effort of the will alone comes to the fore only in moments of extreme personal stress. The talent is well hidden indeed; how else could it have remained submerged for centuries with only the tip of the iceberg showing above a sea of quackery?

We have only skimpy hearsay evidence upon which to lay our foundation in this case, but even this is enough to indicate that a "TK" potential of immense magnitude existed within Carrie White. The great tragedy is that we are now all Monday-morning quarterbacks . . .

• • •

5

"Per-iod!"

The catcall came first from Chris Hargensen. It struck the tiled walls, rebounded, and struck again. Sue Snell gasped laughter from her nose and felt an odd, vexing mixture of hate, revulsion, exasperation, and pity. She just looked so *dumb,* standing there, not knowing what was going on. God, you'd think she never—

"PER-iod!"

It was becoming a chant, an incantation. Someone in the background (perhaps Hargensen again, Sue couldn't tell in the jungle of echoes) was yelling, *"Plug it up!"* with hoarse, uninhibited abandon.

"PER-iod, *PER*-iod, *PER*-iod!"

Carrie stood dumbly in the center of a forming circle, water rolling from her skin in beads. She stood like a patient ox, aware that the joke was on her (as always), dumbly embarrassed but unsurprised.

Sue felt welling disgust as the first dark drops of menstrual blood struck the tile in dime-sized drops. "For God's sake, Carrie, you got your period!" she cried. "Clean yourself up!"

"Ohuh?"

She looked around bovinely. Her hair stuck to her cheeks in a curving helmet shape. There was a cluster of acne on one shoulder. At sixteen, the elusive stamp of hurt was already marked clearly in her eyes.

"She thinks they're for lipstick!" Ruth Gogan suddenly shouted with cryptic glee, and then burst into a shriek of laughter. Sue remembered the comment later and fitted it into a general picture, but now it was only another senseless sound in the confusion. *Sixteen?* She was thinking. *She must know what's happening, she—*

More droplets of blood. Carrie still blinked around at her classmates in slow bewilderment.

Helen Shyres turned around and made mock throwing-up gestures.

"You're *bleeding!*" Sue yelled suddenly, furiously. "You're *bleeding,* you big dumb pudding!"

Carrie looked down at herself.

She shrieked.

The sound was very loud in the humid locker room.

A tampon suddenly struck her in the chest and fell with a plop at her feet. A red flower stained the absorbent cotton and spread.

Then the laughter, disgusted, contemptuous, horrified, seemed to rise and bloom into something jagged and ugly, and the girls were bombarding her with tampons and sanitary napkins, some from purses, some from the broken dispenser on the wall. They flew like snow and the chant became: "Plug it *up*, plug it *up*, plug it *up*, plug it—"

Sue was throwing them too, throwing and chanting with the rest, not really sure what she was doing—a charm had occurred to her mind and it glowed there like neon: *There's no harm in it really no harm in it really no harm—* It was still flashing and glowing, reassuringly, when Carrie suddenly began to howl and back away, flailing her arms and grunting and gobbling.

The girls stopped, realizing that fission and explosion had finally been reached. It was at this point, when looking back, that some of them would claim surprise. Yet there had been all these years, all these years of let's short-sheet Carrie's bed at Christian Youth Camp and I found this love letter from Carrie to Flash Bobby Pickett let's copy it and pass it around and hide her underpants somewhere and put this snake in her shoe and duck her *again,* duck her *again;* Carrie tagging along stubbornly on biking trips, known one year as pudd'n and the next year as truck-face, always smelling sweaty, not able to catch up; catching poison ivy from urinating in the bushes and everyone finding out (hey, scratch-ass, your bum itch?); Billy Preston putting peanut butter in her hair that time she fell asleep in study hall; the pinches, the legs outstretched in school aisles to trip her up, the books knocked from her desk, the obscene postcard tucked into her purse; Carrie on the church picnic and kneeling down clumsily to pray and the seam of her old madras skirt splitting along the zipper like the sound of a huge wind-breakage; Carrie always missing the ball, even in kickball, falling on her face in Modern Dance during their sophomore year and chipping a tooth, running into the net during volleyball; wearing stockings that were always run, running, or about to run, always showing sweat stains under the arms of her blouses; even the time Chris Hargensen called up after school from the Kelly Fruit Company downtown and asked her if she knew that *pig poop* was spelled C-A-R-R-I-E: Suddenly all this and the critical mass was reached. The ultimate shit-on, gross-out, put-down, long searched for, was found. Fission.

She backed away, howling in the new silence, fat forearms crossing her face, a tampon stuck in the middle of her pubic hair.

The girls watched her, their eyes shining solemnly.

Carrie backed into the side of one of the four large shower compartments and slowly collapsed into a sitting position. Slow, helpless groans jerked out of her. Her eyes rolled with wet whiteness, like the eyes of a hog in the slaughtering pen.

Sue said slowly, hesitantly: "I think this must be the first time she ever—"

That was when the door pumped open with a flat and hurried bang and Miss Desjardin burst in to see what the matter was.

From *The Shadow Exploded* (p. 41):

Both medical and psychological writers on the subject are in agreement that Carrie White's exceptionally late and traumatic commencement of the menstrual cycle might well have provided the trigger for her latent talent.

It seems incredible that, as late as 1979, Carrie knew nothing of the mature woman's monthly cycle. It is nearly as incredible to believe that the girl's mother would permit her daughter to reach the age of nearly seventeen without consulting a gynecologist concerning the daughter's failure to menstruate.

Yet the facts are incontrovertible. When Carrie White realized she was bleeding from the vaginal opening, she had no idea of what was taking place. She was innocent of the entire concept of menstruation.

One of her surviving classmates, Ruth Gogan, tells of entering the girls' locker room at Ewen High School the year before the events we are concerned with and seeing Carrie using a tampon to blot her lipstick with. At that time Miss Gogan said: "What the hell are you up to?" Miss White replied: "Isn't this right?" Miss Gogan then replied: "Sure. Sure it is." Ruth Gogan let a number of her girl friends in on this (she later told this interviewer she thought it was "sorta cute"), and if anyone tried in the future to inform Carrie of the true purpose of what she was using to make up with, she apparently dismissed the explanation as an attempt to pull her leg. This was a facet of her life that she had become exceedingly wary of. . . .

When the girls were gone to their Period Two classes and the bell had been silenced (several of them had slipped quietly out the back door before Miss Desjardin could begin to take names), Miss Desjardin employed the standard tactic for hysterics: She slapped Carrie smartly across the face. She hardly would have admitted the pleasure the act gave her, and she certainly would have denied that she regarded Carrie as a fat, whiny bag of lard. A first-year teacher, she still believed that she thought all children were good.

Carrie looked up at her dumbly, face still contorted and working. "M-M-Miss D-D-Des-D—"

"Get up," Miss Desjardin said dispassionately. "Get up and tend to yourself."

"I'm bleeding to death!" Carrie screamed, and one blind, searching hand came up and clutched Miss Desjardin's white shorts. It left a bloody handprint.

"I . . . you . . ." The gym teacher's face contorted into a pucker of disgust, and she suddenly hurled Carrie, stumbling, to her feet. *"Get over there!"*

Carrie stood swaying between the showers and the wall with its dime sanitary-napkin dispenser, slumped over, breasts pointing at the floor, her arms dangling limply. She looked like an ape. Her eyes were shiny and blank.

"Now," Miss Desjardin said with hissing, deadly emphasis, "you take one of those napkins out . . . no, never mind the coin slot, it's broken anyway . . . take one and . . . damn it, will you *do* it! You act as if you never had a period before."

"Period?" Carrie said.

Her expression of complete unbelief was too genuine, too full of dumb and hopeless horror, to be ignored or denied. A terrible and black foreknowledge grew in Rita Desjardin's mind. It was incredible, could not be. She herself had begun menstruation shortly after her eleventh birthday and had gone to the head of the stairs to yell down excitedly: "Hey, Mum, I'm on the rag!"

"Carrie?" she said now. She advanced toward the girl. "Carrie?"

Carrie flinched away. At the same instant, a rack of softball bats in the corner fell over with a large, echoing bang. They rolled every which way, making Desjardin jump.

"Carrie, is this your first period?"

But now that the thought had been admitted, she hardly had to ask. The blood was dark and flowing with terrible heaviness. Both of Carrie's legs were smeared and splattered with it, as though she had waded through a river of blood.

"It hurts," Carrie groaned. "My stomach . . ."

"That passes," Miss Desjardin said. Pity and self-shame met in her and mixed uneasily. "You have to . . . uh, stop the flow of blood. You—"

There was a bright flash overhead, followed by a flashgun-like pop as a lightbulb sizzled and went out. Miss Desjardin cried out with surprise, and it occurred to her

(the whole damn place is falling in)

that this kind of thing always seemed to happen around Carrie when she was upset, as if bad luck dogged her every step. The thought was gone almost as quickly as it had come. She took one of the sanitary napkins from the broken dispenser and unwrapped it.

"Look," she said. "Like this—"

From *The Shadow Exploded* (p. 54):

Carrie White's mother, Margaret White, gave birth to her daughter on September 21, 1963, under circumstances which can only be termed bizarre. In fact, an overview of the Carrie White case leaves the careful student with one feeling ascendent over all others: that Carrie was the only issue of a family as odd as any that has ever been brought to popular attention.

As noted earlier, Ralph White died in February of 1963 when a steel girder fell out of a carrying sling on a housing-project job in Portland. Mrs. White continued to live alone in their suburban Chamberlain bungalow.

Due to the Whites' near-fanatical fundamentalist religious beliefs, Mrs. White had no friends to see her through her period of bereavement. And when her labor began seven months later, she was alone.

At approximately 1:30 P.M. on September 21, the neighbors on Carlin Street began to hear screams from the White bungalow. The police, however, were not summoned to the scene until after 6:00 P.M. We are left with two unappetizing alternatives to explain this time lag: Either Mrs. White's neighbors on the street did not wish to become involved in a police investigation, or dislike for her had become so strong that they deliberately adopted a wait-and-see attitude. Mrs. Georgia McLaughlin, the only one of three remaining residents who were on the street at that time and who would talk to me, said that she did not call the police because she thought the screams had something to do with "holy rollin'."

When the police did arrive at 6:22 P.M. the screams had become irregular. Mrs. White was found in her bed upstairs, and the investigating officer, Thomas G. Mearton, at first thought she had been the victim of an assault. The bed was drenched with blood, and a butcher knife lay on the floor. It was only then that he saw the baby, still partially wrapped in the placental membrane, at Mrs. White's breast. She had apparently cut the umbilical cord herself with the knife.

It staggers both imagination and belief to advance the hypothesis that Mrs. Margaret White did not know she was pregnant, or even understand what the word entails, and recent scholars such as J. W. Bankson and George Fielding have made a more reasonable case for the hypothesis that the concept, linked irrevocably in her mind with the "sin" of intercourse, had been blocked entirely from her mind. She may simply have refused to believe that such a thing could happen to her.

We have records of at least three letters to a friend in Kenosha, Wisconsin, that seem to prove conclusively that Mrs. White believed, from her fifth month on, that she had "a cancer of the womanly parts" and would soon join her husband in heaven. . . .

When Miss Desjardin led Carrie up to the office fifteen minutes later, the halls were mercifully empty. Classes droned onward behind closed doors.

Carrie's shrieks had finally ended, but she had continued to weep with steady regularity. Desjardin had finally placed the napkin herself, cleaned the girl up with wet paper towels, and gotten her back into her plain cotton underpants.

She tried twice to explain the commonplace reality of menstruation, but Carrie clapped her hands over her ears and continued to cry.

Mr. Morton, the assistant principal, was out of his office in a flash when they entered. Billy deLois and Henry Trennant, two boys waiting for the lecture due them for cutting French I, goggled around from their chairs.

"Come in," Mr. Morton said briskly. "Come right in." He glared over Desjardin's shoulder at the boys, who were staring at the bloody handprint on her shorts. "What are *you* looking at?"

"Blood," Henry said, and smiled with a kind of vacuous surprise.

"Two detention periods," Morton snapped. He glanced down at the bloody handprint and blinked.

He closed the door behind them and began pawing through the top drawer of his filing cabinet for a school accident form.

"Are you all right, uh—"

"Carrie," Desjardin supplied. "Carrie White." Mr. Morton had finally located an accident form. There was a large coffee stain on it. "You won't need that, Mr. Morton."

"I suppose it was the trampoline. We just . . . I won't?"

"No. But I think Carrie should be allowed to go home for the rest of the day. She's had a rather frightening experience." Her eyes flashed a signal which he caught but could not interpret.

"Yes, okay, if you say so. Good. Fine." Morton crumpled the form back into the filing cabinet, slammed it shut with his thumb in the drawer, and grunted. He whirled gracefully to the door, yanked it open, glared at Billy and Henry, and called: "Miss Fish, could we have a dismissal slip here, please? Carrie Wright."

"White," said Miss Desjardin.

"White," Morton agreed.

Billy deLois sniggered.

"Week's detention!" Morton barked. A blood blister was forming under his thumbnail. Hurt like hell. Carrie's steady, monotonous weeping went on and on.

Miss Fish brought the yellow dismissal slip and Morton scrawled his initials on it with his silver pocket pencil, wincing at the pressure on his wounded thumb.

"Do you need a ride, Cassie?" he asked. "We can call a cab if you need one."

She shook her head. He noticed with distaste that a large bubble of green mucus had formed at one nostril. Morton looked over her head and at Miss Desjardin.

"I'm sure she'll be all right," she said. "Carrie only has to go over to Carlin Street. The fresh air will do her good."

Morton gave the girl the yellow slip. "You can go now, Cassie," he said magnanimously.

"That's not my name!" she screamed suddenly.

Morton recoiled, and Miss Desjardin jumped as if struck from behind. The heavy ceramic ashtray on Morton's desk (it was Rodin's *Thinker* with his head turned into a receptacle for cigarette butts) suddenly toppled to the rug, as if to take cover from the force of her scream. Butts and flakes of Morton's pipe tobacco scattered on the pale-green nylon rug.

"Now, listen," Morton said, trying to muster sternness. "I know you're upset, but that doesn't mean I'll stand for—"

"Please," Miss Desjardin said quietly.

Morton blinked at her and then nodded curtly. He tried to project the image of a lovable John Wayne figure while performing the disciplinary functions that were his main job as Assistant Principal, but did not succeed very well. The administration (usually represented at Jay Cee suppers, P.T.A. functions, and American Legion award ceremonies by Principal Henry Grayle) usually termed him "lovable Mort." The student body was more apt to term him "that crazy ass-jabber from the office." But, as few students such as Billy deLois and Henry Trennant spoke at P.T.A. functions or town meetings, the administration's view tended to carry the day.

Now lovable Mort, still secretly nursing his jammed thumb, smiled at Carrie and said, "Go along then if you like, Miss Wright. Or would you like to sit a spell and just collect yourself?"

"I'll go," she muttered, and swiped at her hair. She got up, then looked around at Miss Desjardin. Her eyes were wide open and dark with knowledge. "They laughed at me. Threw things. They've *always* laughed."

Desjardin could only look at her helplessly.

Carrie left.

For a moment there was silence; Morton and Desjardin watched her go. Then, with an awkward throat-clearing sound, Mr. Morton hunkered down carefully and began to sweep together the debris from the fallen ashtray.

"What was *that* all about?"

She sighed and looked at the drying maroon handprint on her shorts with distaste. "She got her period. Her first period. In the shower."

Morton cleared his throat again and his cheeks went pink. The sheet of paper he was sweeping with moved even faster. "Isn't she a bit, uh—"

"Old for her first? Yes. That's what made it so traumatic for her. Although I can't understand why her mother . . ." The thought trailed off, forgotten for the moment. "I don't think I handled it very well, Morty, but I didn't understand what was going on. She thought she was bleeding to death."

He stared up sharply.

"I don't believe she knew there was such a thing as menstruation until half an hour ago."

"Hand me that little brush there, Miss Desjardin. Yes, that's it." She handed him a little brush with the legend *Chamberlain Hardware and Lumber Company NEVER Brushes You Off* written up the handle. He began to brush his pile of ashes onto the paper. "There's still going to be some for the vacuum cleaner, I guess. This deep pile is miserable. I thought I set that ashtray back on the desk further. Funny how things fall over." He bumped his head on the desk and sat up abruptly. "It's hard for me to believe that a girl in this or any other high school could get through three years and still be alien to the fact of menstruation, Miss Desjardin."

"It's even more difficult for me," she said. "But it's all I can think of to explain her reaction. And she's always been a group scapegoat."

"Um." He funneled the ashes and butts into the wastebasket and dusted his hands. "I've placed her, I think. White. Margaret White's daughter. Must be. That makes it a little easier to believe." He sat down behind his desk and smiled apologetically. "There's so many of them. After five years or so, they all start to merge into one group face. You call boys by their brother's names, that type of thing. It's hard."

"Of course it is."

"Wait 'til you've been in the game twenty years, like me," he said morosely, looking down at his blood blister. "You get kids that look familiar and find out you had their daddy the year you started teaching. Margaret White was before my time, for which I am profoundly grateful. She told Mrs. Bicente, God rest her, that the Lord was reserving a special burning seat in hell for her because she gave the kids an outline of Mr. Darwin's beliefs on evolution. She was suspended twice while she was here—once for beating a classmate with her purse. Legend has it that Margaret saw the classmate smoking a cigarette. Peculiar religious views. Very peculiar." His John Wayne expression suddenly snapped down. "The other girls. Did they really laugh at her?"

"Worse. They were yelling and throwing sanitary napkins at her when I walked in. Throwing them like . . . like peanuts."

"Oh. Oh, dear." John Wayne disappeared. Mr. Morton went scarlet. "You have names?"

"Yes. Not all of them, although some of them may rat on the rest. Christine Hargensen appeared to be the ringleader . . . as usual."

"Chris and her Mortimer Snerds," Morton murmured.

"Yes. Tina Blake, Rachel Spies, Helen Shyres, Donna Thibodeau and her sister Mary Lila Grace, Jessica Upshaw. And Sue Snell." She frowned. "You wouldn't expect a trick like that from Sue. She's never seemed the type for this kind of a—a stunt."

"Did you talk to the girls involved?"

Miss Desjardin chuckled unhappily. "I got them the hell out of there. I was too flustered. And Carrie was having hysterics."

"Um." He steepled his fingers. "Do you plan to talk to them?"

"Yes." But she sounded reluctant.

"Do I detect a note of—"

"You probably do," she said glumly. "I'm living in a glass house, see. I understand how those girls felt. The whole thing just made me want to take the girl and *shake* her. Maybe there's some kind of instinct about menstruation that makes women want to snarl, I don't know. I keep seeing Sue Snell and the way she looked."

"Um," Mr. Morton repeated wisely. He did not understand women and had no urge at all to discuss menstruation.

"I'll talk to them tomorrow," she promised, rising. "Rip them down one side and up the other."

"Good. Make the punishment suit the crime. And if you feel you have to send any of them to, ah, to me, feel free—"

"I will," she said kindly. "By the way, a light blew out while I was trying to calm her down. It added the final touch."

"I'll send a janitor right down," he promised. "And thanks for doing your best, Miss Desjardin. Will you have Miss Fish send in Billy and Henry?"

"Certainly." She left.

He leaned back and let the whole business slide out of his mind. When Billy deLois and Henry Trennant, class-cutters *extraordinaire,* slunk in, he glowered at them happily and prepared to talk tough.

As he often told Hank Grayle, he ate class-cutters for lunch.

Graffiti scratched on a desk in Chamberlain Junior High School:
   Roses are red, violets are blue, sugar is sweet, but Carrie White eats shit.

She walked down Ewen Avenue and crossed over to Carlin at the stoplight on the corner. Her head was down and she was trying to think of nothing. Cramps came and went in great, gripping waves, making her slow down and speed up like a car with carburetor trouble. She stared at the sidewalk. Quartz glittering in the cement. Hopscotch grids scratched in ghostly, rain-faded chalk. Wads of gum stamped flat. Pieces of tinfoil and penny-candy wrappers. *They all hate and they never stop. They never get tired of it.* A penny lodged in a crack. She kicked it. *Imagine Chris Hargensen all bloody and screaming for mercy. With rats crawling all over her face. Good. Good. That would be good. A* dog turd with a foot-track in the middle of it. A roll of black-ened caps that some kid had banged with a stone. Cigarette butts. *Crash in her head with a rock, with a boulder. Crash in all their heads. Good. Good.*

(saviour jesus meek and mild)

That was good for Momma, all right for her. She didn't have to go among the wolves every day of every year, out into a carnival of laughers, joke-tellers, pointers, snickerers. And didn't Momma say there would be a Day of Judgment

(the name of that star shall be wormwood and they shall be scourged with scorpions)

and an angel with a sword?

If only it would be today and Jesus coming not with a lamb and a shepherd's crook, but with a boulder in each hand to crush the laughers and the snickerers, to root out the evil and destroy it screaming—a terrible Jesus of blood and righteousness.

And if only she could be His sword and His arm.

She had tried to fit. She had defied Momma in a hundred little ways, had tried to erase the red-plague circle that had been drawn around her from the first day she had left the controlled environment of the small house on Carlin Street and had walked up to the Barker Street Grammar School with her Bible under her arm. She could still remember that day, the stares, and the sudden, awful silence when she had gotten down on her knees before lunch in the school cafeteria—the laughter had begun on that day and had echoed up through the years.

The red-plague circle was like blood itself—you could scrub and scrub and scrub and still it would be there, not erased, not clean. She had never gotten on her knees in a public place again, although she had not told Momma that. Still, the original memory remained, with her and with *them.* She had fought Momma tooth and nail over the Christian Youth Camp, and had earned the money to go herself by taking in sewing. Momma told her darkly that it was Sin, that it was Methodists and Baptists and Congregationalists and that it was Sin and Back-sliding. She forbade Carrie to swim at the camp. Yet although she *had* swum and *had* laughed when they ducked her (until she couldn't get her breath any more and they kept doing it and she got panicky and began to scream) and had tried to take part in the camp's activities, a thousand practical jokes had been played on ol' prayin' Carrie and she had come home on the bus a week early, her eyes red and socketed from weeping, to be picked up by Momma at the station, and Momma had told her grimly that she should treasure the memory of her scourging as proof that Momma knew, that Momma was right, that the only hope of safety and salvation was inside the red circle. "For strait is the gate," Momma said grimly in the taxi, and at home she had sent Carrie to the closet for six hours.

Momma had, of course, forbade her to shower with the other girls; Carrie had hidden her shower things in her school locker and had showered anyway, taking part in a naked ritual that was shameful and embarrassing to her in hopes that the circle around her might fade a little, just a little—

(but today o today)

Tommy Erbter, age five, was biking up the other side of the street. He was a small, intense-looking boy on a twenty-inch Schwinn with bright-red training wheels. He was humming "Scoobie Doo, where are you?" under his breath. He saw Carrie, brightened, and stuck out his tongue.

"Hey, ol' fart-face! Ol' prayin' Carrie!"

Carrie glared at him with sudden smoking rage. The bike wobbled on its training wheels and suddenly fell over. Tommy screamed. The bike was on top of him. Carrie smiled and walked on. The sound of Tommy's wails was sweet, jangling music in her ears.

If only she could make something like that happen whenever she liked.

(just did)

She stopped dead seven houses up from her own, staring blankly at nothing. Behind her, Tommy was climbing tearfully back onto his bike, nursing a scraped knee. He yelled something at her, but she ignored it. She had been yelled at by experts.

She had been thinking:

(fall off that bike kid push you off that bike and split your rotten head) and something had *happened*.

Her mind had ... had ... she groped for a word. Had *flexed*. That was not just right, but it was very close. There had been a curious mental bending, almost like an elbow curling a dumbbell. That wasn't exactly right either, but it was all she could think of. An elbow with no strength. A weak baby muscle.

Flex.

She suddenly stared fiercely at Mrs. Yorraty's big picture window. She thought:

(stupid frumpy old bitch break that window)

Nothing. Mrs. Yorraty's picture window glittered serenely in the fresh nine o'clock glow of morning. Another cramp gripped Carrie's belly and she walked on.

But . . .

The light. And the ashtray; don't forget the ashtray.

She looked back

(old bitch hates my momma)

over her shoulder. Again it seemed that something flexed . . . but very weakly. The flow of her thoughts shuddered as if there had been a sudden bubbling from a wellspring deeper inside.

The picture window seemed to ripple. Nothing more. It could have been her eyes. *Could* have been.

Her head began to feel tired and fuzzy, and it throbbed with the beginning of a headache. Her eyes were hot, as if she had just sat down and read the Book of Revelations straight through.

She continued to walk down the street toward the small white house with the blue shutters. The familiar hate-love-dread feeling was churning inside her. Ivy had crawled up the west side of the bungalow (they always called it the bungalow because the White house sounded like a political joke and Momma said all politicians were crooks and sinners and would eventually give the country over to the Godless Reds who would put all the believers of Jesus—even the Catholics—up against the wall), and the ivy was picturesque, she *knew* it was, but sometimes she hated it. Sometimes, like now, the ivy looked like a grotesque giant hand ridged with great veins which had sprung up out of the ground to grip the building. She approached it with dragging feet.

Of course, there had been the stones.

She stopped again, blinking vapidly at the day. The stones. Momma never talked about that; Carrie didn't even know if her momma still remembered the day of the stones. It was surprising that she herself still remembered it. She had been a very little girl then. How old? Three? Four? There had been that girl in the white bathing suit, and then the stones came. And things had flown in the house. Here the memory was, suddenly bright and clear. As if it had been here all along, just below the surface, waiting for a kind of mental puberty.

Waiting, maybe, for today.

From *Carrie: The Black Dawn of T.K. (Esquire* magazine, September 12, 1980) by Jack Gaver:

Estelle Horan has lived in the neat San Diego suburb of Parrish for twelve years, and outwardly she is typical Ms. California: She wears bright print shifts and smoked amber sunglasses; her hair is black-streaked blonde; she drives a neat maroon Volkswagen Formula Vee with a smile decal on the gas cap and a green-flag ecology sticker on the back window. Her husband is an executive at the Parrish branch of the Bank of America; her son and daughter are certified members of the Southern California Sun 'n Fun Crowd, burnished-brown beach creatures. There is a hibachi in the small, beautifully kept back yard, and the door chimes play a tinkly phrase from the refrain of "Hey, Jude."

But Ms. Horan still carries the thin, difficult soil of New England somewhere inside her, and when she talks of Carrie White her face takes on an odd, pinched look that is more like Lovecraft out of Arkham than Kerouac out of Southern Cal.

"Of course she was strange," Estelle Horan tells me, lighting a second Virginia Slim a moment after stubbing out her first. "The whole family was strange. Ralph was a construction worker, and people on the street said he carried a Bible and a .38 revolver to work with him every day. The Bible was for his coffee break and lunch. The .38 was in case he met Antichrist on the job. I can remember the Bible myself. The revolver . . . who knows? He was a big olive-skinned man with his hair always shaved into a flattop crewcut. He always looked mean. And you didn't meet his eyes, not ever. They were so intense they actually seemed to glow. When you saw him coming you crossed the street and you never stuck out your tongue at his back, not ever. That's how spooky *he* was."

She pauses, puffing clouds of cigarette smoke toward the pseudo-redwood beams that cross the ceiling. Stella Horan lived on Carlin Street until she was twenty, commuting to day classes at Lewin Business College in Motton. But she remembers the incident of the stones very clearly.

"There are times," she says, "when I wonder if I might have caused it. Their back yard was next to ours, and Mrs. White had put in a hedge but it hadn't grown out yet. She'd called my mother dozens of times about 'the show' I was putting on in my back yard. Well, my bathing suit was perfectly decent—prudish by today's standards—nothing but a plain old one-piece Jantzen. Mrs. White used to go on and on about what a scandal it was for 'her baby.' My mother . . . well, she tries to be polite, but her temper is *so* quick. I don't know what Margaret White said to finally push her over the edge—called me the Whore of Babylon, I suppose—but my mother told her our yard was our yard and I'd go out and dance the hootchie-kootchie buck naked if that was her pleasure and mine. She also told her that she was a dirty old woman with a can of worms for a mind. There was a lot more shouting, but that was the upshot of it.

"I wanted to stop sunbathing right then. I hate trouble. It upsets my stomach. But Mom—when she gets a case, she's a terror. She came home from Jordan Marsh with a little white bikini. Told me I might as well get all the sun I could. 'After all,' she said, 'the privacy of our own back yard and all.' "

Stella Horan smiles a little at the memory and crushes out her cigarette.

"I tried to argue with her, tell her I didn't want any more trouble, didn't want to be a pawn in their back-fence war. Didn't do a bit of good. Trying to stop my mom when she gets a bee in her hat is like trying to stop a Mack truck going downhill with no brakes. Actually, there was more to it. I was scared of the Whites. Real religious nuts are nothing to fool with. Sure, Ralph White was dead, but what if Margaret still had that .38 around?

"But there I was on Saturday afternoon, spread out on a blanket in the back yard, covered with suntan lotion and listening to Top Forty on the radio. Mom hated that stuff and usually she'd yell out at least twice for me to turn it down before she went nuts. But that day she turned it up twice herself. I started to feel like the Whore of Babylon myself.

"But nobody came out of the Whites' place. Not even the old lady to hang her wash. That's something else—she never hung any undies on the back line. Not even Carrie's, and she was only three back then. Always in the house.

"I started to relax. I guess I was thinking Margaret must have taken Carrie to the park to worship God in the raw or something. Anyway, after a little while I rolled on my back, put one arm over my eyes, and dozed off.

"When I woke up, Carrie was standing next to me and looking down at my body."

She breaks off, frowning into space. Outside, the cars are whizzing by endlessly. I can hear the steady little whine my tape recorder makes. But it all seems a little too brittle, too glossy, just a cheap patina over a darker world—a real world where nightmares happen.

"She was such a *pretty* girl," Stella Horan resumes, lighting another cigarette. "I've seen some high school pictures of her, and that horrible fuzzy black-and-white photo on the cover of *Newsweek.* I look at them and all I can think is, Dear God, where did she go? What did that woman do to her? Then I feel sick and sorry. She was so pretty, with pink cheeks and bright brown eyes, and her hair the shade of blonde you know will darken and get mousy. Sweet is the only word that fits. Sweet and bright and innocent. Her mother's sickness hadn't touched her very deeply, not then.

"I kind of started up awake and tried to smile. It was hard to think what to do. I was logy from the sun and my mind felt sticky and slow. I said 'Hi.' She was wearing a little yellow dress, sort of cute but awfully long for a little girl in the summer. It came down to her shins.

"She didn't smile back. She just pointed and said, 'What are those?'

"I looked down and saw that my top had slipped while I was asleep. So I fixed it and said, 'Those are my breasts, Carrie.'

"Then she said—very solemnly: 'I wish I had some.'

"I said: 'You have to wait, Carrie. You won't start to get them for another . . . oh, eight or nine years.'

" 'No, I won't,' she said. 'Momma says good girls don't.' She looked strange for a little girl, half sad and half self-righteous.

"I could hardly believe it, and the first thing that popped into my mind also popped right out my mouth. I said: 'Well, I'm a good girl. And doesn't your mother have breasts?'

"She lowered her head and said something so softly I couldn't hear it. When I asked her to repeat it, she looked at me defiantly and said that her momma had been bad when she made her and that was why she had them. She called them dirtypillows, as if it was all one word.

"I couldn't believe it. I was just dumbfounded. There was nothing at all I could think to say. We just stared at each other, and what I wanted to do was grab that sad little scrap of a girl and run away with her.

"And that was when Margaret White came out of her back door and saw us.

"For a minute she just goggled as if she couldn't believe it. Then she opened her mouth and whooped. That's the ugliest sound I've ever heard in my life. It was like the noise a bull alligator would make in a swamp. She just *whooped*. Rage. Complete, insane rage. Her face went just as red as the side of a fire truck and she curled her hands into fists and whooped at the sky. She was shaking all over. I thought she was having a stroke. Her face was all scrunched up, and it was a gargoyle's face.

"I thought Carrie was going to faint—or die on the spot. She sucked in all her breath and that little face went a cottage-cheesy color.

"Her mother yelled: 'CAAAARRRIEEEEEE!'

"I jumped up and yelled back: 'Don't you yell at her that way! You ought to be ashamed!' Something stupid like that. I don't remember. Carrie started to go back and then she stopped and then she started again, and just before she crossed over from our lawn to theirs she looked back at me and there was a look . . . oh, dreadful. I can't say it. Wanting and hating and fearing . . . and *misery*. As if life itself had fallen on her like stones, all at the age of three.

"My mother came out on the back stoop and her face just crumpled when she saw the child. And Margaret . . . oh, she was screaming things about sluts and strumpets and the sins of the fathers being visited even unto the seventh generation. My tongue felt like a little dried-up plant.

"For just a second Carrie stood swaying back and forth between the two yards, and then Margaret White looked upward and I swear sweet Jesus that woman *bayed* at the sky. And then she started to . . . to hurt herself, scourge herself. She was clawing at her neck and cheeks, making red marks and scratches. She tore her dress.

"Carrie screamed out 'Momma!' and ran to her.

"Mrs. White kind of . . . squatted, like a frog, and her arms swooped wide open. I thought she was going to crush her and I screamed. The woman was grinning. Grinning and drooling right down her chin. Oh, I was sick. Jesus, I was so sick.

"She gathered her up and they went in. I turned off my radio and I could hear her. Some of the words, but not all. You didn't have to hear all the words to know what was going on. Praying and sobbing and screeching. Crazy sounds. And Margaret telling the little girl to get herself into her closet and pray. The little girl crying and screaming that she was sorry, she forgot. Then nothing. And my mother and I just looked at each other. I never saw Mom look so bad, not even when Dad died. She said: 'The child—' and that was all. We went inside."

She gets up and goes to the window, a pretty woman in a yellow no-back sundress. "It's almost like living it all over again, you know," she says, not turning around. "I'm all riled up inside again." She laughs a little and cradles her elbows in her palms.

"Oh, she was so pretty. You'd never know from those pictures."

Cars go by outside, back and forth, and I sit and wait for her to go on. She reminds me of a pole-vaulter eyeing the bar and wondering if it's set too high.

"My mother brewed us scotch tea, strong, with milk, the way she used to when I was tomboying around and someone would push me in the nettle patch or I'd fall off my bicycle. It was awful but we drank it anyway, sitting across from each other in the kitchen nook. She was in some old housedress with the hem falling down in back, and I was in my Whore of Babylon two-piece swimsuit. I wanted to cry but it was too real to cry about, not like the movies. Once when I was in New York I saw an old drunk leading a little girl in a blue dress by the hand. The girl had cried herself into a bloody nose. The drunk had goiter and his neck looked like an inner tube. There was a red bump in the middle of his forehead and a long white string on the blue serge jacket he was wearing. Everyone kept going and coming because, if you did, then pretty soon you wouldn't see them any more. That was real, too.

"I wanted to tell my mother that, and I was just opening my mouth to say it when the other thing happened . . . the thing you want to hear about, I guess. There was a big thump outside that made the glasses rattle in the china cabinet. It was a feeling as well as a sound, thick and solid, as if someone had just pushed an iron safe off the roof."

She lights a new cigarette and begins to puff rapidly.

"I went to the window and looked out, but I couldn't see anything. Then, when I was getting ready to turn around, something else fell. The sun glittered on it. I thought it was a big glass globe for a second. Then it hit the edge of the Whites' roof and shattered, and it wasn't glass at all. It was a big chunk of ice. I was going to turn around and tell Mom, and that's when they started to fall all at once, in a shower.

"They were falling on the Whites' roof, on the back and front lawn, on the outside door to their cellar. That was a sheet-tin bulkhead, and when the first one hit it made a huge *bong* noise, like a church bell. My mother and I both screamed. We were clutching each other like a couple of girls in a thunderstorm.

"Then it stopped. There was no sound at all from their house. You could see the water from the melting ice trickling down their slate shingles in the sunshine. A great big hunk of ice was stuck in the angle of the roof and their little chimney. The light on it was so bright that my eyes hurt to look at it.

"My mother started to ask me if it was over, and then Margaret screamed. The sound came to us very clearly. In a way it was worse than before, because there was terror in this one. Then there were clanging, banging sounds, as if she was throwing every pot and pan in the house at the girl.

"The back door slammed open and slammed closed. No one came out. More screams. Mom said for me to call the police but I couldn't move. I was stuck to the spot. Mr. Kirk and his wife Virginia came out on their lawn to look. The Smiths, too. Pretty soon everyone on the street that was home had come out, even old Mrs. Warwick from up the block, and she was deaf in one ear.

"Things started to crash and tinkle and break. Bottles, glasses, I don't know what all. And then the side window broke open and the kitchen table fell halfway through. With God as my witness. It was a big mahogany thing and it took the screen with it and it must have weighed three hundred pounds. How could a woman—even a big woman—throw that?"

I ask her if she is implying something.

"I'm only *telling* you," she insists, suddenly distraught. "I'm not asking you to believe—"

She seems to catch her breath and then goes on flatly:

"There was nothing for maybe five minutes. Water was dripping out of the gutters over there. And there was ice all over the Whites' lawn. It was melting fast."

She gives a short, chopping laugh and butts her cigarette.

"Why not? It *was* August."

She wanders aimlessly back toward the sofa, then veers away. "Then the stones. Right out of the blue, blue sky. Whistling and screaming like bombs. My mother cried out, 'What, in the name of God!' and put her hands over her head. But I couldn't move. I watched it all and I couldn't move. It didn't matter anyway. They only fell on the Whites' property.

"One of them hit a downspout and knocked it onto the lawn. Others punched holes right through the roof and into the attic. The roof made a big cracking sound each time one hit, and puffs of dust would squirt up. The ones that hit the ground made everything vibrate. You could feel them hitting in your feet.

"Our china was tinkling and the fancy Welsh dresser was shaking and Mom's teacup fell on the floor and broke.

"They made big pits in the Whites' back lawn when they struck. Craters. Mrs. White hired a junkman from across town to cart them away, and Jerry Smith from up the street paid him a buck to let him chip a piece off one. He took it to B.U. and they looked at it and said it was ordinary granite.

"One of the last ones hit a little table they had in their back yard and smashed it to pieces.

"But nothing, nothing that wasn't on their property was hit."

She stops and turns from the window to look at me, and her face is haggard from remembering all that. One hand plays forgetfully with her casually stylish shag haircut. "Not much of it got into the local paper. By the time Billy Harris came around—he reported the Chamberlain news—she had already gotten the roof fixed, and when people told him the stones had gone right through it, I think he thought we were all pulling his leg.

"Nobody wants to believe it, not even now. You and all the people who'll read what you write will wish they could laugh it off and call me just another nut who's been out here in the sun too long. But it *happened.* There were lots of people on the block who *saw* it happen, and it was just as real as that drunk leading the little girl with the bloody nose. And now there's this other thing. No one can laugh that off, either. Too many people are dead.

"And it's not just on the White's property any more."

She smiles, but there's not a drop of humor in it. She says: "Ralph White was insured, and Margaret got a lot of money when he died . . . double indemnity. He left the house insured, too, but she never got a penny of that. The damage was caused by an act of God. Poetic justice, huh?"

She laughs a little, but there's no humor in that, either. . . .

Found written repeatedly on one page of a Ewen Consolidated High School notebook owned by Carrie White:

*Everybody's guessed/that baby can't be blessed/'til she finally sees that she's like all the rest. . . .**

Carrie went into the house and closed the door behind her. Bright daylight disappeared and was replaced by brown shad-

* Lyrics from JUST LIKE A WOMAN by Bob Dylan. Copyright © 1966 Dwarf Music. Used by permission of Dwarf Music.

ows, coolness, and the oppressive smell of talcum powder. The only sound was the ticking of the Black Forest cuckoo clock in the living room. Momma had gotten the cuckoo clock with Green Stamps. Once, in the sixth grade, Carrie had set out to ask Momma if Green Stamps weren't sinful, but her nerve had failed her.

She walked up the hall and put her coat in the closet. A luminous picture above the coathooks limned a ghostly Jesus hovering grimly over a family seated at the kitchen table. Beneath was the caption (also luminous): *The Unseen Guest.*

She went into the living room and stood in the middle of the faded, starting-to-be-threadbare rug. She closed her eyes and watched the little dots flash by in the darkness. Her headache thumped queasily behind her temples.

Alone.

Momma worked on the speed ironer and folder down at the Blue Ribbon Laundry in Chamberlain Center. She had worked there since Carrie was five, when the compensation and insurance that had resulted from her father's accident had begun to run out. Her hours were from seven-thirty in the morning until four in the afternoon. The laundry was Godless. Momma had told her so many times. The foreman, Mr. Elton Mott, was especially Godless. Momma said that Satan had reserved a special blue corner of Hell for Elt, as he was called at the Blue Ribbon.

Alone.

She opened her eyes. The living room contained two chairs with straight backs. There was a sewing table with a light where Carrie sometimes made dresses in the evening while Momma tatted doilies and talked about The Coming. The Black Forest cuckoo clock was on the far wall.

There were many religious pictures, but the one Carrie liked best was on the wall above her chair. It was Jesus leading lambs on a hill that was as green and smooth as the Riverside golf course. The others were not as tranquil: Jesus turning the moneychangers from the temple, Moses throwing the Tablets down upon the worshipers of the golden calf, Thomas the doubter putting his hand in Christ's wounded side (oh, the horrified fascination of that one and the nightmares it had given her as a girl!), Noah's ark floating above the agonized, drowning sinners, Lot and his family fleeing the great burning of Sodom and Gomorrah.

On a small deal table there were a lamp and a stack of tracts. The top pamphlet showed a sinner (his spiritual status was obvious from the agonized expression on his face) trying to crawl beneath a large boulder. The title blared: *Neither shall the rock hide him ON THAT DAY!*

But the room was actually dominated by a huge plaster crucifix on the far wall, fully four feet high. Momma had mail-ordered it special from St. Louis. The Jesus impaled upon it was frozen in a grotesque, muscle-straining rictus of pain, mouth drawn down in a groaning curve. His crown of thorns bled scarlet streams down temples and forehead. The eyes were turned up in a medieval expression of slanted agony. Both hands were also drenched with blood and the feet were nailed to a small plaster platform. This corpus had also given Carrie endless nightmares in which the mutilated Christ chased her through dream corridors, holding a mallet and nails, begging her to take up her cross and follow Him. Just lately these dreams had evolved into something less understandable but more sinister. The object did not seem to be murder but something even more awful.

Alone.

The pain in her legs and belly and privates had drained away a little. She no longer thought she was bleeding to death. The word was *menstruation,* and all at once it seemed logical and inevitable. It was her Time of the Month. She giggled a strange, affrighted giggle in the solemn stillness of the living room. It sounded like a quiz show. You too can win an all-expenses-paid trip to Bermuda on Time of the Month. Like the memory of the stones, the knowledge of menstruation seemed always to have been there, blocked but waiting.

She turned and walked heavily upstairs. The bathroom had a wooden floor that had been scrubbed nearly white (Cleanliness is next to Godliness) and a tub on claw feet. Rust stains dripped down the porcelain below the chrome spout, and there was no shower attachment. Momma said showers were sinful.

Carrie went in, opened the towel cabinet, and began to hunt purposefully but carefully, not leaving anything out of place. Momma's eyes were sharp.

The blue box was in the very back, behind the old towels they didn't use any more. There was a fuzzily silhouetted woman in a long, filmy gown on the side.

She took one of the napkins out and looked at it curiously. She had blotted the lipstick she snuck into her purse quite openly with these—once on a street corner. Now she remembered (or imagined she did) quizzical, shocked looks. Her face flamed. *They* had told her. The flush faded to a milky anger.

She went into her tiny bedroom. There were many more religious pictures here, but there were more lambs and fewer scenes of righteous wrath. A Ewen pennant was tacked over her dresser. On the dresser itself was a Bible and a plastic Jesus that glowed in the dark.

She undressed—first her blouse, then her hateful knee-length skirt, her slip, her girdle, her pettipants, her garter belt, her stockings. She looked at the pile of heavy clothes, their buttons and rubber, with an expression of fierce wretchedness. In the school library there was a stack of back issues of *Seventeen* and often she leafed through them, pasting an expression of idiotic casualness on her face. The models looked so easy and smooth in their short, kicky skirts, pantyhose, and frilly underwear with patterns on them. Of course *easy* was one of Momma's pet words (she knew what Momma would say o no question) to describe *them*. And it would make her dreadfully self-conscious, she knew that. Naked, evil, blackened with the sin of exhibitionism, the breeze blowing lewdly up the backs of her legs, inciting lust. And she knew that *they* would know how she felt. They always did. They would embarrass her somehow, push her savagely back down into clowndom. It was their way.

She could, she knew she could be
(what)
in another place. She was thick through the waist only because sometimes she felt so miserable, empty, bored, that the only way to fill that gaping, whistling hole was to eat and eat and eat—but she was not *that* thick through the middle. Her body chemistry would not allow her to go beyond a certain point.

And she thought her legs were actually pretty, almost as pretty as Sue Snell's or Vicky Hanscom's. She could be

(what o what o what)

could stop the chocolates and her pimples would go down. They always did. She could fix her hair. Buy pantyhose and blue and green tights. Make little skirts and dresses from Butterick and Simplicity patterns. The price of a bus ticket, a train ticket. She could be, could be, could *be*—

Alive.

She unsnapped her heavy cotton bra and let it fall. Her breasts were milk-white, upright and smooth. The nipples were a light coffee color. She ran her hands over them and a little shiver went through her. Evil, bad, oh it was. Momma had told her there was Something. The Something was dangerous, ancient, unutterably evil. It could make you Feeble. *Watch*, Momma said. *It comes at night. It will make you think of the evil that goes on in parking lots and roadhouses.*

But, though this was only nine-twenty in the morning, Carrie thought that the Something had come to her. She ran her hands over her breasts

(dirtypillows)

again, and the skin was cool but the nipples were hot and hard, and when she tweaked one it made her feel weak and dissolving. Yes, this was the Something.

Her underpants were spotted with blood.

Suddenly she felt that she must burst into tears, scream, or rip the Something out of her body whole and beating, crush it, kill it.

The napkin Miss Desjardin had fixed was already wilting and she changed it carefully, knowing how bad she was, how bad *they* were, how she hated them and herself. Only Momma was good. Momma had battled the Black Man and had vanquished him. Carrie had seen it happen in a dream. Momma had driven him out of the front door with a broom, and the Black Man had fled up Carlin Street into the night, his cloven feet striking red sparks from the cement.

Her momma had torn the Something out of herself and was pure.

Carrie hated her.

She caught a glimpse of her own face in the tiny mirror she had hung on the back of the door, a mirror with a cheap green plastic rim, good only for combing hair by.

She hated her face, her dull, stupid, bovine face, the vapid eyes, the red, shiny pimples, the nests of blackheads. She hated her face most of all.

The reflection was suddenly split by a jagged, silvery crack. The mirror fell on the floor and shattered at her feet, leaving only the plastic ring to stare at her like a blinded eye.

From *Ogilvie's Dictionary of Psychic Phenomena:*

Telekinesis is the ability to move objects or to cause changes in objects by force of the mind. The phenomenon has most reliably been reported in times of crisis or in stress situations, when automobiles have been levitated from pinned bodies or debris from collapsed buildings, etc.

The phenomenon is often confused with the work of *poltergeists,* which are playful spirits. It should be noted that poltergeists are astral beings of questionable reality, while telekinesis is thought to be an empiric function of the mind, possibly electrochemical in nature. . . .

When they had finished making love, as she slowly put her clothes in order in the back seat of Tommy Ross's 1963 Ford, Sue Snell found her thoughts turning back to Carrie White.

It was Friday night and Tommy (who was looking pensively out the back window with his pants still down around his ankles; the effect was comic but oddly endearing) had taken her bowling. That, of course, was a mutually accepted excuse. Fornication had been on their minds from the word go.

She had been going out more or less steadily with Tommy ever since October (it was now May) and they had been lovers for only two weeks. Seven times, she amended. Tonight had been the seventh. There had been no fireworks yet, no bands playing "Stars and Stripes Forever," but it had gotten a little better.

The first time had hurt like hell. Her girl friends, Helen Shyres and Jeanne Gault, had both done It, and they both assured her that it only hurt for a minute—like getting a shot of penicillin—and then it was roses. But for Sue, the first time had been like being reamed out with a hoe handle. Tommy had confessed to her since, with a grin, that he had gotten the rubber on wrong, too.

Tonight was only the second time she had begun to feel something like pleasure, and then it was over. Tommy had held out for as long as he could, but then it was just . . . over. It seemed like an awful lot of rubbing for a little warmth.

In the aftermath she felt low and melancholy, and her thoughts turned to Carrie in this light. A wave of remorse caught her with all emotional guards down, and when Tommy turned back from the view of Brickyard Hill, she was crying.

"Hey," he said, alarmed. "Oh, hey." He held her clumsily.

"'S all right," she said, still weeping. "It's not you. I did a not-so-good thing today. I was just thinking of it."

"What?" He patted the back of her neck gently.

So she found herself launching into the story of that morning's incident, hardly believing it was herself she was listening to. Facing the thing frankly, she realized the main reason she had allowed Tommy to have her was because she was in

(love? infatuation? didn't matter results were the same) with him, and now to put herself in this position—cohort in a nasty shower-room joke—was hardly the approved method to hook a fella. And Tommy was, of course, Popular. As someone who had been Popular herself all her life, it had almost seemed written that she would meet and fall in love with someone as Popular as she. They were almost certain to be voted King and Queen of the high school Spring Ball, and the senior class had already voted them class couple for the yearbook. They had become a fixed star in the shifting firmament of the high school's relationships, the acknowledged Romeo and Juliet. And she knew with sudden hatefulness that there was one couple like them in every white suburban high school in America.

And having something she had always longed for—a sense of place, of security, of status—she found that it carried uneasiness with it like a darker sister. It was not the way she had conceived it. There were dark things lumbering around their warm circle of light. The idea that she had let him fuck her

(do you have to say it that way yes this time I do)
simply because he was Popular, for instance. The fact that they fit together walking, or that she could look at their reflection in a store window and think, *There goes a handsome couple.* She was quite sure
(or only hopeful)
that she wasn't that weak, not that liable to fall docilely into the complacent expectations of parents, friends, and even herself. But now there was this shower thing, where she had gone along and pitched in with high, savage glee. The word she was avoiding was expressed *To Conform,* in the infinitive, and it conjured up miserable images of hair in rollers, long afternoons in front of the ironing board in front of the soap operas while hubby was off busting heavies in an anonymous Office; of joining the P.T.A. and then the country club when their income moved into five figures; of pills in circular yellow cases without number to insure against having to move out of the misses' sizes before it became absolutely necessary and against the intrusion of repulsive little strangers who shat in their pants and screamed for help at two in the morning; of fighting with desperate decorum to keep the niggers out of Kleen Korners, standing shoulder to shoulder with Terri Smith (Miss Potato Blossom of 1975) and Vicki Jones (Vice President of the Women's League), armed with signs and petitions and sweet, slightly desperate smiles.

Carrie, it was that goddamned Carrie, this was her fault. Perhaps before today she had heard distant, circling footfalls around their lighted place, but tonight, hearing her own sordid, crummy story, she saw the actual silhouettes of all these things, and yellow eyes that glowed like flashlights in the dark.

She had already bought her prom gown. It was blue. It was beautiful.

"You're right," he said when she was done. "Bad news. Doesn't sound a bit like you." His face was grave and she felt a cool slice of terror. Then he smiled—he had a very jolly smile—and the darkness retreated a bit.

"I kicked a kid in the slats once when he was knocked out. Did I ever tell you about that?"

She shook her head.

"Yeah." He rubbed his nose reminiscently and his cheek gave a small tic, the way it had when he made his confession about getting the rubber wrong the first time. "The kid's name was Danny Patrick. He beat the living shit out of me once when we were in the sixth grade. I hated him, but I was scared, too. I was laying for him. You know how that is?"

She didn't, but nodded anyway.

"Anyway, he finally picked on the wrong kid a year or so later. Pete Taber. He was just a little guy, but he had lots of muscle. Danny got on him about something, I don't know, marbles or something, and finally Peter just rose up righteous and beat the shit out of him. That was on the playground of the old Kennedy Junior High. Danny fell down and hit his head and went out cold. Everybody ran. We thought he might be dead. I ran away too, but first I gave him a good kick in the ribs. Felt really bad about it afterward. You going to apologize to her?"

It caught Sue flat-footed and all she could do was clinch weakly: "Did you?"

"Huh? Hell no! I had better things to do than spend my time in traction. But there's a big difference, Susie."

"There is?"

"It's not seventh grade any more. And I had some kind of reason, even if it was a piss-poor reason. What did that sad, silly bitch ever do to you?"

She didn't answer because she couldn't. She had never passed more than a hundred words with Carrie in her whole life, and three dozen or so had come today. Phys Ed was the only class they'd had in common since they had graduated from Chamberlain Junior High. Carrie was taking the commercial/business courses. Sue, of course, was in the college division.

She thought herself suddenly loathsome.

She found she could not bear that and so she twisted it at him. "When did you start making all these big moral decisions? After you started fucking me?"

She saw the good humor fade from his face and was sorry.

"Guess I should have kept quiet," he said, and pulled up his pants.

"It's not you, it's me." She put a hand on his arm. "I'm ashamed, see?"

"I know," he said. "But I shouldn't be giving advice. I'm not very good at it."

"Tommy, do you ever hate being so . . . well, Popular?"

"Me?" The question wrote surprise on his face. "Do you mean like football and class president and that stuff?"

"Yes."

"No. It's not very important. High school isn't a very important place. When you're going you think it's a big deal, but when it's over nobody really thinks it was great unless they're beered up. That's how my brother and his buddies are, anyway."

It did not soothe her; it made her fears worse. Little Susie mix 'n match from Ewen High School, Head Cupcake of the entire Cupcake Brigade. Prom gown kept forever in the closet, wrapped in protective plastic.

The night pressed dark against the slightly steamed car windows.

"I'll probably end up working at my dad's car lot," he said. "I'll spend my Friday and Saturday nights down at Uncle Billy's or out at The Cavalier drinking beer and talking about the Saturday afternoon I got that fat pitch from Saunders and we upset Dorchester. Get married to some nagging broad and always own last year's model, vote Democrat—"

"Don't," she said, her mouth suddenly full of a dark, sweet horror. She pulled him to her. "Love me. My head is so bad tonight. Love me. Love me."

So he loved her and this time it was different, this time there finally seemed to be room and there was no tiresome rubbing but a delicious friction that went up and up: Twice he had to stop, panting, and held himself back, and then he went again

(he was a virgin before me and admitted it i would have believed a lie)

and went hard and her breath came in short, digging gasps and then she began to yell and hold at his back, helpless to stop, sweating, the bad taste washed away, every cell seeming to have its own climax, body filled with sunlight, musical notes in her mind, butterflies behind her skull in the cage of her mind.

Later, on the way home, he asked her formally if she would go to the Spring Ball with him. She said she would. He asked her if she had decided what to do about Carrie. She said she hadn't. He said that it made no difference, but she thought that it did. It had begun to seem that it meant all the difference.

From "Telekinesis: Analysis and Aftermath" *(Science Yearbook 1981),* by Dean D. L. McGuffin:

There are, of course, still these scientists today—regretfully, the Duke University people are in their forefront—who reject the terrific underlying implications of the Carrie White affair. Like the Flatlands Society, the Rosicrucians, or the Corlies of Arizona, who are positive that the atomic bomb does not work, these unfortunates are flying in the face of logic with their heads in the sand—and beg your pardon for the mixed metaphor.

Of course one is able to understand the consternation, the raised voices, the angry letters and arguments at scientific convocations. The idea of telekinesis itself has been a bitter pill for the scientific community to swallow, with its horror-movie trappings of ouija boards and mediums and table rappings and floating coronets; but understanding will still not excuse scientific irresponsibility.

The outcome of the White affair raises grave and difficult questions. An earthquake has struck our ordered notions of the way the natural world is supposed to act and react. Can you blame even such a renowned physicist as Gerald Luponet for claiming the whole thing is a hoax and a fraud, even in the face of such overwhelming evidence as the White Commission presented? For if Carrie White is the truth, then what of Newton? . . .

They sat in the living room, Carrie and Momma, listening to Tennessee Ernie Ford singing "Let the Lower Lights Be Burning" on a Webcor phonograph (which Momma called the victrola, or, if in a particularly good mood, the vic). Carrie sat at the sewing machine, pumping with her feet as she sewed the sleeves on a new dress. Momma sat beneath the plaster crucifix tatting doilies and bumping her feet in time to the song, which was one of her favorites. Mr. P. P. Bliss, who had written this hymn and others seemingly without number, was one of Momma's shining examples of God at work upon the face of the earth. He had been a sailor and a sinner (two terms that were synonymous in Momma's lexicon), a great blasphemer, a laugher in the face of the Almighty. Then a great storm had come up at sea, the boat had threatened to capsize, and Mr. P. P. Bliss had gotten down on his sin-sickly knees with a vision of Hell yawning beneath the ocean floor to receive him, and he had prayed to God. Mr. P. P. Bliss promised God that if He saved him, he would dedicate the rest of his life to Him. The storm, of course, had cleared immediately.

> Brightly beams our Father's mercy
> From his lighthouse evermore,
> But to us he gives the keeping
> Of the lights along the shore . . .

All of Mr. P. P. Bliss's hymns had a seagoing flavor to them.

The dress she was sewing was actually quite pretty, a dark wine color—the closest Momma would allow her to red—and the sleeves were puffed. She tried to keep her mind strictly on her sewing, but of course it wandered.

The overhead light was strong and harsh and yellow, the small dusty plush sofa was of course deserted (Carrie had never had a boy in To Sit), and on the far wall was a twin shadow: the crucified Jesus, and beneath Him, Momma.

The school had called Momma at the laundry and she had come home at noon. Carrie had watched her come up the walk, and her belly trembled.

Momma was a very big woman, and she always wore a hat. Lately her legs had begun to swell, and her feet always seemed on the point of overflowing her shoes. She wore a black cloth coat with a black fur collar. Her eyes were blue and magnified behind rimless bifocals. She always carried a large black satchel purse and in it was her change purse, her billfold (both black), a large King James Bible (also black) with her name stamped on the front in gold, and a stack of tracts secured with a rubber band. The tracts were usually orange, and smearily printed.

Carrie knew vaguely that Momma and Daddy Ralph had been Baptists once but had left the church when they became convinced that the Baptists were doing the work of the Antichrist. Since that time, all worship had taken place at home. Momma held worship on Sundays, Tuesdays, and Fridays. These were called Holy Days. Momma was the minister, Carrie the congregation. Services lasted from two to three hours.

Momma had opened the door and walked stolidly in. She and Carrie had stared at each other down the short length of the front hall for a moment, like gunfighters before a shoot-out. It was one of those brief moments that seem

(fear could it really have been fear in momma's eyes)

much longer in retrospect.

Momma closed the door behind her. "You're a woman," she said softly.

Carrie felt her face twisting and crumpling and could not help it. "Why didn't you *tell* me?" she cried. "Oh Momma, I was so *scared!* And the girls all made fun and threw things and—"

Momma had been walking toward her, and now her hand flashed with sudden limber speed, a hard hand, laundry-callused and muscled. It struck her backhand across the jaw and Carrie fell down in the doorway between the hall and the living room, weeping loudly.

"And God made Eve from the rib of Adam," Momma said. Her eyes were very large in the rimless glasses; they looked like poached eggs. She thumped Carrie with the side of her foot and Carrie screamed. "Get up, woman. Let's us get in and pray. Let's us pray to Jesus for our woman-weak, wicked, sinning souls."

"Momma—"

The sobs were too strong to allow more. The latent hysterics had come out grinning and gibbering. She could not stand up. She could only crawl into the living room with her hair hanging in her face, braying huge, hoarse sobs. Every now and again Momma would swing her foot. So they progressed across the living room toward the place of the altar, which had once been a small bedroom.

"And Eve was weak and—say it, woman. Say it!"

"No, Momma, please help me—"

The foot swung. Carrie screamed.

"And Eve was weak and loosed the raven on the world," Momma continued, "and the raven was called Sin, and the first

Sin was Intercourse. And the Lord visited Eve with a Curse, and the Curse was the Curse of Blood. And Adam and Eve were driven out of the Garden and into the World and Eve found that her belly had grown big with child."

The foot swung and connected with Carrie's rump. Her nose scraped the wood floor. They were entering the place of the altar. There was a cross on a table covered with an embroidered silk cloth. On either side of the cross there were white candles. Behind this were several paint-by-the-numbers of Jesus and His apostles. And to the right was the worst place of all, the home of terror, the cave where all hope, all resistance to God's will—and Momma's—was extinguished. The closet door leered open. Inside, below a hideous blue bulb that was always lit, was Derrault's conception of Jonathan Edwards' famous sermon, *Sinners in the Hands of an Angry God.*

"And there was a second Curse, and this was the Curse of Childbearing, and Eve brought forth Cain in sweat and blood."

Now Momma dragged her, half-standing and half-crawling, down to the altar, where they both fell on their knees. Momma gripped Carrie's wrist tightly.

"And following Cain, Eve gave birth to Abel, having not yet repented of the Sin of Intercourse. And so the Lord visited Eve with a third Curse, and this was the Curse of Murder. Cain rose up and slew Abel with a rock. And still Eve did not repent, nor all the daughters of Eve, and upon Eve did the Crafty Serpent found a kingdom of whoredoms and pestilences."

"Momma!" she shrieked. "Momma, please listen! *It wasn't my fault!"*

"Bow your head," Momma said. "Let's us pray."

"You should have told me!"

Momma brought her hand down on the back of Carrie's neck, and behind it was all the heavy muscle developed by eleven years of slinging heavy laundry bags and trucking piles of wet sheets. Carrie's eye-bulging face jerked forward and her forehead smacked the altar, leaving a mark and making the candles tremble.

"Let's us pray," Momma said softly, implacably.

Weeping and snuffling, Carrie bowed her head. A runner of snot hung pendulously from her nose and she wiped it away (if i had a nickel for every time she made me cry here) with the back of her hand.

"O Lord," Momma declaimed hugely, her head thrown back, "help this sinning woman beside me here see the sin of her days and ways. Show her that if she had remained sinless the Curse of Blood never would have come on her. She may have committed the Sin of Lustful Thoughts. She may have been listening to rock 'n roll music on the radio. She may have been tempted by the Antichrist. Show her that this is Your kind, vengeful hand at work and—"

"No! Let me go!"

She tried to struggle to her feet and Momma's hand, as strong and pitiless as an iron manacle, forced her back to her knees.

"—and Your sign that she must walk the straight and narrow from here on out if she is to avoid the flaming agonies of the Eternal Pit. Amen."

She turned her glittering, magnified eyes upon her daughter. "Go to your closet now."

"No!" She felt her breath go thick with terror.

"Go to your closet. Pray in secret. Ask forgiveness for your sin."

"I didn't sin, Momma. *You* sinned. You didn't tell me and they laughed."

Again she seemed to see a flash of fear in Momma's eyes, gone as quickly and soundlessly as summer lightning. Momma began to force Carrie toward the blue glare of the closet.

"Pray to God and your sins may be washed away."

"Momma, you let me go."

"Pray, woman."

"I'll make the stones come again, Momma."

Momma halted.

Even her breath seemed to stop in her throat for a moment. And then the hand tightened on her neck, tightened, until Carrie saw red, lurid dots in front of her eyes and felt her brain go fuzzy and far-off.

Momma's magnified eyes swam in front of her.

"You spawn of the devil," she whispered. "Why was I so cursed?"

Carrie's whirling mind strove to find something huge enough to express her agony, shame, terror, hate, fear. It seemed her whole life had narrowed to this miserable, beaten point of rebellion. Her eyes bulged crazily, her mouth, filled with spit, opened wide.

"You SUCK!" she screamed.

Momma hissed like a burned cat. "Sin!" she cried. "O, Sin!" She began to beat Carrie's back, her neck, her head. Carrie was driven, reeling, into the close blue glare of the closet.

"You FUCK!" Carrie screamed.

(there there o there it's out how else do you think she got you o god o good)

She was whirled into the closet headfirst and she struck the far wall and fell on the floor in a semidaze. The door slammed and the key turned.

She was alone with Momma's angry God.

The blue light glared on a picture of a huge and bearded Yahweh who was casting screaming multitudes of humans down through cloudy depths into an abyss of fire. Below them, black horrid figures struggled through the flames of perdition while the Black Man sat on a huge flame-colored throne with a trident in one hand. His body was that of a man, but he had a spiked tail and the head of a jackal.

She would not break this time.

But of course she did break. It took six hours but she broke, weeping and calling Momma to open the door and let her out. The need to urinate was terrible. The Black Man grinned at her with his jackal mouth, and his scarlet eyes knew all the secrets of woman-blood.

An hour after Carrie began to call, Momma let her out. Carrie scrabbled madly for the bathroom.

It was only now, three hours after that, sitting here with her head bowed over the sewing machine like a penitent, that she remembered the fear in Momma's eyes and she thought she knew the reason why.

There had been other times when Momma had kept her in the closet for as long as a day at a stretch—when she stole that forty-nine-cent finger ring from Shuber's Five and Ten, the time she had found that picture of Flash Bobby Pickett under

Carrie's pillow—and Carrie had once fainted from the lack of food and the smell of her own waste. And she had never, never spoken back as she had done today. Today she had even said the Eff Word. Yet Momma had let her out almost as soon as she broke.

There. The dress was done. She removed her feet from the treadle and held it up to look at it. It was long. And ugly. She hated it.

She knew why Momma had let her out.

"Momma, may I go to bed?"

"Yes." Momma did not look up from her doily.

She folded the dress over her arm. She looked down at the sewing machine. All at once the treadle depressed itself. The needle began to dip up and down, catching the light in steely flashes. The bobbin whirred and jerked. The sidewheel spun.

Momma's head jerked up, her eyes wide. The looped matrix at the edge of her doily, wonderfully intricate yet at the same time as precise and even, suddenly fell in disarray.

"Only clearing the thread," Carrie said softly.

"Go to bed," Momma said curtly, and the fear was back in her eyes.

"Yes,

(she was afraid i'd knock the closet door right off its hinges)

Momma."

(and i think i could i think i could yes i think i could)

From *The Shadow Exploded* (p. 58):

Margaret White was born and raised in Motton, a small town which borders Chamberlain and sends its tuition students to Chamberlain's junior and senior high schools. Her parents were fairly well-to-do; they owned a prosperous night spot just outside the Motton town limits called The Jolly Roadhouse. Margaret's father, John Brigham, was killed in a barroom shooting incident in the summer of 1959.

Margaret Brigham, who was then almost thirty, began attending fundamentalist prayer meetings. Her mother had become involved with a new man (Harold Allison, whom she later married) and they both wanted Margaret out of the house—she believed her mother, Judith, and Harold Allison were living in sin and made her views known frequently. Judith Brigham expected her daughter to remain a spinster the rest of her life. In the more pungent phraseology of her soon-to-be stepfather, "Margaret had a face like the ass end of a gasoline truck and a body to match." He also referred to her as "a little prayin' Jesus."

Margaret refused to leave until 1960, when she met Ralph White at a revival meeting. In September of that year she left the Brigham residence in Motton and moved to a small flat in Chamberlain Center.

The courtship of Margaret Brigham and Ralph White terminated in marriage on March 23, 1962. On April 3, 1962, Margaret White was admitted briefly to Westover Doctors Hospital.

"Nope, she wouldn't tell us what was wrong," Harold Allison said. "The one time we went to see her she told us we were living in adultery even though we were hitched, and we were going to hell. She said God had put an invisible mark on our foreheads, but she could see it. Acted crazy as a bat in a henhouse, she did. Her mom tried to be nice, tried to find out what the matter with her was. She got hysterical and started to rave about an angel with a sword who would walk through the parking lots of roadhouses and cut down the wicked. We left."

Judith Allison, however, had at least an idea of what might have been wrong with her daughter; she thought that Margaret had gone through a miscarriage. If so, the baby was conceived out of wedlock. Confirmation of this would shed an interesting light on the character of Carrie's mother.

In a long and rather hysterical letter to her mother dated August 19, 1962, Margaret said that she and Ralph were living sinlessly, without "the Curse of Intercourse." She urged Harold and Judith Allison to close their "abode of wickedness" and do likewise. "It is," Margaret declares near the end of her letter, "the oney [sic] way you & That Man can avoid the Rain of Blood yet to come. Ralph & I, like Mary & Joseph, will neither know or polute [sic] each other's flesh. If there is issue, let it be Divine."

Of course, the calendar tells us that Carrie was conceived later that same year . . .

•   •   •

The girls dressed quietly for their Monday morning Period One gym class, with no horseplay or little screaming catcalls, and none of them were very surprised when Miss Desjardin slammed open the locker-room door and walked in. Her silver whistle dangled between her small breasts, and if her shorts were the ones she had been wearing on Friday, no trace of Carrie's bloody handprint remained.

The girls continued to dress sullenly, not looking at her.

"Aren't you the bunch to send out for graduation," Miss Desjardin said softly. "When is it? A month? And the Spring Ball even less than that. Most of you have your dates and gowns already, I bet. Sue, you'll be going with Tommy Ross. Helen, Roy Evarts. Chris, I imagine that you can take your pick. Who's the lucky guy?"

"Billy Nolan," Chris Hargensen said sullenly.

"Well, isn't he the lucky one?" Desjardin remarked. "What are you going to give him for a party favor, Chris, a bloody Kotex? Or how about some used toilet paper? I understand these things seem to be your sack these days."

Chris went red. "I'm leaving. I don't have to listen to that."

Desjardin had not been able to get the image of Carrie out of her mind all weekend, Carrie screaming, blubbering, a wet napkin plastered squarely in the middle of her pubic hair—and her own sick, angry reaction.

And now, as Chris tried to storm out past her, she reached out and slammed her against a row of dented, olive-colored lockers beside the inner door. Chris's eyes widened with shocked disbelief. Then a kind of insane rage filled her face.

"You can't hit us!" she screamed. "You'll get canned for this! See if you don't, you *bitch!*"

The other girls winced and sucked breath and stared at the floor. It was getting out of hand. Sue noticed out of the corner of her eye that Mary and Donna Thibodeau were holding hands.

"I don't really care, Hargensen," Desjardin said. "If you—or any of you girls—think I'm wearing my teacher hat right now, you're making a bad mistake. I just want you all to know that you did a shitty thing on Friday. A really shitty thing."

Chris Hargensen was sneering at the floor. The rest of the girls were looking miserably at anything but their gym instructor. Sue found herself looking into the shower stall—the scene of the crime—and jerked her glance elsewhere. None of them had ever heard a teacher call anything shitty before.

"Did any of you stop to think that Carrie White has feelings? Do any of you *ever* stop to think? Sue? Fern? Helen? Jessica? Any of you? You think she's ugly. Well, you're all ugly. I saw it on Friday morning."

Chris Hargensen was mumbling about her father being a lawyer.

"*Shut up!*" Desjardin yelled in her face. Chris recoiled so suddenly that her head struck the lockers behind her. She began to whine and rub her head.

"One more remark out of you," Desjardin said softly, "and I'll throw you across the room. Want to find out if I'm telling the truth?"

Chris, who had apparently decided she was dealing with a madwoman, said nothing.

Desjardin put her hands on her hips. "The office has decided on punishment for you girls. Not *my* punishment, I'm sorry to say. My idea was three days' suspension and refusal of your prom tickets."

Several girls looked at each other and muttered unhappily.

"That would have hit you where you live," Desjardin continued. "Unfortunately, Ewen is staffed completely by men in its administration wing. I don't believe they have any real conception of how utterly nasty what you did was. So. One week's detention."

Spontaneous sighs of relief.

"But. It's to be *my* detention. In the gym. And I'm going to run you ragged."

"I won't come," Chris said. Her lips had thinned across her teeth.

"That's up to you, Chris. That's up to all of you. But punishment for skipping detention is going to be three days' suspension and refusal of your prom tickets. Get the picture?"

No one said anything.

"Right. Change up. And think about what I said."

She left.

Utter silence for a long and stricken moment. Then Chris Hargensen said with loud, hysterical stridency:

"She can't get away with it!" She opened a door at random, pulled out a pair of sneakers and hurled them across the room. "I'm going to get her! Goddammit! Goddammit! See if I don't! If we all stick together we can—"

"Shut up, Chris," Sue said, and was shocked to hear a dead, adult lifelessness in her voice. "Just shut up."

"This isn't over," Chris Hargensen said, unzipping her skirt with a rough jab and reaching for her fashionably frayed green gym shorts. "This isn't over by a long way."

And she was right.

From *The Shadow Exploded* (pp. 60–61):

In the opinion of this researcher, a great many of the people who have researched the Carrie White matter—either for the scientific journals or for the popular press—have placed a mistaken emphasis on a relatively fruitless search for incidents of telekinesis in the girl's childhood. To strike a rough analogy, this is like spending years researching the early incidents of masturbation in a rapist's childhood.

The spectacular incident of the stones serves as a kind of red herring in this respect. Many researchers have adopted the erroneous belief that where there has been one incident, there must be others. To offer another analogy, this is like dispatching a crew of meteor watchers to Crater National Park because a huge asteroid struck there two million years ago.

To the best of my knowledge, there are no other *recorded* instances of TK in Carrie's childhood. If Carrie had not been an only child, we might have at least hearsay reports of dozens of other minor occurrences.

In the case of Andrea Kolintz (see Appendix II for a fuller history), we are told that, following a spanking for crawling out on the roof, "The medicine cabinet flew open, bottles fell to the floor or seemed to hurl themselves across the bathroom, doors flew open and slammed shut, and, at the climax of the manifestation, a 300-pound stereo cabinet tipped over and records flew all over the living room, dive-bombing the occupants and shattering against the walls."

Significantly, this report is from one of Andrea's brothers, as quoted in the September 4, 1955, issue of *Life* magazine. *Life* is hardly the most scholarly or unimpeachable source, but there is a great deal of other documentation, and I think that the point of familiar witness-ship is served.

In the case of Carrie White, the only witness to any possible prologue to the final climactic events was Margaret White, and she, of course is dead. . . .

Henry Grayle, principal of Ewen High School, had been expecting him all week, but Chris Hargensen's father didn't show up until Friday—the day after Chris had skipped her detention period with the formidable Miss Desjardin.

"Yes, Miss Fish?" He spoke formally into the intercom, although he could see the man in the outer office through his window, and certainly knew his face from pictures in the local paper.

"John Hargensen to see you, Mr. Grayle."

"Send him in, please." *Goddammit, Fish, do you have to sound so impressed?*

Grayle was an irrepressible paper-clip-bender, napkin-ripper, corner-folder. For John Hargensen, the town's leading legal light, he was bringing up the heavy ammunition—a whole box of heavy-duty clips in the middle of his desk blotter.

Hargensen was a tall, impressive man with a self-confident way of moving and the kind of sure, mobile features that said this was a man superior at the game of one-step-ahead social interaction.

He was wearing a brown Savile Row suit with subtle glints of green and gold running through the weave that put Grayle's local off-the-rack job to shame. His briefcase was thin, real leather, and bound with glittering stainless steel. The smile was faultless and full of many capped teeth—a smile to make the hearts of lady jurors melt like butter in a warm skillet. His grip was major league all the way—firm, warm, long.

"Mr. Grayle. I've wanted to meet you for some time now."

"I'm always glad to see interested parents," Grayle said with a dry smile. "That's why we have Parents Open House every October."

"Of course." Hargensen smiled. "I imagine you're a busy man, and I have to be in court forty-five minutes from now. Shall we get down to specifics?"

"Surely." Grayle dipped into his box of clips and began to mangle the first one. "I suspect you are here concerning the disciplinary action taken against your daughter Christine. You should be informed that school policy on the matter has been set. As a man concerned with the workings of justice yourself, you should realize that bending the rules is hardly possible or—"

Hargensen waved his hand impatiently. "Apparently you're laboring under a misconception, Mr. Grayle. I am here because my daughter was manhandled by your gym teacher, Miss Rita Desjardin. And verbally abused, I'm afraid. I believe the term your Miss Desjardin used in connection with my daughter was 'shitty.' "

Grayle sighed inwardly. "Miss Desjardin has been reprimanded."

John Hargensen's smile cooled thirty degrees. "I'm afraid a reprimand will not be sufficient. I believe this has been the young, ah, lady's first year in a teaching capacity?"

"Yes. We have found her to be eminently satisfactory."

"Apparently your definition of eminently satisfactory includes throwing students up against lockers and the ability to curse like a sailor?"

Grayle fenced: "As a lawyer, you must be aware that this state acknowledges the school's title to *in loco parentis*—along with full responsibility, we succeed to full parental rights during school hours. If you're not familiar, I'd advise you to check *Monondock Consolidated School District vs. Cranepool* or—"

"I'm familiar with the concept," Hargensen said. "I'm also aware that neither the Cranepool case that you administrators are so fond of quoting or the Frick case cover anything remotely concerned with physical or verbal abuse. There is, however, the case of *School District #4 vs. David*. Are you familiar with it?"

Grayle was. George Kramer, the assistant principal of the consolidated high school in S.D. 14 was a poker buddy. George wasn't playing much poker any more. He was working for an insurance company after taking it upon himself to cut a student's hair. The school district had ultimately paid seven thousand dollars in damages, or about a thousand bucks a snip.

Grayle started on another paper clip.

"Let's not quote cases at each other, Mr. Grayle. We're busy men. I don't want a lot of unpleasantness. I don't want a mess. My daughter is at home, and she will stay there Monday and Tuesday. That will complete her three-day suspension. That's all right." Another dismissive wave of the hand.

(catch fido good boy here's a nice bone)

"Here's what *I* want," Hargensen continued. "One, prom tickets for my daughter. A girl's senior prom is important to her, and Chris is very distressed. Two, no contract renewal of the Desjardin woman. That's for me. I believe that if I cared to take the School Department to court, I could walk out with both her dismissal and a hefty damage settlement in my pocket. But I don't want to be vindictive."

"So court is the alternative if I don't agree to your demands?"

"I understand that a School Committee hearing would precede that, but only as a formality. But yes, court would be the final result. Nasty for you."

Another paper clip.

"For physical and verbal abuse, is that correct?"

"Essentially."

"Mr. Hargensen, are you aware that your daughter and about ten of her peers threw sanitary napkins at a girl who was having her first menstrual period? A girl who was under the impression that she was bleeding to death?"

A faint frown creased Hargensen's features, as if someone had spoken in a distant room. "I hardly think such an allegation is at issue. I am speaking of actions following—"

"Never mind," Grayle said. "Never mind what you were speaking of. This girl, Carietta White, was called 'a dumb pudding' and was told to 'plug it up' and was subjected to various obscene gestures. She has not been in school this week at all. Does that sound like physical and verbal abuse to you? It does to me."

"I don't intend," Hargensen said, "to sit here and listen to a tissue of half-truths or your standard schoolmaster lecture, Mr. Grayle. I know my daughter well enough to—"

"Here." Grayle reached into the wire IN basket beside the blotter and tossed a sheaf of pink cards across the desk. "I doubt very much if you know the daughter represented in these cards half so well as you think you do. If you did, you might realize that it was about time for a trip to the woodshed. It's time you snubbed her close before she does someone a major damage."

"You aren't—"

"Ewen, four years," Grayle overrode him. "Graduation slated June seventy-nine; next month. Tested I.Q. of a hundred and forty. Eighty-three average. Nonetheless, I see she's been accepted at Oberlin. I'd guess someone—probably you, Mr. Hargensen—has been yanking some pretty long strings. Seventy-four assigned detentions. *Twenty* of those have been for harassment of misfit pupils, I might add. Fifth wheels. I understand that Chris's clique calls them Mortimer Snerds. They find it all quite hilarious. She skipped out on fifty-one of those assigned detentions. At Chamberlain Junior High, one suspension for putting a firecracker in a girl's shoe . . . the note on the card says that little prank almost cost a little girl named Irma Swope two toes. The Swope girl has a harelip, I understand. I'm talking about your *daughter,* Mr. Hargensen. Does that tell you anything?"

"Yes," Hargensen said, rising. A thin flush had suffused his features. "It tells me I'll see you in court. And when I'm done with you, you'll be lucky to get a job selling encyclopedias door to door."

Grayle also rose, angrily, and the two men faced each other across the desk.

"Let it be court, then," Grayle said.

He noted a faint flick of surprise on Hargensen's face, crossed his fingers, and went in for what he hoped would be a knockout—or at least a TKO that would save Desjardin's job and take this silk-ass son of a bitch down a notch.

"You apparently haven't realized all the implications of *in loco parentis* in this matter, Mr. Hargensen. The same umbrella that covers your daughter also covers Carrie White. And the minute you file for damages on the grounds of physical and verbal abuse, we will cross-file against your daughter on those same grounds for Carrie White."

Hargensen's mouth dropped open, then closed. "You can't get away with a cheap gimmick like that, you—"

"Shyster lawyer? Is that the phrase you were looking for?" Grayle smiled grimly. "I believe you know your way out, Mr. Hargensen. The sanctions against your daughter stand. If you care to take the matter further, that is your right."

Hargensen crossed the room stiffly, paused as if to add something, then left, barely restraining himself from the satisfaction of a hard doorslam.

Grayle blew out breath. It wasn't hard to see where Chris Hargensen came by her self-willed stubbornness.

A. P. Morton entered a minute later. "How did it go?"

"Time'll tell, Morty," Grayle said. Grimacing, he looked at the twisted pile of paper clips. "He was good for seven clips, anyway. That's some kind of record."

"Is he going to make it a civil matter?"

"Don't know. It rocked him when I said we'd cross-sue."

"I bet it did." Morton glanced at the phone on Grayle's desk. "It's time we let the superintendent in on this bag of garbage, isn't it?"

"Yes," Grayle said, picking up the phone. "Thank God my unemployment insurance is paid up."

"Me too," Morton said loyally.

From *The Shadow Exploded* (Appendix III):

Carietta White passed in the following short verse as a poetry assignment in the seventh grade. Mr. Edwin King, who had Carrie for grade seven English, says: "I don't know why I saved it. She certainly doesn't stick out in my mind as a superior pupil, and this isn't a superior verse. She was very quiet and I can't remember her ever raising her hand even once in class. But something in this seemed to cry out."

> Jesus watches from the wall,
> But his face is cold as stone,
> And if he loves me
> As she tells me
> Why do I feel so all alone?

The border of the paper on which this little verse is written is decorated with a great many cruciform figures which almost seem to dance. . . .

Tommy was at baseball practice Monday afternoon, and Sue went down to the Kelly Fruit Company in The Center to wait for him.

Kelly's was the closest thing to a high school hangout the loosely sprawled community of Chamberlain could boast since Sheriff Doyle had closed the rec center following a large drug bust. It was run by a morose fat man named Hubert Kelly who dyed his hair black and complained constantly that his electronic pacemaker was on the verge of electrocuting him.

The place was a combination grocery, soda fountain, and gas station—there was a rusted Jenny gas pump out front that Hubie had never bothered to change when the company merged. He also sold beer, cheap wine, dirty books, and a wide selection of obscure cigarettes such as Murads, King Sano, and Marvel Straights.

The soda fountain was a slab of real marble, and there were four or five booths for kids unlucky enough or friendless enough to have no place to go and get drunk or stoned. An ancient pinball machine that always tilted on the third ball stuttered lights on and off in the back beside the rack of dirty books.

When Sue walked in she saw Chris Hargensen immediately. She was sitting in one of the back booths. Her current amour, Billy Nolan, was looking through the latest issue of *Popular Mechanics* at the magazine rack. Sue didn't know what a rich, Popular girl like Chris saw in Nolan, who was like some strange time traveler from the 1950s with his greased hair, zipper-bejeweled black leather jacket, and manifold-bubbling Chevrolet road machine.

"Sue!" Chris hailed. "Come on over!"

Sue nodded and raised a hand, although dislike rose in her throat like a paper snake. Looking at Chris was like looking through a slanted doorway to a place where Carrie White crouched with hands over her head. Predictably, she found her own hypocrisy (inherent in the wave and the nod) incomprehensible and sickening. Why couldn't she just cut her dead?

"A dime root beer," she told Hubie. Hubie had genuine draft root beer, and he served it in huge, frosted 1890s mugs. She had been looking forward to tipping a long one while she read a paper novel and waited for Tommy—in spite of the havoc the root beers raised with her complexion, she was hooked. But she wasn't surprised to find she'd lost her taste for this one.

"How's your heart, Hubie?" she asked.

"You kids," Hubie said, scraping the head off Sue's beer with a table knife and filling the mug the rest of the way. "You don't understand nothing. I plugged in my electric razor this morning and got a hundred and ten volts right through this pacemaker. You kids don't know what that's like, am I right?"

"I guess not."

"No. Christ Jesus forbid you should ever have to find out. How long can my old ticker take it? You kids'll all find out when I buy the farm and those urban renewal poops turn this place into a parking lot. That's a dime."

She pushed her dime across the marble.

"Fifty million volts right up the old tubes," Hubie said darkly, and stared down at the small bulge in his breast pocket.

Sue went over and slid carefully into the vacant side of Chris's booth. She was looking exceptionally pretty, her black hair held by a shamrock-green band and a tight basque blouse that accentuated her firm, upthrust breasts.

"How are you, Chris?"

"Bitchin' good," Chris said a little too blithely. "You heard the latest? I'm out of the prom. I bet that cocksucker Grayle loses his job, though."

Sue *had* heard the latest. Along with everyone at Ewen.

"Daddy's suing them," Chris went on. Over her shoulder: *"Billeee!* Come over here and say hi to Sue."

He dropped his magazine and sauntered over, thumbs hooked into his side-hitched garrison belt, fingers dangling limply toward the stuffed crotch of his pegged levis. Sue felt a wave of unreality surge over her and fought an urge to put her hands to her face and giggle madly.

"Hi, Suze," Billy said. He slid in beside Chris and immediately began to massage her shoulder. His face was utterly blank. He might have been testing a cut of beef.

"I think we're going to crash the prom anyway," Chris said. "As a protest or something."

"Is that right?" Sue was frankly startled.

"No," Chris replied, dismissing it. "I don't know." Her face suddenly twisted into an expression of fury, as abrupt and surprising as a tornado funnel. "That goddamned Carrie White! I wish she'd take her goddam holy joe routine and stuff it straight up her ass!"

"You'll get over it," Sue said.

"If only the rest of you had walked out with me . . . Jesus, Sue, why didn't you? We could have had them by the balls. I never figured you for an establishment pawn."

Sue felt her face grow hot. "I don't know about anyone else, but I wasn't being anybody's pawn. I took the punishment because I thought I earned it. We did a suck-off thing. End of statement."

"Bullshit. That fucking Carrie runs around saying everyone but her and her gilt-edged momma are going to hell and you can stick up for her? We should have taken those rags and stuffed them down her throat."

"Sure. Yeah. See you around, Chris." She pushed out of the booth.

This time it was Chris who colored; the blood slammed to her face in a sudden rush, as if a red cloud had passed over some inner sun.

"Aren't you getting to be the Joan of Arc around here! I seem to remember you were in there pitching with the rest of us."

"Yes," Sue said, trembling. "But I stopped."

"Oh, aren't you just *it?*" Chris marveled. "Oh my *yes.* Take your root beer with you. I'm afraid I might touch it and turn to gold."

She didn't take her root beer. She turned and half-walked, half-stumbled out. The upset inside her was very great, too great yet for either tears or anger. She was a get-along girl, and it was the first fight she had been in, physical or verbal, since grade-school pigtail pulling. And it was the first time in her life that she had actively espoused a Principle.

And of course Chris had hit her in just the right place, had hit her exactly where she was most vulnerable: She *was* being a hypocrite, there seemed no way to avoid that, and deeply, sheathed within her and hateful, was the knowledge that one of the reasons she had gone to Miss Desjardin's hour of calisthenics and sweating runs around the gym floor had nothing to do with nobility. She wasn't going to miss her last Spring Ball for anything. Not for *anything*.

Tommy was nowhere in sight.

She began to walk back toward the school, her stomach churning unhappily. Little Miss Sorority. Suzy Creemcheese. The Nice Girl who only does It with the boy she plans to marry—with the proper Sunday supplement coverage, of course. Two kids. Beat the living shit out of them if they show any signs of honesty: screwing, fighting, or refusing to grin each time some mythic honcho yelled frog.

Spring Ball. Blue gown. Corsage kept all the afternoon in the fridge. Tommy in a white dinner jacket, cummerbund, black pants, black shoes. Parents taking photos posed by the living-room sofa with Kodak Starflashes and Polaroid Big-Shots. Crepe masking the stark gymnasium girders. Two bands: one rock, one mellow. No fifth wheels need apply. Mortimer Snerd, please keep out. Aspiring country club members and future residents of Kleen Korners only.

The tears finally came and she began to run.

From *The Shadow Exploded* (p. 60):

The following excerpt is from a letter to Donna Kellogg from Christine Hargensen. The Kellogg girl moved from Chamberlain to Providence, Rhode Island, in the fall of 1978. She was apparently one of Chris Hargersen's few close friends and a confidante. The letter is postmarked May 17, 1979:

"So I'm out of the Prom and my yellow-guts father says he won't give them what they deserve. But they're not going to get away with it. I don't know exactly what I'm going to do yet, but I guarantee you everyone is going to get a big fucking surprise . . ."

It was the seventeenth. May seventeenth. She crossed the day off the calendar in her room as soon as she slipped into her long white nightgown. She crossed off each day as it passed with a heavy black felt pen, and she supposed it expressed a very bad attitude toward life. She didn't really care. The only thing she really cared about was knowing that Momma was going to make her go back to school tomorrow and she would have to face all of Them.

She sat down in the small Boston rocker (bought and paid for with her own money) beside the window, closed her eyes, and swept Them and all the clutter of her conscious thoughts from her mind. It was like sweeping a floor. Lift the rug of your subconscious and sweep all the dirt under. Good-bye.

She opened her eyes. She looked at the hairbrush on her bureau.

Flex.

She was lifting the hairbrush. It was heavy. It was like lifting a barbell with very weak arms. Oh. Grunt.

The hairbrush slid to the edge of the bureau, slid out past the point where gravity should have toppled it, and then dangled, as if on an invisible string. Carrie's eyes had closed to slits. Veins pulsed in her temples. A doctor might have been interested in what her body was doing at that instant; it made no rational sense. Respiration had fallen to sixteen breaths per minute. Blood pressure up to 190/100. Heartbeat up to 140—higher than astronauts under the heavy g-load of lift-off. Temperature down to 94.3°. Her body was burning energy that seemed to be coming from nowhere and seemed to be going nowhere. An electroencephalogram would have shown alpha waves that were no longer waves at all, but great, jagged spikes.

She let the hairbrush down carefully. Good. Last night she had dropped it. Lose all your points, go to jail.

She closed her eyes again and rocked. Physical functions began to revert to the norm; her respiration speeded until she was nearly panting. The rocker had a slight squeak. Wasn't annoying, though. Was soothing. Rock, rock. Clear your mind.

"Carrie?" Her mother's voice, slightly disturbed, floated up.

(she's getting interference like the radio when you turn on the blender good good)

"Have you said your prayers, Carrie?"

"I'm saying them," she called back.

Yes. She was saying them, all right.

She looked at her small studio bed.

Flex.

Tremendous weight. Huge. Unbearable.

The bed trembled and then the end came up perhaps three inches.

It dropped with a crash. She waited, a small smile playing about her lips, for Momma to call upstairs angrily. She didn't. So Carrie got up, went to her bed, and slid between the cool sheets. Her head ached and she felt giddy, as she always did after these exercise sessions. Her heart was pounding in a fierce, scary way.

She reached over, turned off the light, and lay back. No pillow. Momma didn't allow her a pillow.

She thought of imps and familiars and witches

(am i a witch momma the devil's whore)

riding through the night, souring milk, overturning butter churns, blighting crops while They huddled inside their houses with hex signs scrawled on Their doors.

She closed her eyes, slept, and dreamed of huge, living stones crashing through the night, seeking out Momma, seeking out Them. They were trying to run, trying to hide. But the rock would not hide them; the dead tree gave no shelter.

From *My Name Is Susan Snell* by Susan Snell (New York: Simon & Schuster, 1986), pp. i–iv:

There's one thing no one has understood about what happened in Chamberlain on Prom Night. The press hasn't understood it, the scientists at Duke University haven't understood it, David Congress hasn't understood it—although his *The Shadow Exploded* is probably the only half-decent book written on the subject—and certainly the White Commission, which used me as a handy scapegoat, did not understand it.

This one thing is the most fundamental fact: We were kids.

Carrie was seventeen, Chris Hargensen was seventeen, I was seventeen, Tommy Ross was eighteen, Billy Nolan (who spent a year repeating the ninth grade, presumably before he learned how to shoot his cuffs during examinations) was nineteen. . . .

Older kids react in more socially acceptable ways than younger kids, but they still have a way of making bad decisions, of overreacting, of underestimating.

In the first section which follows this introduction I must show these tendencies in myself as well as I am able. Yet the matter which I am going to discuss is at the root of my involvement in Prom Night, and if I am to clear my name, I must begin by recalling scenes which I find particularly painful. . . .

I have told this story before, most notoriously before the White Commission, which received it with incredulity. In the wake of two hundred deaths and the destruction of an entire town, it is so easy to forget one thing: We were kids. We were kids. We were kids trying to do our best. . . .

"You must be crazy."

He blinked at her, not willing to believe that he had actually heard it. They were at his house, and the television was on but forgotten. His mother had gone over to visit Mrs. Klein across the street. His father was in the cellar workroom making a birdhouse.

Sue looked uncomfortable but determined. "It's the way I want it, Tommy."

"Well it's not the way I want it. I think it's the craziest goddam thing I ever heard. Like something you might do on a bet."

Her face tightened. "Oh? I thought you were the one making the big speeches the other night. But when it comes to putting your money where your big fat mouth is—"

"Wait, whoa." He was unoffended, grinning. "I didn't say no, did I? Not yet, anyway."

"You—"

"Wait. Just wait. Let me talk. You want me to ask Carrie White to the Spring Ball. Okay, I got that. But there's a couple of things I don't understand."

"Name them." She leaned forward.

"First, what good would it do? And second, what makes you think she'd say yes if I asked her?"

"Not say yes! Why—" She floundered. "You're . . . everybody likes you and—"

"We both know Carrie's got no reason to care much for people that everybody likes."

"She'd go with you."

"Why?"

Pressed, she looked defiant and proud at the same time. "I've seen the way she looks at you. She's got a crush. Like half the girls at Ewen."

He rolled his eyes.

"Well, I'm just telling you," Sue said defensively. "She won't be able to say no."

"Suppose I believe you," he said. "What about the other thing?"

"You mean what good will it do? Why . . . it'll bring her out of her shell, of course. Make her . . ." She trailed off.

"A part of things? Come on, Suze. You don't believe that bullshit."

"All right," she said. "Maybe I don't. But maybe I still think I've got something to make up for."

"The shower room?"

"A lot more than that. Maybe if that was all I could let it go, but the mean tricks have been going on ever since grammar school. I wasn't in on many of them, but I was on some. If I'd been in Carrie's groups, I bet I would have been in on even more. It seemed like . . . oh, a big laugh. Girls can be cat-mean about that sort of thing, and boys don't really understand. The boys would tease Carrie for a little while and then forget, but the girls . . . it went on and on and on and I can't even remember where it started any more. If I were Carrie, I couldn't even face showing myself to the world. I'd just find a big rock and hide under it."

"You were kids," he said. "Kids don't know what they're doing. Kids don't even know their reactions really, actually, hurt other people. They have no, uh, empathy. Dig?"

She found herself struggling to express the thought this called up in her, for it suddenly seemed basic, bulking over the shower-room incident the way sky bulks over mountains.

"But hardly *anybody* ever finds out that their actions really, actually, hurt other people! People don't get better, they just get smarter. When you get smarter you don't stop pulling the wings off flies, you just think of better reasons for doing it. Lots of kids say they feel sorry for Carrie White—mostly girls, and *that's* a laugh—but I bet none of them understand what it's like to *be* Carrie White, every second of every day. And they don't really care."

"Do you?"

"I don't know!" she cried. "But someone ought to try and be sorry in a way that counts . . . in a way that means something."

"All right. I'll ask her."

"You will?" The statement came out in a flat, surprised way. She had not thought he actually would.

"Yes. But I think she'll say no. You've overestimated my box-office appeal. That popularity stuff is bullshit. You've got a bee in your bonnet about that."

"Thank you," she said, and it sounded odd, as if she had thanked an Inquisitor for torture.

"I love you," he said.

She looked at him, startled. It was the first time he had said it.

From *My Name Is Susan Snell* (p. 6):

There are lots of people—mostly men—who aren't surprised that I asked Tommy to take Carrie to the Spring Ball. They are surprised that he did it, though, which shows you that the male mind expects very little in the way of altruism from its fellows.

Tommy took her because he loved me and because it was what I wanted. How, asks the skeptic from the balcony, did you know he loved you? Because he told me so, mister. And if you'd known him, that would have been good enough for you, too. . . .

He asked her on Thursday, after lunch, and found himself as nervous as a kid going to his first ice-cream party.

She sat four rows over from him in Period Five study hall, and when it was over he cut across to her through the mass of rushing bodies. At the teacher's desk Mr. Stephens, a tall man just beginning to run to fat, was folding papers abstractedly back into his ratty brown briefcase.

"Carrie?"

"Ohuh?"

She looked up from her books with a startled wince, as if expecting a blow. The day was overcast and the bank of fluorescents embedded in the ceiling was not particularly kind to her pale complexion. But he saw for the first time (because it was the first time he had really looked) that she was far from repulsive. Her face was round rather than oval, and the eyes were so dark that they seemed to cast shadows beneath them, like bruises. Her hair was darkish blonde, slightly wiry, pulled back in a bun that was not becoming to her. The lips were full, almost lush, the teeth naturally white. Her body, for the most part, was indeterminate. A baggy sweater concealed her breasts except for token nubs. The skirt was colorful but awful all the same: It fell to a 1958 midshin hem in an odd and clumsy A-line. The calves were strong and rounded (the attempt to conceal these with heathery knee-socks was bizarre but unsuccessful) and handsome.

She was looking up with an expression that was slightly fearful, slightly something else. He was quite sure he knew what the something else was. Sue had been right, and being right, he had just time to wonder if this was doing a kindness or making things even worse.

"If you don't have a date for the Ball, would you want to go with me?"

Now she blinked, and as she did so, a strange thing happened. The time it took to happen could have been no more than the doorway to a second, but afterward he had no trouble recalling it, as one does with dreams or the sensation of *déjà vu*. He felt a dizziness as if his mind was no longer controlling his body—the miserable, out-of-control feeling he associated with drinking too much and then coming to the vomiting point.

Then it was gone.

"What? What?"

She wasn't angry, at least. He had expected a brief gust of rage and then a sweeping retreat. But she wasn't angry; she seemed unable to cope with what he had said at all. They were alone in the study hall now, perfectly between the ebb of old students and the flow of new ones.

"The Spring Ball," he said, a little shaken. "It's next Friday and I know this is late notice but—"

"I don't like to be tricked," she said softly, and lowered her head. She hesitated for just a second and then passed him by. She stopped and turned and he suddenly saw dignity in her, something so natural that he doubted if she was even aware of it. "Do You People think you can just go on tricking me forever? I know who you go around with."

"I don't go around with anyone I don't want to," Tommy said patiently. "I'm asking you because I want to ask you." Ultimately, he knew this to be the truth. If Sue was making a gesture of atonement, she was doing it only at secondhand.

The Period Six students were coming in now, and some of them were looking over curiously. Dale Ullman said something to a boy Tommy didn't know and both of them snickered.

"Come on," Tommy said. They walked out into the hall.

They were halfway to Wing Four—his class was the other way—walking together but perhaps only by accident, when she said, almost too quietly to hear: "I'd love to. Love to."

He was perceptive enough to know it was not an acceptance, and again doubt assailed him. Still, it was started. "Do it, then. It will be all right. For both of us. We'll see to it."

"No," she said, and in her sudden pensiveness she could have been mistaken for beautiful. "It will be a nightmare."

"I don't have tickets," he said, as if he hadn't heard. "This is the last day they sell them."

"Hey, Tommy, you're going the wrong way!" Brent Gillian yelled.

She stopped. "You're going to be late."

"Will you?"

"Your class," she said, distraught. "Your class. The bell is going to ring."

"Will you?"

"Yes," she said with angry helplessness. "You knew I would." She swiped at her eyes with the back of her hand.

"No," he said. "But now I do. I'll pick you up at seven-thirty."

"Fine," she whispered. "Thank you." She looked as if she might swoon.

And then, more uncertain than ever, he touched her hand.

• • •

From *The Shadow Exploded* (pp. 74–76):

Probably no other aspect of the Carrie White affair has been so misunderstood, second-guessed, and shrouded in mystery as the part played by Thomas Everett Ross, Carrie's ill-starred escort to the Ewen High School Spring Ball.

Morton Cratzchbarken, in an admittedly sensationalized address to The National Colloquium on Psychic Phenomena last year, said that the two most stunning events of the twentieth century have been the assassination of John F. Kennedy in 1963 and the destruction that came to Chamberlain, Maine, in May of 1979. Cratzchbarken points out that both events were driven home to the citizenry by mass media, and both events have almost shouted the frightening fact that, while something had ended, something else had been irrevocably set in motion, for good or ill. If the comparison can be made, then Thomas Ross played the part of a Lee Harvey Oswald—trigger man in a catastrophe. The question that still remains is: Did he do so wittingly or unwittingly?

Susan Snell, by her own admission, was to have been escorted by Ross to the annual event. She claims that she suggested Ross take Carrie to make up for her part in the shower-room incident. Those who oppose this story, most lately led by George Jerome of Harvard, claim that this is either a highly romantic distortion or an outright lie. Jerome argues with great force and eloquence that it is hardly typical of high-school-age adolescents to feel that they have to "atone" for anything—particularly for an offense against a peer who has been ostracized from existing cliques.

"It would be uplifting if we could believe that adolescent human nature is capable of salvaging the pride and self-image of the low bird in the pecking order with such a gesture," Jerome has said in a recent issue of *The Atlantic Monthly*, "but we know better. The low bird is not picked tenderly out of the dust by its fellows; rather, it is dispatched quickly and without mercy."

Jerome, of course, is absolutely right—about birds, at any rate—and his eloquence is undoubtedly responsible in large part for the advancement of the "practical joker" theory, which the White Commission approached but did not actually state.

This theory hypothesizes that Ross and Christine Hargensen (see pp. 10–18) were at the center of a loose conspiracy to get Carrie White to the Spring Ball, and, once there, complete her humiliation. Some theorists (mostly crime writers) also claim that Sue Snell was an active part of this conspiracy. This casts the mysterious Mr. Ross in the worst possible light, that of a practical joker deliberately maneuvering an unstable girl into a situation of extreme stress.

This author doesn't believe that likely in light of Mr. Ross's character. This is a facet which has remained largely unexplored by his detractors, who have painted him as a rather dull clique-centered athlete; the phrase "dumb jock" expresses this view of Tommy Ross perfectly.

It is true that Ross was an athlete of above-average ability. His best sport was baseball, and he was a member of the Ewen varsity squad from his Sophomore year. Dick O'Connell, general manager of the Boston Red Sox, has indicated that Ross would have been offered a fairly large bonus for signing a contract, had he lived.

But Ross was also a straight-A student (hardly fitting the "dumb jock" image), and his parents have both said that he had decided pro baseball would have to wait until he had finished college, where he planned to study for an English degree. His interests included writing poetry, and a poem written six months prior to his death was published in an established "little magazine" called *Everleaf*. This is available in Appendix V.

His surviving classmates also give him high marks, and this is significant. There were only twelve survivors of what has become known in the popular press as Prom Night. Those who were not in attendance were largely the unpopular members of the Junior and Senior classes. If these "outs" remember Ross as a friendly, good-natured fellow (many referred to him as "a hell of a good shit"), does not Professor Jerome's thesis suffer accordingly?

Ross's school records—which cannot, according to state law, be photostated here—when taken with classmates' recollections and the comments of relatives, neighbors, and teachers, form a picture of an extraordinary young man. This is a fact that jells very badly with Professor Jerome's picture of a peer-worshiping, sly young tough. He apparently had a high enough tolerance to verbal abuse and enough independence from his peer group to ask Carrie in the first place. In fact, Thomas Ross appears to have been something of a rarity: a socially conscious young man.

No case will be made here for his sainthood. There is none to be made. But intensive research has satisfied me that neither was he a human chicken in a public-school barnyard, joining mindlessly in the ruin of a weaker hen . . .

She lay
    (i am not afraid not afraid of her)
on her bed with an arm thrown over her eyes. It was Saturday night. If she was to make the dress she had in mind, she would have to start tomorrow at the
    (i'm not afraid momma)
latest. She had already bought the material at John's in West-over. The heavy, crumpled velvet richness of it frightened her. The price had also frightened her, and she had been intimidated by the size of the place, the chic ladies wandering here and there in their light spring dresses, examining bolts of cloth. There was an echoing strangeness in the atmosphere and it was worlds from the Chamberlain Woolworth's, where she usually bought her material.

She was intimidated but not stopped. Because, if she wanted to, she could send them all screaming into the streets. Mannequins toppling over, light fixtures falling, bolts of cloth shooting through the air in unwinding streamers. Like Samson in the temple, she could rain destruction on their heads if she so desired.

    (i am not afraid)
The package was now hidden on a dry shelf down in the cellar, and she was going to bring it up. Tonight.

She opened her eyes.

Flex.

The bureau rose into the air, trembled for a moment, and then rose until it nearly touched the ceiling. She lowered it. Lifted it. Lowered it. Now the bed, complete with her weight. Up. Down. Up. Down. Just like an elevator.

She was hardly tired at all. Well, a little. Not much. The ability, almost lost two weeks ago, was in full flower. It had progressed at a speed that was—

Well, almost terrifying.

And now, seemingly unbidden—like the knowledge of menstruation—a score of memories had come, as if some mental dam had been knocked down so that strange waters could gush forth. They were cloudy, distorted little-girl memories, but very real for all that. Making the pictures dance on the walls; turning on the water faucets from across the room; Momma asking her

(carrie shut the windows it's going to rain)

to do something and windows suddenly banging down all over the house; giving Miss Macaferty four flat tires all at once by unscrewing the valves in the tires of her Volkswagen; the stones—

(!!!!!!! no no no no no !!!!!!!)

—but now there was no denying the memory, no more than there could be a denying of the monthly flow, and that memory was not cloudy, no, not *that* one; it was harsh and brilliant, like jagged strokes of lightning: the little girl

(momma stop momma don't i can't breathe o my throat o momma i'm sorry i looked momma o my tongue blood in my mouth)

the poor little girl

(screaming: little slut o i know how it is with you i see what has to be done)

the poor little girl lying half in the closet and half out of it, seeing black stars dancing in front of everything, a sweet, far-away buzzing, swollen tongue lolling between her lips, throat circled with a bracelet of puffed, abraded flesh where Momma had throttled her and then Momma coming back, coming for her, Momma holding Daddy Ralph's long butcher knife

(cut it out i have to cut out the evil the nastiness sins of the flesh o i know about that the eyes cut out your eyes)

in her right hand, Momma's face twisted and working, drool on her chin, holding Daddy Ralph's Bible in her other hand

(you'll never look at that naked wickedness again)

and something flexed, not flex but *FLEX*, something huge and unformed and titanic, a wellspring of power that was not hers now and never would be again and then something fell on the roof and Momma screamed and dropped Daddy Ralph's Bible and that was *good,* and then more bumps and thumps and then the house began to throw its furnishings around and Momma dropped the knife and got on her knees and began to pray, holding up her hands and swaying on her knees while chairs whistled down the hall and the beds upstairs fell over and the dining room table tried to jam itself through a window and then Momma's eyes growing huge and crazed, bulging, her finger pointing at the little girl

(it's you it's you devilspawn witch imp of the devil it's *you* doing it)

and then the stones and Momma had fainted as their roof cracked and thumped as if with the footfalls of God and then—

Then she had fainted herself. And after that there were no more memories. Momma did not speak of it. The butcher knife was back in its drawer. Momma dressed the huge black and blue bruises on her neck and Carrie thought she could remember asking Momma how she had gotten them and Momma tightening her lips and saying nothing. Little by little it was forgotten. The eye of memory opened only in dreams. The pictures no longer danced on the walls. The windows did not shut themselves. Carrie did not remember a time when things had been different. Not until now.

She lay on her bed, looking at the ceiling, sweating.

"Carrie! Supper!"

"Thank you,

(i am not afraid)

Momma."

She got up and fixed her hair with a dark-blue headband. Then she went downstairs.

From *The Shadow Exploded* (p. 59):

How apparent was Carrie's "wild talent" and what did Margaret White, with her extreme Christian ethic, think of it? We shall probably never know. But one is tempted to believe that Mrs. White's reaction must have been extreme . . .

*   *   *

"You haven't touched your pie, Carrie." Momma looked up from the tract she had been perusing while she drank her Constant Comment. "It's homemade."

"It makes me have pimples, Momma."

"Your pimples are the Lord's way of chastising you. Now eat your pie."

"Momma?"

"Yes?"

Carrie plunged. "I've been invited to the Spring Ball next Friday by Tommy Ross—"

The tract was forgotten. Momma was staring at her with wide my-ears-are-deceiving-me eyes. Her nostrils flared like those of a horse that has heard the dry rattle of a snake.

Carrie tried to swallow an obstruction and only

(i am not afraid o yes i am)

got rid of part of it.

"—and he's a very nice boy. He's promised to stop in and meet you before and—"

"No."

"—to have me in by eleven. I've—"

"No, no, *no!*"

"—accepted. Momma, please see that I have to start to . . . to try and get along with the world. I'm not like you. I'm funny—I mean, the kids think I'm funny. I don't want to be. I want to try and be a whole person before it's too late to—"

Mrs. White threw her tea in Carrie's face.

It was only lukewarm, but it could not have shut off Carrie's words more suddenly if it had been scalding. She sat numbly, the amber fluid dripping from her chin and cheeks onto her white blouse, spreading. It was sticky and smelled like cinnamon.

Mrs. White sat trembling, her face frozen except for her nostrils, which continued to flare. Abruptly she threw back her head and screamed at the ceiling.

"God! God! God!" Her jaw snapped brutally over each syllable.

Carrie sat without moving.

Mrs. White got up and came around the table. Her hands were hooked into shaking claws. Her face bore a half-mad expression of compassion mixed with hate.

"The closet," she said. "Go to your closet and pray."

"No, Momma."

"Boys. Yes, boys come next. After the blood the boys come. Like sniffing dogs, grinning and slobbering, trying to find out where that smell is. *That . . . smell!*"

She swung her whole arm into the blow, and the sound of her palm against Carrie's face

(o god i am so afraid now)

was like that flat sound of a leather belt being snapped in air. Carrie remained seated, although her upper body swayed. The mark on her cheek was first white, then blood red.

"The mark," Mrs. White said. Her eyes were large but blank; she was breathing in rapid, snatching gulps of air. She seemed to be talking to herself as the claw hand descended onto Carrie's shoulder and pulled her out of her chair.

"I've seen it, all right. Oh yes. But. I. Never. Did. But for him. He. Took. Me . . ." She paused, her eyes wandering vaguely toward the ceiling. Carrie was terrified. Momma seemed in the throes of some great revelation which might destroy her.

"Momma—"

"In cars. Oh, I know where they take you in their cars. City limits. Roadhouses. Whiskey. Smelling . . . *oh they smell it on you!*" Her voice rose to a scream. Tendons stood out on her neck, and her head twisted in a questing upward rotation.

"Momma, you better stop."

This seemed to snap her back to some kind of hazy reality. Her lips twitched in a kind of elementary surprise and she halted, as if groping for old bearings in a new world.

"The closet," she muttered. "Go to your closet and pray."

"No."

Momma raised her hand to strike.

"*No!*"

The hand stopped in the dead air. Momma stared up at it, as if to confirm that it was still there, and whole.

The pie pan suddenly rose from the trivet on the table and hurled itself across the room to impact beside the living-room door in a splash of blueberry drool.

"*I'm going, Momma!*"

Momma's overturned teacup rose and flew past her head to shatter above the stove. Momma shrieked and dropped to her knees with her hands over her head.

"Devil's child," she moaned. "Devil's child, Satan spawn—"

"Momma, stand up."

"Lust and licentiousness, the cravings of the flesh—"

"Stand up!"

Momma's voice failed her but she did stand up, with her hands still on her head, like a prisoner of war. Her lips moved. To Carrie she seemed to be reciting the Lord's Prayer.

"I don't want to fight with you, Momma," Carrie said, and her voice almost broke from her and dissolved. She struggled to control it. "I only want to be let to live my own life. I . . . I don't like yours." She stopped, horrified in spite of herself. The ultimate blasphemy had been spoken, and it was a thousand times worse than the Eff Word.

"Witch," Momma whispered. "It says in the Lord's Book: 'Thou shalt not suffer a witch to live.' Your father did the Lord's work—"

"I don't want to talk about that," Carrie said. It always disturbed her to hear Momma talk about her father. "I just want you to understand that things are going to change around here, Momma." Her eyes gleamed. *"They* better understand it, too."

But Momma was whispering to herself again.

Unsatisfied, with a feeling of anticlimax in her throat and the dismal roiling of emotional upset in her belly, she went to the cellar to get her dress material.

It was better than the closet. There was that. Anything was better than the closet with its blue light and the overpowering stench of sweat and her own sin. Anything. Everything.

She stood with the wrapped package hugged against her breast and closed her eyes, shutting out the weak glow of the cellar's bare, cobweb-festooned bulb. Tommy Ross didn't love her; she knew that. This was some strange kind of atonement, and she could understand that and respond to it. She had lain cheek and jowl with the concept of penance since she had been old enough to reason.

He had said it would be good—that they would see to it. Well, *she* would see to it. They better not start anything. They just better not. She did not know if her gift had come from the lord of light or of darkness, and now, finally finding that she did not care which, she was overcome with an almost indescribable relief, as if a huge weight, long carried, had slipped from her shoulders.

Upstairs, Momma continued to whisper. It was not the Lord's Prayer. It was the Prayer of Exorcism from Deuteronomy.

From *My Name Is Susan Snell* (p. 23):

They finally even made a movie about it. I saw it last April. When I came out, I was sick. Whenever anything important happens in America, they have to gold-plate it, like baby shoes. That way you can forget it. And forgetting Carrie White may be a bigger mistake than anyone realizes. . . .

Monday morning; Principal Grayle and his understudy, Pete Morton, were having coffee in Grayle's office.

"No word from Hargensen yet?" Morty asked. His lips curled into a John Wayne leer that was a little frightened around the edges.

"Not a peep. And Christine has stopped lipping off about how her father is going to send us down the road." Grayle blew on his coffee with a long face.

"You don't exactly seem to be turning cartwheels."

"I'm not. Did you know Carrie White is going to the prom?"

Morty blinked. "With who? The Beak?" The Beak was Freddy Holt, another of Ewen's misfits. He weighed perhaps one hundred pounds soaking wet, and the casual observer might be tempted to believe that sixty of it was nose.

"No," Grayle said. "With Tommy Ross."

Morty swallowed his coffee the wrong way and went into a coughing fit.

"That's the way I felt," Grayle said.

"What about his girl friend? The little Snell girl?"

"I think she put him up to it," Grayle said. "She certainly seemed guilty enough about what happened to Carrie when I talked to her. Now she's on the Decoration Committee, happy as a clam, just as if not going to her Senior prom was nothing at all."

"Oh," Morty said wisely.

"And Hargensen—I think he must have talked to some people and discovered we really could sue him on behalf of Carrie White if we wanted to. I think he's cut his losses. It's the daughter that's worrying me."

"Do you think there's going to be an incident Friday night?"

"I don't know. I do know Chris has got a lot of friends who are going to be there. And she's going around with that Billy Nolan mess; he's got a zooful of friends, too. The kind that make a career out of scaring pregnant ladies. Chris Hargensen has him tied around her finger, from what I've heard."

"Are you afraid of anything specific?"

Grayle made a restless gesture. "Specific? No. But I've been in the game long enough to know it's a bad situation. Do you remember the Stadler game in seventy-six?"

Morty nodded. It would take more than the passage of three years to obscure the memory of the Ewen-Stadler game. Bruce Trevor had been a marginal student but a fantastic basketball player. Coach Gaines didn't like him, but Trevor was going to put Ewen in the area tournament for the first time in ten years. He was cut from the team a week before Ewen's last must-win game against the Stadler Bobcats. A regular announced locker inspection had uncovered a kilo of marijuana behind Trevor's civics book. Ewen lost the game—and their shot at the tourney—104–48. But no one remembered that; what they remembered was the riot that had interrupted the game in the fourth period. Led by Bruce Trevor, who righteously claimed he had been bum rapped, it resulted in four hospital admissions. One of them had been the Stadler coach, who had been hit over the head with a first-aid kit.

"I've got that kind of feeling," Grayle said. "A hunch. Someone's going to come with rotten apples or something."

"Maybe you're psychic," Morty said.

From *The Shadow Exploded* (pp. 92–93):

It is now generally agreed that the TK phenomenon is a genetic-recessive occurrence—but the opposite of a disease like hemophilia, which becomes overt only in males. In that disease, once called "King's Evil," the gene is recessive in the female and is carried harmlessly. Male offspring, however, are "bleeders." This disease is generated only if an afflicted male marries a woman carrying the recessive gene. If the offspring of such union is male, the result will be a hemophiliac son. If the offspring is female, the result will be a daughter who is a carrier. It should be emphasized that the hemophilia gene *may* be carried recessively in the male as a part of his genetic make-up. But if he marries a woman with the same outlaw gene, the result will be hemophilia if the offspring is male.

In the case of royal families, where intermarriage was common, the chance of the gene reproducing once it entered the family tree were high—thus the name King's Evil. Hemophilia also showed up in significant quantities in Appalachia during the earlier part of this century, and is commonly noticed in those cultures where incest and the marriage of first cousins is common.

With the TK phenomenon, the male appears to be the carrier; the TK gene *may* be recessive in the female, but dominates *only* in the female. It appears that Ralph White carried the gene. Margaret Brigham, by purest chance, also carried the outlaw gene sign, but we may be fairly confident that it was recessive, as no information has ever been found to indicate that she had telekinetic powers resembling her daughter's. Investigations are now being conducted into the life of Margaret Brigham's grandmother, Sadie Cochran—for, if the dominant/recessive pattern obtains with TK as it does with hemophilia, Mrs. Cochran may have been TK dominant.

If the issue of the White marriage had been male, the result would have been another carrier. Chances that the mutation would have died with him would have been excellent, as neither side of the Ralph White–Margaret Brigham alliance had cousins of a comparable age for the theoretical male offspring to marry. And the chances of meeting and marrying another woman with the TK gene at random would be small. None of the teams working on the problem have yet isolated the gene.

Surely no one can doubt, in light of the Maine holocaust, that isolating this gene must become one of medicine's number-one priorities. The hemophiliac, or H gene, produces male issue with a lack of blood platelets. The telekinetic, or TK gene, produces female Typhoid Marys capable of destroying almost at will. . . .

Wednesday afternoon.

Susan and fourteen other students—The Spring Ball Decoration Committee, no less—were working on the huge mural that would hang behind the twin bandstands on Friday night. The theme was Springtime in Venice (who picked these hokey themes, Sue wondered. She had been a student at Ewen for four years, had attended two Balls, and she still didn't know. Why did the goddam thing *need* a theme, anyway? Why not just have a sock hop and be done with it?); George Chizmar, Ewen's most artistic student, had done a small chalk sketch of gondolas on a canal at sunset and a gondolier in a huge straw fedora leaning against the tiller as a gorgeous panoply of pinks and reds and oranges stained both sky and water. It *was* beautiful, no doubt about that. He had redrawn it in silhouette on a huge fourteen-by-twenty-foot canvas flat, numbering the various sections to go with the various chalk hues. Now the Committee was patiently coloring it in, like children crawling over a huge page in a giant's coloring book. Still, Sue thought, looking at her hands and forearms, both heavily dusted with pink chalk, it was going to be the prettiest prom ever.

Next to her, Helen Shyres sat up on her haunches, stretched, and groaned as her back popped. She brushed a hank of hair from her forehead with the back of her hand, leaving a rose-colored smear.

"How in hell did you talk me into this?"

"You want it to be nice, don't you?" Sue mimicked Miss Geer, the spinster chairman (apt enough term for Miss Mustache) of the Decoration Committee.

"Yeah, but why not the Refreshment Committee or the Entertainment Committee? Less back, more mind. The mind, that's my area. Besides, you're not even—" She bit down on the words.

"Going?" Susan shrugged and picked up her chalk again. She had a monstrous writer's cramp. "No, but I still want it to be nice." She added shyly: "Tommy's going."

75

They worked in silence for a bit, and then Helen stopped again. No one was near them; the closest was Holly Marshall, on the other end of the mural, coloring the gondola's keel.

"Can I ask you about it, Sue?" Helen asked finally. "God, everybody's talking."

"Sure." Sue stopped coloring and flexed her hand. "Maybe I ought to tell someone, just so the story stays straight. I asked Tommy to take Carrie. I'm hoping it'll bring her out of herself a little . . . knock down some of the barriers. I think I owe her that much."

"Where does that put the rest of us?" Helen asked without rancor.

Sue shrugged. "You have to make up your own mind about what we did, Helen. I'm in no position to throw stones. But I don't want people to think I'm, uh . . ."

"Playing martyr?"

"Something like that."

"And Tommy went along with it?" This was the part that most fascinated her.

"Yes," Sue said, and did not elaborate. After a pause: "I suppose the other kids think I'm stuck up."

Helen thought it over. "Well . . . they're all talking about it. But most of them still think you're okay. Like you said, you make your own decisions. There is, however, a small dissenting faction." She snickered dolefully.

"The Chris Hargensen people?"

"And the Billy Nolan people. God, he's scuzzy."

"She doesn't like me much?" Sue said, making it a question.

"Susie, she hates your guts."

Susan nodded, surprised to find the thought both distressed and excited her.

"I heard her father was going to sue the School Department and then he changed his mind," she said.

Helen shrugged. "She hasn't made any friends out of this," she said. "I don't know what got into us, any of us. It makes me feel like I don't even know my own mind."

They worked on in silence. Across the room, Don Barrett was putting up an extension ladder preparatory to gilding the overhead steel beams with crepe paper.

"Look," Helen said. "There goes Chris now."

Susan looked up just in time to see her walking into the cubbyhole office to the left of the gym entrance. She was wearing wine-colored velvet hot pants and a silky white blouse—no bra, from the way things were jiggling up front—a dirty old man's dream, Sue thought sourly, and then wondered what Chris could want in where the Prom Committee had set up shop. Of course Tina Blake was on the Committee and the two of them were thicker than thieves.

Stop it, she scolded herself. Do you want her in sackcloth and ashes?

Yes, she admitted. A part of her wanted just that.

"Helen?"

"Hmmmm?"

"Are they going to do something?"

Helen's face took on an unwilling masklike quality. "I don't know." The voice was light, overinnocent.

"Oh," Sue said noncommittally.

(you know you know something: accept something goddammit if it's only yourself tell me)

They continued to color, and neither spoke. She knew it wasn't as all right as Helen had said. It couldn't be; she would never be quite the same golden girl again in the eyes of her mates. She had done an ungovernable, dangerous thing—she had broken cover and shown her face.

The late afternoon sunlight, warm as oil and sweet as childhood, slanted through the high, bright gymnasium windows.

From *My Name Is Susan Snell* (p. 40):

I can understand some of what must have led up to the prom. Awful as it was, I can understand how someone like Billy Nolan could go along, for instance. Chris Hargensen led him by the nose—at least, most of the time. His friends were just as easily led by Billy himself. Kenny Garson, who dropped out of high school when he was eighteen, had a tested third-grade reading level. In the clinical sense, Steve Deighan was little more than an idiot. Some of the others had police records; one of them, Jackie Talbot, was first busted at the age of nine for stealing hubcaps. If you've got a social-worker mentality, you can even regard these people as unfortunate victims.

But what can you say for Chris Hargensen herself?

It seems to me that from first to last, her one and only object in view was the complete and total destruction of Carrie White. . . .

"I'm not supposed to," Tina Blake said uneasily. She was a small, pretty girl with a billow of red hair. A pencil was pushed importantly in it. "And if Norma comes back, she'll spill."

"She's in the crapper," Chris said. "Come on."

Tina, a little shocked, giggled in spite of herself. Still, she offered token resistance: "Why do you want to see, anyway? You can't go."

"Never mind," Chris said. As always, she seemed to bubble with dark humor.

"Here," Tina said, and pushed a sheet enclosed in limp plastic across the desk. "I'm going out for a Coke. If that bitchy Norma Watson comes back and catches you, I never saw you."

"Okay," Chris murmured, already absorbed in the floor plan. She didn't hear the door close.

George Chizmar had also done the floor plan, so it was perfect. The dance floor was clearly marked. Twin bandstands. The stage where the King and Queen would be crowned

(i'd like to crown that fucking snell bitch carrie too)

at the end of the evening. Ranged along the three sides of the floor were the prom-goers' tables. Card tables, actually, but covered with a froth of crepe and ribbon, each holding party favors, prom programs, and ballots for King and Queen.

She ran a lacquered, spade-shaped fingernail down the tables to the right of the dance floor, then the left. There: *Tommy R. & Carrie W.* They were really going through with it. She could hardly believe it. Outrage made her tremble. Did they really think they would be allowed to get away with it? Her lips tautened grimly.

She looked over her shoulder. Norma Watson was still nowhere in sight.

Chris put the seating chart back and riffled quickly through the rest of the papers on the pitted and initial-scarred desk.

Invoices (mostly for crepe paper and ha'penny nails), a list of parents who had loaned card tables, petty-cash vouchers, a bill from Star Printers, who had run off the prom tickets, a sample King and Queen ballot—

Ballot! She snatched it up.

No one was supposed to see the actual King and Queen ballot until Friday, when the whole student body would hear the candidates announced over the school's intercom. The King and Queen would be voted in by those attending the prom, but blank nomination ballots had been circulated to home rooms almost a month earlier. The results were supposed to be top secret.

There was a gaining student move afoot to do away with the King and Queen business all together—some of the girls claimed it was sexist, the boys thought it was just plain stupid and a little embarrassing. Chances were good that this would be the last year the dance would be so formal or traditional.

But for Chris, this was the only year that counted. She stared at the ballot with greedy intensity.

George and Frieda. No way. Frieda Jason was a Jew.

Peter and Myra. No way here, either. Myra was one of the female clique dedicated to erasing the whole horse race. She wouldn't serve even if elected. Besides, she was about as good-looking as the ass-end of old drayhorse Ethel.

Frank and Jessica. Quite possible. Frank Grier had made the All New England football team this year, but Jessica was another little sparrowfart with more pimples than brains.

Don and Helen. Forget it. Helen Shyres couldn't get elected dog catcher.

And the last pairing: *Tommy and Sue.* Only Sue, of course, had been crossed out, and Carrie's name had been written in. There was a pairing to conjure with! A kind of strange, shuffling laughter came over her, and she clapped a hand over her mouth to hold it in.

Tina scurried back in. "Jesus, Chris, you still here? She's *coming!*"

"Don't sweat it, doll," Chris said, and put the papers back on the desk. She was still grinning as she walked out, pausing to raise a mocking hand to Sue Snell, who was slaving her skinny butt off on that stupid mural.

In the outer hall, she fumbled a dime from her bag, dropped it into the pay phone, and called Billy Nolan.

From *The Shadow Exploded* (pp. 100–1):

One wonders just how much planning went into the ruination of Carrie White—was it a carefully made plan, rehearsed and gone over many times, or just something that happened in a bumbling sort of way?

... I favor the latter idea. I suspect that Christine Hargensen was the brains of the affair, but that she herself had only the most nebulous of ideas on how one might "get" a girl like Carrie. I rather suspect it was she who suggested that William Nolan and his friends make the trip to Irwin Henty's farm in North Chamberlain. The thought of that trip's imagined result would have appealed to a warped sense of poetic justice, I am sure. ...

The car screamed up the rutted Stack End Road in North Chamberlain at a sixty-five that was dangerous to life and limb on the washboard unpaved hardpan. A low-hanging branch, lush with May leaves, occasionally scraped the roof of the '61 Biscayne, which was fender-dented, rusted out, jacked in the back, and equipped with dual glasspack mufflers. One headlight was out; the other flickered in the midnight dark when the car struck a particularly rough bump.

Billy Nolan was at the pink fuzz-covered wheel. Jackie Talbot, Henry Blake, Steve Deighan, and the Garson brothers, Kenny and Lou, were also squeezed in. Three joints were going, passing through the inner dark like the lambent eyes of some rotating Cerberus.

"You sure Henty ain't around?" Henry asked. "I got no urge to go back up, ole Sweet William. They feed you shit."

Kenny Garson, who was wrecked to the fifth power, found this unutterably funny and emitted a slipstream of high-pitched giggles.

"He ain't around," Billy said. Even those few words seemed to slip out grudgingly, against his will. "Funeral."

Chris had found this out accidentally. Old man Henty ran one of the few successful independent farms in the Chamberlain area. Unlike the crotchety old farmer with a heart of gold that is one of the staples of pastoral literature, old man Henty was as mean as cat dirt. He did not load his shotgun with rock salt at green-apple time, but with birdshot. He had also prosecuted several fellows for pilferage. One of them had been a friend of these boys, a luckless bastard named Freddy Overlock. Freddy had been caught red-handed in old man Henty's henhouse, and had received a double dose of number-six bird where the good Lord had split him. Good ole Fred had spent four raving, cursing hours on his belly in an Emergency Wing examining room while a jovial intern picked tiny pellets out of his butt and dropped them into a steel pan. To add insult to injury, he had been fined two hundred dollars for larceny and trespass. There was no love lost between Irwin Henty and the Chamberlain greaser squad.

"What about Red?" Steve asked.

"He's trying to get into some new waitress at The Cavalier," Billy said, swinging the wheel and pulling the Biscayne through a juddering racing drift and onto the Henty Road. Red Trelawney was ole man Henty's hired hand. He was a heavy drinker and just as handy with the birdshot as his employer. "He won't be back until they close up."

"Hell of a risk for a joke," Jackie Talbot grumbled.

Billy stiffened. "You want out?"

"No, uh-uh," Jackie said hastily. Billy had produced an ounce of good grass to split among the five of them—and besides, it was nine miles back to town. "It's a *good* joke, Billy."

Kenny opened the glove compartment, took out an ornate scrolled roach clip (Chris's), and fixed the smoldering butt-end of a joint in it. This operation struck him as highly amusing, and he let out his high-pitched giggle again.

Now they were flashing past No Trespassing signs on either side of the road, barbed wire, newly turned fields. The smell of fresh earth was heavy and gravid and sweet on the warm May air.

Billy popped the headlights off as they breasted the next hill, dropped the gearshift into neutral and killed the ignition. They rolled, a silent hulk of metal, toward the Henty driveway.

Billy negotiated the turn with no trouble, and most of their speed bled away as they breasted another small rise and passed the dark and empty house. Now they could see the huge bulk of barn and beyond it, moonlight glittering dreamily on the cow pond and the apple orchard.

In the pigpen, two sows poked their flat snouts through the bars. In the barn, one cow lowed softly, perhaps in sleep.

Billy stopped the car with the emergency brake—not really necessary since the ignition was off, but it was a nice Commando touch—and they got out.

Lou Garson reached past Kenny and got something out of the glove compartment. Billy and Henry went around to the trunk and opened it.

"The bastard is going to shit where he stands when he comes back and gets a look," Steve said with soft glee.

"For Freddy," Henry said, taking the hammer out of the trunk.

Billy said nothing, but of course it was not for Freddy Overlock, who was an asshole. It was for Chris Hargensen, just as everything was for Chris, and had been since the day she swept down from her lofty college-course Olympus and made herself vulnerable to him. He would have done murder for her, and more.

Henry was swinging the nine-pound sledge experimentally in one hand. The heavy block of its business end made a portentous swishing noise in the night air, and the other boys gathered around as Billy opened the lid of the ice chest and took out the two galvanized steel pails. They were numbingly cold to the touch, lightly traced with frost.

"Okay," he said.

The six of them walked quickly to the hogpen, their respiration shortening with excitement. The two sows were both as tame as tabbies, and the old boar lay asleep on his side at the far end. Henry swung the sledge once more through the air, but this time with no conviction. He handed it to Billy.

"I can't," he said sickly. "You."

Billy took it and looked questioningly at Lou, who held the broad butcher knife he had taken from the glove compartment.

"Don't worry," he said, and touched the ball of his thumb to the honed edge.

"The throat," Billy reminded.

"I know."

Kenny was crooning and grinning as he fed the remains of a crumpled bag of potato chips to the pigs. "Doan worry, piggies, doan worry, big Bill's gonna bash your fuckin heads in and you woan have to worry about the bomb any more." He scratched their bristly chins, and the pigs grunted and munched contentedly.

"Here it comes," Billy remarked, and the sledge flashed down.

There was a sound that reminded him of the time he and Henry had dropped a pumpkin off Claridge Road overpass which crossed 495 west of town. One of the sows dropped dead with its tongue protruding, eyes still open, potato chip crumbs around its snout.

Kenny giggled. "She didn't even have time to burp."

"Do it quick, Lou," Billy said.

Kenny's brother slid between the slats, lifted the pig's head toward the moon—the glazing eyes regarded the crescent with rapt blankness—and slashed.

The flow of blood was immediate and startling. Several of the boys were splattered and jumped back with little cries of disgust.

Billy leaned through and put one of the buckets under the main flow. The pail filled up rapidly, and he set it aside. The second was half full when the flow trickled and died.

"The other one," he said.

"Jesus, Billy," Jackie whined. "Isn't that en—"

"The other one," Billy repeated.

"Soo-*ee*, pig-pig-pig," Kenny called, grinning and rattling the empty potato-chip bag. After a pause, the sow returned to the fence. The sledge flashed. The second bucket was filled and the remainder of the blood allowed to flow into the ground. A rank, coppery smell hung on the air. Billy found he was slimed in pig blood to the forearms.

Carrying the pails back to the trunk, his mind made a dim, symbolic connection. Pig blood. That was good. Chris was right. It was really good. It made everything solidify.

Pig blood for a pig.

He nestled the galvanized steel pails into the crushed ice, capped them, and slammed the lid of the chest. "Let's go," he said.

Billy got behind the wheel and released the emergency brake. The five boys got behind, put their shoulders into it, and the car turned in a tight, noiseless circle and trundled up past the barn to the crest of the hill across from Henty's house.

When the car began to roll on its own, they trotted up beside the doors and climbed in, puffing and panting.

The car gained speed enough to slew a little as Billy whipped it out of the long driveway and onto the Henty Road. At the bottom of the hill he dropped the transmission into third and popped the clutch. The engine hitched and grunted into life.

Pig blood for a pig. Yes, that was good, all right. That was really good. He smiled, and Lou Garson felt a start of surprise and fear. He was not sure he could recall ever having seen Billy Nolan smile before. There had not even been rumors.

"Whose funeral did ole man Henty go to?" Steve asked.

"His mother's," Billy said.

"His *mother?*" Jackie Talbot said, stunned. "Jesus Christ, she musta been older'n God."

Kenny's high-pitched cackle drifted back on the redolent darkness that trembled at the edge of summer.

PART TWO
PROM NIGHT

She put the dress on for the first time on the morning of May 27, in her room. She had bought a special brassiere to go with it, which gave her breasts the proper uplift (not that they actually needed it) but left their top halves uncovered. Wearing it gave her a weird, dreamy feeling that was half shame and half defiant excitement.

The dress itself was nearly floor length. The skirt was loose, but the waist was snug, the material rich and unfamiliar against her skin, which was used to only cotton and wool.

The hang of it seemed to be right—or would be, with the new shoes. She slipped them on, adjusted the neckline, and went to the window. She could see only a maddening ghost image of herself, but everything seemed to be right. Maybe later she could—

The door swung open behind her with only a soft snick of the latch, and Carrie turned to look at her mother.

She was dressed for work, wearing her white sweater and holding her black pocketbook in one hand. In the other she was holding Daddy Ralph's Bible.

They looked at each other.

Hardly conscious of it, Carrie felt her back straighten until she stood straight in the patch of early spring sunshine that fell through the window.

"Red," Momma murmured. "I might have known it would be red."

Carrie said nothing.

"I can see your dirtypillows. Everyone will. They'll be looking at your body. The Book says—"

"Those are my breasts, Momma. Every woman has them."

"Take off that dress," Momma said.

"No."

"Take it off, Carrie. We'll go down and burn it in the incinerator together, and then pray for forgiveness. We'll do penance." Her eyes began to sparkle with the strange, disconnected zeal that came over her at events which she considered to be tests of faith. "I'll stay home from work and you'll stay home from school. We'll pray. We'll ask for a Sign. We'll get us down on our knees and ask for the Pentecostal Fire."

"No, Momma."

Her mother reached up and pinched her own face. It left a red mark. She looked to Carrie for reaction, saw none, hooked her right hand into claws and ripped it across her own cheek, bringing thin blood. She whined and rocked back on her heels. Her eyes glowed with exaltation.

"Stop hurting yourself, Momma. That's not going to make me stop either."

Momma screamed. She made her right hand a fist and struck herself in the mouth, bringing blood. She dabbled her fingers in it, looked at it dreamily, and daubed a spot on the cover of the Bible.

"Washed in the Blood of the Lamb," she whispered. "Many times. Many times he and I—"

"Go away, Momma."

She looked up at Carrie, her eyes glowing. There was a terrifying expression of righteous anger graven on her face.

"The Lord is not mocked," she whispered. "Be sure your sin will find you out. Burn it, Carrie! Cast that devil's red from you and burn it! Burn it! Burn it! *Burn it!*"

The door slammed open by itself.

"Go away, Momma."

Momma smiled. Her bloody mouth made the smile grotesque, twisted. "As Jezebel fell from the tower, let it be with you," she said. "And the dogs came and licked up the blood. It's in the Bible! It's—"

"Her feet began to slip along the floor and she looked down at them, bewildered. The wood might have turned to ice.

"Stop that!" she screamed.

She was in the hall now. She caught the doorjamb and held on for a moment; then her fingers were torn loose, seemingly by nothing.

"I love you, Momma," Carrie said steadily. "I'm sorry."

She envisioned the door swinging shut, and the door did just that, as if moved by a light breeze. Carefully, so as not to hurt her, she disengaged the mental hands she had pushed her mother with.

A moment later, Margaret was pounding on the door. Carrie held it shut, her lips trembling.

"There's going to be a judgment!" Margaret White raved. "I wash my hands of it! I tried!"

"Pilate said that," Carrie said.

Her mother went away. A minute later Carrie saw her go down the walk and cross the street on her way to work.

"Momma," she said softly, and put her forehead on the glass.

From *The Shadow Exploded* (p. 129):

Before turning to a more detailed analysis of Prom Night itself, it might be well to sum up what we know of Carrie White the person.

We know that Carrie was the victim of her mother's religious mania. We know that she possessed a latent telekinetic talent, commonly referred to as TK. We know that this so-called "wild talent" is really a hereditary trait, produced by a gene that is usually recessive, if present at all. We suspect that the TK ability may be glandular in nature. We know that Carrie produced at least one demonstration of her ability as a small girl when she was put into an extreme situation of guilt and stress. We know that a second extreme situation of guilt and stress arose from a shower-room hazing incident. It has been theorized (especially by William G. Throneberry and Julia Givens, Berkeley) that resurgence of the TK ability at this point was caused by both psychological factors (i.e., the reaction of the other girls and Carrie herself to their first menstrual period) and physiological factors (i.e., the advent of puberty).

And finally, we know that on Prom Night, a third stress situation arose, causing the terrible events which we now must begin to discuss. We will begin with . . .

(i am not nervous not a bit nervous)

Tommy had called earlier with her corsage, and now she was pinning it to the shoulder of her gown herself. There was no momma, of course, to do it for her and make sure it was in the right place. Momma had locked herself in the chapel and had been in there for the last two hours, praying hysterically. Her voice rose and fell in frightening, incoherent cycles.

(i'm sorry momma but I can't be sorry)

When she had it fixed to her satisfaction, she dropped her hands and stood quietly for a moment with her eyes closed. There was no full-length mirror in the house,

(vanity vanity all is vanity)

but she thought she was all right. She *had* to be. She—

She opened her eyes again. The Black Forest cuckoo clock, bought with Green Stamps, said seven-ten.

(he'll be here in twenty minutes)

Would he?

Maybe it was all just an elaborate joke, the final crusher, the ultimate punch line. To leave her sitting here half the night in her crushed-velvet prom gown with its princess waistline, juliet sleeves and simple straight skirt—and her tea roses pinned to her left shoulder.

From the other room, on the rise now: ". . . in hallowed earth! We know thou bring'st the Eye That Watcheth, the hideous three-lobed Eye, and the sound of black trumpets. We most heartily repent—"

Carrie did not think anyone could understand the brute courage it had taken to reconcile herself to this, to leave herself open to whatever fearsome possibilities the night might realize. Being stood up could hardly be the worst of them. In fact, in a kind of sneaking, wishful way she thought it might be for the best if—

(no stop that)

Of course it would be easier to stay here with Momma.
Safer. She knew what They thought of Momma. Well, maybe
Momma was a fanatic, a freak, but at least she was predictable.
The house was predictable. She never came home to laughing,
shrieking girls who threw things.

And if he didn't come, if she drew back and gave up? High
school would be over in a month. Then what? A creeping,
subterranean existence in this house, supported by Momma,
watching game shows and soap operas all day on television at
Mrs. Garrison's house when she had Carrie In To Visit (Mrs.
Garrison was eighty-six), walking down to the Center to get a
malted after supper at the Kelly Fruit when it was deserted,
getting fatter, losing hope, losing even the power to think?

No. Oh dear God, please no.

(please let it be a happy ending)

"—protect us from *he* with the split foot who waits in the
alleys and in the parking lots of roadhouses, O Saviour—"

Seven twenty-five.

Restlessly, without thinking, she began to lift objects with
her mind and put them back down, the way a nervous woman
awaiting someone in a restaurant will fold and unfold her
napkin. She could dangle half a dozen objects in air at one
time, and not a sign of tiredness or headache. She kept waiting
for the power to abate, but it remained at high water with no
sign of waning. The other night on her way home from school,
she had rolled a parked car

(oh please god let it not be a joke)

twenty feet down the main street curb with no strain at all. The
courthouse idlers had stared at it as if their eyes would pop out,
and of course she stared too, but she was smiling inside.

The cuckoo popped out of the clock and spoke once.
Seven-thirty.

She had grown a little wary of the terrific strain using the
power seemed to put on her heart and lungs and internal
thermostat. She suspected it would be all too possible for her
heart to literally burst with the strain. It was like being in another's body and forcing her to run and run and run. You would
not pay the cost yourself; the other body would. She was begin-

ning to realize that her power was perhaps not so different from the powers of Indian fakirs, who stroll across hot coals, run needles into their eyes, or blithely bury themselves for periods up to six weeks. Mind over matter in any form is a terrific drain on the body's resources.

Seven thirty-two.

(he's not coming)

(don't think about it a watched pot doesn't boil he'll come)

(no he won't he's out laughing at you with his friends and after a little bit they'll drive by in one of their fast noisy cars laughing and hooting and yelling)

Miserably, she began lifting the sewing machine up and down, swinging it in widening arcs through the air.

"—and protect us also from rebellious daughters imbued with the willfulness of the Wicked One—"

"*Shut up!*" Carrie screamed suddenly.

There was startled silence for a moment, and then the babbling chant began again.

Seven thirty-three.

Not coming.

(then i'll wreck the house)

The thought came to her naturally and cleanly. First the sewing machine, driven through the living-room wall. The couch through a window. Tables, chairs, books and tracts all flying. The plumbing ripped loose and still spurting, like arteries ripped free of flesh. The roof itself, if that were within her power, shingles exploding upward into the night like startled pigeons—

Lights splashed gaudily across the window.

Others cars had gone by, making her heart leap a little, but this one was going much more slowly.

(o)

She ran to the window, unable to restrain herself, and it was him, Tommy, just climbing out of his car, and even under the street light he was handsome and alive and almost . . . crackling. The odd word made her want to giggle.

Momma had stopped praying.

She grabbed her light silken wrap from where it had lain across the back of her chair and put it around her bare shoulders. She bit her lip, touched her hair, and would have sold her soul for a mirror. The buzzer in the hall made its harsh cry.

She made herself wait, controlling the twitch in her hands, for the second buzz. Then she went slowly, with silken swish.

She opened the door and he was there, nearly blinding in white dinner jacket and dark dress pants.

They looked at each other, and neither said a word.

She felt that her heart would break if he uttered so much as the wrong sound, and if he laughed she would die. She felt—actually, physically—her whole miserable life narrow to a point that might be an end or the beginning of a widening beam.

Finally, helpless, she said: "Do you like me?"

He said: "You're beautiful."

She was.

From *The Shadow Exploded* (p. 131):

While those going to the Ewen Spring Ball were gathering at the high school or just leaving pre-Prom buffets, Christine Hargensen and William Nolan had met in a room above a local town-limits tavern called The Cavalier. We know that they had been meeting there for some time; that is in the records of the White Commission. What we don't know is whether their plans were complete and irrevocable or if they went ahead almost on whim . . .

"Is it time yet?" she asked in the darkness.

He looked at his watch. "No."

Faintly, through the board floor, came the thump of the juke playing "She's Got To Be a Saint," by Ray Price. The Cavalier, Chris reflected, hadn't changed their records since the first time she'd been here with a forged ID two years ago. Of course then she'd been down in the taprooms, not in one of Sam Deveaux's "specials."

Billy's cigarette winked fitfully in the dark, like the eye of an uneasy demon. She watched it introspectively. She hadn't let him sleep with her until last Monday, when he had promised that he and his greaser friends would help her pull the string on Carrie White if she actually dared to go to the prom with

Tommy Ross. But they had been here before, and had had some pretty hot necking sessions—what she thought of as Scotch love and what he would call, in his unfailing ability to pinpoint the vulgar, the dry humps.

She had meant to make him wait until he had actually *done* something

(but of course he did he got the blood)

but it had all begun to slip out of her hands, and it made her uneasy. If she had not given in willingly on Monday, he would have taken her by force.

Billy had not been her first lover, but he was the first she could not dance and dandle at her whim. Before him her boys had been clever marionettes with clear, pimple-free faces and parents with connections and country-club memberships. They drove their own VWs or Javelins or Dodge Chargers. They went to UMass or Boston College. They wore fraternity wind-breakers in the fall and muscle-shirts with bright stripes in the summer. They smoked marijuana a great deal and talked about the funny things that happened to them when they were wrecked. They began by treating her with patronizing good fellowship (all high school girls, no matter how good-looking, were Bush League) and always ended up trotting after her with panting, doglike lust. If they trotted long enough and spent enough in the process, she usually let them go to bed with her. Quite often she lay passively beneath them, not helping or hindering, until it was over. Later, she achieved her own solitary climax while viewing the incident as a single closed loop of memory.

She had met Billy Nolan following a drug bust at a Portland apartment. Four students, including Chris's date for the evening, had been busted for possession. Chris and the other girls were charged with being present there. Her father took care of it with quiet efficiency, and asked her if she knew what would happen to his image and his practice if his daughter was taken up on a drug charge. She told him that she doubted if anything could hurt either one, and he took her car away.

Billy offered her a ride home from school one afternoon a week later and she accepted.

He was what the other kids called a white-soxer or a machine-shop Chuck. Yet something about him excited her and now, lying drowsily in this illicit bed (but with an awakening sense of excitement and pleasurable fear), she thought it might have been his car—at least at the start.

It was a million miles from the machine-stamped, anonymous vehicles of her fraternity dates with their ventless windows, fold-up steering wheels, and vaguely unpleasant smell of plastic seat covers and windshield solvent.

Billy's car was old, dark, somehow sinister. The windshield was milky around the edges, as if a cataract was beginning to form. The seats were loose and unanchored. Beer bottles clicked and rolled in the back (her fraternity dates drank Budweiser; Billy and his friends drank Rheingold), and she had to place her feet around a huge, grease-clotted Craftsman toolkit without a lid. The tools inside were of many different makes, and she suspected that many of them were stolen. The car smelled of oil and gas. The sound of straight pipes came loudly and exhilaratingly through the thin floorboards. A row of dials slung under the dash registered amps, oil pressure, and tach (whatever that was). The back wheels were jacked and the hood seemed to point at the road.

And of course he drove fast.

On the third ride home one of the bald front tires blew at sixty miles an hour. The car went into a screaming slide and she shrieked aloud, suddenly positive of her own death. An image of her broken, bloody corpse, thrown against the base of a telephone pole like a pile of rags, flashed through her mind like a tabloid photograph. Billy cursed and whipped the fuzz-covered steering wheel from side to side.

They came to a stop on the left-hand shoulder, and when she got out of the car on knees that threatened to buckle at every step, she saw that they had left a looping trail of scorched rubber for seventy feet.

Billy was already opening the trunk, pulling out a jack and muttering to himself. Not a hair was out of place.

He passed her, a cigarette already dangling from the corner of his mouth. "Bring that toolkit, babe."

She was flabbergasted. Her mouth opened and closed twice, like a beached fish, before she could get the words out. "I—I will not! You almost k—you—almost—you crazy *bastard!* Besides, it's *dirty!*"

He turned around and looked at her, his eyes flat. "You bring it or I ain't taking you to the fuckin fights tomorrow night."

"I hate the fights!" She had never been, but her anger and outrage required absolutes. Her fraternity dates took her to rock concerts, which she hated. They always ended up next to someone who hadn't bathed in weeks.

He shrugged, went back to the front end, and began jacking.

She brought the toolkit, getting grease all over a brand-new sweater. He grunted without turning around. His tee shirt had pulled out of his jeans, and the flesh of his back was smooth, tanned, alive with muscles. It fascinated her, and she felt her tongue creep into the corner of her mouth. She helped him pull the tire off the wheel, getting her hands black. The car rocked alarmingly on the jack, and the spare was down to the canvas in two places.

When the job was finished and she got back in, there were heavy smears of grease across both the sweater and the expensive red skirt she was wearing.

"If you think—" she began as he got behind the wheel.

He slid across the seat and kissed her, his hands moving heavily on her, from waist to breasts. His breath was redolent of tobacco; there was the smell of Brylcreem and sweat. She broke it at last and stared down at herself, gasping for breath. The sweater was blotted with road grease and dirt now. Twenty-seven-fifty in Jordan Marsh and it was beyond anything but the garbage can. She was intensely, almost painfully excited.

"How are you going to explain that?" he asked, and kissed her again. His mouth felt as if he might be grinning.

"Feel me," she said in his ear. "Feel me all over. Get me dirty."

He did. One nylon split like a gaping mouth. Her skirt, short to begin with, was pushed rudely up to her waist. He groped greedily with no finesse at all. And something—perhaps that, perhaps the sudden brush with death—brought her to sudden, jolting orgasm. She had gone to the fights with him.

"Quarter of eight," he said, and sat up in bed. He put on the lamp and began to dress. His body still fascinated her. She thought of last Monday night, and how it had been. He had—

(no)

Time enough to think of that later, maybe, when it would do something for her besides cause useless arousal. She swung her own legs over the edge of the bed and slid into gossamer panties.

"Maybe it's a bad idea," she said, not sure if she was testing him or herself. "Maybe we ought to just get back into bed and—"

"It's a good idea," he said, and a shadow of humor crossed his face. "Pig blood for a pig."

"What?"

"Nothing. Come on. Get dressed."

She did, and when they left by the back stairs she could feel a large excitement blooming, like a rapacious and night-flowering vine, in her belly.

From *My Name Is Susan Snell* (p. 45):

You know, I'm not as sorry about all of it as people seem to think I should be. Not that they say it right out; *they're* the ones who always say how dreadfully sorry they are. That's usually just before they ask for my autograph. But they expect you to be sorry. They expect you to get weepy, to wear a lot of black, to drink a little too much or take drugs. They say things like: "Oh, it's such a shame. But you know what happened to her—" and blah, blah, blah.

But sorry is the Kool-Aid of human emotions. It's what you say when you spill a cup of coffee or throw a gutterball when you're bowling with the girls in the league. True sorrow is as rare as true love. I'm not sorry that Tommy is dead any more. He seems too much like a daydream I once had. You probably think that's cruel, but there's been a lot of water under the bridge since Prom Night. And I'm not sorry for my appearance before the White Commission. I told the truth—as much of it as I knew.

But I am sorry for Carrie.

They've forgotten her, you know. They've made her into some kind of a symbol and forgotten that she was a human being, as real as you reading this, with hopes and dreams and blah, blah, blah. Useless to tell you that, I suppose. Nothing can change her back now from something made out of newsprint into a person. But she was, and she hurt. More than any of us probably know, she hurt.

And so I'm sorry and I hope it was good for her, that prom. Until the terror began, I hope it was good and fine and wonderful and magic. . . .

Tommy pulled into the parking lot beside the high school's new wing, let the motor idle for just a second, and then switched it off. Carrie sat on her side of the seat, holding her wrap around her bare shoulders. It suddenly seemed to her that she was living in a dream of hidden intentions and had just become aware of the fact. What could she be doing? She had left Momma alone.

"Nervous?" he asked, and she jumped.

"Yes."

He laughed and got out. She was about to open her door when he opened it for her. "Don't be nervous," he said. "You're like Galatea."

"Who?"

"Galatea. We read about her in Mr. Evers' class. She turned from a drudge into a beautiful woman and nobody even knew her."

She considered it. "I want them to know me," she said finally.

"I don't blame you. Come on."

George Dawson and Frieda Jason were standing by the Coke machine. Frieda was in an orange tulle concoction, and looked a little like a tuba. Donna Thibodeau was taking tickets at the door along with David Bracken. They were both National Honor Society members, part of Miss Geer's personal Gestapo, and they wore white slacks and red blazers—the school colors. Tina Blake and Norma Watson were handing out programs and seating people inside according to their chart. Both of them were dressed in black, and Carrie supposed they thought they were very chic, but to her they looked like cigarette girls in an old gangster movie.

All of them turned to look at Tommy and Carrie when they came in, and for a moment there was a stiff, awkward silence.

Carrie felt a strong urge to wet her lips and controlled it. Then George Dawson said:

"Gawd, you look queer, Ross."

Tommy smiled. "When did you come out of the treetops, Bomba?"

Dawson lurched forward with his fists up, and for a moment Carrie felt stark terror. In her keyed-up state, she came within an ace of picking George up and throwing him across the lobby. Then she realized it was an old game, often played, well-loved.

The two of them sparred in a growling circle. Then George, who had been tagged twice in the ribs, began to gobble and yell: "Kill them Congs! Get them Gooks! Pongee sticks! Tiger cages!" and Tommy collapsed his guard, laughing.

"Don't let it bother you," Frieda said, tilting her letter-opener nose and strolling over. "If they kill each other, I'll dance with you."

"They look too stupid to kill," Carrie ventured. "Like dinosaurs." And when Frieda grinned, she felt something very old and rusty loosen inside her. A warmth came with it. Relief. Ease.

"Where'd you buy your dress?" Frieda asked. "I love it."

"I made it."

"Made it?" Frieda's eyes opened in unaffected surprise. "No shit!"

Carrie felt herself blushing furiously. "Yes I did. I . . . I like to sew. I got the material at John's in Westover. The pattern is really quite easy."

"Come on," George said to all of them in general. "Band's gonna start." He rolled his eyes and went through a limber, satiric buck-and-wing. "Vibes, vibes, vibes. Us Gooks love them big Fender viyyybrations."

When they went in, George was doing impressions of Flash Bobby Pickett and mugging, Carrie was telling Frieda about her dress, and Tommy was grinning, hands stuffed in his pockets. Spoiled the lines of his dinner jacket Sue would be telling him, but fuck it, it seem to be working. So far it was working fine.

He and George and Frieda had less than two hours to live.

•   •   •

From *The Shadow Exploded* (p. 132):

The White Commission's stand on the trigger of the whole affair—two buckets of pig blood on a beam over the stage—seems to be overly weak and vacillating, even in light of the scant concrete proof. If one chooses to believe the hearsay evidence of Nolan's immediate circle of friends (and to be brutally frank, they do not seem intelligent enough to lie convincingly), then Nolan took this part of the conspiracy entirely out of Christine Hargensen's hands and acted on his own initiative . . .

He didn't talk when he drove; he liked to drive. The operation gave him a feeling of power that nothing could rival, not even fucking.

The road unrolled before them in photographic blacks and whites, and the speedometer trembled just past seventy. He came from a broken home; his father had taken off after the failure of a badly managed gas-station venture when Billy was twelve, and his mother had four boy friends at last count. Brucie was in greatest favor right now. He was a Seagrams 7 man. She was turning into one ugly bag, too.

But the car: the car fed him power and glory from its own mystic lines of force. It made him someone to be reckoned with, someone with *mana*. It was not by accident that he had done most of his balling in the back seat. The car was his slave and his god. It gave, and it could take away. Billy had used it to take away many times. On long, sleepless nights when his mother and Brucie were fighting, Billy made popcorn and went out cruising for stray dogs. Some mornings he let the car roll, engine dead, into the garage he had constructed behind the house with its front bumper dripping.

She knew his habits well enough by now and did not bother making conversation that would simply be ignored anyway. She sat beside him with one leg curled under her, gnawing a knuckle. The lights of the cars streaking past them on 302 gleamed softly in her hair, streaking it silver.

He wondered how long she would last. Maybe not long after tonight. Somehow it had all led to this, even the early part, and when it was done the glue that had held them together would be thin and might dissolve, leaving them to wonder how it could have been in the first place. He thought she would start to look less like a goddess and more like the typical society bitch again, and that would make him want to belt her around a little. Or maybe a lot. Rub her nose in it.

They breasted the Brickyard Hill and there was the high school below them, the parking lot filled with plump, glistening daddies' cars. He felt the familiar gorge of disgust and hate rise in his throat. We'll give them something

(a night to remember)

all right. We can do that.

The classroom wings were dark and silent and deserted; the lobby was lit with a standard yellow glow, and the bank of glass that was the gymnasium's east side glowed with a soft, orangey light that was ethereal, almost ghostly. Again the bitter taste, and the urge to throw rocks.

"I see the lights, I see the party lights," he murmured.

"Huh?" She turned to him, startled out of her own thoughts.

"Nothing." He touched the nape of her neck. "I think I'm gonna let you pull the string."

Billy did it by himself, because he knew perfectly well that he could trust nobody else. That had been a hard lesson, much harder than the ones they taught you in school, but he had learned it well. The boys who had gone with him to Henty's place the night before had not even known what he wanted the blood for. They probably suspected Chris was involved, but they could not even be sure of that.

He drove to the school minutes after Thursday night had become Friday morning and cruised by twice to make sure it was deserted and neither of Chamberlain's two police cars was in the area.

He drove into the parking lot with his lights off and swung around in back of the building. Further back, the football field glimmered beneath a thin membrane of ground fog.

He opened the trunk and unlocked the ice chest. The blood

had frozen solid, but that was all right. It would have the next twenty-two hours to thaw.

He put the buckets on the ground, then got a number of tools from his kit. He stuck them in his back pocket and grabbed a brown bag from the seat. Screws clinked inside.

He worked without hurry, with the easeful concentration of one who is unable to conceive of interruption. The gym where the dance was to be held was also the school auditorium, and the small row of windows looking toward where he had parked opened on the backstage storage area.

He selected a flat tool with a spatulate end and slid it through the small jointure between the upper and lower panes of one window. It was a good tool. He had made it himself in the Chamberlain metal shop. He wiggled it until the window's slip lock came free. He pushed the window up and slid in.

It was very dark. The predominant odor was of old paint from the Dramatics Club canvas flats. The gaunt shadows of Band Society music stands and instrument cases stood around like sentinels. Mr. Downer's piano stood in one corner.

Billy took a small flashlight out of the bag and made his way to the stage and stepped through the red velvet curtains. The gym floor, with its painted basketball lines and highly varnished surface, glimmered at him like an amber lagoon. He shone his light on the apron in front of the curtain. There, in ghostly chalk lines, someone had drawn the floor silhouette of the King and Queen thrones which would be placed the following day. Then the entire apron would be strewn with paper flowers . . . why, Christ only knew.

He craned his neck and shone the beam of his light up into the shadows. Overhead, girders crisscrossed in shadowy lines. The girders over the dance floor had been sheathed in crepe paper, but the area directly over the apron hadn't been decorated. A short draw curtain obscured the girders up there, and they were invisible from the gym floor. The draw curtain also hid a bank of lights that would highlight the gondola mural.

Billy turned off the flashlight, walked to the left-hand edge of the apron, and mounted a steel-runged ladder bolted to the wall. The contents of his brown bag, which he had tucked into his shirt for safety, jingled with a strange, hollow jolliness in the deserted gymnasium.

At the top of the ladder was a small platform. Now, as he faced outward toward the apron, the stage flies were to his right, the gym itself on his left. In the flies the Dramatics Club props were stored, some of them dating back to the 1920s. A bust of Pallas, used in some ancient dramatic version of Poe's "The Raven," stared at Billy with blind, floating eyes from atop a rusting bedspring. Straight ahead, a steel girder ran out over the apron. Lights to be used against the mural were bolted to the bottom of it.

He stepped out onto it and walked effortlessly, without fear, out over the drop. He was humming a popular tune under his breath. The beam was inch-thick with dust, and he left long, shuffling tracks. Halfway out he stopped, dropped to his knees, and peered down.

Yes. With the help of his light he could make out the chalk lines on the apron directly below. He made a soundless whistling.

(bombs away)

He X'd the precise spot in the dust, then beam-walked back to the platform. No one would be up here between now and the Ball; the lights that shone on the mural and on the apron where the King and Queen would be crowned

(they'll get crowned all right)

were controlled from a box backstage. Anyone looking up from directly below would be blinded by those same lights. His arrangements would be noticed only if someone went up into the flies for something. He didn't believe anyone would. It was an acceptable risk.

He opened the brown bag and took out a pair of Playtex rubber gloves, put them on, and then took out one of two small pullies he had purchased yesterday. He had gotten them at a hardware store in Lewiston, just to be safe. He popped a number of nails into his mouth like cigarettes and got the hammer. Still humming around his mouthful of nails, he fixed the pulley neatly in the corner a foot above the platform. Beside it he fixed a small eyehole screw.

He went back down the ladder, crossed backstage, and climbed another ladder not far from where he had come in. He was in the loft—sort of a catchall school attic. Here there were stacks of old yearbooks, moth-eaten athletic uniforms, and ancient textbooks that had been nibbled by mice.

Looking left, he could shine his light over the stage flies and spotlight the pulley he had just put up. Turning right, cool night air played on his face from a vent in the wall. Still humming, he took out the second pulley and nailed it up.

He went back down, crawled out the window he had forced, and got the two buckets of pig blood. He had been about his business for a half hour, but it showed no signs of thawing. He picked the buckets up and walked back to the window, silhouetted in the darkness like a farmer coming back from the first milking. He lifted them inside and went in after.

Beam-walking was easier with a bucket in each hand for balance. When he reached his dust-marked X, he put the buckets down, peered at the chalk marks on the apron once more, nodded, and walked back to the platform. He thought about wiping the buckets on his last trip out to them—Kenny's prints would be on them, Don's and Steve's as well—but it was better not to. Maybe they would have a little surprise on Saturday morning. The thought made his lips quirk.

The last item in the bag was a coil of jute twine. He walked back out to the buckets and tied the handles of both with running slipknots. He threaded the screw, then the pulley. He threw the uncoiling twine across to the loft, and then threaded that one. He probably would not have been amused to know that, in the gloom of the auditorium, covered and streaked with decades-old dust, gray kitties flying dreamily about his crow's-nest hair, he looked like a hunched, half-mad Rube Goldberg intent upon creating the better mousetrap.

He piled the slack twine on top of a stack of crates within reach of the vent. He climbed down for the last time and dusted off his hands. The thing was done.

He looked out the window, then wriggled through and thumped to the ground. He closed the window, reinserted his jimmy, and closed the lock as far as he could. Then he went back to his car.

Chris said chances were good that Tommy Ross and the White bitch would be the ones under the buckets; she had been doing a little quiet promoting among her friends. That would be good, if it happened. But, for Billy, any of the others would be all right too.

He was beginning to think that it would be all right if it was Chris herself.

He drove away.

From *My Name Is Susan Snell* (p. 48):

Carrie went to see Tommy the day before the prom. She was waiting outside one of his classes and he said she looked really wretched, as if she thought he'd yell at her to stop hanging around and stop bugging him.

She said she had to be in by eleven-thirty at the latest, or her momma would be worried. She said she wasn't going to spoil his time or anything, but it wouldn't be fair to worry her momma.

Tommy suggested they stop at the Kelly Fruit after and grab a root beer and a burger. All the other kids would be going to Westover or Lewiston, and they would have the place to themselves. Carrie's face lit up, he said. She told him that would be fine. Just fine.

This is the girl they keep calling a monster. I want you to keep that firmly in mind. The girl who could be satisfied with a hamburger and a dime root beer after her only school dance so her momma wouldn't be worried . . .

The first thing that struck Carrie when they walked in was Glamor. Not glamor but Glamor. Beautiful shadows rustled about in chiffon, lace, silk, satin. The air was redolent with the odor of flowers; the nose was constantly amazed by it. Girls in dresses with low backs, with scooped bodices showing actual cleavage, with Empire waists. Long skirts, pumps. Blinding white dinner jackets, cummerbunds, black shoes that had been spit-shined.

A few people were on the dance floor, not many yet, and in the soft revolving gloom they were wraiths without substance. She did not really want to see them as her classmates. She wanted them to be beautiful strangers.

Tommy's hand was firm on her elbow. "The mural's nice," he said.

"Yes," she agreed faintly.

It had taken on a soft nether light under the orange spots, the boatman leaning with eternal indolence against his tiller while the sunset blazed around him and the buildings conspired together over urban waters. She knew with suddenness and ease that this moment would be with her always, within hand's reach of memory.

She doubted if they all sensed it—they had seen the world—but even George was silent for a minute as they looked, and the scene, the smell, even the sound of the band playing a faintly recognizable movie theme, was locked forever in her, and she was at peace. Her soul knew a moment's calm, as if it had been uncrumpled and smoothed under an iron.

"Viiiiiybes," George yelled suddenly, and led Frieda out onto the floor. He began to do a sarcastic jitterbug to the old-timey big-band music, and someone catcalled over to him. George blabbered, leered, and went into a brief arms-crossed Cossack routine that nearly landed him on his butt.

Carrie smiled. "George is funny," she said.

"Sure he is. He's a good guy. There are lots of good people around. Want to sit down?"

"Yes," she said gratefully.

He went back to the door and returned with Norma Watson, whose hair had been pulled into a huge, teased explosion for the affair.

"It's on the other SIDE," she said, and her bright gerbel's eyes picked Carrie up and down, looking for an exposed strap, an eruption of pimples, any news to carry back to the door when her errand was done. "That's a LOVELY dress, Carrie. Where did you EVER get it?"

Carrie told her while Norma led them around the dance floor to their table. She exuded odors of Avon soap, Woolworth's perfume, and Juicy Fruit gum.

There were two folding chairs at the table (looped and beribboned with the inevitable crepe paper), and the table itself was decked with crepe paper in the school colors. On top was a candle in a wine bottle, a dance program, a tiny gilded pencil, and two party favors—gondolas filled with Planters Mixed Nuts.

"I can't get OVER it," Norma was saying. "You look so DIFFERENT." She cast an odd, furtive look at Carrie's face and it made her feel nervous. "You're positively GLOWING. What's your SECRET?"

"I'm Don MacLean's secret lover," Carrie said. Tommy sniggered and quickly smothered it. Norma's smile slipped a notch, and Carrie was amazed by her own wit—and audacity. That's what you looked like when the joke was on you. As though a bee had stung your rear end. Carrie found she liked Norma to look that way. It was distinctly unchristian.

"Well, I have to get back," she said. "Isn't it EXCITING, Tommy?" Her smile was sympathetic: *Wouldn't it be exciting if—?*

"Cold sweat is running down my thighs in rivers," Tommy said gravely.

Norma left with an odd, puzzled smile. It had not gone the way things were supposed to go. Everyone knew how things were supposed to go with Carrie. Tommy sniggered again. "Would you like to dance?" he asked.

She didn't know how, but wasn't ready to admit to *that* yet. "Let's just sit down for a minute."

While he held out her chair, she saw the candle and asked Tommy if he would light it. He did. Their eyes met over its flame. He reached out and took her hand. And the band played on.

From *The Shadow Exploded* (pp. 133–34):

Perhaps a complete study of Carrie's mother will be undertaken someday, when the subject of Carrie herself becomes more academic. I myself might attempt it, if only to gain access to the Brigham family tree. It might be extremely interesting to know what odd occurrences one might come across two or three generations back . . .

And there is, of course, the knowledge that Carrie went home on Prom Night. Why? It is hard to tell just how sane Carrie's motives were by that time. She may have gone for absolution and forgiveness, or she may have gone for the express purpose of committing matricide. In any event, the physical evidence seems to indicate that Margaret White was waiting for her. . . .

The house was completely silent.
    She was gone.
    At night.
    Gone.
    Margaret White walked slowly from her bedroom into the living room. First had come the flow of blood and the filthy fantasies the Devil sent with it. Then this hellish Power the Devil had given to her. It came at the time of the blood and the time of hair on the body, of course. Oh, she knew the Devil's Power. Her own grandmother had it. She had been able to light the fireplace without even stirring from her rocker by the window. It made her eyes glow with
    (thou shalt not suffer a witch to live)
a kind of witch's light. And sometimes, at the supper table the sugar bowl would whirl madly like a dervish. Whenever it happened, Gram would cackle crazily and drool and make the sign of the Evil Eye all around her. Sometimes she panted like a dog on a hot day, and when she died of a heart attack at sixty-six, senile to the point of idiocy even at that early age, Carrie had not even been a year old. Margaret had gone into her bedroom not four weeks after Gram's funeral and there her girl-child had lain in her crib, laughing and gurgling, watching a bottle that was dangling in thin air over her head.
    Margaret had almost killed her then. Ralph had stopped her.
    She should not have let him stop her.
    Now Margaret White stood in the middle of the living room. Christ on Calvary looked down at her with his wounded, suffering, reproachful eyes. The Black Forest cuckoo clock ticked. It was ten minutes after eight.
    She had been able to feel, actually *feel*, the Devil's Power working in Carrie. It crawled all over you, lifting and pulling like evil, tickling little fingers. She had set out to do her duty again when Carrie was three, when she had caught her looking in sin at the Devil's slut in the next yard over. Then the

stones had come, and she had weakened. And the power had risen again, after thirteen years. God was not mocked.

First the blood, then the power,

(you sign your name you sign it in blood)

now a boy and dancing and he would take her to a roadhouse after, take her into the parking lot, take her into the back seat, take her—

Blood, fresh blood. Blood was always at the root of it, and only blood could expiate it.

She was a big woman with massive upper arms that had dwarfed her elbows to dimples, but her head was surprisingly small on the end of her strong, corded neck. It had once been a beautiful face. It was still beautiful in a weird, zealous way. But the eyes had taken on a strange, wandering cast, and the lines had deepened cruelly around the denying but oddly weak mouth. Her hair, which had been almost all black a year ago, was now almost white.

The only way to kill sin, true black sin, was to drown it in the blood of

(she must be sacrificed)

a repentant heart. Surely God understood that, and had laid His finger upon her. Had not God Himself commanded Abraham to take his son Isaac up upon the mountain?

She shuffled out into the kitchen in her old and splayed slippers, and opened the kitchen utensil drawer. The knife they used for carving was long and sharp and arched in the middle from constant honing. She sat down on the high stool by the counter, found the sliver of whetstone in its small aluminum dish, and began to scrub it along the gleaming edge of the blade with the apathetic, fixated attention of the damned.

The Black Forest cuckoo clock ticked and ticked and finally the bird jumped out to call once and announce eight-thirty.

In her mouth she tasted olives.

THE SENIOR CLASS PRESENTS SPRING BALL '79

May 27, 1979

Music by The Billy Bosnan Band
Music by Josie and the Moonglows

ENTERTAINMENT
"Cabaret"—Baton Twirling by Sandra Stenchfield
"500 Miles"
"Lemon Tree"
"Mr. Tambourine Man"
     Folk Music by John Swithen and Maureen Cowan
"The Street Where You Live"
"Raindrops Keep Fallin' on My Head"
"Bridge Over Troubled Waters"
     Ewen High School Chorus

CHAPERONES
Mr. Stephens, Miss Geer, Mr. and Mrs. Lublin, Miss Desjardin
Coronation at 10:00 P.M.
Remember, it's YOUR prom; make it one to remember always!

When he asked her the third time, Carrie had to admit that
she didn't know how to dance. She didn't add that, now that the
rock band had taken over for a half-hour set, she would feel
out of place gyrating on the floor,
     (and sinful)
yes, and sinful.
     Tommy nodded, then smiled. He leaned forward and told
her that he hated to dance. Would she like to go around and
visit some of the other tables? Trepidation rose thickly in her
throat, but she nodded. Yes, that would be nice. He was seeing
to her. She must see to him (even if he really did not expect it);
that was part of the deal. And she felt dusted over with the
enchantment of the evening. She was suddenly hopeful that no
one would stick out a foot or slyly paste a kick-me-hard sign on
her back or suddenly squirt water in her face from a novelty

110

carnation and retreat cackling while everyone laughed and pointed and catcalled.

And if there was enchantment, it was not divine but pagan

(momma untie your apron strings i'm getting big)

and she wanted it that way.

"Look," he said as they got up.

Two or three stagehands were sliding the King and Queen thrones from the wings while Mr. Lavoie, the head custodian, directed them with hand motions toward preset marks on the apron. She thought they looked quite Arthurian, those thrones, dressed all in blinding white, strewn with real flowers as well as huge crepe banners.

"They're beautiful," she said.

"You're beautiful," Tommy said, and she became quite sure that nothing bad could happen this night—perhaps they themselves might even be voted King and Queen of the Prom. She smiled at her own folly.

It was nine o'clock.

"Carrie?" a voice said hesitantly.

She had been so wrapped up in watching the band and the dance floor and the other tables that she hadn't seen anyone coming at all. Tommy had gone to get them punch.

She turned around and saw Miss Desjardin.

For a moment the two of them merely looked at each other, and the memory traveled between them, communicated

(she saw me she saw me naked and screaming and bloody)

without words or thought. It was in the eyes.

Then Carrie said shyly: "You look very pretty, Miss Desjardin."

She did. She was dressed in a glimmering silver sheath, a perfect complement to her blonde hair, which was up. A simple pendant hung around her neck. She looked very young, young enough to be attending rather than chaperoning.

"Thank you." She hesitated, then put a gloved hand on Carrie's arm. "You are beautiful," she said, and each word carried a peculiar emphasis.

Carrie felt herself blushing again and dropped her eyes to the table. "It's awfully nice of you to say so. I know I'm not . . . not really . . . but thank you anyway."

"It's true," Desjardin said. "Carrie, anything that happened before . . . well, it's all forgotten. I wanted you to know that."

"I can't forget it," Carrie said. She looked up. The words that rose to her lips were: *I don't blame anyone any more.* She bit them off. It was a lie. She blamed them all and always would, and she wanted more than anything else to be honest. "But it's over with. Now it's over with."

Miss Desjardin smiled, and her eyes seemed to catch and hold the soft mix of lights in an almost liquid sparkling. She looked across toward the dance floor, and Carrie followed her gaze.

"I remember my own prom," Desjardin said softly. "I was two inches taller than the boy I went with when I was in my heels. He gave me a corsage that clashed with my gown. The tailpipe was broken on his car and the engine made . . . oh, an awful racket. But it was magic. I don't know why. But I've never had a date like it, ever again." She looked at Carrie. "Is it like that for you?"

"It's very nice," Carrie said.

"And is that all?"

"No. There's more. I couldn't tell it all. Not to anybody."

Desjardin smiled and squeezed her arm. "You'll never forget it," she said. "Never."

"I think you're right."

"Have a lovely time, Carrie."

"Thank you."

Tommy came up with two Dixie cups of punch as Desjardin left, walking around the dance floor toward the chaperones' table.

"What did she want?" he asked, putting the Dixie cups down carefully.

Carrie, looking after her, said: "I think she wanted to say she was sorry."

Sue Snell sat quietly in the living room of her house, hemming a dress and listening to the Jefferson Airplane *Long John Silver* album. It was old and badly scratched, but soothing.

Her mother and father had gone out for the evening. They knew what was going on, she was sure of that, but they had spared her the bumbling talks about how proud they were of Their Girl, or how glad they were that she was finally Growing Up. She was glad they had decided to leave her alone, because she was still uncomfortable about her own motives and afraid to examine them too deeply, lest she discover a jewel of selfishness glowing and winking at her from the black velvet of her subconscious.

She had done it; that was enough; she was satisfied.

(maybe he'll fall in love with her)

She looked up as if someone had spoken from the hallway, a startled smile curving her lips. That would be a fairy-tale ending, all right. The Prince bends over the Sleeping Beauty, touches his lips to hers.

Sue, I don't know how to tell you this but—

The smile faded.

Her period was late. Almost a week late. And she had always been as regular as an almanac.

The record changer clicked; another record dropped down. In the sudden, brief silence, she heard something within her turn over. Perhaps only her soul.

It was nine-fifteen.

Billy drove to the far end of the parking lot and pulled into a stall that faced the asphalt ramp leading to the highway. Chris started to get out and he jerked her back. His eyes glowed ferally in the dark.

"What?" she said with angry nervousness.

"They use a P.A. system to announce the King and Queen," he said. "Then one of the bands will play the school song. That means they're sitting there in those thrones, on target."

"I know all that. Let go of me. You're hurting."

He squeezed her wrist tighter still and felt small bones grind. It gave him a grim pleasure. Still, she didn't cry out. She was pretty good.

"You listen to me. I want you to know what you're getting into. Pull the rope when the song is playing. Pull it hard. There will be a little slack between the pulleys, but not much. When you pull it and feel those buckets go, *run*. You don't stick around to hear the screams or anything else. This is out of the cute-little-joke league. This is criminal assault, you know? They don't fine you. They put you in jail and throw the key over their shoulder."

It was an enormous speech for him.

Her eyes only glared at him, full of defiant anger.

"Dig it?"

"Yes."

"All right. When the buckets go, I'm going to run. When I get to the car, I'm going to drive away. If you're there, you can come. If you're not, I'll leave you. If I leave you and you spill your guts, I'll kill you. Do you believe me?"

"Yes. Take your fucking hand off me."

He did. An unwilling shadow-grin touched his face. "Okay. It's going to be good."

They got out of the car.

It was almost nine-thirty.

Vic Mooney, President of the Senior Class, was calling jovially into the mike: "All right, ladies and gentlemen. Take your seats, please. It's time for the voting. We're going to vote for the King and Queen."

"This contest insults women!" Myra Crewes called with uneasy good nature.

"It insults men, too!" George Dawson called back, and there was general laughter. Myra was silent. She had made her token protest.

"Take your seats, please!" Vic was smiling into the mike, smiling and blushing furiously, fingering a pimple on his chin. The huge Venetian boatman behind him looked dreamily over Vic's shoulder. "Time to vote."

Carrie and Tommy sat down. Tina Blake and Norma Watson were circulating mimeographed ballots, and when Norma dropped one at their table and breathed "Good LUCK!" Carrie picked up the ballot and studied it. Her mouth popped open.

"Tommy, we're *on* here!"

"Yeah, I saw that," he said. "The school votes for single

candidates and their dates get sort of shanghaied into it. Welcome aboard. Shall we decline?"

She bit her lip and looked at him. "Do you want to decline?"

"Hell, no," he said cheerfully. "If you win, all you do is sit up there for the school song and one dance and wave a scepter and look like a goddam idiot. They take your picture for the yearbook so everyone can see you looked like a goddam idiot."

"Who do we vote for?" She looked doubtfully from the ballot to the tiny pencil by her boatful of nuts. "They're more your crowd than mine." A little chuckle escaped her. "In fact, I don't really have a crowd."

He shrugged. "Let's vote for ourselves. To the devil with false modesty."

She laughed out loud, then clapped a hand over her mouth. The sound was almost entirely foreign to her. Before she could think, she circled their names, third from the top. The tiny pencil broke in her hand, and she gasped. A splinter had scratched the pad of one finger, and a small bead of blood welled.

"You hurt yourself?"

"No." She smiled, but suddenly it was difficult to smile. The sight of the blood was distasteful to her. She blotted it away with her napkin. "But I broke the pencil and it was a souvenir. Stupid me."

"There's your boat," he said, and pushed it toward her. "Toot, toot." Her throat closed, and she felt sure she would weep and then be ashamed. She did not, but her eyes glimmered like prisms and she lowered her head so he would not see.

The band was playing catchy fill-in music while the Honor Society ushers collected the folded-over ballots. They were taken to the chaperones' table by the door, where Vic and Mr. Stephens and the Lublins counted them. Miss Geer surveyed it all with grim gimlet eyes.

Carrie felt an unwilling tension worm into her, tightening muscles in her stomach and back. She held Tommy's hand tightly. It was absurd, of course. No one was going to vote for them. The stallion, perhaps, but not when harnessed in tandem with a she-ox. It would be Frank and Jessica or maybe Don Farnham and Helen Shyres. Or—hell!

Two piles were growing larger than the others. Mr. Stephens finished dividing the slips and all four of them took turns at counting the large piles, which looked about the same. They put their heads together, conferred, and counted once more. Mr. Stephens nodded, thumbed the ballots once more like a man about to deal a hand of poker, and gave them back to Vic. He climbed back on stage and approached the mike. The Billy Bosnan Band played a flourish. Vic smiled nervously, harrumphed into the mike, and blinked at the sudden feedback whine. He nearly dropped the ballots to the floor, which was covered with heavy electrical cables, and somebody snickered.

"We've sort of hit a snag," Vic said artlessly. "Mr. Lublin says this is the first time in the history of the Spring Ball—"

"How far does he go back?" someone behind Tommy grumbled. "Eighteen hundred?"

"We've got a tie."

This got a murmur from the crowd. "Polka dots or striped?" George Dawson called, and there was some laughter. Vic gave a twitchy little smile and almost dropped the ballots again.

"Sixty-three votes for Frank Grier and Jessica MacLean, and sixty-three votes for Thomas Ross and Carrie White."

This was followed by a moment of silence, and then sudden, swelling applause. Tommy looked across at his date. Her head was lowered, as if in shame, but he had a sudden feeling

(carrie carrie carrie)

not unlike the one he had had when he asked her to the prom. His mind felt as if something alien was moving in there, calling Carrie's name over and over again. As if—

"Attention!" Vic was calling. "If I could have your attention, please." The applause quieted. "We're going to have a run-off ballot. When the people passing out the slips of paper get to you, please write the couple you favor on it."

He left the mike, looking relieved.

The ballots were circulated; they had been hastily torn from leftover prom programs. The band played unnoticed and people talked excitedly.

"They weren't applauding for us," Carrie said, looking up. The thing he had felt (or thought he had felt) was gone. "It couldn't have been for us."

"Maybe it was for you."
She looked at him, mute.

"What's taking it so long?" she hissed at him. "I heard them clap. Maybe that was it. If you fucked up—" The length of jute cord hung between them limply, untouched since Billy had poked a screwdriver through the vent and lifted it out.

"Don't worry," he said calmly. "They'll play the school song. They always do."

"But—"

"Shut up. You talk too fucking much." The tip of his cigarette winked peacefully in the dark.

She shut. But

(oh when this is over you're going to get it buddy maybe you'll go to bed with lover's nuts tonight)

her mind ran furiously over his words, storing them. People did not speak to her in such a manner. Her father was a lawyer.

It was seven minutes of ten.

He was holding the broken pencil in his hand, ready to write, when she touched his wrist lightly, tentatively.

"Don't . . ."

"What?"

"Don't vote for us," she said finally.

He raised his eyebrows quizzically. "Why not? In for a penny, in for a pound. That's what my mother always says."

(mother)

A picture rose in her mind instantly, her mother droning endless prayers to a towering, faceless, columnar God who prowled roadhouse parking lots with a sword of fire in one hand. Terror rose in her blackly, and she had to fight with all her spirit to hold it back. She could not explain her dread, her sense of premonition. She could only smile helplessly and repeat: "Don't. Please."

The Honor Society ushers were coming back, collecting folded slips. He hesitated a moment longer, then suddenly scrawled *Tommy and Carrie* on the ragged slip of paper. "For you," he said. "Tonight you go first-class."

She could not reply, for the premonition was on her: her mother's face.

The knife slipped from the whetstone, and in an instant it had sliced the cup of her palm below the thumb.

She looked at the cut. It bled slowly, thickly, from the open lips of the wound, running out of her hand and spotting the worn linoleum of the kitchen floor. Good, then. It was good. The blade had tasted flesh and let blood. She did not bandage it but tipped the flow over the cutting edge, letting the blood dull the blade's sharp glimmer. Then she began to sharpen again, heedless of the droplets which splattered her dress.

If thine right eye offend thee, pluck it out.

If it was a hard scripture, it was also sweet and good. A fitting scripture for those who lurked in the doorway shadows of one-night hotels and in the weeds behind bowling alleys.

Pluck it out.

(oh and the nasty music they play)

Pluck it

(the girls show their underwear how it sweats how it sweats blood)

out.

The Black Forest cuckoo clock began to strike ten *and*

(cut her guts out on the floor)

if thine right eye offend thee, pluck it out.

The dress was done and she could not watch the television or take out her books or call Nancy on the phone. There was nothing to do but sit on the sofa facing the blackness of the kitchen window and feel some nameless sort of fear growing in her like an infant coming to dreadful term.

With a sigh she began to massage her arms absently. They were cold and prickly. It was twelve after ten and there was no reason, really no reason, to feel that the world was coming to an end.

• • •

The stacks were higher this time, but they still looked exactly the same. Again, three counts were taken to make sure. Then Vic Mooney went to the mike again. He paused a moment, relishing the blue feel of tension in the air, and then announced simply:

"Tommy and Carrie win. By one vote."

Dead silence for a moment. Then applause filled the hall again, some of it not without satiric overtones. Carrie drew in a startled, smothered gasp, and Tommy again felt (but for only a second) that weird vertigo in his mind

(carrie carrie carrie carrie)

that seemed to blank out all thought but the name and image of this strange girl he was with. For a fleeting second he was literally scared shitless.

Something fell on the floor with a clink, and at the same instant the candle between them whiffed out.

Then Josie and the Moonglows were playing a rock version of "Pomp and Circumstance," the ushers appeared at their table (almost magically; all this had been rehearsed meticulously by Miss Geer who, according to rumor, ate slow and clumsy ushers for lunch), a scepter wrapped in aluminum foil was thrust into Tommy's hand, a robe with a lush dog-fur collar was thrown over Carrie's shoulders, and they were being led down the center aisle by a boy and a girl in white blazers. The band blared. The audience applauded. Miss Geer looked vindicated. Tommy Ross was grinning bemusedly.

They were ushered up the steps to the apron, led across to the thrones, and seated. Still the applause swelled. The sarcasm in it was lost now; it was honest and deep, a little frightening. Carrie was glad to sit down. It was all happening too fast. Her legs were trembling under her and suddenly, even with the comparatively high neck of her gown, her breasts

(dirtypillows)

felt dreadfully exposed. The sound of the applause in her ears made her feel woozy, almost punch-drunk. Part of her was actually convinced that all this was a dream from which she would wake with mixed feelings of loss and relief.

Vic boomed into the mike: "The King and Queen of the 1979 Spring Ball—Tommy ROSS and Carrie WHITE!"

Still applause, swelling and booming and crackling. Tommy Ross, in the fading moments of his life now, took Carrie's hand and grinned at her, thinking that Suzie's intuition had been very right. Somehow she grinned back. Tommy

(she was right and i love her well i love this one too this carrie she is she is beautiful and it's right and i love all of them the light the light in her eyes)

and Carrie

(can't see them the lights are too bright i can hear them but can't see them the shower remember the shower o momma it's too high i think i want to get down o are they laughing and ready to throw things to point and scream with laughter i can't see them i can't see them it's all too bright)

and the beam above them.

Both bands, in a sudden and serendipitous coalition of rock and brass, swung into the school song. The audience rose to its feet and began to sing, still applauding.

It was ten-o-seven.

Billy had just flexed his knees to make the joints pop. Chris Hargensen stood next to him with increasing signs of nervousness. Her hands played aimlessly along the seams of the jeans she had worn and she was biting the softness of her lower lip, chewing at it, making it a little ragged.

"You think they'll vote for *them?*" Billy said softly.

"They will," she said. "I set it up. It won't even be close. Why do they keep applauding? What's going on in there?"

"Don't ask me, babe. I—"

The school song suddenly roared out, full and strong on the soft May air, and Chris jumped as if stung. A soft gasp of surprise escaped her.

All rise high for Thomas Ewen Hiiiiyyygh . . .

"Go on," he said. "They're there." His eyes glowed softly in the dark. The odd half-grin had touched his features.

She licked her lips. They both stared at the length of jute cord.

We'll raise your banners to the skyyyyyy . . .

"Shut up," she whispered. She was trembling, and he thought that her body had never looked so lush or exciting. When this was over he was going to have her until every other time she'd been had was like two pumps with a fag's little finger. He was going on her like a raw cob through butter.

"No guts, babe?"

He leaned forward. "I won't pull it for you, babe. It can sit there till hell freezes."

With pride we wear the red and whiiyyyyte . . .

A sudden smothered sound that might have been a half-scream came from her mouth, and she leaned forward and pulled violently on the cord with both hands. It came loose with slack for a moment, making her think that Billy had been having her on all this time, that the rope was attached to nothing but thin air. Then it snubbed tight, held for a second, and then came through her palms harshly, leaving a thin burn.

"I—" she began.

The music inside came to a jangling, discordant halt. For a moment ragged voices continued oblivious, and then they stopped. There was a beat of silence, and then someone screamed. Silence again.

They stared at each other in the dark, frozen by the actual act as thought never could have done. Her very breath turned to glass in her throat.

Then, inside, the laughter began.

It was ten twenty-five, and the feeling had been getting worse and worse. Sue stood in front of the gas range on one foot, waiting for the milk to begin steaming so she could dump in the Nestlé's. Twice she had begun to go upstairs and put on a nightgown and twice she had stopped, drawn for no reason at all to the kitchen window that looked down Brickyard Hill and the spiral of Route 6 that led into town.

Now, as the whistle mounted atop the town hall on Main Street suddenly began to shriek into the night, rising and falling in cycles of panic, she did not even turn immediately to the window, but only turned the heat off under the milk so it would not burn.

The town hall whistle went off every day at twelve noon and that was all, except to call the volunteer fire department during grass-fire season in August and September. It was strictly for major disasters, and its sound was dreamy and terrifying in the empty house.

She went to the window, but slowly. The shrieking of the whistle rose and fell, rose and fell. Somewhere, horns were beginning to blat, as if for a wedding. She could see her reflection in the darkened glass, lips parted, eyes wide, and then the condensation of her breath obscured it.

A memory, half-forgotten, came to her. As children in grammar school, they had practiced air-raid drills. When the teacher clapped her hands and said, "The town whistle is blowing," you were supposed to crawl under your desk and put your hands over your head and wait, either for the all-clear or for enemy missiles to blow you to powder. Now, in her mind, as clearly as a leaf pressed in plastic,

(the town whistle is blowing)
she heard the words clang in her mind.

Far below, to the left, where the high school parking lot was—the ring of sodium arc lamps made it a sure landmark, although the school building itself was invisible in the dark—a spark glowed as if God had struck a flint-and-steel.

(that's where the oil tanks are)

The spark hesitated, then bloomed orange. Now you could see the school, and it was on fire.

She was already on her way to the closet to get her coat when the first dull, booming explosion shook the floor under her feet and made her mother's china rattle in the cupboards.

From *We Survived the Black Prom,* by Norma Watson (Published in the August, 1980, issue of *The Reader's Digest* as a "Drama in Real Life" article):

. . . and it happened so quickly that no one really knew what was happening. We were all standing and applauding and singing the school song. Then—I was at the ushers' table just inside the main doors, looking at the stage—there was a sparkle as the big lights over the stage apron reflected on something metallic. I was standing with Tina Blake and Stella Horan, and I think they saw it, too.

All at once there was a huge red splash in the air. Some of it hit the mural and ran in long drips. I knew right away, even before it hit them, that it was blood. Stella Horan thought it was paint, but I had a premonition, just like the time my brother got hit by a hay truck.

They were drenched. Carrie got it the worst. She looked exactly like she had been dipped in a bucket of red paint. She just sat there. She never moved. The band that was closest to the stage, Josie and the Moonglows, got splattered. The lead guitarist had a white instrument, and it splattered all over it.

I said: "My God, that's blood!"

When I said that, Tina screamed. It was very loud, and it rang out clearly in the auditorium.

People had stopped singing and everything was completely quiet. I couldn't move. I was rooted to the spot. I looked up and there were two buckets dangling high over the thrones, swinging and banging together. They were still dripping. All of a sudden they fell, with a lot of loose string paying out behind them. One of them hit Tommy Ross on the head. It made a very loud noise, like a gong.

That made someone laugh. I don't know who it was, but it wasn't the way a person laughs when they see something funny and gay. It was raw and hysterical and awful.

At that same instant, Carrie opened her eyes wide.

That was when they all started laughing. I did too, God help me. It was so . . . so weird.

When I was a little girl I had a Walt Disney storybook called *Song of the South,* and it had that Uncle Remus story about the tarbaby in it. There was a picture of the tarbaby sitting in the middle of the road, looking like one of those old-time Negro minstrels with the blackface and great big white eyes. When Carrie opened her eyes it was like that. They were the only part of her that wasn't completely red. And the light had gotten in them and made them glassy. God help me, but she looked for all the world like Eddie Cantor doing that pop-eyed act of his.

That was what made people laugh. We couldn't help it. It was one of those things where you laugh or go crazy. Carrie had been the butt of every joke for so long, and we all felt that we were part of something special that night. It was as if we were watching a person rejoin the human race, and I for one thanked the Lord for it. And *that* happened. That horror.

And so there was nothing else to do. It was either laugh or cry, and who could bring himself to cry over Carrie after all those years?

She just sat there, staring out at them, and the laughter kept swelling, getting louder and louder. People were holding their bellies and doubling up and pointing at her. Tommy was the only one who wasn't looking at her. He was sort of slumped over in his seat as if he'd gone to sleep. You couldn't tell he was hurt, though; he was splashed too bad.

And then her face . . . broke. I don't know how else to describe it. She put her hands up to her face and half-staggered to her feet. She almost got tangled in her own feet and fell over, and that made people laugh even more. Then she sort of . . . hopped off the stage. It was like watching a big red frog hopping off a lily pad. She almost fell again, but kept on her feet.

Miss Desjardin came running over to her, and she wasn't laughing any more. She was holding out her arms to her. But then she veered off and hit the wall beside the stage. It was the strangest thing. She didn't stumble or anything. It was as if someone had pushed her, but there was no one there.

Carrie ran through the crowd with her hands clutching her face, and somebody put his foot out. I don't know who it was, but she went sprawling on her face, leaving a long red streak on the floor. And she said, "Oof!" I remember that. It made me laugh even harder, hearing Carrie say Oof like that. She started to crawl along the floor and then she got up and ran out. She ran right past me. You could smell the blood. It smelled like something sick and rotted.

She went down the stairs two at a time and then out the doors. And was gone.

The laughter just sort of faded off, a little at a time. Some people were still hitching and snorting. Lennie Brock had taken out a big white handkerchief and was wiping his eyes. Sally McManus looked all white, like she was going to throw up, but she was still giggling and she couldn't seem to stop. Billy Bosnan was just standing there with his little conductor's stick in his hand and shaking his head. Mr. Lublin was sitting by Miss Desjardin and calling for a Kleenex. She had a bloody nose.

You have to understand that all this happened in no more than two minutes. Nobody could put it all together. We were stunned. Some of them were wandering around, talking a little, but not much. Helen Shyres burst into tears, and that made some of the others start up.

Then someone yelled: "Call a doctor! Hey, call a doctor quick!"

It was Josie Vreck. He was up on the stage, kneeling by Tommy Ross, and his face was white as paper. He tried to pick him up, and the throne fell over and Tommy rolled onto the floor.

Nobody moved. They were all just staring. I felt like I was frozen in ice. My God, was all I could think. My God, my God, my God. And then this other thought crept in, and it was as if it wasn't my own at all. I was thinking about Carrie. And about God. It was all twisted up together, and it was awful.

Stella looked over at me and said: "Carrie's back."

And I said: "Yes, that's right."

The lobby doors all slammed shut. The sound was like hands clapping. Somebody in the back screamed, and that started the stampede. They ran for the doors in a rush. I just stood there, not believing it. And when I looked, just before the first of them got there and started to push, I saw Carrie looking in, her face all smeared, like an Indian with war paint on.

She was smiling.

They were pushing at the doors, hammering on them, but they wouldn't budge. As more of them crowded up against them, I could see the first ones to get there being battered against them, grunting and wheezing. They wouldn't open. And those doors are never locked. It's a state law.

Mr. Stephens and Mr. Lublin waded in, and began to pull them away, grabbing jackets, skirts, anything. They were all screaming and burrowing like cattle. Mr. Stephens slapped a couple of girls and punched Vic Mooney in the eye. They were yelling for them to go out the back fire doors. Some did. Those were the ones who lived.

That's when it started to rain ... at least, that's what I thought it was at first. There was water falling all over the place. I looked up and all the sprinklers were on, all over the gym. Water was hitting the basketball court and splashing. Josie Vreck was yelling for the guys in his band to turn off the electric amps and mikes quick, but they were all gone. He jumped down from the stage.

The panic at the doors stopped. People backed away, looking up at the ceiling. I heard somebody—Don Farnham, I think—say: "This is gonna wreck the basketball court."

A few other people started to go over and look at Tommy Ross. All at once I knew I wanted to get out of there. I took Tina Blake's hand and said, "Let's run. Quick."

To get to the fire doors, you had to go down a short corridor to the left of the stage. There were sprinklers there too, but they weren't on. And the doors were open—I could see a few people running out. But most of them were just standing around in little groups, blinking at each other. Some of them were looking at the smear of blood where Carrie fell down. The water was washing it away.

I took Tina's arm and started to pull her toward the exit sign. At that same instant there was a huge flash of light, a scream, and a horrible feedback whine. I looked around and saw Josie Vreck holding onto one of the mike stands. He couldn't let go. His eyes were bugging out and his hair was on end and it looked like he was dancing. His feet were sliding around in the water and smoke started to come out of his shirt.

He fell over on one of the amps—they were big ones, five or six feet high—and it fell into the water. The feedback went up to a scream that was head-splitting, and then there was another sizzling flash and it stopped. Josie's shirt was on fire.

"Run!" Tina yelled at me. "Come on, Norma. *Please!*"

We ran out into the hallway, and something exploded backstage—the main power switches, I guess. For just a second I looked back. You could see right out onto the stage, where Tommy's body was, because the curtain was up. All the heavy light cables were in the air, flowing and jerking and writhing like snakes out of an Indian fakir's basket. Then one of them pulled in two. There was a violet flash when it hit the water, and then everybody was screaming at once.

Then we were out the door and running across the parking lot. I think I was screaming. I don't remember very well. I don't remember anything very well after they started screaming. After those high-voltage cables hit that water-covered floor . . .

For Tommy Ross, age eighteen, the end came swiftly and mercifully and almost without pain.

He was never even aware that something of importance was happening. There was a clanging, clashing noise that he associated momentarily with

(there go the milk buckets)

a childhood memory of his Uncle Galen's farm and then with

(somebody dropped something)

the band below him. He caught a glimpse of Josie Vreck looking over his head

(what have i got a halo or something)

and then the quarter-full bucket of blood struck him. The raised lip along the bottom of the rim struck him on top of the head and

(hey that hur)

he went swiftly down into unconsciousness. He was still sprawled on the stage when the fire originating in the electrical equipment of Josie and the Moonglows spread to the mural of the Venetian boatman, and then to the rat warren of old uniforms, books, and papers backstage and overhead.

He was dead when the oil tank exploded a half hour later.

From the New England AP ticker, 10:46 P.M.:

CHAMBERLAIN, MAINE (AP)

A FIRE IS RAGING OUT OF CONTROL AT EWEN (U-WIN) CON-
SOLIDATED HIGH SCHOOL AT THIS TIME. A SCHOOL DANCE
WAS IN PROGRESS AT THE TIME OF THE OUTBREAK WHICH IS
BELIEVED TO HAVE BEEN ELECTRICAL IN ORIGIN. WITNESSES

SAY THAT THE SCHOOL'S SPRINKLER SYSTEM WENT ON WITH-
OUT WARNING, CAUSING A SHORT-CIRCUIT IN THE EQUIPMENT
OF A ROCK BAND. SOME WITNESSES ALSO REPORT BREAKS IN
MAIN POWER CABLES. IT IS BELIEVED THAT AS MANY AS ONE
HUNDRED AND TEN PERSONS MAY BE TRAPPED IN THE BLAZING
SCHOOL GYMNASIUM. FIRE FIGHTING EQUIPMENT FROM THE
NEIGHBORING TOWNS OF WESTOVER, MOTTON, AND LEWISTON
HAVE REPORTEDLY RECEIVED REQUESTS FOR ASSISTANCE AND
ARE NOW OR SHORTLY WILL BE EN ROUTE. AS YET, NO CASUAL-
TIES HAVE BEEN REPORTED. ENDS.
10:46 PM MAY 27 6904D AP

From the New England AP ticker, 11:22 P.M.

URGENT

CHAMBERLAIN, MAINE (AP)

A TREMENDOUS EXPLOSION HAS ROCKED THOMAS EWIN
(U-WIN) CONSOLIDATED HIGH SCHOOL IN THE SMALL MAINE
TOWN OF CHAMBERLAIN. THREE CHAMBERLAIN FIRE TRUCKS,
DISPATCHED EARLIER TO FIGHT A BLAZE AT THE GYMNASIUM
WHERE A SCHOOL PROM WAS TAKING PLACE, HAVE ARRIVED
TO NO AVAIL. ALL FIRE HYDRANTS IN THE AREA HAVE BEEN
VANDALIZED, AND WATER PRESSURE FROM CITY MAINS IN THE
AREA FROM SPRING STREET TO GRASS PLAZA IS REPORTED TO
BE NIL. ONE FIRE OFFICIAL SAID: "THE DAMN THINGS WERE
STRIPPED OF THEIR NOZZLES. THEY MUST HAVE SPOUTED
LIKE GUSHERS WHILE THOSE KIDS WERE BURNING." THREE
BODIES HAVE BEEN RECOVERED SO FAR. ONE HAS BEEN IDEN-
TIFIED AS THOMAS B. MEARS, A CHAMBERLAIN FIREMAN. THE
TWO OTHERS WERE APPARENT PROM-GOERS. THREE MORE
CHAMBERLAIN FIREMEN HAVE BEEN TAKEN TO MOTTON RE-
CEIVING HOSPITAL SUFFERING FROM MINOR BURNS AND
SMOKE INHALATION. IT IS BELIEVED THAT THE EXPLOSION
OCCURRED WHEN THE FIRE REACHED THE SCHOOL'S FUEL-
OIL TANKS, WHICH ARE SITUATED NEAR THE GYMNASIUM.
THE FIRE ITSELF IS BELIEVED TO HAVE STARTED IN POORLY
INSULATED ELECTRICAL EQUIPMENT FOLLOWING A SPRINKLER
SYSTEM MALFUNCTION. ENDS.
11:22 PM MAY 27 70119E AP

•   •   •

Sue had only a driver's permit, but she took the keys to her mother's car from the pegboard beside the refrigerator and ran to the garage. The kitchen clock read exactly 11:00.

She flooded the car on her first try, and forced herself to wait before trying again. This time the motor coughed and caught, and she roared out of the garage heedlessly, dinging one fender. She turned around, and the rear wheels splurted gravel. Her mother's '77 Plymouth swerved onto the road, almost fishtailing onto the shoulder and making her feel sick to her stomach. It was only at this point that she realized she was moaning deep in her throat, like an animal in a trap.

. She did not pause at the stop sign that marked the intersection of Route 6 and the Back Chamberlain Road. Fire sirens filled the night in the east, where Chamberlain bordered Westover, and from the south behind her—Motton.

She was almost at the base of the hill when the school exploded.

She jammed on the power brakes with both feet and was thrown into the steering wheel like a rag doll. The tires wailed on the pavement. Somehow she fumbled the door open and was out, shading her eyes against the glare.

A gout of flame had ripped skyward, trailing a nimbus of fluttering steel roof panels, wood, and paper. The smell was thick and oily. Main Street was lit as if by a flashgun. In that terrible hallway between seconds, she saw that the entire gymnasium wing of Ewen High was a gutted, flaming ruin.

Concussion struck a moment later, knocking her backward. Road litter blew past her in a sudden and tremendous rush, along with a blast of warm air that reminded her fleetingly of

(the smell of subways)

a trip she had taken to Boston the year before. The windows of Bill's Home Drugstore and the Kelly Fruit Company jingled and fell inward.

She had fallen on her side, and the fire lit the street with hellish noonday. What happened next happened in slow motion as her mind ran steadily onward

(dead are they all dead carrie why think carrie)

at its own clip. Cars were rushing toward the scene, and some people were running in robes, nightshirts, pajamas. She saw a man come out of the front door of Chamberlain's combined police station and courthouse. He was moving slowly. The cars were moving slowly. Even the people running were moving slowly.

She saw the man on the police-station steps cup his hand around his mouth and scream something; unclear over the shrieking town whistle, the fire sirens, the monster-mouth of the fire. Sounded like:

"Heyret! Don't hey that ass!"

The street was all wet down there. The light danced on the water. Down by Teddy's Amoco station.

"—hey, that's—"

And then the world exploded.

From the sworn testimony of Thomas K. Quillan, taken before The State Investigatory Board of Maine in connection with the events of May 27–28 in Chamberlain, Maine (abridged version which follows is from *Black Prom: The White Commission Report*, Signet Books: New York, 1980):

Q. Mr. Quillan, are you a resident of Chamberlain?

A. Yes.

Q. What is your address?

A. I got a room over the pool hall. That's where I work. I mop the floors, vacuum the tables, work on the machines—pinball machines, you know.

Q. Where were you on the night of May twenty-seventh at 10:30 P.M., Mr. Quillan?

A. Well ... actually, I was in a detention cell at the police station. I get paid on Thursdays, see. And I always go out and get bombed. I go out to The Cavalier, drink some Schlitz, play a little poker out back. But I get mean when I drink. Feels like the Roller Derby's going on in my head. Bummer, huh? Once I conked a guy over the head with a chair and—

Q. Was it your habit to go to the police station when you felt these fits of temper coming on?

A. Yeah. Big Otis, he's a friend of mine.

Q. Are you referring to Sheriff Otis Doyle of this county?

A. Yeah. He told me to pop in any time I started feeling mean. The night before the prom, a bunch of us guys were in the back room down at The Cavalier playing stud poker and I got to thinking Fast Marcel Dubay was cheating. I would have known better sober—a Frenchman's idea of pullin' a fast one is to look at his own cards—but that got me going. I'd had a couple of beers, you know, so I folded my hand and went on down to the station. Plessy was catching, and he locked me right up in Holding Cell Number 1. Plessy's a good boy. I knew his mom, but that was many years ago.

Q. Mr. Quillan, do you suppose we could discuss the night of the twenty-seventh? 10:30 P.M.?

A. Ain't we?

Q. I devoutly hope so. Continue.

A. Well, Plessy locked me up around quarter of two on Friday morning, and I popped right off to sleep. Passed out, you might say. Woke up around four o'clock the next afternoon, took three Alka-Seltzers, and went back to sleep. I got a knack that way. I can sleep until my hangover's all gone. Big Otis says I should find out how I do it and take out a patent. He says I could save the world a lot of pain.

Q. I'm sure you could, Mr. Quillan. Now when did you wake up again?

A. Around ten o'clock on Friday night. I was pretty hungry, so I decided to go get some chow down at the diner.

Q. They left you all alone in an open cell?

A. Sure. I'm a fantastic guy when I'm sober. In fact, one time—

Q. Just tell the Committee what happened when you left the cell.

A. The fire whistle went off, that's what happened. Scared the bejesus out of me. I ain't heard that whistle at night since the Viet Nam war ended. So I ran upstairs and sonofabitch, there's no one in the office. I say to myself, hot damn, Plessy's gonna get it for this. There's always supposed to be somebody catching, in case there's a call-in. So I went over to the window and looked out.

Q. Could the school be seen from that window?

A. Sure. It's on the other side of the street, a block and a half down. People were running around and yelling. And that's when I saw Carrie White.

Q. Had you ever seen Carrie White before?

A. Nope.

Q. Then how did you know it was she?

A. That's hard to explain.

Q. Could you see her clearly?

A. She was standing under a street light, by the fire hydrant on the corner of Main and Spring.

Q. Did something happen?

A. I guess to Christ. The whole top of the hydrant exploded off three different ways. Left, right, and straight up to heaven.

Q. What time did this . . . uh . . . malfunction occur?

A. Around twenty to eleven. Couldn't have been no later.

Q. What happened then?

A. She started downtown. Mister, she looked awful. She was wearing some kind of party dress, what was left of it, and she was all wet from that hydrant and covered with blood. She looked like she just crawled out of a car accident. But she was *grinning*. I never saw such a grin. It was like a death's head. And she kept looking at her hands and rubbing them on her dress, trying to get the blood off and thinking she'd never get it off and how she was going to pour blood on the whole town and make them pay. It was awful stuff.

Q. How would you have any idea what she was thinking?

A. I don't know. I can't explain.

Q. For the remainder of your testimony, I wish you would stick to what you *saw*, Mr. Quillan.

A. Okay. There was a hydrant on the corner of Grass Plaza, and that one went, too. I could see that one better. The big lug nuts on the sides were unscrewing themselves. I *saw* that happening. It blew, just like the other one. And she was *happy*. She was saying to herself, *that'll* give 'em a shower, *that'll* . . . whoops, sorry. The fire trucks started to go by then, and I lost track of her. The new pumper pulled up to the school and they started on those hydrants and saw they wasn't going to get no water. Chief Burton was hollering at them, and that's when the school exploded. Je-*sus*.

Q. Did you leave the police station?

A. Yeah. I wanted to find Plessy and tell him about that crazy broad and the fire hydrants. I glanced over at Teddy's Amoco, and I seen something that made my blood run cold. All six gas pumps was off their hooks. Teddy Duchamp's been dead since 1968, God love him, but his boy locked those pumps up every night just like Teddy himself used to do. Every one of them Yale padlocks was hanging busted by their hasps. The nozzles were laying on the tarmac, and the automatic feeds was set on every one. Gas was pouring out onto the sidewalk and into the street. Holy mother of God, when I seen that, my balls drew right up. Then I saw this guy running along with a lighted cigarette.

Q. What did you do?

A. Hollered at him. Something like *Hey! Watch that cigarette! Hey don't, that's gas!* He never heard me. Fire sirens and the town whistle and cars rip-assing up and down the street, I don't wonder. I saw he was going to pitch it, so I started to duck back inside.

Q. What happened next?

A. Next? Why, next thing, the Devil came to Chamberlain . . .

When the buckets fell, she was at first only aware of a loud, metallic clang cutting through the music, and then she was deluged in warmth and wetness. She closed her eyes instinctively. There was a grunt from beside her, and in the part of her mind that had come so recently awake, she sensed brief pain.

(tommy)

The music came to a crashing, discordant halt, a few voices hanging on after it like broken strings, and in the sudden deadness of anticipation, filling the gap between event and realization, like doom, she heard someone say quite clearly:

"My God, that's blood."

A moment later, as if to ram the truth of it home, to make it utterly and exactly clear, someone screamed.

Carrie sat with her eyes closed and felt the black bulge of terror rising in her mind. Momma had been right, after all.

They had taken her again, gulled her again, made her the butt again. The horror of it should have been monotonous, but it was not; they had gotten her up here, up here in front of the whole school, and had repeated the shower-room scene . . . only the voice had said

(my god that's blood)

something too awful to be contemplated. If she opened her eyes and it was true, oh, what then? What then?

Someone began to laugh, a solitary, affrighted hyena sound, and she *did* open her eyes, opened them to see who it was and it *was* true, the final nightmare, she was red and dripping with it, they had drenched her in the very secretness of blood, in front of all of them and her thought

(oh . . . i . . . *COVERED* . . . with it)

was colored a ghastly purple with her revulsion and her shame. She could smell herself and it was the *stink* of blood, the awful wet, coppery smell. In a flickering kaleidoscope of images she saw the blood running thickly down her naked thighs, heard the constant beating of the shower on the tiles, felt the soft patter of tampons and napkins against her skin as voices exhorted her to *plug it UP*, tasted the plump, fulsome bitterness of horror. They had finally given her the shower they wanted.

A second voice joined the first, and was followed by a third—girl's soprano giggle—a fourth, a fifth, six, a dozen, all of them, all laughing. Vic Mooney was laughing. She could see him. His face was utterly frozen, shocked, but that laughter issued forth just the same.

She sat quite still, letting the noise wash over her like surf. They were still all beautiful and there was still enchantment and wonder, but she had crossed a line and now the fairy tale was green with corruption and evil. In this one she would bite a poison apple, be attacked by trolls, be eaten by tigers.

They were laughing at her again.

And suddenly it broke. The horrible realization of how badly she had been cheated came over her, and a horrible, soundless cry

(they're LOOKING at me)

tried to come out of her. She put her hands over her face to hide it and staggered out of the chair. Her only thought was to run, to get out of the light, to let the darkness have her and hide her.

But it was like trying to run through molasses. Her traitor mind had slowed time to a crawl; it was as if God had switched the whole scene from 78 rpm to 33⅓. Even the laughter seemed to have deepened and slowed to a sinister bass rumble.

Her feet tangled in each other, and she almost fell off the edge of the stage. She recovered herself, bent down, and hopped down to the floor. The grinding laughter swelled louder. It was like rocks rubbing together.

She wanted not to see, but she *did* see; the lights were too bright and she could see all their faces. Their mouths, their teeth, their eyes. She could see her own gore-streaked hands in front of her face.

Miss Desjardin was running toward her, and Miss Desjardin's face was filled with lying compassion. Carrie could see beneath the surface to where the real Miss Desjardin was giggling and chuckling with rancid old-maid ribaldry. Miss Desjardin's mouth opened and her voice issued forth, horrible and slow and deep:

"Let me help you, dear. Oh I am so sor—"

She struck out at her

(flex)

and Miss Desjardin went flying to rattle off the wall at the side of the stage and fall into a heap.

Carrie ran. She ran through the middle of them. Her hands were to her face but she could see through the prison of her fingers, could see them, how they were, beautiful, wrapped in light, swathed in the bright, angelic robes of Acceptance. The shined shoes, the clear faces, the careful beauty-parlor hairdos, the glittery gowns. They stepped back from her as if she was plague, but they kept laughing. Then a foot was stuck slyly out

(o yes that comes next o yes)

and she fell over on her hands and knees and began to crawl, to crawl along the floor with her blood-clotted hair hanging in her face, crawling like St. Paul on the Damascus Road, whose eyes had been blinded by the light. Next someone would kick her ass.

But no one did and then she was scrabbling to her feet again. Things began to speed up. She was out through the

door, out into the lobby, then flying down the stairs that she
and Tommy had swept up so grandly two hours ago.

(tommy's dead full price paid full price for bringing a plague
into the place of light)

She went down them in great, awkward leaps, with the
sound of the laughter flapping around her like black birds.

Then, darkness.

She fled across the school's wide front lawn, losing both of
her prom slippers and fleeing barefoot. The closely cut school
lawn was like velvet, lightly dusted with dewfall, and the laughter was behind her. She began to calm slightly.

Then her feet *did* tangle and she fell at full length out by the
flagpole. She lay quiescent, breathing raggedly, her hot face
buried in the cool grass. The tears of shame began to flow, as
hot and as heavy as that first flow of menstrual blood had been.
They had beaten her, bested her, once and for all time. It was
over.

She would pick herself up very soon now, and sneak home
by the back streets, keeping to the shadows in case someone
came looking for her, find Momma, admit she had been wrong—

(!! NO !!)

The steel in her—and there was a great deal of it—suddenly
rose up and cried the word out strongly. The closet? The endless, wandering prayers? The tracts and the cross and only the
mechanical bird in the Black Forest cuckoo clock to mark off
the rest of the hours and days and years and decades of her life?

Suddenly, as if a videotape machine had been turned on in
her mind, she saw Miss Desjardin running toward her, and saw
her thrown out of her way like a rag doll as she used her mind
on her, without even consciously thinking of it.

She rolled over on her back, eyes staring wildly at the stars
from her painted face. She was forgetting

(!! THE POWER !!)

It was time to teach them a lesson. Time to show them a thing
or two. She giggled hysterically. It was one of Momma's pet
phrases.

(momma coming home putting her purse down eyeglasses
flashing well i guess i showed that elt a thing or two at the shop
today)

There was the sprinkler system. She could turn it on, turn it on easily. She giggled again and got up, began to walk barefoot back toward the lobby doors. Turn on the sprinkler system and close all the doors. Look in and let them *see* her looking in, watching and laughing while the shower ruined their dresses and their hairdos and took the shine off their shoes. Her only regret was that it couldn't be blood.

The lobby was empty. She paused halfway up the stairs and *FLEX*, the doors all slammed shut under the concentrated force she directed at them, the pneumatic door-closers snapping off. She heard some of them scream and it was music, sweet soul music.

For a moment nothing changed and then she could feel them pushing against the doors, wanting them to open. The pressure was negligible. They were trapped

(*trapped*)

and the word echoed intoxicatingly in her mind. They were under her thumb, in her power. *Power!* What a word that was!

She went the rest of the way up and looked in and George Dawson was smashed up against the glass, struggling, pushing, his face distorted with effort. There were others behind him, and they all looked like fish in an aquarium.

She glanced up and yes, there were the sprinkler pipes, with their tiny nozzles like metal daisies. The pipes went through small holes in the green cinderblock wall. There were a great many inside, she remembered. Fire laws, or something.

Fire laws. In a flash her mind recalled

(black thick cords like snakes)

the power cords strung all over the stage. They were out of the audience's sight, hidden by the footlights, but she had had to step carefully over them to get to the throne. Tommy had been holding her arm.

(fire and water)

She reached up with her mind, felt the pipes, traced them. Cold, full of water. She tasted iron in her mouth, cold wet metal, the taste of water drunk from the nozzle of a garden hose.

Flex.

For a moment nothing happened. Then they began to back away from the doors, looking around. She walked to the small oblong of glass in the middle door and looked inside.

It was raining in the gym.

Carrie began to smile.

She hadn't gotten all of them, only some. But she found that by looking up at the sprinkler system with her eyes, she could trace its course more easily with her mind. She began to turn on more of the nozzles, and more. Yet it wasn't enough. They weren't crying yet, so it wasn't enough.

(hurt them then hurt them)

There was a boy up on stage by Tommy, gesturing wildly and shouting something. As she watched, he climbed down and ran toward the rock band's equipment. He caught hold of one of the microphone stands and was transfixed. Carrie watched, amazed, as his body went through a nearly motionless dance of electricity. His feet shuffled in the water, his hair stood up in spikes, and his mouth jerked open, like the mouth of a fish. He looked funny. She began to laugh.

(by christ then let them all look funny)

And in a sudden, blind thrust, she yanked at all the power she could feel.

Some of the lights puffed out. There was a dazzling flash somewhere as a live power cord hit a puddle of water. There were dull thumps in her mind as circuit breakers went into hopeless operation. The boy who had been holding the mike stand fell over on one of his amps and there was an explosion of purple sparks and then the crepe bunting that faced the stage was burning.

Just below the thrones, a live 220-volt electricity cable was crackling on the floor and beside it Rhonda Simard was doing a crazed puppet dance in her green tulle formal. Its full skirt suddenly blazed into flame and she fell forward, still jerking.

It might have been at that moment that Carrie went over the edge. She leaned against the doors, her heart pumping wildly, yet her body as cold as ice cubes. Her face was livid, but dull red fever spots stood on each cheek. Her head throbbed thickly, and conscious thought was lost.

She reeled away from the doors, still holding them shut, doing it without thought or plan. Inside the fire was brightening and she realized dimly that the mural must have caught on fire.

She collapsed on the top step and put her head down on her knees, trying to slow her breathing. They were trying to get out the doors again, but she held them shut easily—that alone was no strain. Some obscure sense told her that a few were getting out the fire doors, but let them. She would get them later. She would get all of them. Every last one.

She went down the stairs slowly and out the front doors, still holding the gymnasium doors closed. It was easy. All you had to do was see them in your mind.

The town whistle went off suddenly, making her scream and put her hands in front of her face

(the whistle it's just the fire whistle)

for a moment. Her mind's eye lost sight of the gymnasium doors and some of them almost got out. No, no. Naughty. She slammed them shut again, catching somebody's fingers—it felt like Dale Norbert—in the jamb and severing one of them.

She began to reel across the lawn again, a scarecrow figure with bulging eyes, toward Main Street. On her right was downtown—the department store, the Kelly Fruit, the beauty parlor and barbershop, gas stations, police station, fire station—

(they'll put out my fire)

But they wouldn't. She began to giggle and it was an insane sound: triumphant, lost, victorious, terrified. She came to the first hydrant and tried to twist the huge painted lug nut on the side.

(ohuh)

It was heavy. It was very heavy. Metal twisted tight to balk her. Didn't matter.

She twisted harder and felt it give. Then the other side. Then the top. Then she twisted all three at once, standing back, and they unscrewed in a flash. Water exploded outward and upward, one of the lug nuts flying five feet in front of her at suicidal speed. It hit the street, caromed high into the air, and was gone. Water gushed with white pressure in a cruciform pattern.

Smiling, staggering, her heart beating at over two hundred per minute, she began to walk down toward Grass Plaza. She was unaware that she was scrubbing her bloodied hands against her dress like Lady Macbeth, or that she was weeping even as she laughed, or that one hidden part of her mind was keening over her final and utter ruin.

Because she was going to take them with her, and there was going to be a great burning, until the land was full of its stink.

She opened the hydrant at Grass Plaza, and then began to walk down to Teddy's Amoco. It happened to the first gas station she came to, but it was not the last.

From the sworn testimony of Sheriff Otis Doyle, taken before The State Investigatory Board of Maine (from *The White Commission Report*), p. 29–31:

Q. Sheriff, where were you on the night of May twenty-seventh?

A. I was on Route 179, known as Old Bentown Road, investigating an automobile accident. This was actually over the Chamberlain town line and into Durham, but I was assisting Mel Crager, who is the Durham constable.

Q. When were you first informed that trouble had broken out at Ewen High School?

A. I received a radio transmission from Officer Jacob Plessy at 10:21.

Q. What was the nature of the radio call?

A. Officer Plessy said there was trouble at the school, but he didn't know if it was serious or not. There was a lot of shouting going on, he said, and someone had pulled a couple of fire alarms. He said he was going over to try and determine the nature of the trouble.

Q. Did he say the school was on fire?

A. No, sir.

Q. Did you ask him to report back to you?

A. I did.

Q. Did Officer Plessy report back?

A. No. He was killed in the subsequent explosion of Teddy's Amoco gas station on the corner of Main and Summer.

Q. When did you next have a radio communication concerning Chamberlain?

A. At 10:42. I was at that time returning to Chamberlain with a suspect in the back of my car—a drunk driver. As I have said, the case was actually in Mel Crager's town, but Durham has no jail. When I got him to Chamberlain, we didn't have much of one, either.

Q. What communication did you receive at 10:42?

A. I got a call from the State Police that had been relayed from the Motton Fire Department. The State Police dispatcher said there was a fire and an apparent riot at Ewen High School, and a probable explosion. No one was sure of anything at that time. Remember, it all happened in a space of forty minutes.

Q. We understand that, Sheriff. What happened then?

A. I drove back to Chamberlain with siren and flasher. I was trying to raise Jake Plessy and not having any luck. That's when Tom Quillan came on and started to babble about the whole town going up in flames and no water.

Q. Do you know what time that was?

A. Yes, sir. I was keeping a record by then. It was 10:58.

Q. Quillan claims the Amoco station exploded at 11:00.

A. I'd take the average, sir. Call it 10:59.

Q. At what time did you arrive in Chamberlain?

A. At 11:10 P.M.

Q. What was your immediate impression upon arriving, Sheriff Doyle?

A. I was stunned. I couldn't believe what I was seeing.

Q. What exactly *were* you seeing?

A. The entire upper half of the town's business section was burning. The Amoco station was gone. Woolworth's was nothing but a blazing frame. The fire had spread to three wooden store fronts next to that—Duffy's Bar and Grille, the Kelly Fruit Company, and the billiard parlor. The heat was ferocious. Sparks were flying onto the roofs of the Maitland Real Estate Agency and Doug Brann's Western Auto Store. Fire trucks were coming in, but they could do very little. Every fire hydrant on that side of the street was stripped. The only trucks doing any business at all were two old volunteer fire department pumpers from Westover, and about all they could do was wet the roofs of the surrounding buildings. And of course the high school. It was just . . . gone. Of course it's fairly isolated—nothing close enough to it to burn—but my God, all those kids inside . . . all those kids . . .

Q. Did you meet Susan Snell upon entering town?

A. Yes, sir. She flagged me down.

Q. What time was this?

A. Just as I entered town . . . 11:12, no later.

Q. What did she say?

A. She was distraught. She'd been in a minor car accident—skidding—and she was barely making sense. She asked me if Tommy was dead. I asked her who Tommy was, but she didn't answer. She asked me if we had caught Carrie yet.

Q. The Commission is extremely interested in this part of your testimony, Sheriff Doyle.

A. Yes, sir, I know that.

Q. How did you respond to her question?

A. Well, there's only one Carrie in town as far as I know, and that's Margaret White's daughter. I asked her if Carrie had something to do with the fires. Miss Snell told me Carrie had done it. Those were her words. "Carrie did it. Carrie did it." She said it twice.

Q. Did she say anything else?

A. Yes, sir. She said: "They've hurt Carrie for the last time."

Q. Sheriff, are you sure she didn't say: *"We've* hurt Carrie for the last time"?

A. I am quite sure.

Q. Are you positive? One hundred per cent?

A. Sir, the town was burning around our heads. I—

Q. Had she been drinking?

A. I beg pardon?

Q. Had she been drinking? You said she had been involved in a car smash.

A. I believe I said a minor skidding accident.

Q. And you can't be sure she didn't say *we* instead of *they*?

A. I guess she might have, but—

Q. What did Miss Snell do then?

A. She burst into tears. I slapped her.

Q. Why did you do that?

A. She seemed hysterical.

Q. Did she quiet eventually?

A. Yes, sir. She quieted down and got control of herself pretty well, in light of the fact that her boy friend was probably dead.

Q. Did you interrogate her?

A. Well, not the way you'd interrogate a criminal, if that's what you mean. I asked her if she knew anything about what had happened. She repeated what she had already said, but in a calmer way. I asked her where she had been when the trouble began, and she told me that she had been at home.

Q. Did you interrogate her further?

A. No, sir.

Q. Did she say anything else to you?

A. Yes, sir. She asked me—begged me—to find Carrie White.

Q. What was your reaction to that?

A. I told her to go home.

Q. Thank you, Sheriff Doyle.

Vic Mooney lurched out of the shadows near the Bankers Trust drive-in office with a grin on his face. It was a huge and awful grin, a Cheshire cat grin, floating dreamily in the fireshot darkness like a trace memory of lunacy. His hair, carefully slicked down for his emcee duties, was now sticking up in a crow's nest. Tiny drops of blood were branded across his forehead from some unremembered fall in his mad flight from the Spring Ball. One eye was swelled purple and screwed shut. He walked into Sheriff Doyle's squad car, bounced back like a pool ball, and grinned in at the drunk driver dozing in the back. Then he turned to Doyle, who had just finished with Sue Snell. The fire cast wavering shadows of light across everything, turning the world into the maroon tones of dried blood.

As Doyle turned, Vic Mooney clutched him. He clutched Doyle as an amorous swain might clutch his lady in a hug dance. He clutched Doyle with both arms and squeezed him, all the while goggling upward into Doyle's face with his great crazed grin.

"Vic—" Doyle began.

"She pulled all the plugs," Vic said lightly, grinning. "Pulled all the plugs and turned on the water and buzz, buzz, buzz."

"Vic—"

"We can't let 'em. Oh no. NoNoNo. We can't. Carrie pulled all the plugs. Rhonda Simard burnt up. *Oh Jeeeeeeeeeesuuuuuuuuusss*—"

Doyle slapped him twice, callused palm cracking flatly on the boy's face. The scream died with shocking suddenness, but the grin remained, like an echo of evil. It was loose and terrible.

"What happened?" Doyle said roughly. "What happened at the school?"

"Carrie," Vic muttered. "Carrie happened at the school. She . . ." He trailed off and grinned at the ground.

Doyle gave him three brisk shakes. Vic's teeth clicked together like castanets.

"What about Carrie?"

"Queen of the Prom," Vic muttered. "They dumped blood on her and Tommy."

"What—"

It was 11:15. Tony's Citgo on Summer Street suddenly exploded with a great, coughing roar. The street went daylight that made them both stagger back against the police car and shield their eyes. A huge, oily cloud of fire climbed over the elms in Courthouse Park, lighting the duck pond and the Little League diamond in scarlet. Amid the hungry crackling roar that followed, Doyle could hear glass and wood and hunks of gas-station cinderblock rattling back to earth. A secondary explosion followed, making them wince again. He still couldn't get it straight

(my town this is happening in my town)

that this was happening in Chamberlain, in *Chamberlain*, for God's sake, where he drank iced tea on his mother's sun porch and refereed PAL basketball and made one last cruise out Route 6 past The Cavalier before turning in at 2:30 every morning. His town was burning up.

Tom Quillan came out of the police station and ran down the sidewalk to Doyle's cruiser. His hair was standing up every which way, he was dressed in dirty green work fatigues and an undershirt and he had his loafers on the wrong feet, but Doyle thought he had never been so glad to see anyone in his life.

Tom Quillan was as much Chamberlain as anything, and he was here—intact.

"Holy God," he panted. "Did you see *that?*"

"What's been happening?" Doyle asked curtly.

"I been monitorin' the radio," Quillan said. "Motton and Westover wanted to know if they should send ambulances and I said hell yes, send everything. Hearses too. Did I do right?"

"Yes." Doyle ran his hands through his hair. "Have you seen Harry Block?" Block was the town's Commissioner of Public Utilities, and that included water.

"Nope. But Chief Deighan says they got water in the old Rennett Block across town. They're laying hose now. I collared some kids, and they're settin' up a hospital in the police station. They're good boys, but they're gonna get blood on your floor, Otis."

Otis Doyle felt unreality surge over him. Surely this conversation couldn't be happening in Chamberlain. *Couldn't.*

"That's all right, Tommy. You did right. You go back there and start calling every doctor in the phone book. I'm going over to Summer Street."

"Okay, Otis. If you see that crazy broad, be careful."

"Who?" Doyle was not a barking man, but now he did.

Tom Quillan flinched back. "Carrie. Carrie White."

"Who? How do you know?"

Quillan blinked slowly. "I dunno. It just sort of . . . came to me."

From the national AP ticker, 11:46 P.M.:

CHAMBERLAIN, MAINE (AP)

A DISASTER OF MAJOR PROPORTIONS HAS STRUCK THE TOWN OF CHAMBERLAIN, MAINE, TONIGHT. A FIRE, BELIEVED TO HAVE BEGUN AT EWEN (U-WIN) HIGH SCHOOL DURING A SCHOOL DANCE, HAS SPREAD TO THE DOWNTOWN AREA, RE-SULTING IN MULTIPLE EXPLOSIONS THAT HAVE LEVELED MUCH OF THE DOWNTOWN AREA. A RESIDENTIAL AREA TO THE WEST OF THE DOWNTOWN AREA IS ALSO REPORTED TO BE BURNING. HOWEVER, MOST CONCERN AT THIS TIME IS OVER THE HIGH SCHOOL WHERE A JUNIOR-SENIOR PROM WAS

BEING HELD. IT IS BELIEVED THAT MANY OF THE PROM-GOERS WERE TRAPPED INSIDE. A WESTOVER FIRE OFFICIAL SUMMONED TO THE SCENE SAID THE KNOWN TOTAL OF DEAD STOOD AT SIXTY-SEVEN, MOST OF THEM HIGH SCHOOL STUDENTS. ASKED HOW HIGH THE TOTAL MIGHT GO HE SAID: "WE DON'T KNOW. WE'RE AFRAID TO GUESS. THIS IS GOING TO BE WORSE THAN THE COCONUT GROVE." AT LAST REPORT THREE FIRES WERE RAGING OUT OF CONTROL IN THE TOWN. REPORTS OF POSSIBLE ARSON ARE UNCONFIRMED. ENDS.
11:46 PM MAY 27 8943F AP

There were no more AP reports from Chamberlain. At 12:06 A.M., a Jackson Avenue gas main was opened. At 12:17, an ambulance attendant from Motton tossed out a cigarette butt as the rescue vehicle sped toward Summer Street.

The explosion destroyed nearly half a block at a stroke, including the offices of the Chamberlain *Clarion*. By 12:18 A.M., Chamberlain was cut off from the country that slept in reason beyond.

At 12:10, still seven minutes before the gas-main explosion, the telephone exchange experienced a softer explosion: a complete jam of every town phone line still in operation. The three harried girls on duty stayed at their posts but were utterly unable to cope. They worked with expressions of wooden horror on their faces, trying to place unplaceable calls.

And so Chamberlain drifted into the streets.

They came like an invasion from the graveyard that lay in the elbow crook formed by the intersection of the Bellsqueeze Road and Route 6; they came in white nightgowns and in robes, as if in winding shrouds. They came in pajamas and curlers (Mrs. Dawson, she of the now-deceased son who had been a very funny fellow, came in a mudpack as if dressed for a minstrel show); they came to see what happened to their town, to see if it was indeed lying burned and bleeding. Many of them also came to die.

Carlin Street was thronged with them, a riptide of them, moving downtown through the hectic light in the sky, when

Carrie came out of the Carlin Street Congregational Church, where she had been praying.

She had gone in only five minutes before, after opening the gas main (it had been easy; as soon as she pictured it lying there under the street it had been easy), but it seemed like hours. She had prayed long and deeply, sometimes aloud, sometimes silently. Her heart thudded and labored. The veins on her face and neck bulged. Her mind was filled with the huge knowledge of POWERS, and of an ABYSS. She prayed in front of the altar, kneeling in her wet and torn and bloody gown, her feet bare and dirty and bleeding from a broken bottle she had stepped on. Her breath sobbed in and out of her throat, and the church was filled with groanings and swayings and sunderings as psychic energy sprang from her. Pews fell, hymnals flew, and a silver Communion set cruised silently across the vaulted darkness of the nave to crash into the far wall. She prayed and there was no answer. No one was there—or if there was, He/It was cowering from her. God had turned His face away, and why not? This horror was as much His doing as hers. And so she left the church, left it to go home and find her momma and make destruction complete.

She paused on the lower step, looking at the flocks of people streaming toward the center of town. Animals. Let them burn, then. Let the streets be filled with the smell of their sacrifice. Let this place be called racca, ichabod, wormwood.

Flex.

And power transformers atop lightpoles bloomed into nacreous purple light, spitting catherine-wheel sparks. High-tension wires fell into the streets in pick-up-sticks tangles and some of them ran, and that was bad for them because now the whole street was littered with wires and the stink began, the burning began. People began to scream and back away and some touched the cables and went into jerky electrical dances. Some had already slumped into the street, their robes and pajamas smoldering.

Carrie turned back and looked fixedly at the church she had just left. The heavy door suddenly swung shut, as if in a hurricane wind.

Carrie turned toward home.

• • •

From the sworn testimony of Mrs. Cora Simard, taken before The State Investigatory Board (from *The White Commission Report*), pp. 217–18:

Q. Mrs. Simard, the Board understands that you lost your daughter on Prom Night, and we sympathize with you deeply. We will make this as brief as possible.

A. Thank you. I want to help if I can, of course.

Q. Were you on Carlin Street at approximately 12:12, when Carietta White came out of the First Congregational Church on that street?

A. Yes.

Q. Why were you there?

A. My husband had to be in Boston over the weekend on business and Rhonda was at the Spring Ball. I was home alone watching TV and waiting up for her. I was watching the Friday Night Movie when the town hall whistle went off, but I didn't connect that with the dance. But then the explosion . . . I didn't know what to do. I tried to call the police but got a busy signal after the first three numbers. I . . . I . . . Then . . .

Q. Take your time, Mrs. Simard. All the time you need.

A. I was getting frantic. There was a second explosion— Teddy's Amoco station, I know now—and I decided to go downtown and see what was happening. There was a glow in the sky, an awful glow. That was when Mrs. Shyres pounded on the door.

Q. Mrs. Georgette Shyres?

A. Yes, they live around the corner. 217 Willow. That's just off Carlin Street. She was pounding and calling: "Cora, are you in there? Are you in there?" I went to the door. She was in her bathrobe and slippers. Her feet looked cold. She said they had called Westover to see if they knew anything and they told her the school was on fire. I said: "Oh dear God, Rhonda's at the dance."

Q. Is this when you decided to go downtown with Mrs. Shyres?

A. We didn't decide anything. We just went. I put on a pair of slippers—Rhonda's, I think. They had little white puffballs on them. I should have worn my shoes, but I wasn't thinking. I guess I'm not thinking now. What do you want to hear about my shoes for?

Q. You tell it in your own way, Mrs. Simard.

A. T-Thank you. I gave Mrs. Shyres some old jacket that was around, and we went.

Q. Were there many people walking down Carlin Street?

A. I don't know. I was too upset. Maybe thirty. Maybe more.

Q. What happened?

A. Georgette and I were walking toward Main Street, holding hands just like two little girls walking across a meadow after dark. Georgette's teeth were clicking. I remember that. I wanted to ask her to stop clicking her teeth, but I thought it would be impolite. A block and a half from the Congo Church, I saw the door open and I thought: Someone has gone in to ask God's help. But a second later I knew that wasn't true.

Q. How did you know? It would be logical to assume just what you first assumed, wouldn't it?

A. I just knew.

Q. Did you know the person who came out of the church?

A. Yes. It was Carrie White.

Q. Had you ever seen Carrie White before?

A. No. She was not one of my daughter's friends.

Q. Had you ever seen a picture of Carrie White?

A. No.

Q. And in any case, it was dark and you were a block and a half from the church.

A. Yes, sir.

Q. Mrs. Simard, how did you know it was Carrie White?

A. I just knew.

Q. This *knowing*, Mrs. Simard: was it like a light going on in your head?

A. No, sir.

Q. What *was* it like?

A. I can't tell you. It faded away the way a dream does. An hour after you get up you can only remember you had a dream. But I knew.

Q. Was there an emotional feeling that went with this knowledge?

A. Yes. Horror.

Q. What did you do then?

A. I turned to Georgette and said: "There she is." Georgette said: "Yes, that's her." She started to say something else, and then the whole street was lit up by a bright glow and there were crackling noises and then the power lines started to fall into the street, some of them spitting live sparks. One of them hit a man in front of us and he b-burst into flames. Another man started to run and he stepped on one of them and his body just . . . arched backward, as if his back had turned into elastic. And then *he* fell down. Other people were screaming and running, just running blindly, and more and more cables fell. They were strung all over the place like snakes. And she was glad about it. *Glad!* I could *feel* her being glad. I knew I had to keep my head. The people who were running were getting electrocuted. Georgette said: "Quick, Cora. Oh God, I don't want to get burned alive." I said: "Stop that. We have to use our heads, Georgette, or we'll never use them again." Something foolish like that. But she wouldn't listen. She let go of my hand and started to run for the sidewalk. I screamed at her to stop—there was one of those heavy main cables broken off right in front of us—but she didn't listen. And she . . . she . . . oh, I could smell her when she started to burn. Smoke just seemed to *burst* out of her clothes and I thought: that's what it must be like when someone gets electrocuted. The smell was sweet, like pork. Have any of you ever smelled that? Sometimes I smell it in my dreams. I stood dead still, watching Georgette Shyres turn black. There was a big explosion over in the West End—the gas main, I suppose—but I never even noticed it. I looked around and I was all alone. Everyone else had either run away or was burning. I saw maybe six bodies. They were like piles of old rags. One of the cables had fallen onto the porch of a house to the left, and it was catching on fire. I could hear the old-fashioned shake shingles popping like corn. It seemed like I stood there a long time, telling myself to keep my head. It seemed like hours. I began to be afraid that I would faint and fall on one of the cables, or that I would panic and start to run. Like . . . like Georgette. So I started to walk. One step at a time. The street got even brighter, because of the burning house. I stepped over two live wires and went around a body that wasn't much more than a puddle. I—I—I had to look to see where I was going. There was a wedding ring on the body's hand, but it was all black. All *black*. Jesus, I was thinking. Oh dear Lord. I stepped over another cable and then there were three, all at once. I just stood there looking at them. I thought if I got over those I'd be all right but . . . I didn't dare. Do you know what I kept thinking of? That game you play when you're kids. Giant Step. A voice in my mind was saying, Cora, take one giant step over the live wires in the street. And I was thinking *May I? May I?* One of them was still spitting a few sparks, but the other two looked dead. But you can't tell. The third rail looks dead too. So I stood there, waiting for someone to come and nobody did. The house was still burning and the flames had spread to the lawn and the trees and the hedge beside it. But no fire trucks came. Of course they didn't. The whole west side was burning up by that time. And I felt so *faint*. And at last I knew it was take the giant step or faint and so I took it, as big a giant step as I could, and the heel of my slipper came down not an inch from the last wire. Then I got over and went around the end of one more wire and then I started to run. And that's all I remember. When morning came I was lying on a blanket in the police station with a lot of other people. Some of them—a few—were kids in their prom get-ups and I started to ask them if they had seen Rhonda. And they said . . . they s-s-said . . .

(A short recess)

Q. You are personally sure that Carrie White did this?
A. Yes.
Q. Thank you, Mrs. Simard.
A. I'd like to ask a question, if you please.
Q. Of course.
A. What happens if there are others like her? What happens to the world?

From *The Shadow Exploded* (p. 151):

By 12:45 on the morning of May 28, the situation in Chamberlain was critical. The school had burned itself out on a fairly isolated piece of ground, but the entire downtown area was ablaze. Almost all the city water in that area had been tapped, but enough was available (at low pressure) from Deighan Street water mains to save the business buildings below the intersection of Main and Oak streets.

The explosion of Tony's Citgo on upper Summer Street had resulted in a ferocious fire that was not to be controlled until nearly ten o'clock that morning. There was water on Summer Street; there simply were no firemen or fire-fighting equipment to utilize it. Equipment was then on its way from Lewiston, Auburn, Lisbon, and Brunswick, but nothing arrived until one o'clock.

On Carlin Street, an electrical fire, caused by downed power lines, had begun. It was to eventually gut the entire north side of the street, including the bungalow where Margaret White gave birth to her daughter.

On the West End of town, just below what is commonly called Brickyard Hill, the worst disaster had taken place: the explosion of a gas main and a resulting fire that raged out of control through most of the next day.

And if we look at these flash points on a municipal map (see page facing), we can pick out Carrie's route—a wandering, looping path of destruction through the town, but one with an almost certain destination: home. . . .

Something toppled over in the living room, and Margaret White straightened up, cocking her head to one side. The butcher knife glittered dully in the light of the flames. The electric power had gone off sometime before, and the only light in the house came from the fire up the street.

One of the pictures fell from the wall with a thump. A moment later the Black Forest cuckoo clock fell. The mechanical bird gave a small, strangled squawk and was still.

From the town the sirens whooped endlessly, but she could still hear the footsteps when they turned up the walk.

The door blew open. Steps in the hall.

She heard the plaster plaques in the living room (CHRIST, THE UNSEEN GUEST; WHAT WOULD JESUS DO; THE HOUR DRAWETH NIGH: IF TONIGHT BECAME JUDGMENT, WOULD YOU BE READY) explode one after the other, like plaster birds in a shooting gallery.

(o i've been there and seen the harlots shimmy on wooden stages)

She sat up on her stool like a very bright scholar who has gone to the head of the class. But her eyes were deranged.

The living-room windows blew outward.

The kitchen door slammed and Carrie walked in.

Her body seemed to have become twisted, shrunken, crone-like. The prom dress was in tatters and flaps, and the pig blood had began to clot and streak. There was a smudge of grease on her forehead, and both knees were scraped and raw-looking.

"Momma," she whispered. Her eyes were preternaturally bright, hawklike, but her mouth was trembling. If someone had been there to watch, he would have been struck by the resemblance between them.

Margaret White sat on her kitchen stool, the carving knife hidden among the folds of her dress in her lap.

"I should have killed myself when he put it in me," she said clearly. "After the first time, before we were married, he promised. Never again. He said we just . . . slipped. I believed him. I fell down and I lost the baby and that was God's judgment. I felt that the sin had been expiated. By blood. But sin never dies. *Sin . . . never . . . dies.*" Her eyes glittered.

"Momma, I—"

"At first it was all right. We lived sinlessly. We slept in the same bed, belly to belly sometimes, and o, I could feel the presence of the Serpent, but we. never. did. until." She began to grin, and it was a hard, terrible grin. "And that night I could see him looking at me That Way. We got down on our knees to pray for strength and he . . . touched me. In that place. That woman place. And I sent him out of the house. He was gone for hours, and I prayed for him. I could see him in my mind's eye, walking the midnight streets, wrestling with the devil as Jacob wrestled with the Angel of the Lord. And when he came back, my heart was filled with thanksgiving."

She paused, grinning her dry, spitless grin into the shifting shadows of the room.

"Momma, I don't want to hear it!"

Plates began to explode in the cupboards like clay pigeons.

"It wasn't until he came in that I smelled the whiskey on his breath. And he took me. *Took me!* With the stink of filthy roadhouse whiskey still on him he took me . . . *and I liked it!*" She screamed out the last words at the ceiling. *"I liked it o all that dirty fucking and his hands on me ALL OVER ME!"*

"MOMMA!"

(!! MOMMA !!)

She broke off as if slapped and blinked at her daughter. "I almost killed myself," she said in a more normal tone of voice. "And Ralph wept and talked about atonement and I didn't and then he was dead and then I thought God had visited me with cancer; that He was turning my female parts into something as black and rotten as my sinning soul. But that would have been too easy. The Lord works in mysterious ways His wonders to perform. I see that now. When the pains began I went and got a knife—this knife—" she held it up "—and waited for you to come so I could make my sacrifice. But I was weak and back-sliding. I took this knife in hand again when you were three, and I backslid again. So now the devil has come home."

She held the knife up, and her eyes fastened hypnotically on the glittering hook of its blade.

Carrie took a slow, blundering step forward.

"I came to kill you, Momma. And you were waiting here to kill me. Momma, I . . . it's not right, Momma. It's not . . ."

"Let's pray," Momma said softly. Her eyes fixed on Carrie's and there was a crazed, awful compasssion in them. The fire-light was brighter now, dancing on the walls like dervishes. "For the last time, let us pray."

"Oh Momma help me!" Carrie cried out.

She fell forward on her knees, head down, hands raised in supplication.

Momma leaned forward, and the knife came down in a shining arc.

Carrie, perhaps seeing out of the tail of her eye, jerked back, and instead of penetrating her back, the knife went into her shoulder to the hilt. Momma's feet tangled in the legs of her chair, and she collapsed in a sitting sprawl.

They stared at each other in silent tableau.

Blood began to ooze from around the handle of the knife and to splash onto the floor.

Then Carrie said softly: "I'm going to give you a present, Momma."

Margaret tried to get up, staggered, and fell back on her hands and knees. "What are you doing?" she croaked hoarsely.

"I'm picturing your heart, Momma," Carrie said. "It's easier when you see things in your mind. Your heart is a big red muscle. Mine goes faster when I use my power. But yours is going a little slower now. A little slower."

Margaret tried to get up again, failed, and forked the sign of the evil eye at her daughter.

"A little slower, Momma. Do you know what the present is, Momma? What you always wanted. Darkness. And whatever God lives there."

Margaret White whispered: "Our Father, Who art in heaven—"

"Slower, Momma. Slower."

"—hallowed be Thy name—"

"I can see the blood draining back into you. Slower."

"—Thy kingdom come—"

"Your feet and hands like marble, like alabaster. White."

"—Thy will be done—"

"*My* will, Momma. Slower."

"—on earth—"

"Slower."

"—as . . . as . . . as it . . ."

She collapsed forward, hands twitching.

"—as it is in heaven."

Carrie whispered: "Full stop."

She looked down at herself, and put her hands weakly around the haft of the knife.

(no o no that hurts that's too much hurt)

She tried to get up, failed, then pulled herself up by Momma's stool. Dizziness and nausea washed over her. She could taste blood, bright and slick, in the back of her throat. Smoke, acrid and choking, was drifting in through the windows now. The flames had reached next door; even now sparks would be lighting softly on the roof that rocks had punched brutally through a thousand years before.

Carrie went out the back door, staggered across the lawn, and rested

(where's my momma)

against a tree. There was something she was supposed to do. Something about

(roadhouses parking lots)

the Angel with the Sword. The Fiery Sword.

Never mind. It would come to her.

She crossed by back yards to Willow Street and then crawled up the embankment to Route 6.

It was 1:15 A.M.

It was 11:20 P.M. when Christine Hargensen and Billy Nolan got back to The Cavalier. They went up the back stairs, down the hall, and before she could do more than turn on the lights, he was yanking at her blouse.

"For God's sake let me unbutton it—"

"To hell with that."

He ripped it suddenly down the back. The cloth tore with a sudden hard sound. One button popped free and winked on the bare wood floor. Honky-tonkin' music came faintly up to them, and the building vibrated subtly with the clumsy-enthusiastic dancing of farmers and truckers and millworkers and waitresses and hairdressers, of the greasers and their townie girl friends from Westover and Lewiston.

"Hey—"

"Be quiet."

He slapped her, rocking her head back. Her eyes took on a flat and deadly shine.

"This is the end, Billy." She backed away from him, breasts swelling into her bra, flat stomach pumping, legs long and tapering in her jeans; but she backed toward the bed. "It's over."

"Sure," he said. He lunged for her and she punched him, a surprisingly hard punch that landed on his cheek.

He straightened and twitched his head a little. "You gave me a shiner, you bitch."

"I'll give you more."

"You're goddam right you will."

They stared at each other, panting, glaring. Then he began to unbutton his shirt, a little grin beginning on his face.

"We got it on, Charlie. We really got it on." He called her Charlie whenever he was pleased with her. It seemed to be, she thought with a cold blink of humor, a generic term for good cunt.

She felt a little smile come to her own face, relaxed a little, and that was when he whipped his shirt across her face and came in low, butting her in the stomach like a goat, tipping her onto the bed. The springs screamed. She pounded her fists helplessly on his back.

"Get off me! Get off me! Get off me! You fucking grease-ball, *get off me!*"

He was grinning at her, and with one quick, hard yank her zipper was broken, her hips free.

"Call your daddy?" he was grunting. "That what you gonna do? Huh? Huh? That it, ole Chuckie? Call big ole legal beagle daddy? Huh? I woulda done it to you, you know that? I woulda dumped it all over your fuckin squash. You know it? Huh? Know it? Pig blood for pigs, right? Right on your motherfuckin squash. You—"

She had suddenly ceased to resist. He paused, staring down at her, and she had an odd smile on her face. "You wanted it this way all along, didn't you? You miserable little scumbag. That's right, isn't it? You creepy little one-nut low-cock dinkless wonder."

His grin was slow, crazed. "It doesn't matter."

"No," she said. "It doesn't." Her smile suddenly vanished, the cords on her neck stood out as she hawked back—and spit in his face.

They descended into a red, thrashing unconsciousness.

Downstairs the music thumped and wheezed (*"I'm poppin little white pills an my eyes are open wide/Six days on the road, and I'm gonna make it home tonight"*), c/w, full throttle, very loud, very bad, five-man band wearing sequined cowboy shirts and new pegged jeans with bright rivets, occasionally wiping mixed sweat and Vitalis from their brows, lead guitar, rhythm, steel, dobro guitar, drums: no one heard the town whistle, or the first

157

explosion, or the second; and when the gas main blew and the music stopped and someone drove into the parking lot and began to yell the news, Chris and Billy were asleep.

Chris woke suddenly and the clock on the night table said five minutes of one. Someone was pounding on the door.

"Billy!" the voice was yelling. "Get up! Hey! Hey!"

Billy stirred, rolled over, and knocked the cheap alarm clock onto the floor. "What the Christ?" he said thickly, and sat up. His back stung. The bitch had covered it with long scratches. He'd barely noticed it at the time, but now he decided he was going to have to send her home bowlegged. Just to show her who was b—

Silence struck him. Silence. The Cavalier did not close until two; as a matter of fact, he could still see the neon twinkling and flicking through the dusty garret window. Except for the steady pounding

(something happened)

the place was a graveyard.

"Billy, you in there? Hey!"

"Who is it?" Chris whispered. Her eyes were glittering and watchful in the intermittent neon.

"Jackie Talbot," he said absently, then raised his voice. "What?"

"Lemme in, Billy. I got to talk to you!"

Billy got up and padded to the door, naked. He unlocked the old-fashioned hook-and-eye and opened it.

Jackie Talbot burst in. His eyes were wild and his face was smeared with soot. He had been drinking it up with Steve and Henry when the news came at ten minutes of twelve. They had gone back to town in Henry's elderly Dodge convertible, and had seen the Jackson Avenue gas main explode from the vantage point of Brickyard Hill. When Jackie had borrowed the Dodge and started to drive back at 12:30, the town was a panicky shambles.

"Chamberlain's burning up," he said to Billy. "Whole fuckin town. The school's gone. The Center's gone. West End blew up—gas. And Carlin Street's on fire. And they're saying Carrie White did it!"

"Oh God," Chris said. She started to get out of bed and grope for her clothes. "What did—"

"Shut up," Billy said mildly, "or I'll kick your ass." He looked at Jackie again and nodded for him to go on.

"They seen her. Lots of people seen her. Billy, they say she's all covered with blood. She was at that fuckin prom tonight . . . Steve and Henry didn't get it but . . . Billy, did you . . . that pig blood . . . was it—"

"Yeah," Billy said.

"Oh, no." Jackie stumbled back against the doorframe. His face was a sickly yellow in the light of the one hall lightbulb. "Oh Jesus, Billy, the whole town—"

"Carrie trashed the whole town? Carrie *White*? You're full of shit." He said it calmly, almost serenely. Behind him, Chris was dressing rapidly.

"Go look out the window," Jackie said.

Billy went over and looked out. The entire eastern horizon had gone crimson, and the sky was alight with it. Even as he looked, three fire trucks screamed by. He could make out the names on them in the glow of the street light that marked The Cavalier's parking lot.

"Son of a whore," he said. "Those trucks are from Brunswick."

"Brunswick?" Chris said. "That's forty miles away. That can't be . . ."

Billy turned back to Jackie Talbot. "All right. What happened?"

Jackie shook his head. "Nobody knows, not yet. It started at the high school. Carrie and Tommy Ross got the King and Queen, and then somebody dumped a couple of buckets of blood on them and she ran out. Then the school caught on fire, and they say nobody got out. Then Teddy's Amoco blew up, then that Mobil station on Summer Street—"

"Citgo," Billy corrected. "It's a Citgo."

"*Who the fuck cares?*" Jackie screamed. "It was her, every place something happened it was *her!* And those buckets . . . none of us wore gloves. . . ."

"I'll take care of it," Billy said.

"You don't get it, Billy. Carrie is—"

"Get out."

"Billy—"

"Get out or I'll break your arm and feed it to you."

Jackie backed out of the door warily.

"Go home. Don't talk to nobody. I'm going to take care of everything."

"All right," Jackie said. "Okay. Billy, I just thought—"

Billy slammed the door.

Chris was on him in a second. "Billy what are we going to do that bitch Carrie oh my Lord what are we going to—"

Billy slapped her, getting his whole arm into it, and knocked her onto the floor. Chris sat sprawled in stunned silence for a moment, and then held her face and began to sob.

Billy put on his pants, his tee shirt, his boots. Then he went to the chipped porcelain washstand in the corner, clicked on the light, wet his head, and began to comb his hair, bending down to see his reflection in the spotted, ancient mirror. Behind him, wavy and distorted, Chris Hargensen sat on the floor, wiping blood from her split lip.

"I'll tell you what we're going to do," he said. "We're going into town and watch the fires. Then we're coming home. You're going to tell your dear old daddy that we were out to The Cavalier drinking beers when it happened. I'm gonna tell my dear ole mummy the same thing. Dig?"

"Billy, your fingerprints," she said. Her voice was muffled, but respectful.

"*Their* fingerprints," he said. "*I* wore gloves."

"Would they tell?" she asked. "If the police took them in and questioned them—"

"Sure," he said. "They'd tell." The loops and swirls were almost right. They glistened in the light of the dull, fly-specked globe like eddies in deep water. His face was calm, reposeful. The comb he used was a battered old Ace, clotted with grease. His father had given it to him on his eleventh birthday, and not one tooth was broken in it. Not one.

"Maybe they'll never find the buckets," he said. "If they do, maybe the fingerprints will all be burnt off. I don't know. But if Doyle takes any of 'em in, I'm heading for California. You do what you want."

"Would you take me with you?" she asked. She looked at him from the floor, her lip puffed to negroid size, her eyes pleading.

He smiled. "Maybe." But he wouldn't. Not any more. "Come on. We're going to town."

They went downstairs and through the empty dance hall, where chairs were still pushed back and beers were standing flat on the tables.

As they went out through the fire door Billy said: "This place sucks, anyway."

They got into his car, and he started it up. When he popped on the headlights, Chris began to scream, hands in fists up to her cheeks.

Billy felt it at the same time: Something in his mind,

(carrie carrie carrie carrie)

a presence.

Carrie was standing in front of them, perhaps seventy feet away.

The high beams picked her out in ghastly horror-movie blacks and whites, dripping and clotted with blood. Now much of it was her own. The hilt of the butcher knife still protruded from her shoulder, and her gown was covered with dirt and grass stain. She had crawled much of the distance from Carlin Street, half fainting, to destroy this roadhouse—perhaps the very one where the doom of her creation had begun.

She stood swaying, her arms thrown out like the arms of a stage hypnotist, and she began to totter toward them.

It happened in the blink of a second. Chris had not had time to expend her first scream. Billy's reflexes were very good and his reaction was instantaneous. He shifted into low, popped the clutch, and floored it.

The Chevrolet's tires screamed against the asphalt, and the car sprang forward like some old and terrible man-eater. The figure swelled in the windshield and as it did the presence became louder

(CARRIE CARRIE CARRIE)

and louder

(CARRIE CARRIE CARRIE)

like a radio being turned up to full volume. Time seemed to close around them in a frame and for a moment they were frozen even in motion: Billy

(CARRIE just like the dogs *CARRIE* just like the goddam dogs *CARRIE* brucie i wish it could *CARRIE* be *CARRIE* you)

and Chris

(*CARRIE* jesus not to kill her *CARRIE* didn't mean to kill her *CARRIE* billy i don't *CARRIE* want to *CARRIE* see it *CA*) and Carrie herself.

(see the wheel car wheel gas pedal wheel i see the *WHEEL* o god my heart my heart my heart)

And Billy suddenly felt his car turn traitor, come alive, slither in his hands. The Chevvy dug around in a smoking half-circle, straight pipes racketing, and suddenly the clapboard side of The Cavalier was swelling, swelling, swelling and

(this is)

they slammed into it at forty, still accelerating, and wood sprayed up in a neon-tinted detonation. Billy was thrown forward and the steering column speared him. Chris was thrown into the dashboard.

The gas tank split open, and fuel began to puddle around the rear of the car. Part of one straight pipe fell into it, and the gas bloomed into flame.

Carrie lay on her side, eyes closed, panting thickly. Her chest was on fire.

She began to drag herself across the parking lot, going nowhere.

(momma i'm sorry it all went wrong o momma o please o please i hurt so bad momma what do i do)

And suddenly it didn't seem to matter any more, nothing would matter if she could turn over, turn over and see the stars, turn over and look once and die.

And that was how Sue found her at two o'clock.

When Sheriff Doyle left her, Sue walked down the street and sat on the steps of the Chamberlain U-Wash-It. She stared at the burning sky without seeing it. Tommy was dead. She knew it was true and accepted it with an ease that was dreadful.

And Carrie had done it.

She had no idea how she knew it, but the conviction was as pure and right as arithmetic.

Time passed. It didn't matter. Macbeth hath murdered sleep and Carrie hath murdered time. Pretty good. A *bon mot*. Sue smiled dolefully. Can this be the end of our heroine, Miss Sweet

Little Sixteen? No worries about the country club and Kleen Korners now. Not ever. Gone. Burned out. Someone ran past, blabbering that Carlin Street was on fire. Good for Carlin Street. Tommy was gone. And Carrie had gone home to murder her mother.

(???????????)

She sat bolt upright, staring into the darkness.

(???????????)

She didn't know how she knew. It bore no relationship to anything she had ever read about telepathy. There were no pictures in her head, no great white flashes of revelation, only prosaic knowledge; the way you know summer follows spring, that cancer can kill you, that Carrie's mother was dead already, that—

(!!!!!)

Her heart rose thickly in her chest. Dead? She examined her knowledge of the incident, trying to disregard the insistent weirdness of knowing from nothing.

Yes, Margaret White was dead. Something to do with her heart. But she had stabbed Carrie. Carrie was badly hurt. She was—

There was nothing more.

She got up and ran back to her mother's car. Ten minutes later she parked on the corner of Branch and Carlin Street, which was on fire. No trucks were available to fight the blaze yet, but sawhorses had been put across both ends of the street, and greasily smoking road pots lit a sign which said:

DANGER! LIVE WIRES!

Sue cut through two back yards and forced her way through a budding hedge that scraped at her with short, stiff bristles. She came out one yard from the Whites' house and crossed over.

The house was in flames, the roof blazing. It was impossible to even think about getting close enough to look in. But in the strong firelight she saw something better: the splashed trail of Carrie's blood. She followed it with her head down, past the larger spots where Carrie had rested, through another hedge, across a Willow Street back yard, and then through an undeveloped tangle of scrub pine and oak. Beyond that, a short, unpaved spur—little more than a footpath—wound up the rise of land to the right, angling away from Route 6.

She stopped suddenly as doubt struck her with vicious and corrosive force. Suppose she could find her? What then? Heart failure? Set on fire? Controlled and forced to walk in front of an oncoming car or fire engine? Her peculiar knowledge told her Carrie would be capable of all these things.

(find a policeman)

She giggled a little at that one and sat down in the grass, which was silked with dew. She had already found a policeman. And even supposing Otis Doyle had believed her, what then? A mental picture came to her of a hundred desperate manhunters surrounding Carrie, demanding her to hand over her weapons and give up. Carrie obediently raises her hands and plucks her head from her shoulders. Hands it to Sheriff Doyle, who solemnly puts it in a wicker basket marked People's Exhibit A.

(and tommy's dead)

Well, well. She began to cry. She put her hands over her face and sobbed into them. A soft breeze snuffled through the juniper bushes on top of the hill. More fire engines screamed by on Route 6 like huge red hounds in the night.

(the town's burning down o well)

She had no idea how long she sat there, crying in a grainy half-doze. She was not even aware that she was following Carrie's progress toward The Cavalier, no more than she was aware of the process of respiration unless she thought about it. Carrie was hurt very badly, was going on brute determination alone at this point. It was three miles out to The Cavalier, even cross country, as Carrie was going. Sue

(watched? thought? doesn't matter)

as Carrie fell in a brook and dragged herself out, icy and shivering. It was really amazing that she kept going. But of course it was for Momma. Momma wanted her to be the Angel's Fiery Sword, to destroy—

(she's going to destroy that too)

She got up and began to run clumsily, not bothering to follow the trail of blood. She didn't need to follow it any more.

• • •

From *The Shadow Exploded* (pp. 164–65):

Whatever any of us may think of the Carrie White affair, it is over. It's time to turn to the future. As Dean McGuffin points out, in his excellent *Science Yearbook* article, if we refuse to do this, we will almost certainly have to pay the piper—and the price is apt to be a high one.

A thorny moral question is raised here. Progress is already being made toward complete isolation of the TK gene. It is more or less assumed in the scientific community (see, for instance, Bourke and Hannegan's "A View Toward Isolation of the TK Gene with Specific Recommendations for Control Parameters" in *Microbiology Annual*, Berkeley: 1982) that when a testing procedure is established, all school-age children will undergo the test as routinely as they now undergo the TB skin-patch. Yet TK is not a germ; it is as much a part of the afflicted person as the color of his eyes.

If overt TK ability occurs as a part of puberty, and if this hypothetical TK test is performed on children entering the first grade, we shall certainly be forewarned. But in this case, is forewarned forearmed? If the TB test shows positive, a child can be treated or isolated. If the TK test shows positive, we have no treatment except a bullet in the head. And how is it possible to isolate a person who will eventually have the power to knock down all walls?

And even if isolation could be made successful, would the American people allow a small pretty girl-child to be ripped away from her parents at the first sign of puberty to be locked in a bank vault for the rest of her life? I doubt it. Especially when the White Commission has worked so hard to convince the public that the nightmare in Chamberlain was a complete fluke.

Indeed, we seem to have returned to Square One . . .

From the sworn testimony of Susan Snell, taken before The State Investigatory Board of Maine (from *The White Commission Report*), pp. 306–472:

Q. Now, Miss Snell, the Board would like to go through your testimony concerning your alleged meeting with Carrie White in The Cavalier parking lot—

A. Why do you keep asking the same questions over and over? I've told you twice already.

Q. We want to make sure the record is correct in every—

A. You want to catch me in a lie, isn't that what you really mean? You don't think I'm telling the truth, do you?

Q. You say you came upon Carrie at—

A. Will you answer me?

Q. —at approximately 2:00 on the morning of May 28th. Is that correct?

A. I'm not going to answer any more questions until you answer the one I just asked.

Q. Miss Snell, this body is empowered to cite you for contempt if you refuse to answer on any other grounds than Constitutional ones.

A. I don't care what you're empowered to do. I've lost someone I love. Go and throw me in jail. I don't care. I—I—Oh, go to hell. All of you, go to hell. You're trying to ... to ... I don't know, crucify me or something. Just lay off me!

(A short recess)

Q. Miss Snell, are you willing to continue your testimony at this time?

A. Yes. But I won't be badgered, Mr. Chairman.

Q. Of course not, young lady. No one wants to badger you. Now you claim to have come upon Carrie in the parking lot of this tavern at about 2:00. Is that correct?

A. Yes.

Q. You knew the time.

A. I was wearing the watch you see on my wrist right now.

Q. To be sure. Isn't The Cavalier better than six miles from where you left your mother's car?

A. It is by the road. It's closer to three as the crow flies.

Q. You walked this distance?

A. Yes.

Q. Now you testified earlier that you "knew" you were getting close to Carrie. Can you explain this?

A. No.

Q. Could you smell her?

A. What?

Q. Did you follow your nose?

(Laughter in the galleries)

A. Are you playing games with me?

Q. Answer the question, please.

A. No. I didn't follow my nose.

Q. Could you see her?

A. No.

Q. Hear her?

A. No.

Q. Then how could you possibly know she was there?

A. How did Tom Quillan know? Or Cora Simard? Or poor Vic Mooney? How did any of them know?

Q. Answer the question, miss. This is hardly the place or the time for impertinence.

A. But they did say they "just knew," didn't they? I read Mrs. Simard's testimony in the paper! And what about the fire hydrants that opened themselves? And the gas pumps that broke their own locks and turned themselves on? The power lines that climbed down off their poles! And—

Q. Miss Snell, please—

A. Those things are in the record of this Commission's proceedings!

Q. That is not an issue here.

A. Then what *is*? Are you looking for the truth or just a scapegoat?

Q. You deny you had prior knowledge of Carrie White's whereabouts?

A. Of course I do. It's an absurd idea.

Q. Oh? And why is it absurd?

A. Well, if you're suggesting some kind of conspiracy, it's absurd because Carrie was dying when I found her. It could not have been an easy way to die.

Q. If you had no prior knowledge of her whereabouts, how could you go directly to her location?

A. Oh, you stupid man! Have you listened to anything that's been said here? Everybody knew it was Carrie! Anyone could have found her if they had put their minds to it.

Q. But not just anyone found her. You did. Can you tell us why people did not show up from all over, like iron filings drawn to a magnet?

A. She was weakening rapidly. I think that perhaps the . . . the zone of her influence was shrinking.

Q. I think you will agree that that is a relatively uninformed supposition.

A. Of course it is. On the subject of Carrie White, we're all relatively uninformed.

Q. Have it your way, Miss Snell. Now if we could turn to . . .

At first, when she climbed up the embankment between Henry Drain's meadow and the parking lot of The Cavalier, she thought Carrie was dead. Her figure was halfway across the parking lot, and she looked oddly shrunken and crumpled. Sue was reminded of dead animals she had seen on 95—woodchucks, groundhogs, skunks—that had been crushed by speeding trucks and station wagons.

But the presence was still in her mind, vibrating stubbornly, repeating the call letters of Carrie White's personality over and over. An essence of Carrie, a *gestalt*. Muted now, not strident, not announcing itself with a clarion, but waxing and waning in steady oscillations.

Unconscious.

Sue climbed over the guard rail that bordered the parking lot, feeling the heat of the fire against her face. The Cavalier was a wooden frame building, and it was burning briskly. The charred remains of a car were limned in flame to the right of the back door. Carrie had done that, then. She did not go to look and see if anyone had been in it. It didn't matter, not now.

She walked over to where Carrie lay on her side, unable to hear her own footsteps under the hungry crackle of the fire. She looked down at the curled-up figure with a bemused and bitter pity. The knife hilt protruded cruelly from her shoulder, and she was lying in a small pool of blood—some of it was trickling from her mouth. She looked as if she had been trying to turn herself over when unconsciousness had taken her. Able to start fires, pull down electric cables, able to kill almost by thought alone; lying here unable to turn herself over.

Sue knelt, took her by one arm and the unhurt shoulder, and gently turned her onto her back.

Carrie moaned thickly, and her eyes fluttered. The perception of her in Sue's mind sharpened, as if a mental picture was coming into focus.

(who's there)

And Sue, without thought, spoke in the same fashion:

(me sue snell)

Only there was no need to think of her name. The thought of herself as herself was neither words nor pictures. The realization suddenly brought everything up close, made it real, and compassion for Carrie broke through the dullness of her shock.

And Carrie, with faraway, dumb reproach:

(you tricked me you all tricked me)

(carrie i don't even know what happened is tommy)

(you tricked me that happened trick trick trick o dirty trick)

The mixture of image and emotion was staggering, indescribable. Blood. Sadness. Fear. The latest dirty trick in a long series of dirty tricks: they flashed by in a dizzying shuffle that made Sue's mind reel helplessly, hopelessly. They shared the awful totality of perfect knowledge.

(carrie don't don't don't hurts me)

Now girls throwing sanitary napkins, chanting, laughing, Sue's face mirrored in her own mind: ugly, caricatured, all mouth, cruelly beautiful.

(see the dirty tricks see my whole life one long dirty trick)

(look carrie look inside me)

And Carrie looked.

The sensation was terrifying. Her mind and nervous system had become a library. Someone in desperate need ran through her, fingers trailing lightly over shelves of books, lifting some out, scanning them, putting them back, letting some fall, leaving the pages to flutter wildly

(glimpses that's me as a kid hate him daddy o mommy wide lips o teeth bobby pushed me o my knee car want to ride in the car we're going to see aunt cecily mommy come quick i made pee) in the wind of memory; and still on and on, finally reaching a shelf marked TOMMY, subheaded PROM. Books thrown open, flashes of experience, marginal notations in all the hieroglyphs of emotion, more complex than the Rosetta Stone.

Looking. Finding more than Sue herself had suspected—love for Tommy, jealousy, selfishness, a need to subjugate him to her will on the matter of taking Carrie, disgust for Carrie herself,

(she could take better care of herself she does look just like a GODDAM TOAD)

hate for Miss Desjardin, hate for herself.

But no ill will for Carrie personally, no plan to get her in front of everyone and undo her.

The feverish feeling of being raped in her most secret corridors began to fade. She felt Carrie pulling back, weak and exhausted.

(why didn't you just leave me alone)

(carrie i)

(momma would be alive i killed my momma i want her o it hurts my chest hurts my shoulder o o o i want my momma)

(carrie i)

And there was no way to finish that thought, nothing there to complete it with. Sue was suddenly overwhelmed with terror, the worse because she could put no name to it: The bleeding freak on this oil-stained asphalt suddenly seemed meaningless and awful in its pain and dying.

(o momma i'm scared momma *MOMMA)*

Sue tried to pull away, to disengage her mind, to allow Carrie at least the privacy of her dying, and was unable to. She felt that she was dying herself and did not want to see this preview of her own eventual end.

(carrie let me GO)

(Momma Momma Momma *ooooooooooooooo OOOOOOOOOO*)

The mental scream reached a flaring, unbelievable crescendo and then suddenly faded. For a moment Sue felt as if she were watching a candle flame disappear down a long, black tunnel at a tremendous speed.

(she's dying o my god i'm feeling her die)

And then the light was gone, and the last conscious thought had been

(momma i'm sorry where)

and it broke up and Sue was tuned in only on the blank, idiot frequency of the physical nerve endings that would take hours to die.

She stumbled away from it, holding her arms out in front of her like a blind woman, toward the edge of the parking lot. She tripped over the knee-high guard rail and tumbled down the embankment. She got to her feet and stumbled into the field, which was filling with mystic white pockets of ground mist. Crickets chirruped mindlessly and a whippoorwill

(whippoorwill somebody's dying)

called in the great stillness of morning.

She began to run, breathing deep in her chest, running from Tommy, from the fires and explosions, from Carrie, but mostly from the final horror—that last lighted thought carried swiftly down into the black tunnel of eternity, followed by the blank, idiot hum of prosaic electricity.

The after-image began to fade reluctantly, leaving a blessed, cool darkness in her mind that knew nothing. She slowed, halted, and became aware that something had begun to happen. She stood in the middle of the great and misty field, waiting for realization.

Her rapid breathing slowed, slowed, caught suddenly as if on a thorn—

And suddenly vented itself in one howling, cheated scream.

As she felt the slow course of dark menstrual blood down her thighs.

PART THREE

WRECKAGE

WESTOVER MERCY HOSPITAL/REPORT OF DECEASE

Name White   Carietta   N.   by *RM*
      (Last)   (First)   (Middle)

Address 47 Carlin Street

       Chamberlain, Maine 02249

Emergency Room None   Ambulance #16

Treatment administered None   D.O.A. X
                                          YES   NO

Time of Death May 28, 1979 - 2:00 AM (approx.)

Cause of Death Hemorrhage, shock, coronary occlusion

and/or coronary thrombosis (possible)

Person identifying deceased Susan D. Snell

                                 19 Back Chamberlain Road

                                 Chamberlain, Maine 02249

Next of kin None

Body to be released to State of Maine

Doctor in attendance *Harold Knebler, M.D.*

Pathologist *FM*

From the national AP ticker, Friday, June 5, 1979:

CHAMBERLAIN, MAINE (AP)

STATE OFFICIALS SAY THAT THE DEATH TOLL IN CHAMBER-
LAIN STANDS AT 409, WITH 49 STILL LISTED AS MISSING.
INVESTIGATION CONCERNING CARIETTA WHITE AND THE
SO-CALLED "TK" PHENOMENA CONTINUES AMID PERSISTENT
RUMORS THAT AN AUTOPSY ON THE WHITE GIRL HAS UN-
COVERED CERTAIN UNUSUAL FORMATIONS IN THE CEREBRUM
AND CEREBELLUM OF THE BRAIN. THIS STATE'S GOVERNOR
HAS APPOINTED A BLUE-RIBBON COMMITTEE TO STUDY THE
ENTIRE TRAGEDY. ENDS.
FINAL JUNE 5 0303N AP

From *The Lewiston Daily Sun,* Sunday, September 7 (p. 3):

The Legacy of TK:
Scorched Earth and Scorched Hearts

CHAMBERLAIN—Prom Night is history now. Pundits have been
saying for centuries that time heals all wounds, but the hurt of
this small western Maine town may be mortal. The residential
streets are still there on the town's East Side, guarded by graceful oaks that have stood for two hundred years. The trim
saltboxes and ranch styles on Morin Street and Brickyard Hill
are still neat and undamaged. But this New England pastoral
lies on the rim of a blackened and shattered hub, and many of
the neat houses have FOR SALE signs on their front lawns.
Those still occupied are marked by black wreaths on front
doors. Bright-yellow Allied vans and orange U-Hauls of varying
sizes are a common sight on Chamberlain's streets these days.

The town's major industry, Chamberlain Mills and Weaving,
still stands, untouched by the fire that raged over much of the
town on those two days in May. But it has only been running
one shift since June 4th, and according to mill president William A. Chamblis, further lay-offs are a strong possibility. "We
have the orders," Chamblis said, "but you can't run a mill
without people to punch the time clock. We don't have them.
I've gotten notice from thirty-four men since August 15th. The

only thing we can see to do now is close up the dye house and job our work out. We'd hate to let the men go, but this thing is getting down to a matter of financial survival."

Roger Fearon has lived in Chamberlain for twenty-two years, and has been with the mail for eighteen of those years. He has risen during that time from a third-floor bagger making seventy-three cents an hour to dye-house foreman; yet he seems strangely unmoved by the possibility of losing his job. "I'd lose a damned good wage," Fearon said. "It's not something you take lightly. The wife and I have talked it over. We could sell the house—it's worth $20,000 easy—and although we probably won't realize half of that, we'll probably go ahead and put it up. Doesn't matter. We don't really want to live in Chamberlain any more. Call it what you want, but Chamberlain has gone bad for us."

Fearon is not alone. Henry Kelly, proprietor of a tobacco shop and soda fountain called the Kelly Fruit until Prom Night leveled it, has no plans to rebuild. "The kids are gone," he shrugs. "If I opened up again, there'd be too many ghosts in too many corners. I'm going to take the insurance money and retire to St. Petersburg."

A week after the tornado of '54 had cut its path of death and destruction through Worcester, the air was filled with the sound of hammers, the smell of new timber, and a feeling of optimism and human resilience. There is none of that in Chamberlain this fall. The main road has been cleared of rubble and that is about the extent of it. The faces that you meet are full of dull hopelessness. Men drink beer without talking in Frank's Bar on the corner of Sullivan Street, and women exchange tales of grief and loss in back yards. Chamberlain has been declared a disaster area, and money is available to help put the town back on its feet and begin rebuilding the business district.

But the main business of Chamberlain in the last four months has been funerals.

Four hundred and forty are now known dead, eighteen more still unaccounted for. And sixty-seven of the dead were Ewen High School Seniors on the verge of graduation. It is this, perhaps, more than anythng else, that has taken the guts out of Chamberlain.

They were buried on June 1 and 2 in three mass ceremonies. A memorial service was held on June 3 in the town square. It was the most moving ceremony that this reporter has ever witnessed. Attendance was in the thousands, and the entire assemblage was still as the school band, stripped from fifty-six to a bare forty, played the school song and taps.

There was a somber graduation ceremony the following week at neighboring Motton Academy, but there were only fifty-two Seniors left to graduate. The valedictorian, Henry Stampel, broke into tears halfway through his speech and could not continue. There were no Graduation Night parties following the ceremony; the Seniors merely took their diplomas and went home.

And still, as the summer progressed, the hearses continued to roll as more bodies were discovered. To some residents it seemed that each day the scab was ripped off again, so that the wound could bleed afresh.

If you are one of the many curiosity-seekers who have been through Chamberlain in the last week, you have seen a town that may be suffering from terminal cancer of the spirit. A few people, looking lost, wander through the aisles of the A&P. The Congregational Church on Carlin Street is gone, swept away by fire, but the brick Catholic Church still stands on Elm Street, and the trim Methodist Church on outer Main Street, although singed by fire, is unhurt. Yet attendance has been poor. The old men still sit on the benches in Courthouse Square, but there is little interest in the checkerboards or even in conversation.

The over-all impression is one of a town that is waiting to die. It is not enough, these days, to say that Chamberlain will never be the same. It may be closer to the truth to say that Chamberlain will simply never again be.

Excerpt from a letter dated June ninth from Principal Henry Grayle to Peter Philpott, Superintendent of Schools:

...and so I feel I can no longer continue in my present position, feeling, as I do, that such a tragedy might have been averted if I had only had more foresight. I would like you to accept my resignation effective as of July 1, if this is agreeable to you and your staff. . . .

Excerpt from a letter dated June eleventh from Rita Desjardin, instructor of Physical Education, to Principal Henry Grayle:

. . . am returning my contract to you at this time. I feel that I would kill myself before ever teaching again. Late at night I keep thinking: If I had only reached out to that girl, if only, if only . . .

Found painted on the lawn of the house lot where the White bungalow had been located:

CARRIE WHITE IS BURNING FOR HER SINS
JESUS NEVER FAILS

From "Telekinesis: Analysis and Aftermath" (Science Yearbook, 1981), by Dean D. L. McGuffin:

In conclusion, I would like to point out the grave risk authorities are taking by burying the Carrie White affair under the bureaucratic mat—and I am speaking specifically of the so-called White Commission. The desire among politicians to regard TK as a once-in-a-lifetime phenomenon seems very strong, and while this may be understandable it is not acceptable. The possibility of a recurrence, genetically speaking, is 99 per cent. It's time we planned now for what may be. . . .

From Slang Terms Explained: A Parents' Guide, by John R. Coombs (New York: The Lighthouse Press, 1985), p. 73:

to rip off a Carrie: To cause either violence or destruction; mayhem, confusion; (2) to commit arson (from Carrie White, 1963–1979)

From The Shadow Exploded (p. 201):

Elsewhere in this book mention is made of a page in one of Carrie White's school notebooks where a line from a famous rock poet of the '60s, Bob Dylan, was written repeatedly, as if in desperation.

It might not be amiss to close this book with a few lines from another Bob Dylan song, lines that might serve as Carrie's epitaph: *I wish I could write you a melody so plain/That would save you, dear lady, from going insane/That would ease you and cool you and cease the pain/Of your useless and pointless knowledge . . .**

From *My Name Is Susan Snell* (p. 98):

This little book is done now. I hope it sells well so I can go someplace where nobody knows me. I want to think things over, decide what I'm going to do between now and the time when my light is carried down that long tunnel into blackness. . . .

From the conclusion of The State Investigatory Board of Maine in connection with the events of May 27–28 in Chamberlain, Maine:

. . . and so we must conclude that, while an autopsy performed on the subject indicates some cellular changes which *may* indicate the presence of *some* paranormal power, we find no reason to believe that a recurrence is likely or even possible . . .

Excerpt from a letter dated May 3, 1988, from Amelia Jenks, Royal Knob, Tennessee, to Sandra Jenks, Macon, Georgia:

. . . and your little neece is growin like a weed, awfull big for only 2. She has blue eyes like her daddy and my blond hair but that will porubly go dark. Still she is awfull pretty & I think sometimes when she is asleep how she looks like our momma.

The other day wile she was playin in the dirt beside the house I sneeked around and saw the funnyest thing. Annie was playin with her brothers marbles only they was mooving around all by themselfs. Annie was giggeling and laffing but I was a

* Lyrics from TOMBSTONE BLUES by Bob Dylan. Copyright © 1965 M. Witmark & Sons. All Rights Reserved. Used by permission of WARNER BROS. MUSIC.

little skared. Some of them marbles was going right up & down. It remined me of gramma, do you remember when the law came up that time after Pete and there guns flew out of there hands and grammie just laffed and laffed. And she use to be able to make her rocker go even when she wasen in it. It gave me a reel bad turn to think on it. I shure hope she don't get heartspels like grammie did, remember?

Well I must go & do a wash so give my best to Rich and take care to send us some pitchers when you can. Still our Annie is awfull pretty & her eyes are as brite as buttons. I bet she'll be a world-beeter someday.

All my love,
Melia

'SALEM'S
LOT

For Naomi Rachel King
". . . promises to keep."

CONTENTS

AUTHOR'S NOTE

No one writes a long novel alone, and I would like to take a moment of your time to thank some of the people who helped with this one: G. Everett McCutcheon, of Hampden Academy, for his practical suggestions and encouragement; Dr. John Pearson, of Old Town, Maine, medical examiner of Penobscot County and member in good standing of that most excellent medical specialty, general practice; Father Renald Hallee, of St. John's Catholic Church in Bangor, Maine. And of course my wife, whose criticism is as tough and unflinching as ever.

Although the towns surrounding 'salem's Lot are very real, 'salem's Lot itself exists wholly in the author's imagination, and any resemblance between the people who live there and people who live in the real world is coincidental and unintended.

S.K.

PROLOGUE

Old friend, what are you looking for?
After those many years abroad you come
With images you tended
Under foreign skies
Far away from your own land.

GEORGE SEFERIS

1

Almost everyone thought the man and the boy were father and son.

They crossed the country on a rambling southwest line in an old Citroën sedan, keeping mostly to secondary roads, traveling in fits and starts. They stopped in three places along the way before reaching their final destination: first in Rhode Island, where the tall man with the black hair worked in a textile mill; then in Youngstown, Ohio, where he worked for three months on a tractor assembly line; and finally in a small California town near the Mexican border, where he pumped gas and worked at repairing small foreign cars with an amount of success that was, to him, surprising and gratifying.

Wherever they stopped, he got a Maine newspaper called the Portland *Press-Herald* and watched it for items concerning a small southern Maine town named Jerusalem's Lot and the surrounding area. There were such items from time to time.

He wrote an outline of a novel in motel rooms before they hit Central Falls, Rhode Island, and mailed it to his agent. He had been a mildly successful novelist a million years before, in a time when the darkness had not come over his life. The agent took the outline to his last publisher, who expressed polite interest but no inclination to part with any advance money.

"Please" and "thank you," he told the boy as he tore the agent's letter up, were still free. He said it without too much bitterness and set about the book anyway.

The boy did not speak much. His face retained a perpetual pinched look, and his eyes were dark—as if they always scanned some bleak inner horizon. In the diners and gas stations where they stopped along the way, he was polite and nothing more. He didn't seem to want the tall man out of his sight, and the boy seemed nervous even when the man left him to use the bathroom. He refused to talk about the town of Jerusalem's Lot, although the tall man tried to raise the topic from time to time, and he would not look at the Portland newspapers the man sometimes deliberately left around.

When the book was written, they were living in a beach cottage off the highway, and they both swam in the Pacific a great deal. It was warmer than the Atlantic, and friendlier. It held no memories. The boy began to get very brown.

Although they were living well enough to eat three square meals a day and keep a solid roof over their heads, the man had begun to feel depressed and doubtful about the life they were living. He was tutoring the boy, and he did not seem to be losing anything in the way of education (the boy was bright and easy about books, as the tall man had been himself), but he didn't think that blotting 'salem's Lot out was doing the boy any good. Sometimes at night he screamed in his sleep and thrashed the blankets onto the floor.

A letter came from New York. The tall man's agent said that Random House was offering $12,000 in advance, and a book club sale was almost certain. Was it okay?

It was.

The man quit his job at the gas station, and he and the boy crossed the border.

2

Los Zapatos, which means "the shoes" (a name that secretly pleased the man to no end), was a small village not far from the ocean. It was fairly free of tourists. There was no good road, no ocean view (you had to go five miles further west to get that), and no historical points of interest. Also, the local cantina was infested with cockroaches and the only whore was a fifty-year-old grandmother.

With the States behind them, an almost unearthly quiet dropped over their lives. Few planes went overhead, there were no turnpikes, and no one owned a power lawn mower (or cared to have one) for a hundred miles. They had a radio, but even that was noise without meaning; the news broadcasts were all in Spanish, which the boy began to pick up but which remained—and always would—gibberish to the man. All the music seemed to consist of opera. At night they sometimes got a pop music station from Monterey made frantic with the accents of Wolfman Jack, but it faded in and out. The only motor within hearing distance was a quaint old Rototiller owned by a local farmer. When the wind was right, its irregular burping noise would come to their ears faintly, like an uneasy spirit. They drew their water from the well by hand.

Once or twice a month (not always together) they attended mass at the small church in town. Neither of them understood the ceremony, but they went all the same. The man found himself sometimes drowsing in the suffocating heat to the steady, familiar rhythms and the voices which gave them tongue. One Sunday the boy came out onto the rickety back porch where the man had begun work on a new novel and told him hesitantly that he had spoken to the priest about being taken into the church. The man nodded and asked him if he had enough Spanish to take instruction. The boy said he didn't think it would be a problem.

The man made a forty-mile trip once a week to get the Portland, Maine, paper, which was always at least a week old and was sometimes yellowed with dog urine. Two weeks after the boy had told him of his intentions, he found a featured story about 'salem's Lot and a Vermont town called Momson. The tall man's name was mentioned in the course of the story.

He left the paper around with no particular hope that the boy would pick it up. The article made him uneasy for a number of reasons. It was not over in 'salem's Lot yet, it seemed.

The boy came to him a day later with the paper in his hand, folded open to expose the headline: "Ghost Town in Maine?"

"I'm scared," he said.

"I am, too," the tall man answered.

3

GHOST TOWN IN MAINE?
By John Lewis
Press-Herald Features Editor

JERUSALEM'S LOT—Jerusalem's Lot is a small town east of Cumberland and twenty miles north of Portland. It is not the first town in American history to just dry up and blow away, and will probably not be the last, but it is one of the strangest. Ghost towns are common in the American Southwest, where communities grew up almost overnight around rich gold and silver lodes and then disappeared almost as rapidly when the veins of ore played out, leaving empty stores and hotels and saloons to rot emptily in desert silence.

In New England the only counterpart to the mysterious emptying of Jerusalem's Lot, or 'salem's Lot as the natives often refer to it, seems to be a small town in Vermont called Momson. During the summer of 1923, Momson apparently just dried up and blew away, and all 312 residents went with it. The houses and few small business buildings in the town's center still stand, but since that summer fifty-two years ago, they have been uninhabited. In some cases the furnishings had been removed, but in most the houses were still furnished, as if in the middle of daily life some great wind had blown all the people away. In one house the table had been set for the evening meal, complete with a centerpiece of long-wilted flowers. In another the covers had been turned down neatly in an upstairs bedroom as if for sleep. In the local mercantile store, a rotted bolt of cotton cloth was found on the counter and a price of $1.22 rung up on the cash register. Investigators found almost $50.00 in the cash drawer, untouched.

People in the area like to entertain tourists with the story and to hint that the town is haunted—that, they say, is why it has remained empty ever since. A more likely reason is that Momson is located in a forgotten corner of the state, far from any main road. There is nothing there that could not be duplicated in a hundred other towns—except, of course, the *Mary Celeste*-like mystery of its sudden emptiness.

Much the same could be said for Jerusalem's Lot.

In the census of 1970, 'salem's Lot claimed 1,319 inhabitants—a gain of exactly 67 souls in the ten years since the previous census. It is a sprawling, comfortable township, familiarly called the Lot by its previous inhabitants, where little of any note ever took place. The only thing the oldsters who regularly gathered in the park and around the stove in Crossen's Agricultural Market had to talk about was the Fire of '51, when a carelessly tossed match started one of the largest forest fires in the state's history.

If a man wanted to spin out his retirement in a small country town where everyone minded his own business and the big event of any given week was apt to be the Ladies' Auxiliary Bake-off, then the Lot would have been a good choice. Demographically, the census of 1970 showed a pattern familiar both to rural sociologists and to the long-time resident of any small Maine town: a lot of old folks, quite a few poor folks, and a lot of young folks who leave the area with their diplomas under their arms, never to return again.

But a little over a year ago, something began to happen in Jerusalem's Lot that was not usual. People began to drop out of sight. The larger proportion of these, naturally, haven't disappeared in the real sense of the word at all. The Lot's former constable, Parkins Gillespie, is living with his sister in Kittery. Charles James, owner of a gas station across from the drugstore, is now running a repair shop in neighboring Cumberland. Pauline Dickens has moved to Los Angeles, and Rhoda Curless is working with the St. Matthew's Mission in Portland. The list of "undisappearances" could go on and on.

What is mystifying about these found people is their unanimous unwillingness—or inability—to talk about Jerusalem's Lot and what, if anything, might have happened there. Parkins Gillespie simply looked at this reporter, lit a cigarette, and said, "I just decided to leave." Charles James claims he was forced to leave because his business dried up with the town. Pauline Dickens, who worked as a waitress in the Excellent Café for years, never answered this reporter's letter of inquiry. And Miss Curless refuses to speak of 'salem's Lot at all.

Some of the missing can be accounted for by educated guesswork and a little research. Lawrence Crockett, a local real estate agent who has disappeared with his wife and daughter, has left a

number of questionable business ventures and land deals behind
him, including one piece of Portland land speculation where the
Portland Mall and Shopping Center is now under construction.
The Royce McDougalls, also among the missing, had lost their
infant son earlier in the year and there was little to hold them in
town. They might be anywhere. Others fit into the same category. According to State Police Chief Peter McFee, "We've got
tracers out on a great many people from Jerusalem's Lot—but
that isn't the only Maine town where people have dropped out of
sight. Royce McDougall, for instance, left owing money to one
bank and two finance companies . . . in my judgment, he was just
a fly-by-nighter who decided to get out from under. Someday
this year or next, he'll use one of those credit cards he's got in his
wallet and the repossession men will land on him with both feet.
In America missing persons are as natural as cherry pie. We're
living in an automobile-oriented society. People pick up stakes
and move on every two or three years. Sometimes they forget to
leave a forwarding address. Especially the deadbeats."

Yet for all the hardheaded practicality of Captain McFee's
words, there are unanswered questions in Jerusalem's Lot. Henry
Petrie and his wife and son are gone, and Mr. Petrie, a Prudential Insurance Company executive, could hardly be called a dead-
beat. The local mortician, the local librarian, and the local
beautician are also in the dead-letter file. The list is of a disquieting length.

In the surrounding towns the whispering campaign that is the
beginning of legend has already begun. 'Salem's Lot is reputed to
be haunted. Sometimes colored lights are reported hovering over
the Central Maine Power lines that bisect the township, and if
you suggest that the inhabitants of the Lot have been carried off
by UFOs, no one will laugh. There has been some talk of a "dark
coven" of young people who were practicing the black mass in
town and, perhaps, brought the wrath of God Himself on the
namesake of the Holy Land's holiest city. Others, of a less supernatural bent, remember the young men who "disappeared" in
the Houston, Texas, area some three years ago only to be discovered in grisly mass graves.

An actual visit to 'salem's Lot makes such talk seem less wild.
There is not one business left open. The last one to go under was
Spencer's Sundries and Pharmacy, which closed its doors in Jan-
uary. Crossen's Agricultural Store, the hardware store, Barlow
and Straker's Furniture Shop, the Excellent Café, and even the
Municipal Building are all boarded up. The new grammar school

is empty, and so is the tri-town consolidated high school, built in the Lot in 1967. The school furnishings and the books have been moved to make-do facilities in Cumberland pending a referendum vote in the other towns of the school district, but it seems that no children from 'salem's Lot will be in attendance when a new school year begins. There are no children; only abandoned shops and stores, deserted houses, overgrown lawns, deserted streets, and back roads.

Some of the other people that the state police would like to locate or at least hear from include John Groggins, pastor of the Jerusalem's Lot Methodist Church; Father Donald Callahan, parish priest of St. Andrew's; Mabel Werts, a local widow who was prominent in 'salem's Lot church and social functions; Lester and Harriet Durham, a local couple who both worked at Gates Mill and Weaving; Eva Miller, who ran a local boardinghouse. . . .

4

Two months after the newspaper article, the boy was taken into the church. He made his first confession—and confessed everything.

5

The village priest was an old man with white hair and a face seamed into a net of wrinkles. His eyes peered out of his sun-beaten face with surprising life and avidity. They were blue eyes, very Irish. When the tall man arrived at his house, he was sitting on the porch and drinking tea. A man in a city suit stood beside him. The man's hair was parted in the middle and greased in a manner that reminded the tall man of photograph portraits from the 1890s.

The man said stiffly, "I am Jesús de la rey Muñoz. Father Gracon has asked me to interpret, as he has no English. Father Gracon has done my family a great service which I may not mention. My lips are likewise sealed in the matter he wishes to discuss. Is it agreeable to you?"

"Yes." He shook Muñoz's hand and then Gracon's. Gracon replied in Spanish and smiled. He had only five teeth left in his jaw, but the smile was sunny and glad.

"He asks, Would you like a cup of tea? It is green tea. Very cooling."

"That would be lovely."

When the amenities had passed among them, the priest said, "The boy is not your son."

"No.

"He made a strange confession. In fact, I have never heard a stranger confession in all my days of the priesthood."

"That does not surprise me."

"He wept," Father Gracon said, sipping his tea. "It was a deep and terrible weeping. It came from the cellar of his soul. Must I ask the question this confession raises in my heart?"

"No," the tall man said evenly. "You don't. He is telling the truth."

Gracon was nodding even before Muñoz translated, and his face had grown grave. He leaned forward with his hands clasped between his knees and spoke for a long time. Muñoz listened intently, his face carefully expressionless. When the priest finished, Muñoz said:

"He says there are strange things in the world. Forty years ago a peasant from El Graniones brought him a lizard that screamed as though it were a woman. He has seen a man with stigmata, the marks of Our Lord's passion, and this man bled from his hands and feet on Good Friday. He says this is an awful thing, a dark thing. It is serious for you and the boy. Particularly for the boy. It is eating him up. He says . . ."

Gracon spoke again, briefly.

"He asks if you understand what you have done in this New Jerusalem."

"Jerusalem's Lot," the tall man said. "Yes. I understand."

Gracon spoke again.

"He asks what you intend to do about it."

The tall man shook his head very slowly. "I don't know."

Gracon spoke again.

"He says he will pray for you."

6

A week later he awoke sweating from a nightmare and called out the boy's name.

"I'm going back," he said.

The boy paled beneath his tan.

"Can you come with me?" the man asked.

"Do you love me?"

"Yes. God, yes."

The boy began to weep, and the tall man held him.

7

Still, there was no sleep for him. Faces lurked in the shadows, swirling up at him like faces obscured in snow, and when the wind blew an overhanging tree limb against the roof, he jumped.

Jerusalem's Lot.

He closed his eyes and put his arm across them and it all began to come back. He could almost see the glass paperweight, the kind that will make a tiny blizzard when you shake it.

'Salem's Lot . . .

PART ONE

THE MARSTEN HOUSE

No live organism can continue for long to exist sanely under conditions of absolute reality; even larks and katydids are supposed, by some, to dream. Hill House, not sane, stood by itself against its hills, holding darkness within; it had stood for eighty years and might stand for eighty more. Within, walls continued upright, bricks met neatly, floors were firm, and doors were sensibly shut; silence lay steadily against the wood and stone of Hill House, and whatever walked there, walked alone.

SHIRLEY JACKSON
The Haunting of Hill House

Chapter One
BEN (I)

1

By the time he had passed Portland going north on the turn-pike, Ben Mears had begun to feel a not unpleasurable tingle of excitement in his belly. It was September 5, 1975, and summer was enjoying her final grand fling. The trees were bursting with green, the sky was a high, soft blue, and just over the Falmouth town line he saw two boys walking a road parallel to the expressway with fishing rods settled on their shoulders like carbines.

He switched to the travel lane, slowed to the mimimum turnpike speed, and began to look for anything that would jog his memory. There was nothing at first, and he tried to caution himself against almost sure disappointment. *You were seven then. That's twenty-five years of water under the bridge. Places change. Like people.*

In those days the four-lane 295 hadn't existed. If you wanted to go to Portland from the Lot, you went out Route 12 to Falmouth and then got on Number 1. Time had marched on.

Stop that shit.

But it was hard to stop. It was hard to stop when—

A big BSA cycle with jacked handlebars suddenly roared past him in the passing lane, a kid in a T-shirt driving, a girl in a red cloth jacket and huge mirror-lensed sunglasses riding pillion behind him. They cut in a little too quickly and he overreacted, jamming on his brakes and laying both hands on the horn. The BSA sped up, belching blue smoke from its exhaust, and the girl jabbed her middle finger back at him.

He resumed speed, wishing for a cigarette. His hands were trembling slightly. The BSA was almost out of sight now, moving fast. The kids. The goddamned kids. Memories tried to crowd in on him, memories of a more recent vintage. He pushed them away. He hadn't been on a motorcycle in two years. He planned never to ride on one again.

A flash of red caught his eye off to the left, and when he glanced that way, he felt a burst of pleasure and recognition. A large red barn stood on a hill far across a rising field of timothy and clover, a barn with a cupola painted white—even at this distance he could see the sungleam on the weather vane atop that cupola. It had been there then and was still here now. It looked exactly the same. Maybe it was going to be all right after all. Then the trees blotted it out.

As the turnpike entered Cumberland, more and more things began to seem familiar. He passed over the Royal River, where they had fished for steelies and pickerel as boys. Past a brief, flickering view of Cumberland Village through the trees. In the distance the Cumberland water tower with its huge slogan painted across the side: "Keep Maine Green." Aunt Cindy had always said someone should print "Bring Money" underneath that.

His original sense of excitement grew and he began to speed up, watching for the sign. It came twinkling up out of the distance in reflectorized green five miles later:

ROUTE 12 JERUSALEM'S LOT
CUMBERLAND CUMBERLAND CTR

A sudden blackness came over him, dousing his good spirits like sand on fire. He had been subject to these since (his mind tried to speak Miranda's name and he would not let it) the bad time and was used to fending them off, but this one swept over him with a savage power that was dismaying.

What was he doing, coming back to a town where he had lived for four years as a boy, trying to recapture something that was irrevocably lost? What magic could he expect to recapture by walking roads that he had once walked as a boy and were probably asphalted and straightened and logged off and littered with tourist beer cans? The magic was gone, both white and black. It had all gone down the chutes on that night when the motorcycle had gone out of control and then there was the yellow moving van, growing and growing, his wife Miranda's scream, cut off with sudden finality when—

The exit came up on his right, and for a moment he considered driving right past it, continuing on to Chamberlain or Lewiston, stopping for lunch, and then turning around and going back. But back where? Home? That was a laugh. If there was a home, it had been here. Even if it had only been four years, it was his.

He signaled, slowed the Citroën, and went up the ramp. Toward the top, where the turnpike ramp joined Route 12 (which became Jointner Avenue closer to town), he glanced up toward the horizon. What he saw there made him jam the brakes on with both feet. The Citroën shuddered to a stop and stalled.

The trees, mostly pine and spruce, rose in gentle slopes toward the east, seeming to almost crowd against the sky at the limit of vision. From here the town was not visible. Only the trees, and in the distance, where those trees rose against the sky, the peaked, gabled roof of the Marsten House.

He gazed at it, fascinated. Warring emotions crossed his face with kaleidoscopic swiftness.

"Still here," he murmured aloud. "By God."

He looked down at his arms. They had broken out in goose flesh.

2

He deliberately skirted town, crossing into Cumberland and then coming back into 'salem's Lot from the west, taking the Burns Road. He was amazed by how little things had changed out here. There were a few new houses he didn't remember, there was a tavern called Dell's just over the town line, and a pair of fresh gravel quarries. A good deal of the hardwood had been pulped over. But the old tin sign pointing the way to the town dump was still there, and the road itself was still unpaved, full of chuckholes and washboards, and he could see School-yard Hill through the slash in the trees where the Central Maine Power pylons ran on a northwest to southeast line. The Griffen farm was still there, although the barn had been en-larged. He wondered if they still bottled and sold their own milk. The logo had been a smiling cow under the name brand: "Sunshine Milk from the Griffen Farms!" He smiled. He had splashed a lot of that milk on his corn flakes at Aunt Cindy's house.

He turned left onto the Brooks Road, passed the wrought-iron gates and the low fieldstone wall surrounding Harmony Hill Cemetery, and then went down the steep grade and started up the far side—the side known as Marsten's Hill.

At the top, the trees fell away on both sides of the road. On the right, you could look right down into the town proper—Ben's first view of it. On the left, the Marsten House. He pulled over and got out of the car.

It was just the same. There was no difference, not at all. He might have last seen it yesterday.

The witch grass grew wild and tall in the front yard, obscur-ing the old, frost-heaved flagstones that led to the porch. Chirring crickets sang in it, and he could see grasshoppers jumping in erratic parabolas.

The house itself looked toward town. It was huge and ram-bling and sagging, its windows haphazardly boarded shut, giving it that sinister look of all old houses that have been empty for a long time. The paint had been weathered away, giving the house a uniform gray look. Windstorms had ripped many of the shingles off, and a heavy snowfall had punched in the west corner of the main roof, giving it a slumped, hunched look. A tattered no-trespassing sign was nailed to the right-hand newel post.

He felt a strong urge to walk up that overgrown path, past the crickets and hoppers that would jump around his shoes, climb the porch, peek between the haphazard boards into the hallway or the front room. Perhaps try the front door. If it was unlocked, go in.

He swallowed and stared up at the house, almost hypno-tized. It stared back at him with idiot indifference.

You walked down the hall, smelling wet plaster and rotting wallpaper, and mice would skitter in the walls. There would still be a lot of junk lying around, and you might pick something up, a paperweight maybe, and put it in your pocket. Then, at the end of the hall, instead of going through into the kitchen, you could turn left and go up the stairs, your feet gritting in the plaster dust which had sifted down from the ceiling over the years. There were fourteen steps, exactly fourteen. But the top one was smaller, out of proportion, as if it had been added to avoid the evil number. At the top of the stairs you stand on the landing, looking down the hall toward a closed door. And if you walk down the hall toward it, watching as if from outside yourself as the door gets closer and larger, you can reach out your hand and put it on the tarnished silver knob—

He turned away from the house, a straw-dry whistle of air slipping from his mouth. Not yet. Later, perhaps, but not yet. For now it was enough to know that all of that was still here. It had waited for him. He put his hands on the hood of his car and looked out over the town. He could find out down there who was handling the Marsten House, and perhaps lease it. The kitchen would make an adequate writing room and he could bunk down in the front parlor. But he wouldn't allow himself to go upstairs.

Not unless it had to be done.

He got in his car, started it, and drove down the hill to Jerusalem's Lot.

Chapter Two
SUSAN (I)

1

He was sitting on a bench in the park when he observed the girl watching him. She was a very pretty girl, and there was a silk scarf tied over her light blond hair. She was currently reading a book, but there was a sketch pad and what looked like a charcoal pencil beside her. It was Tuesday, September 16, the first day of school, and the park had magically emptied of the rowdier element. What was left was a scattering of mothers with infants, a few old men sitting by the war memorial, and this girl sitting in the dappled shade of a gnarled old elm.

She looked up and saw him. An expression of startlement crossed her face. She looked down at her book; looked up at him again and started to rise; almost thought better of it; did rise; sat down again.

He got up and walked over, holding his own book, which was a paperback Western. "Hello," he said agreeably. "Do we know each other?"

"No," she said. "That is . . . you're Benjaman Mears, right?"

"Right." He raised his eyebrows.

She laughed nervously, not looking in his eyes except in a quick flash, to try to read the barometer of his intentions. She was quite obviously a girl not accustomed to speaking to strange men in the park.

"I thought I was seeing a ghost." She held up the book in her lap. He saw fleetingly that "Jerusalem's Lot Public Library" was stamped on the thickness of pages between covers. The book was *Air Dance,* his second novel. She showed him the photograph of himself on the back jacket, a photo that was four years old now. The face looked boyish and frighteningly serious— the eyes were black diamonds.

"Of such inconsequential beginnings dynasties are begun," he said, and although it was a joking throwaway remark, it hung oddly in the air, like prophecy spoken in jest. Behind them, a number of toddlers were splashing happily in the wading pool and a mother was telling Roddy not to push his sister so *high.* The sister went soaring up on her swing regardless, dress flying, trying for the sky. It was a moment he remembered for years after, as though a special small slice had been cut from the cake of time. If nothing fires between two people, such an instant simply falls back into the general wrack of memory.

Then she laughed and offered him the book. "Will you autograph it?"

"A library book?"

"I'll buy it from them and replace it."

He found a mechanical pencil in his sweater pocket, opened the book to the flyleaf, and asked, "What's your name?"

"Susan Norton."

He wrote quickly, without thinking: *For Susan Norton, the prettiest girl in the park. Warm regards, Ben Mears.* He added the date below his signature in slashed notation.

"Now you'll have to steal it," he said, handing it back. "*Air Dance* is out of print, alas."

"I'll get a copy from one of those book finders in New York." She hesitated, and this time her glance at his eyes was a little longer. "It's an awfully good book."

"Thanks. When I take it down and look at it, I wonder how it ever got published."

"Do you take it down often?"

"Yeah, but I'm trying to quit."

She grinned at him and they both laughed and that made things more natural. Later he would have a chance to think how easily this had happened, how smoothly. The thought was never a comfortable one. It conjured up an image of fate, not blind at all but equipped with sentient 20/20 vision and intent on grinding helpless mortals between the great millstones of the universe to make some unknown bread.

"I read *Conway's Daughter,* too. I loved that. I suppose you hear that all the time."

"Remarkably little," he said honestly. Miranda had also loved *Conway's Daughter,* but most of his coffeehouse friends had been noncommittal and most of the critics had clobbered it. Well, that was critics for you. Plot was out, masturbation in.

"Well, I did."

"Have you read the new one?"

"Billy Said Keep Going? Not yet. Miss Coogan at the drugstore says it's pretty racy."

"Hell, it's almost puritanical," Ben said. "The language is rough, but when you're writing about uneducated country boys, you can't . . . look, can I buy you an ice-cream soda or something? I was just getting a hanker on for one."

She checked his eyes a third time. Then smiled, warmly. "Sure. I'd love one. They're great in Spencer's."

That was the beginning of it.

2

"Is that Miss Coogan?"

Ben asked it, low-voiced. He was looking at a tall, spare woman who was wearing a red nylon duster over her white uniform. Her blue-rinsed hair was done in a steplike succession of finger waves.

"That's her. She's got a little cart she takes to the library every Thursday night. She fills out reserve cards by the ton and drives Miss Starcher crazy."

They were seated on red leather stools at the soda fountain. He was drinking a chocolate soda; hers was strawberry. Spencer's also served as the local bus depot and from where they sat they could look through an old-fashioned scrolled arch and into the waiting room, where a solitary young man in Air Force blues sat glumly with his feet planted around his suitcase.

"Doesn't look happy to be going wherever he's going, does he?" she said, following his glance.

"Leave's over, I imagine," Ben said. Now, he thought, she'll ask if I've ever been in the service.

But instead: "I'll be on that ten-thirty bus one of these days. Good-by, 'salem's Lot. Probably I'll be looking just as glum as that boy."

"Where?"

"New York, I guess. To see if I can't finally become self-supporting."

"What's wrong with right here?"

"The Lot? I love it. But my folks, you know. They'd always be sort of looking over my shoulder. That's a bummer. And the Lot doesn't really have that much to offer the young career girl." She shrugged and dipped her head to suck at her straw. Her neck was tanned, beautifully muscled. She was wearing a colorful print shift that hinted at a good figure.

"What kind of job are you looking for?"

She shrugged. "I've got a B.A. from Boston University . . . not worth the paper it's printed on, really. Art major, English minor. The original dipso duo. Strictly eligible for the educated idiot category. I'm not even trained to decorate an office. Some of the girls I went to high school with are holding down plump secretarial jobs now. I never got beyond Personal Typing I, myself."

"So what does that leave?"

"Oh . . . maybe a publishing house," she said vaguely. "Or some magazine . . . advertising, maybe. Places like that can always use someone who can draw on command. I can do that. I have a portfolio."

"Do you have offers?" he asked gently.

"No . . . no. But . . ."

"You don't go to New York without offers," he said. "Believe me. You'll wear out the heels on your shoes."

She smiled uneasily. "I guess you should know."

"Have you sold stuff locally?"

"Oh yes." She laughed abruptly. "My biggest sale to date was to the Cinex Corporation. They opened a new triple cinema in Portland and bought twelve paintings at a crack to hang in their lobby. Paid seven hundred dollars. I made a down payment on my little car."

"You ought to take a hotel room for a week or so in New York," he said, "and hit every magazine and publishing house you can find with your portfolio. Make your appointments six months in advance so the editors and personnel guys don't have anything on their calendars. But for God's sake, don't just haul stakes for the big city."

"What about you?" she asked, leaving off the straw and spooning ice cream. "What are you doing in the thriving community of Jerusalem's Lot, Maine, population thirteen hundred?"

He shrugged. "Trying to write a novel."

She was instantly alight with excitement. "In the Lot? What's it about? Why here? Are you—"

He looked at her gravely. "You're dripping."

"I'm—? Oh, I am. Sorry." She mopped the base of her glass with a napkin. "Say, I didn't mean to pry. I'm really not gushy as a rule."

"No apology needed," he said. "All writers like to talk about their books. Sometimes when I'm lying in bed at night I make up a *Playboy* interview about me. Waste of time. They only do authors if their books are big on campus."

The Air Force youngster stood up. A Greyhound was pulling up to the curb out front, air brakes chuffing.

"I lived in 'salem's Lot for four years as a kid. Out on the Burns Road."

"The Burns Road? There's nothing out there now but the Marshes and a little graveyard. Harmony Hill, they call it."

"I lived with my Aunt Cindy. Cynthia Stowens. My dad died, see, and my mom went through a . . . well, kind of a nervous breakdown. So she farmed me out to Aunt Cindy while she got her act back together. Aunt Cindy put me on a bus back to Long Island and my mom just about a month after the big fire." He looked at his face in the mirror behind the soda fountain. "I cried on the bus going away from Mom, and I cried on the bus going away from Aunt Cindy and Jerusalem's Lot."

"I was born the year of the fire," Susan said. "The biggest damn thing that ever happened to this town and I slept through it."

Ben laughed. "That makes you about seven years older than I thought in the park."

"Really?" She looked pleased. "Thank you . . . I think. Your aunt's house must have burned down."

"Yes," he said. "That night is one of my clearest memories. Some men with Indian pumps on their backs came to the door and said we'd have to leave. It was very exciting. Aunt Cindy dithered around, picking things up and loading them into her Hudson. Christ, what a night."

"Was she insured?"

"No, but the house was rented and we got just about everything valuable into the car, except for the TV. We tried to lift it and couldn't even budge it off the floor. It was a Video King with a seven-inch screen and a magnifying glass over the picture tube. Hell on the eyes. We only got one channel anyway—lots of country music, farm reports, and Kitty the Klown."

"And you came back here to write a book," she marveled.

Ben didn't reply at once. Miss Coogan was opening cartons of cigarettes and filling the display rack by the cash register. The pharmacist, Mr. Labree, was puttering around behind the high drug counter like a frosty ghost. The Air Force kid was standing by the door to the bus, waiting for the driver to come back from the bathroom.

"Yes," Ben said. He turned and looked at her, full in the face, for the first time. She had a very pretty face, with candid blue eyes and a high, clear, tanned forehead. "Is this town your childhood?" he asked.

"Yes."

He nodded. "Then you know. I was a kid in 'salem's Lot and it's haunted for me. When I came back, I almost drove right by because I was afraid it would be different."

"Things don't change here," she said. "Not very much."

"I used to play war with the Gardener kids down in the Marshes. Pirates out by Royal's Pond. Capture-the-flag and hide-and-go-seek in the park. My mom and I knocked around some pretty hard places after I left Aunt Cindy. She killed herself when I was fourteen, but most of the magic dust had rubbed off me long before that. What there was of it was here. And it's still here. The town hasn't changed that much. Looking out on Jointner Avenue is like looking through a thin pane of ice—like the one you can pick off the top of the town cistern in November if you knock it around the edges first—looking through that at your childhood. It's wavy and misty and in some places it trails off into nothing, but most of it is still all there."

He stopped, amazed. He had made a speech.

"You talk just like your books," she said, awed.

He laughed. "I never said anything like that before. Not out loud."

"What did you do after your mother . . . after she died?"

"Knocked around," he said briefly. "Eat your ice cream."

She did.

"Some things have changed," she said after a while. "Mr. Spencer died. Do you remember him?"

"Sure. Every Thursday night Aunt Cindy came into town to do her shopping at Crossen's store and she'd send me in here to have a root beer. That was when it was on draft, real Rochester root beer. She'd give me a handkerchief with a nickel wrapped up in it."

"They were a dime when I came along. Do you remember what he always used to say?"

Ben hunched forward, twisted one hand into an arthritic claw, and turned one corner of his mouth down in a paralytic twist. "Your bladder," he whispered. "Those rut beers will destroy your bladder, bucko."

Her laughter pealed upward toward the slowly rotating fan over their heads. Miss Coogan looked up suspiciously. "That's *perfect!* Except he used to call me lassie."

They looked at each other, delighted.

"Say, would you like to go to a movie tonight?" he asked.

"I'd love to."

"What's closest?"

She giggled. "The Cinex in Portland, actually. Where the lobby is decorated with the deathless paintings of Susan Norton."

"Where else? What kind of movies do you like?"

"Something exciting with a car chase in it."

"Okay. Do you remember the Nordica? That was right here in town."

"Sure. It closed in 1968. I used to go on double dates there when I was in high school. We threw popcorn boxes at the screen when the movies were bad." She giggled. "They usually were."

"They used to have those old Republic serials," he said. *"Rocket Man. The Return of Rocket Man. Crash Callahan and the Voodoo Death God."*

"That was before my time."

"Whatever happened to it?"

"That's Larry Crockett's real estate office now," she said. "The drive-in over in Cumberland killed it, I guess. That and TV."

They were silent for a moment, thinking their own thoughts. The Greyhound clock showed 10:45 A.M.

They said in chorus: "Say, do you remember—"

They looked at each other, and this time Miss Coogan looked up at both of them when the laughter rang out. Even Mr. Labree looked over.

They talked for another fifteen minutes, until Susan told him reluctantly that she had errands to run but yes, she could be ready at seven-thirty. When they went different ways, they both marveled over the easy, natural, coincidental impingement of their lives.

Ben strolled back down Jointner Avenue, pausing at the corner of Brock Street to look casually up at the Marsten House. He remembered that the great forest fire of 1951 had burned almost to its very yard before the wind had changed.

He thought: Maybe it should have burned. Maybe that would have been better.

3

Nolly Gardener came out of the Municipal Building and sat down on the steps next to Parkins Gillespie just in time to see Ben and Susan walk into Spencer's together. Parkins was smoking a Pall Mall and cleaning his yellowed fingernails with a pocket knife.

"That's that writer fella, ain't it?" Nolly asked.

"Yep."

"Was that Susie Norton with him?"

"Yep."

"Well, that's interesting," Nolly said, and hitched his garrison belt. His deputy star glittered importantly on his chest. He had sent away to a detective magazine to get it; the town did not provide its deputy constables with badges. Parkins had one, but he carried it in his wallet, something Nolly had never been able to understand. Of course everybody in the Lot knew he was the constable, but there was such a thing as tradition. There was such a thing as responsibility. When you were an officer of the law, you had to think about both. Nolly thought about them both often, although he could only afford to deputy part-time.

Parkins's knife slipped and slit the cuticle of his thumb. "Shit," he said mildly.

"You think he's a real writer, Park?"

"Sure he is. He's got three books right in this library."

"True or made up?"

"Made up." Parkins put his knife away and sighed.

"Floyd Tibbets ain't going to like some guy makin' time with his woman."

"They ain't married," Parkins said. "And she's over eighteen."

"Floyd ain't going to like it."

"Floyd can crap in his hat and wear it backward for all of me," Parkins said. He crushed his smoke on the step, took a Sucrets box out of his pocket, put the dead butt inside, and put the box back in his pocket.

"Where's that writer fella livin'?"

"Down to Eva's," Parkins said. He examined his wounded cuticle closely. "He was up lookin' at the Marsten House the other day. Funny expression on his face."

"Funny? What do you mean?"

"Funny, that's all." Parkins took his cigarettes out. The sun felt warm and good on his face. "Then he went to see Larry Crockett. Wanted to lease the place."

"The *Marsten* place?"

"Yep."

"What is he, crazy?"

"Could be." Parkins brushed a fly from the left knee of his pants and watched it buzz away into the bright morning. "Ole Larry Crockett's been a busy one lately. I hear he's gone and sold the Village Washtub. Sold it awhile back, as a matter of fact."

"What, that old laundrymat?"

"Yep."

"What would anyone want to put in there?"

"Dunno."

"Well." Nolly stood up and gave his belt another hitch. "Think I'll take a turn around town."

"You do that," Parkins said, and lit another cigarette.

"Want to come?"

"No, I believe I'll sit right here for a while."

"Okay. See you."

Nolly went down the steps, wondering (not for the first time) when Parkins would decide to retire so that he, Nolly, could have the job full-time. How in God's name could you ferret out crime sitting on the Municipal Building steps?

Parkins watched him go with a mild feeling of relief. Nolly was a good boy, but he was awfully eager. He took out his pocket knife, opened it, and began paring his nails again.

4

Jerusalem's Lot was incorporated in 1765 (two hundred years later it had celebrated its bicentennial with fireworks and a pageant in the park; little Debbie Forester's Indian princess costume was set on fire by a thrown sparkler and Parkins Gillespie had to throw six fellows in the local cooler for public intoxication), a full fifty-five years before Maine became a state as the result of the Missouri Compromise.

The town took its peculiar name from a fairly prosaic occurrence. One of the area's earliest residents was a dour, gangling farmer named Charles Belknap Tanner. He kept pigs, and one of the large sows was named Jerusalem. Jerusalem broke out of her pen one day at feeding time, escaped into the nearby woods, and went wild and mean. Tanner warned small children off his property for years afterward by leaning over his gate and croaking at them in ominous, gore-crow tones: "Keep 'ee out o' Jerusalem's wood lot, if 'ee want to keep 'ee guts in 'ee belly!" The warning took hold, and so did the name. It proves little, except that perhaps in America even a pig can aspire to immortality.

The main street, known originally as the Portland Post Road, had been named after Elias Jointner in 1896. Jointner, a member of the House of Representatives for six years (up until his death, which was caused by syphilis, at the age of fifty-eight), was the closest thing to a personage that the Lot could boast—with the exception of Jerusalem the pig and Pearl Ann Butts, who ran off to New York City in 1907 to become a Ziegfeld girl.

Brock Street crossed Jointner Avenue dead center and at right angles, and the township itself was nearly circular (although a little flat on the east, where the boundary was the meandering Royal River). On a map, the two main roads gave the town an appearance very much like a telescopic sight.

The northwest quadrant of the sight was north Jerusalem, the most heavily wooded section of town. It was the high ground, although it would not have appeared very high to anyone except perhaps a Midwesterner. The tired old hills, which were honeycombed with old logging roads, sloped down gently toward the town itself, and the Marsten House stood on the last of these.

Much of the northeast quadrant was open land—hay, timothy, and alfalfa. The Royal River ran here, an old river that had cut its banks almost to the base level. It flowed under the small wooden Brock Street Bridge and wandered north in flat, shining arcs until it entered the land near the northern limits of the town, where solid granite lay close under the thin soil. Here it had cut fifty-foot stone cliffs over the course of a million years. The kids called it Drunk's Leap, because a few years back Tommy Rathbun, Virge Rathbun's tosspot brother, staggered over the edge while looking for a place to take a leak. The Royal fed the mill-polluted Androscoggin but had never been polluted itself; the only industry the Lot had ever boasted was a sawmill, long since closed. In the summer months, fishermen casting from the Brock Street Bridge were a common sight. A day when you couldn't take your limit out of the Royal was a rare day.

The southeast quadrant was the prettiest. The land rose again, but there was no ugly blight of fire or any of the topsoil ruin that is a fire's legacy. The land on both sides of the Griffen Road was owned by Charles Griffen, who was the biggest dairy farmer south of Mechanic Falls, and from Schoolyard Hill you could see Griffen's huge barn with its aluminum roof glittering in the sun like a monstrous heliograph. There were other farms in the area, and a good many houses that had been bought by the white-collar workers who commuted to either Portland or Lewiston. Sometimes, in autumn, you could stand on top of Schoolyard Hill and smell the fragrant odor of the field burnings and see the toylike 'salem's Lot Volunteer Fire Department truck, waiting to step in if anything got out of hand. The lesson of 1951 had remained with these people.

It was in the southwest area that the trailers had begun to move in, and everything that goes with them, like an exurban asteroid belt: junked-out cars up on blocks, tire swings hanging on frayed rope, glittering beer cans lying beside the roads, ragged wash hung on lines between makeshift poles, the ripe smell of sewage from hastily laid septic tanks. The houses in the Bend were kissing cousins to woodsheds, but a gleaming TV aerial sprouted from nearly every one, and most of the TVs inside were color, bought on credit from Grant's or Sears. The yards of the shacks and trailers were usually full of kids, toys, pickup trucks, snowmobiles, and motorbikes. In some cases the trailers were well kept, but in most cases it seemed to be too much trouble. Dandelions and witch grass grew ankle-deep. Out near the town line, where Brock Street became Brock Road, there was Dell's, where a rock 'n' roll band played on Fridays and a c/w combo played on Saturdays. It had burned down once in 1971 and was rebuilt. For most of the down-home cowboys and their girl friends, it was the place to go and have a beer or a fight.

Most of the telephone lines were two-, four-, or six-party connections, and so folks always had someone to talk about. In all small towns, scandal is always simmering on the back burner, like your Aunt Cindy's baked beans. The Bend produced most of the scandal, but every now and then someone with a little more status added something to the communal pot.

Town government was by town meeting, and while there had been talk ever since 1965 of changing to the town council form with biannual public budget hearings, the idea gained no way. The town was not growing fast enough to make the old way actively painful, although its stodgy, one-for-one democracy made some of the newcomers roll their eyes in exasperation. There were three selectmen, the town constable, an overseer of the poor, a town clerk (to register your car you have to go far out on the Taggart Stream Road and brave two mean dogs who ran loose in the yard), and the school commissioner. The volunteer Fire Department got a token appropriation of three hundred dollars each year, but it was mostly a social club for old fellows on pensions. They saw a fair amount of excitement during grass fire season and sat around the Reliable tall-taling each other the rest of the year. There was no Public Works Department because there were no public water lines, gas mains, sewage, or light-and-power. The CMP electricity pylons marched across town on a diagonal from northwest to southeast, cutting a huge gash through the timberland 150 feet wide. One of these stood close to the Marsten House, looming over it like an alien sentinel.

What 'salem's Lot knew of wars and burnings and crises in government it got mostly from Walter Cronkite on TV. Oh, the Potter boy got killed in Vietnam and Claude Bowie's son came back with a mechanical foot—stepped on a land mine—but he got a job with the post office helping Kenny Danles and so *that* was all right The kids were wearing their hair longer and not combing it neatly like their fathers, but nobody really noticed anymore. When they threw the dress code out at the Consolidated High School, Aggie Corliss wrote a letter to the Cumberland *Ledger*, but Aggie had been writing to the *Ledger* every week for years, mostly about the evils of liquor and the wonder of accepting Jesus Christ into your heart as your personal savior.

Some of the kids took dope. Horace Kilby's boy Frank went up before Judge Hooker in August and got fined fifty dollars (the judge agreed to let him pay the fine with profits from his paper route), but alcohol was a bigger problem. Lots of kids hung out at Dell's since the liquor age went down to eighteen. They went rip-assing home as if they wanted to resurface the road with rubber, and every now and then someone would get killed. Like when Billy Smith ran into a tree on the Deep Cut Road at ninety and killed both himself and his girl friend, LaVerne Dube.

But except for these things, the Lot's knowledge of the country's torment was academic. Time went on a different schedule there. Nothing too nasty could happen in such a nice little town. Not there.

5

Ann Norton was ironing when her daughter burst in with a bag of groceries, thrust a book with a rather thin-faced young man on the back jacket in her face, and began to babble.

"Slow down," she said. "Turn down the TV and tell me."

Susan choked off Peter Marshall, who was giving away thousands of dollars on "The Hollywood Squares," and told her mother about meeting Ben Mears. Mrs. Norton made herself nod with calm and sympathetic understanding as the story spilled out, despite the yellow warning lights that always flashed when Susan mentioned a new boy—men now, she supposed, although it was hard to think Susie could be old enough for men. But the lights were a little brighter today.

"Sounds exciting," she said, and put another one of her husband's shirts on the ironing board.

"He was really nice," Susan said. "Very natural."

"Hoo, my feet," Mrs. Norton said. She set the iron on its fanny, making it hiss balefully, and eased into the Boston rocker by the picture window. She reached a Parliament out of the pack on the coffee table and lit it. "Are you sure he's all right Susie?"

Susan smiled a little defensively. "Sure, I'm sure. He looks like . . . oh, I don't know—a college instructor or something."

"They say the Mad Bomber looked like a gardener," Mrs. Norton said reflectively.

"Moose shit," Susan said cheerfully. It was an epithet that never failed to irritate her mother.

"Let me see the book." She held a hand out for it.

Susan gave it to her, suddenly remembering the homosexual rape scene in the prison section.

"*Air Dance*," Ann Norton said meditatively, and began to thumb pages at random. Susan waited, resigned. Her mother would birddog it. She always did.

The windows were up, and a lazy forenoon breeze ruffled the yellow curtains in the kitchen—which Mom insisted on calling the pantry, as if they lived in the lap of class. It was a nice house, solid brick, a little hard to heat in the winter but cool as a grotto in the summer. They were on a gentle rise of land on outer Brock Street, and from the picture window where Mrs. Norton sat you could see all the way into town. The view was a pleasant one, and in the winter it could be spectacular with long, twinkling vistas of unbroken snow and distance-dwindled buildings casting yellow oblongs of light on the snow fields.

"Seems I read a review of this in the Portland paper. It wasn't very good."

"I like it," Susan said steadily. "And I like him."

"Perhaps Floyd would like him, too," Mrs. Norton said idly. "You ought to introduce them."

Susan felt a real stab of anger and was dismayed by it. She thought that she and her mother had weathered the last of the adolescent storms and even the aftersqualls, but here it all was. They took up the ancient arguments of her identity versus her mother's experience and beliefs like an old piece of knitting.

"We've talked about Floyd, Mom. You know there's nothing firm there."

"The paper said there were some pretty lurid prison scenes, too. Boys getting together with boys."

"Oh, Mother, for Christ's sake." She helped herself to one of her mother's cigarettes.

"No need to curse," Mrs. Norton said, unperturbed. She handed the book back and tapped the long ash on her cigarette into a ceramic ash tray in the shape of a fish. It had been given to her by one of her Ladies' Auxiliary friends, and it had always irritated Susan in a formless sort of way. There was something obscene about tapping your ashes into a perch's mouth.

"I'll put the groceries away," Susan said, getting up.

Mrs. Norton said quietly, "I only meant that if you and Floyd Tibbits are going to be married—"

The irritation boiled over into the old, goaded anger. "What in the name of *God* ever gave you that idea? Have I ever told you that?"

"I assumed—"

"You assumed wrong," she said hotly and not entirely truthfully. But she had been cooling toward Floyd by slow degrees over a period of weeks.

"I assumed that when you date the same boy for a year and a half," her mother continued softly and implacably, "that it must mean things have gone beyond the hand-holding stage."

"Floyd and I are more than friends," Susan agreed evenly. Let her make something of *that.*

An unspoken conversation hung suspended between them.

Have you been sleeping with Floyd?

None of your business.

What does this Ben Mears mean to you?

None of your business.

Are you going to fall for him and do something foolish?

None of your business.

I love you, Susie. Your dad and I both love you.

And to that no answer. And no answer. And no answer. And that was why New York—or someplace—was imperative. In the end you always crashed against the unspoken barricades of their love, like the walls of a padded cell. The truth of their love rendered further meaningful discussion impossible and made what had gone before empty of meaning.

"Well," Mrs. Norton said softly. She stubbed her cigarette out on the perch's lip and dropped it into his belly.

"I'm going upstairs," Susan said.

"Sure. Can I read the book when you're finished?"

"If you want to."

"I'd like to meet him," she said.

Susan spread her hands and shrugged.

"Will you be late tonight?"

"I don't know."

"What shall I tell Floyd Tibbits if he calls?"

The anger flashed over her again. "Tell him what you want." She paused. "You will anyway."

"Susan!"

She went upstairs without looking back.

Mrs. Norton remained where she was, staring out the window and at the town without seeing it. Overhead she could hear Susan's footsteps and then the clatter of her easel being pulled out.

She got up and began to iron again. When she thought Susan might be fully immersed in her work (although she didn't allow that idea to do more than flitter through a corner of her conscious mind), she went to the telephone in the pantry and called up Mabel Werts. In the course of the conversation she happened to mention that Susie had told her there was a famous author in their midst and Mabel sniffed and said well you must mean that man who wrote *Conway's Daughter* and Mrs. Norton said yes and Mabel said that wasn't writing but just a sexbook, pure and simple. Mrs. Norton asked if he was staying at a motel or—

As a matter of fact, he was staying downtown at Eva's Rooms, the town's only boardinghouse. Mrs. Norton felt a surge of relief. Eva Miller was a decent widow who would put up with no hankypanky. Her rules on women in the rooms were brief and to the point. If she's your mother or your sister, all right. If she's not, you can sit in the kitchen. No negotiation on the rule was entertained.

Mrs. Norton hung up fifteen minutes later, after artfully camouflaging her main objective with small talk.

Susan, she thought, going back to the ironing board. Oh, Susan, I only want what's best for you. Can't you see that?

6

They were driving back from Portland along 295, and it was not late at all—only a little after eleven. The speed limit on the expressway after it got out of Portland's suburbs was fifty-five, and he drove well. The Citroën's headlights cut the dark smoothly.

They had both enjoyed the movie, but cautiously, the way people do when they are feeling for each other's boundaries. Now her mother's question occurred to her and she said, "Where are you staying? Are you renting a place?"

"I've got a third-floor cubbyhole at Eva's Rooms, on Railroad Street."

"But that's awful! It must be a hundred degrees up there!"

"I like the heat," he said. "I work well in it. Strip to the waist, turn up the radio, and drink a gallon of beer. I've been putting out ten pages a day, fresh copy. There's some interesting old codgers there, too. And when you finally go out on the porch and catch the breeze . . . heaven."

"Still," she said doubtfully.

"I thought about renting the Marsten House," he said casually. "Even went so far as to inquire about it. But it's been sold."

"The *Marsten* House?" She smiled. "You're thinking of the wrong place."

"Nope. Sits up on that first hill to the northwest of town. Brooks Road."

"Sold? Who in the name of heaven—?"

"I wondered the same thing. I've been accused of having a screw loose from time to time, but even I only thought of renting it. The real estate man wouldn't tell me. Seems to be a deep, dark secret."

"Maybe some out-of-state people want to turn it into a summer place," she said. "Whoever it is, they're crazy. Renovating a place is one thing—I'd love to try it—but that place is beyond renovation. The place was a wreck even when I was a kid. Ben, why would you ever want to stay there?"

"Were you ever actually inside?"

"No, but I looked in the window on a dare. Were you?"

"Yes. Once."

"Creepy place, isn't it?"

They fell silent, both thinking of the Marsten House. This particular reminiscence did not have the pastel nostalgia of the others. The scandal and violence connected with the house had occurred before their births, but small towns have long memories and pass their horrors down ceremonially from generation to generation.

The story of Hubert Marsten and his wife, Birdie, was the closest thing the town had to a skeleton in its closet. Hubie had been the president of a large New England trucking company in the 1920s—a trucking company which, some said, conducted its most profitable business after midnight, running Canadian whisky into Massachusetts.

He and his wife had retired wealthy to 'salem's Lot in 1928, and had lost a good part of that wealth (no one, not even Mabel Werts, knew exactly how much) in the stock market crash of 1929.

In the ten years between the fall of the market and the rise of Hitler, Marsten and his wife lived in their house like hermits. The only time they were seen was on Wednesday afternoons when they came to town to do their shopping. Larry McLeod, who was the mailman during those years, reported that Marsten got four daily papers, *The Saturday Evening Post, The New Yorker,* and a pulp magazine called *Amazing Stories.* He also got a check once a month from the trucking company, which was based in Fall River, Massachusetts. Larry said he could tell it was a check by bending the envelope and peeking into the address window.

Larry was the one who found them in the summer of 1939. The papers and magazines—five days' worth—had piled up in the mailbox until it was impossible to cram in more. Larry took them all up the walk with the intention of putting them in between the screen door and the main door.

It was August and high summer, the beginning of dog days, and the grass in the Marsten front yard was calf-high, green and rank. Honeysuckle ran wild over the trellis on the west side of the house, and fat bees buzzed indolently around the wax-white, redolent blossoms. In those days the house was still a fine-looking place in spite of the high grass, and it was generally agreed that Hubie had built the nicest house in 'salem's Lot before going soft in the attic.

Halfway up the walk, according to the story that was eventually told with breathless horror to each new Ladies' Auxiliary member, Larry had smelled something bad, like spoiled meat. He knocked on the front door and got no answer. He looked through the door but could see nothing in the thick gloom. He went around to the back instead of walking in, which was lucky for him. The smell was worse in back. Larry tried the back door, found it unlocked, and stepped into the kitchen. Birdie Marsten was sprawled in a corner, legs splayed out, feet bare. Half her head had been blown away by a close-range shot from a thirty-ought-six.

("Flies," Audrey Hersey always said at this point, speaking with calm authority. "Larry said the kitchen was full of 'em. Buzzing around, lighting on the . . . you know, and taking off again. Flies.")

Larry McLeod turned around and went straight back to town. He fetched Norris Varney, who was constable at the time, and three or four of the hangers-on from Crossen's Store—Milt's father was still running the place in those days. Audrey's eldest brother, Jackson, had been among them. They drove back up in Norris's Chevrolet and Larry's mail truck.

No one from town had ever been in the house, and it was a nine days' wonder. After the excitement died down, the Portland *Telegram* had done a feature on it. Hubert Marsten's house was a piled, jumbled, bewildering rat's nest of junk, scavenged items, and narrow, winding passageways which led through yellowing stacks of newspapers and magazines and piles of moldering white-elephant books. The complete sets of Dickens, Scott, and Mariatt had been scavenged for the Jerusalem's Lot Public Library by Loretta Starcher's predecessor and still remained in the stacks.

Jackson Hersey picked up a *Saturday Evening Post,* began to flip through it, and did a double-take. A dollar bill had been taped neatly to each page.

Norris Varney discovered how lucky Larry had been when he went around to the back door. The murder weapon had been lashed to a chair with its barrel pointing directly at the front door, aimed chest-high. The gun was cocked, and a string attached to the trigger ran down the hall to the doorknob.

("Gun was loaded, too," Audrey would say at this point. "One tug and Larry McLeod would have gone straight up to the pearly gates.")

There were other, less lethal booby traps. A forty-pound bundle of newspapers had been rigged over the dining room door. One of the stair risers leading to the second floor had been hinged and could have cost someone a broken ankle. It quickly became apparent that Hubie Marsten had been something more than Soft; he had been a full-fledged Loony.

They found him in the bedroom at the end of the upstairs hall, dangling from a rafter.

(Susan and her girl friends had tortured themselves deliciously with the stories they had gleaned from their elders; Amy Rawcliffe had a log playhouse in her back yard and they would lock themselves in and sit in the dark, scaring each other about the Marsten House, which gained its proper noun status for all time even before Hitler invaded Poland, and repeating their elders' stories with as many grisly embellishments as their minds could conceive. Even now, eighteen years later, she found that just thinking of the Marsten House had acted on her like a wizard's spell, conjuring up the painfully clear images of little girls crouched inside Amy's playhouse, holding hands, and

Amy saying with impressive eeriness: "His face was all swole up and his tongue turned black and popped out and there was flies crawling on it. My momma tole Mrs. Werts.")

". . . place."

"What? I'm sorry." She came back to the present with an almost physical wrench. Ben was pulling off the turnpike and onto the 'salem's Lot exit ramp.

"I said, it was a spooky old place."

"Tell me about when you went in."

He laughed humorlessly and flicked up his high beams. The two-lane blacktop ran straight ahead through an alley of pine and spruce, deserted. "It started as kid's stuff. Maybe that's all it ever was. Remember, this was in 1951, and little kids had to think up something to take the place of sniffing airplane glue out of paper bags, which hadn't been invented yet. I used to play pretty much with the Bend kids, and most of them have probably moved away by now . . . do they still call south 'salem's Lot the Bend?"

"Yes."

"I messed around with Davie Barclay, Charles James—only all the kids used to call him Sonny—Harold Rauberson, Floyd Tibbits—"

"Floyd?" she asked, startled.

"Yes, do you know him?"

"I've dated him," she said, and afraid her voice sounded strange, hurried on: "Sonny James is still around, too. He runs the gas station on Jointner Avenue. Harold Rauberson is dead. Leukemia."

"They were all older than I, by a year or two. They had a club. Exclusive, you know. Only Bloody Pirates with at least three references need apply." He had meant it to be light, but there was a jag of old bitterness buried in the words. "But I was persistent. The one thing in the world I wanted was to be a Bloody Pirate . . . that summer, at least.

"They finally weakened and told me I could come in if I passed the initiation, which Davie thought up on the spot. We were all going up to the Marsten House, and I was supposed to go in and bring something out. As booty." He chuckled but his mouth had gone dry.

"What happened?"

"I got in through a window. The house was *still* full of junk, even after twelve years. They must have taken the newspapers during the war, but they just left the rest of it. There was a table in the front hall with one of those snow globes on it—do you know what I mean? There's a little house inside, and when you shake it, there's snow. I put it in my pocket, but I didn't leave. I really wanted to prove myself. So I went upstairs to where he hung himself."

"Oh my God," she said.

"Reach in the glove box and get me a cigarette, would you? I'm trying to quit, but I need one for this."

She got him one and he punched the dashboard lighter.

"The house smelled. You wouldn't believe how it smelled. Mildew and upholstery rot and a kind of rancid smell like butter that had gone over. And living things—rats or woodchucks or whatever else that had been nesting in the walls or hibernating in the cellar. A yellow, wet smell.

"I crept up the stairs, a little kid nine years old, scared shitless. The house was creaking and settling around me and I could hear things scuttling away from me on the other side of the plaster. I kept thinking I heard footsteps behind me. I was afraid to turn around because I might see Hubie Marsten shambling after me with a hangman's noose in one hand and his face all black."

He was gripping the steering wheel very hard. The levity had gone out of his voice. The *intensity* of his remembering frightened her a little. His face, in the glow of the instrument panel, was set in the long lines of a man who was traveling a hated country he could not completely leave.

"At the top of the stairs I got all my courage and ran down the hall to that room. My idea was to run in, grab something from there, too, and then get the hell out of there. The door at the end of the hall was closed. I could see it getting closer and closer and I could see that the hinges had settled and the bottom edge was resting on the doorjamb. I could see the doorknob, silvery and a little tarnished in the place where palms had gripped it. When I pulled on it, the bottom edge of the door gave a scream against the wood like a woman in pain. If I had been straight, I think I would have turned around and gotten the hell out right then. But I was pumped full of adrenaline, and I grabbed it in both hands and pulled for all I was worth. It flew open. And there was Hubie, hanging from the beam with his body silhouetted against the light from the window."

"Oh, Ben, don't—" she said nervously.

"No, I'm telling you the truth," he insisted. "The truth of what a nine-year-old boy saw and what the man remembers twenty-four years later, anyway. Hubie was hanging there, and his face wasn't black at all. It was green. The eyes were puffed shut. His hands were livid . . . ghastly. And then he opened his eyes."

Ben took a huge drag on his cigarette and pitched it out his window into the dark.

"I let out a scream that probably could have been heard for two miles. And then I ran. I fell halfway downstairs, got up, and ran out the front door and straight down the road. The kids were waiting for me about half a mile down. That's when I noticed I still had the glass snow globe in my hand. And I've still got it."

"You don't really think you saw Hubert Marsten, do you, Ben?" Far up ahead she could see the yellow blinking light that signaled the center of town and was glad for it.

After a long pause, he said, "I don't know." He said it with difficulty and reluctance, as if he would have rather said *no* and closed the subject thereby. "Probably I was so keyed up that I hallucinated the whole thing. On the other hand, there may be some truth in that idea that houses absorb the emotions that are spent in them, that they hold a kind of . . . dry charge. Perhaps the right personality, that of an imaginative boy, for instance, could act as a catalyst on that dry charge, and cause it to produce an active manifestation of . . . of something. I'm not talking about ghosts, precisely. I'm talking about a kind of psychic television in three dimensions. Perhaps even something alive. A monster, if you like."

She took one of his cigarettes and lit it.

"Anyway, I slept with the light on in my bedroom for weeks after, and I've dreamed about opening that door off and on for the rest of my life. Whenever I'm in stress, the dream comes."

"That's terrible."

"No, it's not," he said. "Not very, anyway. We all have our bad dreams." He gestured with a thumb at the silent, sleeping houses they were passing on Jointner Avenue. "Sometimes I wonder that the very boards of those houses don't cry out with the awful things that happen in dreams." He paused. "Come on down to Eva's and sit on the porch for a while, if you like. I can't invite you in—rules of the house—but I've got a couple of Cokes in the icebox and some Bacardi in my room, if you'd like a nightcap."

"I'd like one very much."

He turned onto Railroad Street, popped off the headlights, and turned into the small dirt parking lot which served the rooming house. The back porch was painted white with red trim, and the three wicker chairs lined up on it looked toward the Royal River. The river itself was a dazzling dream. There was a late summer moon caught in the trees on the river's far bank, three-quarters full, and it had painted a silver path across the water. With the town silent, she could hear the faint foaming sound as water spilled down the sluiceways of the dam.

"Sit down. I'll be back."

He went in, closing the screen door softly behind him, and she sat down in one of the rockers.

She liked him in spite of his strangeness. She was not a believer in love at first sight, although she did believe that instant lust (going under the more innocent name of infatuation) occurred frequently. And yet he wasn't a man that would ordinarily encourage midnight entries in a locked diary; he was too thin for his height, a little pale. His face was introspective and bookish, and his eyes rarely gave away the train of his thoughts. All this topped with a heavy pelt of black hair that looked as if it had been raked with the fingers rather than brushed.

And that story—

Neither *Conway's Daughter* nor *Air Dance* hinted at such a morbid turn of mind. The former was about a minister's daughter who runs away, joins the counterculture, and takes a long, rambling journey across the country by thumb. The latter was the story of Frank Buzzey, an escaped convict who begins a new life as a car mechanic in another state, and his eventual recapture. Both of them were bright, energetic books, and Hubie Marsten's dangling shadow, mirrored in the eyes of a nine-year-old boy, did not seem to lie over either of them.

As if by the very suggestion, she found her eyes dragged away from the river and up to the left of the porch, where the last hill before town blotted out the stars.

"Here," he said. "I hope these'll be all right—"

"Look at the Marsten House," she said.

He did. There was a light on up there.

7

The drinks were gone and midnight passed; the moon was nearly out of sight. They had made some light conversation, and then she said into a pause:

"I like you, Ben. Very much."

"I like you, too. And I'm surprised . . . no, I don't mean it that way. Do you remember that stupid crack I made in the park? This all seems too fortuitous."

"I want to see you again, if you want to see me."

"I do."

"But go slow. Remember, I'm just a small-town girl."

He smiled. "It seems so Hollywood. But Hollywood good. Am I supposed to kiss you now?"

"Yes," she said seriously, "I think that comes next."

He was sitting in the rocker next to her, and without stopping its slow movement forth and back, he leaned over and pressed his mouth on hers, with no attempt to draw her tongue or to touch her. His lips were firm with the pressure of his square teeth, and there was a faint taste-odor of rum and tobacco.

She began to rock also, and the movement made the kiss into something new. It waxed and waned, light and then firm. She thought: He's tasting me. The thought wakened a secret, clean excitement in her, and she broke the kiss before it could take her further.

"Wow," he said.

"Would you like to come to dinner at my house tomorrow night?" she asked. "My folks would love to meet you, I bet." In the pleasure and serenity of this moment, she could throw that sop to her mother.

"Home cooking?"

"The homiest."

"I'd love it. I've been living on TV dinners since I moved in."

"Six o'clock? We eat early in Sticksville."

"Sure. Fine. And speaking of home, I better get you there. Come on."

They didn't speak on the ride back until she could see the night light twinkling on top of the hill, the one her mother always left on when she was out.

"I wonder who's up there tonight?" she asked, looking toward the Marsten House.

"The new owner, probably," he said noncommittally.

"It didn't look like electricity, that light," she mused. "Too yellow, too faint. Kerosene lamp, maybe."

"They probably haven't had a chance to have the power turned on yet."

"Maybe. But almost anyone with a little foresight would call up the power company before they moved in."

He didn't reply. They had come to her driveway.

"Ben," she said suddenly, "is your new book about the Marsten House?"

He laughed and kissed the tip of her nose. "It's late."

She smiled at him. "I don't mean to snoop."

"It's all right. But maybe another time . . . in daylight."

"Okay."

"You better get in, girly. Six tomorrow?"

She looked at her watch. "Six today."

"Night, Susan."

"Night."

She got out and ran lightly up the path to the side door, then turned and waved as he drove away. Before she went in, she added sour cream to the milkman's order. With baked potatoes, that would add a little class to supper.

She paused a minute longer before going in, looking up at the Marsten House.

8

In his small, boxlike room he undressed with the light off and crawled into bed naked. She was a nice girl, the first nice one since Miranda had died. He hoped he wasn't trying to turn her into a new Miranda; that would be painful for him and horribly unfair to her.

He lay down and let himself drift. Shortly before sleep took him, he hooked himself up on one elbow, looked past the square shadow of his typewriter and the thin sheaf of manuscript beside it, and out the window. He had asked Eva Miller specifically for this room after looking at several, because it faced the Marsten House directly.

The lights up there were still on.

That night he had the old dream for the first time since he had come to Jerusalem's Lot, and it had not come with such vividness since those terrible maroon days following Miranda's death in the motorcycle accident. The run up the hallway, the horrible scream of the door as he pulled it open, the dangling figure suddenly opening its hideous puffed eyes, himself turning to the door in the slow, sludgy panic of dreams—

And finding it locked.

Chapter Three
THE LOT (I)

1

The town is not slow to wake—chores won't wait. Even while the edge of the sun lies below the horizon and darkness is on the land, activity has begun.

2

4:00 A.M.

The Griffen boys—Hal, eighteen, and Jack, fourteen—and the two hired hands had begun the milking. The barn was a marvel of cleanliness, whitewashed and gleaming. Down the center, between the spotless runways which fronted the stalls on both sides, a cement drinking trough ran. Hal turned on the water at the far end by flicking a switch and opening a valve. The electric pump that pulled water up from one of the two artesian wells that served the place hummed into smooth operation. He was a sullen boy, not bright, and especially irked on this day. He and his father had had it out the night before. Hal wanted to quit school. He hated school. He hated its boredom, its insistence that you sit still for great fifty-minute chunks of time, and he hated all his subjects with the exceptions of Woodshop and Graphic Arts. English was maddening, history was stupid, business math was incomprehensible. And none of it mattered, that was the hell of it. Cows didn't care if you said ain't or mixed your tenses, they didn't care who was the Commander in Chief of the goddamn Army of the Potomac during the goddamn Civil War, and as for math, his own for chrissakes father couldn't add two fifths and one half if it meant the firing squad. That's why he had an accountant. And look at that guy! College-educated and still working for a dummy like his old man. His father had told him many times that book learning wasn't the secret of running a successful business (and daily farming was a business like any other); *knowing* people was the secret of that. His father was a great one to sling all that bullshit about the wonders of education, him and his sixth-grade education. He never read anything but *Reader's Digest* and the farm was making $16,000 a year. Know people. Be able to shake their hands and ask after their wives by name. Well, Hal knew people. There were two kinds: those you could push around and those you couldn't. The former outnumbered the latter ten to one.

Unfortunately, his father was a one.

He looked over his shoulder at Jack, who was forking hay slowly and dreamily into the first four stalls from a broken bale. There was the bookworm, Daddy's pet. The miserable little shit.

"Come on!" He shouted. "Fork that hay!"

He opened the storage lockers and pulled out the first of their four milking machines. He trundled it down the aisle, frowning fiercely over the glittering stainless-steel top.

School. Fucking for chrissakes *school*.

The next nine months stretched ahead of him like an endless tomb.

3

4:30 A.M.

The fruits of yesterday's late milking had been processed and were now on their way back to the Lot, this time in cartons rather than galvanized steel milk cans, under the colorful label of Slewfoot Hill Dairy. Charles Griffen's father had marketed his own milk, but that was no longer practical. The conglomerates had eaten up the last of the independents.

The Slewfoot Hill milkman in west Salem was Irwin Purinton, and he began his run along Brock Street (which was known in the country as the Brock Road or That Christless Washboard). Later he would cover the center of town and then work back out of town along the Brooks Road.

Win had turned sixty-one in August, and for the first time his coming retirement seemed real and possible. His wife, a hateful old bitch named Elsie, had died in the fall of 1973 (predeceasing him was the one considerate thing she had done in twenty-seven years of marriage), and when his retirement finally came he was going to pack up his dog, a half-cocker mongrel named Doc, and move down to Pemaquid Point. He planned to sleep until nine o'clock every day and never look at another sunrise.

He pulled over in front of the Norton house, and filled his carry rack with their order: orange juice, two quarts of milk, a dozen eggs. Climbing out of the cab, his knee gave a twinge, but only a faint one. It was going to be a fine day.

There was an addition to Mrs. Norton's usual order in Susan's round, Palmer-method script: "Please leave one small sour cream, Win. Thanx."

Purinton went back for it, thinking it was going to be one of those days when everyone wanted something special. Sour cream! He had tasted it once and liked to puke.

The sky was beginning to lighten in the east, and on the fields between here and town, heavy dew sparkled like a king's ransom of diamonds.

4

5:15 A.M.

Eva Miller had been up for twenty minutes, dressed in a rag of a housedress and a pair of floppy pink slippers. She was cooking her breakfast—four scrambled eggs, eight rashers of bacon, a skillet of home fries. She would garnish this humble repast with two slices of toast and jam, a ten-ounce tumbler of orange juice, and two cups of coffee with cream to follow. She was a big woman, but not precisely fat; she worked too hard at keeping her place up to ever be fat. The curves of her body were heroic, Rabelaisian. Watching her in motion at her eight-burner electric stove was like watching the restless movements of the tide, or the migration of sand dunes.

She liked to eat her morning meal in this utter solitude, planning the work ahead of her for the day. There was a lot of it: Wednesday was the day she changed the linen. She had nine boarders at present, counting the new one, Mr. Mears. The house had three stories and seventeen rooms and there were also floors to wash, the stairs to be scrubbed, the banister to be waxed, and the rug to be turned in the central common room. She would get Weasel Craig to help her with some of it, unless he was sleeping off a bad drunk.

The back door opened just as she was sitting down to the table.

"Hi, Win. How are you doing?"

"Passable. Knee's kickin' a bit."

"Sorry to hear it. You want to leave an extra quart of milk and a gallon of that lemonade?"

"Sure," he said, resigned. "I knew it was gonna be that kind of day."

She dug into her eggs, dismissing the comment. Win Purinton could always find something to complain about, although God knew he should have been the happiest man alive since that hellcat he had hooked up with fell down the cellar stairs and broke her neck.

At quarter of six, just as she was finishing up her second cup of coffee and smoking a Chesterfield, the *Press-Herald* thumped against the side of the house and dropped into the rosebushes. The third time this week; the Kilby kid was batting a thousand. Probably delivering the papers wrecked out of his mind. Well, let it sit there awhile. The earliest sunshine, thin and precious gold, was slanting in through the east windows. It was the best time of her day, and she would not disturb its moveless peace for anything.

Her boarders had the use of the stove and the refrigerator—that, like the weekly change of linen, came with their rent—and shortly the peace would be broken as Grover Verrill and Mickey Sylvester came down to slop up their cereal before leaving for the textile mill over in Gates Falls where they both worked.

As if her thought had summoned a messenger of their coming, the toilet on the second floor flushed and she heard Sylvester's heavy work boots on the stairs.

She heaved herself up and went to rescue the paper.

5

6:05 A.M.

The baby's thin wails pierced Sandy McDougall's thin morning sleep and she got up to check the baby with her eyes still bleared shut. She barked her shin on the night stand and said, *"Kukka!"*

The baby, hearing her, screamed louder. "Shut up!" she yelled. "I'm coming!"

She walked down the narrow trailer corridor to the kitchen, a slender girl who was losing whatever marginal prettiness she might once have had. She got Randy's bottle out of the refrigerator, thought about warming it, then thought to hell with it. If you want it so bad, buster, you can just drink it cold.

She went down to his bedroom and looked at him coldly. He was ten months old, but sickly and puling for his age. He had only started crawling last month. Maybe he had polio or something. Now there was something on his hands, and on the wall, too. She pushed forward, wondering what in Mary's name he had been into.

She was seventeen years old and she and her husband had celebrated their first wedding anniversary in July. At the time she had married Royce McDougall, six months' pregnant and looking like the Goodyear blimp, marriage had seemed every bit as blessed as Father Callahan said it was—a blessed escape hatch. Now it just seemed like a pile of kukka.

Which was, she saw with dismay, exactly what Randy had smeared all over his hands, on the wall, and in his hair.

She stood looking at him dully, holding the cold bottle in one hand.

This was what she had given up high school for, her friends for, her hopes of becoming a model for. For this crummy trailer stuck out in the Bend, Formica already peeling off the counters in strips, for a husband that worked all day at the mill and went off drinking or playing poker with his no-good gas-station buddies at night. For a kid who looked just like his no-good old man and smeared kukka all over everything.

He was screaming at the top of his lungs.

"You shut up!" she screamed back suddenly, and threw the plastic bottle at him. It struck his forehead and he toppled on his back in the crib, wailing and thrashing his arms. There was a red circle just below the hairline, and she felt a horrid surge of gratification, pity, and hate in her throat. She plucked him out of the crib like a rag.

"Shut up! Shut up! Shut up!" She had punched him twice before she could stop herself and Randy's screams of pain had become too great for sound. He lay gasping in his crib, his face purple.

"I'm sorry," she muttered. "Jesus, Mary, and Joseph. I'm sorry. You okay, Randy? Just a minute, Momma's going to clean you up."

By the time she came back with a wet rag, both of Randy's eyes had swelled shut and were discoloring. But he took the bottle and when she began to wipe his face with a damp rag, he smiled toothlessly at her.

I'll tell Roy he fell off the changing table, she thought. He'll believe that. Oh God, let him believe that.

6

6:45 A.M.

Most of the blue-collar population of 'salem's Lot was on its way to work. Mike Ryerson was one of the few who worked in town. In the annual town report he was listed as a grounds keeper, but he was actually in charge of maintaining the town's three cemeteries. In the summer this was almost a full-time job, but even in the winter it was no walk, as some folks, such as that prissy George Middler down at the hardware store, seemed to think. He worked part-time for Carl Foreman, the Lot's undertaker, and most of the old folks seemed to poop off in the winter.

Now he was on his way out to the Burns Road in his pickup truck, which was loaded down with clippers, a battery-driven hedge-trimmer, a box of flag stands, a crowbar for lifting gravestones that might have fallen over, a ten-gallon gas can, and two Briggs & Stratton lawn mowers.

He would mow the grass at Harmony Hill this morning, and do any maintenance on the stones and the rock wall that was necessary, and this afternoon he would cross town to the Schoolyard Hill Cemetery, where schoolteachers sometimes came to do rubbings, on account of an extinct colony of Shakers who had once buried their dead there. But he liked Harmony Hill best of all three. It was not as old as the Schoolyard Hill bone yard, but it was pleasant and shady. He hoped that someday he could be buried there himself—in a hundred years or so.

He was twenty-seven, and had gone through three years of college in the course of a rather checkered career. He hoped to go back someday and finish up. He was good-looking in an open, pleasant way, and he had no trouble connecting with unattached females on Saturday nights out at Dell's or in Portland. Some of them were turned off by his job, and Mike found this honestly hard to understand. It was pleasant work, there was no boss always looking over your shoulder, and the work was in the open air, under God's sky; and so what if he dug a few graves or on occasion drove Carl Foreman's funeral hack? Somebody had to do it. To his way of thinking, the only thing more natural than death was sex.

Humming, he turned off onto the Burns Road and shifted to second going up the hill. Dry dust spumed out behind him. Through the choked summer greenery on both sides of the road he could see the skeletal, leafless trunks of the trees that had burned in the big fire of '51, like old and moldering bones. There were deadfalls back in there, he knew, where a man could break his leg if he wasn't careful. Even after twenty-five years, the scar of that great burning was there. Well, that was just it. In the midst of life, we are in death.

The cemetery was at the crest of the hill, and Mike turned in think. He worked part-time for Carl Foreman, the Lot's under-taker, and most of the old folks seemed to poop off in the winter.

Now he was on his way out to the Burns Road in his pickup truck, which was loaded down with clippers, a battery-driven hedge-trimmer, a box of flag stands, a crowbar for lifting grave-stones that might have fallen over, a ten-gallon gas can, and two Briggs & Stratton lawn mowers.

He would mow the grass at Harmony Hill this morning, and do any maintenance on the stones and the rock wall that was necessary, and this afternoon he would cross town to the School-yard Hill Cemetery, where schoolteachers sometimes came to do rubbings, on account of an extinct colony of Shakers who had once buried their dead there. But he liked Harmony Hill best of all three. It was not as old as the Schoolyard Hill bone yard, but it was pleasant and shady. He hoped that someday he could be buried there himself—in a hundred years or so.

He was twenty-seven, and had gone through three years of college in the course of a rather checkered career. He hoped to go back someday and finish up. He was good-looking in an open, pleasant way, and he had no trouble connecting with unattached females on Saturday nights out at Dell's or in Port-land. Some of them were turned off by his job, and Mike found this honestly hard to understand. It was pleasant work, there was no boss always looking over your shoulder, and the work was in the open air, under God's sky; and so what if he dug a few graves or on occasion drove Carl Foreman's funeral hack? Somebody had to do it. To his way of thinking, the only thing more natural than death was sex.

Humming, he turned off onto the Burns Road and shifted to second going up the hill. Dry dust spumed out behind him. Through the choked summer greenery on both sides of the road he could see the skeletal, leafless trunks of the trees that had burned in the big fire of '51, like old and molder-ing bones. There were deadfalls back in there, he knew, where a man could break his leg if he wasn't careful. Even after twenty-five years, the scar of that great burning was there. Well, that was just it. In the midst of life, we are in death.

The cemetery was at the crest of the hill, and Mike turned in

Rhodes was driving one of these buses, and his pickup route covered the Taggart Stream Road in east 'salem and the upper half of Jointner Avenue.

The kids who rode Charlie's bus were the best behaved in town—in the entire school district, for that matter. There was no yelling or horseplay or pulling pigtails on Bus 6. They goddamn well sat still and minded their manners, or they could walk the two miles to Stanley Street Elementary and explain why in the office.

He knew what they thought of him, and he had a good idea of what they called him behind his back. But that was all right. He was not going to have a lot of foolishness and shit-slinging on his bus. Let them save that for their spineless teachers.

The principal at Stanley Street had had the nerve to ask him if he hadn't acted "impulsively" when he put the Durham boy off three days' running for just talking a little too loud. Charlie had just stared at him, and eventually the principal, a wet-eared little pipsqueak who had only been out of college four years, had looked away. The man in charge of the S.A.D. 21 motor pool, Dave Felsen, was an old buddy; they went all the way back to Korea together. They understood each other. They understood what was going on in the country. They understood how the kid who had been "just talking a little too loud" on the school bus in 1958 was the kid who had been out pissing on the flag in 1968.

He glanced into the wide overhead mirror and saw Mary Kate Griegson passing a note to her little chum Brent Tenney. Little chum, yeah, right. They were banging each other by the sixth grade these days.

He pulled over, switching on his Stop flashers. Mary Kate and Brent looked up, dismayed.

"Got a lot to talk about?" he asked into the mirror. "Good. You better get started."

He threw open the folding doors and waited for them to get the hell off his bus.

8

9:00 A.M.

Weasel Craig rolled out of bed—literally. The sunshine coming in his second-floor window was blinding. His head thumped queasily. Upstairs that writer fella was already pecking away. Christ, a man would have to be nuttier than a squirrel to tap-tap-tap away like that, day in and day out.

He got up and went over to the calendar in his skivvies to see if this was the day he picked up his unemployment. No. This was Wednesday.

His hangover wasn't as bad as it had been on occasion. He had been out at Dell's until it closed at one, but he had only had two dollars and hadn't been able to cadge many beers after that was gone. Losing my touch, he thought, and scrubbed the side of his face with one hand.

He pulled on the thermal undershirt that he wore winter and summer, pulled on his green work pants, and then opened his closet and got breakfast—a bottle of warm beer for up here and a box of government-donated-commodities oatmeal for downstairs. He hated oatmeal, but he had promised the widow he would help her turn that rug, and she would probably have some other chores lined up.

He didn't mind—not really—but it was a comedown from the days when he had shared Eva Miller's bed. Her husband had died in a sawmill accident in 1959, and it was kind of funny in a way, if you could call any such horrible accident funny. In those days the sawmill had employed sixty or seventy men, and Ralph Miller had been in line for the mill's presidency.

What had happened to him was sort of funny because Ralph Miller hadn't touched a bit of machinery since 1952, seven years before, when he stepped up from foreman to the front office. That was executive gratitude for you, sure enough, and Weasel supposed that Ralph had earned it. When the big fire had swept out of the Marshes and jumped Jointner Avenue under the urging of a twenty-five-mile-an-hour east wind, it had seemed that the sawmill was certain to go. The fire departments of six neighboring townships had enough on their hands trying to save the town without sparing men for such a pissant operation as the Jerusalem's Lot Sawmill. Ralph Miller had organized the whole second shift into a fire-fighting force, and under his direction they wetted the roof and did what the entire combined fire-fighting force had been unable to do west of Jointner Avenue—he had constructed a firebreak that stopped the fire and turned it south, where it was fully contained.

Seven years later he had fallen into a shredding machine while he was talking to some visiting brass from a Massachusetts company. He had been taking them around the plant, hoping to convince them to buy in. His foot slipped in a puddle of water and son of a bitch, right into the shredder before their very eyes. Needless to say, any possibility of a deal went right down the chute with Ralph Miller. The sawmill that he had saved in 1951 closed for good in February of 1960.

Weasel looked in his water-spotted mirror and combed his white hair, which was shaggy, beautiful, and still sexy at sixty-seven. It was the only part of him that seemed to thrive on alcohol. Then he pulled on his khaki work shirt, took his oatmeal box, and went downstairs.

And here he was, almost sixteen years after all of that had happened, hiring out as a frigging housekeeper to a woman he had once bedded—and a woman he still regarded as damned attractive.

The widow fell on him like a vulture as soon as he stepped into the sunny kitchen.

"Say, would you like to wax that front banister for me after you have your breakfast, Weasel? You got time?" They both preserved the gentle fiction that he did these things as favors, and not as pay for his fourteen-dollar-a-week upstairs room.

"Sure would, Eva."

"And that rug in the front room—"

"—has got to be turned. Yeah, I remember."

"How's your head this morning?" She asked the question in a businesslike way, allowing no pity to enter her tone . . . but he sensed its existence beneath the surface.

"Head's fine," he said touchily, putting water on to boil for the oatmeal.

"You were out late, is why I asked."

"You got a line on me, is that right?" He cocked a humorous eyebrow at her and was gratified to see that she could still blush like a schoolgirl, even though they had left off any funny stuff almost nine years ago.

"Now, Ed—"

She was the only one who still called him that. To everyone else in the Lot he was just Weasel. Well, that was all right. Let them call him any old thing they wanted. The bear had caught him, sure enough.

"Never mind," he said gruffly. "I got up on the wrong side of the bed."

"Fell out of it, by the sound." She spoke more quickly than she had intended, but Weasel only grunted. He cooked and ate his hateful oatmeal, then took the can of furniture wax and rags without looking back.

Upstairs, the tap-tap of that guy's typewriter went on and on. Vinnie Upshaw, who had the room upstairs across from him, said he started in every morning at nine, went till noon, started in again at three, went until six, started in *again* at nine and went right through until midnight. Weasel couldn't imagine having that many words in your mind.

Still, he seemed a nice enough sort, and he might be good for a few beers out to Dell's some night. He had heard most of those writers drank like fish.

He began to polish the banister methodically, and fell to thinking about the widow again. She had turned this place into a boardinghouse with her husband's insurance money, and had done quite well. Why shouldn't she? She worked like a dray horse. But she must have been used to getting it regular from her husband, and after the grief had washed out of her, that need had remained. God, she had liked to do it!

In those days, '61 and '62, people had still been calling him Ed instead of Weasel, and he had still been holding the bottle instead of the other way around. He had a good job on the B&M, and one night in January of 1962 it had happened.

He paused in the steady waxing movements and looked thoughtfully out of the narrow Judas window on the second-floor landing. It was filled with the last bright foolishly golden light of summer, a light that laughed at the cold, rattling autumn and the colder winter that would follow it.

It had been part her and part him that night, and after it had happened and they were lying together in the darkness of her bedroom, she began to weep and tell him that what they had done was wrong. He told her it had been right, not knowing if it had been right or not and not caring, and there had been a norther whooping and coughing and screaming around the eaves and her room had been warm and safe and at last they had slept together like spoons in a silverware drawer.

Ah God and sonny Jesus, time was like a river and he wondered if that writer fella knew *that*.

He began to polish the banister again with long, sweeping strokes.

9

10:00 A.M.

It was recess time at Stanley Street Elementary School, which was the Lot's newest and proudest school building. It was a low, glassine four-classroom building that the school district was still paying for, as new and bright and modern as the Brock Street Elementary School was old and dark.

Richie Boddin, who was the school bully and proud of it, stepped out onto the playground grandly, eyes searching for that smart-ass new kid who knew all the answers in math. No new kid came waltzing into *his* school without knowing who was boss. Especially some four-eyes queer-boy teacher's pet like this one.

Richie was eleven years old and weighed 140 pounds. All his life his mother had been calling on people to see what a *huge* young man her son was. And so he knew he was big. Sometimes he fancied that he could feel the ground tremble underneath his feet when he walked. And when he grew up he was going to smoke Camels, just like his old man.

The fourth- and fifth-graders were terrified of him, and the smaller kids regarded him as a schoolyard totem. When he moved on to the seventh grade at Brock Street School, their pantheon would be empty of its devil. All this pleased him immensely.

And there was the Petrie kid, waiting to be chosen up for the recess touch football game.

"Hey!" Richie yelled.

Everyone looked around except Petrie. Every eye had a glassy sheen on it and every pair of eyes showed relief when they saw that Richie's rested elsewhere.

"Hey you! Four-eyes!"

Mark Petrie turned and looked at Richie. His steel-rimmed glasses flashed in the morning sun. He was as tall as Richie, which meant he towered over most of his classmates, but he was slender and his face looked defenseless and bookish.

"Are you speaking to me?"

" 'Are you speaking to me?' " Richie mimicked, his voice a high falsetto. "You sound like a queer, four-eyes. You know that?"

"No, I didn't know that," Mark Petrie said.

Richie took a step forward. "I bet you suck, you know that, four-eyes? I bet you suck the old hairy root."

"Really?" His polite tone was infuriating.

"Yeah, I heard you really suck it. Not just Thursdays for you. You can't wait. Every day for you."

Kids began to drift over to watch Richie stomp the new boy. Miss Holcomb, who was playground monitor this week, was out front watching the little kids on the swings and seesaws.

"What's your racket?" Mark Petrie asked. He was looking at Richie as if he had discovered an interesting new beetle.

" 'What's your racket?' " Richie mimicked falsetto. "I ain't got no racket. I just heard you were a big fat queer, that's all."

"Is that right?" Mark asked, still polite. "I heard that you were a big clumsy stupid turd, that's what I heard."

Utter silence. The other boys gaped (but it was an interested gape; none of them had ever seen a fellow sign his own death warrant before). Richie was caught entirely by surprise and gaped with the rest.

Mark took off his glasses and handed them to the boy next to him. "Hold these, would you?" The boy took them and goggled at Mark silently.

Richie charged. It was a slow, lumbering charge, with not a bit of grace or finesse in it. The ground trembled under his feet. He was filled with confidence and the clear, joyous urge to stomp and break. He swung his haymaker right, which would catch ole four-eyes queer-boy right in the mouth and send his teeth flying like piano keys. Get ready for the dentist, queer-boy. Here I come.

Mark Petrie ducked and sidestepped at the same instant. The haymaker went over his head. Richie was pulled halfway around by the force of his own blow, and Mark had only to stick out a foot. Richie Boddin thumped to the ground. He grunted. The crowd of watching children went "Aaaah."

Mark knew perfectly well that if the big, clumsy boy on the ground regained the advantage, he would be beaten up badly. Mark was agile, but agility could not stand up for long in a schoolyard brawl. In a street situation this would have been the time to run, to outdistance his slower pursuer, then turn and thumb his nose. But this wasn't the street or the city, and he knew perfectly well that if he didn't whip this big ugly turd now the harassment would never stop.

These thoughts went through his mind in a fifth of a second.

He jumped on Richie Boddin's back.

Richie grunted. The crowd went "Aaaah" again. Mark grabbed Richie's arm, careful to get it above the shirt cuff so he couldn't sweat out of his grip, and twisted it behind Richie's back. Richie screamed in pain.

"Say uncle," Mark told him.

Richie's reply would have pleased a twenty-year Navy man.

Mark yanked Richie's arm up to his shoulder blades, and Richie screamed again. He was filled with indignation, fright, and puzzlement. This had never happened to him before. It couldn't be happening now. Surely no four-eyes queer-boy could be sitting on his back and twisting his arm and making him scream before his subjects.

"Say uncle," Mark repeated.

Richie heaved himself to his knees; Mark squeezed his own knees into Richie's sides, like a man riding a horse bareback, and stayed on. They were both covered with dust, but Richie was much the worse for wear. His face was red and straining, his eyes bulged, and there was a scratch on his cheek.

He tried to dump Mark over his shoulders, and Mark yanked upward on the arm again. This time Richie didn't scream. He wailed.

"Say uncle, or so help me God I'll break it."

Richie's shirt had pulled out of his pants. His belly felt hot and scratched. He began to sob and wrench his shoulders from side to side. Yet the hateful four-eyes queer-boy stayed on. His forearm was ice, his shoulder fire.

"Get off me, you son of a whore! You don't fight fair!"

An explosion of pain.

"Say uncle."

"No!"

He overbalanced on his knees and went face-down in the dust. The pain in his arm was paralyzing. He was eating dirt. There was dirt in his eyes. He thrashed his legs helplessly. He had forgotten about being *huge*. He had forgotten about how the ground trembled under his feet when he walked. He had forgotten that he was going to smoke Camels, just like his old man, when he grew up.

"Uncle! Uncle! Uncle!" Richie screamed. He felt that he could go on screaming uncle for hours, for days, if it would get his arm back.

"Say: 'I'm a big ugly turd.' "

"I'm a big ugly turd!" Richie screamed into the dirt.

"Good enough."

Mark Petrie got off him and stepped back warily out of reach as Richie got up. His thighs hurt from squeezing them together. He hoped that all the fight was out of Richie. If not, he was going to get creamed.

Richie got up. He looked around. No one met his eyes. They turned away and went back to whatever they had been doing. That stinking Glick kid was standing next to the queer-boy and looking at him as though he were some kind of God.

Richie stood by himself, hardly able to believe how quickly his ruination had come. His face was dusty except where it had been streaked clean with his tears of rage and shame. He considered launching himself at Mark Petrie. Yet his shame and fear, new and shining and *huge*, would not allow it. Not yet. His arm ached like a rotted tooth. Son of a whoring dirty fighter. If I ever land on you and get you down—

But not today. He turned away and walked off and the ground didn't tremble a bit. He looked at the ground so he wouldn't have to look anyone in the face.

Someone on the girl's side laughed—a high, mocking sound that carried with cruel clarity on the morning air.

He didn't look up to see who was laughing at him.

10

11:15 A.M.

The Jerusalem's Lot Town Dump had been a plain old gravel pit until it struck clay and paid out in 1945. It was at the end of a spur that led off from the Burns Road two miles beyond Harmony Hill Cemetery.

Dud Rogers could hear the faint putter and cough of Mike Ryerson's lawn mower down the road. But that sound would soon be blotted out by the crackle of flames.

Dud had been the dump custodian since 1956, and his reappointment each year at town meeting was routine and by acclamation. He lived at the dump in a neat tarpaper lean-to with a sign reading "Dump Custodian" on the skew-hung door. He had wangled a space heater out of that skinflint board of selectmen three years ago, and had given up his apartment in town for good.

He was a hunchback with a curious cocked head that made him look as if God had given him a final petulant wrench before allowing him out into the world. His arms, which dangled apelike almost to his knees, were amazingly strong. It had taken four men to load the old hardware store floor safe into their panel truck to bring it out here when the store got its new wall job. The tires of the truck had settled appreciably when they put it in. But Dud Rogers had taken it off himself, cords standing out on his neck, veins bulging on his forehead and forearms and biceps like blue cables. He had pushed it over the east edge himself.

Dud *liked* the dump. He liked running off the kids who came here to bust bottles, and he liked directing traffic to wherever the day's dumping was going on. He liked dump-picking, which was his privilege as custodian. He supposed they sneered at him, walking across the mountains of trash in his hip waders and leather gloves, with his pistol in his holster, a sack over his shoulder, and his pocket knife in his hand. Let them sneer. There was copper core wire and sometimes whole motors with their copper wrappings intact, and copper fetched a good price in Portland. There were busted-out bureaus and chairs and sofas, things that could be fixed up and sold to the antique dealers on Route 1. Dud rooked the dealers and the dealers turned around and rooked the summer people, and wasn't it just fine the way the world went round and round. He'd found a splintered spool bed with a busted frame two years back and had sold it to a faggot from Wells for two hundred bucks. The faggot had gone into ecstasies about the New England authenticity of that bed, never knowing how carefully Dud had sanded off the *Made in Grand Rapids* on the back of the headboard.

At the far end of the dump were the junked cars, Buicks and Fords and Chevies and you name it, and my God the parts people left on their machines when they were through with them. Radiators were best, but a good four-barrel carb would fetch seven dollars after it had been soaked in gasoline. Not to mention fan belts, taillights, distributor caps, windshields, steering wheels, and floor mats.

Yes, the dump was fine. The dump was Disneyland and Shangri-La all rolled up into one. But not even the money tucked away in the black box buried in the dirt below his easy chair was the best part.

The best part was the fires—and the rats.

Dud set parts of his dump on fire on Sunday and Wednesday mornings, and on Monday and Friday evenings. Evening fires were the prettiest. He loved the dusky, roseate glow that bloomed out of the green plastic bags of crap and all the newspapers and boxes. But morning fires were better for rats.

Now, sitting in his easy chair and watching the fire catch and begin to send its greasy black smoke into the air, sending the gulls aloft, Dud held his .22 target pistol loosely in his hand and waited for the rats to come out.

When they came, they came in battalions. They were big, dirty gray, pink-eyed. Small fleas and ticks jumped on their hides. Their tails dragged after them like thick pink wires. Dud loved to shoot rats.

"You buy a powerful slug o' shells, Dud," George Middler down at the hardware store would say in his fruity voice, pushing the boxes of Remingtons across. "Town pay for 'em?" This was an old joke. Some years back, Dud had put in a purchase order for two thousand rounds of hollow-point .22 cartridges, and Bill Norton had grimly sent him packing.

"Now," Dud would say, "you know this is purely a public service, George."

There. That big fat one with the gimpy back leg was George Middler. Had something in his mouth that looked like a shredded piece of chicken liver.

"Here you go, George. Here y'are," Dud said, and squeezed off. The .22's report was flat and undramatic, but the rat tumbled over twice and lay twitching. Hollow points, that was the ticket. Someday he was going to get a large-bore .45 or a .357 Magnum and see what that did to the little cock-knockers.

That next one now, that was that slutty little Ruthie Crockett, the one who didn't wear no bra to school and was always elbowing her chums and sniggering when Dud passed on the street. Bang. Goodby, Ruthie.

The rats scurried madly for the protection of the dump's far side, but before they were gone Dud had gotten six of them—a good morning's kill. If he went out there and looked at them, the ticks would be running off the cooling bodies like . . . like . . . why, like rats deserting a sinking ship.

This struck him as deliciously funny and he threw back his queerly cocked head and rocked back on his hump and laughed in great long gusts as the fire crept through the trash with its grasping orange fingers.

Life surely was grand.

11

12:00 noon.

The town whistle went off with a great twelve-second blast, ushering in lunch hour at all three schools and welcoming the afternoon. Lawrence Crockett, the Lot's second selectman and proprietor of Crockett's Southern Maine Insurance and Realty, put away the book he had been reading (*Satan's Sex Slaves*) and set his watch by the whistle. He went to the door and hung the

"Back at One O'clock" sign from the shade pull. His routine was unvarying. He would walk up to the Excellent Café, have two cheeseburgers with the works and a cup of coffee, and watch Pauline's legs while he smoked a William Penn.

He rattled the doorknob once to make sure the lock had caught and moved off down Jointner Avenue. He paused on the corner and glanced up at the Marsten House. There was a car in the driveway. He could just make it out, twinkling and shining. It caused a thread of disquiet somewhere in his chest. He had sold the Marsten House and the long-defunct Village Washtub in a package deal over a year ago. It had been the strangest deal of his life—and he had made some strange ones in his time. The owner of the car up there was, in all probability, a man named Straker. R. T. Straker. And just this morning he had received something in the mail from this Straker.

The fellow in question had driven up to Crockett's office on a shimmering July afternoon just over a year ago. He got out of the car and stood on the sidewalk for a moment before coming inside, a tall man dressed in a sober three-piece suit in spite of the day's heat. He was as bald as a cueball and as sweatless as same. His eyebrows were a straight black slash, and the eye sockets shelved away below them to dark holes that might have been carved into the angular surface of his face with drill bits. He carried a slim black briefcase in one hand. Larry was alone in his office when Straker came in; his part-time secretary, a Falmouth girl with the most delectable set of jahoobies you ever clapped an eye to, worked for a Gates Falls lawyer on her afternoons.

The bald man sat down in the client's chair, put his briefcase in his lap, and stared at Larry Crockett. It was impossible to read the expression in his eyes, and that bothered Larry. He liked to be able to read a man's wants in his baby blues or browns before the man even opened his mouth. This man had not paused to look at the pictures of local properties that were tacked up on the bulletin board, had not offered to shake hands and introduce himself, had not even said hello.

"How can I help you?" Larry asked.

"I have been sent to buy a residence and a business establishment in your so-fair town," the bald man said. He spoke with a flat, uninflected tonelessness that made Larry think of the recorded announcements you got when you dialed the weather.

"Well, hey, wonderful," Larry said. "We have several very nice properties that might—"

"There is no need," the bald man said, and held up his hand to stop Larry's words. Larry noted with fascination that his fingers were amazingly long—the middle finger looked four or five inches from base to tip. "The business establishment is a block beyond the Town Office Building. It fronts on the park."

"Yeah, I can deal with you on that. Used to be a Laundromat. Went broke a year ago. That'd be a real good location if you—"

"The residence," the bald man overrode him, "is the one referred to in town as the Marsten House."

Larry had been in the business too long to show his thunderstruck feelings on his face. "Is that so?"

"Yes. My name is Straker. Richard Throckett Straker. All papers will be in my name."

"Very good," Larry said. The man meant business, that much seemed clear enough. "The asking price on the Marsten House is fourteen thousand, although I think my clients could be persuaded to take a little less. On the old washateria—"

"That is no accord. I have been authorized to pay one dollar."

"One—?" Larry tilted his head forward the way a man will when he has failed to hear something correctly.

"Yes. Attend, please."

Straker's long fingers undid the clasps on his briefcase, opened it, and took out a number of papers bound in a blue transparent folder.

Larry Crockett looked at him, frowning.

"Read, please. That will save time."

Larry thumbed back the folder's plastic cover and glanced down at the first sheet with the air of a man humoring a fool. His eyes moved from left to right randomly for a moment, then riveted on something.

Straker smiled thinly. He reached inside his suit coat, produced a flat gold cigarette case, and selected a cigarette. He tamped it and then lit it with a wooden match. The harsh aroma of a Turkish blend filled the office and was eddied around by the fan.

There had been silence in the office for the next ten minutes, broken only by the hum of the fan and the muted passage of traffic on the street outside. Straker smoked his cigarette down to a shred, crushed the glowing ash between his fingers, and lit another.

Larry looked up, his face pale and shaken. "This is a joke. Who put you up to it? John Kelly?"

"I know no John Kelly. I don't joke."

"These papers . . . quit-claim deed . . . land title search . . . my God, man, don't you know that piece of land is worth one and a half million dollars?"

"You pike," Straker said coldly. "It is worth four million. Soon to be worth more, when the shopping center is built."

"What do you want?" Larry asked. His voice was hoarse.

"I have told you what I want. My partner and I plan to open a business in this town. We plan to live in the Marsten House."

"What sort of business? Murder Incorporated?"

Straker smiled coldly. "A perfectly ordinary furniture business, I am afraid. With a line of rather special antiques for collectors. My partner is something of an expert in that field."

"Shit," Larry said crudely. "The Marsten House you could have for eight and a half grand, the shop for sixteen. Your partner must know that. And you both must know that this town can't support a fancy furniture and antique place."

"My partner is extremely knowledgeable on any subject in which he becomes interested," Straker said. "He knows that your town is on a highway which serves tourists and summer residents. These are the people with whom we expect to do the bulk of our business. However, that is no accord to you. Do you find the papers in order?"

Larry tapped his desk with the blue folder. "They seem to be. But I'm not going to be horse-traded, no matter what you *say* you want."

"No, of course not." Straker's voice was edged with well-bred contempt. "You have a lawyer in Boston, I believe. One Francis Walsh."

"How do you know that?" Larry barked.

"It doesn't matter. Take the papers to him. He will confirm their validity. The land where this shopping center is to be built will be yours, on fulfillment of three conditions."

"Ah," Larry said, and looked relieved. "Conditions." He leaned back and selected a William Penn from the ceramic cigar box on his desk. He scratched a match on shoe leather and puffed. "Now we're getting down to the bone. Fire away."

"Number one. You will sell me the Marsten House and the business establishment for one dollar. Your client in the matter of the house is a land corporation in Bangor. The business establishment now belongs to a Portland bank. I am sure both parties will be agreeable if you make up the difference to the lowest acceptable prices. Minus your commission, of course."

"Where do you get your information?"

"That is not for you to know, Mr. Crockett. Condition two. You will say nothing of our transaction here today. Nothing. If the question ever comes up, all you know is what I have told you—we are two partners beginning a business aimed at tourists and summer people. This is very important."

"I don't blab."

"Nonetheless, I want to impress on you the seriousness of the condition. A time may come, Mr. Crockett, when you will want to tell someone of the wonderful deal you made on this day. If you do so, I will find out. I will ruin you. Do you understand?"

"You sound like one of those cheap spy movies," Larry said. He sounded unruffled, but underneath he felt a nasty tremor of fear. The words *I will ruin you* had come out as flatly as *How are you today.* It gave the statement an unpleasant ring of truth. And how in hell did this joker know about Frank Walsh? Not even his wife knew about Frank Walsh.

"Do you understand me, Mr. Crockett?"

"Yes," Larry said. "I'm used to playing them close to the vest."

Straker offered his thin smile again. "Of course. That is why I am doing business with you."

"The third condition?"

"The house will need certain renovations."

"That's one way of puttin' it," Larry said dryly.

"My partner plans to carry this task out himself. But you will be his agent. From time to time there will be requests. From time to time I will require the services of whatever laborers you employ to bring certain things either to the house or to the shop. You will not speak of such services. Do you understand?"

"Yeah, I understand. But you don't come from these parts, do you?"

"Does that have bearing?" Straker raised his eyebrows.

"Sure it does. This isn't Boston or New York. It's not going to be just a matter of me keepin' my lip buttoned. People are going to talk. Why, there's an old biddy over on Railroad Street, name of Mabel Werts, who spends all day with a pair of binoculars—"

"I don't care about the townspeople. My partner doesn't care about the townspeople. The townspeople always talk. They are no different from the magpies on the telephone wires. Soon they will accept us."

Larry shrugged. "It's your party."

"As you say," Straker agreed. "You will pay for all services and keep all invoices and bills. You will be reimbursed. Do you agree?"

Larry was, as he has told Straker, used to playing them close to the vest, and he had a reputation as one of the best poker players in Cumberland County. And although he had maintained his outward calm through all of this, he was on fire inside. The deal this crazyman was offering him was the kind of thing that came along once, if ever. Perhaps the guy's boss was one of those nutty billionaire recluses who—

"Mr. Crockett? I am waiting."

"There are two conditions of my own," Larry said.

"Ah?" Straker looked politely interested.

He rattled the blue folder. "First, these papers have to check out."

"Of course."

"Second, if you're doing anything illegal up there, I don't want to know about it. By that I mean—"

But he was interrupted. Straker threw his head back and gave vent to a singularly cold and emotionless laugh.

"Did I say somethin' funny?" Larry asked, without a trace of a smile.

"Oh ... ah ... of course not, Mr. Crockett. You must pardon my outburst. I found your comment amusing for reasons of my own. What were you about to add?"

"These renovations. I'm not going to get you anything that would leave my ass out to the wind. If you're fixing up to make moonshine or LSD or explosives for some hippie radical outfit, that's your own lookout."

"Agreed," Straker said. The smile was gone from his face. "Have we a deal?"

And with an odd feeling of reluctance, Larry had said, "If these papers check out, I guess we do at that. Although it seems like you did all the dealin' and I did all the money-makin'."

"This is Monday," Straker said. "Shall I stop by Thursday afternoon?"

"Better make it Friday."

"So. It is very well." He stood. "Good day, Mr. Crockett."

The papers had checked out. Larry's Boston lawyer said the land where the Portland shopping center was to be built had been purchased by an outfit called Continental Land and Realty, which was a dummy company with office space in the Chemical Bank Building in New York. There was nothing in Continental's offices but a few empty filing cabinets and a lot of dust.

Straker had come back that Friday and Larry signed the necessary title papers. He did so with a strong taste of doubt in the back of his mouth. He had overthrown his own personal maxim for the first time: You don't shit where you eat. And although the inducement had been high, he realized as Straker put the ownership papers to the Marsten House and erstwhile Village Washtub into his briefcase that he had put himself at this man's beck and call. And the same went for his partner, the absent Mr. Barlow.

As last August had passed, and as summer had slipped into fall and then fall into winter, he had begun to feel an indefinable sense of relief. By this spring he had almost managed to forget the deal he had made to get the papers which now resided in his Portland safe-deposit box.

Then things began to happen.

That writer, Mears, had come in a week and a half ago, asking if the Marsten House was available for rental, and he had given Larry a peculiar look when he told him it was sold.

Yesterday there had been a long tube in his post office box and a letter from Straker. A note, really. It had been brief: "Kindly have the poster which you will be receiving mounted in the window of the shop—R. T. Straker." The poster itself was common enough, and more subdued than some. It only said: "Opening in one week. Barlow and Straker. Fine furnishings. Selected antiques. Browsers welcome." He had gotten Royal Snow to put it right up.

And now there was a car up there at the Marsten House. He was still looking at it when someone said at his elbow: "Fallin' asleep, Larry?"

He jumped and looked around at Parkins Gillespie, who was standing on the corner next to him and lighting a Pall Mall.

"No," he said, and laughed nervously. "Just thinking."

Parkins glanced up at the Marsten House, where the sun twinkled on chrome and metal in the driveway, then down at the old laundry with its new sign in the window. "And you're not the only one, I guess. Always good to get new folks in town. You've met 'em, ain't you?"

"One of them. Last year."

"Mr. Barlow or Mr. Straker?"

"Straker."

"Seem like a nice enough sort, did he?"

"Hard to tell," Larry said, and found he wanted to lick his lips. He didn't. "We only talked business. He seemed okay."

"Good. That's good. Come on. I'll walk up to the Excellent with you."

When they crossed the street, Lawrence Crockett was thinking about deals with the devil.

12

1:00 P.M.

Susan Norton stepped into Babs' Beauty Boutique, smiled at Babs Griffen (Hal and Jack's eldest sister), and said, "Thank goodness you could take me on such short notice."

"No problem in the middle of the week," Babs said, turning on the fan. "My, ain't it close? It'll thunderstorm this afternoon."

Susan looked at the sky, which was an unblemished blue. "Do you think so?"

"Yeah. How do you want it, hon?"

"Natural," Susan said, thinking of Ben Mears. "Like I hadn't even been near this place."

"Hon," Babs said, closing in on her with a sigh, "that's what they all say."

The sigh wafted the odor of Juicy Fruit gum, and Babs asked Susan if she had seen that some folks were opening up a new furniture store in the old Village Washtub. Expensive stuff by the look of it, but wouldn't it be nice if they had a nice little hurricane lamp to match the one she had in her apartment and getting away from home and living in town was the smartest move she'd ever made and hadn't it been a nice summer? It seemed a shame it ever had to end.

13

3:00 P.M.

Bonnie Sawyer was lying on the big double bed in her house on the Deep Cut Road. It was a regular house, no shanty trailer, and it had a foundation and a cellar. Her husband, Reg, made good money as a car mechanic at Jim Smith's Pontiac in Buxton.

She was naked except for a pair of filmy blue panties, and she looked impatiently over at the clock on the nightstand: 3:02—where was he?

Almost as if the thought had summoned him, the bedroom door opened the tiniest bit, and Corey Bryant peered through.

"Is it okay?" he whispered. Corey was only twenty-two, had been working for the phone company two years, and this affair with a married woman—especially a knockout like Bonnie Sawyer, who had been Miss Cumberland County of 1973—left him feeling weak and nervous and horny.

Bonnie smiled at him with her lovely capped teeth. "If it wasn't, honey," she said, "you'd have a hole in you big enough to watch TV through."

He came tiptoeing in, his utility lineman's belt jingling ridiculously around his waist.

Bonnie giggled and opened her arms. "I really like you, Corey. You're cute."

Corey's eyes happened on the dark shadow beneath the taut blue nylon, and began to feel more horny than nervous. He forgot about tiptoeing and came to her, and as they joined, a cicada began to buzz somewhere in the woods.

14

4:00 P.M.

Ben Mears pushed away from his desk, the afternoon's writing done. He had forgone his walk in the park so he could go to dinner at the Nortons' that night with a clear conscience, and had written for most of the day without a break.

He stood up and stretched, listening to the bones in his spine crackle. His torso was wet with sweat. He went to the cupboard at the head of the bed, pulled out a fresh towel, and went down to the bathroom to shower before everyone else got home from work and clogged the place.

He hung the towel over his shoulder, turned back to the door, and then went to the window, where something had caught his eye. Nothing in town; it was drowsing away the late afternoon under a sky that peculiar shade of deep blue that graces New England on fine late summer days.

He could look across the two-story buildings on Jointner Avenue, could see their flat, asphalted roofs, and across the park where the children now home from school lazed or biked or squabbled, and out to the northwest section of town where Brock Street disappeared behind the shoulder of that first wooded hill. His eyes traveled naturally up to the break in the woods where the Burns Road and the Brooks Road intersected in a T—and on up to where the Marsten House sat overlooking the town.

From here it was a perfect miniature, diminished to the size of a child's doll house. And he liked it that way. From here the Marsten House was a size that could be coped with. You could hold up your hand and blot it out with your palm.

There was a car in the driveway.

He stood with the towel over his shoulder, looking out at it, not moving, feeling a crawl of terror in his belly that he did not try to analyze. Two of the fallen shutters had been replaced, too, giving the house a secretive, blind look that it had not possessed before.

His lips moved silently, as if forming words no one—even himself—could understand.

15

5:00 P.M.

Matthew Burke left the high school carrying his briefcase in his left hand and crossed the empty parking lot to where his old Chevy Biscayne sat, still on last year's snow tires.

He was sixty-three, two years from mandatory retirement, and still carrying a full load of English classes and extracurricular activities. Fall's activity was the school play, and he had just finished readings for a three-act farce called *Charley's Problem*. He had gotten the usual glut of utter impossibles, perhaps a dozen usable warm bodies who would at least memorize their lines (and then deliver them in a deathly, trembling monotone), and three kids who showed flair. He would cast them on Friday and begin blocking next week. They would pull together between then and October 30, which was the play date. It was Matt's theory that a high school play should be like a bowl of Campbell's Alphabet Soup: tasteless but not actively offensive. The relatives would come and love it. The theater critic from the Cumberland *Ledger* would come and go into polysyllabic ecstasies, as he was paid to do over any local play. The female lead (Ruthie Crockett this year, probably) would fall in love with some other cast member and quite possibly lose her virginity after the cast party. And then he would pick up the threads of the Debate Club.

At sixty-three, Matt Burke still enjoyed teaching. He was a lousy disciplinarian, thus forfeiting any chance he might once have had to step up to administration (he was a little too dreamy-eyed to ever serve effectively as an assistant principal), but his lack of discipline had never held him back. He had read the sonnets of Shakespeare in cold, pipe-clanking classrooms full of flying airplanes and spitballs, had sat down upon tacks and thrown them away absently as he told the class to turn to page 467 in their grammars, had opened drawers to get composition paper only to discover crickets, frogs, and once a seven-foot black snake.

He had ranged across the length and breadth of the English language like a solitary and oddly complacent Ancient Mariner: Steinbeck period one, Chaucer period two, the topic sentence period three, and the function of the gerund just before lunch. His fingers were permanently yellowed with chalk dust rather than nicotine, but it was still the residue of an addicting substance.

Children did not revere or love him; he was not a Mr. Chips languishing away in a rustic corner of America and waiting for Ross Hunter to discover him, but many of his students did come to respect him, and a few learned from him that dedication, however eccentric or humble, can be a noteworthy thing. He liked his work.

Now he got into his car, pumped the accelerator too much and flooded it, waited, and started it again. He tuned the radio to a Portland rock 'n' roll station and jacked the volume almost to the speaker's distortion point. He thought rock 'n' roll was fine music. He backed out of his parking slot, stalled, and started the car up again.

He had a small house out on the Taggart Stream Road, and had very few callers. He had never been married, had no family except for a brother in Texas who worked for an oil company and never wrote. He did not really miss the attachments. He was a solitary man, but solitude had in no way twisted him.

He paused at the blinking light at the intersection of Jointner Avenue and Brock Street, then turned toward home. The shadows were long now, and the daylight had taken on a curiously beautiful warmth—flat and golden, like something from a French Impressionist painting. He glanced over to his left, saw the Marsten House, and glanced again.

"The shutters," he said aloud, against the driving beat from the radio. "Those shutters are back up."

He glanced in the rear-view mirror and saw that there was a car parked in the driveway. He had been teaching in 'salem's Lot since 1952, and he had never seen a car parked in that driveway.

"Is someone living up there?" he asked no one in particular, and drove on.

16

6:00 P.M.

Susan's father, Bill Norton, the Lot's first selectman, was surprised to find that he liked Ben Mears—liked him quite a lot. Bill was a big, tough man with black hair, built like a truck, and not fat even after fifty. He had left high school for the Navy in the eleventh grade with his father's permission, and he had clawed his way up from there, picking up his diploma at the age of twenty-four on a high school equivalency test taken almost as an afterthought. He was not a blind, bullish anti-intellectual as some plain workingmen become when they are denied the level of learning that they may have been capable of, either through fate or their own doing, but he had no patience with "art farts," as he termed some of the doe-eyed, long-haired boys Susan had brought home from school. He didn't mind their hair or their dress. What bothered him was that none of them seemed serious-minded. He didn't share his wife's liking for Floyd Tibbits, the boy that Susie had been going around with the most since she graduated, but he didn't actively dislike him, either. Floyd had a pretty good job at the executive level in the Falmouth Grant's, and Bill Norton considered him to be moderately serious-minded. And he was a hometown boy. But so was this Mears, in a manner of speaking.

"Now, you leave him alone about that art fart business," Susan said, rising at the sound of the doorbell. She was wearing a light green summer dress, her new casual hairdo pulled back and tied loosely with a hank of oversized green yarn.

Bill laughed. "I got to call 'em as I see 'em, Susie darlin'. I won't embarrass you . . . never do, do I?"

She gave him a pensive, nervous smile and went to open the door.

The man who came back in with her was lanky and agile-looking, with finely drawn features and a thick, almost greasy shock of black hair that looked freshly washed despite its natural oiliness. He was dressed in a way that impressed Bill favorably: plain blue jeans, very new, and a white shirt rolled to the elbows.

"Ben, this is my dad and mom—Bill and Ann Norton. Mom, Dad, Ben Mears."

"Hello. Nice to meet you."

He smiled at Mrs. Norton with a touch of reserve and she said, "Hello, Mr. Mears. This is the first time we've seen a real live author up close. Susan has been *awfully* excited."

"Don't worry; I don't quote from my own works." He smiled again.

"H'lo," Bill said, and heaved himself up out of his chair. He had worked himself up to the union position he now held on the Portland docks, and his grip was hard and strong. But Mears's hand did not crimp and jellyfish like that of your ordinary, garden-variety art fart, and Bill was pleased. He imposed his second testing criterion.

"Like a beer? Got some on ice out yonder." He gestured toward the back patio, which he had built himself. Art farts invariably said no; most of them were potheads and couldn't waste their valuable consciousness juicing.

"Man, I'd love a beer," Ben said, and the smile became a grin. "Two or three, even."

Bill's laughter boomed out. "Okay, you're my man. Come on."

At the sound of his laughter, an odd communication seemed to pass between the two women, who bore strong resemblance to each other. Ann Norton's brow contracted while Susan's smoothed out—a load of worry seemed to have been transferred across the room by telepathy.

Ben followed Bill out onto the veranda. An ice chest sat on a stool in the corner, stuffed with ring-tab cans of Pabst. Bill pulled a can out of the cooler and tossed it to Ben, who caught it one-hand but lightly, so it wouldn't fizz.

"Nice out here," Ben said, looking toward the barbecue in the back yard. It was a low, businesslike construction of bricks, and a shimmer of heat hung over it.

"Built it myself," Bill said. "Better be nice."

Ben drank deeply and then belched, another sign in his favor.

"Susie thinks you're quite the fella," Norton said.

"She's a nice girl."

"Good practical girl," Norton added, and belched reflectively. "She says you've written three books. Published 'em, too."

"Yes, that's so."

"They do well?"

"The first did," Ben said, and said no more. Bill Norton nodded slightly, in approval of a man who had enough marbles to keep his dollars-and-cents business to himself.

"You like to lend a hand with some burgers and hot dogs?"

"Sure."

"You got to cut the hot dogs to let the squidges out of 'em. You know about that?"

"Yeah." He made diagonal slashes in the air with his right index finger, grinning slightly as he did so. The small slashes in natural-casing franks kept them from blistering.

"You came from this neck of the woods, all right," Bill Norton said. "Goddamn well told. Take that bag of briquettes over there and I'll get the meat. Bring your beer."

"You couldn't part me from it."

Bill hesitated on the verge of going in and cocked an eyebrow at Ben Mears. "You a serious-minded fella?" he asked.

Ben smiled, a trifle grimly. "That I am," he said.

Bill nodded. "That's good," he said, and went inside.

Babs Griffen's prediction of rain was a million miles wrong, and the back yard dinner went well. A light breeze sprang up, combining with the eddies of hickory smoke from the barbecue to keep the worst of the late-season mosquitoes away. The women cleared away the paper plates and condiments, then came back to drink a beer each and laugh as Bill, an old hand at playing the tricky wind currents, trimmed Ben 21–6 at badminton. Ben declined a rematch with real regret, pointing at his watch.

"I got a book on the fire," he said. "I owe another six pages. If I get drunk, I won't even be able to read what I wrote tomorrow morning."

Susan saw him to the front gate—he had walked up from town. Bill nodded to himself as he damped the fire. He had said he was serious-minded, and Bill was ready to take him at his word. He had not come with a big case on to impress anyone, but any man who worked after dinner was out to make his mark on somebody's tree, probably in big letters.

Ann Norton, however, never quite unthawed.

17

7:00 P.M.

Floyd Tibbits pulled into the crushed-stone parking lot at Dell's about ten minutes after Delbert Markey, owner and bartender, had turned on his new pink sign out front. The sign said DELL'S in letters three feet high, and the apostrophe was a highball glass.

Outside, the sunlight had been leached from the sky by gathering purple twilight, and soon ground mist would begin to form in the low-lying pockets of land. The night's regulars would begin to show up in another hour or so.

"Hi, Floyd," Dell said, pulling a Michelob out of the cooler. "Good day?"

"Fair," Floyd said. "That beer looks good."

He was a tall man with a well-trimmed sandy beard, now dressed in double-knit slacks and a casual sports jacket—his Grant's working uniform. He was second in charge of credit, and liked his work in the absent kind of way that can cross the line into boredom almost overnight. He felt himself to be drifting, but the sensation was not actively unpleasant. And there was Suze—a fine girl. She was going to come around before much longer, and then he supposed he would have to make something of himself.

He dropped a dollar bill on the bar, poured beer down the side of his glass, downed it thirstily, and refilled. The bar's only other patron at present was a young fellow in phone-company coveralls—the Bryant kid, Floyd thought. He was drinking beer at a table and listening to a moody love song on the juke.

"So what's new in town?" Floyd asked, knowing the answer already. Nothing new, not really. Someone might have showed up drunk at the high school, but he couldn't think of anything else.

"Well, somebody killed your uncle's dog. That's new."

Floyd paused with his glass halfway to his mouth. "What? Uncle Win's dog Doc?"

"That's right."

"Hit him with a car?"

"Not so you'd notice. Mike Ryerson found him. He was out to Harmony Hill to mow the grass and Doc was hangin' off those spikes atop the cemetery gate. Ripped wide open."

"Son of a bitch!" Floyd said, astounded.

Dell nodded gravely, pleased with the impression he had made. He knew something else that was a fairly hot item in town this evening—that Floyd's girl had been seen with that writer who was staying at Eva's. But let Floyd find that out for himself.

"Ryerson brung the co'pse in to Parkins Gillespie," he told Floyd. "*He* was of the mind that maybe the dog was dead and a bunch of kids hung it up for a joke."

"Gillespie doesn't know his ass from a hole in the ground."

"Maybe not. I'll tell you what *I* think." Dell leaned forward on his thick forearms. "I think it's kids, all right . . . hell, I *know* that. But it might be a smidge more serious than just a joke. Here, looka this." He reached under the bar and slapped a newspaper down on it, turned to an inside page.

Floyd picked it up. The headline read SATAN WORSHIPERS DESECRATE FLA. CHURCH. He skimmed through it. Apparently a bunch of kids had broken into a Catholic Church in Clewiston, Florida, some time after midnight and had held some sort of unholy rites there. The altar had been desecrated, obscene words had been scrawled on the pews, the confessionals, and the holy font, and splatters of blood had been found on steps leading to the nave. Laboratory analysis had confirmed that although some of the blood was animal (goat's blood was suggested), most of it was human. The Clewiston police chief admitted there were no immediate leads.

Floyd put the paper down. "Devil worshipers in the Lot? Come on, Dell. You've been into the cook's pot."

"The kids are going crazy," Dell said stubbornly. "You see if that ain't it. Next thing you know, they'll be doing human sacrifices in Griffen's pasture. Want a refill on that?"

"No thanks," Floyd said, sliding off his stool. "I think I'll go out and see how Uncle Win's getting along. He loved that dog."

"Give him my best," Dell said, stowing his paper back under the bar—Exhibit A for later in the evening. "Awful sorry to hear about it."

Floyd paused halfway to the door and spoke, seemingly to the air. "Hung him up on the spikes, did they? By Christ, I'd like to get hold of the kids who did that."

"Devil worshipers," Dell said. "Wouldn't surprise me a bit. I don't know what's got into people these days."

Floyd left. The Bryant kid put another dime in the juke, and Dick Curless began to sing "Bury the Bottle with Me."

18

7:30 P.M.

"You be home early," Marjorie Glick said to her eldest son, Danny. "School tomorrow. I want your brother in bed by quarter past nine."

Danny shuffled his feet. "I don't see why I have to take him at all."

"You don't," Marjorie said with dangerous pleasantness. "You can always stay home."

She turned back to the counter, where she was freshening fish, and Ralphie stuck out his tongue. Danny made a fist and shook it, but his putrid little brother only smiled.

"We'll be back," he muttered and turned to leave the kitchen, Ralphie in tow.

"By nine."

"Okay, *okay.*"

In the living room Tony Glick was sitting in front of the TV with his feet up, watching the Red Sox and the Yankees. "Where are you going, boys?"

"Over to see that new kid," Danny said. "Mark Petrie."

"Yeah," Ralphie said. "We're gonna look at his . . . *electric trains.*"

Danny cast a baleful eye on his brother, but their father noticed neither the pause nor the emphasis. Doug Griffen had just struck out. "Be home early," he said absently.

Outside, afterlight still lingered in the sky, although sunset had passed. As they crossed the back yard Danny said, "I ought to beat the stuff out of you, punko."

"I'll tell," Ralphie said smugly. "I'll tell why you *really* wanted to go."

"You creep," Danny said hopelessly.

At the back of the mowed yard, a beaten path led down the slope to the woods. The Glick house was on Brock Street, Mark Petrie's on South Jointner Avenue. The path was a short cut that saved considerable time if you were twelve and nine years old and willing to pick your way across the Crockett Brook stepping stones. Pine needles and twigs crackled under their feet. Somewhere in the woods, a whippoorwill sang, and crickets chirred all around them.

Danny had made the mistake of telling his brother that Mark Petrie had the entire set of Aurora plastic monsters—wolfman, mummy, Dracula, Frankenstein, the mad doctor, and even the Chamber of Horrors. Their mother thought all that stuff was bad news, rotted your brains or something, and Danny's brother had immediately turned blackmailer. He was putrid, all right.

"You're putrid, you know that?" Danny said.

"I know," Ralphie said proudly. "What's putrid?"

"It's when you get green and squishy, like boogers."

"Get bent," Ralphie said. They were going down the bank of Crockett Brook, which gurgled leisurely over its gravel bed, holding a faint pearliness on its surface. Two miles east it joined Taggart Stream, which in turn joined the Royal River.

Danny started across the stepping stones, squinting in the gathering gloom to see his footing.

"I'm gonna pushya!" Ralphie cried gleefully behind him. "Look out, Danny, I'm gonna pushya!"

"You push me and I'll push you in the quicksand, ringmeat," Danny said.

They reached the other bank. "There ain't no quicksand around here," Ralphie scoffed, moving closer to his brother nevertheless.

"Yeah?" Danny said ominously. "A kid got killed in the quicksand just a few years ago. I heard those old dudes that hang around the store talkin' about it."

"Really?" Ralphie asked. His eyes were wide.

"Yeah," Danny said. "He went down screamin' and hollerin' and his mouth filled up with quicksand and that was it. *Raaaacccccchhhh.*"

"C'mon," Ralphie said uneasily. It was close to full dark now, and the woods were full of moving shadows. "Let's get out of here."

They started up the other bank, slipping a little in the pine needles. The boy Danny had heard discussed in the store was a ten-year-old named Jerry Kingfield. He might have gone down in the quicksand screaming and hollering, but if he had, no one had heard him. He had simply disappeared in the Marshes six years ago while fishing. Some people thought quicksand, others held that a sex preevert had killed him. There were preeverts everywhere.

"They say his ghost still haunts these woods," Danny said solemnly, neglecting to tell his little brother that the Marshes were three miles south.

"Don't, Danny," Ralphie said uneasily. "Not . . . not in the dark."

The woods creaked secretively around them. The whip-poorwill had ceased his cry. A branch snapped somewhere behind them, almost stealthily. The daylight was nearly gone from the sky.

"Every now and then," Danny went on eerily, "when some ringmeat little kid comes out after dark, it comes flapping out of the trees, the face all putrid and covered with quicksand—"

"Danny, *come on.*"

His little brother's voice held real pleading, and Danny stopped. He had almost scared himself. The trees were dark, bulking presences all around them, moving slowly in the night breeze, rubbing together, creaking in their joints.

Another branch snapped off to their left.

Danny suddenly wished they had gone by the road.

Another branch snapped.

"Danny, I'm scared," Ralphie whispered.

"Don't be stupid," Danny said. "Come on."

They started to walk again. Their feet crackled in the pine needles. Danny told himself that he didn't hear any branches snapping. He didn't hear anything except them. Blood thudded in his temples. His hands were cold. Count steps, he told himself. We'll be at Jointner Avenue in two hundred steps. And when we come back we'll go by the road, so ringmeat won't be scared. In just a minute we'll see the streetlights and feel stupid but it will be *good* to feel stupid so count steps. One . . . two . . . three . . .

Ralphie shrieked.

"I see it! I see the ghost! I SEE IT!"

Terror like hot iron leaped into Danny's chest. Wires seemed to have run up his legs. He would have turned and run, but Ralphie was clutching him.

"Where?" he whispered, forgetting that he had invented the ghost. "Where?" He peered into the woods, half afraid of what he might see, and saw only blackness.

"It's gone now—but I saw him . . . it. Eyes. I saw eyes. Oh, Danneee—" He was blubbering.

"There ain't no ghosts, you fool. Come on."

Danny held his brother's hand and they began to walk. His legs felt as if they were made up of ten thousand pencil erasers. His knees were trembling. Ralphie was crowding against him, almost forcing him off the path.

"It's watchin' us," Ralphie whispered.

"Listen, I'm not gonna—"

"No, Danny. Really. Can't you *feel* it?"

Danny stopped. And in the way of children, he did feel something and knew they were no longer alone. A great hush had fallen over the woods; but it was a malefic hush. Shadows, urged by the wind, twisted languorously around them.

And Danny smelled something savage, but not with his nose.

There were no ghosts, but there *were* preeverts. They stopped in black cars and offered you candy or hung around on street corners or . . . or they followed you into the woods. . . .

And then . . .

Oh and then they . . .

"Run," he said harshly.

But Ralphie trembled beside him in a paralysis of fear. His grip on Danny's hand was as tight as baling wire. His eyes stared into the woods, and then began to widen.

"Danny?"

A branch snapped.

Danny turned and looked where his brother was looking.

The darkness enfolded them.

19

9:00 P.M.

Mabel Werts was a hugely fat woman, seventy-four on her last birthday, and her legs had become less and less reliable. She was a repository of town history and town gossip, and her memory stretched back over five decades of necrology, adultery, thievery, and insanity. She was a gossip but not a deliberately cruel one (although those whose stories she had sped on their back fence way might tend to disagree); she simply lived in and for the town. In a way she *was* the town, a fat widow who now went out very little, and who spent most of her time by her window dressed in a tentlike silk camisole, her yellowish-ivory hair done up in a coronet of thick, braided cables, with the telephone on her right hand and her high-powered Japanese binoculars on the left. The combination of the two—plus the time to use them fully—made her a benevolent spider sitting in the center of a communications web that stretched from the Bend to east 'salem.

She had been watching the Marsten House for want of something better to watch when the shutters to the left of the porch were opened, letting out a golden square of light that was definitely not the steady glow of electricity. She had gotten just a tantalizing glimpse of what might have been a man's head and shoulders silhouetted against the light. It gave her a queer thrill.

There had been no more movement from the house.

She thought: Now, what kind of people is it that only opens up when a body can't catch a decent glimpse of them?

She put the glasses down and carefully picked up the telephone. Two voices—she quickly identified them as Harriet Durham and Glynis Mayberry—were talking about the Ryerson boy finding Irwin Purinton's dog.

She sat quietly, breathing through her mouth, so as to give no sign of her presence on the line.

20

11:59 P.M.

The day trembled on the edge of extinction. The houses slept in darkness. Downtown, night lights in the hardware store and the Foreman Funeral Home and the Excellent Café threw mild electric light onto the pavement. Some lay awake—George Boyer, who had just gotten home from the three-to-eleven shift at the Gates Mill, Win Purinton, sitting and playing solitaire and unable to sleep for thinking of his Doc, whose passing had affected him much more deeply than that of his wife—but most slept the sleep of the just and the hard-working.

In Harmony Hill Cemetery a dark figure stood meditatively inside the gate, waiting for the turn of time. When he spoke, the voice was soft and cultured.

"O my father, favor me now. Lord of Flies, favor me now. Now I bring you spoiled meat and reeking flesh. I have made sacrifice for your favor. With my left hand I bring it. Make a sign for me on this ground, consecrated in your name. I wait for a sign to begin your work."

The voice died away. A wind had sprung up, gentle, bringing with it the sigh and whisper of leafy branches and grasses and a whiff of carrion from the dump up the road.

There was no sound but that brought on the breeze. The figure stood silent and thoughtful for a time. Then it stooped and stood with the figure of a child in his arms.

"I bring you this."

It became unspeakable.

Chapter Four
DANNY GLICK
AND OTHERS

1

Danny and Ralphie Glick had gone out to see Mark Petrie with orders to be in by nine, and when they hadn't come home by ten past, Marjorie Glick called the Petrie house. No, Mrs. Petrie said, the boys weren't there. Hadn't been there. Maybe your husband had better talk to Henry. Mrs. Glick handed the phone to her husband, feeling the lightness of fear in her belly.

The men talked it over. Yes, the boys had gone by the woods path. No, the little brook was very shallow at this time of year, especially after the fine weather. No more than ankle-deep. Henry suggested that he start from his end of the path with a high-powered flashlight and Mr. Glick start from his. Perhaps the boys had found a woodchuck burrow or were smoking cigarettes or something. Tony agreed and thanked Mr. Petrie for his trouble. Mr. Petrie said it was no trouble at all. Tony hung up and comforted his wife a little; she was frightened. He had mentally decided that neither of the boys was going to be able to sit down for a week when he found them.

But before he had even left the yard, Danny stumbled out from the trees and collapsed beside the back yard barbecue. He was dazed and slow-spoken, responding to questions ploddingly and not always sensibly. There was grass in his cuffs and a few autumn leaves in his hair.

He told his father that he and Ralphie had gone down the path through the woods, had crossed Crockett Brook by the stepping stones, and had gotten up the other bank with no trouble. Then Ralphie began to talk about a ghost in the woods (Danny neglected to mention he had put this idea in his brother's head). Ralphie said he could see a face. Danny began to be frightened. He didn't believe in ghosts or in any kid stuff like the bogeyman, but he did think he had heard something in the dark.

What did they do then?

Danny thought they had started to walk again, holding hands. He wasn't sure. Ralphie had been whimpering about the ghost. Danny told him not to cry, because soon they would be able to see the streetlights of Jointner Avenue. It was only two hundred steps, maybe less. Then something bad had happened.

What? What was the bad thing?

Danny didn't know.

They argued with him, grew excited, expostulated. Danny only shook his head slowly and uncomprehendingly. Yes, he knew he should remember, but he couldn't. Honestly, he couldn't. No, he didn't remember falling over anything. Just . . . everything was dark. Very dark. And the next thing he remembered was lying on the path by himself. Ralphie was gone.

Parkins Gillespie said there was no point in sending men into the woods that night. Too many deadfalls. Probably the boy had just wandered off the path. He and Nolly Gardener and Tony Glick and Henry Petrie went up and down the path and along the shoulders of both South Jointner and Brock streets, hailing with battery-powered bullhorns.

Early the next morning, both the Cumberland and the state police began a co-ordinated search of the wood lot. When they found nothing, the search was widened. They beat the bushes for four days, and Mr. and Mrs. Glick wandered through the woods and fields, picking their way around the deadfalls left by the ancient fire, calling their son's name with endless and wrenching hope.

When there was no result, Taggart Stream and the Royal River were dragged. No result.

On the morning of the fifth day, Marjorie Glick woke her husband at 4:00 A.M., terrified and hysterical. Danny had collapsed in the upstairs hallway, apparently on his way to the bathroom. An ambulance bore him away to Central Maine General Hospital. The preliminary diagnosis was severe and delayed emotional shock.

The doctor in charge, a man named Gorby, took Mr. Glick aside.

"Has your boy ever been subject to asthma attacks?"

Mr. Glick, blinking rapidly, shook his head. He had aged ten years in less than a week.

"Any history of rheumatic fever?"

"Danny? No . . . not Danny."

"Has he had a TB skin patch during the last year?"

"TB? My boy got TB?"

"Mr. Glick, we're only trying to find out—"

"Marge! Margie, come down here!"

Marjorie Glick got up and walked slowly down the corridor. Her face was pale, her hair absently combed. She looked like a woman in the grip of a deep migraine headache.

"Did Danny have a TB skin patch at school this year?"

"Yes," she said dully. "When he started school. No reaction."

Gorby asked, "Does he cough in the night?"

"No."

"Complain of aches in the chest or joints?"

"No."

"Painful urination?"

"No."

"Any abnormal bleeding? Bloody noses or bloody stool or even an abnormal number of scrapes and bruises?"

"No."

Gordy smiled and nodded. "We'd like to keep him for tests, if we may."

"Sure," Tony said. "Sure. I got Blue Cross."

"His reactions are very slow," the doctor said. "We're going to do some X rays, a marrow test, a white count—"

Marjorie Glick's eyes had slowly been widening. "Has Danny got leukemia?" she whispered.

"Mrs. Glick, that's hardly—"

But she had fainted.

2

Ben Mears was one of the 'salem's Lot volunteers who beat the bushes for Ralphie Glick, and he got nothing for his pains other than pants cuffs full of cockleburs and an aggravated case of hay fever brought on by late summer goldenrod.

On the third day of the search he came into the kitchen of Eva's ready to eat a can of ravioli and then fall into bed for a nap before writing. He found Susan Norton bustling around the kitchen stove and preparing some kind of hamburger casserole. The men just home from work were sitting around the table, pretending to talk, and ogling her—she was wearing a faded check shirt tied at the midriff and cut-off corduroy shorts. Eva Miller was ironing in a private alcove off the kitchen.

"Hey, what are you doing here?" he asked.

"Cooking you something decent before you fall away to a shadow," she said, and Eva snorted laughter from behind the angle of the wall. Ben felt his ears burn.

"Cooks real good, she does," Weasel said. "I can tell. I been watchin'."

"If you was watchin' any more, your eyes woulda fell outta their sockets," Grover Verrill said, and cackled.

Susan covered the casserole, put it in the oven, and they went out on the back porch to wait for it. The sun was going down red and inflamed.

"Any luck?"

"No. Nothing." He pulled a battered pack of cigarettes out of his breast pocket and lit one.

"You smell like you took a bath in Old Woodsman's," she said.

"Fat lot of good it did." He held out his arm and showed her a number of puffed insect bites and half-healed scratches. "Son of a bitching mosquitoes and goddamn pricker bushes."

"What do you think happened to him, Ben?"

"God knows." He exhaled smoke. "Maybe somebody crept up behind the older brother, coshed him with a sock full of sand or something, and abducted the kid."

"Do you think he's dead?"

Ben looked at her to see if she wanted an honest answer or merely a hopeful one. He took her hand and locked his fingers through hers. "Yes," he said briefly. "I think the kid is dead. No conclusive proof yet, but I think so."

She shook her head slowly. "I hope you're wrong. My mom and some of the other ladies have been in to sit with Mrs. Glick. She's out of her mind and so is her husband. And the other boy just wanders around like a ghost."

"Um," Ben said. He was looking up at the Marsten House, not really listening. The shutters were closed; they would open up later on. After dark. The shutters would open after dark. He felt a morbid chill at the thought and its nearly incantatory quality.

". . . night?"

"Hmm? Sorry." He looked around at her.

"I said, my dad would like you to come over tomorrow night. Can you?"

"Will you be there?"

"Sure, I will," she said, and looked at him.

"All right. Good." He wanted to look at her—she was lovely in the sunset light—but his eyes were drawn toward the Marsten House as if by a magnet.

"It draws you, doesn't it?" she said, and the reading of his thought, right down to the metaphor, was nearly uncanny.

"Yes. It does."

"Ben, what's this new book about?"

"Not yet," he said. "Give it time. I'll tell you as soon as I can. It's . . . got to work itself out."

She wanted to say *I love you* at that precise moment, say it with the ease and lack of self-consciousness with which the thought had risen to the surface of her mind, but she bit the words off behind her lips. She did not want to say it while he was looking . . . looking up there.

She got up. "I'll check the casserole."

When she left him, he was smoking and looking up at the Marsten House.

3

Lawrence Crockett was sitting in his office on the morning of the twenty-second, pretending to read his Monday correspondence and keeping an eye on his secretary's jahoobies, when the telephone rang. He had been thinking about his business career in 'salem's Lot, about that small, twinkling car in the Marsten House driveway, and about deals with the devil.

Even before the deal with Straker had been consummated (that's some word, all right, he thought, and his eyes crawled over the front of his secretary's blouse), Lawrence Crockett was, without doubt, the richest man in 'salem's Lot and one of the richest in Cumberland County, although there was nothing about his office or his person to indicate it. The office was old, dusty, and lighted by two fly-specked yellow globes. The desk was an ancient roll-top, littered with papers, pens, and correspondence. A gluepot stood on one side of it and on the other was a square glass paperweight that showed pictures of his family on its different faces. Poised perilously on top of a stack of ledgers was a glass fish bowl filled with matches, and a sign on the front said, "For Our Matchless Friends." Except for three fireproof steel filing cabinets and the secretary's desk in a small enclosure, the office was barren.

There were, however, pictures.

Snapshots and photos were everywhere—tacked, stapled, or taped to every available surface. Some were new Polaroid prints, others were colored Kodak shots taken a few years back, still more were curled and yellowing black-and-whites, some going back fifteen years. Beneath each was a typed caption: *Fine Country Living! Six Rms.* or *Hilltop Location! Taggart Stream Road, $32,000—Cheap!* or *Fit for a Squire! Ten-Rm. Farmhouse, Burns Road.* It looked like a dismal, fly-by-night operation and so it had been until 1957, when Larry Crockett, who was regarded by the better element in Jerusalem's Lot as only one step above shiftless, had decided that trailers were the wave of the future. In those dim dead days, most people thought of trailers as those cute silvery things you hooked on the back of your car when you wanted to go to Yellowstone National Park and take pictures of your wife and kids standing in front of Old Faithful. In those dim dead days, hardly anyone—even the trailer manufacturers themselves—foresaw a day when the cute silvery things would be replaced by campers, which hooked right over the bed of your Chevy pickup or which could come complete and motorized in themselves.

Larry, however, had not needed to know these things. A bush-league visionary at best, he had simply gone down to the town office (in those days he was not a selectman; in those days he couldn't have gotten elected dog catcher) and looked up the Jerusalem's Lot zoning laws. They were tremendously satisfactory. Peering between the lines, he could see thousands of dollars. The law said you could not maintain a public dumping ground, or have more than three junked cars in your yard unless you also had a junk yard permit, or have a chemical toilet—a fancy and not very accurate term for outhouse—unless it was approved by the Town Health Officer. And that was it.

Larry had mortgaged himself to the hilt, had borrowed more, and had bought three trailers. Not cute little silvery things but long, plush, thyroidal monsters with plastic wood paneling and Formica bathrooms. He bought one-acre plots for each in the Bend, where land was cheap, had set them on cheap foundations, and had gone to work selling them. He had done so in three months, overcoming some initial resistance from people who were dubious about living in a home that resembled a Pullman car, and his profit had been close to ten thousand dollars. The wave of the future had arrived in 'salem's Lot, and Larry Crockett had been right up there shooting the curl.

On the day R. T. Straker had walked into his office, Crockett had been worth nearly two million dollars. He had done this as a result of land speculation in a great many neighboring towns (but not in the Lot; you don't shit where you eat was Lawrence Crockett's motto), based on the conviction that the mobile-home industry was going to grow like a mad bastard. It did, and my God how the money rolled in.

In 1965 Larry Crockett became the silent partner of a contractor named Romeo Poulin, who was building a supermarket plaza in Auburn. Poulin was a veteran corner-cutter, and with his on-the-job know-how and Larry's way with figures, they made $750,000 apiece and only had to report a third of that to Uncle. It was all extremely satisfactory, and if the supermarket roof had a bad case of the leaks, well, that was life.

In 1966–68 Larry bought controlling interests in three Maine mobile-home businesses, going through any number of fancy ownership shuffles to throw the tax people off. To Romeo Poulin he described this process as going into the tunnel of love with girl A, screwing girl B in the car behind you, and ending up holding hands with girl A on the other side. He ended up buying mobile homes from himself, and these incestuous businesses were so healthy they were almost frightening.

Deals with the devil, all right, Larry thought, shuffling his papers. When you deal with him, notes come due in brimstone.

The people who bought trailers were lower-middle-class blue- or white-collar workers, people who could not raise a down payment on a more conventional house, or older people looking for ways to stretch their social security. The idea of a brand-new six-room house was something to conjure with for these people. For the elderly, there was another advantage, something that others missed but Larry, always astute, had noticed: Trailers were all on one level and there were no stairs to climb.

Financing was easy, too. A $500 down payment was usually enough to do business on. And in the bad old barracuda-financing days of the sixties, the fact that the other $9,500 was financed at 24 percent rarely struck these house-hungry people as a pitfall.

And my God! how the money rolled in.

Crockett himself had changed very little, even after playing "Let's Make a Deal" with the unsettling Mr. Straker. No fag decorator came to redo his office. He still got by with the cheap electric fan instead of air conditioning. He wore the same shiny-seat suits or glaring sports jacket combinations. He smoked the same cheap cigars and still dropped by Dell's on Saturday night to have a few beers and shoot some bumper pool with the boys. He had kept his hand in home town real estate, which had borne two fruits: First, it had gotten him elected selectman, and second, it wrote off nicely on his income tax return, because each year's visible operation was one rung below the break-even point. Besides the Marsten House, he was and had been the selling agent for perhaps three dozen other decrepit manses in the area. There were some good deals of course. But Larry didn't push them. The money was, after all, rolling in.

Too much money, maybe. It was possible, he supposed, to outsmart yourself. To go into the tunnel of love with girl A, screw girl B, come out holding hands with girl A, only to have both of them beat the living shit out of you. Straker had said he would be in touch and that had been fourteen months ago. Now what if—

That was when the telephone rang.

4

"Mr. Crockett," the familiar, accentless voice said.

"Straker, isn't it?"

"Indeed."

"I was just thinkin' about you. Maybe I'm psychic."

"How very amusing, Mr. Crockett. I need a service, please."

"I thought you might."

"You will procure a truck, please. A big one. A rental truck, perhaps. Have it at the Portland docks tonight at seven sharp. Custom House Wharf. Two movers will be sufficient, I think."

"Okay." Larry drew a pad over by his right hand and scrawled: *H. Peters, R. Snow. Henry's U-Haul. 6 at latest.* He did not stop to consider how imperative it seemed to follow Straker's orders to the letter.

"There are a dozen boxes to be picked up. All save one go to the shop. The other is an extremely valuable sideboard—a Hepplewhite. Your movers will know it by its size. It is to be taken to the house. You understand?"

"Yeah."

"Have them put it down cellar. Your men can enter through the outside bulkhead below the kitchen windows. You understand?"

"Yeah. Now, this sideboard—"

"One other service, please. You will procure five stout Yale padlocks. You are familiar with the brand Yale?"

"Everybody is. What—"

"Your movers will lock the shop's back door when they leave. At the house, they will leave the keys to all five locks on the basement table. When they leave the house, they will padlock the bulkhead door, the front and back doors, and the shed-garage. You understand?"

"Yeah."

"Thank you, Mr. Crockett. Follow all directions explicitly. Good-by."

"Now, wait just a minute—"

Dead line.

5

It was two minutes of seven when the big orange-and-white truck with "Henry's U-Haul" printed on the sides and back pulled up to the corrugated-steel shack at the end of Custom House Wharf at the Portland docks. The tide was on the turn and the gulls were restless with it, wheeling and crying overhead against the sunset-crimson sky.

"Christ, there's nobody here," Royal Snow said, swigging the last of his Pepsi and dropping the empty to the floor of the cab. "We'll get arrested for burglars."

"There's somebody," Hank Peters said. "Cop."

It wasn't precisely a cop; it was a night watchman. He shone his light in at them. "Either of you guys Lawrence Crewcut?"

"Crockett," Royal said. "We're from him. Come to pick up some boxes."

"Good," the night watchman said. "Come on in the office. I got an invoice for you to sign." He gestured to Peters, who was behind the wheel. "Back up right over there. Those double doors with the light burning. See?"

"Yeah." He put the truck in reverse.

Royal Snow followed the night watchman into the office where a coffee maker was burbling. The clock over the pin-up calendar said 7:04. The night watchman scrabbled through some papers on the desk and came up with a clipboard. "Sign there."

Royal signed his name.

"You want to watch out when you go in there. Turn on the lights. There's rats."

"I've never seen a rat that wouldn't run from one of these," Royal said, and swung his work-booted foot in an arc.

"These are wharf rats, sonny," the watchman said dryly. "They've run off with bigger men than you."

Royal went back out and walked over to the warehouse door. The night watchman stood in the doorway of the shack, watching him. "Look out," Royal said to Peters. "The old guy said there was rats."

"Okay." He sniggered. "Good ole Larry Crewcut."

Royal found the light switch inside the door and turned them on. There was something about the atmosphere, heavy with the mixed aromas of salt and wood rot and wetness, that stifled hilarity. That, and the thought of rats.

The boxes were stacked in the middle of the wide warehouse floor. The place was otherwise empty, and the collection looked a little portentous as a result. The sideboard was in the center, taller than the others, and the only one not stamped "Barlow and Straker, 27 Jointner Avenue, Jer. Lot Maine."

"Well, this don't look too bad," Royal said. He consulted his copy of the invoice and then counted boxes. "Yeah, they're all here."

"There are rats," Hank said. "Hear 'em?"

"Yeah, miserable things. I hate 'em."

They both fell silent for a moment, listening to the squeak and patter coming from the shadows.

"Well, let's get with it," Royal said. "Let's put that big baby on first so it won't be in the way when we get to the store."

"Okay."

They walked over to the box, and Royal took out his pocket knife. With one quick gesture he had slit the brown invoice envelope taped to the side.

"Hey," Hank said. "Do you think we ought to—"

"We gotta make sure we got the right thing, don't we? If we screw up, Larry'll tack our asses to his bulletin board." He pulled the invoice out and looked at it.

"What's it say?" Hank asked.

"Heroin," Royal said judiciously. "Two hundred pounds of

the shit. Also two thousand girlie books from Sweden, three hundred gross of French ticklers—"

"Gimme that." Hank snatched it away. "Sideboard," he said. "Just like Larry told us. From London, England. Portland, Maine, P.O.E. French ticklers, my ass. Put this back."

Royal did. "Something funny about this," he said.

"Yeah, you. Funny like the Italian Army."

"No, no shit. There's no customs stamp on this fucker. Not on the box, not on the invoice envelope, not on the invoice. No stamp."

"They probably do 'em in that ink that only shows up under a special black light."

"They never did when I was on the docks. Christ, they stamped cargo ninety ways for Sunday. You couldn't grab a box without getting blue ink up to your elbows."

"Good. I'm very glad. But my wife happens to go to bed very early and I had hopes of getting some tonight."

"Maybe if we took a look inside—"

"No way. Come on. Grab it."

Royal shrugged. They tipped the box, and something shifted heavily inside. The box was a bitch to lift. It could be one of those fancy dressers, all right. It was heavy enough.

Grunting, they staggered out to the truck and heaved it onto the hydraulic lifter with identical cries of relief. Royal stood back while Hank operated the lift. When it was even with the truck body, they climbed up and walked it inside.

There was something about the box he didn't like. It was more than the lack of customs stamp. An indefinable something. He looked at it until Hank ran down the back gate.

"Come on," he said. "Let's get the rest of them."

The other boxes had regulation customs stamps, except for three that had been shipped here from inside the United States. As they loaded each box onto the truck, Royal checked it off on the invoice form and initialed it. They stacked all of the boxes bound for the new store near the back gate of the truck, away from the sideboard.

"Now, who in the name of God is going to buy all this stuff?" Royal asked when they had finished. "A Polish rocking chair, a German clock, a spinning wheel from Ireland . . . Christ Almighty, I bet they charge a frigging fortune."

"Tourists," Hank said wisely. "Tourists'll buy anything. Some of those people from Boston and New York . . . they'd buy a bag of cowshit if it was an *old* bag."

"I don't like that big box, neither," Royal said. "No customs stamp, that's a hell of a funny thing."

"Well, let's get it where it's going."

They drove back to 'salem's Lot without speaking, Hank driving heavy on the gas. This was one errand he wanted done. He didn't like it. As Royal had said, it was damn peculiar.

He drove around to the back of the new store, and the back door was unlocked, as Larry had said it would be. Royal tried the lightswitch just inside with no result.

"That's nice," he grumbled. "We get to unload this stuff in the goddamn dark . . . say, does it smell a little funny in here to you?"

Hank sniffed. Yes, there was an odor, an unpleasant one, but he could not have said exactly what it reminded him of. It was dry and acrid in the nostrils, like a whiff of old corruption.

"It's just been shut up too long," he said, shining his flashlight around the long, empty room. "Needs a good airing out."

"Or a good burning down," Royal said. He didn't like it. Something about the place put his back up. "Come on. And let's try not to break our legs."

They unloaded the boxes as quickly as they could, putting each one down carefully. A half an hour later, Royal closed the back door with a sigh of relief and snapped one of the new padlocks on it.

"That's half of it," he said.

"The easy half," Hank answered. He looked up toward the Marsten House, which was dark and shuttered tonight. "I don't like goin' up there, and I ain't afraid to say so. If there was ever a haunted house, that's it. Those guys must be crazy, tryin' to live there. Probably queer for each other anyway."

"Like those fag interior decorators," Royal agreed. "Probably trying to turn it into a showplace. Good for business."

"Well, if we got to do it, let's get with it."

They spared a last look for the crated sideboard leaning against the side of the U-Haul and then Hank pulled the back door down with a bang. He got in behind the wheel and they drove up Jointner Avenue onto the Brooks Road. A minute later the Marsten House loomed ahead of them, dark and crepitating, and Royal felt the first thread of real fear worm its way into his belly.

"Lordy, that's a creepy place," Hank murmured. "Who'd want to live there?"

"I don't know. You see any lights on behind those shutters?"

"No."

The house seemed to lean toward them, as if awaiting their arrival. Hank wheeled the truck up the driveway and around to the back. Neither of them looked too closely at what the bouncing headlights might reveal in the rank grass of the back yard. Hank felt a strain of fear enter his heart that he had not even felt in Nam, although he had been scared most of his time there. That was a rational fear. Fear that you might step on a pongee stick and see your foot swell up like some noxious green balloon, fear that some kid in black p.j.'s whose name you couldn't even fit in your mouth might blow your head off with a Russian rifle, fear that you might draw a Crazy Jake on patrol that might want you to blow up everyone in a village where the Cong had been a week before. But this fear was childlike, dreamy. There was no reference point to it. A house was a house—boards and hinges and nails and sills. There was no reason, really no reason, to feel that each splintered crack was exhaling its own chalky aroma of evil. That was just plain stupid thinking. Ghosts? He didn't believe in ghosts. Not after Nam.

He had to fumble twice for reverse, and then backed the truck jerkily up to the bulkhead leading to the cellar. The rusted doors stood open, and in the red glow of the truck's taillights, the shallow stone steps seemed to lead down into hell.

"Man, I don't dig this at *all*," Hank said. He tried to smile and it became a grimace.

"Me either."

They looked at each other in the wan dash lights, the fear heavy on both of them. But childhood was beyond them, and they were incapable of going back with the job undone because of irrational fear—how would they explain it in bright daylight? The job had to be done.

Hank killed the engine and they got out and walked around to the back of the truck. Royal climbed up, released the door catch, and thrust the door up on its tracks.

The box sat there, sawdust still clinging to it, squat and mute.

"God, I don't want to take that down there!" Hank Peters choked out, and his voice was almost a sob.

"Come on up," Royal said. "Let's get rid of it."

They dragged the box onto the lift and let it down with a hiss of escaping air. When it was at waist level, Hank let go of the lever and they gripped it.

"Easy," Royal grunted, backing toward the steps. "Easy does it . . . easy . . ." In the red glow of the taillights his face was constricted and corded like the face of a man having a heart attack.

He backed down the stairs one at a time, and as the box tilted up against his chest, he felt its dreadful weight settle against him like a slab of stone. It was heavy, he would think later, but not that heavy. He and Hank had muscled bigger loads for Larry Crockett, both upstairs and down, but there was something about the atmosphere of this place that took the heart out of you and made you no good.

The steps were slimy-slick and twice he tottered on the precarious edge of balance, crying out miserably, "Hey! For Christ's sake! Watch it!"

And then they were down. The ceiling was low above them and they carried the sideboard bent over like hags.

"Set it here!" Hank gasped. "I can't carry it no further!"

They set it down with a thump and stepped away. They looked into each other's eyes and saw that fear had been changed to near terror by some secret alchemy. The cellar seemed suddenly filled with secret rustling noises. Rats, perhaps, or perhaps something that didn't even bear thinking of.

They bolted, Hank first and Royal Snow right behind him. They ran up the cellar steps and Royal slammed the bulkhead doors with backward sweeps of his arm.

They clambered into the cab of the U-Haul and Hank started it up and put it in gear. Royal grabbed his arm, and in the darkness his face seemed to be all eyes, huge and staring.

"Hank, we never put on those locks."

They both stared at the bundle of new padlocks on the truck's dashboard, held together by a twist of baling wire. Hank grabbed at his jacket pocket and brought out a key ring with five new Yale keys on it, one which would fit the lock on the back door of the shop in town, four for out here. Each was neatly labeled.

"Oh, Christ," he said. "Look, if we come back early tomorrow morning—"

Royal unclamped the flashlight under the dashboard. "That won't work," he said, "and you know it."

They got out of the cab, feeling the cool evening breeze strike the sweat on their foreheads. "Go do the back door," Royal said. "I'll get the front door and the shed."

They separated. Hank went to the back door, his heart thudding heavily in his chest. He had to fumble twice to thread the locking arm through the hasp. This close to the house, the smell of age and wood rot was palpable. All those stories about Hubie Marsten that they had laughed about as kids began to recur, and the chant they had chased the girls with: *Watch out, watch out, watch out! Hubie'll get you if you don't . . . watch . . . OUT—*

"Hank?"

He drew in breath sharply, and the other lock dropped out of his hands. He picked it up. "You oughtta know better than to creep up on a person like that. Did you . . . ?"

"Yeah. Hank, who's gonna go down in that cellar again and put the key ring on the table?"

"I dunno," Hank Peters said. "I dunno."

"Think we better flip for it?"

"Yeah, I guess that's best."

Royal took out a quarter. "Call it in the air." He flicked it.

"Heads."

Royal caught it, slapped it on his forearm, and exposed it. The eagle gleamed at them dully.

"Jesus," Hank said miserably. But he took the key ring and the flashlight and opened the bulkhead doors again.

He forced his legs to carry him down the steps, and when he had cleared the roof overhang he shone his light across the visible cellar, which took an L-turn thirty feet further up and went off God knew where. The flashlight beam picked out the table, with a dusty checked tablecloth on it. A rat sat on the table, a huge one, and it did not move when the beam of light struck it. It sat up on its plump haunches and almost seemed to grin.

He walked past the box toward the table. "Hsst! Rat!"

The rat jumped down and trotted off toward the elbow-bend further up. Hank's hand was trembling now, and the flashlight beam slipped jerkily from place to place, now picking out a dusty barrel, now a decades-old bureau that had been loaded down here, now a stack of old newspapers, now—

He jerked the flashlight beam back toward the newspapers and sucked in breath as the light fell on something to the left side of them.

A shirt . . . was that a shirt? Bundled up like an old rag. Something behind it that might have been blue jeans. And something that looked like . . .

Something snapped behind him.

He panicked, threw the keys wildly on the table, and turned away, shambling into a run. As he passed the box, he saw what had made the noise. One of the aluminum bands had let go, and now pointed jaggedly toward the low roof, like a finger.

He stumbled up the stairs, slammed the bulkhead behind him (his whole body had crawled into goose flesh; he would not be aware of it until later), snapped the lock on the catch, and ran to the cab of the truck. He was breathing in small, whistling gasps like a hurt dog. He dimly heard Royal asking him what had happened, what was going on down there, and then he threw the truck into drive and screamed out, roaring around the corner of the house on two wheels, digging at the soft earth. He did not slow down until the truck was back on the Brooks Road, speeding toward Lawrence Crockett's office in town. And then he began to shake so badly he was afraid he would have to pull over.

"What was down there?" Royal asked. "What did you see?"

"Nothin'," Hank Peters said, and the word came out in sections divided by his clicking teeth. "I didn't see nothin' and I never want to see it again."

6

Larry Crockett was getting ready to shut up shop and go home when there was a perfunctory tap on the door and Hank Peters stepped back in. He still looked scared.

"Forget somethin', Hank?" Larry asked. When they had come back from the Marsten House, both looking like somebody had given their nuts a healthy tweak, he had given them each an extra ten dollars and two six-packs of Black Label and had allowed as how maybe it would be best if none of them said too much about the evening's outing.

"I got to tell you," Hank said now. "I can't help it, Larry. I got to."

"Sure you do," Larry said. He opened the bottom desk drawer, took out a bottle of Johnnie Walker, and poured them each a knock in a couple of Dixie cups. "What's on your mind?"

Hank took a mouthful, grimaced, and swallowed it.

"When I took those keys down to put 'em on the table, I seen something. Clothes, it looked like. A shirt and maybe some dungarees. And a sneaker. I think it was a sneaker, Larry."

Larry shrugged and smiled. "So?" It seemed to him that a large lump of ice was resting in his chest.

"That little Glick boy was wearin' jeans. That's what it said in the *Ledger*. Jeans and a red pull-over shirt and sneaks. Larry, what if—"

Larry kept smiling. The smile felt frozen on.

Hank gulped convulsively. "What if those guys that bought the Marsten House and that store blew up the Glick kid?" There. It was out. He swallowed the rest of the liquid fire in his cup.

Smiling, Larry said, "Maybe you saw a body, too."

"No—no. But—"

"That'd be a matter for the police," Larry Crockett said. He refilled Hank's cup and his hand didn't tremble at all. It was as cold and steady as a rock in a frozen brook. "And I'd drive you right down to see Parkins. But something like this . . ." He shook his head. "A lot of nastiness can come up. Things like you and that waitress out to Dell's . . . her name's Jackie, ain't it?"

"What the hell are you talking about?" His face had gone deadly pale.

"And they'd sure as shit find out about that dishonorable discharge of yours. But you do your duty, Hank. Do it as you see it."

"I didn't see no body," Hank whispered.

"That's good," Larry said, smiling. "And maybe you didn't see any clothes, either. Maybe they were just . . . rags."

"Rags," Hank Peters said hollowly.

"Sure, you know those old places. All kinds of junk in 'em. Maybe you saw some old shirt or something that was torn up for a cleaning rag."

"Sure," Hank said. He drained his glass a second time. "You got a good way of looking at things, Larry."

Crockett took his wallet out of his back pocket, opened it, and counted five ten-dollar bills out on the desk.

"What's that for?"

"Forgot all about paying you for that Brennan job last month. You should prod me about those things, Hank. You know how I forget things."

"But you did—"

"Why," Larry interrupted, smiling, "you could be sitting right here and telling me something, and I wouldn't remember a thing about it tomorrow morning. Ain't that a pitiful way to be?"

"Yeah," Hank whispered. His hand reached out trembling and took the bills; stuffed them into the breast pocket of his denim jacket as if anxious to be rid of the touch of them. He got up with such jerky hurriedness that he almost knocked his chair over. "Listen, I got to go, Larry. I . . . I didn't . . . I got to go."

"Take the bottle," Larry invited, but Hank was already going out the door. He didn't pause.

Larry sat back down. He poured himself another drink. His hand still did not tremble. He did not go on shutting up shop. He had another drink, and then another. He thought about deals with the devil. And at last his phone rang. He picked it up. Listened.

"It's taken care of," Larry Crockett said.

He listened. He hung up. He poured himself another drink.

7

Hank Peters woke up in the early hours of the next morning from a dream of huge rats crawling out of an open grave, a grave which held the green and rotting body of Hubie Marsten, with a frayed length of manila hemp around his neck. Peters lay propped on his elbows, breathing heavily, naked torso slicked with sweat, and when his wife touched his arm he screamed aloud.

8

Milt Crossen's Agricultural Store was located in the angle formed by the intersection of Jointner Avenue and Railroad Street, and most of the town's old codgers went there when it rained and the park was uninhabitable. During the long winters, they were a day-by-day fixture.

When Straker drove up in that '39 Packard—or was it a '40?—it was just misting gently, and Milt and Pat Middler were having a desultory conversation about whether Freddy Overlock's girl Judy run off in 1957 or '58. They both agreed that she had run off with that Saladmaster salesman from Yarmouth, and they both agreed that he hadn't been worth a pisshole in the snow, nor was she, but beyond that they couldn't get together.

All conversation ceased when Straker walked in.

He looked around at them—Milt and Pat Middler and Joe Crane and Vinnie Upshaw and Clyde Corliss—and smiled humorlessly. "Good afternoon, gentlemen," he said.

Milt Crossen stood up, pulling his apron around him almost primly. "Help you?"

"Very good," Straker said. "Attend over at this meat case, please."

He bought a roast of beef, a dozen prime ribs, some hamburger, and a pound of calves' liver. To this he added some dry goods—flour, sugar, beans—and several loaves of ready-made bread.

His shopping took place in utter silence. The store's habitués sat around the large Pearl Kineo stove that Milt's father had converted to range oil, smoked, looked wisely out at the sky, and observed the stranger from the corners of their eyes.

When Milt had finished packing the goods into a large cardboard carton, Straker paid with hard cash—a twenty and a ten. He picked up the carton, tucked it under one arm, and flashed that hard, humorless smile at them again.

"Good day, gentlemen," he said, and left.

Joe Crane tamped a load of Planter's into his corncob. Clyde Corliss hawked back and spat a mass of phlegm and chewing tobacco into the dented pail beside the stove. Vinnie Upshaw produced his old Top cigarette roller from inside his vest, spilled a line of tobacco into it, and inserted a cigarette paper with arthritis-swelled fingers.

They watched the stranger lift the carton into the trunk. All of them knew that the carton must have weighed thirty pounds with the dry goods, and they had all seen him tuck it under his arm like a feather pillow going out. He went around to the driver's side, got in, and drove off up Jointner Avenue. The car went up the hill, turned left onto the Brooks Road, disappeared, and reappeared from behind the screen of trees a few moments later, now toy-sized with distance. It turned into the Marsten driveway and was lost from sight.

"Peculiar fella," Vinnie said. He stuck his cigarette in his mouth, plucked a few bits of tobacco from the end of it, and took a kitchen match from his vest pocket.

"Must be one of the ones got that store," Joe Crane said.

"Marsten House, too," Vinnie agreed.

Clyde Corliss broke wind.

Pat Middler picked at a callus on his left palm with great interest.

Five minutes passed.

"Do you suppose they'll make a go of it?" Clyde asked no one in particular.

"Might," Vinnie said. "They might show up right pert in the summertime. Hard to tell the way things are these days."

A general murmur, sigh almost, of agreement.

"Strong fella," Joe said.

"Ayuh," Vinnie said. "That was a thirty-nine Packard, and not a spot of rust on her."

" 'Twas a forty," Clyde said.

"The forty didn't have runnin' boards," Vinnie said. " 'Twas a thirty-nine."

"You're wrong on that one," Clyde said.

Five minutes passed. They saw Milt was examining the twenty Straker had paid with.

"That funny money, Milt?" Pat asked. "That fella give you some funny money?"

"No; but look." Milt passed it across the counter and they all stared at it. It was much bigger than an ordinary bill.

Pat held it up to the light, examined it, then turned it over. "That's a series E twenty, ain't it, Milt?"

"Yep," Milt said. "They stopped makin' those forty-five or fifty years back. My guess is that'd be worth some money down to Arcade Coin in Portland."

Pat handed the bill around and each examined it, holding it up close or far off depending on the flaws in their eyesight. Joe Crane handed it back, and Milt put it under the cash drawer with the personal checks and the coupons.

"Sure is a funny fella," Clyde mused.

"Ayuh," Vinnie said, and paused. "That was a thirty-nine, though. My half brother Vic had one. Was the first car he ever owned. Bought it used, he did, in 1944. Left the oil out of her one mornin' and burned the goddamn pistons right out of her."

"I believe it was a forty," Clyde said, "because I remember a fella that used to cane chairs down by Alfred, come right to your house he would, and—"

And so the argument was begun, progressing more in the silences than in the speeches, like a chess game played by mail. And the day seemed to stand still and stretch into eternity for them, and Vinnie Upshaw began to make another cigarette with sweet, arthritic slowness.

9

Ben was writing when the tap came at the door, and he marked his place before getting up to open it. It was just after three o'clock on Wednesday, September 24. The rain had ended any plans to search further for Ralphie Glick, and the consensus was that the search was over. The Glick boy was gone . . . solid gone.

He opened the door and Parkins Gillespie was standing there, smoking a cigarette. He was holding a paperback in one hand, and Ben saw with some amusement that it was the Bantam edition of *Conway's Daughter*.

"Come on in, Constable," he said. "Wet out there."

"It is, a trifle," Parkins said, stepping in. "September's grippe weather. I always wear m' galoshes. There's some that laughs, but I ain't had the grippe since St.-Lô, France, in 1944."

"Lay your coat on the bed. Sorry I can't offer you coffee."

"Wouldn't think of wettin' it," Parkins said, and tapped ash in Ben's wastebasket. "And I just had a cup of Pauline's down to the Excellent."

"Can I do something for you?"

"Well, my wife read this. . . ." He held up the book. "She heard you was in town, but she's shy. She kind of thought maybe you might write your name in it, or somethin'."

Ben took the book. "The way Weasel Craig tells it, your wife's been dead fourteen or fifteen years."

"That so?" Parkins looked totally unsurprised. "That Weasel, he does love to talk. He'll open his mouth too wide one day and fall right in."

Ben said nothing.

"Do you s'pose you could sign it for me, then?"

"Delighted to." He took a pen from the desk, opened the book to the flyleaf ("A raw slice of life!"—Cleveland *Plain Dealer*), and wrote: *Best wishes to Constable Gillespie, from Ben Mears, 9/24/75*. He handed it back.

"I appreciate that," Parkins said, without looking at what Ben had written. He bent over and crushed out his smoke on the side of the wastebasket. "That's the only signed book I got."

"Did you come here to brace me?" Ben asked, smiling.

"You're pretty sharp," Parkins said. "I figured I ought to come and ask a question or two, now that you mention it. Waited until Nolly was off somewheres. He's a good boy, but he likes to talk, too. Lordy, the gossip that goes on."

"What would you like to know?"

"Mostly where you were on last Wednesday evenin'."

"The night Ralphie Glick disappeared?"

"Yeah."

"Am I a suspect, Constable?"

"No, sir. I ain't got no suspects. A thing like this is outside my tour, you might say. Catchin' speeders out by Dell's or chasin' kids outta the park before they turn randy is more my line. I'm just nosin' here and there."

"Suppose I don't want to tell you."

Parkins shrugged and produced his cigarettes. "That's your business, son."

"I had dinner with Susan Norton and her folks. Played some badminton with her dad."

"Bet he beat you, too. He always beats Nolly. Nolly raves up and down about how bad he'd like to beat Bill Norton just once. What time did you leave?"

Ben laughed, but the sound did not contain a great deal of humor. "You cut right to the bone, don't you?"

"You know," Parkins said, "if I was one of those New York detectives like on TV, I might think you had somethin' to hide, the way you polka around my questions."

"Nothing to hide," Ben said. "I'm just tired of being the stranger in town, getting pointed at in the streets, being nudged over in the library. Now you come around with this Yankee trader routine, trying to find out if I've got Ralphie Glick's scalp in my closet."

"Now, I don't think that, not at all." He gazed at Ben over his cigarette, and his eyes had gone flinty. "I'm just tryin' to close you off. If I thought you had anything to do with anything, you'd be down in the tank."

"Okay," Ben said. "I left the Nortons around quarter past seven. I took a walk out toward Schoolyard Hill. When it got too dark to see, I came back here, wrote for two hours, and went to bed."

"What time did you get back here?"

"Quarter past eight, I think. Around there."

"Well, that don't clear you as well as I'd like. Did you see anybody?"

"No," Ben said. "No one."

Parkins made a noncommittal grunt and walked toward the typewriter. "What are you writin' about?"

"None of your damn business," Ben said, and his voice had gone tight. "I'll thank you to keep your eyes and your hands off that. Unless you've got a search warrant, of course."

"Kind of touchy, ain't you? For a man who means his books to be read?"

"When it's gone through three drafts, editorial correction, galleyproof corrections, final set and print, I'll personally see that you get four copies. Signed. Right now that comes under the heading of private papers."

Parkins smiled and moved away. "Good enough. I doubt like hell that it's a signed confession to anything, anyway."

Ben smiled back. "Mark Twain said a novel was a confession to everything by a man who had never done anything."

Parkins blew out smoke and went to the door. "I won't drip on your rug anymore, Mr. Mears. Want to thank you for y'time, and just for the record, I don't think you ever saw that Glick boy. But it's my job to kind of ask round about these things."

Ben nodded. "Understood."

"And you oughtta know how things are in places like 'salem's Lot or Milbridge or Guilford or any little pissant burg. You're the stranger in town until you been here twenty years."

"I know. I'm sorry if I snapped at you. But after a week of looking for him and not finding a goddamned thing—" Ben shook his head.

"Yeah," Parkins said. "It's bad for his mother. Awful bad. You take care."

"Sure," Ben said.

"No hard feelin's?"

"No." He paused. "Will you tell me one thing?"

"I will if I can."

"Where did you get that book? Really?"

Parkins Gillespie smiled. "Well, there's a fella over in Cumberland that's got a used-furniture barn. Kind of a sissy fella, he is. Name of Gendron. He sells paperbacks a dime apiece. Had five of these."

Ben threw back his head and laughed, and Parkins Gillespie went out, smiling and smoking. Ben went to the window and watched until he saw the constable come out and cross the street, walking carefully around puddles in his black galoshes.

10

Parkins paused a moment to look in the show window of the new shop before knocking on the door. When the place had been the Village Washtub, a body could look in here and see nothing but a lot of fat women in rollers adding bleach or getting change out of the machine on the wall, most of them chewing gum like cows with mouthfuls of mulch. But an interior decorator's truck from Portland had been here yesterday afternoon and most of today, and the place looked considerably different.

A platform had been shoved up behind the window, and it was covered with a swatch of deep nubby carpet, light green in color. Two spotlights had been installed up out of sight, and they cast soft, highlighting glows on the three objects that had been arranged in the window: a clock, a spinning wheel, and an old-fashioned cherrywood cabinet. There was a small easel in front of each piece, and a discreet price tag on each easel, and my God, would anybody in their right mind actually pay $600 for a spinning wheel when they could go down to the Value House and get a Singer for $48.95?

Sighing, Parkins went to the door and knocked.

It was opened only a second later, almost as if the new fella had been lurking behind it, waiting for him to come to the door.

"Inspector!" Straker said with a narrow smile. "How good of you to drop by!"

"Plain old constable, I guess," Parkins said. He lit a Pall Mall and strolled in. "Parkins Gillespie. Pleased to meet you." He stuck out his hand. It was gripped, squeezed gently by a hand that felt enormously strong and very dry, and then dropped.

"Richard Throckett Straker," the bald man said.

"I figured you was," Parkins said, looking around. The entire shop had been carpeted and was in the process of being painted. The smell of fresh paint was a good one, but there seemed to be another smell underneath it, an unpleasant one. Parkins could not place it; he turned his attention back to Straker.

"What can I do for you on this so-fine day?" Straker asked.

Parkins turned his mild gaze out the window, where the rain continued to pour down.

"Oh, nothing at all, I guess. I just came by to say how-do. More or less welcome you to the town an' wish you good luck, I guess."

"How thoughtful. Would you care for a coffee? Some sherry? I have both out back."

"No thanks, I can't stop. Mr. Barlow around?"

"Mr. Barlow is in New York, on a buying trip. I don't expect him back until at least the tenth of October."

"You'll be openin' without him, then," Parkins said, thinking that if the prices he had seen in the window were any indication, Straker wouldn't exactly be swamped with customers. "What's Mr. Barlow's first name, by the way?"

Straker's smile reappeared, razor-thin. "Are you asking in your official capacity, ah . . . Constable?"

"Nope. Just curious."

"My partner's full name is Kurt Barlow," Straker said. "We have worked together in both London and Hamburg. This"—he swept his arm around him—"this is our retirement. Modest. Yet tasteful. We expect to make no more than a living. Yet we both love old things, fine things, and we hope to make a reputation in the area . . . perhaps even throughout your so-beautiful New England region. Do you think that would be possible, Constable Gillespie?"

"Anything's possible, I guess," Parkins said, looking around for an ash tray. He saw none, and tapped his cigarette ash into his coat pocket. "Anyway, I hope you'll have the best of luck, and tell Mr. Barlow when you see him that I'm gonna try and get around."

"I'll do so," Straker said. "He enjoys company."

"That's fine," Gillespie said. He went to the door, paused, looked back. Straker was looking at him intently. "By the way, how do you like that old house?"

"It needs a great deal of work," Straker said. "But we have time."

"I guess you do," Parkins agreed. "Don't suppose you seen any yow'uns up around there."

Straker's brow creased. "Yowwens?"

"Kids," Parkins explained patiently. "You know how they sometimes like to devil new folks. Throw rocks or ring the bell an' run away . . . that sort of thing."

"No," Straker said. "No children."

"We seem to kind of have misplaced one."

"Is that so?"

"Yes," Parkins said judiciously, "yes, it is. The thinkin' now is that we may not find him. Not alive."

"What a shame," Straker said distantly.

"It is, kinda. If you should see anything . . ."

"I would of course report it to your office, posthaste." He smiled his chilly smile again.

"That's good," Parkins said. He opened the door and looked resignedly out at the pouring rain. "You tell Mr. Barlow that I'm lookin' forward."

"I certainly will, Constable Gillespie. *Ciao.*"

Parkins looked back, startled. "Chow?"

Straker's smile widened. "Good-by, Constable Gillespie. That is the familiar Italian expression for good-by."

"Oh? Well, you learn somethin' new every day, don't you? 'By." He stepped out into the rain and closed the door behind him. "Not familiar to me, it ain't." His cigarette was soaked. He threw it away.

Inside, Straker watched him up the street through the show window. He was no longer smiling.

11

When Parkins got back to his office in the Municipal Building, he called, "Nolly? You here, Nolly?"

No answer. Parkins nodded. Nolly was a good boy, but a little bit short on brains. He took off his coat, unbuckled his galoshes, sat down at his desk, looked up a telephone number in the Portland book, and dialed. The other end picked up on the first ring.

"FBI, Portland. Agent Hanrahan."

"This is Parkins Gillespie. Constable at Jerusalem's Lot township. We've got us a missin' boy up here."

"So I understand," Hanrahan said crisply. "Ralph Glick. Nine years old, four-three, black hair, blue eyes. What is it, kidnap note?"

"Nothin' like that. Can you check on some fellas for me?"

Hanrahan answered in the affirmative.

"First one is Benjaman Mears. M-E-A-R-S. Writer. Wrote a book called *Conway's Daughter*. The other two are sorta stapled together. Kurt Barlow. B-A-R-L-O-W. The other guy—"

"You spell that Kurt with a 'c' or a 'k'?" Hanrahan asked.

"I dunno."

"Okay. Go on."

Parkins did so, sweating. Talking to the real law always made him feel like an asshole. "The other guy is Richard Throckett Straker. Two *t*'s on the end of Throckett, and Straker like it sounds. This guy and Barlow are in the furniture and antique business. They just opened a little shop here in town. Straker claims Barlow's in New York on a buyin' trip. Straker claims the two of them worked together in London an' Hamburg. And I guess that pretty well covers it."

"Do you suspect these people in the Glick case?"

"Right now I don't know if there even is a case. But they all showed up in town about the same time."

"Do you think there's any connection between this guy Mears and the other two?"

Parkins leaned back and cocked an eye out the window. "That," he said, "is one of the things I'd like to find out."

12

The telephone wires make an odd humming on clear, cool days, almost as if vibrating with the gossip that is transmitted through them, and it is a sound like no other—the lonely sound of voices flying over space. The telephone poles are gray and splintery, and the freezes and thaws of winter have heaved them into leaning postures that are casual. They are not businesslike and military, like phone poles anchored in concrete. Their bases are black with tar if they are beside paved roads, and floured with dust if beside the back roads. Old weathered cleat marks show on their surfaces where linemen have climbed to fix something in 1946 or 1952 or 1969. Birds—crows, sparrows, robins, starlings—roost on the humming wires and sit in hunched silence, and perhaps they hear the foreign human sounds through their taloned feet. If so, their beady eyes give no sign. The town has a sense, not of history, but of time, and the telephone poles seem to know this. If you lay your hand against one, you can feel the vibration from the wires deep in the wood, as if souls had been imprisoned in there and were struggling to get out.

". . . and he paid with an old twenty, Mable, one of the big ones. Clyde said he hadn't seen one of those since the run on the Gates Bank and Trust in 1930. He was . . ."

". . . yes, he *is* a peculiar sort of man, Evvie. I've seen him through my binocs, trundling around behind the house with a wheelbarrer. Is he up there alone, I wonder, or . . ."

". . . Crockett might know, but he won't tell. He's keeping shut about it. He always was a . . ."

". . . writer at Eva's. I wonder if Floyd Tibbits knows he's been . . ."

". . . spends an awful lot of time at the library. Loretta Starcher says she never saw a fella who knew so many . . ."

". . . she said his name was . . ."

". . . yes, it's Straker. Mr. R. T. Straker. Kenny Danles's mom said she stopped by that new place downtown and there was a genuine DeBiers cabinet in the window and they wanted *eight hundred dollars* for it. Can you imagine? So I said . . ."

". . . funny, him coming and that little Glick boy . . ."

". . . you don't think . . ."

". . . no, but it *is* funny. By the way, do you still have that recipe for . . ."

The wires hum. And hum. And hum.

13

9/23/75

NAME: Glick, Daniel Francis

ADDRESS: RFD #1, Brock Road, Jerusalem's Lot, Maine 04270

AGE: 12 SEX: Male RACE: Caucasian

ADMITTED: 9/22/75 ADMITTING PERSON: Anthony H. Glick (Father)

SYMPTOMS: Shock, loss of memory (partial), nausea, disinterest in food, constipation, general loginess

TESTS   (see attached sheet):
1. Tuberculosis skin patch: Neg.
2. Tuberculosis sputum and urine: Neg.
3. Diabetes: Neg.
4. White cell count: Neg.
5. Red cell count: 45% hemo.
6. Marrow sample: Neg.
7. Chest X ray: Neg.

POSSIBLE DIAGNOSIS: Pernicious anemia, primary or secondary; previous exam shows 86% hemoglobin. Secondary anemia is unlikely; no history of ulcers, hemorrhoids, bleeding piles, et al. Differential cell count neg. Primary anemia combined with mental shock likely. Recommend barium enema and X rays for internal bleeding on the off-chance, yet no recent accidents, father says. Also recommend daily dosage of vitamin B_{12} (see attached sheet).

Pending further tests, let's release him.

G. M. Gorby
Attending Physician

14

At one o'clock in the morning, September 24, the nurse stepped into Danny Glick's hospital room to give him his medication. She paused in the doorway, frowning. The bed was empty.

Her eyes jumped from the bed to the oddly wasted white bundle that lay collapsed by the foot. "Danny?" she said.

She stepped toward him and thought, He had to go to the bathroom and it was too much for him, that's all.

She turned him over gently, and her first thought before realizing that he was dead was that the B_{12} had been helping; he looked better than he had since his admission.

And then she felt the cold flesh of his wrist and the lack of movement in the light blue tracery of veins beneath her fingers, and she ran for the nurses' station to report a death on the ward.

Chapter Five
BEN (II)

1

On September 25 Ben took dinner with the Nortons again. It was Thursday night, and the meal was traditional—beans and franks. Bill Norton grilled the franks on the outdoor grill, and Ann had had her kidney beans simmering in molasses since nine that morning. They ate at the picnic table and afterward they sat smoking, the four of them, talking desultorily of Boston's fading pennant chances.

There was a subtle change in the air; it was still pleasant enough, even in shirt sleeves, but there was a glint of ice in it now. Autumn was waiting in the wings, almost in sight. The large and ancient maple in front of Eva Miller's boardinghouse had already begun to go red.

There had been no change in Ben's relationship with the Nortons. Susan's liking for him was frank and clear and natural. And he liked her very much. In Bill he sensed a steadily increasing liking, held in abeyance by the subconscious taboo that affects all fathers when in the presence of men who are there because of their daughters rather than themselves. If you like another man and you are honest, you speak freely, discuss women over beer, shoot the shit about politics. But no matter how deep the potential liking, it is impossible to open up completely to a man who is dangling your daughter's potential defloration between his legs. Ben reflected that after marriage the possible had become the actual and could you become complete friends with the man who was banging your daughter night after night? There might be a moral there, but Ben doubted it.

Ann Norton continued cool. Susan had told him a little of the Floyd Tibbits situation the night before—of her mother's assumption that her son-in-law problems had been solved neatly and satisfactorily in that direction. Floyd was a known quantity; he was Steady. Ben Mears, on the other hand, had come out of nowhere and might disappear back there just as quickly, possibly with her daughter's heart in his pocket. She distrusted the creative male with an instinctive small-town dislike (one that Edward Arlington Robinson or Sherwood Anderson would have recognized at once), and Ben suspected that down deep she had absorbed a maxim: either faggots or bull studs; sometimes homicidal, suicidal, or maniacal; tend to send young girls packages containing their left ears. Ben's participation in the search for Ralphie Glick seemed to have increased her suspicions rather than allayed them, and he suspected that winning her over was an impossibility. He wondered if she knew of Parkins Gillespie's visit to his room.

He was chewing these thoughts over lazily when Ann said, "Terrible about the Glick boy."

"Ralphie? Yes," Bill said.

"No, the older one. He's dead."

Ben started. "Who? Danny?"

"He died early yesterday morning." She seemed surprised that the men did not know. It had been all the talk.

"I heard them talking in Milt's," Susan said. Her hand found Ben's under the table and he took it willingly. "How are the Glicks taking it?"

"The same way I would," Ann said simply. "They are out of their minds."

Well they might be, Ben thought. Ten days ago their life had been going about its usual ordained cycle; now their family unit was smashed and in pieces. It gave him a morbid chill.

"Do you think the other Glick boy will ever show up alive?" Bill asked Ben.

"No," Ben said. "I think he's dead, too."

"Like that thing in Houston two years ago," Susan said. "If he's dead, I almost hope they don't find him. Whoever could do something like that to a little, defenseless boy—"

"The police are looking around, I guess," Ben said. "Rounding up known sex offenders and talking to them."

"When they find the guy they ought to hang him up by the thumbs," Bill Norton said. "Badminton, Ben?"

Ben stood. "No thanks. Too much like you playing solitaire with me for the dummy. Thanks for the nice meal. I've got work to do tonight."

Ann Norton lifted her eyebrow and said nothing.

Bill stood. "How's that new book coming?"

"Good," Ben said briefly. "Would you like to walk down the hill with me and have a soda at Spencer's, Susan?"

"Oh, I don't know," Ann interposed swiftly. "After Ralphie Glick and all, I'd feel better if—"

"Momma, I'm a big girl," Susan interposed. "And there are streetlights all the way up Brock Hill."

"I'll walk you back up, of course," Ben said, almost formally. He had left his car at Eva's. The early evening had been too fine to drive.

"They'll be fine," Bill said. "You worry too much, Mother."

"Oh, I suppose I do. Young folks always know best, don't they?" She smiled thinly.

"I'll just get a jacket," Susan murmured to Ben, and turned up the back walk. She was wearing a red play skirt, thigh-high, and she exposed a lot of leg going up the steps to the door. Ben watched, knowing Ann was watching him watch. Her husband was damping the charcoal fire.

"How long do you intend to stay in the Lot, Ben?" Ann asked, showing polite interest.

"Until the book gets written, anyway," he said. "After that, I can't say. It's very lovely in the mornings, and the air tastes good when you breathe it." He smiled into her eyes. "I may stay longer."

She smiled back. "It gets cold in the winters, Ben. Awfully cold."

Then Susan was coming back down the steps with a light jacket thrown over her shoulders. "Ready? I'm going to have a chocolate. Look out, complexion."

"Your complexion will survive," he said, and turned to Mr. and Mrs. Norton. "Thank you again."

"Anytime," Bill said. "Come on over with a six-pack tomorrow night, if you want. We'll make fun of that goddamn Yastrzemski."

"That would be fun," Ben said, "but what'll we do after the second inning?"

His laughter, hearty and full, followed them around the corner of the house.

2

"I don't really want to go to Spencer's," she said as they went down the hill. "Let's go to the park instead."

"What about muggers, lady?" he asked, doing the Bronx for her.

"In the Lot, all muggers have to be in by seven. It's a town ordinance. And it is now exactly eight-oh-three." Darkness had fallen over them as they walked down the hill, and their shadows waxed and waned in the streetlights.

"Agreeable muggers you have," he said. "No one goes to the park after dark?"

"Sometimes the town kids go there to make out if they can't afford the drive-in," she said, and winked at him. "So if you see anyone skulking around in the bushes, look the other way."

They entered from the west side, which faced the Municipal Building. The park was shadowy and a little dreamlike, the concrete walks curving away under the leafy trees, and the wading pool glimmering quietly in the refracted glow from the streetlights. If anyone was here, Ben didn't see him.

They walked around the War Memorial with its long lists of names, the oldest from the Revolutionary War, the newest from Vietnam, carved under the War of 1812. There were six home town names from the most recent conflict, the new cuts in the brass gleaming like fresh wounds. He thought: This town has the wrong name. It ought to be Time. And as if the action was a natural outgrowth of the thought, he looked over his shoulder for the Marsten House, but the bulk of the Municipal Building blocked it out.

She saw his glance and it made her frown. As they spread their jackets on the grass and sat down (they had spurned the park benches without discussion), she said, "Mom said Parkins Gillespie was checking up on you. The new boy in school must have stolen the milk money, or something like that."

"He's quite a character," Ben said.

"Mom had you practically tried and convicted." It was said lightly, but the lightness faltered and let something serious through.

"Your mother doesn't care for me much, does she?"

"No," Susan said, holding his hand. "It was a case of dislike at first sight. I'm very sorry."

"It's okay," he said. "I'm batting five hundred anyway."

"Daddy?" She smiled. "He just knows class when he sees it." The smile faded. "Ben, what's this new book about?"

"That's hard to say." He slipped his loafers off and dug his toes into the dewy grass.

"Subject-changer."

"No, I don't mind telling you." And he found, surprisingly, that this was true. He had always thought of a work in progress as a child, a weak child, that had to be protected and cradled. Too much handling would kill it. He had refused to tell Miranda a word about *Conway's Daughter* or *Air Dance,* although she had been wildly curious about both of them. But Susan was different. With Miranda there had always been a directed sort of probing, and her questions were more like interrogations.

"Just let me think how to put it together," he said.

"Can you kiss me while you think?" she asked, lying back on the grass. He was forcibly aware of how short her skirt was; it had given a lot of ground.

"I think that might interfere with the thought processes," he said softly. "Let's see."

He leaned over and kissed her, placing one hand lightly on her waist. She met his mouth firmly, and her hands closed over his. A moment later he felt her tongue for the first time, and he met it with his own. She shifted to return his kiss more fully, and the soft rustle of her cotton skirt seemed loud, almost maddening.

He slid his hand up and she arched her breast into it, soft and full. For the second time since he had known her he felt sixteen, a head-busting sixteen with everything in front of him six lanes wide and no hard traveling in sight.

"Ben?"

"Yes."

"Make love to me? Do you want to?"

"Yes," he said. "I want that."

"Here on the grass," she said.

"Yes."

She was looking up at him, her eyes wide in the dark. She said, "Make it be good."

"I'll try."

"Slow," she said. "Slow. Slow. Here . . ."

They became shadows in the dark.

"There," he said. "Oh, Susan."

3

They were walking, first aimlessly through the park, and then with more purpose toward Brock Street.

"Are you sorry?" he asked.

She looked up at him and smiled without artifice. "No. I'm glad."

"Good."

They walked hand in hand without speaking.

"The book?" she asked. "You were going to tell me about that before we were so sweetly interrupted."

"The book is about the Marsten House," he said slowly. "Maybe it didn't start out to be, not wholly. I thought it was going to be about this town. But maybe I'm fooling myself. I researched Hubie Marsten, you know. He was a mobster. The trucking company was just a front."

She was looking at him in wonder. "How did you find that out?"

"Some from the Boston police, and more from a woman named Minella Corey, Birdie Marsten's sister. She's seventy-nine now, and she can't remember what she had for breakfast, but she's never forgotten a thing that happened before 1940."

"And she told you—"

"As much as she knew. She's in a nursing home in New Hampshire, and I don't think anyone's really taken the time to listen to her in years. I asked her if Hubert Marsten had really been a contract killer in the Boston area—the police sure thought he was—and she nodded. 'How many?' I asked her. She held her fingers up in front of her eyes and waggled them back and forth and said, 'How many times can you count these?' "

"My God."

The Boston organization began to get very nervous about Hubert Marsten in 1927," Ben went on. "He was picked up for questioning twice, once by the city police and once by the Malden police. The Boston grab was for a gangland killing, and he was back on the street in two hours. The thing in Malden wasn't business at all. It was the murder of an eleven-year-old boy. The child had been eviscerated."

"Ben," she said, and her voice was sick.

"Marsten's employers got him off the hook—I imagine he knew where a few bodies were buried—but that was the end of him in Boston. He moved quietly to 'salem's Lot, just a retired trucking official who got a check once a month. He didn't go out much. At least, not much that we know of."

"What do you mean?"

"I've spent a lot of time in the library looking at old copies of the *Ledger* from 1928 to 1939. Four children disappeared in that period. Not that unusual, not in a rural area. Kids get lost, and they sometimes die of exposure. Sometimes kids get buried in a gravel-pit slide. Not nice, but it happens."

"But you don't think that's what happened?"

"I don't *know*. But I do know that *not one of those four were ever found*. No hunter turning up a skeleton in 1945 or a contractor digging one up while getting a load of gravel to make cement. Hubert and Birdie lived in that house for eleven years and the kids disappeared, and that's all anyone knows. But I keep thinking about that kid in Malden. I think about that a lot. Do you know *The Haunting of Hill House*, by Shirley Jackson?"

"Yes."

He quoted softly, " 'And whatever walked there, walked alone.' You asked what my book was about. Essentially, it's about the recurrent power of evil."

She put her hands on his arm. "You don't think that Ralphie Glick . . ."

"Was gobbled up by the revengeful spirit of Hubert Marsten, who comes back to life on every third year at the full of the moon?"

"Something like that."

"You're asking the wrong person if you want to be reassured. Don't forget, I'm the kid who opened the door to an upstairs bedroom and saw him hanging from a beam."

"That's not an answer."

"No, it's not. Let me tell you one other thing before I tell you exactly what I think. Something Minella Corey said. She said there are evil men in the world, truly evil men. Sometimes we hear of them, but more often they work in absolute darkness. She said she had been cursed with a knowledge of two such men in her lifetime. One was Adolf Hitler. The other was her brother-in-law, Hubert Marsten." He paused. "She said that on the day Hubie shot her sister she was three hundred miles away in Cape Cod. She had taken a job as housekeeper for a rich family that summer. She was making a tossed salad in a large wooden bowl. It was quarter after two in the afternoon. A bolt of pain, 'like lightning,' she said, went through her head and she heard a shotgun blast. She fell on the floor, she claims. When she picked herself up—she was alone in the house—twenty minutes had passed. She looked in the wooden bowl and screamed. It appeared to her that it was full of blood."

"God," Susan murmured.

"A moment later, everything was normal again. No headache, nothing in the salad bowl but salad. But she said she knew—she *knew*—that her sister was dead, murdered with a shotgun."

"That's her unsubstantiated story?"

"Unsubstantiated, yes. But she's not some oily trickster; she's an old woman without enough brains left to lie. That part doesn't bother me, anyway. Not very much, at least. There's a large enough body of ESP data now so that a rational man laughs it off at his own expense. The idea that Birdie transmitted the facts of her death three hundred miles over a kind of psychic telegraph isn't half so hard for me to believe as the face of evil—the really monstrous face—that I sometimes think I can see buried in the outlines of that house.

"You asked me what I think. I'll tell you. I think it's relatively easy for people to accept something like telepathy or precognition or teleplasm because their willingness to believe doesn't cost them anything. It doesn't keep them awake nights. But the idea that the evil that men do lives after them is more unsettling."

He looked up at the Marsten House and spoke slowly.

"I think that house might be Hubert Marsten's monument to evil, a kind of psychic sounding board. A supernatural beacon, if you like. Sitting there all these years, maybe holding the essence of Hubie's evil in its old, moldering bones.

"And now it's occupied again.

"And there's been another disappearance." He turned to her and cradled her upturned face in his hands. "You see, that's something I never counted on when I came back here. I thought the house might have been torn down, but never in my wildest dreams that it had been bought. I saw myself renting it and . . . oh, I don't know. Confronting my own terrors and evils, maybe. Playing ghostbreaker, maybe—be gone in the name of all the saints, Hubie. Or maybe just tapping into the atmosphere of the place to write a book scary enough to make me a million dollars. But no matter what, I felt that I was in control of the situation, and that would make all the difference. I wasn't any nine-year-old kid anymore, ready to run screaming from a magic-lantern show that maybe came out of my own mind and no place else. But now . . ."

"Now what, Ben?"

"Now it's occupied!" he burst out, and beat a fist into his palm. "I'm *not* in control of the situation. A little boy has disappeared and I don't know what to make of it. It could have nothing to do with that house, but . . . I don't believe it." The last four words came out in measured lengths.

"Ghosts? Spirits?"

"Not necessarily. Maybe just some harmless guy who admired the house when he was a kid and bought it and became . . . possessed."

"Do you know something about—" she began, alarmed.

"The new tenant? No. I'm just guessing. But if it is the house, I'd almost rather it was possession than something else."

"What?"

He said simply, "Perhaps it's called another evil man."

4

Ann Norton watched them from the window. She had called the drugstore earlier. No, Miss Coogan said, with something like glee. Not here. Haven't been in.

Where have you been, Susan? Oh, where have you been?

Her mouth twisted down into a helpless ugly grimace.

Go away, Ben Mears. Go away and leave her alone.

5

When she left his arms, she said, "Do something important for me, Ben."

"Whatever I can."

"Don't mention those things to anyone else in town. Anyone."

He smiled humorlessly. "Don't worry. I'm not anxious to have people thinking I've been struck nuts."

"Do you lock your room at Eva's?"

"No."

"I'd start locking it." She looked at him levelly. "You have to think of yourself as under suspicion."

"With you, too?"

"You would be, if I didn't love you."

And then she was gone, hastening up the driveway, leaving him to look after her, stunned by all he had said and more stunned by the four or five words she had said at the end.

6

He found when he got back to Eva's that he could neither write nor sleep. He was too excited to do either. So he warmed up the Citroën, and after a moment of indecision, he drove out toward Dell's place.

It was crowded, and the place was smoky and loud. The band, a country-and-western group on trial called the Rangers, was playing a version of "You've Never Been This Far Before," which made up in volume for whatever it lost in quality. Perhaps forty couples were gyrating on the floor, most of them wearing blue jeans. Ben, a little amused, thought of Edward Albee's line about monkey nipples.

The stools in front of the bar were held down by construction and mill workers, each drinking identical glasses of beer and all wearing nearly identical crepe-soled work boots, laced with rawhide.

Two or three barmaids with bouffant hairdos and their names written in gold thread on their white blouses (Jackie, Toni, Shirley) circulated to the tables and booths. Behind the bar, Dell was drawing beers, and at the far end, a hawklike man with his hair greased back was making mixed drinks. His face remained utterly blank as he measured liquor into shot glasses, dumped it into his silver shaker, and added whatever went with it.

Ben started toward the bar, skirting the dance floor, and someone called out, "Ben! Say, fella! How are you, buddy?"

Ben looked around and saw Weasel Craig sitting at a table close to the bar, a half-empty beer in front of him.

"Hello, Weasel," Ben said, sitting down. He was relieved to see a familiar face, and he liked Weasel.

"Decided to get some night life, did you, buddy?" Weasel smiled and clapped him on the shoulder. Ben thought that his check must have come in; his breath alone could have made Milwaukee famous.

"Yeah," Ben said. He got out a dollar and laid it on the table, which was covered with the circular ghosts of the many beer glasses that had stood there. "How you doing?"

"Just fine. What do you think of that new band? Great, ain't they?"

"They're okay," Ben said. "Finish that thing up before it goes flat. I'm buying."

"I been waitin' to hear somebody say that all night. *Jackie!*" he bawled. "Bring my buddy here a pitcher! Budweiser!"

Jackie brought the pitcher on a tray littered with beer-soaked change and lifted it onto the table, her right arm bulging like a prize fighter's. She looked at the dollar as if it were a new species of cockroach. "That's a buck fawty," she said.

Ben put another bill down. She picked them both up, fished sixty cents out of the assorted puddles on her tray, banged them down on the table, and said, "Weasel Craig, when you yell like that you sound like a rooster gettin' its neck wrung."

"You're beautiful, darlin'," Weasel said. "This is Ben Mears. He writes books."

"Meetcha," Jackie said, and disappeared into the dimness.

Ben poured himself a glass of beer and Weasel followed suit, filling his glass professionally to the top. The foam threatened to overspill and then backed down. "Here's to you, buddy."

Ben lifted his glass and drank.

"So how's that writin' goin'?"

"Pretty good, Weasel."

"I seen you goin' round with that little Norton girl. She's a real peach, she is. You couldn't do no better there."

"Yes, she's—"

"*Matt!*" Weasel bawled, almost startling Ben into dropping his glass. By God, he thought, he *does* sound like a rooster saying good-by to this world.

"Matt Burke!" Weasel waved wildly, and a man with white hair raised his hand in greeting and started to cut through the crowd. "Here's a fella you ought to meet," Weasel told Ben. "Matt Burke's one smart son of a whore."

The man coming toward them looked about sixty. He was tall, wearing a clean flannel shirt open at the throat, and his hair, which was as white as Weasel's, was cut in a flattop.

"Hello, Weasel," he said.

"How are you, buddy?" Weasel said. "Want you to meet a fella stayin' over to Eva's. Ben Mears. Writes books, he does. He's a lovely fella." He looked at Ben. "Me'n Matt grew up together, only he got an education and I got the shaft." Weasel cackled.

Ben stood up and shook Matt Burke's bunched hand gingerly. "How are you?"

"Fine, thanks. I've read one of your books, Mr. Mears. *Air Dance.*"

"Make it Ben, please. I hope you liked it."

"I liked it much better than the critics, apparently," Matt said, sitting down. "I think it will gain ground as time goes by. How are you, Weasel?"

"Perky," Weasel said. "Just as perky as ever I could be. *Jackie!*" he bawled. "Bring Matt a glass!"

"Just wait a minute, y'old fart!" Jackie yelled back, drawing laughter from the nearby tables.

"She's a lovely girl," Weasel said. "Maureen Talbot's girl."

"Yes," Matt said. "I had Jackie in school. Class of '71. Her mother was '51."

"Matt teaches high school English," Weasel told Ben. "You and him should have a lot to talk about."

"I remember a girl named Maureen Talbot," Ben said. "She came and got my aunt's wash and brought it back all folded in a wicker basket. The basket only had one handle."

"Are you from town, Ben?" Matt asked.

"I spent some time here as a boy. With my Aunt Cynthia."

"Cindy Stowens?"

"Yes."

Jackie came with a clean glass, and Matt tipped beer into it. "It really is a small world, then. Your aunt was in a senior class I taught my first year in 'salem's Lot. Is she well?"

"She died in 1972."

"I'm sorry."

"She went very easily," Ben said, and refilled his glass. The band had finished its set, and the members were trouping toward the bar. The level of conversation went down a notch.

"Have you come back to Jerusalem's Lot to write a book about us?" Matt asked.

A warning bell went off in Ben's mind.

"In a way, I suppose," he said.

"This town could do much worse for a biographer. *Air*

Dance was a fine book. I think there might be another fine book in this town. I once thought I might write it."

"Why didn't you?"

Matt smiled—an easy smile with no trace of bitterness, cynicism, or malice. "I lacked one vital ingredient. Talent."

"Don't you believe it," Weasel said, refilling his glass from the dregs of the pitcher. "Ole Matt's got a world of talent. Schoolteachin' is a wonnerful job. Nobody appreciates schoo'-teachers, but they're . . ." He swayed a little in his chair, searching for completion. He was becoming very drunk. "Salt of the earth," he finished, took a mouthful of beer, grimaced, and stood up. "Pardon me while I take a leak."

He wandered off, bumping into people and hailing them by name. They passed him on with impatience or good cheer, and watching his progress to the men's room was like watching a pinball racket and bounce its way down toward the flipper buttons.

"There goes the wreck of a fine man," Matt said, and held up one finger. A waitress appeared almost immediately and addressed him as Mr. Burke. She seemed a trifle scandalized that her old English Classics teacher should be here, boozing it up with the likes of Weasel Craig. When she turned away to bring them another pitcher, Ben thought Matt looked a trifle bemused.

"I like Weasel," Ben said. "I get a feeling there was a lot there once. What happened to him?"

"Oh, there's no story there," Matt said. "The bottle got him. It got him a little more each year and now it's got all of him. He won a Silver Star at Anzio in World War II. A cynic might believe his life would have had more meaning if he had died there."

"I'm not a cynic," Ben said. "I like him still. But I think I better give him a ride home tonight."

"That would be good of you. I come out here now and then to listen to the music. I like loud music. More than ever, since my hearing began to fail. I understand that you're interested in the Marsten House. Is your book about it?"

Ben jumped. "Who told you that?"

Matt smiled. "How does that old Marvin Gaye song put it? I heard it through the grapevine. Luscious, vivid idiom, although the image is a bit obscure if you consider it. One conjures up a picture of a man standing with his ear cocked attentively toward a Concord or Tokay. . . . I'm rambling. I ramble a great deal these days but rarely try to keep it in hand anymore. I heard from what the gentlemen of the press would call an informed source—Loretta Starcher, actually. She's the librarian at our local citadel of literature. You've been in several times to look at the Cumberland *Ledger* articles pertaining to the ancient scandal, and she also got you two true-crime books that had articles on it. By the way, the Lubert one is good—he came to the Lot and researched it himself in 1946—but the Snow chapter is speculative trash."

"I know," Ben said automatically.

The waitress set down a fresh pitcher of beer and Ben suddenly had an uncomfortable image: Here is a fish swimming around comfortably and (he thinks) unobtrusively, flicking here and there amongst the kelp and the plankton. Draw away for the long view and there's the kicker: It's a goldfish bowl.

Matt paid the waitress and said, "Nasty thing that happened up there. It's stayed in the town's consciousness, too. Of course, tales of nastiness and murder are always handed down with slavering delight from generation to generation, while students groan and complain when they're faced with a George Washington Carver or a Jonas Salk. But it's more than that, I think. Perhaps it's due to a geographical freak."

"Yes," Ben said, drawn in spite of himself. The teacher had just stated an idea that had been lurking below the level of his consciousness from the day he had arrived back in town, possibly even before that. "It stands on that hill overlooking the village like—oh, like some kind of dark idol." He chuckled to make the remark seem trivial—it seemed to him that he had said something so deeply felt in an unguarded way that he must have opened a window on his soul to this stranger. Matt Burke's sudden close scrutiny of him did not make him feel any better.

"That is talent," he said.

"Pardon me?"

"You have said it precisely. The Marsten House has looked down on us all for almost fifty years, at all our little peccadilloes and sins and lies. Like an idol."

"Maybe it's seen the good, too," Ben said.

"There's little good in sedentary small towns. Mostly indifference spiced with an occasional vapid evil—or worse, a conscious one. I believe Thomas Wolfe wrote about seven pounds of literature about that."

"I thought you weren't a cynic."

"You said that, not I." Matt smiled and sipped at his beer. The band was moving away from the bar, resplendent in their red shirts and glittering vests and neckerchiefs. The lead singer took his guitar and began to chord it.

"At any rate, you never answered my question. Is your new book about the Marsten House?"

"I suppose it is, in a way."

"I'm pumping you. Sorry."

"It's all right," Ben said, thinking of Susan and feeling uncomfortable. "I wonder what's keeping Weasel? He's been gone a hell of a long time."

"Could I presume on short acquaintanceship and ask a rather large favor? If you refuse, I'll more than understand."

"Sure, ask," Ben said.

"I have a creative writing class," Matt said. "They are intelligent children, eleventh- and twelfth-graders, most of them, and I would like to present someone who makes his living with words to them. Someone who—how shall I say?—has taken the word and made it flesh."

"I'd be more than happy to," Ben said, feeling absurdly flattered. "How long are your periods?"

"Fifty minutes."

"Well, I don't suppose I can bore them too badly in that length of time."

"Oh? I do it quite well, I think," Matt said. "Although I'm sure you wouldn't bore them at all. This next week?"

"Sure. Name a day and a time."

"Tuesday? Period four? That goes from eleven o'clock until ten of twelve. No one will boo you, but I suspect you will hear a great many stomachs rumble."

"I'll bring some cotton for my ears."

Matt laughed. "I'm very pleased. I will meet you at the office, if that's agreeable."

"Fine. Do you—"

"Mr. Burke?" It was Jackie, she of the heavy biceps. "Weasel's passed out in the men's room. Do you suppose—"

"Oh? Goodness, yes. Ben, would you—"

"Sure."

They got up and crossed the room. The band had begun to play again, something about how the kids in Muskogee still respected the college dean.

The bathroom smelled of sour urine and chlorine. Weasel was propped against the wall between two urinals, and a fellow in an army uniform was pissing approximately two inches from his right ear.

His mouth was open and Ben thought how terribly old he looked, old and ravaged by cold, impersonal forces with no gentle touch in them. The reality of his own dissolution, advancing day by day, came home to him, not for the first time, but with shocking unexpectedness. The pity that welled up in his throat like clear, black waters was as much for himself as for Weasel.

"Here," Matt said, "can you get an arm under him when this gentleman finishes relieving himself?"

"Yes," Ben said. He looked at the man in the army uniform, who was shaking off in leisurely fashion. "Hurry it up, can you, buddy?"

"Why? He ain't in no rush."

Nevertheless, he zipped up and stepped away from the urinal so they could get in.

Ben got an arm around Weasel's back, hooked a hand in his armpit, and lifted. For a moment his buttocks pressed against the tiled wall and he could feel the vibrations from the band. Weasel came up with the limp mail sack weight of utter unconsciousness. Matt slid his head under Weasel's other arm, hooked his own arm around Weasel's waist, and they carried him out the door.

"There goes Weasel," someone said, and there was laughter.

"Dell ought to cut him off," Matt said, sounding out of breath. "He knows how this always turns out."

They went through the door into the foyer, and then out onto the wooden steps leading down to the parking lot.

"Easy," Ben grunted. "Don't drop him."

They went down the stairs, Weasel's limp feet clopping on the risers like blocks of wood.

"The Citroën . . . over in the last row."

They carried him over. The coolness in the air was sharper now, and tomorrow the leaves would be blooded. Weasel had begun to grunt deep in his throat and his head jerked weakly on the stalk of his neck.

"Can you put him to bed when you get back to Eva's?" Matt asked.

"Yes, I think so."

"Good. Look, you can just see the roof tree of the Marsten House over the trees."

Ben looked. Matt was right; the top angle just peeked above the dark horizon of pines, blotting out the stars at the rim of the visible world with the regular shape of human construction.

Ben opened the passenger door and said, "Here. Let me have him."

He took Weasel's full weight and slipped him neatly into the passenger seat and closed the door. Weasel's head lolled against the window, giving it a flattened, grotesque look.

"Tuesday at eleven?"

"I'll be there."

"Thanks. And thanks for helping Weasel, too." He held out his hand and Ben shook it.

He got in, started the Citroën, and headed back toward town. Once the roadhouse neon had disappeared behind the trees, the road was deserted and black, and Ben thought, These roads are haunted now.

Weasel gave a snort and a groan beside him and Ben jumped. The Citroën swerved minutely on the road.

Now, why did I think that?

No answer.

7

He opened the wing window so that it scooped cold air directly onto Weasel on the ride home, and by the time he drove into Eva Miller's dooryard, Weasel had attained a soupy semiconsciousness.

Ben led him, half stumbling, up the back porch steps and into the kitchen, which was dimly lit by the stove's fluorescent.

Weasel moaned, then muttered deep in his throat, "She's a lovely girl, Jack, and married women, they know . . . know . . ."

A shadow detached itself from the hall and it was Eva, huge in an old quilted house coat, her hair done up in rollers and covered with a filmy net scarf. Her face was pale and ghostly with night cream.

"Ed," she said. "Oh, Ed . . . you do go on, don't you?"

His eyes opened a little at the sound of her voice, and a smile touched his features. "On and on and on," he croaked. "Wouldn't you know it more than the rest?"

"Can you get him up to his room?" she asked Ben.

"Yes, no sweat."

He tightened his grip on Weasel and somehow got him up the stairs and down to his room. The door was unlocked and he carried him inside. The minute he laid him on the bed, signs of consciousness ceased and he fell into a deep sleep.

Ben paused a moment to look around. The room was clean, almost sterile, things put away with barrackslike neatness. As he began to work on Weasel's shoes, Eva Miller said from behind him, "Never mind that, Mr. Mears. Go on up, if you like."

"But he ought to be—"

"I'll undress him." Her face was grave and full of dignified, measured sadness. "Undress him and give him an alcohol rub to help with his hangover in the morning. I've done it before. Many times."

"All right," Ben said, and went upstairs without looking back. He undressed slowly, thought about taking a shower, and decided not to. He got into bed and lay looking at the ceiling and did not sleep for a long time.

Chapter Six
THE LOT (II)

1

Fall and spring came to Jerusalem's Lot with the same suddenness of sunrise and sunset in the tropics. The line of demarcation could be as thin as one day. But spring is not the finest season in New England—it's too short, too uncertain, too apt to turn savage on short notice. Even so, there are April days which linger in the memory even after one has forgotten the wife's touch, or the feel of the baby's toothless mouth at the nipple. But by mid-May, the sun rises out of the morning's haze with authority and potency, and standing on your top step at seven in the morning with your dinner bucket in your hand, you know that the dew will be melted off the grass by eight and that the dust on the back roads will hang depthless and still in the air for five minutes after a car's passage; and that by one in the afternoon it will be up to ninety-five on the third floor of the mill and the sweat will roll off your arms like oil and stick your shirt to your back in a widening patch and it might as well be July.

But when fall comes, kicking summer out on its treacherous ass as it always does one day sometime after the midpoint of September, it stays awhile like an old friend that you have missed. It settles in the way an old friend will settle into your favorite chair and take out his pipe and light it and then fill the afternoon with stories of places he has been and things he has done since last he saw you.

It stays on through October and, in rare years, on into November. Day after day the skies are a clear, hard blue, and the clouds that float across them, always west to east, are calm white ships with gray keels. The wind begins to blow by the day, and it is never still. It hurries you along as you walk the roads, crunching the leaves that have fallen in mad and variegated drifts. The wind makes you ache in some place that is deeper than your bones. It may be that it touches something old in the human soul, a chord of race memory that says *Migrate or die— migrate or die.* Even in your house, behind square walls, the wind beats against the wood and the glass and sends its fleshless pucker against the eaves and sooner or later you have to put down what you were doing and go out and see. And you can stand on your stoop or in your dooryard at midafternoon and watch the cloud shadows rush across Griffen's pasture and up Schoolyard Hill, light and dark, light and dark, like the shutters of the gods being opened and closed. You can see the golden-rod, that most tenacious and pernicious and beauteous of all New England flora, bowing away from the wind like a great and silent congregation. And if there are no cars or planes, and if no one's Uncle John is out in the wood lot west of town banging away at a quail or pheasant; if the only sound is the slow beat of your own heart, you can hear another sound, and that is the sound of life winding down to its cyclic close, waiting for the first winter snow to perform last rites.

2

That year the first day of fall (real fall as opposed to calendar fall) was September 28, the day that Danny Glick was buried in the Harmony Hill Cemetery.

Church services were private, but the graveside services were open to the town and a good portion of the town turned out—classmates, the curious, and the older people to whom funerals grow nearly compulsive as old age knits their shrouds up around them.

They came up Burns Road in a long line, twisting up and out of sight over the next hill. All the cars had their lights turned on in spite of the day's brilliance. First came Carl Foreman's hearse, its rear windows filled with flowers, then Tony Glick's 1965 Mercury, its deteriorating muffler bellowing and farting. Behind that, in the next four cars, came relatives on both sides of the family, one bunch from as far away as Tulsa, Oklahoma. Others in that long, lights-on parade included: Mark Petrie (the boy Ralphie and Danny had been on their way to see the night Ralphie disappeared) and his mother and father; Richie Boddin and family; Mabel Werts in a car containing Mr. and Mrs. William Norton (sitting in the back seat with her cane planted between her swelled legs, she talked with unceasing constancy about other funerals she had attended all the way back to 1930); Lester Durham and his wife, Harriet; Paul Mayberry and his wife, Glynis; Pat Middler, Joe Crane, Vinnie Upshaw, and Clyde Corliss, all riding in a car driven by Milt Crossen (Milt had opened the beer cooler before they left, and they had all shared out a solemn six-pack in front of the stove); Eva Miller in a car which also contained her close friends Loretta Starcher and Rhoda Curless, who were both maiden ladies; Parkins Gillespie and his deputy, Nolly Gardener, riding in the Jerusalem's Lot police car (Parkins's Ford with a stick-on dashboard bubble); Lawrence Crockett and his sallow wife; Charles Rhodes, the sour bus driver, who went to all funerals on general principles; the Charles Griffen family, including wife and two sons, Hal and Jack, the only offspring still living at home.

Mike Ryerson and Royal Snow had dug the grave early that morning, laying strips of fake grass over the raw soil they had thrown out of the ground. Mike had lighted the Flame of Remembrance that the Glicks had specified. Mike could remember thinking that Royal didn't seem himself this morning. He was usually full of little jokes and ditties about the work at hand (cracked, off-key tenor: "They wrap you up in a big white sheet, an' put you down at least six feet. . . ."), but this morning he had seemed exceptionally quiet, almost sullen. Hung over, maybe, Mike thought. He and that muscle-bound buddy of his, Peters, had certainly been slopping it up down at Dell's the night before.

Five minutes ago, when he had seen Carl's hearse coming over the hill about a mile down the road, he had swung open the wide iron gates, glancing up at the high iron spikes as he always did since he had found Doc up there. With the gates open, he walked back to the newly dug grave where Father Donald Callahan, the pastor of the Jerusalem's Lot parish, waited by the grave. He was wearing a stole about his shoulders and the book he held was open to the children's burial service. This was what they called the third station, Mike knew. The first was the house of the deceased, the second at the tiny Catholic Church, St. Andrew's. Last station, Harmony Hill. Everybody out.

A little chill touched him and he looked down at the bright plastic grass, wondering why it had to be a part of every funeral. It looked like exactly what it was: a cheap imitation of life discreetly masking the heavy brown clods of the final earth.

"They're on their way, Father," he said.

Callahan was a tall man with piercing blue eyes and a ruddy complexion. His hair was a graying steel color. Ryerson, who hadn't been to church since he turned sixteen, liked him the best of all the local witch doctors. John Groggins, the Methodist minister, was a hypocritical old poop, and Patterson, from the Church of the Latter-day Saints and Followers of the Cross, was as crazy as a bear stuck in a honey tree. At a funeral for one of the church deacons two or three years back, Patterson had gotten right down and rolled on the ground. But Callahan seemed nice enough for a Pope-lover; his funerals were calm and comforting and always short. Ryerson doubted if Callahan had gotten all those red and broken veins in his cheeks and around his nose from praying, but if Callahan did a little drinking, who was to blame him? The way the world was, it was a wonder all those preachers didn't end up in looney-bins.

"Thanks, Mike," he said, and looked up at the bright sky. "This is going to be a hard one."

"I guess so. How long?"

"Ten minutes, no more. I'm not going to draw out his parents' agony. There's enough of that still ahead of them."

"Okay," Mike said, and walked toward the rear of the grave-yard. He would jump over the stone wall, go into the woods, and eat a late lunch. He knew from long experience that the last thing the grieving family and friends want to see during the third station is the resident gravedigger in his dirt-stained coveralls; it kind of put a crimp in the minister's glowing pictures of immortality and the pearly gates.

Near the back wall he paused and bent to examine a slate headstone that had fallen forward. He stood it up and again felt a small chill go through him as he brushed the dirt from the inscription:

HUBERT BARCLAY MARSTEN
October 6, 1889
August 12, 1939

The angel of Death who holdeth
The bronze Lamp beyond the golden door
Hath taken thee into dark Waters

And below that, almost obliterated by thirty-six seasons of freeze and thaw:

God Grant He Lie Still

Still vaguely troubled and still not knowing why, Mike Ryerson went back into the woods to sit by the brook and eat his lunch.

3

In the early days at the seminary, a friend of Father Callahan's had given him a blasphemous crewelwork sampler which had sent him into gales of horrified laughter at the time, but which seemed more true and less blasphemous as the years passed: *God grant me the SERENITY to accept what I cannot change, the TENACITY to change what I may, and the GOOD LUCK not to fuck up too often.* This in Old English script with a rising sun in the background.

Now, standing before Danny Glick's mourners, that old credo recurred.

The pallbearers, two uncles and two cousins of the dead boy, had lowered the coffin into the ground. Marjorie Glick, dressed in a black coat and a veiled black hat, her face showing through the mesh in the netting like cottage cheese, stood swaying in the protective curve of her father's arm, clutching a black purse as though it were a life preserver. Tony Glick stood apart from her, his face shocked and wandering. Several times during the church service he had looked around, as if to verify his presence among these people. His face was that of a man who believes he is dreaming.

The church can't stop this dream, Callahan thought. Nor all the serenity, tenacity, or good luck in the world. The fuck-up has already happened.

He sprinkled holy water on the coffin and the grave, sanctifying them for all time.

"Let us pray," he said. The words rolled melodiously from his throat as they always had, in shine and shadow, drunk or sober. The mourners bowed their heads.

"Lord God, through your mercy those who have lived in faith find eternal peace. Bless this grave and send your angel to watch over it. As we bury the body of Daniel Glick, welcome him into your presence, and with your saints let him rejoice in you forever. We ask it through Christ our Lord. Amen."

"Amen," the congregation muttered, and the wind swept it away in rags. Tony Glick was looking around with wide, haunted eyes. His wife was pressing a Kleenex to her mouth.

"With faith in Jesus Christ, we reverently bring the body of this child to be buried in its human imperfection. Let us pray with confidence to God, who gives life to all things, that he will raise up this mortal body to the perfection and company of saints."

He turned the pages of his missal. A woman in the third row of the loose horseshoe grouped around the grave had begun to sob hoarsely. A bird chirruped somewhere back in the woods.

"Let us pray for our brother Daniel Glick to our Lord Jesus Christ," Father Callahan said, "who told us: 'I am the resurrection and the life. The man who believes in me will live even though he dies, and every living person who puts his faith in me will never suffer eternal death.' Lord, you wept at the death of Lazarus, your friend: comfort us in our sorrow. We ask this in faith."

"Lord, hear our prayer," the Catholics answered.

"You raised the dead to life; give our brother Daniel eternal life. We ask this in faith."

"Lord, hear our prayer," they answered. Something seemed to be dawning in Tony Glick's eyes; a revelation, perhaps.

"Our brother Daniel was washed clean in baptism; give him fellowship with all your saints. We ask this in faith."

"Lord, hear our prayer."

"He was nourished with your body and blood; grant him a place at the table in your heavenly kingdom. We ask this in faith."

"Lord, hear our prayer."

Marjorie Glick had begun to rock back and forth, moaning.

"Comfort us in our sorrow at the death of our brother; let our faith be our consolation and eternal life our hope. We ask this in faith."

"Lord, hear our prayer."

He closed his missal. "Let us pray as our Lord taught us," he said quietly. "Our Father who art in heaven—"

"No!" Tony Glick screamed, and propelled himself forward. "You ain't gonna throw no dirt on my boy!"

Hands reached out to stay him, but they were belated. For a moment he tottered on the edge of the grave, and then the fake grass wrinkled and gave way. He fell into the hole and landed on the coffin with a horrid, heavy thump.

"Danny, you come outta there!" he bawled.

"Oh, *my*," Mabel Werts said, and pressed her black silk funeral hankie to her lips. Her eyes were bright and avid, storing this the way a squirrel stores nuts for the winter.

"Danny, goddammit, you stop this fucking around!"

Father Callahan nodded at two of the pallbearers and they stepped forward, but three other men, including Parkins Gillespie and Nolly Gardener, had to step in before Glick could be gotten out of the grave, kicking and screaming and howling.

"Danny, you stop it now! You got your Momma scared! I'm gonna whip your butt for you! Lemme go! Lemme go ... I want m'boy ... let me go, you pricks ... ahhh, *God*—"

"Our Father who art in heaven—" Callahan began again, and other voices joined him, lifting the words toward the indifferent shield of the sky.

"—hallowed be thy name. Thy kingdom come, thy will be done—"

"Danny, you come to me, hear? *You hear me?*"

"—on earth, as it is in heaven. Give us this day our daily bread and forgive us—"

"*Dannneeee—*"

"—our trespasses, as we forgive those who trespass against us—"

"He ain't dead, he ain't dead, let go a me you miserable shitpokes—"

"—and lead us not into temptation, but deliver us from evil. Through Christ our Lord, amen."

"He ain't dead," Tony Glick sobbed. "He can't be. He's only twelve fucking years old." He began to weep heavily and staggered forward in spite of the men who held him, his face ravaged and streaming with tears. He fell on his knees at Callahan's feet and grasped his trousers with muddy hands. "Please give me my boy back. Please don't fool me no more."

Callahan took his head gently with both hands. "Let us pray," he said. He could feel Glick's wracking sobs in his thighs.

"Lord, comfort this man and his wife in their sorrow. You cleansed this child in the waters of baptism and gave him new life. May we one day join him and share heaven's joys forever. We ask this in Jesus' name, amen."

He raised his head and saw that Marjorie Glick had fainted.

4

When they were all gone, Mike Ryerson came back and sat down on the edge of the open grave to eat his last half sandwich and wait for Royal Snow to come back.

The funeral had been at four, and it was now almost five o'clock. The shadows were long and the sun was already slanting through the tall western oaks. That frigging Royal had promised to be back by quarter of five at the latest; now where was he?

The sandwich was bologna and cheese, his favorite. All the sandwiches he made were his favorites; that was one of the advantages to being single. He finished up and dusted his hands, spraying a few bread crumbs down on the coffin.

Someone was watching him.

He felt it suddenly and surely. He stared around at the cemetery with wide, startled eyes.

"Royal? You there, Royal?"

No answer. The wind sighed through the trees, making them rustle mysteriously. In the waving shadows of the elms beyond the stone wall, he could see Hubert Marsten's marker, and suddenly he thought of Win's dog, hanging impaled on the iron front gate.

Eyes. Flat and emotionless. Watching.

Dark, don't catch me here.

He started to his feet as if someone had spoken aloud.

"Goddamn you, Royal." He spoke the words aloud, but quietly. He no longer thought Royal was around, or even coming back. He would have to do it by himself, and it would take a long time alone.

Maybe until dark.

He set to work, not trying to understand the dread that had fallen over him, not wondering why this job that had never bothered him before was bothering him terribly now.

Moving with quick, economical gestures, he pulled the strips of fake grass away from the raw earth and folded them neatly. He laid them over his arm and took them out to his truck, parked beyond the gate, and once out of the graveyard, that nasty feeling of being watched slipped away.

He put the grass in the back of the pickup and took out a spade. He started back, then hesitated. He stared at the open grave and it seemed to mock him.

It occurred to him that the feeling of being watched had stopped as soon as he could no longer see the coffin nestled at the bottom of its hole. He had a sudden mental image of Danny Glick lying on that little satin pillow with his eyes open. No—that was stupid. They closed the eyes. He had watched Carl Foreman do it enough times. *Course we gum 'em,* Carl had said once. *Wouldn't want the corpse winkin' at the congregation, would we?*

He loaded his shovel with dirt and threw it in. It made a heavy, solid thump on the polished mahogany box, and Mike winced. The sound made him feel a little sick. He straightened up and looked around distractedly at the floral displays. A damn waste. Tomorrow the petals would be scattered all over in red and yellow flakes. Why anybody bothered was beyond him. If you were going to spend money, why not give it to the Cancer Society or the March of Dimes or even the Ladies' Aid? Then it went to some good, at least.

He threw in another shovelful and rested again.

That coffin was another waste. Nice mahogany coffin, worth a thousand bucks at least, and here he was shoveling dirt over it. The Glicks didn't have no more money than anyone else, and who puts burial insurance on kids? They were probably six miles in hock, all for a box to shovel in the ground.

He bent down, got another spadeful of earth, and reluctantly threw it in. Again that horrid, final thump. The top of the coffin was sprayed with dirt now, but the polished mahogany gleamed through, almost reproachfully.

Stop looking at me.

He got another spadeful, not a very big one, and threw it in.

Thump.

The shadows were getting very long now. He paused, looked up, and there was the Marsten House, its shutters closed blankly. The east side, the one that bid good day to the light first, looked directly down on the iron gate of the cemetery, where Doc—

He forced himself to get another spadeful of earth and throw it into the hole.

Thump.

Some of it trickled off the sides, creasing into the brass hinges. Now if anyone opened it, there would be a gritting, grating noise like opening the door to a tomb.

Stop looking at me, goddammit.

He began to bend for another spadeful, but the thought seemed too heavy and he rested for a minute. He had read once—in the *National Enquirer* or someplace—about some Texas oilman dude who had specified in his will that he be buried in a brand-new Cadillac Coupe de Ville. They did it, too. Dug the hole with a payloader and lifted the car in with a crane. People all over the country driving around in old cars held together with spit and baling wire and one of these rich pigs gets himself buried sitting behind the wheel of a ten-thousand-dollar car with all the accessories—

He suddenly jerked and took a step backward, shaking his head warily. He had almost—well—had almost been in a trance, it seemed like. That feeling of being watched was much stronger now. He looked at the sky and was alarmed to see how much light had gone out of it. Only the top story of the Marsten House was in bright sunlight now. His watch said ten past six. Christ, it had been an hour and he hadn't thrown half a dozen shovelfuls of dirt down that hole!

Mike bent to his work, trying not to let himself think. *Thump* and *thump* and *thump* and now the sound of dirt striking wood was muffled; the top of the coffin was covered and dirt was running off the sides in brown rivulets, almost up to the lock and catch.

He threw in another two spadefuls and paused.

Lock and catch?

Now, why in the name of God would anyone put a lock into a coffin? Did they think someone was going to try to get in? That had to be it. Surely they couldn't think someone would be trying to get out—

"Stop *staring* at me," Mike Ryerson said aloud, and then felt his heart crawl up into his throat. A sudden urge to run from this place, to run straight down the road to town, filled him. He controlled it only with great effort. Just the heebie-jeebies, that's all it was. Working in a graveyard, who wouldn't get them once in a while? It was like a fucking horror movie, having to cover up that kid, only twelve years old and his eyes wide open—

"Christ, *stop it!*" he cried, and looked wildly up toward the Marsten House. Now only the roof was in sunshine. It was six-fifteen.

After that he began to work more quickly again, bending and shoveling and trying to keep his mind completely blank. But that sense of being watched seemed to grow rather than lessen, and each shovelful of dirt seemed heavier than the last. The top of the coffin was covered now but you could still see the shape, shrouded in earth.

The Catholic prayer for the dead began to run through his mind, the way things like that will for no good reason. He had heard Callahan saying it while he was eating his dinner down by the brook. That, and the father's helpless screaming.

Let us pray for our brother to our Lord Jesus Christ, who said . . .
(O my father, favor me now.)

He paused and looked blankly down into the grave. It was deep, very deep. The shadows of coming night had already pooled into it, like something viscid and alive. It was still deep. He would never be able to fill it by dark. Never.

I am the resurrection and the life. The man who believes in me will live even though he die . . .

(Lord of Flies, favor me now.)

Yes, the eyes were open. That's why he felt watched. Carl hadn't used enough gum on them and they had flown up just like window shades and the Glick kid was staring at him. Something ought to be done about it.

. . . and every living person who puts his faith in me will never suffer eternal death . . .

(Now I bring you spoiled meat and reeking flesh.)

Shovel out the dirt. That was the ticket. Shovel it out and break the lock with the shovel and open the coffin and close those awful staring eyes. He had no mortician's gum, but he had two quarters in his pocket. That would do as well. Silver. Yes, silver was what the boy needed.

The sun was above the roof of the Marsten House now, and only touched the highest and oldest spruces to the west of town. Even with the shutters closed the house seemed to stare at him.

You raised the dead to life; give our brother Daniel eternal life.

(I have made sacrifice for your favor. With my left hand I bring it.)

Mike Ryerson suddenly leaped into the grave and began to shovel madly, throwing dirt up and out in brown explosions. At last the blade of the shovel struck wood and he began to scrape the last of the dirt over the sides and then he was kneeling on the coffin striking at the brass lip of the lock again and again and again.

The frogs down by the brook had begun to thump, a nightjar was singing in the shadows, and somewhere close by a number of whippoorwills had begun to lift their shrilling call.

Six-fifty.

What am I doing? he asked himself. What in God's name am I doing?

He knelt there on top of the coffin and tried to think about it . . . but something on the underside of his mind was urging him to hurry, hurry, the sun was going down—

Dark, don't catch me here.

He lifted the spade over his shoulder, brought it down on the lock once more, and there was a snapping sound. It was broken.

He looked up for a moment, in a last glimmering of sanity, his face streaked and circled with dirt and sweat, the eyes staring from it in bulging white circles.

Venus glowed against the breast of the sky.

Panting, he pulled himself out of the grave, lay down full length, and fumbled for the catches on the coffin lid. He found them and pulled. The lid swung upward, gritting on its hinges just as he had imagined it would, showing at first only pink satin, and then one dark-clad arm (Danny Glick had been buried in his communion suit), then . . . then the face.

Mike's breath clogged and stopped in his throat.

The eyes were open. Just as he had known they would be. Wide open and hardly glazed at all. They seemed to sparkle with hideous life in the last, dying light of day. There was no death pallor in that face; the cheeks seemed rosy, almost juicy with vitality.

He tried to drag his eyes away from that glittering, frozen stare and was unable.

He muttered: "Jesus—"

The sun's diminishing arc passed below the horizon.

5

Mark Petrie was working on a model of Frankenstein's monster in his room and listening to his parents down in the living room. His room was on the second floor of the farmhouse they had bought on South Jointner Avenue, and although the house was heated by a modern oil furnace now, the old second-floor grates were still there. Originally, when the house had been heated by a central kitchen stove, the warm-air grates had kept the second floor from becoming too cold—although the woman who had originally lived in this house with her dour Baptist husband from 1873 to 1896 had still taken a hot brick wrapped in flannel to bed with her—but now the grates served another purpose. They conducted sound excellently.

Although his parents were down in the living room, they might as well have been discussing him right outside the door.

Once, when his father had caught him listening at the door in their old house—Mark had only been six then—his father had told him an old English proverb: Never listen at a knothole lest you be vexed. That meant, his father said, that you may hear something about yourself that you don't like.

Well, there was another one, too. Forewarned is forearmed.

At age twelve, Mark Petrie was a little smaller than the average and slightly delicate-looking. Yet he moved with a grace and litheness that is not the common lot of boys his age, who seem mostly made up of knees and elbows and scabs. His complexion was fair, almost milky, and his features, which would be considered aquiline later in life, now seemed a trifle feminine. It had caused him some trouble even before the Richie Boddin incident in the schoolyard, and he had determined to handle it himself. He had made an analysis of the problem. Most bullies, he had decided, were big and ugly and clumsy. They scared people by being able to hurt them. They fought dirty. Therefore, if you were not afraid of being hurt a little, and if you were willing to fight dirty, a bully might be bested. Richie Boddin had been the first full vindication of his theory. He and the bully at the Kittery Elementary School had come off even (which had been a victory of a kind; the Kittery bully, bloody but unbowed, had proclaimed to the schoolyard community at large that he and Mark Petrie were pals. Mark, who thought the Kittery bully was a dumb piece of shit, did not contradict him. He understood discretion.). Talk did no good with bullies. Hurting was the only language that the Richie Boddins of the world seemed to understand, and Mark supposed that was why the world always had such a hard time getting along. He had been sent from school that day, and his father had been very angry until Mark, resigned to his ritual whipping with a rolled-up magazine, told him that Hitler had just been a Richie Boddin at heart. That had made his father laugh like hell, and even his mother snickered. The whipping had been averted.

Now June Petrie was saying: "Do you think it's affected him, Henry?"

"Hard . . . to tell." And Mark knew by the pause that his father was lighting his pipe. "He's got a hell of a poker face."

"Still waters run deep, though." She paused. His mother was always saying things like still waters run deep or it's a long, long road that has no turning. He loved them both dearly, but sometimes they seemed just as ponderous as the books in the folio section of the library . . . and just as dusty.

"They were on their way to see Mark," she resumed. "To play with his train set . . . now one dead and one missing! Don't fool yourself, Henry. The boy feels something."

"He's got his feet pretty solidly planted on the ground," Mr. Petrie said. "Whatever his feelings are, I'm sure he's got them in hand."

Mark glued the Frankenstein monster's left arm into the shoulder socket. It was a specially treated Aurora model that glowed green in the dark, just like the plastic Jesus he had gotten for memorizing all of the 119th Psalm in Sunday school class in Kittery.

"I've sometimes thought we should have had another," his father was saying. "Among other things, it would have been good for Mark."

And his mother, in an arch tone: "Not for lack of trying, dear."

His father grunted.

There was a long pause in the conversation. His father, he knew, would be rattling through *The Wall Street Journal*. His mother would be holding a novel by Jane Austen on her lap, or perhaps Henry James. She read them over and over again, and Mark was darned if he could see the sense in reading a book more than once. You knew how it was going to end.

"D'you think it's safe to let him go in the woods behind the house?" his mother asked presently. "They say there's quicksand somewhere in town—"

"Miles from here."

Mark relaxed a little and glued the monster's other arm on. He had a whole table of Aurora horror monsters, arranged in a scene that he changed each time a new element was added. It was a pretty good set. Danny and Ralphie had really been coming to see that the night when . . . whatever.

"I think it's okay," his father said. "Not after dark, of course."

"Well, I hope that awful funeral won't give him nightmares."

Mark could almost see his father shrug. "Tony Glick . . .

unfortunate. But death and grief are part of living. Time he got used to the idea."

"Maybe." Another long pause. What was coming now? he wondered. The child is the father of the man, maybe. Or as the twig is bent the tree is shaped. Mark glued the monster onto his base, which was a grave mound with a leaning headstone in the background. "In the midst of life we're in death. But *I* may have nightmares."

"Oh?"

"That Mr. Foreman must be quite an artist, grisly as it sounds. He really looked as if he was just asleep. That any second he might open his eyes and yawn and . . . I don't know why these people insist on torturing themselves with open-coffin services. It's . . . heathenish."

"Well, it's over."

"Yes, I suppose. He's a good boy, isn't he, Henry?"

"Mark? The best."

Mark smiled.

"Is there anything on TV?"

"I'll look."

Mark turned the rest off; the serious discussion was done. He set his model on the window sill to dry and harden. In another fifteen minutes his mother would be calling up for him to get ready for bed. He took his pajamas out of the top dresser drawer and began to undress.

In point of fact, his mother was worrying needlessly about his psyche, which was not tender at all. There was no particular reason why it should have been; he was a typical boy in most ways, despite his economy and his gracefulness. His family was upper middle class and still upwardly mobile, and the marriage of his parents was sound. They loved each other firmly, if a little stodgily. There had never been any great trauma in Mark's life. The few school fights had not scarred him. He got along with his peers and in general wanted the same things they wanted.

If there was anything that set him apart, it was a reservoir of remoteness, of cool self-control. No one had inculcated it in him; he seemed to have been born with it. When his pet dog, Chopper, had been hit by a car, he had insisted on going with his mother to the vet's. And when the vet had said, The dog has got to be put to sleep, my boy. Do you understand why? Mark said, You're not going to put him to sleep. You're going to gas him to death, aren't you? The vet said yes. Mark told him to go ahead, but he had kissed Chopper first. He had felt sorry but he hadn't cried and tears had never been close to the surface. His mother had cried but three days later Chopper was in the dim past to her, and he would never be in the dim past for Mark. That was the value in not crying. Crying was like pissing everything out on the ground.

He had been shocked by the disappearance of Ralphie Glick, and shocked again by Danny's death, but he had not been frightened. He had heard one of the men in the store say that probably a sex pervert had gotten Ralphie. Mark knew what perverts were. They did something to you that got their rocks off and when they were done they strangled you (in the comic books, the guy getting strangled always said *Arrrgggh*) and buried you in a gravel pit or under the boards of a deserted shed. If a sex pervert ever offered him candy, he would kick him in the balls and then run like a split streak.

"Mark?" His mother's voice, drifting up the stairs.

"I am," he said, and smiled again.

"Don't forget your ears when you wash."

"I won't."

He went downstairs to kiss them good night, moving lithely and gracefully, sparing one glance backward to the table where his monsters rested in tableau: Dracula with his mouth open, showing his fangs, was menacing a girl lying on the ground while the Mad Doctor was torturing a lady on the rack and Mr. Hyde was creeping up on an old guy walking home.

Understand death? Sure. That was when the monsters got you.

6

Roy McDougall pulled into the driveway of his trailer at half past eight, gunned the engine of his old Ford twice, and turned the engine off. The header pipe was just about shot, the blinkers didn't work, and the sticker came up next month. Some car.

Some life. The kid was howling in the house and Sandy was screaming at him. Great old marriage.

He got out of the car and fell over one of the flagstones he had been meaning to turn into a walk from the driveway to the steps since last summer.

"Shitfire," he muttered, glowering balefully at the piece of flagging and rubbing his shin.

He was quite drunk. He had gotten off work at three and had been drinking down at Dell's ever since with Hank Peters and Buddy Mayberry. Hank had been flush just lately, and seemed intent on drinking up the whole of his dividend, whatever it had been. He knew what Sandy thought of his buddies. Well, let her get tight-assed. Begrudge a man a few beers on Saturday and Sunday even though he spent the whole week breaking his back on the goddamn picker—and getting weekend overtime to boot. Who was she to get so holy? She spent all day sitting in the house with nothing to do but take care of the place and shoot the shit with the mailman and see that the kid didn't crawl into the oven. She hadn't been watching him too close lately, anyway. Goddamn kid even fell off the changing table the other day.

Where were you?

I was holding him, Roy. He just wriggles so.

Wriggles. Yeah.

He went up to the door, still steaming. His leg hurt where he had bumped it. Not that he'd get any sympathy from *her*. So what was she doing while he was sweating his guts out for that prick of a foreman? Reading confession magazines and eating chocolate-covered cherries or watching the soap operas on the TV and eating chocolate-covered cherries or gabbing to her friends on the phone and eating chocolate-covered cherries. She was getting pimples on her ass as well as her face. Pretty soon you wouldn't be able to tell the two of them apart.

He pushed open the door and walked in.

The scene struck him immediately and forcibly, cutting through the beer haze like the flick of a wet towel: the baby, naked and screaming, blood running from his nose; Sandy holding him, her sleeveless blouse smeared with blood, looking at him over her shoulder, her face contracting with surprise and fear; the diaper on the floor.

Randy, with the discolored marks around his eyes barely fading, raised his hands as if in supplication.

"What's going on around here?" Roy asked slowly.

"Nothing, Roy. He just—"

"You hit him," he said tonelessly. "He wouldn't hold still for the diapers so you smacked him."

"No," she said quickly. "He rolled over and bumped his nose, that's all. That's all."

"I ought to beat the shit out of you," he said.

"Roy, he just bumped his *nose*—"

His shoulders slumped. "What's for dinner?"

"Hamburgs. They're burnt," she said petulantly, and pulled the bottom of her blouse out of her Wranglers to wipe under Randy's nose. Roy could see the roll of fat she was getting. She'd never bounced back after the baby. Didn't care.

"Shut him up."

"He isn't—"

"*Shut him up!*" Roy yelled, and Randy, who had actually been quieting down to snuffles, began to scream again.

"I'll give him a bottle," Sandy said, getting up.

"And get my dinner." He started to take off his denim jacket. "*Christ,* isn't this place a mess. What do you do all day, beat off?"

"*Roy!*" she said, sounding shocked. Then she giggled. Her insane burst of anger at the baby who would not hold still on his diapers so she could pin them began to be far away, hazy. It might have happened on one of her afternoon stories, or "Medical Center."

"Get my dinner and then pick this frigging place up."

"All right. All right, sure." She got a bottle out of the refrigerator and put Randy down in the playpen with it. He began to suck it apathetically, his eyes moving from mother to father in small, trapped circles.

"Roy?"

"Hmmm? What?"

"It's all over."

"What is?"

"You know what. Do you want to? Tonight?"

"Sure," he said. "Sure." And thought again: Isn't this some life. Isn't this just *some* life.

7

Nolly Gardener was listening to rock 'n' roll music on WLOB and snapping his fingers when the telephone rang. Parkins put down his crossword magazine and said, "Cut that some, will you?"

"Sure, Park." Nolly turned the radio down and went on snapping his fingers.

"Hello?" Parkins said.

"Constable Gillespie?"

"Yeah."

"Agent Tom Hanrahan here, sir. I've got the information you requested."

"Good of you to get back so quick."

"We haven't got much of a hook for you."

"That's okay," Parkins said. "What have you got?"

"Ben Mears investigated as a result of a traffic fatality in upstate New York, May 1973. No charges brought. Motorcycle smash. His wife Miranda was killed. Witnesses said he was moving slowly and a breath test was negative. Apparently just hit a wet spot. His politics are leftish. He was in a peace march at Princeton in 1966. Spoke at an antiwar rally in Brooklyn in 1967. March on Washington in 1968 and 1970. Arrested during a San Francisco peace march November 1971. And that's all there is on him."

"What else?"

"Kurt Barlow, that's Kurt with a 'k'. He's British, but by naturalization rather than birth. Born in Germany, fled to England in 1938, apparently just ahead of the Gestapo. His earlier records just aren't available, but he's probably in his seventies. The name he was born with was Breichen. He's been in the import-export business in London since 1945, but he's elusive. Straker has been his partner since then, and Straker seems to be the fellow who deals with the public."

"Yeah?"

"Straker is British by birth. Fifty-eight years old. His father was a cabinetmaker in Manchester. Left a fair amount of money to his son, apparently, and this Straker has done all right, too. Both of them applied for visas to spend an extended amount of time in the United States eighteen months ago. That's all we have. Except that they may be queer for each other."

"Yeah," Parkins said, and sighed. "About what I thought."

"If you'd like further assistance, we can query CID and Scotland Yard about your two new merchants."

"No, that's fine."

"No connection between Mears and the other two, by the way. Unless it's deep undercover."

"Okay. Thanks."

"It's what we're here for. If you want assistance, get in touch."

"I will. Thank you now."

He put the receiver back in its cradle and looked at it thoughtfully.

"Who was that, Park?" Nolly asked, turning up the radio.

"The Excellent Café. They ain't got any ham on rye. Nothin' but toasted cheese and egg salad."

"I got some raspberry fluff in my desk if you want it."

"No thanks," Parkins said, and sighed again.

8

The dump was still smoldering.

Dud Rogers walked along the edge, smelling the fragrance of smoldering offal. Underfoot, small bottles crunched and powdery black ash puffed up at every step. Out in the dump's wasteland, a wide bed of coals waxed and waned with the vagaries of the wind, reminding him of a huge red eye opening and closing . . . the eye of a giant. Every now and then there was a muffled small explosion as an aerosol can or light bulb blew up. A great many rats had come out of the dump when he lit it that morning, more rats than he had ever seen before. He had shot fully three dozen, and his pistol had been hot to the touch when he finally tucked it back in its holster. They were big bastards, too, some of them fully two feet long stretched end to end. Funny how their numbers seemed to grow or shrink depending on the year. Had something to do with the weather, probably. If it kept up, he would have to start salting poison bait around, something he hadn't had to do since 1964.

There was one now, creeping under one of the yellow saw-horses that served as fire barriers.

Dud pulled out his pistol, clicked off the safety, aimed, and fired. The shot kicked dirt in front of the rat, spraying its fur. But instead of running, it only rose up on its hind legs and looked at him, beady little eyes glittering red in the fire glow. Jesus, but some of them were bold!

"By-by, Mr. Rat," Dud said, and took careful aim.

Kapow. The rat flopped over, twitching.

Dud walked across and prodded it with one heavy work boot. The rat bit weakly at the shoe leather, its sides aspirating weakly.

"Bastard," Dud said mildly, and crushed its head.

He hunkered down, looked at it, and found himself think-ing of Ruthie Crockett, who wore no bra. When she wore one of those clingy cardigan sweaters, you could see her little nip-ples just as clear, made erect by the friction as they rubbed against the wool, and if a man could get ahold of those tits and rub them just a little, just a little, mind you, a slut like that would go off just like a rocket. . . .

He picked the rat up by its tail and swung it like a pendu-lum. "How'd you like ole Mr. Rat in your pencil box, Ruthie?" The thought with its unintentional double-entendre amused him, and he uttered a high-pitched giggle, his oddly off-center head nodding and dipping.

He slung the rat far out into the dump. As he did so, he swung around and caught sight of a figure—a tall, extremely thin silhouette about fifty paces to the right.

Dud wiped his hands on his green pants, hitched them up, and strolled over.

"Dump's closed, mister."

The man turned toward him. The face that was discovered in the red glow of the dying fire was high-cheekboned and thoughtful. The hair was white, streaked with oddly virile slashes of iron gray. The guy had it swept back from his high, waxy fore-head like one of those fag concert pianists. The eyes caught and held the red glow of the embers and made them look bloodshot.

"Is it?" the man asked politely, and there was a faint accent in the words, although they were perfectly spoken. The guy might be a frog, or maybe a bohunk. "I came to watch the fire. It is beautiful."

"Yeah," Dud said. "You from around here?"

"I am a recent resident of your lovely town, yes. Do you shoot many rats?"

"Quite a few, yeah. Just lately there's millions of the little sonsawhores. Say, you ain't the fella who bought the Marsten place, are you?"

"Predators," the man said, crossing his hands behind his back. Dud noticed with surprise that the guy was all tricked out in a suit, vest and all. "I love the predators of the night. The rats . . . the owls . . . the wolves. Are there wolves in this area?"

"Naw," Dud said. "Guy up in Durham bagged a coyote two years ago. And there's a wild-dog pack that's been runnin' deer—"

"Dogs," the stranger said, and gestured with contempt. "Low animals that cringe and howl at the sound of a strange step. Fit only to whine and grovel. Gut them all, I say. Gut them all!"

"Well, I never thought of it that way," Dud said, taking a shuffling step backward. "It's always nice to have someone come out and, you know, shoot the shit, but the dump closes at six on Sundays and it's happast nine now—"

"To be sure."

Yet the stranger showed no sign of moving away. Dud was thinking that he had stolen a march on the rest of the town. They were all wondering who was behind that Straker guy, and he was the first to know—except maybe for Larry Crockett, who was a deep one. The next time he was in town buying shells from that prissy-faced George Middler, he would just happen to say casually: Happened to meet that new fella the other night. Who? Oh, you know. Fella that took the Marsten House. Nice enough fella. Talked a little like a bohunk.

"Any ghosts up in that old house?" he asked, when the old party showed no signs of hauling ass.

"Ghosts!" The old party smiled, and there was something very disquieting about that smile. A barracuda might smile like that. "No; no ghosts." He placed a faint emphasis on that last word, as if there might be something up there that was even worse.

"Well . . . gettin' late and all . . . you really ought to go now, Mister—?"

"But it's so pleasant speaking with you," the old party said, and for the first time he turned his full face to Dud and looked in his eyes. The eyes were wide-set, and still rimmed with the dump's sullen fire. There was no way you could look away from them, although it wasn't polite to stare. "You don't mind if we converse a bit longer, do you?"

"No, I guess not," Dud said, and his voice sounded far away. Those eyes seemed to be expanding, growing, until they were like dark pits ringed with fire, pits you could fall into and drown in.

"Thank you," he said. "Tell me . . . does the hump on your back discommode you in your job?"

"No," Dud said, still feeling far away. He thought faintly: I be buggered if he ain't hypnotizin' me. Just like that fella at Topsham Fair . . . what was his name? Mr. Mephisto. He'd put you to sleep and make you do all kinds of comical things—act like a chicken or run around like a dog or tell what happened at the birthday party you had when you were six. He hypnotized ole Reggie Sawyer and Gawd didn't we laugh. . . .

"Does it perhaps inconvenience you in other ways?"

"No . . . well . . ." He looked into the eyes, fascinated.

"Come, come," the old party's voice cajoled gently. "We are friends, are we not? Speak to me, tell me."

"Well . . . girls . . . you know, girls . . ."

"Of course," the old party said soothingly. "The girls laugh at you, do they not? They have no knowing of your manhood. Of your strength."

"That's right" Dud whispered. "They laugh. *She* laughs."

"Who is this she?"

"Ruthie Crockett. She . . . she . . ." The thought flew away. He let it. It didn't matter. Nothing mattered except this peace. This cool and complete peace.

"She makes the jokes perhaps? Snickers behind her hand? Nudges her friends when you pass?"

"Yes . . ."

"But you want her," the voice insisted. "Is it not so?"

"Oh yes . . ."

"You shall have her. I am sure of it."

There was something . . . pleasant about this. Far away he seemed to hear sweet voices singing foul words. Silver chimes . . . white faces . . . Ruthie Crockett's voice. He could almost see her, hands cupping her titties, making them bulge into the V of her cardigan sweater in ripe white half-globes, whispering: *Kiss them, Dud . . . bite them . . . suck them. . . .*

It was like drowning. Drowning in the old man's red-rimmed eyes.

As the stranger came closer, Dud understood everything and welcomed it, and when the pain came, it was as sweet as silver, as green as still water at dark fathoms.

9

His hand was unsteady and instead of gripping the bottle the fingers knocked it off the desk and to the carpet with a heavy thump, where it lay gurgling good scotch into the green nap.

"Shit!" said Father Donald Callahan, and reached down to pick it up before all was lost. There was, in fact, not much to lose. He set what was left on the desk again (well back from the edge) and wandered into the kitchen to look for a rag under the sink and a bottle of cleaning fluid. It would never do to let Mrs. Curless find a patch of spilled scotch by the leg of his study desk. Her kind, pitying looks were too hard to take on the long, grainy mornings when you were feeling a little low—

Hung over, you mean.

Yes, hung over, very good. Let's have a little truth around here, by all means. Know the truth and it will set you free. Bully for the truth.

He found a bottle of something called E-Vap, which was not too far from the sound of violent regurgitation ("E-Vap!" croaked the old drunk, simultaneously crapping himself and blowing lunch), and took it back to the study. He was not weaving at all. Hardly at all. Watch this, Ossifer, I'm going to walk right up this white line to the stop light.

Callahan was an imposing fifty-three. His hair was silvery, his eyes a direct blue (now threaded with tiny snaps of red) surrounded by Irish laugh wrinkles, his mouth firm, his slightly cleft chin firmer still. Some mornings, looking at himself in the mirror, he thought that when he reached sixty he would throw over the priesthood, go to Hollywood, and get a job playing Spencer Tracy.

"Father Flanagan, where are you when we need you?" he muttered, and hunkered down by the stain. He squinted, read the instructions on the label of the bottle, and poured two capfuls of E-Vap onto the stain. The patch immediately turned white and began to bubble. Callahan viewed this with some alarm, and consulted the label again.

"For really tough stains," he read aloud in the rich, rolling voice that had made him so welcome in this parish after the long, denture-clicking peregrinations of poor old Father Hume, "allow to set for seven to ten minutes."

He went over to the study window, which fronted on Elm Street and St. Andrew's on the far side.

Well, well, he thought. Here I am, Sunday night and drunk again.

Bless me, Father, for I have sinned.

If you went slow and if you continued to work (on his long, solitary evenings, Father Callahan worked on his Notes. He had been working on the Notes for nearly seven years, supposedly for a book on the Catholic Church in New England, but he suspected now and then that the book would never be written. In point of fact, the Notes and his drinking problem had begun at the same time. Genesis 1:1—"In the beginning there was scotch, and Father Callahan said, Let there be Notes."), you were hardly aware of the slow growth of drunkenness. You could educate your hand not to be aware of the bottle's lessening weight.

It has been at least one day since my last confession.

It was eleven-thirty, and looking out the window he saw uniform darkness, broken only by the spotlight circle of the streetlight in front of the church. At any moment Fred Astaire would dance into it, wearing a top hat, tails, spats, and white shoes, twirling a cane. He is met by Ginger Rogers. They waltz to the tune of "I Got Dem Ol' Kozmic E-Vap Blues Again."

He leaned his forehead against the glass, allowing the handsome face that had been, in some measure at least, his curse sag into drawn lines of distracted weariness.

I'm a drunk and I'm a lousy priest, Father.

With his eyes closed he could see the darkness of the confessional booth, could feel his fingers sliding back the window and rolling up the shade on all the secrets of the human heart, could smell varnish and old velvet from the kneeling benches and the sweat of old men; could taste alkali traces in his saliva.

Bless me, Father,

(I broke my brother's wagon, I hit my wife, I peeked in Mrs. Sawyer's window when she was undressing, I lied, I cheated, I have had lustful thoughts, I, I, I)

for I have sinned.

He opened his eyes and Fred Astaire had not appeared yet. On the stroke of midnight, perhaps. His town was asleep. Except—

He glanced up. Yes, the lights were on up *there.*

He thought of the Bowie girl—no, McDougall, her name was McDougall now—saying in her breathy little voice that she had hit her baby and when he asked how often, he could sense (could almost hear) the wheels turning in her mind, making a dozen times five, or a hundred a dozen. Sad excuse for a human being. He had baptized the baby. Randall Fratus McDougall. Conceived in the back seat of Royce McDougall's car, probably during the second feature of a drive-in double bill. Tiny screaming little thing. He wondered if she knew or guessed that he would like to reach through the little window with both hands and grasp the soul on the other side as it fluttered and twisted and squeeze it until it screamed. Your penance is six head-knocks and a good swift kick in the ass. Go your way and sin no more.

"Dull," he said.

But there was more than dullness in the confessional; it was not that by itself that had sickened him or propelled him toward that always widening club, Associated Catholic Priests of the Bottle and Knights of the Cutty Sark. It was the steady, dead, onrushing engine of the church, bearing down all petty sins on its endless shuttle to heaven. It was the ritualistic acknowledgment of evil by a church now more concerned with social evils; atonement told in beads for elderly ladies whose parents had spoken European tongues. It was the actual presence of evil in the confessional, as real as the smell of old velvet.

But it was a mindless, moronic evil from which there was no mercy or reprieve. The fist crashing into the baby's face, the tire cut open with a jackknife, the barroom brawl, the insertion of razor blades into Halloween apples, the constant, vapid qualifiers which the human mind, in all its labyrinthine twists and turns, is able to spew forth. Gentlemen, better prisons will cure this. Better cops. Better social services agencies. Better birth control. Better sterilization techniques. Better abortions. Gentlemen, if we rip this fetus from the womb in a bloody tangle of unformed arms and legs, it will never grow up to beat an old lady to death with a hammer. Ladies, if we strap this man into a specially wired chair and fry him like a pork chop in a microwave oven, he will never have an opportunity to torture any more boys to death. Countrymen, if this eugenics bill is passed, I can guarantee you that never again—

Shit.

The truth of his condition had been becoming clearer and clearer to him for some time now, perhaps for as long as three years. It had gained clarity and resolution like an out-of-focus motion picture being adjusted until every line is sharp and defined. He had been pining for a Challenge. The new priests had theirs: racial discrimination, women's liberation, even gay liberation; poverty, insanity, illegality. They made him uncomfortable. The only socially conscious priests he felt at ease with were the ones who had been militantly opposed to the war in Vietnam. Now that their cause had become obsolete, they sat around and discussed marches and rallies the way old married couples discuss their honeymoons or their first train rides. But Callahan was neither a new priest nor an old one; he found himself cast in the role of a traditionalist who can no longer even trust his basic postulates. He wanted to lead a division in the army of—who? God, right, goodness, they were names for the same thing—into battle against EVIL. He wanted issues and battle lines and never mind standing in the cold outside supermarkets handing out leaflets about the lettuce boycott or the grape strike. He wanted to see EVIL with its cerements of deception cast aside, with every feature of its visage clear. He wanted to slug it out toe to toe with EVIL, like Muhammad Ali against Joe Frazier, the Celtics against the Knicks, Jacob against the Angel. He wanted this struggle to be pure, unhindered by

the politics that rode the back of every social issue like a de-
formed Siamese twin. He had wanted all this since he had
wanted to be a priest, and that call had come to him at the age
of fourteen, when he had been inflamed by the story of St.
Stephen, the first Christian martyr, who had been stoned to
death and who had seen Christ at the moment of his death.
Heaven was a dim attraction compared to that of fighting—and
perhaps perishing—in the service of the Lord.

But there were no battles. There were only skirmishes of
vague resolution. And EVIL did not wear one face but many,
and all of them were vacuous and more often than not the chin
was slicked with drool. In fact, he was being forced to the
conclusion that there was no EVIL in the world at all but only
evil—or perhaps (evil). At moments like this he suspected that
Hitler had been nothing but a harried bureaucrat and Satan
himself a mental defective with a rudimentary sense of humor—
the kind that finds feeding firecrackers wrapped in bread to
seagulls unutterably funny.

The great social, moral, and spiritual battles of the ages
boiled down to Sandy McDougall slamming her snot-nosed kid
in the corner and the kid would grow up and slam his own kid
in the corner, world without end, hallelujah, chunky peanut
butter. Hail Mary, full of grace, help me win this stock-car race.

It was more than dull. It was terrifying in its consequences
for any meaningful definition of life, and perhaps of heaven.
What there? An eternity of church bingo, amusement park
rides, and celestial drag strips?

He looked over at the clock on the wall. It was six minutes
past midnight and still no sign of Fred Astaire or Ginger Rogers. Not even Mickey Rooney. But the E-Vap had had time to
set. Now he would vacuum it up and Mrs. Curless would not
look at him with that expression of pity, and life would go on.
Amen.

Chapter Seven
MATT

At the end of period three on Tuesday, Matt walked up to the office and Ben Mears was there waiting for him.

"Hi," Matt said. "You're early."

Ben stood up and shook hands. "Family curse, I guess. Say, these kids aren't going to eat me, are they?"

"Positive," Matt said. "Come on."

He was a little surprised. Ben had dressed in a nice-looking sport coat and a pair of gray double-knit slacks. Good shoes that looked as if they hadn't been worn much. Matt had had other literary types into his classes and they were usually dressed in casual clothes or something downright weird. A year ago he had asked a rather well known female poet who had done a reading at the University of Maine at Portland if she would come in the following day and talk to a class about poetry. She had shown up in pedal pushers and high heels. It seemed to be a subconscious way of saying: Look at me, I've beaten the system at its own game. I come and go like the wind.

His admiration for Ben went up a notch in comparison. After thirty-plus years of teaching, he believed that nobody beat the system or won the game, and only suckers ever thought they were ahead.

"It's a nice building," Ben said, looking around as they walked down the hall. "Helluva lot different from where I went to high school. Most of the windows in that place looked like loopholes."

"First mistake," Matt said. "You must never call it a building. It's a 'plant.' Blackboards are 'visual aids.' And the kids are a 'homogenous mid-teen coeducational student body.' "

"How wonderful for them," Ben said, grinning.

"It is, isn't it? Did you go to college, Ben?"

"I tried. Liberal arts. But everybody seemed to be playing an intellectual game of capture-the-flag—you too can find an ax and grind it, thus becoming known and loved. Also, I flunked out. When *Conway's Daughter* sold, I was bucking cases of Coca-Cola onto delivery trucks."

"Tell the kids that. They'll be interested."

"You like teaching?" Ben said.

"Sure I like it. It would have been a busted-axle forty years if I didn't."

The late bell rang, echoing loudly in the corridor, which was empty now except for one loitering student who was wandering slowly past a painted arrow under a sign which read "Wood Shop."

"How's drugs here?" Ben asked.

"All kinds. Like every school in America. Ours is booze more than anything else."

"Not marijuana?"

"I don't consider pot a problem and neither does the administration, when it speaks off the record with a few knocks of Jim Beam under its belt. I happen to know that our guidance counselor, who is one of the best in his line, isn't averse to toking up and going to a movie. I've tried it myself. The effect is fine, but it gives me acid indigestion."

"*You* have?"

"Shhh," Matt said. "Big Brother is listening everywhere. Besides, this is my room."

"Oh boy."

"Don't be nervous," Matt said, and led him in. "Good morning, folks," he said to the twenty or so students, who were eying Ben closely. "This is Mr. Ben Mears."

2

At first Ben thought he had the wrong house.

When Matt Burke invited him for supper he was quite sure he had said the house was the small gray one after the red brick, but there was rock 'n' roll music pouring from this one in a steady stream.

He used the tarnished brass knocker, got no answer, and rapped again. This time the music was turned down and a voice that was unmistakably Matt's yelled, "It's open! Come on in!"

He did, looking around curiously. The front door opened directly on a small living room furnished in Early American Junk Shop and dominated by an incredibly ancient Motorola TV. A KLH sound system with quad speakers was putting out the music.

Matt came out of the kitchen, outfitted in a red-and-white-checked apron. The odor of spaghetti sauce wandered out after him.

"Sorry about the noise," Matt said. "I'm a little deaf. I turn it up."

"Good music."

"I've been a rock fan ever since Buddy Holly. Lovely music. Are you hungry?"

"Yeah," Ben said. "Thanks again for asking me. I've eaten out more since I came back to 'salem's Lot than I have in the last five years, I guess."

"It's a friendly town. Hope you don't mind eating in the kitchen. An antique man came by a couple of months ago and offered me two hundred dollars for my dining room table. I haven't gotten around to getting another one."

"I don't mind. I'm a kitchen eater from a long line of kitchen eaters."

The kitchen was astringently neat. On the small four-burner stove, a pot of spaghetti sauce simmered and a colander full of spaghetti stood steaming. A small drop-leaf table was set with a couple of mismatched plates and glasses which had animated cartoon figures dancing around the rims—jelly glasses, Ben thought with amusement. The last constraint of being with a stranger dropped away and he began to feel at home.

"There's bourbon, rye, and vodka in the cupboard over the sink," Matt said, pointing. "There's some mixers in the fridge. Nothing too fancy, I'm afraid."

"Bourbon and tap water will do me."

"Go to it. I'm going to serve this mess up."

Mixing his drink, Ben said, "I liked your kids. They asked good questions. Tough, but good."

"Like where do you get your ideas?" Matt asked, mimicking Ruthie Crockett's sexy little-girl lisp.

"She's quite a piece."

"She is indeed. There's a bottle of Lancers in the icebox behind the pineapple chunks. I got it special."

"Say, you shouldn't—"

"Oh come, Ben. We hardly see best-selling authors in the Lot every day."

"That's a little extravagant."

Ben finished the rest of his drink, took a plate of spaghetti from Matt, ladled sauce over it, and twirled a forkful against his spoon. "Fantastic," he said. "Mamma mia."

"But of course," Matt said.

Ben looked down at his plate, which had emptied with amazing rapidity. He wiped his mouth a little guiltily.

"More?"

"Half a plate, if it's okay. It's great spaghetti."

Matt brought him a whole plate. "If we don't eat it, my cat will. He's a miserable animal. Weighs twenty pounds and waddles to his dish."

"Lord, how did I miss him?"

Matt smiled. "He's cruising. Is your new book a novel?"

"A fictionalized sort of thing," Ben said. "To be honest, I'm writing it for money. Art is wonderful, but just once I'd like to pull a big number out of the hat."

"What are the prospects?"

"Murky," Ben said.

"Let's go in the living room," Matt said. "The chairs are lumpy but more comfortable than these kitchen horrors. Did you get enough to eat?"

"Does the Pope wear a tall hat?"

In the living room Matt put on a stack of albums and went to work firing up a huge, knotted calabash pipe. After he had it going to his satisfaction (sitting in the middle of a huge raft of smoke), he looked up at Ben.

"No," he said. "You can't see it from here."

Ben looked around sharply. "What?"

"The Marsten House. I'll bet you a nickel that's what you were looking for."

Ben laughed uneasily. "No bet."

"Is your book set in a town like 'salem's Lot?"

"Town and people," Ben nodded. "There are a series of sex murders and mutilations. I'm going to open with one of them and describe it in progress, from start to finish, in minute detail. Rub the reader's nose in it. I was outlining that part when Ralphie Glick disappeared and it gave me . . . well, it gave me a nasty turn."

"You're basing all of this on the disappearances of the thirties in the township?"

Ben looked at him closely. "You know about that?"

"Oh yes. A good many of the older residents do, too. I wasn't in the Lot then, but Mabel Werts and Glynis Mayberry and Milt Crossen were. Some of them have made the connection already."

"What connection?"

"Come now, Ben. The connection is pretty obvious, isn't it?"

"I suppose so. The last time the house was occupied, four kids disappeared over a period of ten years. Now it's occupied again after a thirty-six-year period, and Ralphie Glick disappears right off the bat."

"Do you think it's a coincidence?"

"I suppose so," Ben said cautiously. Susan's words of caution were very much in his ears. "But it's funny. I checked through the copies of the *Ledger* from 1939 to 1970 just to get a comparison. Three kids disappeared. One ran off and was later found working in Boston—he was sixteen and looked older. Another one was fished out of the Androscoggin a month later. And one was found buried off Route 116 in Gates, apparently the victim of a hit-and-run. All explained."

"Perhaps the Glick boy's disappearance will be explained, too."

"Maybe."

"But you don't think so. What do you know about this man Straker?"

"Nothing at all," Ben said. "I'm not even sure I want to meet him. I've got a viable book working right now, and it's bound up in a certain concept of the Marsten House and inhabitants of that house. Discovering Straker to be a perfectly ordinary businessman, as I'm sure he is, might knock me off kilter."

"I don't think that would be the case. He opened the store today, you know. Susie Norton and her mother dropped by, I understand . . . hell, most of the women in town got in long enough to get a peek. According to Dell Markey, an unimpeachable source, even Mabel Werts hobbled down. The man is supposed to be quite striking. A dandy dresser, extremely graceful, totally bald. And charming. I'm told he actually sold some pieces."

Ben grinned. "Wonderful. Has anyone seen the other half of the team?"

"He's on a buying trip, supposedly."

"Why supposedly?"

Matt shrugged restlessly. "I don't know. The whole thing is probably perfectly on the level, but the house makes me nervous. Almost as if the two of them had sought it out. As you said, it's like an idol, squatting there on top of its hill."

Ben nodded.

"And on top of everything else, we have another child disappearance. And Ralphie's brother, Danny. Dead at twelve. Cause of death pernicious anemia."

"What's odd about that? It's unfortunate, of course—"

"My doctor is a young fellow named Jimmy Cody, Ben. I had him in school. He was a little heller then, a good doctor now. This is gossip, mind you. Hearsay."

"Okay."

"I was in for a check-up, and happened to mention that it was a shame about the Glick boy, dreadful for his parents on top of the other one's vanishing act. Jimmy said he had consulted with George Gorby on the case. The boy was anemic, all right. He said that a red cell count on a boy Danny's age should run anywere from eighty-five to ninety-eight per cent. Danny's was down to forty-five per cent."

"Wow," Ben said.

"They were giving him B$_{12}$ injections and calf liver and it seemed to be working fine. They were going to release him the next day. And boom, he dropped dead."

"You don't want to let Mabel Werts get that," Ben said. "She'll be seeing natives with poison blowguns in the park."

"I haven't mentioned it to anyone but you. And I don't intend to. And by the way, Ben, I believe I'd keep the subject matter of your book quiet, if I were you. If Loretta Starcher asks what you're writing about, tell her it's architecture."

"I've already been given that advice."

"By Susan Norton, no doubt."

Ben looked at his watch and stood up. "Speaking of Susan—"

"The courting male in full plumage," Matt said. "As it happens, I have to go up to the school. We are reblocking the third act of the school play, a comedy of great social significance called *Charley's Problem.*"

"What is his problem?"

"Pimples," Matt said, and grinned.

They walked to the door together, Matt pausing to pull on a faded school letter jacket. Ben thought he had the figure of an aging track coach rather than that of a sedentary English teacher—if you ignored his face, which was intelligent yet dreamy, and somehow innocent.

"Listen," Matt said as they went out onto the stoop, "what have you got on the stove for Friday night?"

"I don't know," Ben said. "I thought Susan and I might go to a movie. That's about the long and short of it around here."

"I can think of something else," Matt said. "Perhaps we should form a committee of three and take a drive up to the Marsten House and introduce ourselves to the new squire. On behalf of the town, of course."

"Of course," Ben said. "It would be only common courtesy, wouldn't it?"

"A rustic welcome wagon," Matt agreed.

"I'll mention it to Susan tonight. I think she'll go for it."

"Good."

Matt raised his hand and waved as Ben's Citroën purred away. Ben tooted twice in acknowledgment, and then his tail-lights disappeared over the hill.

Matt stood on his stoop for almost a full minute after the sound of the car had died away, his hands poked into his jacket pockets, his eyes turned toward the house on the hill.

3

There was no play practice Thursday night, and Matt drove over to Dell's around nine o'clock for two or three beers. If that damn snip Jimmy Cody wouldn't prescribe for his insomnia, he would prescribe for himself.

Dell's was sparsely populated on nights when no band played. Matt saw only three people he knew: Weasel Craig, nursing a beer along in the corner; Floyd Tibbits, with thunderclouds on his brow (he had spoken to Susan three times this week, twice on the phone and once in person, in the Norton living room, and none of the conversations had gone well); and Mike Ryerson, who was sitting in one of the far booths against the wall.

Matt walked over to the bar, where Dell Markey was polishing glasses and watching "Ironside" on a portable TV.

"Hi, Matt. How's it going?"

"Fair. Slow night."

Dell shrugged. "Yeah. They got a couple of motorcycle pictures over to the drive-in in Gates. I can't compete with that. Glass or pitcher?"

"Make it a pitcher."

Dell drew it, cut the foam off, and added another two inches. Matt paid, and after a moment's hesitation, walked over to Mike's booth. Mike had filtered through one of Matt's English classes, like almost all the young people in the Lot, and Matt had enjoyed him. He had done above-average work with an average intelligence because he worked hard and had asked over and over about things he didn't understand until he got them. In addition to that, he had a clear, free-running sense of humor and a pleasant streak of individualism that made him a class favorite.

"Hi, Mike," he said. "Mind if I join you?"

Mike Ryerson looked up and Matt felt shock hit him like a live wire. His first reaction: *Drugs. Heavy drugs.*

"Sure, Mr. Burke. Sit down." His voice was listless. His complexion was a horrid, pasty white, darkening to deep shadows under his eyes. The eyes themselves seemed overlarge and hectic. His hands moved slowly across the table in the tavern's semigloom like ghosts. A glass of beer stood untouched before him.

"How are you doing, Mike?" Matt poured himself a glass of beer, controlling his hands, which wanted to shake.

His life had always been one of sweet evenness, a graph with modulate highs and lows (and even those had sunk to foothills since the death of his mother thirteen years before), and one of the things that disturbed it was the miserable ends some of his students came to. Billy Royko dying in a Vietnam helicopter crash two months before the cease-fire; Sally Greer, one of the brightest and most vivacious girls he had ever had, killed by her drunken boy friend when she told him she wanted to break up; Gary Coleman, who had gone blind due to some mysterious optic nerve degeneration; Buddy Mayberry's brother Doug, the only good kid in that whole half-bright clan, drowning at Old Orchard Beach; and drugs, the little death. Not all of them who waded into the waters of Lethe found it necessary to take a bath in it, but there were enough—kids who had made dreams their protein.

"Doing?" Mike said slowly. "I don't know, Mr. Burke. Not so good."

"What kind of shit are you on, Mike?" Matt asked gently.

Mike looked at him uncomprehendingly.

"Dope," Matt said. "Bennies? Reds? Coke? Or is it—"

"I'm not on dope," Mike said. "I guess I'm sick."

"Is that the truth?"

"I never did no heavy dope in my life," Mike said, and the words seemed to be costing him a dreadful effort. "Just grass, and I ain't had any of that for four months. I'm sick . . . been sick since Monday, I think it was. I fell asleep out at Harmony Hill Sunday night, see. Never even woke up until Monday morning." He shook his head slowly. "I felt crappy. I've felt crappy ever since. Worse every day, it seems like." He sighed, and the whistle of air seemed to shake his frame like a dead leaf on a November maple.

Matt leaned forward, concerned. "This happened after Danny Glick's funeral?"

"Yeah." Mike looked at him again. "I came back to finish up after everybody went home but that fucking—excuse me, Mr. Burke—that Royal Snow never showed up. I waited for him a long time, and that's when I must have started to get sick, because everything after that is . . . oh, it hurts my head. It's hard to think."

"What do you remember, Mike?"

"Remember?" Mike looked into the golden depths of his beer glass and watched the bubbles detaching themselves from the sides and floating to the surface to release their gas.

"I remember singing," he said. "The sweetest singing I ever heard. And a feeling like . . . like drowning. Only it was nice. Except for the eyes. The *eyes.*"

He clutched his elbows and shuddered.

"Whose eyes?" Matt asked, leaning forward.

"They were red. Oh, scary eyes."

"Whose?"

"I don't remember. No eyes. I dreamed it all." He pushed it away from himself. Matt could almost see him do it. "I don't remember anything else about Sunday night. I woke up Monday morning on the ground, and at first I couldn't even get up I was so tired. But I finally did. The sun was coming up and I was afraid I'd get a sunburn. So I went down in the woods by the brook. Tired me out. Oh, awful tired. So I went back to sleep. Slept till . . . oh, four or five o'clock." He offered a papery little chuckle. "I was all covered with leaves when I woke up. I felt a little better, though. I got up and went back to my truck." He passed a slow hand over his face. "I must have finished up with the little Glick boy Sunday night, though. Funny. I don't even remember."

"Finished up?"

"Grave was all filled in, Royal or no Royal. Sods tamped in and all. A good job. Don't remember doing it. Must have been really sick."

"Where did you spend Monday night?"

"At my place. Where else?"

"How did you feel Tuesday morning?"

"I never woke up Tuesday morning. Slept through the whole day. Never woke up until Tuesday night."

"How did you feel then?"

"Terrible. Legs like rubber. I tried to go get a drink of water and almost fell down. I had to go into the kitchen holding on to things. Weak as a kitten." He frowned. "I had a can of stew for my dinner—you know, that Dinty Moore stuff—but I couldn't eat it. Seemed like just looking at it made me feel sick to my stomach. Like when you've got an awful hangover and someone shows you food."

"You didn't eat anything?"

"I tried, but I threw it up. But I felt a little better. I went out and walked around for a while. Then I went back to bed." His fingers traced old beer rings on the table. "I got scared before I went to bed. Just like a little kid afraid of the Allamagoosalum. I went around and made sure all the windows were locked. And I went to sleep with all the lights on."

"And yesterday morning?"

"Hmmm? No . . . never got up until nine o'clock last night." He offered the papery little chuckle again. "I remember think-ing if it kept up I'd be sleeping the clock right around. And that's what you do when you're dead."

Matt regarded him somberly. Floyd Tibbits got up and put a quarter in the juke and began to punch up songs.

"Funny," Mike said. "My bedroom window was open when I got up. I must have done it myself. I had a dream . . . someone was at the window and I got up . . . got up to let him in. Like you'd get up to let in an old friend who was cold or . . . or hungry."

"Who was it?"

"It was just a dream, Mr. Burke."

"But in the dream who was it?"

"I don't know. I was going to try and eat, but the thought of it made me want to puke."

"What did you do?"

"I watched TV until Johnny Carson went off. I felt a lot better. Then I went to bed."

"Did you lock the windows?"

"No."

"And slept all day?"

"I woke up around sundown."

"Weak?"

"I hope to tell." He passed a hand over his face. "I feel so low!" he cried out in a breaking voice. "It's just the flu or something, isn't it, Mr. Burke? I'm not really sick, am I?"

"I don't know," Matt said.

"I thought a few beers would cheer me up, but I can't drink it. I took one sip and it like to gag me. The last week . . . it all seems like a bad dream. And I'm scared. I'm awful scared." He put his thin hands to his face and Matt saw that he was crying.

"Mike?"

No response.

"Mike." Gently, he pulled Mike's hands away from his face. "I want you to come home with me tonight. I want you to sleep in my guest room. Will you do that?"

"All right. I don't care." He wiped his sleeve across his eyes with lethargic slowness.

"And tomorrow I want you to come see Dr. Cody with me."

"All right."

"Come on. Let's go."

He thought of calling Ben Mears and didn't.

4

When Matt knocked on the door, Mike Ryerson said, "Come in."

Matt came in with a pair of pajamas. "These are going to be a little big—"

"That's all right, Mr. Burke. I sleep in my skivvies."

He was standing in his shorts now, and Matt saw that his entire body was horribly pale. His ribs stood out in circular ridges.

"Turn your head, Mike. This way."

Mike turned his head obediently.

"Mike, where did you get those marks?"

Mike's hand touched his throat below the angle of the jaw. "I don't know."

Matt stood restively. Then he went to the window. The catch was securely fastened, yet he rattled it back and forth with hands that were distraught. Beyond, the dark pressed against the glass heavily. "Call me in the night if you want anything. *Anything*. Even if you have a bad dream. Will you do that, Mike?"

"Yes."

"I mean it. *Anything*. I'm right down the hall."

"I will."

Hesitating, feeling there were other things he should do, he went out.

5

He didn't sleep at all, and the only thing now that kept him from calling Ben Mears was knowing that everyone at Eva's would be in bed. The boardinghouse was filled with old men, and when the phone rang late at night, it meant that someone had died.

He lay restively, watching the luminous hands of his alarm clock move from eleven-thirty to twelve. The house was preternaturally silent—perhaps because his ears were consciously attuned to catch the slightest noise. The house was an old one and built solidly, and its settling groans had mostly ceased long before. There were no sounds but the clock and the faint passage of the wind outside. No cars passed on Taggart Stream Road late on week nights.

What you're thinking is madness.

But step by step he had been forced backward toward belief. Of course, being a literary man, it had been the first thing that had come to mind when Jimmy Cody had thumbnailed Danny Glick's case. He and Cody had laughed over it. Maybe this was his punishment for laughing.

Scratches? Those marks weren't scratches. They were punctures.

One was taught that such things could not be; that things like Coleridge's "Cristabel" or Bram Stoker's evil fairy tale were only the warp and woof of fantasy. Of course monsters existed; they were the men with their fingers on the thermonuclear triggers in six countries, the hijackers, the mass murderers, the child molesters. But not this. One knows better. The mark of the devil on a woman's breast is only a mole, the man who came back from the dead and stood at his wife's door dressed in the cerements of the grave was only suffering from locomotor ataxia, the bogeyman who gibbers and capers in the corner of a child's bedroom is only a heap of blankets. Some clergymen had proclaimed that even God, that venerable white warlock, was dead.

He was bled almost white.

No sound from up the hall. Matt thought: He is sleeping like the stones himself. Well, why not? Why had he invited Mike back to the house, if not for a good night's sleep, uninterrupted by . . . by bad dreams? He got out of bed and turned on the lamp and went to the window. From here one could just see the roof tree of the Marsten House, frosted in moonlight.

I'm frightened.

But it was worse than that; he was dead scared. His mind ran over the old protections for an unmentionable disease: garlic, holy wafer and water, crucifix, rose, running water. He had none of the holy things. He was a nonpracticing Methodist, and privately thought that John Groggins was the asshole of the Western world.

The only religious object in the house was—

Softly yet clearly in the silent house the words came, spoken in Mike Ryerson's voice, spoken in the dead accents of sleep:

"Yes. Come in."

Matt's breath stopped, then whistled out in a soundless scream. He felt faint with fear. His belly seemed to have turned to lead. His testicles had drawn up. What in God's name had been invited into his house?

Stealthily, the sound of the hasp on the guest room window being turned back. Then the grind of wood against wood as the window was forced up.

He could go downstairs. Run, get the Bible from the dresser in the dining room. Run back up, jerk open the door to the guest room, hold the Bible high: *In the name of the Father, the Son, and the Holy Ghost, I command you to be gone—*

But who was in there?

Call me in the night if you want anything.

But I can't, Mike. I'm an old man. I'm afraid.

Night invaded his brain and made it a circus of terrifying images which danced in and out of the shadows. Clown-white faces, huge eyes, sharp teeth, forms that slipped from the shadows with long white hands that reached for . . . for . . .

A shuddering groan escaped him, and he put his hands over his face.

I can't. I am afraid.

He could not have risen even if the brass knob on his own door had begun to turn. He was paralyzed with fear and wished crazily that he had never gone out to Dell's that night.

I am afraid.

And in the awful heavy silence of the house, as he sat impotently on his bed with his face in his hands, he heard the high, sweet, evil laugh of a child—

—and then the sucking sounds.

PART TWO

THE EMPEROR
OF ICE CREAM

Call the roller of big cigars,
The muscular one, and bid him whip
In kitchen cups concupiscent curds.
Let the wenches dawdle in such dress
As they are used to wear, and let the boys
Bring flowers in last month's newspapers.
Let be be finale of seem.
The only emperor is the emperor of ice cream.

Take from the dresser of deal,
Lacking the three glass knobs, that sheet
On which she embroidered three fantails once
And spread it so as to cover her face.
If her horny feet protrude, they come
To show how cold she is, and dumb.
Let the lamp affix its beam.
The only emperor is the emperor of ice cream.

WALLACE STEVENS

This column has
A hole. Can you see
The Queen of the Dead?

GEORGE SEFERIS

Chapter Eight
BEN (III)

1

The knocking must have been going on for a long time, because it seemed to echo far down the avenues of sleep as he slowly struggled up to wakefulness. It was dark outside, but when he turned to grasp the clock and bring it to his face, he knocked it onto the floor. He felt disoriented and frightened.

"Who is it?" he called out.

"It's Eva, Mr. Mears. There's a phone call for you."

He got up, pulled on his pants, and opened the door bare-chested. Eva Miller was in a white terry-cloth robe, and her face was full of the slow vulnerability of a person still two-fifths asleep. They looked at each other nakedly, and he was thinking: *Who's sick? Who's died?*

"Long-distance?"

"No, it's Matthew Burke."

The knowledge did not relieve him as it should have done. "What time is it?"

"Just after four. Mr. Burke sounds very upset."

Ben went downstairs and picked the phone up. "This is Ben, Matt."

Matt was breathing rapidly into the phone, the sound of his respiration coming in harsh little blurts. "Can you come, Ben? Right now?"

"Yes, all right. What's the matter? Are you sick?"

"Not on the phone. Just come."

"Ten minutes."

"Ben?"

"Yes."

"Have you got a crucifix? A St. Christopher's medallion? Anything like that?"

"Hell no. I'm—was—a Baptist."

"All right. Come fast."

Ben hung up and went back upstairs quickly. Eva was standing with one hand on the newel post, her face filled with worry and indecision—on one hand wanting to know, on the other, not wanting to mix in the tenant's business.

"Is Mr. Burke sick, Mr. Mears?"

"He says not. He just asked me . . . say, you aren't Catholic?"

"My husband was."

"Do you have a crucifix or a rosary or a St. Christopher's medallion?"

"Well . . . my husband's crucifix is in the bedroom. . . . I could . . ."

"Yes, would you?"

She went up the hall, her furry slippers scuffing at the faded strip of carpet. Ben went into his room, pulled on yesterday's shirt and slipped his bare feet into a pair of loafers. When he came out again, Eva was standing by his door, holding the crucifix. It caught the light and threw back dim silver.

"Thank you," he said, taking it.

"Did Mr. Burke ask you for this?"

"Yes, he did."

She was frowning, more awake now. "He's not Catholic. I don't believe he goes to church."

"He didn't explain to me."

"Oh." She nodded in a charade of understanding and gave him the crucifix. "Please be careful of it. It has great value for me."

"I understand that. I will."

"I hope Mr. Burke is all right. He's a fine man."

He went downstairs and out onto the porch. He could not hold the crucifix and dig for his car keys at the same time, and instead of simply transferring it from his right hand to his left, he slipped it over his neck. The silver slipped comfortably against his shirt, and getting into the car he was hardly aware that he felt comforted.

2

Every window on the lower floor of Matt's house was lit up, and when Ben's headlights splashed across the front as he turned into the driveway, Matt opened the door and waited for him.

He came up the walk ready for almost anything, but Matt's face was still a shock. It was deadly pale, and the mouth was trembling. His eyes were wide, and they didn't seem to blink.

"Let's go in the kitchen," he said.

Ben came in, and as he stepped inside, the hall light caught the cross lying against his chest.

"You brought one."

"It belongs to Eva Miller. What's the matter?"

Matt repeated: "In the kitchen." As they passed the stairs leading to the second floor, he glanced upward and seemed to flinch away at the same time.

The kitchen table where they had eaten spaghetti was bare now except for three items, two of them peculiar: a cup of coffee, an old-fashioned clasp Bible, and a .38 revolver.

"Now, what's up, Matt? You look awful."

"And maybe I dreamed the whole thing, but thank God you're here." He had picked up the revolver and was turning it over restively in his hands.

"Tell me. And stop playing with that thing. Is it loaded?"

Matt put the pistol down and ran a hand through his hair. "Yes, it's loaded. Although I don't think it would do any good . . . unless I used it on myself." He laughed, a jagged, unhealthy sound like grinding glass.

"Stop that."

The harshness in his voice broke the queer, fixed look in his eyes. He shook his head, not like a man propounding a negative, but the way some animals will shake themselves coming out of cold water.

"There's a dead man upstairs," he said.

"Who?"

"Mike Ryerson. He works for the town. He's a grounds keeper."

"Are you sure he's dead?"

"I am in my guts, even though I haven't looked in on him. I haven't dared. Because, in another way, he may not be dead at all."

"Matt, you're not talking good sense."

"Don't you think I know that? I'm talking nonsense and I'm thinking madness. But there was no one to call but you. In all of 'salem's Lot you're the only person that might . . . might . . ." He shook his head and began again. "We talked about Danny Glick."

"Yes."

"And how he might have died of pernicious anemia . . . what our grandfathers would have called 'just wasting away.' "

"Yes."

"Mike buried him. And Mike found Win Purinton's dog impaled on the Harmony Hill Cemetery gates. I met Mike Ryerson in Dell's last night, and—"

3

"—and I couldn't go in," he finished. "Couldn't. I sat on my bed for nearly four hours. Then I crept downstairs like a thief and called you. What do you think?"

Ben had taken the crucifix off; now he poked at the glimmering heap of fine-link chain with a reflective finger. It was almost five o'clock and the eastern sky was rose with dawn. The fluorescent bar overhead had gone pallid.

"I think we'd better go up to your guest room and look. That's all, I think, right now."

"The whole thing seems like a madman's nightmare now, with the light coming in the window." He laughed shakily. "I hope it is. I hope Mike is sleeping like a baby."

"Well, let's go see."

Matt firmed his lips with an effort. "Okay." He dropped his eyes to the table and then looked at Ben questioningly.

"Sure," Ben said, and slipped the crucifix over Matt's neck.

"It actually does make me feel better." He laughed self-consciously. "Do you suppose they'll let me wear it when they cart me off to Augusta?"

Ben said, "Do you want the gun?"

"No, I guess not. I'd stick it in the top of my pants and blow my balls off."

They went upstairs, Ben in the lead. There was a short hall at the top, running both ways. At one end, the door to Matt's bedroom stood open, a pale sheaf of lamplight spilling out onto the orange runner.

"Down at the other end," Matt said.

Ben walked down the hall and stood in front of the guest room door. He did not believe the monstrosity Matt had implied, but nonetheless he found himself engulfed by a wave of the blackest fright he had ever known.

You open the door and he's hanging from the beam, the face swelled and puffed and black, and then the eyes open and they're bulging in the sockets but they're SEEING you and they're glad you came—

The memory rose up in almost total sensory reference, and for the moment of its totality he was paralyzed. He could even smell the plaster and the wild odor of nesting animals. It seemed to him that the plain varnished wood door of Matt Burke's guest room stood between him and all the secrets of hell.

Then he twisted the knob and pushed the door inward. Matt was at his shoulder, and he was holding Eva's crucifix tightly.

The guest room window faced directly east, and the top arc of the sun had just cleared the horizon. The first pellucid rays shone directly through the window, isolating a few golden motes as it fell in a shaft to the white linen sheet that was pulled up to Mike Ryerson's chest.

Ben looked at Matt and nodded. "He's all right," he whispered. "Sleeping."

Matt said tonelessly, "The window's open. It was closed and locked. I made sure of it."

Ben's eyes centered on the upper hem of the flawlessly laundered sheet that covered Mike. There was a single small drop of blood on it, dried to maroon.

"I don't think he's breathing," Matt said.

Ben took two steps forward and then stopped. "Mike? Mike Ryerson. Wake up, Mike!"

No response. Mike's lashes lay cleanly against his cheeks. His hair was tousled loosely across his brow, and Ben thought that in the first delicate light he was more than handsome; he was as beautiful as the profile of a Greek statue. Light color bloomed in his cheeks, and his body held none of the deathly pallor Matt had mentioned—only healthy skin tones.

"Of course he's breathing," he said a trifle impatiently. "Just fast asleep. Mike—" He stretched out a hand and shook Ryerson slightly. Mike's left arm, which had been crossed loosely on his chest, fell limply over the side of the bed and the knuckles rapped on the floor, like a request for entry.

Matt stepped forward and picked up the limp arm. He pressed his index finger over the wrist. "No pulse."

He started to drop it, remembered the grisly knocking noise the knuckles had made, and put the arm across Ryerson's chest. It started to fall anyway, and he put it back more firmly with a grimace.

Ben couldn't believe it. He was sleeping, had to be. The good color, the obvious suppleness of the muscles, the lips half parted as if to draw breath . . . unreality washed over him. He placed his wrist against Ryerson's shoulder and found the skin cool.

He moistened his finger and held it in front of those half-open lips. Nothing. Not a feather of breath.

He and Matt looked at each other.

"The marks on the neck?" Matt asked.

Ben took Ryerson's jaw in his hands and turned it gently until the exposed cheek lay against the pillow. The movement dislodged the left arm, and the knuckles rapped the floor again.

There were no marks on Mike Ryerson's neck.

4

They were at the kitchen table again. It was 5:35 A.M. They could hear the lowing of the Griffen cows as they were let into their east pasturage down the hill and beyond the belt of shrubbery and underbrush that screened Taggart Stream from view.

"According to folklore, the marks disappear," Matt said suddenly. "When the victim dies, the marks disappear."

"I know that," Ben said. He remembered it both from Stoker's *Dracula* and from the Hammer films starring Christopher Lee.

"We have to put an ash stake through his heart."

"You better think again," Ben said, and sipped his coffee. "That would be damned hard to explain to a coroner's jury. You'd go to jail for desecrating a corpse at the very least. More likely to the funny farm."

"Do you think I'm crazy?" Matt asked quietly.

With no discernible hesitation, Ben said, "No."

"Do you believe me about the marks?"

"I don't know. I guess I have to. Why would you lie to me? I can't see any gain for you in a lie. I suppose you'd lie if you had killed him."

"Perhaps I did, then," Matt said, watching him.

"There are three things going against it. First, what's your motive? Pardon me, Matt, but you're just too old for the classic ones like jealousy and money to fit very well. Second, what was your method? If it was poison, he must have gone very easily. He certainly looks peaceful enough. And that eliminates most of the common poisons right there."

"What's your third reason?"

"No murderer in his right mind would invent a story like yours to cover up murder. It would be insane."

"We keep coming back to my mental health," Matt said. He sighed. "I knew we would."

"I don't think you're crazy," Ben said, accenting the first word slightly. "You seem rational enough."

"But you're not a doctor, are you?" Matt asked. "And crazy people are sometimes able to counterfeit sanity remarkably well."

Ben agreed. "So where does that put us?"

"Back to square one."

"No. Neither one of us can afford that, because there's a dead man upstairs and pretty soon he's going to have to be explained. The constable is going to want to know what happened, and so is the medical examiner, and so is the county sheriff. Matt, could it be that Mike Ryerson was just sick with some virus all week and happened to drop dead in your house?"

For the first time since they had come back down, Matt showed signs of agitation. "Ben, I told you what he said! I saw the marks on his neck! And I heard him invite someone into my house! Then I heard . . . God, I heard that laugh!" His eyes had taken on that peculiar blank look again.

"All right," Ben said. He got up and went to the window, trying to set his thoughts in order. They didn't go well. As he had told Susan, things seemed to have a way of getting out of hand.

He was looking toward the Marsten House.

"Matt, do you know what's going to happen to you if you even let out a whisper of what you've told me?"

Matt didn't answer.

"People are going to start tapping their foreheads behind your back when you go by in the street. Little kids are going to get out their Halloween wax teeth when they see you coming and jump out and yell *Boo!* when you walk by their hedge. Somebody will invent a rhyme like *One, two, three, four, I'm gonna suck your blood some more.* The high school kids will pick it up and you'll hear it in the halls when you pass. Your colleagues will begin looking at you strangely. There's apt to be anonymous phone calls from people purporting to be Danny Glick or Mike Ryerson. They'll turn your life into a nightmare. They'll hound you out of town in six months."

"They wouldn't. They know me."

Ben turned from the window. "Who do they know? A funny old duck who lives alone out on Taggart Stream Road. Just the fact that you're not married is apt to make them believe you've got a screw loose anyway. And what backup can I give you? I saw the body but nothing else. Even if I had, they would just say I was an outsider. They would even get around to telling each other we were a couple of queers and this was the way we got our kicks."

Matt was looking at him with slowly dawning horror.

"One word, Matt. That's all it will take to finish you in 'salem's Lot."

"So there's nothing to be done."

"Yes, there is. You have a certain theory about who—or what—killed Mike Ryerson. The theory is relatively simple to prove or disprove, I think. I'm in a hell of a fix. I can't believe you're crazy, but I can't believe that Danny Glick came back from the dead and sucked Mike Ryerson's blood for a whole week before killing him, either. But I'm going to put the idea to the test. And you've got to help."

"How?"

"Call your doctor, Cody is his name? Then call Parkins Gillespie. Let the machinery take over. Tell your story just as though you'd never heard a thing in the night. You went into Dell's and sat down with Mike. He said he'd been feeling sick since last Sunday. You invited him home with you. You went in to check him around three-thirty this morning, couldn't wake him, and called me."

"That's all?"

"That's it. When you speak to Cody, don't even say he's dead."

"Not dead—"

"Christ, how do we know he *is*?" Ben exploded. "You took his pulse and couldn't find it; I tried to find his breath and couldn't do it. If I thought someone was going to shove me into my grave on that basis, I'd damn well pack a lunch. Especially if I looked as lifelike as he does."

"That bothers you as much as it does me, doesn't it?"

"Yes, it bothers me," Ben admitted. "He looks like a goddamn waxwork."

"All right," Matt said. "You're talking sense . . . as much as anyone can in a business like this. I guess I sounded nuts, at that."

Ben started to deprecate, but Matt waved it off. "But suppose . . . just hypothetically . . . that my first suspicion is right? Would you want even the remotest possibility in the back of your mind? The possibility that Mike might . . . come back?"

"As I said, that theory is easy enough to prove or disprove. And it isn't what bothers me about all this."

"What is?"

"Just a minute. First things first. Proving or disproving it ought to be no more than an exercise in logic—ruling out possibilities. First possibility: Mike died of some disease—a virus or something. How do you confirm that or rule it out?"

Matt shrugged. "Medical examination, I suppose."

"Exactly. And the same method to confirm or rule out foul

play. If somebody poisoned him or shot him or got him to eat a piece of fudge with a bundle of wires in it—"

"Murder has gone undetected before."

"Sure it has. But I'll bet on the medical examiner."

"And if the medical examiner's verdict is 'unknown cause'?"

"Then," Ben said deliberately, "we can visit the grave after the funeral and see if he rises. If he does—which I can't conceive of—we'll know. If he doesn't, we're faced with the thing that bothers me."

"The fact of my insanity," Matt said slowly. "Ben, I swear on my mother's name that those marks were there, that I heard the window go up, that—"

"I believe you," Ben said quietly.

Matt stopped. His expression was that of a man who has braced himself for a crash that never came.

"You do?" he said uncertainly.

"To put it another way, I refuse to believe that you're crazy or had a hallucination. I had an experience once . . . an experience that had to do with that damned house on the hill . . . that makes me extremely sympathetic to people whose stories seem utterly insane in light of rational knowledge. I'll tell you about that, one day."

"Why not now?"

"There's no time. You have those calls to make. And I have one more question. Think about it carefully. Do you have any enemies?"

"No one who qualifies for something like this."

"An ex-student, maybe? One with a grudge?"

Matt, who knew exactly to what extent he influenced the lives of his students, laughed politely.

"Okay," Ben said. "I'll take your word for it." He shook his head. "I don't like it. First that dog shows up on the cemetery gates. Then Ralphie Glick disappears, his brother dies, and Mike Ryerson. Maybe they all tie in somehow. But this . . . I can't believe it."

"I better call Cody's home," Matt said, getting up. "Parkins will be at home."

"Call in sick at school, too."

"Right." Matt laughed without force. "It will be my first sick day in three years. A real occasion."

He went into the living room and began to make his calls, waiting at the end of each number sequence for the bell to prod sleepers awake. Cody's wife apparently referred him to Cumberland Receiving, for he dialed another number, asked for Cody, and went into his story after a short wait.

He hung up and called into the kitchen: "Jimmy will be here in an hour."

"Good," Ben said. "I'm going upstairs."

"Don't touch anything."

"No."

By the time he reached the second-floor landing he could hear Matt on the phone to Parkins Gillespie, answerimg questions. The words melted into a background murmur as he went down the hall.

That feeling of half-remembered, half-imagined terror washed over him again as he contemplated the door to the guest room. In his mind's eye he could see himself stepping forward, pushing it open. The room looks larger, seen from a child's eye view. The body lies as they left it, left arm dangling to the floor, left cheek pressed against the pillow which still shows the fold lines from the linen closet. The eyes suddenly open, and they are filled with blank, animalistic triumph. The door slams shut. The left arm comes up, the hand hooked into a claw, and the lips twist into a vulpine smile that shows incisors grown wondrously long and sharp—

He stepped forward and pushed the door with tented fingers. The lower hinges squeaked slightly.

The body lay as they had left it, left arm fallen, left cheek pressed against the pillowcase—

"Parkins is coming," Matt said from the hallway behind him, and Ben nearly screamed.

5

Ben thought how apt his phrase had been: *Let the machinery take over.* It was very much like a machine—one of those elaborate German contraptions constructed of clockwork and cogs; figures moving in an elaborate dance.

Parkins Gillespie arrived first, wearing a green tie set off by a VFW tie tack. There were still sleepy seeds in his eyes. He told them he had notified the county M.E.

"He won't be out himself, the son of a bitch," Parkins said, tucking a Pall Mall into the corner of his seamed mouth, "but he'll send out a deputy and a fella to take pitchers. You touch the cawpse?"

"His arm fell out of bed," Ben said. "I tried to put it back, but it wouldn't stay."

Parkins looked him up and down and said nothing. Ben thought of the grisly sound the knuckles had made on the hardwood floor of Matt's guest room and felt a queasy laughter in his belly. He swallowed to keep it there.

Matt led the way upstairs, and Parkins walked around the body several times. "Say, you sure he's dead?" he asked finally. "You tried to wake him up?"

James Cody, M.D., arrived next, fresh from a delivery in Cumberland. After the amenities had passed among them ("Good t'seeya," Parkins Gillespie said, and lit a fresh cigarette), Matt led them all upstairs again. Now, if we all only played instruments, Ben thought, we could give the guy a real send-off. He felt the laughter trying to come up his throat again.

Cody turned back the sheet and frowned down at the body for a moment. With a calmness that astounded Ben, Matt Burke said, "It reminded me of what you said about the Glick boy, Jimmy."

"That was a privileged communication, Mr. Burke," Jimmy Cody said mildly. "If Danny Glick's folks found out you'd said that, they could sue me."

"Would they win?"

"No, probably not," Jimmy said, and sighed.

"What's this about the Glick boy?" Parkins asked, frowning.

"Nothing," Jimmy said. "No connection." He used his stethoscope, muttered, rolled back an eyelid, and shone a light into the glassy orb beneath.

Ben saw the pupil contract and said quite audibly, "Christ!"

"Interesting reflex, isn't it?" Jimmy said. He let the eyelid go and it rolled shut with grotesque slowness, as if the corpse had winked at them. "David Prine at Johns Hopkins reports pupillary contraction in some cadavers up to nine hours."

"Now he's a scholar," Matt said gruffly. "Used to pull C's in Expository Writing."

"You just didn't like to read about dissections, you old grump," Jimmy said absently, and produced a small hammer. Nice, Ben thought. He retains his bedside manner even when the patient is, as Parkins would say, a cawpse. The dark laughter welled inside him again.

"He dead?" Parkins asked, and tapped the ash of his cigarette into an empty flower vase. Matt winced.

"Oh, he's dead," Jimmy told him. He got up, turned the sheet back to Ryerson's feet, and tapped the right knee. The toes were moveless. Ben noticed that Mike Ryerson had yellow rings of callus on the bottoms of his feet, at the ball of the heel and at the instep. It made him think of that Wallace Stevens poem about the dead woman. "Let it be the finale of seem," he misquoted. "The only emperor is the emperor of ice cream."

Matt looked at him sharply, and for a moment his control seemed to waver.

"What's that?" Parkins asked.

"A poem," Matt said. "It's from a poem about death."

"Sounds more like the Good Humor man to me," Parkins said, and tapped his ash into the vase again.

6

"Have we been introduced?" Jimmy asked, looking up at Ben.

"You were, but only in passing," Matt said. "Jimmy Cody, local quack, meet Ben Mears, local hack. And vice versa."

"He's always been clever that way," Jimmy said. "That's how he made all his money."

They shook hands over the body.

"Help me turn him over, Mr. Mears."

A little squeamishly, Ben helped him turn the body on its belly. The flesh was cool, not yet cold, still pliant. Jimmy stared closely at the back, then pulled the jockey shorts down from the buttocks.

"What's that for?" Parkins asked.

"I'm trying to place the time of death by skin lividity,"

Jimmy said. "Blood tends to seek its lowest level when pumping action ceases, like any other fluid."

"Yeah, sort of like that Drāno commercial. That's the examiner's job, ain't it?"

"He'll send out Norbert, you know that," Jimmy said. "And Brent Norbert was never averse to a little help from his friends."

"Norbert couldn't find his own ass with both hands and a flashlight," Parkins said, and flipped his cigarette butt out the open window. "You lost your screen offa this window, Matt. I seen it down on the lawn when I drove in."

"That so?" Matt asked, his voice carefully controlled.

"Yeah."

Cody had taken a thermometer from his bag and now he slid it into Ryerson's anus and laid his watch on the crisp sheet, where it glittered in the strong sunlight. It was quarter of seven.

"I'm going downstairs," Matt said in a slightly strangled voice.

"You might as well all go," Jimmy said. "I'll be a little while longer. Would you put on coffee, Mr. Burke?"

"Sure."

They all went out and Ben closed the door on the scene. His last glance back would remain with him: the bright, sun-washed room, the clean sheet turned back, the gold wristwatch heliographing bright arrows of light onto the wallpaper, and Cody himself, with his swatch of flaming red hair, sitting beside the body like a steel engraving.

Matt was making coffee when Brenton Norbert, the assistant medical examiner, arrived in an elderly gray Dodge. He came in with another man who was carrying a large camera.

"Where is it?" Norbert asked.

Gillespie gestured with his thumb toward the stairs. "Jim Cody's up there."

"Good deal," Norbert said. "The guy's probably jitterbugging by now." He and the photographer went upstairs.

Parkins Gillespie poured cream into his coffee until it slopped into his saucer, tested it with his thumb, wiped his thumb on his pants, lit another Pall Mall, and said, "How did you get into this, Mr. Mears?"

And so Ben and Matt started their little song and dance and none of what they said was precisely a lie, but enough was left unsaid to link them together in a tenuous bond of conspiracy, and enough to make Ben wonder uneasily if he wasn't in the process of abetting either a harmless bit of kookery or something more serious, something dark. He thought of Matt saying that he had called Ben because he was the only person in 'salem's Lot who might listen to such a story. Whatever Matt Burke's mental failings might be, Ben thought, inability to read character was not one of them. And that also made him nervous.

7

By nine-thirty it was over.

Carl Foreman's funeral wagon had come and taken Mike Ryerson's body away, and the fact of his passing left the house with him and belonged to the town. Jimmy Cody had gone back to his office; Norbert and the photographer had gone to Portland to talk with the county M.E.

Parkins Gillespie stood on the stoop for a moment and watched the hearse trundle slowly up the road, a cigarette dangling between his lips. "All the times Mike drove that, I bet he never guessed how soon he'd be ridin' in the back." He turned to Ben. "You ain't leavin' the Lot just yet, are you? Like you to testify for the coroner's jury, if that's okay by you."

"No, I'm not leaving."

The constable's faded blue eyes measured him. "I checked you through with the feds and the Maine State Police R&I in Augusta," he said. "You've got a clean rep."

"That's good to know," Ben said evenly.

"I hear it around that you're sparkin' Bill Norton's girl."

"Guilty," Ben said.

"She's a fine lass," Parkins said without smiling. The hearse was out of sight now; even the hum of its engine had dwindled to a drone that faded altogether. "Guess she don't see much of Floyd Tibbits these days."

"Haven't you some paper work to do, Park?" Matt prodded gently.

He sighed and cast the butt of his cigarette away. "Sure do. Duplicate, triplicate, don't-punch-spindle-or-mutilate. This job's been more trouble than a she-bitch with crabs the last couple of weeks. Maybe that old Marsten House has got a curse on it."

Ben and Matt kept poker faces.

"Well, s'long." He hitched his pants and walked down to his car. He opened the driver's side door and then turned back to them. "You two ain't holdin' nothin' back on me, are you?"

"Parkins," Matt said, "there's nothing to hold back. He's dead."

He looked at them a moment longer, the faded eyes sharp and glittering under his hooked brows, and then he sighed. "I suppose," he said. "But it's awful goddamn funny. The dog, the Glick boy, then t'other Glick boy, now Mike. That's a year's run for a pissant little burg like this one. My old grammy used to say things ran in threes, not fours."

He got in, started the engine, and backed out of the driveway. A moment later he was gone over the hill, tralling one farewell honk.

Matt let out a gusty sigh. "That's over."

"Yes," Ben said. "I'm beat. Are you?"

"I am, but I feel . . . weird. You know that word, the way the kids use it?"

"Yes."

"They've got another one: spaced out. Like coming down from an acid trip or speed, when even being normal is crazy." He scrubbed a hand across his face. "God, you must think I'm a lunatic. It all sounds like a madman's raving in the daylight, doesn't it?"

"Yes and no," Ben said. He put a diffident hand on Matt's shoulder. "Gillespie is right, you know. There is something going on. And I'm thinking more and more that it has to do with the Marsten House. Other than myself, the people up there are the only new people in town. And I know I haven't done anything. Is our trip up there tonight still on? The rustic welcome wagon?"

"If you like."

"I do. You go in and get some sleep. I'll get in touch with Susan and we'll drop by this evening."

"All right." He paused. "There's one other thing. It's been bothering me ever since you mentioned autopsies."

"What?"

"The laugh I heard—or thought I heard—was a child's laugh. Horrible and soulless, but still a child's laugh. Connected to Mike's story, does that make you think of Danny Glick?"

"Yes, of course it does."

"Do you know what the embalming procedure is?"

"Not specifically. The blood is drained from the cadaver and replaced with some fluid. They used to use formaldehyde, but I'm sure they've got more sophisticated methods now. And the corpse is eviscerated."

"I wonder if all that was done to Danny?" Matt said, looking at him.

"Do you know Carl Foreman well enough to ask him in confidence?"

"Yes, I think I could find a way to do that."

"Do it, by all means."

"I will."

They looked at each other a moment longer, and the glance that passed between them was friendly but indefinable; on Matt's part the uneasy defiance of the rational man who has been forced to speak irrationalities, on Ben's a kind of ill-defined fright of forces he could not understand enough to define.

8

Eva was ironing and watching "Dialing for Dollars" when he came in. The jackpot was currently up to forty-five dollars, and the emcee was picking telephone numbers out of a large glass drum.

"I heard," she said as he opened the refrigerator and got a Coke. "Awful. Poor Mike."

"It's too bad." He reached into his breast pocket and fished out the crucifix on its fine-link chain.

"Do they know what—"

"Not yet," Ben said. "I'm very tired, Mrs. Miller. I think I'll sleep for a while."

"Of course you should. That upstairs room is hot at midday, even this late in the year. Take the one in the downstairs hall if you like. The sheets are fresh."

"No, that's all right. I know all the squeaks in the one upstairs."

"Yes, a person does get used to their own," she said matter-of-factly. "Why in the world did Mr. Burke want Ralph's crucifix?"

Ben paused on his way to the stairs, momentarily at a loss. "I think he must have thought Mike Ryerson was a Catholic."

Eva slipped a new shirt on the end of her ironing board. "He should have known better than that. After all, he had Mike in school. All his people were Lutherans."

Ben had no answer for that. He went upstairs, pulled his clothes off, and got into bed. Sleep came rapidly and heavily. He did not dream.

9

When he woke up, it was quarter past four. His body was beaded with sweat, and he had kicked the upper sheet away. Still, he felt clear-headed again. The events of that early morning seemed to be far away and dim, and Matt Burke's fancies had lost their urgency. His job for tonight was only to humor him out of them if he could.

10

He decided that he would call Susan from Spencer's and have her meet him there. They could go to the park and he would tell her the whole thing from beginning to end. He could get her opinion on their way out to see Matt, and at Matt's house she could listen to his version and complete her judgment. Then, on to the Marsten House. The thought caused a ripple of fear in his midsection.

He was so involved in his own thoughts that he never noticed that someone was sitting in his car until the door opened and the tall form accordioned out. For a moment his mind was too stunned to command his body; it was busy boggling at what it first took to be an animated scarecrow. The slanting sun picked the figure out in detail that was sharp and cruel: the old fedora hat pulled low around the ears; the wrap-around sunglasses; the ragged overcoat with the collar turned up; the heavy industrial green rubber gloves on the hands.

"Who—" was all Ben had time to get out.

The figure moved closer. The fists bunched. There was an old yellow smell that Ben recognized as that of mothballs. He could hear breath slobbering in and out.

"You're the son of a bitch that stole my girl," Floyd Tibbits said in a grating, toneless voice. "I'm going to kill you."

And while Ben was still trying to clear all this through his central switchboard, Floyd Tibbits waded in.

Chapter Nine
SUSAN (II)

1

Susan arrived home from Portland a little after three in the afternoon, and came into the house carrying three crackling brown department-store bags—she had sold two paintings for a sum totaling just over eighty dollars and had gone on a small spree. Two new skirts and a cardigan top.

"Suze?" Her mother called. "Is that you?"

"I'm home. I got—"

"Come in here, Susan. I want to talk to you."

She recognized the tone instantly, although she had not heard it to that precise degree since her high school days, when the arguments over hem lines and boy friends had gone on day after bitter day.

She put down her bags and went into the living room. Her mother had grown colder and colder on the subject of Ben Mears, and Susan supposed this was to be her Final Word.

Her mother was sitting in the rocker by the bay window, knitting. The TV was off. The two in conjunction were an ominous sign.

"I suppose you haven't heard the latest," Mrs. Norton said. Her needles clicked rapidly, meshing the dark green yarn she was working with into neat rows. Someone's winter scarf. "You left too early this morning."

"Latest?"

"Mike Ryerson died at Matthew Burke's house last night, and who should be in attendance at the deathbed but your writer friend, Mr. Ben Mears!"

"Mike . . . Ben . . . what?"

Mrs. Norton smiled grimly. "Mabel called around ten this morning and told me. Mr. Burke *says* he met Mike down at Delbert Markey's tavern last night—although what a teacher is doing bar-hopping I don't know—and brought him home with him because Mike didn't look well. He died in the night. And no one seems to know just what Mr. Mears was doing there!"

"They know each other," Susan said absently. "In fact, Ben says they hit it off really well . . . what happened to Mike, Mom?"

But Mrs. Norton was not to be sidetracked so quickly. "Nonetheless, there's some that think we've had a little too much excitement in 'salem's Lot since Mr. Ben Mears showed his face. A little too much altogether."

"That's foolishness!" Susan said, exasperated. "Now, what did Mike—"

"They haven't decided that yet," Mrs. Norton said. She twirled her ball of yarn and let out slack. "There's some that think he may have caught a disease from the little Glick boy."

"If so, why hasn't anyone else caught it? Like his folks?"

"Some young people think they know everything," Mrs. Norton remarked to the air. Her needles flashed up and down.

Susan got up. "I think I'll go downstreet and see if—"

"Sit back down a minute," Mrs. Norton said. "I have a few more things to say to you."

Susan sat down again, her face neutral.

"Sometimes young people don't know all there is to know," Ann Norton said. A spurious tone of comfort had come into her voice that Susan distrusted immediately.

"Like what, Mom?"

"Well, it seems that Mr. Ben Mears had an accident a few years ago. Just after his second book was published. A motorcycle accident. He was drunk. His wife was killed."

Susan stood up. "I don't want to hear any more."

"I'm telling you for your own good," Mrs. Norton said calmly.

"Who told you?" Susan asked. She felt none of the old hot and impotent anger, or the urge to run upstairs away from that calm, knowing voice and weep. She only felt cold and distant, as if drifting in space. "It was Mabel Werts, wasn't it?"

"That doesn't matter. It's true."

"Sure it is. And we won in Vietnam and Jesus Christ drives through the center of town in a gocart every day at high noon."

"Mabel thought he looked familiar," Ann Norton said, "and so she went through the back issues of her newspapers box by box—"

"You mean the scandal sheets? The ones that specialize in astrology and pictures of car wrecks and starlets' tits? Oh, what an informed source." She laughed harshly.

"No need to be obscene. The story was right there in black and white. The woman—his wife if she really was—was riding on the back seat and he skidded on the pavement and they went smack into the side of a moving van. They gave him a breathalyzer test on the spot, the article said. Right . . . on . . . the spot." She emphasized intensifier, preposition, and object by tapping a knitting needle against the arm of her rocker.

"Then why isn't he in prison?"

"These famous fellows always know people," she said with calm certainty. "There are ways to get out of everything, if you're rich enough. Just look at what those Kennedy boys have gotten away with."

"Was he tried in court?"

"I told you, they gave him a—"

"You said that, Mother. But was he drunk?"

"I told you he was drunk!" Spots of color had begun to creep into her cheeks. "They don't give you a breathalyzer test if you're sober! His wife died! It was just like that Chappaquiddick business! Just like it!"

"I'm going to move into town," Susan said slowly. "I've been meaning to tell you. I should have done it a long time ago, Mom. For both of us. I was talking to Babs Griffen, and she says there's a nice little four-room place on Sister's Lane—"

"Oh, she's offended!" Mrs. Norton remarked to the air. "Someone just spoiled her pretty picture of Mr. Ben Big-shot Mears and she's just so mad she could *spit*." This line had been particularly effective some years back.

"Mom, what's happened to you?" Susan asked a little despairingly. "You never used to . . . to get this low—"

Ann Norton's head jerked up. Her knitting slid off her lap as she stood up, clapped her hands to Susan's shoulders, and gave her a smart shake.

"You listen to me! I won't have you running around like a common trollop with some sissy boy who's got your head all filled up with moonlight. *Do you hear me?*"

Susan slapped her across the face.

Ann Norton's eyes blinked and then opened wide in stunned surprise. They looked at each other for a moment in silence, shocked. A tiny sound came and died in Susan's throat.

"I'm going upstairs," she said. "I'll be out by Tuesday at the latest."

"Floyd was here," Mrs. Norton said. Her face was still rigid from the slap. Her daughter's finger marks stood out in red, like exclamation points.

"I'm through with Floyd," Susan said tonelessly. "Get used to the idea. Tell your harpy friend Mabel all about it on the telephone, why don't you? Maybe then it will seem real to you."

"Floyd loves you, Susan. This is . . . ruining him. He broke down and told me everything. He poured out his heart to me." Her eyes shone with the memory of it. "He broke down at the end and cried like a baby."

Susan thought how unlike Floyd that was. She wondered if her mother could be making it up, and knew by her eyes that she was not.

"Is that what you want for me, Mom? A crybaby? Or did you just fall in love with the idea of blond-haired grandchildren? I suppose I bother you—you can't feel your job is complete until you see me married and settled down to a good man you can put your thumb on. Settled down with a fellow who'll get me pregnant and turn me into a matron in a hurry. That's the scoop, isn't it? Well, what about what *I* want?"

"Susan, you don't know what you want."

And she said it with such absolute, convinced certainty that for a moment Susan was tempted to believe her. An image came to her of herself and her mother, standing here in set positions, her mother by her rocker and she by the door; only they were tied together by a hank of green yarn, a cord that had grown frayed and weak from many restless tuggings. Image transformed into her mother in a nimrod's hat, the band sportily pierced with many different flies. Trying desperately to reel in a large trout wearing a yellow print shift. Trying to reel it in for the last time and pop it away in the wicker creel. But for what purpose? To mount it? To eat it?

"No, Mom. I know exactly what I want. Ben Mears."

She turned and went up the stairs.

Her mother ran after her and called up shrilly: "You can't get a room! You haven't any money!"

"I've got a hundred in checking and three hundred in savings," Susan replied calmly. "And I can get a job down at Spencer's, I think. Mr. Labree has offered several times."

"All he'll care about is looking up your dress," Mrs. Norton said, but her voice had gone down an octave. Much of her anger had left her and she felt a little frightened.

"Let him," Susan said. "I'll wear bloomers."

"Honey, don't be mad." She came two steps up the stairs. "I only want what's best for—"

"Spare it, Mom. I'm sorry I slapped you. That was awful of me. I do love you. But I'm moving out. It's way past time. You must see that."

"You think it over," Mrs. Norton said, now clearly sorry as well as frightened. "I still don't think I spoke out of turn. That Ben Mears, I've seen showboats like him before. All he's interested in is—"

"No. No more."

She turned away.

Her mother came up another step and called after her: "When Floyd left here he was in an awful state. He—"

But the door to Susan's room closed and cut off her words.

She lay down on her bed—which had been decorated with stuffed toys and a poodle dog with a transistor radio in its belly not so long ago—and lay looking at the wall, trying not to think. There were a number of Sierra Club posters on the wall, but not so long ago she had been surrounded by posters clipped from *Rolling Stone* and *Creem* and *Crawdaddy*, pictures of her idols—Jim Morrison and John Lennon and Dave van Ronk and Chuck Berry. The ghost of those days seemed to crowd in on her like bad time exposures of the mind.

She could almost see the newsprint, standing out on the cheap pulp stock. GOING-PLACES YOUNG WRITER AND YOUNG WIFE INVOLVED IN "MAYBE" MOTORCYCLE FATALITY. The rest in carefully couched innuendoes. Perhaps a picture taken at the scene by a local photographer, too gory for the local paper, just right for Mabel's kind.

And the worst was that a seed of doubt had been planted. Stupid. Did you think he was in cold storage before he came back here? That he came wrapped in a germ-proof cellophane bag, like a motel drinking glass? Stupid. Yet the seed had been planted. And for that she could feel something more than adolescent pique for her mother—she could feel something black that bordered on hate.

She shut the thoughts—not out but away—and put an arm over her face and drifted into an uncomfortable doze that was broken by the shrill of the telephone downstairs, then more sharply by her mother's voice calling, "Susan! It's for you!"

She went downstairs, noticing it was just after five-thirty. The sun was in the west. Mrs. Norton was in the kitchen, beginning supper. Her father wasn't home yet.

"Hello?"

"Susan?" The voice was familiar, but she could not put a name to it immediately.

"Yes, who's this?"

"Eva Miller, Susan. I've got some bad news."

"Has something happened to Ben?" All the spit seemed to have gone out of her mouth. Her hand came up and touched her throat. Mrs. Norton had come to the kitchen door and was watching, a spatula held in one hand.

"Well, there was a fight. Floyd Tibbits showed up here this afternoon—"

"Floyd!"

Mrs. Norton winced at her tone.

"—and I said Mr. Mears was sleeping. He said all right, just as polite as ever, but he was dressed awful funny. I asked him if he felt all right. He had on an old-fashioned overcoat and a funny hat and he kept his hands in his pockets. I never thought to mention it to Mr. Mears when he got up. There's been so much excitement—"

"What happened?" Susan nearly screamed.

"Well, Floyd beat him up," Eva said unhappily. "Right out in my parking lot. Sheldon Corson and Ed Craig went out and dragged him off."

"Ben. Is Ben all right?"

"I guess not."

"What is it?" She was holding the phone very tightly.

"Floyd got in one last crack and sent Mr. Mears back against that little foreign car of his, and he hit his head. Carl Foreman took him over to Cumberland Receiving, and he was unconscious. I don't know anything else. If you—"

She hung up, ran to the closet, and pulled her coat off the hanger.

"Susan, what is it?"

"That nice boy Floyd Tibbits," Susan said, hardly aware that she had begun to cry. "He's put Ben in the hospital."

She ran out without waiting for a reply.

2

She got to the hospital at six-thirty and sat in an uncomfortable plastic contour chair, staring blankly at a copy of *Good Housekeeping*. And I'm the only one, she thought. How damned awful. She had thought of calling Matt Burke, but the thought of the doctor coming back and finding her gone had stopped her.

The minutes crawled by on the waiting room clock, and at ten minutes of seven, a doctor with a sheaf of papers in one hand stepped through the door and said, "Miss Norton?"

"That's right. Is Ben all right?"

"That's not an answerable question at this point." He saw the dread come into her face and added: "He seems to be, but we'll want him here for two or three days. He's got a hairline fracture, multiple bruises, contusions, and one hell of a black eye."

"Can I see him?"

"No, not tonight. He's been sedated."

"For a minute? Please? One minute?"

He sighed. "You can look in on him, if you like. He'll probably be asleep. I don't want you to say anything to him unless he speaks to you."

He took her up to the third floor and then down to a room at the far end of a medicinal-smelling corridor. The man in the other bed was reading a magazine and looked up at them desultorily.

Ben was lying with his eyes closed, a sheet pulled up to his chin. He was so pale and still that for one terrified moment Susan was sure he was dead; that he had just slipped away while she and the doctor had been talking downstairs. Then she marked the slow, steady rise and fall of his chest and felt a relief so great that she swayed a little on her feet. She looked at his face closely, hardly noticing the way it had been marked. Sissy boy, her mother had called him, and Susan could see how she might have gotten that idea. His features were strong but sensitive (she wished there was a better word than "sensitive"; that was the word you used to describe the local librarian who wrote stilted Spenserian sonnets to daffodils in his spare time; but it was the only word that fit). Only his hair seemed virile in the traditional sense. Black and heavy, it seemed almost to float above his face. The white bandage on the left side above the temple stood out in sharp, telling contrast.

I love the man, she thought. Get well, Ben. Get well and finish your book so we can go away from the Lot together, if you want me. The Lot has turned bad for both of us.

"I think you'd better leave now," the doctor said. "Perhaps tomorrow—"

Ben stirred and made a thick sound in his throat. His eyelids opened slowly, closed, opened again. His eyes were dark with sedation, but the knowledge of her presence was in them. He moved his hand over hers. Tears spilled out of her eyes and she smiled and squeezed his hand.

He moved his lips and she bent to hear.

"They're real killers in this town, aren't they?"

"Ben, I'm so sorry."

"I think I knocked out two of his teeth before he decked me," Ben whispered. "Not bad for a writer fella."

"Ben—"

"I think that will be enough, Mr. Mears," the doctor said. "Give the airplane glue a chance to set."

Ben shifted his eyes to the doctor. "Just a minute."

The doctor rolled his eyes. "That's what *she* said."

Ben's eyelids slipped down again, then came up with difficulty. He said something unintelligible.

Susan bent closer. "What, darling?"

"Is it dark yet?"

"Yes."

"Want you to go see . . ."

"Matt?"

He nodded. "Tell him . . . I said for you to be told everything. Ask him if he . . . knows Father Callahan. He'll understand."

"Okay," Susan said. "I'll give him the message. You sleep now. Sleep well, Ben."

" 'Kay. Love you." He muttered something else, twice, and then his eyes closed. His breathing deepened.

"What did he say?" the doctor asked.

Susan was frowning. "It sounded like 'Lock the windows,' " she said.

3

Eva Miller and Weasel Craig were in the waiting room when she went back to get her coat. Eva was wearing an old fall coat with a rusty fur collar, obviously kept for best, and Weasel was floating in an outsized motorcycle jacket. Susan warmed at the sight of both of them.

"How is he?" Eva asked.

"Going to be all right, I think." She repeated the doctor's diagnosis, and Eva's face relaxed.

"I'm so glad. Mr. Mears seems like a very nice man. Nothing like this has ever happened at my place. And Parkins Gillespie had to lock Floyd up in the drunk tank. He didn't act drunk, though. Just sort of . . . dopey and confused."

Susan shook her head. "It doesn't sound like Floyd at all."

There was a moment of uncomfortable silence.

"Ben's a lovely fella," Weasel said, and patted Susan's hand. "He'll be up and about in no time. You wait and see."

"I'm sure he will be," Susan said, and squeezed his hand in both of hers. "Eva, isn't Father Callahan the priest at St. Andrew's?"

"Yes, why?"

"Oh . . . curious. Listen, thank you both for coming. If you could come back tomorrow—"

"We'll do that," Weasal said. "Sure we will, won't we, Eva?" He slipped an arm about her waist. It was a long reach, but he got there eventually.

"Yes, we will."

Susan walked out to the parking lot with them and then drove back to Jerusalem's Lot.

4

Matt did not answer at her knock or yell *Come in!* as he usually did. Instead, a very careful voice which she hardly recognized said, "Who is it?" very quietly from the other side.

"Susie Norton, Mr. Burke."

He opened the door and she felt real shock at the change in him. He looked old and haggard. A moment after that, she saw that he was wearing a heavy gold crucifix. There was something so strange and ludicrous about that ornate five-and-dime corpus lying against his checked flannel shirt that she almost laughed—but didn't.

"Come in. Where's Ben?"

She told him and his face grew long. "So Floyd Tibbits of all people decides to play wronged lover, is that it? Well, it couldn't have happened at a more inopportune time. Mike Ryerson was brought back from Portland late this afternoon for burial preparations at Foreman's. And I suppose our trip up to the Marsten House will have to be put off—"

"What trip? What's this about Mike?"

"Would you like coffee?" he asked absently.

"No. I want to find out what's going on. Ben said you know."

"That," he said, "is a very tall order. Easy for Ben to say I'm to tell you everything. Harder to do. But I will try."

"What—"

He held up one hand. "One thing first, Susan. You and your mother went down to the new shop the other day."

Susan's brow furrowed. "Sure. Why?"

"Can you give me your impressions of the place, and more specifically, of the man who runs it?"

"Mr. Straker?"

"Yes."

"Well, he's quite charming," she said. "Courtly might be an even better word. He complimented Glynis Mayberry on her dress and she blushed like a schoolgirl. And asked Mrs. Boddin about the bandage on her arm . . . she spilled some hot fat on it, you know. He gave her a recipe for a poultice. Wrote it right down. And when Mabel came in . . ." She laughed a bit at the memory.

"Yes?"

"He got her a chair," Susan said. "Not a chair, actually, but a *chair*. More like a throne. A great carved mahogany thing. He brought it out of the back room all by himself, smiling and chatting with the other ladies all the time. But it must have weighed at least three hundred pounds. He plonked it down in the middle of the floor and escorted Mabel to it. Took her arm, you know. And she was *giggling*. If you've seen Mabel giggling, you've seen everything. And he served coffee. Very strong but very good."

"Did you like him?" Matt asked, watching her closely.

"This is all a part of it, isn't it?" she asked.

"It might be, yes."

"All right, then. I'll give you a woman's reaction. I did and I didn't. I was attracted to him in a mildly sexual way, I guess. Older man, very urbane, very charming, very courtly. You know looking at him that he could order from a French menu and know what wine would go with what, not just red or white but the year and even the vineyard. Very defintely not the run of fellow you see around here. But not effeminate in the least. Lithe, like a dancer. And of course there's something attractive about a man who is so unabashedly bald." She smiled a little defensively, knowing there was color in her cheeks, wondering if she had said more than she intended.

"But then you didn't," Matt said.

She shrugged. "That's harder to put my finger on. I think . . . I think I sensed a certain contempt under the surface. A cynicism. As if he were playing a certain part, and playing it well, but as if he knew he wouldn't have to pull out all the stops to fool us. A touch of condescension." She looked at him uncertainly. "And there seemed to be something a little bit cruel about him. I don't really know why."

"Did anyone buy anything?"

"Not much, but he didn't seem to mind. Mom bought a little knickknack shelf from Yugoslavia, and that Mrs. Petrie bought a lovely little drop-leaf table, but that was all I saw. He didn't seem to mind. Just urged people to tell their friends he was open, to come back by and not be strangers. Very Old World charming."

"And do you think people were charmed?"

"By and large, yes," Susan said, mentally comparing her mother's enthusiastic impression of R. T. Straker to her immediate dislike of Ben.

"You didn't see his partner?"

"Mr. Barlow? No, he's in New York, on a buying trip."

"Is he?" Matt said, speaking to himself. "I wonder. The elusive Mr. Barlow."

"Mr. Burke, don't you think you better tell me what all this is about?"

He sighed heavily.

"I suppose I must try. What you've just told me is disturbing. Very disturbing. It all fits so well. . . ."

"What? What does?"

"I have to start," he began, "with meeting Mike Ryerson in Dell's tavern last night . . . which already seems a century ago."

5

It was twenty after eight by the time he had finished, and they had both drunk two cups of coffee.

"I believe that's everything," Matt said. "And now shall I do my Napoleon imitation? Tell you about my astral conversations with Toulouse-Lautrec?"

"Don't be silly," she said. "There's something going on, but not what you think. You must *know* that."

"I did until last night."

"If no one has it in for you, as Ben suggested, then maybe Mike did it himself. In a delirium or something." That sounded thin, but she pushed ahead anyway. "Or maybe you fell asleep without knowing and dreamed the whole thing. I've dozed off without knowing it before and lost a whole fifteen or twenty minutes."

He shrugged tiredly. "How does a person defend testimony no rational mind will accept at face value? I heard what I heard. I was not asleep. And something has me worried . . . rather badly worried. According to the old literature, a vampire cannot simply walk into a man's house and suck his blood. No. He has to be invited. But Mike Ryerson invited Danny Glick in last night. *And I invited Mike myself!*"

"Matt, has Ben told you about his new book?"

He fiddled with his pipe but didn't light it. "Very little. Only that it's somehow connected with the Marsten House."

"Has he told you he had a very traumatic experience in the Marsten House as a boy?"

He looked up sharply. *"In* it? No."

"He went in on a dare. He wanted to join a club, and the initiation was for him to go into the Marsten House and bring something out. He did, as a matter of fact—but before he left, he went up to the second-floor bedroom where Hubie Marsten hung himself. When he opened the door, he saw Hubie hanging there. He opened his eyes. Ben ran. That's festered in him for twenty-four years. He came back to the Lot to try to write it out of his system."

"Christ," Matt said.

"He has . . . a certain theory about the Marsten House. It springs partly from his own experience and partly from some rather amazing research he's done on Hubert Marsten—"

"His penchant for devil worship?"

She started. "How did you know that?"

He smiled a trifle grimly. "Not all the gossip in a small town is open gossip. There are secrets. Some of the secret gossip in 'salem's Lot has to do with Hubie Marsten. It's shared among perhaps only a dozen or so of the older people now—Mabel Werts is one of them. It was a long time ago, Susan. But even so, there is no statute of limitations on some stories. It's strange, you know. Even Mabel won't talk about Hubert Marsten with anyone but her own circle. They'll talk about his death, of course. About the murder. But if you ask about the ten years he and his wife spent up there in their house, doing God knows what, a sort of governor comes into play—perhaps the closest thing to a taboo our Western civilization knows. There have even been whispers that Hubert Marsten kidnapped and sacrificed small children to his infernal gods. I'm surprised Ben found out as much as he did. The secrecy concerning that aspect of Hubie and his wife and his house is almost tribal."

"He didn't come by it in the Lot."

"That explains it, then. I suspect his theory is a rather old parapsychological wheeze—that humans manufacture evil just as they manufacture snot or excrement or fingernail parings. That it doesn't go away. Specifically, that the Marsten House may have become a kind of evil dry-cell; a malign storage battery."

"Yes. He expressed it in exactly those terms." She looked at him wonderingly.

He gave a dry chuckle. "We've read the same books. And what do you think, Susan? Is there more than heaven and earth in your philosophy?"

"No," she said with quiet firmness. "Houses are only houses. Evil dies with the perpetration of evil acts."

"You're suggesting that Ben's instability may enable me to lead him down the path to insanity that I am already traversing?"

"No, of course not. I don't think you're insane. But Mr. Burke, you must realize—"

"*Be quiet.*"

He had cocked his head forward. She stopped talking and listened. Nothing . . . except perhaps a creaky board. She looked at him questioningly, and he shook his head. "You were saying?"

"Only that coincidence has made this a poor time for him to exercise the demons of his youth. There's been a lot of cheap talk going around town since the Marsten House was reoccupied and that store was opened . . . there's been talk about Ben himself, for that matter. Rites of exorcism have been known to get out of hand and turn on the exorcist. I think Ben needs to get out of this town and I think maybe you could use a vacation from it, Mr. Burke."

Exorcism made her think of Ben's request to mention the Catholic priest to Matt. On impulse, she decided not to. The reason he had asked was now clear enough, but it would only be adding fuel to a fire that was, in her opinion, already dangerously high. When Ben asked her—if he ever did—she would say she had forgotten.

"I know how mad it must sound," Matt said. "Even to me, who heard the window go up, and that laugh, and saw the screen lying beside the driveway this morning. But if it will allay your fears any, I must say that Ben's reaction to the whole thing was very sensible. He suggested we put the thing on the basis of a theory to be proved or disproved, and begin by—" He ceased again, listening.

This time the silence spun out, and when he spoke again, the soft certainty in his voice frightened her. "There's someone upstairs."

She listened. Nothing.

"You're imagining things."

"I know my house," he said softly. "Someone is in the guest bedroom . . . there, you hear?"

And this time she did hear. The audible creak of a board, creaking the way boards in old houses do, for no good reason at all. But to Susan's ears there seemed to be something more— something unutterably sly—in that sound.

"I'm going upstairs," he said.

"No!"

The word came out with no thought. She told herself: *Now who's sitting in the chimney corner, believing the wind in the eaves is a banshee?*

"I was frightened last night and did nothing and things grew worse. Now I am going upstairs."

"Mr. Burke—"

They had both begun to speak in undertones. Tension had wormed into her veins, making her muscles stiff. Maybe there *was* someone upstairs. A prowler.

"Talk," he said. "After I go, continue speaking. On any subject."

And before she could argue, he was out of his seat and moving toward the hall, moving with a grace that was nearly astounding. He looked back once, but she couldn't read his eyes. He began to go up the stairs.

Her mind felt dazed into unreality by the swift turn-around

things had taken. Less than two minutes ago they had been discussing this business calmly, under the rational light of electric bulbs. And now she was afraid. Question: If you put a psychologist in a room with a man who thinks he's Napoleon and leave them there for a year (or ten or twenty), will you end up with two Skinner men or two guys with their hands in their shirts? Answer: Insufficient data.

She opened her mouth and said, "Ben and I were going to drive up Route 1 to Camden on Sunday—you know, the town where they filmed *Peyton Place*—but now I guess we'll have to wait. They have the most darling little church . . ."

She found herself droning along with great facility, even though her hands were clenched together in her lap tightly enough to whiten the knuckles. Her mind was clear, still unimpressed with this talk of bloodsuckers and the undead. It was from her spinal cord, a much older network of nerves and ganglia, that the black dread emanated in waves.

6

Going up the stairs was the hardest thing Matt Burke had ever done in his life. That was all; that was it. Nothing else even came close. Except perhaps one thing.

As a boy of eight, he had been in a Cub Scout pack. The den mother's house was a mile up the road and going was fine, yes, excellent, because you walked in the late afternoon daylight. But coming home twilight had begun to fall, freeing the shadows to yawn across the road in long, twisty patterns—or, if the meeting was particularly enthusiastic and ran late, you had to walk home in the dark. Alone.

Alone. Yes, that's the key word, the most awful word in the English tongue. Murder doesn't hold a candle to it and hell is only a poor synonym. . . .

There was a ruined church along the way, an old Methodist meeting house, which reared its shambles at the far end of a frost-heaved and hummocked lawn, and when you walked past the view of its glaring, senseless windows your footsteps became very loud in your ears and whatever you had been whistling died on your lips and you thought about how it must be inside—the overturned pews, the rotting hymnals, the crumbling altar where only mice now kept the sabbath, and you wondered what might be in there besides mice—what madmen, what monsters. Maybe they were peering out at you with yellow reptilian eyes. And maybe one night watching would not be enough; maybe some night that splintered, crazily hung door would be thrown open, and what you saw standing there would drive you to lunacy at one look.

And you couldn't explain that to your mother and father, who were creatures of the light. No more than you could explain to them how, at the age of three, the spare blanket at the foot of the crib turned into a collection of snakes that lay staring at you with flat and lidless eyes. No child ever conquers those fears, he thought. If a fear cannot be articulated, it can't be conquered. And the fears locked in small brains are much too large to pass through the orifice of the mouth. Sooner or later you found someone to walk past all the deserted meeting houses you had to pass between grinning babyhood and grunting senility. Until tonight. Until tonight when you found out that none of the old fears had been staked—only tucked away in their tiny, child-sized coffins with a wild rose on top.

He didn't turn on the light. He mounted the steps, one by one, avoiding the sixth, which creaked. He held on to the crucifix, and his palm was sweaty and slick.

He reached the top and turned soundlessly to look down the hall. The guest room door was ajar. He had left it shut. From downstairs came the steady murmur of Susan's voice.

Walking carefully to avoid squeaks, he went down to the door and stood in front of it. The basis of all human fears, he thought. A closed door, slightly ajar.

He reached out and pushed it open.

Mike Ryerson was lying on the bed.

Moonlight flooded in the windows and silvered the room, turning it into a lagoon of dreams. Matt shook his head, as if to clear it. Almost it seemed as though he had moved backward in time, that it was the night before. He would go downstairs and call Ben because Ben wasn't in the hospital yet—

Mike opened his eyes.

They glittered for just a moment in the moonlight, silver rimmed with red. They were as blank as washed blackboards. There was no human thought or feeling in them. *The eyes are the windows of the soul,* Wordsworth had said. If so, these windows looked in on an empty room.

Mike sat up, the sheet falling from his chest, and Matt saw the heavy industrial stitchwork where the M.E. or pathologist had repaired the work of his autopsy, perhaps whistling as he sewed.

Mike smiled, and his canines and incisors were white and sharp. The smile itself was a mere flexing of the muscles around the mouth; it never touched the eyes. They retained their original dead blankness.

Mike said very clearly, *"Look at me."*

Matt looked. Yes, the eyes were utterly blank. But very deep. You could almost see little silver cameos of yourself in those eyes, drowning sweetly, making the world seem unimportant, making fears seem unimportant—

He stepped backward and cried out, "No! No!"

And held the crucifix out.

Whatever had been Mike Ryerson hissed as if hot water had been thrown in its face. Its arms went up as if to ward off a blow. Matt took a step into the room; Ryerson took a compensatory one backward.

"Get out of here!" Matt croaked. "I revoke my invitation!"

Ryerson screamed, a high, ululating sound full of hate and pain. He took four shambling steps backward. The backs of the knees struck the ledge of the open window, and Ryerson tottered past the edge of balance.

"I will see you sleep like the dead, teacher."

It fell outward into the night, going backward with its hands thrown out above its head, like a diver going off a high board. The pallid body gleamed like marble, in hard and depthless contrast to the black stitches that crisscrossed the torso in a Y pattern.

Matt let out a crazed, terrified wail and rushed to the window and peered out. There was nothing to be seen but the moon-gilded night—and suspended in the air below the window and above the spill of light that marked the living room, a dancing pattern of motes that might have been dust. They whirled, coalesced in a pattern that was hideously humanoid, and then dissipated into nothing.

He turned to run, and that was when the pain filled his chest and made him stagger. He clutched at it and doubled over. The pain seemed to be coming up his arm in steady, pulsing waves. The crucifix swung below his eyes.

He walked out the door holding his forearms crossed before his chest, the chain of the crucifix still caught in his right hand. The image of Mike Ryerson hanging in the dark air like some pallid high-diver hung before him.

"Mr. Burke!"

"My doctor is James Cody," he said through lips that were as cold as snow. "It's on the phone reminder. I'm having a heart attack, I think."

He collapsed in the upper hall, face down.

7

She dialed the number marked beside JIMMY CODY, PILLPUSHER. The legend was written in the neat block capitals she remembered so well from her school days. A woman's voice answered and Susan said, "Is the doctor home? Emergency!"

"Yes," the woman said calmly. "Here he is."

"Dr. Cody speaking."

"This is Susan Norton. I'm at Mr. Burke's house. He's had a heart attack."

"Who? *Matt* Burke?"

"Yes. He's unconscious. What should I—"

"Call an ambulance," he said. "In Cumberland that's 841–4000. Stay with him. Put a blanket over him but don't move him. Do you understand?"

"Yes."

"I'll be there in twenty minutes."

"Will you—"

But the phone clicked, and she was alone.

She called for an ambulance and then she was alone again, faced with going back upstairs to him.

8

She stared at the stairwell with a trepidation which was amazing to her. She found herself wishing that none of it had happened, not so that Matt could be all right, but so she would not have to feel this sick, shaken fear. Her unbelief had been total—she saw Matt's perceptions of the previous night as something to be defined in terms of her accepted realities, nothing more or less. And now that firm unbelief was gone from beneath her and she felt herself falling.

She had heard Matt's voice and had heard a terrible toneless incantation: *I will see you sleep like the dead, teacher.* The voice that had spoken those words had no more human quality than a dog's bark.

She went back upstairs, forcing her body through every step. Even the hall light did not help much. Matt lay where she had left him, his face turned sideways so the right cheek lay against the threadbare nap of the hall runner, breathing in harsh, tearing gasps. She bent and undid the top two buttons of his shirt and his breathing seemed to ease a little. Then she went into the guest bedroom to get a blanket.

The room was cool. The window stood open. The bed had been stripped except for the mattress pad, but there were blankets stacked on the top shelf of the closet. As she turned back to the hall, something on the floor near the window glittered in the moonlight and she stooped and picked it up. She recognized it immediately. A Cumberland Consolidated High School class ring. The initials engraved on the inner curve were M.C.R.

Michael Corey Ryerson.

For the moment, in the dark, she believed. She believed it all. A scream rose in her throat and she choked it unvoiced, but the ring tumbled from her fingers and lay on the floor below the window, glinting in the moonlight that rode the autumn dark.

Chapter Ten
THE LOT (III)

1

The town knew about darkness.

It knew about the darkness that comes on the land when rotation hides the land from the sun, and about the darkness of the human soul. The town is an accumulation of three parts which, in sum, are greater than the sections. The town is the people who live there, the buildings which they have erected to den or do business in, and it is the land. The people are Scotch-English and French. There are others, of course—a smattering, like a fistful of pepper thrown in a pot of salt but not many. This melting pot never melted very much. The buildings are nearly all constructed of honest wood. Many of the older houses are saltboxes and most of the stores are false-fronted, although no one could have said why. The people know there is nothing behind those false façades just as most of them know that Loretta Starcher wears falsies. The land is granite-bodied and covered with a thin, easily ruptured skin of topsoil. Farming it is a thankless, sweaty, miserable, crazy business. The harrow turns up great chunks of the granite under-layer and breaks on them. In May you take out your truck as soon as the ground is dry enough to support it, and you and your boys fill it up with rocks perhaps a dozen times before harrowing and dump them in the great weed-choked pile where you have dumped them since 1955, when you first took this tiger by the balls. And when you have picked them until the dirt won't come out from under your nails when you wash and your fingers feel huge and numb and oddly large-pored, you hitch your harrow to your tractor and before you've broken two rows you bust one of the blades on a rock you missed. And putting on a new blade, getting your oldest boy to hold up the hitch so you can get at it, the first mosquito of the new season buzzes blood-thirstily past your ear with that eye-watering hum that always makes you think it's the sound loonies must hear just before they kill all their kids or close their eyes on the Interstate and put the gas pedal to the floor or tighten their toe on the trigger of the .30-.30 they just jammed into their quackers; and then your boy's sweat-slicked fingers slip and one of the other round harrow blades scrapes skin from your arm and looking around in that kind of despairing, heartless flicker of time, when it seems you could just give it all over and take up drinking or go down to the bank that holds your mortgage and declare bankruptcy, at that moment of hating the land and the soft suck of gravity that holds you to it, you also love it and understand how it knows darkness and has always known it. The land has got you, locked up solid got you, and the house, and the woman you fell in love with when you started high school (only she was a girl then, and you didn't know for shit about girls except you got one and hung on to her and she wrote your name all over her book covers and first you broke her in and then she broke you in and then neither one of you had to worry about *that* mess anymore), and the kids have got you, the kids that were started in the creaky double bed with the splintered headboard. You and she made the kids after the darkness fell—six kids, or seven, or ten. The bank has you, and the car dealership, and the Sears store in Lewiston, and John Deere in Brunswick. But most of all the town has you because you know it the way you know the shape of your wife's breast. You know who will be hanging around Crossen's store in the daytime because Knapp Shoe laid him off and you know who is having woman trouble even before *he* knows it, the way Reggie Sawyer is having it, with that phone-company kid dipping his wick in Bonnie Sawyer's barrel; you know where the roads go and where, on Friday afternoon, you and Hank and Nolly

Gardener can go and park and drink a couple of six-packs or a couple of cases. You know how the ground lies and you know how to get through the Marshes in April without getting the tops of your boots wet. You know it all. And it knows you, how your crotch aches from the tractor saddle when the day's harrowing is done and how the lump on your back was just a cyst and nothing to worry about like the doctor said at first it might be, and how your mind works over the bills that come in during the last week of the month. It sees through your lies, even the ones you tell yourself, like how you are going to take the wife and the kids to Disneyland next year or the year after that, like how you can afford the payments on a new color TV if you cut cordwood next fall, like how everything is going to come out all right. Being in the town is a daily act of utter intercourse, so complete that it makes what you and your wife do in the squeaky bed look like a handshake. Being in the town is prosaic, sensuous, alcoholic. And in the dark, the town is yours and you are the town's and together you sleep like the dead, like the very stones in your north field. There is no life here but the slow death of days, and so when the evil falls on the town, its coming seems almost preordained, sweet and morphic. It is almost as though the town knows the evil was coming and the shape it would take.

The town has its secrets, and keeps them well. The people don't know them all. They know old Albie Crane's wife ran off with a traveling man from New York City—or they think they know it. But Albie cracked her skull open after the traveling man had left her cold and then he tied a block on her feet and tumbled her down the old well and twenty years later Albie died peacefully in his bed of a heart attack, just as his son Joe will die later in this story, and perhaps someday a kid will stumble on the old well where it is hidden by choked blackberry creepers and pull back the whitened, weather-smoothed boards and see that crumbling skeleton staring blankly up from the bottom of that rock-lined pit, the sweet traveling man's necklace still dangling, green and mossy, over her rib cage.

They know that Hubie Marsten killed his wife, but they don't know what he made her do first, or how it was with them in that sun-sticky kitchen in the moments before he blew her head in, with the smell of honeysuckle hanging in the hot air like the gagging sweetness of an uncovered charnel pit. They don't know that she begged him to do it.

Some of the older women in town—Mabel Werts, Glynis Mayberry, Audrey Hersey—remember that Larry McLeod found some charred papers in the upstairs fireplace, but none of them know that the papers were the accumulation of twelve years' correspondence between Hubert Marsten and an amusingly antique Austrian nobleman named Breichen, or that the correspondence of these two had commenced through the offices of a rather peculiar Boston book merchant who died an extremely nasty death in 1933, or that Hubie had burned each and every letter before hanging himself, feeding them to the fire one at a time, watching the flames blacken and char the thick, cream-colored paper and obliterate the elegant, spider-thin calligraphy. They don't know he was smiling as he did it, the way Larry Crockett now smiles over the fabulous land-title papers that reside in the safe-deposit box of his Portland bank.

They know that Coretta Simons, old Jumpin' Simons's widow, is dying slowly and horribly of intestinal cancer, but they don't know that there is better than thirty thousand dollars cash tucked away behind the dowdy sitting room wallpaper, the results of an insurance policy she collected but never invested and now, in her last extremity, has forgotten entirely.

They know that a fire burned up half of the town in that smoke-hazed September of 1951, but they don't know that it was set, and they don't know that the boy who set it graduated valedictorian of his class in 1953 and went on to make a hundred thousand dollars on Wall Street, and even if they *had* known, they would not have known the compulsion that drove him to it or the way it ate at his mind for the next twenty years of his life, until a brain embolism hustled him into his grave at the age of forty-six.

They don't know that the Reverend John Groggins has sometimes awakened in the midnight hour with horrible dreams still vivid beneath his bald pate—dreams in which he preaches to the Little Misses' Thursday Night Bible Class naked and slick, and they ready for him;

or that Floyd Tibbits wandered around for all of that Friday in a sickly daze, feeling the sun lie hatefully against his strangely pallid skin, remembering going to Ann Norton only cloudily, not remembering his attack on Ben Mears at all, but remembering the cool gratitude with which he greeted the setting of the sun, the gratitude and the anticipation of something great and good;

or that Hal Griffen has six hot books hidden in the back of his closet which he masturbates over at every opportunity;

or that George Middler has a suitcase full of silk slips and bras and panties and stockings and that he sometimes pulls down the shades of his apartment over the hardware store and locks the door with both the bolt and the chain and then stands in front of the full-length mirror in the bedroom until his breath comes in short stitches and then he falls to his knees and masturbates;

or that Carl Foreman tried to scream and was unable when Mike Ryerson began to tremble coldly on the metal worktable in the room beneath the mortuary and the scream was as sightless and soundless as glass in his throat when Mike opened his eyes and sat up;

or that ten-month-old Randy McDougall did not even struggle when Danny Glick slipped through his bedroom window and plucked the baby from his crib and sank his teeth into a neck still bruised from a mother's blows.

These are the town's secrets, and some will later be known and some will never be known. The town keeps them all with the ultimate poker face.

The town cares for devil's work no more than it cares for God's or man's. It knew darkness. And darkness was enough.

2

Sandy McDougall knew something was wrong when she woke up, but couldn't tell what. The other side of the bed was empty; it was Roy's day off, and he had gone fishing with some friends. Would be back around noon. Nothing was burning and she didn't hurt anywhere. So what could be wrong?

The sun. The sun was wrong.

It was high up on the wallpaper, dancing through the shadows cast by the maple outside the window. But Randy always woke her before the sun got up high enough to throw the maple's shadow on the wall—

Her startled eyes jumped to the clock on the dresser. It was ten minutes after nine.

Trepidation rose in her throat.

"Randy?" she called, her dressing gown billowing out behind her as she flew down the narrow hall of the trailer. "Randy, *honey?*"

The baby's bedroom was bathed in submerged light from the one small window above the crib . . . open. But she had closed it when she went to bed. She always closed it.

The crib was empty.

"Randy?" she whispered.

And saw him.

The small body, still clad in wash-faded Dr. Dentons, had been flung into the corner like a piece of garbage. One leg stuck up grotesquely, like an inverted exclamation point.

"Randy!"

She fell on her knees by the body, her face marked with the harsh lines of shock. She cradled the child. The body was cool to the touch.

"Randy, honey-baby, wake up, Randy, Randy, wake up—"

The bruises were gone. All gone. They had faded overnight, leaving the small face and form flawless. His color was good. For the only time since his coming she found him beautiful, and she screamed at the sight of the beauty—a horrible, desolate sound.

"Randy! *Wake up!* Randy? Randy? Randy?"

She got up with him and ran back down the hall, the dressing gown slipping off one shoulder. The high chair still stood in the kitchen, the tray encrusted with Randy's supper of the night before. She slipped Randy into the chair, which stood in a patch of morning sunlight. Randy's head lolled against his chest and he slid sideways with a slow and terrible finality until he was lodged in the angle between the tray and one of the chair's high arms.

"Randy?" she said, smiling. Her eyes bulged from their sockets like flawed blue marbles. She patted his cheeks. "Wake up now, Randy. Breakfast, Randy. Is oo hungwy? Please—oh Jesus, please—"

She whirled away from him and pulled open one of the cabinets over the stove and pawed through it, spilling a box of Rice Chex, a can of Chef Boy-ar-dee ravioli, a bottle of Wesson oil. The Wesson oil bottle shattered, spraying heavy liquid across the stove and floor. She found a small jar of Gerber's chocolate custard and grabbed one of the plastic Dairy Queen spoons out of the dish drainer.

"Look, Randy. Your favorite. Wake up and see the nice custard. Chocka, Randy. Chocka, chocka." Rage and terror swept her darkly. *"Wake up!"* she screamed at him, her spittle beading the translucent skin of his brow and cheeks. *"Wake up wake up for the love of God you little shit WAKE UP!"*

She pulled the cover off the jar and spooned out some of the chocolate-flavored custard. Her hand, which knew the truth already, was shaking so badly that most of it spilled. She pushed what was left between the small slack lips, and more fell off onto the tray, making horrid plopping sounds. The spoon clashed against his teeth.

"Randy," she pleaded. "Stop fooling your momma."

Her other hand stretched out, and she pulled his mouth open with a hooked finger and pushed the rest of the custard into his mouth.

"There," said Sandy McDougall. A smile, indescribable in its cracked hope, touched her lips. She settled back in her kitchen chair, relaxing muscle by muscle. Now it would be all right. Now he would know she still loved him and he would stop this cruel trickery.

"Good?" she murmured. "Chocka good, Wandy? Will oo make a smile for Mommy? Be Mommy's good boy and give her a smile."

She reached out with trembling fingers and pushed up the corners of Randy's mouth.

The chocolate fell out onto the tray—plop.

She began to scream.

3

Tony Glick woke up on Saturday morning when his wife, Marjorie, fell down in the living room.

"Margie?" he called, swinging his feet out onto the floor. "Marge?"

And after a long, long pause, she answered, "I'm okay, Tony."

He sat on the edge of the bed, looking blankly down at his feet. He was bare-chested and wearing striped pajama bottoms with the drawstring dangling between his legs. The hair on his head stood up in a crow's nest. It was thick black hair, and both of his sons had inherited it. People thought he was Jewish, but that dago hair should have been a giveaway, he often thought. His grandfather's name had been Gliccucchi. When someone had told him it was easier to get along in America if you had an American name, something short and snappy, Gramps had had it legally changed to Glick, unaware that he was trading the reality of one minority for the appearance of another. Tony Glick's body was wide and dark and heavily corded with muscle. His face bore the dazed expression of a man who has been punched out leaving a bar.

He had taken a leave of absence from his job, and during the past work week he had slept a lot. It went away when you slept. There were no dreams in his sleep. He turned in at seven-thirty and got up at ten the next morning and took a nap in the afternoon from two to three. The time he had gone through between the scene he had made at Danny's funeral and this sunny Saturday morning almost a week later seemed hazy and not real at all. People kept bringing food. Casseroles, preserves, cakes, pies. Margie said she didn't know what they were going to do with it. Neither of them was hungry. On Wednesday night he had tried to make love to his wife and they had both begun to cry.

Margie didn't look good at all. Her own method of coping had been to clean the house from top to bottom, and she had cleaned with a maniacal zeal that precluded all other thought.

The days resounded with the clash of cleaning buckets and the whirr of the vacuum cleaner, and the air was always redolent with the sharp smells of ammonia and Lysol. She had taken all the clothes and toys, packed neatly into cartons, to the Salvation Army and the Goodwill store. When he had come out of the bedroom on Thursday morning, all those cartons had been lined up by the front door, each neatly labeled. He had never seen anything so horrible in his life as those mute cartons. She had dragged all the rugs out into the back yard, had hung them over the clothes line, and had beaten the dust out of them unmercifully. And even in Tony's bleary state of consciousness, he had noticed how pale she had seemed since last Tuesday or Wednesday; even her lips seemed to have lost their natural color. Brown shadows had insinuated themselves beneath her eyes.

These thoughts passed through his mind in less time than it takes to tell them, and he was on the verge of tumbling back into bed when she fell down again and this time did not answer his call.

He got up and padded down to the living room and saw her lying on the floor, breathing shallowly and staring with dazed eyes at the ceiling. She had been changing the living room furniture around, and everything was pulled out of position, giving the room an odd disjointed look.

Whatever was wrong with her had advanced during the night, and her appearance was bad enough to cut through his daze like a sharp knife. She was still in her robe and it had split up to midthigh. Her legs were the color of marble; all the tan she had picked up that summer on their vacation had faded out of them. Her hands moved like ghosts. Her mouth gaped, as if her lungs could not get enough air, and he noticed the odd prominence of her teeth but thought nothing of it. It could have been the light.

"Margie? Honey?"

She tried to answer, couldn't, and real fear shot through him. He got up to call the doctor.

He was turning to the phone when she said, "No . . . no." The word was repeated between a harsh gasp for air. She had struggled up to a sitting position, and the whole sun-silent house was filled with her rasping struggle for breath.

"Pull me . . . help me . . . the sun is so hot. . . ."

He went to her and picked her up, shocked by the lightness of his burden. She seemed to weigh no more than a bundle of sticks.

". . . sofa . . ."

He laid her on it, with her back propped against the arm-rest. She was out of the patch of sun that fell in a square through the front window and onto the rug, and her breath seemed to come a little easier. She closed her eyes for a moment, and again he was impressed by the smooth whiteness of her teeth in contrast to her lips. He felt an urge to kiss her.

"Let me call the doctor," he said.

"No. I'm better. The sun was . . . burning me. Made me feel faint. Better now." A little color had come back into her cheeks.

"Are you sure?"

"Yes. I'm okay."

"You've been working too hard, honey."

"Yes," she said passively. Her eyes were listless.

He ran a hand through his hair, tugging at it. "We've got to snap out of this, Margie. We've got to. You look . . ." He paused, not wanting to hurt her.

"I look awful," she said. "I know. I looked at myself in the bathroom mirror before I went to bed last night, and I hardly seemed to be there. For a minute I . . ." A smile touched her lips. "I thought I could see the tub behind me. Like there was only a little of myself left and it was . . . oh, so *pale* . . ."

"I want Dr. Reardon to look at you."

But she seemed not to hear. "I've had the most lovely dream the last three or four nights, Tony. So real. Danny comes to me in the dream. He says, 'Mommy, Mommy, I'm so glad to be home!' And he says . . . says . . ."

"What does he say?" he asked her gently.

"He says . . . that he's my baby again. My own son, at my breast again. And I give him to suck and . . . and then a feeling of sweetness with an undertone of bitterness, so much like it was before he was weaned but after he was beginning to get teeth and he would nip—oh, this must sound *awful*. Like one of those psychiatrist things."

"No," he said. "No."

He knelt beside her and she put her arms around his neck and wept weakly. Her arms were cold. "No doctor, Tony, please. I'll rest today."

"All right," he said. Giving in to her made him feel uneasy.

"It's such a lovely dream, Tony," she said, speaking against his throat. The movement of her lips, the muffled hardness of her teeth beneath them, was amazingly sensual. He was getting an erection. "I wish I could have it again tonight."

"Maybe you will," he said, stroking her hair. "Maybe you will at that."

4

"My God, don't you look good," Ben said.

Against the hospital world of solid whites and anemic greens, Susan Norton looked very good indeed. She was wearing a bright yellow blouse with black vertical stripes and a short blue denim skirt.

"You, too," she said, and crossed the room to him.

He kissed her deeply, and his hand slid to the warm curve of her hip and rubbed.

"Hey," she said, breaking the kiss. "They kick you out for that."

"Not me."

"No, me."

They looked at each other.

"I love you, Ben."

"I love you, too."

"If I could jump in with you right now—"

"Just a second, let me pull back the spread."

"How would I explain it to those little candy-stripers?"

"Tell them you're giving me the bedpan."

She shook her head, smiling, and pulled up a chair. "A lot has happened in town, Ben."

He sobered. "Like what?"

She hesitated. "I hardly know how to tell you, or what I believe myself. I'm mixed up, to say the least."

"Well, spill it and let me sort it out."

"What's your condition, Ben?"

"Mending. Not serious. Matt's doctor, a guy named Cody—"

"No. Your mind. How much of this Count Dracula stuff do you believe?"

"Oh. That. Matt told you everything?"

"Matt's here in the hospital. One floor up in Intensive Care."

"What?" He was up on his elbows. "What's the matter with him?"

"Heart attack."

"Heart attack!"

"Dr. Cody says his condition is stable. He's listed as serious, but that's mandatory for the first forty-eight hours. I was there when it happened."

"Tell me everything you remember, Susan."

The pleasure had gone out of his face. It was watchful, intent, fine-drawn. Lost in the white room and the white sheets and the white hospital johnny, he again struck her as a man drawn to a taut, perhaps fraying edge.

"You didn't answer my question, Ben."

"About how I took Matt's story?"

"Yes."

"Let me answer you by saying what you think. You think the Marsten House has buggered my brain to the point where I'm seeing bats in my own belfry, to coin a phrase. Is that a fair estimate?"

"Yes, I suppose that's it. But I never thought about it in such . . . such harsh terms."

"I know that, Susan. Let me trace the progression of my thoughts for you, if I can. It may do me some good to sort them out. I can tell from your own face that something has knocked you back a couple of steps. Is that right?"

"Yes . . . but I don't believe, *can't*—"

"Stop a minute. That word *can't* blocks up everything. That's where I was stuck. That absolute, goddamned imperative word. *Can't.* I didn't believe Matt, Susan, because such things can't be true. But I couldn't find a hole in his story any way I looked at it. The most obvious conclusion was that he had jumped the tracks somewhere, right?"

"Yes."

"Did he seem crazy to you?"

"No. No, but—"

"Stop." He held up his hand. "You're thinking *can't* thoughts, aren't you?"

"I suppose I am," she said.

"He didn't seem crazy or irrational to me, either. And we both know that paranoid fantasies or persecution complexes just don't appear overnight. They grow over a period of time. They need careful watering, care, and feeding. Have you ever heard any talk in town about Matt having a screw loose? Ever heard Matt say that someone had the knife out for him? Has he ever been involved with any dubious causes—fluoridation causes brain cancer or Sons of the American Patriots or the NLF? Has he ever expressed an inordinate amount of interest in things such as séances or astral projection or reincarnation? Ever been arrested that you know of?"

"No," she said. "No to everything. But Ben . . . it hurts me to say this about Matt, even to suggest it, but some people go crazy very quietly. They go crazy inside."

"I don't think so," he said quietly. "There are signs. Sometimes you can't read them before, but you can afterward. If you were on a jury, would you believe Matt's testimony about a car crash?"

"Yes . . ."

"Would you believe him if he had told you he saw a prowler kill Mike Ryerson?"

"Yes, I guess I would."

"But not this."

"Ben, I just can't—"

"There, you said it again." He saw her ready to protest and held up a forestalling hand. "I'm not arguing his case, Susan. I'm only laying out my own train of thought. Okay?"

"Okay. Go on."

"My second thought was that somebody set him up. Someone with bad blood, or a grudge."

"Yes, that occurred to me."

"Matt says he has no enemies. I believe him."

"Everybody has enemies."

"There are degrees. Don't forget the most important thing—there's a dead man wrapped up in this mess. If someone was out to get Matt, then someone must have murdered Mike Ryerson to do it."

424

"Why?"

"Because the whole song and dance doesn't make much sense without a body. And yet, according to Matt's story, he met Mike purely by chance. No one led him to Dell's last Thursday night. There was no anonymous call, no note, no nothing. The coincidence of the meeting was enough to rule out a setup."

"What does that leave for rational explanations?"

"That Matt dreamed the sounds of the window going up, the laugh, and the sucking sounds. That Mike died of some natural but unknown causes."

"You don't believe that, either."

"I don't believe that he dreamed hearing the window go up. It was open. And the outside screen was lying on the lawn. I noticed it and Parkins Gillespie noticed it. And I noticed something else. Matt has latch-type screens on his house—they lock on the outside, not the inside. You can't get them off from the inside unless you pry them off with a screw driver or a paint scraper. Even then it would be tough. It would leave marks. I didn't see any marks. And here's another thing: The ground below that window was relatively soft. If you wanted to take off a second-floor screen, you'd need to use a ladder, and that would leave marks. There weren't any. That's what bothers me the most. A second-floor screen removed from the outside and no ladder marks beneath."

They looked at each other somberly.

He resumed: "I was running this through my head this morning. The more I thought about it, the better Matt's story looked. So I took a chance. I took the *can't* away for a while. Now, tell me what happened at Matt's last night. If it will knock all this into a cocked hat, no one is going to be happier than I."

"It doesn't," she said unhappily. "It makes it worse. He had just finished telling me about Mike Ryerson. He said he heard someone upstairs. He was scared, but he went." She folded her hands in her lap and was now holding them tightly, as if they might fly away. "Nothing else happened for a little while . . . and then Matt called out, something like he was revoking his invitation. Then . . . well, I don't really know how to . . ."

"Go on. Don't agonize over it."

"I think someone—someone *else*—made a kind of hissing noise. There was a bump, as if something had fallen." She looked at him bleakly. "And then I heard a voice say: *I will see you sleep like the dead, teacher.* That's word for word. And when I went in later to get a blanket for Matt I found this."

She took the ring out of her blouse pocket and dropped it into his hand.

Ben turned it over, then tilted it toward the window to let the light pick out the initials. "M.C.R. Mike Ryerson?"

"Mike Corey Ryerson. I dropped it and then made myself pick it up again—I thought you or Matt would want to see it. You keep it. I don't want it back."

"It makes you feel—?"

"Bad. Very bad." She raised her head defiantly. "But all rational thought goes against this, Ben. I'd rather believe that Matt somehow murdered Mike Ryerson and invented that crazy vampire story for reasons of his own. Rigged the screen to fall off. Did a ventriloquist act in that guest room while I was downstairs, planted Mike's ring—"

"And gave himself a heart attack to make it all seem more real," Ben said dryly. "I haven't given up hope of rational explanations, Susan. I'm hoping for one. Almost praying for one. Monsters in the movies are sort of fun, but the thought of them actually prowling through the night isn't fun at all. I'll even grant you that the screen could have been rigged—a simple rope sling anchored on the roof would do the trick. Let's go further. Matt is something of a scholar. I suppose there are poisons that would cause the symptoms that Mike had—maybe undetectable poisons. Of course, the idea of poison is a little hard to believe because Mike ate so little—"

"You only have Matt's word for that," she pointed out.

"He wouldn't lie, because he would know that an examination of the victim's stomach is an important part of any autopsy. And a hypo would leave tracks. But for the sake of argument, let's say it could be done. And a man like Matt could surely take something that would fake a heart attack. But where is the motive?"

She shook her head helplessly.

"Even granting some motive we don't suspect, why would he go to such Byzantine lengths, or invent such a wild cover story? I suppose Ellery Queen could explain it somehow, but life isn't an Ellery Queen plot."

"But this . . . this other is lunacy, Ben."

"Yes, like Hiroshima."

"Will you stop doing that!" she whipcracked at him suddenly. "Don't go playing the phony intellectual! It doesn't fit you! We're talking about wives' tales, bad dreams, psychosis, anything you want to call it—"

"That's shit," he said. "Make connections. The world is coming down around our ears and you're sticking at a few vampires."

" 'Salem's Lot is my town," she said stubbornly. "If something is happening there, it's real. Not philosophy."

"I couldn't agree with you more," he said, and touched the bandage on his head with a rueful finger. "And your ex packs a hell of a right."

"I'm sorry. That's a side of Floyd I never saw. I can't understand it."

"Where is he now?"

"In the town drunk tank. Parkins Gillespie told my mom he should turn him over to the county—to Sheriff McCaslin, that is—but he thought he'd wait and see if you wanted to prefer charges."

"Do you have any feelings in the matter?"

"None whatever," she said steadily. "He's out of my life."

"I'm not going to."

She raised her eyebrows.

"But I want to talk to him."

"About us?"

"About why he came at me wearing an overcoat, a hat, sunglasses . . . and Playtex rubber gloves."

"*What?*"

"Well," he said, looking at her, "the sun was out. It was shining on him. And I don't think he liked that."

They looked at each other wordlessly. There seemed to be nothing else on the subject to say.

5

When Nolly brought Floyd his breakfast from the Excellent Café, Floyd was fast asleep. It seemed to Nolly that it would be a meanness to wake him up just to eat a couple of Pauline Dickens's hard-fried eggs and five or six pieces of greasy bacon, so Nolly disposed of it himself in the office and drank the coffee, too. Pauline did make nice coffee—you could say that for her. But when he brought in Floyd's lunch and Floyd was still sleeping and still in the same position, Nolly got a little scared and set the tray on the floor and went over and banged on the bars with a spoon.

"Hey! Floyd! Wake up, I got y'dinner."

Floyd didn't wake up, and Nolly took his key ring out of his pocket to open the drunk-tank door. He paused just before inserting the key. Last week's *"Gunsmoke"* had been about a hard guy who pretended to be sick until he jumped the turnkey. Nolly had never thought of Floyd Tibbits as a particularly hard guy, but he hadn't exactly rocked that Mears guy to sleep.

He paused indecisively, holding the spoon in one hand and the key ring in the other, a big man whose open-throat white shirts always sweat-stained around the armpits by noon of a warm day. He was a league bowler with an average of 151 and a weekend bar-hopper with a list of Portland red-light bars and motels in his wallet right behind his Lutheran Ministry pocket calendar. He was a friendly man, a natural fall guy, slow of reaction and also slow to anger. For all these not inconsiderable advantages, he was not particularly agile on his mental feet and for several minutes he stood wondering how to proceed, beating on the bars with the spoon, hailing Floyd, wishing he would move or snore or do something. He was just thinking he better call Parkins on the citizen's band and get instructions when Parkins himself said from the office doorway:

"What in hell are you doin', Nolly? Callin' the hogs?"

Nolly blushed. "Floyd won't move, Park. I'm afraid that maybe he's . . . you know, sick."

"Well, do you think beatin' the bars with that goddamn

spoon will make him better?" Parkins stepped by him and unlocked the cell.

"Floyd?" He shook Floyd's shoulder. "Are you all r—"

Floyd fell off the chained bunk and onto the floor.

"Goddamn," said Nolly. "He's dead, ain't he?"

But Parkins might not have heard. He was staring down at Floyd's uncannily reposeful face. The fact slowly dawned on Nolly that Parkins looked as if someone had scared the bejesus out of him.

"What's the matter, Park?"

"Nothin'," Parkins said. "Just . . . let's get out of here." And then, almost to himself, he added: "Christ, I wish I hadn't touched him."

Nolly looked down at Floyd's body with dawning horror.

"Wake up," Parkins said. "We've got to get the doctor down here."

6

It was midafternoon when Franklin Boddin and Virgil Rathbun drove up to the slatted wooden gate at the end of the Burns Road fork, two miles beyond Harmony Hill Cemetery. They were in Franklin's 1957 Chevrolet pickup, a vehicle that had been Corinthian ivory back in the first year of Ike's second term but which was now a mixture of shit brown and primer-paint red. The back of the truck was filled with what Franklin called Crappie. Once every month or so, he and Virgil took a load of Crappie to the dump, and a great deal of said Crappie consisted of empty beer bottles, empty beer cans, empty half-kegs, empty wine bottles, and empty Popov vodka bottles.

"Closed," Franklin Boddin said, squinting to read the sign nailed to the gate. "Well I'll be dipped in shit." He took a honk off the bottle of Dawson's that had been resting comfortably against the bulge of his crotch and wiped his mouth with his arm. "This is Saturday, ain't it?"

"Sure is," Virgil Rathbun said. Virgil had no idea if it was Saturday or Tuesday. He was so drunk he wasn't even sure what month it was.

"Dump ain't closed on Saturday, is it?" Franklin asked. There was only one sign, but he was seeing three. He squinted again. All three signs said "Closed." The paint was barn-red and had undoubtedly come out of the can of paint that rested inside the door of Dud Rogers's caretaker shack.

"Never was closed on Saturday," Virgil said. He swung his bottle of beer toward his face, missed his mouth, and poured a blurt of beer on his left shoulder. "God, that hits the spot."

"Closed," Franklin said, with mounting irritation. "That son of a whore is off on a toot, that's what. I'll close *him*." He threw the truck into first gear and popped the clutch. Beer foamed out of the bottle between his legs and ran over his pants.

"Wind her, Franklin!" Virgil cried, and let out a massive belch as the pickup crashed through the gate, knocking it onto the can-littered verge of the road. Franklin shifted into second and shot up the rutted, chuck-holed road. The truck bounced madly on its worn springs. Bottles fell off the back end and smashed. Sea gulls took to the air in screaming, circling waves.

A quarter of a mile beyond the gate, the Burns Road fork (now known as the Dump Road) ended in a widening clearing that was the dump. The close-pressing alders and maples gave way to reveal a great flat area of raw earth which had been scored and runneled by the constant use of the old Case bull-dozer which was now parked by Dud's shack. Beyond this flat area was the gravel pit where current dumping went on. The trash and garbage, glitter-shot with bottles and aluminum cans, stretched away in gigantic dunes.

"Goddamn no-account hunchbacked pisswah, looks like he ain't plowed nor burned all the week long," Franklin said. He jammed both feet on the brake pedal, which sank all the way to the floor with a mechanical scream. After a while the truck stopped. "He's laid up with a case, that's what."

"I never knew Dud to drink much," Virgil said, tossing his empty out the window and pulling another from the brown bag on the floor. He opened it on the door latch, and the beer, crazied up from the bumps, bubbled out over his hand.

"All them hunchbacks do," Franklin said wisely. He spat out the window, discovered it was closed, and swiped his shirt sleeve across the scratched and cloudy glass. "We'll go see him. Might be somethin' in it."

He backed the truck around in a huge, wandering circle and pulled up with the tailgate hanging over the latest accumulation of the Lot's accumulated throwaway. He switched off the ignition, and silence pressed in on them suddenly. Except for the restless calling of the gulls, it was complete.

"Ain't it *quiet*," Virgil muttered.

They got out of the truck and went around to the back. Franklin unhooked the S-bolts that held the tailgate and let it drop with a crash. The gulls that had been feeding at the far end of the dump rose in a cloud, squalling and scolding.

The two of them climbed up without a word and began heaving the Crappie off the end. Green plastic bags spun through the clear air and smashed open as they hit. It was an old job for them. They were a part of the town that few tourists ever saw (or cared to)—firstly, because the town ignored them by tacit agreement, and secondly, because they had developed their own protective coloration. If you met Franklin's pickup on the road, you forgot it the instant it was gone from your rear-view mirror. If you happened to see their shack with its tin chimney sending a pencil line of smoke into the white November sky, you overlooked it. If you met Virgil coming out of the Cumberland greenfront with a bottle of welfare vodka in a brown bag, you said hi and then couldn't quite remember who it was you had spoken to; the face was familiar but the name just slipped your mind. Franklin's brother was Derek Boddin, father of Richie (lately deposed king of Stanley Street Elementary School), and Derek had nearly forgotten that Franklin was still alive and in town. He had progressed beyond black sheepdom; he was totally gray.

Now, with the truck empty, Franklin kicked out a last can—*clink!*—and hitched up his green work pants. "Let's go see Dud," he said.

They climbed down from the truck and Virgil tripped over one of his own rawhide lacings and sat down hard. "Christ, they don't make these things half-right," he muttered obscurely.

They walked across to Dud's tarpaper shack. The door was closed.

"Dud!" Franklin bawled. "Hey, Dud Rogers!" He thumped the door once, and the whole shack trembled. The small hook-and-eye lock on the inside of the door snapped off, and the door tottered open. The shack was empty but filled with a sickish-sweet odor that made them look at each other and grimace—and they were barroom veterans of a great many fungoid smells. It reminded Franklin fleetingly of pickles that had lain in a dark crock for many years, until the fluid seeping out of them had turned white.

"Son of a whore," Virgil said. "Worse than gangrene."

Yet the shack was astringently neat. Dud's extra shirt was hung on a hook over the bed, the splintery kitchen chair was pushed up to the table, and the cot was made up Army-style. The can of red paint, with fresh drips down the sides, was placed on a fold of newspaper behind the door.

"I'm about to puke if we don't get out of here," Virgil said. His face had gone a whitish-green.

Franklin, who felt no better, backed out and shut the door.

They surveyed the dump, which was as deserted and sterile as the mountains of the moon.

"He ain't here," Franklin said. "He's back in the woods someplace, laying up snookered."

"Frank?"

"What," Franklin said shortly. He was out of temper.

"That door was latched on the inside. If he ain't there, how did he get out?"

Startled, Franklin turned around and regarded the shack. *Through the window,* he started to say, and then didn't. The window was nothing but a square cut into the tarpaper and buttoned up with all-weather plastic. The window wasn't large enough for Dud to squirm through, not with the hump on his back.

"Never mind," Franklin said gruffly. "If he don't want to share, fuck him. Let's get out of here."

They walked back to the truck, and Franklin felt something seeping through the protective membrane of drunkenness—something he would not remember later, or want to: a creeping feeling; a feeling that something here had gone terribly awry. It was as if the dump had gained a heartbeat and that beat was slow yet full of terrible vitality. He suddenly wanted to go away very quickly.

"I don't see any rats," Virgil said suddenly.

And there were none to be seen; only the gulls. Franklin tried to remember a time when he had brought the Crappie to the dump and seen no rats. He couldn't. And he didn't like that, either.

"He must have put out poison bait, huh, Frank?"

"Come on, let's go," Franklin said. "Let's get the hell out of here."

7

After supper, they let Ben go up and see Matt Burke. It was a short visit; Matt was sleeping. The oxygen tent had been taken away, however, and the head nurse told Ben that Matt would almost certainly be awake tomorrow morning and able to see visitors for a short time.

Ben thought his face looked drawn and cruelly aged, for the first time an old man's face. Lying still, with the loosened flesh of his neck rising out of the hospital johnny, he seemed vulnerable and defenseless. If it's all true, Ben thought, these people are doing you no favors, Matt. If it's all true, then we're in the citadel of unbelief, where nightmares are dispatched with Lysol and scalpels and chemotherapy rather than with stakes and Bibles and wild mountain thyme. They're happy with their life support units and hypos and enema bags filled with barium solution. If the column of truth has a hole in it, they neither know nor care.

He walked to the head of the bed and turned Matt's head with gentle fingers. There were no marks on the skin of his neck; the flesh was blameless.

He hesitated a moment longer, then went to the closet and opened it. Matt's clothes hung there, and hooked over the closet door's inside knob was the crucifix he had been wearing when Susan visited him. It hung from a filigreed chain that gleamed softly in the room's subdued light.

Ben took it back to the bed and put it around Matt's neck.

"Here, what are you doing?"

A nurse had come in with a pitcher of water and a bedpan with a towel spread decorously over the opening.

"I'm putting his cross around his neck," Ben said.

"Is he a Catholic?"

"He is now," Ben said somberly.

8

Night had fallen when a soft rap came at the kitchen door of the Sawyer house on the Deep Cut Road. Bonnie Sawyer, with a small smile on her lips, went to answer it. She was wearing a short ruffled apron tied at the waist, high heels, and nothing else.

When she opened the door, Corey Bryant's eyes widened and his mouth dropped open. "Buh," he said. "Buh . . . Buh . . . Bonnie?"

"What's the matter, Corey?" She put a hand on the door-jamb with light deliberation, pulling her bare breasts up to their sauciest angle. At the same time she crossed her feet demurely, modeling her legs for him.

"Jeez, Bonnie, what if it had been—"

"The man from the telephone company?" she asked, and giggled. She took one of his hands and placed it on the firm flesh of her right breast. "Want to read my meter?"

With a grunt that held a note of desperation (the drowning man going down for the third time, clutching a mammary instead of a straw), he pulled her to him. His hands cupped her buttocks, and the starched apron crackled briskly between them.

"Oh my," she said, wiggling against him. "Are you going to test my receiver, Mr. Telephone Man? I've been waiting for an important call all day—"

He picked her up and kicked the door shut behind him. She did not need to direct him to the bedroom. He knew his way.

"You're sure he's not going to be home?" he asked.

Her eyes gleamed in the darkness. "Why, who can you mean, Mr. Telephone Man? Not my handsome hubby . . . he's in Burlington, Vermont."

He put her down on the bed crossways, with her legs dangling off the side.

"Turn on the light," she said, her voice suddenly slow and heavy. "I want to see what you're doing."

He turned on the bedside lamp and looked down at her.

The apron had been pulled away to one side. Her eyes were heavy-lidded and warm, the pupils large and brilliant.

"Take that thing off," he said, gesturing.

"You take it off," she said. "You can figure out the knots, Mr. Telephone Man."

He bent to do it. She always made him feel like a dry-mouth kid stepping up to the plate for the first time, and his hands always trembled when they got near her, as if her very flesh was transmitting a strong current into the air all around her. She never left his mind completely anymore. She was lodged in there like a sore inside the cheek which the tongue keeps poking and testing. She even cavorted through his dreams, golden-skinned, blackly exciting. Her invention knew no bounds.

"No, on your knees," she said. "Get on your knees for me."

He dropped clumsily onto his knees and crawled toward her, reaching for the apron ties. She put one high-heeled foot on each shoulder. He bent to kiss the inside of her thigh, the flesh firm and slightly warm under his lips.

"That's right, Corey, that's just right, keep going up, keep—"

"Well, this is cute, ain't it?"

Bonnie Sawyer screamed.

Corey Bryant looked up, blinking and confused.

Reggie Sawyer was leaning in the bedroom doorway. He was holding a shotgun cradled loosely over his forearm, barrels pointed at the floor.

Corey felt a warm gush as his bladder let go.

"So it's true," Reggie marveled. He stepped into the room. He was smiling. "How about that? I owe that tosspot Mickey Sylvester a case of Budweiser. Goddamn."

Bonnie found her voice first.

"Reggie, listen. It isn't what you think. He broke in, he was like a crazyman, he, he was—"

"Shut up, cunt." He was still smiling. It was a gentle smile. He was quite big. He was wearing the same steel-colored suit he had been wearing when she had kissed him good-by two hours before.

"Listen," Corey said weakly. His mouth felt full of loose spit. "Please. Please don't kill me. Not even if I deserve it. You don't want to go to jail. Not over this. Beat me up, I got that coming, but please don't—"

"Get up off your knees, Perry Mason," Reggie Sawyer said, still smiling his gentle smile. "Your fly's unzipped."

"Listen, Mr. Sawyer—"

"Oh, call me Reggie," Reggie said, smiling gently. "We're almost best buddies. I've even been getting your sloppy seconds, isn't that right?"

"Reggie, this isn't what you think, he raped me—"

Reggie looked at her and his smile was gentle and benign. "If you say another word, I'm going to jam this up inside you and let you have some special airmail."

Bonnie began to moan. Her face had gone the color of unflavored yogurt.

"Mr. Sawyer . . . Reggie . . ."

"Your name's Bryant, ain't it? Your daddy's Pete Bryant, ain't he?"

Corey's head bobbed madly in agreement. "Yeah, that's right. That's just right. Listen—"

"I used to sell him number two fuel oil when I was driving for Jim Webber," Reggie said, smiling with gentle reminiscence. "That was four or five years before I met this high-box bitch here. Your daddy know you're here?"

"No, sir, it'd break his heart. You can beat me up, I got that coming, but if you kill me my daddy'd find out and I bet it'd kill him dead as shit and then you'd be responsible for two—"

"No, I bet he don't know. Come on out in the living room a minute. We got to talk this over. Come on." He smiled gently at Corey to show him that he meant him no harm and then his eyes flicked to Bonnie, who was staring at him with bulging eyes. "You stay right there, puss, or you ain't never going to know how 'Secret Storm' comes out. Come on, Bryant." He gestured with the shotgun.

Corey walked out into the living room ahead of Reggie, staggering a little. His legs were rubber. A patch between his shoulder blades began to itch insanely. That's where he's going to put it, he thought, right between the shoulder blades. I wonder if I'll live long enough to see my guts hit the wall—

"Turn around," Reggie said.

Corey turned around. He was beginning to blubber. He didn't want to blubber, but he couldn't seem to help it. He supposed it didn't matter if he blubbered or not. He had already wet himself.

The shotgun was no longer dangling casually over Reggie's forearm. The double barrels were pointing directly at Corey's face. The twin bores seemed to swell and yawn until they were bottomless wells.

"You know what you been doin'?" Reggie asked. The smile was gone. His face was very grave.

Corey didn't answer. It was a stupid question. He did keep on blubbering, however.

"You slept with another guy's wife, Corey. That your name?"

Corey nodded, tears streaming down his cheeks.

"You know what happens to guys like that if they get caught?"

Corey nodded.

"Grab the barrel of this shotgun, Corey. Very easy. It's got a five-pound pull and I got about three on it now. So pretend . . . oh, pretend you're grabbing my wife's tit."

Corey reached out one shaking hand and placed it on the barrel of the shotgun. The metal was cool against his flushed palm. A long, agonized groan came out of his throat. Nothing else was left. Pleading was done.

"Put it in your mouth, Corey. Both barrels. Yes, that's right. Easy! . . . that's okay. Yes, your mouth's big enough. Slip it right in there. You know all about slipping it in, don't you?"

Corey's jaws were open to their widest accommodation. The barrels of the shotgun were pushed back nearly to his palate, and his terrified stomach was trying to retch. The steel was oily against his teeth.

"Close your eyes, Corey."

Corey only stared at him, his swimming eyes as big as tea saucers.

Reggie smiled his gentle smile again. "Close those baby blue eyes, Corey."

Corey closed them.

His sphincter let go. He was only dimly aware of it.

Reggie pulled both triggers. The hammers fell on empty chambers with a double *click-click*.

Corey fell onto the floor in a dead faint.

Reggie looked down at him for a moment, smiling gently, and then reversed the shotgun so the butt end was up. He turned to the bedroom. "Here I come, Bonnie. Ready or not."

Bonnie Sawyer began to scream.

9

Corey Bryant was stumbling up the Deep Cut Road toward where he had left his phone truck parked. He stank. His eyes were bloodshot and glassy. There was a large bump on the back of his head where he had struck it on the floor when he fainted. His boots made dragging, scuffing sounds on the soft shoulder. He tried to think about the scuffing sounds and nothing else, most notably about the sudden and utter ruin of his life. It was quarter past eight.

Reggie Sawyer had still been smiling gently when he ushered Corey out the kitchen door. Bonnie's steady, racking sobs had come from the bedroom, counterpointing his words. "You go on up the road like a good boy, now. Get in your truck and go back to town. There's a bus that comes in from Lewiston for Boston at quarter to ten. From Boston you can get a bus to anywhere in the country. That bus stops at Spencer's. You be on it. Because if I ever see you again, I'm going to kill you. She'll be all right now. She's broke in now. She's gonna have to wear pants and long-sleeve blouses for a couple of weeks, but I didn't mark her face. You just want to get out of 'salem's Lot before you clean yourself up and start thinking you are a man again."

And now here he was, walking up this road, about to do just what Reggie Sawyer said. He could go south from Boston . . . somewhere. He had a little over a thousand dollars saved in the bank. His mother had always said he was a very saving soul. He could wire for the money, live on it until he could get a job and begin the years-long job of forgetting this night—the taste of the gun barrel, the smell of his own shit satcheled in his trousers.

"Hello, Mr. Bryant."

Corey gave a stifled scream and stared wildly into the dark, at first seeing nothing. The wind was moving in the trees, making shadows jump and dance across the road. Suddenly his eyes made out a more solid shadow, standing by the stone wall that ran between the road and Carl Smith's back pasture. The shadow had a manlike form, but there was something . . . something . . .

"Who are you?"

"A friend who sees much, Mr. Bryant."

The form shifted and came from the shadows. In the faint light, Corey saw a middle-aged man with a black mustache and deep, bright eyes.

"You've been ill used, Mr. Bryant."

"How do you know my business?"

"I know a great deal. It's my business to know. Smoke?"

"Thanks." He took the offered cigarette gratefully. He put it between his lips. The stranger struck a light, and in the glow of the wooden match he saw that the stranger's cheekbones were high and Slavic, his forehead pale and bony, his dark hair swept straight back. Then the light was gone and Corey was dragging harsh smoke into his lungs. It was a dago cigarette, but any cigarette was better than none. He began to feel a little calmer.

"Who are you?" he asked again.

The stranger laughed, a startlingly rich and full-bodied sound that drifted off on the slight breeze like the smoke of Corey's cigarette.

"Names!" he said. "Oh, the American insistence on names! Let me sell you an auto because I am Bill Smith! Eat at this one! Watch that one on television! My name is Barlow, if that eases you." And he burst into laughter again, his eyes twinkling and shining. Corey felt a smile creep onto his own lips and could scarcely believe it. His troubles seemed distant, unimportant, in comparison to the derisive good humor in those dark eyes.

"You're a foreigner, aren't you?" Corey asked.

"I am from many lands; but to me this country . . . this town . . . seems full of foreigners. You see? Eh? Eh?" He burst into that full-throated crow of laughter again, and this time Corey found himself joining in. The laughter escaped his throat under full pressure, rising a bit with delayed hysteria.

"Foreigners, yes," he resumed, "but beautiful, enticing foreigners, bursting with vitality, full-blooded and full of life. Do you know how beautiful the people of your country and your town are, Mr. Bryant?"

Corey only chuckled, slightly embarrassed. He did not look away from the stranger's face, however. It held him rapt.

"They have never known hunger or want, the people of this country. It has been two generations since they knew anything close to it, and even then it was like a voice in a distant room. They think they have known sadness, but their sadness is that of a child who has spilled his ice cream on the grass at a birthday party. There is no . . . how is the English? . . . attenuation in them. They spill each other's blood with great vigor. Do you believe it? Do you see?"

"Yes," Corey said. Looking into the stranger's eyes, he could see a great many things, all of them wonderful.

"The country is an amazing paradox. In other lands, when a man eats to his fullest day after day, that man becomes fat . . . sleepy . . . piggish. But in this land . . . it seems the more you have the more aggressive you become. You see? Like Mr. Sawyer. With so much; yet he begrudges you a few crumbs from his table. Also like a child at a birthday party, who will push away another baby even though he himself can eat no more. Is it not so?"

"Yes," Corey said. Barlow's eyes were so large, and so understanding. It was all a matter of—

"It is all a matter of perspective, is it not?"

"Yes!" Corey exclaimed. The man had put his finger on the right, the exact, the perfect, word. The cigarette dropped unnoticed from his fingers and lay smoldering on the road.

"I might have bypassed such a rustic community as this," the stranger said reflectively. "I might have gone to one of your great and teeming cities. Bah!" He drew himself up suddenly, and his eyes flashed. "What do I know of cities? I should be run over by a hansom crossing the street! I should choke on nasty air! I should come in contact with sleek, stupid dilettantes whose concerns are . . . what do you say? inimical? . . . yes, inimical to me. How should a poor rustic like myself deal with the hollow sophistication of a great city . . . even an American city? No! And no and no! I *spit* on your cities!"

"Oh yes!" Corey whispered.

"So I have come here, to a town which was first told of to me by a most brilliant man, a former townsman himself, now lamentably deceased. The folk here are still rich and full-blooded, folk who are stuffed with the aggression and darkness so necessary to . . . there is no English for it. *Pokol; vurderlak; eyalik.* Do you follow?"

"Yes," Corey whispered.

"The people have not cut off the vitality which flows from their mother, the earth, with a shell of concrete and cement. Their hands are plunged into the very waters of life. They have ripped the life from the earth, whole and beating! Is it not true?"

"Yes!"

The stranger chuckled kindly and put a hand on Corey's shoulder. "You are a good boy. A fine, strong boy. I don't think you want to leave this so-perfect town, do you?"

"No . . ." Corey whispered, but he was suddenly doubtful. Fear was returning. But surely it was unimportant. This man would allow no harm to come to him.

"And so you shall not. Ever again."

Corey stood trembling, rooted to the spot, as Barlow's head inclined toward him.

"And you shall yet have your vengeance on those who would fill themselves while others want."

Corey Bryant sank into a great forgetful river, and that river was time, and its waters were red.

10

It was nine o'clock and the Saturday night movie was coming on the hospital TV bolted to the wall when the phone beside Ben's bed rang. It was Susan, and her voice was barely under control.

"Ben, Floyd Tibbits is dead. He died in his cell some time last night. Dr. Cody says acute anemia—but I *went* with Floyd! He had high blood pressure. That's why the Army wouldn't take him!"

"Slow down," Ben said, sitting up.

"There's more. A family named McDougall out in the Bend. A little ten months baby died out there. They took Mrs. McDougall away in restraints."

"Have you heard how the baby died?"

"My mother said Mrs. Evans came over when she heard Sandra McDougall screaming, and Mrs. Evans called old Dr. Plowman. Plowman didn't say anything, but Mrs. Evans told my mother that she couldn't see a thing wrong with the baby . . . except it was dead."

"And both Matt and I, the crackpots, just happen to be out of town and out of action," Ben said, more to himself than to Susan. "Almost as if it were planned."

"There's more."

"What?"

"Carl Foreman is missing. And so is the body of Mike Ryerson."

"I think that's it," he heard himself saying. "That has to be it. I'm getting out of here tomorrow."

"Will they let you go so soon?"

"They aren't going to have anything to say about it." He spoke the words absently; his mind had already moved on to another subject. "Have you got a crucifix?"

"Me?" She sounded startled and a little amused. "Gosh, no."

"I'm not joking with you, Susan—I was never more serious. Is there anyplace where you can get one at this hour?"

"Well, there's Marie Boddin. I could walk—"

"No. Stay off the streets. Stay in the house. Make one yourself, even if it only means gluing two sticks together. Leave it by your bed."

"Ben, I still don't believe this. A maniac, maybe, someone who *thinks* he's a vampire, but—"

"Believe what you want, but make the cross."

"But—"

"Will you do it? Even if it only means humoring me?"

Reluctantly: "Yes, Ben."

"Can you come to the hospital tomorrow around nine?"

"Yes."

"Okay. We'll go upstairs and fill in Matt together. Then you and I are going to talk to Dr. James Cody."

She said, "He's going to think you're crazy, Ben. Don't you know that?"

"I suppose I do. But it all seems more real after dark, doesn't it?"

"Yes," she said softly. "God, yes."

For no reason at all he thought of Miranda and Miranda's dying: the motorcycle hitting the wet patch, going into a skid, the sound of her scream, his own brute panic, and the side of the truck growing and growing as they approached it broadside.

"Susan?"

"Yes."

"Take good care of yourself. Please."

After she hung up, he put the phone back in the cradle and stared at the TV, barely seeing the Doris Day–Rock Hudson comedy that had begun to unreel up there. He felt naked, exposed. He had no cross himself. His eyes strayed to the windows, which showed only blackness. The old, childlike terror of the dark began to creep over him and he looked at the television where Doris Day was giving a shaggy dog a bubble bath and was afraid.

11

The county morgue in Portland is a cold and antiseptic room done entirely in green tile. The floors and walls are a uniform medium green, and the ceiling is a lighter green. The walls are lined with square doors which look like large bus-terminal coin lockers. Long parallel fluorescent tubes shed a chilly neutral light over all of this. The decor is hardly inspired, but none of the clientele have ever been known to complain.

At quarter to ten on this Saturday night, two attendants were wheeling in the sheet-covered body of a young homosexual who had been shot in a downtown bar. It was the first stiff they had received that night; the highway fatals usually came in between 1:00 and 3:00 A.M.

Buddy Bascomb was in the middle of a Frenchman joke that had to do with vaginal deodorant spray when he broke off in midsentence and stared down the line of locker doors M–Z. Two of them were standing open.

He and Bob Greenberg left the new arrival and hurried down quickly. Buddy glanced at the tag on the first door he came to while Bob went down to the next.

TIBBETS, FLOYD MARTIN
SEX: M
ADMITTED: 10/4/75
AUTOPS. SCHED.: 10/5/75
SIGNATOR: J. M. Cody, M.D.

He yanked the handle set inside the door, and the slab rolled out on silent casters.

Empty.

"Hey!" Greenberg yelled up to him. "This fucking thing is empty! Whose idea of a joke—"

"I was on the desk all the time," Buddy said. "No one went by me. I'd swear to it. It must have happened on Carty's shift. What's the name on that one?"

"McDougall, Randall Fratus. What does this abbreviation *inf.* mean?"

"Infant," Buddy said dully. "Jesus Christ, I think we're in trouble."

12

Something had awakened him.

He lay still in the ticking dark, looking at the ceiling.

A noise. Some noise. But the house was silent.

There it was again. Scratching.

Mark Petrie turned over in bed and looked through the window and Danny Glick was staring in at him through the glass, his skin grave-pale, his eyes reddish and feral. Some dark substance was smeared about his lips and chin, and when he saw Mark looking at him, he smiled and showed teeth grown hideously long and sharp.

"Let me in," the voice whispered, and Mark was not sure if the words had crossed dark air or were only in his mind.

He became aware that he was frightened—his body had known before his mind. He had never been so frightened, not even when he got tired swimming back from the float at Popham Beach and thought he was going to drown. His mind, still that of a child in a thousand ways, made an accurate judgment of his position in seconds. He was in peril of more than his life.

"Let me in, Mark. I want to play with you."

There was nothing for that hideous entity outside the window to hold onto; his room was on the second floor and there was no ledge. Yet somehow it hung suspended in space . . . or perhaps it was clinging to the outside shingles like some dark insect.

"Mark . . . I finally came, Mark. Please . . ."

Of course. You have to invite them inside. He knew that from his monster magazines, the ones his mother was afraid might damage or warp him in some way.

He got out of bed and almost fell down. It was only then that he realized fright was too mild a word for this. Even terror did not express what he felt. The pallid face outside the window tried to smile, but it had lain in darkness too long to remember precisely how. What Mark saw was a twitching grimace—a bloody mask of tragedy.

Yet if you looked in the eyes, it wasn't so bad. If you looked in the eyes, you weren't so afraid anymore and you saw that all you had to do was open the window and say, "C'mon in, Danny," and then you wouldn't be afraid at all because you'd be at one with Danny and all of them and at one with *him.* You'd be—

No! That's how they get you!

He dragged his eyes away, and it took all of his will power to do it.

"Mark, let me in! I command it! *He* commands it!"

Mark began to walk toward the window again. There was no help for it. There was no possible way to deny that voice. As he drew closer to the glass, the evil little boy's face on the other side began to twitch and grimace with eagerness. Fingernails, black with earth, scratched across the windowpane.

Think of something. Quick! Quick!

"The rain," he whispered hoarsely. "The rain in Spain falls mainly on the plain. In vain he thrusts his fists against the posts and still insists he sees the ghosts."

Danny Glick hissed at him.

"Mark! Open the window!"

"Betty Bitter bought some butter—"

"The window, Mark, *he* commands it!"

"—but, says Betty, this butter's bitter."

He was weakening. That whispering voice was seeing through his barricade, and the command was imperative. Mark's eyes fell on his desk, littered with his model monsters, now so bland and foolish—

His eyes fixed abruptly on part of the display, and widened slightly.

The plastic ghoul was walking through a plastic graveyard and one of the monuments was in the shape of a cross.

With no pause for thought or consideration (both would have come to an adult—his father, for instance—and both would have undone him), Mark swept up the cross, curled it into a tight fist, and said loudly: "Come on in, then."

The face became suffused with an expression of vulpine triumph. The window slid up and Danny stepped in and took two paces forward. The exhalation from that opening mouth was fetid, beyond description: a smell of charnel pits. Cold, fish-white hands descended on Mark's shoulders. The head cocked, doglike, the upper lip curled away from those shining canines.

Mark brought the plastic cross around in a vicious swipe and laid it against Danny Glick's cheek.

His scream was horrible, unearthly . . . and silent. It echoed only in the corridors of his brain and the chambers of his soul. The smile of triumph on the Glick-thing's mouth became a yawning grimace of agony. Smoke spurted from the pallid flesh, and for just a moment, before the creature twisted away and half dived, half fell out the window, Mark felt the flesh yield like smoke.

And then it was over, as if it had never happened.

But for a moment the cross shone with a fierce light, as if an inner wire had been ignited. Then it dwindled away, leaving only a blue after-image in front of his eyes.

Through the grating in the floor, he heard the distinctive click of the lamp in his parents' bedroom and his father's voice: "What in hell was that?"

13

His bedroom door opened two minutes later, but that was still time enough to set things to rights.

"Son?" Henry Petrie asked softly. "Are you awake?"

"I guess so," Mark answered sleepily.

"Did you have a bad dream?"

"I . . . think so. I don't remember."

"You called out in your sleep."

"Sorry."

"No, don't be sorry." He hesitated and then spoke from earlier memories of his son, a small child in a blue blanket-suit that had been much more trouble but infinitely more explicable: "Do you want a drink of water?"

"No thanks, Dad."

Henry Petrie surveyed the room briefly, unable to understand the trembling feeling of dread he had wakened with, and which lingered still—a feeling of disaster averted by cold inches. Yes, everything seemed all right. The window was shut. Nothing was knocked over.

"Mark, is anything wrong?"

"No, Dad."

"Well . . . g'night, then."

"Night."

The door shut softly and his father's slippered feet descended the stairs. Mark let himself go limp with relief and delayed reaction. An adult might have had hysterics at this point, and a slightly younger or older child might also have done. But Mark felt the terror slip from him in almost imperceptible degrees, and the sensation reminded him of letting the wind dry you after you had been swimming on a cool day. And as the terror left, drowsiness began to come in its place.

Before drifting away entirely, he found himself reflecting—not for the first time—on the peculiarity of adults. They took laxatives, liquor, or sleeping pills to drive away their terrors so that sleep would come, and their terrors were so tame and domestic: the job, the money, what the teacher will think if I

447

can't get Jennie nicer clothes, does my wife still love me, who are my friends. They were pallid compared to the fears every child lies cheek and jowl with in his dark bed, with no one to confess to in hope of perfect understanding but another child. There is no group therapy or psychiatry or community social services for the child who must cope with the thing under the bed or in the cellar every night, the thing which leers and capers and threatens just beyond the point where vision will reach. The same lonely battle must be fought night after night and the only cure is the eventual ossification of the imaginary faculties, and this is called adulthood.

In some shorter, simpler mental shorthand, these thoughts passed through his brain. The night before, Matt Burke had faced such a dark thing and had been stricken by a heart seizure brought on by fright; tonight Mark Petrie had faced one, and ten minutes later lay in the lap of sleep, the plastic cross still grasped loosely in his right hand like a child's rattle. Such is the difference between men and boys.

Chapter Eleven
BEN (IV)

1

It was ten past nine on Sunday morning—a bright, sun-washed Sunday morning—and Ben was beginning to get seriously worried about Susan when the phone by his bed rang. He snatched it up.

"Where are you?"

"Relax. I'm upstairs with Matt Burke. Who requests the pleasure of your company as soon as you're able."

"Why didn't you come—"

"I looked in on you earlier. You were sleeping like a lamb."

"They give you knockout stuff in the night so they can steal different organs for mysterious billionaire patients," he said. "How's Matt?"

"Come up and see for yourself," she said, and before she could do more than hang up, he was getting into his robe.

2

Matt looked much better, rejuvenated, almost. Susan was sitting by his bed in a bright blue dress, and Matt raised a hand in salute when Ben walked in. "Drag up a rock."

Ben pulled over one of the hideously uncomfortable hospital chairs and sat down. "How you feeling?"

"A lot better. Weak, but better. They took the I.V. out of my arm last night and gave me a poached egg for breakfast this morning. Gag. Previews of the old folks home."

Ben kissed Susan lightly and saw a strained kind of composure on her face, as if everything was being held together by fine wire.

"Is there anything new since you called last night?"

"Nothing I've heard. But I left the house around seven and the Lot wakes up a little later on Sunday."

Ben shifted his gaze to Matt. "Are you up to talking this thing over?"

"Yes, I think so," he said, and shifted slightly. The gold cross Ben had hung around his neck flashed prominently. "By the way, thank you for this. It's a great comfort, even though I bought it on the remaindered shelf at Woolworth's Friday afternoon."

"What's your condition?"

" 'Stabilized' is the fulsome term young Dr. Cody used when he examined me late yesterday afternoon. According to the EKG he took, it was strictly a minor-league heart attack . . . no clot formation." He harrumphed. "Should hope for his sake it wasn't. Coming just a week after the check-up he gave me, I'd sue his sheepskin off the wall for breach of promise." He broke off and looked levelly at Ben. "He said he'd seen such cases brought on by massive shock. I kept my lip zipped. Did I do right?"

"Just right. But things have developed. Susan and I are going to see Cody today and spill everything. If he doesn't sign the committal papers on me right away, we'll send him to you."

"I'll give him an earful," Matt said balefully. "Snot-nosed little son of a bitch won't let me have my pipe."

"Has Susan told you what's been happening in Jerusalem's Lot since Friday night?"

"No. She said she wanted to wait until we were all together."

"Before she does, will you tell me exactly what happened at your house?"

Matt's face darkened, and for a moment the mask of convalescence fluttered. Ben glimpsed the old man he had seen sleeping the day before.

"If you're not up to it—"

"No, of course I am. I must be, if half of what I suspect is true." He smiled bitterly. "I've always considered myself a bit of a free thinker, not easily shocked. But it's amazing how hard the mind can try to block out something it doesn't like or finds threatening. Like the magic slates we had as boys. If you didn't like what you had drawn, you had only to pull the top sheet up and it would disappear."

"But the line stayed on the black stuff underneath forever," Susan said.

"Yes." He smiled at her. "A lovely metaphor for the interaction of the conscious and unconscious mind. A pity Freud was stuck with onions. But we wander." He looked at Ben. "You've heard this once from Susan?"

"Yes, but—"

"Of course. I only wanted to be sure I could dispense with the background."

He told the story in a nearly flat, inflectionless voice, pausing only when a nurse entered on whisper-soft crepe soles to ask him if he would like a glass of ginger ale. Matt told her it would be wonderful to have a ginger ale, and he sucked on the flexible straw at intervals as he finished. Ben noticed that when he got to the part about Mike going out the window backward, the ice cubes clinked slightly in the glass as he held it. Yet his voice did not waver; it retained the same even, slightly inflected tones that he undoubtedly used in his classes. Ben thought, not for the first time, that he was an admirable man.

There was a brief pause when he had finished, and Matt broke it himself.

"And so," he said. "You who have seen nothing with your own eyes, what think you of this hearsay?"

"We talked that over for quite a while yesterday," Susan said. "I'll let Ben tell you."

A little shy, Ben advanced each of the reasonable explanations and then knocked it down. When he mentioned the screen that fastened on the outside, the soft ground, the lack of ladder feet impressions, Matt applauded.

"Bravo! A sleuth!"

Matt looked at Susan. "And you, Miss Norton, who used to write such well-organized themes with paragraphs like building blocks and topic sentences for mortar? What do you think?"

She looked down at her hands, which were folding a pleat of her dress, and then back up at him. "Ben lectured me on the linguistic meanings of *can't* yesterday, so I won't use that word. But it's very difficult for me to believe that vampires are stalking 'salem's Lot, Mr. Burke."

"If it can be arranged so that secrecy will not be breached, I will take a polygraph test," he said softly.

She colored a little. "No, no—don't misunderstand me, please. I'm convinced that something is going on in town. Something . . . horrible. But . . . this . . ."

He put his hand out and covered hers with it. "I understand that, Susan. But will you do something for me?"

"If I can."

"Let us . . . the three of us . . . proceed on the premise that all of this is real. Let us keep that premise before us as fact until—and *only* until—it can be disproved. The scientific method, you see? Ben and I have already discussed ways and means of putting the premise to the test. And no one hopes more than I that it can be disproved."

"But you don't think it will be, do you?"

"No," he said softly. "After a long conversation with myself, I've reached my decision. I believe what I saw."

"Let's put questions of belief and unbelief behind us for the minute," Ben said. "Right now they're moot."

"Agreed," Matt said. "What are your ideas about procedure?"

"Well," Ben said, "I'd like to appoint you Researcher General. With your background, you're uniquely well fitted for the job. And you're off your feet."

Matt's eyes gleamed as they had over Cody's perfidy in declaring his pipe off limits. "I'll have Loretta Starcher on the phone when the library opens. She'll have to bring the books down in a wheelbarrow."

"It's Sunday," Susan reminded. "Library's closed."

"She'll open it for me," Matt said, "or I'll know the reason why."

"Get anything and everything that bears on the subject," Ben said. "Psychological as well as pathological and mythic. You understand? The whole works."

"I'll start a notebook," Matt rasped. "Before God, I will!" He looked at them both. "This is the first time since I woke up in here that I feel like a man. What will you be doing?"

"First, Dr. Cody. He examined both Ryerson and Floyd Tibbits. Perhaps we can persuade him to exhume Danny Glick."

"Would he do that?" Susan asked Matt.

Matt sucked at his ginger ale before answering. "The Jimmy Cody I had in class would have, in a minute. He was an imaginative, open-minded boy who was remarkably resistant to cant. How much of an empiricist college and med school may have made of him, I don't know."

"All of this seems roundabout to me," Susan said. "Especially going to Dr. Cody and risking a complete rebuff. Why don't Ben and I just go up to the Marsten House and have done with it? That was on the docket just last week."

"I'll tell you why," Ben said. "Because we are proceeding on the premise that all this is real. Are you so anxious to put your head in the lion's mouth?"

"I thought vampires slept in the daytime."

"Whatever Straker may be, he's not a vampire," Ben said, "unless the old legends are completely wrong. He's been highly visible in the daytime. At best we'd be turned away as trespassers with nothing learned. At worst, he might overpower us and keep us there until dark. A wake-up snack for Count Comic Book."

"Barlow?" Susan asked.

Ben shrugged. "Why not? That story about the New York buying expedition is a little too good to be true."

The expression in her eyes remained stubborn, but she said nothing more.

"What will you do if Cody laughs you off?" Matt asked. "Always assuming he doesn't call for the restraints immediately."

"Off to the graveyard at sunset," Ben said. "To watch Danny Glick's grave. Call it a test case."

Matt half rose from his reclining position. "Promise me that you'll be careful. Ben, promise me!"

"We will," Susan said soothingly. "We'll both positively clank with crosses."

"Don't joke," Matt muttered. "If you'd seen what I have—" He turned his head and looked out the window, which showed the sun-shanked leaves of an alder and the autumn-bright sky beyond.

"If she's joking, I'm not," Ben said. "We'll take all precautions."

"See Father Callahan," Matt said. "Make him give you some holy water . . . and if possible, some of the wafer."

"What kind of man is he?" Ben asked.

Matt shrugged. "A little strange. A drunk, maybe. If he is, he's a literate, polite one. Perhaps chafing a little under the yoke of enlightened Popery."

"Are you sure that Father Callahan is a . . . that he drinks?" Susan asked, her eyes a trifle wide.

"Not positive," Matt said. "But an ex-student of mine, Brad Campion, works in the Yarmouth liquor store and he says Callahan's a regular customer. A Jim Beam man. Good taste."

"Could he be talked to?" Ben asked.

"I don't know. I think you must try."

"Then you don't know him at all?"

"No, not really. He's writing a history of the Catholic Church in New England, and he knows a great deal about the poets of our so-called golden age—Whittier, Longfellow, Russell, Holmes, that lot. I had him in to speak to my American Lit students late last year. He has a quick, acerbic mind—the students enjoyed him."

"I'll see him," Ben said, "and follow my nose."

A nurse peeked in, nodded, and a moment later Jimmy Cody entered with a stethoscope around his neck.

"Disturbing my patient?" he asked amiably.

"Not half so much as you are," Matt said. "I want my pipe."

"You can't have it," Cody said absently, reading Matt's chart.

"Goddamn quack," Matt muttered.

Cody put the chart back and drew the green curtain that went around the bed on a C-shaped steel runner overhead. "I'm afraid I'll have to ask you two to step out in a moment. How is your head, Mr. Mears?"

"Well, nothing seems to have leaked out."

"You heard about Floyd Tibbits?"

"Susan told me. I'd like to speak to you, if you have a moment after your rounds."

"I can make you the last patient on my rounds, if you like. Around eleven."

"Fine."

Cody twitched the curtain again. "And now, if you and Susan would excuse us—"

"Here we go, friends, into isolation," Matt said. "Say the secret word and win a hundred dollars."

The curtain came between Ben and Susan and the bed. From beyond it they heard Cody say: "The next time I have you under gas I think I'll take out your tongue and about half of your prefrontal lobe."

They smiled at each other, the way young couples will when they are in sunshine and there is nothing seriously the matter with their works, and the smiles faded almost simultaneously. For a moment they both wondered if they might not be crazy.

3

When Jimmy Cody finally came into Ben's room, it was twenty after eleven and Ben began, "What I wanted to talk to you about—"

"First the head, then the talk." He parted Ben's hair gently, looked at something, and said, "This'll hurt." He pulled off the adhesive bandage and Ben jumped. "Hell of a lump," Cody said conversationally, and then covered the wound with a slightly smaller dressing.

He shone a light into Ben's eyes, then tapped his left knee with a rubber hammer. With sudden morbidity, Ben wondered if it was the same one he had used on Mike Ryerson.

"All that seems to be satisfactory," he said, putting his things away. "What's your mother's maiden name?"

"Ashford," Ben said. They had asked him similar questions when he had first recovered consciousness.

"First-grade teacher?"

"Mrs. Perkins. She rinsed her hair."

"Father's middle name?"

"Merton."

"Any dizziness or nausea?"

"No."

"Experience of strange odors, colors, or—"

"No, no, and no. I feel fine."

"I'll decide that," Cody said primly. "Any instance of double vision?"

"Not since the last time I bought a gallon of Thunderbird."

"All right," Cody said. "I pronounce you cured through the wonders of modern science and by virtue of a hard head. Now, what was on your mind? Tibbits and the little McDougall boy, I suppose. I can only tell you what I told Parkins Gillespie. Number one, I'm glad they've kept it out of the papers; one scandal per century is enough in a small town. Number two, I'm damned if I know who'd want to do such a twisted thing. It can't have been a local person. We've got our share of the weirdies, but—"

He broke off, seeing the puzzled expressions on their faces. "You don't know? Haven't heard?"

"Heard what?" Ben demanded.

"It's rather like something by Boris Karloff out of Mary Shelley. Someone snatched the bodies from the Cumberland County Morgue in Portland last night."

"Jesus Christ," Susan said. Her lips made the words stiffly.

"What's the matter?" Cody asked, suddenly concerned. "Do you know something about this?"

"I'm starting to really think we do," Ben said.

4

It was ten past noon when they had finished telling everything. The nurse had brought Ben a lunch tray, and it stood untouched by his bed.

The last syllable died away, and the only sound was the rattle of glasses and cutlery coming through the half-open door as hungrier patients on the ward ate.

"Vampires," Jimmy Cody said. Then: "Matt Burke, of all people. That makes it awfully hard to laugh off."

Ben and Susan kept silent.

"And you want me to exhume the Glick kid," he ruminated. "Jesus jumped-up Christ in a sidecar."

Cody took a bottle out of his bag and tossed it to Ben, who caught it. "Aspirin," he said. "Ever use it?"

"A lot."

"My dad used to call it the good doctor's best nurse. Do you know how it works?"

"No," Ben said. He turned the bottle of aspirin idly in his hands, looking at it. He did not know Cody well enough to know what he usually showed or kept hidden, but he was sure that few of his patients saw him like this—the boyish, Norman Rockwell face overcast with thought and introspection. He didn't want to break Cody's mood.

"Neither do I. Neither does anybody else. But it's good for headache and arthritis and the rheumatism. We don't know what any of those are, either. Why should your head ache? There are no nerves in your brain. We know that aspirin is very close in chemical composition to LSD, but why should one cure the ache in the head and the other cause the head to fill up with flowers? Part of the reason we don't understand is because we don't really know what the brain is. The best-educated doctor in the world is standing on a low island in the middle of a sea of ignorance. We rattle our medicine sticks and kill our chickens and read messages in blood. All of that works a surprising amount of time. White magic. *Bene gris-gris.* My med school profs would tear their hair if they could hear me say that. Some of them tore it when I told them I was going into general practice in rural Maine. One of them told me that Marcus Welby always lanced the boils on the patient's ass during station identification. But I never wanted to be Marcus Welby." He smiled. "They'd roll on the ground and have fits if they knew I was going to request an exhumation order on the Glick boy."

"You'll do it?" Susan said, frankly amazed.

"What can it hurt? If he's dead, he's dead. If he's not, then I'll have something to stand the AMA convention on its ear next time. I'm going to tell the county M.E. that I want to look for signs of infectious encephalitis. It's the only sane explanation I can think of."

"Could that actually be it?" she asked hopefully.

"Damned unlikely."

"What's the earliest you could do it?" Ben asked.

"Tomorrow, tops. If I have to hassle around, Tuesday or Wednesday."

"What should he look like?" Ben asked. "I mean . . ."

"Yes, I know what you mean. The Glicks wouldn't have the boy embalmed, would they?"

"No."

"It's been a week?"

"Yes."

"When the coffin is opened, there's apt to be a rush of gas and a rather offensive smell. The body may be bloated. The hair will have grown down over his collar—it continues to grow for an amazing period of time—and the fingernails will also be quite long. The eyes will almost certainly have fallen in."

Susan was trying to maintain an expression of scientific impartiality and not succeeding very well. Ben was glad he hadn't eaten lunch.

"The corpse will not have begun radical mortification," Cody went on in his best recitation voice, "but enough moisture may be present to encourage growth on the exposed cheeks and hands, possibly a mossy substance called—" He broke off. "I'm sorry. I'm grossing you out."

"Some things may be worse than decay," Ben remarked, keeping his voice carefully neutral. "Suppose you find none of those signs? Suppose the body is as natural-looking as the day it was buried? What then? Pound a stake through his heart?"

"Hardly," Cody said. "In the first place, either the M.E. or his assistant will have to be there. I don't think even Brent Norbert would regard it professional of me to take a stake out of my bag and hammer it through a child's corpse."

"What will you do?" Ben asked curiously.

"Well, begging Matt Burke's pardon, I don't think that will come up. If the body was in such a condition, it would undoubtedly be brought to the Maine Medical Center for an extensive post. Once there, I would dally about my examination until dark . . . and observe any phenomena that might occur."

"And if he rises?"

"Like you, I can't conceive of that."

"I'm finding it more conceivable all the time," Ben said grimly. "Can I be present when all this happens—if it does?"

"That might be arranged."

"All right," Ben said. He got out of bed and walked toward the closet where his clothes were hanging. "I'm going to—"

Susan giggled, and Ben turned around. "What?"

Cody was grinning. "Hospital johnnies have a tendency to flap in the back, Mr. Mears."

"Oh hell," Ben said, and instinctively reached around to pull the johnny together. "You better call me Ben."

"And on that note," Cody said, rising, "Susan and I will exit. Meet us downstairs in the coffee shop when you're decent. You and I have some business this afternoon."

"We do?"

"Yes. The Glicks will have to be told the encephalitis story. You can be my colleague if you like. Don't say anything. Just stroke your chin and look wise."

"They're not going to like it, are they?"

"Would you?"

"No," Ben said. "I wouldn't."

"Do you need their permission to get an exhumation order?" Susan asked.

"Technically, no. Realistically, probably. My only experience with the question of exhuming corpses has been in Medical Law II. But I think if the Glicks are set strongly enough against it, they could force us to a hearing. That would lose us two weeks to a month, and once we got there I doubt if my encephalitis theory would hold up." He paused and looked at them both. "Which leads us to the thing that disturbs me most about this, Mr. Burke's story aside. Danny Glick is the only corpse we have a marker for. All the others have disappeared into thin air."

5

Ben and Jimmy Cody got to the Glick home around one-thirty. Tony Glick's car was sitting in the driveway, but the house was silent. When no one answered the third knock, they crossed the road to the small ranch-style house that sat there—a sad, prefab refugee of the 1950s held up on one end by a rusty pair of house jacks. The name on the mailbox was Dickens. A pink lawn flamingo stood by the walk, and a small cocker spaniel thumped his tail at their approach.

Pauline Dickens, waitress and part owner of the Excellent Café, opened the door a moment or two after Cody rang the bell. She was wearing her uniform.

"Hi, Pauline," Jimmy said. "Do you know where the Glicks are?"

"You mean you don't *know?*"

"Know what?"

"Mrs. Glick died early this morning. They took Tony Glick to Central Maine General. He's in shock."

Ben looked at Cody. Jimmy looked like a man who had been kicked in the stomach.

Ben took up the slack quickly. "Where did they take her body?"

Pauline ran her hands across her hips to make sure her uniform was right. "Well, I spoke to Mabel Werts on the phone an hour ago, and she said Parkins Gillespie was going to take the body right up to that Jewish fellow's funeral home in Cumberland. On account of no one knows where Carl Foreman is."

"Thank you," Cody said slowly.

"Awful thing," she said, her eyes straying to the empty house across the road. Tony Glick's car sat in the driveway like a large and dusty dog that had been chained and then abandoned. "If I was a superstitious person, I'd be afraid."

"Afraid of what, Pauline?" Cody asked.

"Oh . . . things." She smiled vaguely. Her fingers touched a small chain hung around her neck.

A St. Christopher's medal.

6

They were sitting in the car again. They had watched Pauline drive off to work without speaking.

"Now what?" Ben asked finally.

"It's a balls-up," Jimmy said. "The Jewish fellow is Maury Green. I think maybe we ought to drive over to Cumberland. Nine years ago Maury's boy almost drowned at Sebago Lake. I happened to be there with a girl friend, and I gave the kid artificial respiration. Got his motor going again. Maybe this is one time I ought to trade on somebody's good will."

"What good will it do? The M.E. will have taken her body for autopsy or post-mortem or whatever they call it."

"I doubt it. It's Sunday, remember? The M.E. will be out in the woods someplace with a rock hammer—he's an amateur geologist. Norbert—do you remember Norbert?"

Ben nodded.

"Norbert is supposed to be on call, but he's erratic. He's probably got the phone off the hook so he can watch the Packers and the Patriots. If we go up to Maury Green's funeral parlor now, there's a pretty fair chance the body will be there unclaimed until after dark."

"All right," Ben said. "Let's go."

He remembered the call he was to have made on Father Callahan, but it would have to wait. Things were going very fast now. Too fast to suit him. Fantasy and reality had merged.

7

They drove in silence until they were on the turnpike, each lost in his own thoughts. Ben was thinking about what Cody had said at the hospital. Carl Foreman gone. The bodies of Floyd Tibbits and the McDougall baby gone—disappeared from under the noses of two morgue attendants. Mike Ryerson was also gone, and God knew who else. How many people in 'salem's Lot could drop out of sight and not be missed for a week . . . two weeks . . . a month? Two hundred? Three? It made the palms of his hands sweaty.

"This is beginning to seem like a paranoid's dream," Jimmy said, "or a Gahan Wilson cartoon. The scariest part of this whole thing, from an academic point of view, is the relative ease with which a vampire colony could be founded—always if you grant the first one. It's a bedroom town for Portland and Lewiston and Gates Falls, mostly. There's no in-town industry where a rise in absenteeism would be noticed. The schools are three-town consolidated, and if the absence list starts getting a little longer, who notices? A lot of people go to church over in Cumberland, a lot more don't go at all. And TV has pretty well put the kibosh on the old neighborhood get-togethers, except for the duffers who hang around Milt's store. All this could be going on with great effectiveness behind the scenes."

"Yeah," Ben said. "Danny Glick infects Mike. Mike infects . . . oh, I don't know. Floyd, maybe. The McDougall baby infects . . . his father? Mother? How are they? Has anyone checked?"

"Not my patients. I assume Dr. Plowman would have been the one to call them this morning and tell them about their son's disappearance. But I have no real way of knowing if he actually called or actually got in contact with them if he did."

"They should be checked on," Ben said. He began to feel harried. "You see how easily we could end up chasing our tails? A person from out of town could drive through the Lot and not know a thing was wrong. Just another one-horse town where they roll up the sidewalks at nine. But who knows what's going on in the houses, behind drawn shades? People could be lying in their beds . . . or propped in closets like brooms . . . down in cellars . . . waiting for the sun to go down. And each sunrise, less people out on the streets. Less every day." He swallowed and heard a dry click in his throat.

"Take it easy," Jimmy said. "None of this is proven."

"The proof is piling up in drifts," Ben retorted. "If we were dealing in an accepted frame of reference—with a possible outbreak of typhoid or A2 flu, say—the whole town would be in quarantine by now."

"I doubt that. You don't want to forget that only one person has actually *seen* anything."

"Hardly the town drunk."

"He'd be crucified if a story like this got out," Jimmy said.

"By whom? Not by Pauline Dickens, that's for sure. She's ready to start nailing hex signs on her door."

"In an era of Watergate and oil depletion, she's an exception," Jimmy said.

They drove the rest of the way without conversation. Green's Mortuary was at the north end of Cumberland, and two hearses were parked around back, between the rear door of the nonde-nominational chapel and a high board fence. Jimmy turned off the ignition and looked at Ben. "Ready?"

"I guess."

They got out.

8

The rebellion had been growing in her all afternoon, and around two o'clock it burst its bonds. They were going at it stupidly, taking the long way around the barn to prove something that was (sorry, Mr. Burke) probably a lot of horseshit anyway. Susan decided to go up to the Marsten House now, this afternoon.

She went downstairs and picked up her pocketbook. Ann Norton was baking cookies and her father was in the living room, watching the Packers-Patriots game.

"Where are you going?" Mrs. Norton asked.

"For a drive."

"Supper's at six. See if you can be back on time."

"Five at the latest."

She went out and got into her car, which was her proudest possession—not because it was the first one she'd ever owned outright (although it was), but because she had paid for it (almost, she amended; there were six payments left) from her own work, her own talent. It was a Vega hatchback, now almost two years old. She backed it carefully out of the garage and lifted a hand briefly to her mother, who was looking out the kitchen window at her. The break was still between them, not spoken of, not healed. The other quarrels, no matter how bitter, had always knit up in time; life simply went on, burying the hurts under a bandage of days, not ripped off again until the next quarrel, when all the old grudges and grievances would be brought out and counted up like high-scoring cribbage hands. But this one seemed complete, it had been a total war. The wounds were beyond bandaging. Only amputation remained. She had already packed most of her things, and it felt right. This had been long overdue.

She drove out along Brock Street, feeling a growing sense of pleasure and purpose (and a not unpleasant underlayer of absurdity) as the house dropped behind her. She was going to take positive action, and the thought was a tonic to her. She was a forthright girl, and the events of the weekend had bewildered her, left her drifting at sea. Now she would row!

She pulled over onto the soft shoulder outside the village limits, and walked out into Carl Smith's west pasture to where a roll of red-painted snow fence was curled up, waiting for winter. The sense of absurdity was magnified now, and she couldn't help grinning as she bent one of the pickets back and forth until the flexible wire holding it to the others snapped. The picket formed a natural stake, about three feet long, tapering to a point. She carried it back to the car and put it in the back seat, knowing intellectually what it was for (she had seen enough Hammer films at the drive-in on double dates to know you had to pound a stake into a vampire's heart), but never pausing to wonder if she would be able to hammer it through a man's chest if the situation called for it.

She drove on, past the town limits and into Cumberland. On the left was a small country store that stayed open on Sundays, where her father got the Sunday *Times*. Susan remembered a small display case of junk jewelry beside the counter.

She bought the *Times*, and then picked out a small gold crucifix. Her purchases came to four-fifty, and were rung up by a fat counterman who hardly turned from the TV, where Jim Plunkett was being thrown for a loss.

She turned north on the County Road, a newly surfaced stretch of two-lane blacktop. Everything seemed fresh and crisp and alive in the sunny afternoon, and life seemed very dear. Her thoughts jumped from that to Ben. It was a short jump.

The sun came out from behind a slowly moving cumulus cloud, flooding the road with brilliant patches of dark and light as it streamed through the overhanging trees. On a day like this, she thought, it was possible to believe there would be happy endings all around.

About five miles up County, she turned off onto the Brooks Road, which was unpaved once she recrossed the town line into 'salem's Lot. The road rose and fell and wound through the heavily wooded area northwest of the village, and much of the bright afternoon sunlight was cut off. There were no houses or trailers out here. Most of the land was owned by a paper company most renowned for asking patrons not to squeeze their toilet paper. The verge of the road was marked every one hundred feet with no-hunting and no-trespassing signs. As she passed the turnoff which led to the dump, a ripple of unease went through her. On this gloomy stretch of road, nebulous possibilities seemed more real. She found herself wondering— not for the first time—why any normal man would buy the wreck of a suicide's house and then keep the windows shuttered against the sunlight.

The road dipped sharply and then rose steeply up the western flank of Marsten's Hill. She could make out the peak of the Marsten House roof through the trees.

She parked at the head of a disused wood-road at the bottom of the dip and got out of the car. After a moment's hesitation, she took the stake and hung the crucifix around her neck. She still felt absurd, but not half so absurd as she was going to feel if someone she knew happened to drive by and see her marching up the road with a snow-fence picket in her hand.

Hi, Suze, where you headed?

Oh, just up to the old Marsten place to kill a vampire. But I have to hurry because supper's at six.

She decided to cut through the woods.

She stepped carefully over a ruinous rock wall at the foot of the road's ditch, and was glad she had worn slacks. Very much *haute couture* for fearless vampire killers. There were nasty brambles and deadfalls before the woods actually started.

In the pines it was at least ten degrees cooler, and gloomier still. The ground was carpeted with old needles, and the wind hissed through the trees. Somewhere, some small animal crashed off through the underbrush. She suddenly realized that if she turned to her left, a walk of no more than half a mile would bring her into the Harmony Hill Cemetery, if she were agile enough to scale the back wall.

She toiled steadily upward, going as quietly as possible. As she neared the brow of the hill, she began to catch glimpses of the house through the steadily thinning screen of branches— the blind side of the house in relation to the village below. And she began to be afraid. She could not put her finger on any precise reason, and in that way it was like the fear she had felt (but had already largely forgotten) at Matt Burke's house. She was fairly sure that no one could hear her, and it was broad daylight—but the fear was there, a steadily oppressive weight. It seemed to be welling into her consciousness from a part of her brain that was usually silent and probably as obsolete as her appendix. Her pleasure in the day was gone. The sense that she was playing was gone. The feeling of decisiveness was gone. She found herself thinking of those same drive-in horror movie epics where the heroine goes venturing up the narrow attic stairs to see what's frightened poor old Mrs. Cobham so, or down into some dark, cobwebby cellar where the walls are rough, sweating stone—symbolic womb—and she, with her date's arm comfortably around her, thinking: *What a silly bitch . . . I'd never do that!* And here she was, doing it, and she began to grasp how deep the division between the human cerebrum and the human midbrain had become; how the cerebrum can force one on and on in spite of the warnings given by that instinctive part, which is so similar in physical construction to the brain of the alligator. The cerebrum could force one on and on, until the attic door was flung open in the face of some grinning horror or one looked into a half-bricked alcove in the cellar and saw—

STOP!

She threw the thoughts off and found that she was sweating. All at the sight of an ordinary house with its shutters closed. You've got to stop being stupid, she told herself. You're going to go up there and spy the place out, that's all. From the front yard you can see your own house. Now, what in God's name could happen to you in sight of your own house?

Nonetheless, she bent over slightly and took a tighter grip on the stake, and when the screening trees became too thin to offer much protection, she dropped to her hands and knees and crawled. Three or four minutes later, she had come as far as it was possible without breaking cover. From her spot behind a final stand of pines and a spray of junipers, she could see the west side of the house and the creepered tangle of honeysuckle, now autumn-barren. The grass of summer was yellow but still knee-high. No effort had been made to cut it.

A motor roared suddenly in the stillness, making her heart rise into her throat, She controlled herself by hooking her fingers into the ground and biting hard on her lower lip. A moment later an old black car backed into sight, paused at the head of the driveway, and then turned out onto the road and started away toward town. Before it drew out of sight, she saw the man quite clearly: large bald head, eyes sunken so deeply you could really see nothing of them but the sockets, and the lapels and collar of a dark suit. Straker. On his way in to Crossen's store, perhaps.

She could see that most of the shutters had broken slats. All right, then. She would creep up and peek through and see what there was to see. Probably nothing but a house in the first stages of a long renovation process, new plastering under way, new papering perhaps, tools and ladders and buckets. All about as romantic and supernatural as a TV football game.

But still: the fear.

It rose suddenly, emotion overspilling logic and the bright Formica reason of the cerebrum, filling her mouth with a taste like black copper.

And she knew someone was behind her even before the hand fell on her shoulder.

9

It was almost dark.

Ben got up from the wooden folding chair, walked over to the window that looked out on the funeral parlor's back lawn, and saw nothing in particular. It was quarter to seven, and evening's shadows were very long. The grass was still green despite the lateness of the year, and he supposed that the thoughtful mortician would endeavor to keep it so until snow covered it. A symbol of continuing life in the midst of the death of the year. He found the thought inordinately depressing and turned from the view.

"I wish I had a cigarette," he said.

"They're killers," Jimmy told him without turning around. He was watching a Sunday night wildlife program on Maury Green's small Sony. "Actually, so do I. I quit when the surgeon general did his number on cigarettes ten years ago. Bad P.R. not to. But I always wake up grabbing for the pack on the night stand."

"I thought you quit."

"I keep it there for the same reason some alcoholics keep a bottle of scotch on the kitchen shelf. Will power, son."

Ben looked at the clock: 6:47. Maury Green's Sunday paper said sundown would officially arrive at 7:02 EST.

Jimmy had handled everything quite neatly. Maury Green was a small man who had answered the door in an unbuttoned black vest and an open-collar white shirt. His sober, inquiring expression had changed to a broad smile of welcome.

"*Shalom,* Jimmy!" He cried. "It's good to see you! Where you been keeping yourself?"

"Saving the world from the common cold," Jimmy said, smiling, as Green wrung his hand. "I want you to meet a very good friend of mine. Maury Green, Ben Mears."

Ben's hand was enveloped in both of Maury's. His eyes glistened behind the black-rimmed glasses he wore. "*Shalom,* also. Any friend of Jimmy's, and so on. Come on in, both of you. I could call Rachel—"

"Please don't," Jimmy said. "We've come to ask a favor. A rather large one."

Green glanced more closely at Jimmy's face. "'A rather large one,'" he jeered softly. "And why? What have you ever done for me, that my son should graduate third in his class from Northwestern? Anything, Jimmy."

Jimmy blushed. "I did what anyone would have done, Maury."

"I'm not going to argue with you," Green said. "Ask. What is it that has you and Mr. Mears so worried? Have you been in an accident?"

"No. Nothing like that."

He had taken them into a small kitchenette behind the chapel, and as they talked, he brewed coffee in a battered old pot that sat on a hot plate.

"Has Norbert come after Mrs. Glick yet?" Jimmy asked.

"No, and not a sign of him," Maury said, putting sugar and cream on the table. "That one will come by at eleven tonight and wonder why I'm not here to let him in." He sighed. "Poor lady. Such tragedy in one family. And she looks so sweet, Jimmy. That old poop Reardon brought her in. She was your patient?"

"No," Jimmy said. "But Ben and I . . . we'd like to sit up with her this evening, Maury. Right downstairs."

Green paused in the act of reaching for the coffeepot. "Sit up with her? Examine her, you mean?"

"No," Jimmy said steadily. "Just sit up with her."

"You're joking?" He looked at them closely. "No, I see you're not. Why would you want to do that?"

"I can't tell you that, Maury."

"Oh." He poured the coffee, sat down with them, and sipped. "Not too strong. Very nice. Has she got something? Something infectious?"

Jimmy and Ben exchanged a glance.

"Not in the accepted sense of the word," Jimmy said finally.

"You'd like me to keep my mouth shut about this, eh?"

"Yes."

"And if Norbert comes?"

"I can handle Norbert," Jimmy said. "I'll tell him Reardon asked me to check her for infectious encephalitis. He'll never check."

Green nodded. "Norbert doesn't know enough to check his watch, unless someone asks him."

"Is it okay, Maury?"

"Sure, sure. I thought you said a big favor."

"It's bigger than you think, maybe."

"When I finish my coffee, I'll go home and see what horror Rachel has produced for my Sunday dinner. Here is the key. Lock up when you go, Jimmy."

Jimmy tucked it away in his pocket. "I will. Thanks again, Maury."

"Anything. Just do me one favor in return."

"Sure. What?"

"If she says anything, write it down for posterity." He began to chuckle, saw the identical look on their faces, and stopped.

10

It was five to seven. Ben felt tension begin to seep into his body.

"Might as well stop staring at the clock," Jimmy said. "You can't make it go any faster by looking at it."

Ben started guiltily.

"I doubt very much that vampires—if they exist at all—rise at almanac sunset," Jimmy said. "It's never full dark."

Nonetheless he got up and shut off the TV, catching a wood duck in mid-squawk.

Silence descended on the room like a blanket. They were in Green's workroom, and the body of Marjorie Glick was on a stainless-steel table equipped with gutters and foot stirrups that could be raised or depressed. It reminded Ben of the tables in hospital delivery rooms.

Jimmy had turned back the sheet that covered her body when they entered and had made a brief examination. Mrs. Glick was wearing a burgundy-colored quilted house coat and knitted slippers. There was a Band-Aid on her left shin, perhaps covering a shaving nick. Ben looked away from it, but his eyes were drawn back again and again.

"What do you think?" Ben had asked.

"I'm not going to commit myself when another three hours will probably decide one way or the other. But her condition is strikingly similar to that of Mike Ryerson—no surface lividity, no sign of rigor or incipient rigor." And he had pulled the sheet back and would say no more.

It was 7:02.

Jimmy suddenly said, "Where's your cross?"

Ben started. "Cross? Jesus, I don't have one!"

"You were never a Boy Scout," Jimmy said, and opened his bag. "I, however, always come prepared."

He brought out two tongue depressors, stripped off the protective cellophane, and bound them together at right angles with a twist of Red Cross tape.

"Bless it," he said to Ben.

"What? I can't . . . I don't know how."

"Then make it up," Jimmy said, and his pleasant face suddenly appeared strained. "You're the writer; you'll have to be the metaphysician. For Christ's sake, hurry. I think something is going to happen. Can't you feel it?"

And Ben could. Something seemed to be gathering in the slow purple twilight, unseen as yet, but heavy and electric. His mouth had gone dry, and he had to wet his lips before he could speak.

"In the name of the Father, the Son, and the Holy Ghost." Then he added, as an afterthought: "In the name of the Virgin Mary, too. Bless this cross and . . . and . . ."

Words rose to his lips with sudden, eerie surety.

"The Lord is my shepherd," he spoke, and the words fell into the shadowy room as stones would have fallen into a deep lake, sinking out of sight without a ripple. "I shall not want. He maketh me to lie down in green pastures: He leadeth me beside the still waters. He restoreth my soul."

Jimmy's voice joined his own, chanting.

"He leadeth me in the paths of righteousness for his name's sake. Yea, though I walk through the valley of the shadow of death, I will fear no evil—"

It seemed hard to breathe properly. Ben found that his whole body had crawled into goose flesh, and the short hairs on the nape of his neck had begun to prickle, as if they were rising into hackles.

"Thy rod and thy staff they comfort me. Thou preparest a table before me in the presence of mine enemies: thou anointest my head with oil; my cup runneth over. Surely goodness and mercy shall—"

The sheet covering Marjorie Glick's body had begun to tremble. A hand fell out below the sheet and the fingers began to dance jaggedly on the air, twisting and turning.

"My Christ, am I *seeing* this?" Jimmy whispered. His face had gone pale and his freckles stood out like spatters on a windowpane.

"—follow me all the days of my life," Ben finished. "Jimmy, look at the cross."

The cross was glowing. The light spilled over his hand in an elvish flood.

A slow, choked voice spoke in the stillness, as grating as shards of broken crockery: *"Danny?"*

Ben felt his tongue cleave to the roof of his mouth. The form under the sheet was sitting up. Shadows in the darkening room moved and slithered.

"Danny, where are you, darling?"

The sheet fell from her face and crumpled in her lap.

The face of Marjorie Glick was a pallid, moonlike circle in the semidark, punched only by the black holes of her eyes. She saw them, and her mouth juddered open in an awful, cheated snarl. The fading glow of daylight flashed against her teeth.

She swung her legs over the side of the table; one of the slippers fell off and lay unheeded.

"Sit right there!" Jimmy told her. "Don't try to move."

Her answer was a snarl, a dark silver sound, doglike. She slid off the table, staggered, and walked toward them. Ben caught himself looking into those punched eyes and wrenched his gaze away. There were black galaxies shot with red in there. You could see yourself, drowning and liking it.

"Don't look in her face," he told Jimmy.

They were retreating from her without thought, allowing her to force them toward the narrow hall which led to the stairs.

"Try the cross, Ben."

He had almost forgotten he had it. Now he held it up, and the cross seemed to flash with brilliance. He had to squint against it. Mrs. Glick made a hissing, dismayed noise and threw her hands up in front of her face. Her features seemed to draw together, twitching and writhing like a nest of snakes. She tottered a step backward.

"That's got her!" Jimmy yelled.

Ben advanced on her, holding the cross out before him. She hooked one hand into a claw and made a swipe at it. Ben dipped it below her hand and then thrust it at her. A ululating scream came from her throat.

For Ben, the rest took on the maroon tones of nightmare. Although worse horrors were to come, the dreams of the following days and nights were always of driving Marjorie Glick back toward that mortician's table, where the sheet that had covered her lay crumpled beside one knitted slipper.

She retreated unwillingly, her eyes alternating between the hateful cross and an area on Ben's neck to the right of the chin. The sounds that were wrenched out of her were inhuman gibberings and hissings and glottals, and there was something so blindly reluctant in her withdrawal that she began to seem like some giant, lumbering insect. Ben thought: If I didn't have this cross out front, she would rip my throat open with her nails and gulp down the blood that spurted out of the jugular and carotid like a man just out of the desert and dying of thirst. She would bathe in it.

Jimmy had cut away from his side, and was circling her to the left. She didn't see him. Her eyes were fixed only on Ben, dark and filled with hatred . . . filled with fear.

Jimmy circled the mortician's table, and when she backed around it, he threw both arms around her neck with a convulsive yell.

She gave a high, whistling cry and twisted in his grip. Ben saw Jimmy's nails pull away a flap of her skin at the shoulder, and nothing welled out—the cut was like a lipless mouth. And then, incredibly, she threw him across the room. Jimmy crashed into the corner, knocking Maury Green's portable TV off its stand.

She was on him in a flash, moving in a hunched, scrabbling run that was nearly spiderlike. Ben caught a shadow-scrawled glimpse of her falling on top of him, ripping at his collar, and then the sideward predatory lunge of her head, the yawning of her jaws, as she battened on him.

Jimmy Cody screamed—the high, despairing scream of the utterly damned.

Ben threw himself at her, stumbling and nearly falling over the shattered television on the floor. He could hear her harsh breathing, like the rattle of straw, and below that, the revolting sound of smacking, champing lips.

He grabbed her by the collar of her house coat and yanked her upward, forgetting the cross momentarily. Her head came around with frightening swiftness. Her eyes were dilated and glittering, her lips and chin slicked with blood that was black in this near-total darkness.

Her breath in his face was foul beyond measure, the breath of tombs. As if in slow motion, he could see her tongue lick across her teeth.

He brought the cross up just as she jerked him forward into her embrace, her strength making him feel like something made of rags. The rounded point of the tongue depressor that formed the cross's downstroke struck her under the chin—and then continued upward with no fleshy resistance. Ben's eyes were stunned by a flash of not-light that happened not before his eyes but seemingly behind them. There was the hot and porcine smell of burning flesh. Her scream this time was full-throated and agonized. He sensed rather than saw her throw herself backward, stumble over the television, and fall on the floor, one white arm thrown outward to break her fall. She was up again with wolflike agility, her eyes narrowed in pain, yet still filled with her insane hunger. The flesh of her lower jaw was smoking and black. She was snarling at him.

"Come on, you bitch," he panted. "Come on, come on."

He held the cross out before him again, and backed her into the corner at the far left of the room. When he got her there, he was going to jam the cross through her forehead.

But even as her back pressed the narrowing walls, she uttered a high, squealing giggle that made him wince. It was like the sound of a fork being dragged across a porcelain sink.

"Even now one laughs! Even now your circle is smaller!"

And before his eyes her body seemed to elongate and become translucent. For a moment he thought she was still there, laughing at him, and then the white glow of the street lamp outside was shining on bare wall, and there was only a fleeting sensation on his nerve endings, which seemed to be reporting that she had seeped into the very pores of the wall, like smoke.

She was gone.

And Jimmy was screaming.

11

He flicked on the overhead bar of fluorescents and turned to look at Jimmy, but Jimmy was already on his feet, holding his hands to the side of his neck. The fingers were sparkling scarlet.

"She *bit* me!" Jimmy howled. "Oh God-Jesus, she *bit* me!"

Ben went to him, tried to take him in his arms, and Jimmy pushed him away. His eyes rolled madly in their sockets.

"Don't touch me. I'm unclean."

"Jimmy—"

"Give me my bag. Jesus, Ben, I can feel it in there. I can feel it working in me. *For Christ's sake, give me my bag!*"

It was in the corner. Ben got it, and Jimmy snatched it. He went to the mortician's table and set the bag on it. His face was death pale, shining with sweat. The blood pulsed remorselessly from the torn gash in the side of his neck. He sat down on the table and opened the bag and swept through it, his breath coming in whining gasps through his open mouth.

"She *bit* me," he muttered into the bag. "Her mouth . . . oh God, her dirty filthy *mouth* . . ."

He pulled a bottle of disinfectant out of the bag and sent the cap spinning across the tiled floor. He leaned back, supporting himself on one arm, and upended the bottle over his throat, and it splashed the wound, his slacks, the table. Blood washed away in threads. His eyes closed and he screamed once, then again. The bottle never wavered.

"Jimmy, what can I—"

"In a minute," Jimmy muttered. "Wait. It's better, I think. Wait, just wait—"

He tossed the bottle away and it shattered on the floor. The wound, washed clean of the tainted blood, was clearly visible. Ben saw there was not one but two—puncture wounds not far from the jugular, one of them horribly mangled.

Jimmy had pulled an ampoule and a hypo from the bag. He stripped the protective covering from the needle and jabbed it through the ampoule. His hands were shaking so badly he had to make two thrusts at it. He filled the needle and held it out to Ben.

"Tetanus," he said. "Give it to me. Here." He held his arm out, rotated to expose the armpit.

"Jimmy, that'll knock you out."

"No. No, it won't. Do it."

Ben took the needle and looked questioningly into Jimmy's eyes. He nodded. Ben injected the needle.

Jimmy's body tensed like spring steel. For a moment he was a sculpture in agony, every tendon pulled out into sharp relief. Little by little he began to relax. His body shuddered in reaction, and Ben saw that tears had mixed with the sweat on his face.

"Put the cross on me," he said. "If I'm still dirty from her, it'll . . . it'll do something to me."

"Will it?"

"I'm sure it will. When you were going after her, I looked up and I wanted to go after *you*. God help me, I did. And I looked at that cross and I . . . my belly wanted to heave up."

Ben put the cross on his neck. Nothing happened. Its glow—if there had been a glow at all—was entirely gone. Ben took the cross away.

"Okay," Jimmy said. "I think that's all we can do." He rummaged in his bag again, found an envelope containing two pills, and crushed them into his mouth. "Dope," he said. "Great invention. Thank God I used the john before that . . . before it happened. I think I pissed myself, but it only came to about six drops. Can you bandage my neck?"

"I think so," Ben said.

Jimmy handed him gauze, adhesive tape, and a pair of surgical scissors. Bending to put the bandage on, he saw that the skin around the wounds had gone an ugly, congealed red. Jimmy flinched when he pressed the bandage gently into place.

He said: "For a couple of minutes there, I thought I was going to go nuts. Really, clinically nuts. Her lips on me . . . biting me . . ." His throat rippled as he swallowed. "And when she was doing it, I *liked* it, Ben. That's the hellish part. I actually had an erection. Can you believe it? If you hadn't been here to pull her off, I would have . . . would have let her . . ."

"Never mind," Ben said.

"There's one more thing I have to do that I don't like."

"What's that?"

"Here. Look at me a minute."

Ben finished the bandage and drew back a little to look at Jimmy. "What—"

And suddenly Jimmy slugged him. Stars rocketed up in his brain and he took three wandering steps backward and sat down heavily. He shook his head and saw Jimmy getting carefully down from the table and coming toward him. He groped madly for the cross, thinking: This is what's known as an O. Henry ending, you stupid shit, you stupid, stupid—

"You all right?" Jimmy was asking him. "I'm sorry, but it's a little easier when you don't know it's coming."

"What the Christ—?"

Jimmy sat down beside him on the floor. "I'm going to tell you our story," he said. "It's a damned poor one, but I'm pretty sure Maury Green will back it up. It will keep my practice, and keep us both out of jail or some asylum . . . and at this point, I'm not so concerned about those things as I am about staying free to fight these . . . things, whatever you want to call them, another day. Do you understand that?"

"The thrust of it," Ben said. He touched his jaw and winced. There was a knot to the left of his chin.

"Somebody barged in on us while I was examining Mrs. Glick," Jimmy said. "The somebody cold-cocked you and then used me for a punching bag. During the struggle, the somebody bit me to make me let him go. That's all either of us remembers. *All.* Understand?"

Ben nodded.

"The guy was wearing a dark CPO coat, maybe blue, maybe black, and a green or gray knitted cap. That's all you saw. Okay?"

"Have you ever thought about giving up doctoring in favor of a career in creative writing?"

Jimmy smiled. "I'm only creative in moments of extreme self-interest. Can you remember the story?"

"Sure. And I don't think it's as poor as you might believe. After all, hers isn't the first body that's disappeared lately."

"I'm hoping they'll add that up. But the county sheriff is a lot more on the ball than Parkins Gillespie ever thought of being. We have to watch our step. Don't embellish the story."

"Do you suppose anyone in officialdom will begin to see the pattern in all this?"

Jimmy shook his head. "Not a chance in the world. We're going to have to bumble through this on our own. And remember that from this point on, we're criminals."

Shortly after, he went to the phone and called Maury Green, then County Sheriff Homer McCaslin.

12

Ben got back to Eva's at about fifteen minutes past midnight and made himself a cup of coffee in the deserted downstairs kitchen. He drank it slowly, reviewing the night's events with all the intense recall of a man who has just escaped falling from a high ledge.

The county sheriff was a tall, balding man. He chewed tobacco. He moved slowly, but his eyes were bright with observation. He had pulled an enormous battered notebook on a chain from his hip pocket, and an old thick-barreled fountain pen from under his green wool vest. He had questioned Ben and Jimmy while two deputies dusted for fingerprints and took pictures. Maury Green stood quietly in the background, throwing a puzzled look at Jimmy from time to time.

What had brought them to Green's Mortuary?

Jimmy took that one, reciting the encephalitis story.

Did old Doc Reardon know about it?

Well, no. Jimmy thought it would be best to make a quiet check before mentioning it to anyone. Doc Reardon had been known to be, well, overly chatty on occasion.

What about this encephawhatzis? Did the woman have it?

No, almost certainly not. He had finished his examination before the man in the CPO coat burst in. He (Jimmy) would not be willing—or able—to state just how the woman *had* died, but it certainly wasn't of encephalitis.

Could they describe this fella?

They answered in terms of the story they had worked out. Ben added a pair of brown work boots just so they wouldn't sound too much like Tweedledum and Tweedledee.

McCaslin asked a few more questions, and Ben was just beginning to feel that they were going to get out of it unscathed when McCaslin turned to him and asked:

"What are you doing in this, Mears? You ain't no doctor."

His watchful eyes twinkled benignly. Jimmy opened his mouth to answer, but the sheriff quieted him with a single hand gesture.

If the purpose of McCaslin's sudden shot had been to startle Ben into a guilty expression or gesture, it failed. He was too emotionally wrung out to react much. Being caught in a misstatement did not seem too shattering after what had gone before. "I'm a writer, not a doctor. I write novels. I'm writing one currently where one of the important secondary characters is a mortician's son. I just wanted a look into the back room. I hitched a ride with Jimmy here. He told me he would rather not reveal his business, and I didn't ask." He rubbed his chin, where a small, knotted bump had risen. "I got more than I bargained for."

McCaslin looked neither pleased nor disappointed in Ben's answer. "I should say you did. You're the fella that wrote *Conway's Daughter,* ain't you?"

"Yes."

"My wife read part of that in some woman's magazine. *Cosmopolitan*, I think. Laughed like hell. I took a look and couldn't see nothing funny in a little girl strung out on drugs."

"No," Ben said, looking McCaslin in the eye. "I didn't see anything funny about it, either."

"This new book the one they say you been workin' on up to the Lot?"

"Yes."

"P'raps you'd like Moe Green here to read it over," McCaslin remarked. "See if you got the undertakin' parts right."

"That section isn't written yet," Ben said. "I always research before I write. It's easier."

McCaslin shook his head wonderingly. "You know, your story sounds just like one of those Fu Manchu books. Some guy breaks in here an' overpowers two strong men an' makes off with the body of some poor woman who died of unknown causes."

"Listen, Homer—" Jimmy began.

"Don't you Homer me," McCaslin said. "I don't like it. I don't like any part of it. This encephalitis is catchin', ain't it?"

"Yes, it's infectious," Jimmy said warily.

"An' you still brought this writer along? Knowin' she might be infected with somethin' like that?"

Jimmy shrugged and looked angry. "I don't question your professional judgments, Sheriff. You'll just have to bear with mine. Encephalitis is a fairly low-grade infection which gains slowly in the human blood stream. I felt there would be no danger to either of us. Now, wouldn't you be better off trying to find out who carted away Mrs. Glick's body—Fu Manchu or otherwise—or are you just having fun questioning us?"

McCaslin fetched a deep sigh from his not inconsiderable belly, flipped his notebook closed, and stored it in the depths of his hip pocket again. "Well, we'll put the word out, Jimmy. Doubt if we'll get much on this unless the kook comes out of the woodwork again—if there ever was a kook, which I doubt."

Jimmy raised his eyebrows.

"You're lyin' to me," McCaslin said patiently. "I know it, these deputies know it, prob'ly even ole Moe knows it. I don't know how much you're lyin'—a little or a lot—but I know I can't *prove* you're lyin' as long as you both stick to the same story. I could take you both down to the cooler, but the rules say I gotta give you one phone call, an' even the greenest kid fresh out of law school could spring you on what I got, which could best be described as Suspicion of Unknown Hanky-panky. An' I bet your lawyer ain't fresh out of law school, is he?"

"No," Jimmy said. "He's not."

"I'd take you down just the same and put you to the inconvenience except I get a feelin' you ain't lyin' because you did somethin' against the law." He hit the pedal at the foot of the stainless-steel waste can by the mortician's table. The top banged up and McCaslin shot a brown stream of tobacco juice into it. Maury Green jumped. "Would either of you like to sort of revise your story?" he asked quietly, and the back-country twang was gone from his voice. "This is serious business. We've had four deaths in the Lot, and all four bodies are gone, I want to know what's happening."

"We've told you everything we know," Jimmy said with quiet firmness. He looked directly at McCaslin. "If we could tell you more, we would."

McCaslin looked back at him, just as keenly. "You're scared shitless," he said. "You and this writer, both of you. You look the way some of the guys in Korea looked when they brought 'em back from the front lines."

The deputies were looking at them. Ben and Jimmy said nothing.

McCaslin sighed again. "Go on, get out of here. I want you both down to my office tomorrow by ten to make statements. If you ain't there by ten, I'll send a patrol car out to get you."

"You won't have to do that," Ben said.

McCaslin looked at him mournfully and shook his head. "You ought to write books with better sense. Like the guy who writes those Travis McGee stories. A man can sink his teeth into one of those."

13

Ben got up from the table and rinsed his coffee cup at the sink, pausing to look out the window into the night's blackness. What was out there tonight? Marjorie Glick, reunited with her son at last? Mike Ryerson? Floyd Tibbits? Carl Foreman?

He turned away and went upstairs.

He slept the rest of the night with the desk lamp on and left the tongue-depressor cross that had vanquished Mrs. Glick on the table by his right hand. His last thought before sleep took him was to wonder if Susan was all right, and safe.

Chapter Twelve
MARK

1
___

When he first heard the distant snapping of twigs, he crept behind the trunk of a large spruce and stood there, waiting to see who would show up. *They* couldn't come out in the daytime, but that didn't mean *they* couldn't get people who could; giving them money was one way, but it wasn't the only way. Mark had seen that guy Straker in town, and his eyes were like the eyes of a toad sunning itself on a rock. He looked like he could break a baby's arm and smile while he did it.

He touched the heavy shape of his father's target pistol in his jacket pocket. Bullets were no good against *them*—except maybe silver ones—but a shot between the eyes would punch that Straker's ticket, all right.

His eyes shifted downward momentarily to the roughly cylindrical shape propped against the tree, wrapped in an old piece of toweling. There was a woodpile behind his house, half a cord of yellow ash stove lengths which he and his father had cut with the McCulloch chain saw in July and August. Henry Petrie was methodical, and each length, Mark knew, would be within an inch of three feet, one way or the other. His father knew the proper length just as he knew that winter followed fall and that yellow ash would burn longer and cleaner in the living room fireplace.

His son, who knew other things, knew that ash was for men—things—like *him*. This morning, while his mother and father were out on their Sunday bird walk, he had taken one of the lengths and whacked one end into a rough point with his Boy Scout hatchet. It was rough, but it would serve.

He saw a flash of color and shrank back against the tree, peering around the rough bark with one eye. A moment later he got his first clear glimpse of the person climbing the hill. It was a girl. He felt a sense of relief mingled with disappointment. No henchman of the devil there; that was Mr. Norton's daughter.

His gaze sharpened again. She was carrying a stake of her own! As she drew closer, he felt an urge to laugh bitterly—a piece of snow fence, that's what she had. Two swings with an ordinary tool box hammer would split it right in two.

She was going to pass his tree on the right. As she drew closer, he began to slide carefully around his tree to the left, avoiding any small twigs that might pop and give him away. At last the synchronized little movement was done; her back was to him as she went on up the hill toward the break in the trees. She was going very carefully, he noted with approval. That was good. In spite of the silly snow fence stake, she apparently had some idea of what she was getting into. Still, if she went much further, she was going to be in trouble. Straker was at home. Mark had been here since twelve-thirty, and he had seen Straker go out to the driveway and look down the road and then go back into the house. Mark had been trying to make up his mind on what to do himself when this girl had entered things, upsetting the equation.

Perhaps she was going to be all right. She had stopped behind a screen of bushes and was crouching there, just looking at the house. Mark turned it over in his mind. Obviously she knew. How didn't matter, but she would not have had even that pitiful stake with her if she didn't know. He supposed he would have to go up and warn her that Straker was still around, and on guard. She probably didn't have a gun, not even a little one like his.

He was pondering how to make his presence known to her without having her scream her head off when the motor of Straker's car roared into life. She jumped visibly, and at first he was afraid she was going to break and run, crashing through the woods and advertising her presence for a hundred miles. But then she hunkered down again, holding on to the ground like she was afraid it would fly away from her. She's got guts even if she is stupid, he thought approvingly.

Straker's car backed down the driveway—she would have a much better view from where she was; he could only see the Packard's black roof—hesitated for a moment, and then went off down the road toward town.

He decided they had to team up. Anything would be better than going up to that house alone. He had already sampled the poison atmosphere that enveloped it. He had felt it from a half a mile away, and it thickened as you got closer.

Now he ran lightly up the carpeted incline and put his hand on her shoulder. He felt her body tense, knew she was going to scream, and said, "Don't yell. It's all right. It's me."

She didn't scream. What escaped was a terrified exhalation of air. She turned around and looked at him, her face white. "W-Who's me?"

He sat down beside her. "My name is Mark Petrie. I know you; you're Sue Norton. My dad knows your dad."

"Petrie . . . ? Henry Petrie?"

"Yes, that's my father."

"What are you doing here?" Her eyes were moving continually over him, as if she hadn't been able to take in his actuality yet.

"The same thing you are. Only that stake won't work. It's too . . ." He groped for a word that had checked into his vocabulary through sight and definition but not by use. "It's too flimsy."

She looked down at her piece of snow fence and actually blushed. "Oh, that. Well, I found that in the woods and . . . and thought someone might fall over it, so I just—"

He cut her adult temporizing short impatiently: "You came to kill the vampire, didn't you?"

"Wherever did you get that idea? Vampires and things like that?"

He said somberly, "A vampire tried to get me last night. It almost did, too."

"That's absurd. A big boy like you should know better than to make up—"

"It was Danny Glick."

She recoiled, her eyes wincing as if he had thrown a mock punch instead of words. She groped out, found his arm, and held it. Their eyes locked. "Are you making this up, Mark?"

"No," he said, and told his story in a few simple sentences.

"And you came here alone?" she asked when he had finished. "You believed it and came up here alone?"

"Believed it?" He looked at her, honestly puzzled. "Sure I believed it. I saw it, didn't I?"

There was no response to that, and suddenly she was ashamed of her instant doubt (no, doubt was too kind a word) of Matt's story and of Ben's tentative acceptance.

"How come you're here?"

She hesitated a moment and then said, "There are some men in town who suspect that there is a man in that house whom no one has seen. That he might be a . . . a . . ." Still she could not say the word, but he nodded his understanding. Even on short acquaintance, he seemed quite an extraordinary little boy.

Abridging all that she might have added, she said simply, "So I came to look and find out."

He nodded at the stake. "And brought that to pound through him?"

"I don't know if I could do that."

"I could," he said calmly. "After what I saw last night. Danny was outside my window, holding on like a great big fly. And his teeth . . ." He shook his head, dismissing the nightmare as a businessman might dismiss a bankrupt client.

"Do your parents know you're here?" she asked, knowing they must not.

"No," he said matter-of-factly. "Sunday is their nature day. They go on bird walks in the mornings and do other things in the afternoon. Sometimes I go and sometimes I don't. Today they went for a ride up the coast."

"You're quite a boy," she said.

"No, I'm not," he said, his composure unruffled by the praise. "But I'm going to get rid of *him.*" He looked up at the house.

"Are you sure—"

"Sure I am. So're you. Can't you *feel* how bad he is? Doesn't that house make you afraid, just looking at it?"

"Yes," she said simply, giving in to him. His logic was the logic of nerve endings, and unlike Ben's or Matt's, it was resistless.

"How are we going to do it?" she asked, automatically giving over the leadership of the venture to him.

"Just go up there and break in," he said. "Find him, pound the stake—*my* stake—through his heart, and get out again. He's probably down cellar. They like dark places. Did you bring a flashlight?"

"No."

"Damn it, neither did I." He shuffled his sneakered feet aimlessly in the leaves for a moment. "Probably didn't bring a cross either, did you?"

"Yes, I did," Susan said. She pulled the link chain out of her blouse and showed him. He nodded and then pulled a chain out of his own shirt.

"I hope I can get this back before my folks come home," he said gloomily. "I crooked it from my mother's jewelry box. I'll catch hell if she finds out." He looked around. The shadows had lengthened even as they talked, and they both felt an impulse to delay and delay.

"When we find him, don't look in his eyes," Mark told her. "He can't move out of his coffin, not until dark, but he can still hook you with his eyes. Do you know anything religious by heart?"

They had started through the bushes between the woods and the unkempt lawn of the Marsten House.

"Well, the Lord's Prayer—"

"Sure, that's good. I know that one, too. We'll both say it while I pound the stake in."

He saw her expression, revolted and half flagging, and he took her hand and squeezed it. His self-possession was disconcerting. "Listen, we have to. I bet he's got half the town after last night. If we wait any longer, he'll have it all. It will go fast, now."

"After last night?"

"I dreamed it," Mark said. His voice was still calm, but his eyes were dark. "I dreamed of them going to houses and calling on phones and begging to be let in. Some people knew, way down deep they knew, but they let them in just the same. Because it was easier to do that than to think something so bad might be real."

"Just a dream," she said uneasily.

"I bet there's a lot of people lying around in bed today with the curtains closed or the shades drawn, wondering if they've got a cold or the flu or something. They feel all weak and fuzzy-headed. They don't want to eat. The idea of eating makes them want to puke."

"How do you know so much?"

"I read the monster magazines," he said, "and go to see the movies when I can. Usually I have to tell my mom I'm going to see Walt Disney. And you can't trust all of it. Sometimes they just make stuff up so the story will be bloodier."

They were at the side of the house. Say, we're quite a crew, we believers, Susan thought. An old teacher half-cracked with books, a writer obsessed with his childhood nightmares, a little boy who has taken a postgraduate course in vampire lore from the films and the modern penny-dreadfuls. And me? Do I really believe? Are paranoid fantasies catching?

She believed.

As Mark had said, this close to the house it was just not possible to scoff. All the thought processes, the act of conversation itself, were overshadowed by a more fundamental voice that was screaming *danger! danger!* in words that were not words at all. Her heartbeat and respiration were up, yet her skin was cold with the capillary-dilating effect of adrenaline, which keeps the blood hiding deep in the body's wells during moments of stress. Her kidneys were tight and heavy. Her eyes seemed preternaturally sharp, taking in every splinter and paint flake on the side of the house. And all of this had been triggered by no external stimuli at all: no men with guns, no large and snarling dogs, no smell of fire. A deeper watchman than her five senses had been wakened after a long season of sleep. And there was no ignoring it.

She peered through a break in the lower shutters. "Why, they haven't done a thing to it," she said almost angrily. "It's a mess."

"Let me see. Boost me up."

She laced her fingers together so he could look through the broken slats and into the crumbling living room of the Marsten House. He saw a deserted, boxy parlor with a thick patina of dust on the floor (many footprints had been tracked through it), peeling wallpaper, two or three old easy chairs, a scarred table. There were cobwebs festooned in the room's upper corners, near the ceiling.

Before she could protest, he had rapped the hook-and-eye combination that held the shutter closed with the blunt end of his stake. The lock fell to the ground in two rusty pieces, and the shutters creaked outward an inch or two.

"Hey!" she protested. "You shouldn't—"

"What do you want to do? Ring the doorbell?"

He accordioned back the right-hand shutter and rapped one of the dusty, wavy panes of glass. It tinkled inward. The fear leaped up in her, hot and strong, making a coppery taste in her mouth.

"We can still run," she said, almost to herself.

He looked down at her and there was no contempt in his glance—only an honesty and a fear that was as great as her own. "You go if you have to," he said.

"No. I don't have to." She tried to swallow away the obstruction in her throat and succeeded not at all. "Hurry it up. You're getting heavy."

He knocked the protruding shards of glass out of the pane he had broken, switched the stake to his other hand, then reached through and unlatched the window. It moaned slightly as he pushed it up, and then the way was open.

She let him down and they looked wordlessly at the window for a moment. Then Susan stepped forward, pushed the right-hand shutter open all the way, and put her hands on the splintery windowsill preparatory to boosting herself up. The fear in her was sickening with its greatness, settled in her belly like a horrid pregnancy. At last, she understood how Matt Burke had felt as he had gone up the stairs to whatever waited in his guest room.

She had always consciously or unconsciously formed fear into a simple equation: fears = unknown. And to solve the equation, one simply reduced the problem to simple algebraic terms, thus: unknown = creaky board (or whatever), creaky board = nothing to be afraid of. In the modern world all terrors could be gutted by simple use of the transitive axiom of equality. Some fears were justified, of course (you don't drive when you're too plowed to see, don't extend the hand of friendship to snarling dogs, don't go parking with boys you don't know—how did the old joke go? Screw or walk?), but until now she had not believed that some fears were larger than comprehension, apocalyptic and nearly paralyzing. This equation was insoluble. The act of moving forward at all became heroism.

She boosted herself with a smooth flex of muscles, swung one leg over the sill, and then dropped to the dusty parlor floor and looked around. There was a smell. It oozed out of the walls in an almost visible miasma. She tried to tell herself it was only plaster rot, or the accumulated damp guano of all the animals that had nested behind those broken lathings—woodchucks, rats, perhaps even a raccoon or two. But it was more. The smell was deeper than animal-stink, more entrenched. It made her think of tears and vomit and blackness.

"Hey," Mark called softly. His hands waved above the windowsill. "A little help."

She leaned out, caught him under the armpits, and dragged him up until he had caught a grip on the windowsill. Then he jackknifed himself in neatly. His sneakered feet thumped the carpet, and then the house was still again.

They found themselves listening to the silence, fascinated by it. There did not even seem to be the faint, high hum that comes in utter stillness, the sound of nerve endings idling in neutral. There was only a great dead soundlessness and the beat of blood in their own ears.

And yet they both knew, of course. They were not alone.

2

"Come on," he said. "Let's look around." He clutched the stake very tightly and for just a moment looked longingly back at the window.

She moved slowly toward the hall and he came after her. Just outside the door there was a small end table with a book on it. Mark picked it up.

"Hey," he said. "Do you know Latin?"

"A little, from high school."

"What's this mean?" He showed her the binding.

She sounded the words out, a frown creasing her forehead. Then she shook her head. "Don't know."

He opened the book at random, and flinched. There was a picture of a naked man holding a child's gutted body toward something you couldn't see. He put the book down, glad to let go of it—the stretched binding felt uncomfortably familiar under his hand—and they went down the hallway toward the kitchen together. The shadows were more prominent here. The sun had gotten around to the other side of the house.

"Do you smell it?" he asked.

"Yes."

"It's worse back here, isn't it?"

"Yes."

He was remembering the cold-pantry his mother had kept in the other house, and how one year three bushel baskets of tomatoes had gone bad down there in the dark. This smell was like that, like the smell of tomatoes decaying into putrescence.

Susan whispered: "God, I'm so scared."

His hand groped out, found hers, and they locked tightly.

The kitchen linoleum was old and gritty and pocked, worn black in front of the old porcelain-tub sink. A large, scarred table stood in the middle of the floor, and on it was a yellow plate, a knife and fork, and a scrap of raw hamburger.

The cellar door was standing ajar.

"That's where we have to go," he said.

"Oh," she said weakly.

The door was open just a crack, and the light did not penetrate at all. The tongue of darkness seemed to lick hungrily at the kitchen, waiting for night to come so it could swallow it whole. That quarter inch of darkness was hideous, unspeakable in its possibilities. She stood beside Mark, helpless and moveless.

Then he stepped forward and pulled the door open and stood for a moment, looking down. She saw a muscle jump beneath his jaw.

"I think—" he began, and she heard something behind her and turned, suddenly feeling slow, feeling too late. It was Straker. He was grinning.

Mark turned, saw, and tried to dive around him. Straker's fist crashed into his chin and he knew no more.

3

When Mark came to, he was being carried up a flight of stairs—not the cellar stairs, though. There was not that feeling of stone enclosure, and the air was not so fetid. He allowed his eyelids to unclose themselves a tiny fraction, letting his head still loll limply on his neck. A stair landing coming up . . . the second floor. He could see quite clearly. The sun was not down yet. Thin hope, then.

They gained the landing, and suddenly the arms holding him were gone. He thumped heavily onto the floor, hitting his head.

"Do you not think I know when someone is playing the possum, young master?" Straker asked him. From the floor he seemed easily ten feet tall. His bald head glistened with a subdued elegance in the gathering gloom. Mark saw with growing terror that there was a coil of rope around his shoulder.

He grabbed for the pocket where the pistol had been.

Straker threw back his head and laughed. "I have taken the liberty of removing the gun, young master. Boys should not be allowed weapons they do not understand . . . any more than they should lead young ladies to houses where their commerce has not been invited."

"What did you do with Susan Norton?"

Straker smiled. "I have taken her where she wished to go, my boy. Into the cellar. Later, when the sun goes down, she will meet the man she came here to meet. You will meet him yourself, perhaps later tonight, perhaps tomorrow night. He may give you to the girl, of course . . . but I rather think he'll want to deal with you himself. The girl will have friends of her own, some of them perhaps meddlers like yourself."

Mark lashed out with both feet at Straker's crotch, and Straker side-stepped liquidly, like a dancer. At the same moment he kicked his own foot out, connecting squarely with Mark's kidneys.

Mark bit his lips and writhed on the floor.

Straker chuckled. "Come, young master. To your feet."

"I . . . I can't."

"Then crawl," Straker said contemptuously. He kicked again, this time striking the large muscle of the thigh. The pain was dreadful, but Mark clenched his teeth together. He got to his knees, and then to his feet.

They progressed down the hall toward the door at the far end. The pain in his kidneys was subsiding to a dull ache. "What are you going to do with me?"

"Truss you like a spring turkey, young master. Later, after my Master holds intercourse with you, you will be set free."

"Like the others?"

Straker smiled.

As Mark pushed open the door and stepped into the room where Hubert Marsten had committed suicide, something odd seemed to happen in his mind. The fear did not fall away from it, but it seemed to stop acting as a brake on his thoughts, jamming all productive signals. His thoughts began to flicker past with amazing speed, not in words or precisely in images, but in a kind of symbolic shorthand. He felt like a light bulb that has suddenly received a surge of power from no known source.

The room itself was utterly prosaic. The wallpaper hung in strips, showing the white plaster and sheet rock beneath. The floor was heavily dusted with time and plaster, but there was only one set of footprints in it, suggesting someone had come up once, looked around, and left again. There were two stacks of magazines, a cast-iron cot with no spring or mattress, and a small tin plate with a faded Currier & Ives design that had once blocked the stove hole in the chimney. The window was shuttered, but enough light filtered dustily through the broken slats to make Mark think there might be an hour of daylight left. There was an aura of old nastiness about the room.

It took perhaps five seconds to open the door, see these things, and cross to the center of the room where Straker told him to stop. In that short period, his mind raced along three tracks and saw three possible outcomes to the situation he found himself in.

On one, he suddenly sprinted across the room toward the shuttered window and tried to crash through both glass and shutter like a Western movie hero, taking the drop to whatever lay below with blind hope. In one mental eye he saw himself crashing through only to fall onto a rusty pile of junked farm machinery, twitching away the last seconds of his life impaled on blunt harrow blades like a bug on a pin. In the other eye he saw himself crashing through the glass and into the shutter which trembled but did not break. He saw Straker pulling him back, his clothes torn, his body lacerated and bleeding in a dozen places.

On the second track, he saw Straker tie him up and leave. He saw himself trussed on the floor, saw the light fading, saw his struggles become more frenzied (but just as useless), and heard, finally, the steady tread on the stairs of one who was a million times worse than Straker.

On the third track, he saw himself using a trick he had read about last summer in a book on Houdini. Houdini had been a famous magician who had escaped jail cells, chained boxes, bank vaults, steamer trunks thrown into rivers. He could get out of ropes, police handcuffs, and Chinese finger-pullers. And one of the things the book said he did was hold his breath and tighten his hands into fists when a volunteer from the audience was tying him up. You bulged your thighs and forearms and neck muscles, too. If your muscles were big, you had a little slack when you relaxed them. The trick then was to relax completely, and go at your escape slowly and surely, never letting panic hurry you up. Little by little, your body would give you sweat for grease, and that helped, too. The book made it sound very easy.

"Turn around," Straker said. "I am going to tie you up. While I tie you up, you will not move. If you move, I take this"—he cocked his thumb before Mark like a hitchhiker—"and pop your right eye out. Do you understand?"

Mark nodded. He took a deep breath, held it, and bunched all his muscles.

Straker threw his coil of rope over one of the beams.

"Lie down," he said.

Mark did.

He crossed Mark's hands behind his back and bound them tightly with the rope. He made a loop, slipped it around Mark's neck, and tied it in a hangman's knot. "You're made fast to the very beam my Master's friend and sponsor in this country hung himself from, young master. Are you flattered?"

Mark grunted, and Straker laughed. He passed the rope through Mark's crotch, and he groaned as Straker took up the slack with a brutal jerk.

He chuckled with monstrous good nature. "So your jewels hurt? They will not for long. You are going to lead an ascetic's life, my boy—a long, long life."

He banded the rope over Mark's taut thighs, made the knot tight, banded it again over his knees, and again over his ankles. Mark needed to breathe very badly now, but he held on stubbornly.

"You're trembling, young master," Straker said mockingly. "Your body is all in hard little knots. Your flesh is white—but it will be whiter! Yet you need not be so afraid. My Master has the capacity for kindness. He is much loved, right here in your own town. There is only a little sting, like the doctor's needle, and then sweetness. And later on you will be let free. You will go see your mother and father, yes? You will see them after they sleep."

He stood up and looked down at Mark benignly. "I will say good-by for a bit now, young master. Your lovely consort is to be made comfortable. When we meet again, you will like me better."

He left, slamming the door behind him. A key rattled in the lock. And as his feet descended the stairs, Mark let out his breath and relaxed his muscles with a great, whooping sigh.

The ropes holding him loosened—a little.

He lay moveless, collecting himself. His mind was still flying with that same unnatural, exhilarating speed. From his position, he looked across the swelled, uneven floor to the iron cot frame. He could see the wall beyond it. The wallpaper was peeled away from that section and lay beneath the cot frame like a discarded snakeskin. He focused on a small section of the wall and examined it closely. He flushed everything else from his mind. The book on Houdini said that concentration was all-important. No fear or taint of panic must be allowed in the mind. The body must be completely relaxed. And the escape must take place in the mind before a single finger did so much as twitch. Every step must exist concretely in the mind.

He looked at the wall, and minutes passed.

The wall was white and bumpy, like an old drive-in movie screen. Eventually, as his body relaxed to its greatest degree, he began to see himself projected there, a small boy wearing a blue T-shirt and Levi's jeans. The boy was on his side, arms pulled behind him, wrists nestling the small of the back above the buttocks. A noose looped around his neck, and any hard struggling would tighten that running slipknot inexorably until enough air was cut off to black out the brain.

He looked at the wall.

The figure there had begun to move cautiously, although he himself lay perfectly still. He watched all the movements of the simulacrum raptly. He had achieved a level of concentration necessary to the Indian fakirs and yogis, who are able to contemplate their toes or the tips of their noses for days, the state of certain mediums who levitate tables in a state of unconsciousness or extrude long tendrils of teleplasm from the nose, the mouth, the fingertips. His state was close to sublime. He did not think of Straker or the fading daylight. He no longer saw the gritty floor, the cot frame, or even the wall. He only saw the boy, a perfect figure which went through a tiny dance of carefully controlled muscles.

He looked at the wall.

And at last he began to move his wrists in half circles, toward each other. At the limit of each half circle, the thumb sides of his palms touched. No muscles moved but those in his lower forearms. He did not hurry. He looked at the wall.

As sweat rose through his pores, his wrists began to turn more freely. The half circles became three-quarters. At the limit of each, the backs of his hands pressed together. The loops holding them had loosened a tiny bit more.

He stopped.

After a moment had passed, he began to flex his thumbs against his palms and press his fingers together in a wriggling motion. His face was utterly expressionless, the plaster face of a department store dummy.

Five minutes passed. His hands were sweating freely now. The extreme level of his concentration had put him in partial control of his own sympathetic nervous system, another device of yogis and fakirs, and he had, unknowingly, gained some control over his body's involuntary functions. More sweat trickled from his pores than his careful movements could account for. His hands had become oily. Droplets fell from his forehead, darkening the white dust on the floor.

He began to move his arms in an up-and-down piston motion, using his biceps and back muscles now. The noose tightened a little, but he could feel one of the loops holding his hands beginning to drag lower on his right palm. It was sticking against the pad of the thumb now, and that was all. Excitement shot through him and he stopped at once until the emotion had passed away completely. When it had, he began again. Up-down. Up-down. Up-down. He gained an eighth of an inch at a time. And suddenly, shockingly, his right hand was free.

He left it where it was, flexing it. When he was sure it was limber, he eased the fingers under the loop holding the left wrist and tented them. The left hand slid free.

He brought both hands around and put them on the floor. He closed his eyes for a moment. The trick now was to not think he had it made. The trick was to move with great deliberation.

Supporting himself with his left hand, he let his right roam over the bumps and valleys of the knot which secured the noose at his neck. He saw immediately that he would have to nearly choke himself to free it—and he was going to tighten the pressure on his testicles, which already throbbed dully.

He took a deep breath and began to work on the knot. The rope tightened by steady degrees, pressing into his neck and crotch. Prickles of coarse hemp dug into his throat like miniature tattoo needles. The knot defied him for what seemed an endless time. His vision began to fade under the onslaught of large black flowers that burst into soundless bloom before his eyes. He refused to hurry. He wiggled the knot steadily, and at last felt new slack in it. For a moment the pressure on his groin tightened unbearably, and then with a convulsive jerk, he threw the noose over his head and the pain lessened.

He sat up and hung his head over, breathing raggedly, cradling his wounded testicles in both hands. The sharp pain became a dull, pervading ache that made him feel nauseated.

When it began to abate a little, he looked over at the shuttered window. The light coming through the broken slats had faded to a dull ocher—it was almost sundown. And the door was locked.

He pulled the loose loop of rope over the beam, and set to work on the knots that held his legs. They were maddeningly tight, and his concentration had begun to slip away from him as reaction set in.

He freed his thighs, the knees, and after a seemingly endless struggle, his ankles. He stood up weakly among the harmless loops of rope and staggered. He began to rub his thighs.

There was a noise from below: footsteps.

He looked up, panicky, nostrils dilating. He hobbled over to the window and tried to lift it. Nailed shut, with rusted tenpennies bent over the cheap wood of the half sill like staples.

The feet were coming up the stairs.

He wiped his mouth with his hand and stared wildly around the room. Two bundles of magazines. A small tin plate with a picture of an 1890s summer picnic on the back. The iron cot frame.

He went to it despairingly and pulled up one end. And some distant gods, perhaps seeing how much luck he had manufactured by himself, doled out a little of their own.

The steps had begun down the hall toward the door when he unscrewed the steel cot leg to its final thread and pulled it free.

4

When the door opened, Mark was standing behind it with the bed leg upraised, like a wooden Indian with a tomahawk.

"Young master, I've come to—"

He saw the empty coils of rope and froze for perhaps one full second in utter surprise. He was halfway through the door.

To Mark, things seemed to have slowed to the speed of a football maneuver seen in instant replay. He seemed to have minutes rather than bare seconds to aim at the one-quarter skull circumference visible beyond the edge of the door.

He brought the leg down with both hands, not as hard as he could—he sacrificed some force for better aim. It struck Straker just above the temple, as he started to turn to look behind the door. His eyes, open wide, squeezed shut in pain. Blood flew from the scalp wound in an amazing spray.

Straker's body recoiled and he stumbled backward into the room. His face was twisted into a terrifying grimace. He reached out and Mark hit him again. This time the pipe struck his bald skull just above the bulge of the forehead, and there was another gout of blood.

He went down bonelessly, his eyes rolling up in his head.

Mark skirted the body, looking at it with eyes that were bulging and wide. The end of the bed leg was painted with blood. It was darker than Technicolor movie blood. Looking at it made him feel sick, but looking at Straker made him feel nothing.

I killed him, he thought. And on the heels of that: *Good. Good.*

Straker's hand closed around his ankle.

Mark gasped and tried to pull his foot away. The hand held fast like a steel trap and now Straker was looking up at him, his eyes cold and bright through a dripping mask of blood. His lips were moving, but no sound came out. Mark pulled harder, to no avail. With a half groan, he began to hammer at Straker's clutching hand with the bed leg. Once, twice, three times, four. There was the awful pencil sound of snapping fingers. The hand loosened, and he pulled free with a yank that sent him stumbling out through the doorway and into the hall.

Straker's head had dropped to the floor again, but his mangled hand opened and closed on the air with tenebrous vitality, like the jerking of a dog's paws in dreams of cat-chasing.

The bed leg fell from his nerveless fingers and he backed away, trembling. Then panic took him and he turned and fled down the stairs, leaping two or three at a time on his numb legs, his hand skimming the splintered banister.

The front hall was shadow-struck, horribly dark.

He went into the kitchen, casting lunatic, shying glances at the open cellar door. The sun was going down in a blazing mullion of reds and yellows and purples. In a funeral parlor sixteen miles distant, Ben Mears was watching the clock as the hands hesitated between 7:01 and 7:02.

Mark knew nothing of that, but he knew the vampire's time was imminent. To stay longer meant confrontation on top of confrontation; to go back down into that cellar and try to save Susan meant induction into the ranks of the Undead.

Yet he went to the cellar door and actually walked down the

first three steps before his fear wrapped him in almost physical bonds and would allow him to go no further. He was weeping, and his body was trembling wildly, as if with ague.

"Susan!" he screamed. "Run!"

"M-Mark?" Her voice, sounding weak and dazed. "I can't see. It's dark—"

There was a sudden booming noise, like a hollow gunshot, followed by a profound and soulless chuckle.

Susan screamed . . . a sound that trailed away to a moan and then to silence.

Still he paused, on feather-feet that trembled to blow him away.

And from below came a friendly voice, amazingly like his father's: "Come down, my boy. I admire you."

The power in the voice alone was so great that he felt the fear ebbing from him, the feathers in his feet turning to lead. He actually began to grope down another step before he caught hold of himself—and the catching hold took all the ragged discipline he had left.

"Come down," the voice said, closer now. It held, beneath the friendly fatherliness, the smooth steel of command.

Mark shouted down: "I know your name! It's Barlow!"

And fled.

By the time he reached the front hall the fear had come on him full again, and if the door had not been unlocked he might have burst straight through the center of it, leaving a cartoon cutout of himself behind.

He fled down the driveway (much like that long-ago boy Benjaman Mears) and then straight down the center of the Brooks Road toward town and dubious safety. Yet might not the king vampire come after him, even now?

He swerved off the road and made his way blunderingly through the woods, splashing through Taggart Stream and falling in a tangle of burdocks on the other side, and finally out into his own back yard.

He walked through the kitchen door and looked through the arch into the living room to where his mother, with worry written across her face in large letters, was talking into the telephone with the directory open on her lap.

She looked up and saw him, and relief spread across her face in a physical wave.

"—here he is—"

She set the phone into its cradle without waiting for a response and walked toward him. He saw with greater sorrow than she would have believed that she had been crying.

"Oh, Mark . . . where have you been?"

"He's home?" His father called from the den. His face, unseen, was filling with thunder.

"Where have you been?" She caught his shoulders and shook them.

"Out," he said wanly. "I fell down running home."

There was nothing else to say. The essential and defining characteristic of childhood is not the effortless merging of dream and reality, but only alienation. There are no words for childhood's dark turns and exhalations. A wise child recognizes it and submits to the necessary consequences. A child who counts the cost is a child no longer.

He added: "The time got away from me. It—"

Then his father, descending upon him.

5

Some time in the darkness before Monday's dawn.

Scratching at the window.

He came up from sleep with no pause, no intervening period of drowsiness or orientation. The insanities of sleep and waking had become remarkably similar.

The white face in the darkness outside the glass was Susan's.

"Mark . . . let me in."

He got out of bed. The floor was cold under his bare feet. He was shivering.

"Go away," he said tonelessly. He could see that she was still wearing the same blouse, the same slacks. I wonder if *her* folks are worried, he thought. If they've called the police.

"It's not so bad, Mark," she said, and her eyes were flat and obsidian. She smiled, showing her teeth, which shone in sharp relief below her pale gums. "It's ever so nice. Let me in, I'll show you. I'll kiss you, Mark. I'll kiss you all over like your mother never did."

"Go away," he repeated.

"One of us will get you sooner or later," she said. "There are lots more of us now. Let it be me, Mark. I'm . . . I'm hungry." She tried to smile, but it turned into a nightshade grimace that made his bones cold.

He held up his cross and pressed it against the window.

She hissed, as if scalded, and let go of the window frame. For a moment she hung suspended in air, her body becoming misty and indistinct. Then, gone. But not before he saw (or thought he saw) a look of desperate unhappiness on her face.

The night was still and silent again.

There are lots more of us now.

His thoughts turned to his parents, sleeping in thoughtless peril below him, and dread gripped his bowels.

Some men knew, she had said, or suspected.

Who?

The writer, of course. The one she dated. Mears, his name was. He lived at Eva's boardinghouse. Writers knew a lot. It would be him. And he would have to get to Mears before she did—

He stopped on his way back to bed.

If she hadn't already.

Chapter Thirteen
FATHER CALLAHAN

1

On that same Sunday evening, Father Callahan stepped hesitantly into Matt Burke's hospital room at quarter to seven by
Matt's watch. The bedside table and the counterpane itself were
littered with books, some of them dusty with age. Matt had
called Loretta Starcher at her spinster's apartment and had not
only gotten her to open the library on Sunday, but had gotten
her to deliver the books in person. She had come in at the head
of a procession made up of three hospital orderlies, each loaded
down. She had left in something of a huff because he refused
to answer questions about the strange conglomeration.

Father Callahan regarded the schoolteacher curiously. He
looked worn, but not so worn or wearily shocked as most of the
parishioners he visited in similar circumstances. Callahan found
that the common first reaction to news of cancer, strokes, heart
attacks, or the failure of some major organ was one of betrayal.
The patient was astounded to find that such a close (and, up to
now at least, fully understood) friend as one's own body could
be so sluggard as to lie down on the job. The reaction which
followed close on the heels of the first was the thought that a
friend who would let one down so cruelly was not worth having. The conclusion that followed these reactions was that it
didn't matter if *this* friend was worth having or not. One could

not refuse to speak to one's traitorous body, or get up a petition against it, or pretend that one was not at home when it called. The final thought in this hospital-bed train of reasoning was the hideous possibility that one's body might not be a friend at all, but an enemy implacably dedicated to destroying the superior force that had used it and abused it ever since the disease of reason set in.

Once, while in a fine drunken frenzy, Callahan had sat down to write a monograph on the subject for *The Catholic Journal*. He had even illustrated it with a fiendish editorial-page cartoon, which showed a brain poised on the highest ledge of a skyscraper. The building (labeled "The Human Body") was in flames (which were labeled "Cancer"—although they might have been a dozen others). The cartoon was titled "Too Far to Jump." During the next day's enforced bout with sobriety, he had torn the prospective monograph to shreds and burned the cartoon—there was no place in Catholic doctrine for either, unless you wanted to add a helicopter labeled "Christ" that was dangling a rope ladder. Nonetheless, he felt that his insights had been true ones, and the result of such sickbed logic on the part of the patient was usually acute depression. The symptoms included dulled eyes, slow responses, sighs fetched from deep within the chest cavity, and sometimes tears at the sight of the priest, that black crow whose function was ultimately predicated on the problem the fact of mortality presented to the thinking being.

Matt Burke showed none of this depression. He held out his hand, and when Callahan shook it, he found the grip surprisingly strong.

"Father Callahan. Good of you to come."

"Pleased to. Good teachers, like a wife's wisdom, are pearls beyond price."

"Even agnostic old bears like myself?"

"Especially those," Callahan said, riposting with pleasure. "I may have caught you at a weak moment. There are no atheists in the foxholes, I've been told, and precious few agnostics in the Intensive Care ward."

"I'm being moved soon, alas."

"Pish-posh," Callahan said. "We'll have you Hail Marying and Our Fathering yet."

"That," Matt said, "is not as far-fetched as you might think."

Father Callahan sat down, and his knee bumped the bedstand as he drew his chair up. A carelessly piled stack of books cascaded into his lap. He read the titles aloud as he put them back.

"*Dracula. Dracula's Guest. The Search for Dracula. The Golden Bough. The Natural History of the Vampire*—natural? *Hungarian Folk Tales. Monsters of the Darkness. Monsters in Real Life. Peter Kurtin, Monster of Düsseldorf.* And ..." He brushed a thick patina of dust from the last cover and revealed a spectral figure poised menacingly above a sleeping damsel. "*Varney the Vampyre, or, The Feast of Blood.* Goodness—required reading for convalescent heart attack patients?"

Matt smiled. "Poor old *Varney.* I read it a long time ago for a class report in Eh-279 at the university . . . Romantic Lit. The professor, whose idea of fantasy began with *Beowulf* and ended with *The Screwtape Letters,* was quite shocked. I got a D plus on the report and a written command to elevate my sights."

"The case of Peter Kurtin is interesting enough, though," Callahan said. "In a repulsive sort of way."

"You know his history?"

"Most of it, yes. I took an interest in such things as a divinity student. My excuse to the highly skeptical elders was that, in order to be a successful priest, one had to plumb the depths of human nature as well as aspire to its heights. All eyewash, actually. I just liked a shudder as well as the next one. Kurtin, I believe, murdered two of his playmates as a young boy by drowning them—he simply gained possession of a small float anchored in the middle of a wide river and kept pushing them away until they tired and went under."

"Yes," Matt said. "As a teen-ager, he twice tried to kill the parents of a girl who refused to go walking with him. He later burned down their house. But that is not the part of his, uh, career that I'm interested in."

"I guessed not, from the trend of your reading matter." He picked a magazine off the coverlet which showed an incredibly endowed young woman in a skintight costume who was sucking the blood of a young man. The young man's expression seemed to be an uneasy combination of extreme terror and extreme lust. The name of the magazine—and of the young woman, apparently—was *Vampirella.* Callahan put it down, more intrigued than ever.

"Kurtin attacked and killed over a dozen women," Callahan said. "Mutilated many more with a hammer. If it was their time of the month, he drank their discharge."

Matt Burke nodded again. "What's not so generally known," he said, "is that he also mutilated animals. At the height of his obsession, he ripped the heads from the bodies of two swans in Düsseldorf's central park and drank the blood which gushed from their necks."

"Has all this to do with why you wanted to see me?" Callahan asked. "Mrs. Curless told me you said it was a matter of some importance."

"Yes, it does and it is."

"What might it be, then? If you've meant to intrigue me, you've certainly succeeded."

Matt looked at him calmly. "A good friend of mine, Ben Mears, was to have gotten in touch with you today. Your housekeeper said he had not."

"That's so. I've seen no one since two o'clock this afternoon."

"I have been unable to reach him. He left the hospital in the company of my doctor, James Cody. I have also been unable to reach him. I have likewise been unable to reach Susan Norton, Ben's lady friend. She went out early this afternoon, promising her parents she would be in by five. They are worried."

Callahan sat forward at this. He had a passing acquaintance with Bill Norton, who had once come to see him about a problem that had to do with some Catholic co-workers.

"You suspect something?"

"Let me ask you a question," Matt said. "Take it very seriously and think it over before you answer. Have you noticed anything out of the ordinary in town just lately?"

Callahan's original impression, now almost a certainty, was that this man was proceeding very carefully indeed, not wanting to frighten him off by whatever was on his mind. Something sufficiently outrageous was suggested by the litter of books.

"Vampires in 'salem's Lot?" he asked.

He was thinking that the deep depression which followed grave illness could sometimes be avoided if the person afflicted had a deep enough investment in life: artists, musicians, a carpenter whose thoughts centered on some half-completed building. The interest could just as well be linked to some harmless (or not so harmless) psychosis, perhaps incipient before the illness.

He had spoken at some length with an elderly man named Horris from Schoolyard Hill who had been in the Maine Medical Center with advanced cancer of the lower intestine. In spite of pain which must have been excruciating, he had discoursed with Callahan in great and lucid detail concerning the creatures from Uranus who were infiltrating every walk of American life. "One day the fella who fills your gas tank down at Sonny's Amoco is just Joe Blow from Falmouth," this bright-eyed, talking skeleton told him, "and the next day it's a Uranian who just *looks* like Joe Blow. He even has Joe Blow's memories and speech patterns, you see. Because Uranians eat alpha waves . . . smack, smack, smack!" According to Horris, he did not have cancer at all, but an advanced case of laser poisoning. The Uranians, alarmed at his knowledge of their machinations, had decided to put him out of the way. Horris accepted this, and was prepared to go down fighting. Callahan made no effort to disabuse him. Leave that to well-meaning but thick-headed relatives. Callahan's experience was that psychosis, like a good knock of Cutty Sark, could be extremely beneficial.

So now he simply folded his hands and waited for Matt to continue.

Matt said, "It's difficult to proceed as it is. It's going to be more difficult still if you think I'm suffering from sickbed dementia."

Startled by hearing his thoughts expressed just as he had finished thinking them, Callahan kept his poker face only with difficulty—although the emotion that would have come through would not have been disquiet but admiration.

"On the contrary, you seem extremely lucid," he said.

Matt sighed. "Lucidity doesn't presuppose sanity—as you well know." He shifted in bed, redistributing the books that lay around him. "If there is a God, He must be making me do penance for a life of careful academicism—of refusing to plant an intellectual foot on any ground until it had been footnoted in triplicate. Now for the second time in one day, I'm compelled to make the wildest declarations without a shred of proof to back them up. All I can say in defense of my own sanity is that my statements can be either proved or disproved without too much difficulty, and hope that you will take me seriously enough to make the test before it's too late." He chuckled. *"Before it's too late.* Sounds straight out of the thirties' pulp magazines, doesn't it?"

"Life is full of melodrama," Callahan remarked, reflecting that if it were so, he had seen precious little of it lately.

"Let me ask you again if you have noticed anything— *anything*—out of the way or peculiar this weekend."

"To do with vampires, or—"

"To do with anything."

Callahan thought it over. "The dump's closed," he said finally. "But the gate was broken off, so I drove in anyway." He smiled. "I rather enjoy taking my own garbage to the dump. It's so practical and humble that I can indulge my elitist fantasies of a poor but happy proletariat to the fullest. Dud Rogers wasn't around, either."

"Anything else?"

"Well . . . the Crocketts weren't at mass this morning, and Mrs. Crockett hardly ever misses."

"More?"

"Poor Mrs. Glick, of course—"

Matt got up on one elbow. "Mrs. Glick? What about her?"

"She's dead."

"Of what?"

"Pauline Dickens seemed to think it was a heart attack," Callahan said, but hesitatingly.

"Has anyone else died in the Lot today?" Ordinarily, it would have been a foolish question. Deaths in a small town like 'salem's Lot were generally spread apart, in spite of the higher proportion of elderly in the population.

"No," Callahan said slowly. "But the mortality rate has certainly been high lately, hasn't it? Mike Ryerson . . . Floyd Tibbits . . . the McDougall baby . . ."

Matt nodded, looking tired. "Passing strange," he said. "Yes. But things are reaching the point where they'll be able to cover up for each other. A few more nights and I'm afraid . . . afraid . . ."

"Let's stop beating around the bush," Callahan said.

"All right. There's been rather too much of that already, hasn't there?"

He began to tell his story from beginning to end, weaving in Ben's and Susan's and Jimmy's additions as he went along, holding back nothing. By the time he had finished, the evening's horror had ended for Ben and Jimmy. Susan Norton's was just beginning.

2

When he had finished, Matt allowed a moment of silence and then said, "So. Am I crazy?"

"You're determined that people will think you so, anyway," Callahan said, "in spite of the fact that you seem to have convinced Mr. Mears and your own doctor. No, I don't think you're crazy. After all, I am in the business of dealing with the supernatural. If I may be allowed a small pun, it is my bread and wine."

"But—"

"Let me tell you a story. I won't vouch for its truth, but I will vouch for my own belief that it *is* true. It concerns a good friend of mine, Father Raymond Bissonette, who has been ministering to a parish in Cornwall for some years now—along the so-called Tin Coast. Do you know of it?"

"Through reading, yes."

"Some five years ago he wrote me that he had been called to an out-of-the-way corner of his parish to conduct a funeral service for a girl who had just 'pined away.' The girl's coffin was filled with wild roses, which struck Ray as unusual. What he found downright grotesque was the fact that her mouth had been propped open with a stick and then filled with garlic and wild thyme."

"But those are—"

"Traditional protections against the rising of the Undead, yes. Folk remedies. When Ray inquired, he was told quite matter-of-factly by the girl's father that she had been killed by an incubus. You know the meaning?"

"A sexual vampire."

"The girl had been betrothed to a young man named Bannock, who had a large strawberry-colored birthmark on the side of his neck. He was struck and killed by a car on his way home from work two weeks before the wedding. Two years later, the girl became engaged to another man. She broke it off quite suddenly during the week before the banns were to be cried for the second time. She told her parents and friends that John Bannock had been coming to her in the night and she had been unfaithful with him. Her present lover, according to Ray, was more distressed by the thought that she might have become mentally unbalanced than by the possibility of demon visitation. Nonetheless, she wasted away, died, and was buried in the old ways of the church.

"All of that did not occasion Ray's letter. What did was an occurrence some two months after the girl's burial. While he was on an early morning walk, Ray spied a young man standing by the girl's grave—a young man with a strawberry-colored birthmark on his neck. Nor is that the end of the story. He had gotten a Polaroid camera from his parents the Christmas before and had amused himself by snapping various views of the Cornish countryside. I have some of them in a picture album at the rectory—they're quite good. The camera was around his neck that morning, and he took several snaps of the young man. When he showed them around the village, the reaction was quite amazing. One old lady fell down in a faint, and the dead girl's mother began to pray in the street.

"But when Ray got up the next morning, the young man's figure had completely faded out of the pictures, and all that was left were several views of the local churchyard."

"And you believe that?" Matt asked.

"Oh yes. And I suspect most people would. The ordinary fellow isn't half so leery of the supernatural as the fiction writers like to make out. Most writers who deal in that particular subject, as a matter of fact, are more hardheaded about spirits and demons and boogies than your ordinary man in the street. Lovecraft was an atheist. Edgar Allen Poe was sort of a half-assed transcendentalist. And Hawthorne was only conventionally religious."

"You're amazingly conversant on the subject," Matt said.

The priest shrugged. "I had a boy's interest in the occult and the outré," he said, "and as I grew older, my calling to the priesthood enhanced rather than retarded it." He sighed deeply. "But lately I've begun to ask myself some rather hard questions about the nature of evil in the world." With a twisted smile he added, "It's spoiled a lot of the fun."

"Then . . . would you investigate a few things for me? And would you be averse to taking along some holy water and a bit of the Host?"

"You're treading on uneasy theological ground now," Callahan said with genuine gravity.

"Why?"

"I'm not going to say no, not at this point," Callahan said. "And I ought to tell you that if you'd gotten a younger priest, he probably would have said yes almost at once, with few if any qualms at all." He smiled bitterly. "They view the trappings of the church as symbolic rather than practical—like a shaman's headdress and medicine stick. This young priest might decide you were crazy, but if shaking a little holy water around would ease your craziness, fine and dandy. I can't do that. If I should proceed to make your investigations in a neat Harris tweed with nothing under my arm but a copy of Sybil Leek's *The Sensuous Exorcist* or whatever, that would be between you and me. But if I go with the Host . . . then I go as an agent of the Holy Catholic Church, prepared to execute what I would consider the most spiritual rites of my office. Then I go as Christ's representative on earth." He was now looking at Matt seriously, solemnly. "I may be a poor excuse for a priest—at times I've thought so—a bit jaded, a bit cynical, and just lately suffering a crisis of . . . what? faith? identity? . . . but I still believe enough in the awesome, mystical, and apotheotic power of the church which stands behind me to tremble a bit at the thought of accepting your request lightly. The church is more than a bundle of ideals, as these younger fellows seem to believe. It's more than a spiritual Boy Scout troop. The church is a Force . . . and one does not set a Force in motion lightly." He frowned severely at Matt. "Do you understand that? Your understanding is vitally important."

"I understand."

"You see, the over-all concept of evil in the Catholic Church has undergone a radical change in this century. Do you know what caused it?"

"I imagine it was Freud."

"Very good. The Catholic Church began to cope with a new concept as it marched into the twentieth century: evil with a small 'e.' With a devil that was not a red-horned monster complete with spiked tail and cloven hooves, or a serpent crawling through the garden—although that is a remarkably apt psychological image. The devil, according to the Gospel According to Freud, would be a gigantic composite id, the subconscious of all of us."

"Surely a more stupendous concept than red-tailed boogies or demons with such sensitive noses that they can be banished with one good fart from a constipated churchman," Matt said.

"Stupendous, of course. But impersonal. Merciless. Untouchable. Banishing Freud's devil is as impossible as Shylock's bargain—to extract a pound of flesh without spilling a drop of blood. The Catholic Church has been forced to reinterpret its whole approach to evil—bombers over Cambodia, the war in Ireland and the Middle East, cop-killings and ghetto riots, the billion smaller evils loosed on the world each day like a plague of gnats. It is in the process of shedding its old medicine-man skin and re-emerging as a socially active, socially conscious body. The inner city rap-center ascendant over the confessional. Communion playing second fiddle to the civil rights movement and urban renewal. The church has been in the process of planting both feet in this world."

"Where there are no witches or incubi or vampires," Matt said, "but only child-beating, incest, and the rape of the environment."

"Yes."

Matt said deliberately, "And you hate it, don't you?"

"Yes," Callahan said quietly. "I think it's an abomination. It's the Catholic Church's way of saying that God isn't dead, only a little senile. And I guess that's my answer, isn't it? What do you want me to do?"

Matt told him.

Callahan thought it over and said, "You realize it flies in the face of everything I just told you?"

"On the contrary, I think it's your chance to put your church—*your* church—to the test."

Callahan took a deep breath. "Very well, I agree. On one condition."

"What would that be?"

"That all of us who go on this little expedition first go to the shop this Mr. Straker is managing. That Mr. Mears, as spokesman, should speak to him frankly about all of this. That we all have a chance to observe his reactions. And finally, that he should have his chance to laugh in our faces."

Matt was frowning. "It would be warning him."

Callahan shook his head. "I believe the warning would be of no avail if the three of us—Mr. Mears, Dr. Cody, and myself—still agreed that we should move ahead regardless."

"All right," Matt said. "I agree, contingent on the approval of Ben and Jimmy Cody."

"Fine." Callahan sighed. "Will it hurt you if I tell you that I hope this is all in your mind? That I hope this man Straker does laugh in our faces, and with good reason?"

"Not in the slightest."

"I do hope it. I have agreed to more than you know. It frightens me."

"I am frightened, too," Matt said softly.

3

But walking back to St. Andrew's, he did not feel frightened at all. He felt exhilarated, renewed. For the first time in years he was sober and did not crave a drink.

He went into the rectory, picked up the telephone, and dialed Eva Miller's boardinghouse. "Hello? Mrs. Miller? May I speak with Mr. Mears? . . . He's not. Yes, I see. . . . No, no message. I'll call tomorrow. Yes, good-by."

He hung up and went to the window.

Was Mears out there someplace, drinking beer on a country road, or could it be that everything the old schoolteacher had told him was true?

If so . . . if so . . .

He could not stay in the house. He went out on the back porch, breathing in the brisk, steely air of October, and looked into the moving darkness. Perhaps it wasn't all Freud after all. Perhaps a large part of it had to do with the invention of the electric light, which had killed the shadows in men's minds much more effectively than a stake through a vampire's heart— and less messily, too.

The evil still went on, but now it went on in the hard, soulless glare of parking-lot fluorescents, of neon tubing, of hundred-watt bulbs by the billions. Generals planned strategic air strikes beneath the no-nonsense glow of alternating current, and it was all out of control, like a kid's soapbox racer going downhill with no brakes: *I was following my orders.* Yes, that was true, patently true. We were all soldiers, simply following what was written on our walking papers. But where were the orders coming from, ultimately? *Take me to your leader.* But where is his office? *I was just following orders. The people elected me.* But who elected the people?

Something flapped overhead and Callahan looked up, startled out of his confused revery. A bird? A bat? Gone. Didn't matter.

He listened for the town and heard nothing but the whine of telephone wires.

The night the kudzu gets your fields, you sleep like the dead.

Who wrote that? Dickey?

No sound; no light but the fluorescent in front of the church where Fred Astaire had never danced and the faint waxing and waning of the yellow warning light at the crossroads of Brock Street and Jointner Avenue. No baby cried.

The night the kudzu gets your fields, you sleep like—

The exultation had faded away like a bad echo of pride. Terror struck him around the heart like a blow. Not terror for his life or his honor or that his housekeeper might find out about his drinking. It was a terror he had never dreamed of, not even in the tortured days of his adolescence.

The terror he felt was for his immortal soul.

PART THREE

THE DESERTED VILLAGE

I heard a voice, crying from the deep:
Come join me, baby, in my endless sleep.

—Old rock 'n' roll song

And travelers now within that valley
    Through the red-litten windows see
Vast forms that move fantastically
    To a discordant melody;
While, like a rapid ghastly river,
    Through the pale door,
A hideous throng rush out forever
    And laugh—but smile no more.

—EDGAR ALLAN POE
"The Haunted Palace"

Tell you now that the whole town is empty.

—BOB DYLAN

Chapter Fourteen
THE LOT (IV)

1

From the "Old Farmer's Almanac":

Sunset on Sunday, October 5, 1975, at 7:02 P.M., sunrise on Monday, October 6, 1975, at 6:49 A.M. The period of darkness on Jerusalem's Lot during that particular rotation of the Earth, thirteen days after the vernal equinox, lasted eleven hours and forty-seven minutes. The moon was new. The day's verse from the Old Farmer was: "See less sun, harvest's nigh done."

From the Portland Weather Station:

High temperature for the period of darkness was 62°, reported at 7:05 P.M. Low temperature was 47°, reported at 4:06 A.M. Scattered clouds, precipitation zero. Winds from the northwest at five to ten miles per hour.

From the Cumberland County police blotter:

Nothing.

2

No one pronounced Jerusalem's Lot dead on the morning of October 6; no one knew it was. Like the bodies of previous days, it retained every semblance of life.

Ruthie Crockett, who had lain pale and ill in bed all weekend, was gone on Monday morning. The disappearance went unreported. Her mother was down cellar, lying behind her shelves of preserves with a canvas tarpaulin pulled over her body, and Larry Crockett, who woke up very late indeed, simply assumed that his daughter had gotten herself off to school. He decided not to go into the office that day. He felt weak and washed out and lightheaded. Flu, or something. The light hurt his eyes. He got up and pulled down the shades, yelping once when the sunlight fell directly on his arm. He would have to replace that window some day when he felt better. Defective window glass was no joke. You could come home on a sunshiny day, find your house burning away six licks to the minute, and those insurance pricks in the home office called it spontaneous combustion and wouldn't pay up. When he felt better was time enough. He thought about a cup of coffee and felt sick to his stomach. He wondered vaguely where his wife was, and then the subject slipped out of his mind. He went back to bed, fingering a funny little shaving nick just under his chin, pulled the sheet over his wan cheek, and went back to sleep.

His daughter, meanwhile, slept in enameled darkness within an abandoned freezer close to Dud Rogers—in the night world of her new existence, she found his advances among the heaped mounds of garbage very acceptable.

Loretta Starcher, the town librarian, had also disappeared, although there was no one in her disconnected spinster's life to remark it. She now resided on the dark and musty third floor of the Jerusalem's Lot Public Library. The third floor was always kept locked (she had the only key, always worn on a chain around her neck) except when some special supplicant could convince her that he was strong enough, intelligent enough, and *moral* enough to receive a special dispensation.

Now she rested there herself, a first edition of a different kind, as mint as when she had first entered the world. Her binding, so to speak, had never even been cracked.

The disappearance of Virgil Rathbun also went unnoticed. Franklin Boddin woke up at nine o'clock in their shack, noticed vaguely that Virgil's pallet was empty, thought nothing of it, and started to get out of bed and see if there was a beer. He fell back, all rubber legs and reeling head.

Christ, he thought, drifting into sleep again. *What was we in to last night? Sterno?*

And beneath the shack, in the cool of twenty seasons' fallen leaves and among a galaxy of rusted beer cans popped down through the gaping floorboards in the front room, Virgil lay waiting for night. In the dark clay of his brain there were perhaps visions of a liquid more fiery than the finest scotch, more quenching than the finest wine.

Eva Miller missed Weasel Craig at breakfast but thought little of it. She was too busy directing the flow to and from the stove as her tenants rustled up their breakfasts and then stumbled forth to look another work week in the eye. Then she was too busy putting things to rights and washing the plates of that damned Grover Verrill and that no good Mickey Sylvester, both of whom had been consistently ignoring the "Please wash up your dishes" sign taped over the sink for years.

But as the silence crept back into the day and the frantic bulge of breakfast work merged into the steady routine of things to be done, she missed him again. Monday was garbage-collection day on Railroad Street, and Weasel always took the big green bags of rubbish out to the curb for Royal Snow to pick up in his dilapidated old International Harvester truck. Today the green bags were still out on the back steps.

She went to his room and knocked gently. "Ed?"

There was no response. On another day she would have assumed his drunkenness and simply have put the bags out herself, her lips slightly more compressed than usual. But this morning a faint thread of disquiet wormed into her, and she turned the doorknob and poked her head in. "Ed?" she called softly.

The room was empty. The window by the head of the bed was open, the curtains fluttering randomly in and out with the vagaries of the light breeze. The bed was wrinkled and she made it without thinking, her hands doing their own work. Stepping over to the other side, her right loafer crunched in something. She looked down and saw Weasel's horn-backed mirror, shattered on the floor. She picked it up and turned it over in her hands, frowning. It had been his mother's, and he had once turned down an antique dealer's offer of ten dollars for it. And that had been after he started drinking.

She got the dustpan from the hall closet and brushed up the glass with slow, thoughtful gestures. She knew Weasel had been sober when he went to bed the night before, and there was no place he could buy beer after nine o'clock, unless he had hitched a ride out to Dell's or into Cumberland.

She dumped the fragments of broken mirror into Weasel's wastebasket, seeing herself reflected over and over for a brief second. She looked into the wastebasket but saw no empty bottle there. Secret drinking was really not Ed Craig's style, anyway.

Well. He'll turn up.

But going downstairs, the disquiet remained. Without consciously admitting it to herself she knew that her feelings for Weasel went a bit deeper than friendly concern.

"Ma'am?"

She started from her thoughts and regarded the stranger in her kitchen. The stranger was a little boy, neatly dressed in corduroy pants and a clean blue T-shirt. *Looks like he fell off his bike.* He looked familiar, but she couldn't quite pin him down. From one of the new families out on Jointner Avenue, most likely.

"Does Mr. Ben Mears live here?"

Eva began to ask why he wasn't in school, then didn't. His expression was very serious, even grave. There were blue hollows under his eyes.

"He's sleeping."

"May I wait?"

Homer McCaslin had gone directly from Green's Mortuary to the Norton home on Brock Street. It was eleven o'clock by the time he got there. Mrs. Norton was in tears, and while Bill Norton seemed calm enough, he was chain smoking and his face looked drawn.

McCaslin agreed to put the girl's description on the wire. Yes, he would call as soon as he heard something. Yes, he would check the hospitals in the area, it was part of the routine (so was the morgue). He privately thought the girl might have gone off in a tiff. The mother admitted they had quarreled and that the girl had been talking of moving out.

Nonetheless, he cruised some of the back roads, one ear comfortably cocked to the crackle of static coming from the radio slung under the dash. At a few minutes past midnight, coming up the Brooks Road toward town, the spotlight he had trained on the soft shoulder of the road glinted off metal—a car parked in the woods.

He stopped, backed up, got out. The car was parked partway up an old disused wood-road. Chevy Vega, light brown, two years old. He pulled his heavy chained notebook out of his back pocket, paged past the interview with Ben and Jimmy, and trained his light on the license number Mrs. Norton had given him. It matched. The girl's car, all right. That made things more serious. He laid his hand on the hood. Cool. It had been parked for a while.

"Sheriff?"

A light, carefree voice, like tinkling bells. Why had his hand dropped to the butt of his gun?

He turned and saw the Norton girl, looking incredibly beautiful, walking toward him hand in hand with a stranger—a young man with black hair unfashionably combed straight back from his forehead. McCaslin shone the flashlight at his face and had the oddest impression that the light was shining right through it without illuminating it in the slightest. And although they were walking, they left no tracks in the soft dirt. He felt fear and warning kindle in his nerves, his hand tightened on his revolver . . . and then loosened. He clicked off his flashlight and waited passively.

"Sheriff," she said, and now her voice was low, caressing.

"How good of you to come," the stranger said.

They fell on him.

Now his patrol car was parked far out on the rutted and brambled dead end of the Deep Cut Road, with hardly a twinkle of chrome showing through the heavy strands of juniper, bracken, and Lolly-come-see-me. McCaslin was curled up in the trunk. The radio called him at regular intervals unheeded.

Later that same morning Susan paid a short visit to her mother but did little damage; like a leech that had fed well on a slow swimmer, she was satisfied. Still, she had been invited in and now she could come and go as she pleased. There would be a new hunger tonight . . . every night.

Charles Griffen had wakened his wife at a little after five on that Monday morning, his face long and chiseled into sardonic lines by his anger. Outside, the cows were bawling unmilked with full udders. He summed up the work of the night in six words:

"Those damned boys have run off."

But they had not. Danny Glick had found and battened upon Jack Griffen and Jack had gone to his brother Hal's room and had finally ended his worries of school and books and unyielding fathers forever. Now both of them lay in the center of a huge pile of loose hay in the upper mow, with chaff in their hair and sweet motes of pollen dancing in the dark and tideless channels of their noses. An occasional mouse scampered across their faces.

Now the light had spilled across the land, and all evil things slept. It was to be a beautiful autumn day, crisp and clear and filled with sunshine. By and large the town (not knowing it was dead) would go off to their jobs with no inkling of the night's work. According to the Old Farmer, sunset Monday night would come at 7:00 P.M. sharp.

The days shortened, moving toward Halloween, and beyond that, winter.

3

When Ben came downstairs at quarter to nine, Eva Miller said from the sink, "There's someone waiting to see you on the porch."

He nodded and went out the back door, still in his slippers, expecting to see either Susan or Sheriff McCaslin. But the visitor was a small, economical boy sitting on the top step of the porch and looking out over the town, which was coming slowly to its Monday morning vitality.

"Hello?" Ben said, and the boy turned around quickly.

They looked at each other for no great space of time, but for Ben the moment seemed to undergo a queer stretching, and a feeling of unreality swept him. The boy reminded him physically of the boy he himself had been, but it was more than that. He seemed to feel a weight settle onto his neck, as if in a curious way he sensed the more-than-chance coming together of their lives. It made him think of the day he had met Susan in the park, and how their light, get-acquainted conversation had seemed queerly heavy and fraught with intimations of the future.

Perhaps the boy felt something similar, for his eyes widened slightly and his hand found the porch railing, as if for support.

"You're Mr. Mears," the boy said, not questioning.

"Yes. You have the advantage, I'm afraid."

"My name is Mark Petrie," the boy said. "I have some bad news for you."

And I bet he does, too, Ben thought dismally, and tried to tighten his mind against whatever it might be—but when it came, it was a total, shocking surprise.

"Susan Norton is one of *them,*" the boy said. "Barlow got her at the house. But I killed Straker. At least, I think I did."

Ben tried to speak and couldn't. His throat was locked.

The boy nodded, taking charge effortlessly. "Maybe we could go for a ride in your car and talk. I don't want anyone to see me around. I'm playing hooky and I'm already in dutch with my folks."

Ben said something—he didn't know what. After the motorcycle accident that had killed Miranda, he had picked himself up off the pavement shaken but unhurt (except for a small scratch across the back of his left hand, mustn't forget that, Purple Hearts had been awarded for less) and the truck driver had walked over to him, casting two shadows in the glow of the streetlight and the head lamps of the truck—he was a big, balding man with a pen in the breast pocket of his white shirt, and stamped in gold letters on the barrel of the pen he could read "Frank's Mobil Sta" and the rest was hidden by the pocket, but Ben had guessed shrewdly that the final letters were "tion," elementary, my dear Watson, elementary. The truck driver had said something to Ben, he didn't remember what, and then he took Ben's arm gently, trying to lead him away. He saw one of Miranda's flat-heeled shoes lying near the large rear wheels of the moving van and had shaken the trucker off and started toward it and the trucker had taken two steps after him and said, *I wouldn't do that, buddy.* And Ben had looked up at him dumbly, unhurt except for the small scratch across the back of his left hand, wanting to tell the trucker that five minutes ago this hadn't happened, wanting to tell the trucker that in some parallel world he and Miranda had taken a left at the corner one block back and were riding into an entirely different future. A crowd was gathering, coming out of a liquor store on one corner and a small milk-and-sandwich bar on the other. And he had begun to feel then what he was feeling now: the complex and awful mental and physical interaction that is the beginning of acceptance, and the only counterpart to that feeling is rape. The stomach seems to drop. The lips become numb. A thin foam forms on the roof of the mouth. There is a ringing noise in the ears. The skin on the testicles seems to crawl and tighten. The mind goes through a turning away, a hiding of its face, as from a light too brilliant to bear. He had shaken off the well-meaning truck driver's hands a second time and had walked over to the shoe. He picked it up. He turned it over. He placed his hand inside it, and the insole was still warm from her foot. Carrying it, he had gone two steps further and had seen her sprawled legs under the truck's front wheels, clad in the yellow Wranglers she had pulled on with such careless and laughing ease back at the apartment. It was impossible to believe that the girl who had pulled on those slacks was dead, yet the acceptance was there, in his belly, his mouth, his balls. He had groaned aloud, and that was when the tabloid photographer had snapped his picture for Mabel's paper. One shoe off, one shoe on. People looking at her bare foot as if they had never seen one before. He had taken two steps away and leaned over and—

"I'm going to be sick," he said.

"That's all right."

Ben stepped behind his Citroën and doubled over, holding on to the door handle. He closed his eyes, feeling darkness wash over him, and in the darkness Susan's face appeared, smiling at him and looking at him with those lovely deep eyes. He opened his eyes again. It occurred to him that the kid might be lying, or mixed up, or an out-and-out psycho. Yet the thought brought him no hope. The kid was not set up like that. He turned back and looked into the kid's face and read concern there—nothing else.

"Come on," he said.

The boy got in the car and they drove off. Eva Miller watched them go from the kitchen window, her brow creased. Something bad was happening. She felt it, was filled with it, the same way she had been filled with an obscure and cloudy dread on the day her husband died.

She got up and dialed Loretta Starcher. The phone rang over and over without answer until she put it back in the cradle.

Where could she be? Certainly not at the library. It was closed Mondays.

She sat, looking pensively at the telephone. She felt that some great disaster was in the wind—perhaps something as terrible as the fire of '51.

At last she picked up the phone again and called Mabel Werts, who was filled with the gossip of the hour and eager for more. The town hadn't known such a weekend in years.

4

Ben drove aimlessly and without direction as Mark told his story. He told it well, beginning with the night Danny Glick had come to his window and ending with his nocturnal visitor early this morning.

"Are you sure it was Susan?" he asked.

Mark Petrie nodded.

Ben pulled an abrupt U-turn and accelerated back up Jointner Avenue.

"Where are you going? To the—"

"Not there. Not yet."

5

"Wait. Stop."

Ben pulled over and they got out together. They had been driving slowly down the Brooks Road, at the bottom of Marsten's Hill. The wood-road where Homer McCaslin had spotted Susan's Vega. They had both caught the glint of sun on metal. They walked up the disused road together, not speaking. There were deep and dusty wheel ruts, and the grass grew high between them. A bird twitted somewhere.

They found the car shortly.

Ben hesitated, then halted. He felt sick to his stomach again. The sweat on his arms was cold.

"Go look," he said.

Mark went down to the car and leaned in the driver's side window. "Keys are in it," he called back.

Ben began to walk toward the car and his foot kicked something. He looked down and saw a .38 revolver lying in the dust. He picked it up and turned it over in his hands. It looked very much like a police issue revolver.

"Whose gun?" Mark asked, walking toward him. He had Susan's keys in his hand.

"I don't know." He checked the safety to be sure it was on, and then put the gun in his pocket.

Mark offered him the keys and Ben took them and walked toward the Vega, feeling like a man in a dream. His hands were shaking and he had to poke twice before he could get the right key into the trunk slot. He twisted it and pulled the back deck up without allowing himself to think.

They looked in together. The trunk held a spare tire, a jack, and nothing else. Ben felt his breath come out in a rush.

"Now?" Mark asked.

Ben didn't answer for a moment. When he felt that his voice would be under control, he said, "We're going to see a friend of mine named Matt Burke, who is in the hospital. He's been researching vampires."

The urgency in the boy's gaze remained. "Do you believe me?"

"Yes," Ben said, and hearing the word on the air seemed to confirm it and give it weight. It was beyond recall. "Yes, I believe you."

"Mr. Burke is from the high school, isn't he? Does he know about this?"

"Yes. So does his doctor."

"Dr. Cody?"

"Yes."

They were both looking at the car as they spoke, as if it were a relic of some dark, lost race which they had discovered in these sunny woods to the west of town. The trunk gaped open like a mouth, and as Ben slammed it shut, the dull thud of its latching echoed in his heart.

"And after we talk," he said, "we're going up to the Marsten House and get the son of a bitch who did this."

Mark looked at him without moving. "It may not be as easy as you think. She will be there, too. She's *his* now."

"He's going to wish he never saw 'salem's Lot," he said softly. "Come on."

6

They arrived at the hospital at nine-thirty, and Jimmy Cody was in Matt's room. He looked at Ben, unsmiling, and then his eyes flicked to Mark Petrie with curiosity.

"I've got some bad news for you, Ben. Sue Norton has disappeared."

"She's a vampire," Ben said flatly, and Matt grunted from his bed.

"Are you sure of that?" Jimmy asked sharply.

Ben cocked his thumb at Mark Petrie and introduced him. "Mark here had a little visit from Danny Glick on Saturday night. He can tell you the rest."

Mark told it from beginning to end, just as he had told Ben earlier.

Matt spoke first when he had finished. "Ben, there are no words to say how sorry I am."

"I can give you something if you need it," Jimmy said.

"I know what medicine I need, Jimmy. I want to move against this Barlow today. Now. Before dark."

"All right," Jimmy said. "I've canceled all my calls. And I phoned the county sheriff's office. McCaslin is gone, too."

"Maybe that explains this," Ben said, and took the pistol out of his pocket and dropped it onto Matt's bedside table. It looked strange and out of place in the hospital room.

"Where did you get this?" Jimmy asked, picking it up.

"Out by Susan's car."

"Then I can guess. McCaslin went to the Norton house sometime after he left us. He got the story on Susan, including the make, model, and license number of her car. Went out cruising some of the back roads, just on the off-chance. And—"

Broken silence in the room. None of them needed it filled.

"Foreman's is still closed," Jimmy said. "And a lot of the old men who hang around Crossen's have been complaining about the dump. No one has seen Dud Rogers for a week."

They looked at each other bleakly.

"I spoke with Father Callahan last night," Matt said. "He has agreed to go along, providing you two—plus Mark, of course—will stop at this new shop and talk to Straker first."

"I don't think he'll be talking to anyone today," Mark said quietly.

"What did you find out about *them?*" Jimmy asked Matt. "Anything useful?"

"Well, I think I've put some of the pieces together. Straker must be this thing's human watchdog and bodyguard . . . a kind of human familiar. He must have been in town long before Barlow appeared. There were certain rites to be performed, in propitiation of the Dark Father. Even Barlow has his Master, you see." He looked at them somberly. "I rather suspect no one will ever find a trace of Ralphie Glick. I think he was Barlow's ticket of admission. Straker took him and sacrificed him."

"Bastard," Jimmy said distantly.

"And Danny Glick?" Ben asked.

"Straker bled him first," Matt said. "His Master's gift. First blood for the faithful servant. Later, Barlow would have taken over that job himself. But Straker performed another service for his Master before Barlow ever arrived. Do any of you know what?"

For a moment there was silence, and then Mark said quite distinctly, "The dog that man found on the cemetery gate."

"What?" Jimmy said. "Why? Why would he do that?"

"The white eyes," Mark said, and then looked questioningly at Matt, who was nodding with some surprise.

"All last night I nodded over these books, not knowing we had a scholar in our midst." The boy blushed a little. "What Mark says is exactly right. According to several of the standard references on folklore and the supernatural, one way to frighten a vampire away is to paint white 'angel eyes' over the real eyes of a black dog. Win's Doc was all black except for two white patches. Win used to call them his headlights—they were directly over his eyes. He let the dog run at night. Straker must have spotted it, killed it, and then hung it on the cemetery gate."

"And how about this Barlow?" Jimmy asked. "How did he get to town?"

Matt shrugged. "I have no way of telling. I think that we must assume, in line with the legends, that he is old . . . very old. He may have changed his name a dozen times, or a thousand. He may have been a native of almost every country in the world at one time or another, although I suspect his origins may have been Romanian or Magyar or Hungarian. It doesn't really matter how he got to town anyway . . . although I wouldn't be surprised to find out Larry Crockett had a hand in it. He's here. That's the important thing.

"Now, here is what you must do: Take a stake when you go. And a gun, in case Straker is still alive. Sheriff McCaslin's revolver will serve the purpose. The stake must pierce the heart or the vampire may rise again. Jimmy, you can check that. When you have staked him you must cut off his head, stuff the mouth with garlic, and turn it face down in the coffin. In most vampire fiction, Hollywood and otherwise, the staked vampire mortifies almost instantly into dust. This may not happen in real life. If it doesn't, you must weight the coffin and throw it into running water. I would suggest the Royal River. Do you have questions?"

There were none.

"Good. You must each carry a vial of holy water and a bit of the Host. And you must each have Father Callahan hear your confession before you go."

"I don't think any of us are Catholic," Ben said.

"I am," Jimmy said. "Nonpracticing."

"Nonetheless, you will make a confession and an act of contrition. Then you go pure, washed in Christ's blood . . . clean blood, not tainted."

"All right," Ben said.

"Ben, had you slept with Susan? Forgive me, but—"

"Yes," he said.

"Then you must pound the stake—first into Barlow, then into *her*. You are the only person in this little party who has been hurt personally. You will act as her husband. And you mustn't falter. You'll be releasing her."

"All right," he said again.

"Above all"—his glance swept all of them—"*you must not look in his eyes!* If you do, he'll catch you and turn you against the others, even at the expense of your own life. Remember Floyd Tibbits! That makes it dangerous to carry a gun, even if it's necessary. Jimmy, you take it, and hang back a little. If you have to examine either Barlow or Susan, give it to Mark."

"Understood," Jimmy said.

"Remember to buy garlic. And roses, if you can. Is that little flower shop in Cumberland still open, Jimmy?"

"The Northern Belle? I think so."

"A white rose for each of you. Tie them in your hair or around your neck. And I'll repeat myself—don't look in his eyes! I could keep you here and tell you a hundred other things, but you better go along. It's ten o'clock already, and Father Callahan may be having second thoughts. My best wishes and my prayers go with you. Praying is quite a trick for an old agnostic like me, too. But I don't think I'm as agnostic as I once was. Was it Carlyle who said that if a man dethrones God in his heart, then Satan must ascend to His position?"

No one answered, and Matt sighed. "Jimmy, I want a closer look at your neck."

Jimmy stepped to the bedside and lifted his chin. The wounds were obviously punctures, but they had both scabbed over and seemed to be healing nicely.

"Any pain? Itching?" Matt asked.

"No."

"You were very lucky," he said looking at Jimmy soberly.

"I'm starting to think I was luckier than I'll ever know."

Matt leaned back in his bed. His face looked drawn, the eyes deeply socketed. "I will take the pill Ben refused, if you please."

"I'll tell one of the nurses."

"I'll sleep while you go about your work," Matt said. "Later there is another matter . . . well, enough of that." His eyes shifted to Mark. "You did a remarkable thing yesterday, boy. Foolish and reckless, but remarkable."

"*She* paid for it," Mark said quietly, and clasped his hands together in front of him. They were trembling.

"Yes, and you may have to pay again. Any of you, or all of you. Don't underestimate him! And now, if you don't mind, I'm very tired. I was reading most of the night. Call me the very minute the work is done."

They left. In the hall Ben looked at Jimmy and said, "Did he remind you of anyone?"

"Yes," Jimmy said. "Van Helsing."

7

At quarter past ten, Eva Miller went down cellar to get two jars of corn to take to Mrs. Norton who, according to Mabel Werts, was in bed. Eva had spent most of September in a steamy kitchen, toiling over her canning operations, blanching vegetables and putting them up, putting paraffin plugs in the tops of Ball jars to cover homemade jelly. There were well over two hundred glass jars neatly shelved in her spick-and-span dirt-floored basement—canning was one of her great joys. Later in the year, as fall drifted into winter and the holidays neared, she would add mincemeat.

The smell struck her as soon as she opened the cellar door.

"Gosh'n fishes," she muttered under her breath, and went down gingerly, as if wading into a polluted pool. Her husband had built the cellar himself, rock-walling it for coolness. Every now and then a muskrat or woodchuck or mink would crawl into one of the wide chinks and die there. That was what must have happened, although she could never recall a stink this strong.

She reached the lower floor and went along the walls, squinting in the faint overhead glow of the two fifty-watt bulbs. Those should be replaced with seventy-fives, she thought. She got her preserves, neatly labeled CORN in her own careful blue script (a slice of red pepper on the top of every one), and continued her inspection, even squeezing into the space behind the huge, multi-duct furnace. Nothing.

She arrived back at the steps leading up to her kitchen and stared around, frowning, hands on hips. The large cellar was much neater since she had hired two of Larry Crockett's boys to build a tool shed behind her house two years ago. There was the furnace, looking like an Impressionist sculpture of the goddess Kali with its score of pipes twisting off in all directions; the storm windows that she would have to get on soon now that October had come and heating was so dear; the tarpaulin-covered pool table that had been Ralph's. She had the felt carefully vacuumed each May, although no one had played on it since Ralph had died in 1959. Nothing much else down here now. A box of paperbacks she had collected for the Cumberland Hospital, a snow shovel with a broken handle, a pegboard with some of Ralph's old tools hanging from it, a trunk containing drapes that were probably all mildewed by now.

Still, the stink persisted.

Her eyes fixed on the small half-door that led down to the root cellar, but she wasn't going down there, not today. Besides, the walls of the root cellar were solid concrete. Unlikely that an animal could have gotten in there. Still—

"Ed?" she called suddenly, for no reason at all. The flat sound of her voice scared her.

The word died in the dimly lit cellar. Now, why had she done that? What in God's name would Ed Craig be doing down here, even if there *was* a place to hide? Drinking? Offhand, she couldn't think of a more depressing place in town to drink than here in her cellar. More likely he was off in the woods with that good-for-nothing friend of his, Virge Rathbun, guzzling someone's dividend.

Yet she lingered a moment longer, sweeping her gaze around. The rotten stink was awful, just awful. She hoped she wouldn't have to have the place fumigated.

With a last glance at the root cellar door, she went back upstairs.

8

Father Callahan heard them out, all three, and by the time he was brought up to date, it was a little after eleven-thirty. They were sitting in the cool and spacious sitting room of the rectory, and the sun flooded in the large front windows in bars that looked thick enough to slice. Watching the dust motes that danced dreamily in the sun shafts, Callahan was reminded of an old cartoon he had seen somewhere. Cleaning woman with a broom is staring in surprise down at the floor; she has swept away part of her shadow. He felt a little like that now. For the second time in twenty-four hours he had been confronted with a stark impossibility—only now the impossibility had corroboration from a writer, a seemingly levelheaded little boy, and a doctor whom the town respected. Still, an impossibility was an impossibility. You couldn't sweep away your own shadow. Except that it seemed to have happened.

"This would be much easier to accept if you could have arranged for a thunderstorm and a power failure," he said.

"It's quite true," Jimmy said. "I assure you." His hand went to his neck.

Father Callahan got up and pulled something out of Jimmy's black bag—two truncated baseball bats with sharpened points. He turned one of them over in his hands and said, "Just a moment, Mrs. Smith. This won't hurt a bit."

No one laughed.

Callahan put the stakes back, went to the window, and looked out at Jointner Avenue. "You are all very persuasive," he said. "And I suppose I must add one little piece which you now do not have in your possession."

He turned back to them.

"There is a sign in the window of the Barlow and Straker Furniture Shop," he said. "It says, 'Closed Until Further Notice.' I went down this morning myself promptly at nine o'clock to discuss Mr. Burke's allegations with your mysterious Mr. Straker. The shop is locked, front and back."

"You have to admit that jibes with what Mark says," Ben remarked.

"Perhaps. And perhaps it's only chance. Let me ask you again: Are you sure you must have the Catholic Church in this?"

"Yes," Ben said. "But we'll proceed without you if we have to. If it comes to that, I'll go alone."

"No need of that," Father Callahan said, rising. "Follow me across to the church, gentlemen, and I will hear your confessions."

9

Ben knelt awkwardly in the darkened mustiness of the confessional, his mind whirling, his thoughts inchoate. Flicking through them was a succession of surreal images: Susan in the park; Mrs. Glick backing away from the makeshift tongue-depressor cross, her mouth an open, writhing wound; Floyd Tibbits coming out of his car in a lurch, dressed like a scarecrow, charging him; Mark Petrie leaning in the window of Susan's car. For the first and only time, the possibility that all of this might be a dream occurred to him, and his tired mind clutched at it eagerly.

His eye fell on something in the corner of the confessional, and he picked it up curiously. It was an empty Junior Mints box, fallen from the pocket of some little boy, perhaps. A touch of reality that was undeniable. The cardboard was real and tangible under his fingers. This nightmare was real.

The little sliding door opened. He looked at it but could see nothing beyond. There was a heavy screen in the opening.

"What should I do?" He asked the screen.

"Say, 'Bless me, Father, for I have sinned.' "

"Bless me, Father, for I have sinned," Ben said, his voice sounding strange and heavy in the enclosed space.

"Now tell me your sins."

"All of them?" Ben asked, appalled.

"Try to be representative," Callahan said, his voice dry. "I know we have something to do before dark."

Thinking hard and trying to keep the Ten Commandments before him as a kind of sorting screen, Ben began. It didn't become easier as he went along. There was no sense of catharsis—only the dull embarrassment that went with telling a stranger the mean secrets of his life. Yet he could see how this ritual could become compulsive: as bitterly compelling as strained rubbing alcohol for the chronic drinker or the pictures behind the loose board in the bathroom for an adolescent boy. There was something medieval about it, something accursed—a ritual act of regurgitation. He found himself remembering a scene from the Bergman picture *The Seventh Seal*, where a crowd of ragged penitents proceeds through a town stricken with the black plague. The penitents were scourging themselves with birch branches, making themselves bleed. The hatefulness of baring himself this way (and perversely, he would not allow himself to lie, although he could have done so quite convincingly) made the day's purpose real in the final sense, and he could almost see the word "vampire" printed on the black screen of his mind, not in scare movie-poster print, but in small, economical letters that were made to be a woodcut or scratched on a scroll. He felt helpless in the grip of this alien ritual, out of joint with his time. The confessional might have been a direct pipeline to the days when werewolves and incubi and witches were an accepted part of the outer darkness and the church the only beacon of light. For the first time in his life he felt the slow, terrible beat and swell of the ages and saw his life as a dim and glimmering spark in an edifice which, if seen clearly, might drive all men mad. Matt had not told them of Father Callahan's conception of his church as a Force, but Ben would have understood that now. He could feel the Force in this fetid little box, beating in on him, leaving him naked and contemptible. He felt it as no Catholic, raised to confession since earliest childhood, could have.

When he stepped out, the fresh air from the open doors struck him thankfully. He wiped at his neck with the palm of his hand and it came away sweaty.

Callahan stepped out. "You're not done yet," he said.

Wordlessly, Ben stepped back inside, but did not kneel. Callahan gave him an act of contrition—ten Our Fathers and ten Hail Marys.

"I don't know that one," Ben said.

"I'll give you a card with the prayer written on it," the voice on the other side of the screen said. "You can say them to yourself while we ride over to Cumberland."

Ben hesitated a moment. "Matt was right, you know. When he said it was going to be harder than we thought. We're going to sweat blood before this is over."

"Yes?" Callahan said—polite or just dubious? Ben couldn't tell. He looked down and saw he was still holding the Junior Mints box. He had crushed it to a shapeless pulp with the convulsive squeezing of his right hand.

10

It was nearing one o'clock when they all got in Jimmy Cody's large Buick and set off. None of them spoke. Father Donald Callahan was wearing his full gown, a surplice, and a white stole bordered with purple. He had given them each a small tube of water from the Holy Font, and had blessed them each with the sign of the cross. He held a small silver pyx on his lap which contained several pieces of the Host.

They stopped at Jimmy's Cumberland office first, and Jimmy left the motor idling while he went inside. When he came out, he was wearing a baggy sport coat that concealed the bulge of McCaslin's revolver and carrying an ordinary Craftsman hammer in his right hand.

Ben looked at it with some fascination and saw from the tail of his eye that Mark and Callahan were also staring. The hammer had a blue steel head and a perforated rubber handgrip.

"Ugly, isn't it?" Jimmy remarked.

Ben thought of using that hammer on Susan, using it to ram a stake between her breasts, and felt his stomach flip over slowly, like an airplane doing a slow roll.

"Yes," he said, and moistened his lips. "It's ugly, all right."

They drove to the Cumberland Stop and Shop. Ben and Jimmy went into the supermarket and picked up all the garlic that was displayed along the vegetable counter—twelve boxes of the whitish-gray bulbs. The check-out girl raised her eyebrows and said, "Glad I ain't going on a long ride with you boys t'night."

Going out, Ben said idly, "I wonder what the basis of garlic's effectiveness against them is? Something in the Bible, or an ancient curse, or—"

"I suspect it's an allergy," Jimmy said.

"Allergy?"

Callahan caught the last of it and asked for a repetition as they drove toward the Northern Belle Flower Shop.

"Oh yes, I agree with Dr. Cody," he said. "Probably is an allergy . . . if it works as a deterrent at all. Remember, that's not proved yet."

"That's a funny idea for a priest," Mark said.

"Why? If I must accept the existence of vampires (and it seems I must, at least for the time being), must I also accept them as creatures beyond the bounds of all natural laws? Some, certainly. Folklore says they can't be seen in mirrors, that they can transform themselves into bats or wolves or birds—the so-called psychopompos—that they can narrow their bodies and slip through the tiniest cracks. Yet we know they see, and hear, and speak . . . and they most certainly taste. Perhaps they also know discomfort, pain—"

"And love?" Ben asked, looking straight ahead.

"No," Jimmy answered. "I suspect that love is beyond them." He pulled into a small parking lot beside an L-shaped flower shop with an attached greenhouse.

A small bell tinkled over the door when they went in, and the heavy aroma of flowers struck them. Ben felt sickened by the cloying heaviness of their mixed perfumes, and was reminded of funeral parlors.

"Hi there." A tall man in a canvas apron came toward them, holding an earthen flowerpot in one hand.

Ben had only started to explain what they wanted when the man in the apron shook his head and interrupted.

"You're late, I'm afraid. A man came in last Friday and bought every rose I had in stock—red, white, and yellow. I'll have no more until Wednesday at least. If you'd care to order—"

"What did this man look like?"

"Very striking," the proprietor said, putting his pot down. "Tall, totally bald. Piercing eyes. Smoked foreign cigarettes, by the smell. He had to take the flowers out in three armloads. He put them in the back of a very old car, a Dodge, I think—"

"Packard," Ben said. "A black Packard."

"You know him, then."

"In a manner of speaking."

"He paid cash. Very unusual, considering the size of the order. But perhaps if you get in touch with him, he would sell you—"

"Perhaps," Ben said.

In the car again, they talked it over.

"There's a shop in Falmouth—" Father Callahan began doubtfully.

"No!" Ben said. "No!" And the raw edge of hysteria in his voice made them all look around. "And when we got to Falmouth and found that Straker had been there, too? What then? Portland? Kittery? *Boston?* Don't you realize what's happening? He's foreseen us! *He's leading us by the nose!*"

"Ben, be reasonable," Jimmy said. "Don't you think we ought to at least—"

"Don't you remember what Matt said? 'You mustn't go into this feeling that because he can't rise in the daytime he can't harm you.' Look at your watch, Jimmy."

Jimmy did. "Two-fifteen," he said slowly, and looked up at the sky as if doubting the truth on the dial. But it was true; now the shadows were going the other way.

"He's anticipated us," Ben said. "He's been four jumps ahead every mile of the way. Did we—could we—actually think that *he* would be blissfully unaware of us? That *he* never took the possibility of discovery and opposition into account? We have to go *now,* before we waste the rest of the day arguing about how many angels can dance on the head of a pin."

"He's right," Callahan said quietly. "I think we had better stop talking and get going."

"Then *drive,*" Mark said urgently.

Jimmy pulled out of the flower-shop parking lot fast, screeching the tires on the pavement. The proprietor stared after them, three men, one of them a priest, and a little boy who sat in a car with M.D. plates and shouted at each other of total lunacies.

11

Cody came at the Marsten House from the Brooks Road, on the village's blind side, and Donald Callahan, looking at it from this new angle, thought: Why, it actually *looms* over the town. Strange I never saw it before. It must have perfect elevation there, perched on its hill high above the crossroads of Jointner Avenue and Brock Street. Perfect elevation and a very nearly 360° view of the township itself. It was a huge and rambling place, and with the shutters closed it took on an uncomfortable, overlarge configuration in the mind; it became a sarcophaguslike monolith, an evocation of doom.

And it was the site of both suicide and murder, which meant it stood on unhallowed ground.

He opened his mouth to say so, and then thought better of it.

Cody turned off onto the Brooks Road, and for a moment the house was blotted out by trees. Then they thinned, and Cody was turning into the driveway. The Packard was parked just outside the garage, and when Jimmy turned off the car, he drew McCaslin's revolver.

Callahan felt the atmosphere of the place seize him at once. He took a crucifix—his mother's—from his pocket and slipped it around his neck with his own. No bird sang in these fall-denuded trees. The long and ragged grass seemed even drier and more dehydrated than the end of the season warranted; the ground itself seemed gray and used up.

The steps leading up to the porch were warped crazily, and there was a brighter square of paint on one of the porch posts where a no-trespassing sign had recently been taken down. A new Yale lock glittered brassily below the old rusted bolt on the front door.

"A window, maybe, like Mark—" Jimmy began hesitantly.

"No," Ben said. "Right through the front door. We'll break it down if we have to."

"I don't think that will be necessary," Callahan said, and his voice did not seem to be his own. When they got out, he led them without stopping to think about it. An eagerness—the old eagerness he was sure had gone forever—seemed to seize him as he approached the door. The house seemed to lean around them, to almost ooze its evil from the cracked pores of its paint. Yet he did not hesitate. Any thought of temporizing was gone. In the last moments he did not lead them so much as he was impelled.

"In the name of God the Father!" he cried, and his voice took on a hoarse, commanding note that made them all draw closer to him. "I command the evil to be gone from this house! Spirits, depart!" And without being aware he was going to do it, he smote the door with the crucifix in his hand.

There was a flash of light—afterward they all agreed there had been—a pungent whiff of ozone, and a crackling sound, as if the boards themselves had screamed. The curved fanlight above the door suddenly exploded outward, and the large bay window to the left that overlooked the lawn coughed its glass onto the grass at the same instant. Jimmy cried out. The new Yale lock lay on the boards at their feet, welded into an almost unrecognizable mass. Mark bent to poke it and then yelped.

"Hot," he said.

Callahan withdrew from the door, trembling. He looked down at the cross in his hand. "This is, without a doubt, the most amazing thing that's ever happened to me in my life," he said. He glanced up at the sky, as if to see the very face of God, but the sky was indifferent.

Ben pushed at the door and it swung open easily. But he waited for Callahan to go in first. In the hall Callahan looked at Mark.

"The cellar," he said. "You get to it through the kitchen. Straker's upstairs. But—" He paused, frowning. "Something's different. I don't know what. Something's not the same as it was."

They went upstairs first, and even though Ben was not in the lead, he felt a prickle of very old terror as they approached the door at the end of the hall. Here, almost a month to the day after he had come back to 'salem's Lot, he was to get his second look into that room. When Callahan pushed the door open, he glanced upward . . . and felt the scream well up in his throat and out of his mouth before he could stop it. It was high, womanish, hysterical.

But it was not Hubert Marsten hanging from the overhead beam, or his spirit.

It was Straker, and he had been hung upside down like a pig in a slaughtering pen, his throat ripped wide open. His glazed eyes stared at them, through them, past them.

He had been bled white.

12

"Dear God," Father Callahan said. "Dear God."

They advanced slowly into the room, Callahan and Cody a bit in the lead, Ben and Mark behind, pressed together.

Straker's feet had been bound together; then he had been hauled up and tied there. It occurred to Ben in a distant part of his brain that it must have taken a man with enormous strength to haul Straker's dead weight up to a point where his dangling hands did not quite touch the floor.

Jimmy touched the forehead with his inner wrist, then held one of the dead hands in his own. "He's been dead for maybe eighteen hours," he said. He dropped the hand with a shudder. "My God, what an awful way to ... I can't figure this out. Why—who—"

"Barlow did it," Mark said. He looked at Straker's corpse with unflinching eyes.

"And Straker screwed up," Jimmy said. "No eternal life for him. But why like this? Hung upside down?"

"It's as old as Macedonia," Father Callahan said. "Hanging the body of your enemy or betrayer upside down so his head faces earth instead of heaven. St. Paul was crucified that way, on an X-shaped cross with his legs broken."

Ben spoke, and his voice sounded old and dusty in his throat. "He's still diverting us. He has a hundred tricks. Let's go."

They followed him back down the hall, back down the stairs, into the kitchen. Once there, he deferred to Father Callahan again. For a moment they just looked at each other, and then at the cellar door that led downward, just as twenty-five-odd years ago he had taken a set of stairs upward, to face an overwhelming question.

13

When the priest opened the door, Mark felt the rank, rotten odor assail his nostrils again—but that was also different. Not so strong. Less malevolent.

The priest started down the stairs. Still, it took all his will power to continue down after Father Callahan into that pit of the dead.

Jimmy had produced a flashlight from his bag and clicked it on. The beam illuminated the floor, crossed to one wall, and swung back. It paused for a moment on a long crate, and then the beam fell on a table.

"There," he said. "Look."

It was an envelope, clean and shining in all this dingy darkness, a rich yellow vellum.

"It's a trick," Father Callahan said. "Better not touch it."

"No," Mark spoke up. He felt both relief and disappointment. "He's not here. He's gone. That's for us. Full of mean things, probably."

Ben stepped forward and picked the envelope up. He turned it over in his hands twice—Mark could see in the glow of Jimmy's flashlight that his fingers were trembling—and then he tore it open.

There was one sheet inside, rich vellum like the envelope, and they crowded around. Jimmy focused his flashlight on the page, which was closely written in an elegant, spider-thin hand. They read it together, Mark a little more slowly than the others.

October 4.

My Dear Young Friends,

How lovely of you to have stopped by!

I am never averse to company; it has been one of my great joys in a long and often lonely life. Had you come in the evening, I should have welcomed you in person with the greatest of pleasure. However, since I suspected you might choose to arrive during daylight hours, I thought it best to be out.

I have left you a small token of my appreciation; someone very near and dear to one of you is now in the place where I occupied my days until I decided that other quarters might be more congenial. She is very lovely, Mr. Mears—very *toothsome,* if I may be permitted a small *bon mot.* I have no further need of her and so I have left her for you to—how is your idiom?—to warm up for the main event. To whet your appetites, if you like. Let us see how well you like the appetizer to the main course you contemplate, shall we?

Master Petrie, you have robbed me of the most faithful and resourceful servant I have ever known. You have caused me, in an indirect fashion, to take part in his ruination; have caused my own appetites to betray me. You sneaked up behind him, doubtless. I am going to enjoy dealing with you. Your parents first, I think. Tonight . . . or tomorrow night . . . or the next. And then you. But you shall enter my church as choirboy *castratum.*

And Father Callahan—have they persuaded you to come? I thought so. I have observed you at some length since I arrived in Jerusalem's Lot . . . much as a good chess player will study the games of his opposition, am I correct? The Catholic Church is not the oldest of my opponents, though! I was old when it was young, when its members hid in the catacombs of Rome and painted fishes on their chests so they could tell one from another. I was strong when this simpering club of bread-eaters and wine-drinkers who venerate the sheep-savior was weak. My rites were old when the rites of your church were unconceived. Yet I do not underestimate. I am wise in the ways of goodness as well as those of evil. I am not jaded.

And I will best you. *How?* you say. Does not Callahan bear the symbol of White? Does not Callahan move in the day as well as the night? Are there not charms and potions, both Christian and pagan, which my so-good friend Matthew Burke has informed me and my compatriots of? Yes, yes, and yes. But I have lived longer than you. I am crafty. I am not the serpent, but the father of serpents.

Still, you say, this is not enough. And it is not. In the end, "Father" Callahan, you will undo yourself. Your faith in the White is weak and soft. Your talk of love is presumption. Only when you speak of the bottle are you informed.

My good, good friends—Mr. Mears; Mr. Cody; Master Petrie; Father Callahan—enjoy your stay. The Médoc is excellent, procured for me especially by the late owner of this house, whose personal company I was never able to enjoy. Please be my guests if you still have a taste for wine after you have finished the work at hand. We will meet again, in person, and I shall convey my felicitations to each of you at that time in a more personal way.

Until then, adieu.

BARLOW.

Trembling, Ben let the letter fall to the table. He looked at the others. Mark stood with his hands clenched into fists, his mouth frozen in the twist of someone who has bitten something rotten; Jimmy, his oddly boyish face drawn and pale; Father Donald Callahan, his eyes alight, his mouth drawn down in a trembling bow.

And one by one, they looked up at him.

"Come on," he said.

They went around the corner together.

14

Parkins Gillespie was standing on the front step of the brick Municipal Building, looking through his high-powered Zeiss binoculars when Nolly Gardener drove up in the town's police car and got out, hitching up his belt and picking out his seat at the same time.

"What's up, Park?" he asked, walking up the steps.

Parkins gave him the glasses wordlessly and flicked one callused thumb at the Marsten House.

Nolly looked. He saw that old Packard, and parked in front of it, a new tan Buick. The gain on the binoculars wasn't quite high enough to pick off the plate number. He lowered his glasses. "That's Doc Cody's car, ain't it?"

"Yes, I believe it is." Parkins inserted a Pall Mall between his lips and scratched a kitchen match on the brick wall behind him.

"I never seen a car up there except that Packard."

"Yes, that's so," Parkins said meditatively.

"Think we ought to go up there and have a look?" Nolly spoke with a marked lack of his usual enthusiasm. He had been a lawman for five years and was still entranced with his own position.

"No," Parkins said, "I believe we'll just leave her alone." He took his watch out of his vest and clicked up the scrolled silver cover like a trainman checking an express. Just 3:41. He checked his watch against the clock on the town hall and then tucked it back into place.

"How'd all that come out with Floyd Tibbits and the little McDougall baby?" Nolly asked.

"Dunno."

"Oh," Nolly said, momentarily nonplussed. Parkins was always taciturn, but this was a new high for him. He looked through the glasses again: no change.

"Town seems quiet today," Nolly volunteered.

"Yes," Parkins said. He looked across Jointner Avenue and the park with his faded blue eyes. Both the avenue and the park were deserted. They had been deserted most of the day. There was a remarkable lack of mothers strolling babies or idlers around the War Memorial.

"Funny things been happening," Nolly ventured.

"Yes," Parkins said, considering.

As a last gasp, Nolly fell back on the one bit of conversational bait that Parkins had never failed to rise to: the weather. "Clouding up," he said. "Be rain by tonight."

Parkins studied the sky. There were mackerel scales directly overhead and a building bar of clouds to the southwest. "Yes," he said, and threw the stub of his cigarette away.

"Park, you feelin' all right?"

Parkins Gillespie considered it.

"Nope," he said.

"Well, what in hell's the matter?"

"I believe," Gillespie said, "that I'm scared shitless."

"What?" Nolly floundered. "Of what?"

"Dunno," Parkins said, and took his binoculars back. He began to scan the Marsten House again while Nolly stood speechless beside him.

15

Beyond the table where the letter had been propped, the cellar made an L-turn, and they were now in what once had been a wine cellar. Hubert Marsten must have been a bootlegger indeed, Ben thought. There were small and medium casks covered with dust and cobwebs. One wall was covered with a crisscrossed wine rack, and ancient magnums still peered forth from some of the diamond-shaped pigeonholes. Some of them had exploded, and where sparkling burgundy had once waited for some discerning palate, the spider now made his home. Others had undoubtedly turned to vinegar; that sharp odor drifted in the air, mingled with that of slow corruption.

"No," Ben said, speaking quietly, as a man speaks a fact. "I can't."

"You must," Father Callahan said. "I'm not telling you it will be easy, or for the best. Only that you must."

"I *can't!*" Ben cried, and this time the words echoed in the cellar.

In the center, on a raised dais and spotlighted by Jimmy's flashlight, Susan Norton lay still. She was covered from shoulders to feet in a drift of simple white linen, and when they reached her, none of them had been able to speak. Wonder had swallowed words.

In life she had been a cheerfully pretty girl who had missed the turn to beauty somewhere (perhaps by inches), not through any lack in her features but—just possibly—because her life had been so calm and unremarkable. But now she had achieved beauty. Dark beauty.

Death had not put its mark on her. Her face was blushed with color, and her lips, innocent of make-up, were a deep and glowing red. Her forehead was pale but flawless, the skin like cream. Her eyes were closed, and the dark lashes lay sootily against her cheeks. One hand was curled at her side, and the other was thrown lightly across her waist. Yet the total impression was not of angelic loveliness but a cold, disconnected beauty. Something in her face—not stated but hinted at—made Jimmy think of the young Saigon girls, some not yet thirteen, who would kneel before soldiers in the alleys behind the bars, not for the first time or the hundredth. Yet with those girls, the corruption hadn't been evil but only a knowledge of the world that had come too soon. The change in Susan's face was quite different—but he could not have said just how.

Now Callahan stepped forward and pressed his fingers against the springiness of her left breast. "Here," he said. "The heart."

"No," Ben repeated. "I can't."

"Be her lover," Father Callahan said softly. "Better, be her husband. You won't hurt her, Ben. You'll free her. The only one hurt will be you."

Ben looked at him dumbly. Mark had taken the stake from Jimmy's black bag and held it out wordlessly. Ben took it in a hand that seemed to stretch out for miles.

If I don't think about it when I do it, then maybe—

But it would be impossible not to think about it. And suddenly a line came to him from *Dracula*, that amusing bit of fiction that no longer amused him in the slightest. It was Van Helsing's speech to Arthur Holmwood when Arthur had been faced with this same dreadful task: *We must go through bitter waters before we reach the sweet.*

Could there be sweetness for any of them, ever again?

"Take it away!" he groaned. "Don't make me do this—"

No answer.

He felt a cold, sick sweat spring out on his brow, his cheeks, his forearms. The stake that had been a simple baseball bat four hours before seemed infused with eerie heaviness, as if invisible yet titanic lines of force had converged on it.

He lifted the stake and pressed it against her left breast, just above the last fastened button of her blouse. The point made a dimple in her flesh, and he felt the side of his mouth begin to twitch in an uncontrollable tic.

"She's not dead," he said. His voice was hoarse and thick. It was his last line of defense.

"No," Jimmy said implacably. "She's Undead, Ben." He had shown them; had wrapped the blood-pressure cuff around her still arm and pumped it. The reading had been 00/00. He had put his stethoscope on her chest, and each of them had listened to the silence inside her.

Something was put into Ben's other hand—years later he still did not remember which of them had put it there. The hammer. The Craftsman hammer with the rubber perforated grip. The head glimmered in the flashlight's glow.

"Do it quickly," Callahan said, "and go out into the daylight. We'll do the rest."

We must go through bitter waters before we reach the sweet.

"God forgive me," Ben whispered.

He raised the hammer and brought it down.

The hammer struck the top of the stake squarely, and the gelatinous tremor that vibrated up the length of ash would haunt him forever in his dreams. Her eyes flew open, wide and blue, as if from the very force of the blow. Blood gushed upward from the stake's point of entry in a bright and astonishing flood, splashing his hands, his shirt, his cheeks. In an instant the cellar was filled with its hot, coppery odor.

She writhed on the table. Her hands came up and beat madly at the air like birds. Her feet thumped an aimless, rattling tattoo on the wood of the platform. Her mouth yawned open, revealing shocking, wolflike fangs, and she began to peal forth shriek after shriek, like hell's clarion. Blood gushed from the corners of her mouth in freshets.

The hammer rose and fell: again . . . again . . . again.

Ben's brain was filled with the shrieks of large black crows. It whirled with awful, unremembered images. His hands were scarlet, the stake was scarlet, the remorselessly rising and falling hammer was scarlet. In Jimmy's trembling hands the flashlight became stroboscopic, illuminating Susan's crazed, lashing face in spurts and flashes. Her teeth sheared through the flesh of her lips, tearing them to ribbons. Blood splattered across the fresh linen sheet which Jimmy had so neatly turned back, making patterns like Chinese idiograms.

And then, suddenly, her back arched like a bow, and her mouth stretched open until it seemed her jaws must break. A huge explosion of darker blood issued forth from the wound the stake had made—almost black in this chancy, lunatic light: heart's blood. The scream that welled from the sounding chamber of that gaping mouth came from all the subcellars of deepest race memory and beyond that, to the moist darknesses of the human soul. Blood suddenly boiled from her mouth and nose in a tide . . . and something else. In the faint light it was only a suggestion, a shadow, of something leaping up and out, cheated and ruined. It merged with the darkness and was gone.

She settled back, her mouth relaxing, closing. The mangled lips parted in a last, susurating pulse of air. For a moment the eyelids fluttered and Ben saw, or fancied he saw, the Susan he had met in the park, reading his book.

It was done.

He backed away, dropping the hammer, holding his hands out before him, a terrified conductor whose symphony has run riot.

Callahan put a hand on his shoulder. "Ben—"

He fled.

He stumbled going up the stairs, fell, and crawled toward the light at the top. Childhood horror and adult horror had merged. If he looked over his shoulder, he would see Hubie Marsten (or perhaps Straker) only a hand's breadth behind, grinning out of his puffed and greenish face, the rope embedded deep into his neck—the grin revealing fangs instead of teeth. He screamed once, miserably.

Dimly, he heard Callahan cry out, "No, let him go—"

He burst through the kitchen and out the back door. The back porch steps were gone under his feet and he pitched headlong into the dirt. He got to his knees, crawled, got to his feet, and cast a glance behind him.

Nothing.

The house loomed without purpose, the last of its evil stolen away. It was just a house again.

Ben Mears stood in the great silence of the weed-choked back yard, his head thrown back, breathing in great white snuffles of air.

16

In the fall, night comes like this in the Lot:

The sun loses its thin grip on the air first, turning it cold, making it remember that winter is coming and winter will be long. Thin clouds form, and the shadows lengthen out. They have no breadth, as summer shadows have; there are no leaves on the trees or fat clouds in the sky to make them thick. They are gaunt, mean shadows that bite the ground like teeth.

As the sun nears the horizon, its benevolent yellow begins to deepen, to become infected, until it glares an angry inflamed orange. It throws a variegated glow over the horizon—a cloud-congested caul that is alternately red, orange, vermilion, purple. Sometimes the clouds break apart in great, slow rafts, letting through beams of innocent yellow sunlight that are bitterly nostalgic for the summer that has gone by.

This is six o'clock, the supper hour (in the Lot, dinner is eaten at noon and the lunch buckets that men grab from counters before going out the door are known as dinner pails). Mabel Werts, the unhealthy fat of old age hanging doughily on her bones, is sitting down to a broiled breast of chicken and a cup of Lipton tea, the phone by her elbow. In Eva's the men are getting together whatever they have to get together: TV dinners, canned corned beef, canned beans which are woefully unlike the beans their mothers used to bake all Saturday morning and afternoon years ago, spaghetti dinners, or reheated hamburgers picked up at the Falmouth McDonald's on the way home from work. Eva sits at the table in the front room, irritably playing gin rummy with Grover Verrill, and snapping at the others to wipe up their grease and to stop that damn slopping around. They cannot remember ever having seen her this way, cat-nervous and feisty. But they know what the matter is, even if she does not.

Mr. and Mrs. Petrie eat sandwiches in their kitchen, trying to puzzle out the call they have just received, a call from the local Catholic priest, Father Callahan: *Your son is with me. He's fine. I will have him home shortly. Good-by.* They have debated calling the local lawman, Parkins Gillespie, and have decided to wait a bit longer. They have sensed some sort of change in their son, who has always been what his mother likes to call A Deep One. Yet the specters of Ralphie and Danny Glick hang over them, unacknowledged.

Milt Crossen is having bread and milk in the back of his store. He has had damned little appetite since his wife died back in '68. Delbert Markey, proprietor of Dell's, is working his way methodically through the five hamburgers which he has fried himself on the grill. He eats them with mustard and heaps of raw onions, and will complain most of the night to anyone who will listen that his goddamn acid indigestion is killing him. Father Callahan's housekeeper, Rhoda Curless, eats nothing. She is worried about the Father, who is out someplace ramming the roads. Harriet Durham and her family are eating pork chops. Carl Smith, a widower since 1957, has one boiled potato and a bottle of Moxie. The Derek Boddins are having an Armour Star ham and brussels sprouts. *Yechhh,* says Richie Boddin, the deposed bully. Brussels sprouts. You eat 'em or I'll clout your ass backward, Derek says. He hates them himself.

Reggie and Bonnie Sawyer are having a rib roast of beef, frozen corn, french-fried potatoes, and for dessert a chocolate bread pudding with hard sauce. These are all Reggie's favorites. Bonnie, her bruises just beginning to fade, serves silently with downcast eyes. Reggie eats with steady, serious attention, killing three cans of Bud with the meal. Bonnie eats standing up. She is still too sore to sit down. She hasn't much appetite, but she eats anyway, so Reggie won't notice and say something. After he beat her up on that night, he flushed all her pills down the toilet and raped her. And has raped her every night since then.

By quarter of seven, most meals have been eaten, most after-dinner cigarettes and cigars and pipes smoked, most tables cleared. Dishes are being washed, rinsed, and stacked in drainers. Young children are being packed into Dr. Dentons and sent into the other room to watch game shows on TV until bedtime.

Roy McDougall, who has burned the shit out of a fry pan full of veal steaks, curses and throws them—fry pan and all—into the swill. He puts on his denim jacket and sets out for Dell's, leaving his goddamn good-for-nothing pig of a wife to sleep in the bedroom. Kid's dead, wife's slacking off, supper's burned to hell. Time to get drunk. And maybe time to haul stakes and roll out of this two-bit town.

In a small upstairs flat on Taggart Street, which runs a short distance from Jointner Avenue to a dead end behind the Municipal Building, Joe Crane is given a left-handed gift from the gods. He has finished a small bowl of Shredded Wheat and is sitting down to watch the TV when he feels a large and sudden pain paralyze the left side of his chest and his left arm. He thinks: *What's this? Ticker?* As it happens, this is exactly right. He gets up and makes it halfway to the telephone before the pain suddenly swells and drops him in his tracks like a steer hit with a hammer. His small color TV babbles on and on, and it will be twenty-four hours before anyone finds him. His death, which occurs at 6:51 P.M., is the only natural death to occur in Jerusalem's Lot on October 6.

By 7:00 the panoply of colors on the horizon has shrunk to a bitter orange line on the western horizon, as if furnace fires had been banked beyond the edge of the world. In the east the stars are already out. They gleam steadily, like fierce diamonds. There is no mercy in them at this time of year, no comfort for lovers. They gleam in beautiful indifference.

For the small children, bedtime is come. Time for the babies to be packed into their beds and cribs by parents who smile at their cries to be let up a little longer, to leave the light on. They indulgently open closet doors to show there is nothing in there.

And all around them, the bestiality of the night rises on tenebrous wings. The vampire's time has come.

17

Matt was dozing lightly when Jimmy and Ben came in, and he snapped awake almost immediately, his hand tightening on the cross he held in his right hand.

His eyes touched Jimmy's, moved to Ben's . . . and lingered.

"What happened?"

Jimmy told him briefly. Ben said nothing.

"Her body?"

"Callahan and I put it face down in a crate that was down cellar, maybe the same crate Barlow came to town in. We threw it into the Royal River not an hour ago. Filled the box with stones. We used Straker's car. If anyone noticed it by the bridge, they'll think of him."

"You did well. Where's Callahan? And the boy?"

"Gone to Mark's house. His parents have to be told everything. Barlow threatened them specifically."

"Will they believe?"

"If they don't, Mark will have his father call you."

Matt nodded. He looked very tired.

"And Ben," he said. "Come here. Sit on my bed."

Ben came obediently, his face blank and dazed. He sat down and folded his hands neatly in his lap. His eyes were burned cigarette holes.

"There's no comfort for you," Matt said. He took one of Ben's hands in his own. Ben let him, unprotesting. "It doesn't matter. Time will comfort you. She is at rest."

"He played us for fools," Ben said hollowly. "He mocked us, each in turn. Jimmy, give him the letter."

Jimmy gave Matt the envelope. He stripped the heavy sheet of stationery from the envelope and read it carefully, holding the paper only inches from his nose. His lips moved slightly. He put it down and said, "Yes. It is him. His ego is larger than even I imagined. It makes me want to shiver."

"He left her for a joke," Ben said hollowly. "*He* was gone, long before. Fighting him is like fighting the wind. We must seem like bugs to him. Little bugs scurrying around for his amusement."

Jimmy opened his mouth to speak, but Matt shook his head slightly.

"That is far from the truth," he said. "If he could have taken Susan with him, he would have. He wouldn't give up his Undead just for jokes when there are so few of them! Step back a minute, Ben, and consider what you've done to him. Killed his familiar, Straker. By his own admission, even forced him to participate in the murder by reason of his insatiable appetite! How it must have terrified him to wake from his dreamless sleep and find that a young boy, unarmed, had slain such a fearsome creature."

He sat up in bed with some difficulty. Ben had turned his head and was looking at him with the first interest he had shown since the others had come out of the house to find him in the back yard.

"Maybe that's not the greatest victory," Matt mused. "You've driven him from his house, his chosen home. Jimmy said that Father Callahan sterilized the cellar with holy water and has sealed all the doors with the Host. If he goes there again, he'll die . . . *and he knows it.*"

"But he got away," Ben said. "What does it matter?"

"He got away," Matt echoed softly. "And where did he sleep today? In the trunk of a car? In the cellar of one of his victims? Perhaps in the basement of the old Methodist Church in the Marshes which burned down in the fire of '51? Wherever it was, do you think he liked it, or felt safe there?"

Ben didn't answer.

"Tomorrow, you'll begin to hunt," Matt said, and his hands tightened over Ben's. "Not just for Barlow, but for all the little fish—and there will be a great many little fish after tonight. *Their* hunger is never satisfied. They'll eat until they're glutted. The nights are his, but in the daytime you will hound him and hound him until he takes fright and flees or until you drag him, staked and screaming, into the sunlight!"

Ben's head had come up at this speech. His face had taken on an animation that was close to ghastly. Now a small smile touched his mouth. "Yes, that's good," he whispered. "Only tonight instead of tomorrow. Right now—"

Matt's hand shot out and clutched Ben's shoulder with surprising, sinewy strength. "Not tonight. Tonight we're going to spend together—you and I and Jimmy and Father Callahan and Mark and Mark's parents. *He* knows now . . . he's afraid. Only a madman or a saint would dare to approach Barlow when he is awake in his mother-night. And none of us are either." He closed his eyes and said softly, "I'm beginning to know him, I think. I lie in this hospital bed and play Mycroft Holmes, trying to outguess him by putting myself in his place. He has lived for centuries, and he is brilliant. But he is also an egocentric, as his letter shows. Why not? His ego has grown the way a pearl does, layer by layer, until it is huge and poisonous. He's filled with pride. It must be vaunting indeed. And his thirst for revenge must be overmastering, a thing to be trembled at, but perhaps also a thing to be used."

He opened his eyes and looked solemnly at them both. He raised the cross before him. "This will stop *him*, but it may not stop someone he can use, the way he used Floyd Tibbits. I think he may try to eliminate some of us tonight . . . some of us or all of us."

He looked at Jimmy.

"I think bad judgment was used in sending Mark and Father Callahan to the house of Mark's parents. They could have been called from here and summoned, knowing nothing. Now we are split . . . and I am especially worried for the boy. Jimmy, you had better call them . . . call them now."

"All right." He got up.

Matt looked at Ben. "And you will stay with us? Fight with us?"

"Yes," Ben said hoarsely. "Yes."

Jimmy left the room, went down the hall to the nurse's station, and found the Petries' number in the book. He dialed it rapidly and listened with sick horror as the sirening sound of a line out of service came through the earpiece instead of a ringing tone.

"He's got them," he said.

The head nurse glanced up at the sound of his voice and was frightened by the look on his face.

18

Henry Petrie was an educated man. He had a B.S. from Northeastern, a master's from Massachusetts Tech, and a Ph.D. in economics. He had left a perfectly good junior college teaching position to take an administration post with the Prudential Insurance Company, as much out of curiosity as from any hope of monetary gain. He had wanted to see if certain of his economic ideas worked out as well in practice as they did in theory. They did. By the following summer, he hoped to be able to take the CPA test, and two years after that, the bar examination. His current goal was to begin the 1980s in a high federal government economics post. His son's fey streak had not come from Henry Petrie; his father's logic was complete and seamless, and his world was machined to a point of almost total precision. He was a registered Democrat who had voted for Nixon in the 1972 elections not because he believed Nixon was honest—he had told his wife many times that he considered Richard Nixon to be an unimaginative little crook with all the finesse of a shoplifter in Woolworth's—but because the opposition was a crack-brained sky pilot who would bring down economic ruin on the country. He had viewed the counterculture of the late sixties with calm tolerance born of the belief that it would collapse harmlessly because it had no monetary base upon which to stand. His love for his wife and son was not beautiful—no one would ever write a poem to the passion of a man who balled his socks before his wife—but it was sturdy and unswerving. He was a straight arrow, confident in himself and in the natural laws of physics, mathematics, economics, and (to a slightly lesser degree) sociology.

He listened to the story told by his son and the village abbé, sipping a cup of coffee and prompting them with lucid questions at points where the thread of narration became tangled or unclear. His calmness increased, it seemed, in direct ratio to the story's grotesqueries and to his wife June's growing agitation. When they had finished it was almost five minutes of seven. Henry Petrie spoke his verdict in four calm, considered syllables.

"Impossible."

Mark sighed and looked at Callahan and said, "I told you."
He *had* told him, as they drove over from the rectory in Callahan's
old car.

"Henry, don't you think we—"

"Wait."

That and his hand held up (almost casually) stilled her at
once. She sat down and put her arm around Mark, pulling him
slightly away from Callahan's side. The boy submitted.

Henry Petrie looked at Father Callahan pleasantly. "Let's
see if we can't work this delusion or whatever it is out like two
reasonable men."

"That may be impossible," Callahan said with equal pleasantness, "but we'll certainly try. We are here, Mr. Petrie, specifically because Barlow has threatened you and your wife."

"Did you actually pound a stake through that girl's body this
afternoon?"

"I did not. Mr. Mears did."

"Is the corpse still there?"

"They threw it in the river."

"If that much is true," Petrie said, "you have involved my
son in a crime. Are you aware of that?"

"I am. It was necessary. Mr. Petrie, if you'll simply call Matt
Burke's hospital room—"

"Oh, I'm sure your witnesses will back you up," Petrie said,
still smiling that faint, maddening smile. "That's one of the
fascinating things about this lunacy. May I see the letter this
Barlow left you?"

Callahan cursed mentally. "Dr. Cody has it." He added as an
afterthought: "We really ought to ride over to the Cumberland
Hospital. If you talk to—"

Petrie was shaking his head.

"Let's talk a little more first. I'm sure your witnesses are
reliable, as I've indicated. Dr. Cody is our family physician, and
we all like him very much. I've also been given to understand
that Matthew Burke is above reproach . . . as a teacher, at
least."

"But in spite of that?" Callahan asked.

"Father Callahan, let me put it to you. If a dozen reliable
witnesses told you that a giant ladybug had lumbered through

the town park at high noon singing 'Sweet Adeline' and waving a Confederate flag, would you believe it?"

"If I was sure the witnesses were reliable, and if I was sure they weren't joking, I would be far down the road to belief, yes."

Still with the faint smile, Petrie said, "That is where we differ."

"Your mind is closed," Callahan said.

"No—simply made up."

"It amounts to the same thing. Tell me, in the company you work for do they approve of executives making decisions on the basis of internal beliefs rather than external facts? That's not logic, Petrie; that's cant."

Petrie stopped smiling and stood up. "Your story is disturbing, I'll grant you that. You've involved my son in something deranged, possibly dangerous. You'll all be lucky if you don't stand in court for it. I'm going to call your people and talk to them. Then I think we had all better go to Mr. Burke's hospital room and discuss the matter further."

"How good of you to bend a principle," Callahan said dryly.

Petrie went into the living room and picked up the telephone. There was no answering open hum; the line was bare and silent. Frowning slightly, he jiggled the cut-off buttons. No response. He set the phone in its cradle and went back to the kitchen.

"The phone seems to be out of order," he said.

He saw the instant look of fearful understanding that passed between Callahan and his son, and was irritated by it.

"I can assure you," he said a little more sharply than he had intended, "that the Jerusalem's Lot telephone service needs no vampires to disrupt it."

The lights went out.

19

Jimmy ran back to Matt's room.

"The line's out at the Petrie house. I think he's there. Goddamn, we were so *stupid*—"

Ben got off the bed. Matt's face seemed to squeeze and crumple. "You see how he works?" he muttered. "How smoothly?

If only we had another hour of daylight, we could . . . but we don't. It's done."

"We have to go out there," Jimmy said.

"No! You must not! For fear of your lives and mine, you must not."

"But they—"

"They are on their own! What is happening—or has happened—will be done by the time you get out there!"

They stood near the door, indecisive.

Matt struggled, gathered his strength, and spoke to them quietly but with force.

"His ego is great, and his pride is great. These might be flaws we can put to our use. But his mind is also great, and we must respect it and allow for it. You showed me his letter—he speaks of chess. I've no doubt he's a superb player. Don't you realize that he could have done his work at that house without cutting the telephone line? He did it because he wants you to know one of white's pieces is in check! He understands forces, and he understands that it becomes easier to conquer if the forces are split and in confusion. You gave him the first move by default because you forgot that—the original group was split in two. If you go haring off to the Petries' house, the group is split in three. I'm alone and bedridden; easy game in spite of crosses and books and incantations. All he needs to do is send one of his almost-Undead here to kill me with a gun or a knife. And that leaves only you and Ben, rushing pell-mell through the night to your own doom. Then 'salem's Lot is his. Don't you see it?"

Ben spoke first. "Yes," he said.

Matt slumped back. "I'm not speaking out of fear for my life, Ben. You have to believe that. Not even for fear of your lives. I'm afraid for the town. No matter what else happens, someone must be left to stop him tomorrow."

"Yes. And he's not going to have me until I've had revenge for Susan."

A silence fell among them.

Jimmy Cody broke it. "They may get away anyway," he said meditatively. "I think he's underestimated Callahan, and I know damned well he's underestimated the boy. That kid is one cool customer."

"We'll hope," Matt said, and closed his eyes.

They settled down to wait.

20

Father Donald Callahan stood on one side of the spacious Petrie kitchen, holding his mother's cross high above his head, and it spilled its ghostly effulgence across the room. Barlow stood on the other side, near the sink, one hand pinning Mark's hands behind his back, the other slung around his neck. Between them, Henry and June Petrie lay sprawled on the floor in the shattered glass of Barlow's entry.

Callahan was dazed. It had all happened with such swiftness that he could not take it in. At one moment he had been discussing the matter rationally (if maddeningly) with Petrie, under the brisk, no-nonsense glow of the kitchen lights. At the next, he had been plunged into the insanity that Mark's father had denied with such calm and understanding firmness.

His mind tried to reconstruct what had happened.

Petrie had come back and told them the phone was out. Moments later they had lost the lights. June Petrie screamed. A chair fell over. For several moments all of them had stumbled around in the new dark, calling out to each other. Then the window over the sink had crashed inward, spraying glass across the kitchen counter and onto the linoleum floor. All this had happened in a space of thirty seconds.

Then a shadow had moved in the kitchen, and Callahan had broken the spell that held him. He clutched at the cross that hung around his neck, and even as his flesh touched it, the room was lit with its unearthly light.

He saw Mark, trying to drag his mother toward the arch which led into the living room. Henry Petrie stood beside them, his head turned, his calm face suddenly slack-jawed with amazement at this totally illogical invasion. And behind him, looming over them, a white, grinning face like something out of a Frazetta painting, which split to reveal long, sharp fangs—and red, lurid eyes like furnace doors to hell. Barlow's hands flew out (Callahan had just time to see how long and sensitive those livid fingers were, like a concert pianist's) and then he had seized Henry Petrie's head in one hand, June's in the other, and had brought them together with a grinding, sickening crack. They had both dropped down like stones, and Barlow's first threat had been carried out.

Mark had uttered a high, keening scream and threw himself at Barlow without thought.

"And here you are!" Barlow had boomed good-naturedly in his rich, powerful voice. Mark attacked without thought and was captured instantly.

Callahan moved forward, holding his cross up.

Barlow's grin of triumph was instantly transformed into a rictus of agony. He fell back toward the sink, dragging the boy in front of him. Their feet crunched in the broken glass.

"In God's name—" Callahan began.

At the name of the Deity, Barlow screamed aloud as if he had been struck by a whip, his mouth open in a downward grimace, the needle fangs glimmering within. The cords of muscle on his neck stood out in stark, etched relief. "No closer!" he said. "No closer, shaman! Or I sever the boy's jugular and carotid before you can draw a breath!" As he spoke, his upper lip lifted from those long, needlelike teeth, and as he finished, his head made a predatory downward pass with adder's speed, missing Mark's flesh by a quarter-inch.

Callahan stopped.

"Back up," Barlow commanded, now grinning again. "You on your side of the board and I on mine, eh?"

Callahan backed up slowly, still holding the cross before him at eye level, so that he looked over its arms. The cross seemed to thrum with chained fire, and its power coursed up his forearm until the muscles bunched and trembled.

They faced each other.

"Together at last!" Barlow said, smiling. His face was strong and intelligent and handsome in a sharp, forbidding sort of way—yet, as the light shifted, it seemed almost effeminate. Where had he seen a face like that before? And it came to him, in this moment of the most extreme terror he had ever known. It was the face of Mr. Flip, his own personal bogeyman, the thing that hid in the closet during the days and came out after his mother closed the bedroom door. He was not allowed a night light—both his mother and his father had agreed that the way to conquer these childish fears was to face them, not toady to them—and every night, when the door snicked shut and his mother's footsteps padded off down the hall, the closet door slid open a crack and he could sense (or actually *see?*) the thin white face and burning eyes of Mr. Flip. And here he was again, out of the closet, staring over Mark's shoulder with his clown-white face and glowing eyes and red, sensual lips.

"What now?" Callahan said, and his voice was not his own at all. He was looking at Barlow's fingers, those long, sensitive fingers, which lay against the boy's throat. There were small blue blotches on them.

"That depends. What will you give for this miserable wretch?" He suddenly jerked Mark's wrists high behind his back, obviously hoping to punctuate his question with a scream, but Mark would not oblige. Except for the sudden whistle of air between his set teeth, he was silent.

"You'll scream," Barlow whispered, and his lips had twisted into a grimace of animal hate. "You'll scream until your throat *bursts!*"

"Stop that!" Callahan cried.

"And should I?" The hate was wiped from his face. A darkly charming smile shone forth in its place. "Should I reprieve the boy, save him for another night?"

"Yes!"

Softly, almost purring, Barlow said, "Then will you throw away your cross and face me on even terms—black against white? Your faith against my own?"

"Yes," Callahan said, but a trifle less firmly.

"Then do it!" Those full lips became pursed, anticipatory. The high forehead gleamed in the weird fairy light that filled the room.

"And trust you to let him go? I would be wiser to put a rattlesnake in my shirt and trust it not to bite me."

"But I trust you . . . look!"

He let Mark go and stood back, both hands in the air, empty.

Mark stood still, unbelieving for a moment, and then ran to his parents without a backward look at Barlow.

"Run, Mark!" Callahan cried. "Run!"

Mark looked up at him, his eyes huge and dark. "I think they're dead—"

"RUN!"

Mark got slowly to his feet. He turned around and looked at Barlow.

"Soon, little brother," Barlow said, almost benignly. "Very soon now you and I will—"

Mark spit in his face.

Barlow's breath stopped. His brow darkened with a depth of fury that made his previous expressions seem like what they might well have been: mere play-acting. For a moment Callahan saw a madness in his eyes blacker than the soul of murder.

"You spit on me," Barlow whispered. His body was trembling, nearly rocking with his rage. He took a shuddering step forward like some awful blind man.

"Get back!" Callahan screamed, and thrust the cross forward.

Barlow cried out and threw his hands in front of his face. The cross flared with preternatural, dazzling brilliance, and it was at that moment that Callahan might have banished him if he had dared to press forward.

"I'm going to kill you," Mark said.

He was gone, like a dark eddy of water.

Barlow seemed to grow taller. His hair, swept back from his brow in the European manner, seemed to float around his skull. He was wearing a dark suit and a wine-colored tie, impeccably knotted, and to Callahan he seemed part and parcel of the darkness that surrounded him. His eyes glared out of their sockets like sly and sullen embers.

"Then fulfill your part of the bargain, shaman."

"I'm a *priest!*" Callahan flung at him.

Barlow made a small, mocking bow. *"Priest,"* he said, and the word sounded like a dead haddock in his mouth.

Callahan stood indecisive. Why throw it down? Drive him off, settle for a draw tonight, and tomorrow—

But a deeper part of his mind warned. To deny the vampire's challenge was to risk possibilities far graver than any he had considered. If he dared not throw the cross aside, it would be as much as admitting . . . admitting . . . what? If only things weren't going so fast, if one only had time to think, to reason it out—

The cross's glow was dying.

He looked at it, eyes widening. Fear leaped into his belly like a confusion of hot wires. His head jerked up and he stared at

Barlow. He was walking toward him across the kitchen and his smile was wide, almost voluptuous.

"Stay back," Callahan said hoarsely, retreating a step. "I command it, in the name of God."

Barlow laughed at him.

The glow in the cross was only a thin and guttering light in a cruciform shape. The shadows had crept across the vampire's face again, masking his features in strangely barbaric lines and triangles under the sharp cheekbones.

Callahan took another step backward, and his buttocks bumped the kitchen table, which was set against the wall.

"Nowhere left to go," Barlow murmured sadly. His dark eyes bubbled with infernal mirth. "Sad to see a man's faith fail. Ah, well . . ."

The cross trembled in Callahan's hand and suddenly the last of its light vanished. It was only a piece of plaster that his mother had bought in a Dublin souvenir shop, probably at a scalper's price. The power it had sent ramming up his arm, enough power to smash down walls and shatter stone, was gone. The muscles remembered the thrumming but could not duplicate it.

Barlow reached from the darkness and plucked the cross from his fingers. Callahan cried out miserably, the cry that had vibrated in the soul—but never the throat—of that long-ago child who had been left alone each night with Mr. Flip peering out of the closet at him from between the shutters of sleep. And the next sound would haunt him for the rest of his life: two dry snaps as Barlow broke the arms of the cross, and a meaningless thump as he threw it on the floor.

"God *damn* you!" he cried out.

"It's too late for such melodrama," Barlow said from the darkness. His voice was almost sorrowful. "There is no need of it. You have forgotten the doctrine of your own church, is it not so? The cross . . . the bread and wine . . . the confessional . . . only symbols. Without faith, the cross is only wood, the bread baked wheat, the wine sour grapes. If you had cast the cross away, you should have beaten me another night. In a way, I hoped it might be so. It has been long since I have met an opponent of any real worth. The boy makes ten of you, false priest."

Suddenly, out of the darkness, hands of amazing strength gripped Callahan's shoulders.

"You would welcome the oblivion of my death now, I think. There is no memory for the Undead; only the hunger and the need to serve the Master. I could make use of you. I could send you among your friends. Yet is there need of that? Without you to lead them, I think they are little. And the boy will tell them. One moves against them at this time. There is, perhaps, a more fitting punishment for you, false priest."

He remembered Matt saying: *Some things are worse than death.*

He tried to struggle away, but the hands held him in a viselike grip. Then one hand left him. There was the sound of cloth moving across bare skin, and then a scraping sound.

The hands moved to his neck.

"Come, false priest. Learn of a true religion. Take *my* communion."

Understanding washed over Callahan in a ghastly flood.

"No! Don't . . . don't—"

But the hands were implacable. His head was drawn forward, forward, forward.

"Now, priest," Barlow whispered.

And Callahan's mouth was pressed against the reeking flesh of the vampire's cold throat, where an open vein pulsed. He held his breath for what seemed like aeons, twisting his head wildly and to no avail, smearing the blood across his cheeks and forehead and chin like war paint.

Yet at last, he drank.

21

Ann Norton got out of her car without bothering to take the keys, and began to walk across the hospital parking lot toward the bright lights of the lobby. Overhead, clouds had blotted out the stars and soon it would begin to rain. She didn't look up to see the clouds. She walked stolidly, looking straight in front of her.

She was a very different-looking woman from the lady Ben Mears had met on that first evening Susan had invited him to take dinner with her family. That lady had been medium-tall, dressed in a green wool dress that did not scream of money but spoke of material comfort. That lady had not been beautiful but she had been well groomed and pleasant to look at; her graying hair had been permed not long since.

This woman wore only carpet slippers on her feet. Her legs were bare, and with no Supp-hose to mask them, the varicose veins bulged prominently (although not as prominently as before; some of the pressure had been taken off them). She was wearing a ragged yellow dressing gown over her negligee; her hair was blown in errant sheafs by the rising wind. Her face was pallid, and heavy brown circles lay beneath her eyes.

She had told Susan, had warned her about that man Mears and his friends, had warned her about the man who had murdered her. Matt Burke had put him up to it. They had been in cahoots. Oh yes. She knew. *He* had told her.

She had been sick all day, sick and sleepy and nearly unable to get out of bed. And when she had fallen into a heavy slumber after noon, while her husband was off answering questions for a silly missing persons report, *he* had come to her in a dream. His face was handsome and commanding and arrogant and compelling. His nose was hawklike, his hair swept back from his brow, and his heavy, fascinating mouth masked strangely exciting white teeth that showed when *he* smiled. And his eyes . . . they were red and hypnotic. When *he* looked at you with those eyes, you could not look away . . . and you didn't want to.

He had told her everything, and what she must do—and how she could be with her daughter when it was done, and with so many others . . . and with *him*. Despite Susan, it was *him* she wanted to please, so *he* would give her the thing she craved and needed: the touch; the penetration.

Her husband's .38 was in her pocket.

She entered the lobby and looked toward the reception desk. If anyone tried to stop her, she would take care of them. Not by shooting, no. No shot must be fired until she was in Burke's room. *He* had told her so. If they got to her and stopped her before she had done the job, *he* would not come to her, to give her burning kisses in the night.

There was a young girl at the desk in a white cap and uniform, working a crossword in the soft glow of the lamp over her main console. An orderly was just going down the hall, his back to them.

The duty nurse looked up with a trained smile when she heard Ann's footsteps, but it faded when she saw the hollow-eyed woman who was approaching her in night clothes. Her eyes were blank yet oddly shiny, as if she were a wind-up toy someone had set in motion. A patient, perhaps, who had gone wandering.

"Ma'am, if you—"

Ann Norton drew the .38 from the pocket of her wrapper like some creaky gunslinger from beyond time. She pointed it at the duty nurse's head and told her, "Turn around."

The nurse's mouth worked silently. She drew in breath with a convulsive heave.

"Don't scream. I'll kill you if you do."

The air wheezed out. The nurse had gone very pale.

"Turn around now."

The nurse got up slowly and turned around. Ann Norton reversed the .38 and prepared to bring the butt down on the nurse's head with all the strength she had.

At that precise moment, her feet were kicked out from under her.

22

The gun went flying.

The woman in the ragged yellow dressing gown did not scream but began to make a high whining noise in her throat, almost keening. She scrambled after it like a crab, and the man who was behind her, looking bewildered and frightened, also darted after it. When he saw that she would get to it first, he kicked it across the lobby rug.

"Hey!" he yelled. "Hey, help!"

Ann Norton looked over her shoulder and hissed at him, her face pulled into a cheated scrawl of hate, and then scrambled after the gun again. The orderly had come back, on the run. He looked at the scene with blank amazement for a moment, and then picked up the gun that lay almost at his feet.

"For Christ's sake," he said. "This thing is load—"

She attacked him. Her hands, hooked into claws, pinwheeled across his face, dragging red stripes across the surprised orderly's forehead and right cheek. He held the gun up out of her reach. Still keening, she clawed for it.

The bewildered man came up from behind and grabbed her. He would say later that it was like grabbing a bag of snakes. The body beneath the dressing gown was hot and repulsive, every muscle twitching and writhing.

As she struggled to get free, the orderly popped her one flush on the jaw. Her eyes rolled up to the whites and she collapsed.

The orderly and the bewildered man looked at each other.

The nurse at the reception desk was screaming. Her hands were clapped to her mouth, giving the screams a unique foghorn effect.

"What kind of a hospital do you people run here, anyhow?" the bewildered man asked.

"Christ if I know," the orderly said. "What the hell happened?"

"I was just coming in to visit my sister. She had a baby. And this kid walks up to me and says a woman just went in with a gun. And—"

"What kid?"

The bewildered man who had come to visit his sister looked around. The lobby was filling with people, but all of them were above drinking age.

"I don't see him now. But he was here. That gun loaded?"

"It sure is," the orderly said.

"What kind of a hospital do you people run here, anyhow?" the bewildered man asked again.

23

They had seen two nurses run past the door toward the elevators and heard a vague shout down the stairwell. Ben glanced at Jimmy and Jimmy shrugged imperceptibly. Matt was dozing with his mouth open.

Ben closed the door and turned off the lights. Jimmy crouched by the foot of Matt's bed, and when they heard footsteps hesitate outside the door, Ben stood beside it, ready. When it opened and a head poked through, he grabbed it in a half nelson and jammed the cross he held in the other hand into the face.

"Let me *go!*"

A hand reached up and beat futilely at his chest. A moment later the overhead light went on. Matt was sitting up in bed, blinking at Mark Petrie, who was struggling in Ben's arms.

Jimmy came out of his crouch and ran across the room. He seemed almost ready to embrace the boy when he hesitated. "Lift your chin."

Mark did, showing all three of them his unmarked neck.

Jimmy relaxed. "Boy, I've never been so glad to see anyone in my life. Where's the Father?"

"Don't know," Mark said somberly. "Barlow caught me . . . killed my folks. They're dead. My folks are dead. He beat their heads together. He killed my folks. Then he had me and he said to Father Callahan that he would let me go if Father Callahan would promise to throw away his cross. He promised. I ran. But before I ran, I spit on him. I spit on him and I'm going to kill him."

He swayed in the doorway. There were bramble marks on his forehead and cheeks. He had run through the forest along the path where Danny Glick and his brother had come to grief so long before. His pants were wet to the knees from his flight through Taggart Stream. He had hitched a ride, but couldn't remember who he had hitched it with. The radio had been playing, he remembered that.

Ben's tongue was frozen. He did not know what to say.

"You poor boy," Matt said softly. "You poor, brave boy."

Mark's face began to break up. His eyes closed and his mouth twisted and strained. "My muh-muh-*mother*—"

He staggered blindly and Ben caught him in his arms, enfolded him, rocked him as the tears came and raged against his shirt.

24

Father Donald Callahan had no idea how long he walked in the dark. He stumbled back toward the downtown area along Jointner Avenue, never heeding his car, which he had left parked in the Petries' driveway. Sometimes he wandered in the middle of the road, and sometimes he staggered along the sidewalk. Once a car bore down on him, its headlights great shining circles; its horn began to blare and it swerved at the last instant, tires screaming on the pavement. Once he fell in the ditch. As he approached the yellow blinking light, it began to rain.

There was no one on the streets to mark his passage; 'salem's Lot had battened down for the night, even tighter than usual. The diner was empty, and in Spencer's Miss Coogan was sitting by her cash register and reading a confession magazine off the rack in the frosty glow of the overhead fluorescents. Outside, under the lighted sign showing the blue dog in mid-flight, a red neon sign said:

BUS

They were afraid, he supposed. They had every reason to be. Some inner part of themselves had absorbed the danger, and tonight doors were locked in the Lot that had not been locked in years . . . if ever.

He was on the streets alone. And he alone had nothing to fear. It was funny. He laughed aloud, and the sound of it was like wild, lunatic sobbing. No vampire would touch him. Others, perhaps, but not him. The Master had marked him, and he would walk free until the Master claimed his own.

St. Andrew's loomed above him.

He hesitated, then walked up the path. He would pray. Pray all night if necessary. Not to the new God, the God of ghettos and social conscience and free lunches, but the old God, who had proclaimed through Moses not to suffer a witch to live and who had given it unto His own son to raise from the dead. A second chance, God. All my life for penance. Only . . . a second chance.

He stumbled up the wide steps, his gown muddy and bedraggled, his mouth smeared with Barlow's blood.

At the top he paused a moment, and then reached for the handle of the middle door.

As he touched it, there was a blue flash of light and he was thrown backward. Pain lanced his back, then his head, then his chest and stomach and shins as he fell head over heels down the granite steps to the walk.

He lay trembling in the rain, his hand afire.

He lifted it before his eyes. It was burned.

"Unclean," he muttered. "Unclean, unclean, O God, so unclean."

He began to shiver. He slid his arms around his shoulders and shivered in the rain and the church loomed behind him, its doors shut against him.

25

Mark Petrie sat on Matt's bed, in exactly the spot Ben had occupied when Ben and Jimmy had come in. Mark had dried his tears with his shirt sleeve, and although his eyes were puffy and bloodshot, he seemed to have himself in control.

"You know, don't you," Matt asked him, "that 'salem's Lot is in a desperate situation?"

Mark nodded.

"Even now, *his* Undead are crawling over it," Matt said somberly. "Taking others to themselves. They won't get them all—not tonight—but there is dreadful work ahead of you tomorrow."

"Matt, I want you to get some sleep," Jimmy said. "We'll be here, don't worry. You don't look good. This has been a horrible strain on you—"

"My town is disintegrating almost before my eyes and you want me to sleep?" His eyes, seemingly tireless, flashed out of his haggard face.

Jimmy said stubbornly, "If you want to be around for the

finish, you better save something back. I'm telling you that as your physician, goddammit."

"All right. In a minute." He looked at all of them. "Tomorrow the three of you must go back to Mark's house. You're going to make stakes. A great many of them."

The meaning sank home to them.

"How many?" Ben asked softly.

"I would say you'll need three hundred at least. I advise you to make five hundred."

"That's impossible," Jimmy said flatly. "There can't be that many of them."

"The Undead are thirsty," Matt said simply. "It's best to be prepared. You will go together. You dare not split up, even in the daytime. It will be like a scavenger hunt. You must start at one end of town and work toward the other."

"We'll never be able to find them all," Ben objected. "Not even if we could start at first light and work through until dark."

"You've got to do your best, Ben. People may begin to believe you. Some will help, if you show them the truth of what you say. And when dark comes again, much of *his* work will be undone." He sighed. "We have to assume that Father Callahan is lost to us. That's bad. But you must press on, regardless. You'll have to be careful, all of you. Be ready to lie. If you're locked up, that will serve *his* purpose well. And if you haven't considered it, you might do well to consider it now: There is every possibility that some of us or all of us may live and triumph only to stand trial for murder."

He looked each of them in the face. What he saw there must have satisfied him, because he turned his attention wholly to Mark again.

"You know what the most important job is, don't you?"

"Yes," Mark said. "Barlow has to be killed."

Matt smiled a trifle thinly. "That's putting the cart before the horse, I'm afraid. First we have to find him." He looked closely at Mark. "Did you see anything tonight, hear anything, smell anything, touch anything, that might help us locate him? Think carefully before you answer! You know better than any of us how important it is!"

Mark thought. Ben had never seen anyone take a command quite so literally. He lowered his chin into the palm of his hand

and shut his eyes. He seemed to be quite deliberately going over every nuance of the night's encounter.

At last he opened his eyes, looked around at them briefly, and shook his head. "Nothing."

Matt's face fell, but he did not give up. "A leaf clinging to his coat, maybe? A cattail in his pants cuff? Dirt on his shoes? Any loose thread that he has allowed to dangle?" He smote the bed helplessly. "Jesus Christ Almighty, is he seamless like an egg?"

Mark's eyes suddenly widened.

"What?" Matt said. He grasped the boy's elbow. "What is it? What have you thought of?"

"Blue chalk," Mark said. "He had one arm hooked around my neck, like this, and I could see his hand. He had long white fingers and there were smears of blue chalk on two of them. Just little ones."

"Blue chalk," Matt said thoughtfully.

"A school," Ben said. "It must be."

"Not the high school," Matt said. "All our supplies come from Dennison and Company in Portland. They supply only white and yellow. I've had it under my fingernails and on my coats for years."

"Art classes?" Ben asked.

"No, only graphic arts at the high school. They use inks, not chalk. Mark, are you sure it was—"

"Chalk," he said, nodding.

"I believe some of the science teachers use colored chalk, but where is there to hide at the high school? You saw it—all on one level, all enclosed in glass. People are in and out of the supply closets all day. That is also true of the furnace room."

"Backstage?"

Matt shrugged. "It's dark enough. But if Mrs. Rodin takes over the class play for me—the students call her Mrs. Rodan after a quaint Japanese science fiction film—that area would be used a great deal. It would be a horrible risk for him."

"What about the grammar schools?" Jimmy asked. "They must teach drawing in the lower grades. And I'd bet a hundred dollars that colored chalk is one of the things they keep on hand."

Matt said, "The Stanley Street Elementary School was built with the same bond money as the high school. It is also modernistic, filled to capacity, and built on one level. Many glass windows to let in the sun. Not the kind of building our target would want to frequent at all. They like old buildings, full of tradition, dark, dingy, like—"

"Like the Brock Street School," Mark said.

"Yes." Matt looked at Ben. "The Brock Street School is a wooden frame building, three stories and a basement, built at about the same time as the Marsten House. There was much talk in the town when the school bond issue was up for a vote that the school was a fire hazard. It was one reason our bond issue passed. There had been a schoolhouse fire in New Hampshire two or three years before—"

"I remember," Jimmy murmured. "In Cobbs' Ferry, wasn't it?"

"Yes. Three children were burned to death."

"Is the Brock Street School still used?" Ben asked.

"Only the first floor. Grades one through four. The entire building is due to be phased out in two years, when they put the addition on the Stanley Street School."

"Is there a place for Barlow to hide?"

"I suppose so," Matt said, but he sounded reluctant. "The second and third floors are full of empty classrooms. The windows have been boarded over because so many children threw stones through them."

"That's it, then," Ben said. "It must be."

"It sounds good," Matt admitted, and he looked very tired indeed now. "But it seems too simple. Too transparent."

"Blue chalk," Jimmy murmured. His eyes were far away.

"I don't know," Matt said, sounding distracted. "I just don't know."

Jimmy opened his black bag and brought out a small bottle of pills. "Two of these with water," he said. "Right now."

"No. There's too much to go over. There's too much—"

"Too much for us to risk losing you," Ben said firmly. "If Father Callahan *is* gone, you're the most important of all of us now. Do as he says."

Mark brought a glass of water from the bathroom, and Matt gave in with some bad grace.

It was quarter after ten.

Silence fell in the room. Ben thought that Matt looked fearfully old, fearfully used. His white hair seemed thinner, drier, and a lifetime of care seemed to have stamped itself on his face in a matter of days. In a way, Ben thought, it was fitting that when trouble finally came to him—great trouble—it should come in this dreamlike, darkly fantastical form. A lifetime's existence had prepared him to deal in symbolic evils that sprang to light under the reading lamp and disappeared at dawn.

"I'm worried about him," Jimmy said softly.

"I thought the attack was mild," Ben said. "Not really a heart attack at all."

"It was a mild occlusion. But the next one won't be mild. It'll be major. This business is going to kill him if it doesn't end quickly." He took Matt's hand and fingered the pulse gently, with love. "That," he said, "would be a tragedy."

They waited around his bedside, sleeping and watching by turns. He slept the night away, and Barlow did not put in an appearance. He had business elsewhere.

26

Miss Coogan was reading a story called "I Tried to Strangle Our Baby" in *Real Life Confessions* when the door opened and her first customer of the evening came in.

She had never seen things so slow. Ruthie Crockett and her friends hadn't even been in for a soda at the fountain—not that she missed *that* crowd—and Loretta Starcher hadn't stopped in for *The New York Times*. It was still under the counter, neatly folded. Loretta was the only person in Jerusalem's Lot who bought the *Times* (she pronounced it that way, in italics) regularly. And the next day she would put it out in the reading room.

Mr. Labree hadn't come back from his supper, either, although there was nothing unusual about that. Mr. Labree was a widower with a big house out on Schoolyard Hill near the Griffens, and Miss Coogan knew perfectly well that he didn't go home for his supper. He went out to Dell's and ate hamburgers and drank beer. If he wasn't back by eleven (and it was quarter of now), she would get the key out of the cash drawer and lock up herself. Wouldn't be the first time, either. But they would all be in a pretty pickle if someone came in needing medicine badly.

She sometimes missed the after-movie rush that had always come about this time before they had demolished the old Nordica across the street—people wanting ice-cream sodas and frappés and malteds, dates holding hands and talking about homework assignments. It had been hard, but it had been *wholesome,* too. Those children hadn't been like Ruthie Crockett and her crowd, sniggering and flaunting their busts and wearing jeans tight enough to show the line of their panties—if they were wearing any. The reality of her feelings for those bygone patrons (who, although she had forgotten it, had irritated her just as much) was fogged by nostalgia, and she looked up eagerly when the door opened, as if it might be a member of the class of '64 and his girl, ready for a chocolate fudge sundae with extra nuts.

But it was a man, a grown-up man, someone she knew but could not place. As he carried his suitcase down to the counter, something in his walk or the motion of his head identified him for her.

"Father Callahan!" she said, unable to keep the surprise out of her voice. She had never seen him without his priest suit on. He was wearing plain dark slacks and a blue chambray shirt, like a common millworker.

She was suddenly frightened. The clothes he wore were clean and his hair was neatly combed, but there was something in his face, something—

She suddenly remembered the day, twenty years ago, when she had come from the hospital where her mother had died of a sudden stroke—what the old-timers called a shock. When she had told her brother, he had looked something like Father Callahan did now. His face had a haggard, doomed look, and his eyes were blank and stunned. There was a burned-out look in them that made her uncomfortable. And the skin around his mouth looked red and irritated, as if he had overshaved or rubbed it for a long period of time with a washcloth, trying to get rid of a bad stain.

"I want to buy a bus ticket," he said.

That's it, she thought. Poor man, someone's died and he just got the call down at the directory, or whatever they call it.

"Certainly," she said. "Where—"

"What's the first bus?"

"To where?"

"Anywhere," he said, throwing her theory into shambles.

"Well . . . I don't . . . let me see . . ." She fumbled out the schedule and looked at it, flustered. "There's a bus at eleven-ten that connects with Portland, Boston, Hartford, and New Y—"

"That one," he said. "How much?"

"For how long—I mean, how far?" She was thoroughly flustered now.

"All the way," he said hollowly, and smiled. She had never seen such a dreadful smile on a human face, and she flinched from it. *If he touches me,* she thought, *I'll scream. Scream blue murder.*

"T-th-that would be to New York City," she said. "Twenty-nine dollars and seventy-five cents."

He dug his wallet out of his back pocket with some difficulty, and she saw that his right hand was bandaged. He put a twenty and two ones before her, and she knocked a whole pile of blank tickets onto the floor taking one off the top of the stack. When she finished picking them up, he had added five more ones and a pile of change.

She wrote the ticket as fast as she could, but nothing would have been fast enough. She could feel his dead gaze on her. She stamped it and pushed it across the counter so she wouldn't have to touch his hand.

"Y-you'll have to wait outside, Father C-Callahan. I've got to close in about five minutes." She scraped the bills and change into the cash drawer blindly, making no attempt to count it.

"That's fine," he said. He stuffed the ticket into his breast pocket. Without looking at her he said, "And the Lord set a mark upon Cain, that whosoever found him should not kill him. And Cain went out from the face of the Lord, and dwelt as a fugitive on the earth, at the east side of Eden. That's Scripture, Miss Coogan. The hardest scripture in the Bible."

"Is that so?" she said. "I'm afraid you'll have to go outside, Father Callahan. I . . . Mr. Labree is just in back a minute and he doesn't like . . . doesn't like me to . . . to . . ."

"Of course," he said, and turned to go. He stopped and looked around at her. She flinched before those wooden eyes. "You live in Falmouth, don't you, Miss Coogan?"

"Yes—"

"Have your own car?"

"Yes, of course. I really have to ask you to wait for the bus outside—"

"Drive home quickly tonight, Miss Coogan. Lock all your car doors and don't stop for anybody. *Anybody.* Don't even stop if it's someone you know."

"I *never* pick up hitchhikers," Miss Coogan said righteously.

"And when you get home, stay away from Jerusalem's Lot," Callahan went on. He was looking at her fixedly. "Things have gone bad in the Lot now."

She said faintly, "I don't know what you're talking about, but you'll have to wait for the bus outside."

"Yes. All right."

He went out.

She became suddenly aware of how quiet the drugstore was, how utterly quiet. Could it be that no one—*no* one—had come in since it got dark except Father Callahan? It was. No one at all.

Things have gone bad in the Lot now.

She began to go around and turn off the lights.

27

In the Lot the dark held hard.

At ten minutes to twelve, Charlie Rhodes was awakened by a long, steady honking. He came awake in his bed and sat bolt upright.

His bus!

And on the heels of that:

The little bastards!

The children had tried things like this before. He knew them, the miserable little sneaks. They had let the air out of his tires with matchsticks once. He hadn't seen who did it, but he had a damned good idea. He had gone to that damned wet-ass principal and reported Mike Philbrook and Audie James. He had known it was them—who had to see?

Are you sure it was them, Rhodes?

I told you, didn't I?

And there was nothing that fucking molly-coddle could do; he *had* to suspend them. Then the bastard had called him to the office a week later.

Rhodes, we suspended Andy Garvey today.

Yeah? Not surprised. What was he up to?

Bob Thomas caught him letting the air out of his bus tires. And he had given Charlie Rhodes a long, cold, measuring look.

Well, so what if it had been Garvey instead of Philbrook and James? They all hung around together, they were all creeps, they all deserved to have their nuts in the grinder.

Now, from outside, the maddening sound of his horn, running down the battery, really laying on it:

WHONK, WHONNK, WHOONNNNNNNNK—

"You sons of whores," he whispered, and slid out of bed. He dragged his pants on without using the light. The light would scare the little scumbags away, and he didn't want that.

Another time, someone had left a cow pie on his driver's seat, and he had a pretty good idea of who had done that, too. You could read it in their eyes. He had learned that standing guard at the repple depple in the war. He had taken care of the cow-pie business in his own way. Kicked the little son of a whore off the bus three days' running, four miles from home. The kid finally came to him crying.

I ain't done nothin', Mr. Rhodes. Why you keep kickin' me off?

You call puttin' a cow flop on my seat nothin'?

No, that wasn't me. Honest to God it wasn't.

Well, you had to hand it to them. They could lie to their own mothers with a clear and smiling face, and they probably did it, too. He had kicked the kid off two more nights and then he had confessed, by the Jesus. Charlie kicked him off once more—one to grow on, you might say—and then Dave Felsen down at the motor pool told him he better cool it for a while.

WHONNNNNNNNNNNNNNNNNK—

He grabbed his shirt and then got the old tennis racket standing in the corner. By Christ, he was going to whip some ass tonight!

He went out the back door and around the house to where he kept the big yellow bus parked. He felt tough and coldly competent. This was infiltration, just like the Army.

He paused behind the oleander bush and looked at the bus. Yes, he could see them, a whole bunch of them, darker shapes behind the night-darkened glass. He felt the old red rage, the hate of them like hot ice, and his grip on the tennis racket tightened until it trembled in his hand like a tuning fork. They had busted out—six, seven, eight—eight windows on *his* bus!

He slipped behind it and then crept up the long yellow side to the passenger door. It was folded open. He tensed, and suddenly sprang up the steps.

"All right! Stay where you are! Kid, lay off that goddamn horn or I'll—"

The kid sitting in the driver's seat with both hands plastered on the horn ring turned to him and smiled crazily. Charlie felt a sickening drop in his gut. It was Richie Boddin. He was white—just as white as a sheet—except for the black chips of coal that were his eyes, and his lips, which were ruby red.

And his teeth—

Charlie Rhodes looked down the aisle.

Was that Mike Philbrook? Audie James? God Almighty, the Griffen boys were down there! Hal and Jack, sitting near the back with hay in their hair. *But they don't ride on my bus!* Mary Kate Greigson and Brent Tenney, sitting side by side. She was in a nightgown, he in blue jeans and a flannel shirt that was on backward and inside out, as if he had forgotten how to dress himself.

And Danny Glick. But—oh, Christ—he was *dead;* dead for *weeks!*

"You," he said through numb lips. "You kids—"

The tennis racket slid from his hand. There was a wheeze and a thump as Richie Boddin, still smiling that crazy smile, worked the chrome lever that shut the folding door. They were getting out of their seats now, all of them.

"No," he said, trying to smile. "You kids . . . you don't understand. It's me. It's Charlie Rhodes. You . . . you . . ." He grinned at them without meaning, shook his head, held out his hands to show them they were just ole Charlie Rhodes's hands, blameless, and backed up until his back was jammed against the wide tinted glass of the windshield.

"Don't," he whispered.

They came on, grinning.

"Please don't."

And fell on him.

28

Ann Norton died on the short elevator trip from the first floor of the hospital to the second. She shivered once, and a small trickle of blood ran from the corner of her mouth.

"Okay," one of the orderlies said. "You can turn off the siren now."

29

Eva Miller had been dreaming.

It was a strange dream, not quite a nightmare. The fire of '51 was raging under an unforgiving sky that shaded from pale blue at the horizons to a hot and merciless white overhead. The sun glared from this inverted bowl like a glinting copper coin. The acrid smell of smoke was everywhere; all business activity had stopped and people stood in the streets, looking southwest, toward the Marshes, and northwest, toward the woods. The smoke had been in the air all morning, but now, at one in the afternoon, you could see the bright arteries of fire dancing in the green beyond Griffen's pasture. The steady breeze that had allowed the flames to jump one firebreak now brought a steady fall of white ash over the town like summer snow.

Ralph was alive, off trying to save the sawmill. But it was all mixed up because Ed Craig was with her and she had never even met Ed until the fall of 1954.

She was watching the fire from her upstairs bedroom window, and she was naked. Hands touched her from behind, rough brown hands on the smooth whiteness of her hips, and she knew it was Ed, although she could not see even a ghost of his reflection in the glass.

Ed, she tried to say. Not now. *It's too early. Not for almost nine years.*

But his hands were insistent, running over her belly, one finger toying with the cup of her navel, then both hands slipping up to catch her breasts with brazen knowledge.

She tried to tell him they were in the window, anyone out there in the street could look over his shoulder and see them, but the words would not come out and then his lips were on her arm, her shoulder, then fastening with firm and lustful insistence on her neck. She felt his teeth and he was biting her, sucking and biting, drawing blood, and she tried to protest again: *Don't give me a hickey, Ralph will see—*

But it was impossible to protest and she no longer even wanted to. She no longer cared who looked around and saw them, naked and brazen.

Her eyes drifted dreamily to the fire as his lips and teeth worked against her neck, and the smoke was very black, as black as night, obscuring that hot gun-metal sky, turning day to night; yet the fire moved inside it in those pulsing scarlet threads and blossoms—rioting flowers in a midnight jungle.

And then it *was* night and the town was gone but the fire still raged in the blackness, shifting through fascinating, kaleidoscopic shapes until it seemed that it limned a face in blood—a face with a hawk nose, deep-set, fiery eyes, full and sensuous lips partially hidden by a heavy mustache, and hair swept back from the brow like a musician's.

"The Welsh dresser," a voice said distantly, and she knew it was *his*. "The one in the attic. That will do nicely, I think. And then we'll fix the stairs . . . it's wise to be prepared."

The voice faded. The flames faded.

There was only the darkness, and she in it, dreaming or beginning to dream. She thought dimly that the dream would be sweet and long, but bitter underneath and without light, like the waters of Lethe.

Another voice—Ed's voice. "Come on, darlin'. Get up. We have to do as he says."

"Ed? Ed?"

His face looked over hers, not drawn in fire, but looking terribly pale and strangely empty. Yet she loved him again . . . more than ever. She yearned for his kiss.

"Come on, Eva."

"Is it a dream, Ed?"

"No . . . not a dream."

For a moment she was frightened, and then there was no

more fear. There was knowing instead. With the knowing came the hunger.

She glanced into the mirror and saw only her bedroom reflected, empty and still. The attic door was locked and the key was in the bottom drawer of the dresser, but it didn't matter. No need for keys now.

They slipped between the door and the jamb like shades.

30

At three in the morning the blood runs slow and thick, and slumber is heavy. The soul either sleeps in blessed ignorance of such an hour or gazes about itself in utter despair. There is no middle ground. At three in the morning the gaudy paint is off that old whore, the world, and she has no nose and a glass eye. Gaiety becomes hollow and brittle, as in Poe's castle surrounded by the Red Death. Horror is destroyed by boredom. Love is a dream.

Parkins Gillespie shambled from his office desk to the coffeepot, looking like a very thin ape that had been sick with a wasting illness. Behind him, a game of solitaire was laid out like a clock. He had heard several screams in the night, the strange, jagged beating of a horn on the air, and once, running feet. He had not gone out to investigate any of these things. His lined and socketed face was haunted by the things he thought were going on out there. He was wearing a cross, a St. Christopher's medal, and a peace sign around his neck. He didn't know exactly why he had put them on, but they comforted him. He was thinking that if he could get through this night, he would go far away tomorrow and leave his badge on the shelf, by his key ring.

Mabel Werts was sitting at her kitchen table, a cold cup of coffee in front of her, the shades pulled down for the first time in years, the lens caps on her binoculars. For the first time in sixty years she did not want to see things, or hear them. The night was rife with a deadly gossip she did not want to listen to.

Bill Norton was on his way to the Cumberland Hospital in response to a telephone call (made while his wife was still alive), and his face was wooden and unmoving. The windshield wipers clicked steadily against the rain, which was coming down more heavily now. He was trying not to think about anything.

There were others in the town who were either sleeping or waking untouched. Most of the untouched were single people without relatives or close friends in the town. Many of them were unaware that anything had been happening.

Those that were awake, however, had turned on all their lights, and a person driving through town (and several cars did pass, headed for Portland or points south) might have been struck by this small village, so much like the others along the way, with its odd salting of fully lit dwellings in the very grave-yard of morning. The passer-by might have slowed to look for a fire or an accident, and seeing neither, speeded up and dismissed it from mind.

Here is the peculiar thing: None of those awake in Jerusalem's Lot knew the truth. A handful might have suspected, but even their suspicions were as vague and unformed as three-month fetuses. Yet they had gone unhesitatingly to bureau drawers, attic boxes, or bedroom jewel collections to find whatever religious hex symbols they might possess. They did this without thinking, the way a man driving a long distance alone will sing without knowing he sings. They walked slowly from room to room, as if their bodies had become glassy and fragile, and they turned on all the lights, and they did not look out their windows.

That above all else. They did not look out their windows.

No matter what noises or dreadful possibilities, no matter how awful the unknown, there was an even worse thing: to look the Gorgon in the face.

31

The noise penetrated his sleep like a nail being bludgeoned into heavy oak; with exquisite slowness, seemingly fiber by fiber. At first Reggie Sawyer thought he was dreaming of carpentry, and his brain, in the shadow land between sleeping and waking, obliged with a slow-motion memory fragment of him and his father nailing clapboards to the sides of the camp they had built on Bryant Pond in 1960.

This faded into a muddled idea that he was not dreaming at all, but actually hearing a hammer at work. Disorientation followed, and then he was awake and the blows were falling on the front door, someone dropping his fist against the wood with metronomelike regularity.

His eyes first jerked to Bonnie, who was lying on her side, an S-shaped hump under the blankets. Then to the clock: 4:15.

He got up, slipped out of the bedroom, and closed the door behind him. He turned on the hall light, started down toward the door, and then paused. An internal set of hackles had risen.

Sawyer regarded his front door with mute, head-cocked curiosity. No one knocked at 4:15. If someone in the family croaked, they called on the telephone, but they didn't come knocking.

He had been in Vietnam for seven months in 1968, a very hard year for American boys in Vietnam, and he had seen combat. In those days, coming awake had been as sudden as the snapping of fingers or the clicking on of a lamp; one minute you were a stone, the next you were awake in the dark. The habit had died in him almost as soon as he had been shipped back to the States, and he had been proud of that, although he never spoke of it. He was no machine, by Jesus. Push button A and Johnny wakes up, push button B and Johnny kills some slants.

But now, with no warning at all, the muzziness and cottonheadedness of sleep fell off him like a snakeskin and he was cold and blinking.

Someone out there. The Bryant kid, likely, liquored up and packing iron. Ready to do or die for the fair maiden.

He went into the living room and crossed to the gunrack over the fake fireplace. He didn't turn on a light; he knew his way around by touch perfectly well. He took down his shotgun, broke it, and the hall light gleamed dully on brass casings. He went back to the living room doorway and poked his head out into the hall. The pounding went on monotonously, with regularity but no rhythm.

"Come on in," Reggie Sawyer called.

The pounding stopped.

There was a long pause and then the doorknob turned, very slowly, until it had reached full cock. The door opened and Corey Bryant stood there.

Reggie felt his heart falter for an instant. Bryant was dressed in the same clothes he had been wearing when Reggie sent him down the road, only now they were ripped and mud-stained. Leaves clung to his pants and shirt. A streak of dirt across his forehead accentuated his pallor.

"Stop right there," Reggie said, lifting the shotgun and clicking off the safety. "This time it's loaded."

But Corey Bryant plodded forward, his dull eyes fixed on Reggie's face with an expression that was worse than hate. His tongue slid out and slicked his lips. His shoes were clotted with heavy mud that had been mixed to a black glue by the rain, and clods dropped off onto the hall floor as he came forward. There was something unforgiving and remorseless in that walk, something that impressed the watching eye with a cold and dreadful lack of mercy. The mud-caked heels clumped. There was no command that would stop them or plea that would stay them.

"Take two more steps and I'll blow your fucking head off," Reggie said. The words came out hard and dry. The guy was worse than drunk. He was off his rocker. He knew with sudden clarity that he was going to have to shoot him.

"Stop," he said again, but in a casual, offhand way.

Corey Bryant did not stop. His eyes were fixed on Reggie's face with the dead and sparkling avidity of a stuffed moose. His heels clumped solemnly on the floor.

Bonnie screamed behind him.

"Go on in the bedroom," Reggie said. He stepped out into the hallway to get between them. Bryant was only two paces away now. One limp, white hand was reaching out to grasp the twin barrels of the Stevens.

Reggie pulled both triggers.

The blast was like a thunderclap in the narrow hallway. Fire licked momentarily from both barrels. The stink of burned powder filled the air. Bonnie screamed again, piercingly. Corey's shirt shredded and blackened and parted, not so much perforated as disintegrated. Yet when it blew open, divorced from its buttons, the fish whiteness of his chest and abdomen was incredibly unmarked. Reggie's frozen eyes received an impression that the flesh was not really flesh at all, but something as insubstantial as a gauze curtain.

Then the shotgun was slapped from his hands, as if from the hands of a child. He was gripped and thrown against the wall with teeth-rattling force. His legs refused to support him and he fell down, dazed. Bryant walked past him, toward Bonnie. She was cringing in the doorway, but her eyes were on his face, and Reggie could see the heat in them.

Corey looked back over his shoulder and grinned at Reggie, a huge and moony grin, like that offered to tourists by cow skulls in the desert. Bonnie was holding her arms out. They trembled. Over her face, terror and lust seemed to pass like alternating flashes of sunshine and shadow.

"Darling," she said.

Reggie screamed.

32

"Hey," the bus driver said. "This is Hartford, Mac."

Callahan looked out the wide, polarized window at the strange country, made even stranger by the first seeping light of morning. In the Lot they would be going back now, back into their holes.

"I know," he said.

"We got a twenty-minute rest stop. Don't you want to go in and get a sandwich or something?"

Callahan fumbled his wallet out of his pocket with his bandaged hand and almost dropped it. Oddly, the burned hand didn't seem to hurt much anymore; it was only numb. It would have been better if there had been pain. Pain was at least real. The taste of death was in his mouth, a moronic, mealy taste like a spoiled apple. Was that all? Yes. That was bad enough.

He held out a twenty. "Can you get me a bottle?"

"Mister, the rules—"

"And keep the change, of course. A pint would be fine."

"I don't need nobody cutting up on my bus, mister. We'll be in New York in two hours. You can get what you want there. Anything."

I think you are wrong, friend, Callahan thought. He looked into the wallet again to see what was there. A ten, two fives, a single. He added the ten to the twenty and held it out in his bandaged hand.

"A pint would be fine," he said. "And keep the change, of course."

The driver looked from the thirty dollars to the dark, socketed eyes, and for one terrible moment thought he was holding conversation with a living skull, a skull that had somehow forgotten how to grin.

"Thirty dollars for a pint? Mister, you're crazy." But he took the money, walked to the front of the empty bus, then turned back. The money had disappeared. "But don't you go cutting up on me. I don't need nobody cutting up on my bus."

Callahan nodded like a very small boy accepting a deserved reprimand.

The bus driver looked at him a moment longer, then got off.

Something cheap, Callahan thought. Something that will burn the tongue and sizzle the throat. Something to take away that bland, sweet taste . . . or at least allay it until he could find a place to begin drinking in earnest. To drink and drink and drink—

He thought then that he might break down, begin to cry. There were no tears. He felt very dry, and completely empty. There was only . . . that taste.

Hurry, driver.

He went on looking out the window. Across the street, a teenaged boy was sitting on a porch stoop with his head folded into his arms. Callahan watched him until the bus pulled out again, but the boy never moved.

33

Ben felt a hand on his arm and swam upward to wakefulness. Mark, near his right ear, said, "Morning."

He opened his eyes, blinked twice to clear the gum out of them, and looked out the window at the world. Dawn had come stealing through a steady autumn rain that was neither heavy nor light. The trees which ringed the grassy pavilion on the hospital's north side were half denuded now, and the black branches were limned against the gray sky like giant letters in an unknown alphabet. Route 30, which curved out of town to the east, was as shiny as sealskin—a car passing with its taillights still on left baleful red reflections on the macadam.

Ben stood up and looked around. Matt was sleeping, his chest rising and falling in regular but shallow respiration. Jimmy was also asleep, stretched out in the room's one lounge chair. There was an undoctorlike stubble on the planes of his cheeks, and Ben ran a palm across his own face. It rasped.

"Time to get going, isn't it?" Mark asked.

Ben nodded. He thought of the day ahead of them and all its potential hideousness, and shied away from it. The only way to get through it would be without thinking more than ten minutes ahead. He looked into the boy's face, and the stony eagerness he saw there made him feel queasy. He went over and shook Jimmy.

"Huh!" Jimmy said. He thrashed in his chair like a swimmer coming up from deep water. His face twitched, his eyes fluttered open, and for a moment they showed blank terror. He looked at them both unreasoningly, without recognition.

Then recognition came, and his body relaxed. "Oh. Dream."

Mark nodded in perfect understanding.

Jimmy looked out the window and said "Daylight" the way a miser might say *money*. He got up and went over to Matt, took his wrist and held it.

"Is he all right?" Mark asked.

"I think he's better than he was last night," Jimmy said. "Ben, I want the three of us to leave by way of the service elevator in case someone noticed Mark last night. The less risk, the better."

"Will Mr. Burke be okay alone?" Mark asked.

"I think so," Ben said. "We'll have to trust to his ingenuity, I guess. Barlow would like nothing better than to have us tied up another day."

They tiptoed down the corridor and used the service elevator. The kitchen was just cranking up at this hour—almost quarter past seven. One of the cooks looked up, waved a hand, and said, "Hi, Doc." No one else spoke to them.

"Where first?" Jimmy asked. "The Brock Street School?"

"No," Ben said. "Too many people until this afternoon. Do the little ones get out early, Mark?"

"They go until two o'clock."

"That leaves plenty of daylight," Ben said. "Mark's house first. Stakes."

34

As they drew closer to the Lot, an almost palpable cloud of dread formed in Jimmy's Buick, and conversation lagged. When Jimmy pulled off the turnpike at the large green reflectorized sign that read ROUTE 12 JERUSALEM'S LOT CUMBERLAND CUMBERLAND CTR, Ben thought that this was the way he and Susan had come home after their first date—she had wanted to see something with a car chase in it.

"It's gone bad," Jimmy said. His boyish face looked pale and frightened and angry. "Christ, you can almost smell it."

And you could, Ben thought, although the smell was mental rather than physical: a psychic whiff of tombs.

Route 12 was nearly deserted. On the way in they passed Win Purinton's milk truck, parked off the road and deserted. The motor was idling, and Ben turned it off after looking in the back. Jimmy glanced at him inquiringly as he got back in. Ben shook his head. "He's not there. The engine light was on, and it was almost out of gas. Been idling there for hours." Jimmy pounded his leg with a closed fist.

But as they entered town, Jimmy said in an almost absurdly relieved tone, "Look there. Crossen's is open."

It was. Milt was out front, fussing a plastic drop cover over his rack of newspapers, and Lester Silvius was standing next to him, dressed in a yellow slicker.

"Don't see the rest of the crew, though," Ben said.

Milt glanced up at them and waved, and Ben thought he saw lines of strain on both men's faces. The "Closed" sign was still posted inside the door of Foreman's Mortuary. The hardware store was also closed, and Spencer's was locked and dark. The diner was open, and after they had passed it, Jimmy pulled his Buick up to the curb in front of the new shop. Above the show window, simple gold-faced letters spelled out the name: "Barlow and Straker—Fine Furnishings." And taped to the door, as Callahan had said, a sign which had been hand-lettered in a fine script which they all recognized from the note they had seen the day before: "Closed until further notice."

"Why are you stopping here?" Mark asked.

"Just on the off-chance that he might be holing up inside," Jimmy said. "It's so obvious he might figure we'd overlook it. And I think that sometimes customs men put an okay on boxes they've checked through. They write it on with chalk."

They went around to the back, and while Ben and Mark hunched their shoulders against the rain, Jimmy poked one overcoated elbow through the glass in the back door until they could all climb inside.

The air was noxious and stale, the air of a room shut up for centuries rather than days. Ben poked his head out into the show-room, but there was no place to hide out there. Sparsely furnished, there was no sign that Straker had been replenishing his stock.

"Come here!" Jimmy called hoarsely, and Ben's heart leaped into his throat.

Jimmy and Mark were standing by a long crate which Jimmy had partly pried open with the claw end of his hammer. Looking in, they could see one pale hand and a dark sleeve.

Without thinking, Ben attacked the crate. Jimmy was fumbling at the far end with the hammer.

"Ben," Jimmy said, "you're going to cut your hands. You—"

He hadn't heard. He snapped boards off the crate, regardless of nails and splinters. They had him, they had the slimy night-thing, and he would pound the stake into him as he had pounded it into Susan, he would—

He snapped back another piece of the cheap wooden crating and looked into the dead, moon-pallid face of Mike Ryerson.

For a moment there was utter silence, and then they all let out their breath . . . it was as if a soft wind had coursed through the room.

"What do we do now?" Jimmy asked.

"We better get out to Mark's house first," Ben said. His voice was dull with disappointment. "We know where he is. We don't even have a finished stake yet."

They put the splintered strips of wood back helter-skelter.

"Better let me look at those hands," Jimmy said. "They're bleeding."

"Later," Ben said. "Come on."

They went back around the building, all of them wordlessly glad to be back in the open air, and Jimmy drove the Buick up Jointner Avenue and into the residential part of town, just outside the skimpy business district. They arrived at Mark's house perhaps sooner than any of them would have liked.

Father Callahan's old sedan was parked behind Henry Petrie's sensible Pinto runabout in the circular Petrie driveway. At the sight of it, Mark sucked in his breath and looked away. All color had drained out of his face.

"I can't go in there," he muttered. "I'm sorry. I'll wait in the car."

"Nothing to be sorry for, Mark," Jimmy said.

He parked, turned off the ignition, and got out. Ben hesitated a minute, then put a hand on Mark's shoulder. "Are you going to be all right?"

"Sure." But he did not look all right. His chin was trembling and his eyes looked hollow. He suddenly turned to Ben and the hollowness was gone from the eyes and they were filled with simple pain, swimming with tears. "Cover them up, will you? If they're dead, cover them up."

"Sure I will," Ben said.

"It's better this way," Mark said. "My father . . . he would have made a very successful vampire. Maybe as good as Barlow, in time. He . . . he was good at everything he tried. Maybe too good."

"Try not to think too much," Ben said, hating the lame sound of the words as they left his mouth. Mark looked up at him and smiled wanly.

"The woodpile's around in the back," Mark said. "You can go faster if you use my father's lathe down in the basement."

"All right," Ben said. "Be easy, Mark. As easy as you can."

But the boy was looking away now, swiping at his eyes with his arm.

He and Jimmy went up the back steps and inside.

35

"Callahan's not here," Jimmy said flatly. They had gone through the entire house.

Ben forced himself to say it. "Barlow must have gotten him."

He looked at the broken cross in his hand. It had been around Callahan's neck yesterday. It was the only trace of him they had found. It had been lying next to the bodies of the Petries, who were very dead indeed. Their heads had been crushed together with force enough to literally shatter the skulls. Ben remembered the unnatural strength Mrs. Glick had displayed and felt sick.

"Come on," he said to Jimmy. "We've got to cover them up. I promised."

36

They took the dust cover from the couch in the living room and covered them with that. Ben tried not to look at or think about what they were doing, but it was impossible. When the job was done, one hand—the cultivated, lacquered nails revealed it to be June Petrie's—protruded from under the gaily patterned dust cover, and he poked it underneath with his toe, grimacing in an effort to keep his stomach under control. The shapes of the bodies under the cover were undeniable and unmistakable, making him think of news photos from Vietnam— battlefield dead and soldiers carrying dreadful burdens in black rubber sacks that looked absurdly like golf bags.

They went downstairs, each with an armload of yellow ash stove lengths.

The cellar had been Henry Petrie's domain, and it reflected his personality perfectly: Three high-intensity lights had been hung in a straight line over the work area, each shaded with a wide metal shell that allowed the light to fall with strong brilliance on the planer, the jigsaw, the bench saw, the lathe, the electric sander. Ben saw that he had been building a bird hotel, probably to place in the back yard next spring, and the blueprint he had been working from was neatly laid out and held at each corner with machined metal paperweights. He had been doing a competent but uninspired job, and now it would never be finished. The floor was neatly swept, but a pleasantly nostalgic odor of sawdust hung in the air.

"This isn't going to work at all," Jimmy said.

"I know that," Ben said.

"The woodpile," Jimmy snorted, and let the wood fall from his arms in a lumbering crash. The stove lengths rolled wildly on the floor like jackstraws. He uttered a high, hysterical laugh.

"Jimmy—"

But his laugh cut across Ben's attempt to speak like jags of piano wire. "We're going to go out and end the scourge with a pile of wood from Henry Petrie's back lot. How about some chair legs or baseball bats?"

"Jimmy, what else can we do?"

Jimmy looked at him and got himself under control with a visible effort. "Some treasure hunt," he said. "Go forty paces into Charles Griffen's north pasture and look under the large rock. Ha. Jesus. We can get out of town. We can do that."

"Do you want to quit? Is that what you want?"

"No. But it isn't going to be just today, Ben. It's going to be weeks before we get them all, if we ever do. Can you stand that? Can you stand doing . . . doing what you did to Susan a thousand times? Pulling them out of their closets and their stinking little bolt holes screaming and struggling, only to pound a stake into their chest cavities and smash their hearts? Can you keep that up until November without going nuts?"

Ben thought about it and met a blank wall: utter incomprehension.

"I don't know," he said.

"Well, what about the kid? Do you think he can take it? He'll be ready for the fucking nut hatch. And Matt will be dead. I'll guarantee you that. And what do we do when the state cops start nosing around to find out what in hell happened to 'salem's Lot? What do we tell them? 'Pardon me while I stake this bloodsucker'? What about that, Ben?"

"How the hell should I know? Who's had a chance to stop and think this thing out?"

They realized simultaneously that they were standing nose to nose, yelling at each other. "Hey," Jimmy said. "Hey."

Ben dropped his eyes. "I'm sorry."

"No, my fault. We're under pressure . . . what Barlow would undoubtedly call an end game." He ran a hand through his carroty hair and looked around aimlessly. His eye suddenly lit on something beside Petrie's blueprint and he picked it up. It was a black grease pencil.

"Maybe this is the best way," he said.

"What?"

"You stay here, Ben. Start turning out stakes. If we're going to do this, it's got to be scientific. You're the production department. Mark and I will be research. We'll go through the town, looking for them. We'll find them, too, just the way we found Mike. I can mark the locations with this grease pencil. Then, tomorrow, the stakes."

"Won't they see the marks and move?"

"I don't think so. Mrs. Glick didn't look as though she was connecting too well. I think they move more on instinct than real thought. They might wise up after a while, start hiding better, but I think at first it would be like shooting fish in a barrel."

"Why don't I go?"

"Because I know the town, and the town knows me—like they knew my father. The live ones in the Lot are hiding in their houses today. If you come knocking, they won't answer. If I come, most of them will. I know some of the hiding places. I know where the winos shack up out in the Marshes and where the pulp roads go. You don't. Can you run that lathe?"

"Yes," Ben said.

Jimmy was right, of course. Yet the relief he felt at not having to go out and face *them* made him feel guilty.

"Okay. Get going. It's after noon now."

Ben turned to the lathe, then paused. "If you want to wait a half hour, I can give you maybe half a dozen stakes to take with you."

Jimmy paused a moment, then dropped his eyes. "Uh, I think tomorrow . . . tomorrow would be . . ."

"Okay," Ben said. "Go on. Listen, why don't you come back around three? Things ought to be quiet enough around that school by then so we can check it out."

"Good."

Jimmy stepped away from Petrie's shop area and started for the stairs. Something—a half thought or perhaps inspiration—made him turn. He saw Ben across the basement, working under the bright glare of those three lights, hung neatly in a row.

Something . . . and it was gone.

He walked back.

Ben shut off the lathe and looked at him. "Something else?"

"Yeah," Jimmy said. "On the tip of my tongue. But it's stuck there."

Ben raised his eyebrows.

"When I looked back from the stairs and saw you, something clicked. It's gone now."

"Important?"

"I don't know." He shuffled his feet purposelessly, wanting it to come back. Something about the image Ben had made, standing under those work lights, bent over the lathe. No good. Thinking about it only made it seem more distant.

He went up the stairs, but paused once more to look back. The image was hauntingly familiar, but it wouldn't come. He went through the kitchen and out to the car. The rain had faded to drizzle.

37

Roy McDougall's car was standing in the driveway of the trailer lot on the Bend Road, and seeing it there on a weekday made Jimmy suspect the worst.

He and Mark got out, Jimmy carrying his black bag. They mounted the steps and Jimmy tried the bell. It didn't work and so he knocked instead. The pounding roused no one in the McDougall trailer or in the neighboring one twenty yards down the road. There was a car in that driveway, too.

Jimmy tried the storm door and it was locked. "There's a hammer in the back seat of the car," he said.

Mark got it, and Jimmy smashed the glass of the storm door beside the knob. He reached through and unsnapped the catch. The inside door was unlocked. They went in.

The smell was definable instantly, and Jimmy felt his nostrils cringe against it and try to shut it out. The smell was not as strong as it had been in the basement of the Marsten House, but it was just as basically offensive—the smell of rot and deadness. A wet, putrified stink. Jimmy found himself remembering when, as boys, he and his buddies had gone out on their bikes during spring vacation to pick up the returnable beer and soft-drink bottles the retreating snows had uncovered. In one of those (an Orange Crush bottle) he saw a small, decayed field mouse which had been attracted by the sweetness and had then been unable to get out. He had gotten a whiff of it and had immediately turned away and thrown up. This smell was plangently like that—sickish sweet and decayed sour, mixed together and fermenting wildly. He felt his gorge rise.

"They're here," Mark said. "Somewhere."

They went through the place methodically—kitchen, dining nook, living room, the two bedrooms. They opened closets as they went. Jimmy thought they had found something in the master bedroom closet, but it was only a heap of dirty clothes.

"No cellar?" Mark asked.

"No, but there might be a crawl space."

They went around to the back and saw a small door that swung inward, set into the trailer's cheap concrete foundation. It was fastened with an old padlock. Jimmy knocked it off with five hard blows of the hammer, and when he pushed the half-trap open, the smell hit them in a ripe wave.

"There they are," Mark said.

Peering in, Jimmy could see three sets of feet, like corpses lined up on a battlefield. One set wore work boots, one wore knitted bedroom slippers, and the third set—tiny feet indeed—were bare.

Family scene, Jimmy thought crazily. *Reader's Digest,* where are you when we need you? Unreality washed over him. The baby, he thought. How are we supposed to do that to a little baby?

He made a mark with the black grease pencil on the trap and picked up the broken padlock. "Let's go next door," he said.

"Wait," Mark said. "Let me pull one of them out."

"Pull . . . ? Why?"

"Maybe the daylight will kill them," Mark said. "Maybe we won't have to do that with the stakes."

Jimmy felt hope. "Yeah, okay. Which one?"

"Not the baby," Mark said instantly. "The man. You catch one foot."

"All right," Jimmy said. His mouth had gone cotton-dry, and when he swallowed there was a click in his throat.

Mark wriggled in on his stomach, the dead leaves that had drifted in crackling under his weight. He seized one of Roy McDougall's workboots and pulled. Jimmy squirmed in beside him, scraping his back on the low overhang, fighting claustrophobia. He got hold of the other boot and together they pulled him out into the lessening drizzle and white light.

What followed was almost unbearable. Roy McDougall began to writhe as soon as the light struck him full, like a man who has been disturbed in sleep. Steam and moisture came from his pores, and the skin underwent a slight sagging and yellowing. Eyeballs rolled behind the thin skin of his closed lids. His feet kicked slowly and dreamily in the wet leaves. His upper lip curled back, showing upper incisors like those of a large dog—a German shepherd or a collie. His arms thrashed slowly, the hands clenching and unclenching, and when one of them brushed Mark's shirt, he jerked back with a disgusted cry.

Roy turned over and began to hunch slowly back into the crawl space, arms and knees and face digging grooves in the rain-softened humus. Jimmy noted that a hitching, Cheyne-Stokes type of respiration had begun as soon as the light struck the body; it stopped as soon as McDougall was wholly in shadow again. So did the moisture extrusion.

When he had reached his previous resting place, McDougall turned over and lay still.

"Shut it," Mark said in a strangled voice. "Please shut it."

Jimmy closed the trap and replaced the hammered lock as well as he could. The image of McDougall's body, struggling in the wet, rotted leaves like a dazed snake, remained in his mind. He did not think there would ever be a time when it was not within hand's reach of his memory—even if he lived to be a hundred.

38

They stood in the rain, trembling, looking at each other. "Next door?" Mark asked.

"Yes. They'd be the logical ones for the McDougalls to attack first."

They went across, and this time their nostrils picked up the telltale odor of rot in the dooryard. The name below the doorbell was Evans. Jimmy nodded. David Evans and family. He worked as a mechanic in the auto department of Sears in Gates Falls. He had treated him a couple of years ago, for a cyst or something.

This time the bell worked, but there was no response. They found Mrs. Evans in bed. The two children were in a bunk bed in a single bedroom, dressed in identical pajamas that featured characters from the Pooh stories. It took longer to find Dave Evans. He had hidden himself away in the unfinished storage space over the small garage.

Jimmy marked a check inside a circle on the front door and the garage door. "We're doing good," he said. "Two for two."

Mark said diffidently, "Could you hold on a minute or two? I'd like to wash my hands."

"Sure," Jimmy said. "I'd like that, too. The Evanses won't mind if we use their bathroom."

They went inside, and Jimmy sat down in one of the living room chairs and closed his eyes. Soon he heard Mark running water in the bathroom.

On the darkened screen of his eyes he saw the mortician's table, saw the sheet covering Marjorie Glick's body start to tremble, saw her hand fall out and begin its delicate toe dance on the air—

He opened his eyes.

This trailer was in nicer condition than the McDougalls', neater, taken care of. He had never met Mrs. Evans, but it seemed she must have taken pride in her home. There was a neat pile of the dead children's toys in a small storage room, a room that had probably been called the laundry room in the mobile home dealer's original brochure. Poor kids, he hoped they'd enjoyed the toys while there had still been bright days and sunshine to enjoy them in. There was a tricycle, several large plastic trucks and a play gas station, one of those caterpillars on wheels (there must have been some dandy fights over that), a toy pool table.

He started to look away and then looked back, startled.

Blue chalk.

Three shaded lights in a row.

Men walking around the green table under the bright lights, cueing up, brushing the grains of blue chalk off their fingertips—

"Mark!" he shouted, sitting bolt upright in the chair. *"Mark!"* And Mark came running with his shirt off, to see what the matter was.

39

An old student of Matt's (class of '64, A's in literature, C's in composition) had dropped by to see him around two-thirty, had commented on the stacks of arcane literature, and had asked Matt if he was studying for a degree in the occult. Matt couldn't remember if his name was Herbert or Harold.

Matt, who had been reading a book called *Strange Disappearances* when Herbert-or-Harold walked in, welcomed the interruption. He was waiting for the phone to ring even now, although he knew the others could not safely enter the Brock Street School until after three o'clock. He was desperate to know what had happened to Father Callahan. And the day seemed to be passing with alarming rapidity—he had always heard that time passed slowly in the hospital. He felt slow and foggy, an old man at last.

He began telling Herbert-or-Harold about the town of Momson, Vermont, whose history he had just been reading. He had found it particularly interesting because he thought the story, if true, might be a precursor of the Lot's fate.

"Everyone disappeared," he told Herbert-or-Harold, who was listening with polite but not very well masked boredom. "Just a small town in the upcountry of northern Vermont, accessible by Interstate Route 2 and Vermont Route 19. Population of 312 in the census of 1920. In August of 1923 a woman in New York got worried because her sister hadn't written her for two months. She and her husband took a ride out there, and they were the first to break the story to the newspapers, although I don't doubt that the locals in the surrounding area had known about the disappearance for some time. The sister and her husband were gone, all right, and so was everyone else in Momson. The houses and the barns were all standing, and in one place supper had been put on the table. The case was rather sensational at the time. I don't believe that I would care to stay there overnight. The author of this book claims the people in the neighboring townships tell some odd stories . . . ha'ants and goblins and all that. Several of the outlying barns have hex signs and large crosses painted on them, even to this day. Look, here's a photograph of the general store and ethyl station and feed-and-grain store—what served in Momson as downtown. What do you suppose ever happened there?"

Herbert-or-Harold looked at the picture politely. Just a little town with a few stores and a few houses. Some of them were falling down, probably from the weight of snow in the winter. Could be any town in the country. Driving through most of them, you wouldn't know if anyone was alive after eight o'clock when they rolled up the sidewalks. The old man had certainly gone dotty in his old age. Herbert-or-Harold thought about an old aunt of his who had become convinced in the last two years of her life that her daughter had killed her pet parakeet and was feeding it to her in the meat loaf. Old people got funny ideas.

"Very interesting," he said, looking up. "But I don't think . . . Mr. Burke? Mr. Burke, is something wrong? Are you . . . nurse! Hey, *nurse!*"

Matt's eyes had grown very fixed. One hand gripped the top sheet of the bed. The other was pressed against his chest. His face had gone pallid, and a pulse beat in the center of his forehead.

Too soon, he thought. *No, too soon—*

Pain, smashing into him in waves, driving him down into darkness. Dimly he thought: *Watch that last step, it's a killer.*

Then, falling.

Herbert-or-Harold ran out of the room, knocking over his chair and spilling a pile of books. The nurse was already coming, nearly running herself.

"It's Mr. Burke," Herbert-or-Harold told her. He was still holding the book, with his index finger inserted at the picture of Momson, Vermont.

The nurse nodded curtly and entered the room. Matt was lying with his head half off the bed, his eyes closed.

"Is he—?" Herbert-or-Harold asked timidly. It was a complete question.

"Yes, I think so," the nurse answered, at the same time pushing the button that would summon the ECV unit. "You'll have to leave now."

She was calm again now that all was known, and had time to regret her lunch, left half-eaten.

40

"But there's no pool hall in the Lot," Mark said. "The closest one is over in Gates Falls. Would he go there?"

"No," Jimmy said. "I'm sure he wouldn't. But some people have pool tables or billiard tables in their houses."

"Yes, I know that."

"There's something else," Jimmy said. "I can almost get it."

He leaned back, closed his eyes, and put his hands over them. There was something else, and in his mind he associated it with plastic. Why plastic? There were plastic toys and plastic utensils for picnics and plastic drop covers to put over your boat when winter came—

And suddenly a picture of a pool table draped in a large plastic dust cover formed in his mind, complete with sound track, a voice-over that was saying, *I really ought to sell it before the felt gets mildew or something—Ed Craig says it might mildew—but it was Ralph's* . . .

He opened his eyes. "I know where he is," he said. "I know where Barlow is. He's in the basement of Eva Miller's boardinghouse." And it was true; he knew it was. It felt incontrovertibly right in his mind.

Mark's eyes flashed brilliantly. "Let's go get him."

"Wait."

He went to the phone, found Eva's number in the book, and dialed it swiftly. It rang with no answer. Ten rings, eleven, a dozen. He put it back in its cradle, frightened. There had been at least ten roomers at Eva's, many of them old men, retired. There was always someone around. Always before this.

He looked at his watch. It was quarter after three and time was racing, racing.

"Let's go," he said.

"What about Ben?"

Jimmy said grimly, "We can't call. The line's out at your house. If we go straight to Eva's, there'll be plenty of daylight left if we're wrong. If we're right, we'll come back and get Ben and stop his fucking clock."

"Let me put my shirt on again," Mark said, and ran down the hall to the bathroom.

41

Ben's Citroën was still sitting in Eva's parking lot, now plastered with wet leaves from the elms that shaded the square of gravel. The wind had picked up but the rain had stopped. The sign that said "Eva's Rooms" swung and squeaked in the gray afternoon. The house had an eerie silence about it, a waiting quality, and Jimmy made a mental connection and was chilled by it. It was just like the Marsten House. He wondered if anyone had ever committed suicide here. Eva would know, but he didn't think Eva would be talking . . . not anymore.

"It would be perfect," he said aloud. "Take up residence in the local boardinghouse and then surround yourself with your children."

"Are you sure we shouldn't get Ben?"

"Later. Come on."

They got out of the car and walked toward the porch. The wind pulled at their clothes, riffled their hair. All the shades were drawn, and the house seemed to brood over them.

"Can you smell it?" Jimmy asked.

"Yes. Thicker than ever."

"Are you up to this?"

"Yes," Mark said firmly. "Are you?"

"I hope to Christ I am," Jimmy said.

They went up the porch steps and Jimmy tried the door. It was unlocked. When they stepped into Eva Miller's compulsively neat big kitchen, the odor smote them both, like an open garbage pit—yet dry, as with the smoke of years.

Jimmy remembered his conversation with Eva—it had been almost four years ago, just after he had begun practicing. Eva had come in for a check-up. His father had had her for a patient for years, and when Jimmy took his place, even running things out of the same Cumberland office, she had come to him without embarrassment. They had spoken of Ralph, dead twelve years even then, and she had told him that Ralph's ghost was still in the house—every now and then she would turn up something new and temporarily forgotten in the attic or a bureau drawer. And of course there was the pool table in the basement. She said that she really ought to get rid of it; it was just taking up space she could use for something else. But it had been Ralph's, and she just couldn't bring herself to take out an ad in the paper or call up the local radio "Yankee Trader" program.

Now they walked across the kitchen to the cellar door, and Jimmy opened it. The stench was thick, nearly overpowering. He thumbed the light switch but got no response. He would have broken that, of course.

"Look around," he told Mark. "She's got to have a flashlight, or candles."

Mark began nosing around, pulling open drawers and looking into them. He noticed that the knife rack over the sink was empty, but thought nothing of it at the time. His heart was thudding with painful slowness, like a muffled drum. He recognized the fact that he was now on the far, ragged edges of his endurance, at the outer limits. His mind did not seem to be thinking, but only reacting. He kept seeing movement at the corners of his eyes and jerking his head around to look, seeing nothing. A war veteran might have recognized the symptoms which signaled the onset of battle fatigue.

He went out into the hall and looked through the dresser

there. In the third drawer he found a long four-cell flashlight. He took it back to the kitchen. "Here it is, J—"

There was a rattling noise, followed by a heavy thump.

The cellar door stood open.

And the screams began.

42

When Mark stepped back into the kitchen of Eva's Rooms, it was twenty minutes of five. His eyes were hollow, and his T-shirt was smeared with blood. His eyes were stunned and slow.

Suddenly he shrieked.

The sound came roaring out of his belly, up the dark passage of his throat, and through his distended jaws. He shrieked until he felt some of the madness begin to leave his brain. He shrieked until his throat cracked and an awful pain lodged in his vocal cords like a sliver of bone. And even when he had externalized all the fear, the horror, the rage, the disappointment that he could, that awful pressure remained, coming up out of the cellar in waves—the knowledge of Barlow's presence somewhere down there—and now it was close to dark.

He went outside onto the porch and breathed great gasps of the windy air. Ben. He had to get Ben. But an odd sort of lethargy seemed to have wrapped his legs in lead. What was the use? Barlow was going to win. They had been crazy to go against him. And now Jimmy had paid the full price, as well as Susan and the Father.

The steel in him came up. *No. No. No.*

He went down the porch steps on trembling legs and got into Jimmy's Buick. The keys hung in the ignition.

Get Ben. Try once more.

His legs were too short to reach the pedals. He pulled the seat up and twisted the key. The engine roared. He put the gearshift lever in drive and put his foot on the gas. The car leaped forward. He slammed his foot down on the power brake and was thrown painfully into the steering wheel. The horn honked.

I can't drive it!

And he seemed to hear his father saying in his logical, pedantic voice: You must be careful when you learn to drive, Mark. Driving is the only means of transportation that is not fully regulated by federal law. As a result, all the operators are amateurs. Many of these amateurs are suicidal. Therefore, you must be *extremely* careful. You use the gas pedal like there was an egg between it and your foot. When you're driving a car with an automatic transmission, like ours, the left foot is not used at all. Only the right is used; first brake and then gas.

He let his foot off the brake and the car crawled forward down the driveway. It bumped over the curb and he brought it to a jerky stop. The windshield had fogged up. He rubbed it with his arm and only smeared it more.

"Screw it," he muttered.

He started up jerkily and performed a wide, drunken U-turn, driving over the far curb in the process, and set off for his house. He had to crane his neck to see over the steering wheel. He fumbled out with his right hand and turned on the radio and played it loud. He was crying.

43

Ben was walking down Jointner Avenue toward town when Jimmy's tan Buick came up the road, moving in jerks and spasms, weaving drunkenly. He waved at it and it pulled over, bounced the left front wheel over the curb, and came to a stop.

He had lost track of time making the stakes, and when he looked at his watch, he had been startled to see that it was nearly ten minutes past four. He had shut down the lathe, taken a couple of the stakes, put them in his belt, and gone upstairs to use the telephone. He had only put his hand on it when he remembered it was out.

Badly worried now, he ran outside and looked in both cars, Callahan's and Petrie's. No keys in either. He could have gone back and searched Henry Petrie's pockets, but the thought was too much. He had set off for town at a fast walk, keeping an eye peeled for Jimmy's Buick. He had been intending to go straight to the Brock Street School when Jimmy's car came into sight.

He ran around to the driver's seat and Mark Petrie was sitting behind the wheel . . . alone. He looked at Ben numbly. His lips worked but no sound came out.

"What's the matter? Where's Jimmy?"

"Jimmy's dead," Mark said woodenly. "Barlow thought ahead of us again. He's in the basement of Mrs. Miller's boardinghouse somewhere. Jimmy's there, too. I went down to help him and I couldn't get back out. Finally I got a board that I could crawl up, but at first I thought I was going to be trapped down there . . . until s-s-sunset. . . ."

"What happened? What are you talking about?"

"Jimmy figured out the blue chalk, you see? While we were at a house in the Bend. Blue chalk. Pool tables. There's a pool table in the cellar at Mrs. Miller's, it belonged to her husband. Jimmy called the boardinghouse and there was no answer so we drove over."

He lifted his tearless face to Ben's.

"He told me to look around for a flashlight because the cellar light switch was broken, just like at the Marsten House. So I started to look around. I . . . I noticed that all the knives in the rack over the sink were gone, but I didn't think anything of it. So in a way I killed him. I did it. It's my fault, all my fault, all my—"

Ben shook him: two brisk snaps. "Stop it, Mark. Stop it!"

Mark put his hands to his mouth, as if to catch the hysterical babble before it could flow out. His eyes stared hugely at Ben over his hands.

At last he went on: "I found a flashlight in the hall dresser, see. And that was when Jimmy fell, and he started to scream. He—I would have fallen, too, but he warned me. The last thing he said was *Look out, Mark.*"

"What was it?" Ben demanded.

"Barlow and the others just took the stairs away," Mark said in a dead, listless voice. "Sawed the stairs off after the second one going down. They left a little more of the railing so it looked like . . . looked like . . ." He shook his head. "In the dark, Jimmy just thought they were there. You see?"

"Yes," Ben said. He saw. It made him feel sick. "And the knives?"

"Set all around on the floor underneath," Mark whispered. "*They* pounded the blades through these thin plywood squares and then knocked off the handles so they would sit flat with the blades pointing . . . pointing."

"Oh," Ben said helplessly. "Oh, Christ." He reached down and took Mark by the shoulders. "Are you sure he's dead, Mark?"

"Yes. He . . . he was stuck in half a dozen places. The blood . . ."

Ben looked at his watch. It was ten minutes of five. Again he had that feeling of being crowded, of running out of time.

"What are we going to do now?" Mark asked remotely.

"Go into town. Talk to Matt on the phone and then talk to Parkins Gillespie. We'll finish Barlow before dark. We've got to."

Mark smiled a small, morbid smile. "Jimmy said that, too. He said we were going to stop his clock. But he keeps beating us. Better guys than us must have tried, too."

Ben looked down at the boy and got ready to do something nasty.

"You sound scared," he said.

"I *am* scared," Mark said, not rising to it. "Aren't you?"

"I'm scared," Ben said, "but I'm mad, too. I lost a girl I liked one hell of a lot. I loved her, I guess. We both lost Jimmy. You lost your mother and father. They're lying in your living room under a dust cover from your sofa." He pushed himself to a final brutality. "Want to go back and look?"

Mark winced away from him, his face horrified and hurting.

"I want you with me," Ben said more softly. He felt a germ of self-disgust in his stomach. He sounded like a football coach before the big game. "I don't care who's tried to stop him before. I don't care if Attila the Hun played him and lost. I'm going to have my shot. I want you with me. I need you." And that was the truth, pure and naked.

"Okay," Mark said. He looked down into his lap, and his hands found each other and entwined in distraught pantomime.

"Dig your feet in," Ben said.

Mark looked at him hopelessly. "I'm trying," he said.

44

Sonny's Exxon station on outer Jointner Avenue was open and Sonny James (who exploited his country-music namesake with a huge color poster in the window beside a pyramid of oil cans) came out to wait on them himself. He was a small, gnomelike man whose receding hair was lawn-mowered into a perpetual crew cut that showed his pink scalp.

"Hey there, Mr. Mears, howya doin'? Where's your Citrowan?"

"Laid up, Sonny. Where's Pete?" Pete Cook was Sonny's part-time help, and lived in town. Sonny did not.

"Never showed up today. Don't matter. Things been slow, anyway. Town seems downright dead."

Ben felt dark, hysterical laughter in his belly. It threatened to boil out of his mouth in a great and rancid wave.

"Want to fill it up?" he managed. "Want to use your phone."

"Sure. Hi, kid. No school today?"

"I'm on a field trip with Mr. Mears," Mark said. "I had a bloody nose."

"I guess to God you did. My brother used to get 'em. They're a sign of high blood pressure, boy. You want to watch out." He strolled to the back of Jimmy's car and took off the gas cap.

Ben went inside and dialed the pay phone beside the rack of New England road maps.

"Cumberland Hospital, which department?"

"I'd like to speak with Mr. Burke, please. Room 402."

There was an uncharacteristic hesitation, and Ben was about to ask if the room had been changed when the voice said:

"Who is this, please?"

"Benjaman Mears." The possibility of Matt's death suddenly loomed up in his mind like a long shadow. Could that be? Surely not—that would be too much. "Is he all right?"

"Are you a relative?"

"No, a close friend. He isn't—"

"Mr. Burke died at 3:07 this afternoon, Mr. Mears. If you'd like to hold for just a minute, I'll see if Dr. Cody has come in yet. Perhaps he could . . ."

The voice went on but Ben had ceased hearing it, although the receiver was still glued to his ear. The realization of how much he had been depending on Matt to get them through the rest of this nightmare afternoon crashed home with sickening weight. Matt was dead. Congestive heart failure. Natural causes. It was as if God Himself had turned His face away from them.

Just Mark and I now.

Susan, Jimmy, Father Callahan, Matt. All gone.

Panic seized him and he grappled with it silently.

He put the receiver back into its cradle without thinking about it, guillotining a question half-asked.

He walked back outside. It was ten after five. In the west the clouds were breaking up.

"Comes to just three dollars even," Sonny told him brightly. "That's Doc Cody's car, ain't it? I see them M.D. plates and it always makes me think of this movie I seen, this story about a bunch of crooks and one of them would always steal cars with M.D. plates because—"

Ben gave him three one-dollar bills. "I've got to split, Sonny. Sorry. I've got trouble."

Sonny's face crinkled up. "Gee, I'm sorry to hear that, Mr. Mears. Bad news from your editor?"

"I guess you could say that." He got behind the wheel, shut the door, pulled out, and left Sonny looking after him in his yellow foul-weather slicker.

"Matt's dead, isn't he?" Mark asked, watching him.

"Yes. Heart attack. How did you know?"

"Your face. I saw your face."

It was 5:15.

45

Parkins Gillespie was standing on the small covered porch of the Municipal Building, smoking a Pall Mall and looking out at the western sky. He turned his attention to Ben Mears and Mark Petrie reluctantly. His face looked sad and old, like the glasses of water they bring you in cheap diners.

"How are you, Constable?" Ben asked.

"Tolerable," Parkins allowed. He considered a hangnail on the leathery arc of skin that bordered his thumbnail. "Seen you truckin' back and forth. Looked like the kid was drivin' up from Railroad Street by hisself this last time. That so?"

"Yes," Mark said.

"Almost got clipped. Fella goin' the other way missed you by a whore's hair."

"Constable," Ben said, "we want to tell you what's been happening around here."

Parkins Gillespie spat out the stub of his cigarette without raising his hands from the rail of the small covered porch. Without looking at either of them, he said calmly, "I don't want to hear it."

They looked at him dumbfounded.

"Nolly didn't show up today," Parkins said, still in that calm, conversational voice. "Somehow don't think he will. He called in late last night and said he'd seen Homer McCaslin's car out on the Deep Cut Road—I think it was the Deep Cut he said. He never called back in." Slowly, sadly, like a man under water, he dipped into his shirt pocket and reached another Pall Mall out of it. He rolled it reflectively between his thumb and finger. "These fucking things are going to be the death of me," he said.

Ben tried again. "The man who took the Marsten House, Gillespie. His name is Barlow. He's in the basement of Eva Miller's boardinghouse right now."

"That so?" Parkins said with no particular surprise. "Vampire, ain't he? Just like in all the comic books they used to put out twenty years ago."

Ben said nothing. He felt more and more like a man lost in a great and grinding nightmare where clockwork ran on and on endlessly, unseen, but just below the surface of things.

"I'm leavin' town," Parkins said. "Got my stuff all packed up in the back of the car. I left my gun and the bubble and my badge in on the shelf. I'm done with lawin'. Goin' t'see my sister in Kittery, I am. Figure that's far enough to be safe."

Ben heard himself say remotely, "You gutless creep. You cowardly piece of shit. This town is still alive and you're running out on it."

"It ain't alive," Parkins said, lighting his smoke with a wooden kitchen match. "That's why *he* came here. It's dead, like him.

Has been for twenty years or more. Whole country's goin' the same way. Me and Nolly went to a drive-in show up in Falmouth a couple of weeks ago, just before they closed her down for the season. I seen more blood and killin's in that first Western than I seen both years in Korea. Kids was eatin' popcorn and cheerin' 'em on." He gestured vaguely at the town, now lying unnaturally gilded in the broken rays of the westering sun, like a dream village. "They prob'ly like bein' vampires. But not me; Nolly'd be in after me tonight. I'm goin'."

Ben looked at him helplessly.

"You two fellas want to get in that car and hit it out of here," Parkins said. "This town will go on without us . . . for a while. Then it won't matter."

Yes, Ben thought. *Why don't we do that?*

Mark spoke the reason for both of them. "Because he's bad, mister. He's really bad. That's all."

"Is that so?" Parkins said. He nodded and puffed his Pall Mall. "Well, okay." He looked up toward the Consolidated High School. "Piss-poor attendance today, from the Lot, anyway. Buses runnin' late, kids out sick, office phonin' houses and not gettin' any answer. The attendance officer called me, and I soothed him some. He's a funny little bald-headed fella who thinks he knows what he's doing. Well, the teachers are there, anyway. They come from out of town, mostly. They can teach each other."

Thinking of Matt, Ben said, "Not all of them are from out of town."

"It don't matter," Parkins said. His eyes dropped to the stakes in Ben's belt. "You going to try to do that fella up with one of those?"

"Yes."

"You can have my riot gun if you want it. That gun, it was Nolly's idear. Nolly liked to go armed, he did. Not even a bank in town so's he could hope someone would rob it. He'll make a good vampire though, once he gets the hang of it."

Mark was looking at him with rising horror, and Ben knew he had to get him away. This was the worst of all.

"Come on," he said to Mark. "He's done."

"I guess that's it," Parkins said. His pale, crinkle-caught eyes surveyed the town. "Surely is quiet. I seen Mabel Werts, peekin' out with her glasses, but I don't guess there's much to peek at, today. There'll be more tonight, likely."

They went back to the car. It was almost 5:30.

46

They pulled up in front of St. Andrew's at quarter of six. Lengthening shadows fell from the church across the street to the rectory, covering it like a prophecy. Ben pulled Jimmy's bag out of the back seat and dumped it out. He found several small ampoules, and dumped their contents out the window, saving the bottles.

"What are you doing?"

"We're going to put holy water in these," Ben said. "Come on."

They went up the walk to the church and climbed the steps. Mark, about to open the middle door, paused and pointed. "Look at that."

The handle was blackened and pulled slightly out of shape, as if a heavy electric charge had been pushed through it.

"Does that mean anything to you?" Ben asked.

"No. No, but ..." Mark shook his head, pushing an unformed thought away. He opened the door and they went in. The church was cool and gray and filled with the endless pregnant pause that all empty altars of faith, white and black, have in common.

The two ranks of pews were split by a wide central aisle, and flanking this, two plaster angels stood cradling bowls of holy water, their calm and sweetly knowing faces bent, as if to catch their own reflections in the still water.

Ben put the ampoules in his pocket. "Bathe your face and hands," he said.

Mark looked at him, troubled. "That's sac—sacri—"

"Sacrilege? Not this time. Go ahead."

They dunked their hands in the still water and then splashed it over their faces, the way a man who has just wakened will splash cold water into his eyes to shock the world back into them.

Ben took the first ampoule out of his pocket and was filling it when a shrill voice cried, "Here! Here now! What are you doing?"

Ben turned around. It was Rhoda Curless, Father Callahan's housekeeper, who had been sitting in the first pew and twisting a rosary helplessly between her fingers. She was wearing a black dress, and her slip hung below the hem. Her hair was in disarray; she had been pulling her fingers through it.

"Where's the Father? What are you doing?" Her voice was reedy and thin, close to hysteria.

"Who are you?" Ben asked.

"Mrs. Curless. I'm Father Callahan's housekeeper. Where's the Father? What are you doing?" Her hands came together and began to war with each other.

"Father Callahan is gone," Ben said, as gently as he could.

"Oh." She closed her eyes. "Was he getting after whatever ails this town?"

"Yes," Ben said.

"I knew it," she said. "I didn't have to ask. He's a strong, good man of the cloth. There were always those who said he'd never be man enough to fill Father Bergeron's shoes, but he filled 'em. They were too small for him, as it turned out."

She opened her eyes wide and looked at them. A tear spilled from her left, and ran down her cheek. "He won't be back, will he?"

"I don't know," Ben said.

"They talked about his drinkin'," she said, as though she hadn't heard. "Was there ever an Irish priest worth his keep who didn't tip the bottle? None of that mollycoddlin' wet-nursin' church-bingo-prayer-basket for him. He was more'n that!" Her voice rose toward the vaulted ceiling in a hoarse, almost challenging cry. "He was a *priest*, not some holy alderman!"

Ben and Mark listened without speech or surprise. There was no surprise left on this dream-struck day; there was not even the capacity for it. They no longer saw themselves as doers or avengers or saviors; the day had absorbed them. Helplessly, they were only living.

"Was he strong when last you saw him?" she demanded, peering at them. The tears magnified the gimlet lack of compromise in her eyes.

"Yes," Mark said, remembering Callahan in his mother's kitchen, holding his cross aloft.

"And are you about his work now?"

"Yes," Mark said again.

"Then be about it," she snapped at them. "What are you waiting for?" And she left them, walking down the center aisle in her black dress, the solitary mourner at a funeral that hadn't been held here.

47

Eva's again—and at the last. It was ten minutes after six. The sun hung over the western pines, peering out of the broken clouds like blood.

Ben drove into the parking lot and looked curiously up at his room. The shade was not drawn and he could see his typewriter standing sentinel, and beside it, his pile of manuscript and the glass globe paperweight on top of it. It seemed amazing that he could see all those things from here, see them clearly, as if everything in the world was sane and normal and ordered.

He let his eyes drop to the back porch. The rocking chairs where he and Susan had shared their first kiss stood side by side, unchanged. The door which gave ingress to the kitchen stood open, as Mark had left it.

"I can't," Mark muttered. "I just can't." His eyes were wide and white. He had drawn up his knees and was now crouched on the seat.

"It's got to be both of us," Ben said. He held out two of the ampoules filled with holy water. Mark twitched away from them in horror, as if touching them would admit poison through his skin. "Come on," Ben said. He had no arguments left. "Come on, come on."

"No."

"Mark?"

"No!"

"Mark, I need you. You and me, that's all that's left."

"I've done enough!" Mark cried. "I can't do any more! *Can't you understand I can't look at him?*"

"Mark, it has to be the two of us. Don't you know that?"

Mark took the ampoules and curled them slowly against his chest. "Oh boy," he whispered. "Oh boy, oh boy." He looked at Ben and nodded. The movement of his head was jerky and agonized. "Okay," he said.

"Where's the hammer?" he asked as they got out.

"Jimmy had it."

"Okay."

They walked up the porch steps in the strengthening wind. The sun glared red through the clouds, dyeing everything. Inside, in the kitchen, the stink of death was palpable and wet, pressing against them like granite. The cellar door stood open.

"I'm so scared," Mark said, shuddering.

"You better be. Where's that flashlight?"

"In the cellar. I left it when . . ."

"Okay." They stood at the mouth of the cellar. As Mark had said, the stairs looked intact in the sunset light. "Follow me," Ben said.

48

Ben thought quite easily: *I'm going to my death.*

The thought came naturally, and there was no fear or regret in it. Inward-turning emotions were lost under the overwhelming atmosphere of evil that hung over this place. As he slipped and scraped his way down the board Mark had set up to get out of the cellar, all he felt was an unnatural glacial calm. He saw that his hands were glowing, as if wreathed in ghost gloves. It did not surprise him.

Let be be finale of seem. The only emperor is the emperor of ice cream. Who had said that? Matt? Matt was dead. Susan was dead. Miranda was dead. Wallace Stevens was dead, too. *I wouldn't look at that, if I were you.* But he had looked. That's what you looked like when it was over. Like something smashed and broken that had been filled with different-colored fluids. It wasn't so bad. Not so bad as *his* death. Jimmy had been carrying McCaslin's pistol; it would still be in his coat pocket. He would take it, and if sunset came before they could get to Barlow

. . . first the boy, and then himself. Not good, but better than *his* death.

He dropped to the cellar floor and then helped Mark down. The boy's eyes flashed to the dark, curled thing on the floor and then skipped away.

"I can't look at that," he said huskily.

"That's all right."

Mark turned away and Ben knelt down. He swept away a number of the lethal plywood squares, the knife blades thrust through them glittering like dragon's teeth. Gently, then, he turned Jimmy over.

I wouldn't look at that, if I were you.

"Oh, Jimmy," he tried to say, and the words broke open and bled in his throat. He cradled Jimmy in the curve of his left arm and pulled Barlow's blades out of him with his right hand. There were six of them, and Jimmy had bled a great deal.

There was a neatly folded stack of living room drapes on a corner shelf. He took them over to Jimmy and spread them over his body after he had the gun and the flashlight and the hammer.

He stood up and tried the flashlight. The plastic lens cover had cracked, but the bulb still worked. He flashed it around. Nothing. He shone it under the pool table. Bare. Nothing behind the furnace. Racks of preserves, and a wallboard hung with tools. The amputated stairs, pushed over in the far corner so they would be out of sight from the kitchen. They looked like a scaffold leading nowhere.

"Where is he?" Ben muttered. He glanced at his watch, and the hands stood at 6:23. When was sunset? He couldn't remember. Surely no later than 6:55. That gave them a bare half hour.

"Where is he?" he cried out. "I can *feel* him, but where is he?"

"There!" Mark cried, pointing with one glowing hand. "What's that?"

Ben centered the light on it. A Welsh dresser. "It's not big enough," he said to Mark. "And it's flush against the wall."

"Let's look behind it."

Ben shrugged. They crossed the room to the Welsh dresser and each took a side. He felt a trickle of building excitement.

Surely the odor or aura or atmosphere or whatever you wanted to call it was thicker here, more offensive?

Ben glanced up at the open kitchen door. The light was dimmer now. The gold was fading out of it.

"It's too heavy for me," Mark panted.

"Never mind," Ben said. "We're going to tip it over. Get your best hold."

Mark bent over it, his shoulder against the wood. His eyes looked fiercely out of his glowing face. "Okay."

They threw their combined weight against it and the Welsh dresser went over with a bonelike crash as Eva Miller's long-ago wedding china shattered inside.

"I *knew* it!" Mark cried triumphantly.

There was a small door, chest-high, set into the wall where the Welsh dresser had been. A new Yale padlock secured the hasp.

Two hard swings of the hammer convinced him that the lock wasn't going to give. "Jesus Christ," he muttered softly. Frustration welled up bitterly in his throat. To be balked like this at the end, balked by a five-dollar padlock—

No. He would bite through the wood with his teeth if he had to.

He shone the flashlight around, and its beam fell on the neatly hung tool board to the right of the stairs. Hung on two of its steel pegs was an ax with a rubber cover masking its blade.

He ran across, snatched it off the wallboard, and pulled the rubber cover from the blade. He took one of the ampoules from his pocket and dropped it. The holy water ran out on the floor, beginning to glow immediately. He got another one, twisted the small cap off, and doused the blade of the ax. It began to glimmer with eldritch fairy-light. And when he set his hands on the wooden haft, the grip felt incredibly good, incredibly *right*. Power seemed to have welded his flesh into its present grip. He stood holding it for a moment, looking at the shining blade, and some curious impulse made him touch it to his forehead. A hard sense of sureness clasped him, a feeling of inevitable rightness, of *whiteness*. For the first time in weeks he felt he was no longer groping through fogs of belief and unbelief, sparring with a partner whose body was too insubstantial to sustain blows.

Power, humming up his arms like volts.

The blade glowed brighter.

"Do it!" Mark pleaded. "Quick! Please!"

Ben Mears spread his feet, slung the ax back, and brought it down in a gleaming arc that left an after-image on the eye. The blade bit wood with a booming, portentous sound and sunk to the haft. Splinters flew.

He pulled it out, the wood screaming against the steel. He brought it down again . . . again . . . again. He could feel the muscles of his back and arms flexing and meshing, moving with a sureness and a studied heat that they had never known before. Each blow sent chips and splinters flying like shrapnel. On the fifth blow the blade crashed through to emptiness and he began hacking the hole wider with a speed that approached frenzy.

Mark stared at him, amazed. The cold blue fire had crept down the ax handle and spread up his arms until he seemed to be working in a column of fire. His head was twisted to one side, the muscles of his neck corded with strain, one eye open and glaring, the other squeezed shut. The back of his shirt had split between the straining wings of his shoulder blades, and the muscles writhed beneath the skin like ropes. He was a man taken over, possessed, and Mark saw without knowing (or having to know) that the possession was not in the least Christian; the good was more elemental, less refined. It was ore, like something coughed up out of the ground in naked chunks. There was nothing finished about it. It was Force; it was Power; it was whatever moved the greatest wheels of the universe.

The door to Eva Miller's root cellar could not stand before it. The ax began to move at a nearly blinding speed; it became a ripple, a descending arc, a rainbow from over Ben's shoulder to the splintered wood of the final door.

He dealt it a final blow and slung the ax away. He held his hands up before his eyes. They blazed.

He held them out to Mark, and the boy flinched.

"I love you," Ben said.

They clasped hands.

49

The root cellar was small and cell-like, empty except for a few dusty bottles, some crates, and a dusty bushel basket of very old potatoes that were sprouting eyes in every direction—and the bodies. Barlow's coffin stood at the far end, propped up against the wall like a mummy's sarcophagus, and the crest on it blazed coldly in the light they carried with them like St. Elmo's fire.

In front of the coffin, leading up to it like railroad ties, were the bodies of the people Ben had lived with and broken bread with: Eva Miller, and Weasel Craig beside her; Mabe Mullican from the room at the end of the second-floor hall; John Snow, who had been on the county and could barely walk down to the breakfast table with his arthritis; Vinnie Upshaw; Grover Verrill.

They stepped over them and stood by the coffin. Ben glanced down at his watch; it was 6:40.

"We're going to take it out there," he said. "By Jimmy."

"It must weigh a ton," Mark said.

"We can do it." He reached out, almost tentatively, and then grasped the upper right corner of the coffin. The crest glittered like an impassioned eye. The wood was crawlingly unpleasant to the touch, smooth and stonelike with years. There seemed to be no pores in the wood, no small imperfections for the fingers to recognize and mold to. Yet it rocked easily. One hand did it.

He tipped it forward with a small push, feeling the great weight held in check as if by invisible counterweights. Something thumped inside. Ben took the weight of the coffin on one hand.

"Now," he said. "Your end."

Mark lifted and the end of the coffin came up easily. The boy's face filled with pleased amazement. "I think I could do it with one finger."

"You probably could. Things are finally running our way. But we have to be quick."

They carried the coffin through the shattered door. It threatened to stick at its widest point, and Mark lowered his head and shoved. It went through with a wooden scream.

They carried it across to where Jimmy lay, covered with Eva Miller's drapes.

"Here he is, Jimmy," Ben said. "Here the bastard is. Set it down, Mark."

He glanced at his watch again. 6:45. Now the light coming through the kitchen door above them was an ashy gray.

"Now?" Mark asked.

They looked at each other over the coffin.

"Yes," Ben said.

Mark came around and they stood together in front of the coffin's locks and seals. They bent together, and the locks split as they touched them, making a sound like thin, snapping clapboards. They lifted.

Barlow lay before them, his eyes glaring upward.

He was a young man now, his black hair vibrant and lustrous, flowing over the satin pillow at the head of his narrow apartment. His skin glowed with life. The cheeks were as ruddy as wine. His teeth curved out over his full lips, white with strong streaks of yellow, like ivory.

"He—" Mark began, and never finished.

Barlow's red eyes rolled in their sockets, filling with a hideous life and mocking triumph. They locked with Mark's eyes and Mark gaped down into them, his own eyes growing blank and far away.

"Don't look at him!" Ben cried, but it was too late.

He knocked Mark away. The boy whined deep in his throat and suddenly attacked Ben. Taken by surprise, Ben staggered backward. A moment later the boy's hands were in his coat pocket, digging for Homer McCaslin's pistol.

"Mark! Don't—"

But the boy didn't hear. His face was as blank as a washed blackboard. The whining went on and on in his throat, the sound of a very small trapped animal. He had both hands around the pistol. They struggled for it, Ben trying to rip it from the boy's grasp and keep it pointed away from both of them.

"Mark!" he bellowed. "Mark, wake up! For Christ's sake—"

The muzzle jerked down toward his head and the gun went off. He felt the slug pass by his temple. He wrapped his hands around Mark's and kicked out with one foot. Mark staggered backward, and the gun clattered on the floor between them. The boy leaped at it, whining, and Ben punched him in the mouth with all the strength he had. He felt the boy's lips mash back against his teeth and cried out as if he himself had been hit. Mark slipped to his knees, and Ben kicked the gun away. Mark tried to go after it crawling, and Ben hit him again.

With a tired sigh, the boy collapsed.

The strength had left him now, and the sureness. He was only Ben Mears again, and he was afraid.

The square of light in the kitchen doorway had faded to thin purple; his watch said 6:51.

A huge force seemed to be dragging at his head, commanding him to look at the rosy, gorged parasite in the coffin beside him.

Look and see me, puny man. Look upon Barlow, who has passed the centuries as you have passed hours before a fireplace with a book. Look and see the great creature of the night whom you would slay with your miserable little stick. Look upon me, scribbler. I have written in human lives, and blood has been my ink. Look upon me and despair!

Jimmy, I can't do it. It's too late, he's too strong for me—

LOOK AT ME!

It was 6:53.

Mark groaned on the floor. "Mom? Momma, where are you? My head hurts . . . it's dark . . ."

He shall enter my service castratum. . . .

Ben fumbled one of the stakes from his belt and dropped it. He cried out miserably, in utter despair. Outside, the sun had deserted Jerusalem's Lot. Its last rays lingered on the roof of the Marsten House.

He snatched the stake up. But where was the hammer? *Where was the fucking hammer?*

By the root cellar door. He had swung at the padlock with it.

He scrambled across the cellar and picked it up where it lay.

Mark was half sitting, his mouth a bloody gash. He wiped a hand across it and looked dazedly at the blood. "Momma!" he cried. "Where's my mother?"

6:55 now. Light and darkness hung perfectly balanced.

Ben ran back across the darkening cellar, the stake clutched in his left hand, the hammer in his right.

There was a booming, triumphant laugh. Barlow was sitting up in his coffin, those red eyes flashing with hellish triumph. They locked with Ben's, and he felt the will draining away from him.

With a mad, convulsive yell, he raised the stake over his head and brought it down in a whistling arc. Its razored point sheared through Barlow's shirt, and he felt it strike into the flesh beneath.

Barlow screamed. It was an eerie, hurt sound, like the howl of a wolf. The force of the stake slamming home drove him back into the coffin on his back. His hands rose out of it, hooked into claws, waving crazily.

Ben brought the hammer down on the top of the stake, and Barlow screamed again. One of his hands, as cold as the grave, seized Ben's left hand, which was locked around the stake.

Ben wriggled into the coffin, his knees planted on Barlow's knees. He stared down into the hate and pain-driven face.

"Let me GO!" Barlow cried.

"Here it comes, you bastard," Ben sobbed. "Here it is, leech. Here it is for you."

He brought the hammer down again. Blood splashed upward in a cold gush, blinding him momentarily. Barlow's head lashed from side to side on the satin pillow.

"Let me go, you dare not, you dare not, you dare not do this—"

He brought the hammer down again and again. Blood burst from Barlow's nostrils. His body began to jerk in the coffin like a stabbed fish. The hands clawed at Ben's cheeks, pulling long gouges in his skin.

"LET ME GOOOOOOOOOOOOOOOO—"

He brought the hammer down on the stake once more, and the blood that pulsed from Barlow's chest turned black.

Then, dissolution.

It came in the space of two seconds, too fast to ever be believed in the daylight of later years, yet slow enough to recur again and again in nightmares, with awful stop-motion slowness.

The skin yellowed, coarsened, blistered like old sheets of canvas. The eyes faded, filmed white, fell in. The hair went white and fell like a drift of feathers. The body inside the dark suit shriveled and retreated. The mouth widened gapingly as the lips drew back and drew back, meeting the nose and disappearing in an oral ring of jutting teeth. The fingernails went black and peeled off, and then there were only bones, still dressed with rings, clicking and clenching like castanets. Dust puffed through the fibers of the linen shirt. The bald and wrinkled head became a skull. The pants, with nothing to fill them out, fell away to broomsticks clad in black silk. For a moment a hideously animated scarecrow writhed beneath him, and Ben lunged out of the coffin with a strangled cry of horror. But it was impossible to tear the gaze away from Barlow's last metamorphosis; it hypnotized. The fleshless skull whipped from side to side on the satin pillow. The nude jawbone opened in a soundless scream that had no vocal cords to power it. The skeletal fingers danced and clicked on the dark air like marionettes.

Smells struck his nose and then vanished, each in a tight little puff: gas; putrescence, horrid and fleshy; a moldy library smell; acrid dust; then nothing. The twisting, protesting finger bones shredded and flaked away like pencils. The nasal cavity of the skull widened and met the oral cavity. The empty eye sockets widened in a fleshless expression of surprise and horror, met, and were no more. The skull caved in like an ancient Ming vase. The clothes settled flat and became as neutral as dirty laundry.

And still there was no end to its tenacious hold on the world—even the dust billowed and writhed in tiny dust devils within the coffin. And then, suddenly, he felt the passage of something which buffeted past him like a strong wind, making him shudder. At the same instant, every window of Eva Miller's boardinghouse blew outward.

"Look out, Ben!" Mark screamed. "Look out!"

He whirled over on his back and saw them coming out of the root cellar—Eva, Weasel, Mabe, Grover, and the others. Their time was on the world.

Mark's screams echoed in his ears like great fire bells, and he grabbed the boy by the shoulders.

"The holy water!" he yelled into Mark's tormented face. *"They can't touch us!"*

Mark's cries turned to whimpers.

"Go up the board," Ben said. "Go on." He had to turn the boy to face it, and then slap his bottom to make him climb.

When he was sure the boy was going up, he turned back and looked at them, the Undead.

They were standing passively some fifteen feet away, looking at him with a flat hate that was not human.

"You killed the Master," Eva said, and he could almost believe there was grief in her voice. "How could you kill the Master?"

"I'll be back," he told her. "For all of you."

He went up the board, climbing bent over, using his hands. It groaned under his weight, but held. At the top, he spared one glance back down. They were gathered around the coffin now, looking in silently. They reminded him of the people who had gathered around Miranda's body after the accident with the moving van.

He looked around for Mark, and saw him lying by the porch door, on his face.

50

Ben told himself that the boy had just fainted, and nothing more. It might be true. His pulse was strong and regular. He gathered him in his arms and carried him out to the Citroën.

He got behind the wheel and started the engine. As he pulled out onto Railroad Street, delayed reaction struck him like a physical blow, and he had to stifle a scream.

They were in the streets, the walking dead.

Cold and hot, his head full of a wild roaring sound, he turned left on Jointner Avenue and drove out of 'salem's Lot.

Chapter Fifteen
BEN AND MARK

1

Mark woke up a little at a time, letting the Citroën's steady hum bring him back without thought or memory. At last he looked out the window, and fright took him in rough hands. It was dark. The trees at the sides of the road were vague blurs, and the cars that passed them had their parking lights and headlights on. A gagging, inarticulate groan escaped him, and he clawed at his neck for the cross that still hung there.

"Relax," Ben said. "We're out of town. It's twenty miles behind us."

The boy reached over him, almost making him swerve, and locked the driver's side door. Whirling, he locked his own door. Then he crouched slowly down in a ball on his side of the seat. He wished the nothingness would come back. The nothingness was nice. Nice nothingness with no nasty pictures in it.

The steady sound of the Citroën's engine was soothing. *Mmmmmmmmmmm*. Nice. He closed his eyes.

"Mark?"

Safer not to answer.

"Mark, are you all right?"

Mmmmmmmmmmmmmmmmm.

"—mark—"

Far away. That was all right. Nice nothingness came back, and shades of gray swallowed him.

2

Ben checked them into a motel just across the New Hampshire state line, signing the register Ben Cody and Son, scrawling it. Mark walked into the room holding his cross out. His eyes darted from side to side in their sockets like small, trapped beasts. He held the cross until Ben had closed the door, locked it, and hung his own cross from the doorknob. There was a color TV and Ben watched it for a while. Two African nations had gone to war. The President had a cold but it wasn't considered serious. And a man in Los Angeles had gone berserk and shot fourteen people. The weather forecast was for rain—snow flurries in northern Maine.

3

'Salem's Lot slept darkly, and the vampires walked its streets and country roads like a trace memory of evil. Some of them had emerged enough from the shadows of death to have regained some rudimentary cunning. Lawrence Crockett called up Royal Snow and invited him over to the office to play some cribbage. When Royal pulled up front and walked in, Lawrence and his wife fell on him. Glynis Mayberry called Mabel Werts, said she was frightened, and asked if she could come over and spend the evening with her until her husband got back from Waterville. Mabel agreed with almost pitiful relief, and when she opened the door ten minutes later, Glynis was standing there stark naked, her purse over her arm, grinning with huge, ravenous incisors. Mabel had time to scream, but only once. When Delbert Markey stepped out of his deserted tavern just after eight o'clock, Carl Foreman and a grinning Homer McCaslin stepped out of the shadows and said they had come for a drink. Milt Crossen was visited at his store just after closing time by a number of his most faithful customers and oldest cronies. And George Middler visited several of the high school boys who bought things at his store and always had looked at him with a mixture of scorn and knowledge; and his darkest fantasies were satisfied.

Tourists and through-travelers still passed by on Route 12, seeing nothing of the Lot but an Elks billboard and a thirty-five-mile-an-hour speed sign. Outside of town they went back up to sixty and perhaps dismissed it with a single thought: Christ, what a dead little place.

The town kept its secrets, and the Marsten House brooded over it like a ruined king.

4

Ben drove back the next day at dawn, leaving Mark in the motel room. He stopped at a busy hardware store in Westbrook and bought a spade and a pick.

'Salem's Lot lay silent under a dark sky from which rain had not yet begun to fall. Few cars moved on the streets. Spencer's was open but now the Excellent Café was shut up, all the green blinds drawn, the menus removed from the windows, the small daily special chalk board erased clean.

The empty streets made him feel cold in his bones, and an image came to mind, an old rock 'n' roll album with a picture of a transvestite on the front, profile shot against a black back-ground, the strangely masculine face bleeding with rouge and paint; title: "They Only Come Out at Night."

He went to Eva's first, climbed the stairs to the second floor, and pushed the door to his room open. Just the same as he had left it, the bed unmade, an open roll of Life Savers on his desk. There was an empty tin wastebasket under the desk and he pulled it out into the middle of the floor.

He took his manuscript, threw it in, and made a paper spill of the title page. He lit it with his Cricket, and when it flared up he tossed it in on top of the drift of typewritten pages. The flame tasted them, found them good, and began to crawl eagerly over the paper. Corners charred, turned upward, blackened. Whitish smoke began to billow out of the wastebasket, and without thinking about it, he leaned over his desk and opened the window.

His hand found the paperweight—the glass globe that had been with him since his boyhood in his nighted town—grabbed unknowing in a dreamlike visit to a monster's house. Shake it up and watch the snow float down.

He did it now, holding it up before his eyes as he had as a boy, and it did its old, old trick. Through the floating snow you could see a little gingerbread house with a path leading up to it. The gingerbread shutters were closed, but as an imaginative boy (as Mark Petrie was now), you could fancy that one of the shutters was being folded back (as indeed, one of them seemed to be folding back now) by a long white hand, and then a pallid face would be looking out at you, grinning with long teeth, inviting you into this house beyond the world in its slow and endless fantasy-land of false snow, where time was a myth. The face was looking out at him now, pallid and hungry, a face that would never look on daylight or blue skies again.

It was his own face.

He threw the paperweight into the corner and it shattered.

He left without waiting to see what might leak out of it.

5

He went down into the cellar to get Jimmy's body, and that was the hardest trip of all. The coffin lay where it had the night before, empty even of dust. Yet . . . not entirely empty. The stake was in there, and something else. He felt his gorge rise. Teeth. Barlow's teeth—all that was left of him. Ben reached down, picked them up—and they twisted in his hand like tiny white animals, trying to come together and bite.

With a disgusted cry he threw them outward, scattering them.

"God," he whispered, rubbing his hand against his shirt. "Oh, my dear God. Please let that be the end. Let it be the end of him."

6

Somehow he managed to get Jimmy, still bundled up in Eva's drapes, out of the cellar. He tucked the bundle into the trunk of Jimmy's Buick and then drove out to the Petrie house, the pick and shovel resting next to Jimmy's black bag in the back seat. In a wooded clearing behind the Petrie house and close to the babble of Taggart Stream, he spent the rest of the morning and half the afternoon digging a wide grave four feet deep. Into it he put Jimmy's body and the Petries, still wrapped in the sofa dust cover.

He began filling in the grave of these clean ones at two-thirty. He began to shovel faster and faster as the light began its long drain from the cloudy sky. Sweat that was not wholly from exertion condensed on his skin.

The hole was filled in by four. He tamped in the sods as well as he could, and drove back to town with the earth-clotted pick and shovel in the trunk of Jimmy's car. He parked it in front of the Excellent Café, leaving the keys in the ignition.

He paused for a moment, looking around. The deserted business buildings with their false fronts seemed to lean crepitatingly over the street. The rain, which had started around noon, fell softly and slowly, as if in mourning. The little park where he had met Susan Norton was empty and forlorn. The shades of the Municipal Building were drawn. A "Be back soon" sign hung in the window of Larry Crockett's Insurance and Real Estate office with hollow jauntiness. And the only sound was soft rain.

He walked up toward Railroad Street, his heels clicking emptily on the sidewalk. When he got to Eva's, he paused by his car for a moment, looking around for the last time. Nothing moved.

The town was dead. All at once he knew it for sure and true, just as he had known for sure that Miranda was dead when he had seen her shoe lying in the road.

He began to cry.

He was still crying when he drove past the Elks sign, which read: "You are now leaving Jerusalem's Lot, a nice little town. Come again!"

He got on the turnpike. The Marsten House was blotted out by the trees as he went down the feeder ramp. He began to drive south toward Mark, toward his life.

EPILOGUE

Among these decimated villages
Upon this headland naked to the south wind
With the trail of mountains before us,
    hiding you,
Who will reckon up our decision to forget?
Who will accept our offering at this end
    of autumn?

—GEORGE SEFERIS

Now she's eyeless.
The snakes she held once
Eat up her hands.

—GEORGE SEFERIS

1

From a scrapbook kept by Ben Mears (all clippings from the Portland "Press-Herald"):

November 19, 1975 (p. 27).

JERUSALEM'S LOT—The Charles V. Pritchett family, who bought a farm in the Cumberland County town of Jerusalem's Lot only a month ago, are moving out because things keep going bump in the night, according to Charles and Amanda Pritchett, who moved here from Portland. The farm, a local landmark on Schoolyard Hill, was previously owned by Charles Griffen. Griffen's father was the owner of Sunshine Dairy, Inc., which was absorbed by the Slewfoot Dairy Corporation in 1962. Charles Griffen, who sold the farm through a Portland realtor for what Pritchett called "a bargain basement price," could not be reached for comment. Amanda Pritchett first told her husband about the "funny noises" in the hayloft shortly after . . .

January 4, 1976 (p. 1):

JERUSALEM'S LOT—A bizarre car crash occurred last night or early this morning in the small southern Maine town of Jerusalem's Lot. Police theorize from skid marks found near the scene that the car, a late-model sedan, was traveling at an excessive speed when it left the road and struck a Central Maine Power utility pole. The car was a total wreck, but although blood was found on the front seat and the dashboard, no passengers have yet been found. Police say that the car was registered to Mr. Gordon Phillips of Scarborough. According to a neighbor, Phillips and his family had been on their way to see relatives in Yarmouth. Police theorize that Phillips, his wife, and their two children may have wandered off in a daze and become lost. Plans for a search have been . . .

February 14, 1976 (p. 4):

CUMBERLAND—Mrs. Fiona Coggins, a widow who lived alone on the Smith Road in West Cumberland, was reported missing this morning to the Cumberland County sheriff's office by her niece, Mrs. Gertrude Hersey. Mrs. Hersey told police officers that her aunt was a shut-in and is in poor health. Sheriff's deputies are investigating, but claim that at this point it is impossible to say what . . .

February 27, 1976 (p. 6):

FALMOUTH—John Farrington, an elderly farmer and lifelong Falmouth resident, was found dead in his barn early this morning by his son-in-law, Frank Vickery. Vickery said Farrington was lying face down outside a low haymow, a pitchfork near one hand. County Medical Examiner David Rice says Farrington apparently died of a massive hemorrhage, or perhaps internal bleeding . . .

May 20, 1976 (p. 17):

PORTLAND—Cumberland County game wardens have been instructed by the Maine State Wildlife Service to be on the lookout for a wild dog pack that may be running in the Jerusalem's Lot-Cumberland-Falmouth area. During the last month, several sheep have been found dead with their throats and bellies mangled. In some cases, sheep have been disemboweled. Deputy Game Warden Upton Pruitt said, "As you know, this situation has worsened a good deal in southern Maine . . .

May 29, 1976 (p. 1):

JERUSALEM'S LOT—Possible foul play is suspected in the disappearance of the Daniel Holloway family, who had moved into a house on the Taggart Stream Road in this small Cumberland County township recently. Police were alerted by Daniel Holloway's grandfather, who became alarmed at the repeated failure of anyone to answer his telephone calls.

The Holloways and their two children moved onto the Taggart Stream Road in April, and had complained to both friends and relatives of hearing "funny noises" after dark.

Jerusalem's Lot has been at the center of several strange occurrences during the last several months, and a great many families have . . .

June 4, 1976 (p. 2):

CUMBERLAND—Mrs. Elaine Tremont, a widow who owns a small house on the Back Stage Road in the western part of this small Cumberland County village, was admitted to Cumberland Receiving Hospital early this morning with a heart attack. She told a reporter from this paper that she had heard a scratching noise at her bedroom window while she was watching television, and looked up to see a face peering in at her.

"It was grinning," Mrs. Tremont said. "It was horrible. I've never been so frightened in my life. And since that family was killed just a mile away on the Taggart Stream Road, I've been frightened all the time."

Mrs. Tremont referred to the Daniel Holloway family, who disappeared from their Jerusalem's Lot residence some time early last week. Police said the connection was being investigated, but . . .

2

The tall man and the boy arrived in Portland in mid-September and stayed at a local motel for three weeks. They were used to heat, but after the dry climate of Los Zapatos, they both found the high humidity enervating. They both swam in the motel pool a great deal and watched the sky a great deal. The man got the Portland *Press-Herald* every day, and now the copies were fresh, unmarked by time or dog urine. He read the weather forecasts and he watched for items concerning Jerusalem's Lot. On the ninth day of their stay in Portland, a man in Falmouth disappeared. His dog was found dead in the yard. Police were looking into it.

The man rose early on October 6 and stood in the forecourt of the motel. Most of the tourists were gone now, back to New York and New Jersey and Florida, to Ontario and Nova Scotia, to Pennsylvania and California. The tourists left their litter and their summer dollars and the natives to enjoy their state's most beautiful season.

This morning there was something new in the air. The smell of exhaust from the main road was not so great. There was no haze on the horizon, and no ground fog lying milkily around the legs of the billboard in the field across the way. The morning sky was very clear, and the air was chill. Indian summer seemed to have left overnight.

The boy came out and stood beside him.

The man said: "Today."

3

It was almost noon when they got to the 'salem's Lot turnoff, and Ben was reminded achingly of the day he had arrived here determined to exorcise all the demons that had haunted him, and confident of his success. That day had been warmer than this, the wind had not been so strong out of the west, and Indian summer had only been beginning. He remembered two boys with fishing poles. The sky today was a harder blue, colder.

The car radio proclaimed that the fire index was at five, its second-highest reading. There had been no significant rainfall in southern Maine since the first week of September. The deejay on WJAB cautioned drivers to crush their smokes and then played a record about a man who was going to jump off a water tower for love.

They drove down Route 12 past the Elks sign and were on Jointner Avenue. Ben saw at once that the blinker was dark. No need of a warning light now.

Then they were in town. They drove through it slowly, and Ben felt the old fear drop over him, like a coat found in the attic which has grown tight but still fits. Mark sat rigidly beside him, holding a vial of holy water brought all the way from Los Zapatos. Father Gracon had presented him with it as a going-away present.

With the fear came memories: almost heartbreaking.

They had changed Spencer's Sundries to a LaVerdiere's, but it had fared no better. The closed windows were dirty and bare. The Greyhound bus sign was gone. A for-sale sign had fallen askew in the window of the Excellent Café, and all the counter stools had been uprooted and ferried away to some more prosperous lunchroom. Up the street the sign over what had once been a Laundromat still read "Barlow and Straker—Fine Furnishings," but now the gilt letters were tarnished and they looked out on empty sidewalks. The show window was empty, the deep-pile carpet dirty. Ben thought of Mike Ryerson and wondered if he was still lying in the crate in the back room. The thought made his mouth dry.

Ben slowed at the crossroads. Up the hill he could see the Norton house, the grass grown long and yellow in front and behind it, where Bill Norton's brick barbecue had stood. Some of the windows were broken.

Further up the street he pulled in to the curb and looked into the park. The War Memorial presided over a junglelike growth of bushes and grass. The wading pool had been choked by summer waterweeds. The green paint on the benches was flaked and peeling. The swing chains had rusted, and to ride in one would produce squealing noises unpleasant enough to spoil the fun. The slippery slide had fallen over and lay with its legs sticking stiffly out, like a dead antelope. And perched in one corner of the sandbox, a floppy arm trailing on the grass, was some child's forgotten Raggedy Andy doll. Its shoe-button eyes seemed to reflect a black, vapid horror, as if it had seen all the secrets of darkness during its long stay in the sandbox. Perhaps it had.

He looked up and saw the Marsten House, its shutters still closed, looking down on the town with rickety malevolence. It was harmless now, but after dark . . . ?

The rains would have washed away the wafer with which Callahan had sealed it. It could be theirs again if they wanted it, a shrine, a dark lighthouse overlooking this shunned and deadly town. Did they meet up there? he wondered. Did they wander, pallid, through its nighted halls and hold revels, twisted services to the Maker of their Maker?

He looked away, cold.

Mark was looking at the houses. In most of them the shades were drawn; in others, uncovered windows looked in on empty rooms. They were worse than those decently closed, Ben thought. They seemed to look out at these daylight interlopers with the vapid stares of mental defectives.

"They're in those houses," Mark said tightly. "Right now, in all those houses. Behind the shades. In beds and closets and cellars. Under the floors. Hiding."

"Take it easy," Ben said.

The village dropped behind them. Ben turned onto the Brooks Road and they drove past the Marsten House—its shutters still sagging, its lawn a complex maze of knee-high witch grass and goldenrod.

Mark pointed, and Ben looked. A path had been beaten across the grass, beaten white. It cut across the lawn from the road to the porch. Then it was behind them, and he felt a loosening in his chest. The worst had been faced and was behind them.

Far out on the Burns Road, not too far distant from the Harmony Hill graveyard, Ben stopped the car and they got out. They walked into the woods together. The undergrowth snapped harshly, dryly, under their feet. There was a gin-sharp smell of juniper berries and the sound of late locusts. They came out on a small, knoll-like prominence of land that looked down on a slash through the woods where the Central Maine Power lines twinkled in the day's cool windiness. Some of the trees were beginning to show color.

"The old-timers say this is where it started," Ben said. "Back in 1951. The wind was blowing from the west. They think maybe a guy got careless with a cigarette. One little cigarette. It took off across the Marshes and no one could stop it."

He took a package of Pall Malls from his pocket, looked at the emblem thoughtfully—*in hoc signo vinces*—and then tore the cellophane top off. He lit one and shook out the match. The cigarette tasted surprisingly good, although he had not smoked in months.

"They have their places," he said. "But they could lose them. A lot of them could be killed . . . or destroyed. That's a better word. But not all of them. Do you understand?"

"Yes," Mark said.

"They're not very bright. If they lose their hiding places, they'll hide badly the second time. A couple of people just looking in obvious places could do well. Maybe it could be finished in 'salem's Lot by the time the first snow flew. Maybe it would never be finished. No guarantee, one way or the other. But without . . . something . . . to drive them out, to upset them, there would be no chance at all."

"Yes."

"It would be ugly and dangerous."

"I know that."

"But they say fire purifies," Ben said reflectively. "Purification should count for something, don't you think?"

"Yes," Mark said again.

Ben stood up. "We ought to go back."

He flicked the smoldering cigarette into a pile of dead brush and old brittle leaves. The white ribbon of smoke rose thinly against the green background of junipers for two or three feet, and then was pulled apart by the wind. Twenty feet away, downwind, was a large, jumbled deadfall.

They watched the smoke, transfixed, fascinated.

It thickened. A tongue of flame appeared. A small popping noise issued from the pile of dead brush as twigs caught.

"Tonight they won't be running sheep or visiting farms," Ben said softly. "Tonight they'll be on the run. And tomorrow—"

"You and me," Mark said, and closed his fist. His face was no longer pale; bright color glowed there. His eyes flashed.

They went back to the road and drove away.

In the small clearing overlooking the power lines, the fire in the brush began to burn more strongly, urged by the autumn wind that blew from the west.

October 1972
June 1975

THE
SHINING

This is for Joe Hill King, who shines on.

My editor on this book, as on the previous two, was Mr. William G. Thompson, a man of wit and good sense. His contribution to this book has been large, and for it, my thanks.

S.K.

Some of the most beautiful
resort hotels in the world
are located in Colorado, but
the hotel in these pages
is based on none of them.
The Overlook and the people
associated with it exist
              wholly within
              the author's
              imagination.

It was in this apartment, also, that there stood . . . a gigantic clock of ebony. Its pendulum swung to and fro with a dull, heavy, monotonous clang; and when . . . the hour was to be stricken, there came from the brazen lungs of the clock a sound which was clear and loud and deep and exceedingly musical, but of so peculiar a note and emphasis that, at each lapse of an hour, the musicians of the orchestra were constrained to pause . . . to hearken to the sound; and thus the waltzers perforce ceased their evolutions; and there was a brief disconcert of the whole gay company; and, while the chimes of the clock yet rang, it was observed that the giddiest grew pale, and the more aged and sedate passed their hands over their brows as if in confused reverie or meditation. But when the echoes had fully ceased, a light laughter at once pervaded the assembly . . . and [they] smiled as if at their own nervousness . . . and made whispering vows, each to the other, that the next chiming of the clock should produce in them no similar emotion; and then, after the lapse of sixty minutes . . . there came yet another chiming of the clock, and then were the same disconcert and tremulousness and meditation as before.

But in spite of these things, it was a gay and magnificent revel . . .

E. A. Poe
"The Masque of the Red Death"

The sleep of reason breeds monsters.
Goya

It'll shine when it shines.
Folk saying

PART ONE

PREFATORY MATTERS

JOB INTERVIEW

Jack Torrance thought: *Officious little prick.*

Ullman stood five-five, and when he moved, it was with the prissy speed that seems to be the exclusive domain of all small plump men. The part in his hair was exact, and his dark suit was sober but comforting. I am a man you can bring your problems to, that suit said to the paying customer. To the hired help it spoke more curtly: This had better be good, you. There was a red carnation in the lapel, perhaps so that no one on the street would mistake Stuart Ullman for the local undertaker.

As he listened to Ullman speak, Jack admitted to himself that he probably could not have liked any man on that side of the desk—under the circumstances.

Ullman had asked a question he hadn't caught. That was bad; Ullman was the type of man who would file such lapses away in a mental Rolodex for later consideration.

"I'm sorry?"

"I asked if your wife fully understood what you would be taking on here. And there's your son, of course." He glanced down at the application in front of him. "Daniel. Your wife isn't a bit intimidated by the idea?"

"Wendy is an extraordinary woman."

"And your son is also extraordinary?"

Jack smiled, a big wide PR smile. "We like to think so, I suppose. He's quite self-reliant for a five-year-old."

No returning smile from Ullman. He slipped Jack's application back into a file. The file went into a drawer. The desk top was now completely bare except for a blotter, a telephone, a Tensor lamp, and an in/out basket. Both sides of the in/out were empty, too.

Ullman stood up and went to the file cabinet in the corner. "Step around the desk, if you will, Mr. Torrance. We'll look at the hotel floor plans."

He brought back five large sheets and set them down on the glossy walnut plain of the desk. Jack stood by his shoulder, very much aware of the scent of Ullman's cologne. *All my men wear English Leather or they wear nothing at all* came into his mind for no reason at all, and he had to clamp his tongue between his teeth to keep in a bray of laughter. Beyond the wall, faintly, came the sounds of the Overlook Hotel's kitchen, gearing down from lunch.

"Top floor," Ullman said briskly. "The attic. Absolutely nothing up there now but bric-a-brac. The Overlook has changed hands several times since World War II and it seems that each successive manager has put everything they don't want up in the attic. I want rattraps and poison bait sowed around in it. Some of the third-floor chambermaids say they have heard rustling noises. I don't believe it, not for a moment, but there mustn't even be that one-in-a-hundred chance that a single rat inhabits the Overlook Hotel."

Jack, who suspected that every hotel in the world had a rat or two, held his tongue.

"Of course you wouldn't allow your son up in the attic under any circumstances."

"No," Jack said, and flashed the big PR smile again. Humiliating situation. Did this officious little prick actually think he would allow his son to goof around in a rattrap attic full of junk furniture and God knew what else?

Ullman whisked away the attic floor plan and put it on the bottom of the pile.

"The Overlook has one hundred and ten guest quarters," he said in a scholarly voice. "Thirty of them, all suites, are here on the third floor. Ten in the west wing (including the Presidential Suite), ten in the center, ten more in the east wing. All of them command magnificent views."

Could you at least spare the salestalk?

But he kept quiet. He needed the job.

Ullman put the third floor on the bottom of the pile and they studied the second floor.

"Forty rooms," Ullman said, "thirty doubles and ten singles. And on the first floor, twenty of each. Plus three linen closets on each floor, and a storeroom which is at the extreme east end of the hotel on the second floor and the extreme west end on the first. Questions?"

Jack shook his head. Ullman whisked the second and first floors away.

"Now. Lobby level. Here in the center is the registration desk. Behind it are the offices. The lobby runs for eighty feet in either direction from the desk. Over here in the west wing is the Overlook Dining Room and the Colorado Lounge. The banquet and ballroom facility is in the east wing. Questions?"

"Only about the basement," Jack said. "For the winter care-taker, that's the most important level of all. Where the action is, so to speak."

"Watson will show you all that. The basement floor plan is on the boiler room wall." He frowned impressively, perhaps to show that as manager, he did not concern himself with such mundane aspects of the Overlook's operation as the boiler and the plumbing. "Might not be a bad idea to put some traps down there too. Just a minute . . ."

He scrawled a note on a pad he took from his inner coat pocket (each sheet bore the legend *From the Desk of Stuart Ullman* in bold black script), tore it off, and dropped it into the out basket. It sat there looking lonesome. The pad disappeared back into Ullman's jacket pocket like the conclusion of a magi-cian's trick. Now you see it, Jacky-boy, now you don't. This guy is a real heavyweight.

They had resumed their original positions, Ullman behind the desk and Jack in front of it, interviewer and interviewee, supplicant and reluctant patron. Ullman folded his neat little hands on the desk blotter and looked directly at Jack, a small, balding man in a banker's suit and a quiet gray tie. The flower in his lapel was balanced off by a small lapel pin on the other side. It read simply STAFF in small gold letters.

"I'll be perfectly frank with you, Mr. Torrance. Albert Shockley is a powerful man with a large interest in the Overlook, which showed a profit this season for the first time in its history. Mr. Shockley also sits on the Board of Directors, but he is not a hotel man and he would be the first to admit this. But he has made his wishes in this caretaking matter quite obvious. He wants you hired. I will do so. But if I had been given a free hand in this matter, I would not have taken you on."

Jack's hands were clenched tightly in his lap, working against each other, sweating. *Officious little prick, officious little prick, officious—*

"I don't believe you care much for me, Mr. Torrance. I don't care. Certainly your feelings toward me play no part in my own belief that you are not right for the job. During the season that runs from May fifteenth to September thirtieth, the Overlook employs one hundred and ten people full-time; one for every room in the hotel, you might say. I don't think many of them like me and I suspect that some of them think I'm a bit of a bastard. They would be correct in their judgment of my character. I have to be a bit of a bastard to run this hotel in the manner it deserves."

He looked at Jack for comment, and Jack flashed the PR smile again, large and insultingly toothy.

Ullman said: "The Overlook was built in the years 1907 to 1909. The closest town is Sidewinder, forty miles east of here over roads that are closed from sometime in late October or November until sometime in April. A man named Robert Townley Watson built it, the grandfather of our present maintenance man. Vanderbilts have stayed here, and Rockefellers, and Astors, and Du Ponts. Four Presidents have stayed in the Presidential Suite. Wilson, Harding, Roosevelt, and Nixon."

"I wouldn't be too proud of Harding and Nixon," Jack murmured.

Ullman frowned but went on regardless. "It proved too much for Mr. Watson, and he sold the hotel in 1915. It was sold again in 1922, in 1929, in 1936. It stood vacant until the end of World War II, when it was purchased and completely renovated by Horace Derwent, millionaire inventor, pilot, film producer, and entrepreneur."

"I know the name," Jack said.

"Yes. Everything he touched seemed to turn to gold . . . except the Overlook. He funneled over a million dollars into it before the first postwar guest ever stepped through its doors, turning a decrepit relic into a showplace. It was Derwent who added the roque court I saw you admiring when you arrived."

"Roque?"

"A British forebear of our croquet, Mr. Torrance. Croquet is bastardized roque. According to legend, Derwent learned the game from his social secretary and fell completely in love with it. Ours may be the finest roque court in America."

"I wouldn't doubt it," Jack said gravely. A roque court, a topiary full of hedge animals out front, what next? A life-sized Uncle Wiggily game behind the equipment shed? He was getting very tired of Mr. Stuart Ullman, but he could see that Ullman wasn't done. Ullman was going to have his say, every last word of it.

"When he had lost three million, Derwent sold it to a group of California investors. Their experience with the Overlook was equally bad. Just not hotel people.

"In 1970, Mr. Shockley and a group of his associates bought the hotel and turned its management over to me. We have also run in the red for several years, but I'm happy to say that the trust of the present owners in me has never wavered. Last year we broke even. And this year the Overlook's accounts were written in black ink for the first time in almost seven decades."

Jack supposed that this fussy little man's pride was justified, and then his original dislike washed over him again in a wave.

He said: "I see no connection between the Overlook's admittedly colorful history and your feeling that I'm wrong for the post, Mr. Ullman."

"One reason that the Overlook has lost so much money lies in the depreciation that occurs each winter. It shortens the profit margin a great deal more than you might believe, Mr. Torrance. The winters are fantastically cruel. In order to cope with the problem, I've installed a full-time winter caretaker to run the boiler and to heat different parts of the hotel on a daily rotating basis. To repair breakage as it occurs and to do repairs, so the elements can't get a foothold. To be constantly alert to any and every contingency. During our first winter I hired a family instead of a single man. There was a tragedy. A horrible tragedy."

Ullman looked at Jack coolly and appraisingly.

"I made a mistake. I admit it freely. The man was a drunk."

Jack felt a slow, hot grin—the total antithesis of the toothy PR grin—stretch across his mouth. "Is that it? I'm surprised Al didn't tell you. I've retired."

"Yes, Mr. Shockley told me you no longer drink. He also told me about your last job . . . your last position of trust, shall we say? You were teaching English in a Vermont prep school. You lost your temper, I don't believe I need to be any more specific than that. But I do happen to believe that Grady's case has a bearing, and that is why I have brought the matter of your . . . uh, previous history into the conversation. During the winter of 1970–71, after we had refurbished the Overlook but before our first season, I hired this . . . this unfortunate named Delbert Grady. He moved into the quarters you and your wife and son will be sharing. He had a wife and two daughters. I had reservations, the main ones being the harshness of the winter season and the fact that the Gradys would be cut off from the outside world for five to six months."

"But that's not really true, is it? There are telephones here, and probably a citizen's band radio as well. And the Rocky Mountain National Park is within helicopter range and surely a piece of ground that big must have a chopper or two."

"I wouldn't know about that," Ullman said. "The hotel does have a two-way radio that Mr. Watson will show you, along with a list of the correct frequencies to broadcast on if you need help. The telephone lines between here and Sidewinder are still aboveground, and they go down almost every winter at some point or other and are apt to stay down for three weeks to a month and a half. There is a snowmobile in the equipment shed also."

"Then the place really isn't cut off."

Mr. Ullman looked pained. "Suppose your son or your wife tripped on the stairs and fractured his or her skull, Mr. Torrance. Would you think the place was cut off then?"

Jack saw the point. A snowmobile running at top speed could get you down to Sidewinder in an hour and a half . . . maybe. A helicopter from the Parks Rescue Service could get up here in three hours ... under optimum conditions. In a blizzard it would never even be able to lift off and you couldn't hope to run a snowmobile at top speed, even if you dared take a seriously injured person out into temperatures that might be twenty-five below—or forty-five below, if you added in the wind chill factor.

"In the case of Grady," Ullman said, "I reasoned much as Mr. Shockley seems to have done in your case. Solitude can be damaging in itself. Better for the man to have his family with him. If there was trouble, I thought, the odds were very high that it would be something less urgent than a fractured skull or an accident with one of the power tools or some sort of convulsion. A serious case of the flu, pneumonia, a broken arm, even appendicitis. Any of those things would have left enough time.

"I suspect that what happened came as a result of too much cheap whiskey, of which Grady had laid in a generous supply, unbeknownst to me, and a curious condition which the old-timers call cabin fever. Do you know the term?" Ullman offered a patronizing little smile, ready to explain as soon as Jack admitted his ignorance, and Jack was happy to respond quickly and crisply.

"It's a slang term for the claustrophobic reaction that can occur when people are shut in together over long periods of time. The feeling of claustrophobia is externalized as dislike for the people you happen to be shut in with. In extreme cases it can result in hallucinations and violence—murder has been done over such minor things as a burned meal or an argument about whose turn it is to do the dishes."

Ullman looked rather nonplussed, which did Jack a world of good. He decided to press a little further, but silently promised Wendy he would stay cool.

"I suspect you did make a mistake at that. Did he hurt them?"

"He killed them, Mr. Torrance, and then committed suicide. He murdered the little girls with a hatchet, his wife with a shotgun, and himself the same way. His leg was broken. Undoubtedly so drunk he fell downstairs."

Ullman spread his hands and looked at Jack self-righteously.

"Was he a high school graduate?"

"As a matter of fact, he wasn't," Ullman said a little stiffly. "I thought a, shall we say, less imaginative individual would be less susceptible to the rigors, the loneliness—"

"That was your mistake," Jack said. "A stupid man is more prone to cabin fever just as he's more prone to shoot someone over a card game or commit a spur-of-the-moment robbery. He gets bored. When the snow comes, there's nothing to do but watch TV or play solitaire and cheat when he can't get all the aces out. Nothing to do but bitch at his wife and nag at the kids and drink. It gets hard to sleep because there's nothing to hear. So he drinks himself to sleep and wakes up with a hangover. He gets edgy. And maybe the telephone goes out and the TV aerial blows down and there's nothing to do but think and cheat at solitaire and get edgier and edgier. Finally . . . boom, boom, boom."

"Whereas a more educated man, such as yourself?"

"My wife and I both like to read. I have a play to work on, as Al Shockley probably told you. Danny has his puzzles, his coloring books, and his crystal radio. I plan to teach him to read, and I also want to teach him to snowshoe. Wendy would like to learn how, too. Oh yes, I think we can keep busy and out of each other's hair if the TV goes on the fritz." He paused. "And Al was telling the truth when he told you I no longer drink. I did once, and it got to be serious. But I haven't had so much as a glass of beer in the last fourteen months. I don't intend to bring any alcohol up here, and I don't think there will be an opportunity to get any after the snow flies."

"In that you would be quite correct," Ullman said. "But as long as the three of you are up here, the potential for problems is multiplied. I have told Mr. Shockley this, and he told me he would take the responsibility. Now I've told you, and apparently you are also willing to take the responsibility—"

"I am."

"All right. I'll accept that, since I have little choice. But I would still rather have an unattached college boy taking a year off. Well, perhaps you'll do. Now I'll turn you over to Mr. Watson, who will take you through the basement and around the grounds. Unless you have further questions?"

"No. None at all."

Ullman stood. "I hope there are no hard feelings, Mr. Torrance. There is nothing personal in the things I have said to you. I only want what's best for the Overlook. It is a great hotel. I want it to stay that way."

"No. No hard feelings." Jack flashed the PR grin again, but he was glad Ullman didn't offer to shake hands. There were hard feelings. All kinds of them.

2

BOULDER

She looked out the kitchen window and saw him just sitting there on the curb, not playing with his trucks or the wagon or even the balsa glider that had pleased him so much all the last week since Jack had brought it home. He was just sitting there, watching for their shopworn VW, his elbows planted on his thighs and his chin propped in his hands, a five-year-old kid waiting for his daddy.

Wendy suddenly felt bad, almost crying bad.

She hung the dish towel over the bar by the sink and went downstairs, buttoning the top two buttons of her house dress. Jack and his pride! *Hey no, Al, I don't need an advance. I'm okay for a while.* The hallway walls were gouged and marked with crayons, grease pencil, spray paint. The stairs were steep and splintery. The whole building smelled of sour age, and what sort of place was this for Danny after the small neat brick house in Stovington? The people living above them on the third floor weren't married, and while that didn't bother her, their constant, rancorous fighting did. It scared her. The guy up there was Tom, and after the bars had closed and they had returned home, the fights would start in earnest—the rest of the week was just a prelim in comparison. The Friday Night Fights, Jack called them, but it wasn't funny. The woman—her name was Elaine—would at last be reduced to tears and to repeating over and over again: "Don't, Tom. Please don't. Please don't." And he would shout at her. Once they had even awakened Danny, and Danny slept like a corpse. The next morning Jack caught Tom going out and had spoken to him on the sidewalk at some length. Tom started to bluster and Jack had said something else to him, too quietly for Wendy to hear, and Tom had only shaken his head sullenly and walked away. That had been a week ago and for a few days things had been better, but since the weekend things had been working back to normal—excuse me, abnormal. It was bad for the boy.

Her sense of grief washed over her again but she was on the walk now and she smothered it. Sweeping her dress under her and sitting down on the curb beside him, she said: "What's up, doc?"

He smiled at her but it was perfunctory. "Hi, Mom."

The glider was between his sneakered feet, and she saw that one of the wings had started to splinter.

"Want me to see what I can do with that, honey?"

Danny had gone back to staring up the street. "No. Dad will fix it."

"Your daddy may not be back until suppertime, doc. It's a long drive up into those mountains."

"Do you think the bug will break down?"

"No, I don't think so." But he had just given her something new to worry about. *Thanks, Danny. I needed that.*

"Dad said it might," Danny said in a matter-of-fact, almost bored manner. "He said the fuel pump was all shot to shit."

"Don't say that, Danny."

"Fuel pump?" he asked her with honest surprise.

She sighed. "No, 'All shot to shit.' Don't say that."

"Why?"

"It's vulgar."

"What's vulgar, Mom?"

"Like when you pick your nose at the table or pee with the bathroom door open. Or saying things like 'All shot to shit.' Shit is a vulgar word. Nice people don't say it."

"Dad says it. When he was looking at the bugmotor he said, 'Christ this fuel pump's all shot to shit.' Isn't Dad nice?"

How do you get into these things, Winnifred? Do you practice?

"He's nice, but he's also a grown-up. And he's very careful not to say things like that in front of people who wouldn't understand."

"You mean like Uncle Al?"

"Yes, that's right."

"Can I say it when I'm grown-up?"

"I suppose you will, whether I like it or not."

"How old?"

"How does twenty sound, doc?"

"That's a long time to have to wait."

"I guess it is, but will you try?"

"Hokay."

He went back to staring up the street. He flexed a little, as if to rise, but the beetle coming was much newer, and much brighter red. He relaxed again. She wondered just how hard this move to Colorado had been on Danny. He was close-mouthed about it, but it bothered her to see him spending so much time by himself. In Vermont three of Jack's fellow faculty members had had children about Danny's age—and there had been the preschool—but in this neighborhood there was no one for him to play with. Most of the apartments were occupied by students attending CU, and of the few married couples here on Arapahoe Street, only a tiny percentage had children. She had spotted perhaps a dozen of high school or junior high school age, three infants, and that was all.

"Mommy, why did Daddy lose his job?"

She was jolted out of her reverie and floundering for an answer. She and Jack had discussed ways they might handle just such a question from Danny, ways that had varied from evasion to the plain truth with no varnish on it. But Danny had never asked. Not until now, when she was feeling low and least prepared for such a question. Yet he was looking at her, maybe reading the confusion on her face and forming his own ideas about that. She thought that to children adult motives and actions must seem as bulking and ominous as dangerous animals seen in the shadows of a dark forest. They were jerked about like puppets, having only the vaguest notions why. The thought brought her dangerously close to tears again, and while she fought them off she leaned over, picked up the disabled glider, and turned it over in her hands.

"Your daddy was coaching the debate team, Danny. Do you remember that?"

"Sure," he said. "Arguments for fun, right?"

"Right." She turned the glider over and over, looking at the trade name (SPEEDOGLIDE) and the blue star decals on the wings, and found herself telling the exact truth to her son.

"There was a boy named George Hatfield that Daddy had to cut from the team. That means he wasn't as good as some of the others. George said your daddy cut him because he didn't like him and not because he wasn't good enough. Then George did a bad thing. I think you know about that."

"Was he the one who put holes in our bug's tires?"

"Yes, he was. It was after school and your daddy caught him doing it." Now she hesitated again, but there was no question of evasion now; it was reduced to tell the truth or tell a lie.

"Your daddy . . . sometimes he does things he's sorry for later. Sometimes he doesn't think the way he should. That doesn't happen very often, but sometimes it does."

"Did he hurt George Haffield like the time I spilled all his papers?"

Sometimes—

(Danny with his arm in a cast)

—he does things he's sorry for later.

Wendy blinked her eyes savagely hard, driving her tears all the way back.

"Something like that, honey. Your daddy hit George to make him stop cutting the tires and George hit his head. Then the men who are in charge of the school said that George couldn't go there anymore and your daddy couldn't teach there anymore." She stopped, out of words, and waited in dread for the deluge of questions.

"Oh," Danny said, and went back to looking up the street. Apparently the subject was closed. If only it could be closed that easily for her—

She stood up. "I'm going upstairs for a cup of tea, doc. Want a couple of cookies and a glass of milk?"

"I think I'll watch for Dad."

"I don't think he'll be home much before five."

"Maybe he'll be early."

"Maybe," she agreed. "Maybe he will."

She was halfway up the walk when he called, "Mommy?"

"What, Danny?"

"Do you want to go and live in that hotel for the winter?"

Now, which of five thousand answers should she give to that one? The way she had felt yesterday or last night or this morning? They were all different, they crossed the spectrum from rosy pink to dead black.

She said: "If it's what your father wants, it's what I want." She paused. "What about you?"

"I guess I do," he said finally. "Nobody much to play with around here."

"You miss your friends, don't you?"

"Sometimes I miss Scott and Andy. That's about all."

She went back to him and kissed him, rumpled his light-colored hair that was just losing its baby-fineness. He was such a solemn little boy, and sometimes she wondered just how he was supposed to survive with her and Jack for parents. The high hopes they had begun with came down to this unpleasant apartment building in a city they didn't know. The image of Danny in his cast rose up before her again. Somebody in the Divine Placement Service had made a mistake, one she sometimes feared could never be corrected and which only the most innocent bystander could pay for.

"Stay out of the road, doc," she said, and hugged him tight.

"Sure, Mom."

She went upstairs and into the kitchen. She put on the teapot and laid a couple of Oreos on a plate for Danny in case he decided to come up while she was lying down. Sitting at the table with her big pottery cup in front of her, she looked out the window at him, still sitting on the curb in his bluejeans and his oversized dark green Stovington Prep sweatshirt, the glider now lying beside him. The tears which had threatened all day now came in a cloudburst and she leaned into the fragrant, curling steam of the tea and wept. In grief and loss for the past, and terror of the future.

3

WATSON

You lost your temper, Ullman had said.

"Okay, here's your furnace," Watson said, turning on a light in the dark, musty-smelling room. He was a beefy man with fluffy popcorn hair, white shirt, and dark green chinos. He swung open a small square grating in the furnace's belly and he and Jack peered in together. "This here's the pilot light." A steady blue-white jet hissing steadily upward channeled destructive force, but the key word, Jack thought was *destructive* and not *channeled:* if you stuck your hand in there, the barbecue would happen in three quick seconds.

Lost your temper.

(Danny, are you all right?)

The furnace filled the entire room, by far the biggest and oldest Jack had ever seen.

"The pilot's got a fail-safe," Watson told him. "Little sensor in there measures heat. If the heat falls below a certain point, it sets off a buzzer in your quarters. Boiler's on the other side of the wall. I'll take you around." He slammed the grating shut and led Jack behind the iron bulk of the furnace toward another door. The iron radiated a stuporous heat at them, and for some reason Jack thought of a large, dozing cat. Watson jingled his keys and whistled.

Lost your—

(When he went back into his study and saw Danny standing there, wearing nothing but his training pants and a grin, a slow, red cloud of rage had eclipsed Jack's reason. It had seemed slow subjectively, inside his head, but it must have all happened in less than a minute. It only seemed slow the way some dreams seem slow. The bad ones. Every door and drawer in his study seemed to have been ransacked in the time he had been gone. Closet, cupboards, the sliding bookcase. Every desk drawer yanked out to the stop. His manuscript, the three-act play he had been slowly developing from a novelette he had written seven years ago as an undergraduate, was scattered all over the floor. He had been drinking a beer and doing the Act II corrections when Wendy said the phone was for him, and Danny had poured the can of beer all over the pages. Probably to see it foam. *See it foam, see it foam,* the words played over and over in his mind like a single sick chord on an out-of-tune piano, completing the circuit of his rage. He stepped deliberately toward his three-year-old son, who was looking up at him with that pleased grin, his pleasure at the job of work so successfully and recently completed in Daddy's study; Danny began to say something and that was when he had grabbed Danny's hand and bent it to make him drop the typewriter eraser and the mechanical pencil he was clenching in it. Danny had cried out a little . . . no . . . no . . . tell the truth . . . he screamed. It was all hard to remember through the fog of anger, the sick single thump of that one Spike Jones chord. Wendy somewhere, asking what was wrong. Her voice faint, damped by the inner mist. This was between the two of them. He had whirled Danny around to spank him, his big adult fingers digging into the scant meat of the boy's forearm, meeting around it in a closed fist, and the snap of the breaking bone had not been loud, not loud but it had been *very* loud, *HUGE,* but not loud. Just enough of a sound to slit through the red fog like an arrow— but instead of letting in sunlight, that sound let in the dark clouds of shame and remorse, the terror, the agonizing convulsion of the spirit. A clean sound with the past on one side of it and all the future on the other, a sound like a breaking pencil lead or a small piece of kindling when you brought it down over your knee. A moment of utter silence on the other side, in respect to the beginning future maybe, all the rest of his life. Seeing Danny's face drain of color until it was like cheese, seeing his eyes, always large, grow larger still, and glassy, Jack sure the boy was going to faint dead away into the puddle of beer and papers; his own voice, weak and drunk, slurry, trying to take it all back, to find *a way* around that not too loud sound of bone cracking and into the past—is there a status quo in the house?—saying: *Danny, are you all right?* Danny's answering shriek, then Wendy's shocked gasp as she came around them and saw the peculiar angle Danny's forearm had to his elbow; no arm was meant to hang quite that way in a world of normal families. Her own scream as she swept him into her arms, and a nonsense babble: *Oh God Danny oh dear God oh sweet God your poor sweet arm;* and Jack was standing there, stunned and stupid, trying to understand how a thing like this could have happened. He was standing there and his eyes met the eyes of his wife and he saw that Wendy hated him. It did not occur to him what the hate might mean in practical terms; it was only later that he realized she might have left him that night, gone to a motel, gotten a divorce lawyer in the morning; or called the police. He saw only that his wife hated him and he felt staggered by it, all alone. He felt awful. This was what oncoming death felt like. Then she fled for the telephone and dialed the hospital with their screaming boy wedged in the crook of her arm and Jack did not go after her, he only stood in the ruins of his office, smelling beer and thinking—)

You lost your temper.

He rubbed his hand harshly across his lips and followed Watson into the boiler room. It was humid in here, but it was more than the humidity that brought the sick and slimy sweat onto his brow and stomach and legs. The remembering did that, it was a total thing that made that night two years ago seem like two hours ago. There was no lag. It brought the shame and revulsion back, the sense of having no worth at all, and that feeling always made him want to have a drink, and the wanting of a drink brought still blacker despair—would he ever have an hour, not a week or even a day, mind you, but just one waking hour when the craving for a drink wouldn't surprise him like this?

"The boiler," Watson announced. He pulled a red and blue bandanna from his back pocket, blew his nose with a decisive honk, and thrust it back out of sight after a short peek into it to see if he had gotten anything interesting.

The boiler stood on four cement blocks, a long and cylindrical metal tank, copper-jacketed and often patched. It squatted beneath a confusion of pipes and ducts which zigzagged upward into the high, cobweb-festooned basement ceiling. To Jack's right, two large heating pipes came through the wall from the furnace in the adjoining room.

"Pressure gauge is here." Watson tapped it. "Pounds per square inch, psi. I guess you'd know that. I got her up to a hundred now, and the rooms get a little chilly at night. Few guests complain, what the fuck. They're crazy to come up here in September anyway. Besides, this is an old baby. Got more patches on her than a pair of welfare overalls." Out came the bandanna. A honk. A peek. Back it went.

"I got me a fuckin cold," Watson said conversationally. "I get one every September. I be tinkering down here with this old whore, then I be out cuttin the grass or rakin that roque court. Get a chill and catch a cold, my old mum used to say. God bless her, she been dead six year. The cancer got her. Once the cancer gets you, you might as well make your will.

"You'll want to keep your press up to no more than fifty, maybe sixty. Mr. Ullman, he says to heat the west wing one day, central wing the next, east wing the day after that. Ain't he a crazyman? I hate that little fucker. Yap-yap-yap, all the livelong day, he's just like one a those little dogs that bites you on the ankle then run around an pee all over the rug. If brains was black powder he couldn't blow his own nose. It's a pity the things you see when you ain't got a gun.

"Look here. You open an close these ducks by pullin these rings. I got em all marked for you. The blue tags all go to the rooms in the east wing. Red tags is the middle. Yellow is the west wing. When you go to heat the west wing, you got to remember that's the side of the hotel that really catches the weather. When it whoops, those rooms get as cold as a frigid woman with an ice cube up her works. You can run your press all the way to eighty on west wing days. I would, anyway."

"The thermostats upstairs—" Jack began.

Watson shook his head vehemently, making his fluffy hair bounce on his skull. "They ain't hooked up. They're just there for show. Some of these people from California, they don't think things is right unless they got it hot enough to grow a palm tree in their fuckin bedroom. All the heat comes from down here. Got to watch the press, though. See her creep?"

He tapped the main dial, which had crept from a hundred pounds per square inch to a hundred and two as Watson soliloquized. Jack felt a sudden shiver cross his back in a hurry and thought: *The goose just walked over my grave.* Then Watson gave the pressure wheel a spin and dumped the boiler off. There was a great hissing, and the needle dropped back to ninety-one. Watson twisted the valve shut and the hissing died reluctantly.

"She creeps," Watson said. "You tell that fat little peckerwood Ullman, he drags out the account books and spends three hours showing how we can't afford a new one until 1982. I tell you, this whole place is gonna go sky-high someday, and I just hope that fat fuck's here to ride the rocket. God, I wish I could be as charitable as my mother was. She could see the good in everyone. Me, I'm just as mean as a snake with the shingles. What the fuck, a man can't help his nature.

"Now you got to remember to come down here twice a day and once at night before you rack in. You got to check the press. If you forget, it'll just creep and creep and like as not you an your fambly'll wake up on the fuckin moon. You just dump her off a little and you'll have no trouble."

"What's top end?"

"Oh, she's rated for two-fifty, but she'd blow long before that now. You couldn't get me to come down an stand next to her when that dial was up to one hundred and eighty."

"There's no automatic shutdown?"

"No, there ain't. This was built before such things were required. Federal government's into everything these days, ain't it? FBI openin mail, CIA buggin the goddam phones . . . and look what happened to that Nixon. Wasn't that a sorry sight?

"But if you just come down here regular an check the press, you'll be fine. An remember to switch those ducks around like he wants. Won't none of the rooms get much above forty-five unless we have an amazin warm winter. And you'll have your own apartment just as warm as you like it."

"What about the plumbing?"

"Okay, I was just getting to that. Over here through this arch."

They walked into a long, rectangular room that seemed to stretch for miles. Watson pulled a cord and a single seventy-five-watt bulb cast a sickish, swinging glow over the area they were standing in. Straight ahead was the bottom of the elevator shaft, heavy greased cables descending to pulleys twenty feet in diameter and a huge, grease-clogged motor. Newspapers were everywhere, bundled and banded and boxed. Other cartons were marked *Records* or *Invoices* or *Receipts*—SAVE! The smell was yellow and moldy. Some of the cartons were falling apart, spilling yellow flimsy sheets that might have been twenty years old out onto the floor. Jack stared around, fascinated. The Overlook's entire history might be here, buried in these rotting cartons.

"That elevator's a bitch to keep runnin," Watson said, jerking his thumb at it. "I *know* Ullman's buying the state elevator inspector a few fancy dinners to keep the repairman away from that fucker.

"Now, here's your central plumbin core." In front of them five large pipes, each of them wrapped in insulation and cinched with steel bands, rose into the shadows and out of sight.

Watson pointed to a cobwebby shelf beside the utility shaft. There were a number of greasy rags on it, and a loose-leaf binder. "That there is all your plumbin schematics," he said. "I don't think you'll have any trouble with leaks—never has been— but sometimes the pipes freeze up. Only way to stop that is to run the faucets a little bit durin the nights, but there's over four hundred taps in this fuckin palace. That fat fairy upstairs would scream all the way to Denver when he saw the water bill. Ain't that right?"

"I'd say that's a remarkably astute analysis."

Watson looked at him admiringly. "Say, you really are a college fella, aren't you? Talk just like a book. I admire that, as long as the fella ain't one of those fairy-boys. Lots of em are. You know who stirred up all those college riots a few years ago? The hommasexshuls, that's who. They get frustrated an have to cut loose. Comin out of the closet, they call it. Holy shit, I don't know what the world's comin to.

"Now, if she freezes, she most likely gonna freeze right up in this shaft. No heat, you see. If it happens, use this." He reached into a broken orange crate and produced a small gas torch.

"You just unstrap the insulation when you find the ice plug and put the heat right to her. Get it?"

"Yes. But what if a pipe freezes outside the utility core?"

"That won't happen if you're doin your job and keepin the place heated. You can't get to the other pipes anyway. Don't you fret about it. You'll have no trouble. Beastly place down here. Cobwebby. Gives me the horrors, it does."

"Ullman said the first winter caretaker killed his family and himself."

"Yeah, that guy Grady. He was a bad actor, I knew that the minute I saw him. Always grinnin like an egg-suck dog. That was when they were just startin out here and that fat fuck Ullman, he woulda hired the Boston Strangler if he'd've worked for minimum wage. Was a ranger from the National Park that found em; the phone was out. All of em up in the west wing on the third floor, froze solid. Too bad about the little girls. Eight and six, they was. Cute as cut-buttons. Oh, that was a hell of a mess. That Ullman, he manages some honky-tonky resort place down in Florida in the off-season, and he caught a plane up to Denver and hired a sleigh to take him up here from Sidewinder because the roads were closed—a *sleigh,* can you believe that? He about split a gut tryin to keep it out of the papers. Did pretty well, I got to give him that. There was an item in the Denver *Post,* and of course the bituary in that pissant little rag they have down in Estes Park, but that was just about all. Pretty good, considerin the reputation this place has got. I expected some reporter would dig it all up again and just sorta put Grady in it as an excuse to rake over the scandals."

"What scandals?"

Watson shrugged. "Any big hotels have got scandals," he said. "Just like every big hotel has got a ghost. Why? Hell, people come and go. Sometimes one of em will pop off in his room, heart attack or stroke or something like that. Hotels are superstitious places. No thirteenth floor or room thirteen, no mirrors on the back of the door you come in through, stuff like that. Why, we lost a lady just this last July. Ullman had to take care of that, and you can bet your ass he did. That's what they pay him twenty-two thousand bucks a season for, and as much as I dislike the little prick, he earns it. It's like some people just come here to throw up and they hire a guy like Ullman to clean up the messes. Here's this woman, must be sixty fuckin years old—my age!—and her hair's dyed just as red as a whore's stoplight, tits saggin just about down to her belly button on account of she ain't wearin no brassy-ear, big varycoarse veins all up and down her legs so they look like a couple of goddam roadmaps, the jools drippin off her neck and arms an hangin out her ears. And she's got this kid with her, he can't be no more than seventeen, with hair down to his asshole and his crotch bulgin like he stuffed it up with the funnypages. So they're here a week, ten days maybe, and every night it's the same drill. Down in the Colorado Lounge from five to seven, her suckin up singapore slings like they're gonna outlaw em tomorrow and him with just the one bottle of Olympia, suckin it, makin it last. And she'd be makin jokes and sayin all these witty things, and every time she said one he'd grin just like a fuckin ape, like she had strings tied to the corners of his mouth. Only after a few days you could see it was gettin harder an harder for him to grin, and God knows what he had to think about to get his pump primed by bedtime. Well, they'd go in for dinner, him walkin and her staggerin, drunk as a coot, you know, and he'd be pinchin the waitresses and grinnin at em when she wasn't lookin. Hell, we even had bets on how long he'd last."

Watson shrugged.

"Then he comes down one night around ten, sayin his 'wife' is 'indisposed'—which meant she was passed out again like every other night they was there—and he's goin to get her some stomach medicine. So off he goes in the little Porsche they come in, and that's the last we see of him. Next morning she comes down and tries to put on this big act, but all day she's gettin paler an paler, and Mr. Ullman asks her, sorta diplomatic-like, would she like him to notify the state cops, just in case maybe he had a little accident or something. She's on him like a cat. No-no-no, he's a fine driver, she isn't worried, everything's under control, he'll be back for dinner. So that afternoon she steps into the Colorado around three and never has no dinner at all. She goes up to her room around ten-thirty, and that's the last time anybody saw her alive."

"What happened?"

"County coroner said she took about thirty sleepin pills on top of all the booze. Her husband showed up the next day, some bigshot lawyer from New York. He gave old Ullman four different shades of holy hell. I'll sue this an I'll sue that an when I'm through you won't even be able to find a clean pair of underwear, stuff like that. But Ullman's good, the sucker. Ullman got him quieted down. Probably asked that bigshot how he'd like to see his wife splashed all over the New York papers: Wife of Prominent New York Blah Blah Found Dead With Bellyful of Sleeping Pills. After playing hide-the-salami with a kid young enough to be her grandson.

"The state cops found the Porsche in back of this all-night burger joint down in Lyons, and Ullman pulled a few strings to get it released to that lawyer. Then both of them ganged up on old Archer Houghton, which is the county coroner, and got him to change the verdict to accidental death. Heart attack. Now ole Archer's driving a Chrysler. I don't begrudge him. A man's got to take it where he finds it, especially when he starts gettin along in years."

Out came the bandanna. Honk. Peek. Out of sight.

"So what happens? About a week later this stupid cunt of a chambermaid, Delores Vickery by name, she gives out with a helluva shriek while she's makin up the room where those two stayed, and she faints dead away. When she comes to she says she seen the dead woman in the bathroom, layin naked in the tub. 'Her face was all purple an puffy,' she says, 'an she was grinnin at me.' So Ullman gave her two weeks' worth of walking papers and told her to get lost. I figure there's maybe forty–fifty people died in this hotel since my grandfather opened it for business in 1910."

He looked shrewdly at Jack.

"You know how most of em go? Heart attack or stroke, while they're bangin the lady they're with. That's what these resorts get a lot of, old types that want one last fling. They come up here to the mountains to pretend they're twenty again. Sometimes somethin gives, and not all the guys who ran this place was as good as Ullman is at keepin it out of the papers. So the Overlook's got a reputation, yeah. I'll bet the fuckin Biltmore in New York City has got a reputation, if you ask the right people."

"But no ghosts?"

"Mr. Torrance, I've worked here all my life. I played here when I was a kid no older'n your boy in that wallet snapshot you showed me. I never seen a ghost yet. You want to come out back with me, I'll show you the equipment shed."

"Fine."

As Watson reached up to turn off the light, Jack said, "There sure are a lot of papers down here."

"Oh, you're not kiddin. Seems like they go back a thousand years. Newspapers and old invoices and bills of lading and Christ knows what else. My dad used to keep up with them pretty good when we had the old wood-burning furnace, but now they've got all out of hand. Some year I got to get a boy to haul them down to Sidewinder and burn em. If Ullman will stand the expense. I guess he will if I holler 'rat' loud enough."

"Then there are rats?"

"Yeah, I guess there's some. I got the traps and the poison Mr. Ullman wants you to use up in the attic and down here. You keep a good eye on your boy, Mr. Torrance. You wouldn't want nothing to happen to him."

"No, I sure wouldn't." Coming from Watson the advice didn't sting.

They went to the stairs and paused there for a moment while Watson blew his nose again.

"You'll find all the tools you need out there and some you don't, I guess. And there's the shingles. Did Ullman tell you about that?"

"Yes, he wants part of the west roof reshingled."

"He'll get all the for-free out of you that he can, the fat little prick, and then whine around in the spring about how you didn't do the job half right. I told him once right to his face, I said . . ."

Watson's words faded away to a comforting drone as they mounted the stairs. Jack Torrance looked back over his shoulder once into the impenetrable, musty-smelling darkness and thought that if there was ever a place that should have ghosts, this was it. He thought of Grady, locked in by the soft, implacable snow, going quietly berserk and committing his atrocity. Did they scream? he wondered. Poor Grady, feeling it close in on him more every day, and knowing at last that for him spring would never come. He shouldn't have been here. And he shouldn't have lost his temper.

As he followed Watson through the door, the words echoed back to him like a knell, accompanied by a sharp snap—like a breaking pencil lead. Dear God, he could use a drink. Or a thousand of them.

4

SHADOWLAND

Danny weakened and went up for his milk and cookies at quarter past four. He gobbled them while looking out the window, then went in to kiss his mother, who was lying down. She suggested that he stay in and watch "Sesame Street"—the time would pass faster—but he shook his head firmly and went back to his place on the curb.

Now it was five o'clock, and although he didn't have a watch and couldn't tell time too well yet anyway, he was aware of passing time by the lengthening of the shadows, and by the golden cast that now tinged the afternoon light.

Turning the glider over in his hands, he sang under his breath: "Skip to m Lou, n I don't care . . . skip to m Lou, n I don't care . . . my master's gone away . . . Lou, Lou, skip to m Lou . . ."

They had sung that song all together at the Jack and Jill Nursery School he had gone to back in Stovington. He didn't go to nursery school out here because Daddy couldn't afford to send him anymore. He knew his mother and father worried about that, worried that it was adding to his loneliness (and even more deeply, unspoken between them, that Danny blamed them), but he didn't really want to go to that old Jack and Jill anymore. It was for babies. He wasn't quite a big kid yet, but he wasn't a baby anymore. Big kids went to the big school and got a hot lunch. First grade. Next year. This year was someplace between being a baby and a real kid. It was all right. He did miss Scott and Andy—mostly Scott—but it was still all right. It seemed best to wait alone for whatever might happen next.

He understood a great many things about his parents, and he knew that many times they didn't like his understandings and many other times refused to believe them. But someday they would have to believe. He was content to wait.

It was too bad they couldn't believe more, though, especially at times like now. Mommy was lying on her bed in the apart-

672

ment, just about crying she was so worried about Daddy. Some of the things she was worried about were too grown-up for Danny to understand—vague things that had to do with security, with Daddy's *selfimage,* feelings of guilt and anger and the fear of what was to become of them—but the two main things on her mind right now were that Daddy had had a breakdown in the mountains *(then why doesn't he call?)* or that Daddy had gone off to do the Bad Thing. Danny knew perfectly well what the Bad Thing was since Scotty Aaronson, who was six months older, had explained it to him. Scotty knew because his daddy did the Bad Thing, too. Once, Scotty told him, his daddy had punched his mom right in the eye and knocked her down. Finally, Scotty's dad and mom had gotten a DIVORCE over the Bad Thing, and when Danny had known him, Scotty lived with his mother and only saw his daddy on weekends. The greatest terror of Danny's life was DIVORCE, a word that always appeared in his mind as a sign painted in red letters which were covered with hissing, poisonous snakes. In DIVORCE, your parents no longer lived together. They had a tug of war over you in a court (tennis court? badminton court? Danny wasn't sure which or if it was some other, but Mommy and Daddy had played both tennis and badminton at Stovington, so he assumed it could be either) and you had to go with one of them and you practically never saw the other one, and the one you were with could marry somebody you didn't even know if the urge came on them. The most terrifying thing about DIVORCE was that he had sensed the word—or concept, or whatever it was that came to him in his understandings—floating around in his own parents' heads, sometimes diffuse and relatively distant, sometimes as thick and obscuring and frightening as thunderheads. It had been that way after Daddy punished him for messing the papers up in his study and the doctor had to put his arm in a cast. That memory was already faded, but the memory of the DIVORCE thoughts was clear and terrifying. It had mostly been around his mommy that time, and he had been in constant terror that she would pluck the word from her brain and drag it out of her mouth, making it real. DIVORCE. It was a constant undercurrent in their thoughts, one of the few he could always pick up, like the beat of simple music. But like a beat, the central thought formed only the spine of more complex thoughts, thoughts he could not as yet even begin to interpret. They came to him only as colors and moods. Mommy's DIVORCE thoughts centered around what Daddy had done to his arm, and what had happened at Stovington when Daddy lost his job. That boy. That George Haffield who got pissed off at Daddy and put the holes in their bug's feet. Daddy's DIVORCE thoughts were more complex, colored dark violet and shot through with frightening veins of pure black. He seemed to think they would be better off if he left. That things would stop hurting. His daddy hurt almost all the time, mostly about the Bad Thing. Danny could almost always pick that up too: Daddy's constant craving to go into a dark place and watch a color TV and eat peanuts out of a bowl and do the Bad Thing until his brain would be quiet and leave him alone.

But this afternoon his mother had no need to worry and he wished he could go to her and tell her that. The bug had not broken down. Daddy was not off somewhere doing the Bad Thing. He was almost home now, put-putting along the highway between Lyons and Boulder. For the moment his daddy wasn't even thinking about the Bad Thing. He was thinking about . . . about . . .

Danny looked furtively behind him at the kitchen window. Sometimes thinking very hard made something happen to him. It made things—real things—go away, and then he saw things that weren't there. Once, not long after they put the cast on his arm, this had happened at the supper table. They weren't talking much to each other then. But they were thinking. Oh yes. The thoughts of DIVORCE hung over the kitchen table like a cloud full of black rain, pregnant, ready to burst. It was so bad he couldn't eat. The thought of eating with all that black DIVORCE around made him want to throw up. And because it had seemed desperately important, he had thrown himself fully into concentration and something had happened. When he came back to real things, he was lying on the floor with beans and mashed potatoes in his lap and his mommy was holding him and crying and Daddy had been on the phone. He had been frightened, had tried to explain to them that there was nothing wrong, that this sometimes happened to him when he concentrated on understanding more than what normally came to him. He tried to explain about Tony, who they called his "invisible playmate."

His father had said: "He's having a Ha Loo Sin Nation. He seems okay, but I want the doctor to look at him anyway."

After the doctor left, Mommy had made him promise to never do that again, to *never* scare them that way, and Danny had agreed. He was frightened himself. Because when he had concentrated his mind, it had flown out to his daddy, and for just a moment, before Tony had appeared (far away, as he always did, calling distantly) and the strange things had blotted out their kitchen and the carved roast on the blue plate, for just a moment his own consciousness had plunged through his daddy's darkness to an incomprehensible word much more frightening than DIVORCE, and that word was SUICIDE. Danny had never come across it again in his daddy's mind, and he had certainly not gone looking for it. He didn't care if he never found out exactly what that word meant.

But he did like to concentrate, because sometimes Tony would come. Not every time. Sometimes things just got woozy and swimmy for a minute and then cleared—most times, in fact—but at other times Tony would appear at the very limit of his vision, calling distantly and beckoning . . .

It had happened twice since they moved to Boulder, and he remembered how surprised and pleased he had been to find Tony had followed him all the way from Vermont. So all his friends hadn't been left behind after all.

The first time he had been out in the back yard and nothing much had happened. Just Tony beckoning and then darkness and a few minutes later he had come back to real things with a few vague fragments of memory, like a jumbled dream. The second time, two weeks ago, had been more interesting. Tony, beckoning, calling from four yards over: *"Danny . . . come see . . ."* It seemed that he was getting up, then falling into a deep hole, like Alice into Wonderland. Then he had been in the basement of the apartment house and Tony had been beside him, pointing into the shadows at the trunk his daddy carried all his important papers in, especially "THE PLAY."

"See?" Tony had said in his distant, musical voice. "It's under the stairs. Right under the stairs. The movers put it right . . . under . . . the stairs."

Danny had stepped forward to look more closely at this marvel and then he was falling again, this time out of the back-yard swing, where he had been sitting all along. He had gotten the wind knocked out of himself, too.

Three or four days later his daddy had been stomping around, telling Mommy furiously that he had been all over the goddam basement and the trunk wasn't there and he was going to sue the goddam movers who had left it somewhere between Vermont and Colorado. How was he supposed to be able to finish "THE PLAY" if things like this kept cropping up?

Danny said, "No, Daddy. It's under the stairs. The movers put it right under the stairs."

Daddy had given him a strange look and had gone down to see. The trunk had been there, just where Tony had shown him. Daddy had taken him aside, had sat him on his lap, and had asked Danny who let him down the cellar. Had it been Tom from upstairs? The cellar was dangerous, Daddy said. That was why the landlord kept it locked. If someone was leaving it unlocked, Daddy wanted to know. He was glad to have his papers and his "PLAY" but it wouldn't be worth it to him, he said, if Danny fell down the stairs and broke his . . . his leg. Danny told his father earnestly that he hadn't been down in the cellar. That door was always locked. And Mommy agreed. Danny never went down in the back hall, she said, because it was damp and dark and spidery. And he didn't tell lies.

"Then how did you know, doc?" Daddy asked.

"Tony showed me."

His mother and father had exchanged a look over his head. This had happened before, from time to time. Because it was frightening, they swept it quickly from their minds. But he knew they worried about Tony, Mommy especially, and he was careful about thinking the way that could make Tony come where she might see. But now he thought she was lying down, not moving about in the kitchen yet, and so he concentrated hard to see if he could understand what Daddy was thinking about.

His brow furrowed and his slightly grimy hands clenched into tight fists on his jeans. He did not close his eyes—that wasn't necessary—but he squinched them down to slits and imagined Daddy's voice, Jack's voice, John Daniel Torrance's voice, deep and steady, sometimes quirking up with amusement or deepening even more with anger or just staying steady because he was thinking. Thinking of. Thinking about. Thinking . . .

(thinking)

Danny sighed quietly and his body slumped on the curb as if all the muscles had gone out of it. He was fully conscious; he saw the street and the girl and boy walking up the sidewalk on the other side, holding hands because they were

(?in love?)

so happy about the day and themselves together in the day. He saw autumn leaves blowing along the gutter, yellow cartwheels of irregular shape. He saw the house they were passing and noticed how the roof was covered with

*(shingles. i guess it'll be no problem if the flashing's ok yeah that'll be all right. that watson. christ what a character. wish there was a place for him in "*THE PLAY.*" i'll end up with the whole fucking human race in it if i don't watch out. yeah. shingles. are there nails out there? oh shit forgot to ask him well they're simple to get. sidewinder hardware store. wasps. they're nesting this time of year. i might want to get one of those bug bombs in case they're there when i rip up the old shingles. new shingles. old)*

shingles. So that's what he was thinking about. He had gotten the job and was thinking about shingles. Danny didn't know who Watson was, but everything else seemed clear enough. And he might get to see a wasps' nest. Just as sure as his name was

"Danny . . . Dannee . . ."

He looked up and there was Tony, far up the street, standing by a stop sign and waving. Danny, as always, felt a warm burst of pleasure at seeing his old friend, but this time he seemed to feel a prick of fear, too, as if Tony had come with some darkness hidden behind his back. A jar of wasps which when released would sting deeply.

But there was no question of not going.

He slumped further down on the curb, his hands sliding laxly from his thighs and dangling below the fork of his crotch. His chin sank onto his chest. Then there was a dim, painless tug as part of him got up and ran after Tony into funneling darkness.

"Dannee—"

Now the darkness was shot with swirling whiteness. A coughing, whooping sound and bending, tortured shadows that resolved themselves into fir trees at night, being pushed by a screaming gale. Snow swirled and danced. Snow everywhere.

"Too deep," Tony said from the darkness, and there was a sadness in his voice that terrified Danny. "Too deep to get out."

Another shape, looming, rearing. Huge and rectangular. A sloping roof. Whiteness that was blurred in the stormy darkness. Many windows. A long building with a shingled roof. Some of the shingles were greener, newer. His daddy put them on. With nails from the Sidewinder hardware store. Now the snow was covering the shingles. It was covering everything.

A green witchlight glowed into being on the front of the building, flickered, and became a giant, grinning skull over two crossed bones.

"Poison," Tony said from the floating darkness. "Poison."

Other signs flickered past his eyes, some in green letters, some of them on boards stuck at leaning angles into the snowdrifts. NO SWIMMING. DANGER! LIVE WIRES. THIS PROPERTY CONDEMNED. HIGH VOLTAGE. THIRD RAIL. DANGER OF DEATH. KEEP OFF. KEEP OUT. NO TRESPASSING. VIOLATERS WILL BE SHOT ON SIGHT. He understood none of them completely—he couldn't read!—but got a sense of all, and a dreamy terror floated into the dark hollows of his body like light brown spores that would die in sunlight.

They faded. Now he was in a room filled with strange furniture, a room that was dark. Snow spattered against the windows like thrown sand. His mouth was dry, his eyes like hot marbles, his heart triphammering in his chest. Outside there was a hollow booming noise, like a dreadful door being thrown wide. Footfalls. Across the room was a mirror, and deep down in its silver bubble a single word appeared in green fire and that word was: REDRUM.

The room faded. Another room. He knew
(would know)
this one. An overturned chair. A broken window with snow swirling in; already it had frosted the edge of the rug. The drapes had been pulled free and hung on their broken rod at an angle. A low cabinet lying on its face.

More hollow booming noises, steady, rhythmic, horrible. Smashing glass. Approaching destruction. A hoarse voice, the voice of a madman, made the more terrible by its familiarity:

Come out! Come out, you little shit! Take your medicine!

Crash. Crash. Crash. Splintering wood. A bellow of rage and satisfaction. REDRUM. Coming.

Drifting across the room. Pictures torn off the walls. A record player

(?Mommy's record player?)

overturned on the floor. Her records, Grieg, Handel, the Beatles, Art Garfunkel, Bach, Liszt, thrown everywhere. Broken into jagged black pie wedges. A shaft of light coming from another room, the bathroom, harsh white light and a word flickering on and off in the medicine cabinet mirror like a red eye, REDRUM, REDRUM, REDRUM—

"No," he whispered. "No, Tony please—"

And, dangling over the white porcelain lip of the bathtub, a hand. Limp. A slow trickle of blood (REDRUM) trickling down one of the fingers, the third, dripping onto the tile from the carefully shaped nail—

No oh no oh no—

(oh please, Tony, you're scaring me)

REDRUM REDRUM REDRUM

(stop it, Tony, stop it)

Fading.

In the darkness the booming noises grew louder, louder still, echoing, everywhere, all around.

And now he was crouched in a dark hallway, crouched on a blue rug with a riot of twisting black shapes woven into its pile, listening to the booming noises approach, and now a Shape turned the corner and began to come toward him, lurching, smelling of blood and doom. It had a mallet in one hand and it was swinging it (REDRUM) from side to side in vicious arcs, slamming it into the walls, cutting the silk wallpaper and knocking out ghostly bursts of plasterdust:

Come on and take your medicine! Take it like a man!

The Shape advancing on him, reeking of that sweet-sour odor, gigantic, the mallet head cutting across the air with a wicked hissing whisper, then the great hollow boom as it crashed into the wall, sending the dust out in a puff you could smell, dry and itchy. Tiny red eyes glowed in the dark. The monster was upon him, it had discovered him, cowering here with a blank wall at his back. And the trapdoor in the ceiling was locked.

Darkness. Drifting.

"Tony, please take me back, please, please—"

And he *was* back, sitting on the curb of Arapahoe Street, his shirt sticking damply to his back, his body bathed in sweat. In his ears he could still hear that huge, contrapuntal booming sound and smell his own urine as he voided himself in the extremity of his terror. He could see that limp hand dangling over the edge of the tub with blood running down one finger, the third, and that inexplicable word so much more horrible than any of the others: REDRUM.

And now sunshine. Real things. Except for Tony, now six blocks up, only a speck, standing on the corner, his voice faint and high and sweet. "Be careful, doc . . ."

Then, in the next instant, Tony was gone and Daddy's battered red bug was turning the corner and chattering up the street, farting blue smoke behind it. Danny was off the curb in a second, waving, jiving from one foot to the other, yelling: "Daddy! Hey, Dad! Hi! Hi!"

His daddy swung the VW into the curb, killed the engine, and opened the door. Danny ran toward him and then froze, his eyes widening. His heart crawled up into the middle of his throat and froze solid. Beside his daddy, in the other front seat, was a short-handled mallet, its head clotted with blood and hair.

Then it was just a bag of groceries.

"Danny . . . you okay, doc?"

"Yeah. I'm okay." He went to his daddy and buried his face in Daddy's sheepskin-lined denim jacket and hugged him tight tight tight. Jack hugged him back, slightly bewildered.

"Hey, you don't want to sit in the sun like that, doc. You're drippin sweat."

"I guess I fell asleep a little. I love you, Daddy. I been waiting."

"I love you too, Dan. I brought home some stuff. Think you're big enough to carry it upstairs?"

"Sure am!"

"Doc Torrance, the world's strongest man," Jack said, and ruffled his hair. "Whose hobby is falling asleep on street corners."

Then they were walking up to the door and Mommy had come down to the porch to meet them and he stood on the second step and watched them kiss. They were glad to see each other. Love came out of them the way love had come out of the boy and girl walking up the street and holding hands. Danny was glad.

The bag of groceries—*just* a bag of groceries—crackled in his arms. Everything was all right. Daddy was home. Mommy was loving him. There were no bad things. And not everything Tony showed him always happened.

But fear had settled around his heart, deep and dreadful, around his heart and around that indecipherable word he had seen in his spirit's mirror.

5

PHONEBOOTH

Jack parked the VW in front of the Rexall in the Table Mesa shopping center and let the engine die. He wondered again if he shouldn't go ahead and get the fuel pump replaced, and told himself again that they couldn't afford it. If the little car could keep running until November, it could retire with full honors anyway. By November the snow up there in the mountains would be higher than the beetle's roof . . . maybe higher than three beetles stacked on top of each other.

"Want you to stay in the car, doc. I'll bring you a candy bar."

"Why can't I come in?"

"I have to make a phone call. It's private stuff."

"Is that why you didn't make it at home?"

"Check."

Wendy had insisted on a phone in spite of their unraveling finances. She had argued that with a small child—especially a boy like Danny, who sometimes suffered from fainting spells—they couldn't afford not to have one. So Jack had forked over the thirty-dollar installation fee, bad enough, and a ninety-dollar security deposit, which really hurt. And so far the phone had been mute except for two wrong numbers.

"Can I have a Baby Ruth, Daddy?"

"Yes. You sit still and don't play with the gearshift, right?"

"Right. I'll look at the maps."

"You do that."

As Jack got out, Danny opened the bug's glovebox and took out the five battered gas station maps: Colorado, Nebraska, Utah, Wyoming, New Mexico. He loved road maps, loved to trace where the roads went with his finger. As far as he was concerned, new maps were the best part of moving West.

Jack went to the drugstore counter, got Danny's candy bar, a newspaper, and a copy of the October *Writer's Digest.* He gave the girl a five and asked for his change in quarters. With the silver in his hand he walked over to the telephone booth by the key-making machine and slipped inside. From here he could see Danny in the bug through three sets of glass. The boy's head was bent studiously over his maps. Jack felt a wave of nearly desperate love for the boy. The emotion showed on his face as a stony grimness.

He supposed he could have made this obligatory thank-you call to Al from home; he certainly wasn't going to say anything Wendy would object to. It was his pride that said no. These days he almost always listened to what his pride told him to do, because along with his wife and son, six hundred dollars in a checking account, and one weary 1968 Volkswagen, his pride was all that was left. The only thing that was his. Even the checking account was joint. A year ago he had been teaching English in one of the finest prep schools in New England. There had been friends—although not exactly the same ones he'd had before going on the wagon—some laughs, fellow faculty members who admired his deft touch in the classroom and his private dedication to writing. Things had been very good six months ago. All at once there was enough money left over at the end of each two-week pay period to start a little savings account. In his drinking days there had never been a penny left over, even though Al Shockley had stood a great many of the rounds. He and Wendy had begun to talk cautiously about finding a house and making a down payment in a year or so. A farmhouse in the country, take six or eight years to renovate it completely, what the hell, they were young, they had time.

Then he had lost his temper.

George Hatfield.

The smell of hope had turned to the smell of old leather in Crommert's office, the whole thing like some scene from his own play: the old prints of previous Stovington headmasters on the walls, steel engravings of the school as it had been in 1879, when it was first built, and in 1895, when Vanderbilt money had enabled them to build the field house that still stood at the west end of the soccer field, squat, immense, dressed in ivy. April ivy had been rustling outside Crommert's slit window and the drowsy sound of steam heat came from the radiator. It was no set, he remembered thinking. It was real. His life. How could he have fucked it up so badly?

"This is a serious situation, Jack. Terribly serious. The Board has asked me to convey its decision to you."

The Board wanted Jack's resignation and Jack had given it to them. Under different circumstances, he would have gotten tenure that June.

What had followed that interview in Crommert's office had been the darkest, most dreadful night of his life. The wanting, the *needing* to get drunk had never been so bad. His hands shook. He knocked things over. And he kept wanting to take it out on Wendy and Danny. His temper was like a vicious animal on a frayed leash. He had left the house in terror that he might strike them. Had ended up outside a bar, and the only thing that had kept him from going in was the knowledge that if he did, Wendy would leave him at last, and take Danny with her. He would be dead from the day they left.

Instead of going into the bar, where dark shadows sat sampling the tasty waters of oblivion, he had gone to Al Shockley's house. The Board's vote had been six to one. Al had been the one.

Now he dialed the operator and she told him that for a dollar eighty-five he could be put in touch with Al two thousand miles away for three minutes. Time is relative, baby, he thought, and stuck in eight quarters. Faintly he could hear the electronic boops and beeps of his connection sniffing its way eastward.

Al's father had been Arthur Longley Shockley, the steel baron. He had left his only son, Albert, a fortune and a huge range of investments and directorships and chairs on various boards. One of these had been on the Board of Directors for Stovington Preparatory Academy, the old man's favorite charity. Both Arthur and Albert Shockley were alumni and Al lived in Barre, close enough to take a personal interest in the school's affairs. For several years Al had been Stovington's tennis coach.

Jack and Al had become friends in a completely natural and uncoincidental way: at the many school and faculty functions they attended together, they were always the two drunkest people there. Shockley was separated from his wife, and Jack's own marriage was skidding slowly downhill, although he still loved Wendy and had promised sincerely (and frequently) to reform, for her sake and for baby Danny's.

The two of them went on from many faculty parties, hitting the bars until they closed, then stopping at some mom 'n' pop store for a case of beer they would drink parked at the end of some back road. There were mornings when Jack would stumble into their leased house with dawn seeping into the sky and find Wendy and the baby asleep on the couch, Danny always on the inside, a tiny fist curled under the shelf of Wendy's jaw. He would look at them and the self-loathing would back up his throat in a bitter wave, even stronger than the taste of beer and cigarettes and martinis—martians, as Al called them. Those were the times that his mind would turn thoughtfully and sanely to the gun or the rope or the razor blade.

If the bender had occurred on a weeknight, he would sleep for three hours, get up, dress, chew four Excedrins, and go off to teach his nine o'clock American Poets still drunk. Good morning, kids, today the Red-Eyed Wonder is going to tell you about how Longfellow lost his wife in the big fire.

He hadn't believed he was an alcoholic, Jack thought as Al's telephone began ringing in his ear. The classes he had missed or taught unshaven, still reeking of last night's martians. Not me, I can stop anytime. The nights he and Wendy had passed in separate beds. Listen, I'm fine. Mashed fenders. Sure I'm okay to drive. The tears she always shed in the bathroom. Cautious looks from his colleagues at any party where alcohol was served, even wine. The slowly dawning realization that he was being talked about. The knowledge that he was producing nothing at his Underwood but balls of mostly blank paper that ended up in the wastebasket. He had been something of a catch for Stovington, a slowly blooming American writer perhaps, and certainly a man well qualified to teach that great mystery, creative writing. He had published two dozen short stories. He was working on a play, and thought there might be a novel incubating in some mental back room. But now he was not producing and his teaching had become erratic.

It had finally ended one night less than a month after Jack had broken his son's arm. That, it seemed to him, had ended his marriage. All that remained was for Wendy to gather her will ... if her mother hadn't been such a grade A bitch, he knew, Wendy would have taken a bus back to New Hampshire as soon as Danny had been okay to travel. It was over.

It had been a little past midnight. Jack and Al were coming into Barre on U.S. 31, Al behind the wheel of his Jag, shifting fancily on the curves, sometimes crossing the double yellow line. They were both very drunk; the martians had landed that night in force. They came around the last curve before the bridge at seventy, and there was a kid's bike in the road, and then the sharp, hurt squealing as rubber shredded from the Jag's tires, and Jack remembered seeing Al's face looming over the steering wheel like a round white moon. Then the jingling crashing sound as they hit the bike at forty, and it had flown up like a bent and twisted bird, the handlebars striking the windshield, and then it was in the air again, leaving the starred safety glass in front of Jack's bulging eyes. A moment later he heard the final dreadful smash as it landed on the road behind them. Something thumped underneath them as the tires passed over it. The Jag drifted around broadside, Al still jockeying the wheel, and from far away Jack heard himself saying: "Jesus, Al. We ran him down. I felt it."

In his ear the phone kept ringing. *Come on, Al. Be home. Let me get this over with.*

Al had brought the car to a smoking halt not more than three feet from a bridge stanchion. Two of the Jag's tires were flat. They had left zigzagging loops of burned rubber for a hundred and thirty feet. They looked at each other for a moment and then ran back in the cold darkness.

The bike was completely ruined. One wheel was gone, and looking back over his shoulder Al had seen it lying in the middle of the road, half a dozen spokes sticking up like piano wire. Al had said hesitantly: "I think that's what we ran over, Jacky-boy."

"Then where's the kid?"

"Did you *see* a kid?"

Jack frowned. It had all happened with such crazy speed. Coming around the corner. The bike looming in the Jag's headlights. Al yelling something. Then the collision and the long skid.

They moved the bike to one shoulder of the road. Al went back to the Jag and put on its four-way flashers. For the next two hours they searched the sides of the road, using a powerful four-cell flashlight. Nothing. Although it was late, several cars passed the beached Jaguar and the two men with the bobbing flashlight. None of them stopped. Jack thought later that some queer providence, bent on giving them both a last chance, had kept the cops away, had kept any of the passers-by from calling them.

At quarter past two they returned to the Jag, sober but queasy. "If there was nobody riding it, what was it doing in the middle of the road?" Al demanded. "It wasn't parked on the side; it was right out in the fucking *middle!*"

Jack could only shake his head.

"Your party does not answer," the operator said. "Would you like me to keep on trying?"

"A couple more rings, operator. Do you mind?"

"No, sir," the voice said dutifully.

Come on, Al!

Al had hiked across the bridge to the nearest pay phone, called a bachelor friend and told him it would be worth fifty dollars if the friend would get the Jag's snow tires out of the garage and bring them down to the Highway 31 bridge outside of Barre. The friend showed up twenty minutes later, wearing a pair of jeans and his pajama top. He surveyed the scene.

"Kill anybody?" he asked.

Al was already jacking up the back of the car and Jack was loosening lug nuts. "Providentially, no one," Al said.

"I think I'll just head on back anyway. Pay me in the morning."

"Fine," Al said without looking up.

The two of them had gotten the tires on without incident, and together they drove back to Al Shockley's house. Al put the Jag in the garage and killed the motor.

In the dark quiet he said: "I'm off drinking, Jacky-boy. It's all over. I've slain my last martian."

And now, sweating in this phonebooth, it occurred to Jack that he had never doubted Al's ability to carry through. He had driven back to his own house in the VW with the radio turned up, and some disco group chanted over and over again, talismanic in the house before dawn: *Do it anyway . . . you wanta do it . . . do it anyway you want . . .* No matter how loud he heard the squealing tires, the crash. When he blinked his eyes shut, he saw that single crushed wheel with its broken spokes pointing at the sky.

When he got in, Wendy was asleep on the couch. He looked in Danny's room and Danny was in his crib on his back, sleeping deeply, his arm still buried in the cast. In the softly filtered glow from the streetlight outside he could see the dark lines on its plastered whiteness where all the doctors and nurses in pediatrics had signed it.

It was an accident. He fell down the stairs.

(o you dirty liar)

It was an accident. I lost my temper.

(you fucking drunken waste god wiped snot out of his nose and that was you)

Listen, hey, come on, please, just an accident—

But the last plea was driven away by the image of that bobbing flashlight as they hunted through the dry late November weeds, looking for the sprawled body that by all good rights should have been there, waiting for the police. It didn't matter that Al had been driving. There had been other nights when he had been driving.

He pulled the covers up over Danny, went into their bedroom, and took the Spanish Llama .38 down from the top shelf of the closet. It was in a shoe box. He sat on the bed with it for nearly an hour, looking at it, fascinated by its deadly shine.

It was dawn when he put it back in the box and put the box back in the closet.

That morning he had called Bruckner, the department head, and told him to please post his classes. He had the flu. Bruckner agreed, with less good grace than was common. Jack Torrance had been extremely susceptible to the flu in the last year.

Wendy made him scrambled eggs and coffee. They ate in silence. The only sound came from the back yard, where Danny was gleefully running his trucks across the sand pile with his good hand.

She went to do the dishes. Her back to him, she said: "Jack. I've been thinking."

"Have you?" He lit a cigarette with trembling hands. No hangover this morning, oddly enough. Only the shakes. He blinked. In the instant's darkness the bike flew up against the windshield, starring the glass. The tires shrieked. The flashlight bobbed.

"I want to talk to you about . . . about what's best for me and Danny. For you too, maybe. I don't know. We should have talked about it before, I guess."

"Would you do something for me?" he asked, looking at the wavering tip of his cigarette. "Would you do me a favor?"

"What?" Her voice was dull and neutral. He looked at her back.

"Let's talk about it a week from today. If you still want to."

Now she turned to him, her hands lacy with suds, her pretty face pale and disillusioned. "Jack, promises don't work with you. You just go right on with—"

She stopped, looking in his eyes, fascinated, suddenly uncertain.

"In a week," he said. His voice had lost all its strength and dropped to a whisper. "Please. I'm not promising anything. If you still want to talk then, we'll talk. About anything you want."

They looked across the sunny kitchen at each other for a long time, and when she turned back to the dishes without saying anything more, he began to shudder. God, he needed a drink. Just a little pick-me-up to put things in their true perspective—

"Danny said he dreamed you had a car accident," she said abruptly. "He has funny dreams sometimes. He said it this morning, when I got him dressed. Did you, Jack? Did you have an accident?"

"No."

By noon the craving for a drink had become a low-grade fever. He went to Al's.

"You dry?" Al asked before letting him in. Al looked horrible.

"Bone dry. You look like Lon Chaney in *Phantom of the Opera*."

"Come on in."

They played two-handed whist all afternoon. They didn't drink.

A week passed. He and Wendy didn't speak much. But he knew she was watching, not believing. He drank coffee black and endless cans of Coca-Cola. One night he drank a whole six-pack of Coke and then ran into the bathroom and vomited it up. The level of the bottles in the liquor cabinet did not go down. After his classes he went over to Al Shockley's—she hated Al Shockley worse than she had ever hated anyone— and when he came home she would swear she smelled scotch or gin on his breath, but he would talk lucidly to her before supper, drink coffee, play with Danny after supper, sharing a Coke with him, read him a bedtime story, then sit and correct themes with cup after cup of black coffee by his hand, and she would have to admit to herself that she had been wrong.

Weeks passed and the unspoken word retreated further from the back of her lips. Jack sensed its retirement but knew it would never retire completely. Things began to get a little easier. Then George Hatfield. He had lost his temper again, this time stone sober.

"Sir, your party still doesn't—"

"Hello?" Al's voice, out of breath.

"Go ahead," the operator said dourly.

"Al, this is Jack Torrance."

"Jacky-boy!" Genuine pleasure. "How are you?"

"Good. I just called to say thanks. I got the job. It's perfect. If I can't finish that goddam play snowed in all winter, I'll never finish it."

"You'll finish."

"How are things?" Jack asked hesitantly.

"Dry," Al responded. "You?"

"As a bone."

"Miss it much?"

"Every day."

Al laughed. "I know that scene. But I don't know how you stayed dry after that Hatfield thing, Jack. That was above and beyond."

"I really bitched things up for myself," he said evenly.

"Oh, hell. I'll have the Board around by spring. Effinger's already saying they might have been too hasty. And if that play comes to something—"

"Yes. Listen, my boy's out in the car, Al. He looks like he might be getting restless—"

"Sure. Understand. You have a good winter up there, Jack. Glad to help."

"Thanks again, Al." He hung up, closed his eyes in the hot booth, and again saw the crashing bike, the bobbing flashlight. There had been a squib in the paper the next day, no more than a space-filler really, but the owner had not been named. Why it had been out there in the night would always be a mystery to them, and perhaps that was as it should be.

He went back out to the car and gave Danny his slightly melted Baby Ruth.

"Daddy?"

"What, doc?"

Danny hesitated, looking at his father's abstracted face.

"When I was waiting for you to come back from that hotel, I had a bad dream. Do you remember? When I fell asleep?"

"Um-hm."

But it was no good. Daddy's mind was someplace else, not with him. Thinking about the Bad Thing again.

(I dreamed that you hurt me, Daddy)

"What was the dream, doc?"

"Nothing," Danny said as they pulled out into the parking lot. He put the maps back into the glove compartment.

"You sure?"

"Yes."

Jack gave his son a faint, troubled glance, and then his mind turned to his play.

6

NIGHT THOUGHTS

Love was over, and her man was sleeping beside her.

Her man.

She smiled a little in the darkness, his seed still trickling with slow warmth from between her slightly parted thighs, and her smile was both rueful and pleased, because the phrase *her man* summoned up a hundred feelings. Each feeling examined alone was a bewilderment. Together, in this darkness floating to sleep, they were like a distant blues tune heard in an almost deserted night club, melancholy but pleasing.

> *Lovin' you baby, is just like rollin' off a log,*
> *But if I can't be your woman, I sure ain't goin' to be your dog.*

Had that been Billie Holiday? Or someone more prosaic like Peggy Lee? Didn't matter. It was low and torchy, and in the silence of her head it played mellowly, as if issuing from one of those old-fashioned jukeboxes, a Wurlitzer, perhaps, half an hour before closing.

Now, moving away from her consciousness, she wondered how many beds she had slept in with this man beside her. They had met in college and had first made love in his apartment . . . that had been less than three months after her mother drove her from the house, told her never to come back, that if she wanted to go somewhere she could go to her father since she had been responsible for the divorce. That had been in 1970. So long ago? A semester later they had moved in together, had found jobs for the summer, and had kept the apartment when their senior year began. She remembered that bed the most clearly, a big double that sagged in the middle. When they made love, the rusty box spring had counted the beats. That fall she had finally managed to break from her mother. Jack had helped her. She wants to keep beating you, Jack had said. The more times you phone her, the more times you crawl back begging forgiveness, the more she can beat you with your father. It's good for her, Wendy, because she can go on making believe it was your fault. But it's not good for you. They had talked it over again and again in that bed, that year.

(Jack sitting up with the covers pooled around his waist, a cigarette burning between his fingers, looking her in the eye—he had a half-humorous, half-scowling way of doing that—telling her: *She told you never to come back, right? Never to darken her door again, right? Then why doesn't she hang up the phone when she knows it's you? Why does she only tell you that you can't come in if I'm with you? Because she thinks I might cramp her style a little bit. She wants to keep putting the thumbscrews right to you, baby. You're a fool if you keep letting her do it. She told you never to come back, so why don't you take her at her word? Give it a rest.* And at last she'd seen it his way.)

It had been Jack's idea to separate for a while—to get perspective on the relationship, he said. She had been afraid he had become interested in someone else. Later she found it wasn't so. They were together again in the spring and he asked her if she had been to see her father. She had jumped as if he'd struck her with a quirt.

How did you know that?

The Shadow knows.

Have you been spying on me?

And his impatient laughter, which had always made her feel so awkward—as if she were eight and he was able to see her motivations more clearly than she.

You needed time, Wendy.

For what?

I guess . . . to see which one of us you wanted to marry.

Jack, what are you saying?

I think I'm proposing marriage.

The wedding. Her father had been there, her mother had not been. She discovered she could live with that, if she had Jack. Then Danny had come, her fine son.

That had been the best year, the best bed. After Danny was born, Jack had gotten her a job typing for half a dozen English Department profs—quizzes, exams, class syllabi, study notes, reading lists. She ended up typing a novel for one of them, a novel that never got published . . . much to Jack's very irreverent and very private glee. The job was good for forty a week, and skyrocketed all the way up to sixty during the two months she spent typing the unsuccessful novel. They had their first car, a five-year-old Buick with a baby seat in the middle. Bright, upwardly mobile young marrieds. Danny forced a reconciliation between her and her mother, a reconciliation that was always tense and never happy, but a reconciliation all the same. When she took Danny to the house, she went without Jack. And she didn't tell Jack that her mother always remade Danny's diapers, frowned over his formula, could always spot the accusatory first signs of a rash on the baby's bottom or privates. Her mother never said anything overtly, but the message came through anyway: the price she had begun to pay (and maybe always would) for the reconciliation was the feeling that she was an inadequate mother. It was her mother's way of keeping the thumbscrews handy.

During the days Wendy would stay home and housewife, feeding Danny his bottles in the sunwashed kitchen of the four-room second-story apartment, playing her records on the battered portable stereo she had had since high school. Jack would come home at three (or at two if he felt he could cut his last class), and while Danny slept he would lead her into the bedroom and fears of inadequacy would be erased.

At night while she typed, he would do his writing and his assignments. In those days she sometimes came out of the bedroom where the typewriter was to find both of them asleep on the studio couch, Jack wearing nothing but his underpants, Danny sprawled comfortably on her husband's chest with his thumb in his mouth. She would put Danny in his crib, then read whatever Jack had written that night before waking him up enough to come to bed.

The best bed, the best year.

Sun gonna shine in my backyard someday . . .

In those days, Jack's drinking had still been well in hand. On Saturday nights a bunch of his fellow students would drop over and there would be a case of beer and discussions in which she seldom took part because her field had been sociology and his was English: arguments over whether Pepys's diaries were literature or history; discussions of Charles Olson's poetry; sometimes the reading of works in progress. Those and a hundred others. No, a thousand. She felt no real urge to take part; it was enough to sit in her rocking chair beside Jack, who sat cross-legged on the floor, one hand holding a beer, the other gently cupping her calf or braceleting her ankle.

The competition at UNH had been fierce, and Jack carried an extra burden in his writing. He put in at least an hour at it every night. It was his routine. The Saturday sessions were necessary therapy. They let something out of him that might otherwise have swelled and swelled until he burst.

At the end of his grad work he had landed the job at Stovington, mostly on the strength of his stories—four of them published at that time, one of them in *Esquire*. She remembered that day clearly enough; it would take more than three years to forget it. She had almost thrown the envelope away, thinking it was a subscription offer. Opening it, she had found instead that it was a letter saying that *Esquire* would like to use Jack's story "Concerning the Black Holes" early the following year. They would pay nine hundred dollars, not on publication but on acceptance. That was nearly half a year's take typing papers and she had flown to the telephone, leaving Danny in his high chair to goggle comically after her, his face lathered with creamed peas and beef purée.

Jack had arrived from the university forty-five minutes later, the Buick weighted down with seven friends and a keg of beer. After a ceremonial toast (Wendy also had a glass, although she ordinarily had no taste for beer), Jack had signed the acceptance letter, put it in the return envelope, and went down the block to drop it in the letter box. When he came back he stood gravely in the door and said, *"Veni, vidi, vici."* There were cheers and applause. When the keg was empty at eleven that night, Jack and the only two others who were still ambulatory went on to hit a few bars.

She had gotten him aside in the downstairs hallway. The other two were already out in the car, drunkenly singing the New Hampshire fight song. Jack was down on one knee, owlishly fumbling with the lacings of his moccasins.

"Jack," she said, "you shouldn't. You can't even tie your shoes, let alone drive."

He stood up and put his hands calmly on her shoulders. "Tonight I could fly to the moon if I wanted to."

"No," she said. "Not for all the *Esquire* stories in the world."

"I'll be home early."

But he hadn't been home until four in the morning, stumbling and mumbling his way up the stairs, waking Danny up when he came in. He had tried to soothe the baby and dropped him on the floor. Wendy had rushed out, thinking of what her mother would think if she saw the bruise before she thought of anything else—God help her, God help them both—and then picked Danny up, sat in the rocking chair with him, soothed him. She had been thinking of her mother for most of the five hours Jack had been gone, her mother's prophecy that Jack would never come to anything. *Big ideas,* her mother had said. *Sure. The welfare lines are full of educated fools with big ideas.* Did the *Esquire* story make her mother wrong or right? *Winnifred, you're not holding that baby right. Give him to me.* And was she not holding her husband right? Why else would he take his joy out of the house? A helpless kind of terror had risen up in her and it never occurred to her that he had gone out for reasons that had nothing to do with her.

"Congratulations," she said, rocking Danny—he was almost asleep again. "Maybe you gave him a concussion."

"It's just a bruise." He sounded sulky, wanting to be repentant: a little boy. For an instant she hated him.

"Maybe," she said tightly. "Maybe not." She heard so much of her mother talking to her departed father in her own voice that she was sickened and afraid.

"Like mother like daughter," Jack muttered.

"Go to bed!" she cried, her fear coming out sounding like anger. "Go to bed, you're drunk!"

"Don't tell me what to do."

"Jack . . . please, we shouldn't . . . it . . ." There were no words.

"Don't tell me what to do," he repeated sullenly, and then went into the bedroom. She was left alone in the rocking chair with Danny, who was sleeping again. Five minutes later Jack's snores came floating out to the living room. That had been the first night she had slept on the couch.

Now she turned restlessly on the bed, already dozing. Her mind, freed of any linear order by encroaching sleep, floated past the first year at Stovington, past the steadily worsening times that had reached low ebb when her husband had broken Danny's arm, to that morning in the breakfast nook.

Danny outside playing trucks in the sandpile, his arm still in the cast. Jack sitting at the table, pallid and grizzled, a cigarette jittering between his fingers. She had decided to ask him for a divorce. She had pondered the question from a hundred different angles, had been pondering it in fact for the six months before the broken arm. She told herself she would have made the decision long ago if it hadn't been for Danny, but not even that was necessarily true. She dreamed on the long nights when Jack was out, and her dreams were always of her mother's face and of her own wedding.

(Who giveth this woman? Her father standing in his best suit which was none too good—he was a traveling salesman for a line of canned goods that even then was going broke—and his tired face, how old he looked, how pale: *I do.)*

Even after the accident—if you could call it an accident—she had not been able to bring it all the way out, to admit that her marriage was a lopsided defeat. She had waited, dumbly hoping that a miracle would occur and Jack would see what was happening, not only to him but to her. But there had been no slowdown. A drink before going off to the Academy. Two or three beers with lunch at the Stovington House. Three or four martinis before dinner. Five or six more while grading papers. The weekends were worse. The nights out with Al Shockley were worse still. She had never dreamed there could be so much pain in a life when there was nothing physically wrong. She hurt all the time. How much of it was her fault? That question haunted her. She felt like her mother. Like her father. Sometimes, when she felt like herself she wondered what it would be like for Danny, and she dreaded the day when he grew old enough to lay blame. And she wondered where they would go. She had no doubt her mother would take her in, and no doubt that after half a year of watching her diapers remade, Danny's meals recooked and/or redistributed, of coming home to find his clothes changed or his hair cut or the books her mother found unsuitable spirited away to some limbo in the attic ... after half a year of that, she would have a complete nervous breakdown. And her mother would pat her hand and say comfortingly, *Although it's not your fault, it's all your own fault. You were never ready. You showed your true colors when you came between your father and me.*

My father, Danny's father. Mine, his.

(Who giveth this woman? I do. Dead of a heart attack six months later.)

The night before that morning she had lain awake almost until he came in, thinking, coming to her decision.

The divorce was necessary, she told herself. Her mother and father didn't belong in the decision. Neither did her feelings of guilt over their marriage nor her feelings of inadequacy over her own. It was necessary for her son's sake, and for herself, if she was to salvage anything at all from her early adulthood. The handwriting on the wall was brutal but clear. Her husband was a lush. He had a bad temper, one he could no longer keep wholly under control now that he was drinking so heavily and his writing was going so badly. Accidentally or not accidentally, he had broken Danny's arm. He was going to lose his job, if not this year then the year after. Already she had noticed the sympathetic looks from the other faculty wives. She told herself that she had stuck with the messy job of her marriage for as long as she could. Now she would have to leave it. Jack could have full visitation rights, and she would want support from him only until she could find something and get on her feet—and that would have to be fairly rapidly because she didn't know how long Jack would be able to pay support money. She would do it with as little bitterness as possible. But it had to end.

So thinking, she had fallen off into her own thin and unrestful sleep, haunted by the faces of her own mother and father. *You're nothing but a home-wrecker,* her mother said. *Who giveth this woman?* the minister said. *I do,* her father said. But in the bright and sunny morning she felt the same. Her back to him, her hands plunged in warm dishwater up to the wrists, she had commenced with the unpleasantness.

"I want to talk to you about something that might be best for Danny and I. For you too, maybe. We should have talked about it before, I guess."

And then he had said an odd thing. She had expected to discover his anger, to provoke the bitterness, the recriminations. She had expected a mad dash for the liquor cabinet. But not this soft, almost toneless reply that was so unlike him. It was almost as though the Jack she had lived with for six years had never come back last night—as if he had been replaced by some unearthly doppelgänger that she would never know or be quite sure of.

"Would you do something for me? A favor?"

"What?" She had to discipline her voice strictly to keep it from trembling.

"Let's talk about it in a week. If you still want to."

And she had agreed. It remained unspoken between them. During that week he had seen Al Shockley more than ever, but he came home early and there was no liquor on his breath. She imagined she smelled it, but knew it wasn't so. Another week. And another.

Divorce went back to committee, unvoted on.

What had happened? She still wondered and still had not the slightest idea. The subject was taboo between them. He was like a man who had leaned around a corner and had seen an unexpected monster lying in wait, crouching among the dried bones of its old kills. The liquor remained in the cabinet, but he didn't touch it. She had considered throwing them out a dozen times but in the end always backed away from the idea, as if some unknown charm would be broken by the act.

And there was Danny's part in it to consider.

If she felt she didn't know her husband, then she was in awe of her child—awe in the strict meaning of that word: a kind of undefined superstitious dread.

Dozing lightly, the image of the instant of his birth was presented to her. She was again lying on the delivery table, bathed in sweat, her hair in strings, her feet splayed out in the stirrups

(and a little high from the gas they kept giving her whiffs of; at one point she had muttered that she felt like an advertisement for gang rape, and the nurse, an old bird who had assisted at the births of enough children to populate a high school, found that extremely funny)

the doctor between her legs, the nurse off to one side, arranging instruments and humming. The sharp, glassy pains had been coming at steadily shortening intervals, and several times she had screamed in spite of her shame.

Then the doctor told her quite sternly that she must *PUSH*, and she did, and then she felt something being taken from her. It was a clear and distinct feeling, one she would never forget— the thing *taken*. Then the doctor held her son up by the legs—she had seen his tiny sex and known he was a boy immediately—and as the doctor groped for the airmask, she had seen something else, something so horrible that she found the strength to scream again after she had thought all screams were used up:

He has no face!

But of course there had been a face, Danny's own sweet face, and the caul that had covered it at birth now resided in a small jar which she had kept, almost shamefully. She did not hold with old superstition, but she had kept the caul nevertheless. She did not hold with wives' tales, but the boy had been unusual from the first. She did not believe in second sight but—

Did Daddy have an accident? I dreamed Daddy had an accident.

Something had changed him. She didn't believe it was just her getting ready to ask for a divorce that had done it. Something had happened before that morning. Something that had happened while she slept uneasily. Al Shockley said that nothing had happened, nothing at all, but he had averted his eyes when he said it, and if you believed faculty gossip, Al had also climbed aboard the fabled wagon.

Did Daddy have an accident?

Maybe a chance collision with fate, surely nothing much more concrete. She had read that day's paper and the next day's with a closer eye than usual, but she saw nothing she could connect with Jack. God help her, she had been looking for a hit-and-run accident or a barroom brawl that had resulted in serious injuries or . . . who knew? Who wanted to? But no policeman came to call, either to ask questions or with a warrant empowering him to take paint scrapings from the VW's bumpers. Nothing. Only her husband's one hundred and eighty degree change and her son's sleepy question on waking:

Did Daddy have an accident? I dreamed . . .

She had stuck with Jack more for Danny's sake than she would admit in her waking hours, but now, sleeping lightly, she could admit it: Danny had been Jack's for the asking, almost from the first. Just as she had been her father's, almost from the first. She couldn't remember Danny ever spitting a bottle back on Jack's shirt. Jack could get him to eat after she had given up in disgust, even when Danny was teething and it gave him visible pain to chew. When Danny had a stomachache, she would rock him for an hour before he began to quiet; Jack had only to pick him up, walk twice around the room with him, and Danny would be asleep on Jack's shoulder, his thumb securely corked in his mouth.

He hadn't minded changing diapers, even those he called the special deliveries. He sat with Danny for hours on end, bouncing him on his lap, playing finger games with him, making faces at him while Danny poked at his nose and then collapsed with the giggles. He made formulas and administered them faultlessly, getting up every last burp afterward. He would take Danny with him in the car to get the paper or a bottle of milk or nails at the hardware store even when their son was still an infant. He had taken Danny to a Stovington-Keene soccer match when Danny was only six months old, and Danny had sat motionlessly on his father's lap through the whole game, wrapped in a blanket, a small Stovington pennant clutched in one chubby fist.

He loved his mother but he was his father's boy.

And hadn't she felt, time and time again, her son's wordless opposition to the whole idea of divorce? She would be thinking about it in the kitchen, turning it over in her mind as she turned the potatoes for supper over in her hands for the peeler's blade. And she would turn around to see him sitting cross-legged in a kitchen chair, looking at her with eyes that seemed both frightened and accusatory. Walking with him in the park, he would suddenly seize both her hands and say— almost demand: "Do you love me? Do you love Daddy?" And, confused, she would nod or say, "Of course I do, honey." Then he would run to the duck pond, sending them squawking and scared to the other end, flapping their wings in a panic before the small ferocity of his charge, leaving her to stare after him and wonder.

There were even times when it seemed that her determination to at least discuss the matter with Jack dissolved, not out of her own weakness, but under the determination of her son's will.

I don't believe such things.

But in sleep she did believe them, and in sleep, with her husband's seed still drying on her thighs, she felt that the three of them had been permanently welded together—that if their three/oneness was to be destroyed, it would not be destroyed by any of them but from outside.

Most of what she believed centered around her love for Jack. She had never stopped loving him, except maybe for that dark period immediately following Danny's "accident." And she loved her son. Most of all she loved them together, walking or riding or only sitting, Jack's large head and Danny's small one poised alertly over the fans of old maid hands, sharing a bottle of Coke, looking at the funnies. She loved having them with her, and she hoped to dear God that this hotel caretaking job Al had gotten for Jack would be the beginning of good times again.

> *And the wind gonna rise up, baby,*
> *and blow my blues away . . .*

Soft and sweet and mellow, the song came back and lingered, following her down into a deeper sleep where thought ceased and the faces that came in dreams went unremembered.

7

IN ANOTHER
BEDROOM

Danny awoke with the booming still loud in his ears, and the drunk, savagely pettish voice crying hoarsely: *Come out here and take your medicine! I'll find you! I'll find you!*

But now the booming was only his racing heart, and the only voice in the night was the faraway sound of a police siren.

He lay in bed motionlessly, looking up at the wind-stirred shadows of the leaves on his bedroom ceiling. They twined sinuously together, making shapes like the vines and creepers in a jungle, like patterns woven into the nap of a thick carpet. He was clad in Doctor Denton pajamas, but between the pajama suit and his skin he had grown a more closely fitting singlet of perspiration.

"Tony?" he whispered. "You there?"

No answer.

He slipped out of bed and padded silently across to the window and looked out on Arapahoe Street, now still and silent. It was two in the morning. There was nothing out there but empty sidewalks drifted with fallen leaves, parked cars, and the long-necked streetlight on the corner across from the Cliff Brice gas station. With its hooded top and motionless stance, the streetlight looked like a monster in a space show.

He looked up the street both ways, straining his eyes for Tony's slight, beckoning form, but there was no one there.

The wind sighed through the trees, and the fallen leaves rattled up the deserted walks and around the hubcaps of parked cars. It was a faint and sorrowful sound, and the boy thought that he might be the only one in Boulder awake enough to hear it. The only human being, at least. There was no way of knowing what else might be out in the night, slinking hungrily through the shadows, watching and scenting the breeze.

I'll find you! I'll find you!

"Tony?" he whispered again, but without much hope.

Only the wind spoke back, gusting more strongly this time, scattering leaves across the sloping roof below his window. Some of them slipped into the raingutter and came to rest there like tired dancers.

Danny . . . Danneee . . .

He started at the sound of that familiar voice and craned out the window, his small hands on the sill. With the sound of Tony's voice the whole night seemed to have come silently and secretly alive, whispering even when the wind quieted again and the leaves were still and the shadows had stopped moving. He thought he saw a darker shadow standing by the bus stop a block down, but it was hard to tell if it was a real thing or an eye-trick.

Don't go, Danny . . .

Then the wind gusted again, making him squint, and the shadow by the bus stop was gone . . . if it had ever been there at all. He stood by his window for

(a minute? an hour?)

some time longer, but there was no more. At last he crept back into his bed and pulled the blankets up and watched the shadows thrown by the alien streetlight turn into a sinuous jungle filled with flesh-eating plants that wanted only to slip around him, squeeze the life out of him, and drag him down into a blackness where one sinister word flashed in red:

REDRUM.

PART TWO

CLOSING DAY

8

A VIEW OF
THE OVERLOOK

Mommy was worried.

She was afraid the bug wouldn't make it up and down all these mountains and that they would get stranded by the side of the road where somebody might come ripping along and hit them. Danny himself was more sanguine; if Daddy thought the bug would make this one last trip, then probably it would.

"We're just about there," Jack said.

Wendy brushed her hair back from her temples. "Thank God."

She was sitting in the right-hand bucket, a Victoria Holt paperback open but face down in her lap. She was wearing her blue dress, the one Danny thought was her prettiest. It had a sailor collar and made her look very young, like a girl just getting ready to graduate from high school. Daddy kept putting his hand high up on her leg and she kept laughing and brushing it off, saying Get away, fly.

Danny was impressed with the mountains. One day Daddy had taken them up in the ones near Boulder, the ones they called the Flatirons, but these were much bigger, and on the tallest of them you could see a fine dusting of snow, which Daddy said was often there year-round.

And they were actually *in* the mountains, no goofing around. Sheer rock faces rose all around them, so high you could barely see their tops even by craning your neck out the window. When they left Boulder, the temperature had been in the high seventies. Now, just after noon, the air up here felt crisp and cold like November back in Vermont and Daddy had the heater going . . . not that it worked all that well. They had passed several signs that said FALLING ROCK ZONE (Mommy read each one to him), and although Danny had waited anxiously to see some rock fall, none had. At least not yet.

Half an hour ago they had passed another sign that Daddy said was very important. This sign said ENTERING SIDEWINDER PASS, and Daddy said that sign was as far as the snowplows went in the wintertime. After that the road got too steep. In the winter the road was closed from the little town of Sidewinder, which they had gone through just before they got to that sign, all the way to Buckland, Utah.

Now they were passing another sign.

"What's that one, Mom?"

"That one says SLOWER VEHICLES USE RIGHT LANE. That means us."

"The bug will make it," Danny said.

"Please, God," Mommy said, and crossed her fingers. Danny looked down at her open-toed sandals and saw that she had crossed her toes as well. He giggled. She smiled back, but he knew that she was still worried.

The road wound up and up in a series of slow S curves, and Jack dropped the bug's stick shift from fourth gear to third, then into second. The bug wheezed and protested, and Wendy's eye fixed on the speedometer needle, which sank from forty to thirty to twenty, where it hovered reluctantly.

"The fuel pump . . ." she began timidly.

"The fuel pump will go another three miles," Jack said shortly.

The rock wall fell away on their right, disclosing a slash valley that seemed to go down forever, lined a dark green with Rocky Mountain pine and spruce. The pines fell away to gray cliffs of rock that dropped for hundreds of feet before smoothing out. She saw a waterfall spilling over one of them, the early afternoon sun sparkling in it like a golden fish snared in a blue net. They were beautiful mountains but they were hard. She did not think they would forgive many mistakes. An unhappy foreboding rose in her throat. Further west in the Sierra Nevada the Donner Party had become snowbound and had resorted to cannibalism to stay alive. The mountains did not forgive many mistakes.

With a punch of the clutch and a jerk, Jack shifted down to first gear and they labored upward, the bug's engine thumping gamely.

"You know," she said, "I don't think we've seen five cars since we came through Sidewinder. And one of them was the hotel limousine."

Jack nodded. "It goes right to Stapleton Airport in Denver. There's already some icy patches up beyond the hotel, Watson says, and they're forecasting more snow for tomorrow up higher. Anybody going through the mountains now wants to be on one of the main roads, just in case. That goddam Ullman better still be up there. I guess he will be."

"You're sure the larder is fully stocked?" she asked, still thinking of the Donners.

"He said so. He wanted Hallorann to go over it with you. Hallorann's the cook."

"Oh," she said faintly, looking at the speedometer. It had dropped from fifteen to ten miles an hour.

"There's the top," Jack said, pointing three hundred yards ahead. "There's a scenic turnout and you can see the Overlook from there. I'm going to pull off the road and give the bug a chance to rest." He craned over his shoulder at Danny, who was sitting on a pile of blankets. "What do you think, doc? We might see some deer. Or caribou."

"Sure, Dad."

The VW labored up and up. The speedometer dropped to just above the five-mile-an-hour hashmark and was beginning to hitch when Jack pulled off the road

("What's that sign, Mommy?" "SCENIC TURNOUT," she read dutifully.)

and stepped on the emergency brake and let the VW run in neutral.

"Come on," he said, and got out.

They walked to the guardrail together.

"That's it," Jack said, and pointed at eleven o'clock.

For Wendy, it was discovering truth in a cliché: her breath was taken away. For a moment she was unable to breathe at all; the view had knocked the wind from her. They were standing near the top of one peak. Across from them—who knew how far?—an even taller mountain reared into the sky, its jagged tip only a silhouette that was now nimbused by the sun, which was beginning its decline. The whole valley floor was spread out below them, the slopes that they had climbed in the laboring bug falling away with such dizzying suddenness that she knew to look down there for too long would bring on nausea and eventual vomiting. The imagination seemed to spring to full life in the clear air, beyond the rein of reason, and to look was to helplessly see one's self plunging down and down and down, sky and slopes changing places in slow cartwheels, the scream drifting from your mouth like a lazy balloon as your hair and your dress billowed out . . .

She jerked her gaze away from the drop almost by force and followed Jack's finger. She could see the highway clinging to the side of this cathedral spire, switching back on itself but always tending northwest, still climbing but at a more gentle angle. Further up, seemingly set directly into the slope itself, she saw the grimly clinging pines give way to a wide square of green lawn and standing in the middle of it, overlooking all this, the hotel. The Overlook. Seeing it, she found breath and voice again.

"Oh, Jack, it's gorgeous!"

"Yes, it is," he said. "Ullman says he thinks it's the single most beautiful location in America. I don't care much for him, but I think he might be . . . Danny! Danny, are you all right?"

She looked around for him and her sudden fear for him blotted out everything else, stupendous or not. She darted toward him. He was holding onto the guardrail and looking up at the hotel, his face a pasty gray color. His eyes had the blank look of someone on the verge of fainting.

She knelt beside him and put steadying hands on his shoulders. "Danny, what's—"

Jack was beside her. "You okay, doc?" He gave Danny a brisk little shake and his eyes cleared.

"I'm okay, Daddy. I'm fine."

"What was it, Danny?" she asked. "Were you dizzy, honey?"

"No, I was just . . . thinking. I'm sorry. I didn't mean to scare you." He looked at his parents, kneeling in front of him, and offered them a small puzzled smile. "Maybe it was the sun. The sun got in my eyes."

"We'll get you up to the hotel and give you a drink of water," Daddy said.

"Okay."

And in the bug, which moved upward more surely on the gentler grade, he kept looking out between them as the road unwound, affording occasional glimpses of the Overlook Hotel, its massive bank of westward-looking windows reflecting back the sun. It was the place he had seen in the midst of the blizzard, the dark and booming place where some hideously familiar figure sought him down long corridors carpeted with jungle. The place Tony had warned him against. It was here. It was here. Whatever Redrum was, it was here.

9

CHECKING IT OUT

Ullman was waiting for them just inside the wide, old-fashioned front doors. He shook hands with Jack and nodded coolly at Wendy, perhaps noticing the way heads turned when she came through into the lobby, her golden hair spilling across the shoulders of the simple navy dress. The hem of the dress stopped a modest two inches above the knee, but you didn't have to see more to know they were good legs.

Ullman seemed truly warm toward Danny only, but Wendy had experienced that before. Danny seemed to be a child for people who ordinarily held W. C. Fields' sentiments about children. He bent a little from the waist and offered Danny his hand. Danny shook it formally, without a smile.

"My son Danny," Jack said. "And my wife Winnifred."

"I'm happy to meet you both," Ullman said. "How old are you, Danny?"

"Five, sir."

"*Sir,* yet." Ullman smiled and glanced at Jack. "He's well mannered."

"Of course he is," Jack said.

"And Mrs. Torrance." He offered the same little bow, and for a bemused instant Wendy thought he would kiss her hand. She half-offered it and he did take it, but only for a moment, clasped in both of his. His hands were small and dry and smooth, and she guessed that he powdered them.

The lobby was a bustle of activity. Almost every one of the old-fashioned high-backed chairs was taken. Bellboys shuttled in and out with suitcases and there was a line at the desk, which was dominated by a huge brass cash register. The BankAmericard and Master Charge decals on it seemed jarringly anachronistic.

To their right, down toward a pair of tall double doors that were pulled closed and roped off, there was an old-fashioned fireplace now blazing with birch logs. Three nuns sat on a sofa that was drawn up almost to the hearth itself. They were talking and smiling with their bags stacked up to either side, waiting for the check-out line to thin a little. As Wendy watched them they burst into a chord of tinkling, girlish laughter. She felt a smile touch her own lips; not one of them could be under sixty.

In the background was the constant hum of conversation, the muted *ding!* of the silver-plated bell beside the cash register as one of the two clerks on duty struck it, the slightly impatient call of "Front, please!" It brought back strong, warm memories of her honeymoon in New York with Jack, at the Beekman Tower. For the first time she let herself believe that this might be exactly what the three of them needed: a season together away from the world, a sort of family honeymoon. She smiled affectionately down at Danny, who was goggling around frankly at everything. Another limo, as gray as a banker's vest, had pulled up out front.

"The last day of the season," Ullman was saying. "Closing day. Always hectic. I had expected you more around three, Mr. Torrance."

"I wanted to give the Volks time for a nervous breakdown if it decided to have one," Jack said. "It didn't."

"How fortunate," Ullman said. "I'd like to take the three of you on a tour of the place a little later, and of course Dick Hallorann wants to show Mrs. Torrance the Overlook's kitchen. But I'm afraid—"

One of the clerks came over and almost tugged his forelock.

"Excuse me, Mr. Ullman—"

"Well? What is it?"

"It's Mrs. Brant," the clerk said uncomfortably. "She refuses to pay her bill with anything but her American Express card. I told her we stopped taking American Express at the end of the season last year, but she won't . . ." His eyes shifted to the Torrance family, then back to Ullman. He shrugged.

"I'll take care of it."

"Thank you, Mr. Ullman." The clerk crossed back to the desk, where a dreadnought of a woman bundled into a long fur coat and what looked like a black feather boa was remonstrating loudly.

"I have been coming to the Overlook Hotel since 1955," she was telling the smiling, shrugging clerk. "I continued to come even after my second husband died of a stroke on that tiresome roque court—I told him the sun was too hot that day—and I have *never* . . . I repeat: *never* . . . paid with anything but my American Express credit card. Call the police if you like! Have them drag me away! I will still refuse to pay with anything but my American Express credit card. I repeat: . . ."

"Excuse me," Mr. Ullman said.

They watched him cross the lobby, touch Mrs. Brant's elbow deferentially, and spread his hands and nod when she turned her tirade on him. He listened sympathetically, nodded again, and said something in return. Mrs. Brant smiled triumphantly, turned to the unhappy desk clerk, and said loudly: "Thank God there is one employee of this hotel who hasn't become an utter Philistine!"

She allowed Ullman, who barely came to the bulky shoulder of her fur coat, to take her arm and lead her away, presumably to his inner office.

"Whooo!" Wendy said, smiling. "There's a dude who earns his money."

"But he didn't like that lady," Danny said immediately. "He was just pretending to like her."

Jack grinned down at him. "I'm sure that's true, doc. But flattery is the stuff that greases the wheels of the world."

"What's flattery?"

"Flattery," Wendy told him, "is when your daddy says he likes my new yellow slacks even if he doesn't or when he says I don't need to take off five pounds."

"Oh. Is it lying for fun?"

"Something very like that."

He had been looking at her closely and now said: "You're pretty, Mommy." He frowned in confusion when they exchanged a glance and then burst into laughter.

"Ullman didn't waste much flattery on me," Jack said. "Come on over by the window, you guys. I feel conspicuous standing out here in the middle with my denim jacket on. I honest to God didn't think there'd be anybody much here on closing day. Guess I was wrong."

"You look very handsome," she said, and then they laughed again, Wendy putting a hand over her mouth. Danny still didn't understand, but it was okay. They were loving each other. Danny thought this place reminded her of somewhere else

(the beak-man place)

where she had been happy. He wished he liked it as well as she did, but he kept telling himself over and over that the things Tony showed him didn't always come true. He would be careful. He would watch for something called Redrum. But he would not say anything unless he absolutely had to. Because they were happy, they had been laughing, and there were no bad thoughts.

"Look at this view," Jack said.

"Oh, it's gorgeous! Danny, look!"

But Danny didn't think it was particularly gorgeous. He didn't like heights; they made him dizzy. Beyond the wide front porch, which ran the length of the hotel, a beautifully manicured lawn (there was a putting green on the right) sloped away to a long, rectangular swimming pool. A CLOSED sign stood on a little tripod at one end of the pool; *closed* was one sign he could read by himself, along with *Stop, Exit, Pizza,* and a few others.

Beyond the pool a graveled path wound off through baby pines and spruces and aspens. Here was a small sign he didn't know: ROQUE. There was an arrow below it.

"What's R-O-Q-U-E, Daddy?"

"A game," Daddy said. "It's a little bit like croquet, only you play it on a gravel court that has sides like a big billiard table instead of grass. It's a very old game, Danny. Sometimes they have tournaments here."

"Do you play it with a croquet mallet?"

"Like that," Jack agreed. "Only the handle's a little shorter and the head has two sides. One side is hard rubber and the other side is wood."

(Come out, you little shit!)

"It's pronounced *roke*," Daddy was saying. "I'll teach you how to play, if you want."

"Maybe," Danny said in an odd colorless little voice that made his parents exchange a puzzled look over his head. "I might not like it, though."

"Well if you don't like it, doc, you don't have to play. All right?"

"Sure."

"Do you like the animals?" Wendy asked. "That's called a topiary." Beyond the path leading to *roque* there were hedges clipped into the shapes of various animals. Danny, whose eyes were sharp, made out a rabbit, a dog, a horse, a cow, and a trio of bigger ones that looked like frolicking lions.

"Those animals were what made Uncle Al think of me for the job," Jack told him. "He knew that when I was in college I used to work for a landscaping company. That's a business that fixes people's lawns and bushes and hedges. I used to trim a lady's topiary."

Wendy put a hand over her mouth and snickered. Looking at her, Jack said, "Yes, I used to trim her topiary at least once a week."

"Get away, fly," Wendy said, and snickered again.

"Did she have nice hedges, Dad?" Danny asked, and at this they both stifled great bursts of laughter. Wendy laughed so hard that tears streamed down her cheeks and she had to get a Kleenex out of her handbag.

"They weren't animals, Danny," Jack said when he had control of himself. "They were playing cards. Spades and hearts and clubs and diamonds. But the hedges grow, you see—"

(They creep, Watson had said ... no, not the hedges, the

boiler. *You have to watch it all the time or you and your fambly will end up on the fuckin moon.)*

They looked at him, puzzled. The smile had faded off his face.

"Dad?" Danny asked.

He blinked at them, as if coming back from far away. "They grow, Danny, and lose their shape. So I'll have to give them a haircut once or twice a week until it gets so cold they stop growing for the year."

"And a playground, too," Wendy said. "My lucky boy."

The playground was beyond the *topiary*. Two slides, a big swing set with half a dozen swings set at varying heights, a jungle gym, a tunnel made of cement rings, a sandbox, and a playhouse that was an exact replica of the Overlook itself.

"Do you like it, Danny?" Wendy asked.

"I sure do," he said, hoping he sounded more enthused than he felt. "It's neat."

Beyond the playground there was an inconspicuous chain link security fence, beyond that the wide, macadamized drive that led up to the hotel, and beyond that the valley itself, dropping away into the bright blue haze of afternoon. Danny didn't know the word *isolation*, but if someone had explained it to him he would have seized on it. Far below, lying in the sun like a long black snake that had decided to snooze for a while, was the road that led back through Sidewinder Pass and eventually to Boulder. The road that would be closed all winter long. He felt a little suffocated at the thought, and almost jumped when Daddy dropped his hand on his shoulder.

"I'll get you that drink as soon as I can, doc. They're a little busy right now."

"Sure, Dad."

Mrs. Brant came out of the inner office looking vindicated. A few moments later two bellboys, struggling with eight suitcases between them, followed her as best they could as she strode triumphantly out the door. Danny watched through the window as a man in a gray uniform and a hat like a captain in the Army brought her long silver car around to the door and got out. He tipped his cap to her and ran around to open the trunk.

And in one of those flashes that sometimes came, he got a complete thought from her, one that floated above the confused, low-pitched babble of emotions and colors that he usually got in crowded places.

(i'd like to get into his pants)

Danny's brow wrinkled as he watched the bellboys put her cases into the trunk. She was looking rather sharply at the man in the gray uniform, who was supervising the loading. Why would she want to get that man's pants? Was she cold, even with that long fur coat on? And if she was that cold, why hadn't she just put on some pants of her own? His mommy wore pants just about all winter.

The man in the gray uniform closed the trunk and walked back to help her into the car. Danny watched closely to see if she would say anything about his pants, but she only smiled and gave him a dollar bill—a tip. A moment later she was guiding the big silver car down the driveway.

He thought about asking his mother why Mrs. Brant might want that car-man's pants, and decided against it. Sometimes questions could get you in a whole lot of trouble. It had happened to him before.

So instead he squeezed in between them on the small sofa they were sharing and watched all the people check out at the desk. He was glad his mommy and daddy were happy and loving each other, but he couldn't help being a little worried. He couldn't help it.

10

HALLORANN

The cook didn't conform to Wendy's image of the typical resort hotel kitchen personage at all. To begin with, such a personage was called a *chef*, nothing so mundane as a cook—cooking was what she did in her apartment kitchen when she threw all the leftovers into a greased Pyrex casserole dish and added noodles. Further, the culinary wizard of such a place as the Overlook, which advertised in the resort section of the New York Sunday *Times*, should be small, rotund, and pasty-faced (rather like the Pillsbury Dough-Boy); he should have a thin pencil-line mustache like a forties musical comedy star, dark eyes, a French accent, and a detestable personality.

Hallorann had the dark eyes and that was all. He was a tall black man with a modest afro that was beginning to powder white. He had a soft southern accent and he laughed a lot, disclosing teeth too white and too even to be anything but 1950-vintage Sears and Roebuck dentures. Her own father had had a pair, which he called Roebuckers, and from time to time he would push them out at her comically at the supper table . . . always, Wendy remembered now, when her mother was out in the kitchen getting something else or on the telephone.

Danny had stared up at this black giant in blue serge, and then had smiled when Hallorann picked him up easily, set him in the crook of his elbow, and said: "You ain't gonna stay up here all winter."

"Yes I am," Danny said with a shy grin.

"No, you're gonna come down to St. Pete's with me and learn to cook and go out on the beach every damn evenin watchin for crabs. Right?"

Danny giggled delightedly and shook his head no. Hallorann set him down.

"If you're gonna change your mind," Hallorann said, bending over him gravely, "you better do it quick. Thirty minutes from now and I'm in my car. Two and a half hours after that, I'm sitting at Gate 32, Concourse B, Stapleton International Airport, in the mile-high city of Denver, Colorado. Three hours after *that*, I'm rentin a car at the Miama Airport and on my way to sunny St. Pete's, waiting to get inta my swimtrunks and just laaafin up my sleeve at anybody stuck and caught in the snow. Can you dig it, my boy?"

"Yes, sir," Danny said, smiling.

Hallorann turned to Jack and Wendy. "Looks like a fine boy there."

"We think he'll do," Jack said, and offered his hand. Hallorann took it. "I'm Jack Torrance. My wife Winnifred. Danny you've met."

"And a pleasure it was. Ma'am, are you a Winnie or a Freddie?"

"I'm a Wendy," she said, smiling.

"Okay. That's better than the other two, I think. Right this way. Mr. Ullman wants you to have the tour, the tour you'll get." He shook his head and said under his breath: "And won't I be glad to see the last of *him*."

Hallorann commenced to tour them around the most immense kitchen Wendy had ever seen in her life. It was sparkling clean. Every surface was coaxed to a high gloss. It was more than just big; it was intimidating. She walked at Hallorann's side while Jack, wholly out of his element, hung back a little with Danny. A long wallboard hung with cutting instruments which went all the way from paring knives to two-handed cleavers hung beside a four-basin sink. There was a breadboard as big as their Boulder apartment's kitchen table. An amazing array of stainless-steel pots and pans hung from floor to ceiling, covering one whole wall.

"I think I'll have to leave a trail of breadcrumbs every time I come in," she said.

"Don't let it get you down," Hallorann said. "It's big, but it's still only a kitchen. Most of this stuff you'll never even have to touch. Keep it clean, that's all I ask. Here's the stove I'd be using, if I was you. There are three of them in all, but this is the smallest."

Smallest, she thought dismally, looking at it. There were twelve burners, two regular ovens and a Dutch oven, a heated well on top in which you could simmer sauces or bake beans, a broiler, and a warmer—plus a million dials and temperature gauges.

"All gas," Hallorann said. "You've cooked with gas before, Wendy?"

"Yes . . ."

"I love gas," he said, and turned on one of the burners. Blue flame popped into life and he adjusted it down to a faint glow with a delicate touch. "I like to be able to see the flame you're cookin with. You see where all the surface burner switches are?"

"Yes."

"And the oven dials are all marked. Myself, I favor the middle one because it seems to heat the most even, but you use whichever one you like—or all three, for that matter."

"A TV dinner in each one," Wendy said, and laughed weakly.

Hallorann roared. "Go right ahead, if you like. I left a list of everything edible over by the sink. You see it?"

"Here it is, Mommy!" Danny brought over two sheets of paper, written closely on both sides.

"Good boy," Hallorann said, taking it from him and ruffling his hair. "You sure you don't want to come to Florida with me, my boy? Learn to cook the sweetest shrimp creole this side of paradise?"

Danny put his hands over his mouth and giggled and retreated to his father's side.

"You three folks could eat up here for a year, I guess," Hallorann said. "We got a cold-pantry, a walk-in freezer, all sorts of vegetable bins, and two refrigerators. Come on and let me show you."

For the next ten minutes Hallorann opened bins and doors, disclosing food in such amounts as Wendy had never seen before. The food supplies amazed her but did not reassure her as much as she might have thought: the Donner Party kept recurring to her, not with thoughts of cannibalism (with all this food it would indeed be a long time before they were reduced to such poor rations as each other), but with the reinforced idea that this was indeed a serious business: when snow fell, getting out of here would not be a matter of an hour's drive to Sidewinder but a major operation. They would sit up here in this deserted grand hotel, eating the food that had been left them like creatures in a fairy tale and listening to the bitter wind around their snowbound eaves. In Vermont, when Danny had broken his arm

(when *Jack* broke Danny's arm)

she had called the emergency Medix squad, dialing the number from the little card attached to the phone. They had been at the house only ten minutes later. There were other numbers written on that little card. You could have a police car in five minutes and a fire truck in even less time than that, because the fire station was only three blocks away and one block over. There was a man to call if the lights went out, a man to call if the shower stopped up, a man to call if the TV went on the fritz. But what would happen up here if Danny had one of his fainting spells and swallowed his tongue?

(oh God what a thought!)

What if the place caught on fire? If Jack fell down the elevator shaft and fractured his skull? What if—?

(what if we have a wonderful time now stop *it, Winnifred!)*

Hallorann showed them into the walk-in freezer first, where their breath puffed out like comic strip balloons. In the freezer it was as if winter had already come.

Hamburger in big plastic bags, ten pounds in each bag, a dozen bags. Forty whole chickens hanging from a row of hooks in the wood-planked walls. Canned hams stacked up like poker chips, a dozen of them. Below the chickens, ten roasts of beef, ten roasts of pork, and a huge leg of lamb.

"You like lamb, doc?" Hallorann asked, grinning.

"I love it," Danny said immediately. He had never had it.

"I knew you did. There's nothin like two good slices of lamb on a cold night, with some mint jelly on the side. You got the mint jelly here, too. Lamb eases the belly. It's a noncontentious sort of meat."

From behind them Jack said curiously: "How did you know we called him doc?"

Hallorann turned around. "Pardon?"

"Danny. We call him doc sometimes. Like in the Bugs Bunny cartoons."

"Looks sort of like a doc, doesn't he?" He wrinkled his nose at Danny, smacked his lips, and said, "Ehhhh, what's up, doc?"

Danny giggled and then Hallorann said something

(Sure you don't want to go to Florida, doc?)

to him, very clearly. He heard every word. He looked at Hallorann, startled and a little scared. Hallorann winked solemnly and turned back to the food.

Wendy looked from the cook's broad, serge-clad back to her son. She had the oddest feeling that something had passed between them, something she could not quite follow.

"You got twelve packages of sausage, twelve packages of bacon," Hallorann said. "So much for the pig. In this drawer, twenty pounds of butter."

"*Real* butter?" Jack asked.

"The A-number-one."

"I don't think I've had real butter since I was a kid back in Berlin, New Hampshire."

"Well, you'll eat it up here until oleo seems a treat," Hallorann said, and laughed. "Over in this bin you got your bread—thirty loaves of white, twenty of dark. We try to keep racial balance at the Overlook, don't you know. Now I know fifty loaves won't take you through, but there's plenty of makings and fresh is better than frozen any day of the week.

"Down here you got your fish. Brain food, right, doc?"

"Is it, Mom?"

"If Mr. Hallorann says so, honey." She smiled.

Danny wrinkled his nose. "I don't like fish."

"You're dead wrong," Hallorann said. "You just never had any fish that liked *you*. This fish here will like you fine. Five pounds of rainbow trout, ten pounds of turbot, fifteen cans of tuna fish—"

"Oh yeah, I like tuna."

"and five pounds of the sweetest-tasting sole that ever swam in the sea. My boy, when next spring rolls around, you're gonna thank old ..." He snapped his fingers as if he had forgotten something. "What's my name, now? I guess it just slipped my mind."

"Mr. Hallorann," Danny said, grinning. "Dick, to your friends."

"That's right! And you bein a friend, you make it Dick."

As he led them into the far corner, Jack and Wendy exchanged a puzzled glance, both of them trying to remember if Hallorann had told them his first name.

"And this here I put in special," Hallorann said. "Hope you folks enjoy it."

"Oh really, you shouldn't have," Wendy said, touched. It was a twenty-pound turkey wrapped in a wide scarlet ribbon with a bow on top.

"You got to have your turkey on Thanksgiving, Wendy," Hallorann said gravely. "I believe there's a capon back here somewhere for Christmas. Doubtless you'll stumble on it. Let's come on out of here now before we all catch the pee-numonia. Right, doc?"

"Right!"

There were more wonders in the cold-pantry. A hundred boxes of dried milk (Hallorann advised her gravely to buy fresh milk for the boy in Sidewinder as long as it was feasible), five twelve-pound bags of sugar, a gallon jug of blackstrap molasses, cereals, glass jugs of rice, macaroni, spaghetti; ranked cans of fruit and fruit salad; a bushel of fresh apples that scented the whole room with autumn; dried raisins, prunes, and apricots ("You got to be regular if you want to be happy," Hallorann said, and pealed laughter at the cold-pantry ceiling, where one old-fashioned light globe hung down on an iron chain); a deep bin filled with potatoes; and smaller caches of tomatoes, onions, turnips, squashes, and cabbages.

"My word," Wendy said as they came out. But seeing all that fresh food after her thirty-dollar-a-week grocery budget so stunned her that she was unable to say just what her word was.

"I'm runnin a bit late," Hallorann said, checking his watch, "so I'll just let you go through the cabinets and the fridges as you get settled in. There's cheeses, canned milk, sweetened condensed milk, yeast, bakin soda, a whole bagful of those Table Talk pies, a few bunches of bananas that ain't even near to ripe yet—"

"Stop," she said, holding up a hand and laughing. "I'll never remember it all. It's super. And I promise to leave the place clean."

"That's all I ask." He turned to Jack. "Did Mr. Ullman give you the rundown on the rats in his belfry?"

Jack grinned. "He said there were possibly some in the attic, and Mr. Watson said there might be some more down in the basement. There must be two tons of paper down there, but I didn't see any shredded, as if they'd been using it to make nests."

"That Watson," Hallorann said, shaking his head in mock sorrow. "Ain't he the foulest-talking man you ever ran on?"

"He's quite a character," Jack agreed. His own father had been the foulest-talking man Jack had ever run on.

"It's sort of a pity," Hallorann said, leading them back toward the wide swinging doors that gave on the Overlook dining room. "There was money in that family, long ago. It was Watson's granddad or great-granddad—I can't remember which—that built this place."

"So I was told," Jack said.

"What happened?" Wendy asked.

"Well, they couldn't make it go," Hallorann said. "Watson will tell you the whole story—twice a day, if you let him. The old man got a bee in his bonnet about the place. He let it drag him down, I guess. He had two boys and one of them was killed in a riding accident on the grounds while the hotel was still a-building. That would have been 1908 or '09. The old man's wife died of the flu, and then it was just the old man and his youngest son. They ended up getting took on as caretakers in the same hotel the old man had built."

"It is sort of a pity," Wendy said.

"What happened to him? The old man?" Jack asked.

"He plugged his finger into a light socket by mistake and that was the end of him," Hallorann said. "Sometime in the early thirties before the Depression closed this place down for ten years.

"Anyway, Jack, I'd appreciate it if you and your wife would keep an eye out for rats in the kitchen, as well. If you should see them . . . traps, not poison."

Jack blinked. "Of course. Who'd want to put rat poison in the kitchen?"

Hallorann laughed derisively. "Mr. Ullman, that's who. That was his bright idea last fall. I put it to him, I said: 'What if we all get up here next May, Mr. Ullman, and I serve the traditional opening night dinner'—which just happens to be salmon in a very nice sauce—'and everybody gits sick and the doctor comes and says to you, "Ullman, what have you been doing up here? You've got eighty of the richest folks in America suffering from rat poisoning!" ' "

Jack threw his head back and bellowed laughter. "What did Ullman say?"

Hallorann tucked his tongue into his cheek as if feeling for a bit of food in there. "He said: 'Get some traps, Hallorann.' "

This time they all laughed, even Danny, although he was not completely sure what the joke was, except it had something to do with Mr. Ullman, who didn't know everything after all.

The four of them passed through the dining room, empty and silent now, with its fabulous western exposure on the snow-dusted peaks. Each of the white linen tablecloths had been covered with a sheet of tough clear plastic. The rug, now rolled up for the season, stood in one corner like a sentinel on guard duty.

Across the wide room was a double set of batwing doors, and over them an old-fashioned sign lettered in gilt script: *The Colorado Lounge.*

Following his gaze, Hallorann said, "If you're a drinkin man, I hope you brought your own supplies. That place is picked clean. Employees' party last night, you know. Every maid and bellhop in the place is goin around with a headache today, me included."

"I don't drink," Jack said shortly. They went back to the lobby.

It had cleared greatly during the half hour they'd spent in the kitchen. The long main room was beginning to take on the quiet, deserted look that Jack supposed they would become familiar with soon enough. The high-backed chairs were empty. The nuns who had been sitting by the fire were gone, and the fire itself was down to a bed of comfortably glowing coals. Wendy glanced out into the parking lot and saw that all but a dozen cars had disappeared.

She found herself wishing they could get back in the VW and go back to Boulder . . . or anywhere else.

Jack was looking around for Ullman, but he wasn't in the lobby.

A young maid with her ash-blond hair pinned up on her neck came over. "Your luggage is out on the porch, Dick."

"Thank you, Sally." He gave her a peck on the forehead. "You have yourself a good winter. Getting married, I hear."

He turned to the Torrances as she strolled away, backside twitching pertly. "I've got to hurry along if I'm going to make that plane. I want to wish you all the best. Know you'll have it."

"Thanks," Jack said. "You've been very kind."

"I'll take good care of your kitchen," Wendy promised again. "Enjoy Florida."

"I always do," Hallorann said. He put his hands on his knees and bent down to Danny. "Last chance, guy. Want to come to Florida?"

"I guess not," Danny said, smiling.

"Okay. Like to give me a hand out to my car with my bags?"

"If my mommy says I can."

"You can," Wendy said, "but you'll have to have that jacket buttoned." She leaned forward to do it but Hallorann was ahead of her, his large brown fingers moving with smooth dexterity.

725

"I'll send him right back in," Hallorann said.

"Fine," Wendy said, and followed them to the door. Jack was still looking around for Ullman. The last of the Overlook's guests were checking out at the desk.

11

THE SHINING

There were four bags in a pile just outside the door. Three of them were giant, battered old suitcases covered with black imitation alligator hide. The last was an oversized zipper bag with a faded tartan skin.

"Guess you can handle that one, can't you?" Hallorann asked him. He picked up two of the big cases in one hand and hoisted the other under his arm.

"Sure," Danny said. He got a grip on it with both hands and followed the cook down the porch steps, trying manfully not to grunt and give away how heavy it was.

A sharp and cutting fall wind had come up since they had arrived; it whistled across the parking lot, making Danny wince his eyes down to slits as he carried the zipper bag in front of him, bumping on his knees. A few errant aspen leaves rattled and turned across the now mostly deserted asphalt, making Danny think momentarily of that night last week when he had wakened out of his nightmare and had heard—or thought he heard, at least—Tony telling him not to go.

Hallorann set his bags down by the trunk of a beige Plymouth Fury. "This ain't much car," he confided to Danny, "just a rental job. My Bessie's on the other end. She's a car. 1950 Cadillac, and does she run sweet? I'll tell the world. I keep her in Florida because she's too old for all this mountain climbing. You need a hand with that?"

"No, sir," Danny said. He managed to carry it the last ten or twelve steps without grunting and set it down with a large sigh of relief.

"Good boy," Hallorann said. He produced a large key ring from the pocket of his blue serge jacket and unlocked the trunk. As he lifted the bags in he said: "You shine on, boy. Harder than anyone I ever met in my life. And I'm sixty years old this January."

"Huh?"

"You got a knack," Hallorann said, turning to him. "Me, I've always called it shining. That's what my grandmother called it, too. She had it. We used to sit in the kitchen when I was a boy no older than you and have long talks without even openin our mouths."

"Really?"

Hallorann smiled at Danny's openmouthed, almost hungry expression and said, "Come on up and sit in the car with me for a few minutes. Want to talk to you." He slammed the trunk.

In the lobby of the Overlook, Wendy Torrance saw her son get into the passenger side of Hallorann's car as the big black cook slid in behind the wheel. A sharp pang of fear struck her and she opened her mouth to tell Jack that Hallorann had not been lying about taking their son to Florida—there was a kidnaping afoot. But they were only sitting there. She could barely see the small silhouette of her son's head, turned attentively toward Hallorann's big one. Even at this distance that small head had a set to it that she recognized—it was the way her son looked when there was something on the TV that particularly fascinated him, or when he and his father were playing old maid or idiot cribbage. Jack, who was still looking around for Ullman, hadn't noticed. Wendy kept silent, watching Hallorann's car nervously, wondering what they could possibly be talking about that would make Danny cock his head that way.

In the car Hallorann was saying: "Get you kinda lonely, thinkin you were the only one?"

Danny, who had been frightened as well as lonely sometimes, nodded. "Am I the only one you ever met?" he asked.

Hallorann laughed and shook his head. "No, child, no. But you shine the hardest."

"Are there lots, then?"

"No," Hallorann said, "but you do run across them. A lot of folks, they got a little bit of shine to them. They don't even know it. But they always seem to show up with flowers when their wives are feelin blue with the monthlies, they do good on school tests they don't even study for, they got a good idea how people are feelin as soon as they walk into a room. I come across fifty or sixty like that. But maybe only a dozen, countin my gram, that *knew* they was shinin."

"Wow," Danny said, and thought about it. Then: "Do you know Mrs. Brant?"

"Her?" Hallorann asked scornfully. "She don't shine. Just sends her supper back two-three times every night."

"I know she doesn't," Danny said earnestly. "But do you know the man in the gray uniform that gets the cars?"

"Mike? Sure, I know Mike. What about him?"

"Mr. Hallorann, why would she want his pants?"

"What are you talking about, boy?"

"Well, when she was watching him, she was thinking she would sure like to get into his pants and I just wondered why—"

But he got no further. Hallorann had thrown his head back, and rich, dark laughter issued from his chest, rolling around in the car like cannonfire. The seat shook with the force of it. Danny smiled, puzzled, and at last the storm subsided by fits and starts. Hallorann produced a large silk handkerchief from his breast pocket like a white flag of surrender and wiped his streaming eyes.

"Boy," he said, still snorting a little, "you are gonna know everything there is to know about the human condition before you make ten. I dunno if to envy you or not."

"But Mrs. Brant—"

"You never mind her," he said. "And don't go askin your mom, either. You'd only upset her, dig what I'm sayin?"

"Yes, sir," Danny said. He dug it perfectly well. He had upset his mother that way in the past.

"That Mrs. Brant is just a dirty old woman with an itch, that's all you have to know." He looked at Danny speculatively. "How hard can you hit, doc?"

"Huh?"

"Give me a blast. Think at me. I want to know if you got as much as I think you do."

"What do you want me to think?"

"Anything. Just think it *hard.*"

"Okay," Danny said. He considered it for a moment, then

gathered his concentration and flung it out at Hallorann. He had never done anything precisely like this before, and at the last instant some instinctive part of him rose up and blunted some of the thought's raw force—he didn't want to hurt Mr. Hallorann. Still the thought arrowed out of him with a force he never would have believed. It went like a Nolan Ryan fastball with a little extra on it.

(Gee I hope I don't hurt him)

And the thought was:

(!!! HI, DICK!!!)

Hallorann winced and jerked backward on the seat. His teeth came together with a hard click, drawing blood from his lower lip in a thin trickle. His hands flew up involuntarily from his lap to the level of his chest and then settled back again. For a moment his eyelids fluttered limply, with no conscious control, and Danny was frightened.

"Mr. Hallorann? Dick? Are you okay?"

"I don't know," Hallorann said, and laughed weakly. "I honest to God don't. My God, boy, you're a pistol."

"I'm sorry," Danny said, more alarmed. "Should I get my daddy? I'll run and get him."

"No, here I come. I'm okay, Danny. You just sit right there. I feel a little scrambled, that's all."

"I didn't go as hard as I could," Danny confessed. "I was scared to, at the last minute."

"Probably my good luck you did ... my brains would be leakin out my ears." He saw the alarm on Danny's face and smiled. "No harm done. What did it feel like to you?"

"Like I was Nolan Ryan throwing a fastball," he replied promptly.

"You like baseball, do you?" Hallorann was rubbing his temples gingerly.

"Daddy and me like the Angels," Danny said. "The Red Sox in the American League East and the Angels in the West. We saw the Red Sox against Cincinnati in the World Series. I was a lot littler then. And Daddy was ..." Danny's face went dark and troubled.

"Was what, Dan?"

"I forget," Danny said. He started to put his thumb in his

mouth to suck it, but that was a baby trick. He put his hand back in his lap.

"Can you tell what your mom and dad are thinking, Danny?" Hallorann was watching him closely.

"Most times, if I want to. But usually I don't try."

"Why not?"

"Well . . ." he paused a moment, troubled. "It would be like peeking into the bedroom and watching while they're doing the thing that makes babies. Do you know that thing?"

"I have had acquaintance with it," Hallorann said gravely.

"They wouldn't like that. And they wouldn't like me peeking at their thinks. It would be dirty."

"I see."

"But I know how they're feeling," Danny said. "I can't help that. I know how you're feeling, too. I hurt you. I'm sorry."

"It's just a headache. I've had hangovers that were worse. Can you read other people, Danny?"

"I can't read yet at all," Danny said, "except a few words. But Daddy's going to teach me this winter. My daddy used to teach reading and writing in a big school. Mostly writing, but he knows reading, too."

"I mean, can you tell what anybody is thinking?"

Danny thought about it.

"I can if it's *loud*," he said finally. "Like Mrs. Brant and the pants. Or like once, when me and Mommy were in this big store to get me some shoes, there was this big kid looking at radios, and he was thinking about taking one without buying it. Then he'd think, what if I get caught? Then he'd think, I really want it. Then he'd think about getting caught again. He was making himself sick about it, and he was making *me* sick. Mommy was talking to the man who sells the shoes so I went over and said, 'Kid, don't take that radio. Go away.' And he got really scared. He went away fast."

Hallorann was grinning broadly. "I bet he did. Can you do anything else, Danny? Is it only thoughts and feelings, or is there more?"

Cautiously: "Is there more for you?"

"Sometimes," Hallorann said. "Not often. Sometimes . . . sometimes there are dreams. Do you dream, Danny?"

"Sometimes," Danny said, "I dream when I'm awake. After Tony comes." His thumb wanted to go into his mouth again. He had never told anyone but Mommy and Daddy about Tony. He made his thumb-sucking hand go back into his lap.

"Who's Tony?"

And suddenly Danny had one of those flashes of understanding that frightened him most of all; it was like a sudden glimpse of some incomprehensible machine that might be safe or might be deadly dangerous. He was too young to know which. He was too young to understand.

"What's wrong?" he cried. "You're asking me all this because you're worried, aren't you? Why are you worried about me? Why are you worried about *us?*"

Hallorann put his large dark hands on the small boy's shoulders. "Stop," he said. "It's probably nothin. But if it is somethin . . . well, you've got a large thing in your head, Danny. You'll have to do a lot of growin yet before you catch up to it, I guess. You got to be brave about it."

"But I don't *understand* things!" Danny burst out. "I *do* but I *don't!* People . . . they feel things and I feel them, but I don't know what I'm feeling!" He looked down at his lap wretchedly. "I wish I could read. Sometimes Tony shows me signs and I can hardly read any of them."

"Who's Tony?" Hallorann asked again.

"Mommy and Daddy call him my 'invisible playmate,' " Danny said, reciting the words carefully. "But he's really real. At least, I think he is. Sometimes, when I try real hard to understand things, he comes. He says, 'Danny, I want to show you something.' And it's like I pass out. Only . . . there are dreams, like you said." He looked at Hallorann and swallowed. "They used to be nice. But now . . . I can't remember the word for dreams that scare you and make you cry."

"Nightmares?" Hallorann asked.

"Yes. That's right. Nightmares."

"About this place? About the Overlook?"

Danny looked down at his thumb-sucking hand again. "Yes," he whispered. Then he spoke shrilly, looking up into Hallorann's face: "But I can't tell my daddy, and you can't, either! He has to have this job because it's the only one Uncle Al could get for him and he has to finish his play or he might start doing the

Bad Thing again and I know what that is, it's getting *drunk*, that's what it is, it's when he used to always be *drunk* and that was a Bad Thing to do!" He stopped, on the verge of tears.

"Shh," Hallorann said, and pulled Danny's face against the rough serge of his jacket. It smelled faintly of mothballs. "That's all right, son. And if that thumb likes your mouth, let it go where it wants." But his face was troubled.

He said: "What you got, son, I call it shinin on, the Bible calls it having visions, and there's scientists that call it precognition. I've read up on it, son. I've studied on it. They all mean seeing the future. Do you understand that?"

Danny nodded against Hallorann's coat.

"I remember the strongest shine I ever had that way . . . I'm not liable to forget. It was 1955. I was still in the Army then, stationed overseas in West Germany. It was an hour before supper, and I was standin by the sink, givin one of the KPs hell for takin too much of the potato along with the peel. I says, 'Here, lemme show you how that's done.' He held out the potato and the peeler and then the whole kitchen was gone. Bang, just like that. You say you see this guy Tony before . . . before you have dreams?"

Danny nodded.

Hallorann put an arm around him. "With me it's smellin oranges. All that afternoon I'd been smellin them and thinkin nothin of it, because they were on the menu for that night—we had thirty crates of Valencias. Everybody in the damn kitchen was smellin oranges that night.

"For a minute it was like I had just passed out. And then I heard an explosion and saw flames. There were people screaming. Sirens. And I heard this hissin noise that could only be steam. Then it seemed like I got a little closer to whatever it was and I saw a railroad car off the tracks and laying on its side with *Georgia and South Carolina Railroad* written on it, and I knew like a flash that my brother Carl was on that train and it jumped the tracks and Carl was dead. Just like that. Then it was gone and here's this scared, stupid little KP in front of me, still holdin out that potato and the peeler. He says, 'Are you okay, Sarge?' And I says, 'No. My brother's just been killed down in Georgia.' And when I finally got my momma on the overseas telephone, she told me how it was.

"But see, boy, I already knew how it was."

He shook his head slowly, as if dismissing the memory, and looked down at the wide-eyed boy.

"But the thing you got to remember, my boy, is this: *Those things don't always come true.* I remember just four years ago I had a job cookin at a boys' camp up in Maine on Long Lake. So I am sittin by the boarding gate at Logan Airport in Boston, just waiting to get on my flight, and I start to smell oranges. For the first time in maybe five years. So I say to myself, 'My God, what's comin on this crazy late show now?' and I got down to the bathroom and sat on one of the toilets to be private. I never did black out, but I started to get this feelin, stronger and stronger, that my plane was gonna crash. Then the feeling went away, and the smell of oranges, and I knew it was over. I went back to the Delta Airlines desk and changed my flight to one three hours later. And do you know what happened?"

"What?" Danny whispered.

"*Nothin!*" Hallorann said, and laughed. He was relieved to see the boy smile a little, too. "Not one single thing! That old plane landed right on time and without a single bump or bruise. So you see . . . sometimes those feelins don't come to anything."

"Oh," Danny said.

"Or you take the race track. I go a lot, and I usually do pretty well. I stand by the rail when they go by the starting gate, and sometimes I get a little shine about this horse or that one. Usually those feelins help me get real well. I always tell myself that someday I'm gonna get three at once on three long shots and make enough on the trifecta to retire early. It ain't happened yet. But there's plenty of times I've come home from the track on shank's mare instead of in a taxicab with my wallet swollen up. Nobody shines on all the time, except maybe for God up in heaven."

"Yes, sir," Danny said, thinking of the time almost a year ago when Tony had showed him a new baby lying in a crib at their house in Stovington. He had been very excited about that, and had waited, knowing that it took time, but there had been no new baby.

"Now you listen," Hallorann said, and took both of Danny's hands in his own. "I've had some bad dreams here, and I've had some bad feelins. I've worked here two seasons now and maybe a dozen times I've had . . . well, nightmares. And maybe half a dozen times I've thought I've seen things. No, I won't say what. It ain't for a little boy like you. Just nasty things. Once it had something to do with those damn hedges clipped to look like animals. Another time there was a maid, Delores Vickery her name was, and she had a little shine to her, but I don't think she knew it. Mr. Ullman fired her . . . do you know what that is, doc?"

"Yes, sir," Danny said candidly, "my daddy got fired from his teaching job and that's why we're in Colorado, I guess."

"Well, Ullman fired her on account of her saying she'd seen something in one of the rooms where . . . well, where a bad thing happened. That was in Room 217, and I want you to promise me you won't go in there, Danny. Not all winter. Steer right clear."

"All right," Danny said. "Did the lady—the maiden—did she ask you to go look?"

"Yes, she did. And there was a bad thing there. But . . . I don't think it was a bad thing that could *hurt* anyone, Danny, that's what I'm tryin to say. People who shine can sometimes see things that are *gonna* happen, and I think sometimes they can see things that *did* happen. But they're just like pictures in a book. Did you ever see a picture in a book that scared you, Danny?"

"Yes," he said, thinking of the story of *Bluebeard* and the picture where *Bluebeard*'s new wife opens the door and sees all the heads.

"But you knew it couldn't hurt you, didn't you?"

"Ye—ess . . ." Danny said, a little dubious.

"Well, that's how it is in this hotel. I don't know why, but it seems that all the bad things that ever happened here, there's little pieces of those things still layin around like fingernail clippins or the boogers that somebody nasty just wiped under a chair. I don't know why it should just be here, there's bad goings-on in just about every hotel in the world, I guess, and I've worked in a lot of them and had no trouble. Only here. But Danny, I don't think those things can hurt anybody." He emphasized each word in the sentence with a mild shake of the boy's shoulders. "So if you should see something, in a hallway or a room or outside by those hedges . . . just look the other way and when you look back, it'll be gone. Are you diggin me?"

"Yes," Danny said. He felt much better, soothed. He got up on his knees, kissed Hallorann's cheek, and gave him a big hard hug. Hallorann hugged him back.

When he released the boy he asked: "Your folks, they don't shine, do they?"

"No, I don't think so."

"I tried them like I did you," Hallorann said. "Your momma jumped the tiniest bit. I think all mothers shine a little, you know, at least until their kids grow up enough to watch out for themselves. Your dad . . ."

Hallorann paused momentarily. He had probed at the boy's father and he just didn't know. It wasn't like meeting someone who had the shine, or someone who definitely did not. Poking at Danny's father had been . . . strange, as if Jack Torrance had something—*something*—that he was hiding. Or something he was holding in so deeply submerged in himself that it was impossible to get to.

"I don't think he shines at all," Hallorann finished. "So you don't worry about them. You just take care of you. *I don't think there's anything here that can hurt you.* So just be cool, okay?"

"Okay."

"Danny! Hey, doc!"

Danny looked around. "That's Mom. She wants me. I have to go."

"I know you do," Hallorann said. "You have a good time here, Danny. Best you can, anyway."

"I will. Thanks, Mr. Hallorann. I feel a lot better."

The smiling thought came in his mind:

(Dick, to my friends)

(Yes, Dick, okay)

Their eyes met, and Dick Hallorann winked.

Danny scrambled across the seat of the car and opened the passenger side door. As he was getting out, Hallorann said, "Danny?"

"What?"

"If there *is* trouble . . . you give a call. A big loud holler like the one you gave a few minutes ago. I might hear you even way down in Florida. And if I do, I'll come on the run."

"Okay," Danny said, and smiled.

"You take care, big boy."

"I will."

Danny slammed the door and ran across the parking lot toward the porch, where Wendy stood holding her elbows against the chill wind. Hallorann watched, the big grin slowly fading.

I don't think there's anything here that can hurt you.

I don't think.

But what if he was wrong? He had known that this was his last season at the Overlook ever since he had seen that thing in the bathtub of Room 217. It had been worse than any picture in any book, and from here the boy running to his mother looked so *small . . .*

I don't think—

His eyes drifted down to the topiary animals.

Abruptly he started the car and put it in gear and drove away, trying not to look back. And of course he did, and of course the porch was empty. They had gone back inside. It was as if the Overlook had swallowed them.

12

THE GRAND TOUR

"What were you talking about, hon?" Wendy asked him as they went back inside.

"Oh, nothing much."

"For nothing much it sure was a long talk."

He shrugged and Wendy saw Danny's paternity in the gesture; Jack could hardly have done it better himself. She would get no more out of Danny. She felt strong exasperation mixed with an even stronger love: the love was helpless, the exasperation came from a feeling that she was deliberately being excluded. With the two of them around she sometimes felt like an outsider, a bit player who had accidentally wandered back onstage while the main action was taking place. Well, they wouldn't be able to exclude her this winter, her two exasperating males;

quarters were going to be a little too close for that. She suddenly realized she was feeling jealous of the closeness between her husband and her son, and felt ashamed. That was too close to the way her own mother might have felt . . . too close for comfort.

The lobby was now empty except for Ullman and the head desk clerk (they were at the register, cashing up), a couple of maids who had changed to warm slacks and sweaters, standing by the front door and looking out with their luggage pooled around them, and Watson, the maintenance man. He caught her looking at him and gave her a wink . . . a decidedly lecherous one. She looked away hurriedly. Jack was over by the window just outside the restaurant, studying the view. He looked rapt and dreamy.

The cash register apparently checked out, because now Ullman ran it shut with an authoritative snap. He initialed the tape and put it in a small zipper case. Wendy silently applauded the head clerk, who looked greatly relieved. Ullman looked like the type of man who might take any shortage out of the head clerk's hide . . . without ever spilling a drop of blood. Wendy didn't much care for Ullman or his officious, ostentatiously bustling manner. He was like every boss she'd ever had, male or female. He would be saccharin sweet with the guests, a petty tyrant when he was backstage with the help. But now school was out and the head clerk's pleasure was written large on his face. It was out for everyone but she and Jack and Danny, anyway.

"Mr. Torrance," Ullman called peremptorily. "Would you come over here, please?"

Jack walked over, nodding to Wendy and Danny that they were to come too.

The clerk, who had gone into the back, now came out again wearing an overcoat. "Have a pleasant winter, Mr. Ullman."

"I doubt it," Ullman said distantly. "May twelfth, Braddock. Not a day earlier. Not a day later."

"Yes, sir."

Braddock walked around the desk, his face sober and dignified, as befitted his position, but when his back was entirely to Ullman, he grinned like a schoolboy. He spoke briefly to the two girls still waiting by the door for their ride, and he was followed out by a brief burst of stifled laughter.

Now Wendy began to notice the silence of the place. It had fallen over the hotel like a heavy blanket muffling everything but the faint pulse of the afternoon wind outside. From where she stood she could look through the inner office, now neat to the point of sterility with its two bare desks and two sets of gray filing cabinets. Beyond that she could see Hallorann's spotless kitchen, the big portholed double doors propped open by rubber wedges.

"I thought I would take a few extra minutes and show you through the Hotel," Ullman said, and Wendy reflected that you could always hear that capital *H* in Ullman's voice. You were supposed to hear it. "I'm sure your husband will get to know the ins and outs of the Overlook quite well, Mrs. Torrance, but you and your son will doubtless keep more to the lobby level and the first floor, where your quarters are."

"Doubtless," Wendy murmured demurely, and Jack shot her a private glance.

"It's a beautiful place," Ullman said expansively. "I rather enjoy showing it off."

I'll bet you do, Wendy thought.

"Let's go up to third and work our way down," Ullman said. He sounded positively enthused.

"If we're keeping you—" Jack began.

"Not at all," Ullman said. "The shop is shut. *Tout fini,* for this season, at least. And I plan to overnight in Boulder—at the Boulderado, of course. Only decent hotel this side of Denver . . . except for the Overlook itself, of course. This way."

They stepped into the elevator together. It was ornately scrolled in copper and brass, but it settled appreciably before Ullman pulled the gate across. Danny stirred a little uneasily, and Ullman smiled down at him. Danny tried to smile back without notable success.

"Don't you worry, little man," Ullman said. "Safe as houses."

"So was the *Titanic,*" Jack said, looking up at the cut-glass globe in the center of the elevator ceiling. Wendy bit the inside of her cheek to keep the smile away.

Ullman was not amused. He slid the inner gate across with a rattle and a bang. "The *Titanic* made only one voyage, Mr. Torrance. This elevator has made thousands of them since it was installed in 1926."

"That's reassuring," Jack said. He ruffled Danny's hair. "The plane ain't gonna crash, doc."

Ullman threw the lever over, and for a moment there was nothing but a shuddering beneath their feet and the tortured whine of the motor below them. Wendy had a vision of the four of them being trapped between floors like flies in a bottle and found in the spring . . . with little bits and pieces gone . . . like the Donner Party . . .

(Stop it!)

The elevator began to rise, with some vibration and clashing and banging from below at first. Then the ride smoothed out. At the third floor Ullman brought them to a bumpy stop, retracted the gate, and opened the door. The elevator car was still six inches below floor level. Danny gazed at the difference in height between the third-floor hall and the elevator floor as if he had just sensed the universe was not as sane as he had been told. Ullman cleared his throat and raised the car a little, brought it to a stop with a jerk (still two inches low), and they all climbed out. With their weight gone the car rebounded almost to floor level, something Wendy did not find reassuring at all. Safe as houses or not, she resolved to take the stairs when she had to go up or down in this place. And under no conditions would she allow the three of them to get into the rickety thing together.

"What are you looking at, doc?" Jack inquired humorously. "See any spots there?"

"Of course not," Ullman said, nettled. "All the rugs were shampooed just two days ago."

Wendy glanced down at the hall runner herself. Pretty, but definitely not anything she would choose for her own home, if the day ever came when she had one. Deep blue pile, it was entwined with what seemed to be a surrealistic jungle scene full of ropes and vines and trees filled with exotic birds. It was hard to tell just what sort of birds, because all the interweaving was done in unshaded black, giving only silhouettes.

"Do you like the rug?" Wendy asked Danny.

"Yes, Mom," he said colorlessly.

They walked down the hall, which was comfortably wide. The wallpaper was silk, a lighter blue to go against the rug. Electric flambeaux stood at ten-foot intervals at a height of about seven feet. Fashioned to look like London gas lamps, the bulbs were masked behind cloudy, cream-hued glass that was bound with crisscrossing iron strips.

"I like those very much," she said.

Ullman nodded, pleased. "Mr. Derwent had those installed throughout the Hotel after the war—number Two, I mean. In fact most—although not all—of the third-floor decorating scheme was his idea. This is 300, the Presidential Suite."

He twisted his key in the lock of the mahogany double doors and swung them wide. The sitting room's wide western exposure made them all gasp, which had probably been Ullman's intention. He smiled. "Quite a view, isn't it?"

"It sure is," Jack said.

The window ran nearly the length of the sitting room, and beyond it the sun was poised directly between two sawtoothed peaks, casting golden light across the rock faces and the sugared snow on the high tips. The clouds around and behind this picture-postcard view were also tinted gold, and a sunbeam glinted duskily down into the darkly pooled firs below the timberline.

Jack and Wendy were so absorbed in the view that they didn't look down at Danny, who was staring not out the window but at the red-and-white-striped silk wallpaper to the left, where a door opened into an interior bedroom. And his gasp, which had been mingled with theirs, had nothing to do with beauty.

Great splashes of dried blood, flecked with tiny bits of grayish-white tissue, clotted the wallpaper. It made Danny feel sick. It was like a crazy picture drawn in blood, a surrealistic etching of a man's face drawn back in terror and pain, the mouth yawning and half the head pulverized—

(So if you should see something . . . just look the other way and when you look back, it'll be gone. Are you diggin me?)

He deliberately looked out the window, being careful to show no expression on his face, and when his mommy's hand closed over his own he took it, being careful not to squeeze it or give her a signal of any kind.

The manager was saying something to his daddy about making sure to shutter that big window so a strong wind wouldn't blow it in. Jack was nodding. Danny looked cautiously back at the wall. The big dried bloodstain was gone. Those little gray-white flecks that had been scattered all through it, they were gone, too.

Then Ullman was leading them out. Mommy asked him if he thought the mountains were pretty. Danny said he did, although he didn't really care for the mountains, one way or the other. As Ullman was closing the door behind them, Danny looked back over his shoulder. The bloodstain had returned, only now it was fresh. It was running. Ullman, looking directly at it, went on with his running commentary about the famous men who had stayed here. Danny discovered that he had bitten his lip hard enough to make it bleed, and he had never even felt it. As they walked on down the corridor, he fell a little bit behind the others and wiped the blood away with the back of his hand and thought about

(blood)

(Did Mr. Hallorann see blood or was it something worse?)

(I don't think those things can hurt you.)

There was an iron scream behind his lips, but he would not let it out. His mommy and daddy could not see such things; they never had. He would keep quiet. His mommy and daddy were loving each other, and that was a real thing. The other things were just like pictures in a book. Some pictures were scary, but they couldn't hurt you. *They ... couldn't ... hurt you.*

Mr. Ullman showed them some other rooms on the third floor, leading them through corridors that twisted and turned like a maze. They were all sweets up here, Mr. Ullman said, although Danny didn't see any candy. He showed them some rooms where a lady named Marilyn Monroe once stayed when she was married to a man named Arthur Miller (Danny got a vague understanding that Marilyn and Arthur had gotten a DIVORCE not long after they were in the Overlook Hotel).

"Mommy?"

"What, honey?"

"If they were married, why did they have different names? You and Daddy have the same names."

"Yes, but we're not famous, Danny," Jack said. "Famous women keep their same names even after they get married because their names are their bread and butter."

"Bread and butter," Danny said, completely mystified.

"What Daddy means is that people used to like to go to the movies and see Marilyn Monroe," Wendy said, "but they might not like to go to see Marilyn Miller."

"Why not? She'd still be the same lady. Wouldn't everyone know that?"

"Yes, but—" She looked at Jack helplessly.

"Truman Capote once stayed in this room," Ullman interrupted impatiently. He opened the door. "That was in my time. An awfully nice man. Continental manners."

There was nothing remarkable in any of these rooms (except for the absence of sweets, which Mr. Ullman kept calling them), nothing that Danny was afraid of. In fact, there was only one other thing on the third floor that bothered Danny, and he could not have said why. It was the fire extinguisher on the wall just before they turned the corner and went back to the elevator, which stood open and waiting like a mouthful of gold teeth.

It was an old-fashioned extinguisher, a flat hose folded back a dozen times upon itself, one end attached to a large red valve, the other ending in a brass nozzle. The folds of the hose were secured with a red steel slat on a hinge. In case of a fire you could knock the steel slat up and out of the way with one hard push and the hose was yours. Danny could see that much; he was good at seeing how things worked. By the time he was two and a half he had been unlocking the protective gate his father had installed at the top of the stairs in the Stovington house. He had seen how the lock worked. His daddy said it was a NACK. Some people had the NACK and some people didn't.

This fire extinguisher was a little older than others he had seen—the one in the nursery school, for instance—but that was not so unusual. Nonetheless it filled him with faint unease, curled up there against the light blue wallpaper like a sleeping snake. And he was glad when it was out of sight around the corner.

"Of course all the windows have to be shuttered," Mr. Ullman said as they stepped back into the elevator. Once again the car sank queasily beneath their feet. "But I'm particularly concerned about the one in the Presidential Suite. The original bill on that window was four hundred and twenty dollars, and that was over thirty years ago. It would cost eight times that to replace today."

"I'll shutter it," Jack said.

They went down to the second floor where there were more rooms and even more twists and turns in the corridor. The light from the windows had begun to fade appreciably now as the sun went behind the mountains. Mr. Ullman showed them one or two rooms and that was all. He walked past 217, the one Dick Hallorann had warned him about, without slowing. Danny looked at the bland number-plate on the door with uneasy fascination.

Then down to the first floor. Mr. Ullman didn't show them into any rooms here until they had almost reached the thickly carpeted staircase that led down into the lobby again. "Here are your quarters," he said. "I think you'll find them adequate."

They went in. Danny was braced for whatever might be there. There was nothing.

Wendy Torrance felt a strong surge of relief. The Presidential Suite, with its cold elegance, had made her feel awkward and clumsy—it was all very well to visit some restored historical building with a bedroom plaque that announced Abraham Lincoln or Franklin D. Roosevelt had slept there, but another thing entirely to imagine you and your husband lying beneath acreages of linen and perhaps making love where the greatest men in the world had once lain (the most powerful, anyway, she amended). But this apartment was simpler, homier, almost inviting. She thought she could abide this place for a season with no great difficulty.

"It's very pleasant," she said to Ullman, and heard the gratitude in her voice.

Ullman nodded. "Simple but adequate. During the season, this suite quarters the cook and his wife, or the cook and his apprentice."

"Mr. Hallorann lived here?" Danny broke in.

Mr. Ullman inclined his head to Danny condescendingly. "Quite so. He and Mr. Nevers." He turned back to Jack and Wendy. "This is the sitting room."

There were several chairs that looked comfortable but not expensive, a coffee table that had once been expensive but now had a long chip gone from the side, two bookcases (stuffed full of Reader's Digest Condensed Books and Detective Book Club trilogies from the forties, Wendy saw with some amusement), and an anonymous hotel TV that looked much less elegant than the buffed wood consoles in the rooms.

"No kitchen, of course," Ullman said, "but there is a dumb-waiter. This apartment is directly over the kitchen." He slid aside a square of paneling and disclosed a wide, square tray. He gave it a push and it disappeared, trailing rope behind it.

"It's a secret passage!" Danny said excitedly to his mother, momentarily forgetting all fears in favor of that intoxicating shaft behind the wall. "Just like in *Abbott and Costello Meet the Monsters!*"

Mr. Ullman frowned but Wendy smiled indulgently. Danny ran over to the dumb-waiter and peered down the shaft.

"This way, please."

He opened the door on the far side of the living room. It gave on the bedroom, which was spacious and airy. There were twin beds. Wendy looked at her husband, smiled, shrugged.

"No problem," Jack said. "We'll push them together."

Mr. Ullman looked over his shoulder, honestly puzzled. "Beg pardon?"

"The beds," Jack said pleasantly. "We can push them together."

"Oh, quite," Ullman said, momentarily confused. Then his face cleared and a red flush began to creep up from the collar of his shirt. "Whatever you like."

He led them back into the sitting room, where a second door opened on a second bedroom, this one equipped with bunk beds. A radiator clanked in one corner, and the rug on the floor was a hideous embroidery of western sage and cactus— Danny had already fallen in love with it, Wendy saw. The walls of this smaller room were paneled in real pine.

"Think you can stand it in here, doc?" Jack asked.

"Sure I can. I'm going to sleep in the top bunk. Okay?"

"If that's what you want."

"I like the rug, too. Mr. Ullman, why don't you have all the rugs like that?"

Mr. Ullman looked for a moment as if he had sunk his teeth into a lemon. Then he smiled and patted Danny's head "Those are your quarters," he said, "except for the bath, which opens off the main bedroom. It's not a huge apartment, but of course you'll have the rest of the hotel to spread out in. The lobby fireplace is in good working order, or so Watson tells me, and you must feel free to eat in the dining room if the spirit moves you to do so." He spoke in the tone of a man conferring a great favor.

"All right," Jack said.

"Shall we go down?" Mr. Ullman asked.

"Fine," Wendy said.

They went downstairs in the elevator, and now the lobby was wholly deserted except for Watson, who was leaning against the main doors in a rawhide jacket, a toothpick between his lips.

"I would have thought you'd be miles from here by now," Mr. Ullman said, his voice slightly chill.

"Just stuck around to remind Mr. Torrance here about the boiler," Watson said, straightening up. "Keep your good weather eye on her, fella, and she'll be fine. Knock the press down a couple of times a day. She creeps."

She creeps, Danny thought, and the words echoed down a long and silent corridor in his mind, a corridor lined with mirrors where people seldom looked.

"I will," his daddy said.

"You'll be fine," Watson said, and offered Jack his hand. Jack shook it. Watson turned to Wendy and inclined his head. "Ma'am," he said.

"I'm pleased," Wendy said, and thought it would sound absurd. It didn't. She had come out here from New England, where she had spent her life, and it seemed to her that in a few short sentences this man Watson, with his fluffy fringe of hair, had epitomized what the West was supposed to be all about. And never mind the lecherous wink earlier.

"Young master Torrance," Watson said gravely, and put out his hand. Danny, who had known all about handshaking for almost a year now, put his own hand out gingerly and felt it swallowed up. "You take good care of em, Dan."

"Yes, sir."

Watson let go of Danny's hand and straightened up fully. He looked at Ullman. "Until next year, I guess," he said, and held his hand out.

Ullman touched it bloodlessly. His pinky ring caught the lobby's electric lights in a baleful sort of wink.

"May twelfth, Watson," he said. "Not a day earlier or later."

"Yes, sir," Watson said, and Jack could almost read the codicil in Watson's mind: . . . *you fucking little faggot.*

"Have a good winter, Mr. Ullman."

"Oh, I doubt it," Ullman said remotely.

Watson opened one of the two big main doors; the wind whined louder and began to flutter the collar of his jacket. "You folks take care now," he said.

It was Danny who answered. "Yes, sir, we will."

Watson, whose not-so-distant ancestor had owned this place, slipped humbly through the door. It closed behind him, muffling the wind. Together they watched him clop down the porch's broad front steps in his battered black cowboy boots. Brittle yellow aspen leaves tumbled around his heels as he crossed the lot to his International Harvester pickup and climbed in. Blue smoke jetted from the rusted exhaust pipe as he started it up. The spell of silence held among them as he backed, then pulled out of the parking lot. His truck disappeared over the brow of the hill and then reappeared, smaller, on the main road, heading west.

For a moment Danny felt more lonely than he ever had in his life.

13

THE FRONT PORCH

The Torrance family stood together on the long front porch of the Overlook Hotel as if posing for a family portrait, Danny in the middle, zippered into last year's fall jacket which was now too small and starting to come out at the elbow, Wendy behind him with one hand on his shoulder, and Jack to his left, his own hand resting lightly on his son's head.

Mr. Ullman was a step below them, buttoned into an expensive-looking brown mohair overcoat. The sun was entirely behind the mountains now, edging them with gold fire, making the shadows around things look long and purple. The only three vehicles left in the parking lots were the hotel truck, Ullman's Lincoln Continental, and the battered Torrance VW.

"You've got your keys, then," Ullman said to Jack, "and you understand fully about the furnace and the boiler?"

Jack nodded, feeling some real sympathy for Ullman. Everything was done for the season, the ball of string was neatly wrapped up until next May 12—not a day earlier or later—and Ullman, who was responsible for all of it and who referred to the hotel in the unmistakable tones of infatuation, could not help looking for loose ends.

"I think everything is well in hand," Jack said.

"Good. I'll be in touch." But he still lingered for a moment, as if waiting for the wind to take a hand and perhaps gust him down to his car. He sighed. "All right. Have a good winter, Mr. Torrance, Mrs. Torrance. You too, Danny."

"Thank you, sir," Danny said. "I hope you do, too."

"I doubt it," Ullman repeated, and he sounded sad. "The place in Florida is a dump, if the out-and-out truth is to be spoken. Busywork. The Overlook is my real job. Take good care of it for me, Mr. Torrance."

"I think it will be here when you get back next spring," Jack said, and a thought flashed through Danny's mind

(but will we?)

and was gone.

"Of course. Of course it will."

Ullman looked out toward the playground where the hedge animals were clattering in the wind. Then he nodded once more in a businesslike way.

"Good-by, then."

He walked quickly and prissily across to his car—a ridiculously big one for such a little man—and tucked himself into it. The Lincoln's motor purred into life and the taillights flashed as he pulled out of his parking stall. As the car moved away, Jack could read the small sign at the head of the stall: RESERVED FOR MR. ULLMAN, MGR.

"Right," Jack said softly.

They watched until the car was out of sight, headed down the eastern slope. When it was gone, the three of them looked at each other for a silent, almost frightened moment. They were alone. Aspen leaves whirled and skittered in aimless packs across the lawn that was now neatly mowed and tended for no guest's eyes. There was no one to see the autumn leaves steal across the grass but the three of them. It gave Jack a curious shrinking feeling, as if his life force had dwindled to a mere spark while the hotel and the grounds had suddenly doubled in size and become sinister, dwarfing them with sullen, inanimate power.

Then Wendy said: "Look at you, doc. Your nose is running like a fire hose. Let's get inside."

And they did, closing the door firmly behind them against the restless whine of the wind.

PART THREE
THE WASPS' NEST

UP ON THE ROOF

"Oh you goddam fucking son of a bitch!"

Jack Torrance cried these words out in both surprise and agony as he slapped his right hand against his blue chambray workshirt, dislodging the big, slow-moving wasp that had stung him. Then he was scrambling up the roof as fast as he could, looking back over his shoulder to see if the wasp's brothers and sisters were rising from the nest he had uncovered to do battle. If they were, it could be bad; the nest was between him and his ladder, and the trap door leading down into the attic was locked from the inside. The drop was seventy feet from the roof to the cement patio between the hotel and the lawn.

The clear air above the nest was still and undisturbed.

Jack whistled disgustedly between his teeth, sat straddling the peak of the roof, and examined his right index finger. It was swelling already, and he supposed he would have to try and creep past that nest to his ladder so he could go down and put some ice on it.

It was October 20. Wendy and Danny had gone down to Sidewinder in the hotel truck (an elderly, rattling Dodge that was still more trustworthy than the VW, which was now wheezing gravely and seemed terminal) to get three gallons of milk and do some Christmas shopping. It was early to shop, but there was no telling when the snow would come to stay. There had already been flurries, and in some places the road down from the Overlook was slick with patch ice.

So far the fall had been almost preternaturally beautiful. In the three weeks they had been here, golden day had followed golden day. Crisp, thirty-degree mornings gave way to afternoon temperatures in the low sixties, the perfect temperature for climbing around on the Overlook's gently sloping western roof and doing the shingling. Jack had admitted freely to Wendy that he could have finished the job four days ago, but he felt no real urge to hurry. The view from up here was spectacular, even putting the vista from the Presidential Suite in the shade. More important, the work itself was soothing. On the roof he felt himself healing from the troubled wounds of the last three years. On the roof he felt at peace. Those three years began to seem like a turbulent nightmare.

The shingles had been badly rotted, some of them blown entirely away by last winter's storms. He had ripped them all up, yelling "Bombs away!" as he dropped them over the side, not wanting Danny to get hit in case he had wandered over. He had been pulling out bad flashing when the wasp had gotten him.

The ironic part was that he warned himself each time he climbed onto the roof to keep an eye out for nests; he had gotten that bug bomb just in case. But this morning the stillness and peace had been so complete that his watchfulness had lapsed. He had been back in the world of the play he was slowly creating, roughing out whatever scene he would be working on that evening in his head. The play was going very well, and although Wendy had said little, he knew she was pleased. He had been roadblocked on the crucial scene between Denker, the sadistic headmaster, and Gary Benson, his young hero, during the last unhappy six months at Stovington, months when the craving for a drink had been so bad that he could barely concentrate on his in-class lectures, let alone his extracurricular literary ambitions.

But in the last twelve evenings, as he actually sat down in front of the office-model Underwood he had borrowed from the main office downstairs, the roadblock had disappeared under his fingers as magically as cotton candy dissolves on the lips. He had come up almost effortlessly with the insights into Denker's character that had always been lacking, and he had rewritten most of the second act accordingly, making it revolve around the new scene. And the progress of the third act, which he had been turning over in his mind when the wasp put an end to cogitation, was coming clearer all the time. He thought he could rough it out in two weeks, and have a clean copy of the whole damned play by New Year's.

He had an agent in New York, a tough red-headed woman named Phyllis Sandler who smoked Herbert Tareytons, drank Jim Beam from a paper cup, and thought the literary sun rose and set on Sean O'Casey. She had marketed three of Jack's short stories, including the *Esquire* piece. He had written her about the play, which was called *The Little School,* describing the basic conflict between Denker, a gifted student who had failed into becoming the brutal and brutalizing headmaster of a turn-of-the-century New England prep school, and Gary Benson, the student he sees as a younger version of himself. Phyllis had written back expressing interest and admonishing him to read O'Casey before sitting down to it. She had written again earlier that year asking where the hell was the play? He had written back wryly that *The Little School* had been indefinitely—and perhaps infinitely—delayed between hand and page "in that interesting intellectual Gobi known as the writer's block." Now it looked as if she might actually get the play. Whether or not it was any good or if it would ever see actual production was another matter. And he didn't seem to care a great deal about those things. He felt in a way that the play itself, the whole thing, was the roadblock, a colossal symbol of the bad years at Stovington Prep, the marriage he had almost totaled like a nutty kid behind the wheel of an old jalopy, the monstrous assault on his son, the incident in the parking lot with George Hatfield, an incident he could no longer view as just another sudden and destructive flare of temper. He now thought that part of his drinking problem had stemmed from an unconscious desire to be free of Stovington and the security he felt was stifling whatever creative urge he had. He had stopped drinking, but the need to be free had been just as great. Hence George Hatfield. Now all that remained of those days was the play on the desk in his and Wendy's bedroom, and when it was done and sent off to Phyllis's hole-in-the-wall New York agency, he could turn to other things. Not a novel, he was not ready to stumble into the swamp of another three-year undertaking, but surely more short stories. Perhaps a book of them.

Moving warily, he scrambled back down the slope of the roof on his hands and knees past the line of demarcation where the fresh green Bird shingles gave way to the section of roof he had just finished clearing. He came to the edge on the left of the wasps' nest he had uncovered and moved gingerly toward it, ready to backtrack and bolt down his ladder to the ground if things looked too hot.

He leaned over the section of pulled-out flashing and looked in.

The nest was in there, tucked into the space between the old flashing and the final roof undercoating of three-by-fives. It was a damn big one. The grayish paper ball looked to Jack as if it might be nearly two feet through the center. Its shape was not perfect because the space between the flashing and the boards was too narrow, but he thought the little buggers had still done a pretty respectable job. The surface of the nest was acrawl with the lumbering, slow-moving insects. They were the big mean ones, not yellow jackets, which are smaller and calmer, but wall wasps. They had been rendered sludgy and stupid by the fall temperatures, but Jack, who knew about wasps from his child-hood, counted himself lucky that he had been stung only once. And, he thought, if Ullman had hired the job done in the height of summer, the workman who tore up that particular section of the flashing would have gotten one hell of a surprise. Yes indeedy. When a dozen wall wasps land on you all at once and start stinging your face and hands and arms, stinging your legs right through your pants, it would be entirely possible to forget you were seventy feet up. You might just charge right off the edge of the roof while you were trying to get away from them. All from those little things, the biggest of them only half the length of a pencil stub.

He had read someplace—in a Sunday supplement piece or a back-of-the-book newsmagazine article—that 7 per cent of all automobile fatalities go unexplained. No mechanical failure, no excessive speed, no booze, no bad weather. Simply one-car crashes on deserted sections of road, one dead occupant, the driver, unable to explain what had happened to him. The article had included an interview with a state trooper who theorized that many of these so-called "foo crashes" resulted from insects in the car. Wasps, a bee, possibly even a spider or moth. The driver gets panicky, tries to swat it or unroll a window to let it out. Possibly the insect stings him. Maybe the driver just loses control. Either way it's bang! . . . all over. And the insect, usually completely unharmed, would buzz merrily out of the smoking wreck, looking for greener pastures. The trooper had been in favor of having pathologists look for insect venom while autopsying such victims, Jack recalled.

Now, looking down into the nest, it seemed to him that it could serve as both a workable symbol for what he had been through (and what he had dragged his hostages to fortune through) and an omen for a better future. How else could you explain the things that had happened to him? For he still felt that the whole range of unhappy Stovington experiences had to be looked at with Jack Torrance in the passive mode. He had not done things; things had been done to him. He had known plenty of people on the Stovington faculty, two of them right in the English Department, who were hard drinkers. Zack Tunney was in the habit of picking up a full keg of beer on Saturday afternoon, plonking it in a backyard snowbank overnight, and then killing damn near all of it on Sunday watching football games and old movies. Yet through the week Zack was as sober as a judge—a weak cocktail with lunch was an occasion.

He and Al Shockley had been alcoholics. They had sought each other out like two castoffs who were still social enough to prefer drowning together to doing it alone. The sea had been whole-grain instead of salt, that was all. Looking down at the wasps, as they slowly went about their instinctual business before winter closed down to kill all but their hibernating queen, he would go further. He was *still* an alcoholic, always would be, perhaps had been since Sophomore Class Night in high school when he had taken his first drink. It had nothing to do with willpower, or the morality of drinking, or the weakness or strength of his own character. There was a broken switch somewhere inside, or a circuit breaker that didn't work, and he had been propelled down the chute willy-nilly, slowly at first, then accelerating as Stovington applied its pressures on him. A big greased slide and at the bottom had been a shattered, ownerless bicycle and a son with a broken arm. Jack Torrance in the passive mode. And his temper, same thing. All his life he had been trying unsuccessfully to control it. He could remember himself at seven, spanked by a neighbor lady for playing with matches. He had gone out and hurled a rock at a passing car. His father had seen that, and he had descended on little Jacky, roaring. He had reddened Jack's behind . . . and then blacked his eye. And when his father had gone into the house, muttering, to see what was on television, Jack had come upon a stray dog and had kicked it into the gutter. There had been two dozen fights in grammar school, even more of them in high school, warranting two suspensions and uncounted detentions in spite of his good grades. Football had provided a partial safety valve, although he remembered perfectly well that he had spent almost every minute of every game in a state of high piss-off, taking every opposing block and tackle personally. He had been a fine player, making All-Conference in his junior and senior years, and he knew perfectly well that he had his own bad temper to thank . . . or to blame. He had not enjoyed football. Every game was a grudge match.

And yet, through it all, he hadn't *felt* like a son of a bitch. He hadn't felt mean. He had always regarded himself as Jack Torrance, a really nice guy who was just going to have to learn how to cope with his temper someday before it got him in trouble. The same way he was going to have to learn how to cope with his drinking. But he had been an emotional alcoholic just as surely as he had been a physical one—the two of them were no doubt tied together somewhere deep inside him, where you'd just as soon not look. But it didn't much matter to him if the root causes were interrelated or separate, sociological or psychological or physiological. He had had to deal with the results: the spankings, the beatings from his old man, the suspensions, with trying to explain the school clothes torn in playground brawls, and later the hangovers, the slowly dissolving glue of his marriage, the single bicycle wheel with its bent spokes pointing into the sky, Danny's broken arm. And George Hatfield, of course.

He felt that he had unwittingly stuck his hand into The

Great Wasps' Nest of Life. As an image it stank. As a cameo of reality, he felt it was serviceable. He had stuck his hand through some rotted flashing in high summer and that hand and his whole arm had been consumed in holy, righteous fire, destroying conscious thought, making the concept of civilized behavior obsolete. Could you be expected to behave as a thinking human being when your hand was being impaled on red-hot darning needles? Could you be expected to live in the love of your nearest and dearest when the brown, furious cloud rose out of the hole in the fabric of things (the fabric you thought was so innocent) and arrowed straight at you? Could you be held responsible for your own actions as you ran crazily about on the sloping roof seventy feet above the ground, not knowing where you were going, not remembering that your panicky, stumbling feet could lead you crashing and blundering right over the rain gutter and down to your death on the concrete seventy feet below? Jack didn't think you could. When you unwittingly stuck your hand into the wasps' nest, you hadn't made a covenant with the devil to give up your civilized self with its trappings of love and respect and honor. It just happened to you. Passively, with no say, you ceased to be a creature of the mind and became a creature of the nerve endings; from college-educated man to wailing ape in five easy seconds.

He thought about George Hatfield.

Tall and shaggily blond, George had been an almost insolently beautiful boy. In his tight faded jeans and Stovington sweatshirt with the sleeves carelessly pushed up to the elbows to disclose his tanned forearms, he had reminded Jack of a young Robert Redford, and he doubted that George had much trouble scoring—no more than that young football-playing devil Jack Torrance had it ten years earlier. He could say that he honestly didn't feel jealous of George, or envy him his good looks; in fact, he had almost unconsciously begun to visualize George as the physical incarnation of his play hero, Gary Benson—the perfect foil for the dark, slumped, and aging Denker, who grew to hate Gary so much. But he, Jack Torrance, had never felt that way about George. If he had, he would have known it. He was quite sure of that.

George had floated through his classes at Stovington. A soccer and baseball star, his academic program had been fairly undemanding and he had been content with C's and an occasional B in history or botany. He was a fierce field contender but a lackadaisical, amused sort of student in the classroom. Jack was familiar with the type, more from his own days as a high school and college student than from his teaching experience, which was at second hand. George Hatfield was a jock. He could be a calm, undemanding figure in the classroom, but when the right set of competitive stimuli was applied (like electrodes to the temples of Frankenstein's monster, Jack thought wryly), he could become a juggernaut.

In January, George had tried out with two dozen others for the debate team. He had been quite frank with Jack. His father was a corporation lawyer, and he wanted his son to follow in his footsteps. George, who felt no burning call to do anything else, was willing. His grades were not top end, but this was, after all, only prep school and it was still early times. If should be came to must be, his father could pull some strings. George's own athletic ability would open still other doors. But Brian Hatfield thought his son should get on the debate team. It was good practice, and it was something that law-school admissions boards always looked for. So George went out for debate, and in late March Jack cut him from the team.

The late winter inter-squad debates had fired George Hatfield's competitive soul. He became a grimly determined debater, prepping his pro or con position fiercely. It didn't matter if the subject was legalization of marijuana, reinstating the death penalty, or the oil-depletion allowance. George became conversant, and he was just jingoist enough to honestly not care which side he was on—a rare and valuable trait even in high-level debaters, Jack knew. The souls of a true carpetbagger and a true debater were not far removed from each other; they were both passionately interested in the main chance. So far, so good.

But George Hatfield stuttered.

This was not a handicap that had even shown up in the classroom, where George was always cool and collected (whether he had done his homework or not), and certainly not on the Stovington playing fields, where talk was not a virtue and they sometimes even threw you out of the game for too much discussion.

When George got tightly wound up in a debate, the stutter would come out. The more eager he became, the worse it was. And when he felt he had an opponent dead in his sights, an intellectual sort of buck fever seemed to take place between his speech centers and his mouth and he would freeze solid while the clock ran out. It was painful to watch.

"S-S-So I th-th-think we have to say that the fuh-fuh-facts in the c-case Mr. D-D-D-Dorsky cities are ren-ren-rendered obsolete by the ruh-recent duh-duh-decision handed down in-in-in . . ."

The buzzer would go off and George would whirl around to stare furiously at Jack, who sat beside it. George's face at those moments would be flushed, his notes crumpled spasmodically in one hand.

Jack had held on to George long after he had cut most of the obvious flat tires, hoping George would work out. He remembered one late afternoon about a week before he had reluctantly dropped the ax. George had stayed after the others had filed out, and then had confronted Jack angrily.

"You s-set the timer ahead."

Jack looked up from the papers he was putting back into his briefcase.

"George, what are you talking about?"

"I d-didn't get my whole five mih-minutes. You set it ahead. I was wuh-watching the clock."

"The clock and the timer may keep slightly different times, George, but I never touched the dial on the damned thing. Scout's honor."

"Yuh-yuh-you *did!*"

The belligerent, I'm-sticking-up-for-my-rights way George was looking at him had sparked Jack's own temper. He had been off the sauce for two months, two months too long, and he was ragged. He made one last effort to hold himself in. "I assure you I did not, George. It's your stutter. Do you have any idea what causes it? You don't stutter in class."

"*I duh-duh-don't s-s-st-st-stutter!*"

"Lower your voice."

"*You w-want to g-get me! You duh-don't w-want me on your g-g-goddam team!*"

"Lower your voice, I said. Let's discuss this rationally."

"F-fuh-fuck th-that!"

"George, if you can control your stutter, I'd be glad to have you. You're well prepped for every practice and you're good at the background stuff, which means you're rarely surprised. But all that doesn't mean much if you can't control that—"

"I've neh-neh-never stuttered!" He cried out. "It's yuh-you! I-i-if suh-someone else had the d-d-deb-debate t-team, I could—"

Jack's temper slipped another notch.

"George, you're never going to make much of a lawyer, corporation or otherwise, if you can't control that. Law isn't like soccer. Two hours of practice every night won't cut it. What are you going to do, stand up in front of a board meeting and say, 'Nuh-nuh-now, g-gentlemen, about this t-t-tort'?"

He suddenly flushed, not with anger but with shame at his own cruelty. This was not a man in front of him but a seventeen-year-old boy who was facing the first major defeat of his life, and maybe asking in the only way he could for Jack to help him find a way to cope with it.

George gave him a final, furious glance, his lips twisting and bucking as the words bottled up behind them struggled to find their way out.

"Yuh-yuh-you s-s-set it ahead! You huh-hate me b-because you nuh-nuh-nuh-know . . . you know . . . nuh-nuh—"

With an inarticulate cry he had rushed out of the classroom, slamming the door hard enough to make the wire-reinforced glass rattle in its frame. Jack had stood there, feeling, rather than hearing, the echo of George's Adidas in the empty hall. Still in the grip of his temper and his shame at mocking George's stutter, his first thought had been a sick sort of exultation: For the first time in his life George Hatfield had wanted something he could not have. For the first time there was something wrong that all of Daddy's money could not fix. You couldn't bribe a speech center. You couldn't offer a tongue an extra fifty a week and a bonus at Christmas if it would agree to stop flapping like a record needle in a defective groove. Then the exultation was simply buried in shame, and he felt the way he had after he had broken Danny's arm.

Dear God, I am not a son of a bitch. Please.

That sick happiness at George's retreat was more typical of Denker in the play than of Jack Torrance the playwright.

You hate me because you know . . .

Because he knew what?

What could he possibly know about George Hatfield that would make him hate him? That his whole future lay ahead of him? That he looked a little bit like Robert Redford and all conversation among the girls stopped when he did a double gainer from the pool diving board? That he played soccer and baseball with a natural, unlearned grace?

Ridiculous. Absolutely absurd. He envied George Hatfield nothing. If the truth was known, he felt worse about George's unfortunate stutter than George himself, because George really would have made an excellent debater. And if Jack had set the timer ahead—and of course he hadn't—it would have been because both he and the other members of the squad were embarrassed for George's struggle, they had agonized over it the way you agonize when the Class Night speaker forgets some of his lines. If he had set the timer ahead, it would have been just to . . . to put George out of his misery.

But he hadn't set the timer ahead. He was quite sure of it.

A week later he had cut him, and that time he had kept his temper. The shouts and the threats had all been on George's side. A week after that he had gone out to the parking lot halfway through practice to get a pile of sourcebooks that he had left in the trunk of the VW and there had been George, down on one knee with his long blond hair swinging in his face, a hunting knife in one hand. He was sawing through the VW's right front tire. The back tires were already shredded, and the bug sat on the flats like a small, tired dog.

Jack had seen red, and remembered very little of the encounter that followed. He remembered a thick growl that seemed to issue from his own throat: "All right, George. If that's how you want it, just come here and take your medicine."

He remembered George looking up, startled and fearful. He had said: "Mr. Torrance—" as if to explain how all this was just a mistake, the tires had been flat when he got there and he was just cleaning dirt out of the front treads with the tip of this gutting knife he just happened to have with him and—

Jack had waded in, his fists held up in front of him, and it seemed that he had been grinning. But he wasn't sure of that.

The last thing he remembered was George holding up the knife and saying: "You better not come any closer—"

And the next thing was Miss Strong, the French teacher, holding Jack's arms, crying, screaming: "Stop it, Jack! Stop it! You're going to kill him!"

He had blinked around stupidly. There was the hunting knife, glittering harmlessly on the parking lot asphalt four yards away. There was his Volkswagen, his poor old battered bug, veteran of many wild midnight drunken rides, sitting on three flat shoes. There was a new dent in the right front fender, he saw, and there was something in the middle of the dent that was either red paint or blood. For a moment he had been confused, his thoughts

(jesus christ al we hit him after all)

of that other night. Then his eyes had shifted to George, George lying dazed and blinking on the asphalt. His debate group had come out and they were huddled together by the door, staring at George. There was blood on his face from a scalp laceration that looked minor, but there was also blood running out of one of George's ears and that probably meant a concussion. When George tried to get up, Jack shook free of Miss Strong and went to him. George cringed.

Jack put his hands on George's chest and pushed him back down. "Lie still," he said. "Don't try to move." He turned to Miss Strong, who was staring at them both with horror.

"Please go call the school doctor, Miss Strong," he told her. She turned and fled toward the office. He looked at his debate class then, looked them right in the eye because he was in charge again, fully himself, and when he was himself there wasn't a nicer guy in the whole state of Vermont. Surely they knew that.

"You can go home now," he told them quietly. "We'll meet again tomorrow."

But by the end of that week six of his debaters had dropped out, two of them the class of the act, but of course it didn't matter much because he had been informed by then that he would be dropping out himself.

Yet somehow he had stayed off the bottle, and he supposed that was something.

And he had not hated George Hatfield. He was sure of that. He had not acted but had been acted upon.

You hate me because you know . . .

But he had known nothing. *Nothing.* He would swear that before the Throne of Almighty God, just as he would swear that he had set the timer ahead no more than a minute. And not out of hate but out of pity.

Two wasps were crawling sluggishly about on the roof beside the hole in the flashing.

He watched them until they spread their aerodynamically unsound but strangely efficient wings and lumbered off into the October sunshine, perchance to sting someone else. God had seen fit to give them stingers and Jack supposed they had to use them on somebody.

How long had he been sitting here, looking at that hole with its unpleasant surprise down inside, raking over old coals? He looked at his watch. Almost half an hour.

He let himself down to the edge of the roof, dropped one leg over, and felt around until his foot found the top rung of the ladder just below the overhang. He would go down to the equipment shed where he had stored the bug bomb on a high shelf out of Danny's reach. He would get it, come back up, and then they would be the ones surprised. You could be stung, but you could also sting back. He believed that sincerely. Two hours from now the nest would be just so much chewed paper and Danny could have it in his room if he wanted to—Jack had had one in his room when he was just a kid, it had always smelled faintly of woodsmoke and gasoline. He could have it right by the head of his bed. It wouldn't hurt him.

"I'm getting better."

The sound of his own voice, confident in the silent afternoon, reassured him even though he hadn't meant to speak aloud. He *was* getting better. It was possible to graduate from passive to active, to take the thing that had once driven you nearly to madness as a neutral prize of no more than occasional academic interest. And if there was a place where the thing could be done, this was surely it.

He went down the ladder to get the bug bomb. They would pay. They would pay for stinging him.

15

DOWN IN THE FRONT YARD

Jack had found a huge white-painted wicker chair in the back of the equipment shed two weeks ago, and had dragged it around to the porch over Wendy's objections that it was really the ugliest thing she had ever seen in her whole life. He was sitting in it now, amusing himself with a copy of E. L. Doctorow's *Welcome to Hard Times,* when his wife and son rattled up the driveway in the hotel truck.

Wendy parked it in the turn-around, raced the engine sportily, and then turned it off. The truck's single taillight died. The engine rumbled grumpily with post-ignition and finally stopped. Jack got out of his chair and ambled down to meet them.

"Hi, Dad!" Danny called, and raced up the hill. He had a box in one hand. "Look what Mommy bought me!"

Jack picked his son up, swung him around twice, and kissed him heartily on the mouth.

"Jack Torrance, the Eugene O'Neill of his generation, the American Shakespeare!" Wendy said, smiling. "Fancy meeting you here, so far up in the mountains."

"The common ruck became too much for me, dear lady," he said, and slipped his arms around her. They kissed. "How was your trip?"

"Very good. Danny complains that I keep jerking him but I didn't stall the truck once and ... oh, Jack, you finished it!"

She was looking at the roof, and Danny followed her gaze. A faint frown touched his face as he looked at the wide swatch of fresh shingles atop the Overlook's west wing, a lighter green than the rest of the roof. Then he looked down at the box in his hand and his face cleared again. At night the pictures Tony had showed him came back to haunt in all their original clarity, but in sunny daylight they were easier to disregard.

"Look, Daddy, look!"

Jack took the box from his son. It was a model car, one of the Big Daddy Roth caricatures that Danny had expressed an admiration for in the past. This one was the Violent Violet Volkswagen, and the picture on the box showed a huge purple VW with long '59 Cadillac Coupe de Ville taillights burning up a dirt track. The VW had a sunroof, and poking up through it, clawed hands on the wheel down below, was a gigantic warty monster with popping bloodshot eyes, a maniacal grin, and a gigantic English racing cap turned around backward.

Wendy was smiling at him, and Jack winked at her.

"That's what I like about you, doc," Jack said, handing the box back. "Your taste runs to the quiet, the sober, the intro-spective. You are definitely the child of my loins."

"Mommy said you'd help me put it together as soon as I could read all of the first Dick and Jane."

"That ought to be by the end of the week," Jack said. "What else have you got in that fine-looking truck, ma'am?"

"Uh-uh." She grabbed his arm and pulled him back. "No peeking. Some of that stuff is for you. Danny and I will take it in. You can get the milk. It's on the floor of the cab."

"That's all I am to you," Jack cried, clapping a hand to his forehead. "Just a dray horse, a common beast of the field. Dray here, dray there, dray everywhere."

"Just dray that milk right into the kitchen, mister."

"It's too much!" he cried, and threw himself on the ground while Danny stood over him and giggled.

"Get up, you ox," Wendy said, and prodded him with the toe of her sneaker.

"See?" he said to Danny. "She called me an ox. You're a witness."

"Witness, witness!" Danny concurred gleefully, and broad-jumped his prone father.

Jack sat up. "That reminds me, chumly. I've got something for you, too. On the porch by my ashtray."

"What is it?"

"Forgot. Go and see."

Jack got up and the two of them stood together, watching Danny charge up the lawn and then take the steps to the porch two by two. He put an arm around Wendy's waist.

"You happy, babe?"

765

She looked up at him solemnly. "This is the happiest I've been since we were married."

"Is that the truth?"

"God's honest."

He squeezed her tightly. "I love you."

She squeezed him back, touched. Those had never been cheap words with John Torrance; she could count the number of times he had said them to her, both before and after marriage, on both her hands.

"I love you too."

"Mommy! Mommy!" Danny was on the porch now, shrill and excited. "Come and see! Wow! It's neat!"

"What is it?" Wendy asked him as they walked up from the parking lot, hand in hand.

"Forgot," Jack said.

"Oh, you'll get yours," she said, and elbowed him. "See if you don't."

"I was hoping I'd get it tonight," he remarked, and she laughed. A moment later he asked, "Is Danny happy, do you think?"

"You ought to know. You're the one who has a long talk with him every night before bed."

"That's usually about what he wants to be when he grows up or if Santa Claus is really real. That's getting to be a big thing with him. I think his old buddy Scott let some pennies drop on that one. No, he hasn't said much of anything about the Overlook to me."

"Me either," she said. They were climbing the porch steps now. "But he's very quiet a lot of the time. And I think he's lost weight, Jack, I really do."

"He's just getting tall."

Danny's back was to them. He was examining something on the table by Jack's chair, but Wendy couldn't see what it was.

"He's not eating as well, either. He used to be the original steam shovel. Remember last year?"

"They taper off," he said vaguely. "I think I read that in Spock. He'll be using two forks again by the time he's seven."

They had stopped on the top step.

"He's pushing awfully hard on those readers, too," she said. "I know he wants to learn how, to please us . . . to please you," she added reluctantly.

"To please himself most of all," Jack said. "I haven't been pushing him on that at all. In fact, I do wish he wouldn't go quite so hard."

"Would you think I was foolish if I made an appointment for him to have a physical? There's a G.P. in Sidewinder, a young man from what the checker in the market said—"

"You're a little nervous about the snow coming, aren't you?"

She shrugged. "I suppose. If you think it's foolish—"

"I don't. In fact, you can make appointments for all three of us. We'll get our clean bills of health and then we can sleep easy at night."

"I'll make the appointments this afternoon," she said.

"Mom! Look, Mommy!"

He came running to her with a large gray thing in his hands, and for one comic-horrible moment Wendy thought it was a brain. She saw what it really was and recoiled instinctively.

Jack put an arm around her. "It's all right. The tenants who didn't fly away have been shaken out. I used the bug bomb."

She looked at the large wasps' nest her son was holding but would not touch it. "Are you sure it's safe?"

"Positive. I had one in my room when I was a kid. My dad gave it to me. Want to put it in your room, Danny?"

"Yeah! Right now!"

He turned around and raced through the double doors. They could hear his muffled, running feet on the main stairs.

"There *were* wasps up there," she said. "Did you get stung?"

"Where's my purple heart?" he asked, and displayed his finger. The swelling had already begun to go down, but she ooohed over it satisfyingly and gave it a small, gentle kiss.

"Did you pull the stinger out?"

"Wasps don't leave them in. That's bees. They have barbed stingers. Wasp stingers are smooth. That's what makes them so dangerous. They can sting again and again."

"Jack, are you sure that's safe for him to have?"

"I followed the directions on the bomb. The stuff is guaranteed to kill every single bug in two hours' time and then dissipate with no residue."

"I hate them," she said.

"What . . . wasps?"

"Anything that stings," she said. Her hands went to her elbows and cupped them, her arms crossed over her breasts.

"I do too," he said, and hugged her.

16

DANNY

Down the hall, in the bedroom, Wendy could hear the typewriter Jack had carried up from downstairs burst into life for thirty seconds, fall silent for a minute or two, and then rattle briefly again. It was like listening to machine-gun fire from an isolated pillbox. The sound was music to her ears; Jack had not been writing so steadily since the second year of their marriage, when he wrote the story that *Esquire* had purchased. He said he thought the play would be done by the end of the year, for better or worse, and he would be moving on to something new. He said he didn't care if *The Little School* stirred any excitement when Phyllis showed it around, didn't care if it sank without a trace, and Wendy believed that, too. The actual act of his writing made her immensely hopeful, not because she expected great things from the play but because her husband seemed to be slowly closing a huge door on a roomful of monsters. He had had his shoulder to that door for a long time now, but at last it was swinging shut.

Every key typed closed it a little more.

"Look, Dick, look."

Danny was hunched over the first of the five battered primers Jack had dug up by culling mercilessly through Boulder's myriad secondhand bookshops. They would take Danny right up to the second-grade reading level, a program she had told Jack she thought was much too ambitious. Their son was intelligent, they knew that, but it would be a mistake to push him too far too fast. Jack had agreed. There would be no pushing involved. But if the kid caught on fast, they would be prepared. And now she wondered if Jack hadn't been right about that, too.

Danny, prepared by four years of "Sesame Street" and three years of "Electric Company," seemed to be catching on with almost scary speed. It bothered her. He hunched over the innocuous little books, his crystal radio and balsa glider on the shelf above him, as though his life depended on learning to read. His small face was more tense and paler than she liked in the close and cozy glow of the goosenecked lamp they had put in his room. He was taking it very seriously, both the reading and the workbook pages his father made up for him every afternoon. Picture of an apple and a peach. The word *apple* written beneath in Jack's large, neatly made printing. Circle the right picture, the one that went with the word. And their son would stare from the word to the pictures, his lips moving, sounding out, actually *sweating* it out. And with his double-sized red pencil curled into his pudgy right fist, he could now write about three dozen words on his own.

His finger traced slowly under the words in the reader. Above them was a picture Wendy half-remembered from her own grammar school days, nineteen years before. A laughing boy with brown curly hair. A girl in a short dress, her hair in blond ringlets, one hand holding a jump rope. A prancing dog running after a large red rubber ball. The first-grade trinity. Dick, Jane, and Jip.

"See Jip run," Danny read slowly. "Run, Jip, run. Run, run, run." He paused, dropping his finger down a line. "See the . . ." He bent closer, his nose almost touching the page now. "See the . . ."

"Not so close, doc," Wendy said quietly. "You'll hurt your eyes. It's—"

"Don't tell me!" he said, sitting up with a jerk. His voice was alarmed. "Don't tell me, Mommy, I can get it!"

"All right, honey," she said. "But it's not a big thing. Really it's not."

Unheeding, Danny bent forward again. On his face was an expression that might be more commonly seen hovering over a graduate record exam in a college gym somewhere. She liked it less and less.

"See the . . . buh. Aw. El. El. See the buhaw-el-el? See the buhawl. *Ball!*" Suddenly triumphant. Fierce. The fierceness in his voice scared her. *"See the ball!"*

"That's right," she said. "Honey, I think that's enough for tonight."

"A couple more pages, Mommy? Please?"

"No, doc." She closed the red-bound book firmly. "It's bedtime."

"Please?"

"Don't tease me about it, Danny. Mommy's tired."

"Okay." But he looked longingly at the primer.

"Go kiss your father and then wash up. Don't forget to brush."

"Yeah."

He slouched out, a small boy in pajama bottoms with feet and a large flannel top with a football on the front and NEW ENGLAND PATRIOTS written on the back.

Jack's typewriter stopped, and she heard Danny's hearty smack. "Night, Daddy."

"Goodnight, doc. How'd you do?"

"Okay, I guess. Mommy made me stop."

"Mommy was right. It's past eight-thirty. Going to the bathroom?"

"Yeah."

"Good. There's potatoes growing out of your ears. And onions and carrots and chives and—"

Danny's giggle, fading, then cut off by the firm click of the bathroom door. He was private about his bathroom functions, while both she and Jack were pretty much catch-as-catch-can. Another sign—and they were multiplying all the time—that there was another human being in the place, not just a carbon copy of one of them or a combination of both. It made her a little sad. Someday her child would be a stranger to her, and she would be strange to him . . . but not as strange as her own mother had become to her. Please don't let it be that way, God. Let him grow up and still love his mother.

Jack's typewriter began its irregular bursts again.

Still sitting in the chair beside Danny's reading table, she let her eyes wander around her son's room. The glider's wing had been neatly mended. His desk was piled high with picture books, coloring books, old Spiderman comic books with the covers half torn off, Crayolas, and an untidy pile of Lincoln Logs. The VW model was neatly placed above these lesser things, its shrink-wrap still undisturbed. He and his father would be putting it together tomorrow night or the night after if Danny went on at this rate, and never mind the end of the week. His pictures of Pooh and Eyore and Christopher Robin were tacked neatly to the wall, soon enough to be replaced with pin-ups and photographs of dope-smoking rock singers, she supposed. Innocence to experience. Human nature, baby. Grab it and growl. Still it made her sad. Next year he would be in school and she would lose at least half of him, maybe more, to his friends. She and Jack had tried to have another one for a while when things had seemed to be going well at Stovington, but she was on the pill again now. Things were too uncertain. God knew where they would be in nine months.

Her eyes fell on the wasps' nest.

It held the ultimate high place in Danny's room, resting on a large plastic plate on the table by his bed. She didn't like it, even if it was empty. She wondered vaguely if it might have germs, thought to ask Jack, then decided he would laugh at her. But she would ask the doctor tomorrow, if she could catch him with Jack out of the room. She didn't like the idea of that thing, constructed from the chewings and saliva of so many alien creatures, lying within a foot of her sleeping son's head.

The water in the bathroom was still running, and she got up and went into the big bedroom to make sure everything was okay. Jack didn't look up; he was lost in the world he was making, staring at the typewriter, a filter cigarette clamped in his teeth.

She knocked lightly on the closed bathroom door. "You okay, doc? You awake?"

No answer.

"Danny?"

No answer. She tried the door. It was locked.

"Danny?" She was worried now. The lack of any sound beneath the steadily running water made her uneasy. "Danny? Open the door, honey."

No answer.

"Danny!"

"Jesus Christ, Wendy, I can't think if you're going to pound on the door all night."

"Danny's locked himself in the bathroom and he doesn't answer me!"

Jack came around the desk, looking put out. He knocked on the door once, hard. "Open up, Danny. No games."

No answer.

Jack knocked harder. "Stop fooling, doc. Bedtime's bedtime. Spanking if you don't open up."

He's losing his temper, she thought, and was more afraid. He had not touched Danny in anger since that evening two years ago, but at this moment he sounded angry enough to do it.

"Danny, honey—" she began.

No answer. Only running water.

"Danny, if you make me break this lock I can guarantee you you'll spend the night sleeping on your belly," Jack warned.

Nothing.

"Break it," she said, and suddenly it was hard to talk. "Quick."

He raised one foot and brought it down hard against the door to the right of the knob. The lock was a poor thing; it gave immediately and the door shuddered open, banging the tiled bathroom wall and rebounding halfway.

"Danny!" she screamed.

The water was running full force in the basin. Beside it, a tube of Crest with the cap off. Danny was sitting on the rim of the bathtub across the room, his toothbrush clasped limply in his left hand, a thin foam of toothpaste around his mouth. He was staring, trancelike, into the mirror on the front of the medicine cabinet above the washbasin. The expression on his face was one of drugged horror, and her first thought was that he was having some sort of epileptic seizure, that he might have swallowed his tongue.

"Danny!"

Danny didn't answer. Guttural sounds came from his throat.

Then she was pushed aside so hard that she crashed into the towel rack, and Jack was kneeling in front of the boy.

"Danny," he said. "Danny, Danny!" He snapped his fingers in front of Danny's blank eyes.

"Ah-sure," Danny said. "Tournament play. Stroke. Nurrrrr . . ."

"Danny—"

"Roque!" Danny said, his voice suddenly deep, almost manlike. "Roque. Stroke. The roque mallet . . . has two sides. *Gaaaaaa—"*

"Oh Jack my God *what's wrong with him?*"

Jack grabbed the boy's elbows and shook him hard. Danny's head rolled limply backward and then snapped forward like a balloon on a stick.

"Roque. Stroke. Redrum."

Jack shook him again, and Danny's eyes suddenly cleared. His toothbrush fell out of his hand and onto the tiled floor with a small click.

"What?" he asked, looking around. He saw his father kneeling before him, Wendy standing by the wall. "What?" Danny asked again, with rising alarm. "W-W-Wuh-What's wr-r-r—"

"Don't stutter!" Jack suddenly screamed into his face. Danny cried out in shock, his body going tense, trying to draw away from his father, and then he collapsed into tears. Stricken, Jack pulled him close. "Oh, honey, I'm sorry. I'm sorry, doc. Please. Don't cry. I'm sorry. Everything's okay."

The water ran ceaselessly in the basin, and Wendy felt that she had suddenly stepped into some grinding nightmare where time ran backward, backward to the time when her drunken husband had broken her son's arm and had then mewled over him in almost the exact same words.

(*Oh honey. I'm sorry. I'm sorry, doc. Please. So sorry.*)

She ran to them both, pried Danny out of Jack's arms somehow (she saw the look of angry reproach on his face but filed it away for later consideration), and lifted him up. She walked him back into the small bedroom, Danny's arms clasped around her neck, Jack trailing them.

She sat down on Danny's bed and rocked him back and forth, soothing him with nonsensical words repeated over and over. She looked up at Jack and there was only worry in his eyes now. He raised questioning eyebrows at her. She shook her head faintly.

"Danny," she said. "Danny, Danny, Danny. 'S okay, doc. 'S fine."

At last Danny was quiet, only faintly trembling in her arms. Yet it was Jack he spoke to first, Jack who was now sitting beside them on the bed, and she felt the old faint pang

(It's him first and it's always been him first)

of jealousy. Jack had shouted at him, she had comforted him, yet it was to his father that Danny said,

"I'm sorry if I was bad."

"Nothing to be sorry for, doc." Jack ruffled his hair. "What the hell happened in there?"

Danny shook his head slowly, dazedly. "I . . . I don't know. Why did you tell me to stop stuttering, Daddy? I don't stutter."

"Of course not," Jack said heartily, but Wendy felt a cold finger touch her heart. Jack suddenly looked scared, as if he'd seen something that might just have been a ghost.

"Something about the timer . . ." Danny muttered.

"What?" Jack was leaning forward, and Danny flinched in her arms.

"Jack, you're scaring him!" she said, and her voice was high, accusatory. It suddenly came to her that they were all scared. But of what?

"I don't know, I don't know," Danny was saying to his father. "What . . . what did I say, Daddy?"

"Nothing," Jack muttered. He took his handkerchief from his back pocket and wiped his mouth with it. Wendy had a moment of that sickening time-is-running-backward feeling again. It was a gesture she remembered well from his drinking days.

"Why did you lock the door, Danny?" she asked gently. "Why did you do that?"

"Tony," he said. "Tony told me to."

They exchanged a glance over the top of his head.

"Did Tony say why, son?" Jack asked quietly.

"I was brushing my teeth and I was thinking about my reading," Danny said. "Thinking real hard. And . . . and I saw Tony way down in the mirror. He said he had to show me again."

"You mean he was behind you?" Wendy asked.

"No, he was *in* the mirror." Danny was very emphatic on this point. "Way down deep. And then I went through the mirror. The next thing I remember Daddy was shaking me and I thought I was being bad again."

Jack winced as if struck.

"No, doc," he said quietly.

"Tony told you to lock the door?" Wendy asked, brushing his hair.

"Yes."

"And what did he want to show you?"

Danny tensed in her arms; it was as if the muscles in his body had turned into something like piano wire. "I don't remember," he said, distraught. "I don't remember. Don't ask me. I . . . *I don't remember nothing!*"

"Shh," Wendy said, alarmed. She began to rock him again. "It's all right if you don't remember, hon. Sure it is."

At last Danny began to relax again.

"Do you want me to stay a little while? Read you a story?"

"No. Just the night light." He looked shyly at his father. "Would you stay, Daddy? For a minute?"

"Sure, doc."

Wendy sighed. "I'll be in the living room, Jack."

"Okay."

She got up and watched as Danny slid under the covers. He seemed very small.

"Are you sure you're okay, Danny?"

"I'm okay. Just plug in Snoopy, Mom."

"Sure."

She plugged in the night light, which showed Snoopy lying fast asleep on top of his doghouse. He had never wanted a night light until they moved into the Overlook, and then he had specifically requested one. She turned off the lamp and the overhead and looked back at them, the small white circle of Danny's face, and Jack's above it. She hesitated a moment

(and then I went through the mirror)

and then left them quietly.

"You sleepy?" Jack asked, brushing Danny's hair off his forehead.

"Yeah."

"Want a drink of water?"

"No . . ."

There was silence for five minutes. Danny was still beneath his hand. Thinking the boy had dropped off, he was about to get up and leave quietly when Danny said from the brink of sleep:

"Roque."

Jack turned back, all zero at the bone.

"Danny—?"

"You'd never hurt Mommy, would you, Daddy?"

"No."

"Or me?"

"No."

Silence again, spinning out.

"Daddy?"

"What?"

"Tony came and told me about roque."

"Did he, doc? What did he say?"

"I don't remember much. Except he said it was in innings. Like baseball. Isn't that funny?"

"Yes." Jack's heart was thudding dully in his chest. How could the boy possibly know a thing like that? Roque was played by innings, not like baseball but like cricket.

"Daddy . . . ?" He was almost asleep now.

"What?"

"What's redrum?"

"Red drum? Sounds like something an Indian might take on the warpath."

Silence.

"Hey, doc?"

But Danny was asleep, breathing in long, slow strokes. Jack sat looking down at him for a moment, and a rush of love pushed through him like tidal water. Why had he yelled at the boy like that? It was perfectly normal for him to stutter a little. He had been coming out of a daze or some weird kind of trance, and stuttering was perfectly normal under those circumstances. Perfectly. And he hadn't said *timer* at all. It had been something else, nonsense, gibberish.

How had he known roque was played in innings? Had someone told him? Ullman? Hallorann?

He looked down at his hands. They were made into tight, clenched fists of tension

(*god how i need a drink*)

and the nails were digging into his palms like tiny brands. Slowly he forced them to open.

"I love you, Danny," he whispered. "God knows I do."

He left the room. He had lost his temper again, only a little, but enough to make him feel sick and afraid. A drink would blunt that feeling, oh yes. It would blunt that

(Something about the timer)

and everything else. There was no mistake about those words at all. None. Each had come out clear as a bell. He paused in the hallway, looking back, and automatically wiped his lips with his handkerchief.

• • •

Their shapes were only dark silhouettes in the glow of the night light. Wendy, wearing only panties, went to his bed and tucked him in again; he had kicked the covers back. Jack stood in the doorway, watching as she put her inner wrist against his forehead.

"Is he feverish?"

"No." She kissed his cheek.

"Thank God you made that appointment," he said as she came back to the doorway. "You think that guy knows his stuff?"

"The checker said he was very good. That's all I know."

"If there's something wrong, I'm going to send you and him to your mother's, Wendy."

"No."

"I know," he said, putting an arm around her, "how you feel."

"You don't know how I feel at all about her."

"Wendy, there's no place else I can send you. You know that."

"If you came—"

"Without this job we're done," he said simply. "You know that."

Her silhouette nodded slowly. She knew it.

"When I had that interview with Ullman, I thought he was just blowing off his bazoo. Now I'm not so sure. Maybe I really shouldn't have tried this with you two along. Forty miles from nowhere."

"I love you," she said. "And Danny loves you even more, if that's possible. He would have been heartbroken, Jack. He will be, if you send us away."

"Don't make it sound that way."

"If the doctor says there's something wrong, I'll look for a job in Sidewinder," she said. "If I can't get one in Sidewinder, Danny and I will go to Boulder. I can't go to my mother, Jack. Not on those terms. Don't ask me. I . . . I just can't."

"I guess I know that. Cheer up. Maybe it's nothing."

"Maybe."

"The appointment's at two?"

"Yes."

"Let's leave the bedroom door open, Wendy."

"I want to. But I think he'll sleep through now."

But he didn't.

Boom . . . boom . . . boomboomBOOMBOOM——

He fled the heavy, crashing, echoing sounds through twist-ing, mazelike corridors, his bare feet whispering over a deep-pile jungle of blue and black. Each time he heard the roque mallet smash into the wall somewhere behind him he wanted to scream aloud. But he mustn't. He mustn't. A scream would give him away and then

(then *REDRUM*)

(Come out here and take your medicine, you fucking crybaby!)

Oh and he could hear the owner of that voice coming, coming for him, charging up the hall like a tiger in an alien blue-black jungle. A man-eater.

(Come out here, you little son of a bitch!)

If he could get to the stairs going down, if he could get off this third floor, he might be all right. Even the elevator. If he could remember what had been forgotten. But it was dark and in his terror he had lost his orientation. He had turned down one corridor and then another, his heart leaping into his mouth like a hot lump of ice, fearing that each turn would bring him face to face with the human tiger in these halls.

The booming was right behind him now, the awful hoarse shouting.

The whistle the head of the mallet made cutting through the air

(roque . . . stroke . . . roque . . . stroke . . . REDRUM)

before it crashed into the wall. The soft whisper of feet on the jungle carpet. Panic squirting in his mouth like bitter juice.

(You will remember what was forgotten . . . but would he? What was it?)

He fled around another corner and saw with creeping, utter horror that he was in a cul-de-sac. Locked doors frowned down at him from three sides. The west wing. He was in the west wing and outside he could hear the storm whooping and scream-ing, seeming to choke on its own dark throat filled with snow.

He backed up against the wall, weeping with terror now, his heart racing like the heart of a rabbit caught in a snare. When his back was against the light blue silk wallpaper with the embossed pattern of wavy lines, his legs gave way and he collapsed to the carpet, hands splayed on the jungle of woven vines and creepers, the breath whistling in and out of his throat.

Louder. Louder.

There was a tiger in the hall, and now the tiger was just around the corner, still crying out in that shrill and petulant and lunatic rage, the roque mallet slamming, because this tiger walked on two legs and it was—

He woke with a sudden indrawn gasp, sitting bolt upright in bed, eyes wide and staring into the darkness, hands crossed in front of his face.

Something on one hand. Crawling.

Wasps. Three of them.

They stung him then, seeming to needle all at once, and that was when all the images broke apart and fell on him in a dark flood and he began to shriek into the dark, the wasps clinging to his left hand, stinging again and again.

The lights went on and Daddy was standing there in his shorts, his eyes glaring. Mommy behind him, sleepy and scared.

"Get them off me!" Danny screamed.

"Oh my God," Jack said. He saw.

"Jack, what's wrong with him? *What's wrong?*"

He didn't answer her. He ran to the bed, scooped up Danny's pillow, and slapped Danny's thrashing left hand with it. Again. Again. Wendy saw lumbering, insectile forms rise into the air, droning.

"Get a magazine!" he yelled over his shoulder. "Kill them!"

"Wasps?" she said, and for a moment she was inside herself, almost detached in her realization. That her mind cross-patched, and knowledge was connected to emotion. "Wasps, oh Jesus, Jack, you said—"

"Shut the fuck up and kill them!" he roared. *"Will you do what I say!"*

One of them had landed on Danny's reading desk. She took a coloring book off his worktable and slammed it down on the wasp. It left a viscous brown smear.

"There's another one on the curtain," he said, and ran out past her with Danny in his arms.

He took the boy into their bedroom and put him on Wendy's side of the makeshift double. "Lie right there, Danny. Don't come back until I tell you. Understand?"

His face puffed and streaked with tears, Danny nodded.

"That's my brave boy."

Jack ran back down the hall to the stairs. Behind him he heard the coloring book slap twice, and then his wife screamed in pain. He didn't slow but went down the stairs two by two into the darkened lobby. He went through Ullman's office into the kitchen, slamming the heavy part of his thigh into the corner of Ullman's oak desk, barely feeling it. He slapped on the kitchen overheads and crossed to the sink. The washed dishes from supper were still heaped up in the drainer, where Wendy had left them to drip-dry. He snatched the big Pyrex bowl off the top. A dish fell to the floor and exploded. Ignoring it, he turned and ran back through the office and up the stairs.

Wendy was standing outside Danny's door, breathing hard. Her face was the color of table linen. Her eyes were shiny and flat; her hair hung damply against her neck. "I got all of them," she said dully, "but one stung me. Jack, you said they were all dead." She began to cry.

He slipped past her without answering and carried the Pyrex bowl over to the nest by Danny's bed. It was still. Nothing there. On the outside, anyway. He slammed the bowl down over the nest.

"There," he said. "Come on."

They went back into their bedroom.

"Where did it get you?" he asked her.

"My . . . on my wrist."

"Let's see."

She showed it to him. Just above the bracelet of lines between wrist and palm, there was a small circular hole. The flesh around it was puffing up.

"Are you allergic to stings?" he asked. "Think hard! If you are, Danny might be. The fucking little bastards got him five or six times."

"No," she said, more calmly. "I . . . I just hate them, that's all. *Hate* them."

Danny was sitting on the foot of the bed, holding his left hand and looking at them. His eyes, circled with the white of shock, looked at Jack reproachfully.

"Daddy, you said you killed them all. My hand . . . it really hurts."

"Let's see it, doc . . . no, I'm not going to touch it. That would make it hurt even more. Just hold it out."

He did and Wendy moaned. "Oh Danny . . . oh, your poor hand!"

Later the doctor would count eleven separate stings. Now all they saw was a dotting of small holes, as if his palm and fingers had been sprinkled with grains of red paper. The swelling was bad. His hand had begun to look like one of those cartoon images where Bugs Bunny or Daffy Duck has just slammed himself with a hammer.

"Wendy, go get that spray stuff in the bathroom," he said.

She went after it, and he sat down next to Danny and slipped an arm around his shoulders.

"After we spray your hand, I want to take some Polaroids of it, doc. Then you sleep the rest of the night with us, 'kay?"

"Sure," Danny said. "But why are you going to take pictures?"

"So maybe we can sue the ass out of some people."

Wendy came back with a spray tube in the shape of a chemical fire extinguisher.

"This won't hurt, honey," she said, taking off the cap.

Danny held out his hand and she sprayed both sides until it gleamed. He let out a long, shuddery sigh.

"Does it smart?" she asked.

"No. Feels better."

"Now these. Crunch them up." She held out five orange-flavored baby aspirin. Danny took them and popped them into his mouth one by one.

"Isn't that a lot of aspirin?" Jack asked.

"It's a lot of stings," she snapped at him angrily. "You go and get rid of that nest, John Torrance. Right now."

"Just a minute."

He went to the dresser and took his Polaroid Square Shooter out of the top drawer. He rummaged deeper and found some flashcubes.

"Jack, what are you doing?" she asked, a little hysterically.

"He's gonna take some pictures of my hand," Danny said gravely, "and then we're gonna sue the ass out of some people. Right, Dad?"

"Right," Jack said grimly. He had found the flash attachment, and he jabbed it onto the camera. "Hold it out, son. I figure about five thousand dollars a sting."

"What are you *talking* about?" Wendy nearly screamed.

"I'll tell you what," he said. "I followed the directions on that fucking bug bomb. We're going to sue them. The damn thing was defective. Had to have been. How else can you explain this?"

"Oh," she said in a small voice.

He took four pictures, pulling out each covered print for Wendy to time on the small locket watch she wore around her neck. Danny, fascinated with the idea that his stung hand might be worth thousands and thousands of dollars, began to lose some of his fright and take an active interest. The hand throbbed dully, and he had a small headache.

When Jack had put the camera away and spread the prints out on top of the dresser to dry, Wendy said: "Should we take him to the doctor tonight?"

"Not unless he's really in pain," Jack said. "If a person has a strong allergy to wasp venom, it hits within thirty seconds."

"Hits? What do you—"

"A coma. Or convulsions."

"Oh. Oh my Jesus." She cupped her hands over her elbows and hugged herself, looking pale and wan.

"How do you feel, son? Think you could sleep?"

Danny blinked at them. The nightmare had faded to a dull, featureless background in his mind, but he was still frightened.

"If I can sleep with you."

"Of course," Wendy said. "Oh honey, I'm so sorry."

"It's okay, Mommy."

She began to cry again, and Jack put his hands on her shoulders. "Wendy, I swear to you that I followed the directions."

"Will you get rid of it in the morning? Please?"

"Of course I will."

The three of them got in bed together, and Jack was about to snap off the light over the bed when he paused and pushed the covers back instead. "Want a picture of the nest, too."

"Come right back."

"I will."

He went to the dresser, got the camera and the last flash-cube, and gave Danny a closed thumb-and-forefinger circle. Danny smiled and gave it back with his good hand.

Quite a kid, he thought as he walked down to Danny's room. *All of that and then some.*

The overhead was still on. Jack crossed to the bunk setup, and as he glanced at the table beside it, his skin crawled into goose flesh. The short hairs on his neck prickled and tried to stand erect.

He could hardly see the nest through the clear Pyrex bowl. The inside of the glass was crawling with wasps. It was hard to tell how many. Fifty at least. Maybe a hundred.

His heart thudding slowly in his chest, he took his pictures and then set the camera down to wait for them to develop. He wiped his lips with the palm of his hand. One thought played over and over in his mind, echoing with

(You lost your temper. You lost your temper. You lost your temper.)

an almost superstitious dread. They had come back. He had killed the wasps but they had come back.

In his mind he heard himself screaming into his frightened, crying son's face: *Don't stutter!*

He wiped his lips again.

He went to Danny's worktable, rummaged in its drawers, and came up with a big jigsaw puzzle with a fiberboard backing. He took it over to the bedtable and carefully slid the bowl and the nest onto it. The wasps buzzed angrily inside their prison. Then, putting his hand firmly on top of the bowl so it wouldn't slip, he went out into the hall.

"Coming to bed, Jack?" Wendy asked.

"Coming to bed, Daddy?"

"Have to go downstairs for a minute," he said, making his voice light.

How had it happened? How in God's name?

The bomb sure hadn't been a dud. He had seen the thick white smoke start to puff out of it when he had pulled the ring. And when he had gone up two hours later, he had shaken a drift of small dead bodies out of the hole in the top.

Then how? Spontaneous regeneration?

That was crazy. Seventeenth-century bullshit. Insects didn't regenerate. And even if wasp eggs could mature full-grown insects in twelve hours, this wasn't the season in which the queen laid. That happened in April or May. Fall was their dying time.

A living contradiction, the wasps buzzed furiously under the bowl.

He took them downstairs and through the kitchen. In back there was a door which gave on the outside. A cold night wind blew against his nearly naked body, and his feet went numb almost instantly against the cold concrete of the platform he was standing on, the platform where milk deliveries were made during the hotel's operating season. He put the puzzle and the bowl down carefully, and when he stood up he looked at the thermometer nailed outside the door. FRESH UP WITH 7-UP, the thermometer said, and the mercury stood at an even twenty-five degrees. The cold would kill them by morning. He went in and shut the door firmly. After a moment's thought he locked it, too.

He crossed the kitchen again and shut off the lights. He stood in the darkness for a moment, thinking, wanting a drink. Suddenly the hotel seemed full of a thousand stealthy sounds: creakings and groans and the sly sniff of the wind under the eaves where more wasps' nests might be hanging like deadly fruit.

They had come back.

And suddenly he found that he didn't like the Overlook so well anymore, as if it wasn't wasps that had stung his son, wasps that had miraculously lived through the bug bomb assault, but the hotel itself.

His last thought before going upstairs to his wife and son (*from now on you will hold your temper. No Matter What.*) was firm and hard and sure.

As he went down the hall to them he wiped his lips with the back of his hand.

17

THE DOCTOR'S OFFICE

Stripped to his underpants, lying on the examination table, Danny Torrance looked very small. He was looking up at Dr. ("Just call me Bill") Edmonds, who was wheeling a large black machine up beside him. Danny rolled his eyes to get a better look at it.

"Don't let it scare you, guy," Bill Edmonds said. "It's an electroencephalograph, and it doesn't hurt."

"Electro—"

"We call it EEG for short. I'm going to hook a bunch of wires to your head—no, not stick them in, only tape them—and the pens in this part of the gadget will record your brain waves."

"Like on 'The Six Million Dollar Man'?"

"About the same. Would you like to be like Steve Austin when you grow up?"

"No way," Danny said as the nurse began to tape the wires to a number of tiny shaved spots on his scalp. "My daddy says that someday he'll get a short circuit and then he'll be up sh . . . he'll be up the creek."

"I know that creek well," Dr. Edmonds said amiably. "I've been up it a few times myself, *sans* paddle. An EEG can tell us lots of things, Danny."

"Like what?"

"Like for instance if you have epilepsy. That's a little problem where—"

"Yeah, I know what epilepsy is."

"Really?"

"Sure. There was a kid in my nursery school back in Vermont—I went to nursery school when I was a little kid—and he had it. He wasn't supposed to use the flashboard."

"What was that, Dan?" He had turned on the machine. Thin lines began to trace their way across graph paper.

"It had all these lights, all different colors. And when you turned it on, some colors would flash but not all. And you had to count the colors and if you pushed the right button, you could turn it off. Brent couldn't use that."

"That's because bright flashing lights sometimes cause an epileptic seizure."

"You mean using the flashboard might've made Brent pitch a fit?"

Edmonds and the nurse exchanged a brief, amused glance. "Inelegantly but accurately put, Danny."

"What?"

"I said you're right, except you should say 'seizure' instead of 'pitch a fit.' That's not nice . . . okay, lie just as still as a mouse now."

"Okay."

"Danny, when you have these . . . whatever they ares, do you ever recall seeing bright flashing lights before?"

"No."

"Funny noises? Ringing? Or chimes like a doorbell?"

"Huh-uh."

"How about a funny smell, maybe like oranges or sawdust? Or a smell like something rotten?"

"No, sir."

"Sometimes do you feel like crying before you pass out? Even though you don't feel sad?"

"No way."

"That's fine, then."

"Have I got epilepsy, Dr. Bill?"

"I don't think so, Danny. Just lie still. Almost done."

The machine hummed and scratched for another five minutes and then Dr. Edmonds shut it off.

"All done, guy," Edmonds said briskly. "Let Sally get those electrodes off you and then come into the next room. I want to have a little talk with you. Okay?"

"Sure."

"Sally, you go ahead and give him a tine test before he comes in."

"All right."

Edmonds ripped off the long curl of paper the machine had extruded and went into the next room, looking at it.

"I'm going to prick your arm just a little," the nurse said after Danny had pulled up his pants. "It's to make sure you don't have TB."

"They gave me that at my school just last year," Danny said without much hope.

"But that was a long time ago and you're a big boy now, right?"

"I guess so," Danny sighed, and offered his arm up for sacrifice.

When he had his shirt and shoes on, he went through the sliding door and into Dr. Edmonds's office. Edmonds was sitting on the edge of his desk, swinging his legs thoughtfully.

"Hi, Danny."

"Hi."

"How's that hand now?" He pointed at Danny's left hand, which was lightly bandaged.

"Pretty good."

"Good. I looked at your EEG and it seems fine. But I'm going to send it to a friend of mine in Denver who makes his living reading those things. I just want to make sure."

"Yes, sir."

"Tell me about Tony, Dan."

Danny shuffled his feet. "He's just an invisible friend," he said. "I made him up. To keep me company."

Edmonds laughed and put his hands on Danny's shoulders. "Now that's what your Mom and Dad say. But this is just between us, guy. I'm your doctor. Tell me the truth and I'll promise not to tell them unless you say I can."

Danny thought about it. He looked at Edmonds and then, with a small effort of concentration, he tried to catch Edmonds's thoughts or at least the color of his mood. And suddenly he got an oddly comforting image in his head: file cabinets, their doors sliding shut one after another, locking with a click. Written on the small tabs in the center of each door was: A–C, SECRET; D–G, SECRET; and so on. This made Danny feel a little easier.

Cautiously he said: "I don't know who Tony is."

"Is he your age?"

"No. He's at least eleven. I think he might be even older. I've never seen him right up close. He might be old enough to drive a car."

"You just see him at a distance, huh?"

"Yes, sir."

"And he always comes just before you pass out?"

"Well, I don't pass out. It's like I go with him. And he shows me things."

"What kind of things?"

"Well . . ." Danny debated for a moment and then told Edmonds about Daddy's trunk with all his writing in it, and about how the movers hadn't lost it between Vermont and Colorado after all. It had been right under the stairs all along.

"And your daddy found it where Tony said he would?"

"Oh yes, sir. Only Tony didn't *tell* me. He showed me."

"I understand. Danny, what did Tony show you last night? When you locked yourself in the bathroom?"

"I don't remember," Danny said quickly.

"Are you sure?"

"Yes, sir."

"A moment ago I said *you* locked the bathroom door. But that wasn't right, was it? *Tony* locked the door."

"No, sir. Tony couldn't lock the door because he isn't real. He wanted me to do it, so I did. I locked it."

"Does Tony always show you where lost things are?"

"No, sir. Sometimes he shows me things that are going to happen."

"Really?"

"Sure. Like one time Tony showed me the amusements and wild animal park in Great Barrington. Tony said Daddy was going to take me there for my birthday. He did, too."

"What else does he show you?"

Danny frowned. "Signs. He's always showing me stupid old *signs*. And I can't read them, hardly ever."

"Why do you suppose Tony would do that, Danny?"

"I don't know." Danny brightened. "But my daddy and mommy are teaching me to read, and I'm trying real hard."

"So you can read Tony's signs."

"Well, I really want to learn. But that too, yeah."

"Do you like Tony, Danny?"

Danny looked at the tile floor and said nothing.

"Danny?"

"It's hard to tell," Danny said. "I used to. I used to hope

he'd come every day, because he always showed me good things, especially since Mommy and Daddy don't think about DIVORCE anymore." Dr. Edmonds's gaze sharpened, but Danny didn't notice. He was looking hard at the floor, concentrating on expressing himself. "But now whenever he comes he shows me bad things. *Awful* things. Like in the bathroom last night. The things he shows me, they sting me like those wasps stung me. Only Tony's things sting me up here." He cocked a finger gravely at his temple, a small boy unconsciously burlesquing suicide.

"What things, Danny?"

"I can't remember!" Danny cried out, agonized. "I'd tell you if I could! It's like I can't remember because it's so bad I don't *want* to remember. All I can remember when I wake up is REDRUM."

"Red *drum* or red *rum?*"

"Rum."

"What's that, Danny?"

"I don't know."

"Danny?"

"Yes, sir?"

"Can you make Tony come now?"

"I don't know. He doesn't always come. I don't even know if I want him to come anymore."

"Try, Danny. I'll be right here."

Danny looked at Edmonds doubtfully. Edmonds nodded encouragement.

Danny let out a long, sighing breath and nodded. "But I don't know if it will work. I never did it with anyone looking at me before. And Tony doesn't always come, anyway."

"If he doesn't, he doesn't," Edmonds said. "I just want you to try."

"Okay."

He dropped his gaze to Edmonds's slowly swinging loafers and cast his mind outward toward his mommy and daddy. They were here someplace . . . right beyond that wall with the picture on it, as a matter of fact. In the waiting room where they had come in. Sitting side by side but not talking. Leafing through magazines. Worried. About him.

He concentrated harder, his brow furrowing, trying to get into the feeling of his mommy's thoughts. It was always harder when they weren't right there in the room with him. Then he began to get it. Mommy was thinking about a sister. Her sister. The sister was dead. His mommy was thinking that was the main thing that turned her mommy into such a

(bitch?)

into such an old biddy. Because her sister had died. As a little girl she was

(hit by a car oh god i could never stand anything like that again like aileen but what if he's sick really sick cancer spinal meningitis leukemia brain tumor like john gunther's son or muscular dystrophy oh jeez kids his age get leukemia all the time radium treatments chemotherapy we couldn't afford anything like that but of course they just can't turn you out to die on the street can they and anyway he's all right all right all right you really shouldn't let yourself think)

(Danny—)

(about aileen and)

(Dannee—)

(that car)

(Dannee—)

But Tony wasn't there. Only his voice. And as it faded, Danny followed it down into darkness, falling and tumbling down some magic hole between Dr. Bill's swinging loafers, past a loud knocking sound, further, a bathtub cruised silently by in the darkness with some horrible thing lolling in it, past a sound like sweetly chiming church bells, past a clock under a dome of glass.

Then the dark was pierced feebly by a single light, festooned with cobwebs. The weak glow disclosed a stone floor that looked damp and unpleasant. Somewhere not far distant was a steady mechanical roaring sound, but muted, not frightening. Soporific. It was the thing that would be forgotten, Danny thought with dreamy surprise.

As his eyes adjusted to the gloom he could see Tony just ahead of him, a silhouette. Tony was looking at something and Danny strained his eyes to see what it was.

(Your daddy. See your daddy?)

Of course he did. How could he have missed him, even in the basement light's feeble glow? Daddy was kneeling on the floor, casting the beam of a flashlight over old cardboard boxes and wooden crates. The cardboard boxes were mushy and old;

some of them had split open and spilled drifts of paper onto the floor. Newspapers, books, printed pieces of paper that looked like bills. His daddy was examining them with great interest. And then Daddy looked up and shone his flashlight in another direction. Its beam of light impaled another book, a large white one bound with gold string. The cover looked like white leather. It was a scrapbook. Danny suddenly needed to cry out to his daddy, to tell him to leave that book alone, that some books should not be opened. But his daddy was climbing toward it.

The mechanical roaring sound, which he now recognized as the boiler at the Overlook which Daddy checked three or four times every day, had developed an ominous, rhythmic hitching. It began to sound like ... like pounding. And the smell of mildew and wet, rotting paper was changing to something else—the high, junipery smell of the Bad Stuff. It hung around his daddy like a vapor as he reached for the book ... and grasped it.

Tony was somewhere in the darkness

(This inhuman place makes human monsters. This inhuman place) repeating the same incomprehensible thing over and over.

(makes human monsters.)

Falling through darkness again, now accompanied by the heavy, pounding thunder that was no longer the boiler but the sound of a whistling mallet striking silk-papered walls, knocking out whiffs of plaster dust. Crouching helplessly on the blue-black woven jungle rug.

(Come out)

(This inhuman place)

(and take your medicine!)

(makes human monsters.)

With a gasp that echoed in his own head he jerked himself out of the darkness. Hands were on him and at first he shrank back, thinking that the dark thing in the Overlook of Tony's world had somehow followed him back into the world of real things—and then Dr. Edmonds was saying: "You're all right, Danny. You're all right. Everything is fine."

Danny recognized the doctor, then his surroundings in the office. He began to shudder helplessly. Edmonds held him.

When the reaction began to subside, Edmonds asked, "You said something about monsters, Danny—what was it?"

"This inhuman place," he said gutturally. "Tony told me . . . this inhuman place . . . makes . . . makes . . ." He shook his head. "Can't remember."

"Try!"

"I can't."

"Did Tony come?"

"Yes."

"What did he show you?"

"Dark. Pounding. I don't remember."

"Where were you?"

"Leave me alone! I don't remember! Leave me alone!" He began to sob helplessly in fear and frustration. It was all gone, dissolved into a sticky mess like a wet bundle of paper, the memory unreadable.

Edmonds went to the water cooler and got him a paper cup of water. Danny drank it and Edmonds got him another one.

"Better?"

"Yes."

"Danny, I don't want to badger you . . . tease you about this, I mean. But can you remember anything about *before* Tony came?"

"My mommy," Danny said slowly. "She's worried about me."

"Mothers always are, guy."

"No . . . she had a sister that died when she was a little girl. Aileen. She was thinking about how Aileen got hit by a car and that made her worried about me. I don't remember anything else."

Edmonds was looking at him sharply. "Just now she was thinking that? Out in the waiting room?"

"Yes, sir."

"Danny, how would you know that?"

"I don't know," Danny said wanly. "The shining, I guess."

"The what?"

Danny shook his head very slowly. "I'm awful tired. Can't I go see my mommy and daddy? I don't want to answer any more questions. I'm tired. And my stomach hurts."

"Are you going to throw up?"

"No, sir. I just want to go see my mommy and daddy."

"Okay, Dan." Edmonds stood up. "You go on out and see them for a minute, then send them in so I can talk to them. Okay?"

"Yes, sir."

"There are books out there to look at. You like books, don't you?"

"Yes, sir," Danny said dutifully.

"You're a good boy, Danny."

Danny gave him a faint smile.

"I can't find a thing wrong with him," Dr. Edmonds said to the Torrances. "Not physically. Mentally, he's bright and rather too imaginative. It happens. Children have to grow into their imaginations like a pair of oversized shoes. Danny's is still way too big for him, ever had his IQ tested?"

"I don't believe in them," Jack said. "They strait-jacket the expectations of both parents and teachers."

Dr. Edmonds nodded. "That may be. But if you did test him, I think you'd find he's right off the scale for his age group. His verbal ability, for a boy who is five going on six, is amazing."

"We don't talk down to him," Jack said with a trace of pride.

"I doubt if you've ever had to in order to make yourself understood." Edmonds paused, fiddling with a pen. "He went into a trance while I was with him. At my request. Exactly as you described him in the bathroom last night. All his muscles went lax, his body slumped, his eyeballs rotated outward. Text-book auto-hypnosis. I was amazed. I still am."

The Torrances sat forward. "What happened?" Wendy asked tensely, and Edmonds carefully related Danny's trance, the muttered phrase from which Edmonds had only been able to pluck the word "monsters," the "dark," the "pounding." The aftermath of tears, near-hysteria, and nervous stomach.

"Tony again," Jack said.

"What does it mean?" Wendy asked. "Have you any idea?"

"A few. You might not like them."

"Go ahead anyway," Jack told him.

"From what Danny told me, his 'invisible friend' was truly a friend until you folks moved out here from New England. Tony has only become a threatening figure since that move. The pleasant interludes have become nightmarish, even more frightening to your son because he can't remember exactly what the nightmares are about. That's common enough. We all remember our pleasant dreams more clearly than the scary ones. There seems to be a buffer somewhere between the conscious and the subconscious, and one hell of a bluenose lives in there. This censor only lets through a small amount, and often what does come through is only symbolic. That's oversimplified Freud, but it does pretty much describe what we know of the mind's interaction with itself."

"You think moving has upset Danny that badly?" Wendy asked.

"It may have, if the move took place under traumatic circumstances," Edmonds said. "Did it?"

Wendy and Jack exchanged a glance.

"I was teaching at a prep school," Jack said slowly. "I lost my job."

"I see," Edmonds said. He put the pen he had been playing with firmly back in its holder. "There's more here, I'm afraid. It may be painful to you. Your son seems to believe you two have seriously contemplated divorce. He spoke of it in an offhand way, but only because he believes you are no longer considering it."

Jack's mouth dropped open, and Wendy recoiled as if slapped. The blood drained from her face.

"We never even discussed it!" she said. "Not in front of him, not even in front of each other! We—"

"I think it's best if you understand everything, Doctor," Jack said. "Shortly after Danny was born, I became an alcoholic. I'd had a drinking problem all the way through college, it subsided a little after Wendy and I met, cropped up worse than ever after Danny was born and the writing I consider to be my real work was going badly. When Danny was three and a half, he spilled some beer on a bunch of papers I was working on . . . papers I was shuffling around, anyway . . . and I . . . well . . . oh shit." His voice broke, but his eyes remained dry and unflinching. "It sounds so goddam beastly said out loud. I broke his arm turning him around to spank him. Three months later I gave up drinking. I haven't touched it since."

"I see," Edmonds said neutrally. "I knew the arm had been broken, of course. It was set well." He pushed back from his desk a little and crossed his legs. "If I may be frank, it's obvious that he's been in no way abused since then. Other than the stings, there's nothing on him but the normal bruises and scabs that any kid has in abundance."

"Of course not," Wendy said hotly. "Jack didn't mean—"

"No, Wendy," Jack said. "I meant to do it. I guess someplace inside I really did mean to do that to him. Or something even worse." He looked back at Edmonds again. "You know something, Doctor? This is the first time the word divorce has been mentioned between us. And alcoholism. And child-beating. Three firsts in five minutes."

"That may be at the root of the problem," Edmonds said. "I am not a psychiatrist. If you want Danny to see a child psychiatrist, I can recommend a good one who works out of the Mission Ridge Medical Center in Boulder. But I am fairly confident of my diagnosis. Danny is an intelligent, imaginative, perceptive boy. I don't believe he would have been as upset by your marital problems as you believed. Small children are great accepters. They don't understand shame, or the need to hide things."

Jack was studying his hands. Wendy took one of them and squeezed it.

"But he sensed the things that were wrong. Chief among them from his point of view was not the broken arm but the broken—or breaking—link between you two. He mentioned divorce to me, but not the broken arm. When my nurse mentioned the set to him, he simply shrugged it off. It was no pressure thing. 'It happened a long time ago' is what I think he said."

"That kid," Jack muttered. His jaws were clamped together, the muscles in the cheeks standing out. "We don't deserve him."

"You have him, all the same," Edmonds said dryly. "At any rate, he retires into a fantasy world from time to time. Nothing unusual about that; lots of kids do. As I recall, I had my own invisible friend when I was Danny's age, a talking rooster named Chug-Chug. Of course no one could see Chug-Chug but me. I had two older brothers who often left me behind, and in such a situation Chug-Chug came in mighty handy. And of course you two must understand why Danny's invisible friend is named Tony instead of Mike or Hal or Dutch."

"Yes," Wendy said.

"Have you ever pointed it out to him?"

"No," Jack said. "Should we?"

"Why bother? Let him realize it in his own time, by his own logic. You see, Danny's fantasies were considerably deeper than those that grow around the ordinary invisible friend syndrome, but he felt he needed Tony that much more. Tony would come and show him pleasant things. Sometimes amazing things. Always good things. Once Tony showed him where Daddy's lost trunk was . . . under the stairs. Another time Tony showed him that Mommy and Daddy were going to take him to an amusement park for his birthday—"

"At Great Barrington!" Wendy cried. "But how could he *know* those things? It's eerie, the things he comes out with sometimes. Almost as if—"

"He had second sight?" Edmonds asked, smiling.

"He was born with a caul," Wendy said weakly.

Edmonds's smile became a good, hearty laugh. Jack and Wendy exchanged a glance and then also smiled, both of them amazed at how easy it was. Danny's occasional "lucky guesses" about things was something else they had not discussed much.

"Next you'll be telling me he can levitate," Edmonds said, still smiling. "No, no, no, I'm afraid not. It's not extrasensory but good old human perception, which in Danny's case is unusually keen. Mr. Torrance, he knew your trunk was under the stairs because you had looked everywhere else. Process of elimination, what? It's so simple Ellery Queen would laugh at it. Sooner or later you would have thought of it yourself.

"As for the amusement park at Great Barrington, whose idea was that originally? Yours or his?"

"His, of course," Wendy said. "They advertised on all the morning children's programs. He was wild to go. But the thing is, Doctor, we couldn't afford to take him. And we had told him so."

"Then a men's magazine I'd sold a story to back in 1971 sent a check for fifty dollars," Jack said. "They were reprinting the story in an annual, or something. So we decided to spend it on Danny."

Edmonds shrugged. "Wish fulfillment plus a lucky coincidence."

"Goddammit, I bet that's just right," Jack said.

Edmonds smiled a little. "And Danny himself told me that Tony often showed him things that never occurred. Visions based on faulty perception, that's all. Danny is doing subconsciously what these so-called mystics and mind readers do quite consciously and cynically. I admire him for it. If life doesn't cause him to retract his antennae, I think he'll be quite a man."

Wendy nodded—of course she thought Danny would be quite a man—but the doctor's explanation struck her as glib. It tasted more like margarine than butter. Edmonds had not lived with them. He had not been there when Danny found lost buttons, told her that maybe the *TV Guide* was under the bed, that he thought he better wear his rubbers to nursery school even though the sun was out ... and later that day they had walked home under her umbrella through the pouring rain. Edmonds couldn't know of the curious way Danny had of preguessing them both. She would decide to have an unusual evening cup of tea, go out in the kitchen and find her cup out with a tea bag in it. She would remember that the books were due at the library and find them all neatly piled up on the hall table, her library card on top. Or Jack would take it into his head to wax the Volkswagen and find Danny already out there, listening to tinny top-forty music on his crystal radio as he sat on the curb to watch.

Aloud she said, "Then why the nightmares now? Why did Tony tell him to lock the bathroom door?"

"I believe it's because Tony has outlived his usefulness," Edmonds said. "He was born—Tony, not Danny—at a time when you and your husband were straining to keep your marriage together. Your husband was drinking too much. There was the incident of the broken arm. The ominous quiet between you."

Ominous quiet, yes, that phrase was the real thing, anyway. The stiff, tense meals where the only conversation had been please pass the butter or Danny, eat the rest of your carrots or may I be excused, please. The nights when Jack was gone and she had lain down, dry-eyed, on the couch while Danny watched TV. The mornings when she and Jack had stalked around each other like two angry cats with a quivering, frightened mouse between them. It all rang true;

(dear God, do old scars ever stop hurting?)

horribly, horribly true.

Edmonds resumed, "But things have changed. You know, schizoid behavior is a pretty common thing in children. It's accepted, because all we adults have this unspoken agreement that children are lunatics. They have invisible friends. They may go and sit in the closet when they're depressed, withdrawing from the world. They attach talismanic importance to a special blanket, or a teddy bear, or a stuffed tiger. They suck their thumbs. When an adult sees things that aren't there, we consider him ready for the rubber room. When a child says he's seen a troll in his bedroom or a vampire outside the window, we simply smile indulgently. We have a one-sentence explanation that explains the whole range of such phenomena in children—"

"He'll grow out of it," Jack said.

Edmonds blinked. "My very words," he said. "Yes. Now I would guess that Danny was in a pretty good position to develop a full-fledged psychosis. Unhappy home life, a big imagination, the invisible friend who was so real to him that he nearly became real to you. Instead of 'growing out of' his childhood schizophrenia, he might well have grown into it."

"And become autistic?" Wendy asked. She had read about autism. The word itself frightened her; it sounded like dread and white silence.

"Possible but not necessarily. He might simply have entered Tony's world someday and never come back to what he calls 'real things.'"

"God," Jack said.

"But now the basic situation has changed drastically. Mr. Torrance no longer drinks. You are in a new place where conditions have forced the three of you into a tighter family unit than ever before—certainly tighter than my own, where my wife and kids may see me for only two or three hours a day. To my mind, he is in the perfect healing situation. And I think the very fact that he is able to differentiate so sharply between Tony's world and 'real things' says a lot about the fundamentally healthy state of his mind. He says that you two are no longer considering divorce. Is he as right as I think he is?"

"Yes," Wendy said, and Jack squeezed her hand tightly, almost painfully. She squeezed back.

Edmonds nodded. "He really doesn't need Tony anymore. Danny is flushing him out of his system. Tony no longer brings pleasant visions but hostile nightmares that are too frightening for him to remember except fragmentarily. He internalized Tony during a difficult—desperate—life situation, and Tony is not leaving easily. But he *is* leaving. Your son is a little like a junkie kicking the habit."

He stood up, and the Torrances stood also.

"As I said, I'm not a psychiatrist. If the nightmares are still continuing when your job at the Overlook ends next spring, Mr. Torrance, I would strongly urge you to take him to this man in Boulder."

"I will."

"Well, let's go out and tell him he can go home," Edmonds said.

"I want to thank you," Jack told him painfully. "I feel better about all this than I have in a very long time."

"So do I," Wendy said.

At the door, Edmonds paused and looked at Wendy. "Do you or did you have a sister, Mrs. Torrance? Named Aileen?"

Wendy looked at him, surprised. "Yes, I did. She was killed outside our home in Somersworth, New Hampshire, when she was six and I was ten. She chased a ball into the street and was struck by a delivery van."

"Does Danny know that?"

"I don't know. I don't think so."

"He says you were thinking about her in the waiting room."

"I was," Wendy said slowly. "For the first time in . . . oh, I don't know how long."

"Does the word 'redrum' mean anything to either of you?"

Wendy shook her head but Jack said, "He mentioned that word last night, just before he went to sleep. Red drum."

"No, *rum*," Edmonds corrected. "He was quite emphatic about that. *Rum.* As in the drink. The alcoholic drink."

"Oh," Jack said. "It fits in, doesn't it?" He took his handkerchief out of his back pocket and wiped his lips with it.

"Does the phrase 'the shining' mean anything to you?"

This time they both shook their heads.

"Doesn't matter, I guess," Edmonds said. He opened the door into the waiting room. "Anybody here named Danny Torrance that would like to go home?"

"Hi, Daddy! Hi, Mommy!" He stood up from the small table where he had been leafing slowly through a copy of *Where the Wild Things Are* and muttering the words he knew aloud.

He ran to Jack, who scooped him up. Wendy ruffled his hair.

Edmonds peered at him. "If you don't love your mommy and daddy, you can stay with good old Bill."

"No, sir!" Danny said emphatically. He slung one arm around Jack's neck, one arm around Wendy's, and looked radiantly happy.

"Okay," Edmonds said, smiling. He looked at Wendy. "You call if you have any problems."

"Yes."

"I don't think you will," Edmonds said, smiling.

18

THE SCRAPBOOK

Jack found the scrapbook on the first of November, while his wife and son were hiking up the rutted old road that ran from behind the roque court to a deserted sawmill two miles further up. The fine weather still held, and all three of them had acquired improbable autumn suntans.

He had gone down in the basement to knock the press down on the boiler and then, on impulse, he had taken the flashlight from the shelf where the plumbing schematics were and decided to look at some of the old papers. He was also looking for good places to set his traps, although he didn't plan to do that for another month—I want them all to be home from vacation, he had told Wendy.

Shining the flashlight ahead of him, he stepped past the elevator shaft (at Wendy's insistence they hadn't used the elevator since they moved in) and through the small stone arch. His nose wrinkled at the smell of rotting paper. Behind him the boiler kicked on with a thundering *whoosh*, making him jump.

He flickered the light around, whistling tunelessly between his teeth. There was a scale-model Andes range down here:

dozens of boxes and crates stuffed with papers, most of them white and shapeless with age and damp. Others had broken open and spilled yellowed sheaves of paper onto the stone floor. There were bales of newspaper tied up with hayrope. Some boxes contained what looked like ledgers, and others contained invoices bound with rubber bands. Jack pulled one out and put the flashlight beam on it.

ROCKY MOUNTAIN EXPRESS, INC.
To: OVERLOOK HOTEL
From: SIDEY'S WAREHOUSE, 1210 16th Street, Denver, CO.
Via: CANADIAN PACIFIC RR
Contents: 400 CASES DELSEY TOILET TISSUE,
       1 GROSS/CASE

Signed *D E F*
Date *August 24, 1954*

Smiling, Jack let the paper drop back into the box.

He flashed the light above it and it speared a hanging lightbulb, almost buried in cobwebs. There was no chain pull.

He stood on tiptoe and tried screwing the bulb in. It lit weakly. He picked up the toilet-paper invoice again and used it to wipe off some of the cobwebs. The glow didn't brighten much.

Still using the flashlight, he wandered through the boxes and bales of paper, looking for rat spoor. They had been here, but not for quite a long time . . . maybe years. He found some droppings that were powdery with age, and several nests of neatly shredded paper that were old and unused.

Jack pulled a newspaper from one of the bundles and glanced down at the headline.

JOHNSON PROMISES ORDERLY TRANSITION
Says Work Begun by JFK Will Go Forward in Coming Year

The paper was the *Rocky Mountain News,* dated December 19, 1963. He dropped it back onto its pile.

He supposed he was fascinated by that commonplace sense of history that anyone can feel glancing through the fresh news of ten or twenty years ago. He found gaps in the piled newspapers and records; nothing from 1937 to 1945, from 1957 to 1960, from 1962 to 1963. Periods when the hotel had been closed, he guessed. When it had been between suckers grabbing for the brass ring.

Ullman's explanations of the Overlook's checkered career still didn't ring quite true to him. It seemed that the Overlook's spectacular location alone should have guaranteed its continuing success. There had always been an American jet-set, even before jets were invented, and it seemed to Jack that the Overlook should have been one of the bases they touched in their migrations. It even sounded right. The Waldorf in May, the Bar Harbor House in June and July, the Overlook in August and early September, before moving on to Bermuda, Havana, Rio, wherever. He found a pile of old desk registers and they bore him out. Nelson Rockefeller in 1950. Henry Ford & Fam. in 1927. Jean Harlow in 1930. Clark Gable and Carole Lombard. In 1956 the whole top floor had been taken for a week by "Darryl F. Zanuck & Party." The money must have rolled down the corridors and into the cash registers like a twentieth-century Comstock Lode. The management must have been spectacularly bad.

There was history here, all right, and not just in newspaper headlines. It was buried between the entries in these ledgers and account books and room-service chits where you couldn't quite see it. In 1922 Warren G. Harding had ordered a whole salmon at ten o'clock in the evening, and a case of Coors beer. But whom had he been eating and drinking with? Had it been a poker game? A strategy session? What?

Jack glanced at his watch and was surprised to see that forty-five minutes had somehow slipped by since he had come down here. His hands and arms were grimy, and he probably smelled bad. He decided to go up and take a shower before Wendy and Danny got back.

He walked slowly between the mountains of paper, his mind alive and ticking over possibilities in a speedy way that was exhilarating. He hadn't felt this way in years. It suddenly seemed that the book he had semijokingly promised himself might really happen. It might even be right here, buried in these untidy heaps of paper. It could be a work of fiction, or history, or both—a long book exploding out of this central place in a hundred directions.

He stood beneath the cobwebby light, took his handkerchief from his back pocket without thinking, and scrubbed at his lips with it. And that was when he saw the scrapbook.

A pile of five boxes stood on his left like some tottering Pisa. The one on top was stuffed with more invoices and ledgers. Balanced on top of those, keeping its angle of repose for who knew how many years, was a thick scrapbook with white leather covers, its pages bound with two hanks of gold string that had been tied along the binding in gaudy bows.

Curious, he went over and took it down. The top cover was thick with dust. He held it on a plane at lip level, blew the dust off in a cloud, and opened it. As he did so a card fluttered out and he grabbed it in mid-air before it could fall to the stone floor. It was rich and creamy, dominated by a raised engraving of the Overlook with every window alight. The lawn and playground were decorated with glowing Japanese lanterns. It looked almost as though you could step right into it, an Overlook Hotel that had existed thirty years ago.

Horace M. Derwent Requests
The Pleasure of Your Company
At a Masked Ball to Celebrate
The Grand Opening of

THE OVERLOOK HOTEL

Dinner Will Be Served At 8 P.M.
Unmasking And Dancing At Midnight
August 29, 1945   RSVP

Dinner at eight! Unmasking at midnight!

He could almost see them in the dining room, the richest men in America and their women. Tuxedos and glimmering starched shirts; evening gowns; the band playing; gleaming high-heeled pumps. The clink of glasses, the jocund pop of champagne corks. The war was over, or almost over. The future lay ahead, clean and shining. America was the colossus of the world and at last she knew it and accepted it.

And later, at midnight, Derwent himself crying: "Unmask! Unmask!" The masks coming off and . . .

(The Red Death held sway over all!)

He frowned. What left field had that come out of? That was Poe, the Great American Hack. And surely the Overlook—this shining, glowing Overlook on the invitation he held in his hands—was the farthest cry from E. A. Poe imaginable.

He put the invitation back and turned to the next page. A paste-up from one of the Denver papers, and scratched beneath it the date: May 15, 1947.

POSH MOUNTAIN RESORT REOPENS WITH
STELLAR GUEST REGISTER
Derwent Says Overlook Will Be "Showplace of the World"

By David Felton, Features Editor

The Overlook Hotel has been opened and reopened in its thirty-eight-year history, but rarely with such style and dash as that promised by Horace Derwent, the mysterious California millionaire who is the latest owner of the hostelry.

Derwent, who makes no secret of having sunk more than one million dollars into his newest venture—and some say the figure is closer to three million—says that "The new Overlook will be one of the world's showplaces, the kind of hotel you will remember overnighting in thirty years later."

When Derwent, who is rumored to have substantial Las Vegas holdings, was asked if his purchase and refurbishing of the Overlook signaled the opening gun in a battle to legalize casino-style gambling in Colorado, the aircraft, movie, munitions, and shipping magnate denied it . . . with a smile. "The Overlook would be cheapened by gambling," he said, "and don't think I'm knocking Vegas! They've got too many of my markers out there for me to do that! I have no interest in lobbying for legalized gambling in Colorado. It would be spitting into the wind."

When the Overlook opens officially (there was a gigantic and hugely successful party there some time ago when the actual work was finished), the newly painted, papered, and decorated rooms will be occupied by a stellar guest list, ranging from Chic designer Corbat Stani to . . .

Smiling bemusedly, Jack turned the page. Now he was looking at a full-page ad from the New York Sunday *Times* travel section. On the page after that a story on Derwent himself, a balding man with eyes that pierced you even from an old newsprint photo. He was wearing rimless spectacles and a forties-style pencil-line mustache that did nothing at all to make him look like Errol Flynn. His face was that of an accountant. It was the eyes that made him look like someone or something else.

Jack skimmed the article rapidly. He knew most of the

information from a *Newsweek* story on Derwent the year before. Born poor in St. Paul, never finished high school, joined the Navy instead. Rose rapidly, then left in a bitter wrangle over the patent on a new type of propeller that he had designed. In the tug of war between the Navy and an unknown young man named Horace Derwent, Uncle Sam came off the predictable winner. But Uncle Sam had never gotten another patent, and there had been a lot of them.

In the late twenties and early thirties, Derwent turned to aviation. He bought out a bankrupt cropdusting company, turned it into an airmail service, and prospered. More patents followed: a new monoplane wing design, a bomb carriage used on the Flying Fortresses that had rained fire on Hamburg and Dresden and Berlin, a machine gun that was cooled by alcohol, a prototype of the ejection seat later used in United States jets.

And along the line, the accountant who lived in the same skin as the inventor kept piling up the investments. A piddling string of munitions factories in New York and New Jersey. Five textile mills in New England. Chemical factories in the bankrupt and groaning South. At the end of the Depression his wealth had been nothing but a handful of controlling interests, bought at abysmally low prices, salable only at lower prices still. At one point Derwent boasted that he could liquidate completely and realize the price of a three-year-old Chevrolet.

There had been rumors, Jack recalled, that some of the means employed by Derwent to keep his head above water were less than savory. Involvement with bootlegging. Prostitution in the Midwest. Smuggling in the coastal areas of the South where his fertilizer factories were. Finally an association with the nascent western gambling interests.

Probably Derwent's most famous investment was the purchase of the foundering Top Mark Studios, which had not had a hit since their child star, Little Margery Morris, had died of a heroin overdose in 1934. She was fourteen. Little Margery, who had specialized in sweet seven-year-olds who saved marriages and the lives of dogs unjustly accused of killing chickens, had been given the biggest Hollywood funeral in history by Top Mark—the official story was that Little Margery had contracted a "wasting disease" while entertaining at a New York orphanage—and some cynics suggested the studio had laid out all that long green because it knew it was burying itself.

Derwent hired a keen businessman and raging sex maniac named Henry Finkel to run Top Mark, and in the two years before Pearl Harbor the studio ground out sixty movies, fifty-five of which glided right into the face of the Hayes Office and spit on its large blue nose. The other five were government training films. The feature films were huge successes. During one of them an unnamed costume designer had jury-rigged a strapless bra for the heroine to appear in during the Grand Ball scene, where she revealed everything except possibly the birthmark just below the cleft of her buttocks. Derwent received credit for this invention as well, and his reputation—or notoriety—grew.

The war had made him rich and he was still rich. Living in Chicago, seldom seen except for Derwent Enterprises board meetings (which he ran with an iron hand), it was rumored that he owned United Air Lines, Las Vegas (where he was known to have controlling interests in four hotel-casinos and some involvement in at least six others), Los Angeles, and the U.S.A. itself. Reputed to be a friend of royalty, presidents, and underworld kingpins, it was supposed by many that he was the richest man in the world.

But he had not been able to make a go of the Overlook, Jack thought. He put the scrapbook down for a moment and took the small notebook and mechanical pencil he always kept with him out of his breast pocket. He jotted "Look into H. Derwent, Sidwndr lbry?" He put the notebook back and picked up the scrapbook again. His face was preoccupied, his eyes distant. He wiped his mouth constantly with his hand as he turned the pages.

He skimmed the material that followed, making a mental note to read it more closely later. Press releases were pasted into many of the pages. So-and-so was expected at the Overlook next week, thus-and-such would be entertaining in the lounge (in Derwent's time it had been the Red-Eye Lounge). Many of the entertainers were Vegas names, and many of the guests were Top Mark executives and stars.

Then, in a clipping marked February 1, 1952:

MILLIONAIRE EXEC TO SELL COLORADO INVESTMENTS
Deal Made with California Investors on
Overlook, Other Investments, Derwent Reveals

By Rodney Conklin, Financial Editor

In a terse communique yesterday from the Chicago offices of the monolithic Derwent Enterprises, it was revealed that millionaire (perhaps billionaire) Horace Derwent has sold out of Colorado in a stunning financial power play that will be completed by October 1, 1954. Derwent's investments include natural gas, coal, hydro-electric power, and a land development company called Colorado Sunshine, Inc., which owns or holds options on better than 500,000 acres of Colorado land.

The most famous Derwent holding in Colorado, the Overlook Hotel, has already been sold, Derwent revealed in a rare interview yesterday. The buyer was a California group of investors headed by Charles Grondin, a former director of the California Land Development Corporation. While Derwent refused to discuss price, informed sources . . .

He had sold out everything, lock, stock, and barrel. It wasn't just the Overlook. But somehow . . . somehow . . .

He wiped his lips with his hand and wished he had a drink. This would go better with a drink. He turned more pages.

The California group had opened the hotel for two seasons, and then sold it to a Colorado group called Mountainview Resorts. Mountainview went bankrupt in 1957 amid charges of corruption, nest-feathering, and cheating the stockholders. The president of the company shot himself two days after being subpoenaed to appear before a grand jury.

The hotel had been closed for the rest of the decade. There was a single story about it, a Sunday feature headlined FORMER GRAND HOTEL SINKING INTO DECAY. The accompanying photos wrenched at Jack's heart: the paint on the front porch peeling, the lawn a bald and scabrous mess, windows broken by storms and stones. This would be a part of the book, if he actually wrote it, too—the phoenix going down into the ashes to be reborn. He promised himself he would take care of the place, very good care. It seemed that before today he had never really understood the breadth of his responsibility to the Overlook. It was almost like having a responsibility to history.

In 1961 four writers, two of them Pulitzer Prize winners, had leased the Overlook and reopened it as a writers' school. That had lasted one year. One of the students had gotten drunk in his third-floor room, crashed out of the window somehow, and fell to his death on the cement terrace below. The paper hinted that it might have been suicide.

Any big hotels have got scandals, Watson had said, *just like every big hotel has got a ghost. Why? Hell, people come and go . . .*

Suddenly it seemed that he could almost feel the weight of the Overlook bearing down on him from above, one hundred and ten guest rooms, the storage rooms, kitchen, pantry, freezer, lounge, ballroom, dining room . . .

(In the room the women come and go)

(. . . and the Red Death held sway over all.)

He rubbed his lips and turned to the next page in the scrapbook. He was in the last third of it now, and for the first time he wondered consciously whose book this was, left atop the highest pile of records in the cellar.

A new headline, this one dated April 10, 1963.

LAS VEGAS GROUP BUYS FAMED COLORADO HOTEL
Scenic Overlook to Become Key Club

Robert T. Leffing, spokesman for a group of investors going under the name of High Country Investments, announced today in Las Vegas that High Country has negotiated a deal for the famous Overlook Hotel, a resort located high in the Rockies. Leffing declined to mention the names of specific investors, but said the hotel would be turned into an exclusive "key club." He said that the group he represents hopes to sell memberships to high-echelon executives in American and foreign companies.

High Country also owns hotels in Montana, Wyoming, and Utah.

The Overlook became world-known in the years 1946 to 1952 when it was owned by elusive mega-millionaire Horace Derwent, who . . .

The item on the next page was a mere squib, dated four months later. The Overlook had opened under its new management. Apparently the paper hadn't been able to find out or wasn't interested in who the key holders were, because no name was mentioned but High Country Investments—the most anonymous-sounding company name Jack had ever heard except for a chain of bike and appliance shops in western New England that went under the name of Business, Inc.

He turned the page and blinked down at the clipping pasted there.

MILLIONAIRE DERWENT BACK IN COLORADO VIA BACK DOOR?
High Country Exec Revealed to be Charles Grondin

By Rodney Conklin, Financial Editor

The Overlook Hotel, a scenic pleasure palace in the Colorado high country and once the private plaything of millionaire Horace Derwent, is at the center of a financial tangle which is only now beginning to come to light.

On April 10 of last year the hotel was purchased by a Las Vegas firm, High Country Investments, as a key club for wealthy executives of both foreign and domestic breeds. Now informed sources say that High Country is headed by Charles Grondin, 53, who was the head of California Land Development Corp. until 1959, when he resigned to take the position of executive veep in the Chicago home office of Derwent Enterprises.

This has led to speculation that High Country Investments may be controlled by Derwent, who may have acquired the Overlook for the second time, and under decidedly peculiar circumstances.

Grondin, who was indicted and acquitted on charges of tax evasion in 1960, could not be reached for comment, and Horace Derwent, who guards his own privacy jealously, had no comment when reached by telephone. State Representative Dick Bows of Golden has called for a complete investigation into . . .

That clipping was dated July 27, 1964. The next was a column from a Sunday paper that September. The byline belonged to Josh Brannigar, a muck-raking investigator of the Jack Anderson breed. Jack vaguely recalled that Brannigar had died in 1968 or '69.

MAFIA FREE-ZONE COLORADO?

By Josh Brannigar

It now seems possible that the newest r&r spot of Organization overlords in the U.S. is located at an out-of-the-way hotel nestled in the center of the Rockies. The Overlook Hotel, a white elephant that has been run lucklessly by almost a dozen different groups and individuals since it first opened its doors in 1910, is now being operated as a security-jacketed "key club," ostensibly for unwinding businessmen. The question is, what business are the Overlook's key holders *really* in?

The members present during the week of August 16–23 may give us an idea. The list below was obtained by a former employee of High Country Investments, a company first believed to be a dummy company owned by Derwent Enterprises. It now seems more likely that Derwent's interest in High Country (if any) is outweighed by those of several Las Vegas gambling barons. And these same gaming honchos have been linked in the past to both suspected and convicted underworld kingpins.

Present at the Overlook during that sunny week in August were:

Charles Grondin, President of High Country Investments. When it became known in July of this year that he was running the High Country ship it was announced—considerably after the fact—that he had resigned his position in Derwent Enterprises previously. The silver-maned Grondin, who refused to talk to me for this column, has been tried once and acquitted on tax evasion charges (1960).

Charles "Baby Charlie" Battaglia, a 60-year-old Vegas impresario (controlling interests in The Greenback and The Lucky Bones on the Strip). Battaglia is a close personal friend of Grondin. His arrest record stretches back to 1932, when he was tried and acquitted in the gangland-style murder of Jack "Dutchy" Morgan. Federal authorities suspect his involvement in the drug traffic, prostitution, and murder for hire, but "Baby Charlie" has only been behind bars once, for income tax evasion in 1955–56.

Richard Scarne, the principal stockholder of Fun Time Automatic Machines. Fun Time makes slot machines for the Nevada crowd, pinball machines, and jukeboxes (Melody-Coin) for the rest of the country. He has done time for assault with a deadly weapon (1940), carrying a concealed weapon (1948), and conspiracy to commit tax fraud (1961).

Peter Zeiss, a Miami-based importer, now nearing 70. For the last five years Zeiss has been fighting deportation as an undesirable person. He has been convicted on charges of receiving and concealing stolen property (1958), and conspiracy to commit tax fraud (1954). Charming, distinguished, and courtly, Pete Zeiss is called "Poppa" by his intimates and has been tried on charges of murder and accessory to murder. A large stockholder in Scarne's

Fun Time company, he also has known interests in four Las Vegas casinos.

Vittorio Gienelli, also known as "Vito the Chopper," tried twice for gangland-style murders, one of them the ax-murder of Boston vice overlord Frank Scoffy. Gienelli has been indicted twenty-three times, tried fourteen times, and convicted only once, for shoplifting in 1940. It has been said that in recent years Gienelli has become a power in the organization's western operation, which is centered in Las Vegas.

Carl "Jimmy-Ricks" Prashkin, a San Francisco investor, reputed to be the heir apparent of the power Gienelli now wields. Prashkin owns large blocks of stock in Derwent Enterprises, High Country Investments, Fun Time Automatic Machines, and three Vegas casinos. Prashkin is clean in America, but was indicted in Mexico on fraud charges that were dropped quickly three weeks after they were brought. It has been suggested that Prashkin may be in charge of laundering money skimmed from Vegas casino operations and funneling the big bucks back into the organization's legitimate western operations. And such operations may now include the Overlook Hotel in Colorado.

Other visitors during the current season include . . .

There was more but Jack only skimmed it, constantly wiping his lips with his hand. A banker with Las Vegas connections. Men from New York who were apparently doing more in the Garment District than making clothes. Men reputed to be involved with drugs, vice, robbery, murder.

God, what a story! And they had all been here, right above him, in those empty rooms. Screwing expensive whores on the third floor, maybe. Drinking magnums of champagne. Making deals that would turn over millions of dollars, maybe in the very suite of rooms where Presidents had stayed. There was a story, all right. One hell of a story. A little frantically, he took out his notebook and jotted down another memo to check all of these people out at the library in Denver when the caretaking job was over. Every hotel has its ghost? The Overlook had a whole coven of them. First suicide, then the Mafia, what next?

The next clipping was an angry denial of Brannigar's charges by Charles Grondin. Jack smirked at it.

The clipping on the next page was so large that it had been folded. Jack unfolded it and gasped harshly. The picture there seemed to leap out at him: the wallpaper had been changed since June of 1966, but he knew that window and the view perfectly well. It was the western exposure of the Presidential Suite. Murder came next. The sitting room wall by the door leading into the bedroom was splashed with blood and what could only be white flecks of brain matter. A blank-faced cop was standing over a corpse hidden by a blanket. Jack stared, fascinated, and then his eyes moved up to the headline.

GANGLAND-STYLE SHOOTING AT COLORADO HOTEL
Reputed Crime Overlord Shot at Mountain Key Club
Two Others Dead

SIDEWINDER, COLO (UPI)—Forty miles from this sleepy Colorado town, a gangland-style execution has occurred in the heart of the Rocky Mountains. The Overlook Hotel, purchased three years ago as an exclusive key club by a Las Vegas firm, was the site of a triple shotgun slaying. Two of the men were either the companions or bodyguards of Vittorio Gienelli, also known as "The Chopper" for his reputed involvement in a Boston slaying twenty years ago.

Police were summoned by Robert Norman, manager of the Overlook, who said he heard shots and that some of the guests reported two men wearing stockings on their faces and carrying guns had fled down the fire escape and driven off in a late-model tan convertible.

State Trooper Benjamin Moorer discovered two dead men, later identified as Victor T. Boorman and Roger Macassi, both of Las Vegas, outside the door of the Presidential Suite where two American Presidents have stayed. Inside, Moorer found the body of Gienelli sprawled on the floor. Gienelli was apparently fleeing his attackers when he was cut down. Moorer said Gienelli had been shot with heavy-gauge shotguns at close range.

Charles Grondin, the representative of the company which now owns the Overlook, could not be reached for . . .

Below the clipping, in heavy strokes of a ball-point pen, someone had written: *They took his balls along with them.* Jack stared at that for a long time, feeling cold. Whose book was this?

He turned the page at last, swallowing a click in his throat. Another column from Josh Brannigar, this one dated early 1967. He only read the headline: NOTORIOUS HOTEL SOLD FOLLOWING MURDER OF UNDERWORLD FIGURE.

The sheets following that clipping were blank.

(They took his balls along with them.)

He flipped back to the beginning, looking for a name or address. Even a room number. Because he felt quite sure that whoever had kept this little book of memories had stayed at the hotel. But there was nothing.

He was getting ready to go through all the clippings, more closely this time, when a voice called down the stairs: "Jack? Hon?"

Wendy.

He started, almost guiltily, as if he had been drinking secretly and she would smell the fumes on him. Ridiculous. He scrubbed his lips with his hand and called back, "Yeah, babe. Lookin for rats."

She was coming down. He heard her on the stairs, then crossing the boiler room. Quickly, without thinking why he might be doing it, he stuffed the scrapbook under a pile of bills and invoices. He stood up as she came through the arch.

"What in the world have you been doing down here? It's almost three o'clock!"

He smiled. "Is it that late? I got rooting around through all this stuff. Trying to find out where the bodies are buried, I guess."

The words clanged back viciously in his mind.

She came closer, looking at him, and he unconsciously retreated a step, unable to help himself. He knew what she was doing. She was trying to smell liquor on him. Probably she wasn't even aware of it herself, but he was, and it made him feel both guilty and angry.

"Your mouth is bleeding," she said in a curiously flat tone.

"Huh?" He put his hand to his lips and winced at the thin stinging. His index finger came away bloody. His guilt increased.

"You've been rubbing your mouth again," she said.

He looked down and shrugged. "Yeah, I guess I have."

"It's been hell for you, hasn't it?"

"No, not so bad."

"Has it gotten any easier?"

He looked up at her and made his feet start moving. Once they were actually in motion it was easier. He crossed to his wife and slipped an arm around her waist. He brushed aside a sheaf of her blond hair and kissed her neck. "Yes," he said. "Where's Danny?"

"Oh, he's around somewhere. It's started to cloud up outside. Hungry?"

He slipped a hand over her taut, jeans-clad bottom with counterfeit lechery. "Like ze bear, madame."

"Watch out, slugger. Don't start something you can't finish."

"Fig-fig, madame?" he asked, still rubbing. "Dirty peectures? Unnatural positions?" As they went through the arch, he threw one glance back at the box where the scrapbook

(whose?)

was hidden. With the light out it was only a shadow. He was relieved that he had gotten Wendy away. His lust became less acted, more natural, as they approached the stairs.

"Maybe," she said. "After we get you a sandwich—*yeek!*" She twisted away from him, giggling. "That tickles!"

"It teekles nozzing like Jock Torrance would like to teekle you, madame."

"Lay off, Jock. How about a ham and cheese . . . for the first course?"

They went up the stairs together, and Jack didn't look over his shoulder again. But he thought of Watson's words:

Every big hotel has got a ghost. Why? Hell, people come and go . . .

Then Wendy shut the basement door behind them, closing it into darkness.

19

OUTSIDE 217

Danny was remembering the words of someone else who had worked at the Overlook during the season:

Her saying she'd seen something in one of the rooms where . . . a bad thing happened. That was in Room 217 and I want you to promise me you won't go in there, Danny . . . steer right clear . . .

It was a perfectly ordinary door, no different from any other door on the first two floors of the hotel. It was dark gray, halfway down a corridor that ran at right angles to the main second-floor hallway. The numbers on the door looked no different from the house numbers on the Boulder apartment building they had lived in. A 2, a 1, and a 7. Big deal. Just below them was a tiny glass circle, a peephole. Danny had tried several of them. From the inside you got a wide, fish-eye view of the corridor. From outside you could screw up your eye seven ways to Sunday and still not see a thing. A dirty gyp.

(Why are you here?)

After the walk behind the Overlook, he and Mommy had come back and she had fixed him his favorite lunch, a cheese and bologna sandwich plus Campbell's Bean Soup. They ate in Dick's kitchen and talked. The radio was on, getting thin and crackly music from the Estes Park station. The kitchen was his favorite place in the hotel, and he guessed that Mommy and Daddy must feel the same way, because after trying their meals in the dining room for three days or so, they had begun eating in the kitchen by mutual consent, setting up chairs around Dick Hallorann's butcher block, which was almost as big as their dining room table back in Stovington, anyway. The dining room had been too depressing, even with the lights on and the music playing from the tape cassette system in the office. You were still just one of three people sitting at a table surrounded by dozens of other tables, all empty, all covered with those transparent plastic dustcloths. Mommy said it was like having dinner in the middle of a Horace Walpole novel, and Daddy had laughed and agreed. Danny had no idea who Horace Walpole was, but he did know that Mommy's cooking had begun to taste better as soon as they began to eat it in the kitchen. He kept discovering little flashes of Dick Hallorann's personality lying around, and they reassured him like a warm touch.

Mommy had eaten half a sandwich, no soup. She said Daddy must have gone out for a walk of his own since both the VW and the hotel truck were in the parking lot. She said she was tired and might lie down for an hour or so, if he thought he could amuse himself and not get into trouble. Danny told her around a mouthful of cheese and bologna that he thought he could.

"Why don't you go out into the playground?" she asked him. "I thought you'd love that place, with a sandbox for your trucks and all."

He swallowed and the food went down his throat in a lump that was dry and hard. "Maybe I will," he said, turning to the radio and fiddling with it.

"And all those neat hedge animals," she said, taking his empty plate. "Your father's got to get out and trim them pretty soon."

"Yeah," he said.

(Just nasty things ... once it had to do with those damn hedges clipped to look like animals ...)

"If you see your father before I do, tell him I'm lying down."

"Sure, Mom."

She put the dirty dishes in the sink and came back over to him. "Are you happy here, Danny?"

He looked at her guilelessly, a milk mustache on his lip. "Uh-huh."

"No more bad dreams?"

"No." Tony had come to him once, one night while he was lying in bed, calling his name faintly and from far away. Danny had squeezed his eyes tightly shut until Tony had gone.

"You sure?"

"Yes, Mom."

She seemed satisfied. "How's your hand?"

He flexed it for her. "All better."

She nodded. Jack had taken the nest under the Pyrex bowl, full of frozen wasps, out to the incinerator in back of the equipment shed and burned it. They had seen no more wasps since. He had written to a lawyer in Boulder, enclosing the snaps of Danny's hand, and the lawyer had called back two days ago—that had put Jack in a foul temper all afternoon. The lawyer doubted if the company that had manufactured the bug bomb could be sued successfully because there was only Jack to testify that he had followed directions printed on the package. Jack had asked the lawyer if they couldn't purchase some others and test them for the same defect. Yes, the lawyer said, but the results were highly doubtful even if all the test bombs malfunctioned. He told Jack of a case that involved an extension ladder company and a man who had broken his back. Wendy had commiserated with Jack, but privately she had just been glad that Danny had gotten off as cheaply as he had. It was best to leave lawsuits to people who understood them, and that did not include the Torrances. And they had seen no more wasps since.

"Go and play, doc. Have fun."

But he hadn't had fun. He had wandered aimlessly around the hotel, poking into the maid's closets and the janitor's rooms, looking for something interesting, not finding it, a small boy padding along a dark blue carpet woven with twisting black lines. He had tried a room door from time to time, but of course they were all locked. The passkey was hanging down in the office, he knew where, but Daddy had told him he shouldn't touch that. And he didn't want to. Did he?

(Why are you here?)

There was nothing aimless about it after all. He had been drawn to Room 217 by a morbid kind of curiosity. He remembered a story Daddy had read to him once when he was drunk. That had been a long time ago, but the story was just as vivid now as when Daddy had read it to him. Mommy had scolded Daddy and asked what he was doing, reading a three-year-old baby something so horrible. The name of the story was *Bluebeard*. That was clear in his mind too, because he had thought at first Daddy was saying *Bluebird,* and there were no bluebirds in the story, or birds of any kind for that matter. Actually the story was about *Bluebeard*'s wife, a pretty lady that had corn-colored hair like Mommy. After *Bluebeard* married her, they lived in a big and ominous castle that was not unlike the Overlook. And every day *Bluebeard* went off to work and every day he would tell his pretty little wife not to look in a certain room, although the key to that room was hanging right on a hook, just like the passkey was hanging on the office wall downstairs. *Bluebeard*'s wife had gotten more and more curious about the locked room. She tried to peep through the keyhole the way Danny had tried to look through Room 217's peephole with similar unsatisfying results. There was even a picture of her getting down on her knees and trying to look *under* the door, but the crack wasn't wide enough. The door swung wide and . . .

The old fairy tale book had depicted her discovery in ghastly, loving detail. The image was burned on Danny's mind. The severed heads of *Bluebeard*'s seven previous wives were in the room, each one on its own pedestal, the eyes turned up to whites, the mouths unhinged and gaping in silent screams. They were somehow balanced on necks ragged from the broadsword's decapitating swing, and there was blood running down the pedestals.

Terrified, she had turned to flee from the room and the castle, only to discover *Bluebeard* standing in the doorway, his terrible eyes blazing. "I told you not to enter this room," *Bluebeard* said, unsheathing his sword. "Alas, in your curiosity you are like the other seven, and though I loved you best of all, your ending shall be as was theirs. Prepare to die, wretched woman!"

It seemed vaguely to Danny that the story had had a happy ending, but that had paled to insignificance beside the two dominant images: the taunting, maddening locked door with some great secret behind it, and the grisly secret itself, repeated more than half a dozen times. The locked door and behind it the heads, the severed heads.

His hand reached out and stroked the room's doorknob, almost furtively. He had no idea how long he had been here, standing hypnotized before the bland gray locked door.

(And maybe three times I've thought I've seen things . . . nasty things . . .)

But Mr. Hallorann—Dick—had also said he didn't think those things could hurt you. They were like scary pictures in a book, that was all. And maybe he wouldn't see anything. On the other hand . . .

He plunged his left hand into his pocket and it came out holding the passkey. It had been there all along, of course.

He held it by the square metal tab on the end which had OFFICE printed on it in Magic Marker. He twirled the key on its chain, watching it go around and around. After several minutes of this he stopped and slipped the passkey into the lock. It slid in smoothly, with no hitch, as if it had wanted to be there all along.

(I've thought I've seen things . . . nasty things . . . promise me you won't go in there.)

(I promise.)

And a promise was, of course, very important. Still, his curiosity itched at him as maddeningly as poison ivy in a place you aren't supposed to scratch. But it was a dreadful kind of curiosity, the kind that makes you peek through your fingers during the scariest parts of a scary movie. What was beyond that door would be no movie.

(I don't think those things can hurt you . . . like scary pictures in a book . . .)

Suddenly he reached out with his left hand, not sure of what it was going to do until it had removed the passkey and stuffed it back into his pocket. He stared at the door a moment longer, blue-gray eyes wide, then turned quickly and walked back down the corridor toward the main hallway that ran at right angles to the corridor he was in.

Something made him pause there and he wasn't sure what for a moment. Then he remembered that directly around this corner, on the way back to the stairs, there was one of those old-fashioned fire extinguishers curled up against the wall. Curled there like a dozing snake.

They weren't chemical-type extinguishers at all, Daddy said, although there were several of those in the kitchen. These were the forerunner of the modern sprinkler systems. The long canvas hoses hooked directly into the Overlook's plumbing system, and by turning a single valve you could become a one-man fire department. Daddy said that the chemical extinguishers, which sprayed foam or CO_2, were much better. The chemicals smothered fires, took away the oxygen they needed to burn, while a high-pressure spray might just spread the flames around. Daddy said that Mr. Ullman should replace the old-fashioned hoses right along with the old-fashioned boiler, but Mr. Ullman would probably do neither because he was a CHEAP PRICK. Danny knew that this was one of the worst epithets his father could summon. It was applied to certain doctors, dentists, and appliance repairmen, and also to the head of his English Department at Stovington, who had disallowed some of Daddy's book orders because he said the books would put them over budget. "Over budget, hell," he had fumed to Wendy—Danny had been listening from his bedroom where he was supposed to be asleep. "He's just saving the last five hundred bucks for himself, the CHEAP PRICK."

Danny looked around the corner.

The extinguisher was there, a flat hose folded back a dozen times on itself, the red tank attached to the wall. Above it was an ax in a glass case like a museum exhibit, with white words printed on a red background: IN CASE OF EMERGENCY, BREAK GLASS. Danny could read the word EMERGENCY, which was also the name of one of his favorite TV shows, but was unsure of the rest. But he didn't like the way the word was used in connection with that long flat hose. EMERGENCY was fire, explosions, car crashes, hospitals, sometimes death. And he didn't like the way that hose hung there so blandly on the wall. When he was alone, he always skittered past these extinguishers as fast as he could. No particular reason. It just felt better to go fast. It felt safer.

Now, heart thumping loudly in his chest, he came around the corner and looked down the hall past the extinguisher to the stairs. Mommy was down there, sleeping. And if Daddy was back from his walk, he would probably be sitting in the kitchen, eating a sandwich and reading a book. He would just walk right past that old extinguisher and go downstairs.

He started toward it, moving closer to the far wall until his right arm was brushing the expensive silk paper. Twenty steps away. Fifteen. A dozen.

When he was ten steps away, the brass nozzle suddenly rolled off the fat loop it had been lying

(sleeping?)

on and fell to the hall carpet with a dull thump. It lay there, the dark bore of its muzzle pointing at Danny. He stopped immediately, his shoulders twitching forward with the suddenness of his scare. His blood thumped thickly in his ears and temples. His mouth had gone dry and sour, his hands curled into fists. Yet the nozzle of the hose only lay there, its brass casing glowing mellowly, a loop of flat canvas leading back up to the red-painted frame bolted to the wall.

So it had fallen off, so what? It was only a fire extinguisher, nothing else. It was stupid to think that it looked like some poison snake from "Wide World of Animals" that had heard him and woken up. Even if the stitched canvas did look a little bit like scales. He would just step over it and go down the hall to the stairs, walking a little bit fast, maybe, to make sure it didn't snap out after him and curl around his foot . . .

He wiped his lips with his left hand, in unconscious imitation of his father, and took a step forward. No movement from the hose. Another step. Nothing. There, see how stupid you are? You got all worked up thinking about that dumb room and that dumb *Bluebeard* story and that hose was probably ready to fall off for the last five years. That's all.

Danny stared at the hose on the floor and thought of wasps.

Eight steps away, the nozzle of the hose gleamed peacefully at him from the rug as if to say: *Don't worry. I'm just a hose, that's all. And even if that isn't all, what I do to you won't be much worse than a bee sting. Or a wasp sting. What would I want to do to a nice little boy like you . . . except bite . . . and bite . . . and bite?*

Danny took another step, and another. His breath was dry and harsh in his throat. Panic was close now. He began to wish the hose *would* move, then at last he would know, he would be sure. He took another step and now he was within striking distance. But it's not going to *strike* at you, he thought hysterically. How can it *strike* at you, *bite* at you, when it's just a hose?

Maybe it's full of wasps.

His internal temperature plummeted to ten below zero. He stared at the black bore in the center of the nozzle, nearly hypnotized. Maybe it *was* full of wasps, secret wasps, their brown bodies bloated with poison, so full of autumn poison that it dripped from their stingers in clear drops of fluid.

Suddenly he knew that he was nearly frozen with terror; if he did not make his feet go now, they would become locked to the carpet and he would stay here, staring at the black hole in the center of the brass nozzle like a bird staring at a snake, he would stay here until his daddy found him and then what would happen?

With a high moan, he made himself run. As he reached the hose, some trick of the light made the nozzle seem to move, to revolve as if to strike, and he leaped high in the air above it; in his panicky state it seemed that his legs pushed him nearly all the way to the ceiling, that he could feel the stiff back hairs that formed his cowlick brushing the hallway's plaster ceiling, although later he knew that couldn't have been so.

He came down on the other side of the hose and ran, and suddenly he heard it behind him, coming for him, the soft dry whicker of that brass snake's head as it slithered rapidly along the carpet after him like a rattlesnake moving swiftly through a dry field of grass. It was coming for him, and suddenly the stairs seemed very far away; they seemed to retreat a running step into the distance for each running step he took toward them.

Daddy! he tried to scream, but his closed throat would not allow a word to pass. He was on his own. Behind him the sound grew louder, the dry sliding sound of the snake slipping swiftly over the carpet's dry hackles. At his heels now, perhaps rising up with clear poison dribbling from its brass snout.

Danny reached the stairs and had to pinwheel his arms crazily for balance. For one moment it seemed sure that he would cartwheel over and go head-for-heels to the bottom.

He threw a glance back over his shoulder.

The hose had not moved. It lay as it had lain, one loop off the frame, the brass nozzle on the hall floor, the nozzle pointing disinterestedly away from him. You see, stupid? he berated himself. You made it all up, scaredy-cat. It was all your imagination, scaredy-cat, scaredy-cat.

He clung to the stairway railing, his legs trembling in reaction.

(It never chased you)

his mind told him, and seized on that thought, and played it back.

(never chased you, never chased you, never did, never did)

It was nothing to be afraid of. Why, he could go back and put that hose right into its frame, if he wanted to. He could, but he didn't think he would. Because what if it had chased him and had gone back when it saw that it couldn't . . . quite . . . catch him?

The hose lay on the carpet, almost seeming to ask him if he would like to come back and try again.

Panting, Danny ran downstairs.

20

TALKING
TO MR. ULLMAN

The Sidewinder Public Library was a small, retiring building one block down from the town's business area. It was a modest, vine-covered building, and the wide concrete walk up to the door was lined with the corpses of last summer's flowers. On the lawn was a large bronze statue of a Civil War general Jack had never heard of, although he had been something of a Civil War buff in his teenage years.

The newspaper files were kept downstairs. They consisted of the Sidewinder *Gazette* that had gone bust in 1963, the Estes Park daily, and the Boulder *Camera*. No Denver papers at all.

Sighing, Jack settled for the *Camera*.

When the files reached 1965, the actual newspapers were replaced by spools of microfilm. ("A federal grant," the librarian told him brightly. "We hope to do 1958 to '64 when the next check comes through, but they're so slow, aren't they? You will be careful, won't you? I just know you will. Call if you need me.") The only reading machine had a lens that had somehow gotten warped, and by the time Wendy put her hand on his shoulder some forty-five minutes after he had switched from the actual papers, he had a juicy thumper of a headache.

"Danny's in the park," she said, "but I don't want him outside too long. How much longer do you think you'll be?"

"Ten minutes," he said. Actually he had traced down the last of the Overlook's fascinating history—the years between the gangland shooting and the takeover by Stuart Ullman & Co. But he felt the same reticence about telling Wendy.

"What are you up to, anyway?" she asked. She ruffled his hair as she said it, but her voice was only half-teasing.

"Looking up some old Overlook history," he said.

"Any particular reason?"

"No,

(and why the hell are you so interested anyway?)
just curiosity."

"Find anything interesting?"

"Not much," he said, having to strive to keep his voice pleasant now. She was prying, just the way she had always pried and poked at him when they had been at Stovington and Danny was still a crib-infant. *Where are you going, Jack? When will you be back? How much money do you have with you? Are you going to take the car? Is Al going to be with you? Will one of you stay sober?* On and on. She had, pardon the expression, driven him to drink. Maybe that hadn't been the only reason, but by Christ let's tell the truth here and admit it was one of them. Nag and nag and nag until you wanted to clout her one just to shut her up and stop the

(Where? When? How? Are you? Will you?)
endless flow of questions. It could give you a real
(headache? hangover?)
headache. The reader. The damned reader with its distorted print. That was why he had such a cunt of a headache.

"Jack, are you all right? You look pale—"

He snapped his head away from her fingers. *"I am fine!"*

She recoiled from his hot eyes and tried on a smile that was a size too small. "Well . . . if you are . . . I'll just go and wait in the park with Danny . . ." She was starting away now, her smile dissolving into a bewildered expression of hurt.

He called to her: "Wendy?"

She looked back from the foot of the stairs. "What, Jack?"

He got up and went over to her. "I'm sorry, babe. I guess I'm really not all right. That machine . . . the lens is distorted. I've got a really bad headache. Got any aspirin?"

"Sure." She pawed in her purse and came up with a tin of Anacin. "You keep them."

He took the tin. "No Excedrin?" He saw the small recoil on her face and understood. It had been a bitter sort of joke between them at first, before the drinking had gotten too bad for jokes. He had claimed that Excedrin was the only nonprescription drug ever invented that could stop a hangover dead in its tracks. Absolutely the only one. He had begun to think of his morning-after thumpers as Excedrin Headache Number Vat 69.

"No Excedrin," she said. "Sorry."

"That's okay," he said, "these'll do just fine." But of course they wouldn't, and she should have known it, too. At times she could be the stupidest bitch . . .

"Want some water?" she asked brightly.

(No I just want you to GET THE FUCK OUT OF HERE!)

"I'll get some at the drinking fountain when I go up. Thanks."

"Okay." She started up the stairs, good legs moving gracefully under a short tan wool skirt. "We'll be in the park."

"Right." He slipped the tin of Anacin absently into his pocket, went back to the reader, and turned it off. When he was sure she was gone, he went upstairs himself. God, but it was a lousy headache. If you were going to have a vise-gripper like this one, you ought to at least be allowed the pleasure of a few drinks to balance it off.

He tried to put the thought from his mind, more ill tempered than ever. He went to the main desk, fingering a matchbook cover with a telephone number on it.

"Ma'am, do you have a pay telephone?"

"No, sir, but you can use mine if it's local."

"It's long-distance, sorry."

"Well then, I guess the drugstore would be your best bet. They have a booth."

"Thanks."

He went out and down the walk, past the anonymous Civil War general. He began to walk toward the business block, hands stuffed in his pockets, head thudding like a leaden bell. The sky was also leaden; it was November 7, and with the new month the weather had become threatening. There had been a number of snow flurries. There had been snow in October too, but that had melted. The new flurries had stayed, a light frosting over everything—it sparkled in the sunlight like fine crystal. But there had been no sunlight today, and even as he reached the drugstore it began to spit snow again.

The phone booth was at the back of the building, and he was halfway down an aisle of patent medicines, jingling his change in his pocket, when his eyes fell on the white boxes with their green print. He took one of them to the cashier, paid, and went back to the telephone booth. He pulled the door closed, put his change and matchbook cover on the counter, and dialed 0.

"Your call, please?"

"Fort Lauderdale, Florida, operator." He gave her the number there and the number in the booth. When she told him it would be a dollar ninety for the first three minutes, he dropped eight quarters into the slot, wincing each time the bell bonged in his ear.

Then, left in limbo with only the faraway clickings and gabblings of connection-making, he took the green bottle of Excedrin out of its box, pried up the white cap, and dropped the wad of cotton batting to the floor of the booth. Cradling the phone receiver between his ear and shoulder, he shook out three of the white tablets and lined them up on the counter beside his remaining change. He recapped the bottle and put it in his pocket.

At the other end, the phone was picked up on the first ring.

"Surf-Sand Resort, how may we help you?" the perky female voice asked.

"I'd like to speak with the manager, please."

"Do you mean Mr. Trent or—"

"I mean Mr. Ullman."

"I believe Mr. Ullman is busy, but if you would like me to check—"

"I would. Tell him it's Jack Torrance calling from Colorado."

"One moment, please." She put him on hold.

Jack's dislike for that cheap, self-important little prick Ullman came flooding back. He took one of the Excedrins from the counter, regarded it for a moment, then put it into his mouth and began to chew it, slowly and with relish. The taste flooded back like memory, making his saliva squirt in mingled pleasure and unhappiness. A dry, bitter taste, but a compelling one. He swallowed with a grimace. Chewing aspirin had been a habit with him in his drinking days; he hadn't done it at all since then. But when your headache was bad enough, a hangover headache or one like this one, chewing them seemed to make them get to work quicker. He had read somewhere that chewing aspirin could become addictive. Where had he read that, anyway? Frowning, he tried to think. And then Ullman came on the line.

"Torrance? What's the trouble?"

"No trouble," he said. "The boiler's okay and I haven't even gotten around to murdering my wife yet. I'm saving that until after the holidays, when things get dull."

"Very funny. Why are you calling? I'm a busy—"

"Busy man, yes, I understand that. I'm calling about some things that you didn't tell me during your history of the Overlook's great and honorable past. Like how Horace Derwent sold it to a bunch of Las Vegas sharpies who dealt it through so many dummy corporations that not even the IRS knew who really owned it. About how they waited until the time was right and then turned it into a playground for Mafia bigwigs, and about how it had to be shut down in 1966 when one of them got a little bit dead. Along with his bodyguards, who were standing outside the door to the Presidential Suite. Great place, the Overlook's Presidential Suite. Wilson, Harding, Roosevelt, Nixon, and Vito the Chopper, right?"

There was a moment of surprised silence on the other end of the line, and then Ullman said quietly: "I don't see how that can have any bearing on your job, Mr. Torrance. It—"

"The best part happened after Gienelli was shot, though, don't you think? Two more quick shuffles, now you see it and now you don't, and then the Overlook is suddenly owned by a private citizen, a woman named Sylvia Hunter . . . who just happened to be Sylvia Hunter Derwent from 1942 to 1948."

"Your three minutes are up," the operator said. "Signal when through."

"My dear Mr. Torrance, all of this is public knowledge . . . and ancient history."

"It formed no part of my knowledge," Jack said. "I doubt if many other people know it, either. Not all of it. They remember the Gienelli shooting, maybe, but I doubt if anybody has put together all the wondrous and strange shuffles the Overlook has been through since 1945. And it always seems like Derwent or a Derwent associate comes up with the door prize. What was Sylvia Hunter running up there in '67 and '68, Mr. Ullman? It was a whorehouse, wasn't it?"

"Torrance!" His shock crackled across two thousand miles of telephone cable without losing a thing.

Smiling, Jack popped another Excedrin into his mouth and chewed it.

"She sold out after a rather well-known U.S. senator died of a heart attack up there. There were rumors that he was found naked except for black nylon stockings and a garter belt and a pair of high-heeled pumps. Patent-leather pumps, as a matter of fact."

"That's a vicious, damnable lie!" Ullman cried.

"Is it?" Jack asked. He was beginning to feel better. The headache was draining away. He took the last Excedrin and chewed it up, enjoying the bitter, powdery taste as the tablet shredded in his mouth.

"It was a very unfortunate occurrence," Ullman said. "Now what is the point, Torrance? If you're planning to write some ugly smear article . . . if this is some ill-conceived, stupid black-mail idea . . ."

"Nothing of the sort," Jack said. "I called because I didn't think you played square with me. And because—"

"Didn't play *square?*" Ullman cried. "My God, did you think I was going to share a large pile of dirty laundry with the hotel's *caretaker?* Who in heaven's name do you think you are? And how could those old stories possibly affect you anyway? Or do you think there are ghosts parading up and down the halls of the west wing wearing bedsheets and crying 'Woe!'?"

"No, I don't think there are any ghosts. But you raked up a lot of my personal history before you gave me the job. You had me on the carpet, quizzing me about my ability to take care of your hotel like a little boy in front of the teacher's desk for peeing in the coatroom. You embarrassed me."

"I just do not believe your cheek, your bloody damned impertinence," Ullman said. He sounded as if he might be choking. "I'd like to sack you. And perhaps I will."

"I think Al Shockley might object. Strenuously."

"And I think you may have finally overestimated Mr. Shockley's commitment to you, Mr. Torrance."

For a moment Jack's headache came back in all its thudding glory, and he closed his eyes against the pain. As if from a distance away he heard himself ask: "Who owns the Overlook now? Is it still Derwent Enterprises? Or are you too smallfry to know?"

"I think that will do, Mr. Torrance. You are an employee of the hotel, no different from a busboy or a kitchen pot scrubber. I have no intention of—"

"Okay, I'll write Al," Jack said. "He'll know; after all, he's on the Board of Directors. And I might just add a little P.S. to the effect that—"

"Derwent doesn't own it."

"What? I couldn't quite make that out."

"I said Derwent doesn't own it. The stockholders are all Easterners. Your friend Mr. Shockley owns the largest block of stock himself, better than thirty-five per cent. You would know better than I if he has any ties to Derwent."

"Who else?"

"I have no intention of divulging the names of the other stockholders to you, Mr. Torrance. I intend to bring this whole matter to the attention of—"

"One other question."

"I am under no obligation to you."

"Most of the Overlook's history—savory and unsavory alike—I found in a scrapbook that was in the cellar. Big thing with white leather covers. Gold thread for binding. Do you have any idea whose scrapbook that might be?"

"None at all."

"Is it possible it could have belonged to Grady? The caretaker who killed himself?"

"Mr. Torrance," Ullman said in tones of deepest frost, "I am by no means sure that Mr. Grady could read, let alone dig out the rotten apples you have been wasting my time with."

"I'm thinking of writing a book about the Overlook Hotel. I thought if I actually got through it, the owner of the scrapbook would like to have an acknowledgment at the front."

"I think writing a book about the Overlook would be very unwise," Ullman said. "Especially a book done from your ... uh, point of view."

"Your opinion doesn't surprise me." His headache was all gone now. There had been that one flash of pain, and that was all. His mind felt sharp and accurate, all the way down to millimeters. It was the way he usually felt only when the writing was going extremely well or when he had a three-drink buzz on. That was another thing he had forgotten about Excedrin; he didn't know if it worked for others, but for him crunching three tablets was like an instant high.

Now he said: "What you'd like is some sort of commissioned guidebook that you could hand out free to the guests when they checked in. Something with a lot of glossy photos of the mountains at sunrise and sunset and a lemon-meringue text to go with it. Also a section on the colorful people who have stayed there, of course excluding the really colorful ones like Gienelli and his friends."

"If I felt I could fire you and be a hundred per cent certain of my own job instead of just ninety-five per cent," Ullman said in clipped, strangled tones, "I would fire you right this minute, over the telephone. But since I feel that five per cent of uncertainty, I intend to call Mr. Shockley the moment you're off the line . . . which will be soon, or so I devoutly hope."

Jack said, "There isn't going to be anything in the book that isn't true, you know. There's no need to dress it up."

(Why are you baiting him? Do you want to be fired?)

"I don't care if Chapter Five is about the Pope of Rome screwing the shade of the Virgin Mary," Ullman said, his voice rising. "I want you out of my hotel!"

"It's not your hotel!" Jack screamed, and slammed the receiver into its cradle.

He sat on the stool breathing hard, a little scared now,

(a little? hell, a lot)

wondering why in the name of God he had called Ullman in the first place.

(You lost your temper again, Jack.)

Yes. Yes, he had. No sense trying to deny it. And the hell of it was, he had no idea how much influence that cheap little prick had over Al, no more than he knew how much bullshit Al would take from him in the name of auld lang syne. If Ullman was as good as he claimed to be, and if he gave Al a he-goes-or-I-go ultimatum, might not Al be forced to take it? He closed his eyes and tried to imagine telling Wendy. Guess what, babe? I lost another job. This time I had to go through two thousand miles of Bell Telephone cable to find someone to punch out, but I managed it.

He opened his eyes and wiped his mouth with his handkerchief. He wanted a drink. Hell, he *needed* one. There was a café just down the street, surely he had time for a quick beer on his way up to the park, just one to lay the dust . . .

He clenched his hands together helplessly.

The question recurred: Why had he called Ullman in the first place? The number of the Surf-Sand in Lauderdale had been written in a small notebook by the phone and the CB radio in the office—plumbers' numbers, carpenters, glaziers, electricians, others. Jack had copied it onto the matchbook cover shortly after getting out of bed, the idea of calling Ullman full-blown and gleeful in his mind. But to what purpose? Once, during the drinking phase, Wendy had accused him of desiring his own destruction but not possessing the necessary moral fiber to support a full-blown deathwish. So he manufactured ways in which other people could do it, lopping a piece at a time off himself and their family. Could it be true? Was he afraid somewhere inside that the Overlook might be just what he needed to finish his play and generally collect up his shit and get it together? Was he blowing the whistle on himself? Please God no, don't let it be that way. Please.

He closed his eyes and an image immediately arose on the darkened screen of his inner lids: sticking his hand through that hole in the shingles to pull out the rotted flashing, the sudden needling sting, his own agonized, startled cry in the still and unheeding air: *Oh you goddam fucking son of a bitch . . .*

Replaced with an image two years earlier, himself stumbling into the house at three in the morning, drunk, falling over a table and sprawling full-length on the floor, cursing, waking Wendy up on the couch. Wendy turning on the light, seeing his clothes ripped and smeared from some cloudy parking-lot scuffle that had occurred at a vaguely remembered honky-tonk just over the New Hampshire border hours before, crusted blood under his nose, now looking up at his wife, blinking stupidly in the light like a mole in the sunshine, and Wendy saying dully, *You son of a bitch, you woke Danny up. If you don't care about yourself, can't you care a little bit about us? Oh, why do I even bother talking to you?*

The telephone rang, making him jump. He snatched it off the cradle, illogically sure it must be either Ullman or Al Shockley. "What?" he barked.

"Your overtime, sir. Three dollars and fifty cents."

"I'll have to break some ones," he said. "Wait a minute."

He put the phone on the shelf, deposited his last six quarters, then went out to the cashier to get more. He performed the transaction automatically, his mind running in a single closed circle like a squirrel on an exercise wheel.

Why had he called Ullman?

Because Ullman had embarrassed him? He had been embarrassed before, and by real masters—the Grand Master, of course, being himself. Simply to crow at the man, expose his hypocrisy? Jack didn't think he was that petty. His mind tried to seize on the scrapbook as a valid reason, but that wouldn't hold water either. The chances of Ullman knowing who the owner was were no more than two in a thousand. At the interview, he had treated the cellar as another country—a nasty underdeveloped one at that. If he had really wanted to know, he would have called Watson, whose winter number was also in the office notebook. Even Watson would not have been a sure thing, but surer than Ullman.

And telling him about the book idea, that had been another stupid thing. Incredibly stupid. Besides jeopardizing his job, he could be closing off wide channels of information once Ullman called around and told people to beware of New Englanders bearing questions about the Overlook Hotel. He could have done his researches quietly, mailing off polite letters, perhaps even arranging some interviews in the spring . . . and then laughed up his sleeve at Ullman's rage when the book came out and he was safely away—The Masked Author Strikes Again. Instead he had made that damned senseless call, lost his temper, antagonized Ullman, and brought out all of the hotel manager's Little Caesar tendencies. Why? If it wasn't an effort to get himself thrown out of the good job Al had snagged for him, then what was it?

He deposited the rest of the money in the slots and hung up the phone. It really was the senseless kind of thing he might have done if he had been drunk. But he had been sober; dead cold sober.

Walkin out of the drugstore he crunched another Excedrin into his mouth, grimacing yet relishing the bitter taste.

On the walk outside he met Wendy and Danny.

"Hey, we were just coming after you," Wendy said. "Snowing, don't you know."

Jack blinked up. "So it is." It was snowing hard. Sidewinder's main street was already heavily powdered, the center line obscured. Danny had his head tilted up to the white sky, his mouth open and his tongue out to catch some of the fat flakes drifting down.

"Do you think this is it?" Wendy asked.

Jack shrugged. "I don't know. I was hoping for another week or two of grace. We still might get it."

Grace, that was it.

(I'm sorry, Al. Grace, your mercy. For your mercy. One more chance. I am heartily sorry—)

How many times, over how many years, had he—a grown man—asked for the mercy of another chance? He was suddenly so sick of himself, so revolted, that he could have groaned aloud.

"How's your headache?" she asked, studying him closely.

He put an arm around her and hugged her tight. "Better. Come on, you two, let's go home while we still can."

They walked back to where the hotel truck was slant-parked against the curb, Jack in the middle, his left arm around Wendy's shoulders, his right hand holding Danny's hand. He had called it home for the first time, for better or worse.

As he got behind the truck's wheel it occurred to him that while he was fascinated by the Overlook, he didn't much like it. He wasn't sure it was good for either his wife or his son or himself. Maybe that was why he had called Ullman.

To be fired while there was still time.

He backed the truck out of its parking space and headed them out of town and up into the mountains.

21

NIGHT THOUGHTS

It was ten o'clock. Their quarters were filled with counterfeit sleep.

Jack lay on his side facing the wall, eyes open, listening to Wendy's slow and regular breathing. The taste of dissolved aspirin was still on his tongue, making it feel rough and slightly numb. Al Shockley had called at quarter of six, quarter of eight back East. Wendy had been downstairs with Danny, sitting in front of the lobby fireplace and reading.

"Person to person," the operator said, "for Mr. Jack Torrance."

"Speaking." He had switched the phone to his right hand, had dug his handkerchief out of his back pocket with his left, and had wiped his tender lips with it. Then he lit a cigarette.

Al's voice then, strong in his ear: "Jacky-boy, what in the name of God are you up to?"

"Hi, Al." He snuffed the cigarette and groped for the Excedrin bottle.

"What's going on, Jack? I got this *weird* phone call from Stuart Ullman this afternoon. And when Stu Ullman calls long-distance out of his own pocket, you know the shit has hit the fan."

"Ullman has nothing to worry about, Al. Neither do you."

"What exactly is the nothing we don't have to worry about? Stu made it sound like a cross between blackmail and a *National Enquirer* feature on the Overlook. Talk to me, boy."

"I wanted to poke him a little," Jack said. "When I came up here to be interviewed, he had to drag out all my dirty laundry. Drinking problem. Lost your last job for racking over a student. Wonder if you're the right man for this. Et cetera. The thing that bugged me was that he was bringing all this up because he loved the goddam hotel so much. The beautiful Overlook. The traditional Overlook. The bloody sacred Overlook. Well, I found a scrapbook in the basement. Somebody had put together all the less savory aspects of Ullman's cathedral, and it looked to me like a little black mass had been going on after hours."

"I hope that's metaphorical, Jack." Al's voice sounded frighteningly cold.

"It is. But I did find out—"

"I know the hotel's history."

Jack ran a hand through his hair. "So I called him up and poked him with it. I admit it wasn't very bright, and I sure wouldn't do it again. End of story."

"Stu says you're planning to do a little dirty-laundry-airing yourself."

"Stu is an asshole!" he barked into the phone. "I told him I had an idea of writing about the Overlook, yes. I do. I think this place forms an index of the whole post-World War II American character. That sounds like an inflated claim, stated so baldly . . . I know it does . . . but it's all here, Al! My God, it could be a *great* book. But it's far in the future, I can promise you that, I've got more on my plate right now than I can eat, and—"

"Jack, that's not good enough."

He found himself gaping at the black receiver of the phone, unable to believe what he had surely heard. "What? Al, did you say—?"

"I said what I said. How long is far in the future, Jack? For you it may be two years, maybe five. For me it's thirty or forty, because I expect to be associated with the Overlook for a long time. The thought of you doing some sort of a scum-job on my hotel and passing it off as a great piece of American writing, that makes me sick."

Jack was speechless.

"I tried to help you, Jacky-boy. We went through the war together, and I thought I owed you some help. You remember the war?"

"I remember it," he muttered, but the coals of resentment had begun to glow around his heart. First Ullman, then Wendy, now Al. What was this? National Let's Pick Jack Torrance Apart Week? He clamped his lips more tightly together, reached for his cigarettes, and knocked them off onto the floor. Had he ever liked this cheap prick talking to him from his mahogany-lined den in Vermont? Had he really?

"Before you hit that Hatfield kid," Al was saying, "I had talked the Board out of letting you go and even had them swung around to considering tenure. You blew that one for yourself. I got you this hotel thing, a nice quiet place for you to get yourself together, finish your play, and wait it out until Harry Effinger and I could convince the rest of those guys that they made a big mistake. Now it looks like you want to chew my arm off on your way to a bigger killing. Is that the way you say thanks to your friends, Jack?"

"No," he whispered.

He didn't dare say more. His head was throbbing with the hot, acid-etched words that wanted to get out. He tried desperately to think of Danny and Wendy, depending on him, Danny and Wendy sitting peacefully downstairs in front of the fire and working on the first of the second-grade reading primers, thinking everything was A-OK. If he lost this job, what then? Off to California in that tired old VW with the distintegrating fuel pump like a family of dustbowl Okies? He told himself he would get down on his knees and beg Al before he let that happen, but still the words struggled to pour out, and the hand holding the hot wires of his rage felt greased.

"What?" Al said sharply.

"No," he said. "That is not the way I treat my friends. And you know it."

"How do I know it? At the worst, you're planning to smear my hotel by digging up bodies that were decently buried years ago. At the best, you call up my temperamental but extremely competent hotel manager and work him into a frenzy as part of some . . . some stupid kid's game."

"It was more than a game, Al. It's easier for you. You don't have to take some rich friend's charity. You don't need a friend in court because you *are* the court. The fact that you were one step from a brown-bag lush goes pretty much unmentioned, doesn't it?"

"I suppose it does," Al said. His voice had dropped a notch and he sounded tired of the whole thing. "But Jack, Jack . . . I can't help that. I can't change that."

"I know," Jack said emptily. "Am I fired? I guess you better tell me if I am."

"Not if you'll do two things for me."

"All right."

"Hadn't you better hear the conditions before you accept them?"

"No. Give me your deal and I'll take it. There's Wendy and Danny to think about. If you want my balls, I'll send them airmail."

"Are you sure self-pity is a luxury you can afford, Jack?"

He had closed his eyes and slid an Excedrin between his dry lips. "At this point I feel it's the only one I can afford. Fire away . . . no pun intended."

Al was silent for a moment. Then he said: "First, no more calls to Ullman. Not even if the place burns down. If that happens, call the maintenance man, that guy who swears all the time, you know who I mean . . ."

"Watson."

"Yes."

"Okay. Done."

"Second, you promise me, Jack. Word of honor. No book about a famous Colorado mountain hotel with a history."

For a moment his rage was so great that he literally could not speak. The blood beat loudly in his ears. It was like getting a call from some twentieth-century Medici prince . . . no portraits of my family with their warts showing, please, or back to the rabble you'll go. I subsidize no pictures but pretty pictures. When you paint the daughter of my good friend and business partner, please omit birthmark or back to the rabble you'll go. Of course we're friends . . . we are both civilized men, aren't we? We've shared bed and board and bottle. We'll always be friends, and the dog collar I have on you will always be ignored by mutual consent, and I'll take good and benevolent care of you. All I ask in return is your soul. Small item. We can even ignore the fact that you've handed it over, the way we ignore the dog collar. Remember, my talented friend, there are Michelangelos begging everywhere in the streets of Rome . . .

"Jack? You there?"

He made a strangled noise that was intended to be the word yes.

Al's voice was firm and very sure of itself. "I really don't think I'm asking so much, Jack. And there will be other books. You just can't expect me to subsidize you while you . . ."

"All right, agreed."

"I don't want you to think I'm trying to control your artistic life, Jack. You know me better than that. It's just that—"

"Al?"

"What?"

"Is Derwent still involved with the Overlook? Somehow?"

"I don't see how that can possibly be any concern of yours, Jack."

"No," he said distantly. "I suppose it isn't. Listen, Al, I think I hear Wendy calling me for something. I'll get back to you."

"Sure thing, Jacky-boy. We'll have a good talk. How are things? Dry?"

(YOU'VE GOT YOUR POUND OF FLESH BLOOD AND ALL NOW CAN'T YOU LEAVE ME ALONE?)

"As a bone."

"Here too. I'm actually beginning to enjoy sobriety. If—"

"I'll get back, Al. Wendy—"

"Sure. Okay."

And so he had hung up and that was when the cramps had come, hitting him like lightning bolts, making him curl up in front of the telephone like a penitent, hands over his belly, head throbbing like a monstrous bladder.

The moving wasp, having stung, moves on . . .

It had passed a little when Wendy came upstairs and asked him who had been on the phone.

"Al," he said. "He called to ask how things were going. I said they were fine."

"Jack, you look terrible. Are you sick?"

"Headache's back. I'm going to bed early. No sense trying to write."

"Can I get you some warm milk?"

He smiled wanly. "That would be nice."

And now he lay beside her, feeling her warm and sleeping thigh against his own. Thinking of the conversation with Al, how he had groveled, still made him hot and cold by turns. Someday there would be a reckoning. Someday there would be a book, not the soft and thoughtful thing he had first considered, but a gem-hard work of research, photo section and all, and he would pull apart the entire Overlook history, nasty, incestuous ownership deals and all. He would spread it all out for the reader like a dissected crayfish. And if Al Shockley had connections with the Derwent empire, then God help him.

Strung up like piano wire, he lay staring into the dark, knowing it might be hours yet before he could sleep.

Wendy Torrance lay on her back, eyes closed, listening to the sound of her husband's slumber—the long inhale, the brief hold, the slightly guttural exhale. Where did he go when he slept, she wondered. To some amusement park, a Great Barrington of dreams where all the riders were free and there was no wife mother along to tell them they'd had enough hotdogs or that they'd better be going if they wanted to get home by dark? Or was it some fathoms-deep bar where the drinking never stopped and the batwings were always propped open and all the old companions were gathered around the electronic hockey game, glasses in hand, Al Shockley prominent among them with his tie loosened and the top button of his shirt undone? A place where both she and Danny were excluded and the boogie went on endlessly?

Wendy was worried about him, the old, helpless worry that she had hoped was behind her forever in Vermont, as if worry could somehow not cross state lines. She didn't like what the Overlook seemed to be doing to Jack and Danny.

The most frightening thing, vaporous and unmentioned, perhaps unmentionable, was that all of Jack's drinking symptoms had come back, one by one . . . all but the drink itself. The constant wiping of the lips with hand or handkerchief, as if to rid them of excess moisture. Long pauses at the typewriter, more balls of paper in the wastebasket. There had been a bottle of Excedrin on the telephone table tonight after Al had called him, but no water glass. He had been chewing them again. He got irritated over little things. He would unconsciously start snapping his fingers in a nervous rhythm when things got too quiet. Increased profanity. She had begun to worry about his temper, too. It would almost come as a relief if he would lose it, blow off steam, in much the same way that he went down to the basement first thing in the morning and last thing at night to dump the press on the boiler. It would almost be good to see him curse and kick a chair across the room or slam a door. But those things, always an integral part of his temperament, had almost wholly ceased. Yet she had the feeling that Jack was more and more often angry with her or Danny, but was refusing to let it out. The boiler had a pressure gauge: old, cracked, clotted with grease, but still workable. Jack had none. She had never been able to read him very well. Danny could, but Danny wasn't talking.

And the call from Al. At about the same time it had come, Danny had lost all interest in the story they had been reading. He left her to sit by the fire and crossed to the main desk where Jack had constructed a roadway for his matchbox cars and trucks. The Violent Violet Volkswagen was there and Danny had begun to push it rapidly back and forth. Pretending to read her own book but actually looking at Danny over the top of it, she had seen an odd amalgam of the ways she and Jack expressed anxiety. The wiping of the lips. Running both hands nervously through his hair, as she had done while waiting for Jack to come home from his round of the bars. She couldn't believe Al had called just to "ask how things were going." If you wanted to shoot the bull, you called Al. When Al called you, that was business.

Later, when she had come back downstairs, she had found Danny curled up by the fire again, reading the second-grade-primer adventures of Joe and Rachel at the circus with their daddy in complete, absorbed attention. The fidgety distraction had completely disappeared. Watching him, she had been struck again by the eerie certainty that Danny knew more and understood more than there was room for in Dr. ("Just call me Bill") Edmonds's philosophy.

"Hey, time for bed, doc," she'd said.

"Yeah, okay." He marked his place in the book and stood up.

"Wash up and brush your teeth."

"Okay."

"Don't forget to use the floss."

"I won't."

They stood side by side for a moment, watching the wax and wane of the coals of the fire. Most of the lobby was chilly and drafty, but this circle around the fireplace was magically warm, and hard to leave.

"It was Uncle Al on the phone," she said casually.

"Oh yeah?" Totally unsurprised.

"I wonder if Uncle Al was mad at Daddy," she said, still casually.

"Yeah, he sure was," Danny said, still watching the fire. "He didn't want Daddy to write the book."

"What book, Danny?"

"About the hotel."

The question framed on her lips was one she and Jack had asked Danny a thousand times: *How do you know that?* she hadn't asked him. She didn't want to upset him before bed, or make him aware that they were casually discussing his knowledge of things he had no way of knowing at all. And he *did* know, she was convinced of that. Dr. Edmonds's patter about inductive reasoning and subconscious logic was just that: patter. Her sister . . . how had Danny known she was thinking about Aileen in the waiting room that day? And

(I dreamed Daddy had an accident.)

She shook her head, as if to clear it. "Go wash up, doc."

"Okay." He ran up the stairs toward their quarters. Frowning, she had gone into the kitchen to warm Jack's milk in a saucepan.

And now, lying wakeful in her bed and listening to her husband's breathing and the wind outside (miraculously, they'd had only another flurry that afternoon; still no heavy snow), she let her mind turn fully to her lovely, troubling son, born with a caul over his face, a simple tissue of membrane that doctors saw perhaps once in every seven hundred births, a tissue that the old wives' tales said betokened the second sight.

She decided that it was time to talk to Danny about the Overlook . . . and high time she tried to get Danny to talk to her. Tomorrow. For sure. The two of them would be going down to the Sidewinder Public Library to see if they could get him some second-grade-level books on an extended loan through the winter, and she would talk to him. And frankly. With that thought she felt a little easier, and at last began to drift toward sleep.

• • •

Danny lay awake in his bedroom, eyes open, left arm encircling his aged and slightly worse-for-wear Pooh (Pooh had lost one shoe-button eye and was oozing stuffing from half a dozen sprung seams), listening to his parents sleep in their bedroom. He felt as if he were standing unwilling guard over them. The nights were the worst of all. He hated the nights and the constant howl of the wind around the west side of the hotel.

His glider floated overhead from a string. On his bureau the VW model, brought up from the roadway setup downstairs, glowed a dimly fluorescent purple. His books were in the bookcase, his coloring books on the desk. *A place for everything and everything in its place,* Mommy said. *Then you know where it is when you want it.* But now things had been misplaced. Things were missing. Worse still, things had been *added,* things you couldn't quite see, like in one of those pictures that said CAN YOU SEE THE INDIANS? And if you strained and squinted, you could see some of them—the thing you had taken for a cactus at first glance was really a brave with a knife clamped in his teeth, and there were others hiding in the rocks, and you could even see one of their evil, merciless faces peering through the spokes of a covered wagon wheel. But you could never see all of them, and that was what made you uneasy. Because it was the ones you couldn't see that would sneak up behind you, a tomahawk in one hand and a scalping knife in the other . . .

He shifted uneasily in his bed, his eyes searching out the comforting glow of the night light. Things were worse here. He knew that much for sure. At first they hadn't been so bad, but little by little . . . his daddy thought about drinking a lot more. Sometimes he was angry at Mommy and didn't know why. He went around wiping his lips with his handkerchief and his eyes were far away and cloudy. Mommy was worried about him and Danny, too. He didn't have to shine into her to know that; it had been in the anxious way she had questioned him on the day the fire hose had seemed to turn into a snake. Mr. Hallorann said he thought all mothers could shine a little bit, and she had known on that day that something had happened. But not what.

He had almost told her, but a couple of things had held him back. He knew that the doctor in Sidewinder had dismissed Tony and the things that Tony showed him as perfectly

(well almost)

normal. His mother might not believe him if he told her about the hose. Worse, she might believe him in the wrong way, might think he was LOSING HIS MARBLES. He understood a little about LOSING YOUR MARBLES, not as much as he did about GETTING A BABY, which his mommy had explained to him the year before at some length, but enough.

Once, at nursery school, his friend Scott had pointed out a boy named Robin Stenger, who was moping around the swings with a face almost long enough to step on. Robin's father taught arithmetic at Daddy's school, and Scott's daddy taught history there. Most of the kids at the nursery school were associated either with Stovington Prep or with the small IBM plant just outside of town. The prep kids chummed in one group, the IBM kids in another. There were cross-friendships, of course, but it was natural enough for the kids whose fathers knew each other to more or less stick together. When there was an adult scandal in one group, it almost always filtered down to the children in some wildly mutated form or other, but it rarely jumped to the other group.

He and Scotty were sitting in the play rocketship when Scotty jerked his thumb at Robin and said: "You know that kid?"

"Yeah," Danny said.

Scott leaned forward. "His dad LOST HIS MARBLES last night. They took him away."

"Yeah? Just for losing some marbles?"

Scotty looked disgusted. "He went crazy. You know." Scott crossed his eyes, flopped out his tongue, and twirled his index fingers in large elliptical orbits around his ears. "They took him to THE BUGHOUSE."

"Wow," Danny said. "When will they let him come back?"

"Never-never-never," Scotty said darkly.

In the course of that day and the next, Danny heard that

a.) Mr. Stenger had tried to kill everybody in his family, including Robin, with his World War II souvenir pistol;

b.) Mr. Stenger ripped the house to pieces while he was STINKO;

c.) Mr. Stenger had been discovered eating a bowl of dead bugs and grass like they were cereal and milk and crying while he did it;

d.) Mr. Stenger had tried to strangle his wife with a stocking when the Red Sox lost a big ball game.

Finally, too troubled to keep it to himself, he had asked Daddy about Mr. Stenger. His daddy had taken him on his lap and had explained that Mr. Stenger had been under a great deal of strain, some of it about his family and some about his job and some of it about things that nobody but doctors could understand. He had been having crying fits, and three nights ago he had gotten crying and couldn't stop it and had broken a lot of things in the Stenger home. It wasn't LOSING YOUR MAR-BLES, Daddy said, it was HAVING A BREAKDOWN, and Mr. Stenger wasn't in a BUGHOUSE but in a SANNY-TARIUM. But despite Dad-dy's careful explanations, Danny was scared. There didn't seem to be any difference at all between LOSING YOUR MARBLES and HAVING A BREAKDOWN, and whether you called it a BUGHOUSE or a SANNY-TARIUM, there were still bars on the windows and they wouldn't let you out if you wanted to go. And his father, quite innocently, had confirmed another of Scotty's phrases unchanged, one that filled Danny with a vague and unformed dread. In the place where Mr. Stenger now lived, there were THE MEN IN THE WHITE COATS. They came to get you in a truck with no windows, a truck that was gravestone gray. It rolled up to the curb in front of your house and THE MEN IN THE WHITE COATS got out and took you away from your family and made you live in a room with soft walls. And if you wanted to write home, you had to do it with Crayolas.

"When will they let him come back?" Danny asked his father.

"Just as soon as he's better, doc."

"But when will that be?" Danny had persisted.

"Dan," Jack said, "NO ONE KNOWS."

And that was the worst of all. It was another way of saying never-never-never. A month later, Robin's mother took him out of nursery school and they moved away from Stovington with-out Mr. Stenger.

That had been over a year ago, after Daddy stopped taking the Bad Stuff but before he had lost his job. Danny still thought about it often. Sometimes when he fell down or bumped his head or had a bellyache, he would begin to cry and the memory would flash over him, accompanied by the fear that he would not be able to stop crying, that he would just go on and on, weeping and wailing, until his daddy went to the phone, dialed it, and said: "Hello? This is Jack Torrance at 149 Mapleline Way. My son here can't stop crying. Please send THE MEN IN THE WHITE COATS to take him to the SANNY-TARIUM. That's right, he's LOST HIS MARBLES. Thank you." And the gray truck with no windows would come rolling up to *his* door, they would load him in, still weeping hysterically, and take him away. When would he see his mommy and daddy again? NO ONE KNOWS.

It was this fear that had kept him silent. A year older, he was quite sure that his daddy and mommy wouldn't let him be taken away for thinking a fire hose was a snake, his *rational* mind was sure of that, but still, when he thought of telling them, that old memory rose up like a stone filling his mouth and blocking words. It wasn't like Tony; Tony had always seemed perfectly natural (until the bad dreams, of course), and his parents had also seemed to accept Tony as a more or less natural phenomenon. Things like Tony came from being BRIGHT, which they both assumed he was (the same way they assumed they were BRIGHT), but a fire hose that turned into a snake, or seeing blood and brains on the wall of the Presidential Sweet when no one else could, those things would not be natural. They had already taken him to see a regular doctor. Was it not reasonable to assume that THE MEN IN THE WHITE COATS might come next?

Still he might have told them except he was sure, sooner or later, that they would want to take him away from the hotel. And he wanted desperately to get away from the Overlook. But he also knew that this was his daddy's last chance, that he was here at the Overlook to do more than take care of the place. He was here to work on his papers. To get over losing his job. To love Mommy/Wendy. And until very recently, it had seemed that all those things were happening. It was only lately that Daddy had begun to have trouble. Since he found those papers.

(This inhuman place makes human monsters.)

What did that mean? He had prayed to God, but God hadn't told him. And what would Daddy do if he stopped working here? He had tried to find out from Daddy's mind, and had become more and more convinced that Daddy didn't know. The strongest proof had come earlier this evening when

Uncle Al had called his daddy up on the phone and said mean things and Daddy didn't dare say anything back because Uncle Al could fire him from this job just the way that Mr. Crommert, the Stovington headmaster, and the Board of Directors had fired him from his schoolteaching job. And Daddy was scared to death of that, for him and Mommy as well as himself.

So he didn't dare say anything. He could only watch help-lessly and hope that there really weren't any Indians at all, or if there were that they would be content to wait for bigger game and let their little three-wagon train pass unmolested.

But he couldn't believe it, no matter how hard he tried.

Things were worse at the Overlook now.

The snow was coming, and when it did, any poor options he had would be abrogated. And after the snow, what? What then, when they were shut in and at the mercy of whatever might have only been toying with them before?

(Come out here and take your medicine!)

What then? REDRUM.

He shivered in his bed and turned over again. He could read more now. Tomorrow maybe he would try to call Tony, he would try to make Tony show him exactly what REDRUM was and if there was any way he could prevent it. He would risk the nightmares. He had to *know*.

Danny was still awake long after his parents' false sleep had become the real thing. He rolled in his bed, twisting the sheets, grappling with a problem years too big for him, awake in the night like a single sentinel on picket. And sometime after mid-night, he slept too and then only the wind was awake, prying at the hotel and hooting in its gables under the bright gimlet gaze of the stars.

22

IN THE TRUCK

> I see a bad moon a-rising.
> I see trouble on the way.
> I see earthquakes and lightnin'.
> I see bad times today.
> Don't go 'round tonight,
> It's bound to take your life,
> There's a bad moon on the rise.*

Someone had added a very old Buick car radio under the hotel truck's dashboard, and now, tinny and choked with static, the distinctive sound of John Fogerty's Creedence Clearwater Revival band came out of the speaker. Wendy and Danny were on their way down to Sidewinder. The day was clear and bright. Danny was turning Jack's orange library card over and over in his hands and seemed cheerful enough, but Wendy thought he looked drawn and tired, as if he hadn't been sleeping enough and was going on nervous energy alone.

The song ended and the disc jockey came on. "Yeah, that's Creedence. And speakin of bad moon, it looks like it may be risin over the KMTX listening area before long, hard as it is to believe with the beautiful, springlike weather we've enjoyed for the last couple-three days. The KMTX Fearless Forecaster says high pressure will give way by one o'clock this afternoon to a widespread low-pressure area which is just gonna grind to a stop in our KMTX area, up where the air is rare. Temperatures will fall rapidly, and precipitation should start around dusk. Elevations under seven thousand feet, including the metro-Denver area, can expect a mixture of sleet and snow, perhaps

---

---

freezing on some roads, and nothin but snow up here, cuz. We're lookin at one to three inches below seven thousand and possible accumulations of six to ten inches in Central Colorado and on the Slope. The Highway Advisory Board says that if you're plannin to tour the mountains in your car this afternoon or tonight, you should remember that the chain law will be in effect. And don't go nowhere unless you have to. Remember," the announcer added jocularly, "that's how the Donners got into trouble. They just weren't as close to the nearest Seven-Eleven as they thought."

A Clairol commercial came on, and Wendy reached down and snapped the radio off. "You mind?"

"Huh-uh, that's okay." He glanced out at the sky, which was bright blue. "Guess Daddy picked just the right day to trim those hedge animals, didn't he?"

"I guess he did," Wendy said.

"Sure doesn't look much like snow, though," Danny added hopefully.

"Getting cold feet?" Wendy asked. She was still thinking about that crack the disc jockey had made about the Donner Party.

"Nah, I guess not."

Well, she thought, this is the time. If you're going to bring it up, do it now or forever hold your peace.

"Danny," she said, making her voice as casual as possible, "would you be happier if we went away from the Overlook? If we didn't stay the winter?"

Danny looked down at his hands. "I guess so," he said. "Yeah. But it's Daddy's job."

"Sometimes," she said carefully, "I get the idea that Daddy might be happier away from the Overlook, too." They passed a sign which read SIDEWINDER 18 MI. and then she took the truck cautiously around a hairpin and shifted up into second. She took no chances on these downgrades; they scared her silly.

"Do you really think so?" Danny asked. He looked at her with interest for a moment and then shook his head. "No, I don't think so."

"Why not?"

"Because he's worried about us," Danny said, choosing his words carefully. It was hard to explain, he understood so little of it himself. He found himself harking back to an incident he had told Mr. Hallorann about, the big kid looking at department store TV sets and wanting to steal one. That had been distressing, but at least it had been clear what was going on, even to Danny, then little more than an infant. But grownups were always in a turmoil, every possible action muddied over by thoughts of the consequences, by self-doubt, by *selfimage,* by feelings of love and responsibility. Every possible choice seemed to have drawbacks, and sometimes he didn't understand why the drawbacks *were* drawbacks. It was very hard.

"He thinks . . ." Danny began again, and then looked at his mother quickly. She was watching the road, not looking at him, and he felt he could go on.

"He thinks maybe we'll be lonely. And then he thinks that he likes it here and it's a good place for us. He loves us and doesn't want us to be lonely . . . or sad . . . but he thinks even if we are, it might be okay in the LONGRUN. Do you know LONGRUN?"

She nodded. "Yes, dear. I do."

"He's worried that if we left he couldn't get another job. That we'd have to beg, or something."

"Is that all?"

"No, but the rest is all mixed up. Because he's different now."

"Yes," she said, almost sighing. The grade eased a little and she shifted cautiously back to third gear.

"I'm not making this up, Mommy. Honest to God."

"I know that," she said, and smiled. "Did Tony tell you?"

"No," he said. "I just know. That doctor didn't believe in Tony, did he?"

"Never mind that doctor," she said. "I believe in Tony. I don't know what he is or who he is, if he's a part of you that's special or if he comes from . . . somewhere outside, but I do believe in him, Danny. And if you . . . he . . . think we should go, we will. The two of us will go and be together with Daddy again in the spring."

He looked at her with sharp hope. "Where? A motel?"

"Hon, we couldn't afford a motel. It would have to be at my mother's."

The hope in Danny's face died out. "I know—" he said, and stopped.

"What?"

"Nothing," he muttered.

She shifted back to second as the grade steepened again. "No, doc, please don't say that. This talk is something we should have had weeks ago, I think. So please. What is it you know? I won't be mad. I can't be mad, because this is too important. Talk straight to me."

"I know how you feel about her," Danny said, and sighed.

"How do I feel?"

"Bad," Danny said, and then rhyming, singsong, frightening her: "Bad. Sad. Mad. It's like she wasn't your mommy at all. Like she wanted to eat you." He looked at her, frightened. "And I don't like it there. She's always thinking about how she would be better for me than you. And how she could get me away from you. Mommy, I don't want to go there. I'd rather be at the Overlook than there."

Wendy was shaken. Was it that bad between her and her mother? God, what hell for the boy if it was and he could really read their thoughts for each other. She suddenly felt more naked than naked, as if she had been caught in an obscene act.

"All right," she said. "All right, Danny."

"You're mad at me," he said in a small, near-to-tears voice.

"No, I'm not. Really I'm not. I'm just sort of shook up." They were passing a SIDEWINDER 15 MI. sign, and Wendy relaxed a little. From here on in the road was better.

"I want to ask you one more question, Danny. I want you to answer it as truthfully as you can. Will you do that?"

"Yes, Mommy," he said, almost whispering.

"Has your daddy been drinking again?"

"No," he said, and smothered the two words that rose behind his lips after that simple negative: *Not yet.*

Wendy relaxed a little more. She put a hand on Danny's jeans-clad leg and squeezed it. "Your daddy has tried very hard," she said softly. "Because he loves us. And we love him, don't we?"

He nodded gravely.

Speaking almost to herself she went on: "He's not a perfect man, but he has tried . . . Danny, he's tried to hard! When he . . . stopped . . . he went through a kind of hell. He's still going through it. I think if it hadn't been for us, he would have just let go. I want to do what's right. And I don't know. Should we go? Stay? It's like a choice between the fat and the fire."

"I know."

"Would you do something for me, doc?"

"What?"

"Try to make Tony come. Right now. Ask him if we're safe at the Overlook."

"I already tried," Danny said slowly. "This morning."

"What happened?" Wendy asked. "What did he say?"

"He didn't come," Danny said. "Tony didn't come." And he suddenly burst into tears.

"Danny," she said, alarmed. "Honey, don't do that. Please—" The truck swerved across the double yellow line and she pulled it back, scared.

"Don't take me to Gramma's," Danny said through his tears. "Please, Mommy, I don't want to go there, I want to stay with Daddy—"

"All right," she said softly. "All right, that's what we'll do." She took a Kleenex out of the pocket of her Western-style shirt and handed it to him. "We'll stay. And everything will be fine. Just fine."

23

IN THE PLAYGROUND

Jack came out onto the porch, tugging the tab of his zipper up under his chin, blinking into the bright air. In his left hand he was holding a battery-powered hedge-clipper. He tugged a fresh handkerchief out of his back pocket with his right hand, swiped his lips with it, and tucked it away. Snow, they had said on the radio. It was hard to believe, even though he could see the clouds building up on the far horizon.

He started down the path to the topiary, switching the hedge-clipper over to the other hand. It wouldn't be a long job, he thought; a little touch-up would do it. The cold nights had surely stunted their growth. The rabbit's ears looked a little fuzzy, and two of the dog's legs had grown fuzzy green bonespurs, but the lions and the buffalo looked fine. Just a little haircut would do the trick, and then let the snow come.

The concrete path ended as abruptly as a diving board. He stepped off it and walked past the drained pool to the gravel path which wound through the hedge sculptures and into the playground itself. He walked over to the rabbit and pushed the button on the handle of the clippers. It hummed into quiet life.

"Hi, Br'er Rabbit," Jack said. "How are you today? A little off the top and get some of the extra off your ears? Fine. Say, did you hear the one about the traveling salesman and the old lady with a pet poodle?"

His voice sounded unnatural and stupid in his ears, and he stopped. It occurred to him that he didn't care much for these hedge animals. It had always seemed slightly perverted to him to clip and torture a plain old hedge into something that it wasn't. Along one of the highways in Vermont there had been a hedge billboard on a high slope overlooking the road, advertising some kind of ice cream. Making nature peddle ice cream, that was just wrong. It was grotesque.

(You weren't hired to philosophize, Torrance.)

Ah, that was true. So true. He clipped along the rabbit's ears, brushing a small litter of sticks and twigs off onto the grass. The hedge-clipper hummed in that low and rather disgustingly metallic way that all battery-powered appliances seem to have. The sun was brilliant but it held no warmth, and now it wasn't so hard to believe that snow was coming.

Working quickly, knowing that to stop and think when you were at this kind of a task usually meant making a mistake, Jack touched up the rabbit's "face" (up this close it didn't look like a face at all, but he knew that at a distance of twenty paces or so light and shadow would seem to suggest one; that, and the viewer's imagination) and then zipped the clippers along its belly.

That done, he shut the clippers off, walked down toward the playground, and then turned back abruptly to get it all at once, the entire rabbit. Yes, it looked all right. Well, he would do the dog next.

"But if it was my hotel," he said, "I'd cut the whole damn bunch of you down." He would, too. Just cut them down and resod the lawn where they'd been and put in half a dozen small metal tables with gaily colored umbrellas. People could have cocktails on the Overlook's lawn in the summer sun. Sloe gin fizzes and margaritas and pink ladies and all those sweet tourist drinks. A rum and tonic, maybe. Jack took his handkerchief out of his back pocket and slowly rubbed his lips with it.

"Come on, come on," he said softly. That was nothing to be thinking about.

He was going to start back, and then some impulse made him change his mind and he went down to the playground instead. It was funny how you never knew kids, he thought. He and Wendy had expected Danny would love the playground; it had everything a kid could want. But Jack didn't think the boy had been down half a dozen times, if that. He supposed if there had been another kid to play with, it would have been different.

The gate squeaked slightly as he let himself in, and then there was crushed gravel crunching under his feet. He went first to the playhouse, the perfect scale model of the Overlook itself. It came up to his lower thigh, just about Danny's height when he was standing up. Jack hunkered down and looked in the third-floor windows.

"The giant has come to eat you all up in your beds," he said hollowly. "Kiss your Triple A rating goodbye." But that wasn't funny, either. You could open the house simply by pulling it apart—it opened on a hidden hinge. The inside was a disappointment. The walls were painted, but the place was mostly hollow. But of course it would have to be, he told himself, or how else could the kids get inside? What play furniture might go with the place in the summer was gone, probably packed away in the equipment shed. He closed it up and heard the small click as the latch closed.

He walked over to the slide, set the hedge-clipper down, and after a glance back at the driveway to make sure Wendy and Danny hadn't returned, he climbed to the top and sat down. This was the big kids' slide, but the fit was still uncomfortably tight for his grownup ass. How long had it been since he had been on a slide? Twenty years? It didn't seem possible it could be that long, it didn't *feel* that long, but it had to be that, or more. He could remember his old man taking him to the park in Berlin when he had been Danny's age, and he had done the whole bit—slide, swings, teeter-totters, everything. He and the old man would have a hotdog lunch and buy peanuts from the man with the cart afterward. They would sit on a bench to eat them and dusky clouds of pigeons would flock around their feet.

"Goddam scavenger birds," his dad would say, "don't you feed them, Jacky." But they would both end up feeding them, and giggling at the way they ran after the nuts, the greedy way they ran after the nuts. Jack didn't think the old man had ever taken his brothers to the park. Jack had been his favorite, and even so Jack had taken his lumps when the old man was drunk, which was a lot of the time. But Jack had loved him for as long as he was able, long after the rest of the family could only hate and fear him.

He pushed off with his hands and went to the bottom, but the trip was unsatisfying. The slide, unused, had too much friction and no really pleasant speed could be built up. And his ass was just too big. His adult feet thumped into the slight dip where thousands of children's feet had landed before him. He stood up, brushed at the seat of his pants, and looked at the hedge-clipper. But instead of going back to it he went to the swings, which were also a disappointment. The chains had built up rust since the close of the season, and they squealed like things in pain. Jack promised himself he would oil them in the spring.

You better stop it, he advised himself. You're not a kid anymore. You don't need this place to prove it.

But he went on to the cement rings—they were too small for him and he passed them up—and then to the security fence which marked the edge of the grounds. He curled his fingers through the links and looked through, the sun crosshatching shadow-lines on his face like a man behind bars. He recognized the similarity himself and he shook the chain link, put a harried expression on his face, and whispered: "Lemme outta here! Lemme outta here!" But for the third time, not funny. It was time to get back to work.

That was when he heard the sound behind him.

He turned around quickly, frowning, embarrassed, wondering if someone had seen him fooling around down here in kiddie country. His eyes ticked off the slides, the opposing angles of the seesaws, the swings in which only the wind sat.

Beyond all that to the gate and the low fence that divided the playground from the lawn and the topiary—the lions gathered protectively around the path, the rabbit bent over as if to crop grass, the buffalo ready to charge, the crouching dog. Beyond them, the putting green and the hotel itself. From here he could even see the raised lip of the roque court on the Overlook's western side.

Everything was just as it had been. So why had the flesh of his face and hands begun to creep, and why had the hair along the back of his neck begun to stand up, as if the flesh back there had suddenly tightened?

He squinted up at the hotel again, but that was no answer. It simply stood there, its windows dark, a tiny thread of smoke curling from the chimney, coming from the banked fire in the lobby.

(Buster, you better get going or they're going to come back and wonder if you were doing anything all the while.)

Sure, get going. Because the snow was coming and he had to get the damn hedges trimmed. It was part of the agreement. Besides, they wouldn't dare—

(Who wouldn't? What wouldn't? Dare do what?)

He began to walk back toward the hedge-clipper at the foot of the big kids' slide, and the sound of his feet crunching on the crushed stone seemed abnormally loud. Now the flesh on his testicles had begun to creep too, and his buttocks felt hard and heavy, like stone.

(*Jesus, what is this?*)

He stopped by the hedge-clipper, but made no move to pick it up. Yes, there was something different. In the topiary. And it was so simple, so easy to see, that he just wasn't picking it up. Come on, he scolded himself, you just trimmed the fucking rabbit, so what's the

(that's it)

His breath stopped in his throat.

The rabbit was down on all fours, cropping grass. Its belly was against the ground. But not ten minutes ago it had been up on its hind legs, of course it had been, he had trimmed its ears ... and its belly.

His eyes darted to the dog. When he had come down the path it had been sitting up, as if begging for a sweet. Now it was crouched, head tilted, the clipped wedge of mouth seeming to snarl silently. And the lions—

(oh no, baby, oh no, uh-uh, no way)

the lions were closer to the path. The two on his right had subtly changed positions, had drawn closer together. The tail of the one on the left now almost jutted out over the path. When he had come past them and through the gate, that lion had been on the right and he was quite sure its tail had been curled around it.

They were no longer protecting the path; they were blocking it.

Jack put his hand suddenly over his eyes and then took it away. The picture didn't change. A soft sigh, too quiet to be a groan, escaped him. In his drinking days he had always been afraid of something like this happening. But when you were a heavy drinker you called it the DTs—good old Ray Milland in *Lost Weekend*, seeing the bugs coming out of the walls.

What did you call it when you were cold sober?

The question was meant to be rhetorical, but his mind answered it

(you call it insanity)

nevertheless.

Staring at the hedge animals, he realized something *had* changed while he had his hand over his eyes. The dog had moved closer. No longer crouching, it seemed to be in a running posture, haunches flexed, one front leg forward, the other back. The hedge mouth yawned wider, the pruned sticks looked sharp and vicious. And now he fancied he could see faint eye indentations in the greenery as well. Looking at him.

Why do they have to be trimmed? he thought hysterically. *They're perfect.*

Another soft sound. He involuntarily backed up a step when he looked at the lions. One of the two on the right seemed to have drawn slightly ahead of the other. Its head was lowered. One paw had stolen almost all the way to the low fence. Dear God, what next?

(*next it leaps over and gobbles you up like something in an evil nursery fable*)

It was like that game they had played when they were kids, red light. One person was "it," and while he turned his back and counted to ten, the other players crept forward. When "it" got to ten, he whirled around and if he caught anyone moving, they were out of the game. The others remained frozen in statue postures until "it" turned his back and counted again. They got closer and closer, and at last, somewhere between five and ten, you would feel a hand on your back . . .

Gravel rattled on the path.

He jerked his head around to look at the dog and it was halfway down the pathway, just behind the lions now, its mouth wide and yawning. Before, it had only been a hedge clipped in the general shape of a dog, something that lost all definition when you got up close to it. But now Jack could see that it had been clipped to look like a German shepherd, and shepherds could be mean. You could train shepherds to kill.

A low rustling sound.

The lion on the left had advanced all the way to the fence now; its muzzle was touching the boards. It seemed to be grinning at him. Jack backed up another two steps. His head was thudding crazily and he could feel the dry rasp of his breath in his throat. Now the buffalo had moved, circling to the right, behind and around the rabbit. The head was lowered, the green hedge horns pointing at him. The thing was, you couldn't watch all of them. Not all at once.

He began to make a whining sound, unaware in his locked concentration that he was making any sound at all. His eyes darted from one hedge creature to the next, trying to *see* them move. The wind gusted, making a hungry rattling sound in the close-matted branches. What kind of sound would there be if they got him? But of course he knew. A snapping, rending, breaking sound. It would be—

(no no NO NO I WILL NOT BELIEVE THIS   NOT   AT ALL!)

He clapped his hands over his eyes, clutching at his hair, his forehead, his throbbing temples. And he stood like that for a long time, dread building until he could stand it no longer and he pulled his hands away with a cry.

By the putting green the dog was sitting up, as if begging for a scrap. The buffalo was gazing with disinterest back toward the roque court, as it had been when Jack had come down with the clippers. The rabbit stood on its hind legs, ears up to catch the faintest sound, freshly clipped belly exposed. The lions, rooted into place, stood beside the path.

He stood frozen for a long time, the harsh breath in his throat finally slowing. He reached for his cigarettes and shook four of them out onto the gravel. He stooped down and picked them up, groped for them, never taking his eyes from the topiary for fear the animals would begin to move again. He picked them up, stuffed three carelessly back into the pack, and lit the fourth. After two deep drags he dropped it and crushed it out. He went to the hedge-clipper and picked it up.

"I'm very tired," he said, and now it seemed okay to talk out loud. It didn't seem crazy at all. "I've been under a strain. The wasps . . . the play . . . Al calling me like that. But it's all right."

He began to trudge back up to the hotel. Part of his mind tugged fretfully at him, tried to make him detour around the hedge animals, but he went directly up the gravel path, through them. A faint breeze rattled through them, that was all. He had imagined the whole thing. He had had a bad scare but it was over now.

In the Overlook's kitchen he paused to take two Excedrin and then went downstairs and looked at papers until he heard the dim sound of the hotel truck rattling into the driveway. He went up to meet them. He felt all right. He saw no need to mention his hallucination. He'd had a bad scare but it was over now.

24

SNOW

It was dusk.

They stood on the porch in the fading light, Jack in the middle, his left arm around Danny's shoulders and his right arm around Wendy's waist. Together they watched as the decision was taken out of their hands.

The sky had been completely clouded over by two-thirty and it had begun to snow an hour later, and this time you didn't need a weatherman to tell you it was serious snow, no flurry that was going to melt or blow away when the evening wind started to whoop. At first it had fallen in perfectly straight lines, building up a snowcover that coated everything evenly, but now, an hour after it had started, the wind had begun to blow from the northwest and the snow had begun to drift against the porch and the sides of the Overlook's driveway. Beyond the grounds the highway had disappeared under an even blanket of white. The hedge animals were also gone, but when Wendy and Danny had gotten home, she had commended him on the good job he had done. Do you think so? he had asked, and said no more. Now the hedges were buried under amorphous white cloaks.

Curiously, all of them were thinking different thoughts but feeling the same emotion: relief. The bridge had been crossed.

"Will it ever be spring?" Wendy murmured.

Jack squeezed her tighter. "Before you know it. What do you say we go in and have some supper? It's cold out here."

She smiled. All afternoon Jack had seemed distant and . . . well, odd. Now he sounded more like his normal self. "Fine by me. How about you, Danny?"

"Sure."

So they went in together, leaving the wind to build to the low-pitched scream that would go on all night—a sound they would get to know well. Flakes of snow swirled and danced across the porch. The Overlook faced it as it had for nearly three quarters of a century, its darkened windows now bearded with snow, indifferent to the fact that it was now cut off from the world. Or possibly it was pleased with the prospect. Inside its shell the three of them went about their early evening routine, like microbes trapped in the intestine of a monster.

25

INSIDE 217

A week and a half later two feet of snow lay white and crisp and even on the grounds of the Overlook Hotel. The hedge menagerie was buried up to its haunches; the rabbit, frozen on its hind legs, seemed to be rising from a white pool. Some of the drifts were over five feet deep. The wind was constantly changing them, sculpting them into sinuous, dunelike shapes. Twice Jack had snowshoed clumsily around to the equipment shed for his shovel to clear the porch, the third time he shrugged, simply cleared a path through the towering drift lying against the door, and let Danny amuse himself by sledding to the right and left of the path. The truly heroic drifts lay against the Overlook's west side; some of them towered to a height of twenty feet, and beyond them the ground was scoured bare to the grass by the constant windflow. The first-floor windows were covered, and the view from the dining room which Jack had so admired on closing day was now no more exciting than a view of a blank movie screen. Their phone had been out for the last eight days, and the CB radio in Ullman's office was now their only communications link with the outside world.

It snowed every day now, sometimes only brief flurries that powdered the glittering snow crust, sometimes for real, the low whistle of the wind cranking up to a womanish shriek that made the old hotel rock and groan alarmingly even in its deep cradle of snow. Night temperatures had not gotten above 10°, and although the thermometer by the kitchen service entrance sometimes got as high as 25° in the early afternoons, the steady knife edge of the wind made it uncomfortable to go out without a ski mask. But they all did go out on the days when the sun shone, usually wearing two sets of clothing and mittens on over their gloves. Getting out was almost a compulsive thing; the hotel was circled with the double track of Danny's Flexible Flyer. The permutations were nearly endless: Danny riding while his parents pulled; Daddy riding and laughing while Wendy and Danny tried to pull (it was just possible for them to pull him on the icy crust, and flatly impossible when powder covered it); Danny and Mommy riding; Wendy riding by herself while her menfolk pulled and puffed white vapor like drayhorses, pretending she was heavier than she was. They laughed a great deal on these sled excursions around the house, but the whooping and impersonal voice of the wind, so huge and hollowly sincere, made their laughter seem tinny and forced.

They had seen caribou tracks in the snow and once the caribou themselves, a group of five standing motionlessly below the security fence. They had all taken turns with Jack's Zeiss-Ikon binoculars to see them better, and looking at them had given Wendy a weird, unreal feeling: they were standing leg-deep in the snow that covered the highway, and it came to her that between now and the spring thaw, the road belonged more to the caribou than it did to them. Now the things that men had made up here were neutralized. The caribou understood that, she believed. She had put the binoculars down and had said something about starting lunch and in the kitchen she had cried a little, trying to rid herself of the awful pent-up feeling that sometimes fell on her like a large, pressing hand over her heart. She thought of the caribou. She thought of the wasps Jack had put out on the service entrance platform, under the Pyrex bowl, to freeze.

There were plenty of snowshoes hung from nails in the equipment shed, and Jack found a pair to fit each of them, although Danny's pair was quite a bit outsized. Jack did well with them. Although he had not snowshoed since his boyhood in Berlin, New Hampshire, he retaught himself quickly. Wendy didn't care much for it—even fifteen minutes of tramping around on the outsized laced paddles made her legs and ankles ache outrageously—but Danny was intrigued and working hard to pick up the knack. He still fell often, but Jack was pleased with his progress. He said that by February Danny would be skipping circles around both of them.

This day was overcast, and by noon the sky had already begun to spit snow. The radio was promising another eight to twelve inches and chanting hosannas to Precipitation, that great god of Colorado skiers. Wendy, sitting in the bedroom and knitting a scarf, thought to herself that she knew exactly what the skiers could do with all that snow. She knew exactly where they could put it.

Jack was in the cellar. He had gone down to check the furnace and boiler—such checks had become a ritual with him since the snow had closed them in—and after satisfying himself that everything was going well he had wandered through the arch, screwed the lightbulb on, and had seated himself in an old and cobwebby camp chair he had found. He was leafing through the old records and papers, constantly wiping his mouth with his handkerchief as he did so. Confinement had leached his skin of its autumn tan, and as he sat hunched over the yellowed, crackling sheets, his reddish-blond hair tumbling untidily over his forehead, he looked slightly lunatic. He had found some odd things tucked in among the invoices, bills of lading, receipts. Disquieting things. A bloody strip of sheeting. A dismembered teddy bear that seemed to have been slashed to pieces. A crumpled sheet of violet ladies' stationery, a ghost of perfume still clinging to it beneath the musk of age, a note begun and left unfinished in faded blue ink: *"Dearest Tommy, I can't think so well up here as I'd hoped, about us I mean, of course, who else? Ha. Ha. Things keep getting in the way. I've had strange dreams about things going bump in the night, can you believe that and"* That was all. The note was dated June 27, 1934. He found a hand puppet that seemed to be either a witch or a warlock . . . something with long teeth and a pointy hat, at any rate. It had been improbably tucked between a bundle of natural-gas receipts and a bundle of receipts for Vichy water. And something that seemed to be a poem, scribbled on the back of a menu in dark pencil: *"Medoc/are you here?/I've been sleepwalking again, my dear. /The plants are moving under the rug."* No date on the menu, and no name on the poem, if it was a poem. Elusive, but fascinating. It seemed to him that these things were like pieces in a jigsaw, things that would eventually fit together if he could find the right linking pieces. And so he kept looking, jumping and wiping his lips every time the furnace roared into life behind him.

Danny was standing outside Room 217 again.

The passkey was in his pocket. He was staring at the door with a kind of drugged avidity, and his upper body seemed to twitch and jiggle beneath his flannel shirt. He was humming softly and tunelessly.

He hadn't wanted to come here, not after the fire hose. He was scared to come here. He was scared that he had taken the passkey again, disobeying his father.

He *had* wanted to come here. Curiosity
(killed the cat; satisfaction brought him back)
was like a constant fishhook in his brain, a kind of nagging siren song that would not be appeased. And hadn't Mr. Hallorann said, "I don't think there's anything here that can hurt you?"
(You promised.)
(Promises were made to be broken.)
He jumped at that. It was as if that thought had come from outside, insectile, buzzing, softly cajoling.
(Promises were made to be broken my dear redrum, to be broken. splintered. shattered. hammered apart. FORE!)
His nervous humming broke into low, atonal song: "Lou, Lou, skip to m' Lou, skip to m' Lou my daaarlin . . ."

Hadn't Mr. Hallorann been right? Hadn't that been, in the end, the reason why he had kept silent and allowed the snow to close them in?
Just close your eyes and it will be gone.
What he had seen in the Presidential Sweet had gone away. And the snake had only been a fire hose that had fallen onto the rug. Yes, even the blood in the Presidential Sweet had been harmless, something old, something that had happened long before he was born or even thought of, something that was done with. Like a movie that only he could see. There was nothing, really nothing, in this hotel that could hurt him, and if he had to prove that to himself by going into this room, shouldn't he do so?

"Lou, Lou, skip to m' Lou . . ."
(Curiosity killed the cat my dear redrum, redrum my dear, sat- isfaction brought him back safe and sound, from toes to crown; from head to ground he was safe and sound. He knew that those things)
(are like scary pictures, they can't hurt you, but oh my god)
(what big teeth you have grandma and is that a wolf in a BLUE- BEARD suit or a BLUEBEARD in a wolf suit and i'm so)
(glad you asked because curiosity killed that cat and it was the HOPE of satisfaction that brought him)

up the hall, treading softly over the blue and twisting jungle carpet. He had stopped by the fire extinguisher, had put the brass nozzle back in the frame, and then had poked it repeatedly with his finger, heart thumping, whispering: "Come on and hurt me. Come on and hurt me, you cheap prick. Can't do it, can you? Huh? You're nothing but a cheap fire hose. Can't do nothin but lie there. Come on, come on!" He had felt insane with bravado. And nothing had happened. It was only a hose after all, only canvas and brass, you could hack it to pieces and it would never complain, never twist and jerk and bleed green slime all over the blue carpet, because it was only a hose, not a nose and not a rose, not glass buttons or satin bows, not a snake in a sleepy doze . . . and he had hurried on, had hurried on because he was

("late, I'm late," said the white rabbit.)

the white rabbit. Yes. Now there was a white rabbit out by the playground, once it had been green but now it was white, as if something had shocked it repeatedly on the snowy, windy nights and turned it old . . .

Danny took the passkey from his pocket and slid it into the lock.

"Lou, Lou . . ."

(the white rabbit had been on its way to a croquet party to the Red Queen's croquet party storks for mallets hedgehogs for balls)

He touched the key, let his fingers wander over it. His head felt dry and sick. He turned the key and the tumblers thumped back smoothly.

(OFF WITH HIS HEAD! OFF WITH HIS HEAD! OFF WITH HIS HEAD!)

(this game isn't croquet though the mallets are too short this game is)

(WHACK-BOOM! Straight through the wicket.)

(OFF WITH HIS HEEEEEAAAAAAAD—)

Danny pushed the door open. It swung smoothly, without a creak. He was standing just outside a large combination bed-sitting room, and although the snow had not reached up this far—the highest drifts were still a foot below the second-floor windows—the room was dark because Daddy had closed all the shutters on the western exposure two weeks ago.

He stood in the doorway, fumbled to his right, and found the switch plate. Two bulbs in an overhead cut-glass fixture came on. Danny stepped further in and looked around. The rug was deep and soft, a quiet rose color. Soothing. A double bed with a white coverlet. A writing desk

(Pray tell me: Why is a raven like a writing desk?)

by the large shuttered window. During the season the Constant Writer

(having a wonderful time, wish you were fear)

would have a pretty view of the mountains to describe to the folks back home.

He stepped further in. Nothing here, nothing at all. Only an empty room, cold because Daddy was heating the east wing today. A bureau. A closet, its door open to reveal a clutch of hotel hangers, the kind you can't steal. A Gideon Bible on an endtable. To his left was the bathroom door, a full-length mirror on it reflecting his own white-faced image. That door was ajar and—

He watched his double nod slowly.

Yes, that's where it was, whatever it was. In there. In the bathroom. His double walked forward, as if to escape the glass. It put its hand out, pressed it against his own. Then it fell away at an angle as the bathroom door swung open. He looked in.

A long room, old-fashioned, like a Pullman car. Tiny white hexagonal tiles on the floor. At the far end, a toilet with the lid up. At the right, a washbasin and another mirror above it, the kind that hides a medicine cabinet. To the left, a huge white tub on claw feet, the shower curtain pulled closed. Danny stepped into the bathroom and walked toward the tub dreamily, as if propelled from outside himself, as if this whole thing were one of the dreams Tony had brought him, that he would perhaps see something nice when he pulled the shower curtain back, something Daddy had forgotten or Mommy had lost, something that would make them both happy—

So he pulled the shower curtain back.

The woman in the tub had been dead for a long time. She was bloated and purple, her gas-filled belly rising out of the cold, ice-rimmed water like some fleshy island. Her eyes were fixed on Danny's, glassy and huge, like marbles. She was grinning, her purple lips pulled back in a grimace. Her breasts lolled. Her pubic hair floated. Her hands were frozen on the knurled porcelain sides of the tub like crab claws.

Danny shrieked. But the sound never escaped his lips; turning inward and inward, it fell down in his darkness like a stone in a well. He took a single blundering step backward, hearing his heels clack on the white hexagonal tiles, and at the same moment his urine broke, spilling effortlessly out of him.

The woman was sitting up.

Still grinning, her huge marble eyes fixed on him, she was sitting up. Her dead palms made squittering noises on the porcelain. Her breasts swayed like ancient cracked punching bags. There was the minute sound of breaking ice shards. She was not breathing. She was a corpse, and dead long years.

Danny turned and ran. Bolting through the bathroom door, his eyes starting from their sockets, his hair on end like the hair of a hedgehog about to be turned into a sacrificial

(croquet? or roque?)

ball, his mouth open and soundless. He ran full-tilt into the outside door of 217, which was now closed. He began hammering on it, far beyond realizing that it was unlocked, and he had only to turn the knob to let himself out. His mouth pealed forth deafening screams that were beyond human auditory range. He could only hammer on the door and hear the dead woman coming for him, bloated belly, dry hair, outstretched hands— something that had lain slain in that tub for perhaps years, embalmed there in magic.

The door would not open, would not, would not, would not.

And then the voice of Dick Hallorann came to him, so sudden and unexpected, so calm, that his locked vocal cords opened and he began to cry weakly—not with fear but with blessed relief.

(I don't think they can hurt you . . . they're like pictures in a book . . . close your eyes and they'll be gone.)

His eyelids snapped down. His hands curled into balls. His shoulders hunched with the effort of his concentration:

(Nothing there nothing there not there at all NOTHING THERE THERE IS NOTHING!)

Time passed. And he was just beginning to relax, just beginning to realize that the door must be unlocked and he could go, when the years-damp, bloated, fish-smelling hands closed softly around his throat and he was turned implacably around to stare into that dead and purple face.

PART FOUR

SNOWBOUND

26
DREAMLAND

Knitting made her sleepy. Today even Bartók would have made her sleepy, and it wasn't Bartók on the little phonograph, it was Bach. Her hands grew slower and slower, and at the time her son was making the acquaintance of Room 217's long-term resident, Wendy was asleep with her knitting on her lap. The yarn and needles rose in the slow time of her breathing. Her sleep was deep and she did not dream.

Jack Torrance had fallen asleep too, but his sleep was light and uneasy, populated by dreams that seemed too vivid to be mere dreams—they were certainly more vivid than any dreams he had ever had before.

His eyes had begun to get heavy as he leafed through packets of milk bills, a hundred to a packet, seemingly tens of thousands all together. Yet he gave each one a cursory glance, afraid that by not being thorough he might miss exactly the piece of Overlookiana he needed to make the mystic connection that he was sure must be here somewhere. He felt like a man with a power cord in one hand, groping around a dark and unfamiliar room for a socket. If he could find it he would be rewarded with a view of wonders.

He had come to grips with Al Shockley's phone call and his request; his strange experience in the playground had helped him to do that. That had been too damned close to some kind of breakdown, and he was convinced that it was his mind in revolt against Al's high-goddam-handed request that he chuck his book project. It had maybe been a signal that his own sense of self-respect could only be pushed so far before disintegrating entirely. He would write the book. If it meant the end of his association with Al Shockley, that would have to be. He would write the hotel's biography, write it straight from the shoulder, and the introduction would be his hallucination that the topiary animals had moved. The title would be uninspired but workable: *Strange Resort, The Story of the Overlook Hotel.* Straight from the shoulder, yes, but it would not be written vindictively, in any effort to get back at Al or Stuart Ullman or George Hatfield or his father (miserable, bullying drunk that he had been) or anyone else, for that matter. He would write it because the Overlook had enchanted him—could any other explanation be so simple or so true? He would write it for the reason he felt that all great literature, fiction and nonfiction, was written: truth comes out, in the end it always comes out. He would write it because he felt he had to.

Five hundred gals whole milk. One hundred gals skim milk. Pd. Billed to acc't. Three hundred pts orange juice. Pd.

He slipped down further in his chair, still holding a clutch of the receipts, but his eyes no longer looking at what was printed there. They had come unfocused. His lids were slow and heavy. His mind had slipped from the Overlook to his father, who had been a male nurse at the Berlin Community Hospital. Big man. A fat man who had towered to six feet two inches, he had been taller than Jack even when Jack got his full growth of six feet even—not that the old man had still been around then. "Runt of the litter," he would say, and then cuff Jack lovingly and laugh. There had been two other brothers, both taller than their father, and Becky, who at five-ten had only been two inches shorter than Jack and taller than he for most of their childhood.

His relationship with his father had been like the unfurling of some flower of beautiful potential, which, when wholly opened, turned out to be blighted inside. Until he had been seven he had loved the tall, big-bellied man uncritically and strongly in spite of the spankings, the black-and-blues, the occasional black eye.

He could remember velvet summer nights, the house quiet, oldest brother Brett out with his girl, middle brother Mike studying something, Becky and their mother in the living room, watching something on the balky old TV; and he would sit in the hall dressed in a pajama singlet and nothing else, ostensibly playing with his trucks, actually waiting for the moment when the silence would be broken by the door swinging open with a large bang, the bellow of his father's welcome when he saw Jacky was waiting, his own happy squeal in answer as this big man came down the hall, his pink scalp glowing beneath his crewcut in the glow of the hall light. In that light he always looked like some soft and flapping oversized ghost in his hospital whites, the shirt always untucked (and sometimes bloody), the pants cuffs drooping down over the black shoes.

His father would sweep him into his arms and Jacky would be propelled deliriously upward, so fast it seemed he could feel air pressure settling against his skull like a cap made out of lead, up and up, both of them crying "Elevator! Elevator!"; and there had been nights when his father in his drunkenness had not stopped the upward lift of his slabmuscled arms soon enough and Jacky had gone right over his father's flattopped head like a human projectile to crash-land on the hall floor behind his dad. But on other nights his father would only sweep him into a giggling ecstasy, through the zone of air where beer hung around his father's face like a mist of raindrops, to be twisted and turned and shaken like a laughing rag, and finally to be set down on his feet, hiccupping with reaction.

The receipts slipped from his relaxing hand and seesawed down through the air to land lazily on the floor; his eyelids, which had settled shut with his father's image tattooed on their backs like stereopticon images, opened a little bit and then slipped back down again. He twitched a little. Consciousness, like the receipts, like autumn aspen leaves, seesawed lazily downward.

That had been the first phase of his relationship with his father, and as it was drawing to its end he had become aware that Becky and his brothers, all of them older, hated the father and that their mother, a nondescript woman who rarely spoke above a mutter, only suffered him because her Catholic upbringing said that she must. In those days it had not seemed strange to Jack that the father won all his arguments with his children by use of his fists, and it had not seemed strange that his own love should go hand-in-hand with his fear: fear of the elevator game which might end in a splintering crash on any given night; fear that his father's bearish good humor on his day off might suddenly change to boarish bellowing and the smack of his *"good right hand";* and sometimes, he remembered, he had even been afraid that his father's shadow might fall over him while he was at play. It was near the end of this phase that he began to notice that Brett never brought his dates home, or Mike and Becky their chums.

Love began to curdle at nine, when his father put his mother into the hospital with his cane. He had begun to carry the cane a year earlier, when a car accident had left him lame. After that he was never without it, long and black and thick and gold-headed. Now, dozing, Jack's body twitched in a remembered cringe at the sound it made in the air, a murderous swish, and its heavy crack against the wall . . . or against flesh. He had beaten their mother for no good reason at all, suddenly and without warning. They had been at the supper table. The cane had been standing by his chair. It was a Sunday night, the end of a three-day weekend for Daddy, a weekend which he had boozed away in his usual inimitable style. Roast chicken. Peas. Mashed potatoes. Daddy at the head of the table, his plate heaped high, snoozing or nearly snoozing. His mother passing plates. And suddenly Daddy had been wide awake, his eyes set deeply into their fat eyesockets, glittering with a kind of stupid, evil petulance. They flickered from one member of the family to the next, and the vein in the center of his forehead was standing out prominently, always a bad sign. One of his large freckled hands had dropped to the gold knob of his cane, caressing it. He said something about coffee—to this day Jack was sure it had been "coffee" that his father said. Momma had opened her mouth to answer and then the cane was whickering through the air, smashing against her face. Blood spurted from her nose. Becky screamed. Momma's spectacles dropped into her gravy. The cane had been drawn back, had come down again, this time on top of her head, splitting the scalp. Momma had dropped to the floor. He had been out of his chair and around to where she lay dazed on the carpet, brandishing the cane, moving with a fat man's grotesque speed and agility, little eyes flashing, jowls quivering as he spoke to her just as he had always spoken to his children during such outbursts. "Now. Now by Christ. I guess you'll take your medicine now. Goddam puppy. Whelp. Come on and take your medicine." The cane had gone up and down on her seven more times before Brett and Mike got hold of him, dragged him away, wrestled the cane out of his hand. Jack

(little Jacky now he was little Jacky now dozing and mumbling on a cobwebby camp chair while the furnace roared into hollow life behind him)

knew exactly how many blows it had been because each soft *whump* against his mother's body had been engraved on his memory like the irrational swipe of a chisel on stone. Seven *whumps.* No more, no less. He and Becky crying, unbelieving, looking at their mother's spectacles lying in her mashed potatoes, one cracked lens smeared with gravy. Brett shouting at Daddy from the back hall, telling him he'd kill him if he moved. And Daddy saying over and over: "Damn little puppy. Damn little whelp. Give me my cane, you damn little pup. Give it to me." Brett brandishing it hysterically, saying yes, yes, I'll give it to you, just you move a little bit and I'll give you all you want and two extra. I'll give you *plenty.* Momma getting slowly to her feet, dazed, her face already puffed and swelling like an old tire with too much air in it, bleeding in four or five different places, and she had said a terrible thing, perhaps the only thing Momma had ever said which Jacky could recall word for word: "Who's got the newspaper? Your daddy wants the funnies. Is it raining yet?" And then she sank to her knees again, her hair hanging in her puffed and bleeding face. Mike calling the doctor, babbling into the phone. Could he come right away? It was their mother. No, he couldn't say what the trouble was, not over the phone, not over a party line he couldn't. Just *come.* The doctor came and took Momma away to the hospital where Daddy had worked all of his adult life. Daddy, sobered up some (or perhaps only with the stupid cunning of any hard-pressed animal), told the doctor she had fallen downstairs. There was blood on the tablecloth because he had tried to wipe her dear face with it. Had her glasses flown all the way through the living room and into the dining room to land in her mashed potatoes and gravy? the doctor asked with a kind of horrid, grinning sarcasm. Is that what happened, Mark? I have heard of folks who can get a radio station on their gold fillings and I have seen a man get shot between the eyes and live to tell about it, but that is a new one on me. Daddy had merely shook his head and said he didn't know; they must have fallen off her face when he brought her through into the dining room. The four children had been stunned to silence by the calm stupendousness of the lie. Four days later Brett quit his job in the mill and joined the Army. Jack had always felt it was not just the sudden and irrational beating his father had administered at the dinner table but the fact that, in the hospital, their mother had corroborated their father's story while holding the hand of the parish priest. Revolted, Brett had left them to whatever might come. He had been killed in Dong Ho province in 1965, the year when Jack Torrance, undergraduate, had joined the active college agitation to end the war. He had waved his brother's bloody shirt at rallies that were increasingly well attended, but it was not Brett's face that hung before his eyes when he spoke—it was his mother's, dazed, uncomprehending face, his mother saying: "Who's got the newspaper?"

Mike escaped three years later when Jack was twelve—he went to UNH on a hefty Merit Scholarship. A year after that their father died of a sudden, massive stroke which occurred while he was prepping a patient for surgery. He had collapsed in his flapping and untucked hospital whites, dead possibly even before he hit the industrial black-and-red hospital tiles, and three days later the man who had dominated Jacky's life, the irrational white ghost-god, was under ground.

The stone read *Mark Anthony Torrance, Loving Father*. To that Jack would have added one line: *He Knew How to Play Elevator*.

There had been a great lot of insurance money. There are people who collect insurance as compulsively as others collect coins and stamps, and Mark Torrance had been that type. The insurance money came in at the same time the monthly policy payments and liquor bills stopped. For five years they had been rich. Nearly rich . . .

In his shallow, uneasy sleep his face rose before him as if in a glass, his face but not his face, the wide eyes and innocent bowed mouth of a boy sitting in the hall with his trucks, waiting for his daddy, waiting for the white ghost-god, waiting for the elevator to rise up with dizzying, exhilarating speed through the salt-and-sawdust mist of exhaled taverns, waiting perhaps for it to go crashing down, spilling old clocksprings out of his ears while his daddy roared with laughter, and it

(transformed into Danny's face, so much like his own had been, his eyes had been light blue while Danny's were cloudy gray, but the lips still made a bow and the complexion was fair; Danny in his study, wearing training pants, all his papers soggy and the fine misty smell of beer rising . . . a dreadful batter all in ferment, rising on the wings of yeast, the breath of taverns . . . snap of bone . . . his own voice, mewling drunkenly *Danny, you okay doc?* . . . *Oh God oh God your poor sweet arm* . . . and that face transformed into)

(momma's dazed face rising up from below the table, punched and bleeding, and momma was saying)

(*"—from your father. I repeat, an enormously important announcement from your father. Please stay tuned or tune immediately to the Happy Jack frequency. Repeat, tune immediately to the Happy Hour frequency. I repeat—"*)

A slow dissolve. Disembodied voices echoing up to him as if along an endless, cloudy hallway.

(Things keep getting in the way, dear Tommy . . .)

(Medoc, are you here? I've been sleepwalking again, my dear. It's the inhuman monsters that I fear . . .)

("Excuse me, Mr. Ullman, but isn't this the . . .")

. . . office, with its file cabinets, Ullman's big desk, a blank reservations book for next year already in place—never misses a trick, that Ullman—all the keys hanging neatly on their hooks

(except for one, which one, which key, passkey—passkey, passkey, who's got the passkey? if we went upstairs perhaps we'd see)

and the big two-way radio on its shelf.

He snapped it on. CB transmissions coming in short, crackly bursts. He switched the band and dialed across bursts of music, news, a preacher haranguing a softly moaning congregation, a weather report. And another voice which he dialed back to. It was his father's voice.

"—kill him. You have to kill him, Jacky, and her, too. Because a real artist must suffer. Because each man kills the thing he loves. Because they'll always be conspiring against you, trying to hold you back and drag you down. Right this minute that boy of yours is in where he shouldn't be. Trespassing. That's what he's doing. He's a goddam little pup. Cane him for it, Jacky, cane him within an inch of his life. Have a drink, Jacky my boy, and we'll play the elevator game. Then I'll go with you while you give him his medicine. I know you can do it, of course you can. You must kill him. You have to kill him, Jacky, and her, too. Because a real artist must suffer. Because each man—"

His father's voice, going up higher and higher, becoming something maddening, not human at all, something squealing and petulant and maddening, the voice of the Ghost-God, the Pig-God, coming dead at him out of the radio and

"No!" he screamed back. "You're *dead,* you're in your *grave,* you're not in me at all!" Because he had cut all the father out of him and it was not right that he should come back, creeping through this hotel two thousand miles from the New England town where his father had lived and died.

He raised the radio up and brought it down, and it smashed on the floor spilling old clocksprings and tubes like the result of some crazy elevator game gone awry, making his father's voice gone, leaving only his voice, Jack's voice, Jacky's voice, chanting in the cold reality of the office:

"—dead, you're dead, you're dead!"

And the startled sound of Wendy's feet hitting the floor over his head, and Wendy's startled, frightened voice: "Jack? *Jack!"*

He stood, blinking down at the shattered radio. Now there was only the snowmobile in the equipment shed to link them to the outside world.

He put his hands over his eyes and clutched at his temples. He was getting a headache.

27

CATATONIC

Wendy ran down the hall in her stocking feet and ran down the main stairs to the lobby two at a time. She didn't look up at the carpeted flight that led to the second floor, but if she had, she would have seen Danny standing at the top of them, still and silent, his unfocused eyes directed out into indifferent space, his thumb in his mouth, the collar and shoulders of his shirt damp. There were puffy bruises on his neck and just below his chin.

Jack's cries had ceased, but that did nothing to ease her fear. Ripped out of her sleep by his voice, raised in that old hectoring pitch she remembered so well, she still felt that she was dreaming—but another part knew she was awake, and that terrified her more. She half-expected to burst into the office and find him standing over Danny's sprawled-out body, drunk and confused.

She pushed through the door and Jack was standing there, rubbing at his temples with his fingers. His face was ghost-white. The two-way CB radio lay at his feet in a sprinkling of broken glass.

"Wendy?" He asked uncertainly. "Wendy—?"

The bewilderment seemed to grow and for a moment she saw his true face, the one he ordinarily kept so well hidden, and it was a face of desperate unhappiness, the face of an animal caught in a snare beyond its ability to decipher and render harmless. Then the muscles began to work, began to writhe under the skin, the mouth began to tremble infirmly, the Adam's apple began to rise and fall.

Her own bewilderment and surprise were overlaid by shock: he was going to cry. She had seen him cry before, but never since he stopped drinking . . . and never in those days unless he was very drunk and pathetically remorseful. He was a tight man, drum-tight, and his loss of control frightened her all over again.

He came toward her, the tears brimming over his lower lids now, his head shaking involuntarily as if in a fruitless effort to ward off this emotional storm, and his chest drew in a convulsive gasp that was expelled in a huge, racking sob. His feet, clad in Hush Puppies, stumbled over the wreck of the radio and he almost fell into her arms, making her stagger back with his weight. His breath blew into her face and there was no smell of liquor on it. Of course not; there was no liquor up here.

"What's wrong?" She held him as best she could. "Jack, what is it?"

But he could do nothing at first but sob, clinging to her, almost crushing the wind from her, his head turning on her shoulder in that helpless, shaking, warding-off gesture. His sobs were heavy and fierce. He was shuddering all over, his muscles jerking beneath his plaid shirt and jeans.

"Jack? What? Tell me what's wrong!"

At last the sobs began to change themselves into words, most of them incoherent at first, but coming clearer as his tears began to spend themselves.

". . . dream, I guess it was a dream, but it was so real, I . . . it was my mother saying that Daddy was going to be on the radio and I . . . he was . . . he was telling me to . . . I don't know, he was *yelling* at me . . . and so I broke the radio . . . to shut him up. To shut him up. He's dead. I don't even want to dream about him. He's dead. My God, Wendy, my God. I never had a nightmare like that. I never want to have another one. Christ! It was awful."

"You just fell asleep in the office?"

"No . . . not here. Downstairs." He was straightening a little now, his weight coming off her, and the steady back-and-forth motion of his head first slowed and then stopped.

"I was looking through those old papers. Sitting on a chair I set up down there. Milk receipts. Dull stuff. And I guess I just drowsed off. That's when I started to dream. I must have sleepwalked up here." He essayed a shaky little laugh against her neck. "Another first."

"Where is Danny, Jack?"

"I don't know. Isn't he with you?"

"He wasn't . . . downstairs with you?"

He looked over his shoulder and his face tightened at what he saw on her face.

"Never going to let me forget that, are you, Wendy?"

"Jack—"

"When I'm on my deathbed you'll lean over and say, 'It serves you right, remember the time you broke Danny's arm?' "

"Jack!"

"Jack what?" he asked hotly, and jumped to his feet. "Are you denying that's what you're thinking? That I hurt him? That I hurt him once before and I could hurt him again?"

"I want to know where he is, that's all!"

"Go ahead, yell your fucking head off, that'll make everything okay, won't it?"

She turned and walked out the door.

He watched her go, frozen for a moment, a blotter covered with fragments of broken glass in one hand. Then he dropped it into the wastebasket, went after her, and caught her by the lobby desk. He put his hands on her shoulders and turned her around. Her face was carefully set.

"Wendy, I'm sorry. It was the dream. I'm upset. Forgive?"

"Of course," she said, her face not changing expression. Her wooden shoulders slipped out of his hands. She walked to the middle of the lobby and called: *"Hey, doc! Where are you?"*

Silence came back. She walked toward the double lobby doors, opened one of them, and stepped out onto the path Jack had shoveled. It was more like a trench; the packed and drifted snow through which the path was cut came to her shoulders. She called him again, her breath coming out in a white plume. When she came back in she had begun to look scared.

Controlling his irritation with her, he said reasonably: "Are you *sure* he's not sleeping in his room?"

"I told you, he was playing somewhere when I was knitting. I could hear him downstairs."

"Did you fall asleep?"

"What's that got to do with it? Yes. *Danny?*"

"Did you look in his room when you came downstairs just now?"

"I—" She stopped.

He nodded. "I didn't really think so."

He started up the stairs without waiting for her. She followed him, half-running, but he was taking the risers two at a time. She almost crashed into his back when he came to a dead stop on the first-floor landing. He was rooted there, looking up, his eyes wide.

"What—?" she began, and followed his gaze.

Danny still stood there, his eyes blank, sucking his thumb. The marks on his throat were cruelly visible in the light of the hall's electric flambeaux.

"Danny!" she shrieked.

It broke Jack's paralysis and they rushed up the stairs together to where he stood. Wendy fell on her knees beside him and swept the boy into her arms. Danny came pliantly enough, but he did not hug her back. It was like hugging a padded stick, and the sweet taste of horror flooded her mouth. He only sucked his thumb and stared with indifferent blankness out into the stairwell beyond both of them.

"Danny, what happened?" Jack asked. He put out his hand to touch the puffy side of Danny's neck. "Who did this to y—"

"Don't you touch him!" Wendy hissed. She clutched Danny in her arms, lifted him, and had retreated halfway down the stairs before Jack could do more than stand up, confused.

"What? Wendy, what the hell are you t—"

"Don't you touch him! I'll kill you if you lay your hands on him again!"

"Wendy—"

"You bastard!"

She turned and ran down the rest of the stairs to the first floor. Danny's head jounced mildly up and down as she ran. His thumb was lodged securely in his mouth. His eyes were soaped windows. She turned right at the foot of the stairs, and Jack heard her feet retreat to the end of it. Their bedroom door slammed. The bolt was run home. The lock turned. Brief silence. Then the soft, muttered sounds of comforting.

He stood for an unknown length of time, literally paralyzed by all that had happened in such a short space of time. His dream was still with him, painting everything a slightly unreal shade. It was as if he had taken a very mild mescaline hit. Had he maybe hurt Danny as Wendy thought? Tried to strangle his son at his dead father's request? No. He would never hurt Danny.

(He fell down the stairs, Doctor.)

He would never hurt Danny *now.*

(How could I know the bug bomb was defective?)

Never in his life had he been willfully vicious when he was sober.

(Except when you almost killed George Hatfield.)

"No!" he cried into the darkness. He brought both fists crashing down on his legs, again and again and again.

Wendy sat in the overstuffed chair by the window with Danny on her lap, holding him, crooning the old meaningless words, the ones you never remember afterward no matter how a thing turns out. He had folded onto her lap with neither protest nor gladness, like a paper cutout of himself, and his eyes didn't even shift toward the door when Jack cried out "No!" somewhere in the hallway.

The confusion had receded a little bit in her mind, but she now discovered something even worse behind it. Panic.

Jack had done this, she had no doubt of it. His denials meant nothing to her. She thought it was perfectly possible that Jack had tried to throttle Danny in his sleep just as he had smashed the CB radio in his sleep. He was having a breakdown of some kind. But what was she going to do about it? She couldn't stay locked in here forever. They would have to eat.

There was really only one question, and it was asked in a mental voice of utter coldness and pragmatism, the voice of her maternity, a cold and passionless voice once it was directed away from the closed circle of mother and child and out toward Jack. It was a voice that spoke of self-preservation only after son-preservation and its question was:

(Exactly how dangerous is he?)

He had denied doing it. He had been horrified at the bruises, at Danny's soft and implacable disconnection. If he had done it, a separate section of himself had been responsible. The fact that he had done it when he was asleep was—in a terrible, twisted way—encouraging. Wasn't it possible that he could be trusted to get them out of here? To get them down and away. And after that . . .

But she could see no further than she and Danny arriving safe at Dr. Edmonds's office in Sidewinder. She had no particular need to see further. The present crisis was more than enough to keep her occupied.

She crooned to Danny, rocking him on her breasts. Her fingers, on his shoulder, had noticed that his T-shirt was damp, but they had not bothered reporting the information to her brain in more than a cursory way. If it had been reported, she might have remembered that Jack's hands, as he had hugged her in the office and sobbed against her neck, had been dry. It might have given her pause. But her mind was still on other things. The decision had to be made—to approach Jack or not?

Actually it was not much of a decision. There was nothing she could do alone, not even carry Danny down to the office and call for help on the CB radio. He had suffered a great shock. He ought to be taken out quickly before any permanent damage could be done. She refused to let herself believe that permanent damage might already have been done.

And still she agonized over it, looking for another alternative. She did not want to put Danny back within Jack's reach. She was aware now that she had made one bad decision when she had gone against her feelings (and Danny's) and allowed the snow to close them in . . . for Jack's sake. Another bad decision when she had shelved the idea of divorce. Now she was nearly paralyzed by the idea that she might be making another mistake, one she would regret every minute of every day of the rest of her life.

There was not a gun in the place. There were knives hanging from the magnetized runners in the kitchen, but Jack was between her and them.

In her striving to make the right decision, to find the alternative, the bitter irony of her thoughts did not occur: an hour ago she had been asleep, firmly convinced that things were all right and soon would be even better. Now she was considering the possibility of using a butcher knife on her husband if he tried to interfere with her and her son.

At last she stood up with Danny in her arms, her legs trembling. There was no other way. She would have to assume that Jack awake was Jack sane, and that he would help her get Danny down to Sidewinder and Dr. Edmonds. And if Jack tried to do anything *but* help, God help *him*.

She went to the door and unlocked it. Shifting Danny up to her shoulder, she opened it and went out into the hall.

"Jack?" she called nervously, and got no answer.

With growing trepidation she walked down to the stairwell, but Jack was not there. And as she stood there on the landing, wondering what to do next, the singing came up from below, rich, angry, bitterly satiric:

> *"Roll me over*
> *In the clo-ho-ver,*
> *Roll me over, lay me down and do it again."*

She was frightened even more by the sound of him than she had been by his silence, but there was still no alternative. She started down the stairs.

28

''IT WAS HER!''

Jack had stood on the stairs, listening to the crooning, comforting sounds coming muffled through the locked door, and slowly his confusion had given way to anger. Things had never really changed. Not to Wendy. He could be off the juice for twenty years and still when he came home at night and she embraced him at the door, he would see/sense that little flare of her nostrils as she tried to divine scotch or gin fumes riding the outbound train of his exhalation. She was always going to assume the worst; if he and Danny got in a car accident with a drunken blindman who had had a stroke just before the collision, she would silently blame Danny's injuries on him and turn away.

Her face as she had snatched Danny away—it rose up before him and he suddenly wanted to wipe the anger that had been on it out with his fist.

She had no goddam right!

Yes, maybe at first. He had been a lush, he had done terrible things. Breaking Danny's arm had been a terrible thing. But if a man reforms, doesn't he deserve to have his reformation credited sooner or later? And if he doesn't get it, doesn't

883

he deserve the game to go with the name? If a father constantly accuses his virginal daughter of screwing every boy in junior high, must she not at last grow weary (enough) of it to earn her scoldings? And if a wife secretly—and not so secretly—continues to believe that her teetotaling husband is a drunk . . .

He got up, walked slowly down to the first-floor landing, and stood there for a moment. He took his handkerchief from his back pocket, wiped his lips with it, and considered going down and pounding on the bedroom door, demanding to be let in so he could see his son. She had no right to be so goddam highhanded.

Well, sooner or later she'd have to come out, unless she planned a radical sort of diet for the two of them. A rather ugly grin touched his lips at the thought. Let her come to him. She would in time.

He went downstairs to the ground floor, stood aimlessly by the lobby desk for a moment, then turned right. He went into the dining room and stood just inside the door. The empty tables, their white linen cloths neatly cleaned and pressed beneath their clear plastic covers glimmered up at him. All was deserted now but

(Dinner Will Be Served At 8 P.M.
Unmasking and Dancing At Midnight)

Jack walked among the tables, momentarily forgetting his wife and son upstairs, forgetting the dream, the smashed radio, the bruises. He trailed his fingers over the slick plastic dustcovers, trying to imagine how it must have been on that hot August night in 1945, the war won, the future stretching ahead so various and new, like a land of dreams. The bright and parti-colored Japanese lanterns hung the whole length of the circular drive, the golden-yellow light spilling from these high windows that were now drifted over with snow. Men and women in costume, here a glittering princess, there a high-booted cavalier, flashing jewelry and flashing wit everywhere, dancing, liquor flowing freely, first wine and then cocktails and then perhaps boilermakers, the level of conversation going up and up and up until the jolly cry rang out from the bandmaster's podium, the cry of "Unmask! Unmask!"

(And the Red Death held sway . . .)

He found himself standing on the other side of the dining room, just outside the stylized batwing doors of the Colorado Lounge where, on that night in 1945, all the booze would have been free.

(Belly up to the bar, pardner, the drinks're on the house.)

He stepped through the batwings and into the deep, folded shadows of the bar. And a strange thing occurred. He had been in here before, once to check the inventory sheet Ullman had left, and he knew the place had been stripped clean. The shelves were totally bare. But now, lit only murkily by the light which filtered through from the dining room (which was itself only dimly lit because of the snow blocking the windows), he thought he saw ranks and ranks of bottles twinkling mutedly behind the bar, and syphons, and even beer dripping from the spigots of all three highly polished taps. Yes, he could even *smell* beer, that damp and fermented and yeasty odor, no different from the smell that had hung finely misted around his father's face every night when he came home from work.

Eyes widening, he fumbled for the wall switch, and the low, intimate bar-lighting came on, circles of twenty-watt bulbs emplanted on the tops of the three wagon-wheel chandeliers overhead.

The shelves were all empty. They had not even as yet gathered a good coat of dust. The beer taps were dry, as were the chrome drains beneath them. To his left and right, the velvet-upholstered booths stood like men with high backs, each one designed to give a maximum of privacy to the couple inside. Straight ahead, across the red-carpeted floor, forty barstools stood around the horseshoe-shaped bar. Each stool was upholstered in leather and embossed with cattle brands—Circle H, Bar D Bar (that was fitting), Rocking W, Lazy B.

He approached it, giving his head a little shake of bewilderment as he did so. It was like that day on the playground when . . . but there was no sense in thinking about that. Still he could have sworn he had seen those bottles, vaguely, it was true, the way you see the darkened shapes of furniture in a room where the curtains have been drawn. Mild glints on glass. The only thing that remained was that smell of beer, and Jack knew that was a smell that faded into the woodwork of every bar in the world after a certain period of time, not to be eradicated by any cleaner invented. Yet the smell here seemed sharp . . . almost fresh.

He sat down on one of the stools and propped his elbows on the bar's leather-cushioned edge. At his left hand was a bowl for peanuts—now empty, of course. The first bar he'd been in for nineteen months and the damned thing was dry—just his luck. All the same, a bitterly powerful wave of nostalgia swept over him, and the physical craving for a drink seemed to work itself up from his belly to his throat to his mouth and nose, shriveling and wrinkling the tissues as it went, making them cry out for something wet and long and cold.

He glanced at the shelves again in wild, irrational hope but the shelves were just as empty as before. He grinned in pain and frustration. His fists, clenching slowly, made minute scratchings on the bar's leather-padded edge.

"Hi, Lloyd," he said. "A little slow tonight, isn't it?"

Lloyd said it was. Lloyd asked him what it would be.

"Now I'm really glad you asked me that," Jack said, "really glad. Because I happen to have two twenties and two tens in my wallet and I was afraid they'd be sitting right there until sometime next April. There isn't a Seven-Eleven around here, would you believe it? And I thought they had Seven-Elevens on the fucking *moon*."

Lloyd sympathized.

"So here's what," Jack said. "You set me up an even twenty martinis. An even twenty, just like that, kazang. One for every month I've been on the wagon and one to grow on. You can do that, can't you? You aren't too busy?"

Lloyd said he wasn't busy at all.

"Good man. You line those martians up right along the bar and I'm going to take them down, one by one. White man's burden, Lloyd my man."

Lloyd turned to do the job. Jack reached into his pocket for his money clip and came out with an Excedrin bottle instead. His money clip was on the bedroom bureau, and of course his skinny-shanks wife had locked him out of the bedroom. Nice going, Wendy. You bleeding bitch.

"I seem to be momentarily light," Jack said. "How's my credit in this joint, anyhow?"

Lloyd said his credit was fine.

"That's super. I like you, Lloyd. You were always the best of them. Best damned barkeep between Barre and Portland, Maine. Portland, *Oregon,* for that matter."

Lloyd thanked him for saying so.

Jack thumped the cap from his Excedrin bottle, shook two tablets out, and flipped them into his mouth. The familiar acid-compelling taste flooded in.

He had a sudden sensation that people were watching him, curiously and with some contempt. The booths behind him were full—there were graying, distinguished men and beautiful young girls, all of them in costume, watching this sad exercise in the dramatic arts with cold amusement.

Jack whirled on his stool.

The booths were all empty, stretching away from the lounge door to the left and right, the line on his left cornering to flank the bar's horseshoe curve down the short length of the room. Padded leather seats and backs. Gleaming dark Formica tables, an ashtray on each one, a book of matches in each ashtray, the words *Colorado Lounge* stamped on each in gold leaf above the batwing-door logo.

He turned back, swallowing the rest of the dissolving Excedrin with a grimace.

"Lloyd, you're a wonder," he said. "Set up already. Your speed is only exceeded by the soulful beauty of your Neapolitan eyes. *Salud.*"

Jack contemplated the twenty imaginary drinks, the martini glasses blushing droplets of condensation, each with a swizzle poked through a plump green olive. He could almost smell gin on the air.

"The wagon," he said. "Have you ever been acquainted with a gentleman who has hopped up on the wagon?"

Lloyd allowed as how he had met such men from time to time.

"Have you ever renewed acquaintances with such a man after he hopped back off?"

Lloyd could not, in all honesty, recall.

"You never did, then," Jack said. He curled his hand around the first drink, carried his fist to his mouth, which was open, and turned his fist up. He swallowed and then tossed the imaginary glass over his shoulder. The people were back again, fresh from their costume ball, studying him, laughing behind their hands. He could feel them. If the backbar had featured a mirror instead of those damn stupid empty shelves, he could have seen them. Let them stare. Fuck them. Let anybody stare who wanted to stare.

"No, you never did," he told Lloyd. "Few men ever return from the fabled Wagon, but those who do come with a fearful tale to tell. When you jump on, it seems like the brightest, cleanest Wagon you ever saw, with ten-foot wheels to keep the bed of it high out of the gutter where all the drunks are laying around with their brown bags and their Thunderbird and their Granddad Flash's Popskull Bourbon. You're away from all the people who throw you nasty looks and tell you to clean up your act or go put it on in another town. From the gutter, that's the finest-lookin Wagon you ever saw, Lloyd my boy. All hung with bunting and a brass band in front and three majorettes to each side, twirling their batons and flashing their panties at you. Man, you got to get on that Wagon and away from the juicers that are straining canned heat and smelling their own puke to get high again and poking along the gutter for butts with half an inch left below the filter."

He drained two more imaginary drinks and tossed the glasses back over his shoulder. He could almost hear them smashing on the floor. And goddam if he wasn't starting to feel high. It was the Excedrin.

"So you climb up," he told Lloyd, "and ain't you glad to be there. My God yes, that's affirmative. That Wagon is the biggest and best float in the whole parade, and everybody is lining the streets and clapping and cheering and waving, all for you. Except for the winos passed out in the gutter. Those guys used to be your friends, but that's all behind you now."

He carried his empty fist to his mouth and sluiced down another—four down, sixteen to go. Making excellent progress. He swayed a little on the stool. Let em stare, if that was how they got off. Take a picture, folks, it'll last longer.

"Then you start to see things, Lloydy-my-boy. Things you missed from the gutter. Like how the floor of the Wagon is nothing but straight pine boards, so fresh they're still bleeding sap, and if you took your shoes off you'd be sure to get a splinter. Like how the only furniture in the Wagon is these long benches with high backs and no cushions to sit on, and in fact they are nothing but pews with a songbook every five feet or so. Like how all the people sitting in the pews on the Wagon are these flatchested el birdos in long dresses with a little lace around the collar and their hair pulled back into buns until it's so tight you can almost hear it screaming. And every face is flat and pale and shiny, and they're all singing 'Shall we gather at the riiiiver, the beautiful, the beautiful, the *riiiiver,*' and up front there's this reekin bitch with blond hair playing the organ and tellin em to sing louder, sing louder. And somebody slams a songbook into your hands and says, 'Sing it out, brother. If you expect to stay on this Wagon, you got to sing morning, noon, and night. Especially at night.' And that's when you realize what the Wagon really is, Lloyd. It's a church with bars on the windows, a church for women and a prison for you."

He stopped. Lloyd was gone. Worse still, he had never been there. The drinks had never been there. Only the people in the booths, the people from the costume party, and he could almost hear their muffled laughter as they held their hands to their mouths and pointed, their eyes sparkling with cruel pinpoints of light.

He whirled around again. "Leave me—"

(alone?)

All the booths were empty. The sound of laughter had died like a stir of autumn leaves. Jack stared at the empty lounge for a tick of time, his eyes wide and dark. A pulse beat noticeably in the center of his forehead. In the very center of him a cold certainty was forming and the certainty was that he was losing his mind. He felt an urge to pick up the bar stool next to him, reverse it, and go through the place like an avenging whirlwind. Instead he whirled back around to the bar and began to bellow:

> "Roll me over
> In the clo-ho-ver,
> Roll me over, lay me down and do it again."

Danny's face rose before him, not Danny's normal face, lively and alert, the eyes sparkling and open, but the catatonic, zombielike face of a stranger, the eyes dull and opaque, the mouth pursed babyishly around his thumb. What was he doing, sitting here and talking to himself like a sulky teen-ager when his son was upstairs someplace, acting like something that belonged in a padded room, acting the way Wally Hollis said Vic Stenger had been before the men in the white coats had to come and take him away?

(But I never put a hand on him! Goddammit, I didn't!)

"Jack?" The voice was timid, hesitant.

He was so startled he almost fell off the stool whirling it around. Wendy was standing just inside the batwing doors, Danny cradled in her arms like some waxen horror show dummy. The three of them made a tableau that Jack felt very strongly: it was just before the curtain of Act II in some old-time temperance play, one so poorly mounted that the prop man had forgotten to stock the shelves of the Den of Iniquity.

"I never touched him," Jack said thickly. "I never have since the night I broke his arm. Not even to spank him."

"Jack, that doesn't matter now. What matters is—"

"This matters!" he shouted. He brought one fist crashing down on the bar, hard enough to make the empty peanut dishes jump. *"It matters, goddammit, it matters!"*

"Jack, we have to get him off the mountain. He's—"

Danny began to stir in her arms. The slack, empty expression on his face had begun to break up like a thick matte of ice over some buried surface. His lips twisted, as if at some weird taste. His eyes widened. His hands came up as if to cover them and then dropped back.

Abruptly he stiffened in her arms. His back arched into a bow, making Wendy stagger. And he suddenly began to shriek, mad sounds that escaped his straining throat in bolt after crazy, echoing bolt. The sound seemed to fill the empty downstairs and come back at them like banshees. There might have been a hundred Dannys, all screaming at once.

"Jack!" she cried in terror. *"Oh God Jack what's wrong with him?"*

He came off the stool, numb from the waist down, more frightened than he had ever been in his life. What hole had his son poked through and into? What dark nest? And what had been in there to sting him?

"Danny!" he roared. *"Danny!"*

Danny saw him. He broke his mother's grip with a sudden, fierce strength that gave her no chance to hold him. She stumbled back against one of the booths and nearly fell into it.

"Daddy!" he screamed, running to Jack, his eyes huge and affrighted. *"Oh Daddy Daddy, it was her! Her! Her! Oh Daaaaah-deee—"*

He slammed into Jack's arms like a blunt arrow, making Jack rock on his feet. Danny clutched at him furiously, at first seeming to pummel him like a fighter, then clutching his belt and sobbing against his shirt. Jack could feel his son's face, hot and working, against his belly.

Daddy, it was her.

Jack looked slowly up into Wendy's face. His eyes were like small silver coins.

"Wendy?" Voice soft, nearly purring. "Wendy, what did you do to him?"

Wendy stared back at him in stunned disbelief, her face pallid. She shook her head.

"Oh Jack, you must know—"

Outside it had begun to snow again.

29

KITCHEN TALK

Jack carried Danny into the kitchen. The boy was still sobbing wildly, refusing to look up from Jack's chest. In the kitchen he gave Danny back to Wendy, who still seemed stunned and disbelieving.

"Jack, I don't know what he's talking about. Please, you must believe that."

"I do believe it," he said, although he had to admit to himself that it gave him a certain amount of pleasure to see the shoe switched to the other foot with such dazzling, unexpected speed. But his anger at Wendy had been only a passing gut twitch. In his heart he knew Wendy would pour a can of gasoline over herself and strike a match before harming Danny.

The large tea kettle was on the back burner, poking along on low heat. Jack dropped a teabag into his own large ceramic cup and poured hot water halfway.

"Got cooking sherry, don't you?" he asked Wendy.

"What? . . . oh, sure. Two or three bottles of it."

"Which cupboard?"

She pointed, and Jack took one of the bottles down. He poured a hefty dollop into the teacup, put the sherry back, and filled the last quarter of the cup with milk. Then he added three tablespoons of sugar and stirred. He brought it to Danny, whose sobs had tapered off to snifflings and hitchings. But he was trembling all over, and his eyes were wide and starey.

"Want you to drink this, doc," Jack said. "It's going to taste frigging awful, but it'll make you feel better. Can you drink it for your daddy?"

Danny nodded that he could and took the cup. He drank a little, grimaced, and looked questioningly at Jack. Jack nodded, and Danny drank again. Wendy felt the familiar twist of jealousy somewhere in her middle, knowing the boy would not have drunk it for her.

On the heels of that came an uncomfortable, even startling thought: Had she *wanted* to think Jack was to blame? Was she that jealous? It was the way her mother would have thought, that was the really horrible thing. She could remember a Sunday when her Dad had taken her to the park and she had toppled from the second tier of the jungle gym, cutting both knees. When her father brought her home, her mother had shrieked at him: *What did you do? Why weren't you watching her? What kind of a father are you?*

(She hounded him to his grave; by the time he divorced her it was too late.)

She had never even given Jack the benefit of the doubt. Not the smallest. Wendy felt her face burn yet knew with a kind of helpless finality that if the whole thing were to be played over again, she would do and think the same way. She carried part of her mother with her always, for good or bad.

"Jack—" she began, not sure if she meant to apologize or justify. Either, she knew, would be useless.

"Not now," he said.

It took Danny fifteen minutes to drink half of the big cup's contents, and by that time he had calmed visibly. The shakes were almost gone.

Jack put his hands solemnly on his son's shoulders. "Danny, do you think you can tell us exactly what happened to you? It's very important."

Danny looked from Jack to Wendy, then back again. In the silent pause, their setting and situation made themselves known: the whoop of the wind outside, driving fresh snow down from the northwest; the creaking and groaning of the old hotel as it settled into another storm. The fact of their disconnect came to Wendy with unexpected force as it sometimes did, like a blow under the heart.

"I want . . . to tell you everything," Danny said. "I wish I had before." He picked up the cup and held it, as if comforted by the warmth.

"Why didn't you, son?" Jack brushed Danny's sweaty, tumbled hair back gently from his brow.

"Because Uncle Al got you the job. And I couldn't figure out how it was good for you here and bad for you here at the same time. It was . . ." He looked at them for help. He did not have the necessary word.

"A dilemma?" Wendy asked gently. "When neither choice seems any good?"

"Yes, that." He nodded, relieved.

Wendy said: "The day that you trimmed the hedges, Danny and I had a talk in the truck. The day the first real snow came. Remember?"

Jack nodded. The day he had trimmed the hedges was very clear in his mind.

Wendy sighed. "I guess we didn't talk enough. Did we, doc?"

Danny, the picture of woe, shook his head.

"Exactly what did you talk about?" Jack asked. "I'm not sure how much I like my wife and son—"

"—discussing how much they love you?"

"Whatever it was, I don't understand it. I feel like I came into a movie just after the intermission."

"We were discussing you," Wendy said quietly. "And maybe we didn't say it all in words, but we both knew. Me because I'm your wife and Danny because he . . . just understands things."

Jack was silent.

"Danny said it just right. The place seemed good for you. You were away from all the pressures that made you so unhappy at Stovington. You were your own boss, working with your hands so you could save your brain—all of your brain—for your evenings writing. Then . . . I don't know just when . . . the place began to seem bad for you. Spending all that time down in the cellar, sifting through those old papers, all that old history. Talking in your sleep—"

"In my sleep?" Jack asked. His face wore a cautious, startled expression. "I talk in my sleep?"

"Most of it is slurry. Once I got up to use the bathroom and· you were saying, 'To hell with it, bring in the slots at least, no one will know, no one will ever know.' Another time you woke me right up, practically yelling, 'Unmask, unmask, unmask.' "

"Jesus Christ," he said, and rubbed a hand over his face. He looked ill.

"All your old drinking habits, too. Chewing Excedrin. Wiping your mouth all the time. Cranky in the morning. And you haven't been able to finish the play yet, have you?"

"No. Not yet, but it's only a matter of time. I've been thinking about something else . . . a new project—"

"This hotel. The project Al Shockley called you about. The one he wanted you to drop."

"How do you know about that?" Jack barked. "Were you listening in? You—"

"No," she said. "I couldn't have listened in if I'd wanted to, and you'd know that if you were thinking straight. Danny and I were downstairs that night. The switchboard is shut down. Our phone upstairs was the only one in the hotel that was working, because it's patched directly into the outside line. You told me so yourself."

"Then how could you know what Al told me?"

"Danny told me. Danny knew. The same way he sometimes knows when things are misplaced, or when people are thinking about divorce."

"The doctor said—"

She shook her head impatiently. "The doctor was full of shit and we both know it. We've known it all the time. Remember when Danny said he wanted to see the firetrucks? That was no hunch. *He was just a baby.* He *knows* things. And now I'm afraid . . ." She looked at the bruises on Danny's neck.

"Did you really know Uncle Al had called me, Danny?"

Danny nodded. "He was really mad, Daddy. Because you called Mr. Ullman and Mr. Ullman called him. Uncle Al didn't want you to write anything about the hotel."

"Jesus," Jack said again. "The bruises, Danny. Who tried to strangle you?"

Danny's face went dark. *"Her,"* he said. "The woman in that room. In 217. The dead lady." His lips began to tremble again, and he seized the teacup and drank.

Jack and Wendy exchanged a scared look over his bowed head.

"Do you know anything about this?" he asked her.

She shook her head. "Not about this, no."

"Danny?" He raised the boy's frightened face. "Try, son. We're right here."

"I knew it was bad here," Danny said in a low voice. "Ever since we were in Boulder. Because Tony gave me dreams about it."

"What dreams?"

"I can't remember everything. He showed me the Overlook at night, with a skull and crossbones on the front. And there was pounding. Something . . . I don't remember what . . . chasing after me. A monster. Tony showed me about redrum."

"What's that, doc?" Wendy asked.

He shook his head. "I don't know."

"Rum, like yo-ho-ho and a bottle of rum?" Jack asked.

Danny shook his head again. "I don't know. Then we got here, and Mr. Hallorann talked to me in his car. Because he has the shine, too."

"Shine?"

"It's . . ." Danny made a sweeping, all-encompassing gesture with his hands. "It's being able to understand things. To know things. Sometimes you see things. Like me knowing Uncle Al called. And Mr. Hallorann knowing you call me doc. Mr. Hallorann, he was peeling potatoes in the Army when he knew his brother got killed in a train crash. And when he called home it was true."

"Holy God," Jack whispered. "You're not making this up, are you, Dan?"

Danny shook his head violently. "No, I swear to God." Then, with a touch of pride he added: "Mr. Hallorann said I had the best shine of anyone he ever met. We could talk back and forth to each other without hardly opening our mouths."

His parents looked at each other again, frankly stunned.

"Mr. Hallorann got me alone because he was worried," Danny went on. "He said this was a bad place for people who shine. He said he'd seen things. I saw something, too. Right after I talked to him. When Mr. Ullman was taking us around."

"What was it?" Jack asked.

"In the Presidential Sweet. On the wall by the door going into the bedroom. A whole lot of blood and some other stuff. Gushy stuff. I think . . . that the gushy stuff must have been brains."

"Oh my God," Jack said.

Wendy was now very pale, her lips nearly gray.

"This place," Jack said. "Some pretty bad types owned it awhile back. Organization people from Las Vegas."

"Crooks?" Danny asked.

"Yeah, crooks." He looked at Wendy. "In 1966 a big-time hood named Vito Gienelli got killed up there, along with his two bodyguards. There was a picture in the newspaper. Danny just described the picture."

"Mr. Hallorann said he saw some other stuff," Danny told them. "Once about the playground. And once it was something bad in that room. 217. A maid saw it and lost her job because she talked about it. So Mr. Hallorann went up and he saw it too. But he didn't talk about it because he didn't want to lose his job. Except he told me never to go in there. But I did. Because I believed him when he said the things you saw here couldn't hurt you." This last was nearly whispered in a low, husky voice, and Danny touched the puffed circle of bruises on his neck.

"What about the playground?" Jack asked in a strange, casual voice.

"I don't know. The playground, he said. And the hedge animals."

Jack jumped a little, and Wendy looked at him curiously.

"Have you seen anything down there, Jack?"

"No," he said. "Nothing."

Danny was looking at him.

"Nothing," he said again, more calmly. And that was true. He had been the victim of an hallucination. And that was *all*.

"Danny, we have to hear about the woman," Wendy said gently.

So Danny told them, but his words came in cyclic bursts, sometimes almost verging on incomprehensible garble in his hurry to spit it out and be free of it. He pushed tighter and tighter against his mother's breasts as he talked.

"I went in," he said. "I stole the passkey and went in. It was like I couldn't help myself. I had to know. And she . . . the lady . . . was in the tub. She was dead. All swelled up. She was nuh-nuh . . . didn't have no clothes on." He looked miserably at his mother. "And she started to get up and she wanted me. I know she did because I could feel it. She wasn't even thinking, not the way you and Daddy think. It was black . . . it was hurt-think . . . like . . . like the wasps that night in my room! Only wanting to hurt. Like the wasps."

He swallowed and there was silence for a moment, all quiet while the image of the wasps sank into them.

"So I ran," Danny said. "I ran but the door was closed. I left it open but it was closed. I didn't think about just opening it again and running out. I was scared. So I just . . . I leaned against the door and closed my eyes and thought of how Mr. Hallorann said the things here were just like pictures in a book and if I . . . kept saying to myself . . . *you're not there, go away, you're not there* . . . she would go away. But it didn't work."

His voice began to rise hysterically.

"She grabbed me . . . turned me around . . . I could see her eyes . . . how her eyes were . . . and she started to choke me . . . I could smell her . . . *I could smell how dead she was . . .*"

"Stop now, shhh," Wendy said, alarmed. "Stop, Danny. It's all right. It—"

She was getting ready to go into her croon again. The Wendy Torrance All-purpose Croon. Pat. Pending.

"Let him finish," Jack said curtly.

"There isn't any more," Danny said. "I passed out. Either because she was choking me or just because I was scared. When I came to, I was dreaming you and Mommy were fighting over me and you wanted to do the Bad Thing again, Daddy. Then I knew it wasn't a dream at all . . . and I was awake . . . and . . . I wet my pants. I wet my pants like a baby." His head fell back against Wendy's sweater and he began to cry with horrible weakness, his hands lying limp and spent in his lap.

Jack got up. "Take care of him."

"What are you going to do?" Her face was full of dread.

"I'm going up to that room, what did you think I was going to do? Have coffee?"

"No! Don't, Jack, please *don't!*"

"Wendy, if there's someone else in the hotel, we have to know."

"Don't you dare leave us alone!" she shrieked at him. Spittle flew from her lips with the force of her cry.

Jack said: "Wendy, that's a remarkable imitation of your mom."

She burst into tears then, unable to cover her face because Danny was on her lap.

"I'm sorry," Jack said. "But I have to, you know. I'm the goddam caretaker. It's what I'm paid for."

She only cried harder and he left her that way, going out of the kitchen, rubbing his mouth with his handkerchief as the door swung shut behind him.

"Don't worry, mommy," Danny said. "He'll be all right. He doesn't shine. Nothing here can hurt him."

Through her tears she said, "No, I don't believe that."

30

217 REVISITED

He took the elevator up and it was strange, because none of them had used the elevator since they moved in. He threw the brass handle over and it wheezed vibratoriously up the shaft, the brass grate rattling madly. Wendy had a true claustrophobe's horror of the elevator, he knew. She envisioned the three of them trapped in it between floors while the winter storms raged outside, she could see them growing thinner and weaker, starving to death. Or perhaps dining on each other, the way those Rugby players had. He remembered a bumper sticker he had seen in Boulder, RUGBY PLAYERS EAT THEIR OWN DEAD. He could think of others. YOU ARE WHAT YOU EAT. Or menu items. Welcome to the Overlook Dining Room, Pride of the Rockies. Eat in Splendor at the Roof of the World. Human Haunch Broiled Over Matches *La Spécialité de la Maison*. The contemptuous smile flicked over his features again. As the number 2 rose on the shaft wall, he threw the brass handle back to the home position and the elevator car creaked to a stop. He took his Excedrin from his pocket, shook three of them into his hand, and opened the elevator door. Nothing in the Overlook frightened him. He felt that he and it were *simpático*.

He walked up the hall flipping his Excedrin into his mouth and chewing them one by one. He rounded the corner into the short corridor off the main hall. The door to Room 217 was ajar, and the passkey hung from the lock on its white paddle.

He frowned, feeling a wave of irritation and even real anger. Whatever had come of it, the boy had been trespassing. He had been told, and told bluntly, that certain areas of the hotel were off limits: the equipment shed, the basement, and all of the guest rooms. He would talk to Danny about that just as soon as the boy was over his fright. He would talk to him reasonably but sternly. There were plenty of fathers who would have done more than just talk. They would have administered a good shaking, and perhaps that was what Danny needed. If the boy had gotten a scare, wasn't that at least his just deserts?

He walked down to the door, removed the passkey, dropped it into his pocket, and stepped inside. The overhead light was on. He glanced at the bed, saw it was not rumpled, and then walked directly across to the bathroom door. A curious certainty had grown in him. Although Watson had mentioned no names or room numbers, Jack felt sure that this was the room the lawyer's wife and her stud had shared, that this was the bathroom where she had been found dead, full of barbiturates and Colorado Lounge booze.

He pushed the mirror-backed bathroom door open and stepped through. The light in here was off. He turned it on and observed the long, Pullman-car room, furnished in the distinctive early nineteen-hundreds-remodeled-in-the-twenties style that seemed common to all Overlook bathrooms, except for the ones on the third floor—those were properly Byzantine, as befitted the royalty, politicians, movie stars, and capos who had stayed there over the years.

The shower curtain, a pallid pastel pink, was drawn protectively around the long claw-footed tub.

(nevertheless they *did* move)

And for the first time he felt his new sense of sureness (almost cockiness) that had come over him when Danny ran to him shouting *It was her! It was her!* deserting him. A chilled finger pressed gently against the base of his spine, cooling him off ten degrees. It was joined by others and they suddenly rippled all the way up his back to his medulla oblongata, playing his spine like a jungle instrument.

His anger at Danny evaporated, and as he stepped forward and pushed the shower curtain back his mouth was dry and he felt only sympathy for his son and terror for himself.

The tub was dry and empty.

Relief and irritation vented in a sudden *"Pah!"* sound that escaped his compressed lips like a very small explosive. The tub had been scrubbed clean at the end of the season; except for the rust stain under the twin faucets, it sparkled. There was a faint but definable smell of cleanser, the kind that can irritate your nose with the smell of its own righteousness for weeks, even months, after it has been used.

He bent down and ran his fingertips along the bottom of the tub. Dry as a bone. Not even a hint of moisture. The boy had been either hallucinating or outright lying. He felt angry again. That was when the bathmat on the floor caught his attention. He frowned down at it. What was a bathmat doing in here? It should be down in the linen cupboard at the end of the wing with the rest of the sheets and towels and pillow slips. All the linen was supposed to be there. Not even the beds were really made up in these guest rooms; the mattresses had been zipped into clear plastic and then covered with bedspreads. He supposed Danny might have gone down and gotten it—the passkey would open the linen cupboard—but why? He brushed the tips of his fingers back and forth across it. The bathmat was bone dry.

He went back to the bathroom door and stood in it. Everything was all right. The boy had been dreaming. There was not a thing out of place. It was a little puzzling about the bathmat, granted, but the logical explanation was that some chambermaid, hurrying like mad on the last day of the season, had just forgotten to pick it up. Other than that, everything was—

His nostrils flared a little. Disinfectant, that self-righteous smell, cleaner-than-thou. And—

Soap?

Surely not. But once the smell had been identified, it was too clear to dismiss. Soap. And not one of those postcard-size bars of Ivory they provide you with in hotels and motels, either. This scent was light and perfumed, a lady's soap. It had a pink sort of smell. Camay or Lowila, the brand that Wendy had always used in Stovington.

(It's nothing. It's your imagination.)
(yes like the hedges nevertheless they did move)
(They did not move!)

He crossed jerkily to the door which gave on the hall, feeling the irregular thump of a headache beginning at his temples. Too much had happened today, too much by far. He wouldn't spank the boy or shake him, just talk to him, but by God, he wasn't going to add Room 217 to his problems. Not on the basis of a dry bathmat and a faint smell of Lowila soap. He—

There was a sudden rattling, metallic sound behind him. It came just as his hand closed around the doorknob, and an observer might have thought the brushed steel of the knob carried an electric charge. He jerked convulsively, eyes widening, other facial features drawing in, grimacing.

Then he had control of himself, a little, anyway, and he let go of the doorknob and turned carefully around. His joints creaked. He began to walk back to the bathroom door, step by leaden step.

The shower curtain, which he had pushed back to look into the tub, was now drawn. The metallic rattle, which had sounded to him like a stir of bones in a crypt, had been the curtain rings on the overhead bar. Jack stared at the curtain. His face felt as if it had been heavily waxed, all dead skin on the outside, live, hot rivulets of fear on the inside. The way he had felt on the playground.

There was something behind the pink plastic shower curtain. There was something in the tub.

He could see it, ill defined and obscure through the plastic, a nearly amorphous shape. It could have been anything. A trick of the light. The shadow of the shower attachment. A woman long dead and reclining in her bath, a bar of Lowila in one stiffening hand as she waited patiently for whatever lover might come.

Jack told himself to step forward boldly and rake the shower curtain back. To expose whatever might be there. Instead he turned with jerky, marionette strides, his heart whamming frightfully in his chest, and went back into the bed/sitting room.

The door to the hall was shut.

He stared at it for a long, immobile second. He could taste his terror now. It was in the back of his throat like a taste of gone-over cherries.

He walked to the door with that same jerky stride and forced his fingers to curl around the knob.

(*It won't open.*)

But it did.

He turned off the light with a fumbling gesture, stepped out into the hall, and pulled the door shut without looking back. From inside, he seemed to hear an odd wet thumping sound, far off, dim, as if something had just scrambled belatedly out of the tub, as if to greet a caller, as if it had realized the caller was leaving before the social amenities had been completed and so it was now rushing to the door, all purple and grinning, to invite the caller back inside. Perhaps forever.

Footsteps approaching the door or only the heartbeat in his ears?

He fumbled at the passkey. It seemed sludgy, unwilling to turn in the lock. He attacked the passkey. The tumblers suddenly fell and he stepped back against the corridor's far wall, a little groan of relief escaping him. He closed his eyes and all the old phrases began to parade through his mind, it seemed there must be hundreds of them,

(cracking up not playing with a full deck lostya marbles guy just went loony tunes he went up and over the high side went bananas lost his football crackers nuts half a seabag)

all meaning the same thing: *losing your mind.*

"No," he whimpered, hardly aware that he had been reduced to this, whimpering with his eyes shut like a child. "Oh no, God. Please, God, no."

But below the tumble of his chaotic thoughts, below the triphammer beat of his heart, he could hear the soft and futile sound of the doorknob being turned to and fro as something locked in tried helplessly to get out, something that wanted to meet him, something that would like to be introduced to his family as the storm shrieked around them and white daylight became black night. If he opened his eyes and saw that doorknob moving he would go mad. So he kept them shut, and after an unknowable time, there was stillness.

Jack forced himself to open his eyes, half-convinced that when he did, she would be standing before him. But the hall was empty.

He felt watched just the same.

He looked at the peephole in the center of the door and wondered what would happen if he approached it, stared into it. What would he be eyeball to eyeball with?

His feet were moving
(feets don't fail me now)
before he realized it. He turned them away from the door and walked down to the main hall, his feet whispering on the blue-black jungle carpet. He stopped halfway to the stairs and looked at the fire extinguisher. He thought that the folds of canvas were arranged in a slightly different manner. And he was quite sure that the brass nozzle had been pointing toward the elevator when he came up the hall. Now it was pointing the other way.

"I didn't see that at all," Jack Torrance said quite clearly. His face was white and haggard and his mouth kept trying to grin.

But he didn't take the elevator back down. It was too much like an open mouth. Too much by half. He took the stairs.

31

THE VERDICT

He stepped into the kitchen and looked at them, bouncing the passkey a few inches up off his left hand, making the chain on the white metal tongue jingle, then catching it again. Danny was pallid and worn out. Wendy had been crying, he saw; her eyes were red and darkly circled. He felt a sudden burst of gladness at this. He wasn't suffering alone, that was sure.

They looked at him without speaking.

"Nothing there," he said, astounded by the heartiness of his voice. "Not a thing."

He bounced the passkey up and down, up and down, smiling reassuringly at them, watching the relief spread over their faces, and thought he had never in his life wanted a drink so badly as he did right now.

32

THE BEDROOM

Late that afternoon Jack got a cot from the first-floor storage room and put it in the corner of their bedroom. Wendy had expected that the boy would be half the night getting to sleep, but Danny was nodding before "The Waltons" was half over, and fifteen minutes after they had tucked him in he was far down in sleep, moveless, one hand tucked under his cheek. Wendy sat watching him, holding her place in a fat paperback copy of *Cashelmara* with one finger. Jack sat at his desk, looking at his play.

"Oh shit," Jack said.

Wendy looked up from her contemplation of Danny. "What?"

"Nothing."

He looked down at the play with smoldering ill-temper. How could he have thought it was good? It was puerile. It had been done a thousand times. Worse, he had no idea how to finish it. Once it had seemed simple enough. Denker, in a fit of rage, seizes the poker from beside the fireplace and beats saintly Gary to death. Then, standing spread-legged over the body, the bloody poker in one hand, he screams at the audience: "It's here somewhere and I *will* find it!" Then, as the lights dim and the curtain is slowly drawn, the audience sees Gary's body face down on the forestage as Denker strides to the upstage bookcase and feverishly begins pulling books from the shelves, looking at them, throwing them aside. He had thought it was something old enough to be new, a play whose novelty alone might be enough to see it through a successful Broadway run: a tragedy in five acts.

But, in addition to his sudden diversion of interest to the Overlook's history, something else had happened. He had developed opposing feelings about his characters. This was something quite new. Ordinarily he liked all of his characters, the good and the bad. He was glad he did. It allowed him to try to see all of their sides and understand their motivations more clearly. His favorite story, sold to a small southern Maine magazine called *Contraband* for copies, had been a piece called "The Monkey Is Here, Paul DeLong." It had been about a child molester about to commit suicide in his furnished room. The child molester's name had been Paul DeLong, Monkey to his friends. Jack had liked Monkey very much. He sympathized with Monkey's bizarre needs, knowing that Monkey was not the only one to blame for the three rape-murders in his past. There had been bad parents, the father a beater as his own father had been, the mother a limp and silent dishrag as his mother had been. A homosexual experience in grammar school. Public humiliation. Worse experiences in high school and college. He had been arrested and sent to an institution after exposing himself to a pair of little girls getting off a school bus. Worst of all, he had been dismissed from the institution, let back out onto the streets, because the man in charge had decided he was all right. This man's name had been Grimmer. Grimmer had known that Monkey DeLong was exhibiting deviant symptoms, but he had written the good, hopeful report and had let him go anyway. Jack liked and sympathized with Grimmer, too. Grimmer had to run an understaffed and underfunded institution and try to keep the whole thing together with spit, baling wire, and nickel-and-dime appropriations from a state legislature who had to go back and face the voters. Grimmer knew that Monkey could interact with other people, that he did not soil his pants or try to stab his fellow inmates with the scissors. He did not think he was Napoleon. The staff psychiatrist in charge of Monkey's case thought there was a better-than-even chance that Monkey could make it on the street, and they both knew that the longer a man is in an institution the more he comes to need that closed environment, like a junkie with his smack. And meanwhile, people were knocking down the doors. Paranoids, schizoids, cycloids, semicatatonics, men who claimed to have gone to heaven in flying saucers, women who had burned their children's sex organs off with Bic lighters, alcoholics, pyromaniacs, kleptomaniacs, manic-depressives, suicidals. Tough old world, baby. If you're not bolted together tightly, you're gonna shake, rattle, and roll before you turn thirty. Jack could sympathize with Grimmer's problem. He could sympathize with the parents of the murder victims. With the murdered children themselves, of course. And with Monkey DeLong. Let the reader lay blame. In those days he hadn't wanted to judge. The cloak of the moralist sat badly on his shoulders.

He had started *The Little School* in the same optimistic vein. But lately he had begun to choose up sides, and worse still, he had come to loathe his hero, Gary Benson. Originally conceived as a bright boy more cursed with money than blessed with it, a boy who wanted more than anything to compile a good record so he could go to a good university because he had earned admission and not because his father had pulled strings, he had become to Jack a kind of simpering Goody Two-shoes, a postulant before the altar of knowledge rather than a sincere acolyte, an outward paragon of Boy Scout virtues, inwardly cynical, filled not with real brilliance (as he had first been conceived) but only with sly animal cunning. All through the play he unfailingly addressed Denker as "sir," just as Jack had taught his own son to address those older and those in authority as "sir." He thought that Danny used the word quite sincerely, and Gary Benson as originally conceived had too, but as he had begun Act V, it had come more and more strongly to him that Gary was using the word satirically, outwardly straight-faced while the Gary Benson inside was mugging and leering at Denker. Denker, who had never had any of the things Gary had. Denker, who had had to work all his life just to become head of a single little school. Who was now faced with ruin over this handsome, innocent-seeming rich boy who had cheated on his Final Composition and had then cunningly covered his tracks. Jack had seen Denker the teacher as not much different from the strutting South American little Caesars in their banana kingdoms, standing dissidents up against the wall of the handiest squash or handball court, a super-zealot in a comparatively small puddle, a man whose every whim becomes a crusade. In the beginning he had wanted to use his play as a microcosm to say something about the abuse of power. Now he tended more and more to see Denker as a Mr. Chips figure, and the tragedy was not the intellectual racking of Gary Benson but rather the destruction of a kindly old teacher and headmaster unable to see through the cynical wiles of this monster masquerading as a boy.

He hadn't been able to finish the play.

Now he sat looking down at it, scowling, wondering if there was any way he could salvage the situation. He didn't really think there was. He had begun with one play and it had somehow turned into another, presto-chango. Well, what the hell. Either way it had been done before. Either way it was a load of shit. And why was he driving himself crazy about it tonight anyway? After the day just gone by it was no wonder he couldn't think straight.

"—get him down?"

He looked up, trying to blink the cobwebs away. "Huh?"

"I said, how are we going to get him down? We've got to get him out of here, Jack."

For a moment his wits were so scattered that he wasn't even sure what she was talking about. Then he realized and uttered a short, barking laugh.

"You say that as if it were so easy."

"I didn't mean—"

"No problem, Wendy. I'll just change clothes in that telephone booth down in the lobby and fly him to Denver on my back. Superman Jack Torrance, they called me in my salad days."

Her face registered slow hurt.

"I understand the problem, Jack. The radio is broken. The snow ... but you have to understand Danny's problem. My God, don't you? He was nearly catatonic, Jack! What if he hadn't come out of that?"

"But he did," Jack said, a trifle shortly. He had been frightened at Danny's blank-eyed, slack-faced state too, of course he had. At first. But the more he thought about it, the more he wondered if it hadn't been a piece of play-acting put on to escape his punishment. He had, after all, been trespassing.

"All the same," she said. She came to him and sat on the end of the bed by his desk. Her face was both surprised and worried. "Jack, the bruises on his neck! Something got at him! And I want him away from it!"

"Don't shout," he said. "My head aches, Wendy. I'm as worried about this as you are, so please ... don't ... shout."

"All right," she said, lowering her voice. "I won't shout. But I don't understand you, Jack. Someone is in here with us. And not a very nice someone, either. We have to get down to Sidewinder, not just Danny but all of us. Quickly. And you ... you're sitting there reading your *play!*"

"'We have to get down, we have to get down,' you keep saying that. You must think I really am Superman."

"I think you're my husband," she said softly, and looked down at her hands.

His temper flared. He slammed the playscript down, knocking the edges of the pile out of true again and crumpling the sheets on the bottom.

"It's time you got some of the home truths into you, Wendy. You don't seem to have internalized them, as the sociologists say. They're knocking around up in your head like a bunch of loose cueballs. You need to shoot them into the pockets. You need to understand that *we are snowed in.*"

Danny had suddenly become active in his bed. Still sleeping, he had begun to twist and turn. The way he always did when we fought, Wendy thought dismally. And we're doing it again.

"Don't wake him up, Jack. Please."

He glanced over at Danny and some of the flush went out of his cheeks. "Okay. I'm sorry. I'm sorry I sounded mad, Wendy. It's not really for you. But I broke the radio. If it's anybody's fault it's mine. That was our big link to the outside. Olly-olly-in-for-free. Please come get us, Mister Ranger. We can't stay out this late."

"Don't," she said, and put a hand on his shoulder. He leaned his head against it. She brushed his hair with her other hand. "I guess you've got a right, after what I accused you of. Sometimes I am like my mother. I can be a bitch. But you have to understand that some things . . . are hard to get over. You have to understand that."

"Do you mean his arm?" His lips had thinned.

"Yes," Wendy said, and then she rushed on: "But it's not just you. I worry when he goes out to play. I worry about him wanting a two-wheeler next year, even one with training wheels. I worry about his teeth and his eyesight and about this thing, what he calls his shine. I worry. Because he's little and he seems very fragile and because . . . because something in this hotel seems to want him. And it will go through us to get him if it has to. That's why we must get him out, Jack. I know that! I feel that! *We must get him out!*"

Her hand had tightened painfully on his shoulder in her agitation, but he didn't move away. One hand found the firm weight of her left breast and he began to stroke it through her shirt.

"Wendy," he said, and stopped. She waited for him to rearrange whatever he had to say. His strong hand on her breast felt good, soothing. "I could maybe snowshoe him down. He could walk part of the way himself, but I would mostly have to carry him. It would mean camping out one, two, maybe three nights. That would mean building a travois to carry supplies and bedrolls on. We have the AM/FM radio, so we could pick a day when the weather forecast called for a three-day spell of good weather. But if the forecast was wrong," he finished, his voice soft and measured, "I think we might die."

Her face had paled. It looked shiny, almost ghostly. He continued to stroke her breast, rubbing the ball of his thumb gently over the nipple.

She made a soft sound—from his words or in reaction to his

gentle pressure on her breast, he couldn't tell. He raised his hand slightly and undid the top button of her shirt. Wendy shifted her legs slightly. All at once her jeans seemed too tight, slightly irritating in a pleasant sort of way.

"It would mean leaving you alone because you can't snow-shoe worth beans. It would be maybe three days of not know-ing. Would you want that?" His hand dropped to the second button, slipped it, and the beginning of her cleavage was exposed.

"No," she said in a voice that was slightly thick. She glanced over at Danny. He had stopped twisting and turning. His thumb had crept back into his mouth. So that was all right. But Jack was leaving something out of the picture. It was too bleak. There was something else . . . what?

"If we stay put," Jack said, unbuttoning the third and fourth buttons with that same deliberate slowness, "a ranger from the park or a game warden is going to poke in here just to find out how we're doing. At that point we simply tell him we want down. He'll see to it." He slipped her naked breasts into the wide V of the open shirt, bent, and molded his lips around the stem of a nipple. It was hard and erect. He slipped his tongue slowly back and forth across it in a way he knew she liked. Wendy moaned a little and arched her back.

(?Something I've forgotten?)

"Honey?" she asked. On their own her hands sought the back of his head so that when he answered his voice was muffled against her flesh.

"How would the ranger take us out?"

He raised his head slightly to answer and then settled his mouth against the other nipple.

"If the helicopter was spoken for I guess it would have to be by snowmobile."

(!!!)

"But we have one of those! Ullman said so!"

His mouth froze against her breast for a moment, and then he sat up. Her own face was slightly flushed, her eyes overbright. Jack's, on the other hand, was calm, as if he had been reading a rather dull book instead of engaging in foreplay with his wife.

"If there's a snowmobile there's no problem," she said excit-edly. "We can all three go down together."

"Wendy, I've never driven a snowmobile in my life."

"It can't be that hard to learn. Back in Vermont you see ten-year-olds driving them in the fields . . . although what their parents can be thinking of I don't know. And you had a motor-cycle when we met." He had, a Honda 350cc. He had traded it in on a Saab shortly after he and Wendy took up residence together.

"I suppose I could," he said slowly. "But I wonder how well it's been maintained. Ullman and Watson . . . they run this place from May to October. They have summertime minds. I know it won't have gas in it. There may not be plugs or a battery, either. I don't want you to get your hopes up over your head, Wendy."

She was totally excited now, leaning over him, her breasts tumbling out of her shirt. He had a sudden impulse to seize one and twist it until she shrieked. Maybe that would teach her to shut up.

"The gas is no problem," she said. "The VW and the hotel truck are both full. There's gas for the emergency generator downstairs, too. And there must be a gascan out in that shed so you could carry extra."

"Yes," he said. "There is." Actually there were three of them, two five-gallons and a two-gallon.

"I'll bet the sparkplugs and the battery are out there too. Nobody would store their snowmobile in one place and the plugs and battery someplace else, would they?"

"Doesn't seem likely, does it?" He got up and walked over to where Danny lay sleeping. A spill of hair had fallen across his forehead and Jack brushed it away gently. Danny didn't stir.

"And if you can get it running you'll take us out?" she asked from behind him. "On the first day the radio says good weather?"

For a moment he didn't answer. He stood looking down at his son, and his mixed feelings dissolved in a wave of love. He was the way she had said, vulnerable, fragile. The marks on his neck were very prominent.

"Yes," he said. "I'll get it running and we'll get out as quick as we can."

"Thank God!"

He turned around. She had taken off her shirt and lay on the bed, her belly flat, her breasts aimed perkily at the ceiling. She was playing with them lazily, flicking at the nipples. "Hurry up, gentlemen," she said softly, "time."

* * *

After, with no light burning in the room but the night light that Danny had brought with him from his room, she lay in the crook of his arm, feeling deliciously at peace. She found it hard to believe they could be sharing the Overlook with a murderous stowaway.

"Jack?"

"Hmmmm?"

"What got at him?"

He didn't answer her directly. "He does have something. Some talent the rest of us are missing. The most of us, beg pardon. And maybe the Overlook has something, too."

"Ghosts?"

"I don't know. Not in the Algernon Blackwood sense, that's for sure. More like the residues of the feelings of the people who have stayed here. Good things and bad things. In that sense, I suppose that every big hotel has got its ghosts. Especially the old ones."

"But a dead woman in the tub . . . Jack, he's not losing his mind, is he?"

He gave her a brief squeeze. "We know he goes into . . . well, trances, for want of a better word . . . from time to time. We know that when he's in them he sometimes . . . sees? . . . things he doesn't understand. If precognitive trances are possible, they're probably functions of the subconscious mind. Freud said that the subconscious never speaks to us in literal language. Only in symbols. If you dream about being in a bakery where no one speaks English, you may be worried about your ability to support your family. Or maybe just that no one understands you. I've read that the falling dream is a standard outlet for feelings of insecurity. Games, little games. Conscious on one side of the net, subconscious on the other, serving some cocka-mamie image back and forth. Same with mental illness, with hunches, all of that. Why should precognition be any different? Maybe Danny really did see blood all over the walls of the Presidential Suite. To a kid his age, the image of blood and the concept of death are nearly interchangeable. To kids, the image is always more accessible than the concept, anyway. William Carlos Williams knew that, he was a pediatrician. When we grow up, concepts gradually get easier and we leave the images to the poets . . . and I'm just rambling on."

"I like to hear you ramble."

"She said it, folks. She said it. You all heard it."

"The marks on his neck, Jack. Those are real."

"Yes."

There was nothing else for a long time. She had begun to think he must have gone to sleep and she was slipping into a drowse herself when he said:

"I can think of two explanations for those. And neither of them involves a fourth party in the hotel."

"What?" She came up on one elbow.

"Stigmata, maybe," he said.

"Stigmata? Isn't that when people bleed on Good Friday or something?"

"Yes. Sometimes people who believe deeply in Christ's divinity exhibit bleeding marks on their hands and feet during the Holy Week. It was more common in the Middle Ages than now. In those days such people were considered blessed by God. I don't think the Catholic Church proclaimed any of it as out-and-out miracles, which was pretty smart of them. Stigmata isn't much different from some of the things the yogis can do. It's better understood now, that's all. The people who understand the interaction between the mind and the body—study it, I mean, no one understands it—believe we have a lot more control over our involuntary functions than they used to think. You can slow your heartbeat if you think about it enough. Speed up your own metabolism. Make yourself sweat more. Or make yourself bleed."

"You think Danny *thought* those bruises onto his neck? Jack, I just can't believe that."

"I can believe it's possible, although it seems unlikely to me, too. What's more likely is that he did it to himself."

"To himself?"

"He's gone into these 'trances' and hurt himself in the past. Do you remember the time at the supper table? About two years ago, I think. We were super-pissed at each other. Nobody talking very much. Then, all at once, his eyes rolled up in his head and he went face-first into his dinner. Then onto the floor. Remember?"

"Yes," she said. "I sure do. I thought he was having a convulsion."

"Another time we were in the park," he said. "Just Danny and I. Saturday afternoon. He was sitting on a swing, coasting back and forth. He collapsed onto the ground. It was like he'd been shot. I ran over and picked him up and all of a sudden he just came around. He sort of blinked at me and said, 'I hurt my tummy. Tell Mommy to close the bedroom windows if it rains.' And that night it rained like hell."

"Yes, but—"

"And he's always coming in with cuts and scraped elbows. His shins look like a battlefield in distress. And when you ask him how he got this one or that one, he just says 'Oh, I was playing,' and that's the end of it."

"Jack, all kids get bumped and bruised up. With little boys it's almost constant from the time they learn to walk until they're twelve or thirteen."

"And I'm sure Danny gets his share," Jack responded. "He's an active kid. But I remember that day in the park and that night at the supper table. And I wonder if some of our kid's bumps and bruises come from just keeling over. That Dr. Edmonds said Danny did it right in his office, for Christ's sake!"

"All right. But those bruises were *fingers*. I'd swear to it. He didn't get them falling down."

"He goes into a trance," Jack said. "Maybe he sees something that happened in that room. An argument. Maybe a suicide. Violent emotions. It isn't like watching a movie; he's in a highly suggestible state. He's right in the damn thing. His subconscious is maybe visualizing whatever happened in a symbolic way . . . as a dead woman who's alive again, zombie, undead, ghoul, you pick your term."

"You're giving me goose-bumps," she said thickly.

"I'm giving myself a few. I'm no psychiatrist, but it seems to fit so well. The walking dead woman as a symbol for dead emotions, dead lives, that just won't give up and go away . . . but because she's a subconscious figure, she's also *him*. In the trance state, the conscious Danny is submerged. The subconscious figure is pulling the strings. So Danny put his hands around his own neck and—"

"Stop," she said. "I get the picture. I think that's more frightening than having a stranger creeping around the halls, Jack. You can move away from a stranger. You can't move away from yourself. You're talking about schizophrenia."

"Of a very limited type," he said, but a trifle uneasily. "And of a very special nature. Because he does seem able to read thoughts, and he really does seem to have precognitive flashes from time to time. I can't think of that as mental illness no matter how hard I try. We all have schizo deposits in us anyway. I think as Danny gets older, he'll get this under control."

"If you're right, then it's imperative that we get him out. Whatever he has, this hotel is making it worse."

"I wouldn't say that," he objected. "If he'd done as he was told, he never would have gone up to that room in the first place. It never would have happened."

"My God, Jack! Are you implying that being half-strangled was a . . . a fitting punishment for being off limits?"

"No . . . no. Of course not. But—"

"No buts," she said, shaking her head violently. "The truth is, we're guessing. We don't have any idea when he might turn a corner and run into one of those . . . air pockets, one-reel horror movies, whatever they are. We have to get him *away*." She laughed a little in the darkness. "Next thing we'll be seeing things."

"Don't talk nonsense," he said, and in the darkness of the room he saw the hedge lions bunching around the path, no longer flanking it but guarding it, hungry November lions. Cold sweat sprang out on his brow.

"You didn't really see anything, did you?" she was asking. "I mean, when you went up to that room. You didn't see anything?"

The lions were gone. Now he saw a pink pastel shower curtain with a dark shape lounging behind it. The closed door. That muffled, hurried thump, and sounds after it that might have been running footsteps. The horrible, lurching beat of his own heart as he struggled with the passkey.

"Nothing," he said, and that was true. He had been strung up, not sure of what was happening. He hadn't had a chance to sift through his thoughts for a reasonable explanation concerning the bruises on his son's neck. He had been pretty damn suggestible himself. Hallucinations could sometimes be catching.

"And you haven't changed your mind? About the snowmobile, I mean?"

His hands clamped into sudden tight fists

(Stop nagging me!)

by his sides. "I said I would, didn't I? I will. Now go to sleep. It's been a long hard day."

"And how," she said. There was a rustle of bedclothes as she turned toward him and kissed his shoulder. "I love you, Jack."

"I love you too," he said, but he was only mouthing the words. His hands were still clenched into fists. They felt like rocks on the ends of his arms. The pulse beat prominently in his forehead. She hadn't said a word about what was going to happen to them *after* they got down, when the party was over. Not one word. It had been Danny this and Danny that and Jack I'm so scared. Oh yes, she was scared of a lot of closet boogeymen and jumping shadows, plenty scared. But there was no lack of real ones, either. When they got down to Sidewinder they would arrive with sixty dollars and the clothes they stood up in. Not even a car. Even if Sidewinder had a pawnshop, which it didn't, they had nothing to hock but Wendy's ninety-dollar diamond engagement ring and the Sony AM/FM radio. A pawnbroker might give them twenty bucks. A *kind* pawnbroker. There would be no job, not even part-time or seasonal, except maybe shoveling out driveways for three dollars a shot. The piture of John Torrance, thirty years old, who had once published in *Esquire* and who had harbored dreams—not at all unreasonable dreams, he felt—of becoming a major American writer during the next decade, with a shovel from the Sidewinder Western Auto on his shoulder, ringing doorbells . . . that picture suddenly came to him much more clearly than the hedge lions and he clenched his fists tighter still, feeling the fingernails sink into his palms and draw blood in mystic quartermoon shapes. John Torrance, standing in line to change his sixty dollars into food stamps, standing in line again at the Sidewinder Methodist Church to get donated commodities and dirty looks from the locals. John Torrance explaining to Al that they'd just had to leave, had to shut down the boiler, had to leave the Overlook and all it contained open to vandals or thieves on snow machines because, you see, Al, *attendez-vous*, Al, there are ghosts up there and they have it in for my boy.

Good-by, Al. Thoughts of Chapter Four, Spring Comes for John Torrance. What then? Whatever then? They might be able to get to the West Coast in the VW, he supposed. A new fuel pump would do it. Fifty miles west of here and it was all downhill, you could damn near put the bug in neutral and coast to Utah. On to sunny California, land of oranges and opportunity. A man with his sterling record of alcoholism, student-beating, and ghost-chasing would undoubtedly be able to write his own ticket. Anything you like. Custodial engineer— swamping out Greyhound buses. The automotive business— washing cars in a rubber suit. The culinary arts, perhaps, washing dishes in a diner. Or possibly a more responsible position, such as pumping gas. A job like that even held the intellectual stimulation of making change and writing out credit slips. *I can give you twenty-five hours a week at the minimum wage.* That was heavy tunes in a year when Wonder bread went for sixty cents a loaf.

Blood had begun to trickle down from his palms. Like stigmata, oh yes. He squeezed tighter, savaging himself with pain. His wife was asleep beside him, why not? There were no problems. He had agreed to take her and Danny away from the big bad boogeyman and there were no problems. *So you see, Al, I thought the best thing to do would be to—*

(kill her.)

The thought rose up from nowhere, naked and unadorned. The urge to tumble her out of bed, naked, bewildered, just beginning to wake up; to pounce on her, seize her neck like the green limb of a young aspen and to throttle her, thumbs on windpipe, fingers pressing against the top of her spine, jerking her head up and ramming it back down against the floor-boards, again and again, whamming, whacking, smashing, crashing. Jitter and jive, baby. Shake, rattle, and roll. He would make her take her medicine. Every drop. Every last bitter drop.

He was dimly aware of a muffled noise somewhere, just outside his hot and racing inner world. He looked across the room and Danny was thrashing again, twisting in his bed and rumpling the blankets. The boy was moaning deep in his throat, a small, caged sound. What nightmare? A purple woman, long dead, shambling after him down twisting hotel corridors? Somehow he didn't think so. Something else chased Danny in his dreams. Something worse.

The bitter lock of his emotions was broken. He got out of bed and went across to the boy, feeling sick and ashamed of himself. It was Danny he had to think of, not Wendy, not himself. Only Danny. And no matter what shape he wrestled the facts into, he knew in his heart that Danny must be taken out. He straightened the boy's blankets and added the quilt from the foot of the bed. Danny had quieted again now. Jack touched the sleeping forehead

(what monsters capering just behind that ridge of bone?)

and found it warm, but not overly so. And he was sleeping peacefully again. Queer.

He got back into bed and tried to sleep. It eluded him.

It was so unfair that things should turn out this way—bad luck seemed to stalk them. They hadn't been able to shake it by coming up here after all. By the time they arrived in Side-winder tomorrow afternoon, the golden opportunity would have evaporated—gone the way of the blue suede shoe, as an old roommate of his had been wont to say. Consider the difference if they didn't go down, if they could somehow stick it out. The play would get finished. One way or the other, he would tack an ending onto it. His own uncertainty about his characters might add an appealing touch of ambiguity to his original ending. Perhaps it would even make him some money, it wasn't impossible. Even lacking that, Al might well convince the Stovington Board to rehire him. He would be on pro of course, maybe for as long as three years, but if he could stay sober and keep writing, he might not have to stay at Stovington for three years. Of course he hadn't cared much for Stovington before, he had felt stifled, buried alive, but that had been an immature reaction. Furthermore, how much could a man enjoy teaching when he went through his first three classes with a skull-busting hangover every second or third day? It wouldn't be that way again. He would be able to handle his responsibilities much better. He was sure of it.

Somewhere in the midst of that thought, things began to break up and he drifted down into sleep. His last thought followed him down like a sounding bell:

It seemed that he might be able to find peace here. At last. If they would only let him.

When he woke up he was standing in the bathroom of 217.

(been walking in my sleep again—why?—no radios to break up here)

The bathroom light was on, the room behind him in darkness. The shower curtain was drawn around the long clawfooted tub. The bathmat beside it was wrinkled and wet.

He began to feel afraid, but the very dreamlike quality of his fear told him this was not real. Yet that could not contain the fear. So many things at the Overlook seemed like dreams.

He moved across the floor to the tub, not wanting to but helpless to turn his feet back.

He flung the curtain open.

Lying in the tub, naked, lolling almost weightless in the water, was George Hatfield, a knife stuck in his chest. The water around him was stained a bright pink. George's eyes were closed. His penis floated limply, like kelp.

"George—" he heard himself say.

At the word, George's eyes snapped open. They were silver, not human eyes at all. George's hands, fish-white, found the sides of the tub and he pulled himself up to a sitting position. The knife stuck straight out from his chest, equidistantly placed between nipples. The wound was lipless.

"You set the timer ahead," silver-eyed George told him.

"No, George, I didn't. I—"

"I don't stutter."

George was standing now, still fixing him with that inhuman silver glare, but his mouth had drawn back in a dead and grimacing smile. He threw one leg over the porcelained side of the tub. One white and wrinkled foot placed itself on the bathmat.

"First you tried to run me over on my bike and then you set the timer ahead and then you tried to stab me to death but *I still don't stutter.*" George was coming for him, his hands out, the fingers slightly curled. He smelled moldy and wet, like leaves that had been rained on.

"It was for your own good," Jack said, backing up. "I set it ahead for your own good. Furthermore, I happen to know you cheated on your Final Composition."

"I don't cheat . . . and I don't stutter."

George's hands touched his neck.

Jack turned and ran, ran with the floating, weightless slowness that is so common to dreams.

"You did! You did cheat!" he screamed in fear and anger as he crossed the darkened bed/sitting room. "I'll prove it!"

George's hands were on his neck again. Jack's heart swelled with fear until he was sure it would burst. And then, at last, his hand curled around the doorknob and it turned under his hand and he yanked the door open. He plunged out, not into the second-floor hallway, but into the basement room beyond the arch. The cobwebby light was on. His campchair, stark and geometrical, stood beneath it. And all around it was a miniature mountain range of boxes and crates and banded bundles of records and invoices and God knew what. Relief surged through him.

"I'll find it!" he heard himself screaming. He seized a damp and moldering cardboard box; it split apart in his hands, spilling out a waterfall of yellow flimsies. "It's here somewhere! *I will find it!*" He plunged his hands deep into the pile of papers and came up with a dry, papery wasps' nest in one hand and a timer in the other. The timer was ticking. Attached to its back was a length of electrical cord and attached to the other end of the cord was a bundle of dynamite. *"Here!"* he screamed. *"Here, take it!"*

His relief became absolute triumph. He had done more than escape George; he had conquered. With these talismanic objects in his hands, George would never touch him again. George would flee in terror.

He began to turn so he could confront George, and that was when George's hands settled around his neck, squeezing, stopping his breath, damming up his respiration entirely after one final dragging gasp.

"I don't stutter," whispered George from behind him.

He dropped the wasps' nest and wasps boiled out of it in a furious brown and yellow wave. His lungs were on fire. His wavering sight fell on the timer and the sense of triumph returned, along with a cresting wave of righteous wrath. Instead of connecting the timer to dynamite, the cord ran to the gold knob of a stout black cane, like the one his father had carried after the accident with the milk truck.

He grasped it and the cord parted. The cane felt heavy and right in his hands. He swung it back over his shoulder. On the way up it glanced against the wire from which the light bulb depended and the light began to swing back and forth, making the room's hooded shadows rock monstrously against the floor and walls. On the way down the cane struck something much harder. George screamed. The grip on Jack's throat loosened.

He tore free of George's grip and whirled. George was on his knees, his head drooping, his hands laced together on top of it. Blood welled through his fingers.

"Please," George whispered humbly. "Give me a break, Mr. Torrance."

"Now you'll take your medicine," Jack grunted. "Now by God, won't you. Young pup. Young worthless cur. Now by God, right now. Every drop. Every single damn drop!"

As the light swayed above him and the shadows danced and flapped, he began to swing the cane, bringing it down again and again, his arm rising and falling like a machine. George's bloody protecting fingers fell away from his head and Jack brought the cane down again and again, and on his neck and shoulders and back and arms. Except that the cane was no longer precisely a cane; it seemed to be a mallet with some kind of brightly striped handle. A mallet with a hard side and soft side. The business end was clotted with blood and hair. And the flat, whacking sound of the mallet against flesh had been replaced with a hollow booming sound, echoing and reverberating. His own voice had taken on this same quality, bellowing, disembodied. And yet, paradoxically, it sounded weaker, slurred, petulant . . . as if he were drunk.

The figure on its knees slowly raised its head, as if in supplication. There was not a face, precisely, but only a mask of blood through which eyes peered. He brought the mallet back for a final whistling downstroke and it was fully launched before he saw that the supplicating face below him was not George's but Danny's. It was the face of his son.

"*Daddy*—"

And then the mallet crashed home, striking Danny right between the eyes, closing them forever. And something somewhere seemed to be laughing—

(*! No !*)

He came out of it standing naked over Danny's bed, his hands empty, his body sheened with sweat. His final scream had only been in his mind. He voiced it again, this time in a whisper.

"No. No, Danny. Never."

He went back to bed on legs that had turned to rubber. Wendy was sleeping deeply. The clock on the nightstand said it was quarter to five. He lay sleepless until seven, when Danny began to stir awake. Then he put his legs over the edge of the bed and began to dress. It was time to go downstairs and check the boiler.

33

THE SNOWMOBILE

Sometime after midnight, while they all slept uneasily, the snow had stopped after dumping a fresh eight inches on the old crust. The clouds had broken, a fresh wind had swept them away, and now Jack stood in a dusty ingot of sunlight, which slanted through the dirty window set into the eastern side of the equipment shed.

The place was about as long as a freight car, and about as high. It smelled of grease and oil and gasoline and—faint, nostalgic smell—sweet grass. Four power lawnmowers were ranked like soldiers on review against the south wall, two of them the riding type that look like small tractors. To their left were posthole diggers, round-bladed shovels made for doing surgery on the putting green, a chain saw, the electric hedge-clippers, and a long thin steel pole with a red flag at the top. Caddy, fetch my ball in under ten seconds and there's a quarter in it for you. Yes, *sir*.

Against the eastern wall, where the morning sun slanted in most strongly, three Ping-Pong tables leaned one against the other like a drunken house of cards. Their nets had been removed and flopped down from the shelf above. In the corner was a stack of shuffleboard weights and a roque set—the wickets banded together with twists of wire, the brightly painted balls in an egg-carton sort of thing (strange hens you have up here, Watson . . . yes, and you should see the animals down on the front lawn, ha-ha), and the mallets, two sets of them, standing in their racks.

He walked over to them, stepping over an old eight-cell battery (which had once sat beneath the hood of the hotel truck, no doubt) and a battery charger and a pair of J. C. Penney jumper cables coiled between them. He slipped one of the short-handled mallets out of the front rack and held it up in front of his face, like a knight bound for battle saluting his king.

Fragments of his dream (it was all jumbled now, fading) recurred, something about George Hatfield and his father's cane, just enough to make him uneasy and, absurdly enough, a trifle guilty about holding a plain old garden-variety roque mallet. Not that roque was such a common garden-variety game anymore; its more modern cousin, croquet, was much more popular now . . . and a child's version of the game at that. Roque, however . . . that must have been quite a game. Jack had found a mildewed rule book down in the basement, from one of the years in the early twenties when a North American Roque Tournament had been held at the Overlook. Quite a game.

(schizo)

He frowned a little, then smiled. Yes, it was a schizo sort of game at that. The mallet expressed that perfectly. A soft end and a hard end. A game of finesse and aim, and a game of raw, bludgeoning power.

He swung the mallet through the air . . . *whhhooop.* He smiled a little at the powerful, whistling sound it made. Then he replaced it in the rack and turned to his left. What he saw there made him frown again.

The snowmobile sat almost in the middle of the equipment shed, a fairly new one, and Jack didn't care for its looks at all.

Bombardier Skidoo was written on the side of the engine cowling facing him in black letters which had been raked backward, presumably to connote speed. The protruding skis were also black. There was black piping to the right and left of the cowling, what they would call racing stripes on a sports car. But the actual paintjob was a bright, sneering yellow, and that was what he didn't like about it. Sitting there in its shaft of morning sun, yellow body and black piping, black skis and black upholstered open cockpit, it looked like a monstrous mechanized wasp. When it was running it would sound like that too. Whining and buzzing and ready to sting. But then, what else should it look like? It wasn't flying under false colors, at least. Because after it had done its job, they were going to be hurting plenty. All of them. By spring the Torrance family would be hurting so badly that what those wasps had done to Danny's hand would look like a mother's kisses.

He pulled his handkerchief from his back pocket, wiped his mouth with it, and walked over to the Skidoo. He stood looking down at it, the frown very deep now, and stuffed his handkerchief back into his pocket. Outside a sudden gust of wind slammed against the equipment shed, making it rock and creak. He looked out the window and saw the gust carrying a sheet of sparkling snow crystals toward the drifted-in rear of the hotel, whirling them high into the hard blue sky.

The wind dropped and he went back to looking at the machine. It was a disgusting thing, really. You almost expected to see a long, limber stinger protruding from the rear of it. He had always disliked the goddam snowmobiles. They shivered the cathedral silence of winter into a million rattling fragments. They startled the wildlife. They sent out huge and pollutive clouds of blue and billowing oilsmoke behind them—cough, cough, gag, gag, let me breathe. They were perhaps the final grotesque toy of the unwinding fossil fuel age, given to ten-year-olds for Christmas.

He remembered a newspaper article he had read in Stovington, a story datelined someplace in Maine. A kid on a snowmobile, barrel-assing up a road he'd never traveled before at better than thirty miles an hour. Night. His headlight off. There had been a heavy chain strung between two posts with a NO TRESPASSING sign hung from the middle. They said that in all probability the kid never saw it. The moon might have gone behind a cloud. The chain had decapitated him. Reading the story Jack had been almost glad, and now, looking down at this machine, the feeling recurred.

(If it wasn't for Danny, I would take great pleasure in grabbing one of those mallets, opening the cowling, and just pounding until)

He let his pent-up breath escape him in a long slow sigh. Wendy was right. Come hell, high water, or the welfare line, Wendy was right. Pounding this machine to death would be the height of folly, no matter how pleasant an aspect that folly made. It would almost be tantamount to pounding his own son to death.

"Fucking Luddite," he said aloud.

He went to the back of the machine and unscrewed the gascap. He found a dipstick on one of the shelves that ran at chest-height around the walls and slipped it in. The last eighth of an inch came out wet. Not very much, but enough to see if the damn thing would run. Later he could siphon more from the Volks and the hotel truck.

He screwed the cap back on and opened the cowling. No sparkplugs, no battery. He went to the shelf again and began to poke along it, pushing aside screwdrivers and adjustable wrenches, a one-lung carburetor that had been taken out of an old lawn mower, plastic boxes of screws and nails and bolts of varying sizes. The shelf was thick and dark with old grease, and the years' accumulation of dust had stuck to it like fur. He didn't like touching it.

He found a small, oil-stained box with the abbreviation *Skid.* laconically marked on it in pencil. He shook it and something rattled inside. Plugs. He held one of them up to the light, trying to estimate the gap without hunting around for the gapping tool. Fuck it, he thought resentfully, and dropped the plug back into the box. If the gap's wrong, that's just too damn bad. Tough fucking titty.

There was a stool behind the door. He dragged it over, sat down, and installed the four sparkplugs, then fitted the small rubber caps over each. That done, he let his fingers play briefly over the magneto. They laughed when I sat down at the piano.

Back to the shelves. This time he couldn't find what he wanted, a small battery. A three- or four-cell. There were socket wrenches, a case filled with drills and drillbits, bags of lawn fertilizer and Vigoro for the flower beds, but no snowmobile battery. It didn't bother him in the slightest. In fact, it made him feel glad. He was relieved. *I did my best, Captain, but I could not get through. That's fine, son. I'm going to put you in for the Silver Star and the Purple Snowmobile. You're a credit to your regiment. Thank you, sir. I did try.*

He began to whistle "Red River Valley" uptempo as he poked along the last two or three feet of shelf. The notes came out in little puffs of white smoke. He had made a complete circuit of the shed and the thing wasn't there. Maybe somebody had lifted it. Maybe Watson had. He laughed aloud. The old office bootleg trick. *A few paperclips, a couple of reams of paper, nobody will miss this tablecloth or this Golden Regal place setting . . . and what about this fine snowmobile battery? Yes, that might come in handy. Toss it in the sack.* White-collar crime, Baby. Everybody has sticky fingers. Under-the-jacket discount, we used to call it when we were kids.

He walked back to the snowmobile and gave the side of it a good healthy kick as he went by. Well, that was the end of it. He would just have to tell Wendy sorry, baby, but—

There was a box sitting in the corner by the door. The stool had been right over it. Written on the top, in pencil, was the abbreviation *Skid.*

He looked at it, the smile drying up on his lips. *Look, sir, it's the cavalry. Looks like your smoke signals must have worked after all.*

It wasn't fair.

Goddammit, it just wasn't fair.

Something—luck, fate, providence—had been trying to save him. Some other luck, white luck. And at the last moment bad old Jack Torrance luck had stepped back in. The lousy run of cards wasn't over yet.

Resentment, a gray, sullen wave of it, pushed up his throat. His hands had clenched into fists again.

(Not fair, goddammit, not fair!)

Why couldn't he have looked someplace else? Anyplace! Why hadn't he had a crick in his neck or an itch in his nose or the need to blink? Just one of those little things. He never would have seen it.

Well, he hadn't. That was all. It was an hallucination, no different from what had happened yesterday outside that room on the second floor or the goddam hedge menagerie. A momentary strain, that was all. Fancy, I thought I saw a snowmobile battery in that corner. Nothing there now. Combat fatigue, I guess, sir. Sorry. Keep your pecker up, son. It happens to all of us sooner or later.

He yanked the door open almost hard enough to snap the hinges and pulled his snowshoes inside. They were clotted with snow and he slapped them down hard enough on the floor to raise a cloud of it. He put his left foot on the left shoe . . . and paused.

Danny was out there, by the milk platform. Trying to make a snowman, by the looks. Not much luck; the snow was too cold to stick together. Still, he was giving it the old college try, out there in the flashing morning, a speck of a bundled-up boy above the brilliant snow and below the brilliant sky. Wearing his hat turned around backward like Carlton Fiske.

(What in the name of God were you thinking of?)

The answer came back with no pause.

(Me. I was thinking of me.)

He suddenly remembered lying in bed the night before, lying there and suddenly he had been contemplating the murder of his wife.

In that instant, kneeling there, everything came clear to him. It was not just Danny the Overlook was working on. It was working on him, too. It wasn't Danny who was the weak link, it was him. He was the vulnerable one, the one who could be bent and twisted until something snapped.

(until i let go and sleep . . . and when i do that if i do that)

He looked up at the banks of windows and the sun threw back an almost blinding glare from their many-paned surfaces but he looked anyway. For the first time he noticed how much they seemed like eyes. They reflected away the sun and held their own darkness within. It was not Danny they were looking at. It was him.

In those few seconds he understood everything. There was a certain black-and-white picture he remembered seeing as a child, in catechism class. The nun had presented it to them on an easel and called it a miracle of God. The class had looked at it blankly, seeing nothing but a jumble of whites and blacks, senseless and patternless. Then one of the children in the third row had gasped, "It's Jesus!" and that child had gone home with a brand-new Testament and also a calendar because he had been first. The others stared even harder, Jacky Torrance among them. One by one the other kids had given a similar gasp, one little girl transported in near-ecstasy, crying out shrilly: "I *see* Him! I *see* Him!" She had also been rewarded with a Testament. At last everyone had seen the face of Jesus in the jumble of blacks and whites except Jacky. He strained harder and harder, scared now, part of him cynically thinking that everyone else was simply putting on to please Sister Beatrice, part of him secretly convinced that he wasn't seeing it because God had decided he was the worst sinner in the class. "Don't you see it, Jacky?" Sister Beatrice had asked him in her sad, sweet manner. I see your *tits*, he had thought in vicious desperation. He began to shake his head, then faked excitement and said: "Yes, I do! Wow! It *is* Jesus!" And everyone in class had laughed and applauded him, making him feel triumphant, ashamed, and scared. Later, when everyone else had tumbled their way up from the church basement and out onto the street he had lingered behind, looking at the meaningless black-and-white jumble that Sister Beatrice had left on the easel. He hated it. They had all made it up the way he had, even Sister herself. It was a big fake. "Shitfire-hellfire-shitfire," he had whispered under his breath, and as he turned to go he had seen the face of Jesus from the corner of his eye, sad and wise. He turned back, his heart in his throat. Everything had suddenly clicked into place and he had stared at the picture with fearful wonder, unable to believe he had missed it. The eyes, the zigzag of shadow across the care-worn brow, the fine nose, the compassionate lips. Looking at Jacky Torrance. What had only been a meaningless sprawl had suddenly been transformed into a stark black-and-white etching of the face of Christ-Our-Lord. Fearful wonder became terror. He had cussed in front of a picture of Jesus. He would be damned. He would be in hell with the sinners. The face of Christ had been in the picture all along. All along.

Now, kneeling in the sun and watching his son playing in the shadow of the hotel, he knew that it was all true. The hotel wanted Danny, maybe all of them but Danny for sure. The hedges had really walked. There was a dead woman in 217, a woman that was perhaps only a spirit and harmless under most circumstances, but a woman who was now an active danger. Like some malevolent clockwork toy she had been wound up and set in motion by Danny's own odd mind . . . and his own. Had it been Watson who had told him a man had dropped dead of a stroke one day on the roque court? Or had it been Ullman? It didn't matter. There had been an assassination on the third floor. How many old quarrels, suicides, strokes? How many murders? Was Grady lurking somewhere in the west wing with his ax, just waiting for Danny to start him up so he could come back out of the woodwork?

The puffed circle of bruises around Danny's neck.

The twinkling, half-seen bottles in the deserted lounge.

The radio.

The dreams.

The scrapbook he had found in the cellar.

(*Medoc, are you here? I've been sleepwalking again, my dear . . .*)

He got up suddenly, thrusting the snowshoes back out the door. He was shaking all over. He slammed the door and picked up the box with the battery in it. It slipped through his shaking fingers

(*oh christ what if i cracked it*)

and thumped over on its side. He pulled the flaps of the carton open and yanked the battery out, heedless of the acid that might be leaking through the battery's casing if it had cracked. But it hadn't. It was whole. A little sigh escaped his lips.

Cradling it, he took it over to the Skidoo and put it on its platform near the front of the engine. He found a small adjustable wrench on one of the shelves and attached the battery cables quickly and with no trouble. The battery was live; no need to use the charger on it. There had been a crackle of electricity and a small odor of ozone when he slipped the positive cable onto its terminal. The job done, he stood away, wiping his hands nervously on his faded denim jacket. There. It should work. No reason why not. No reason at all except that it was part of the Overlook and the Overlook really didn't want them out of here. Not at all. The Overlook was having one hell of a good time. There was a little boy to terrorize, a man and his woman to set one against the other, and if it played its cards right they could end up flitting through the Overlook's halls like insubstantial shades in a Shirley Jackson novel, whatever walked in Hill House walked alone, but you wouldn't be alone in the Overlook, oh no, there would be plenty of company here. But there was really no reason why the snowmobile shouldn't start. Except of course

(Except he still didn't really want to go.)

yes, except for that.

He stood looking at the Skidoo, his breath puffing out in frozen little plumes. He wanted it to be the way it had been. When he had come in here he'd had no doubts. Going down would be the wrong decision, he had known that then. Wendy was only scared of the boogeyman summoned up by a single hysterical little boy. Now, suddenly, he could see her side. It was like his play, his damnable play. He no longer knew which side he was on, or how things should come out. Once you saw the face of a god in those jumbled blacks and whites, it was everybody out of the pool—you could never unsee it. Others might laugh and say it's nothing, just a lot of splotches with no meaning, give me a good old Craftmaster paint-by-the-numbers any day, but *you* would always see the face of Christ-Our-Lord looking out at you. You had seen it in one gestalt leap, the conscious and unconscious melding in that one shocking moment of understanding. You would always see it. You were damned to always see it.

(I've been sleepwalking again, my dear . . .)

It had been all right until he had seen Danny playing in the snow. It was Danny's fault. Everything had been Danny's fault. He was the one with the shining, or whatever it was. It wasn't a shining, it was a curse. If he and Wendy had been here alone, they could have passed the winter quite nicely. No pain, no strain on the brain.

(Don't want to leave. ?Can't?)

The Overlook didn't want them to go and he didn't want them to go either. Not even Danny. Maybe he was a part of it, now. Perhaps the Overlook, large and rambling Samuel Johnson that it was, had picked him to be its Boswell. You say the new caretaker writes? Very good, sign him on. Time we told our side. Let's get rid of the woman and his snotnosed kid first, however. We don't want him to be distracted. We don't—

He was standing by the snowmobile's cockpit, his head starting to ache again. What did it come down to? Go or stay. Very simple. Keep it simple. Shall we go or shall we stay?

If we go, how long will it be before you find the local hole in Sidewinder? a voice inside him asked. The dark place with the lousy color TV that unshaven and unemployed men spend the day watching game shows on? Where the piss in the men's room smells two thousand years old and there's always a sodden Camel butt unraveling in the toilet bowl? Where the beer is thirty cents a glass and you cut it with salt and the jukebox is loaded with seventy country oldies?

How long? Oh Christ, he was so afraid it wouldn't be long at all.

"I can't win," he said, very softly. That was it. It was like trying to play solitaire with one of the aces missing from the deck.

Abruptly he leaned over the Skidoo's motor compartment and yanked off the magneto. It came off with sickening ease. He looked at it for a moment, then went to the equipment shed's back door and opened it.

From here the view of the mountains was unobstructed, picture-postcard beautiful in the twinkling brightness of morning. An unbroken field of snow rose to the first pines about a mile distant. He flung the magneto as far out into the snow as he could. It went much further than it should have. There was a light puff of snow when it fell. The light breeze carried the snow granules away to fresh resting places. Disperse there, I say. There's nothing to see. It's all over. Disperse.

He felt at peace.

He stood in the doorway for a long time, breathing the good mountain air, and then he closed it firmly and went back out the other door to tell Wendy they would be staying. On the way, he stopped and had a snowball fight with Danny.

34

THE HEDGES

It was November 29, three days after Thanksgiving. The last week had been a good one, the Thanksgiving dinner the best they'd ever had as a family. Wendy had cooked Dick Hallorann's turkey to a turn and they had all eaten to bursting without even coming close to demolishing the jolly bird. Jack had groaned that they would be eating turkey for the rest of the winter—creamed turkey, turkey sandwiches, turkey and noodles, turkey surprise.

No, Wendy told him with a little smile. Only until Christmas. Then we have the capon.

Jack and Danny groaned together.

The bruises on Danny's neck had faded, and their fears seemed to have faded with them. On Thanksgiving afternoon Wendy had been pulling Danny around on his sled while Jack worked on the play, which was now almost done.

"Are you still afraid, doc?" she had asked, not knowing how to put the question less baldly.

"Yes," he answered simply. "But now I stay in the safe places."

"Your daddy says that sooner or later the forest rangers will wonder why we're not checking in on the CB radio. They'll come to see if anything is wrong. We might go down then. You and I. And let your daddy finish the winter. He has good reasons for wanting to. In a way, doc . . . I know this is hard for you to understand . . . our backs are against the wall."

"Yes," he had answered noncommittally.

On this sparkling afternoon the two of them were upstairs, and Danny knew that they had been making love. They were dozing now. They were happy, he knew. His mother was still a little bit afraid, but his father's attitude was strange. It was a feeling that he had done something that was very hard and had done it right. But Danny could not seem to see exactly what the something was. His father was guarding that carefully, even in his own mind. Was it possible, Danny wondered, to be glad you had done something and still be so ashamed of that something that you tried not to think of it? The question was a disturbing one. He didn't think such a thing was possible . . . in a normal mind. His hardest probings at his father had only brought him a dim picture of something like an octopus, whirling up into the hard blue sky. And on both occasions that he had concentrated hard enough to get this, Daddy had suddenly been staring at him in a sharp and frightening way, as if he knew what Danny was doing.

Now he was in the lobby, getting ready to go out. He went out a lot, taking his sled or wearing his snowshoes. He liked to get out of the hotel. When he was out in the sunshine, it seemed like a weight had slipped from his shoulders.

He pulled a chair over, stood on it, and got his parka and snow pants out of the ballroom closet, and then sat down on the chair to put them on. His boots were in the boot box and he pulled them on, his tongue creeping out into the corner of his mouth in concentration as he laced them and tied the rawhide into careful granny knots. He pulled on his mittens and his ski mask and was ready.

He tramped out through the kitchen to the back door, then paused. He was tired of playing out back, and at this time of day the hotel's shadow would be cast over his play area. He didn't even like being in the Overlook's shadow. He decided he would put on his snowshoes and go down to the playground instead. Dick Hallorann had told him to stay away from the topiary, but the thought of the hedge animals did not bother him much. They were buried under snowdrifts now, nothing showing but a vague hump that was the rabbit's head and the lions' tails. Sticking out of the snow the way they were, the tails looked more absurd than frightening.

Danny opened the back door and got his snowshoes from the milk platform. Five minutes later he was strapping them to his feet on the front porch. His daddy had told him that he (Danny) had the hang of using the snowshoes—the lazy, shuffling stride, the twist of ankle that shook the powdery snow from the lacings just before the boot came back down—and all that remained was for him to build up the necessary muscles in his thighs and calves and ankles. Danny found that his ankles got tired the fastest. Snowshoeing was almost as hard on your ankles as skating, because you had to keep clearing the lacings. Every five minutes or so he had to stop with his legs spread and the snowshoes flat on the snow to rest them.

But he didn't have to rest on his way down to the playground because it was all downhill. Less than ten minutes after he struggled up and over the monstrous snow-dune that had drifted in on the Overlook's front porch he was standing with his mittened hand on the playground slide. He wasn't even breathing hard.

The playground seemed much nicer in the deep snow than it ever had during the autumn. It looked like a fairyland sculpture. The swing chains had been frozen in strange positions, the seats of the big kids' swings resting flush against the snow. The jungle gym was an ice-cave guarded by dripping icicle teeth. Only the chimneys of the play-Overlook stuck up over the snow

(wish the other one was buried that way only not with us in it)

and the tops of the cement rings protruded in two places like Eskimo igloos. Danny tramped over there, squatted, and began to dig. Before long he had uncovered the dark mouth of one of them and he slipped into the cold tunnel. In his mind he was Patrick McGoohan, the Secret Agent Man (they had shown the reruns of that program twice on the Burlington TV channel and his daddy never missed them; he would skip a party to stay home and watch "Secret Agent" or "The Avengers," and Danny had always watched with him), on the run from KGB agents in the mountains of Switzerland. There had been avalanches in the area and the notorious KGB agent Slobbo had killed his girlfriend with a poison dart, but somewhere near was the Russian antigravity machine. Perhaps at the end of this very tunnel. He drew his automatic and went along the concrete tunnel, his eyes wide and alert, his breath pluming out.

The far end of the concrete ring was solidly blocked with snow. He tried digging through it and was amazed (and a little uneasy) to see how solid it was, almost like ice from the cold and the constant weight of more snow on top of it.

His make-believe game collapsed around him and he was suddenly aware that he felt closed in and extremely nervous in this tight ring of cement. He could hear his breathing; it sounded dank and quick and hollow. He was under the snow, and hardly any light filtered down the hole he had dug to get in here. Suddenly he wanted to be out in the sunlight more than anything, suddenly he remembered his daddy and mommy were sleeping and didn't know where he was, that if the hole he dug caved in he would be trapped, and the Overlook didn't like him.

Danny got turned around with some difficulty and crawled back along the length of the concrete ring, his snowshoes clacking woodenly together behind him, his palms crackling in last fall's dead aspen leaves beneath him. He had just reached the end and the cold spill of light coming down from above when the snow *did* give in, a minor fall, but enough to powder his face and clog the opening he had wriggled down through and leave him in darkness.

For a moment his brain froze in utter panic and he could not think. Then, as if from far off, he heard his daddy telling him that he must never play at the Stovington dump, because sometimes stupid people hauled old refrigerators off to the dump without removing the doors and if you got in one and the door happened to shut on you, there was no way to get out. You would die in the darkness.

(You wouldn't want a thing like that to happen to you, would you, doc?)

(No, Daddy.)

But it *had* happened, his frenzied mind told him, it *had* happened, he was in the dark, he was closed in, and it was as cold as a refrigerator. And—

(something is in here with me.)

His breath stopped in a gasp. An almost drowsy terror stole through his veins. Yes. Yes. There was something in here with him, some awful thing the Overlook had saved for just such a chance as this. Maybe a huge spider that had burrowed down under the dead leaves, or a rat . . . or maybe the corpse of some little kid that had died here on the playground. Had that ever happened? Yes, he thought maybe it had. He thought of the woman in the tub. The blood and brains on the wall of the Presidential Sweet. Of some little kid, its head split open from a fall from the monkey bars or a swing, crawling after him in the dark, grinning, looking for one final playmate in its endless playground. Forever. In a moment he would hear it coming.

At the far end of the concrete ring, Danny heard the stealthy crackle of dead leaves as something came for him on its hands and knees. At any moment he would feel its cold hand close over his ankle—

That thought broke his paralysis. He was digging at the loose fall of snow that choked the end of the concrete ring, throwing it back between his legs in powdery bursts like a dog digging for a bone. Blue light filtered down from above and Danny thrust himself up at it like a diver coming out of deep water. He scraped his back on the lip of the concrete ring. One of his snowshoes twisted behind the other. Snow spilled down inside his ski mask and into the collar of his parka. He dug at the snow, clawed at it. It seemed to be trying to hold him, to suck him back down, back into the concrete ring where that unseen, leaf-crackling *thing* was, and keep him there. Forever.

Then he was out, his face was turned up to the sun, and he was crawling through the snow, crawling away from the half-buried cement ring, gasping harshly, his face almost comically white with powdered snow—a living fright-mask. He hobbled over to the jungle gym and sat down to readjust his snowshoes and get his breath. As he set them to rights and tightened the straps again, he never took his eyes from the hole at the end of the concrete ring. He waited to see if something would come out. Nothing did, and after three or four minutes, Danny's breathing began to slow down. Whatever it was, it couldn't stand the sunlight. It was cooped up down there, maybe only able to come out when it was dark . . . or when both ends of its circular prison were plugged with snow.

(*but i'm safe now i'm safe i'll just go back because now i'm*)

Something thumped softly behind him.

He turned around, toward the hotel, and looked. But even before he looked

(*Can you see the Indians in this picture?*)

he knew what he would see, because he knew what that soft thumping sound had been. It was the sound of a large clump of snow falling, the way it sounded when it slid off the roof of the hotel and fell to the ground.

(*Can you see—?*)

Yes. He could. The snow had fallen off the hedge dog. When he came down it had only been a harmless lump of snow outside the playground. Now it stood revealed, an incongruous splash of green in all the eye-watering whiteness. It was sitting up, as if to beg a sweet or a scrap.

But this time he wouldn't go crazy, he wouldn't blow his cool. Because at least he wasn't trapped in some dark old hole. He was in the sunlight. And it was just a dog. It's pretty warm out today, he thought hopefully. Maybe the sun just melted enough snow off that old dog so the rest fell off in a bunch. Maybe that's all it is.

(Don't go near that place . . . steer right clear.)

His snowshoe bindings were as tight as they were ever going to be. He stood up and stared back at the concrete ring, almost completely submerged in the snow, and what he saw at the end he had exited from froze his heart. There was a circular patch of darkness at the end of it, a fold of shadow that marked the hole he'd dug to get down inside. Now, in spite of the snow-dazzle, he thought he could see something there. Something moving. A hand. The waving hand of some desperately un-happy child, waving hand, pleading hand, drowning hand.

(Save me O please save me If you can't save me at least come play with me . . . Forever. And Forever. And Forever.)

"No," Danny whispered huskily. The word fell dry and bare from his mouth, which was stripped of moisture. He could feel his mind wavering now, trying to go away the way it had when the woman in the room had . . . no, better not think of that.

He grasped at the strings of reality and held them tightly. He had to get out of here. Concentrate on that. Be cool. Be like the Secret Agent Man. Would Patrick McGoohan be crying and peeing in his pants like a little baby?

Would his daddy?

That calmed him somewhat.

From behind him, that soft *flump* sound of falling snow came again. He turned around and the head of one of the hedge lions was sticking out of the snow now, snarling at him. It was closer than it should have been, almost up to the gate of the playground.

Terror tried to rise up and he quelled it. He was the Secret Agent Man, and he *would* escape.

He began to walk out of the playground, taking the same roundabout course his father had taken on the day that the snow flew. He concentrated on operating the snowshoes. Slow, flat strides. Don't lift your foot too high or you'll lose your balance. Twist your ankle and spill the snow off the crisscrossed lacings. It seemed so *slow*. He reached the corner of the playground. The snow was drifted high here and he was able to step over the fence. He got halfway over and then almost fell flat when the snowshoe on his behind foot caught on one of the fence posts. He leaned on the outside edge of gravity, pinwheeling his arms, remembering how hard it was to get up once you fell down.

From his right, that soft sound again, falling clumps of snow. He looked over and saw the other two lions, clear of snow now down to their forepaws, side by side, about sixty paces away. The green indentations that were their eyes were fixed on him. The dog had turned its head.

(*It only happens when you're not looking.*)

"Oh! Hey—"

His snowshoes had crossed and he plunged forward into the snow, arms waving uselessly. More snow got inside his hood and down his neck and into the tops of his boots. He struggled out of the snow and tried to get the snowshoes under him, heart hammering crazily now

(*Secret Agent Man remember you're the Secret Agent*)

and overbalanced backward. For a moment he lay there looking at the sky, thinking it would be simpler to just give up.

Then he thought of the thing in the concrete tunnel and knew he could not. He gained his feet and stared over at the topiary. All three lions were bunched together now, not forty feet away. The dog had ranged off to their left, as if to block Danny's retreat. They were bare of snow except for powdery ruffs around their necks and muzzles. They were all staring at him.

His breath was racing now, and the panic was like a rat behind his forehead, twisting and gnawing. He fought the panic and he fought the snowshoes.

(*Daddy's voice: No, don't fight them, doc. Walk on them like they were your own feet. Walk with them.*)

(*Yes, Daddy.*)

He began to walk again, trying to regain the easy rhythm he had practiced with his daddy. Little by little it began to come, but with the rhythm came an awareness of just how tired he was, how much his fear had exhausted him. The tendons of his thighs and calves and ankles were hot and trembly. Ahead he could see the Overlook, mockingly distant, seeming to stare at him with its many windows, as if this were some sort of contest in which it was mildly interested.

Danny looked back over his shoulder and his hurried breathing caught for a moment and then hurried on even faster. The nearest lion was now only twenty feet behind, breasting through the snow like a dog paddling in a pond. The two others were to its right and left, pacing it. They were like an army platoon on patrol, the dog, still off to their left, the scout. The closest lion had its head down. The shoulders bunched powerfully above its neck. The tail was up, as if in the instant before he had turned to look it had been swishing back and forth, back and forth. He thought it looked like a great big housecat that was having a good time playing with a mouse before killing it.

(—*falling*—)

No, if he fell he was dead. They would never let him get up. They would pounce. He pinwheeled his arms madly and lunged ahead, his center of gravity dancing just beyond his nose. He caught it and hurried on, snapping glances back over his shoulder. The air whistled in and out of his dry throat like hot glass.

The world closed down to the dazzling snow, the green hedges, and the whispery sound of his snowshoes. And something else. A soft, muffled padding sound. He tried to hurry faster and couldn't. He was walking over the buried driveway now, a small boy with his face almost buried in the shadow of his parka hood. The afternoon was still and bright.

When he looked back again, the point lion was only five feet behind. It was grinning. Its mouth was open, its haunches tensed down like a clockspring. Behind it and the others he could see the rabbit, its head now sticking out of the snow, bright green, as if it had turned its horrid blank face to watch the end of the stalk.

Now, on the Overlook's front lawn between the circular drive and the porch, he let the panic loose and began to run clumsily in the snowshoes, not daring to look back now, tilting further and further forward, his arms out ahead of him like a blind man feeling for obstacles. His hood fell back, revealing his complexion, paste white giving way to hectic red blotches on his cheeks, his eyes bulging with terror. The porch was very close now.

Behind him he heard the sudden hard crunch of snow as something leaped.

He fell on the porch steps, screaming without sound, and scrambled up them on his hands and knees, snowshoes clattering and askew behind him.

There was a slashing sound in the air and sudden pain in his leg. The ripping sound of cloth. Something else that might have—*must* have—been in his mind.

Bellowing, angry roar.

Smell of blood and evergreen.

He fell full-length on the porch, sobbing hoarsely, the rich, metallic taste of copper in his mouth. His heart was thundering in his chest. There was a small trickle of blood coming from his nose.

He had no idea how long he lay there before the lobby doors flew open and Jack ran out, wearing just his jeans and a pair of slippers. Wendy was behind him.

"Danny!" she screamed.

"Doc! Danny, for Christ's sake! What's wrong? What happened?"

Daddy was helping him up. Below the knee his snowpants were ripped open. Inside, his woollen ski sock had been ripped open and his calf had been shallowly scratched . . . as if he had tried to push his way through a closely grown evergreen hedge and the branches had clawed him.

He looked over his shoulder. Far down the lawn, past the putting green, were a number of vague, snow-cowled humps. The hedge animals. Between them and the playground. Between them and the road.

His legs gave way. Jack caught him. He began to cry.

35

THE LOBBY

He had told them everything except what had happened to him when the snow had blocked the end of the concrete ring. He couldn't bring himself to repeat that. And he didn't know the right words to express the creeping, lassitudinous sense of terror he had felt when he heard the dead aspen leaves begin to crackle furtively down there in the cold darkness. But he told them about the soft sound of snow falling in clumps. About the lion with its head and its bunched shoulders working its way up and out of the snow to chase him. He even told them about how the rabbit had turned its head to watch near the end.

The three of them were in the lobby. Jack had built a roaring blaze in the fireplace. Danny was bundled up in a blanket on the small sofa where once, a millon years ago, three nuns had sat laughing like girls while they waited for the line at the desk to thin out. He was sipping hot noodle soup from a mug. Wendy sat beside him, stroking his hair. Jack had sat on the floor, his face seeming to grow more and more still, more and more set as Danny told his story. Twice he pulled his handkerchief out of his back pocket and rubbed his sore-looking lips with it.

"Then they chased me," he finished. Jack got up and went over to the window, his back to them. He looked at his mommy. "They chased me all the way up to the porch." He was struggling to keep his voice calm, because if he stayed calm maybe they would believe him. Mr. Stenger hadn't stayed calm. He had started to cry and hadn't been able to stop so THE MEN IN THE WHITE COATS had come to take him away because if you couldn't stop crying it meant you had LOST YOUR MARBLES and when would you be back? NO ONE KNOWS. His parka and snowpants and the clotted snowshoes lay on the rug just inside the big double doors.

(I won't cry I won't let myself cry)

And he thought he could do that, but he couldn't stop shaking. He looked into the fire and waited for Daddy to say something. High yellow flames danced on the dark stone hearth. A pine-knot exploded with a bang and sparks rushed up the flue.

"Danny, come over here." Jack turned around. His face still had that pinched, deathly look. Danny didn't like to look at it.

"Jack—"

"I just want the boy over here for a minute."

Danny slipped off the sofa and came over beside his daddy.

"Good boy. Now what do you see?"

Danny had known what he would see even before he got to the window. Below the clutter of boot tracks, sled tracks, and snowshoe tracks that marked their usual exercise area, the snowfield that covered the Overlook's lawns sloped down to the topiary and the playground beyond. It was marred by two sets of tracks, one of them in a straight line from the porch to the playground, the other a long, looping line coming back up.

"Only my tracks, Daddy. But—"

"What about the hedges, Danny?"

Danny's lips began to tremble. He was going to cry. What if he couldn't stop?

(*i won't cry I Won't Cry Won't Won't WON'T*)

"All covered with snow," he whispered. "But, Daddy—"

"What? I couldn't hear you!"

"Jack, you're cross-examining him! Can't you see he's upset, he's—"

"Shut up! Well, Danny?"

"They scratched me, Daddy. My leg—"

"You must have cut your leg on the crust of the snow."

Then Wendy was between them, her face pale and angry. "What are you trying to make him do?" she asked him. "Confess to murder? *What's wrong with you?*"

The strangeness in his eyes seemed to break then. "I'm trying to help him find the difference between something real and something that was only an hallucination, that's all." He squatted by Danny so they were on an eye-to-eye level, and then hugged him tight. "Danny, it didn't really happen. Okay? It was like one of those trances you have sometimes. That's all."

"Daddy?"

"What, Dan?"

"I didn't cut my leg on the crust. There isn't any crust. It's all powdery snow. It won't even stick together to make snowballs. Remember we tried to have a snowball fight and couldn't?"

He felt his father stiffen against him. "The porch step, then."

Danny pulled away. Suddenly he had it. It had flashed into his mind all at once, the way things sometimes did, the way it had about the woman wanting to be in that gray man's pants. He stared at his father with widening eyes.

"You know I'm telling the truth," he whispered, shocked.

"Danny—" Jack's face, tightening.

"You know because you saw—"

The sound of Jack's open palm striking Danny's face was flat, not dramatic at all. The boy's head rocked back, the palmprint reddening on his cheek like a brand.

Wendy made a moaning noise.

For a moment they were still, the three of them, and then Jack grabbed for his son and said, "Danny, I'm sorry, you okay, doc?"

"You hit him, you bastard!" Wendy cried. "You dirty bastard!"

She grabbed his other arm and for a moment Danny was pulled between them.

"Oh please stop pulling me!" he screamed at them, and there was such agony in his voice that they both let go of him, and then the tears had to come and he collapsed, weeping, between the sofa and the window, his parents staring at him helplessly, the way children might stare at a toy broken in a furious tussle over to whom it belonged. In the fireplace another pineknot exploded like a hand grenade, making them all jump.

Wendy gave him baby aspirin and Jack slipped him, unprotesting, between the sheets of his cot. He was asleep in no time with his thumb in his mouth.

"I don't like that," she said. "It's a regression."

Jack didn't reply.

She looked at him softly, without anger, without a smile, either. "You want me to apologize for calling you a bastard? All right, I apologize. I'm sorry. You still shouldn't have hit him."

"I know," he muttered. "I know that. I don't know what the hell came over me."

"You promised you'd never hit him again."

He looked at her furiously, and then the fury collapsed. Suddenly, with pity and horror, she saw what Jack would look like as an old man. She had never seen him look that way before.

(?what way?)

Defeated, she answered herself. *He looks beaten.*

He said: "I always thought I could keep my promises."

She went to him and put her hands on his arm. "All right, it's over. And when the ranger comes to check us, we'll tell him we all want to go down. All right?"

"All right," Jack said, and at that moment, at least, he meant it. The same way he had always meant it on those mornings after, looking at his pale and haggard face in the bathroom mirror. *I'm going to stop, going to cut it off flat.* But morning gave way to afternoon, and in the afternoons he felt a little better. And afternoon gave way to night. As some great twentieth-century thinker had said, night must fall.

He found himself wishing that Wendy would ask him about the hedges, would ask him what Danny meant when he said *You know because you saw—* If she did, he would tell her everything. Everything. The hedges, the woman in the room, even about the fire hose that seemed to have switched positions. But where did confession stop? Could he tell her he'd thrown the magneto away, that they could all be down in Sidewinder right now if he hadn't done that?

What she said was, "Do you want tea?"

"Yes. A cup of tea would be good."

She went to the door and paused there, rubbing her forearms through her sweater. "It's my fault as much as yours," she said. "What were we doing while he was going through that . . . dream, or whatever it was?"

"Wendy—"

"We were sleeping," she said. "Sleeping like a couple of teenage kids with their itch nicely scratched."

"Stop it," he said. "It's over."

"No," Wendy answered, and gave him a strange, restless smile. "It's not over."

She went out to make tea, leaving him to keep watch over their son.

36

THE ELEVATOR

Jack awoke from a thin and uneasy sleep where huge and ill-defined shapes chased him through endless snowfields to what he first thought was another dream: darkness, and in it, a sudden mechanical jumble of noises—clicks and clanks, hummings, rattlings, snaps and whooshes.

Then Wendy sat up beside him and he knew it was no dream.

"What's that?" Her hand, cold marble, gripped his wrist. He restrained an urge to shake it off—how in the hell was he supposed to know what it was? The illuminated clock on his nightstand said it was five minutes to twelve.

The humming sound again. Loud and steady, varying the slightest bit. Followed by a clank as the humming ceased. A rattling bang. A thump. Then the humming resumed.

It was the elevator.

Danny was sitting up. "Daddy? *Daddy?*" His voice was sleepy and scared.

"Right here, doc," Jack said. "Come on over and jump in. Your mom's awake, too."

The bedclothes rustled as Danny got on the bed between them. "It's the elevator," he whispered.

"That's right," Jack said. "Just the elevator."

"What do you mean, *just?*" Wendy demanded. There was an ice-skim of hysteria on her voice. "It's the middle of the night. *Who's running it?*"

Hummmmmmm. Click/clank. Above them now. The rattle of the gate accordioning back, the bump of the doors opening and closing. Then the hum of the motor and the cables again.

Danny began to whimper.

Jack swung his feet out of bed and onto the floor. "It's probably a short. I'll check."

"Don't you dare go out of this room!"

"Don't be stupid," he said, pulling on his robe. "It's my job."

She was out of bed herself a moment later, pulling Danny with her.

"We'll go, too."

"Wendy—"

"What's wrong?" Danny asked somberly. "What's wrong, Daddy?"

Instead of answering he turned away, his face angry and set. He belted his robe around him at the door, opened it, and stepped out into the dark hall.

Wendy hesitated for a moment, and it was actually Danny who began to move first. She caught up quickly, and they went out together.

Jack hadn't bothered with the lights. She fumbled for the switch that lit the four spaced overheads in the hallway that led to the main corridor. Up ahead, Jack was already turning the corner. This time Danny found the switchplate and flicked all three switches up. The hallway leading down to the stairs and the elevator shaft came alight.

Jack was standing at the elevator station, which was flanked by benches and cigarette urns. He was standing motionless in front of the closed elevator door. In his faded tartan bathrobe and brown leather slippers with the rundown heels, his hair all in sleep corkscrews and Alfalfa cowlicks, he looked to her like an absurd twentieth-century Hamlet, an indecisive figure so mesmerized by onrushing tragedy that he was helpless to divert its course or alter it in any way.

(jesus stop thinking so crazy—)

Danny's hand had tightened painfully on her own. He was looking up at her intently, his face strained and anxious. He had been catching the drift of her thoughts, she realized. Just how much or how little of them he was getting was impossible to say, but she flushed, feeling much the same as if he had caught her in a masturbatory act.

"Come on," she said, and they went down the hall to Jack.

The hummings and clankings and thumpings were louder here, terrifying in a disconnected, benumbed way. Jack was staring at the closed door with feverish intensity. Through the diamond-shaped window in the center of the elevator door she thought she could make out the cables, thrumming slightly. The elevator clanked to a stop below them, at lobby level. They heard the doors thump open. And . . .

(party)

Why had she thought party? The word had simply jumped into her head for no reason at all. The silence in the Overlook was complete and intense except for the weird noises coming up the elevator shaft.

(must have been quite a party)

(???WHAT PARTY???)

For just a moment her mind had filled with an image so real that it seemed to be a memory . . . not just any memory but one of those you treasure, one of those you keep for very special occasions and rarely mention aloud. Lights . . . hundreds, maybe thousands of them. Lights and colors, the pop of champagne corks, a forty-piece orchestra playing Glenn Miller's "In the Mood." But Glenn Miller had gone down in his bomber before she was born, how could she have a memory of Glenn Miller?

She looked down at Danny and saw his head had cocked to one side, as if he was hearing something she couldn't hear. His face was very pale.

Thump.

The door had slid shut down there. A humming whine as the elevator began to rise. She saw the engine housing on top of the car first through the diamond-shaped window, then the interior of the car, seen through the further diamond shapes made by the brass gate. Warm yellow light from the car's overhead. It was empty. The car was empty. It was empty but

(on the night of the party they must have crowded in by the dozens, crowded the car way beyond its safety limit but of course it had been new then and all of them wearing masks)

(????WHAT MASKS????)

The car stopped above them, on the third floor. She looked at Danny. His face was all eyes. His mouth was pressed into a frightened, bloodless slit. Above them, the brass gate rattled back. The elevator door thumped open, it thumped open because it was time, the time had come, it was time to say

(Goodnight . . . goodnight . . . yes, it was lovely . . . no, i really can't stay for the unmasking . . . early to bed, early to rise . . . . oh, was that Sheila? . . . the monk? . . . isn't that witty, Sheila coming as a monk? . . . yes, goodnight . . . good)

Thump.

Gears clashed. The motor engaged. The car began to whine back down.

"Jack," she whispered. "What is it? What's wrong with it?"

"A short circuit," he said. His face was like wood. "I told you, it was a short circuit."

"I keep hearing voices in my head!" she cried. "What is it? What's wrong? I feel like I'm going crazy!"

"What voices?" He looked at her with deadly blandness.

She turned to Danny. "Did you—?"

Danny nodded slowly. "Yes. And music. Like from a long time ago. In my head."

The elevator car stopped again. The hotel was silent, creaking, deserted. Outside, the wind whined around the eaves in the darkness.

"Maybe you are both crazy," Jack said conversationally. "I don't hear a goddamned thing except that elevator having a case of the electrical hiccups. If you two want to have duet hysterics, fine. But count me out."

The elevator was coming down again.

Jack stepped to the right, where a glass-fronted box was mounted on the wall at chest height. He smashed his bare fist against it. Glass tinkled inward. Blood dripped from two of his knuckles. He reached in and took out a key with a long, smooth barrel.

"Jack, no. Don't."

"I am going to do my job. Now leave me alone, Wendy!"

She tried to grab his arm. He pushed her backward. Her feet tangled in the hem of her robe and she fell to the carpet with an ungainly thump. Danny cried out shrilly and fell on his knees beside her. Jack turned back to the elevator and thrust the key into the socket.

The elevator cables disappeared and the bottom of the car came into view in the small window. A second later Jack turned the key hard. There was a grating, screeching sound as the elevator car came to an instant standstill. For a moment the declutched motor in the basement whined even louder, and then its circuit breaker cut in and the Overlook went unearthly still. The night wind outside seemed very loud by comparison. Jack looked stupidly at the gray metal elevator door. There was three splotches of blood below the keyhole from his lacerated knuckles.

He turned back to Wendy and Danny for a moment. She was sitting up, and Danny had his arm around her. They were both staring at him carefully, as if he was a stranger they had never seen before, possibly a dangerous one. He opened his mouth, not sure what was going to come out.

"It . . . Wendy, it's my job."

She said clearly: "Fuck your job."

He turned back to the elevator, worked his fingers into the crack that ran down the right side of the door, and got it to open a little way. Then he was able to get his whole weight on it and threw the door open.

The car had stopped halfway, its floor at Jack's chest level. Warm light still spilled out on it, contrasting with the oily darkness of the shaft below.

He looked in for what seemed a long time.

"It's empty," he said then. "A short circuit, like I said." He hooked his fingers into the slot behind the door and began to pull it closed . . . then her hand was on his shoulder, surprisingly strong, yanking him away.

"Wendy!" he shouted. But she had already caught the car's bottom edge and pulled herself up enough so she could look in. Then, with a convulsive heave of her shoulder and belly muscles, she tried to boost herself all the way up. For a moment the issue was in doubt. Her feet tottered over the blackness of the shaft and one pink slipper fell from her foot and slipped out of sight.

"Mommy!" Danny screamed.

Then she was up, her cheeks flushed, her forehead as pale and shining as a spirit lamp. "What about this, Jack? Is this a short circuit?" She threw something and suddenly the hall was full of drifting confetti, red and white and blue and yellow. "Is *this*?" A green party streamer, faded to a pale pastel color with age.

"And *this*?"

She tossed it out and it came to rest on the blue-black jungle carpet, a black silk cat's-eye mask, dusted with sequins at the temples.

"Does that look like a short circuit to you, Jack?" she screamed at him.

Jack stepped slowly away from it, shaking his head mechanically back and forth. The cat's-eye mask stared up blankly at the ceiling from the confetti-strewn hallway carpet.

37

THE BALLROOM

It was the first of December.

Danny was in the east-wing ballroom, standing on an over-stuffed, high-backed wing chair, looking at the clock under glass. It stood in the center of the ballroom's high, ornamental mantelpiece, flanked by two large ivory elephants. He almost expected the elephants would begin to move and try to gore him with their tusks as he stood there, but they were moveless. They were "safe." Since the night of the elevator he had come to divide all things at the Overlook into two categories. The elevator, the basement, the playground, Room 217, and the Presidential Suite (it was Suite, not Sweet; he had seen the correct spelling in an account book Daddy had been reading at supper last night and had memorized it carefully)—those places were "unsafe." Their quarters, the lobby, and the porch were "safe." Apparently the ballroom was, too.

(The elephants are, anyway.)

He was not sure about other places and so avoided them on general principle.

He looked at the clock inside the glass dome. It was under glass because all its wheels and cogs and springs were showing. A chrome or steel track ran around the outside of these works, and directly below the clockface there was a small axis bar with a pair of meshing cogs at either end. The hands of the clock stood at quarter past XI, and although he didn't know Roman numerals he could guess by the configuration of the hands at what time the clock had stopped. The clock stood on a velvet base. It front of it, slightly distorted by the curve of the dome, was a carefully carved silver key.

He supposed that the clock was one of the things he wasn't supposed to touch, like the decorative fire-tools in their brass-bound cabinet by the lobby fireplace or the tall china highboy at the back of the dining room.

A sense of injustice and a feeling of angry rebellion suddenly rose in him and

(never mind what i'm not supposed to touch, just never mind. touched me, hasn't it? played with me, hasn't it?)

It had. And it hadn't been particularly careful not to break him, either.

Danny put his hands out, grasped the glass dome, and lifted it aside. He let one finger play over the works for a moment, the pad of his index finger denting against the cogs, running smoothly over the wheels. He picked up the silver key. For an adult it would have been uncomfortably small, but it fitted his own fingers perfectly. He placed it in the keyhole at the center of the clockface. It went firmly home with a tiny click, more felt than heard. It wound to the right, of course: clockwise.

Danny turned the key until it would turn no more and then removed it. The clock began to tick. Cogs turned. A large balance wheel rocked back and forth in semicircles. The hands were moving. If you kept your head perfectly motionless and your eyes wide open, you could see the minute hand inching along toward its meeting some forty-five minutes from now with the hour hand. At XII.

(And the Red Death held sway over all.)

He frowned, and then shook the thought away. It was a thought with no meaning or reference for him.

He reached his index finger out again and pushed the minute hand up to the hour, curious about what might happen. It obviously wasn't a cuckoo clock, but that steel rail had to have some purpose.

There was a small, ratcheting series of clicks, and then the clock began to tinkle Strauss's "Blue Danube Waltz." A punched roll of cloth no more than two inches in width began to unwind. A small series of brass strikers rose and fell. From behind the clockface two figures glided into view along the steel track, ballet dancers, on the left a girl in a fluffy skirt and white stockings, on the right a boy in a black leotard and ballet slippers. Their hands were held in arches over their heads. They came together in the middle, in front of VI.

Danny espied tiny grooves in their sides, just below their armpits. The axis bar slipped into these grooves and he heard another small click. The cogs at either end of the bar began to turn. "The Blue Danube" tinkled. The dancers' arms came down around each other. The boy flipped the girl up over his head and then whirled over the bar. They were now lying prone, the boy's head buried beneath the girl's short ballet skirt, the girl's face pressed against the center of the boy's leotard. They writhed in a mechanical frenzy.

Danny's nose wrinkled. They were kissing peepees. That made him feel sick.

A moment later and things began to run backward. The boy whirled back over the axis bar. He flipped the girl into an upright position. They seemed to nod knowingly at each other as their hands arched back over their heads. They retreated the way they had come, disappearing just as "The Blue Danube" finished. The clock began to strike a count of silver chimes.

(Midnight! Stroke of midnight!)

(Hooray for masks!)

Danny whirled on the chair, almost falling down. The ballroom was empty. Beyond the double cathedral window he could see fresh snow beginning to sift down. The huge ballroom rug (rolled up for dancing, of course), a rich tangle of red and gold embroidery, lay undisturbed on the floor. Spaced around it were small, intimate tables for two, the spidery chairs that went with each upended with legs pointing at the ceiling.

The whole place was empty.

But it wasn't really empty. Because here in the Overlook things just went on and on. Here in the Overlook all times were one. There was an endless night in August of 1945, with laughter and drinks and a chosen shining few going up and coming down in the elevator, drinking champagne and popping party favors in each other's faces. It was a not-yet-light morning in June some twenty years later and the organization hitters endlessly pumped shotgun shells into the torn and bleeding bodies of three men who went through their agony endlessly. In a room on the second floor a woman lolled in her tub and waited for visitors.

In the Overlook all things had a sort of life. It was as if the whole place had been wound up with a silver key. The clock was running. The clock was running.

He was that key, Danny thought sadly. Tony had warned him and he had just let things go on.

(I'm just five!)

he cried to some half-felt presence in the room.

(Doesn't it make any difference that I'm just five?)

There was no answer.

He turned reluctantly back to the clock.

He had been putting it off, hoping that something would happen to help him avoid trying to call Tony again, that a ranger would come, or a helicopter, or the rescue team; they always came in time on his TV programs, the people were saved. On TV the rangers and the SWAT squad and the paramedics were a friendly white force counterbalancing the confused evil that he perceived in the world; when people got in trouble they were helped out of it, they were fixed up. They did not have to help themselves out of trouble.

(Please?)

There was no answer.

No answer, and if Tony came would it be the same nightmare? The blooming, the hoarse and petulant voice, the blue-black rug like snakes? *Redrum?*

But what else?

(Please oh please)

No answer.

With a trembling sigh, he looked at the clockface. Cogs turned and meshed with other cogs. The balance wheel rocked hypnotically back and forth. And if you held your head perfectly still, you could see the minute hand creeping inexorably down from XII to V. If you held your head perfectly still you could see that—

The clockface was gone. In its place was a round black hole. It led down into forever. It began to swell. The clock was gone. The room behind it. Danny tottered and then fell into the darkness that had been hiding behind the clockface all along.

The small boy in the chair suddenly collapsed and lay in it at a crooked unnatural angle, his head thrown back, his eyes staring sightlessly at the high ballroom ceiling.

Down and down and down and down to—

—the hallway, crouched in the hallway, and he had made a wrong turn, trying to get back to the stairs he had made a wrong turn and now AND NOW—

—he saw he was in the short dead-end corridor that led only to the Presidential Suite and the booming sound was coming closer, the roque mallet whistling savagely through the air, the head of it embedding itself into the wall, cutting the silk paper, letting out small puffs of plaster dust.

(Goddammit, come out here! Take your)

But there was another figure in the hallway. Slouched nonchalantly against the wall just behind him. Like a ghost.

No, not a ghost, but all dressed in white. Dressed in whites.

(I'll find you, you goddam little whoremastering RUNT!)

Danny cringed back from the sound. Coming up the main third-floor hall now. Soon the owner of that voice would round the corner.

(Come here! Come here, you little shit!)

The figure dressed in white straightened up a little, removed a cigarette from the corner of his mouth, and plucked a shred of tobacco from his full lower lip. It was Hallorann, Danny saw. Dressed in his cook's whites instead of the blue suit he had been wearing on closing day.

"If there *is* trouble," Hallorann said, "you give a call. A big loud holler like the one that knocked me back a few minutes ago. I might hear you even way down in Florida. And if I do, I'll come on the run. I'll come on the run. I'll come on the—"

(Come now, then! Come now, come NOW! Oh Dick I need you we all need)

"—run. Sorry, but I got to run. Sorry, Danny ole kid ole doc, but I got to run. It's sure been fun, you son of a gun, but I got to hurry, I got to run."

(No!)

But as he watched, Dick Hallorann turned, put his cigarette back into the corner of his mouth, and stepped nonchalantly through the wall.

Leaving him alone.

And that was when the shadow-figure turned the corner, huge in the hallway's gloom, only the reflected red of its eyes clear.

(There you are! Now I've got you, you fuck! Now I'll teach you!)

It lurched toward him in a horrible, shambling run, the roque mallet swinging up and up and up. Danny scrambled backward, screaming, and suddenly he was through the wall and falling, tumbling over and over, down the hole, down the rabbit hole and into a land full of sick wonders.

Tony was far below him, also falling.

(I can't come anymore, Danny . . . he won't let me near you . . . none of them will let me near you . . . get Dick . . . get Dick . . .)

"Tony!" he screamed.

But Tony was gone and suddenly he was in a dark room. But not entirely dark. Muted light spilling from somewhere. It was Mommy and Daddy's bedroom. He could see Daddy's desk. But the room was a dreadful shambles. He had been in this room before. Mommy's record player overturned on the floor. Her records scattered on the rug. The mattress half off the bed. Pictures ripped from the walls. His cot lying on its side like a dead dog, the Violent Violet Volkswagen crushed to purple shards of plastic.

The light was coming from the bathroom door, half-open. Just beyond it a hand dangled limply, blood dripping from the tips of the fingers. And in the medicine cabinet mirror, the word REDRUM flashing off and on.

Suddenly a huge clock in a glass bowl materialized in front of it. There were no hands or numbers on the clockface, only a date written in red: DECEMBER 2. And then, eyes widening in horror, he saw the word REDRUM reflecting dimly from the glass dome, now reflected twice. And he saw that it spelled MURDER.

Danny Torrance screamed in wretched terror. The date was gone from the clockface. The clockface itself was gone, replaced by a circular black hole that swelled and swelled like a dilating iris. It blotted out everything and he fell forward, beginning to fall, falling, he was—

—falling off the chair.

For a moment he lay on the ballroom floor, breathing hard.

REDRUM.
MURDER.
REDRUM.
MURDER.

(The Red Death held sway over all!)
(Unmask! Unmask!)

And behind each glittering, lovely mask, the as-yet unseen face of the shape that chased him down these dark hallways, its red eyes widening, blank and homicidal.

Oh, he was afraid of what face might come to light when the time for unmasking came around at last.

(DICK!)

he screamed with all his might. His head seemed to shiver with the force of it.

(!!! OH DICK OH PLEASE PLEASE PLEASE COME   !!!)

Above him the clock he had wound with the silver key continued to mark off the seconds and minutes and hours.

PART FIVE

MATTERS OF LIFE AND DEATH

38

FLORIDA

Mrs. Hallorann's third son, Dick, dressed in his cook's whites, a Lucky Strike parked in the corner of his mouth, backed his reclaimed Cadillac limo out of its space behind the One-A Wholesale Vegetable Mart and drove slowly around the building. Masterton, part owner now but still walking with the patented shuffle he had adopted back before World War II, was pushing a bin of lettuces into the high, dark building.

Hallorann pushed the button that lowered the passenger side window and hollered: "Those avocados is too damn high, you cheapskate!"

Masterton looked back over his shoulder, grinned widely enough to expose all three gold teeth, and yelled back, "And I know exactly where you can put em, my good buddy."

"Remarks like that I keep track of, *bro*."

Masterton gave him the finger. Hallorann returned the compliment.

"Get your cukes, did you?" Masterton asked.

"I did."

"You come back early tomorrow, I gonna give you some of the nicest new potatoes you ever seen."

"I send the boy," Hallorann said. "You comin up tonight?"

"You supplyin the juice, *bro?*"

"That's a big ten-four."

"I be there. You keep that thing off the top end goin home, you hear me? Every cop between here an St. Pete knows your name."

"You know all about it, huh?" Hallorann asked, grinning.

"I know more than you'll ever learn, my man."

"Listen to this sassy nigger. Would you listen?"

"Go on, get outta here fore I start throwin these lettuces."

"Go on an throw em. I'll take anything for free."

Masterton made as if to throw one. Hallorann ducked, rolled up the window, and drove on. He was feeling fine. For the last half hour or so he had been smelling oranges, but he didn't find that queer. For the last half hour he had been in a fruit and vegetable market.

It was 4:30 P.M., EST, the first day of December, Old Man Winter settling his frostbitten rump firmly onto most of the country, but down here the men wore open-throated short-sleeve shirts and the women were in light summer dresses and shorts. On top of the First Bank of Florida building, a digital thermometer bordered with huge grapefruits was flashing 79° over and over. Thank God for Florida, Hallorann thought, mosquitoes and all.

In the back of the limo were two dozen avocados, a crate of cucumbers, ditto oranges, ditto grapefruit. Three shopping sacks filled with Bermuda onions, the sweetest vegetable a loving God ever created, some pretty good sweet peas, which would be served with the entree and come back uneaten nine times out of ten, and a single blue Hubbard squash that was strictly for personal consumption.

Hallorann stopped in the turn lane at the Vermont Street light, and when the green arrow showed he pulled out onto state highway 219, pushing up to forty and holding it there until the town began to trickle away into an exurban sprawl of gas stations, Burger Kings, and McDonalds. It was a small order today, he could have sent Baedecker after it, but Baedecker had been chafing for his chance to buy the meat, and besides, Hallorann never missed a chance to bang it back and forth with Frank Masterton if he could help it. Masterton might show up tonight to watch some TV and drink Hallorann's Bushmill's, or he might not. Either way was all right. But seeing him mattered. Every time it mattered now, because they weren't young anymore. In the last few days it seemed he was thinking of that very fact a great deal. Not so young anymore, when you got up near sixty years old (or—tell the truth and save a lie—past it) you had to start thinking about stepping out. You could go anytime. And that had been on his mind this week, not in a heavy way but as a fact. Dying was a part of living. You had to keep tuning in to that if you expected to be a whole person. And if the fact of your own death was hard to understand, at least it wasn't impossible to accept.

Why this should have been on his mind he could not have said, but his other reason for getting this small order himself was so he could step upstairs to the small office over Frank's Bar and Grill. There was a lawyer up there now (the dentist who had been there last year had apparently gone broke), a young black fellow named McIver. Hallorann had stepped in and told this McIver that he wanted to make a will, and could McIver help him out? Well, McIver asked, how soon do you want the document? Yesterday, said Hallorann, and threw his head back and laughed. Have you got anything complicated in mind? was McIver's next question. Hallorann did not. He had his Cadillac, his bank account—some nine thousand dollars—a piddling checking account, and a closet of clothes. He wanted it all to go to his sister. And if your sister predeceases you? McIver asked. Never mind, Hallorann said. If that happens, I'll make a new will. The document had been completed and signed in less than three hours—fast work for a shyster—and now resided in Hallorann's breast pocket, folded into a stiff blue envelope with the word WILL on the outside in Old English letters.

He could not have said why he had chosen this warm sunny day when he felt so well to do something he had been putting off for years, but the impulse had come on him and he hadn't said no. He was used to following his hunches.

He was pretty well out of town now. He cranked the limo up to an illegal sixty and let it ride there in the left-hand lane, sucking up most of the Petersburg-bound traffic. He knew from experience that the limo would still ride as solid as iron at ninety, and even at a hundred and twenty it didn't seem to lighten up much. But his screamin days were long gone. The thought of putting the limo up to a hundred and twenty on a straight stretch only scared him. He was getting old.

(Jesus, those oranges smell strong. Wonder if they gone over?)

Bugs splattered against the window. He dialed the radio to a Miami soul station and got the soft, wailing voice of Al Green.

> *"What a beautiful time we had together,*
> *Now it's getting late and we must leave each other . . ."*

He unrolled the window, pitched his cigarette butt out, then rolled it further down to clear out the smell of the oranges. He tapped his fingers against the wheel and hummed along under his breath. Hooked over the rearview mirror, his St. Christopher's medal swung gently back and forth.

And suddenly the smell of oranges intensified and he knew it was coming, something was coming at him. He saw his own eyes in the rearview, widening, surprised. And then it came all at once, came in a huge blast that drove out everything else: the music, the road ahead, his own absent awareness of himself as a unique human creature. It was as if someone had put a psychic gun to his head and shot him with a .45 caliber scream.

(!!! OH DICK OH PLEASE PLEASE PLEASE COME !!!)

The limo had just drawn even with a Pinto station wagon driven by a man in workman's clothes. The workman saw the limo drifting into his lane and laid on the horn. When the Cadillac continued to drift he snapped a look at the driver and saw a big black man bolt upright behind the wheel, his eyes looking vaguely upward. Later the workman told his wife that he knew it was just one of those niggery hairdos they were all wearing these days, but at the time it had looked just as if every hair on that coon's head was standing on end. He thought the black man was having a heart attack.

The workman braked hard, dropping back into a luckily-empty space behind him. The rear end of the Cadillac pulled ahead of him, still cutting in, and the workman stared with bemused horror as the long, rocket-shaped rear taillights cut into his lane no more than a quarter of an inch in front of his bumper.

The workman cut to the left, still laying on his horn, and roared around the drunkenly weaving limousine. He invited the driver of the limo to perform an illegal sex act on himself. To engage in oral congress with various rodents and birds. He articulated his own proposal that all persons of Negro blood return to their native continent. He expressed his sincere belief in the position the limo-driver's soul would occupy in the afterlife. He finished by saying that he believed he had met the limo-driver's mother in a New Orleans house of prostitution.

Then he was ahead and out of danger and suddenly aware that he had wet his pants.

In Hallorann's mind the thought kept repeating

(COME DICK PLEASE COME DICK PLEASE)

but it began to fade off the way a radio station will as you approach the limits of its broadcasting area. He became fuzzily aware that his car was tooling along the soft shoulder at better than fifty miles an hour. He guided it back onto the road, feeling the rear end fishtail for a moment before regaining the composition surface.

There was an A/W Rootbeer stand just ahead. Hallorann signaled and turned in, his heart thudding painfully in his chest, his face a sickly gray color. He pulled into a parking slot, took his handkerchief out of his pocket, and mopped his forehead with it.

(Lord God!)

"May I help you?"

The voice startled him again, even though it wasn't the voice of God but that of a cute little carhop, standing by his open window with an order pad.

"Yeah, baby, a rootbeer float. Two scoops of vanilla, okay?"

"Yes, sir." She walked away, hips rolling nicely beneath her red nylon uniform.

Hallorann leaned back against the leather seat and closed his eyes. There was nothing left to pick up. The last of it had faded out between pulling in here and giving the waitress his order. All that was left was a sick, thudding headache, as if his brain had been twisted and wrung out and hung up to dry. Like the headache he'd gotten from letting that boy Danny shine at him up there at Ullman's Folly.

But this had been much louder. Then the boy had only been playing a game with him. This had been pure panic, each word screamed aloud in his head.

He looked down at his arms. Hot sunshine lay on them but they had still goose-bumped. He had told the boy to call him if he needed help, he remembered that. And now the boy was calling.

He suddenly wondered how he could have left that boy up there at all, shining the way he did. There was bound to be trouble, maybe bad trouble.

He suddenly keyed the limo, put it in reverse, and pulled back onto the highway, peeling rubber. The waitress with the rolling hips stood in the A/W stand's archway, a tray with a rootbeer float on it in her hands.

"What is it with you, a fire?" she shouted, but Hallorann was gone.

The manager was a man named Queems, and when Hallorann came in Queems was conversing with his bookie. He wanted the four-horse at Rockaway. No, no parlay, no quinella, no exacta, no goddam futura. Just the little old four, six hundred dollars on the nose. And the Jets on Sunday. What did he mean, the Jets were playing the Bills? Didn't he know who the Jets were playing? Five hundred, seven-point spread. When Queems hung up, looking put-out, Hallorann understood how a man could make fifty grand a year running this little spa and still wear suits with shiny seats. He regarded Hallorann with an eye that was still bloodshot from too many glances into last night's Bourbon bottle.

"Problems, Dick?"

"Yes, sir, Mr. Queems, I guess so. I need three days off."

There was a package of Kents in the breast pocket of Queems's sheer yellow shirt. He reached one out of the pocket without removing the pack, tweezing it out, and bit down morosely on the patented Micronite filter. He lit it with his desktop Cricket.

"So do I," he said. "But what's on your mind?"

"I need three days," Hallorann repeated. "It's my boy."

Queems's eyes dropped to Hallorann's left hand, which was ringless.

"I been divorced since 1964," Hallorann said patiently.

"Dick, you know what the weekend situation is. We're full. To the gunnels. Even the cheap seats. We're even filled up in the Florida Room on Sunday night. So take my watch, my wallet, my pension fund. Hell, you can even take my wife if you can stand the sharp edges. But please don't ask me for time off. What is he, sick?"

"Yes, sir," Hallorann said, still trying to visualize himself twisting a cheap cloth hat and rolling his eyeballs. "He shot."

"Shot!" Queems said. He put his Kent down in an ashtray which bore the emblem of Ole Miss, of which he was a business admin graduate.

"Yes, sir," Hallorann said somberly.

"Hunting accident?"

"No, sir," Hallorann said, and let his voice drop to a lower, huskier note. "Jana, she's been livin with this truck driver. A white man. He shot my boy. He's in a hospital in Denver, Colorado. Critical condition."

"How in hell did you find out? I thought you were buying vegetables."

"Yes, sir, I was." He had stopped at the Western Union office just before coming here to reserve an Avis car at Stapleton Airport. Before leaving he had swiped a Western Union flimsy. Now he took the folded and crumpled blank form from his pocket and flashed it before Queems's bloodshot eyes. He put it back in his pocket and, allowing his voice to drop another notch, said: "Jana sent it. It was waitin in my letter box when I got back just now."

"Jesus. Jesus Christ," Queems said. There was a peculiar tight expression of concern on his face, one Hallorann was familiar with. It was as close to an expression of sympathy as a white man who thought of himself as "good with the coloreds" could get when the object was a black man or his mythical black son.

"Yeah, okay, you get going," Queems said. "Baedecker can take over for three days, I guess. The potboy can help out."

Hallorann nodded, letting his face get longer still, but the thought of the potboy helping out Baedecker made him grin inside. Even on a good day Hallorann doubted if the potboy could hit the urinal on the first squirt.

"I want to rebate back this week's pay," Hallorann said. "The whole thing. I know what a bind this puttin you in, Mr. Queems, sir."

Queems's expression got tighter still; it looked as if he might have a fishbone caught in his throat. "We can talk about that later. You go on and pack. I'll talk to Baedecker. Want me to make you a plane reservation?"

"No, sir, I'll do it."

"All right." Queems stood up, leaned sincerely forward, and inhaled a raft of ascending smoke from his Kent. He coughed heartily, his thin white face turning red. Hallorann struggled hard to keep his somber expression. "I hope everything turns out, Dick. Call when you get word."

"I'll do that."

They shook hands over the desk.

Hallorann made himself get down to the ground floor and across to the hired help's compound before bursting into rich, head-shaking laughter. He was still grinning and mopping his streaming eyes with his handkerchief when the smell of oranges came, thick and gagging, and the bolt followed it, striking him in the head, sending him back against the pink stucco wall in a drunken stagger.

(!!! PLEASE COME DICK PLEASE COME COME QUICK !!!)

He recovered a little at a time and at last felt capable of climbing the outside stairs to his apartment. He kept the latch-key under the rush-plaited doormat, and when he reached down to get it, something fell out of his inner pocket and fell to the second-floor decking with a flat thump. His mind was still so much on the voice that had shivered through his head that for a moment he could only look at the blue envelope blankly, not knowing what it was.

Then he turned it over and the word WILL stared up at him in the black spidery letters.

(Oh my God is it like that?)

He didn't know. But it could be. All week long the thought of his own ending had been on his mind like a . . . well, like a

(Go on, say it)

like a premonition.

Death? For a moment his whole life seemed to flash before him, not in a historical sense, no topography of the ups and downs that Mrs. Hallorann's third son, Dick, had lived through, but his life as it was now. Martin Luther King had told them not long before the bullet took him down to his martyr's grave that he had been to the mountain. Dick could not claim that. No mountain, but he had reached a sunny plateau after years of struggle. He had good friends. He had all the references he would ever need to get a job anywhere. When he wanted fuck, why, he could find a friendly one with no questions asked and no big shitty struggle about what it all meant. He had come to terms with his blackness—happy terms. He was up past sixty and thank God, he was cruising.

Was he going to chance the end of that—the end of *him*—for three white people he didn't even know?

But that was a lie, wasn't it?

He knew the boy. They had shared each other the way good friends can't even after forty years of it. He knew the boy and the boy knew him, because they each had a kind of searchlight in their heads, something they hadn't asked for, something that had just been given.

(Naw, you got a flashlight, he the one with the searchlight.)

And sometimes that light, that shine, seemed like a pretty nice thing. You could pick the horses, or like the boy had said, you could tell your daddy where his trunk was when it turned up missing. But that was only dressing, the sauce on the salad, and down below there was as much bitter vetch in that salad as there was cool cucumber. You could taste pain and death and tears. And now the boy was stuck in that place, and he would go. For the boy. Because, speaking to the boy, they had only been different colors when they used their mouths. So he would go. He would do what he could, because if he didn't, the boy was going to die right inside his head.

But because he was human he could not help a bitter wish that the cup had never been passed his way.

(She had started to get out and come after him.)

He had been dumping a change of clothes into an overnight bag when the thought came to him, freezing him with the

967

power of the memory as it always did when he thought of it. He tried to think of it as seldom as possible.

The maid, Delores Vickery her name was, had been hysterical. Had said some things to the other chambermaids, and worse still, to some of the guests. When the word got back to Ullman, as the silly quiff should have known it would do, he had fired her out of hand. She had come to Hallorann in tears, not about being fired, but about the thing she had seen in that second-floor room. She had gone into 217 to change the towels, she said, and there had been that Mrs. Massey, lying dead in the tub. That, of course, was impossible. Mrs. Massey had been discreetly taken away the day before and was even then winging her way back to New York—in the shipping hold instead of the first class she'd been accustomed to.

Hallorann hadn't liked Delores much, but he had gone up to look that evening. The maid was an olive-complected girl of twenty-three who waited table near the end of the season when things slowed down. She had a small shining, Hallorann judged, really not more than a twinkle; a mousy-looking man and his escort, wearing a faded cloth coat, would come in for dinner and Delores would trade one of her tables for theirs. The mousy little man would leave a picture of Alexander Hamilton under his plate, bad enough for the girl who had made the trade, but worse, Delores would crow over it. She was lazy, a goof-off in an operation run by a man who allowed no goof-offs. She would sit in a linen closet, reading a confession magazine and smoking, but whenever Ullman went on one of his unscheduled prowls (and woe to the girl he caught resting her feet) he found her working industriously, her magazine hidden under the sheets on a high shelf, her ashtray tucked safely into her uniform pocket. Yeah, Hallorann thought, she'd been a goof-off and a sloven and the other girls had resented her, but Delores had had that little twinkle. It had always greased the skids for her. But what she had seen in 217 had scared her badly enough so she was more than glad to pick up the walking papers Ullman had issued her and go.

Why had she come to him? A shine knows a shine, Hallorann thought, grinning at the pun.

So he had gone up that night and had left himself into the room, which was to be reoccupied the next day. He had used the office passkey to get in, and if Ullman had caught him with that key, he would have joined Delores Vickery on the unemployment line.

The shower curtain around the tub had been drawn. He had pushed it back, but even before he did he'd had a premonition of what he was going to see. Mrs. Massey, swollen and purple, lay soggily in the tub, which was half-full of water. He had stood looking down at her, a pulse beating thickly in his throat. There had been other things at the Overlook: a bad dream that recurred at irregular intervals—some sort of costume party and he was catering it in the Overlook's ballroom and at the shout to unmask, everybody exposed faces that were those of rotting insects—and there had been the hedge animals. Twice, maybe three times, he had (or thought he had) seen them move, ever so slightly. That dog would seem to change from his sitting-up posture to a slightly crouched one, and the lions seemed to move forward, as if menacing the little tykes on the playground. Last year in May Ullman had sent him up to the attic to look for the ornate set of firetools that now stood beside the lobby fireplace. While he had been up there the three lightbulbs strung overhead had gone out and he had lost his way back to the trapdoor. He had stumbled around for an unknown length of time, closer and closer to panic, barking his shins on boxes and bumping into things, with a stronger and stronger feeling that something was stalking him in the dark. Some great and frightening creature that had just oozed out of the woodwork when the lights went out. And when he had literally stumbled over the trapdoor's ringbolt he had hurried down as fast as he could, leaving the trap open, sooty and disheveled, with a feeling of disaster barely averted. Later Ullman had come down to the kitchen personally, to inform him he had left the attic trap door open and the lights burning up there. Did Hallorann think the guests wanted to go up there and play treasure hunt? Did he think electricity was free?

And he suspected—no, was nearly positive—that several of the guests had seen or heard things, too. In the three years he had been there, the Presidential Suite had been booked nineteen times. Six of the guests who had put up there had left the hotel early, some of them looking markedly ill. Other guests had left other rooms with the same abruptness. One night in

August of 1974, near dusk, a man who had won the Bronze and Silver Stars in Korea (that man now sat on the boards of three major corporations and was said to have personally pink-slipped a famous TV news anchorman) unaccountably went into a fit of screaming hysterics on the putting green. And there had been dozens of children during Hallorann's association with the Overlook who simply refused to go into the playground. One child had had a convulsion while playing in the concrete rings, but Hallorann didn't know if that could be attributed to the Overlook's deadly siren song or not—word had gone around among the help that the child, the only daughter of a handsome movie actor, was a medically controlled epileptic who had simply forgotten her medicine that day.

And so, staring down at the corpse of Mrs. Massey, he had been frightened but not completely terrified. It was not completely unexpected. Terror came when she opened her eyes to disclose blank silver pupils and began to grin at him. Horror came when

(she had started to get out and come after him.)

He had fled, heart racing, and had not felt safe even with the door shut and locked behind him. In fact, he admitted to himself now as he zipped the flightbag shut, he had never felt safe anywhere in the Overlook again.

And now the boy—calling, screaming for help.

He looked at his watch. It was 5:30 P.M. He went to the apartment's door, remembered it would be heavy winter now in Colorado, especially up in the mountains, and went back to his closet. He pulled his long, sheepskin-lined overcoat out of its polyurethane dry-cleaning bag and put it over his arm. It was the only winter garment he owned. He turned off all the lights and looked around. Had he forgotten anything? Yes. One thing. He took the will out of his breast pocket and slipped it into the margin of the dressing table mirror. With luck he would be back to get it.

Sure, with luck.

He left the apartment, locked the door behind him, put the key under the rush mat, and ran down the outside steps to his converted Cadillac.

•   •   •

Halfway to Miami International, comfortably away from the switchboard where Queems or Queems's toadies were known to listen in, Hallorann stopped at a shopping center Laundromat and called United Air Lines. Flights to Denver?

There was one due out at 6:36 P.M. Could the gentleman make that?

Hallorann looked at his watch, which showed 6:02, and said he could. What about vacancies on the flight?

Just let me check.

A clunking sound in his ear followed by saccharine Montavani, which was supposed to make being on hold more pleasant. It didn't. Hallorann danced from one foot to the other, alternating glances between his watch and a young girl with a sleeping baby in a hammock on her back unloading a coin-op Maytag. She was afraid she was going to get home later than she planned and the roast would burn and her husband—Mark? Mike? Matt?—would be mad.

A minute passed. Two. He had just about made up his mind to drive ahead and take his chances when the canned-sounding voice of the flight reservations clerk came back on. There was an empty seat, a cancellation. It was in first class. Did that make any difference?

No. He wanted it.

Would that be cash or credit card?

Cash, baby, cash. I've got to fly.

And the name was—?

Hallorann, two *l*'s, two *n*'s. Catch you later.

He hung up and hurried toward the door. The girl's simple thought, worry for the roast, broadcast at him over and over until he thought he would go mad. Sometimes it was like that, for no reason at all you would catch a thought, completely isolated, completely pure and clear . . . and usually completely useless.

He almost made it.

He had the limo cranked up to eighty and the airport was actually in sight when one of Florida's Finest pulled him over.

Hallorann unrolled the electric window and opened his mouth at the cop, who was flipping up pages in his citation book.

"I *know*," the cop said comfortingly. "It's a funeral in Cleveland. Your father. It's a wedding in Seattle. Your sister. A fire in San Jose that wiped out your gramp's candy store. Some really fine Cambodian Red just waiting in a terminal locker in New York City. I love this piece of road just outside the airport. Even as a kid, story hour was my favorite part of school."

"Listen, officer, my son is—"

"The only part of the story I can never figure out until the end," the officer said, finding the right page in his citation book, "is the driver's-license number of the offending motorist/storyteller and his registration information. So be a nice guy. Let me peek."

Hallorann looked into the cop's calm blue eyes, debated telling his my-son-is-in-critical-condition story anyway, and decided that would make things worse. This Smokey was no Queems. He dug out his wallet.

"Wonderful," the cop said. "Would you take them out for me, please? I just have to see how it's all going to come out in the end."

Silently, Hallorann took out his driver's license and his Florida registration and gave them to the traffic cop.

"That's very good. That's so good you win a present."

"What?" Hallorann asked hopefully.

"When I finish writing down these numbers, I'm going to let you blow up a little balloon for me."

"Oh, *Jeeeesus!*" Hallorann moaned. "Officer, my flight—"

"Shhh," the traffic cop said. "Don't be naughty."

Hallorann closed his eyes.

He got to the United desk at 6:49, hoping against hope that the flight had been delayed. He didn't even have to ask. The departure monitor over the incoming passengers desk told the story. Flight 901 for Denver, due out at 6:36 EST, had left at 6:40. Nine minutes before.

"Oh shit," Dick Hallorann said.

And suddenly the smell of oranges, heavy and cloying, he had just time to reach the men's room before it came, deafening, terrified:

(*!!! COME PLEASE COME DICK PLEASE PLEASE*
COME !!!)

39

ON THE STAIRS

One of the things they had sold to swell their liquid assets a little before moving from Vermont to Colorado was Jack's collection of two hundred old rock 'n' roll and r & b albums; they had gone at the yard sale for a dollar apiece. One of these albums, Danny's personal favorite, had been an Eddie Cochran double-record set with four pages of bound-in liner notes by Lenny Kaye. Wendy had often been struck by Danny's fascination for this one particular album by a man-boy who had lived fast and died young . . . had died, in fact, when she herself had only been ten years old.

Now, at quarter past seven (mountain time), as Dick Hallorann was telling Queems about his ex-wife's white boyfriend, she came upon Danny sitting halfway up the stairs between the lobby and the first floor, tossing a red rubber ball from hand to hand and singing one of the songs from that album. His voice was low and tuneless.

"So I climb one-two flight three flight four," Danny sang, "five flight six flight seven flight more . . . when I get to the top, I'm too tired to rock . . ."

She came around him, sat down on one of the stair risers, and saw that his lower lip had swelled to twice its size and that there was dried blood on his chin. Her heart took a frightened leap in her chest, but she managed to speak neutrally.

What happened, doc?" she asked, although she was sure she knew. Jack had hit him. Well, of course. That came next, didn't it? The wheels of progress; sooner or later they took you back to where you started from.

"I called Tony," Danny said. "In the ballroom. I guess I fell off the chair. It doesn't hurt anymore. Just feels . . . like my lip's too big."

"Is that what really happened?" she asked, looking at him, troubled.

"Daddy didn't do it," he answered. "Not today."

She gazed at him, feeling eerie. The ball traveled from one

hand to the other. He had read her mind. Her son had read her mind.

"What . . . what did Tony tell you, Danny?"

"It doesn't matter." His face was calm, his voice chillingly indifferent.

"Danny—" She gripped his shoulder, harder than she had intended. But he didn't wince, or even try to shake her off.

(Oh we are wrecking this boy. It's not just Jack, it's me too, and maybe it's not even just us, Jack's father, my mother, are they here too? Sure, why not? The place is lousy with ghosts anyway, why not a couple more? Oh Lord in heaven he's like one of those suitcases they show on TV, run over, dropped from planes, going through factory crushers. Or a Timex watch. Takes a licking and keeps on ticking. Oh Danny I'm so sorry)

"It doesn't matter," he said again. The ball went from hand to hand. "Tony can't come anymore. They won't let him. He's licked."

"Who won't?"

"The people in the hotel," he said. He looked at her then, and his eyes weren't indifferent at all. They were deep and scared. "And the . . . the *things* in the hotel. There's all kinds of them. The hotel is *stuffed* with them."

"You can see—"

"I don't want to see," he said low, and then looked back at the rubber ball, arcing from hand to hand. "But I can hear them sometimes, late at night. They're like the wind, all sighing together. In the attic. The basement. The rooms. All over. I thought it was my fault, because of the way I am. The key. The little silver key."

"Danny, don't . . . don't upset yourself this way."

"But it's *him* too," Danny said. "It's Daddy. And it's you. It wants all of us. It's tricking Daddy, it's fooling him, trying to make him think it wants him the most. It wants me the most, but it will take all of us."

"If only that snowmobile—"

"They wouldn't let him," Danny said in that same low voice. "They made him throw part of it away into the snow. Far away. I dreamed it. And he knows that woman really is in 217." He looked at her with his dark, frightened eyes. "It doesn't matter whether you believe me or not."

She slipped an arm around him.

"I believe you. Danny, tell me the truth. Is Jack . . . is he going to try to hurt us?"

"They'll try to make him," Danny said. "I've been calling for Mr. Hallorann. He said if I ever needed him to just call. And I have been. But it's awful hard. It makes me tired. And the worst part is I don't know if he's hearing me or not. I don't think he can call back because it's too far for him. And I don't know if it's too far for me or not. Tomorrow—"

"What about tomorrow?"

He shook his head. "Nothing."

"Where is he now?" she asked. "Your daddy?"

"He's in the basement. I don't think he'll be up tonight."

She stood up suddenly. "Wait right here for me. Five minutes."

The kitchen was cold and deserted under the overhead fluorescent bars. She went to the rack where the carving knives hung from their magnetized strips. She took the longest and sharpest, wrapped it in a dish towel, and left the kitchen, turning off the lights as she went.

Danny sat on the stairs, his eyes following the course of his red rubber ball from hand to hand. He sang: "She lives on the twentieth floor uptown, the elevator is broken down. So I walk one-two flight three flight four . . ."

(—Lou, Lou, skip to m' Lou—)

His singing broke off. He listened.

(—Skip to m' Lou my daarlin'—)

The voice was in his head, so much a part of him, so frighteningly close that it might have been a part of his own thoughts. It was soft and infinitely sly. Mocking him. Seeming to say:

(Oh yes, you'll like it here. Try it, you'll like it. Try it, you'll liiiiiike it—)

Now his ears were open and he could hear them again, the gathering, ghosts or spirits or maybe the hotel itself, a dreadful funhouse where all the sideshows ended in death, where all the specially painted boogies were really alive, where hedges walked, where a small silver key could start the obscenity. Soft and sighing, rustling like the endless winter wind that played under the eaves at night, the deadly lulling wind the summer tourists never heard. It was like the somnolent hum of summer wasps in a ground nest, sleepy, deadly, beginning to wake up. They were ten thousand feet high.

(Why is a raven like a writing desk? The higher the fewer, of course! Have another cup of tea!)

It was a living sound, but not voices, not breath. A man of a philosophical bent might have called it the sound of souls. Dick Hallorann's Nana, who had grown up on southern roads in the years before the turn of the century, would have called it ha'ants. A psychic investigator might have had a long name for it— psychic echo, psychokinesis, a telesmic sport. But to Danny it was only the sound of the hotel, the old monster, creaking steadily and ever more closely around them: halls that now stretched back through time as well as distance, hungry shadows, unquiet guests who did not rest easy.

In the darkened ballroom the clock under glass struck seven-thirty with a single musical note.

A hoarse voice, made brutal with drink, shouted: *"Unmask and let's fuck!"*

Wendy, halfway across the lobby, jerked to a standstill.

She looked at Danny on the stairs, still tossing the ball from hand to hand. "Did you hear something?"

Danny only looked at her and continued to toss the ball from hand to hand.

There would be little sleep for them that night, although they slept together behind a locked door.

And in the dark, his eyes open, Danny thought:

(He wants to be one of them and live forever. That's what he wants.)

Wendy thought:

(If I have to, I'll take him further up. If we're going to die I'd rather do it in the mountains.)

She had left the butcher knife, still wrapped in the towel, under the bed. She kept her hand close to it. They dozed off and on. The hotel creaked around them. Outside snow had begun to spit down from a sky like lead.

40

IN THE BASEMENT

(!!! The boiler the goddam boiler !!!)

The thought came into Jack Torrance's mind full-blown, edged in bright, warning red. On its heels, the voice of Watson:

(If you forget it'll just creep an creep and like as not you an your fambly will end up on the fuckin moon . . . she's rated for two-fifty but she'd blow long before that now . . . I'd be scared to come down and stand next to her at a hundred and eighty.)

He'd been down here all night, poring over the boxes of old records, possessed by a frantic feeling that time was getting short and he would have to hurry. Still the vital clues, the connections that would make everything clear, eluded him. His fingers were yellow and grimy with crumbling old paper. And he'd become so absorbed he hadn't checked the boiler once. He'd dumped it the previous evening around six o'clock, when he first came down. It was now . . .

He looked at his watch and jumped up, kicking over a stack of old invoices.

Christ, it was quarter of five in the morning.

Behind him, the furnace kicked on. The boiler was making a groaning, whistling sound.

He ran to it. His face, which had become thinner in the last month or so, was now heavily shadowed with beardstubble and he had a hollow concentration-camp look.

The boiler pressure gauge stood at two hundred and ten pounds per square inch. He fancied he could almost see the sides of the old patched and welded boiler heaving out with the lethal strain.

(She creeps . . . I'd be scared to come down and stand next to her at a hundred and eighty . . .)

Suddenly a cold and tempting inner voice spoke to him.

(Let it go. Go get Wendy and Danny and get the fuck out of here. Let it blow sky-high.)

He could visualize the explosion. A double thunderclap that would first rip the heart from this place, then the soul. The boiler would go with an orange-violet flash that would rain hot and burning shrapnel all over the cellar. In his mind he could see the redhot trinkets of metal careening from floor to walls to ceiling like strange billiard balls, whistling jagged death through the air. Some of them, surely, would whizz right through that stone arch, light on the old papers on the other side, and they would burn merry hell. Destroy the secrets, burn the clues, it's a mystery no living hand will ever solve. Then the gas explosion, a great rumbling crackle of flame, a giant pilot light that would turn the whole center of the hotel into a broiler. Stairs and hallways and ceilings and rooms aflame like the castle in the last reel of a Frankenstein movie. The flames spreading into the wings, hurrying up the black-and-blue-twined carpets like eager guests. The silk wallpaper charring and curling. There were no sprinklers, only those outmoded hoses and no one to use them. And there wasn't a fire engine in the world that could get here before late March. Burn, baby, burn. In twelve hours there would be nothing left but the bare bones.

The needle on the gauge had moved up to two-twelve. The boiler was creaking and groaning like an old woman trying to get out of bed. Hissing jets of steam had begun to play around the edges of old patches; beads of solder had begun to sizzle.

He didn't see, he didn't hear. Frozen with his hand on the valve that would dump off the pressure and damp the fire, Jack's eyes glittered from their sockets like sapphires.

(It's my last chance.)

The only thing not cashed in now was the life insurance policy he had taken out jointly with Wendy in the summer between his first and second years at Stovington. Forty-thousand-dollar death benefit, double indemnity if he or she died in a train crash, a plane crash, or a fire. Seven-come-eleven, die the secret death and win a hundred dollars.

(A fire . . . eighty thousand dollars.)

They would have time to get out. Even if they were sleeping, they would have time to get out. He believed that. And he didn't think the hedges or anything else would try to hold them back if the Overlook was going up in flames.

(Flames.)

The needle inside the greasy, almost opaque dial had danced up to two hundred and fifteen pounds per square inch.

Another memory occurred to him, a childhood memory. There had been a wasps' nest in the lower branches of their apple tree behind the house. One of his older brothers—he couldn't remember which one now—had been stung while swinging in the old tire Daddy had hung from one of the tree's lower branches. It had been late summer, when wasps tend to be at their ugliest.

Their father, just home from work, dressed in his whites, the smell of beer hanging around his face in a fine mist, had gathered all three boys, Brett, Mike, and little Jacky, and told them he was going to get rid of the wasps.

"Now watch," he had said, smiling and staggering a little (he hadn't been using the cane then, the collision with the milk truck was years in the future). "Maybe you'll learn something. My father showed me this."

He had raked a big pile of rain-dampened leaves under the branch where the wasps' nest rested, a deadlier fruit than the shrunken but tasty apples their tree usually produced in late September, which was then still half a month away. He lit the leaves. The day was clear and windless. The leaves smoldered but didn't really burn, and they made a smell—a fragrance— that had echoed back to him each fall when men in Saturday pants and light Windbreakers raked leaves together and burned them. A sweet smell with a bitter undertone, rich and evocative. The smoldering leaves produced great rafts of smoke that drifted up to obscure the nest.

Their father had let the leaves smolder all that afternoon, drinking beer on the porch and dropping the empty Black Label cans into his wife's plastic floorbucket while his two older sons flanked him and little Jacky sat on the steps at his feet, playing with his Bolo Bouncer and singing monotonously over and over: "Your cheating heart . . . will make you weep . . . your cheating heart . . . is gonna tell on you."

At quarter of six, just before supper, Daddy had gone out to the apple tree with his sons grouped carefully behind him. In one hand he had a garden hoe. He knocked the leaves apart, leaving little clots spread around to smolder and die. Then he reached the hoe handle up, weaving and blinking, and after two or three tries he knocked the nest to the ground.

The boys fled for the safety of the porch, but Daddy only stood over the nest, swaying and blinking down at it. Jacky crept back to see. A few wasps were crawling sluggishly over the paper terrain of their property, but they were not trying to fly. From the inside of the nest, the black and alien place, came a never-to-be-forgotten sound: a low, somnolent buzz, like the sound of high-tension wires.

"Why don't they try to sting you, Daddy?" he had asked.

"The smoke makes em drunk, Jacky. Go get my gascan."

He ran to fetch it. Daddy doused the nest with amber gasoline.

"Now step away, Jacky, unless you want to lose your eyebrows."

He had stepped away. From somewhere in the voluminous folds of his white overblouse, Daddy had produced a wooden kitchen match. He lit it with his thumbnail and flung it onto the nest. There had been a white-orange explosion, almost soundless in its ferocity. Daddy had stepped away, cackling wildly. The wasps' nest had gone up in no time.

"Fire," Daddy had said, turning to Jacky with a smile. "Fire will kill anything."

After supper the boys had come out in the day's waning light to stand solemnly around the charred and blackened nest. From the hot interior had come the sound of wasp bodies popping like corn.

The pressure gauge stood at two-twenty. A low iron wailing sound was building up in the guts of the thing. Jets of steam stood out erect in a hundred places like porcupine quills.

(Fire will kill anything.)

Jack suddenly started. He had been dozing off . . . and he had almost dozed himself right into kingdom come. What in God's name had he been thinking of? Protecting the hotel was his job. He was the caretaker.

A sweat of terror sprang to his hands so quickly that at first he missed his grip on the large valve. Then he curled his fingers around its spokes. He whirled it one turn, two, three. There was a giant hiss of steam, dragon's breath. A warm tropical mist rose from beneath the boiler and veiled him. For a moment he could no longer see the dial but thought he must have waited too long; the groaning, clanking sound inside the boiler increased, followed by a series of heavy rattling sounds and the wrenching screech of metal.

When some of the steam blew away he saw that the pressure gauge had dropped back to two hundred and was still sinking. The jets of steam escaping around the soldered patches began to lose their force. The wrenching, grinding sounds began to diminish.

One-ninety . . . one-eighty . . . one seventy-five . . .

(He was going downhill, going ninety miles an hour, when the whistle broke into a scream—)

But he didn't think it would blow now. The press was down to one-sixty.

(—they found him in the wreck with his hand on the throttle, he was scalded to death by the steam.)

He stepped away from the boiler, breathing hard, trembling. He looked at his hands and saw that blisters were already rising on his palms. Hell with the blisters, he thought, and laughed shakily. He had almost died with his hand on the throttle, like Casey the engineer in "The Wreck of the Old 97." Worse still, he would have killed the Overlook. The final crashing failure. He had failed as a teacher, a writer, a husband, and a father. He had even failed as a drunk. But you couldn't do much better in the old failure category than to blow up the building you were supposed to be taking care of. And this was no ordinary building, By no means.

Christ, but he needed a drink.

The press had dropped down to eighty psi. Cautiously, wincing a little at the pain in his hands, he closed the dump valve again. But from now on the boiler would have to be watched more closely than ever. It might have been seriously weakened. He wouldn't trust it at more than one hundred psi for the rest of the winter. And if they were a little chilly, they would just have to grin and bear it.

He had broken two of the blisters. His hands throbbed like rotten teeth.

A drink. A drink would fix him up, and there wasn't a thing in the goddamn house besides cooking sherry. At this point a drink would be medicinal. That was just it, by God. An anesthetic. He had done his duty and now he could use a little anesthetic— something stronger than Excedrin. But there was nothing.

He remembered bottles glittering in the shadows.

He had saved the hotel. The hotel would want to reward him. He felt sure of it. He took his handkerchief out of his back pocket and went to the stairs. He rubbed at his mouth. Just a little drink. Just one. To ease the pain.

He had served the Overlook, and now the Overlook would serve him. He was sure of it. His feet on the stair risers were quick and eager, the hurrying steps of a man who has come home from a long and bitter war. It was 5:20 A.M., MST.

41

DAYLIGHT

Danny awoke with a muffled gasp from a terrible dream. There had been an explosion. A fire. The Overlook was burning up. He and his mommy were watching it from the front lawn.

Mommy had said: "Look, Danny, look at the hedges."

He looked at them and they were all dead. Their leaves had turned a suffocant brown. The tightly packed branches showed through like the skeletons of half-dismembered corpses. And then his daddy had burst out of the Overlook's big double doors, and he was burning like a torch. His clothes were in flames, his skin had acquired a dark and sinister tan that was growing darker by the moment, his hair was a burning bush.

That was when he woke up, his throat tight with fear, his hands clutching at the sheet and blankets. Had he screamed? He looked over at his mother. Wendy lay on her side, the blankets up to her chin, a sheaf of straw-colored hair lying against her cheek. She looked like a child herself. No, he hadn't screamed.

Lying in bed, looking upward, the nightmare began to drain away. He had a curious feeling that some great tragedy

(fire? explosion?)

had been averted by inches. He let his mind drift out, searching for his daddy, and found him standing somewhere below. In the lobby. Danny pushed a little harder, trying to get inside his father. It was not good. Because Daddy was thinking about the Bad Thing. He was thinking how

(good just one or two would be i don't care sun's over the yardarm somewhere in the world remember how we used to say that al? gin and tonic bourbon with just a dash of bitters scotch and soda rum and coke tweedledum and tweedledee a drink for me and a drink for thee the martians have landed somewhere in the world princeton or houston or stokely on carmichael some fucking place after all tis the season and none of us are)

(GET OUT OF HIS MIND, YOU LITTLE SHIT!)

He recoiled in terror from that mental voice, his eyes widening, his hands tightening into claws on the counterpane. It hadn't been the voice of his father but a clever mimic. A voice he knew. Hoarse, brutal, yet underpointed with a vacuous sort of humor.

Was it so near, then?

He threw the covers back and swung his feet out onto the floor. He kicked his slippers out from under the bed and put them on. He went to the door and pulled it open and hurried up to the main corridor, his slippered feet whispering on the nap of the carpet runner. He turned the corner.

There was a man on all fours halfway down the corridor, between him and the stairs.

Danny froze.

The man looked up at him. His eyes were tiny and red. He was dressed in some sort of silvery, spangled costume. A dog costume, Danny realized. Protruding from the rump of this strange creation was a long and floppy tail with a puff on the end. A zipper ran up the back of the costume to the neck. To the left of him was a dog's or wolf's head, blank eyesockets above the muzzle, the mouth open in a meaningless snarl that showed the rug's black and blue pattern between fangs that appeared to be papier-mâché.

The man's mouth and chin and cheeks were smeared with blood.

He began to growl at Danny. He was grinning, but the growl was real. It was deep in his throat, a chilling primitive sound. Then he began to bark. His teeth were also stained red. He began to crawl toward Danny, dragging his boneless tail behind him. The costume dog's head lay unheeded on the carpet, glaring vacantly over Danny's shoulder.

"Let me by," Danny said.

"I'm going to eat you, little boy," the dogman answered, and suddenly a fusillade of barks came from his grinning mouth. They were human imitations, but the savagery in them was real. The man's hair was dark, greased with sweat from his confining costume. There was a mixture of scotch and champagne on his breath.

Danny flinched back but didn't run. "Let me by."

"Not by the hair of my chinny-chin-chin," the dogman replied. His small red eyes were fixed attentively on Danny's face. He continued to grin. "I'm going to eat you up, little boy. And I think I'll start with your plump little *cock.*"

He began to prance skittishly forward, making little leaps and snarling.

Danny's nerve broke. He fled back into the short hallway that led to their quarters, looking back over his shoulder. There was a series of mixed howls and barks and growls, broken by slurred mutterings and giggles.

Danny stood in the hallway, trembling.

"Get it up!" the drunken dogman cried out from around the corner. His voice was both violent and despairing. "Get it up, Harry you bitch-bastard! I don't care how many casinos and airlines and movie companies you own! I know what you like in the privacy of your own h-home! Get it up! I'll *huff* . . . and I'll *puff* . . . until Harry Derwent's *all bloowwwwn down!*" He ended with a long, chilling howl that seemed to turn into a scream of rage and pain just before it dwindled off.

Danny turned apprehensively to the closed bedroom door at the end of the hallway and walked quietly down to it. He opened it and poked his head through. His mommy was sleeping in exactly the same position. No one was hearing this but him.

He closed the door softly and went back up to the intersection of their corridor and the main hall, hoping the dogman would be gone, the way the blood on the walls of the Presidential Suite had been gone. He peeked around the corner carefully.

The man in the dog costume was still there. He had put his head back on and was now prancing on all fours by the stairwell, chasing his tail. He occasionally leaped off the rug and came down making dog grunts in his throat.

"Woof! Woof! Bowwowwow! *Grrrrrr!*"

These sounds came hollowly out of the mask's stylized snarling mouth, and among them were sounds that might have been sobs or laughter.

Danny went back to the bedroom and sat down on his cot, covering his eyes with his hands. The hotel was running things now. Maybe at first the things that had happened had only been accidents. Maybe at first the things he had seen really *were* like scary pictures that couldn't hurt him. But now the hotel was controlling those things and they *could* hurt. The Overlook hadn't wanted him to go to his father. That might spoil all the fun. So it had put the dogman in his way, just as it had put the hedge animals between them and the road.

But his daddy could come here. And sooner or later his daddy would.

He began to cry, the tears rolling silently down his cheeks. It was too late. They were going to die, all three of them, and when the Overlook opened next late spring, they would be right here to greet the guests along with the rest of the spooks. The woman in the tub. The dogman. The horrible dark thing that had been in the cement tunnel. They would be—

(Stop! Stop that now!)

He knuckled the tears furiously from his eyes. He would try as hard as he could to keep that from happening. Not to himself, not to his daddy and mommy. He would try as hard as he could.

He closed his eyes and sent his mind out in a high, hard crystal bolt.

*(!!! DICK PLEASE COME QUICK WE'RE IN BAD
TROUBLE DICK WE NEED)*

And suddenly, in the darkness behind his eyes the thing that chased him down the Overlook's dark halls in his dreams was *there*, right *there*, a huge creature dressed in white, its prehistoric club raised over its head:

"I'll make you stop it! You goddam puppy! I'll make you stop it because I am your FATHER!"

"No!" He jerked back to the reality of the bedroom, his eyes wide and staring, the screams tumbling helplessly from his mouth as his mother bolted awake, clutching the sheet to her breasts.

"No Daddy no no no—"

And they both heard the vicious, descending swing of the invisible club, cutting the air somewhere very close, then fading away to silence as he ran to his mother and hugged her, trembling like a rabbit in a snare.

The Overlook was not going to let him call Dick. That might spoil the fun, too.

They were alone.

Outside the snow came harder, curtaining them off from the world.

42

MID-AIR

Dick Hallorann's flight was called at 6:45 A.M., EST, and the boarding clerk held him by Gate 31, shifting his flight bag nervously from hand to hand, until the last call at 6:55. They were both looking for a man named Carlton Vecker, the only passenger on TWA's Flight 196 from Miami to Denver who hadn't checked in.

"Okay," the clerk said, and issued Hallorann a blue first-class boarding pass. "You lucked out. You can board, sir."

Hallorann hurried up the enclosed boarding ramp and let the mechanically grinning stewardess tear his pass off and give him the stub.

"We're serving breakfast on the flight," the stew said. "If you'd like—"

"Just coffee, babe," he said, and went down the aisle to a seat in the smoking section. He kept expecting the no-show Vecker to pop through the door like a jack-in-the-box at the last second. The woman in the seat by the window was reading *You Can Be Your Own Best Friend* with a sour, unbelieving expression on her face. Hallorann buckled his seat belt and then wrapped his large black hands around the seat's armrests and promised the absent Carlton Vecker that it would take him and five strong TWA flight attendants to drag him out of his seat.

He kept his eye on his watch. It dragged off the minutes to the 7:00 takeoff time with maddening slowness.

At 7:05 the stewardess informed them that there would be a slight delay while the ground crew rechecked one of the latches on the cargo door.

"Shit for brains," Dick Hallorann muttered.

The sharp-faced woman turned her sour, unbelieving expression on him and then went back to her book.

He had spent the night at the airport, going from counter to counter—United, American, TWA, Continental, Braniff—haunting the ticket clerks. Sometime after midnight, drinking his eighth or ninth cup of coffee in the canteen, he had decided he was being an asshole to have taken this whole thing on his own shoulders. There were authorities. He had gone down to the nearest bank of telephones, and after talking to three different operators, he had gotten the emergency number of the Rocky Mountain National Park Authority.

The man who answered the telephone sounded utterly worn out. Hallorann had given a false name and said there was trouble at the Overlook Hotel, west of Sidewinder. Bad trouble.

He was put on hold.

The ranger (Hallorann assumed he was a ranger) came back on in about five minutes.

"They've got a CB," the ranger said.

"Sure they've got a CB," Hallorann said.

"We haven't had a Mayday call from them."

"Man, that don't *matter*. They—"

"Exactly what kind of trouble are they in, Mr. Hall?"

"Well, there's a family. The caretaker and his family. I think maybe he's gone a little nuts, you know. I think maybe he might hurt his wife and his little boy."

"May I ask how you've come by this information, sir?"

Hallorann closed his eyes. "What's your name, fellow?"

"Tom Staunton, sir."

"Well, Tom, I *know*. Now I'll be just as straight with you as I can be. There's bad trouble up there. Maybe killin bad, do you dig what I'm sayin?"

"Mr. Hall, I really have to know how you—"

"Look," Hallorann had said. "I'm telling you I *know*. A few years back there was a fellow up there name of Grady. He killed his wife and his two daughters and then pulled the string on himself. I'm telling you it's going to happen again if you guys don't haul your asses out there and stop it!"

"Mr. Hall, you're not calling from Colorado."

"No. But what difference—"

"If you're not in Colorado, you're not in CB range of the Overlook Hotel. If you're not in CB range you can't possibly have been in contact with the, uh . . . ." Faint rattle of papers. "The Torrance family. While I had you on hold I tried to telephone. It's out, which is nothing unusual. There are still twenty-five miles of aboveground telephone lines between the hotel and the Sidewinder switching station. My conclusion is that you must be some sort of crank."

"Oh man, you stupid . . ." But his despair was too great to find a noun to go with the adjective. Suddenly, illumination. "Call them!" he cried.

"Sir?"

"You got the CB, they got the CB. So call them! Call them and ask them what's up!"

There was a brief silence, and the humming of long-distance wires.

"You tried that too, didn't you?" Hallorann asked. "That's why you had me on hold so long. You tried the phone and then you tried the CB and you didn't get *nothing* but you don't think nothing's wrong . . . what are you guys doing up there? Sitting on your asses and playing gin rummy?"

"No, we are not," Staunton said angrily. Hallorann was relieved at the sound of anger in the voice. For the first time he felt he was speaking to a man and not to a recording. "I'm the only man here, sir. Every other ranger in the park, *plus* game wardens, *plus* volunteers, are up in Hasty Notch, risking their lives because three stupid assholes with six months' experience decided to try the north face of King's Ram. They're stuck halfway up there and maybe they'll get down and maybe they won't. There are two choppers up there and the men who are flying them are risking their lives because it's night here and it's starting to snow. So if you're still having trouble putting it all together, I'll give you a hand with it. Number one, I don't have anybody to send to the Overlook. Number two, the Overlook isn't a priority here—what happens in the park is a priority.

Number three, by daybreak neither one of those choppers will be able to fly because it's going to snow like crazy, according to the National Weather Service. Do you understand the situation?"

"Yeah," Hallorann had said softly. "I understand."

"Now my guess as to why I couldn't raise them on the CB is very simple. I don't know what time it is where you are, but out here it's nine-thirty. I think they may have turned it off and gone to bed. Now if you—"

"Good luck with your climbers, man," Hallorann said. "But I want you to know that they are not the only ones who are stuck up high because they didn't know what they were getting into."

He had hung up the phone.

At 7:20 A.M. the TWA 747 backed lumberingly out of its stall, turned, and rolled out toward the runway. Hallorann let out a long, soundless exhale. Carlton Vecker, wherever you are, eat your heart out.

Flight 196 parted company with the ground at 7:28, and at 7:31, as it gained altitude, the thought-pistol went off in Dick Hallorann's head again. His shoulders hunched uselessly against the smell of oranges and then jerked spasmodically. His forehead wrinkled, his mouth drew down in a grimace of pain.

(!!! *DICK PLEASE COME QUICK WE'RE IN BAD TROUBLE DICK WE NEED*)

And that was all. It was suddenly gone. No fading out this time. The communication had been chopped off cleanly, as if with a knife. It scared him. His hands, still clutching the seat rests, had gone almost white. His mouth was dry. Something had happened to the boy. He was sure of it. If anyone had hurt that little child—

"Do you always react so violently to takeoffs?"

He looked around. It was the woman in the horn-rimmed glasses.

"It wasn't that," Hallorann said. "I've got a steel plate in my head. From Korea. Every now and then it gives me a twinge. Vibrates, don't you know. Scrambles the signal."

"Is that so?"

"Yes, ma'am."

"It is the line soldier who ultimately pays for any foreign intervention," the sharp-faced woman said grimly.

"Is that so?"

"It is. This country must swear off its dirty little wars. The CIA has been at the root of every dirty little war America has fought in this century. The CIA and dollar diplomacy."

She opened her book and began to read. The NO SMOKING sign went off. Hallorann watched the receding land and wondered if the boy was all right. He had developed an affectionate feeling for that boy, although his folks hadn't seemed all that much.

He hoped to God they were watching out for Danny.

43

DRINKS ON THE HOUSE

Jack stood in the dining room just outside the batwing doors leading into the Colorado Lounge, his head cocked, listening. He was smiling faintly.

Around him, he could hear the Overlook Hotel coming to life.

It was hard to say just how he knew, but he guessed it wasn't greatly different from the perceptions Danny had from time to time . . . like father, like son. Wasn't that how it was popularly expressed?

It wasn't a perception of sight or sound, although it was very near to those things, separated from those senses by the filmiest of perceptual curtains. It was as if another Overlook now lay scant inches beyond this one, separated from the real world (if there is such a thing as a "real world," Jack thought) but gradually coming into balance with it. He was reminded of the 3-D movies he'd seen as a kid. If you looked at the screen without the special glasses, you saw a double image—the sort of thing he was feeling now. But when you put the glasses on, it made sense.

All the hotel's eras were together now, all but this current one, the Torrance Era. And this would be together with the rest very soon now. That was good. That was very good.

He could almost hear the self-important *ding!ding!* of the silverplated bell on the registration desk, summoning bellboys to the front as men in the fashionable flannels of the 1920s checked in and men in fashionable 1940s double-breasted pin-stripes checked out. There would be three nuns sitting in front of the fireplace as they waited for the check-out line to thin, and standing behind them, nattily dressed with diamond stick-pins holding their blue-and-white-figured ties, Charles Grondin and Vito Gienelli discussed profit and loss, life and death. There was a dozen trucks in the loading bays out back, some laid one over the other like bad time exposures. In the east-wing ballroom, a dozen different business conventions were going on at the same time within temporal centimeters of each other. There was a costume ball going on. There were soirees, wedding receptions, birthday and anniversary parties. Men talking about Neville Chamberlain and the Archduke of Austria. Music. Laughter. Drunkenness. Hysteria. Little love, not here, but a steady undercurrent of sensuousness. And he could almost hear all of them together, drifting through the hotel and making a graceful cacophony. In the dining room where he stood, breakfast, lunch, and dinner for seventy years were all being served simultaneously just behind him. He could almost . . . no, strike the *almost*. He *could* hear them, faintly as yet, but clearly—the way one can hear thunder miles off on a hot summer's day. He could hear all of them, the beautiful strangers. He was becoming aware of them as they must have been aware of him from the very start.

All the rooms of the Overlook were occupied this morning.

A full house.

And beyond the batwings, a low murmur of conversation drifted and swirled like lazy cigarette smoke. More sophisticated, more private. Low, throaty female laughter, the kind that seems to vibrate in a fairy ring around the viscera and the genitals. The sound of a cash register, its window softly lighted in the warm halfdark, ringing up the price of a gin rickey, a Manhattan, a depression bomber, a sloe gin fizz, a zombie. The jukebox, pouring out its drinkers' melodies, each one overlapping the other in time.

He pushed the batwings open and stepped through.

"Hello, boys," Jack Torrance said softly. "I've been away but now I'm back."

"Good evening, Mr. Torrance," Lloyd said, genuinely pleased. "It's good to see you."

"It's good to be back, Lloyd," he said gravely, and hooked his leg over a stool between a man in a sharp blue suit and a bleary-eyed woman in a black dress who was peering into the depths of a singapore sling.

"What will it be, Mr. Torrance?"

"Martini," he said with great pleasure. He looked at the backbar with its rows of dimly gleaming bottles, capped with their silver siphons. Jim Beam. Wild Turkey. Gilby's. Sharrod's Private Label. Toro. Seagram's. And home again.

"One large martian, if you please," he said. "They've landed somewhere in the world, Lloyd." He took his wallet out and laid a twenty carefully on the bar.

As Lloyd made his drink, Jack looked over his shoulder. Every booth was occupied. Some of the occupants were dressed in costumes . . . a woman in gauzy harem pants and a rhinestone-sparkled brassiere, a man with a foxhead rising slyly out of his evening dress, a man in a silvery dog outfit who was tickling the nose of a woman in a sarong with the puff on the end of his long tail, to the general amusement of all.

"No charge to you, Mr. Torrance," Lloyd said, putting the drink down on Jack's twenty. "Your money is no good here. Orders from the manager."

"Manager?"

A faint unease came over him; nevertheless he picked up the martini glass and swirled it, watching the olive at the bottom bob slightly in the drink's chilly depths.

"Of course. The manager." Lloyd's smile broadened, but his eyes were socketed in shadow and his skin was horribly white, like the skin of a corpse. "Later he expects to see to your son's well-being himself. He is very interested in your son. Danny is a talented boy."

The juniper fumes of the gin were pleasantly maddening, but they also seemed to be blurring his reason. Danny? What was all of this about Danny? And what was he doing in a bar with a drink in his hand?

He had TAKEN THE PLEDGE. He had GONE ON THE WAGON. He had SWORN OFF.

What could they want with his son? What could they want with Danny? Wendy and Danny weren't in it. He tried to see into Lloyd's shadowed eyes, but it was too dark, too dark, it was like trying to read emotion into the empty orbs of a skull.

(It's me they must want . . . isn't it? I am the one. Not Danny, not Wendy. I'm the one who loves it here. They wanted to leave. I'm the one who took care of the snowmobile . . . went through the old records . . . dumped the press on the boiler . . . lied . . . practically sold my soul . . . what can they want with him?)

"Where is the manager?" He tried to ask it casually but his words seemed to come out between lips already numbed by the first drink, like words from a nightmare rather than those in a sweet dream.

Lloyd only smiled.

"What do you want with my son? Danny's not in this . . . is he?" He heard the naked plea in his own voice.

Lloyd's face seemed to be running, changing, becoming something pestilent. The white skin becoming a hepatitic yellow, cracking. Red sores erupting on the skin, bleeding foul-smelling liquid. Droplets of blood sprang out on Lloyd's forehead like sweat and somewhere a silver chime was striking the quarter-hour.

(Unmask, unmask!)

"Drink your drink, Mr. Torrance," Lloyd said softly. "It isn't a matter that concerns you. Not at this point."

He picked his drink up again, raised it to his lips, and hesitated. He heard the hard, horrible snap as Danny's arm broke. He saw the bicycle flying brokenly up over the hood of Al's car, starring the windshield. He saw a single wheel lying in the road, twisted spokes pointing into the sky like jags of piano wire.

He became aware that all conversation had stopped.

He looked back over his shoulder. They were all looking at him expectantly, silently. The man beside the woman in the sarong had removed his foxhead and Jack saw that it was Horace Derwent, his pallid blond hair spilling across his forehead. Everyone at the bar was watching, too. The woman beside him was looking at him closely, as if trying to focus. Her

993

dress had slipped off one shoulder and looking down he could see a loosely puckered nipple capping one sagging breast. Looking back at her face he began to think that this might be the woman from 217, the one who had tried to strangle Danny. On his other hand, the man in the sharp blue suit had removed a small pearl-handled .32 from his jacket pocket and was idly spinning it on the bar, like a man with Russian roulette on his mind.

(I want—)

He realized the words were not passing through his frozen vocal cords and tried again.

"I want to see the manager. I . . . I don't think he understands. My son is not a part of this. He . . ."

"Mr. Torrance," Lloyd said, his voice coming with hideous gentleness from inside his plague-raddled face, "you will meet the manager in due time. He has, in fact, decided to make you his agent in this matter. Now drink your drink."

"Drink your drink," they all echoed.

He picked it up with a badly trembling hand. It was raw gin. He looked into it, and looking was like drowning.

The woman beside him began to sing in a flat, dead voice: "Roll . . . out . . . the barrel . . . and we'll have . . . a barrel . . . of fun . . ."

Lloyd picked it up. Then the man in the blue suit. The dogman joined in, thumping one paw against the table

"Now's the time to roll the barrel—"

Derwent added his voice to the rest. A cigarette was cocked in one corner of his mouth at a jaunty angle. His right arm was around the shoulders of the woman in the sarong, and his right hand was gently and absently stroking her right breast. He was looking at the dogman with amused contempt as he sang.

"—because the gang's . . . all . . . here!"

Jack brought the drink to his mouth and downed it in three long gulps, the gin highballing down his throat like a moving van in a tunnel, exploding in his stomach, rebounding up to his brain in one leap where it seized hold of him with a final convulsing fit of the shakes.

When that passed off, he felt fine.

"Do it again, please," he said, and pushed the empty glass toward Lloyd.

"Yes, sir," Lloyd said, taking the glass. Lloyd looked perfectly normal again. The olive-skinned man had put his .32 away. The woman on his right was staring into her singapore sling again. One breast was wholly exposed now, leaning on the bar's leather buffer. A vacuous crooning noise came from her slack mouth. The loom of conversation had begun again, weaving and weaving.

His new drink appeared in front of him.

"*Muchas gracias,* Lloyd," he said, picking it up.

"Always a pleasure to serve you, Mr. Torrance." Lloyd smiled.

"You were always the best of them, Lloyd."

"Why, thank you, sir."

He drank slowly this time, letting it trickle down his throat, tossing a few peanuts down the chute for good luck.

The drink was gone in no time, and he ordered another. Mr. President, I have met the martians and am pleased to report they are friendly. While Lloyd fixed another, he began searching his pockets for a quarter to put in the jukebox. He thought of Danny again, but Danny's face was pleasantly fuzzed and nondescript now. He had hurt Danny once, but that had been before he had learned how to handle his liquor. Those days were behind him now. He would never hurt Danny again.

Not for the world.

44

CONVERSATIONS AT THE PARTY

He was dancing with a beautiful woman.

He had no idea what time it was, how long he had spent in the Colorado Lounge or how long he had been here in the ballroom. Time had ceased to matter.

He had vague memories: listening to a man who had once been a successful radio comic and then a variety star in TV's infant days telling a very long and very hilarious joke about incest between Siamese twins; seeing the woman in the harem pants and the sequined bra do a slow and sinuous striptease to some bumping-and-grinding music from the jukebox (it seemed it had been David Rose's theme music from *The Stripper*); crossing the lobby as one of three, the other two men in evening dress that predated the twenties, all of them singing about the stiff patch on Rosie O'Grady's knickers. He seemed to remember looking out the big double doors and seeing Japanese lanterns strung in graceful, curving arcs that followed the sweep of the driveway—they gleamed in soft pastel colors like dusky jewels. The big glass globe on the porch ceiling was on, and night-insects bumped and flittered against it, and a part of him, perhaps the last tiny spark of sobriety, tried to tell him that it was 6 A.M. on a morning in December. But time had been canceled.

(The arguments against insanity fall through with a soft shurring sound / layer on layer . . .)

Who was that? Some poet he had read as an undergraduate? Some undergraduate poet who was now selling washers in Wausau or insurance in Indianapolis? Perhaps an original thought? Didn't matter.

(The night is dark / the stars are high / a disembodied custard pie / is floating in the sky . . .)

He giggled helplessly.

"What's funny, honey?"

And here he was again, in the ballroom. The chandelier was lit and couples were circling all around them, some in costume and some not, to the smooth sounds of some postwar band— but which war? Can you be certain?

No, of course not. He was certain of only one thing: he was dancing with a beautiful woman.

She was tall and auburn-haired, dressed in clinging white satin, and she was dancing close to him, her breasts pressed softly and sweetly against his chest. Her white hand was entwined in his. She was wearing a small and sparkly cat's-eye mask and her hair had been brushed over to one side in a soft and gleaming fall that seemed to pool in the valley between their touching shoulders. Her dress was full-skirted but he could feel her thighs against his legs from time to time and had become more and more sure that she was smooth-and-powdered naked under her dress,

(the better to feel your erection with, my dear)

and he was sporting a regular railspike. If it offended her she concealed it well; she snuggled even closer to him.

"Nothing funny, honey," he said, and giggled again.

"I like you," she whispered, and he thought that her scent was like lilies, secret and hidden in cracks furred with green moss—places where sunshine is short and shadows long.

"I like you, too."

"We could go upstairs, if you want. I'm supposed to be with Harry, but he'll never notice. He's too busy teasing poor Roger."

The number ended. There was a spatter of applause and then the band swung into "Mood Indigo" with scarcely a pause.

Jack looked over her bare shoulder and saw Derwent standing by the refreshment table. The girl in the sarong was with him. There were bottles of champagne in ice buckets ranged along the white lawn covering the table, and Derwent held a foaming bottle in his hand. A knot of people had gathered, laughing. In front of Derwent and the girl in the sarong, Roger capered grotesquely on all fours, his tail dragging limply behind him. He was barking.

"Speak, boy, speak!" Harry Derwent cried.

"Rowf! Rowf!" Roger responded. Everyone clapped; a few of the men whistled.

"Now sit up. Sit up, doggy!"

Roger clambered up on his haunches. The muzzle of his mask was frozen in its eternal snarl. Inside the eyeholes, Roger's eyes rolled with frantic, sweaty hilarity. He held his arms out, dangling the paws.

"Rowf! Rowf!"

Derwent upended the bottle of champagne and it fell in a foamy Niagara onto the upturned mask. Roger made frantic slurping sounds, and everyone applauded again. Some of the women screamed with laughter.

"Isn't Harry a card?" his partner asked him, pressing close again. "Everyone says so. He's AC/DC, you know. Poor Roger's only DC. He spent a weekend with Harry in Cuba once . . . oh, *months* ago. Now he follows Harry everywhere, wagging his little tail behind him."

She giggled. The shy scent of lilies drifted up.

"But of course Harry never goes back for seconds . . . not on his DC side, anyway . . . and Roger is just *wild*. Harry told him if he came to the masked ball as a doggy, a *cute* little doggy, he might reconsider, and Roger is *such* a silly that he . . ."

The number ended. There was more applause. The band members were filing down for a break.

"Excuse me, sweetness," she said. "There's someone I just *must* . . . Darla! Darla, you *dear girl,* where have you *been?*"

She wove her way into the eating, drinking throng and he gazed after her stupidly, wondering how they had happened to be dancing together in the first place. He didn't remember. Incidents seemed to have occurred with no connections. First here, then there, then everywhere. His head was spinning. He smelled lilies and juniper berries. Up by the refreshment table Derwent was now holding a tiny triangular sandwich over Roger's head and urging him, to the general merriment of the onlookers, to do a somersault. The dogmask was turned upward. The silver sides of the dog costume bellowsed in and out. Roger suddenly leaped, tucking his head under, and tried to roll in mid-air. His leap was too low and too exhausted; he landed awkwardly on his back, rapping his head smartly on the tiles. A hollow groan drifted out of the dogmask.

Derwent led the applause. "Try again, doggy! Try again!"

The onlookers took up the chant—*try again, try again*—and Jack staggered off the other way, feeling vaguely ill.

He almost fell over the drinks cart that was being wheeled along by a low-browed man in a white mess jacket. His foot rapped the lower chromed shelf of the cart; the bottles and siphons on top chattered together musically.

"Sorry," Jack said thickly. He suddenly felt closed in and claustrophobic; he wanted to get out. He wanted the Overlook back the way it had been . . . free of these unwanted guests. His place was not honored, as the true opener of the way; he was only another of the ten thousand cheering extras, a doggy rolling over and sitting up on command.

"Quite all right," the man in the white mess jacket said. The polite, clipped English coming from that thug's face was surreal. "A drink?"

"Martini."

From behind him, another comber of laughter broke; Roger

was howling to the tune of "Home on the Range." Someone was picking out accompaniment on the Steinway baby grand.

"Here you are."

The frosty cold glass was pressed into his hand. Jack drank gratefully, feeling the gin hit and crumble away the first inroads of sobriety.

"Is it all right, sir?"

"Fine."

"Thank you, sir." The cart began to roll again.

Jack suddenly reached out and touched the man's shoulder.

"Yes, sir?"

"Pardon me, but . . . what's your name?"

The other showed no surprise. "Grady, sir. Delbert Grady."

"But you . . . I mean that . . ."

The bartender was looking at him politely. Jack tried again, although his mouth was mushed by gin and unreality; each word felt as large as an ice cube.

"Weren't you once the caretaker here? When you . . . when . . ." But he couldn't finish. He couldn't say it.

"Why no, sir. I don't believe so."

"But your wife . . . your daughters . . ."

"My wife is helping in the kitchen, sir. The girls are asleep, of course. It's much too late for them."

"You were the caretaker. You—" *Oh say it!* "You killed them."

Grady's face remained blankly polite. "I don't have any recollection of that at all, sir." His glass was empty. Grady plucked it from Jack's unresisting fingers and set about making another drink for him. There was a small white plastic bucket on his cart that was filled with olives. For some reason they reminded Jack of tiny severed heads. Grady speared one deftly, dropped it into the glass, and handed it to him.

"But you—"

"*You're* the caretaker, sir," Grady said mildly. "You've *always* been the caretaker. I should know, sir. I've always been here. The same manager hired us both, at the same time. Is it all right, sir?"

Jack gulped at his drink. His head was swirling. "Mr. Ullman—"

"I know no one by that name, sir."

"But he—"

"The manager," Grady said. "The *hotel,* sir. Surely you realize who hired you, sir."

"No," he said thickly. "No, I—"

"I believe you must take it up further with your son, Mr. Torrance, sir. He understands everything, although he hasn't enlightened you. Rather naughty of him, if I may be so bold, sir. In fact, he's crossed you at almost every turn, hasn't he? And him not yet six."

"Yes," Jack said. "He has." There was another wave of laughter from behind them.

"He needs to be corrected, if you don't mind me saying so. He needs a good talking-to, and perhaps a bit more. My own girls, sir, didn't care for the Overlook at first. One of them actually stole a pack of my matches and tried to burn it down. I corrected them. I corrected them most harshly. And when my wife tried to stop me from doing my duty, I corrected her." He offered Jack a bland, meaningless smile. "I find it a sad but true fact that women rarely understand a father's responsibility to his children. Husbands and fathers do have certain responsibilities, don't they, sir?"

"Yes," Jack said.

"They didn't love the Overlook as I did," Grady said, beginning to make him another drink. Silver bubbles rose in the upended gin bottle. "Just as your son and wife don't love it . . . not at present, anyway. But they will come to love it. You must show them the error of their ways, Mr. Torrance. Do you agree?"

"Yes. I do."

He did see. He had been too easy with them. Husbands and fathers did have certain responsibilities. Father Knows Best. They did not understand. That in itself was no crime, but they were *willfully* not understanding. He was not ordinarily a harsh man. But he did believe in punishment. And if his son and his wife had willfully set themselves against his wishes, *against the things he knew were best for them,* then didn't he have a certain duty—?

"A thankless child is sharper than a serpent's tooth," Grady said, handing him his drink. "I do believe that the manager could bring your son into line. And your wife would shortly follow. Do you agree, sir?"

He was suddenly uncertain. "I . . . but . . . if they could just leave . . . I mean, after all, it's me the manager wants, isn't it? It must be. Because—" Because why? He should know but suddenly he didn't. Oh, his poor brain was swimming.

"Bad dog!" Derwent was saying loudly, to a counterpoint of laughter. "Bad dog to piddle on the floor."

"Of course you know," Grady said, leaning confidentially over the cart, "your son is attempting to bring an outside party into it. Your son has a very great talent, one that the manager could use to even further improve the Overlook, to further . . . enrich it, shall we say? But your son is attempting to use that very talent against us. He is willful, Mr. Torrance, sir. Willful."

"Outside party?" Jack asked stupidly.

Grady nodded.

"Who?"

"A nigger," Grady said. "A nigger cook."

"Hallorann?"

"I believe that is his name, sir, yes."

Another burst of laughter from behind them was followed by Roger saying something in a whining, protesting voice.

"Yes! Yes! Yes!" Derwent began to chant. The others around him took it up, but before Jack could hear what they wanted Roger to do now, the band began to play again—the tune was "Tuxedo Junction," with a lot of mellow sax in it but not much soul.

(Soul? Soul hasn't even been invented yet. Or has it?)

(A nigger . . . a nigger cook.)

He opened his mouth to speak, not knowing what might come out. What did was:

"I was told you hadn't finished high school. But you don't talk like an uneducated man."

"It's true that I left organized education very early, sir. But the manager takes care of his help. He finds that it pays. Education always pays, don't you agree, sir?"

"Yes," Jack said dazedly.

"For instance, you show a great interest in learning more about the Overlook Hotel. Very wise of you, sir. Very noble. A certain scrapbook was left in the basement for you to find—"

"By whom?" Jack asked eagerly.

"By the manager, of course. Certain other materials could be put at your disposal, if you wished them . . ."

"I do. Very much." He tried to control the eagerness in his voice and failed miserably.

"You're a true scholar," Grady said. "Pursue the topic to the end. Exhaust all sources." He dipped his low-browed head, pulled out the lapel of his white mess jacket, and buffed his knuckles at a spot of dirt that was invisible to Jack.

"And the manager puts no strings on his largess," Grady went on. "Not at all. Look at me, a tenth-grade dropout. Think how much further you yourself could go in the Overlook's organizational structure. Perhaps ... in time ... to the very top."

"Really?" Jack whispered.

"But that's really up to your son to decide, isn't it?" Grady asked, raising his eyebrows. The delicate gesture went oddly with the brows themselves, which were bushy and somehow savage.

"Up to Danny?" Jack frowned at Grady. "No, of course not. I wouldn't allow my son to make decisions concerning my career. Not at all. What do you take me for?"

"A dedicated man," Grady said warmly. "Perhaps I put it badly, sir. Let us say that your future here is contingent upon how you decide to deal with your son's waywardness."

"I make my own decisions," Jack whispered.

"But you must deal with him."

"I will."

"Firmly."

"I will."

"A man who cannot control his own family holds very little interest for our manager. A man who cannot guide the courses of his own wife and son can hardly be expected to guide himself, let alone assume a position of responsibility in an operation of this magnitude. He—"

"I said I'll handle him!" Jack shouted suddenly, enraged.

"Tuxedo Junction" had just concluded and a new tune hadn't begun. His shout fell perfectly into the gap, and conversation suddenly ceased behind him. His skin suddenly felt hot all over. He became fixedly positive that everyone was staring at him. They had finished with Roger and would now commence with him. Roll over. Sit up. Play dead. If you play the game with us, we'll play the game with you.

Position of responsibility. They wanted him to sacrifice his son.

(—*Now he follows Harry everywhere, wagging his little tail behind him*—)

(*Roll over. Play dead. Chastise your son.*)

"Right this way, sir," Grady was saying. "Something that might interest you."

The conversation had begun again, lifting and dropping in its own rhythm, weaving in and out of the band music, now doing a swing version of Lennon and McCartney's "Ticket to Ride."

(*I've heard better over supermarket loudspeakers.*)

He giggled foolishly. He looked down at his left hand and saw there was another drink in it, half-full. He emptied it at a gulp.

Now he was standing in front of the mantelpiece, the heat from the crackling fire that had been laid in the hearth warming his legs.

(*a fire? . . . in August? . . . yes . . . and no . . . all times are one*)

There was a clock under a glass dome, flanked by two carved ivory elephants. Its hands stood at a minute to midnight. He gazed at it blearily. Had this been what Grady wanted him to see? He turned around to ask, but Grady had left him.

Halfway through "Ticket to Ride," the band wound up in a brassy flourish.

"The hour is at hand!" Horace Derwent proclaimed. "Midnight! Unmask! Unmask!"

He tried to turn again, to see what famous faces were hidden beneath the glitter and paint and masks, but he was frozen now, unable to look away from the clock—its hands had come together and pointed straight up.

"*Unmask! Unmask!*" the chant went up.

The clock began to chime delicately. Along the steel runner below the clockface, from the left and right, two figures advanced. Jack watched, fascinated, the unmasking forgotten. Clockwork whirred. Cogs turned and meshed, brass warmly glowing. The balance wheel rocked back and forth precisely.

One of the figures was a man standing on tiptoe, with what looked like a tiny club clasped in his hands. The other was a small boy wearing a dunce cap. The clockwork figures glittered, fantastically precise. Across the front of the boy's dunce cap he could read the engraved word FOOLE.

The two figures slipped onto the opposing ends of a steel axis bar. Somewhere, tinkling on and on, were the strains of a Strauss waltz. An insane commercial jingle began to run through his mind to the tune: *Buy dog food, rowf-rowf, rowf-rowf, buy dog food . . .*

The steel mallet in the clockwork daddy's hands came down on the boy's head. The clockwork son crumbled forward. The mallet rose and fell, rose and fell. The boy's upstretched, protesting hands began to falter. The boy sagged from his crouch to a prone position. And still the hammer rose and fell to the light, tinkling air of the Strauss melody, and it seemed that he could see the man's face, working and knotting and constricting, could see the clockwork daddy's mouth opening and closing as he berated the unconscious, bludgeoned figure of the son.

A spot of red flew up against the inside of the glass dome. Another followed. Two more splattered beside it.

Now the red liquid was spraying up like an obscene rain shower, striking the glass sides of the dome and running, obscuring what was going on inside, and flecked through the scarlet were tiny gray ribbons of tissue, fragments of bone and brain. And still he could see the hammer rising and falling as the clockwork continued to turn and the cogs continued to mesh the gears and teeth of this cunningly made machine.

"Unmask! Unmask!" Derwent was shrieking behind him, and somewhere a dog was howling in human tones.

(But clockwork can't bleed clockwork can't bleed)

The entire dome was splashed with blood, he could see clotted bits of hair but nothing else thank God he could see nothing else, and still he thought he would be sick because he could hear the hammerblows still falling, could hear them through the glass just as he could hear the phrases of "The Blue Danube." But the sounds were no longer the mechanical *tink-tink-tink* noises of a mechanical hammer striking a mechanical head, but the soft and squashy thudding sounds of a real hammer slicing down and whacking into a spongy, muddy ruin. A ruin that once had been—

"UNMASK!"

(—the Red Death held sway over all!)

With a miserable, rising scream, he turned away from the clock, his hands outstretched, his feet stumbling against one another like wooden blocks as he begged them to stop, to take him, Danny, Wendy, to take the whole world if they wanted it, but only to stop and leave him a little sanity, a little light.

The ballroom was empty.

The chairs with their spindly legs were upended on tables covered with plastic dust drops. The red rug with its golden tracings was back on the dance floor, protecting the polished hardwood surface. The bandstand was deserted except for a disassembled microphone stand and a dusty guitar leaning stringless against the wall. Cold morning light, winterlight, fell languidly through the high windows.

His head was still reeling, he still felt drunk, but when he turned back to the mantelpiece, his drink was gone. There were only the ivory elephants . . . and the clock.

He stumbled back across the cold, shadowy lobby and through the dining room. His foot hooked around a table leg and he fell full-length, upsetting the table with a clatter. He struck his nose hard on the floor and it began to bleed. He got up, snuffling back blood and wiping his nose with the back of his hand. He crossed to the Colorado Lounge and shoved through the batwing doors, making them fly back and bang into the walls.

The place was empty . . . but the bar was fully stocked. God be praised! Glass and the silver edging on labels glowed warmly in the dark.

Once, he remembered, a very long time ago, he had been angry that there was no backbar mirror. Now he was glad. Looking into it he would have seen just another drunk fresh off the wagon: bloody nose, untucked shirt, hair rumpled, cheeks stubbly.

(This is what it's like to stick your whole hand into the nest.)

Loneliness surged over him suddenly and completely. He cried out with sudden wretchedness and honestly wished he were dead. His wife and son were upstairs with the door locked against him. The others had all left. The party was over.

He lurched forward again, reaching the bar.

"Lloyd, where the fuck are you?" he screamed.

There was no answer. In this well-padded
(cell)
room, his words did not even echo back to give the illusion
of company.
"Grady!"
No answer. Only the bottles, standing stiffly at attention.
(Roll over. Play dead. Fetch. Play dead. Sit up. Play dead.)
"Never mind, I'll do it myself, goddammit."

Halfway over the bar he lost his balance and pitched forward, hitting his head a muffled blow on the floor. He got up on his hands and knees, his eyeballs moving disjointed from side to side, fuzzy muttering sounds coming from his mouth. Then he collapsed, his face turned to one side, breathing in harsh snores.

Outside, the wind whooped louder, driving the thickening snow before it. It was 8:30 A.M.

45

STAPLETON AIRPORT, DENVER

At 8:31 A.M., MST, a woman on TWA's Flight 196 burst into tears and began to bugle her own opinion, which was perhaps not unshared among some of the other passengers (or even the crew, for that matter), that the plane was going to crash.

The sharp-faced woman next to Hallorann looked up from her book and offered a brief character analysis: "Ninny," and went back to her book. She had downed two screwdrivers during the flight, but they seemed not to have thawed her at all.

"It's going to crash!" the woman was crying out shrilly. "Oh, I just know it is!"

A stewardess hurried to her seat and squatted beside her. Hallorann thought to himself that only stewardesses and very young housewives seemed able to squat with any degree of grace; it was a rare and wonderful talent. He thought about this while the stewardess talked softly and soothingly to the woman, quieting her bit by bit.

Hallorann didn't know about anyone else on 196, but he personally was almost scared enough to shit peachpits. Outside the window there was nothing to be seen but a buffeting curtain of white. The plane rocked sickeningly from side to side with gusts that seemed to come from everywhere. The engines were cranked up to provide partial compensation and as a result the floor was vibrating under their feet. There were several people moaning in Tourist behind them, one stew had gone back with a handful of fresh airsick bags, and a man three rows in front of Hallorann had whoopsed into his *National Observer* and had grinned apologetically at the stewardess who came to help him clean up. "That's all right," she comforted him, "that's how I feel about the *Reader's Digest*."

Hallorann had flown enough to be able to surmise what had happened. They had been flying against bad headwinds most of the way, the weather over Denver had worsened suddenly and unexpectedly, and now it was just a little late to divert for someplace where the weather was better. *Feets don't fail me now.*

(Buddy-boy, this is some fucked-up cavalry charge.)

The stewardess seemed to have succeeded in curbing the worst of the woman's hysterics. She was snuffling and honking into a lace handkerchief, but had ceased broadcasting her opinions about the flight's possible conclusion to the cabin at large. The stew gave her a final pat on the shoulder and stood up just as the 747 gave its worst lurch yet. The stewardess stumbled backward and landed in the lap of the man who had whoopsed into his paper, exposing a lovely length of nyloned thigh. The man blinked and then patted her kindly on the shoulder. She smiled back, but Hallorann thought the strain was showing. It had been one hell of a hard flight this morning.

There was a little ping as the NO SMOKING light reappeared.

"This is the captain speaking," a soft, slightly southern voice informed them. "We're ready to begin our descent to Stapleton International Airport. It's been a rough flight, for which I apologize. The landing may be a bit rough also, but we anticipate no real difficulty. Please observe the FASTEN SEAT BELTS and NO SMOKING signs, and we hope you enjoy your stay in the Denver metro area. And we also hope—"

Another hard bump rocked the plane and then dropped her with a sickening elevator plunge. Hallorann's stomach did a queasy hornpipe. Several people—not all women by any means—screamed.

"—that we'll see you again on another TWA flight real soon."

"Not bloody likely," someone behind Hallorann said.

"So silly," the sharp-faced woman next to Hallorann remarked, putting a matchbook cover into her book and shutting it as the plane began to descend. "When one has seen the horrors of a dirty little war . . . as you have . . . or sensed the degrading immorality of CIA dollar-diplomacy intervention . . . as I have . . . a rough landing *pales* into *insignificance*. Am I right, Mr. Hallorann?"

"As rain, ma'am," he said, and looked bleakly out into the wildly blowing snow.

"How is your steel plate reacting to all of this, if I might inquire?"

"Oh, my head's fine," Hallorann said. "It's just my stomach that's a mite queasy."

"A shame." She reopened her book.

As they descended through the impenetrable clouds of snow, Hallorann thought of a crash that had occurred at Boston's Logan Airport a few years ago. The conditions had been similar, only fog instead of snow had reduced visibility to zero. The plane had caught its undercarriage on a retaining wall near the end of the landing strip. What had been left of the eighty-nine people aboard hadn't looked much different from a Hamburger Helper casserole.

He wouldn't mind so much if it was just himself. He was pretty much alone in the world now, and attendance at his funeral would be mostly held down to the people he had worked with and that old renegade Masterton, who would at least drink to him. But the boy . . . the boy was depending on him. He was maybe all the help that child could expect, and he didn't like the way the boy's last call had been snapped off. He kept thinking of the way those hedge animals had seemed to move . . .

A thin white hand appeared over his.

The woman with the sharp face had taken off her glasses. Without them her features seemed much softer.

"It will be all right," she said.

Hallorann made a smile and nodded.

As advertised the plane came down hard, reuniting with the earth forcefully enough to knock most of the magazines out of the rack at the front and to send plastic trays cascading out of the galley like oversized playing cards. No one screamed, but Hallorann heard several sets of teeth clicking violently together like gypsy castanets.

Then the turbine engines rose to a howl, braking the plane, and as they dropped in volume the pilot's soft southern voice, perhaps not completely steady, came over the intercom system. "Ladies and gentlemen, we have landed at Stapleton Airport. Please remain in your seats until the plane has come to a complete stop at the terminal. Thank you."

The woman beside Hallorann closed her book and uttered a long sigh. "We live to fight another day, Mr. Hallorann."

"Ma'am, we aren't done with this one, yet."

"True. Very true. Would you care to have a drink in the lounge with me?"

"I would, but I have an appointment to keep."

"Pressing?"

"Very pressing," Hallorann said gravely.

"Something that will improve the general situation in some small way, I hope."

"I hope so too," Hallorann said, and smiled. She smiled back at him, ten years dropping silently from her face as she did so.

Because he had only the flight bag he'd carried for luggage, Hallorann beat the crowd to the Hertz desk on the lower level. Outside the smoked glass windows he could see the snow still falling steadily. The gusting wind drove white clouds of it back and forth, and the people walking across to the parking area were struggling against it. One man lost his hat and Hallorann could commiserate with him as it whirled high, wide, and handsome. The man stared after it and Hallorann thought:

(Aw, just forget it, man. That homburg ain't comin down until it gets to Arizona.)

On the heels of that thought:

(If it's this bad in Denver, what's it going to be like west of Boulder?)

Best not to think about that, maybe.

"Can I help you, sir?" a girl in Hertz yellow asked him.

"If you got a car, you can help me," he said with a big grin.

For a heavier-than-average charge he was able to get a heavier-than-average car, a silver and black Buick Electra. He was thinking of the winding mountain roads rather than style; he would still have to stop somewhere along the way and get chains put on. He wouldn't get far without them.

"How bad is it?" he asked as she handed him the rental agreement to sign.

"They say it's the worst storm since 1969," she answered brightly. "Do you have far to drive, sir?"

"Farther than I'd like."

"If you'd like, sir, I can phone ahead to the Texaco station at the Route 270 junction. They'll put chains on for you."

"That would be a great blessing, dear."

She picked up the phone and made the call. "They'll be expecting you."

"Thank you much."

Leaving the desk, he saw the sharp-faced woman standing on one of the queues that had formed in front of the luggage carousel. She was still reading her book. Halloran winked at her as he went by. She looked up, smiled at him, and gave him a peace sign.

(shine)

He turned up his overcoat collar, smiling, and shifted his flight bag to the other hand. Only a little one, but it made him feel better. He was sorry he'd told her that fish story about having a steel plate in his head. He mentally wished her well and as he went out into the howling wind and snow, he thought she wished him the same in return.

The charge for putting on the chains at the service station was a modest one, but Halloran slipped the man at work in the garage bay an extra ten to get moved up a little way on the waiting list. It was still quarter of ten before he was actually on the road, the windshield wipers clicking and the chains clinking with tuneles monotony on the Buick's big wheels.

The turnpike was a mess. Even with the chains he could go no faster than thirty. Cars had gone off the road at crazy angles, and on several of the grades traffic was barely struggling along, summer tires spinning helplessly in the drifting powder. It was the first big storm of the winter down here in the lowlands (if you could call a mile above sealevel "low"), and it was a mother. Many of them were unprepared, common enough, but Hallorann still found himself cursing them as he inched around them, peering into his snow-clogged outside mirror to be sure nothing was

(Dashing through the snow . . .)

coming up in the left-hand lane to cream his black ass.

There was more bad luck waiting for him at the Route 36 entrance ramp. Route 36, the Denver-Boulder turnpike, also goes west to Estes Park, where it connects with Route 7. That road, also known as the Upland Highway, goes through Sidewinder, passes the Overlook Hotel, and finally winds down the Western Slope and into Utah.

The entrance ramp had been blocked by an overturned semi. Bright-burning flares had been scattered around it like birthday candles on some idiot child's cake.

He came to a stop and rolled his window down. A cop with a fur Cossack hat jammed down over his ears gestured with one gloved hand toward the flow of traffic moving north on I-25.

"You can't get up here!" he bawled to Hallorann over the wind. "Go down two exits, get on 91, and connect with 36 at Broomfield!"

"I think I could get around him on the left!" Hallorann shouted back. "That's twenty miles out of my way, what you're rappin!"

"I'll rap your friggin *head!*" the cop shouted back. "This ramp's closed!"

Hallorann backed up, waited for a break in traffic, and continued on his way up Route 25. The signs informed him it was only a hundred miles to Cheyenne, Wyoming. If he didn't look out for his ramp, he'd wind up there.

He inched his speed up to thirty-five but dared no more; already snow was threatening to clog his wiper blades and the traffic patterns were decidedly crazy. Twenty-mile detour. He cursed, and the feeling that time was growing shorter for the boy welled up in him again, nearly suffocating with its urgency. And at the same time he felt a fatalistic certainty that he would not be coming back from this trip.

He turned on the radio, dialed past Christmas ads, and found a weather forecast.

"—six inches already, and another foot is expected in the Denver metro area by nightfall. Local and state police urge you not to take your car out of the garage unless it's absolutely necessary, and warn that most mountain passes have already been closed. So stay home and wax up your boards and keep tuned to—"

"Thanks, mother," Hallorann said, and turned the radio off savagely.

46

WENDY

Around noon, after Danny had gone into the bathroom to use the toilet, Wendy took the towel-wrapped knife from under her pillow, put it in the pocket of her bathrobe, and went over to the bathroom door.

"Danny?"

"What?"

"I'm going down to make us some lunch. 'Kay?"

"Okay. Do you want me to come down?"

"No, I'll bring it up. How about a cheese omelet and some soup?"

"Sure."

She hesitated outside the closed door a moment longer. "Danny, are you sure it's okay?"

"Yeah," he said. "Just be careful."

"Where's your father? Do you know?"

His voice came back, curiously flat: "No. But it's okay."

She stifled an urge to keep asking, to keep picking around the edges of the thing. The thing was there, they knew what it was, picking at it was only going to frighten Danny more . . . and herself.

Jack had lost his mind. They had sat together on Danny's cot as the storm began to pick up clout and meanness around eight o'clock this morning and had listened to him downstairs, bellowing and stumbling from one place to another. Most of it had seemed to come from the ballroom. Jack singing tuneless bits of song, Jack holding up one side of an argument, Jack screaming loudly at one point, freezing both of their faces as they stared into one another's eyes. Finally they had heard him stumbling back across the lobby, and Wendy thought she had heard a loud banging noise, as if he had fallen down or pushed a door violently open. Since eight-thirty or so—three and a half hours now—there had been only silence.

She went down the short hall, turned into the main first-floor corridor, and went to the stairs. She stood on the first-floor landing looking down into the lobby. It appeared deserted, but the gray and snowy day had left much of the long room in shadow. Danny could be wrong. Jack could be behind a chair or couch . . . maybe behind the registration desk . . . waiting for her to come down . . .

She wet her lips. "Jack?"

No answer.

Her hand found the handle of the knife and she began to go down. She had seen the end of her marriage many times, in divorce, in Jack's death at the scene of a drunken car accident (a regular vision in the dark two o'clock of Stovington mornings), and occasionally in daydreams of being discovered by another man, a soap opera Galahad who would sweep Danny and her onto the saddle of his snow-white charger and take them away. But she had never envisioned herself prowling halls and staircases like a nervous felon, with a knife clasped in one hand to use against Jack.

A wave of despair struck through her at the thought and she had to stop halfway down the stairs and holding the railing, afraid her knees would buckle.

(*Admit it. It isn't just Jack, he's just the one solid thing in all of this you can hang the other things on, the things you can't believe and yet are being forced to believe, that thing about the hedges, the party favor in the elevator, the mask*)

She tried to stop the thought but it was too late.

(and the voices.)

Because from time to time it had not seemed that there was a solitary crazy man below them, shouting at and holding conversations with the phantoms in his own crumbling mind. From time to time, like a radio signal fading in and out, she had heard—or thought she had—other voices, and music, and laughter. At one moment she would hear Jack holding a conversation with someone named Grady (the name was vaguely familiar to her but she made no actual connection), making statements and asking questions into silence, yet speaking loudly, as if to make himself heard over a steady background racket. And then, eerily, other sounds would be there, seeming to slip into place—a dance band, people clapping, a man with an amused yet authoritative voice who seemed to be trying to persuade somebody to make a speech. For a period of thirty seconds to a minute she would hear this, long enough to grow faint with terror, and then it would be gone again and she would only hear Jack, talking in that commanding yet slightly slurred way she remembered as his drunk-speak voice. But there was nothing in the hotel to drink except cooking sherry. Wasn't that right? Yes, but if she could imagine that the hotel was full of voices and music, couldn't Jack imagine that he was drunk?

She didn't like that thought. Not at all.

Wendy reached the lobby and looked around. The velvet rope that had cordoned off the ballroom had been taken down; the steel post it had been clipped to had been knocked over, as if someone had carelessly bumped it going by. Mellow white light fell through the open door onto the lobby rug from the ballroom's high, narrow windows. Heart thumping, she went to the open ballroom doors and looked in. It was empty and silent, the only sound that curious subaural echo that seems to linger in all large rooms, from the largest cathedral to the smallest hometown bingo parlor.

She went back to the registration desk and stood undecided for a moment, listening to the wind howl outside. It was the worst storm so far, and it was still building up force. Somewhere on the west side a shutter latch had broken and the shutter banged back and forth with a steady flat cracking sound, like a shooting gallery with only one customer.

(Jack, you really should take care of that. Before something gets in.)

What would she do if he came at her right now, she wondered. If he should pop up from behind the dark, varnished registration desk with its pile of triplicate forms and its little silver-plated bell, like some murderous jack-in-the-box, pun intended, a grinning jack-in-the-box with a cleaver in one hand and no sense at all left behind his eyes. Would she stand frozen with terror, or was there enough of the primal mother in her to fight him for her son until one of them was dead? She didn't know. The very thought made her sick—made her feel that her whole life had been a long and easy dream to lull her helplessly into this waking nightmare. She was soft. When trouble came, she slept. Her past was unremarkable. She had never been tried in fire. Now the trial was upon her, not fire but ice, and she would not be allowed to sleep through this. Her son was waiting for her upstairs.

Clutching the haft of the knife tighter, she peered over the desk.

Nothing there.

Her relieved breath escaped her in a long, hitching sigh.

She put the gate up and went through, pausing to glance into the inner office before going in herself. She fumbled through the next door for the bank of kitchen light switches, coldly expecting a hand to close over hers at any second. Then the fluorescents were coming on with minuscule ticking and humming sounds and she could see Mr. Hallorann's kitchen— her kitchen now, for better or worse—pale green tiles, gleaming Formica, spotless porcelain, glowing chrome edgings. She had promised him she would keep his kitchen clean, and she had. She felt as if it was one of Danny's safe places. Dick Hallorann's presence seemed to enfold and comfort her. Danny had called for Mr. Hallorann, and upstairs, sitting next to Danny in fear as her husband ranted and raved below, that had seemed like the faintest of all hopes. But standing here, in Mr. Hallorann's place, it seemed almost possible. Perhaps he was on his way now, intent on getting to them regardless of the storm. Perhaps it was so.

She went across to the pantry, shot the bolt back, and stepped inside. She got a can of tomato soup and closed the pantry door again, and bolted it. The door was tight against the floor. If you kept it bolted, you didn't have to worry about rat or mouse droppings in the rice or flour or sugar.

She opened the can and dropped the slightly jellied contents into a saucepan—*plop*. She went to the refrigerator and got milk and eggs for the omelet. Then to the walk-in freezer for cheese. All of these actions, so common and so much a part of her life before the Overlook had been a part of her life, helped to calm her.

She melted butter in the frying pan, diluted the soup with milk, and then poured the beaten eggs into the pan.

A sudden feeling that someone was standing behind her, reaching for her throat.

She wheeled around, clutching the knife. No one there.

(! Get ahold of yourself, girl !)

She grated a bowl of cheese from the block, added it to the omelet, flipped it, and turned the gas ring down to a bare blue flame. The soup was hot. She put the pot on a large tray with silverware, two bowls, two plates, the salt and pepper shakers. When the omelet had puffed slightly, Wendy slid it off onto one of the plates and covered it.

(Now back the way you came. Turn off the kitchen lights. Go through the inner office. Through the desk gate, collect two hundred dollars.)

She stopped on the lobby side of the registration desk and set the tray down beside the silver bell. Unreality would stretch only so far; this was like some surreal game of hide-and-seek.

She stood in the shadowy lobby, frowning in thought.

(Don't push the facts away this time, girl. There are certain realities, as lunatic as this situation may seem. One of them is that you may be the only responsible person left in this grotesque pile. You have a five-going-on-six son to look out for. And your husband, whatever has happened to him and no matter how dangerous he may be . . . maybe he's part of your responsibility, too. And even if he isn't, consider this: Today is December second. You could be stuck up here another four months if a ranger doesn't happen by. Even if they do start to wonder why they haven't heard from us on the CB, no one is going to come today . . . or tomorrow . . . maybe not for weeks. Are you going to spend a month sneaking down to get meals with a knife in your pocket and jumping at every shadow? Do you really think you can avoid Jack for a month? Do you think you can keep Jack out of the upstairs quarters if he wants to get in? He has the passkey and one hard kick would snap the bolt.)

Leaving the tray on the desk, she walked slowly down to the dining room and looked in. It was deserted. There was one table with the chairs set up around it, the table they had tried eating at until the dining room's emptiness began to freak them out.

"Jack?" she called hesitantly.

At that moment the wind rose in a gust, driving snow against the shutters, but it seemed to her that there had been some-thing. A muffled sort of groan.

"Jack?"

No returning sound this time, but her eyes fell on some-thing beneath the batwing doors of the Colorado Lounge, some-thing that gleamed faintly in the subdued light. Jack's cigarette lighter.

Plucking up her courage, she crossed to the batwings and pushed them open. The smell of gin was so strong that her breath snagged in her throat. It wasn't even right to call it a smell; it was a positive reek. But the shelves were empty. Where in God's name had he found it? A bottle hidden at the back of one of the cupboards? *Where?*

There was another groan, low and fuzzy, but perfectly audi-ble this time. Wendy walked slowly to the bar.

"Jack?"

No answer.

She looked over the bar and there he was, sprawled out on the floor in a stupor. Drunk as a lord, by the smell. He must have tried to go right over the top and lost his balance. A wonder he hadn't broken his neck. An old proverb recurred to her: God looks after drunks and little children. Amen.

Yet she was not angry with him; looking down at him she thought he looked like a horribly overtired little boy who had tried to do too much and had fallen asleep in the middle of the living room floor. He had stopped drinking and it was not Jack who had made the decision to start again; there had been no liquor for him to start with . . . so where had it come from?

Resting at every five or six feet along the horseshoe-shaped bar there were wine bottles wrapped in straw, their mouths plugged with candles. Supposed to look bohemian, she sup-posed. She picked one up and shook it, half-expecting to hear the slosh of gin inside it

(new wine in old bottles)
but there was nothing. She set it back down.

Jack was stirring. She went around the bar, found the gate, and walked back on the inside to where Jack lay, pausing only to look at the gleaming chromium taps. They were dry, but when she passed close to them she could smell beer, wet and new, like a fine mist.

As she reached Jack he rolled over, opened his eyes, and looked up at her. For a moment his gaze was utterly blank, and then it cleared.

"Wendy?" he asked. "That you?"

"Yes," she said. "Do you think you can make it upstairs? If you put your arms around me? Jack, where did you—"

His hand closed brutally around her ankle.

"Jack! What are you—"

"Gotcha!" he said, and began to grin. There was a stale odor of gin and olives about him that seemed to set off an old terror in her, a worse terror than any hotel could provide by itself. A distant part of her thought that the worst thing was that it had all come back to this, she and her drunken husband.

"Jack, I want to help."

"Oh yeah. You and Danny only want to *help*." The grip on her ankle was crushing now. Still holding onto her, Jack was getting shakily to his knees. "You wanted to help us all right out of here. But now . . . I . . . *gotcha!*"

"Jack, you're hurting my ankle—"

"I'll hurt more than your ankle, you *bitch*."

The word stunned her so completely that she made no effort to move when he let go of her ankle and stumbled from his knees to his feet, where he stood swaying in front of her.

"You never loved me," he said. "You want us to leave because you know that'll be the end of me. Did you ever think about my re . . . res . . . respons'bilities? No, I guess to fuck you didn't. All you ever think about is ways to drag me down. You're just like my mother, you milksop *bitch!*"

"Stop it," she said, crying. "You don't know what you're saying. You're drunk. I don't know how, but you're drunk."

"Oh, I know. I know now. You and him. That little pup upstairs. The two of you, planning together. Isn't that right?"

"No, no! We never planned anything! What are you—"

"You liar!" he screamed. "Oh, I know how you do it! I guess I know that! When I say, 'We're going to stay here and I'm going to do my job,' you say, 'Yes, dear,' and he says, 'Yes, Daddy,' and then you lay your plans. You planned to use the snowmobile. You planned that. But I knew. I figured it out. *Did you think I wouldn't figure it out? Did you think I was stupid?"*

She stared at him, unable to speak now. He was going to kill her, and then he was going to kill Danny. Then maybe the hotel would be satisfied and allow him to kill himself. Just like that other caretaker. Just like

(*Grady.)*

With almost swooning horror, she realized at last who it was that Jack had been conversing with in the ballroom.

"You turned my son against me. That was the worst." His face sagged into lines of selfpity. "My little boy. Now he hates me, too. You saw to that. That was your plan all along, wasn't it? You've always been jealous, haven't you? Just like your mother. You couldn't be satisfied unless you had all the cake, could you? *Could you?"*

She couldn't talk.

"Well, I'll fix you," he said, and tried to put his hands around her throat.

She took a step backward, then another, and he stumbled against her. She remembered the knife in the pocket of her robe and groped for it, but now his left arm had swept around her, pinning her arm against her side. She could smell sharp gin and the sour odor of his sweat.

"Have to be punished," he was grunting. "Chastised. Chastised . . . harshly."

His right hand found her throat.

As her breath stopped, pure panic took over. His left hand joined his right and now the knife was free to her own hand, but she forgot about it. Both of her hands came up and began to yank helplessly at his larger, stronger ones.

"Mommy!" Danny shrieked from somewhere. *"Daddy, stop! You're hurting Mommy!"* He screamed piercingly, a high and crystal sound that she heard from far off.

Red flashes of light leaped in front of her eyes like ballet dancers. The room grew darker. She saw her son clamber up on the bar and throw himself at Jack's shoulders. Suddenly one of the hands that had been crushing her throat was gone as Jack cuffed Danny away with a snarl. The boy fell back against the empty shelves and dropped to the floor, dazed. The hand was on her throat again. The red flashes began to turn black.

Danny was crying weakly. Her chest was burning. Jack was shouting into her face: "I'll fix you! Goddam you, I'll show you who is boss around here! I'll show you—"

But all sounds were fading down a long dark corridor. Her struggles began to weaken. One of her hands fell away from his and dropped slowly until the arm was stretched out at right angles to her body, the hand dangling limply from the wrist like the hand of a drowning woman.

It touched a bottle—one of the straw-wrapped wine bottles that served as decorative candleholders.

Sightlessly, with the last of her strength, she groped for the bottle's neck and found it, feeling the greasy beads of wax against her hand.

(and O God if it slips)

She brought it up and then down, praying for aim, knowing that if it only struck his shoulder or upper arm she was dead.

But the bottle came down squarely on Jack Torrance's head, the glass shattering violently inside the straw. The base of it was thick and heavy, and it made a sound against his skull like a medicine ball dropped on a hardwood floor. He rocked back on his heels, his eyes rolling up in their sockets. The pressure on her throat loosened, then gave way entirely. He put his hands out, as if to steady himself, and then crashed over on his back.

Wendy drew a long, sobbing breath. She almost fell herself, clutched the edge of the bar, and managed to hold herself up. Consciousness wavered in and out. She could hear Danny crying, but she had no idea where he was. It sounded like crying in an echo chamber. Dimly she saw dime-sized drops of blood falling to the dark surface of the bar—from her nose, she thought. She cleared her throat and spat on the floor. It sent a wave of agony up the column of her throat, but the agony subsided to a steady dull press of pain . . . just bearable.

Little by little, she managed to get control of herself.

She let go of the bar, turned around, and saw Jack lying full-length, the shattered bottle beside him. He looked like a felled giant. Danny was crouched below the lounge's cash register, both hands in his mouth, staring at his unconscious father.

Wendy went to him unsteadily and touched his shoulder. Danny cringed away from her.

"Danny, listen to me—"

"No, no," he muttered in a husky old man's voice. "Daddy hurt you . . . you hurt Daddy . . . Daddy hurt you . . . I want to go to sleep. Danny wants to go to sleep."

"Danny—"

"Sleep, sleep. Nighty-night."

"No!"

Pain ripping up her throat again. She winced against it. But he opened his eyes. They looked at her warily from bluish, shadowed sockets.

She made herself speak calmly, her eyes never leaving his. Her voice was low and husky, almost a whisper. It hurt to talk. "Listen to me, Danny. It wasn't your daddy trying to hurt me. And I didn't want to hurt him. The hotel has gotten into him, Danny. *The Overlook has gotten into your daddy.* Do you understand me?"

Some kind of knowledge came slowly back into Danny's eyes.

"The Bad Stuff," he whispered. "There was none of it here before, was there?"

"No. The hotel put it here. The . . ." She broke off in a fit of coughing and spat out more blood. Her throat already felt puffed to twice its size. "The hotel made him drink it. Did you hear those people he was talking to this morning?"

"Yes . . . the hotel people . . ."

"I heard them too. And that means the hotel is getting stronger. It wants to hurt all of us. But I think . . . I hope . . . that it can only do that through your daddy. He was the only one it could catch. Are you understanding me, Danny? It's desperately important that you understand."

"The hotel caught Daddy." He looked at Jack and groaned helplessly.

"I know you love your daddy. I do too. We have to remember that the hotel is trying to hurt him as much as it is us." And she was convinced that was true. More, she thought that Danny might be the one the hotel really wanted, the reason it was going so far . . . maybe the reason it was *able* to go so far. It might even be that in some unknown fashion it was Danny's shine that was powering it, the way a battery powers the electrical equipment in a car . . . the way a battery gets a car to start. If they got out of here, the Overlook might subside to its old semi-sentient state, able to do no more than present penny-dreadful horror slides to the more psychically aware guests who entered it. Without Danny it was not much more than an amusement park haunted house, where a guest or two might hear rappings or the phantom sounds of a masquerade party, or see an occasional disturbing thing. But if it absorbed Danny . . . Danny's shine or life-force or spirit . . . whatever you wanted to call it . . . into itself—what would it be then?

The thought made her cold all over.

"I wish Daddy was all better," Danny said, and the tears began to flow again.

"Me too," she said, and hugged Danny tightly. "And honey, that's why you've got to help me put your daddy somewhere. Somewhere that the hotel can't make him hurt us and where he can't hurt himself. Then . . . if your friend Dick comes, or a park ranger, we can take him away. And I think he might be all right again. All of us might be all right. I think there's still a chance for that, if we're strong and brave, like you were when you jumped on his back. Do you understand?" She looked at him pleadingly and thought how strange it was; she had never seen him when he looked so much like Jack.

"Yes," he said, and nodded. "I think . . . if we can get away from here . . . everything will be like it was. Where could we put him?"

"The pantry. There's food in there, and a good strong bolt on the outside. It's warm. And we can eat up the things from the refrigerator and the freezer. There will be plenty for all three of us until help comes."

"Do we do it now?"

"Yes, right now. Before he wakes up."

Danny put the bargate up while she folded Jack's hands on his chest and listened to his breathing for a moment. It was slow but regular. From the smell of him she thought he must have drunk a great deal . . . and he was out of the habit. She thought it might be liquor as much as the crack on the head with the bottle that had put him out.

She picked up his legs and began to drag him along the floor. She had been married to him for nearly seven years, he had lain on top of her countless times—in the thousands—but she had never realized how heavy he was. Her breath whistled painfully in and out of her hurt throat. Nevertheless, she felt better than she had in days. She was alive. Having just brushed so close to death, that was precious. And Jack was alive, too. By blind luck rather than plan, they had perhaps found the only way that would bring them all safely out.

Panting harshly, she paused a moment, holding Jack's feet against her hips. The surroundings reminded her of the old seafaring captain's cry in *Treasure Island* after old blind Pew had passed him the Black Spot: *We'll do em yet!*

And then she remembered, uncomfortably, that the old seadog had dropped dead mere seconds later.

"Are you all right, Mommy? Is he . . . is he too heavy?"

"I'll manage." She began to drag him again. Danny was beside Jack. One of his hands had fallen off his chest, and Danny replaced it gently, with love.

"Are you sure, Mommy?"

"Yes. It's the best thing, Danny."

"It's like putting him in jail."

"Only for awhile."

"Okay, then. Are you sure you can do it?"

"Yes."

But it was a near thing, at that. Danny had been cradling his father's head when they went over the doorsills, but his hands slipped in Jack's greasy hair as they went into the kitchen. The back of his head struck the tiles, and Jack began to moan and stir.

"You got to use smoke," Jack muttered quickly. "Now run and get me that gascan."

Wendy and Danny exchanged tight, fearful glances.

"Help me," she said in a low voice.

For a moment Danny stood as if paralyzed by his father's face, and then he moved jerkily to her side and helped her hold the left leg. They dragged him across the kitchen floor in a nightmare kind of slow motion, the only sounds the faint, insectile buzz of the fluorescent lights and their own labored breathing.

When they reached the pantry, Wendy put Jack's feet down and turned to fumble with the bolt. Danny looked down at Jack, who was lying limp and relaxed again. The shirttail had pulled out of the back of his pants as they dragged him and Danny wondered if Daddy was too drunk to be cold. It seemed wrong to lock him in the pantry like a wild animal, but he had seen what he tried to do to Mommy. Even upstairs he had known Daddy was going to do that. He had heard them arguing in his head.

(If only we could all be out of here. Or if it was a dream I was having, back in Stovington. If only.)

The bolt was stuck.

Wendy pulled at it as hard as she could, but it wouldn't move. She couldn't retract the goddam bolt. It was stupid and unfair . . . she had opened it with no trouble at all when she had gone in to get the can of soup. Now it wouldn't move, and what was she going to do? They couldn't put him in the walk-in refrigerator; he would freeze or smother to death. But if they left him out and he woke up . . .

Jack stirred again on the floor.

"I'll take care of it," he muttered. "I understand."

"He's waking up, Mommy!" Danny warned.

Sobbing now, she yanked at the bolt with both hands.

"Danny?" There was something softly menacing, if still blurry, in Jack's voice. "That you, ole doc?"

"Just go to sleep, Daddy," Danny said nervously. "It's bedtime, you know."

He looked up at his mother, still struggling with the bolt, and saw what was wrong immediately. She had forgotten to rotate the bolt before trying to withdraw it. The little catch was stuck in its notch.

"Here," he said low, and brushed her trembling hands aside; his own were shaking almost as badly. He knocked the catch loose with the heel of his hand and the bolt drew back easily.

"Quick," he said. He looked down. Jack's eyes had fluttered open again and this time Daddy was looking directly at him, his gaze strangely flat and speculative.

"You copied it," Daddy told him. "I know you did. But it's here somewhere. And I'll find it. That I promise you. I'll find it ..." His words slurred off again.

Wendy pushed the pantry door open with her knee, hardly noticing the pungent odor of dried fruit that wafted out. She picked up Jack's feet again and dragged him in. She was gasping harshly now, at the limit of her strength. As she yanked the chain pull that turned on the light, Jack's eyes fluttered open again.

"What are you doing? Wendy? What are you doing?"

She stepped over him.

He was quick; amazingly quick. One hand lashed out and she had to sidestep and nearly fall out the door to avoid his grasp. Still, he had caught a handful of her bathrobe and there was a heavy purring noise as it ripped. He was up on his hands and knees now, his hair hanging in his eyes, like some heavy animal. A large dog . . . or a lion.

"Damn you both. I know what you want. But you're not going to get it. This hotel . . . it's mine. It's me they want. Me! Me!"

"The door, Danny!" she screamed. *"Shut the door!"*

He pushed the heavy wooden door shut with a slam, just as Jack leaped. The door latched and Jack thudded uselessly against it.

Danny's small hands groped at the bolt. Wendy was too far away to help; the issue of whether he would be locked in or free was going to be decided in two seconds. Danny missed his grip, found it again, and shot the bolt across just as the latch began to jiggle madly up and down below it. Then it stayed up and there was a series of thuds as Jack slammed his shoulder against the door. The bolt, a quarter inch of steel in diameter, showed no signs of loosening. Wendy let her breath out slowly.

"Let me out of here!" Jack raged. "Let me out! Danny, doggone it, this is your father and I want to get out! *Now do what I tell you!"*

Danny's hand moved automatically toward the bolt. Wendy caught it and pressed it between her breasts.

"You mind your daddy, Danny! You do what I say! You do it or I'll give you a hiding you'll never forget. *Open this door or I'll bash your fucking brains in!"*

Danny looked at her, pale as window glass.

They could hear his breath tearing in and out behind the half inch of solid oak.

"Wendy, you let me out! Let me out right now! You cheap nickel-plated cold-cunt bitch! You let me out! I mean it! Let me out of here and I'll let it go! If you don't, I'll mess you up! I mean it! I'll mess you up so bad your own mother would pass you on the street! *Now open this door!*"

Danny moaned. Wendy looked at him and saw he was going to faint in a moment.

"Come on, doc," she said, surprised at the calmness of her own voice. "It's not your daddy talking, remember. It's the hotel."

"*Come back here and let me out right NOW!*" Jack screamed. There was a scraping, breaking sound as he attacked the inside of the door with his fingernails.

"It's the hotel," Danny said. "It's the hotel. I remember." But he looked back over his shoulder and his face was crumpled and terrified.

47

DANNY

It was three in the afternoon of a long, long day.

They were sitting on the big bed in their quarters. Danny was turning the purple VW model with the monster sticking out of the sun roof over and over in his hands, compulsively.

They had heard Daddy's batterings at the door all the way across the lobby, the batterings and his voice, hoarse and petulantly angry in a weak-king sort of a way, vomiting promises of punishment, vomiting profanity, promising both of them that they would live to regret betraying him after he had slaved his guts out for them over the years.

Danny thought they would no longer be able to hear it upstairs, but the sounds of his rage carried perfectly up the dumb-waiter shaft. Mommy's face was pale, and there were horrible brownish bruises on her neck where Daddy had tried to . . .

He turned the model over and over in his hands, Daddy's prize for having learned his reading lessons.

(*. . . where Daddy had tried to hug her too tight.*)

Mommy put some of her music on the little record player, scratchy and full of horns and flutes. She smiled at him tiredly. He tried to smile back and failed. Even with the volume turned up loud he thought he could still hear Daddy screaming at them and battering the pantry door like an animal in a zoo cage. What if Daddy had to go to the bathroom? What would he do then?

Danny began to cry.

Wendy turned the volume down on the record player at once, held him, rocked him on her lap.

"Danny, love, it will be all right. It will. If Mr. Hallorann didn't get your message, someone else will. As soon as the storm is over. No one could get up here until then anyway. Mr. Hallorann or anyone else. But when the storm is over, everything will be fine again. We'll leave here. And do you know what we'll do next spring? The three of us?"

Danny shook his head against her breasts. He didn't know. It seemed there could never be spring again.

"We'll go fishing. We'll rent a boat and go fishing, just like we did last year on Chatterton Lake. You and me and your daddy. And maybe you'll catch a bass for our supper. And maybe we won't catch anything, but we're sure to have a good time."

"I love you, Mommy," he said, and hugged her.

"Oh, Danny, I love you, too."

Outside, the wind whooped and screamed.

Around four-thirty, just as the daylight began to fail, the screams ceased.

They had both been dozing uneasily, Wendy still holding Danny in her arms, and she didn't wake. But Danny did. Somehow the silence was worse, more ominous than the screams and the blows against the strong pantry door. Was Daddy asleep again? Or dead? Or what?

(*Did he get out?*)

Fifteen minutes later the silence was broken by a hard,

grating, metallic rattle. There was a heavy grinding, then a mechanical humming. Wendy came awake with a cry.

The elevator was running again.

They listened to it, wide-eyed, hugging each other. It went from floor to floor, the grate rattling back, the brass door slamming open. There was laughter, drunken shouts, occasional screams, and the sounds of breakage.

The Overlook was coming to life around them.

48

JACK

He sat on the floor of the pantry with his legs out in front of him, a box of Triscuit crackers between them, looking at the door. He was eating the crackers one by one, not tasting them, only eating them because he had to eat something. When he got out of here, he was going to need his strength. All of it.

At this precise instant, he thought he had never felt quite so miserable in his entire life. His mind and body together made up a large-writ scripture of pain. His head ached terribly, the sick throb of a hangover. The attendant symptoms were there, too: his mouth tasted like a manure rake had taken a swing through it, his ears rang, his heart had an extra-heavy, thudding beat, like a tomtom. In addition, both shoulders ached fiercely from throwing himself against the door and his throat felt raw and peeled from useless shouting. He had cut his right hand on the doorlatch.

And when he got out of here, he was going to kick some ass.

He munched the Triscuits one by one, refusing to give in to his wretched stomach, which wanted to vomit up everything. He thought of the Excedrins in his pocket and decided to wait until his stomach had quieted a bit. No sense swallowing a painkiller if you were going to throw it right back up. Have to use your brain. The celebrated Jack Torrance brain. Aren't you the fellow who once was going to live by his wits? Jack Torrance, best-selling author. Jack Torrance, acclaimed playwright and winner of the New York Critics Circle Award. John

Torrance, man of letters, esteemed thinker, winner of the Pulitzer Prize at seventy for his trenchant book of memoirs, *My Life
in the Twentieth Century.* All any of that shit boiled down to was
living by your wits.

Living by your wits is always knowing where the wasps are.

He put another Triscuit into his mouth and crunched it up.

What it really came down to, he supposed, was their lack of
trust in him. Their failure to believe that he knew what was best
for them and how to get it. His wife had tried to usurp him,
first by fair

(sort of)

means, then by foul. When her little hints and whining
objections had been overturned by his own well-reasoned
arguments, she had turned his boy against him, tried to kill
him with a bottle, and then had locked him, of all places, in the
goddamned fucking *pantry.*

Still, a small interior voice nagged him.

*(Yes but where did the liquor come from? Isn't that really the central
point? You know what happens when you drink, you know it from bitter
experience. When you drink, you lose your wits.)*

He hurled the box of Triscuits across the small room. They
struck a shelf of canned goods and fell to the floor. He looked
at the box, wiped his lips with his hand, and then looked at his
watch. It was almost six-thirty. He had been in here for hours.
His wife had locked him in here and he'd been here for fucking
hours.

He could begin to sympathize with his father.

The thing he'd never asked himself, Jack realized now, was
exactly what had driven his daddy to drink in the first place.
And really ... when you came right down to what his old
students had been pleased to call the nitty-gritty ... hadn't it
been the woman he was married to? A milksop sponge of a
woman, always dragging silently around the house with an
expression of doomed martyrdom on her face? A ball and
chain around Daddy's ankle? No, not ball and chain. She had
never actively tried to make Daddy a prisoner, the way Wendy
had done to him. For Jack's father it must have been more like
the fate of McTeague the dentist at the end of Frank Norris's
great novel: handcuffed to a dead man in the wasteland. Yes,
that was better. Mentally and spiritually dead, his mother had

been handcuffed to his father by matrimony. Still, Daddy had tried to do right as he dragged her rotting corpse through life. He had tried to bring the four children up to know right from wrong, to understand discipline, and above all, to respect their father.

Well, they had been ingrates, all of them, himself included. And now he was paying the price; his own son had turned out to be an ingrate, too. But there was hope. He would get out of here somehow. He would chastise them both, and harshly. He would set Danny an example, so that the day might come when Danny was grown, a day when Danny would know what to do better than he himself had known.

He remembered the Sunday dinner when his father had caned his mother at the table . . . how horrified he and the others had been. Now he could see how necessary that had been, how his father had only been feigning drunkenness, how his wits had been sharp and alive underneath all along, watching for the slightest sign of disrespect.

Jack crawled after the Triscuits and began to eat them again, sitting by the door she had so treacherously bolted. He wondered exactly what his father had seen, and how he had caught her out by his playacting. Had she been sneering at him behind her hand? Sticking her tongue out? Making obscene finger gestures? Or only looking at him insolently and arrogantly, convinced that he was too stupidly drunk to see? Whatever it had been, he had caught her at it, and he had chastised her sharply. And now, twenty years later, he could finally appreciate Daddy's wisdom.

Of course you could say Daddy had been foolish to marry such a woman, to have handcuffed himself to that corpse in the first place . . . and a disrespectful corpse at that. But when the young marry in haste they must repent in leisure, and perhaps Daddy's daddy had married the same type of woman, so that unconsciously Jack's daddy had also married one, as Jack himself had. Except that *his* wife, instead of being satisfied with the passive role of having wrecked one career and crippled another, had opted for the poisonously active task of trying to destroy his last and best chance: to become a member of the Overlook's staff, and possibly to rise . . . all the way to the position of manager, in time. She was trying to deny him

Danny, and Danny was his ticket of admission. That was foolish, of course—why would they want the son when they could have the father?—but employers often had foolish ideas and that was the condition that had been made.

He wasn't going to be able to reason with her, he could see that now. He had tried to reason with her in the Colorado Lounge, and she had refused to listen, had hit him over the head with a bottle for his pains. But there would be another time, and soon. He would get out of here.

He suddenly held his breath and cocked his head. Somewhere a piano was playing boogie-woogie and people were laughing and clapping along. The sound was muffled through the heavy wooden door, but audible. The song was "There'll Be a Hot Time in the Old Town Tonight."

His hands curled helplessly into fists; he had to restrain himself from battering at the door with them. The party had begun again. The liquor would be flowing freely. Somewhere, dancing with someone else, would be the girl who had felt so maddeningly nude under her white silk gown.

"You'll pay for this!" he howled. "Goddam you two, you'll pay! You'll take your goddam medicine for this, I promise you! You—"

"Here, here, now," a mild voice said just outside the door. "No need to shout, old fellow. I can hear you perfectly well."

Jack lurched to his feet.

"Grady? Is that you?"

"Yes, sir. Indeed it is. You appear to have been locked in."

"Let me out, Grady. Quickly."

"I see you can hardly have taken care of the business we discussed, sir. The correction of your wife and son."

"They're the ones who locked me in. Pull the bolt, for God's sake!"

"You let them lock you in?" Grady's voice registered well-bred surprise. "Oh, dear. A woman half your size and a little boy? Hardly sets you off as being of top managerial timber, does it?"

A pulse began to beat in the clockspring of veins at Jack's right temple. "Let me out, Grady. I'll take care of them."

"Will you indeed, sir? I wonder." Well-bred surprise was replaced by well-bred regret. "I'm pained to say that I doubt it.

I—and others—have really come to believe that your heart is not in this, sir. That you haven't the . . . the belly for it."

"*I do!*" Jack shouted. "*I do, I swear it!*"

"You would bring us your son?"

"Yes! Yes!"

"Your wife would object to that very strongly, Mr. Torrance. And she appears to be . . . somewhat stronger than we had imagined. Somewhat more resourceful. She certainly seems to have gotten the better of *you*."

Grady tittered.

"Perhaps, Mr. Torrance, we should have been dealing with her all along."

"I'll bring him, I swear it," Jack said. His face was against the door now. He was sweating. "She won't object. I swear she won't. She won't be able to."

"You would have to kill her, I fear," Grady said coldly.

"I'll do what I have to do. Just *let me out*."

"You'll give your word on it, sir?" Grady persisted.

"My word, my promise, my sacred vow, whatever in hell you want. If you—"

There was a flat snap as the bolt was drawn back. The door shivered open a quarter of an inch. Jack's words and breath halted. For a moment he felt that death itself was outside that door.

The feeling passed.

He whispered: "Thank you, Grady. I swear you won't regret it. I swear you won't."

There was no answer. He became aware that all sounds had stopped except for the cold swooping of the wind outside.

He pushed the pantry door open; the hinges squealed faintly.

The kitchen was empty. Grady was gone. Everything was still and frozen beneath the cold white glare of the fluorescent bars. His eyes caught on the large chopping block where the three of them had eaten their meals.

Standing on top of it was a martini glass, a fifth of gin, and a plastic dish filled with olives.

Leaning against it was one of the roque mallets from the equipment shed.

He looked at it for a long time.

Then a voice, much deeper and much more powerful than Grady's, spoke from somewhere, everywhere . . . from inside him.

(Keep your promise, Mr. Torrance.)

"I will," he said. He heard the fawning servility in his own voice but was unable to control it. "I will."

He walked to the chopping block and put his hand on the handle of the mallet.

He hefted it.

Swung it.

It hissed viciously through the air.

Jack Torrance began to smile.

49

HALLORANN, GOING UP THE COUNTRY

It was quarter of two in the afternoon and according to the snow-clotted signs and the Hertz Buick's odometer, he was less than three miles from Estes Park when he finally went off the road.

In the hills, the Snow was falling faster and more furiously than Hallorann had ever seen (which was, perhaps, not to say a great deal, since Hallorann had seen as little snow as he could manage in his lifetime), and the wind was blowing a capricious gale—now from the west, now backing around to the north, sending clouds of powdery snow across his field of vision, making him coldly aware again and again that if he missed a turn he might well plunge two hundred feet off the road, the Electra cartwheeling ass over teapot as it went down. Making it worse was his own amateur status as a winter driver. It scared him to have the yellow center line buried under swirling, drifting snow, and it scared him when the heavy gusts of wind came unimpeded through the notches in the hills and actually made the heavy Buick slew around. It scared him that the road information signs were mostly masked with snow and you could flip a coin as to whether the road was going to break right or left up ahead in the white drive-in movie screen he seemed to be driving through. He was scared, all right. He had driven in a cold sweat since climbing into the hills west of Boulder and Lyons, handling the accelerator and brake as if they were Ming vases. Between rock 'n' roll tunes on the radio, the disc jockey constantly adjured motorists to stay off the main highways and under no conditions to go into the mountains, because many roads were impassable and all of them were dangerous. Scores of minor accidents had been reported, and two serious ones: a party of skiers in a VW microbus and a family that had been bound for Albuquerque through the Sangre de Cristo Mountains. The combined score on both was four dead and five wounded. "So stay off those roads and get into the good music here at KTLK," the jock concluded cheerily, and then compounded Hallorann's misery by playing "Seasons in the Sun." "We had joy, we had fun, we had—" Terry Jacks gibbered happily, and Hallorann snapped the radio off viciously, knowing he would have it back on in five minutes. No matter how bad it was, it was better than riding alone through this white madness.

(*Admit it. Dis heah black boy has got at least one long stripe of yaller . . . and it runs raht up his ebberlubbin back!*)

It wasn't even funny. He would have backed off before he even cleared Boulder if it hadn't been for his compulsion that the boy was in terrible trouble. Even now a small voice in the back of his skull—more the voice of reason than of cowardice, he thought—was telling him to hole up in an Estes Park motel for the night and wait for the plows to at least expose the center stripe again. That voice kept reminding him of the jet's shaky landing at Stapleton, of that sinking feeling that it was going to come in nose-first, delivering its passengers to the gates of hell rather than at Gate 39, Concourse B. But reason would not stand against the compulsion. It had to be today. The snowstorm was his own bad luck. He would have to cope with it. He was afraid that if he didn't, he might have something much worse to cope with in his dreams.

The wind gusted again, this time from the northeast, a little English on the ball if you please, and he was again cut off from the vague shapes of the hills and even from the embankments on either side of the road. He was driving through white null.

And then the high sodium lights of the snowplow loomed out of the soup, bearing down, and to his horror he saw that instead of being to one side, the Buick's nose was pointed directly between those headlamps. The plow was being none too choosy about keeping its own side of the road, and Hallorann had allowed the Buick to drift.

The grinding roar of the plow's diesel engine intruded over the bellow of the wind, and then the sound of its airhorn, hard, long, almost deafening.

Hallorann's testicles turned into two small wrinkled sacs filled with shaved ice. His guts seemed to have been transformed into a large mass of Silly Putty.

Color was materializing out of the white now, snow-clotted orange. He could see the high cab, even the gesticulating figure of the driver behind the single long wiper blade. He could see the V shape of the plow's wing blades, spewing more snow up onto the road's left-hand embankment like pallid, smoking exhaust.

WHAAAAAAAAA! the airhorn bellowed indignantly.

He squeezed the accelerator like the breast of a much-loved woman and the Buick scooted forward and toward the right. There was no embankment over here; the plows headed up instead of down had only to push the snow directly over the drop.

(The drop, ah yes, the drop—)

The wingblades on Hallorann's left, fully four feet higher than the Electra's roof, flirted by with no more than an inch or two to spare. Until the plow had actually cleared him, Hallorann had thought a crash inevitable. A prayer which was half an inarticulate apology to the boy flitted through his mind like a torn rag.

Then the plow was past, its revolving blue lights glinting and flashing in Hallorann's rearview mirror.

He jockeyed the Buick's steering wheel back to the left, but nothing doing. The scoot had turned into a skid, and the Buick was floating dreamily toward the lip of the drop, spuming snow from under its mudguards.

He flicked the wheel back the other way, in the skid's direction, and the car's front and rear began to swap places. Panicked now, he pumped the brake hard, and then felt a hard bump. In front of him the road was gone ... he was looking into a bottomless chasm of swirling snow and vague greenish-gray pines far away and far below.

(I'm going holy mother of Jesus I'm going off)

And that was where the car stopped, canting forward at a thirty-degree angle, the left fender jammed against a guardrail, the rear wheels nearly off the ground. When Hallorann tried reverse, the wheels only spun helplessly. His heart was doing a Gene Krupa drumroll.

He got out—very carefully he got out—and went around to the Buick's back deck.

He was standing there, looking at the back wheels helplessly, when a cheerful voice behind him said: "Hello there, fella. You must be shit right out of your mind."

He turned around and saw the plow forty yards further down the road, obscured in the blowing snow except for the raftered dark brown streak of its exhaust and the revolving blue lights on top. The driver was standing just behind him, dressed in a long sheepskin coat and a slicker over it. A blue-and-white pinstriped engineer's cap was perched on his head, and Hallorann could hardly believe it was staying on in the teeth of the wind.

(Glue. It sure-God must be glue.)

"Hi," he said. "Can you pull me back onto the road?"

"Oh, I guess I could," the plow driver said. "What the hell you doing way up here, mister? Good way to kill your ass."

"Urgent business."

"Nothin is that urgent," the plow driver said slowly and kindly, as if speaking to a mental defective. "If you'd'a hit that post a leetle mite harder, nobody woulda got you out till All Fools' Day. Don't come from these parts, do you?"

"No. And I wouldn't be here unless my business was as urgent as I say."

"That so?" The driver shifted his stance companionably as if they were having a desultory chat on the back steps instead of standing in a blizzard halfway between hoot and holler, with Hallorann's car balanced three hundred feet above the tops of the trees below.

"Where you headed? Estes?"

"No, a place called the Overlook Hotel," Hallorann said. "It's a little way above Sidewinder—"

But the driver was shaking his head dolefully.

"I guess I know well enough where that is," he said. "Mister, you'll never get up to the old Overlook. Roads between Estes Park and Sidewinder is bloody damn hell. It's driftin in right behind us no matter how hard we push. I come through drifts a few miles back that was damn near six feet through the middle. And even if you could make Sidewinder, why, the road's closed from there all the way across to Buckland, Utah. Nope." He shook his head. "Never make it, mister. Never make it at all."

"I have to try," Hallorann said, calling on his last reserves of patience to keep his voice normal. "There's a boy up there—"

"Boy? Naw. The Overlook closes down at the last end of September. No percentage keepin it open longer. Too many shitstorms like this."

"He's the son of the caretaker. He's in trouble."

"How would you know that?"

His patience snapped.

"For Christ's sake are you going to stand there and flap y'jaw at me the rest of the day? *I know, I know!* Now are you going to pull me back on the road or not?"

"Kind of testy, aren't you?" the driver observed, not particularly perturbed. "Sure, get back in there. I got a chain behind the seat."

Hallorann got back behind the wheel, beginning to shake with delayed reaction now. His hands were numbed almost clear through. He had forgotten to bring gloves.

The plow backed up to the rear of the Buick, and he saw the driver get out with a long coil of chain. Hallorann opened the door and shouted: "What can I do to help?"

"Stay out of the way, is all," the driver shouted back. "This ain't gonna take a blink."

Which was true. A shudder ran through the Buick's frame as the chain pulled tight, and a second later it was back on the road, pointed more or less toward Estes Park. The plow driver walked up beside the window and knocked on the safety glass. Hallorann rolled down the window.

"Thanks," he said. "I'm sorry I shouted at you."

"I been shouted at before," the driver said with a grin. "I guess you're sorta strung up. You take these." A pair of bulky blue mittens dropped into Hallorann's lap. "You'll need em when you go off the road again, I guess. Cold out. You wear em unless you want to spend the rest of your life pickin your nose with a crochetin hook. And you send em back. My wife knitted em and I'm partial to em. Name and address is sewed right into the linin. I'm Howard Cottrell, by the way. You just send em back when you don't need em anymore. And I don't want to have to go payin no postage due, mind."

"All right," Hallorann said. "Thanks. One hell of a lot."

"You be careful. I'd take you myself, but I'm busy as a cat in a mess of guitar strings."

"That's okay. Thanks again."

He started to roll up the window, but Cottrell stopped him.

"When you get to Sidewinder—*if* you get to Sidewinder— you go to Durkin's Conoco. It's right next to the li'brey. Can't miss it. You ask for Larry Durkin. Tell him Howie Cottrell sent you and you want to rent one of his snowmobiles. You mention my name and show those mittens, you'll get the cut rate."

"Thanks again," Hallorann said.

Cottrell nodded. "It's funny. Ain't no way you could know someone's in trouble up there at the Overlook . . . the phone's out, sure as hell. But I believe you. Sometimes I get feelins."

Hallorann nodded. "Sometimes I do, too."

"Yeah. I know you do. But you take care."

"I will."

Cottrell disappeared into the blowing dimness with a final wave, his engineer cap still mounted perkily on his head. Hallorann got going again, the chains flailing at the snowcover on the road, finally digging in enough to start the Buick moving. Behind him, Howard Cottrell gave a final good-luck blast on his plow's airhorn, although it was really unnecessary; Hallorann could feel him wishing him good luck.

That's two shines in one day, he thought, and that ought to be some kind of good omen. But he distrusted omens, good or bad. And meeting two people with the shine in one day (when he usually didn't run across more than four or five in the course of a year) might not mean anything. That feeling of finality, a feeling

(like things are all wrapped up)

he could not completely define was still very much with him. It was—

The Buick wanted to skid sideways around a tight curve and Hallorann jockeyed it carefully, hardly daring to breathe. He turned on the radio again and it was Aretha, and Aretha was just fine. He'd share his Hertz Buick with her any day.

Another gust of wind struck the car, making it rock and slip around. Hallorann cursed it and hunched more closely over the wheel. Aretha finished her song and then the jock was on again, telling him that driving today was a good way to get killed.

Hallorann snapped the radio off.

He did make it to Sidewinder, although he was four and a half hours on the road between Estes Park and there. By the time he got to the Upland Highway it was full dark, but the snowstorm showed no sign of abating. Twice he'd had to stop in front of drifts that were as high as his car's hood and wait for the plows to come along and knock holes in them. At one of the drifts the plow had come up on his side of the road and there had been another close call. The driver had merely swung around his car, not getting out to chew the fat, but he did deliver one of the two finger gestures that all Americans above the age of ten recognize, and it was not the peace sign.

It seemed that as he drew closer to the Overlook, his need to hurry became more and more compulsive. He found himself glancing at his wristwatch almost constantly. The hands seemed to be flying along.

Ten minutes after he had turned onto the Upland, he passed two signs. The whooping wind had cleared both of their snow pack so he was able to read them. SIDEWINDER 10, the first said. The second: ROAD CLOSED 12 MILES AHEAD DURING WINTER MONTHS.

"Larry Durkin," Hallorann muttered to himself. His dark face was strained and tense in the muted green glow of the dashboard instruments. It was ten after six. "The Conoco by the library. Larry—"

And that was when it struck him full-force, the smell of oranges and the thought-force, heavy and hateful, murderous:

(GET OUT OF HERE YOU DIRTY NIGGER THIS IS NONE OF YOUR BUSINESS YOU NIGGER TURN AROUND TURN AROUND OR WE'LL KILL YOU HANG YOU UP FROM A TREE LIMB YOU FUCKING JUNGLEBUNNY COON AND THEN BURN THE BODY THAT'S WHAT WE DO WITH NIGGERS SO TURN AROUND RIGHT NOW)

Halloran screamed in the close confines of the car. The message did not come to him in words but in a series of rebuslike images that were slammed into his head with terrific force. He took his hands from the steering wheel to blot the pictures out.

Then the car smashed broadside into one of the embankments, rebounded, slewed halfway around, and came to a stop. The rear wheels spun uselessly.

Halloran snapped the gearshift into park, and then covered his face with his hands. He did not precisely cry; what escaped him was an uneven huh-huh-huh sound. His chest heaved. He knew that if that blast had taken him on a stretch of road with a dropoff on one side or the other, he might well be dead now. Maybe that had been the idea. And it might hit him again, at any time. He would have to protect against it. He was surrounded by a red force of immense power that might have been memory. He was drowning in instinct.

He took his hands away from his face and opened his eyes cautiously. Nothing. If there was something trying to scare him again, it wasn't getting through. He was closed off.

Had that happened to the boy? Dear God, had that happened to the little boy?

And of all the images, the one that bothered him the most was that dull whacking sound, like a hammer splatting into thick cheese. What did that mean?

(Jesus, not that little boy. Jesus, please.)

He dropped the gearshift lever into low range and fed the engine gas a little at a time. The wheels spun, caught, spun, and caught again. The Buick began to move, its headlights cutting weakly through the swirling snow. He looked at his watch. Almost six-thirty now. And he was beginning to feel that was very late indeed.

50

REDRUM

Wendy Torrance stood indecisive in the middle of the bedroom, looking at her son, who had fallen fast asleep.

Half an hour ago the sounds had ceased. All of them, all at once. The elevator, the party, the sound of room doors opening and closing. Instead of easing her mind it made the tension that had been building in her even worse; it was like a malefic hush before the storm's final brutal push. But Danny had dozed off almost at once; first into a light, twitching doze, and in the last ten minutes or so a heavier sleep. Even looking directly at him she could barely see the slow rise and fall of his narrow chest.

She wondered when he had last gotten a full night's sleep, one without tormenting dreams or long periods of dark wakefulness, listening to revels that had only become audible—and visible—to her in the last couple of days, as the Overlook's grip on the three of them tightened.

(Real psychic phenomena or group hypnosis?)

She didn't know, and didn't think it mattered. What had been happening was just as deadly either way. She looked at Danny and thought

(God grant he lie still)

that if he was undisturbed, he might sleep the rest of the night through. Whatever talent he had, he was still a small boy and he needed his rest.

It was Jack she had begun to worry about.

She grimaced with sudden pain, took her hand away from her mouth, and saw she had torn off one of her fingernails. And her nails were one thing she'd always tried to keep nice. They weren't long enough to be called hooks, but still nicely shaped and

(and what are you worrying about your fingernails for?)

She laughed a little, but it was a shaky sound, without amusement.

First Jack had stopped howling and battering at the door. Then the party had begun again

(or did it ever stop? did it sometimes just drift into a slightly different angle of time where they weren't meant to hear it?)

counterpointed by the crashing, banging elevator. Then that had stopped. In that new silence, as Danny had been falling asleep, she had fancied she heard low, conspiratorial voices coming from the kitchen almost directly below them. At first she had dismissed it as the wind, which could mimic many different human vocal ranges, from a papery deathbed whisper around the doors and window frames to a full-out scream around the eaves . . . the sound of a woman fleeing a murderer in a cheap melodrama. Yet, sitting stiffly beside Danny, the idea that it was indeed voices became more and more convincing.

Jack and someone else, discussing his escape from the pantry.

Discussing the murder of his wife and son.

It would be nothing new inside these walls; murder had been done here before.

She had gone to the heating vent and had placed her ear against it, but at that exact moment the furnace had come on, and any sound was lost in the rush of warm air coming up from the basement. When the furnace had kicked off again, five minutes ago, the place was completely silent except for the wind, the gritty spatter of snow against the building, and the occasional groan of a board.

She looked down at her ripped fingernail. Small beads of blood were oozing up from beneath it.

(Jack's gotten out.)

(Don't talk nonsense.)

(Yes, he's out. He's gotten a knife from the kitchen or maybe the meat cleaver. He's on his way up here right now, walking along the sides of the risers so the stairs won't creak.)

(! You're insane !)

Her lips were trembling, and for a moment it seemed that she must have cried the words out loud. But the silence held.

She felt watched.

She whirled around and stared at the night-blackened window, and a hideous white face with circles of darkness for eyes was gibbering in at her, the face of a monstrous lunatic that had been hiding in these groaning walls all along—

It was only a pattern of frost on the outside of the glass.

She let her breath out in a long, susurrating whisper of fear, and it seemed to her that she heard, quite clearly this time, amused titters from somewhere.

(You're jumping at shadows. It's bad enough without that. By tomorrow morning, you'll be ready for the rubber room.)

There was only one way to allay those fears and she knew what it was.

She would have to go down and make sure Jack was still in the pantry.

Very simple. Go downstairs. Have a peek. Come back up. Oh, by the way, stop and grab the tray on the registration counter. The omelet would be a washout, but the soup could be reheated on the hotplate by Jack's typewriter.

(Oh yes and don't get killed if he's down there with a knife.)

She walked to the dresser, trying to shake off the mantle of fear that lay on her. Scattered across the dresser's top was a pile of change, a stack of gasoline chits for the hotel truck, the two pipes Jack brought with him everywhere but rarely smoked . . . and his keyring.

She picked it up, held it in her hand for a moment, and then put it back down. The idea of locking the bedroom door behind her had occurred, but it just didn't appeal. Danny was asleep. Vague thoughts of fire passed through her mind, and something else nibbled more strongly, but she let it go.

Wendy crossed the room, stood indecisively by the door for a moment, then took the knife from the pocket of her robe and curled her right hand around the wooden haft.

She pulled the door open.

The short corridor leading to their quarters was bare. The electric wall flambeaux all shone brightly at their regular intervals, showing off the rug's blue background and sinuous, weaving pattern.

(See? No boogies here.)

(No, of course not. They want you out. They want you to do something silly and womanish, and that is exactly what you are doing.)

She hesitated again, miserably caught, not wanting to leave Danny and the safety of the apartment and at the same time needing badly to reassure herself that Jack *was* still . . . safely packed away.

(Of course he is.)

(But the voices)

(There were no voices. It was your imagination. It was the wind.)
"It wasn't the wind."

The sound of her own voice made her jump. But the deadly certainty in it made her go forward. The knife swung by her side, catching angles of light and throwing them on the silk wallpaper. Her slippers whispered against the carpet's nap. Her nerves were singing like wires.

She reached the corner of the main corridor and peered around, her mind stiffened for whatever she might see there.

There was nothing to see.

After a moment's hesitation she rounded the corner and began down the main corridor. Each step toward the shadowy stairwell increased her dread and made her aware that she was leaving her sleeping son behind, alone and unprotected. The sound of her slippers against the carpet seemed louder and louder in her ears; twice she looked back over her shoulder to convince herself that someone wasn't creeping up behind her.

She reached the stairwell and put her hand on the cold newel post at the top of the railing. There were nineteen wide steps down to the lobby. She had counted them enough times to know. Nineteen carpeted stair risers, and nary a Jack crouching on any one of them. Of course not. Jack was locked in the pantry behind a hefty steel bolt and a thick wooden door.

But the lobby was dark and oh so full of shadows.

Her pulse thudded steadily and deeply in her throat.

Ahead and slightly to the left, the brass yaw of the elevator stood mockingly open, inviting her to step in and take the ride of her life.

(No thank you)

The inside of the car had been draped with pink and white crepe streamers. Confetti had burst from two tubular party favors. Lying in the rear left corner was an empty bottle of champagne.

She sensed movement above her and wheeled to look up the nineteen steps leading to the dark second-floor landing and saw nothing; yet there was a disturbing corner-of-the-eye sensation that things

(things)

had leaped back into the deeper darkness of the hallway up there just before her eyes could register them.

She looked down the stairs again.

Her right hand was sweating against the wooden handle of the knife; she switched it to her left, wiped her right palm against the pink terrycloth of her robe, and switched the knife back. Almost unaware that her mind had given her body the command to go forward, she began down the stairs, left foot then right, left foot then right, her free hand trailing lightly on the banister.

(Where's the party? Don't let me scare you away, you bunch of moldy sheets! Not one scared woman with a knife! Let's have a little music around here! Let's heave a little life!)

Ten steps down, a dozen, a bakers' dozen.

The light from the first-floor hall filtered a dull yellow down here, and she remembered that she would have to turn on the lobby lights either beside the entrance to the dining room or inside the manager's office.

Yet there was light coming from somewhere else, white and muted.

The fluorescents, of course. In the kitchen.

She paused on the thirteenth step, trying to remember if she had turned them off or left them on when she and Danny left. She simply couldn't remember.

Below her, in the lobby, highbacked chairs hulked in pools of shadow. The glass in the lobby doors was pressed white with a uniform blanket of drifted snow. Brass studs in the sofa cushions gleamed faintly like cat's eyes. There were a hundred places to hide.

Her legs stilted with fear, she continued down.

Now seventeen, now eighteen, now nineteen.

(Lobby level, madam. Step out carefully.)

The ballroom doors were thrown wide, only blackness spilling out. From within came a steady ticking, like a bomb. She stiffened, then remembered the clock on the mantel, the clock under glass. Jack or Danny must have wound it . . . or maybe it had wound itself up, like everything else in the Overlook.

She turned toward the reception desk, meaning to go through the gate and the manager's office and into the kitchen. Gleaming dull silver, she could see the intended lunch tray.

Then the clock began to strike, little tinkling notes.

Wendy stiffened, her tongue rising to the roof of her mouth.

Then she relaxed. It was striking eight, that was all. Eight o'clock . . . *five, six, seven* . . .

She counted the strokes. It suddenly seemed wrong to move again until the clock had stilled.

. . . *eight* . . . *nine* . . .

(?? *Nine* ??)

. . . *ten* . . . *eleven* . . .

Suddenly, belatedly, it came to her. She turned back clumsily for the stairs, knowing already she was too late. But how could she have known?

Twelve.

All the lights in the ballroom went on. There was a huge, shrieking flourish of brass. Wendy screamed aloud, the sound of her cry insignificant against the blare issuing from those brazen lungs.

"Unmask!" the cry echoed. *"Unmask! Unmask!"*

Then they faded, as if down a long corridor of time, leaving her alone again.

No, not alone.

She turned and he was coming for her.

It was Jack and yet not Jack. His eyes were lit with a vacant, murderous glow; his familiar mouth now wore a quivering, joyless grin.

He had the roque mallet in one hand.

"Thought you'd lock me in? Is that what you thought you'd do?"

The mallet whistled through the air. She stepped backward, tripped over a hassock, fell to the lobby rug.

"Jack—"

"You bitch," he whispered. "I know what you are."

The mallet came down again with whistling, deadly velocity and buried itself in her soft stomach. She screamed, suddenly submerged in an ocean of pain. Dimly she saw the mallet rebound. It came to her with sudden numbing reality that he meant to beat her to death with the mallet he held in his hands.

She tried to cry out to him again, to beg him to stop for Danny's sake, but her breath had been knocked loose. She could only force out a weak whimper, hardly a sound at all.

"Now. Now, by Christ," he said, grinning. He kicked the hassock out of his way. "I guess you'll take your medicine now."

The mallet whickered down. Wendy rolled to her left, her robe tangling above her knees. Jack's hold on the mallet was jarred loose when it hit the floor. He had to stoop and pick it up, and while he did she ran for the stairs, the breath at last sobbing back into her. Her stomach was a bruise of throbbing pain.

"Bitch," he said through his grin, and began to come after her. "You stinking bitch, I guess you'll get what's coming to you. I guess you will."

She heard the mallet whistle through the air and then agony exploded on her right side as the mallet-head took her just below the line of her breasts, breaking two ribs. She fell forward on the steps and new agony ripped her as she struck on the wounded side. Yet instinct made her roll over, roll away, and the mallet whizzed past the side of her face, missing by a naked inch. It struck the deep pile of the stair carpeting with a muffled thud. That was when she saw the knife, which had been jarred out of her hand by her fall. It lay glittering on the fourth stair riser.

"Bitch," he repeated. The mallet came down. She shoved herself upward and it landed just below her kneecap. Her lower leg was suddenly on fire. Blood began to trickle down her calf. And then the mallet was coming down again. She jerked her head away from it and it smashed into the stair riser in the hollow between her neck and shoulder, scraping away the flesh from her ear.

He brought the mallet down again and this time she rolled toward him, down the stairs, inside the arc of his swing. A shriek escaped her as her broken ribs thumped and grated. She struck his shins with her body while he was offbalance and he fell backward with a yell of anger and surprise, his feet jigging to keep their purchase on the stair riser. Then he thumped to the floor, the mallet flying from his hand. He sat up, staring at her for a moment with shocked eyes.

"I'll kill you for that," he said.

He rolled over and stretched out for the handle of the mallet. Wendy forced herself to her feet. Her left leg sent bolt after bolt of pain all the way up to her hip. Her face was ashy pale but set. She leaped onto his back as his hand closed over the shaft of the roque mallet.

"Oh dear God!" she screamed to the Overlook's shadowy lobby, and buried the kitchen knife in his lower back up to the handle.

He stiffened beneath her and then shrieked. She thought she had never heard such an awful sound in her whole life; it was as if the very boards and windows and doors of the hotel had screamed. It seemed to go on and on while he remained board-stiff beneath her weight. They were like a parlor charade of horse and rider. Except that the back of his red-and-black-checked flannel shirt was growing darker, sodden, with spreading blood.

Then he collapsed forward on his face, bucking her off on her hurt side, making her groan.

She lay breathing harshly for a time, unable to move. She was an excruciating throb of pain from one end to the other. Every time she inhaled, something stabbed viciously at her, and her neck was wet with blood from her grazed ear.

There was only the sound of her struggle to breathe, the wind, and the ticking clock in the ballroom.

At last she forced herself to her feet and hobbled across to the stairway. When she got there she clung to the newel post, head down, waves of faintness washing over her. When it had passed a little, she began to climb, using her unhurt leg and pulling with her arms on the banister. Once she looked up, expecting to see Danny there, but the stairway was empty.

(Thank God he slept through it thank God thank God)

Six steps up she had to rest, her head down, her blond hair coiled on and over the banister. Air whistled painfully through her throat, as if it had grown barbs. Her right side was a swollen, hot mass.

(Come on Wendy come on old girl get a locked door behind you and then look at the damage thirteen more to go not so bad. And when you get to the upstairs corridor you can crawl. I give my permission.)

She drew in as much breath as her broken ribs would allow and half-pulled, half-fell up another riser. And another.

She was on the ninth, almost halfway up, when Jack's voice came from behind and below her. He said thickly: "You bitch. You killed me."

Terror as black as midnight swept through her. She looked over her shoulder and saw Jack getting slowly to his feet.

His back was bowed over, and she could see the handle of the kitchen knife sticking out of it. His eyes seemed to have contracted, almost to have lost themselves in the pale, sagging folds of the skin around them. He was grasping the roque mallet loosely in his left hand. The end of it was bloody. A scrap of her pink terrycloth robe stuck almost in the center.

"I'll give you your medicine," he whispered, and began to stagger toward the stairs.

Whimpering with fear, she began to pull herself upward again. Ten steps, a dozen, a baker's dozen. But still the first-floor hallway looked as far above her as an unattainable mountain peak. She was panting now, her side shrieking in protest. Her hair swung wildly back and forth in front of her face. Sweat stung her eyes. The ticking of the domed clock in the ballroom seemed to fill her ears, and counterpointing it, Jack's panting, agonized gasps as he began to mount the stairs.

51

HALLORANN ARRIVES

Larry Durkin was a tall and skinny man with a morose face overtopped with a luxuriant mane of red hair. Hallorann had caught him just as he was leaving the Conoco station, the morose face buried deeply inside an army-issue parka. He was reluctant to do any more business that stormy day no matter how far Hallorann had come, and even more reluctant to rent one of his two snowmobiles out to this wild-eyed black man who insisted on going up to the old Overlook. Among people who had spent most of their lives in the little town of Sidewinder, the hotel had a smelly reputation. Murder had been done up there. A bunch of hoods had run the place for a while, and cutthroat businessmen had run it for a while, too. And things had been done up at the old Overlook that never made the papers, because money has a way of talking. But the people in Sidewinder had a pretty good idea. Most of the hotel's chambermaids came from here, and chambermaids see a lot.

But when Hallorann mentioned Howard Cottrell's name and showed Durkin the tag inside one of the blue mittens, the gas station owner thawed.

"Sent you here, did he?" Durkin asked, unlocking one of the garage bays and leading Hallorann inside. "Good to know the old rip's got some sense left. I thought he was plumb out of it." He flicked a switch and a bank of very old and very dirty fluorescents buzzed wearily into life. "Now what in the tarnal creation would you want up at that place, fella?"

Hallorann's nerve had begun to crack. The last few miles into Sidewinder had been very bad. Once a gust of wind that must have been tooling along at better than sixty miles an hour had floated the Buick all the way around in a 360° turn. And there were still miles to travel with God alone knew what at the other end of them. He was terrified for the boy. Now it was almost ten minutes to seven and he had this whole song and dance to go through again.

"Somebody is in trouble up there," he said very carefully. "The son of the caretaker."

"Who? Torrance's boy? Now what kind of trouble could he be in?"

"I don't know," Hallorann muttered. He felt sick with the time this was taking. He was speaking with a country man, and he knew that all country men feel a similar need to approach their business obliquely, to smell around its corners and sides before plunging into the middle of dealing. But there was no time, because now he was one scared nigger and if this went on much longer he just might decide to cut and run.

"Look," he said. "Please. I need to go up there and I have to have a snowmobile to get there. I'll pay your price, but for God's sake let me get on with my business!"

"All right," Durkin said, unperturbed. "If Howard sent you, that's good enough. You take this ArcticCat. I'll put five gallons of gas in the can. Tank's full. She'll get you up and back down, I guess."

"Thank you," Hallorann said, not quite steadily.

"I'll take twenty dollars. That includes the ethyl."

Hallorann fumbled a twenty out of his wallet and handed it over. Durkin tucked it into one of his shirt pockets with hardly a look.

"Guess maybe we better trade jackets, too," Durkin said, pulling off his parka. "That overcoat of yours ain't gonna be worth nothin tonight. You trade me back when you return the snowsled."

"Oh, hey, I couldn't—"

"Don't fuss with me," Durkin interrupted, still mildly. "I ain't sending you out to freeze. I only got to walk down two blocks and I'm at my own supper table. Give it over."

Slightly dazed, Hallorann traded his overcoat for Durkin's furlined parka. Overhead the fluorescents buzzed faintly, reminding him of the lights in the Overlook's kitchen.

"Torrance's boy," Durkin said, and shook his head. "Good-lookin little tyke, ain't he? He n his dad was in here a lot before the snow really flew. Drivin the hotel truck, mostly. Looked to me like the two of em was just about as tight as they could get. That's one little boy that loves his daddy. Hope he's all right."

"So do I." Hallorann zipped the parka and tied the hood.

"Lemme help you push that out," Durkin said. They rolled the snowmobile across the oil-stained concrete and toward the garage bay. "You ever drove one of these before?"

"No."

"Well, there's nothing to it. The instructions are pasted there on the dashboard, but all there really is, is stop and go. Your throttle's here, just like a motorcycle throttle. Brake on the other side. Lean with it on the turns. This baby will do seventy on hardpack, but on this powder you'll get no more than fifty and that's pushing it."

Now they were in the service station's snow-filled front lot, and Durkin had raised his voice to make himself heard over the battering of the wind. "Stay on the road!" he shouted at Hallorann's ear. "Keep your eye on the guardrail posts and the signs and you'll be all right, I guess. If you get off the road, you're going to be dead. Understand?"

Hallorann nodded.

"Wait a minute!" Durkin told him, and ran back into the garage bay.

While he was gone, Hallorann turned the key in the ignition and pumped the throttle a little. The snowmobile coughed into brash, choppy life.

Durkin came back with a red and black ski mask.

"Put this on under your hood!" he shouted.

Hallorann dragged it on. It was a tight fit, but it cut the last of the numbing wind off from his cheeks and forehead and chin.

Durkin leaned close to make himself heard.

"I guess you must know about things the same way Howie does sometimes," he said. "It don't matter, except that place has got a bad reputation around here. I'll give you a rifle if you want it."

"I don't think it would do any good," Hallorann shouted back.

"You're the boss. But if you get that boy, you bring him to Sixteen Peach Lane. The wife'll have some soup on."

"Okay. Thanks for everything."

"You watch out!" Durkin yelled. "Stay on the road!"

Hallorann nodded and twisted the throttle slowly. The snowmobile purred forward, the headlamp cutting a clean cone of light through the thickly falling snow. He saw Durkin's upraised hand in the rearview mirror, and raised his own in return. Then he nudged the handlebars to the left and was traveling up Main Street, the snowmobile coursing smoothly through the white light thrown by the streetlamps. The speedometer stood at thirty miles an hour. It was ten past seven. At the Overlook, Wendy and Danny were sleeping and Jack Torrance was discussing matters of life and death with the previous caretaker.

Five blocks up Main, the streetlamps ended. For half a mile there were small houses, all buttoned tightly up against the storm, and then only wind-howling darkness. In the black again with no light but the thin spear of the snowmobile's headlamp, terror closed in on him again, a childlike fear, dismal and disheartening. He had never felt so alone. For several minutes, as the few lights of Sidewinder dwindled away and disappeared in the rearview, the urge to turn around and go back was almost insurmountable. He reflected that for all of Durkin's concern for Jack Torrance's boy, he had not offered to take the other snowmobile and come with him.

(That place has got a bad reputation around here.)

Clenching his teeth, he turned the throttle higher and watched the needle on the speedometer climb past forty and settle at forty-five. He seemed to be going horribly fast and yet he was afraid it wasn't fast enough. At this speed it would take him almost an hour to get to the Overlook. But at a higher speed he might not get there at all.

He kept his eyes glued to the passing guardrails and the dime-sized reflectors mounted on top of each one. Many of them were buried under drifts. Twice he saw curve signs dangerously late and felt the snowmobile riding up the drifts that masked the dropoff before turning back onto where the road was in the summertime. The odometer counted off the miles at a maddeningly slow clip—five, ten, finally fifteen. Even behind the knitted ski mask his face was beginning to stiffen up and his legs were growing numb.

(*Guess I'd give a hundred bucks for a pair of ski pants.*)

As each mile turned over, his terror grew—as if the place had a poison atmosphere that thickened as you neared it. Had it ever been like this before? He had never really liked the Overlook, and there had been others who shared his feeling, but it had never been like this.

He could feel the voice that had almost wrecked him outside of Sidewinder still trying to get in, to get past his defenses to the soft meat inside. If it had been strong twenty-five miles back, how much stronger would it be now? He couldn't keep it out entirely. Some of it was slipping through, flooding his brain with sinister subliminal images. More and more he got the image of a badly hurt woman in a bathroom, holding her hands up uselessly to ward off a blow, and he felt more and more that the woman must be—

(*Jesus, watch out!*)

The embankment was looming up ahead of him like a freight train. Wool-gathering, he had missed a turn sign. He jerked the snowmobile's steering gear hard right and it swung around, tilting as it did so. From underneath came the harsh grating sound of the snowtread on rock. He thought the snowmobile was going to dump him, and it did totter on the knife-edge of balance before half-driving, half-skidding back down to the more or less level surface of the snow-buried road. Then the dropoff was ahead of him, the headlamp showing an abrupt end to the snowcover and darkness beyond that. He turned the snowmobile the other way, a pulse beating sickly in his throat.

(Keep it on the road Dicky old chum.)

He forced himself to turn the throttle up another notch. Now the speedometer needle was pegged just below fifty. The wind howled and roared. The headlamp probed the dark.

An unknown length of time later, he came around a drift-banked curve and saw a glimmering flash of light ahead. Just a glimpse, and then it was blotted out by a rising fold of land. The glimpse was so brief he was persuading himself it had been wishful thinking when another turn brought it in view again, slightly closer, for another few seconds. There was no question of its reality this time; he had seen it from just this angle too many times before. It was the Overlook. There were lights on the first floor and lobby levels, it looked like.

Some of his terror—the part that had to do with driving off the road or wrecking the snowmobile on an unseen curve—melted entirely away. The snowmobile swept surely into the first half of an S curve that he now remembered confidently foot for foot, and that was when the headlamp picked out the

(oh dear jesus god what is it)

in the road ahead of him. Limned in stark blacks and whites, Hallorann first thought it was some hideously huge timberwolf that had been driven down from the high country by the storm. Then, as he closed on it, he recognized it and horror closed his throat.

Not a wolf but a lion. A hedge lion.

Its features were a mask of black shadow and powdered snow, its haunches wound tight to spring. And it did spring, snow billowing around its pistoning rear legs in a silent burst of crystal glitter.

Hallorann screamed and twisted the handlebars hard right, ducking low at the same time. Scratching, ripping pain scrawled itself across his face, his neck, his shoulders. The ski mask was torn open down the back. He was hurled from the snowmobile. He hit the snow, plowed through it, rolled over.

He could feel it coming for him. In his nostrils there was a bitter smell of green leaves and holly. A huge hedge paw batted him in the small of the back and he flew ten feet through the air, splayed out like a rag doll. He saw the snowmobile, riderless, strike the embankment and rear up, its headlamp searching the sky. It fell over with a thump and stalled.

Then the hedge lion was on him. There was a crackling, rustling sound. Something raked across the front of the parka, shredding it. It might have been stiff twigs, but Hallorann knew it was claws.

"You're not there!" Hallorann screamed at the circling, snarling hedge lion. *"You're not there at all!"* He struggled to his feet and made it halfway to the snowmobile before the lion lunged, batting him across the head with a needle-tipped paw. Hallorann saw silent, exploding lights.

"Not there," he said again, but it was a fading mutter. His knees unhinged and dropped him into the snow. He crawled for the snowmobile, the right side of his face a scarf of blood. The lion struck him again, rolling him onto his back like a turtle. It roared playfully.

Hallorann struggled to reach the snowmobile. What he needed was there. And then the lion was on him again, ripping and clawing.

52

WENDY AND JACK

Wendy risked another glance over her shoulder. Jack was on the sixth riser, clinging to the banister much as she was doing herself. He was still grinning, and dark blood oozed slowly through the grin and slipped down the line of his jaw. He bared his teeth at her.

"I'm going to bash your brains in. Bash them right to fuck in." He struggled up another riser.

Panic spurred her, and the ache in her side diminished a little. She pulled herself up as fast as she could regardless of the pain, yanking convulsively at the banister. She reached the top and threw a glance behind her.

He seemed to be gaining strength rather than losing it. He was only four risers from the top, measuring the distance with the roque mallet in his left hand as he pulled himself up with his right.

"Right behind you," he panted through his bloody grin, as if reading her mind. "Right behind you now, bitch. With your medicine."

She fled stumblingly down the main corridor, hands pressed to her side.

The door to one of the rooms jerked open and a man with a green ghoulmask on popped out. *"Great party, isn't it?"* He screamed into her face, and pulled the waxed string of a party-favor. There was an echoing bang and suddenly crepe streamers were drifting all around her. The man in the ghoulmask cackled and slammed back into his room. She fell forward onto the carpet, full-length. Her right side seemed to explode with pain, and she fought off the blackness of unconsciousness desperately. Dimly she could hear the elevator running again, and beneath her splayed fingers she could see that the carpet pattern appeared to move, swaying and twining sinuously.

The mallet slammed down behind her and she threw herself forward, sobbing. Over her shoulder she saw Jack stumble forward, overbalance, and bring the mallet down just before he crashed to the carpet, expelling a bright splash of blood onto the nap.

The mallet head struck her squarely between the shoulder blades and for a moment the agony was so great that she could only writhe, hands opening and clenching. Something inside her had snapped—she had heard it clearly, and for a few moments she was aware only in a muted, muffled way, as if she were merely observing these things through a cloudy wrapping of gauze.

Then full consciousness came back, terror and pain with it.

Jack was trying to get up so he could finish the job.

Wendy tried to stand and found it was impossible. Electric bolts seemed to course up and down her back at the effort. She began to crawl along in a sidestroke motion. Jack was crawling after her, using the roque mallet as a crutch or a cane.

She reached the corner and pulled herself around it, using her hands to yank at the angle of the wall. Her terror deepened—she would not have believed that possible, but it was. It was a hundred times worse not to be able to see him or know how close he was getting. She tore out fistfuls of the carpet napping pulling herself along, and she was halfway down this short hall before she noticed the bedroom door was standing wide open.

(Danny! O Jesus)

She forced herself to her knees and then clawed her way to her feet, fingers slipping over the silk wallpaper. Her nails pulled little strips of it loose. She ignored the pain and half-walked, half-shambled through the doorway as Jack came around the far corner and began to lunge his way down toward the open door, leaning on the roque mallet.

She caught the edge of the dresser, held herself up against it, and grabbed the doorframe.

Jack shouted at her: "Don't you shut that door! Goddam you, don't you *dare* shut it!"

She slammed it closed and shot the bolt. Her left hand pawed wildly at the junk on the dresser, knocking loose coins onto the floor where they rolled in every direction. Her hand seized the key ring just as the mallet whistled down against the door, making it tremble in its frame. She got the key into the lock on the second stab and twisted it to the right. At the sound of the tumblers falling, Jack screamed. The mallet came down against the door in a volley of booming blows that made her flinch and step back. How could he be doing that with a knife in his back? Where was he finding the strength? She wanted to shriek *Why aren't you dead?* at the locked door.

Instead she turned around. She and Danny would have to go into the attached bathroom and lock that door, too, in case Jack actually could break through the bedroom door. The thought of escaping down the dumb-waiter shaft crossed her mind in a wild burst, and then she rejected it. Danny was small enough to fit into it, but she would be unable to control the rope pull. He might go crashing all the way to the bottom.

The bathroom it would have to be. And if Jack broke through into there—

But she wouldn't allow herself to think of it.

"Danny, honey, you'll have to wake up n—"

But the bed was empty.

When he had begun to sleep more soundly, she had thrown the blankets and one of the quilts over him. Now they were thrown back.

"I'll get you!" Jack howled. "I'll get both of you!" Every other word was punctuated with a blow from the roque hammer, yet Wendy ignored both. All of her attention was focused on that empty bed.

"Come out here! Unlock this goddam door!"

"Danny?" she whispered.

Of course . . . when Jack had attacked her. It had come through to him, as violent emotions always seemed to. Perhaps he'd even seen the whole thing in a nightmare. He was hiding.

She fell clumsily to her knees, enduring another bolt of pain from her swollen and bleeding leg, and looked under the bed. Nothing there but dustballs and Jack's bedroom slippers.

Jack screamed her name, and this time when he swung the mallet, a long splinter of wood jumped from the door and clattered off the hardwood planking. The next blow brought a sickening, splintering crack, the sound of dry kindling under a hatchet. The bloody mallet head, now splintered and gouged in its own right, bashed through the new hole in the door, was withdrawn, and came down again, sending wooden shrapnel flying across the room.

Wendy pulled herself to her feet again using the foot of the bed, and hobbled across the room to the closet. Her broken ribs stabbed at her, making her groan.

"Danny?"

She brushed the hung garments aside frantically; some of them slipped their hangers and ballooned gracelessly to the floor. He was not in the closet.

She hobbled toward the bathroom and as she reached the door she glanced back over her shoulder. The mallet crashed through again, widening the hole, and then a hand appeared, groping for the bolt. She saw with horror that she had left Jack's keyring dangling from the lock.

The hand yanked the bolt back, and as it did so it struck the bunched keys. They jingled merrily. The hand clutched them victoriously.

With a sob, she pushed her way into the bathroom and slammed the door just as the bedroom door burst open and Jack charged through, bellowing.

Wendy ran the bolt and twisted the spring lock, looking around desperately. The bathroom was empty. Danny wasn't here, either. And as she caught sight of her own blood-smeared, horrified face in the medicine cabinet mirror, she was glad. She had never believed that children should be witness to the little quarrels of their parents. And perhaps the thing that was now raving through the bedroom, overturning things and smashing them, would finally collapse before it could go after her son. Perhaps, she thought, it might be possible for her to inflict even more damage on it . . . kill it, perhaps.

Her eyes skated quickly over the bathroom's machine-produced porcelain surfaces, looking for anything that might serve as a weapon. There was a bar of soap, but even wrapped in a towel she didn't think it would be lethal enough. Everything else was bolted down. God, was there nothing she could do?

Beyond the door, the animal sounds of destruction went on and on, accompanied by thick shouts that they would "take their medicine" and "pay for what they'd done to him." He would "show them who's boss." They were "worthless puppies," the both of them.

There was a thump as her record player was overturned, a hollow crash as the secondhand TV's picture tube was smashed, the tinkle of windowglass followed by a cold draft under the bathroom door. A dull thud as the mattresses were ripped from the twin beds where they had slept together, hip to hip. Boomings as Jack struck the walls indiscriminately with the mallet.

There was nothing of the real Jack in that howling, maundering, petulant voice, though. It alternately whined in tones of selfpity and rose in lurid screams; it reminded her chillingly of the screams that sometimes rose in the geriatrics ward of the hospital where she had worked summers as a high school kid. Senile dementia. Jack wasn't out there anymore. She was hearing the lunatic, raving voice of the Overlook itself.

The mallet smashed into the bathroom door, knocking out a huge chunk of the thin paneling. Half of a crazed and working face stared in at her. The mouth and cheeks and throat were lathered in blood, the single eye she could see was tiny and piggish and glittering,

"Nowhere left to run, you cunt," it panted at her through its grin. The mallet descended again, knocking wood splinters into the tub and against the reflecting surface of the medicine cabinet—

(!! The medicine cabinet !!)

A desperate whining noise began to escape her as she whirled, pain temporarily forgotten, and threw the mirror door of the cabinet back. She began to paw through its contents. Behind her that hoarse voice bellowed: "Here I come now! Here I come now, you pig!" It was demolishing the door in a machine-like frenzy.

Bottles and jars fell before her madly searching fingers—cough syrup, Vaseline, Clairol Herbal Essence shampoo, hydrogen peroxide, benzocaine—they fell into the sink and shattered.

Her hand closed over the dispenser of double-edged razor blades just as she heard the hand again, fumbling for the bolt and the spring lock.

She slipped one of the razor blades out, fumbling at it, her breath coming in harsh little gasps. She had cut the ball of her thumb. She whirled around and slashed at the hand, which had turned the lock and was now fumbling for the bolt.

Jack screamed. The hand was jerked back.

Panting, holding the razor blade between her thumb and index finger, she waited for him to try again. He did, and she slashed. He screamed again, trying to grab her hand, and she slashed at him again. The razor blade turned in her hand, cutting her again, and dropped to the the floor by the toilet.

Wendy slipped another blade out of the dispenser and waited.

Movement in the other room—

(?? going away ??)

And a sound coming through the bedroom window. A motor. A high, insectile buzzing sound.

A roar of anger from Jack and then—yes, yes, she was sure of it—he was leaving the caretaker's apartment, plowing through the wreckage and out into the hall.

(?? Someone coming a ranger Dick Hallorann ??)

"Oh God," she muttered brokenly through a mouth that seemed filled with broken sticks and old sawdust. "Oh God, oh please."

She had to leave now, had to go find her son so they could face the rest of this nightmare side by side. She reached out and fumbled at the bolt. Her arm seemed to stretch for miles. At last she got it to come free. She pushed the door open, staggered out, and was suddenly overcome by the horrible certainty that Jack had only pretended to leave, that he was lying in wait for her.

Wendy looked around. The room was empty, the living room too. Jumbled, broken stuff everywhere.

The closet? Empty.

Then the soft shades of gray began to wash over her and she fell down on the mattress Jack had ripped from the bed, semiconscious.

53

HALLORANN LAID LOW

Hallorann reached the overturned snowmobile just as, a mile and a half away, Wendy was pulling herself around the corner and into the short hallway leading to the caretaker's apartment.

It wasn't the snowmobile he wanted but the gascan held onto the back by a pair of elastic straps. His hands, still clad in Howard Cottrell's blue mittens, seized the top strap and pulled it free as the hedge lion roared behind him—a sound that seemed to be more in his head than outside of it. A hard, brambly slap to his left leg, making the knee sing with pain as it was driven in a way the joint had never been expected to bend. A groan escaped Hallorann's clenched teeth. It would come for the kill any time now, tired of playing with him.

He fumbled for the second strap. Sticky blood ran in his eyes.

(Roar! Slap!)

That one raked across his buttocks, almost tumbling him over and away from the snowmobile again. He held on—no exaggeration—for dear life.

Then he had freed the second strap. He clutched the gascan to him as the lion struck again, rolling him over on his back. He saw it again, only a shadow in the darkness and falling snow, as nightmarish as a moving gargoyle. Hallorann twisted at the can's cap as the moving shadow stalked him, kicking up snowpuffs. As it moved in again the cap spun free, releasing the pungent smell of the gasoline.

Hallorann gained his knees and as it came at him, lowslung and incredibly quick, he splashed it with the gas.

There was a hissing, spitting sound and it drew back.

"Gas!" Hallorann cried, his voice shrill and breaking. "Gonna burn you, baby! Dig on it awhile!"

The lion came at him again, still spitting angrily. Hallorann splashed it again but this time the lion didn't give. It charged ahead. Hallorann sensed rather than saw its head angling at his face and he threw himself backward, partially avoiding it. Yet the lion still hit his upper rib cage a glancing blow, and a flare of pain struck there. Gas gurgled out of the can, which he still held, and doused his right hand and arm, cold as death.

Now he lay on his back in a snow angel, to the right of the snowmobile by about ten paces. The hissing lion was a bulking presence to his left, closing in again. Hallorann thought he could see its tail twitching.

He yanked Cottrell's mitten off his right hand, tasting sodden wool and gasoline. He ripped up the hem of the parka and jammed his hand into his pants pocket. Down in there, along with his keys and his change, was a very battered old Zippo lighter. He had bought it in Germany in 1954. Once the hinge had broken and he had returned it to the Zippo factory and they had repaired it without charge, just as advertised.

A nightmare flood of thoughts flooding through his mind in a split second.

(Dear Zippo my lighter was swallowed by a crocodile dropped from an airplane lost in the Pacific trench saved me from a Kraut bullet in the Battle of the Bulge dear Zippo if this fucker doesn't go that lion is going to rip my head off)

The lighter was out. He clicked the hood back. The lion, rushing at him, a growl like ripping cloth, his finger flicking the striker wheel, spark, *flame,*

(my hand)

his gasoline-soaked hand suddenly ablaze, the flames running up the sleeve of the parka, no pain, no pain yet, the lion shying from the torch suddenly blazing in front of it, a hideous flickering hedge sculpture with eyes and a mouth, shying away, too late.

Wincing at the pain, Hallorann drove his blazing arm into its stiff and scratchy side.

In an instant the whole creature was in flames, a prancing, writhing pyre on the snow. It bellowed in rage and pain, seeming to chase its flaming tail as it zigzagged away from Hallorann.

He thrust his own arm deep into the snow, killing the flames, unable to take his eyes from the hedge lion's death agonies for a moment. Then, gasping, he got to his feet. The arm of Durkin's parka was sooty but unburned, and that also described his hand. Thirty yards downhill from where he stood, the hedge lion had turned into a fireball. Sparks flew at the sky and were viciously snatched away by the wind. For a moment its ribs and skull were etched in orange flame and then it seemed to collapse, disintegrate, and fall into separate burning piles.

(Never mind it. Get moving.)

He picked up the gascan and struggled over to the snowmobile. His consciousness seemed to be flickering in and out, offering him cuttings and snippets of home movies but never the whole picture. In one of these he was aware of yanking the snowmobile back onto its tread and then sitting on it, out of breath and incapable of moving for a few moments. In another, he was reattaching the gascan, which was still half-full. His head was thumping horribly from the gasfumes (and in reaction to his battle with the hedge lion, he supposed), and he saw by the steaming hole in the snow beside him that he had vomited, but he was unable to remember when.

The snowmobile, the engine still warm, fired immediately. He twisted the throttle unevenly and started forward with a series of neck-snapping jerks that made his head ache even more fiercely. At first the snowmobile wove drunkenly from side to side, but by half-standing to get his face above the windscreen and into the sharp, needling blast of the wind, he drove some of the stupor out of himself. He opened the throttle wider.

(Where are the rest of the hedge animals?)

He didn't know, but at least he wouldn't be caught unaware again.

The Overlook loomed in front of him, the lighted first-floor windows throwing long yellow rectangles onto the snow. The gate at the foot of the drive was locked and he dismounted after a wary look around, praying he hadn't lost his keys when he pulled his lighter out of his pocket . . . no, they were there. He picked through them in the bright light thrown by the snowmobile head lamp. He found the right one and unsnapped the padlock, letting it drop into the snow. At first he didn't think he was going to be able to move the gate anyway; he pawed frantically at the snow surrounding it, disregarding the throbbing agony in his head and the fear that one of the other lions might be creeping up behind him. He managed to pull it a foot and a half away from the gatepost, squeezed into the gap, and pushed. He got it to move another two feet, enough room for the snowmobile, and threaded it through.

He became aware of movement ahead of him in the dark. The hedge animals, all of them, were clustered at the base of the Overlook's steps, guarding the way in, the way out. The lions prowled. The dog stood with its front paws on the first step.

Hallorann opened the throttle wide and the snowmobile leaped forward, puffing snow up behind it. In the caretaker's apartment, Jack Torrance's head jerked around at the high, wasplike buzz of the approaching engine, and suddenly began to move laboriously toward the hallway again. The bitch wasn't important now. The bitch could wait. Now it was this dirty nigger's turn. This dirty, interfering nigger with his nose in where it didn't belong. First him and then his son. He would show them. He would show them that . . . that he . . . that he was of *managerial timber!*

Outside, the snowmobile rocketed along faster and faster. The hotel seemed to surge toward it. Snow flew in Hallorann's face. The headlamp's oncoming glare spotlighted the hedge shepherd's face, its blank and socketless eyes.

Then it shrank away, leaving an opening. Hallorann yanked at the snowmobile's steering gear with all his remaining strength, and it kicked around in a sharp semicircle, throwing up clouds of snow, threatening to tip over. The rear end struck the foot of the porch steps and rebounded. Hallorann was off in a flash and running up the steps. He stumbled, fell, picked himself up. The dog was growling—again in his head—close behind him. Something ripped at the shoulder of the parka and then he was on the porch, standing in the narrow corridor Jack had shoveled through the snow, and safe. They were too big to fit in here.

He reached the big double doors which gave on the lobby and dug for his keys again. While he was getting them he tried the knob and it turned freely. He pushed his way in.

"Danny!" He cried hoarsely. *"Danny, where are you?"*

Silence came back.

His eyes traveled across the lobby to the foot of the wide stairs and a harsh gasp escaped him. The rug was splashed and matted with blood. There was a scrap of pink terrycloth robe. The trail of blood led up the stairs. The banister was also splashed with it.

"Oh Jesus," he muttered, and raised his voice again. *"Danny! DANNY!"*

The hotel's silence seemed to mock him with echoes which were almost there, sly and oblique.

(Danny? Who's Danny? Anybody here know a Danny? Danny, Danny, who's got the Danny? Anybody for a game of spin the Danny? Pin the tail on the Danny? Get out of here, black boy. No one here knows Danny from Adam.)

Jesus, had he come through everything just to be too late? Had it been done?

He ran up the stairs two at a time and stood at the top of the first floor. The blood led down toward the caretaker's apartment. Horror crept softly into his veins and into his brain as he began to walk toward the short hall. The hedge animals had been bad, but this was worse. In his heart he was already sure of what he was going to find when he got down there.

He was in no hurry to see it.

Jack had been hiding in the elevator when Hallorann came up the stairs. Now he crept up behind the figure in the snow-coated parka, a blood- and gore-streaked phantom with a smile upon its face. The roque mallet was lifted as high as the ugly, ripping pain in his back

(?? did the bitch stick me can't remember ??)

would allow.

"Black boy," he whispered. "I'll teach you to go sticking your nose in other people's business."

Hallorann heard the whisper and began to turn, to duck, and the roque mallet whistled down. The hood of the parka matted the blow, but not enough. A rocket exploded in his head, leaving a contrail of stars . . . and then nothing.

He staggered against the silk wallpaper and Jack hit him again, the roque mallet slicing sideways this time, shattering Hallorann's cheekbone and most of the teeth on the left side of his jaw. He went down limply.

"Now," Jack whispered. "Now, by Christ." Where was Danny? He had business with his trespassing son.

Three minutes later the elevator door banged open on the shadowed third floor. Jack Torrance was in it alone. The car had stopped only halfway into the doorway and he had to boost himself up onto the hall floor, wriggling painfully like a crippled thing. He dragged the splintered roque mallet after him. Outside the eaves, the wind howled and roared. Jack's eyes rolled wildly in their sockets. There was blood and confetti in his hair.

His son was up here, up here somewhere. He could feel it. Left to his own devices, he might do anything: scribble on the expensive silk wallpaper with his crayons, deface the furnishings, break the windows. He was a liar and a cheat and he would have to be chastised . . . harshly.

Jack Torrance struggled to his feet.

"Danny?" he called. "Danny, come here a minute, will you? You've done something wrong and I want you to come and take your medicine like a man. Danny? *Danny!*"

54

TONY

(*Danny* . . .)

    (*Dannneee* . . .)

Darkness and hallways. He was wandering through darkness and hallways that were like those which lay within the body of the hotel but were somehow different. The silk-papered walls stretched up and up, and even when he craned his neck,

Danny could not see the ceiling. It was lost in dimness. All the doors were locked, and they also rose up to dimness. Below the peepholes (in these giant doors they were the size of gunsights), tiny skulls and crossbones had been bolted to each door instead of room numbers.

And somewhere, Tony was calling him.

(*Dannneee . . .*)

There was a pounding noise, one he knew well, and hoarse shouts, faint with distance. He could not make out word for word, but he knew the text well enough by now. He had heard it before, in dreams and awake.

He paused, a little boy not yet three years out of diapers, and tried to decide where he was, where he might be. There was fear, but it was a fear he could live with. He had been afraid every day for two months now, to a degree that ranged from dull disquiet to outright, mind-bending terror. This he could live with. But he wanted to know why Tony had come, why he was making the sound of his name in this hall was neither a part of real things nor of the dreamland where Tony sometimes showed him things. Why, where—

"Danny."

Far down the giant hallway, almost as tiny as Danny himself, was a dark figure. Tony.

"Where am I?" he called softly to Tony.

"Sleeping," Tony said. "Sleeping in your mommy and daddy's bedroom." There was sadness in Tony's voice.

"Danny," Tony said. "Your mother is going to be badly hurt. Perhaps killed. Mr. Hallorann, too."

"No!"

He cried it out in a distant grief, a terror that seemed damped by these dreamy, dreary surroundings. Nonetheless, death images came to him: dead frog plastered to the turnpike like a grisly stamp; Daddy's broken watch lying on top of a box of junk to be thrown out; gravestones with a dead person under every one; dead jay by the telephone pole; the cold junk Mommy scraped off the plates and down the dark maw of the garbage disposal.

Yet he could not equate these simple symbols with the shifting complex reality of his mother; she satisfied his childish definition of eternity. She had been when he was not. She would continue to be when he was not again. He could accept the possibility of his own death, he had dealt with that since the encounter in Room 217.

But not hers.

Not Daddy's.

Not ever.

He began to struggle, and the darkness and the hallway began to waver. Tony's form became chimerical, indistinct.

"Don't!" Tony called. "Don't, Danny, don't do that!"

"She's not going to be dead! *She's not!*"

"Then you have to help her. Danny . . . you're in a place deep down in your own mind. The place where I am. I'm a part of you, Danny."

"You're *Tony*. You're not me. I want my mommy . . . I want my mommy . . ."

"I didn't bring you here, Danny. You brought yourself. Because you knew."

"No—"

"You've always known," Tony continued, and he began to walk closer. For the first time, Tony began to walk closer. "You're deep down in yourself in a place where nothing comes through. We're alone here for a little while, Danny. This is an Overlook where no one can ever come. No clocks work here. None of the keys fit them and they can never be wound up. The doors have never been opened and no one has ever stayed in the rooms. But you can't stay long. Because it's coming."

"It . . ." Danny whispered fearfully, and as he did so the irregular pounding noise seemed to grow closer, louder. His terror, cool and distant a moment ago, became a more immediate thing. Now the words could be made out. Hoarse, huckstering; they were uttered in a coarse imitation of his father's voice, but it wasn't Daddy. He knew that now. He knew

(You brought yourself. Because you knew.)

"Oh Tony, is it my daddy?" Danny screamed. *"Is it my daddy that's coming to get me?"*

Tony didn't answer. But Danny didn't need an answer. He knew. A long and nightmarish masquerade party went on here, and had gone on for years. Little by little a force had accrued, as secret and silent as interest in a bank account. Force, presence, shape, they were all only words and none of them mattered. It wore many masks, but it was all one. Now, somewhere, it was coming for him. It was hiding behind Daddy's face, it was imitating Daddy's voice, it was wearing Daddy's clothes.

But it was not his daddy.

It was not his daddy.

"I've got to help them!" he cried.

And now Tony stood directly in front of him, and looking at Tony was like looking into a magic mirror and seeing himself in ten years, the eyes widely spaced and very dark, the chin firm, the mouth handsomely molded. The hair was light blond like his mother's, and yet the stamp on his features was that of his father, as if Tony—as if the Daniel Anthony Torrance that would someday be—was a halfling caught between father and son, a ghost of both, a fusion.

"You have to try to help," Tony said. "But your father . . . he's with the hotel now, Danny. It's where he wants to be. It wants you too, because it's very greedy."

Tony walked past him, into the shadows.

"Wait!" Danny cried. "What can I—"

"He's close now," Tony said, still walking away. "You'll have to run . . . hide . . . keep away from him. Keep away."

"Tony, I can't!"

"But you've already started," Tony said. "You will remember what your father forgot."

He was gone.

And from somewhere near his father's voice came, coldly wheedling: "Danny? You can come out, doc. Just a little spanking, that's all. Take it like a man and it will be all over. We don't need her, doc. Just you and me, right? When we get this little . . . spanking . . . behind us, it will be just you and me."

Danny ran.

Behind him the thing's temper broke through the shambling charade of normality.

"Come here, you little shit! Right now!"

Down a long hall, panting and gasping. Around a corner. Up a flight of stairs. And as he went, the walls that had been so high and remote began to come down; the rug which had only been a blur beneath his feet took on the familiar black and blue pattern, sinuously woven together; the doors became numbered again and behind them the parties that were all one went on and on, populated by generations of guests. The air seemed to be shimmering around him, the blows of the mallet against the walls echoing and re-echoing. He seemed to be bursting through some thin placental womb from sleep to

the rug outside the Presidential Suite on the third floor; lying near him in a bloody heap were the bodies of two men dressed in suits and narrow ties. They had been taken out by shotgun blasts and now they began to stir in front of him and get up.

He drew in breath to scream but didn't.

(!! FALSE FACES !! NOT REAL !!)

They faded before his gaze like old photographs and were gone.

But below him, the faint sound of the mallet against the walls went on and on, drifting up through the elevator shaft and the stairwell. The controlling force of the Overlook, in the shape of his father, blundering around on the first floor.

A door opened with a thin screeing sound behind him.

A decayed woman in a rotten silk gown pranced out, her yellowed and splitting fingers dressed with verdigris-caked rings. Heavy-bodied wasps crawled sluggishly over her face.

"Come in," she whispered to him, grinning with black lips. "Come in and we will daance the taaaango . . ."

"False face!!" he hissed. "Not real!" She drew back from him in alarm, and in the act of drawing back she faded and was gone.

"Where are you?" it screamed, but the voice was still only in his head. He could still hear the thing that was wearing Jack's face down on the first floor. . . and something else.

The high, whining sound of an approaching motor.

Danny's breath stopped in his throat with a little gasp. Was it just another face of the hotel, another illusion? Or was it Dick? He wanted—wanted desperately—to believe it *was* Dick, but he didn't dare take the chance.

He retreated down the main corridor, and then took one of the offshoots, his feet whispering on the nap of the carpet. Locked doors frowned down at him as they had done in the dreams, the visions, only now he was in the world of real things, where the game was played for keeps.

He turned to the right and came to a halt, his heart thudding heavily in his chest. Heat was blowing around his ankles. From the registers, of course. This must have been Daddy's day to heat the west wing and

(You will remember what your father forgot.)

What was it? He almost knew. Something that might save him and Mommy? But Tony had said he would have to do it himself. What was it?

He sank down against the wall, trying desperately to think. It was so hard ... the hotel kept trying to get into his head ... the image of that dark and slumped form swinging the mallet from side to side, gouging the wallpaper ... sending out puffs of plaster dust.

"Help me," he muttered. "Tony, help me."

And suddenly he became aware that the hotel had grown deathly silent. The whining sound of the motor had stopped.

(must not have been real)

and the sounds of the party had stopped and there was only the wind, howling and whooping endlessly.

The elevator whirred into sudden life.

It was coming up.

And Danny knew who—*what*—was in it.

He bolted to his feet, eyes staring wildly. Panic clutched around his heart. Why had Tony sent him to the third floor? He was trapped up here. All the doors were locked.

The attic!

There was an attic, he knew. He had come up here with Daddy the day he had salted the rattraps around up there. He hadn't allowed Danny to come up with him because of the rats. He was afraid Danny might be bitten. But the trapdoor which led to the attic was set into the ceiling of the last short corridor in this wing. There was a pole leaning against the wall. Daddy had pushed the trapdoor open with the pole, there had been a ratcheting whir of counterweights as the door went up and a ladder had swung down. If he could get up there and pull the ladder after him ...

Somewhere in the maze of corridors behind him, the elevator came to a stop. There was a metallic, rattling crash as the gate was thrown back. And then a voice—not in his head now but terribly real—called out: "Danny? Danny, come here a minute, will you? You've done something wrong and I want you to come and take your medicine like a man. Danny? *Danny!*"

Obedience was so strongly ingrained in him that he actually took two automatic steps toward the sound of that voice before stopping. His hands curled into fists at his sides.

(Not real! False face! I know what you are! Take off your mask!)

"*Danny!*" it roared. "*Come here, you pup! Come here and take it like a man!*" A loud, hollow boom as the mallet struck the wall. When the voice roared out his name again it had changed location. It had come closer.

In the world of real things, the hunt was beginning.

Danny ran. Feet silent on the heavy carpet, he ran past the closed doors, past the silk figured wallpaper, past the fire extinguisher bolted to the corner of the wall. He hesitated, and then plunged down the final corridor. Nothing at the end but a bolted door, and nowhere left to run.

But the pole was still there, still leaning against the wall where Daddy had left it.

Danny snatched it up. He craned his neck to stare up at the trap door. There was a hook on the end of the pole and you had to catch it on a ring set into the trapdoor. You had to—

There was a brand-new Yale padlock dangling from the trapdoor. The lock Jack Torrance had clipped around the hasp after laying his traps, just in case his son should take the notion into his head to go exploring up there someday.

Locked. Terror swept him.

Behind him it was coming, blundering and staggering past the Presidential Suite, the mallet whistling viciously through the air.

Danny backed up against the last closed door and waited for it.

55

THAT WHICH WAS FORGOTTEN

Wendy came to a little at a time, the grayness draining away, pain replacing it: her back, her leg, her side ... she didn't think she would be able to move. Even her fingers hurt, and at first she didn't know why.

(The razor blade, that's why.)

Her blond hair, now dank and matted, hung in her eyes. She brushed it away and her ribs stabbed inside, making her groan. Now she saw a field of blue and white mattress, spotted with blood. Her blood, or maybe Jack's. Either way it was still fresh. She hadn't been out long. And that was important because—

(?Why?)

Because—

It was the insectile, buzzing sound of the motor that she remembered first. For a moment she fixed stupidly on the memory, and then in a single vertiginous and nauseating swoop, her mind seemed to pan back, showing her everything at once.

Hallorann. It must have been Hallorann. Why else would Jack have left so suddenly, without finishing it ... without finishing *her?*

Because he was no longer at leisure. He had to find Danny quickly and ... and do it before Hallorann could put a stop to it.

Or had it happened already?

She could hear the whine of the elevator rising up the shaft.

(No God please no the blood the blood's still fresh don't let it have happened already)

Somehow she was able to find her feet and stagger through the bedroom and across the ruins of the living room to the shattered front door. She pushed it open and made it out into the hall.

"Danny!" she cried, wincing at the pain in her chest. "Mr. Hallorann! Is anybody there? *Anybody?*"

The elevator had been running again and now it came to a stop. She heard the metallic crash of the gate being thrown back and then thought she heard a speaking voice. It might have been her imagination. The wind was too loud to really be able to tell.

Leaning against the wall, she made her way up to the corner of the short hallway. She was about to turn the corner when the scream froze her, floating down the stairwell and the elevator shaft:

"Danny! Come here, you pup! Come here and take it like a man!"

Jack. On the second or third floor. Looking for Danny.

She got around the corner, stumbled, almost fell. Her breath caught in her throat. Something

(someone?)

huddled against the wall about a quarter of the way down from the stairwell. She began to hurry faster, wincing every time her weight came down on her hurt leg. It was a man, she saw, and as she drew closer, she understood the meaning of that buzzing motor.

It was Mr. Hallorann. He had come after all.

She eased to her knees beside him, offering up an incoherent prayer that he was not dead. His nose was bleeding, and a terrible gout of blood had spilled out of his mouth. The side of his face was a puffed purple bruise. But he was breathing, thank God for that. It was coming in long, harsh draws that shook his whole frame.

Looking at him more closely, Wendy's eyes widened. One arm of the parka he was wearing was blackened and singed. One side of it had been ripped open. There was blood in his hair and a shallow but ugly scratch down the back of his neck.

(My God, what's happened to him?)

"Danny!" the hoarse, petulant voice roared from above them. *"Get out here, goddammit!"*

There was no time to wonder about it now. She began to shake him, her face twisting at the flare of agony in her ribs. Her side felt hot and massive and swollen.

(What if they're poking my lung whenever I move?)

There was no help for that, either. If Jack found Danny, he would kill him, beat him to death with that mallet as he had tried to do to her.

So she shook Hallorann, and then began to slap the un-bruised side of his face lightly.

"Wake up," she said. "Mr. Hallorann, you've got to wake up. Please . . . please . . ."

From overhead, the restless booming sounds of the mallet as Jack Torrance looked for his son.

Danny stood with his back against the door, looking at the right angle where the hallways joined. The steady, irregular booming sound of the mallet against the walls grew louder. The thing that was after him screamed and howled and cursed. Dream and reality had joined together without a seam.

It came around the corner.

In a way, what Danny felt was relief. It was not his father. The mask of face and body had been ripped and shredded and made into a bad joke. It was not his daddy, not this Saturday Night Shock Show horror with its rolling eyes and hunched and hulking shoulders and blood-drenched shirt. It was not his daddy.

"Now, by God," it breathed. It wiped its lips with a shaking hand. "Now you'll find out who is the boss around here. You'll see. It's not you they want. It's me. *Me. Me!*"

It slashed out with the scarred hammer, its double head now shapeless and splintered with countless impacts. It struck the wall, cutting a circle in the silk paper. Plaster dust puffed out. It began to grin.

"Let's see you pull any of your fancy tricks now," it muttered. "I wasn't born yesterday, you know. Didn't just fall off the hay truck, by God. I'm going to do my fatherly duty by you, boy."

Danny said: "You're not my daddy."

It stopped. For a moment it actually looked uncertain, as if not sure who or what it was. Then it began to walk again. The hammer whistled out, struck a door panel and made it boom hollowly.

"You're a liar," it said. "Who else would I be? I have the two birthmarks, I have the cupped navel, even the *pecker*, my boy. Ask your mother."

"You're a mask," Danny said. "Just a false face. The only reason the hotel needs to use you is that you aren't as dead as the others. But when it's done with you, you won't be anything at all. You don't scare me."

"I'll scare you!" it howled. The mallet whistled fiercely down, smashing into the rug between Danny's feet. Danny didn't flinch. "You lied about me! You connived with her! You plotted against me! *And you cheated! You copied that final exam!*" The eyes glared out at him from beneath the furred brows. There was an expression of lunatic cunning in them. "I'll find it, too. It's down in the basement somewhere. I'll find it. They promised me I could look all I want." It raised the mallet again.

"Yes, they promise," Danny said, "but they lie."

The mallet hesitated at the top of its swing.

Hallorann had begun to come around, but Wendy had stopped patting his cheeks. A moment ago the words *You cheated! You copied that final exam!* had floated down through the elevator shaft, dim, barely audible over the wind. From somewhere deep in the west wing. She was nearly convinced they were on the third floor and that Jack—whatever had taken possession of Jack—had found Danny. There was nothing she or Hallorann could do now.

"Oh doc," she murmured. Tears blurred her eyes.

"Son of a bitch broke my jaw," Hallorann muttered thickly, "and my *head* . . ." He worked to sit up. His right eye was purpling rapidly and swelling shut. Still, he saw Wendy.

"Missus Torrance—"

"Shhhh," she said.

"Where is the boy, Missus Torrance?"

"On the third floor," she said. "With his father."

"They lie," Danny said again. Something had gone through his mind, flashing like a meteor, too quick, too bright to catch and hold. Only the tail of the thought remained.

(it's down in the basement somewhere)

(you will remember what your father forgot)

"You . . . you shouldn't speak that way to your father," it said hoarsely. The mallet trembled, came down. "You'll only make things worse for yourself. Your . . . your punishment.

Worse." It staggered drunkenly and stared at him with maudlin selfpity that began to turn to hate. The mallet began to rise again.

"You're not my daddy," Danny told it again. "And if there's a little bit of my daddy left inside you, he knows they lie here. Everything is a lie and a cheat. Like the loaded dice my daddy got for my Christmas stocking last Christmas, like the presents they put in the store windows and my daddy says there's nothing in them, no presents, they're just empty boxes. Just for show, my daddy says. You're *it*, not my daddy. You're the hotel. And when you get what you want, you won't give my daddy anything because you're selfish. And my daddy knows that. You had to make him drink the Bad Stuff. That's the only way you could get him, you lying false face."

"Liar! Liar!" The words came in a thin shriek. The mallet wavered wildly in the air.

"Go on and hit me. But you'll never get what you want from me."

The face in front of him changed. It was hard to say how; there was no melting or merging of the features. The body trembled slightly, and then the bloody hands opened like broken claws. The mallet fell from them and thumped to the rug. That was all. But suddenly his daddy *was* there, looking at him in mortal agony, and a sorrow so great that Danny's heart flamed within his chest. The mouth drew down in a quivering bow.

"Doc," Jack Torrance said. "Run away. Quick. And remember how much I love you."

"No," Danny said.

"Oh Danny, for God's sake—"

"No," Danny said. He took one of his father's bloody hands and kissed it. "It's almost over."

Hallorann got to his feet by propping his back against the wall and pushing himself up. He and Wendy stared at each other like nightmare survivors from a bombed hospital.

"We got to get up there," he said. "We have to help him."

Her haunted eyes stared into his from her chalk-pale face. "It's too late," Wendy said. "Now he can only help himself."

A minute passed, then two. Three. And they heard it above

them, screaming, not in anger or triumph now, but in mortal terror.

"Dear God," Hallorann whispered. "What's happening?"

"I don't know," she said.

"Has it killed him?"

"I don't know."

The elevator clashed into life and began to descend with the screaming, raving thing penned up inside.

Danny stood without moving. There was no place he could run where the Overlook was not. He recognized it suddenly, fully, painlessly. For the first time in his life he had an adult thought, an adult feeling, the essence of his experience in this bad place—a sorrowful distillation:

(Mommy and Daddy can't help me and I'm alone.)

"Go away," he said to the bloody stranger in front of him. "Go on. Get out of here."

It bent over, exposing the knife handle in its back. Its hands closed around the mallet again, but instead of aiming at Danny, it reversed the handle, aiming the hard side of the roque mallet at its own face.

Understanding rushed through Danny.

Then the mallet began to rise and descend, destroying the last of Jack Torrance's image. The thing in the hall danced an eerie, shuffling polka, the beat counterpointed by the hideous sound of the mallet head striking again and again. Blood splattered across the wallpaper. Shards of bone leaped into the air like broken piano keys. It was impossible to say just how long it went on. But when it turned its attention back to Danny, his father was gone forever. What remained of the face became a strange, shifting composite, many faces mixed imperfectly into one. Danny saw the woman in 217; the dogman; the hungry boy-thing that had been in the concrete ring.

"Masks off, then," it whispered. "No more interruptions."

The mallet rose for the final time. A ticking sound filled Danny's ears.

"Anything else to say?" it inquired. "Are you sure you wouldn't like to run? A game of tag, perhaps? All we have is time, you know. An eternity of *time*. Or shall we end it? Might as well. After all we're missing the party."

It grinned with broken-toothed greed.

And it came to him. What his father had forgotten.

Sudden triumph filled his face; the thing saw it and hesitated, puzzled.

"The boiler!" Danny screamed. *"It hasn't been dumped since this morning! It's going up! It's going to explode!"*

An expression of grotesque terror and dawning realization swept across the broken features of the thing in front of him. The mallet dropped from its fisted hands and bounced harmlessly on the black and blue rug.

"The boiler!" it cried. "Oh no! That can't be allowed! Certainly not! No! You goddamned little pup! Certainly not! Oh, oh, oh—"

"It is!" Danny cried back at it fiercely. He began to shuffle and shake his fists at the ruined thing before him. "Any minute now! I know it! The boiler, Daddy forgot the boiler! *And you forgot it, too!*"

"No, oh no, it musn't, it can't, you dirty little boy, I'll make you take your medicine, I'll make you take every drop, oh no, oh no—"

It suddenly turned tail and began to shamble away. For a moment its shadow bobbed on the wall, waxing and waning. It trailed cries behind itself like wornout party streamers.

Moments later the elevator crashed into life.

Suddenly the shining was on him

(*mommy mr. hallorann dick to my friends together alive they're alive got to get out it's going to blow going to blow sky-high*)

like a fierce and glaring sunrise and he ran. One foot kicked the bloody, misshapen roque mallet aside. He didn't notice.

Crying, he ran for the stairs.

They had to get out.

56

THE EXPLOSION

Hallorann could never be sure of the progression of things after that. He remembered that the elevator had gone down and past them without stopping, and something had been inside. But he made no attempt to try to see in through the small diamond-shaped window, because what was in there did not sound human. A moment later there were running footsteps on the stairs. Wendy Torrance at first shrank back against him and then began to stumble down the main corridor to the stairs as fast as she could.

"Danny! Danny! Oh, thank God! Thank God!"

She swept him into a hug, groaning with joy as well as her pain.

(Danny.)

Danny looked at him from his mother's arms, and Hallorann saw how the boy had changed. His face was pale and pinched, his eyes dark and fathomless. He looked as if he had lost weight. Looking at the two of them together, Hallorann thought it was the mother who looked younger, in spite of the terrible beating she had taken.

(Dick—we have to go—run—the place—it's going to)

Picture of the Overlook, flames leaping out of its roof. Bricks raining down on the snow. Clang of firebells . . . not that any fire truck would be able to get up here much before the end of March. Most of all what came through in Danny's thought was a sense of urgent immediacy, a feeling that it was going to happen *at any time.*

"All right," Hallorann said. He began to move toward the two of them and at first it was like swimming through deep water. His sense of balance was screwed, and the eye on the right side of his face didn't want to focus. His jaw was sending giant throbbing bursts of pain up to his temple and down his neck, and his cheek felt as large as a cabbage. But the boy's urgency had gotten him going, and it got a little easier.

"All right?" Wendy asked. She looked from Hallorann to her son and back to Hallorann. "What do you mean, all right?"

"We have to go," Hallorann said.

"I'm not dressed . . . my clothes . . ."

Danny darted out of her arms then and raced down the corridor. She looked after him, and as he vanished around the corner, back at Hallorann. "What if he comes back?"

"Your husband?"

"He's not Jack," she muttered. "Jack's dead. This place killed him. *This damned place.*" She struck at the wall with her fist and cried out at the pain in her cut fingers. "It's the boiler, isn't it?"

"Yes, ma'am. Danny says it's going to explode."

"Good." The word was uttered with dead finality. "I don't know if I can get down those stairs again. My ribs . . . he broke my ribs. And something in my back. It hurts."

"You'll make it," Hallorann said. "We'll all make it." But suddenly he remembered the hedge animals, and wondered what they would do if they were guarding the way out.

Then Danny was coming back. He had Wendy's boots and coat and gloves, also his own coat and gloves.

"Danny," she said. "Your boots."

"It's too late," he said. His eyes stared at them with a desperate kind of madness. He looked at Dick and suddenly Hallorann's mind was fixed with an image of a clock under a glass dome, the clock in the ballroom that had been donated by a Swiss diplomat in 1949. The hands of the clock were standing at a minute to midnight.

"Oh my God," Hallorann said. "Oh my dear God."

He clapped an arm around Wendy and picked her up. He clapped his other arm around Danny. He ran for the stairs.

Wendy shrieked in pain as he squeezed the bad ribs, as something in her back ground together, but Hallorann did not slow. He plunged down the stairs with them in his arms. One eye wide and desperate, the other puffed shut to a slit. He looked like a one-eyed pirate abducting hostages to be ransomed later.

Suddenly the shine was on him, and he understood what Danny had meant when he said it was too late. He could feel the explosion getting ready to rumble up from the basement and tear the guts out of this horrid place.

He ran faster, bolting headlong across the lobby toward the double doors.

It hurried across the basement and into the feeble yellow glow of the furnace room's only light. It was slobbering with fear. It had been so close, so close to having the boy and the boy's remarkable power. It could not lose now. It must not happen. It would dump the boiler and then chastise the boy harshly.

"Mustn't happen!" it cried. "Oh no, mustn't happen!"

It stumbled across the floor to the boiler, which glowed a dull red halfway up its long tubular body. It was huffing and rattling and hissing off plumes of steam in a hundred directions, like a monster calliope. The pressure needle stood at the far end of the dial.

"*No, it won't be allowed!*" the manager/caretaker cried.

It laid its Jack Torrance hands on the valve, unmindful of the burning smell which arose or the searing of the flesh as the red-hot wheel sank in, as if into a mudrut.

The wheel gave, and with a triumphant scream, the thing spun it wide open. A giant roar of escaping steam bellowed out of the boiler, a dozen dragons hissing in concert. But before the steam obscured the pressure needle entirely, the needle had visibly begun to swing back.

"*I WIN!*" it cried. It capered obscenely in the hot, rising mist, waving its flaming hands over its head. "*NOT TOO LATE! I WIN! NOT TOO LATE! NOT TOO LATE! NOT—*"

Words turned into a shriek of triumph, and the shriek was swallowed in a shattering roar as the Overlook's boiler exploded.

Hallorann burst out through the double doors and carried the two of them through the trench in the big snowdrift on the porch. He saw the hedge animals clearly, more clearly than before, and even as he realized his worst fears were true, that they were between the porch and the snowmobile, the hotel exploded. It seemed to him that it happened all at once, although later he knew that couldn't have been the way it happened.

There was a flat explosion, a sound that seemed to exist on one low all-pervasive note

(WHUMMMMMMMMMM—)

and then there was a blast of warm air at their backs that seemed to push gently at them. They were thrown from the porch on its breath, the three of them, and a confused thought

(this is what superman must feel like)

slipped through Hallorann's mind as they flew through the air. He lost his hold on them and then he struck the snow in a soft billow. It was down his shirt and up his nose and he was dimly aware that it felt good on his hurt cheek.

Then he struggled to the top of it, for that moment not thinking about the hedge animals, or Wendy Torrance, or even the boy. He rolled over on his back so he could watch it die.

The Overlook's windows shattered. In the ballroom, the dome over the mantelpiece clock cracked, split in two pieces, and fell to the floor. The clock stopped ticking: cogs and gears and balance wheel all became motionless. There was a whispered, sighing noise, and a great billow of dust. In 217 the bathtub suddenly split in two, letting out a small flood of greenish, noxious-smelling water. In the Presidential Suite the wallpaper suddenly burst into flames. The batwing doors of the Colorado Lounge suddenly snapped their hinges and fell to the dining room floor. Beyond the basement arch, the great piles and stacks of old papers caught fire and went up with a blowtorch hiss. Boiling water rolled over the flames but did not quench them. Like burning autumn leaves below a wasps' nest, they whirled and blackened. The furnace exploded, shattering the basement's roofbeams, sending them crashing down like the bones of a dinosaur. The gasjet which had fed the furnace, unstoppered now, rose up in a bellowing pylon of flame through the riven floor of the lobby. The carpeting on the stair risers caught, racing up to the first-floor level as if to tell dreadful good news. A fusillade of explosions ripped the place. The chandelier in the dining room, a two-hundred-pound crystal bomb, fell with a splintering crash, knocking tables every which way. Flame belched out of the Overlook's five chimneys at the breaking clouds.

(No! Mustn't! Mustn't! MUSTN'T!)

It shrieked; it shrieked but now it was voiceless and it was only screaming panic and doom and damnation in its own ear, dissolving, losing thought and will, the webbing falling apart, searching, not finding, going out, going out to, fleeing, going out to emptiness, notness, crumbling.

The party was over.

57

EXIT

The roar shook the whole façade of the hotel. Glass belched out onto the snow and twinkled there like jagged diamonds. The hedge dog, which had been approaching Danny and his mother, recoiled away from it, its green and shadow-marbled ears flattening, its tail coming down between its legs as its haunches flattened abjectly. In his head, Hallorann heard it whine fearfully, and mixed with that sound was the fearful, confused yowling of the big cats. He struggled to his feet to go to the other two and help them, and as he did so he saw something more nightmarish than all the rest: the hedge rabbit, still coated with snow, was battering itself crazily at the chainlink fence at the far end of the playground, and the steel mesh was jingling with a kind of nightmare music, like a spectral zither. Even from here he could hear the sounds of the close-set twigs and branches which made up its body cracking and crunching like breaking bones.

"Dick! Dick!" Danny cried out. He was trying to support his mother, help her over to the snowmobile. The clothes he had carried out for the two of them were scattered between where they had fallen and where they now stood. Hallorann was suddenly aware that the woman was in her nightclothes, Danny jacketless, and it was no more than ten above zero.

(my god she's in her bare feet)

He struggled back through the snow, picking up her coat, her boots, Danny's coat, odd gloves. Then he ran back to them, plunging hip-deep in the snow from time to time, having to flounder his way out.

Wendy was horribly pale, the side of her neck coated with blood, blood that was now freezing,

"I can't," she muttered. She was no more than semiconscious. "No, I . . . can't. Sorry."

Danny looked up at Hallorann pleadingly.

"Gonna be okay," Hallorann said, and gripped her again. "Come on."

The three of them made it to where the snowmobile had slewed around and stalled out. Hallorann sat the woman down on the passenger seat and put her coat on. He lifted her feet up—they were very cold but not frozen yet—and rubbed them briskly with Danny's jacket before putting on her boots. Wendy's face was alabaster pale, her eyes half-lidded and dazed, but she had begun to shiver. Hallorann thought that was a good sign.

Behind them, a series of three explosions rocked the hotel. Orange flashes lit the snow.

Danny put his mouth close to Hallorann's ear and screamed something.

"What?"

"I said do you need that?"

The boy was pointing at the red gascan that leaned at an angle in the snow.

"I guess we do."

He picked it up and sloshed it. Still gas in there, he couldn't tell how much. He attached the can to the back of the snowmobile, fumbling the job several times before getting it right because his fingers were going numb. For the first time he became aware that he'd lost Howard Cottrell's mittens.

(i get out of this i gonna have my sister knit you a dozen pair, howie)

"Get on!" Hallorann shouted at the boy.

Danny shrank back. "We'll freeze!"

"We have to go around to the equipment shed! There's stuff in there . . . blankets . . . stuff like that. Get on behind your mother!"

Danny got on, and Hallorann twisted his head so he could shout into Wendy's face.

"Missus Torrance! Hold onto me! You understand? *Hold on!*"

She put her arms around him and rested her cheek against his back. Hallorann started the snowmobile and turned the throttle delicately so they would start up without a jerk. The woman had the weakest sort of grip on him, and if she shifted backward, her weight would tumble both her and the boy off.

They began to move. He brought the snowmobile around in a circle and then they were traveling west parallel to the hotel. Hallorann cut in more to circle around behind it to the equipment shed.

They had a momentarily clear view into the Overlook's lobby. The gasflame coming up through the shattered floor was like a giant birthday candle, fierce yellow at its heart and blue around its flickering edges. In that moment it seemed only to be lighting, not destroying. They could see the registration desk with its silver bell, the credit card decals, the old-fashioned, scrolled cash register, the small figured throw rugs, the highbacked chairs, horsehair hassocks. Danny could see the small sofa by the fireplace where the three nuns had sat on the day they had come up—closing day. But this was the real closing day.

Then the drift on the porch blotted the view out. A moment later they were skirting the west side of the hotel. It was still light enough to see without the snowmobile's headlight. Both upper stories were flaming now, and pennants of flame shot out the windows. The gleaming white paint had begun to blacken and peel. The shutters which had covered the Presidential Suite's picture window—shutters Jack had carefully fastened as per instructions in mid-October—now hung in flaming brands, exposing the wide and shattered darkness behind them, like a toothless mouth yawing in a final, silent deathrattle.

Wendy had pressed her face against Hallorann's back to cut out the wind, and Danny had likewise pressed his face against his mother's back, and so it was only Hallorann who saw the final thing, and he never spoke of it. From the window of the Presidential Suite he thought he saw a huge dark shape issue, blotting out the snowfield behind it. For a moment it assumed the shape of a huge, obscene manta, and then the wind seemed to catch it, to tear it and shred it like old dark paper. It fragmented, was caught in a whirling eddy of smoke, and a moment later it was gone as if it had never been. But in those few seconds as it whirled blackly, dancing like negative motes of light, he remembered something from his childhood . . . fifty years ago, or more. He and his brother had come upon a huge nest of ground wasps just north of their farm. It had been tucked into a hollow between the earth and an old lightning-blasted tree. His brother had had a big old niggerchaser in the band of his hat, saved all the way from the Fourth of July. He had lighted it and tossed it at the nest. It had exploded with a loud bang, and an angry, rising hum—almost a low shriek— had risen from the blasted nest. They had run away as if demons had been at their heels. In a way, Hallorann supposed that demons had been. And looking back over his shoulder, as he was now, he had on that day seen a large dark cloud of hornets rising in the hot air, swirling together, breaking apart, looking for whatever enemy had done this to their home so that they—the single group intelligence—could sting it to death.

Then the thing in the sky was gone and it might only have been smoke or a great flapping swatch of wallpaper after all, and there was only the Overlook, a flaming pyre in the roaring throat of the night.

There was a key to the equipment shed's padlock on his key ring, but Hallorann saw there would be no need to use it. The door was ajar, the padlock hanging open on its hasp.

"I can't go in there," Danny whispered.

"That's okay. You stay with your mom. There used to be a pile of old horseblankets. Probably all moth-eaten by now, but better than freezin to death. Missus Torrance, you still with us?"

"I don't know," the wan voice answered. "I think so."

"Good. I'll be just a second."

"Come back as quick as you can," Danny whispered. "Please."

Hallorann nodded. He had trained the headlamp on the door and now he floundered through the snow, casting a long shadow in front of himself. He pushed the equipment shed door open and stepped in. The horseblankets were still in the corner, by the roque set. He picked up four of them—they smelled musty and old and the moths certainly had been having a free lunch—and then he paused.

One of the roque mallets was gone.

(Was that what he hit me with?)

Well, it didn't matter what he'd been hit with, did it? Still, his fingers went to the side of his face and began to explore the huge lump there. Six hundred dollars' worth of dental work undone at a single blow. And after all

(maybe he didn't hit me with one of those. Maybe one got lost. Or stolen. Or took for a souvenier. After all)

it didn't really matter. No one was going to be playing roque here next summer. Or any summer in the forseeable future.

No, it didn't really matter, except that looking at the racked mallets with the single missing member had a kind of fascination. He found himself thinking of the hard wooden *whack!* of the mallet head striking the round wooden ball. A nice summery sound. Watching it skitter across the

(bone. blood.)

gravel. It conjured up images of

(bone. blood.)

iced tea, porch swings, ladies in white straw hats, the hum of mosquitoes, and

(bad little boys who don't play by the rules.)

all that stuff. Sure. Nice game. Out of style now, but . . . nice.

"Dick?" The voice was thin, frantic, and, he thought, rather unpleasant. "Are you all right, Dick? Come out now. *Please!*"

("Come on out now nigguh de massa callin youall.")

His hand closed tightly around one of the mallet handles, liking its feel.

(Spare the rod, spoil the child.)

His eyes went blank in the flickering, fire-shot darkness. Really, it would be doing them both a favor. She was messed up . . . in pain . . . and most of it

(all of it)

was that damn boy's fault. Sure. He had left his own daddy in there to burn. When you thought of it, it was damn close to murder. Patricide was what they called it. Pretty goddam low.

"Mr. Hallorann?" Her voice was low, weak, querulous. He didn't much like the sound of it.

"Dick!" The boy was sobbing now, in terror.

Hallorann drew the mallet from the rack and turned toward the flood of white light from the snowmobile headlamp. His feet scratched unevenly over the boards of the equipment shed, like the feet of a clockwork toy that has been wound up and set in motion.

Suddenly he stopped, looked wonderingly at the mallet in his hands, and asked himself with rising horror what it was he had been thinking of doing. Murder? *Had he been thinking of murder?*

For a moment his entire mind seemed filled with an angry, weakly hectoring voice:

(Do it! Do it, you weak-kneed no-balls nigger! Kill them! KILL THEM BOTH!)

Then he flung the mallet behind him with a whispered, terrified cry. It clattered into the corner where the horseblankets had been, one of the two heads pointed toward him in an unspeakable invitation.

He fled.

Danny was sitting on the snowmobile seat and Wendy was holding him weakly. His face was shiny with tears, and he was shaking as if with ague. Between his clicking teeth he said: "Where were you? We were *scared?*"

"It's a good place to be scared of," Hallorann said slowly. "Even if that place burns flat to the foundation, you'll never get me within a hundred miles of here again. Here, Missus Torrance, wrap these around you. I'll help. You too, Danny. Get yourself looking like an Arab."

He swirled two of the blankets around Wendy, fashioning one of them into a hood to cover her head, and helped Danny tie his so they wouldn't fall off.

"Now hold on for dear life," he said. "We got a long way to go, but the worst is behind us now."

He circled the equipment shed and then pointed the snowmobile back along their trail. The Overlook was a torch now, flaming at the sky. Great holes had been eaten into its sides, and there was a red hell inside, waxing and waning. Snowmelt ran down the charred gutters in steaming waterfalls.

They purred down the front lawn, their way well lit. The snowdunes glowed scarlet.

"Look!" Danny shouted as Hallorann slowed for the front gate. He was pointing toward the playground.

The hedge creatures were all in their original positions, but they were denuded, blackened, seared. Their dead branches were a stark interlacing network in the fireglow, their small leaves scattered around their feet like fallen petals.

"They're dead!" Danny screamed in hysterical triumph. *"Dead! They're dead!"*

"Shhh," Wendy said. "All right, honey. It's all right."

"Hey, doc," Hallorann said. "Let's get to someplace warm. You ready?"

"Yes," Danny whispered. "I've been ready for so long—"

Hallorann edged through the gap between gate and post. A moment later they were on the road, pointed back toward Sidewinder. The sound of the snowmobile's engine dwindled until it was lost in the ceaseless roar of the wind. It rattled through the denuded branches of the hedge animals with a low, beating, desolate sound. The fire waxed and waned. Sometime after the sound of the snowmobile's engine had disappeared, the Overlook's roof caved in—first the west wing, then the east, and seconds later the central roof. A huge spiraling gout of sparks and flaming debris rushed up into the howling winter night.

A bundle of flaming shingles and a wad of hot flashing were wafted in through the open equipment shed door by the wind.

After a while the shed began to burn, too.

They were still twenty miles from Sidewinder when Hallorann stopped to pour the rest of the gas into the snowmobile's tank. He was getting very worried about Wendy Torrance, who seemed to be drifting away from them. It was still so far to go.

"Dick!" Danny cried. He was standing up on the seat, pointing. *"Dick, look! Look there!"*

The snow had stopped and a silver-dollar moon had peeked out through the raftering clouds. Far down the road but coming toward them, coming upward through a series of S-shaped switchbacks, was a pearly chain of lights. The wind dropped for a moment and Hallorann heard the faraway buzzing snarl of snowmobile engines.

Hallorann and Danny and Wendy reached them fifteen minutes later. They had brought extra clothes and brandy and Dr. Edmonds.

And the long darkness was over.

58

EPILOGUE / SUMMER

After he had finished checking over the salads his understudy had made and peeked in on the home-baked beans they were using as appetizers this week, Hallorann untied his apron, hung it on a hook, and slipped out the back door. He had maybe forty-five minutes before he had to crank up for dinner in earnest.

The name of this place was the Red Arrow Lodge, and it was buried in the western Maine mountains, thirty miles from the town of Rangely. It was a good gig, Hallorann thought. The trade wasn't too heavy, it tipped well, and so far there hadn't been a single meal sent back. Not bad at all, considering the season was nearly half over.

He threaded his way between the outdoor bar and the swimming pool (although why anyone would want to use the pool with the lake so handy he would never know), crossed a greensward where a party of four was playing croquet and laughing, and crested a mild ridge. Pines took over here, and the wind soughed pleasantly in them, carrying the aroma of fir and sweet resin.

On the other side, a number of cabins with views of the lake were placed discreetly among the trees. The last one was the nicest, and Hallorann had reserved it for a party of two back in April when he had gotten this gig.

The woman was sitting on the porch in a rocking chair, a book in her hands. Hallorann was struck again by the change in her. Part of it was the stiff, almost formal way she sat, in spite of her informal surroundings—that was the back brace, of course. She'd had a shattered vertebra as well as three broken ribs and some internal injuries. The back was the slowest healing, and she was still in the brace . . . hence the formal posture. But the change was more than that. She looked older, and some of the laughter had gone out of her face. Now, as she sat reading her book, Hallorann saw a grave sort of beauty there that had been missing on the day he had first met her, some nine months ago. Then she had still been mostly girl. Now she was a woman, a human being who had been dragged around to the dark side of the moon and had come back able to put the pieces back together. But those pieces, Hallorann thought, they never fit just the same way again. Never in this world.

She heard his step and looked up, closing her book. "Dick! Hi!" She started to rise, and a little grimace of pain crossed her face.

"Nope, don't get up," he said. "I don't stand on no ceremony unless it's white tie and tails."

She smiled as he came up the steps and sat down next to her on the porch.

"How is it going?"

"Pretty fair," he admitted. "You try the shrimp creole tonight. You gonna like it."

"That's a deal."

"Where's Danny?"

"Right down there." She pointed, and Hallorann saw a small figure sitting at the end of the dock. He was wearing jeans rolled up to the knee and a red-striped shirt. Further out on the calm water, a bobber floated. Every now and then Danny would reel it in, examine the sinker and hook below it, and then toss it out again.

"He's gettin brown," Hallorann said.

"Yes. Very brown." She looked at him fondly.

He took out a cigarette, tamped it, lit it. The smoke raftered away lazily in the sunny afternoon. "What about those dreams he's been havin?"

"Better," Wendy said. "Only one this week. It used to be every night, sometimes two and three times. The explosions. The hedges. And most of all . . . you know."

"Yeah. He's going to be okay, Wendy."

She looked at him. "Will he? I wonder."

Hallorann nodded. "You and him, you're coming back. Different, maybe, but okay. You ain't what you were, you two, but that isn't necessarily bad."

They were silent for a while, Wendy moving the rocking chair back and forth a little, Hallorann with his feet up on the porch rail, smoking. A little breeze came up, pushing its secret way through the pines but barely ruffling Wendy's hair. She had cut it short.

"I've decided to take Al—Mr. Shockley—up on his offer," she said.

Hallorann nodded. "It sounds like a good job. Something you could get interested in. When do you start?"

"Right after Labor Day. When Danny and I leave here, we'll be going right on to Maryland to look for a place. It was really the Chamber of Commerce brochure that convinced me, you know. It looks like a nice town to raise a kid in. And I'd like to be working again before we dig too deeply into the insurance money Jack left. There's still over forty thousand dollars. Enough to send Danny to college with enough left over to get him a start, if it's invested right."

Hallorann nodded. "Your mom?"

She looked at him and smiled wanly. "I think Maryland is far enough."

"You won't forget old friends, will you?"

"Danny wouldn't let me. Go on down and see him, he's been waiting all day."

"Well, so have I." He stood up and hitched his cook's whites at the hips. "The two of you are going to be okay," he repeated. "Can't you feel it?"

She looked up at him and this time her smile was warmer. "Yes," she said. She took his hand and kissed it. "Sometimes I think I can."

"The shrimp creole," he said, moving to the steps. "Don't forget."

"I won't."

He walked down the sloping, graveled path that led to the dock and then out along the weather-beaten boards to the end, where Danny sat with his feet in the clear water. Beyond, the lake widened out, mirroring the pines along its verge. The terrain was mountainous around here, but the mountains were old, rounded and humbled by time. Hallorann liked them just fine.

"Catchin much?" Hallorann said, sitting down next to him. He took off one shoe, then the other. With a sigh, he let his hot feet down into the cool water.

"No. But I had a nibble a little while ago."

"We'll take a boat out tomorrow morning. Got to get out in the middle if you want to catch an eatin fish, my boy. Out yonder is where the big ones lay."

"How big?"

Hallorann shrugged. "Oh ... sharks, marlin, whales, that sort of thing."

"There aren't any whales!"

"No *blue* whales, no. Of course not. These ones here run to no more than eighty feet. Pink whales."

"How could they get here from the ocean?"

Hallorann put a hand on the boy's reddish-gold hair and rumpled it. "They swim upstream, my boy. That's how."

"Really?"

"Really."

They were silent for a time, looking out over the stillness of the lake, Hallorann just thinking. When he looked back at Danny, he saw that his eyes had filled with tears.

Putting an arm around him, he said, "What's this?"

"Nothing," Danny whispered.

"You're missin your dad, aren't you?"

Danny nodded. "You always know." One of the tears spilled from the corner of his right eye and trickled slowly down his cheek.

"We can't have any secrets," Hallorann agreed. "That's just how it is."

Looking at his pole, Danny said: "Sometimes I wish it had been me. It was my fault. All my fault."

Hallorann said, "You don't like to talk about it around your mom, do you?"

"No. She wants to forget it ever happened. So do I, but—"

"But you can't."

"No."

"Do you need to cry?"

The boy tried to answer, but the words were swallowed in a sob. He leaned his head against Hallorann's shoulder and wept, the tears now flooding down his face. Hallorann held him and said nothing. The boy would have to shed his tears again and again, he knew, and it was Danny's luck that he was still young enough to be able to do that. The tears that heal are also the tears that scald and scourge.

When he had quieted a little, Hallorann said, "You're gonna get over this. You don't think you are right now, but you will. You got the shi—"

"I wish I didn't!" Danny choked, his voice still thick with tears. "I wish I didn't have it!"

"But you do," Hallorann said quietly. "For better or worse. You didn't get no say, little boy. But the worst is over. You can use it to talk to me when things get rough. And if they get too rough, you just call me and I'll come."

"Even if I'm down in Maryland?"

"Even there."

They were quiet, watching Danny's bobber drift around thirty feet out from the end of the dock. Then Danny said, almost too low to be heard, "You'll be my friend?"

"As long as you want me."

The boy held him tight and Hallorann hugged him.

"Danny? You listen to me. I'm going to talk to you about it this once and never again this same way. There's some things no six-year-old boy in the world should have to be told, but the way things should be and the way things are hardly ever get together. The world's a hard place, Danny. It don't care. It don't hate you and me, but it don't love us, either. Terrible things happen in the world, and they're things no one can explain. Good people die in bad, painful ways and leave the folks that love them all alone. Sometimes it seems like it's only the bad people who stay healthy and prosper. The world don't love you, but your momma does and so do I. You're a good boy. You grieve for your daddy, and when you feel you have to cry over what happened to him, you go into a closet or under your covers and cry until it's all out of you again. That's what a good son has to do. But see that you get on. That's your job in this hard world, to keep your love alive and see that you get on, no matter what. Pull your act together and just go on."

"All right," Danny whispered. "I'll come see you again next summer if you want . . . if you don't mind. Next summer I'm going to be seven."

"And I'll be sixty-two. And I'm gonna hug your brains out your ears. But let's finish one summer before we get on to the next."

"Okay." He looked at Hallorann. "Dick?"

"Hmm?"

"You won't die for a long time, will you?"

"I'm sure not studyin on it. Are you?"

"No, *sir*. I—"

"You got a bite, sonny." He pointed. The red and white bobber had ducked under. It came up again glistening, and then went under again.

"Hey!" Danny gulped.

Wendy had come down and now joined them, standing in back of Danny. "What is it?" she asked. "Pickerel?"

"No, ma'am," Hallorann said, "I believe that's a pink whale."

The tip of the fishing rod bent. Danny pulled it back and a long fish, rainbow-colored, flashed up in a sunny, winking parabola, and disappeared again.

Danny reeled frantically, gulping.

"Help me, Dick! I got him! I got him! Help me!"

Hallorann laughed. "You're doin fine all by yourself, little man. I don't know if it's a pink whale or a trout, but it'll do. It'll do just fine."

He put an arm around Danny's shoulders and the boy reeled the fish in, little by little. Wendy sat down on Danny's other side and the three of them sat on the end of the dock in the afternoon sun.